CECILIA

FRANCES (FANNY) BURNEY (born 1752), the daughter of musicologist Charles Burney, published her highly successful novel *Evelina* in 1778. *Cecilia*, which sealed her mature reputation as a novelist, appeared in 1782. In 1786 Burney was unhappily thrust into a position at court as Second Keeper of the Robes to Queen Charlotte. Her journals and letters, particularly of the court period, have attracted attention from historians, but it is upon her work as a novelist that Burney staked her own claim to fame. After leaving court service in 1791, she met and married Alexandre d'Arblay, an aristocratic liberal, then a penniless émigré in England. Their son, Alexander, was born in 1794. Burney's third novel, the innovative *Camilla* (1796), put a roof over the heads of the new family. While living in France from 1802 to 1812 Burney wrote *The Wanderer*, a novel of the French Revolution, published in 1814. Her last published work was the *Memoirs of Doctor Burney* (1832), which contains much autobiographical material. Frances Burney (Mme d'Arblay) died in 1840.

PETER SABOR is a Professor of English at Queen's University, Ontario. His publications include *Horace Walpole: A Reference Guide*; *Horace Walpole: The Critical Heritage*; and editions of Richardson's *Pamela*, Cleland's *Memoirs of a Woman of Pleasure*, and (in collaboration) Carlyle's *Sartor Resartus*.

MARGARET ANNE DOODY is Andrew W. Mellon Professor of Humanities and Professor of English at Vanderbilt University, where she is currently directing the Comparative Literature Program. Her publications include *A Natural Passion: A Study of the Novels of Samuel Richardson*, *The Daring Muse: Augustan Poetry Reconsidered*, and *Frances Burney: The Life in the Works*, as well as two novels, *Aristotle Detective* and *The Alchemists*. Her most recent work is the *The True Story of the Novel* (1996).

THE WORLD'S CLASSICS

FRANCES BURNEY

Cecilia,
OR
MEMOIRS OF AN HEIRESS

Edited by

PETER SABOR

and

MARGARET ANNE DOODY

with an introduction by
Margaret Anne Doody

Oxford   New York

OXFORD UNIVERSITY PRESS

Oxford University Press, Great Clarendon Street, Oxford OX2 6DP

Oxford New York

Athens Auckland Bangkok Bogota Bombay
Buenos Aires Calcutta Cape Town Dar es Salaam
Delhi Florence Hong Kong Istanbul Karachi
Kuala Lumpur Madras Madrid Melbourne
Mexico City Nairobi Paris Singapore
Taipei Tokyo Toronto Warsaw

and associated companies in
Berlin Ibadan

Oxford is a trade mark of Oxford University Press

First published as a World's Classics paperback 1988

British Library Cataloguing in Publication Data

Data available

Library of Congress Cataloging in Publication Data
Burney, Fanny, 1752-1840.
Cecilia, or, Memories of an heiress.
(The World's classics)
Bibliography: p.
I. Sabor, Peter. II. Doody, Margaret Anne.
III. Title. IV. Title: Cecilia. V. Title: Memoirs
of an heiress.
PR3316.A4C4 1988 823'.6 87-28122
ISBN 0-19-281742-6 (pbk.)

7 9 10 8 6

Printed in Great Britain by
Caledonian International Book Manufacturing Ltd
Glasgow

CONTENTS

VOLUME IV

ACKNOWLEDGEMENTS

WE are grateful to the Frick Collection, New York, for permission to reproduce the cover painting by Thomas Gainsborough. We give thanks to the British Library for permission to transcribe Burney's draft introduction to *Cecilia*. Particular thanks are due to the Henry W. and Albert A. Berg Collection of the New York Public Library and to the curator, Dr Lola Szladits, for permitting Margaret Anne Doody to read the Burney manuscripts in their possession. We are also grateful to librarians of the Bodleian Library, the Firestone Library of Princeton University, and Queen's University Library for their assistance.

We should like to give personal thanks to the following individuals for their interest in and help with the project: Paula Backscheider, Edward A. and Lillian D. Bloom, Fraser Easton, Melinda Finberg, Siobhàn Kilfeather, Marie Legroulx, F. P. Lock, George Logan, Robert Mack, Emmi Sabor, Florian Stuber, Frank Tompa, and Lars Troide.

INTRODUCTION

THE appearance of Frances Burney's second novel, *Cecilia, or Memoirs of an Heiress*, was a public event. Rumours of its advent created long waiting lists at the circulating libraries before the publication date of 12 July 1782. The first edition sold out rapidly. The book was discussed everywhere in London, and contemporaries generally recognized *Cecilia* as the most important novel to be published since Smollett's last appearance with *Humphry Clinker* (1771). The reviews were not only almost entirely favourable, but also unusually lengthy; Burney was accepted as a writer worthy of serious and attentive criticism. The *Critical Review* (December 1782) praised the characters as 'well drawn, and well supported', and the *English Review* (January 1783) agreed: 'All of them [the characters] seem fairly purchased at the great work-shop of life, and not the second-hand, vamped-up shreds and patches of the Monmouth-street of modern romance.'[1] The novel's structural unity was appreciated as well as its characterization and its truthful use of 'common materials'. The *London Magazine* (January 1783) is typical in its praise of the work's organization: 'This novel is planned with great judgment, and executed with great skill.'[2] As Dr Johnson said to Mrs Thrale, 'the grand merit is in the *general Power of the whole*'.[3]

The conditions under which *Cecilia* was written and met its public were very different from those surrounding the birth of Burney's first novel, *Evelina, or, A Young Lady's Entrance into the World*. That novel was written in secrecy, in stolen hours in unheated rooms. The author's father, Dr Charles Burney, was not told about it until months after

---

[1] *Critical Review*, 54 (Dec. 1782), 414; *English Review*, 1 (Jan. 1783), 14.

[2] *London Magazine*, 52 (Jan. 1783), 40.

[3] Letter from Hester Lynch Thrale to Frances Burney, 31 July 1782; the manuscript of this letter is in the Henry W. and Albert A. Berg Collection of the New York Public Library. It is quoted also in Joyce Hemlow, *The History of Fanny Burney* (Oxford: Clarendon Press, 1958), p. 151.

the novel's publication in January 1778, once critical and popular success were assured. Dr Burney then began to take about with him the successful young author he had hitherto seen as his shy girl. 'Fanny' became a member of the group at Streatham, the home of the Thrales where Samuel Johnson was a perpetual guest. The fame of *Evelina* gave Frances at the age of 26 a place within the group that did not depend upon the reputation and merits of her musicologist father. She was now introduced to a large and various world of fashionable people, and the new environment would be reflected in her writing. It would also reflect upon her writing. The production of the next work would inevitably be a public matter, and Burney could no longer hide the fact that she was writing.

The next work planned was not a novel but a play—a kind of work the writing of which, like its final production, is almost necessarily a public affair. Both Arthur Murphy and Richard Brinsley Sheridan, dramatists and men of immense influence in the theatrical world, urged her to write a play, as they had been impressed with the dramatic quality of scenes and dialogues in *Evelina*. At the time Dr Burney seemed delighted by the flattery and the idea. In the winter of 1778–9 and through the next summer Burney worked on her new play, *The Witlings* ('By a Sister of the Order'). The sub-plot concerns a circle of would-be wits who gather around Lady Smatter and her obsequious protégé, the would-be poet Dabler. Lady Smatter's nephew is to marry the orphan Cecilia Stanley, but, at the news that the girl's trustee has gone bankrupt and the money has disappeared, Lady Smatter forbids the match and insults Cecilia. The young woman takes refuge in lodgings with Dabler's vulgar landlady Mrs Voluble and tries to find employment. In the end all comes right, but the moral is to inculcate the value of 'self-dependence'.[4]

The corrected first draft of the new play was submitted to a family play-reading at the home of Burney's old friend

[4] The manuscript of *The Witlings* is in the Henry W. and Albert A. Berg Collection of the New York Public Library.

and literary Mentor, 'Daddy' Samuel Crisp. Young Susanna Burney assured her absent sister that the reading of 2 August had gone very well. Frances must then have been the more shocked to receive a harsh letter from Crisp and Dr Burney forbidding her ever to think of having the play put on. Their 'Fannikin' tried to get them to mollify their judgement, suggesting alterations and changes, but Dr Burney was adamant. 'You have finished it now, in every sense of the word', his daughter wrote in an eloquent and bitter letter.[5] Unless she wanted to separate herself absolutely from her family, a young lady could not have her play produced against such parental prohibition. What made matters harder was that daughterly Fanny was asked to acquiesce in the judgement that the play was simply bad, without submitting it to the more qualified judges, Murphy and Sheridan. Whatever Dr Burney's reasons, he dashed his daughter's hopes, and she found she had wasted a year's work. Dr Burney tried to turn her against theatrical work altogether, and back to the safer (and more ladylike) paths of prose fiction. 'In the Novel way, there is no danger', he pointed out encouragingly.[6] Once the new novel was under way, he constantly tried to push Frances to finish it more quickly, insisting in the spring of 1782 that she needed no more time for a last revision and cutting (Burney herself thought the novel a trifle too long). The new work, which took nearly three years to complete, was published in an exceptionally large edition for the time—2,000 copies. The author was actually underpaid for this large issue, but Samuel Crisp, for one, thought the young woman amazingly lucky: 'If she can coin gold at such a Rate, as to sit by a warm Fire, and in 3 or 4 months . . . gain £250 by scribbling the Inventions of her own Brain—only putting down . . . whatever comes into her own head . . . she need not want

[5] See *Diary and Letters of Madame D'Arblay*, ed. Charlotte Barrett, 7 vols. (London: Henry Colburn, 1854), i. 209.

[6] Letter from Dr Charles Burney to Frances Burney, undated [Aug.–Sept. 1779], British Library, Egerton MS 3690, p. 5.

money.'[7] The Daddies underestimated their Fanny's labour, the true cost of this magical gift of spinning straw into gold like a fairy-tale girl.

It is against this background that the cancelled 'Introduction' to *Cecilia* should be read (see Appendix I). The fable of Genius and Vanity shows how much Burney hopes that it is true genius that drives her. In any case, she knows what it means and what the literary ambition is, as we see when she describes the pilgrimage of the 'youthful Author': 'he [*sic*] wavers—yet he proceeds; he repents—but he never returns! . . . his accustomed occupations become irksome, his former pleasures, insipid'. Anxiously Burney proclaims her own humility as she had been taught to do— her father had teasingly told her that no one ever set up a statue to a novelist.[8] She is frightened of self-delusions; perhaps what she thinks is important is not really so, perhaps she has mistaken 'Inclination' for 'Ability'. Yet within this doubt is the other positive doubt; perhaps what drives her may after all be a muse or beneficent spirit. Self-analysis, in the end, proves bewildering. The 'Mind of Man' is a labyrinth (this is a theme to be repeated in her third novel, *Camilla* (1796), which at the outset states as its subject 'the wilder wonders of the Heart of man').[9] Burney herself cannot know herself, cannot know whether she has genius or delusions; she cannot even know why she writes, or understand 'the interior movements by which I may be impelled: the intricacies of the Human heart are various as innumerable'. The cancelled 'Introduction' to *Cecilia* reflects Burney's anxieties and deepest hopes about the nature and

---

[7] Samuel Crisp to Sophia Gast, *Burford Papers, being Letters of Samuel Crisp to his Sister at Burford*, ed. William Holden Hutton (London: Archibald Constable and Co. Ltd, 1905), p. 74.

[8] *Diary and Letters*, i. 42. See also Madame D'Arblay [Frances Burney], *Memoirs of Doctor Burney*, 3 vols. (London: Edward Moxon, 1832), ii. 148; Burney observes in a footnote 'Sir Walter Scott was then a child', reminding us that during her lifetime the world had at last seen a statue erected to a novelist.

[9] Madame D'Arblay [Frances Burney], *Camilla, or A Picture of Youth*, ed. with introduction by Edward A. Bloom and Lillian D. Bloom (London: Oxford University Press, 1972), p. 7.

value of her writing. Disdaining the mere fashionable success of which she was almost assured, and the money-coining which seemed so remarkable to a man like Crisp, she felt she was doing something of serious importance. She also knew that her writing came from depths within and was too powerful an impulse to be denied. There seemed to be something sacred about it, even though her world (especially the world of the Daddies) would refuse to allow Genius to a young woman merely scribbling 'whatever comes into her head'. The endeavour to make some public statement about private authorial feeling is inevitably awkward, and Burney did well to scrap this Introduction. Still, the piece is an interesting statement—and in part a protest. It is in line with the theme of *Cecilia*, in which we see hopes, ambitions, and even genius (particularly but not only female) deflected and thwarted. After she had seen what 'Daddy' Crisp and her father could do to her in the matter of *The Witlings*, it is no wonder that Burney's new novel concerned a heroine whose talents—symbolically her fortune—are wasted by her male guardians.

Cecilia, like *The Witlings*, deals with an heiress who loses her money. This heroine, however, loses her inheritance not in one abrupt crash but in a series of depredations. It is interesting that in Burney's original concept of her novel the central character may have been designed as an 'unbeautiful, clever heroine, beset all round for the sake of her great fortune'.[10] This heroine was named 'Albina', perhaps after the calumniated heroine of Hannah Cowley's play *Albina* (1779). (The influence of other women dramatists is felt throughout *Cecilia*: the heroine's multiple guardians seem to be adapted from Centlivre's *A Bold Stroke for a Wife* (1718), and the scenes of money-spending and party-giving seem more than a little indebted to Elizabeth Griffith's *The Times* [1779].) The draft manuscript of the novel shows that Albina can be quite tough; she is harsher in her speeches to Mr Arnott about Mr Harrel than Cecilia

[10] Samuel Crisp to Frances Burney, 27 Apr. 1780, *Diary and Letters*, i. 277.

is in the same scene in the published version.[11] It is perhaps a pity that Burney decided against such an original stroke as an 'unbeautiful' heroine (for which the heroine of Sarah Scott's *Agreeable Ugliness* (1754) would have been the only precedent). But the intelligence first associated with the 'clever' heroine is still in evidence, and Cecilia is certainly 'beset' for her great fortune. The heroine herself feels a certain confidence because of that wealth; she is not, she congratulates herself, like other girls, under the humiliating necessity of getting married—she is not 'set up to sale' (p. 468).

Cecilia enters the world of London society as a sort of parodic man, since the will under which she inherits the major part of her estate stipulates that her husband must take her surname at her marriage. The 'name clause' is casually introduced in preliminary description in the first chapter. The reader (like Cecilia) tends to view it as an unimportant matter until its importance becomes glaringly manifest. Cecilia has been put (against her will) in the position of a pseudo-male: standing in for the patriarchal inheritor of name and social identity, she is to impose that name on a consort. For all the appearance of power, she holds her estate on a slender tenure; if she breaks that magical injunction, and her husband does not take her name, then the estate vanishes. If she marries according to the will but has no children, neither she nor her husband can choose who inherits. Richardson had questioned the patriarchal system of inheritance throughout *Clarissa* (1747–8), and in *Sir Charles Grandison* (1753–4) the hero is magnanimous enough to question the justice of the patrilinear system under which he has the advantage: 'For does not tyrant custom make a daughter change *her* name in marriage, and give to a son, for the sake of *name* only, the estate of the common ancestor of both?'[12] Cecilia's uncle

[11] Parts of the manuscript draft of *Cecilia* are to be found in the Berg Collection of the New York Public Library. For a description of this manuscript see Joyce Hemlow, *The History of Fanny Burney*, p. 149.

[12] Samuel Richardson, *The History of Sir Charles Grandison*, ed. with introduction by Jocelyn Harris, 3 vols. (London: Oxford University Press, 1972), i. 398.

may have thought he was defying 'tyrant custom', but his will created a new tyranny in compelling the girl, on pain of loss of the estate, to preserve the masculine tribal portion of her name. For a woman the family name is less significant than it is to a man, as ancestral achievements have little to do with the obscured history of foremothers. A surname is the male portion of a woman's name, a reminder that women are supposed to blend in with a masculine social arrangement. The men in the novel treat 'name' as a magic talisman—an attitude the novel views ironically. The dead Dean (first of the mistaken guardians) begins the process of depredation that leads the heroine to anxiety and distress. In the first part of the novel the guardian Mr Harrel is the chief predator and despoiler, but the concerted attack on the heroine's fortune (and happiness) that continues throughout the novel is the result of social customs and commands.

In a world where nearly everyone is a gambler of some sort, Cecilia is also unwittingly to gamble on the chance of finding a true love who will consent to the conditions of the will and change his name. This wager was placed for her— she did not choose it. She thinks, however, that she may choose not to marry. Her society will hardly allow that, for a female who inherits, an 'heiress', is seen not as an independent person but as a conduit for conveying money from one man's family to another. Cecilia cannot know that as she enters this society she is not seen as a free agent (as she imagines herself) but as a property waiting to be taken. There are a number of men willing to accede to the bargain of changing their name for her fortune. Her guardian Mr Harrel has already in effect sold her to the rake Sir Robert Floyer at the time she comes to London, but her country friend Mr Monckton has long believed her and her estate to be his own property.

The world that Cecilia enters is a complex and greedy society displaying all the attributes of a developing commercialism, including a credit system and a high flush of consumerism. It constantly has its victors and its sacrifices. Fashionable persons attend sales of the effects of those who have financially fallen. There is constant reference to the possibility of 'an execution in the house' which sounds as if lethal pageants were being enacted in drawing-rooms. It is appropriate that Cecilia is at one point forced to step out of the way to avoid the procession to Tyburn. This society plays with real executions as well as with bailiffs and bankruptcies—but to those who must depart from the world of fashion there seems little difference. Those who have not yet broken spend their money lavishly on visiting cards, villas, elaborate desserts, and endless parties. The novel entertains us with its nervous comic scenes of fashionable high life, introducing us to the cults of the 'Insensiblists', the 'Supercilious', and the 'Volubles'. The mannerisms betray the meaningless cultivation of personality as one of the diversions of the high bourgeoisie. Burney not only creates 'characters' (at a time when novel criticism was becoming almost fixated on the idea of 'character' in fiction); she also creates characters trying to be characters—as the masquerade scene indicates in pointed allegory. In this large, ambitious novel Burney is not content, as she had been in *Evelina*, with picking on ostensibly safe and traditional targets—money-grubbing cits, rude sea-captains, old rouged harridans. This novel is nothing less than an examination of a whole society as a structure and a system. Burney gives us a cross-section from the Delviles at the top through the Belfields in the middle to the poor Hill family and the poor pew-opener at the bottom of the economic and social ladder. Throughout, she makes us aware of the power and significance of money.

In three characters of different social positions and outlooks Burney presents particular attitudes to money. Mr Harrel, the guardian at whose home Cecilia unfortunately lives, is a fashion-mad spendthrift. He and his wife Priscilla spend more than they have in a frantic routine that has come to seem normal. The plunge to ruin is perversely determined upon, and Harrel takes that part of Cecilia's fortune that is unreservedly hers with him in the process. Spendthrifts had been portrayed in the drama, but customarily either as lovable bachelors, like Charles Surface in *The School for Scandal* (1777), or as a reformable married pair, like the

Woodleys in Elizabeth Griffith's *The Times* (1779). Mr Harrel is not fundamentally good-natured, nor can he reform. Even the candid heroine soon gives up any sentimental hopes and is knowingly sucked into the disagreeable position of giving her money in a parodic benevolence that goes against her judgement. Cecilia is put into a position in relation to the Harrels where it is impossible to say what the right moral action is. Cecilia herself notes this: in an unusually bitter outburst she exclaims: 'I know no longer what is kind or what is cruel, nor have I known for some time past right from wrong, nor good from evil' (p. 396). This is a startling admission on the part of an eighteenth-century heroine. Cecilia's situation denies the knowability of good, as it does the 'virtue' of immediate kindness. This is not a world that responds warmly to the good-hearted, and a good woman will soon have enough of giving. The reader, like Mr Arnott and Cecilia, becomes tired of Harrel's suicidal exploitative menaces, and we make the mistake of thinking that such foolish levity cannot co-exist with self-destruction, that champagne and despair hold no relation. Burney makes us realize otherwise, without giving any sentimental redemption to the histrionic Harrel.

Mr Harrel's wretched excess exhibits the misery entailed upon too blind and faithful an obedience to society's laws. In the terms of the debate in the very first scene of the novel, Harrel has not been 'guided by the light of his own understanding' but has 'pursu[ed] . . . the track that is already marked out' (p. 14). Even more visibly conformist is Mr Hobson, the man of business who believes in his own right to property and to the comfort money can purchase: 'I'm as willing to spend my money as another man', he boasts (p. 402). He has a simple faith in the virtue of getting and possessing. These are the rights of English men, but he thinks it a fault in the law that women can inherit or own anything at all. Beggars and the needy poor are all alike cheats and scoundrels who should be punished and swept out of sight. Certainly there is nothing wild about Hobson's beliefs, the viability of which is proved by the fact that most of them are still with us, and can be uttered to make a very respectable showing. Such respectability is (unlike the misery of Harrel) impervious to any kind of criticism.

In contrast to Hobson as to Harrel is the man of money-in-itself, the intemperately frugal Mr Briggs. Disdaining the beaten track, he is in his way an original. Appointed one of Cecilia's guardians in order to look after her money, Briggs looks only to the money, in a pure sense, and not to the welfare of Cecilia herself. It is one of the novel's inventive triumphs that Briggs, far from being the stereotyped wretched miser, is one of the most vivacious characters. He lives in perpetual complete enjoyment of himself and what he is worth; his self-love needs no supplement from the comforts or pleasures that lesser men enjoy. It is appropriate that he should not see any need for buying soap—his own physical dirt is part of what has accrued to him, a painless increase from the world of nature. Briggs's every appearance is a revel in dirt of various kinds: rags, sweat, hair, soot, mud—all seem to cling about him. In a sort of constant anal ecstasy he speaks with the energy and joy of one close to some pulse of pure being—for money is pure being. Briggs speaks both profusely and sparingly; his electric impatience is expressed in his short pulsating phrases, almost entirely lacking in connectives, modals, and pronouns. His speech reflects the disconnected world Cecilia moves in, and, like that world, it is much attached to things. Many of Briggs's utterances contain some pungent reference to his own physical experience, as when he describes spitting out Harrel's ice-cream (p. 453). Most of his phrases or truncated clauses pick up some vivid physical object: 'don't trust shoe-buckles, nothing but Bristol stones!'; needy gentlemen asked for their rent-roll will 'stare like stuck pigs' (pp. 95–6). Briggs reflects the world around him, the world of getting and bargains and things, as well as the solipsistic tendency of all advertised satisfactions and pleasures.

In presenting characters such as Harrel, Hobson, and Briggs, Burney is not offering a traditional study of the Use of Riches, though the Pope of the *Epistle to Bathurst* may be among her models. She is not saying just that some typical people misuse money. Rather, she is pointing out the central defects of the money-mad world, of which all these characters are symptoms rather than causes. She resists the customary solution of dramatic plays of the period, in which those characters facing financial ruin through their own carelessness or the wrongdoing of others are rescued by some elderly moneybags, some Uncle Oliver come from the East or West Indies with pots of gold. Burney believes in no such benign paternal figures. In Cumberland's *The Fashionable Lover* (1772), for instance, the heroine is in the care of a bad guardian who has secretly mulcted her of her inheritance. But Augusta's father returns—not in fact being dead as had been thought for eighteen years—so all is well. In *Cecilia* Burney certainly could not show a good daddy turning up at last—there are no good daddies any more. The daddies who shadow *Evelina*—the good if impotent Mr Villars, the rejecting but repentant Sir John—have disappeared. Cecilia has no father surrogates in whom she can confide or to whom she can look for rescue. Father-figures in this novel are not part of a solution, but part of the problem. The heroine's uncle the Dean had tried to control her fate in his strange will. Her three legal guardians ignore her, mistreat her, or despoil her. The older man whom Cecilia does believe to be in something of the paternal or avuncular relationship to her is Mr Monckton, who is far from being a disinterested moral adviser.

Mr Monckton, who might be called an honorary guardian, illustrates most vividly the dirty ways that very respectable and well-born men can choose to go in order to advance themselves. In youth, 'impatient for wealth and ambitious of power', Monckton had married a 'rich dowager of quality' who was 67 years old (evidently something like forty years his senior). He had counted on her rapid demise; unfortunately for him, Lady Margaret is still alive at 77, and Cecilia, his secret intended, may go to another. Society has offered no criticism of Monckton's cynical marriage, with its transparently brutal intention. As so often in this novel, Burney makes the treatment of a woman a test of a character's true worth and also an example of social conditions. That Lady Margaret is of a disagreeable disposition cannot cancel out the continuous abuse of her in Monckton's mind, as he anxiously hopes for her death. Lady Margaret's rude remarks to Cecilia, which seem to the girl only the expression of the lady's innate nastiness, are the expression of a well-founded jealousy. The reader knows what Cecilia does not—Mr Monckton's wishes and plans—and thus sees the irony in her turning to this apparently informative and well-disposed old friend. Monckton suffers hidden pain whenever he sees Cecilia parting with money that he has already counted upon as his own. He is thus in opposition to the other strong male adviser, Albany.

Albany, who also figures as an honorary guardian, is the only character who consistently preaches benevolence and the care of the poor. He is the only one who seems to be outside the socio-economic scheme of things. In taking the advice of this prophetic madman, Cecilia is led to people who really need her help. Albany wants nothing for himself—save power. He is called a madman, as anyone would be called who found wealth disgusting and poverty haunting. Yet Albany is not a trustworthy guide. The reader notices how at all his appearances he insists on making Cecilia feel uncomfortable, and hectors her for doing what she, in her position as a female, cannot help doing—that is, being complaisant to her hosts and guardians. His harshness to her as a woman is of a piece with the history which he finally reveals in Volume IV. He had been the instrument of ruin of a teenage girl; when he had found out her sexual fall, he had brutally rejected and even struck her. Thrown out by him, she had become a prostitute, a state from which he rescued her only to have her die—die without speaking to him, without appearing to hear him, without once taking food under his roof. Her stern-willed penance for her life seems a hostile parody of what men want women to be (deaf, mute, anorexic, motionless). It was her death that led to Albany's madness for a space of about three years. He is devoting himself, he tells Cecilia, to a perpetual penance and to repeated telling of 'my own sad story' to those who may profit (p. 704). His narrative, then, his prophetic speeches, and his odd unsocial behaviour are all alike the creations of guilt—rather like the behaviour of that other guilty party, the Ancient Mariner. What the reader and the heroine have felt at moments to be saintly behaviour in Albany, a prophetic calling, receives a new and less pretty colouring from this narrative. Albany's moral wealth, his capacity to castigate others and to make them give, is founded, like Monckton's economic and social wealth, on mistreatment of a woman.

The exploitation of various women has much to do with their social position as well as their sex. Lady Margaret could preserve Monckton's claim to high status, while Albany's girl was only 'the daughter of a villager' and thus not an appropriate bride. Cecilia is exploited by Mr Harrel both sexually and financially when he turns her into an unwitting prostitute in selling her to Floyer. But Harrel also exploits a woman who is not connected to him by any sexual tie; indeed, he chooses not to see her. The unfortunate Mrs Hill, wife of a carpenter who has suffered incurable injury while working on the Harrels' villa at the prettily named 'Violet Bank', has little power to make her claim for just debts. She is contemptuously referred to as a beggar; Cecilia at first thinks this poor woman is only an object of charity, and is further shocked to learn that money is owed her which is not being paid. Mrs Hill has to waste time hanging about the door of those great folks the Harrels, who owe her husband £22. Mrs Hill's time is truly valuable—all the more since her husband is unemployed. Hers is work time, unlike the empty hours of such as Harrel or the equally idle Delvile who is always proclaiming how precious his time is. In Burney's last novel, *The Wanderer* (1814), the heroine herself will have to hang about rich people's halls, requesting (usually in vain) to be paid what she is owed for her labour. The mature Burney is interested in the working world as it affects women—this can be seen in *The Witlings*, where the heroine tries to find employment in a world where women do work as milliners, landladies, and nursemaids. Burney knows that the real world of the working poor arouses no interest or sympathy among the rich and leisured. Cecilia has that to learn; at first she expects immediate sentimental sympathy for the Hills' plight. She has to find out what people say to poor folk when there are no pretty young ladies around to necessitate politeness. Mr Harrel's callousness is worthy of any Malthusian boor in Dickens: 'when I told him' (Mrs Hill says) 'I had no help now, for I had lost my Billy, he had the heart to say, so much the better, there's one the less of you' (p. 85). Burney wants the reader to understand, as Mrs Hill puts it, 'what the poor go through'. It was a scene between Mrs Hill and Cecilia that Edward Francesco Burney illustrated for *The Norfolk Ladies Memorandum Book* in 1787, and probably this cousin knew how important the author felt the Hills' story to be. The author and the heroine show an understanding not all of Burney's readers would naturally share. Cecilia sympathizes with the Hill family's desire to give the dead eldest son, poor Billy, a good funeral. No strictures are passed on that expense; the author makes a plea for the self-respect of poor people. Nor does Cecilia criticize the injured Mr Hill's desire to leave the hospital and die at home, something which many middle-class persons would have picked on as typical of the folly and ingratitude of the poor. We are to see what class and money divisions mean, what pain the structuring of this society involves. In presenting the Hill family (through Mrs Hill), Burney is subtly undermining the claim that some characters in the novel would make, that there is a true difference between Rank and Money. In *Cecilia* Burney constantly shows how society operates in terms of Rank and Money, and how these two are interrelated.

It was more daring of Burney to pick up the subject of class than it was to attack riches. Satiric criticism of the *nouveaux riches* and of vulgar tradesmen had long been acceptable. In *Evelina*, Burney's memorable portraits of the Branghtons and of Mr Smith had been seized upon by readers who could ignore her representation in that novel of the parallels between the attitudes of the upper classes and the lower middle. In *Cecilia* it is almost impossible to miss such interconnections. A central target in this novel is what might be called 'true' class, real rank as derived from old

family and honourable name. Such rank is illustrated in
Cecilia's third guardian, pompous Compton Delvile.
Delvile sees himself as a total contrast to Briggs, and indeed
the chapter headings apparently emphasize the opposition;
we move from 'A Man of Wealth' to 'A Man of Family'.
Each of these men sees his own source of worth as an
absolute; Delvile values 'Family' above all things. Unlike
Briggs, Delvile has little mental contact with the external
world of objects and people. What comes to his mind is not
the concrete image but the abstraction. His speech is
pompous, careful, guarded, pallidly verbose—a contrast
indeed to that of Briggs. At their first meeting he is offen-
sively condescending to Cecilia. His 'display of importance'
soon makes her regret her visit, but the authorial narrator
notes that her 'inquietude of countenance' is misinterpreted
by Delvile who 'imagined her veneration was every moment
encreasing' and, pitying her gratifying timidity, 'abated
more and more of his greatness' (pp. 97–8). We can see in
such passages the usefulness of the third-person narrator,
whose ironic judgement and tone colour the narrative,
creating ironic emphases not accessible in the epistolary mode
of *Evelina*. The passage on Delvile seems to have about it flecks
of free indirect speech, the 'greatness' of self and manner
being all in Delvile's mind. Most of Mr Delvile exists in his
mind. His repeated 'I' is a proud social 'I', asserting the
fabric of lofty fiction. If he is there, then what he believes in
must be there also. The position of extreme social eminence
that Delvile asserts for himself depends on an elaborate
mental structure whose social power has already begun to
wane. The feudal system really is dead; people may pretend
to value 'Rank' or 'Birth' or 'Family' as a pure idea, but
blue blood and old name are powerless without money.
Briggs's spirited attack on Delvile (pp. 453–6) points out
that the structure on which Delvile relies is a fantastic
fiction—and ultimately (like Briggs's own sources of wealth)
dirty, too. If he is depending on the dust of his ancestors,
Briggs says, Mr Delvile is no more than a 'dustman'—he is
peddling rubbish, the essence of the dead. Delvile, of course,
cannot reply, for his whole being is bent on keeping the

fiction of pure birth going. He always speaks pedagogically, as he has constantly to interpret and explain the values from which his own worth is derived. His utterances are self-supporting little systems, and the 'I' must always be present to authenticate him. He is totally unqualified to endure anonymity, as he proves when he tries to interrogate Mrs Belfield. He cannot bear to hear the satiric fantasia in which Lady Honoria suggests that Delvile Castle should be sold to the local authorities for a gaol. It is a gaol, like the web of abstractions that Delvile devoutly serves. Even to joke about selling the castle is to admit what he cannot admit—that everything he has has a monetary value. Briggs also points out that the dust of the vaults could not buy Delvile's breakfast china or 'fine jemmy tye'.

It is not just the absurd Mr Compton Delvile who is caught in this web of class fiction. Characters whom the reader likes and takes seriously are also caught up in this delusion. Mrs Delvile is an intelligent and forceful woman; very unlike her husband, she acts with elegance and kindness and speaks wisely and wittily. Unlike the raddled Madame Duval of *Evelina*, the rouged grandmother of 50, Mrs Delvile at the same age is truly attractive and elegant. The reader, like Cecilia, may be tempted to see in her an appropriate mother-substitute for the heroine. Like Cecilia, then, we reckon without the mixed qualities of Augusta Delvile's character, which include a very strong class pride, the only justification of her unhappy marriage. The only thing to value in Mr Delvile is his name: 'To love Mr. Delvile she felt was impossible . . . she saw with bitterness the inferiority of his faculties' (p. 461). To endure that marriage, she has always had to make a fetish of the class and 'Family' she is upholding. The manuscript draft indicates that making Mrs Delvile the cousin of Mr Delvile was a fairly late idea in the development of the novel; it is a happy stroke, for in serving 'Family' Augusta is serving her original family, and can believe more readily in the irony of the name. Her name before marriage may have been Augusta Delvile; she would thus be in parallel to Cecilia who has been legally chained to her surname 'Beverley' for life but feels no attachment to it. Augusta Delvile has given way to the religion of 'Family' for which her dull husband serves merely as a symbol or fetish. The introverted nature of that family, the almost incestuous avarice that preys upon itself, locking away its own treasures (in this case, persons)—this sickness is also expressed in that blood relationship.

Burney is one of the first novelists to attribute variety of feelings and important personal qualities to a middle-aged woman. Mrs Delvile, seething with the discontent of many years, with feelings unnaturally repressed, may well be expected to come to some explosive point of crisis. Unaccustomed as we are, however, to thinking of mature matrons as capable of development and surprise, we (like Cecilia) may accept as settled and stable a personality actually dynamic and fluctuating—a readerly obtuseness the author counts upon. Cecilia at 20 is not very likely to think that a woman of 50 will have interesting strengths or disconcerting powers, and we foolishly follow the heroine's misreading.

Hester Lynch Thrale saw in Mrs Delvile a strong resemblance to her own mother.[13] But we may surmise that Burney was drawing upon her knowledge of Hester herself, another proud woman who had been unhappily married off in youth 'without any consultation of her heart or her will'. Mrs Delvile is described as 'high-spirited and fastidious . . . easily wearied and disgusted', yet she is an enthusiast in friendship: 'the chosen few . . . she loved with a zeal all her own . . . she magnified their virtues till she thought them of an higher race of beings' (p. 461). This is the same language that Burney uses later in the *Memoirs* to describe Hester Thrale: 'she had a sweetness of manner, and an activity of service for those she loved, that could ill be appreciated by others . . . she spoke of individuals in general with sarcasm; and of the world at large with sovereign contempt'.[14] Mrs Thrale, like Mrs Delvile, knew pride of

[13] Hester Lynch Thrale to Frances Burney, 25 Apr. 1782, *Diary and Letters*, ii. 110.

[14] *Memoirs of Doctor Burney*, ii. 172.

lineage, as her friend noted.[15] (A good portion of that pride descended to her daughter Queeney, who may have offered Burney one of the models for the 'insensiblist' Miss Leeson; at first encounter Queeney appeared 'a girl of fashion . . . very silent' who 'never looked tired, though she never uttered a syllable'.)[16]

Mrs Delvile represents what the eighteenth-century critics called a 'mixed' character; she is one of the first such characters outside the novels of Richardson. First reactions to *Cecilia* show how unusual such a concept of character still seemed. Readers were puzzled. They liked Mrs Delvile through the first three volumes, appreciating her wit and kindness. How then could a woman so charming become the obstacle to the heroine's happiness, showing herself under pressure a tyrant and an emotional blackmailer? Readers such as Samuel Crisp preferred virtue and vice kept in separate compartments. Burney explained: 'I meant in Mrs. Delvile to draw a great, but not a perfect character; I meant . . . to blend upon paper, as I have frequently seen blended in life, noble and rare qualities with striking and incurable defects.'[17] It is inevitable that Mrs Delvile should respond with irrational intensity to the idea of her son's marrying Cecilia and thus losing the family name. Having sacrificed all her happiness to an ideal—Name and Family—Mrs Delvile must become cruel to the person who threatens that ideal.

Young Mortimer himself has internalized the family ideal so thoroughly that he recoils without prompting from the prospect of marriage to Cecilia and the loss of his name. He makes a laboured anti-proposal on his own initiative, explaining carefully that the 'barbarous and repulsive clause' would 'degrade me for ever' (p. 512). Insulted, Cecilia reacts with sarcastic anger: 'Well, let him keep his name! since so wondrous its properties . . .' But to the Delviles the name's properties truly *are* wondrous. Burney

[15] *Diary and Letters*, ii. 146.
[16] *Memoirs of Doctor Burney*, ii. 88.
[17] Burney to Crisp, 15 Mar. 1782, *Diary and Letters*, ii. 100.

knew better than her father or Crisp, who, newly risen bourgeois that they were with no name to speak of, thought no man would turn down a solid fortune of £3,000 per annum for such a trifle. She pointed out her vindication when she found that Lord De Ferrars said 'old Delvile was in the right not to give up a good family name'.[18] The name issue divided readers' opinions as it divides the opinions of characters in the novel. Burney had hit on a very telling image for patrilinear inheritance and for the class system, in employing an instance in which many in the community could, like Walter Shandy, gravely accept signifier as pure signified. The name issue offers a serious parodic presentation of class considered as pure essence—a last vaporous apparition of the feudal notion imagined as ideal, an intact nominalism unsullied by the material. Characters in the novel believe devoutly in the difference between Wealth and Family, between Money and Class. The Dean had believed in such arbitrary differences, in the fearful symmetry of his design. Cecilia is to have three guardians: Harrel for friendship, Briggs for money, Delvile for class and respectability. It had never occurred to the Dean that the Harrels might affect her money; Briggs, others' views of her class; and the Delviles, as a family, her love and friendship. The compartments of decanal thought, while apparently logical, make little real sense. The entire novel shows that Class and Money are always mingling, and that the apparent opposition between Family and Wealth is really only the movement of an eddy, a fluctuation of power in a society of increasing wealth and irresponsibility.

Burney has no loyalty either to the old system or to the new, to dusty ancestors or to the stock exchange. She shows how all her characters are influenced by a system of power that they cannot control. Those who are trying to rise in the world may try to influence others through obsequiousness and flattery, like Morrice the lawyer. Or, like the attractive and sad young Belfield (whose portrait makes amends for the feeble sycophant Dabler in *The Witlings*), the rising man may try to rise by wit. Both these young men are gauche and both contend against powerful forces. Mrs Belfield's ignorant hopes for her son show her to be pathetically misinformed about social and economic facts. But her wiser son deludes himself too about the route to prosperity and the fulfilment of his talents. Burney shows good men suffering, as good women do, when they come up against the ingenuity and assurance of the powerful within a structure designed to work for the powerful.

Young Delvile is not exempt from such suffering, for he too is 'good'—well-meaning, fair-minded, sweet-tempered. It is not his fault that he has a weight of expectation placed upon him. Burney has been accused of creating too perfect a gentlemanly hero in the Lord Orville of *Evelina*. Although Orville has some less than happy traits, in the main in her first novel Burney had wished to imagine that at some far-off point the system of class, primogeniture, male authority, and money might in a Grandisonian manner be made harmonious with benevolence and feminine development. This hope—tentative even at best in *Evelina*—is denied in *Cecilia*. The author cannot be accused of creating a perfect hero in her second novel. In some respects young Mortimer seems a riposte to Sir Charles Grandison. Never was the hero of a 'love story' (but *Cecilia* is not essentially a love story) more ruthlessly presented in his defects. Upon his marriage Mortimer desperately signalizes his arrival at manhood by a feverish plunge into the manly world of threats and duels. But through most of the novel's action he is indecisive and withdrawn—defects not at all proper to a hero. In his proud statements he anticipates and influences Darcy in *Pride and Prejudice*, but he does not have Darcy's striking virility and sexual flame.

Young Delvile makes his first appearance in the novel at the masquerade, in the midst of a vivid sequence of emblems and metamorphoses. That scene mimics the novel plot itself by showing the difficulty, even the impossibility, of reading character through momentary representation, or of supposing progressive structure where random colourful elements are tending towards collision. Attending the masquerade, young Delvile refuses either to come in his own person (as Cecilia does) or to come in a representative persona, like Belfield who comes as Don Quixote. Mortimer Delvile comes in a white domino—a shapeless androgynous garment, an innocent blank, a complete cover giving nothing away. His garb may be, as Terry Castle says, 'chic (and morally impeccable)'[19] but when he says 'you will find me as inoffensive as the hue of the domino I wear' (p. 116) the remark is tinged with an irony of which he is unaware. Delvile is not going to be 'inoffensive' to Cecilia at all—in fact, he and his are to cause her a great deal of trouble and distress. The trouble is certainly not willed by himself, for he finds it hard to will anything. He wishes to remain innocent, innocuous, an uncommitted blank. Any kind of commitment frightens him, as he is already overcommitted in and by his family to his family name. He cannot come dressed as an emblematic personage because he is already, as young Delvile, burdened by the emblematic persona of his name. The burden of impersonating an abstraction is sapping his vitality. His first name (Mortimer) suggests not only noble French ancestry but death (*mort*); he is mortified and moribund.

Apparently the chief beneficiary of the class system, this only son and heir suffers from being over-determined. He is deprived of emotional health and maturity, a man who has never been permitted to 'act for himself'—as Belfield at the novel's outset suggests that all should do. His sinking into ill-health after giving up the woman he loves is a predictably passive, even 'feminine', reaction, a suppressed inner protest. Lady Honoria mocks him in some of the unkindest true words ever uttered by a fellow-character about the hero of a love story: 'Poor pretty dear Mortimer! what a puppet do they make of him!' (p. 515). She suggests making this over-protected son a present of a 'pap-boat' and 'a *slabbering-bib* . . . lest he should daub his pappy when he is feeding him' (pp. 515–6). Mortimer is his family's 'puppet' or doll, their voiceless infant. He is living in perpetual

<hr>

[19] Terry Castle, *Masquerade and Civilization* (London: Methuen, 1986), p. 263.

babyhood, forced to swallow the pap his daddy feeds him and to bear the repressive exaltation forced on him by a mother who 'rather idolised than loved him' (p. 462). Cecilia may complain of young Delvile's 'hereditary arrogance', but Lady Honoria (who is often used to voice the nasty shrewd remarks that Cecilia cannot make) correctly sees that the passing on of such arrogance involves a process of infantilization. (As she is of the upper class she perhaps understands the process better than the middle-class heroine.)

Young Delvile is very polite and charming, chivalrous under the pain of small accidents (such as being scalded with the contents of a tea-kettle), but is not readily capable of ideas or decisions. Throughout their unsatisfactory courtship he leaves most of the deciding to Cecilia, just as he is used to leaving most family decisions to his mother. There are ironies in his being unable to bear his mother's taunt about becoming '*Mr. Beverley*', since as 'Mr. Delvile' he is so far from being his own man. But few men could readily bear to sink the last name, to become subsumed (as women are required to be) into the identity of a strange family. In Mortimer Delvile's case, his vision of himself has long been enwrapped in the name. To lose it is to be completely castrated, feminized—even annihilated, as he loses his reason for living. His struggle between his mother and Cecilia is from his point of view rending and heroic.

Readers such as Crisp objected to the uncomfortable scene between Mrs Delvile, Cecilia, and Mortimer (pp. 671–80). Burney explained: 'The conflict scene for Cecilia, between the mother and son . . . is the very scene for which I wrote the whole book.'[20] This 'conflict scene' is in its way a revolutionary scene, as Mortimer at last shakes off some of the shackles of prejudice and Cecilia is rescued from yielding to a false obedience and imposed notions of 'Virtue' that had numbed her in the past. But the individual lovers' triumph over pride and prejudice cannot go unpunished— and it is at best a sadly imperfect triumph. Young Delvile

[20] Burney to Crisp, 15 Mar. 1782, *Diary and Letters*, ii. 99.

cannot in the event give up his name—his mother was right, he cannot become '*Mr. Beverley*'. All that wealth with which she had intended to do great things is taken from the heroine. If the 'love story' ends happily with the union of the lovers, it does so ironically. Cecilia has fallen in love with the one man most certain to deprive her of the power to do good in the world. Had she truly understood the significance of the name clause from the outset, and had she originally read the characters of Mrs Delvile and Mortimer aright, she might successfully have resisted the process of falling in love—a process about which she had had incessant doubts.

Cecilia does make a good number of mistakes—though they are so credible, so like the errors that a sophisticated and intelligent young person might still make, that we may not see them as errors. Indeed, the author has created a world in which it becomes impossible clearly to discern right action, to know with certainty 'right from wrong . . . good from evil'. Burney is certainly not employing the conduct-book formula of novel-writing whereby a heroine's errors are incessantly pointed out in order to be corrected. There is nobody in Cecilia's world capable of correcting her; what needs correcting is the society in which she lives. The heroine is ardent but self-controlled, emotionally generous and candid—and she is gifted with a sense of humour as well as some wit. Cecilia is not, however, experienced in emotional relationships (perhaps her orphaned state may be held partly to blame). Where she feels antagonism (as with her three legal guardians) she is not to be taken in by flam and fictions. But where her own emotions are involved she is consistently blind. She misreads most of the people with whom she is connected by the affections. In her school-days she had not seen through the essential shallowness of her friend Priscilla, and she is now willing to expend unreciprocated affection on the basis of that old relationship. As we are informed in the first chapter, Cecilia misreads Mr Monckton. This should warn us that she may not see far into the desires and motives of other characters, as proves to be true in her association with the Delviles. The reader tends to see Mrs Delvile and Mortimer through Cecilia's eyes, despite warnings from the authorial narrator; Burney told Crisp he had been misreading Mrs Delvile: 'You sunk, as . . . I privately noticed to myself . . . all the passages to her disadvantage.'[21] It is a nice point that Cecilia in youthful egotism imagines that kind Mrs Delvile, her friend, might even try to promote a match between her son and Cecilia. The heroine absurdly wastes pride and shame at the apprehension; she is soon humiliatingly undeceived.

There is nothing silly about Cecilia in her mis-understandings. What is hidden from her is usually another person's relation to the structures and modes of power; at first the world of power is a blank to her, and she cannot truly participate in it. Women are supposed to participate only by consuming—by spending on dress, amusements, and fashionable display—that is, in activities and behaviour that Cecilia finds irritating and useless. Cecilia herself is quixotically impatient and ambitious—a matter that others around her cannot fathom, as her kind of ambition is so unorthodox in a female. Not seeing that her being an 'heiress' means to the world that she is an object to be taken, Cecilia thinks that being an heiress allows her to be a subject, to act and change the world. She wants to plan her own life and live in her own manner, which includes making other people's lives systematically better. She treats her majority rather as a man would. In her own way, she is as imperious an Augustan as Augusta Delvile. Cecilia literally has the imperial dream:

In her sleep she bestowed riches, and poured plenty upon the land; she humbled the oppressor, she exalted the oppressed; slaves were raised to dignities, captives restored to liberty . . . and wretchedness was banished the world (p. 711).

The phrases here echo the prophetic injunctions of Anchises to Aeneas in Book VI of the *Aeneid*, as Englished by Dryden:

> To rule Mankind, and make the World obey;
> Disposing Peace, and War, thy own Majestick Way.
> To tame the Proud, the fetter'd Slave to free:
> These are imperial Arts, and worthy thee.[22]

[21] Burney to Crisp, 15 Mar. 1782, *Diary and Letters*, ii. 100.

[22] John Dryden, *The Works of Virgil: Containing His Pastorals, Georgics and Æneis* (London: Jacob Tonson, 1697), p. 397, translation of *Æneid*, Bk. VI, ll. 1175–8.

It is interesting that the ladylike young Cecilia dreams of the same motto that Richardson's rake Lovelace thinks of adopting: 'the *Debellare superbos* should be my motto, were I to have a new one.'[23] Cecilia, however, wants not only to humble the oppressor (though she *does* want that); she desires also to exalt the oppressed, in an echo of the *Magnificat* that goes beyond the more cautious Virgilian injunction to spare the subdued. Such imperial dreams of heroic freedom and virtue are only that, however—mere dreams. Cecilia is awakened from the 'glorious illusion' by the news of her friend Mrs Charlton's death. The illusion of effortless power and easy benevolence is counteracted by the reality of loneliness and suffering, time and death. Far from being able to spread plenty and happiness about the earth, Cecilia can barely make her own life tolerable. Her few months of living on her own are not idyllic; she surrounds herself with women who need kindness and financial support, but they are not comfortable housemates. Priscilla Harrel is bored and boring, while sweet little Henrietta Belfield can be irritating, especially as she starts falling in love with Mortimer. We are a long way from Millenium Hall. Yet Cecilia does manage to create some lasting good for others through her money and exertions. She helps both widowed Mrs Hill and the poor pew-opener. These two poor women and their families will always be better off for Cecilia's having had the money for a brief while. Cecilia believes that her fortune places upon her the duty of Christian stewardship, but nobody else shares this view of money, and most think her giving is unnecessary, even mad.

Like Clarissa, Cecilia is driven into madness and poverty. She who had happily thought herself above being an object advertised for sale is at last only a paragraph of advertisement in a newspaper. Truly nameless herself at this point, unable to be understood, she is rendered pure object. Her struggle with the world of power has been short, and she is a loser. Burney offers us an 'unhappy' ending for

[23] Samuel Richardson, *Clarissa, or The History of a Young Lady*, 8 vols. (London: J. F. and C. Rivington *et al.*, 1785), i. 231.

contemplation, and rejects it for an ending which is not conventionally 'happy'. The author does not have to wrench the preceding comedy by making the heroine die, but neither does she have to accede to the clichés of love-story endings and perfect felicity. Mortimer and Cecilia, living on the legacy of his aunt (another woman who can give to a woman), may personally enjoy an imperfect happiness, but they can do little to make the world better. Their conclusion is a compromise; they have gone only so far in the direction of true change.

In *Cecilia* Burney caught her society slightly off balance, in a historical lurch. There is no reference within the novel to the American War of Independence, yet independence is everywhere a theme. With the advantages of hindsight, we can see that this is a novel of the new decade which was to end with the French Revolution. Even the new slang phrases presage the coming importance of overt ideology; Captain Aresby, for instance, does everything 'upon the principle' or 'upon the system' of something. (Burney's sensitivity to modern language is reflected in the fact that she is frequently cited in the *OED* as the example of first use, and *Cecilia* itself contributes a large number of individual words to the currency of language.)[24] As language changes, so too do old traditions and allegiances which are breaking down—a fact reflected in Compton Delvile's anxious efforts to insist that they are not. We are shown the conflict not only of individuals, but of groups represented in the individual, each group trying to ensure its own survival as a sociological entity. Most characters in the novel seem unconsciously aware of the threat history poses—that they might be dismissed, annihilated. In developing her society through representative (if highly individualized) characters such as Delvile, Briggs, Harrel, and others, Burney anticipates techniques we associate with the historical novel as perfected by Walter Scott. But Burney is writing from the heart of an undecided conflict, not surveying a past era.

[24] See two articles by J. N. Waddell, 'Fanny Burney's Contribution to English Vocabulary', *Neuphilologische Mitteilungen*, 81 (1980), 260–3; 'Additions to *OED* from the Writings of Fanny Burney', *Notes and Queries*, 225 (1980), 27–32.

Contemporary writers seem to have recognized *Cecilia* as an important novel. Its effect can be seen not only in the works of liberal–progressive novelists such as Charlotte Smith but also in the productions of the Jacobin radical writers of the next decade. William Godwin parodied *Cecilia* in *The Herald of Literature* in 1784 (where he paid Burney the compliment of making her the only novelist specifically distinguished by name).[25] But he reread *Cecilia* when he was planning *Caleb Williams* and studying other fictions that analysed society through the story of individual emotions and obsessions.[26] Mary Wollstonecraft read the novel when it first came out, and quoted it with approval: 'Miss Burney's account of high life is *very* just—I have seen the *supercilious* and been pestered to death by the *volubles*.'[27] The influence of *Cecilia*, which set a precedent for mingling the stories of women of different classes in the same narrative, can be felt in Wollstonecraft's *The Wrongs of Woman* (1798). It takes very little stretching to term *Cecilia* the first of the Jacobin novels.

It is no wonder that readers of the 1780s were not entirely comfortable with the work. For all the applause for the wit and characterization, some elements in the novel made readers uneasy; in particular, readers in 1782 were not prepared for such an ending as Burney supplied. As eminent and enthusiastic a reader of the novel as Edmund Burke objected: 'He wished for a conclusion either more happy or more miserable; "for in a work of imagination," said he, "there is no medium".'[28] Three months before the novel's publication Burney had had to repel Samuel Crisp's dissatisfied suggestion that the ending be changed:

[25] [William Godwin], *The Herald of Literature; or, A Review of the most Considerable Publications that will be made in the Course of the Ensuing Winter: with Extracts* (London: John Murray, 1784), 'Article IV. Louisa, or Memoirs of a Lady of Quality. By the Author of Evelina and Cecilia. 3 vols. 12 mo.', pp. 61–76.

[26] See Gary Kelly, *The English Jacobin Novel 1780–1805* (Oxford: Clarendon Press, 1976), pp. 191–2.

[27] Mary Wollstonecraft to her sister Everina, 4 Mar. 1787, *Collected Letters of Mary Wollstonecraft*, ed. Ralph M. Wardle (Ithaca, NY: Cornell University Press, 1979), p. 141.

[28] *Diary and Letters*, ii. 159.

I must frankly confess I shall think I have rather written a farce than a serious history, if the whole is to end, like the hack Italian operas, with a jolly chorus that makes all parties good and all parties happy! . . . if I am made to give up this point, my whole plan is rendered abortive, and the last page of any novel in Mr. Noble's circulating library may serve for the last page of mine . . .[29]

Readers were not quite ready for a structure which intimated that the satire was not incidental, nor for an ending that provoked a sense of the insoluble instead of relief at comic solution. Magazine reviewers, though profuse in praise, worried about the ending, and even spent space imagining devices the author might have employed to kick the Egglestons out of the estate and put Cecilia back in possession. Evidently *Cecilia*'s satire on the money-madness of contemporary life, like Burney's ironic view of the position of women within that money-mad society, had not been fully absorbed. Critics in the *English Review* and the *Critical Review* displayed a lust for tidiness and for optimistic poetical justice that could not meet Burney's aesthetic and moral 'plan'. Readers were more accustomed to open moralizing of the conduct-book kind, which faulted individual behaviour and then drew back and rested on social satisfaction. Burney is a pioneer in creating both mixed character and the mixed ending in the English novel.

Cecilia in these respects looks forward to works such as *Little Dorrit* and *Middlemarch*, though Burney does not share anything like George Eliot's belief in historically appointed progress. Burney's works were important to Jane Austen, but Burney is not truly in the Austenian tradition. Rather she is in a tradition that includes Smollett and Dickens. And not just the early Dickens—the Harrels look forward to the Lammles and the Veneerings of *Our Mutual Friend*. Burney, like Dickens, is not primarily concerned with the development or adventures of a single character within society, but with the relation of a number of individuals to a social world which tends to warp them and press upon them, and which is too great for them to control. Like the

[29] Burney to Crisp, 6 Apr. 1782, ibid., 107–8.

world of the later Dickens, Burney's is a violent and dark world. Neither Mr Harrel nor Augusta Delvile can be considered simply as villainous, though they have great capacities for destruction and share a tendency to self-destruction. Even Mr Monckton, the plot's 'villain' if we want one, has become what he is through attention to society's commands. No happy ending is possible because no character is capable of stepping outside the all-encompassing social structure and finding a possible alternative way of life. Both Albany and Belfield urgently make the attempt, but with indifferent success, equivalent to the heroine's indifferent success. The marriage of the well-meaning if weak hero to the defeated heroine has solved none of the larger problems. In the ending of *Little Dorrit*, hero and heroine, leaving their wedding, step into the streets where the arrogant and the froward and the vain make their usual uproar. At the end of *Cecilia* repetitive activity still swirls as before about the staid couple. Belfield still roves restlessly about the world. Mrs Harrel marries another man of fortune and sets up 'new equipages and new engagements', and the Delvile family complains about Cecilia's lack of money. Beyond the named characters we know the greater routines of pride and prejudice are proceeding in their usual uproar, producing parties and accidents, costumes and crashes. Individual victims such as Mr Harrel, the carpenter Hill, and the wretches going to Tyburn proceed to various destruction. No one, male or female, has the 'imperial arts' to scatter plenty and peace—these are Augustan dreams denied by Georgian realities.

Note: Burney did not publish her novels under a name, and would never have permitted her public authorial self to be called 'Fanny'. Contemporaries referred to her in print as 'Miss Burney' or 'Burney' (and later as 'Madame d'Arblay'); Victorian editors such as Annie Raine Ellis called her 'Frances Burney'. 'Fanny' is largely the invention of the early twentieth century; diminishing the author by suggesting the childlike and harmless, the nickname has impeded serious judgement of the novels. She is therefore referred to as Frances Burney throughout this edition.

xxxix INTRODUCTION

world of the later Dickens, Burney's is a violent and dark
world. Neither Mr Harrel nor Augusta Delvile can be
considered ... capacities ... may have great
capacities for destruction and there a tendency to self-
... meaning if weak hero to the defeat

NOTE ON THE TEXT

This text reproduces the first edition of *Cecilia* published in
five volumes by Payne and Cadell on 12 July 1782. It has
been set from the copy in the Bodleian Library, Oxford.
Obvious misprints have been silently corrected and the long
's' has been modernized, but eccentricities of punctuation,
spelling, and grammar have not been altered. Burney's
notes, indicated here by a dagger, are retained at the foot of
the page; editorial notes, indicated by an asterisk, are placed
at the end of the text.

For the second edition of 1783 Burney redistributed
the book and chapter numbers within the five volumes,
retaining two books per volume but altering the composition
of all but the first and final books. In doing so she enhanced
the novel's physical uniformity by lengthening volume two
and shortening volumes three and five; the revised book and
volume endings are indicated in the notes. She also made
numerous changes to the punctuation and some one
hundred stylistic alterations, nearly all of single words or
short phrases. These stylistic alterations are also recorded in
the notes. In the seven further editions of *Cecilia* published
by Payne and Cadell (Cadell, Davies, and Payne for editions
seven to nine) in Burney's lifetime, a few textual
emendations are made, recorded in the notes below, while
several errors are introduced. The third to the eighth
editions follow the volume, book, and chapter divisions of
the second, while the ninth edition (1809) is in four volumes.
Since this ninth edition was published when Burney was in
France, cut off from communication with England by
Napoleon's continental policy, she was almost certainly not
responsible for the awkward new arrangement, in which
books overlap the individual volumes.

About one-third of the manuscript of *Cecilia*, in the form
of fragments from each of the five volumes, is extant in the
Henry W. and Albert A. Berg Collection of the New York
Public Library. This manuscript, one of the few surviving

manuscripts of eighteenth-century novels, tantalizingly represents the work as it existed for its author in various states before publication.

The nine Payne and Cadell editions published in London are dated 1782, 1783 (second), 1783 (third), 1784 (fourth), 1786 (fifth), 1791 (sixth), 1796 (seventh), 1802 (eighth), and 1809 (ninth). Editions were published in Dublin in 1783, 1784, 1795, and 1801, and in Boston in 1793–4 and 1803. Serialized abridgements were published in the *Universal Magazine* (1783) and *Hibernian Magazine* (1783–4). An abridged French translation by Henri Rieu appeared in 1783, a German translation by C. F. Weisse in 1783–5, a Swedish translation by Sven Dan. Lundmark in 1795–7, and another German translation by W. H. Brömel in 1796. These and many other early editions are listed in Joseph Grau's annotated bibliography; see the Select Bibliography below.

Cecilia was reprinted in England throughout the nineteenth century. The first annotated edition was by Annie Raine Ellis in 1882. The 1904 reprint of this edition, based on one of the texts deriving from the second edition of 1783, was reissued by Virago, with a new introduction by Judy Simons, in 1986. The edition by R. Brimley Johnson (1893) is based on the first edition of 1782. An annotated edition by Virginia Prewitt, a University of Toronto doctoral dissertation (1978), incorporates variants from the second edition in a photocopy of the first.

SELECT BIBLIOGRAPHY

MODERN EDITIONS OF BURNEY'S WORKS

Camilla: or, A Picture of Youth, ed. Edward A. Bloom and Lillian D. Bloom (Oxford, 1972).

Cecilia: or, Memoirs of an Heiress, ed. Annie Raine Ellis, 2 vols. (London, 1882; reprinted with a new introduction by Judy Simons, London, 1986).

Evelina: or, The History of a Young Lady's Entrance into the World, ed. Edward A. Bloom with the assistance of Lillian D. Bloom (Oxford, 1968).

Evelina: or, The History of a Young Lady's Entrance into the World, ed. Frank D. Mackinnon (Oxford, 1938).

The Wanderer; or, Female Difficulties, ed. Margaret Anne Doody, Robert L. Mack, and Peter Sabor, with an Introduction by Margaret Anne Doody (Oxford, 1991)

A Busy Day, ed. Tara G. Wallace (New Brunswick, NJ, 1984).

Edwy and Elgiva, ed. Miriam J. Benkovitz (Hamden, Conn., 1957).

The Early Diary of Frances Burney, 1768–1778, ed. Annie Raine Ellis, 2 vols. (London, 1889; revised edn. 1907).

Diary and Letters of Madame d'Arblay, ed. Charlotte Barrett, 7 vols. (London, 1842–6).

The Journals and Letters of Fanny Burney (Madame d'Arblay), ed. Joyce Hemlow *et al.*, 12 vols. (Oxford, 1972–84).

Fanny Burney: Selected Letters and Journals, ed. Joyce Hemlow (Oxford, 1986).

The Early Journals and Letters of Fanny Burney, ed. Lars E. Troide *et al.* (Oxford, 1988–).

BIOGRAPHICAL AND CRITICAL STUDIES

Michael E. Adelstein, *Fanny Burney* (New York, 1968).

Lillian D. Bloom and Edward A. Bloom, 'Fanny Burney's Novels: the Retreat from Wonder', *Novel: A Forum on Fiction*, 12 (1979), 215–35.

Martha G. Brown, 'Fanny Burney's "Feminism": Gender or Genre', in *Fetter'd or Free: British Women Novelists, 1670–1815*, ed. Mary Anne Schofield and Cecilia Macheski (Athens, Ohio, 1986), pp. 29–39.

Gabrielle Buffet, *Fanny Burney. Sa vie et ses romans*, 2 vols. (Paris, 1962).

Grant D. Campbell, 'Fashionable Suicide: Conspicuous Consumption and the Collapse of Credit in Frances Burney's *Cecilia*', *Studies in Eighteenth-Century Culture*, 20 (1990), 131–45.

Terry Castle, 'Masquerade and Utopia I: Burney's *Cecilia*', in *Masquerade and Civilization: The Carnivalesque in Eighteenth-Century English Culture and Fiction* (London, 1986), pp. 253–89.

Stewart J. Cooke, 'How Much was Frances Burney paid for *Cecilia*?', *Notes and Queries*, 237 (1992), 484–6.

Edward W. Copeland, 'Money in the Novels of Fanny Burney', *Studies in the Novel*, 8 (1976), 24–37.

Rose-Marie Cutting, 'Defiant Women: The Growth of Feminism in Fanny Burney's Novels', *Studies in English Literature*, 17 (1977), 519–30.

D. D. Devlin, *The Novels and Journals of Fanny Burney* (London, 1987).

Marjorie W. Dobbin, 'The Novel, Women's Awareness, and Fanny Burney', *English Language Notes*, 17 (1985), 42–53.

Austin Dobson, *Fanny Burney* (London, 1903).

Margaret Anne Doody, 'George Eliot and the Eighteenth-Century Novel', *Nineteenth-Century Fiction*, 35 (1980), 260–91.

——, 'Fanny Burney', in *Dictionary of Literary Biography 39: British Novelists 1660–1800*, ed. Martin C. Battestin (New York, 1985), pp. 90–101.

——, *Frances Burney: The Life in the Works* (New Brunswick, N.J., 1988).

Julia L. Epstein, 'Fanny Burney's Epistolary Voices', *The Eighteenth Century: Theory and Interpretation*, 27 (1986), 162–79.

——, 'Writing the Unspeakable: Fanny Burney's Mastectomy and the Fictive Body', *Representations*, 16 (1986), 131–66.

——, *The Iron Pen: Frances Burney and the Politics of Women's Writing* (Madison, Wisconsin, 1989).

Jan Fergus, '*Cecilia*', in *Jane Austen and the Didactic Novel* (London, 1983), pp. 62–72.

William Godwin, review and parody of *Cecilia*, in *The Herald of Literature* (1784); reprinted in *Four Early Pamphlets*, ed. Burton R. Pollin (Gainesville, Florida, 1966), pp. 267–82.

Joseph A. Grau, *Fanny Burney: An Annotated Bibliography* (New York, 1981).

Emily Hahn, *A Degree of Prudery: A Biography of Fanny Burney* (New York, 1950).

Joyce Hemlow, 'Fanny Burney and the Courtesy Books', *PMLA*, 65 (1950), 732–61.

——, *The History of Fanny Burney* (Oxford, 1958).

Joyce Hemlow, 'Dr. Johnson and Fanny Burney—Some Additions to the Record', in *Johnsonian Studies*, ed. Magdi Wahba (Cairo, 1962), pp. 173–87.

Kathryn Kris, 'A 70-Year Follow-up of a Childhood Learning Disability: The Case of Fanny Burney', *Psychoanalytic Study of the Child*, 38 (1983), 637–52.

Choderlos de Laclos, review of *Cecilia, ou les Mémoires d'une héritière, Mercure de France*, 17 avril 1784, pp. 103–10; 24 avril, pp. 152–65; 15 mai, pp. 102–20.

Thomas Babington Macaulay, unsigned review of *Diary and Letters of Madame D'Arblay, Edinburgh Review*, 76 (1843), 523–70.

Antoinette A. Overman, *An Investigation into the Character of Fanny Burney* (New York, 1950).

Alvaro Ribeiro, 'The Publication Date of Fanny Burney's *Cecilia*', *Notes and Queries*, 225 (1980), 415–16.

Katharine M. Rogers, 'Fanny Burney: the Private Self and the Public Self', *International Journal of Women's Studies*, 7 (1984), 110–17.

——, 'Burney, Fanny', in *A Dictionary of British and American Women Writers 1660–1800*, ed. Janet Todd (London, 1984).

Judy Simons, *Fanny Burney* (London, 1987).

Kay Rogers, 'Deflation of Male Pretensions in Fanny Burney's *Cecilia*', *Women's Studies: An Interdisciplinary Journal* (15), 87–96.

Margaret M. Smith, 'Fanny Burney', in *English Literary Manuscripts, Volume III 1700–1800* (London, 1986), 83–92.

Patricia M. Spacks, 'Dynamics of Fear: Fanny Burney', in *Imagining a Self: Autobiography and Novel in Eighteenth-Century England* (Cambridge, Mass., 1976), pp. 158–92.

Kristina Straub, *Divided Fictions: Fanny Burney and Feminine Strategy* (Lexington, Kentucky, 1987).

——, 'Frances Burney and the Rise of the Woman Novelist', in *The Columbia History of the British Novel*, ed. John Richetti, John Bender, and Dierdre David (New York, 1994), 199–219.

Arthur B. Tourtellot, *Be Loved No More: the Life and Environment of Fanny Burney* (New York, 1938).

J. N. Waddell, 'Fanny Burney's Contribution to English Vocabulary', *Neuphilologische Mitteilungen*, 81 (1980), 260–3.

——, 'Additions to *OED* from the Writings of Fanny Burney', *Notes and Queries*, 225 (1980), 27–32.

Eugene White, *Fanny Burney, Novelist* (Hamden, Conn., 1960).

A CHRONOLOGY OF FRANCES BURNEY

1780   Visit to Bath with Thrales (Apr.–June); Gordon Riots reach Bath; FB and Thrales escape to Brighton (10 June).

1781   Very ill with 'vile and irksome fever' and depression (Jan.–Mar.); work on new novel retarded; death of Hester Lynch Thrale's husband Henry Thrale (4 Apr.).

1782   Best-loved sister Susanna marries Molesworth Phillips (10 Jan.); *Cecilia, or Memoirs of an Heiress*, sold for £250, published (12 July).

1783   Begins friendship with Mary Delany (Jan.); death of Samuel Crisp (April); troubled by Hester Lynch Thrale's confidences over her suitor Gabriel Piozzi. Second and third editions of *Cecilia* appear, and serialized abridgements in magazines; French translation (abridged), and first part of German translation (completed 1785).

1784   Review of *Cecilia* by Choderlos de Laclos (Apr.–May). Rupture of friendship with Hester Lynch Thrale over marriage to Piozzi (23 July); death of Johnson (13 Dec.).

1783–6 Apparent courtship of Richard Owen Cambridge begins and fades; unrequited love causes FB acute misery.

1786   Largely through Mary Delany, given royal invitation to court service; becomes Second Keeper of the Robes to Queen Charlotte (17 July). Reluctantly agrees to join booksellers in protest against piracy of *Cecilia* (Dec.).

1788–9 King George III's madness forces virtual incarceration upon royal household; FB begins blank-verse tragedy, *Edwy and Elgiva*.

1789–91 Writes three other blank-verse tragedies, never printed or produced; *Hubert de Vere*, *The Siege of Pevensey*, and *Elberta* (draft); health declines.

1791   Leaves service of Queen (7 July), receiving pension of £100 p.a.; tour of West Country with Anna Ord (Aug.–Sept.).

1793   Meets Alexandre d'Arblay, exiled Adjutant-General of the Marquis de Lafayette (Jan.); secret courtship; marriage in Protestant ceremony (28 July) followed by Catholic rite (30 July); pamphlet, *Brief Reflections relative to the Emigrant French Clergy* (19 Nov.), proceeds to charity.

*c.*1792–4   Work on 'Clarinda' novel, to be redesigned and recast as *Camilla*.

1794   Birth of son, Alexander (18 Dec.).

1795   *Edwy and Elgiva* produced at Drury Lane for one night (21 Mar.); 'Proposals for Printing a New Work by the Author of *Evelina* and *Cecilia*' printed in newspapers (July–Aug.).

1796   *Camilla, or, A Picture of Youth* published (?12 July), copyright sold for £1,000. Stepmother dies (20 Oct.).

1797   'Camilla Cottage' in Surrey built with proceeds of *Camilla*.

1798   Writes comedy *Love and Fashion*; Rishtons separate; incestuous elopement of FB's brother James with his half-sister Sarah Harriet (2 Sept.).

1799   Manager of Covent Garden offers £400 to produce *Love and Fashion* in Mar. 1800; continued worry over health of Susanna in Ireland, mistreated by husband.

1800   Susanna dies upon arrival in England; FB keeps this date (6 Jan.) as day of mourning for rest of her life; *Love and Fashion* withdrawn from production (2 Feb.).

1800–2   Dramatic comedies *A Busy Day* and *The Woman-Hater* (not produced).

1802   Heavily revised second edition of *Camilla* published (Feb.); FB and son follow General d'Arblay to France (Apr.).

1811   Diagnosed as having breast cancer; at home in Paris undergoes mastectomy without anaesthetic (30 Sept.).

1812   Returns to England with son.

1814   *The Wanderer, or Female Difficulties*, sold for £1,500 for first edition, published (28 Mar.); Dr Charles Burney dies (12 April); FB returns to France, leaving son at Cambridge.

1815   Moves to Belgium while d'Arblay fights in army opposing Napoleon; FB in Brussels during Battle of Waterloo, bandages the wounded (June); returns to England (Oct.) with wounded husband now Lieutenant-General, with title of *comte* conferred by Louis XVIII.

1817   Reconciliation with Hester Lynch Piozzi at Bath (17 Nov.); death of favourite brother, Charles (28 Dec.).

1818   Death of General d'Arblay (3 May) at home in Bath.

1819   Son Alexander ordained priest in Church of England (11 Apr.).

1821   Brother James appointed Rear-Admiral (July); death of James (Nov.).

1826   Introduced by the poet Samuel Rogers, Sir Walter Scott visits 'the celebrated authoress' at her home at 11 Bolton Street, Piccadilly, London (18 Nov.).

1832   Death of sister Esther (Feb.); *Memoirs of Doctor Burney* published (*c.*23 Nov.).

1837   Death of son Alexander, aged 43 (19 Jan.).

1838   Death of sister Charlotte (12 Sept.).

1840   Death of FB (Mme d'Arblay) in London, 6 Jan.; buried in Wolcot Churchyard, Bath, beside husband and son.

1842–6   Niece and literary executrix Charlotte Barrett publishes *Diary and Letters of Madame d'Arblay*, 7 volumes.

1889   *The Early Diary of Frances Burney 1768–1778*, ed. Annie Raine Ellis, published in 2 volumes.

1972–84   *The Journals and Letters of Fanny Burney (Madame d'Arblay) 1791–1840*, ed. Joyce Hemlow and others, published in 12 volumes.

1988–   *The Early Journals and Letters of Fanny Burney*, ed. Lars E. Troide and others.

CECILIA,

OR

MEMOIRS

OF AN

HEIRESS

BY

THE AUTHOR OF EVELINA

CECILIA,

OR

MEMOIRS

OF AN

HEIRESS

BY

THE AUTHOR OF EVELINA

ADVERTISEMENT

THE indulgence shewn by the Public to EVELINA, which, unpatronized, unaided, and unowned, past through Four Editions in one Year,* has encouraged its Author to risk this SECOND attempt. The animation of success is too universally acknowledged, to make the writer of the following sheets dread much censure of temerity; though the precariousness of any power to give pleasure, suppresses all vanity of confidence, and sends CECILIA into the world with scarce more hope, though far more encouragement, than attended her highly-honoured predecessor, EVELINA.

July, 1782.

VOLUME I

BOOK I

CHAPTER I

A Journey

"PEACE to the spirits of my honoured parents, respected be their remains, and immortalized their virtues! may time, while it moulders their frail relicks to dust, commit to tradition the record of their goodness; and Oh may their orphan-descendant be influenced through life by the remembrance of their purity, and be solaced in death, that by her it was unsullied!"

Such was the secret prayer with which the only survivor of the Beverley family quitted the abode of her youth, and residence of her forefathers; while tears of recollecting sorrow filled her eyes, and obstructed the last view of her native town which had excited them.

Cecilia, this fair traveller, had lately entered into the one-and-twentieth year of her age. Her ancestors had been rich farmers in the county of Suffolk, though her father, in whom a spirit of elegance had supplanted the rapacity of wealth, had spent his time as a private country gentleman, satisfied, without increasing his store, to live upon what he inherited from the labours of his predecessors. She had lost him in her early youth, and her mother had not long survived him. They had bequeathed to her 10,000*l.* and consigned her to the care of the Dean of ——, her uncle. With this gentleman, in whom, by various contingencies, the accumulated possessions of a rising and prosperous family were centred, she had passed the last four years of her life; and a few weeks only had yet elapsed since his death, which, by depriving her of her last relation, made her heiress to an estate of 3000*l.* per annum; with no other restriction than

that of annexing her name, if she married, to the disposal of
her hand and her riches.

But though thus largely indebted to fortune, to nature she
had yet greater obligations: her form was elegant, her heart
was liberal; her countenance announced the intelligence of
her mind, her complexion varied with every emotion of her
soul, and her eyes, the heralds of her speech, now beamed
with understanding and now glistened with sensibility.

For the short period of her minority, the management of
her fortune and the care of her person, had by the Dean been
entrusted* to three guardians, among whom her own choice
was to settle her residence: but her mind, saddened by
the loss of all her natural friends, coveted to regain its
serenity in the quietness of the country, and in the bosom of
an aged and maternal counsellor, whom she loved as her
mother, and to whom she had been known from her
childhood.

The Deanery, indeed, she was obliged to relinquish, a
long repining expectant being eager, by entering it, to
bequeath to another the anxiety and suspence he had
suffered himself; though probably without much impatience
to shorten their duration in favour of the next successor; but
the house of Mrs. Charlton, her benevolent friend, was open
for her reception, and the alleviating tenderness of her
conversation took from her all wish of changing it.

Here she had dwelt since the interment of her uncle; and
here, from the affectionate gratitude of her disposition, she
had perhaps been content to dwell till her own, had not her
guardians interfered to remove her.

Reluctantly she complied; she quitted her early
companions, the friend she most revered, and the spot which
contained the relicks of all she had lived to lament; and,
accompanied by one of her guardians, and attended by two
servants, she began her journey from Bury* to London.

Mr. Harrel, this gentleman, though in the prime of his
life, though gay, fashionable and splendid, had been
appointed by her uncle to be one of her trustees; a choice
which had for object the peculiar gratification of his niece,
whose most favourite young friend Mr. Harrel had married,

and in whose house he therefore knew she would most wish to live.

Whatever good-nature could dictate or politeness suggest to dispel her melancholy, Mr. Harrel failed not to urge; and Cecilia, in whose disposition sweetness was tempered with dignity, and gentleness with fortitude, suffered not his kind offices to seem ineffectual; she kissed her hand at the last glimpse a friendly hill afforded of her native town, and made an effort to forget the regret with which she lost sight of it. She revived her spirits by plans of future happiness, dwelt upon the delight with which she should meet her young friend, and, by accepting his consolation, amply rewarded his trouble.

Her serenity, however, had yet another, though milder trial to undergo, since another friend was yet to be met, and another farewell was yet to be taken.

At the distance of seven miles from Bury resided Mr. Monckton, the richest and most powerful man in that neighbourhood, at whose house Cecilia and her guardian were invited to breakfast in their journey.

Mr. Monckton, who was the younger son of a noble family, was a man of parts, information and sagacity; to great native strength of mind he added a penetrating knowledge of the world, and to faculties the most skilful of investigating the character of every other, a dissimulation the most profound in concealing his own. In the bloom of his youth, impatient for wealth and ambitious of power, he had tied himself to a rich dowager of quality, whose age, though sixty-seven, was but among the smaller species of her evil properties, her disposition being far more repulsive than her wrinkles. An inequality of years so considerable, had led him to expect that the fortune he had thus acquired, would speedily be released from the burthen with which it was at present incumbered; but his expectations proved as vain as they were mercenary, and his lady was not more the dupe of his protestations than he was himself of his own purposes. Ten years he had been married to her, yet her health was good, and her faculties were unimpaired; eagerly he had watched for her dissolution, yet his eagerness had injured no health but his own! So short-sighted is selfish cunning, that in aiming no further than at the gratification of the present moment, it obscures the evils of the future, while it impedes the perception of integrity and honour.

His ardour, however, to attain the blest period of returning liberty, deprived him neither of spirit nor inclination for intermediate enjoyment; he knew the world too well to incur it's censure by ill-treating the woman to whom he was indebted for the rank he held in it; he saw her, indeed, but seldom, yet he had the decency, alike in avoiding as in meeting her, to shew no abatement of civility and good breeding: but, having thus sacrificed to ambition all possibility of happiness in domestic life, he turned his thoughts to those other methods of procuring it, which he had so dearly purchased the power of essaying.

The resources of pleasure to the possessors of wealth are only to be cut off by the satiety of which they are productive: a satiety which the vigorous mind of Mr. Monckton had not yet suffered him to experience; his time, therefore, was either devoted to the expensive amusements of the metropolis, or spent in the country among the gayest of its diversions.

The little knowledge of fashionable manners and of the characters of the times of which Cecilia was yet mistress, she had gathered at the house of this gentleman, with whom the Dean her Uncle had been intimately connected: for as he preserved to the world the same appearance of decency he supported to his wife, he was every where well received, and being but partially known, was extremely respected: the world, with its wonted facility, repaying his circumspect attention to its laws, by silencing the voice of censure, guarding his character from impeachment, and his name from reproach.

Cecilia had been known to him half her life; she had been caressed in his house as a beautiful child, and her presence was now solicited there as an amiable acquaintance. Her visits, indeed, had by no means been frequent, as the ill-humour of Lady Margaret Monckton had rendered them painful to her; yet the opportunities they had afforded her of mixing with people of fashion, had served to prepare her for the new scenes in which she was soon to be a performer.

Mr. Monckton, in return, had always been a welcome guest at the Deanery; his conversation was to Cecilia a never-failing source of information, as his knowledge of life and manners enabled him to start those subjects of which she was most ignorant; and her mind, copious for the admission and intelligent for the arrangement of knowledge, received all new ideas with avidity.

Pleasure given in society, like money lent in usury, returns with interest to those who dispense it: and the discourse of Mr. Monckton conferred not a greater favour upon Cecilia than her attention to it repaid. And thus, the speaker and the hearer being mutually gratified, they had always met with complacency, and commonly parted with regret.

This reciprocation of pleasure had, however, produced different effects upon their minds; the ideas of Cecilia were enlarged, while the reflections of Mr. Monckton were embittered. He here saw an object who to all the advantages of that wealth he had so highly prized, added youth, beauty, and intelligence; though much her senior, he was by no means of an age to render his addressing her an impropriety, and the entertainment she received from his conversation, persuaded him that her good opinion might with ease be improved into a regard the most partial. He regretted the venal rapacity with which he had sacrificed himself to a woman he abhorred, and his wishes for her final decay became daily more fervent. He knew that the acquaintance of Cecilia was confined to a circle of which he was himself the principal ornament, that she had rejected all the proposals of marriage which had hitherto been made to her, and, as he had sedulously watched her from her earliest years, he had reason to believe that her heart had escaped any dangerous impression. This being her situation, he had long looked upon her as his future property; as such he had indulged his admiration, and as such he had already appropriated her estate, though he had not more vigilantly inspected into her sentiments, than he had guarded his own from a similar scrutiny.

The death of the Dean her Uncle* had, indeed, much alarmed him; he grieved at her leaving Suffolk, where he considered himself the first man, alike in parts and in consequence, and he dreaded her residing in London, where he foresaw that numerous rivals, equal to himself in talents and in riches, would speedily surround her; rivals, too, youthful and sanguine, not shackled by present ties, but at liberty to solicit her immediate acceptance. Beauty and independence, rarely found together, would attract a crowd of suitors at once brilliant and assiduous; and the house of Mr. Harrel was eminent for it's elegance and gaiety; but yet, undaunted by danger, and confiding in his own powers, he determined to pursue the project he had formed, not fearing by address and perseverance to ensure its success.

complacency, and continually parted with regret.

This reciprocation of pleasure had, however, produced different effects upon them: the ideas of Cecilia were enlarged, while the reflections of Mr. Monckton were embittered. He here saw Cecilia, who to all the advantages of that wealth he had so highly prized, added youth, beauty,

CHAPTER II

An Argument

MR. Monckton had, at this time, a party of company assembled at his house for the purpose of spending the Christmas holidays. He waited with anxiety the arrival of Cecilia, and flew to hand her from the chaise before Mr. Harrel could alight. He observed the melancholy of her countenance, and was much pleased to find that her London journey had so little power to charm her. He conducted her to the breakfast parlour, where Lady Margaret and his friends expected her.

of Cecilia was confined to a circle.

Lady Margaret received her with a coldness that bordered upon incivility; irascible by nature and jealous by situation, the appearance of beauty alarmed, and of chearfulness disgusted her. She regarded with watchful suspicion whoever was addressed by her husband, and having marked his frequent attendance at the Deanery, she had singled out Cecilia for the object of her peculiar antipathy; while Cecilia, perceiving her aversion though ignorant of its cause, took care to avoid all intercourse with her but what ceremony exacted, and pitied in secret the unfortunate lot of her friend.

The company now present consisted of one lady and several gentlemen.

Miss Bennet, the lady, was in every sense of the phrase, the humble companion* of Lady Margaret; she was low-born, meanly educated, and narrow-minded; a stranger alike to innate merit or acquired accomplishments, yet skilful in the art of flattery, and an adept in every species of low cunning. With no other view in life than the attainment of affluence without labour, she was not more the slave of the mistress of the house, than the tool of it's master; receiving indignity without murmur, and submitting to contempt as a thing of course.

Among the gentlemen, the most conspicuous, by means of his dress, was Mr. Aresby, a captain in the militia; a young man who having frequently heard the words red-coat and gallantry put together, imagined the conjunction not merely customary, but honourable, and therefore, without even pretending to think of the service of his country, he considered a cockade* as a badge of politeness, and wore it but to mark his devotion to the ladies, whom he held himself equipped to conquer, and bound to adore.

The next who by forwardness the most officious took care to be noticed, was Mr. Morrice, a young lawyer, who, though rising in his profession, owed his success neither to distinguished abilities, nor to skill-supplying industry, but to the art of uniting suppleness to others with confidence in himself. To a reverence of rank, talents, and fortune the most profound, he joined an assurance in his own merit, which no superiority could depress; and with a presumption which encouraged him to aim at all things, he blended a good-humour that no mortification could lessen. And while by the pliability of his disposition he avoided making enemies, by his readiness to oblige, he learned the surest way of making friends by becoming useful to them.

There were also some neighbouring squires; and there was one old gentleman, who, without seeming to notice any of the company, sat frowning in a corner.

But the principal figure in the circle was Mr. Belfield, a tall, thin young man, whose face was all animation, and whose eyes sparkled with intelligence. He had been intended by his father for trade, but his spirit, soaring above the occupation for which he was designed, from repining led him to resist, and from resisting, to rebel. He eloped from his friends, and contrived to enter the army. But, fond of the polite arts, and eager for the acquirement of knowledge, he found not this way of life much better adapted to his inclination than that from which he had escaped; he soon grew weary of it, was reconciled to his father, and entered at the Temple.* But here, too volatile for serious study, and too gay for laborious application, he made little progress: and the same quickness of parts and vigour of imagination which united with prudence, or accompanied by judgment, might have raised him to the head of his profession, being unhappily associated with fickleness and caprice, served only to impede his improvement, and obstruct his preferment. And now, with little business, and that little neglected, a small fortune, and that fortune daily becoming less, the admiration of the world, but that admiration ending simply in civility, he lived an unsettled and unprofitable life, generally caressed, and universally sought, yet careless of his interest and thoughtless of the future; devoting his time to company, his income to dissipation, and his heart to the Muses.

"I bring you," said Mr. Monckton, as he attended Cecilia into the room, "a subject of sorrow in a young lady who never gave disturbance to her friends but in quitting them."

"If sorrow," cried Mr. Belfield, darting upon her his piercing eyes, "wears in your part of the world a form such as this, who would wish to change it for a view of joy?"

"She's divinely handsome, indeed!" cried the captain, affecting an involuntary exclamation.

Meantime, Cecilia, who was placed next to the lady of the house, quietly began her breakfast; Mr. Morrice, the young lawyer, with the most easy freedom, seating himself at her side, while Mr. Monckton was elsewhere arranging the rest of his guests, in order to secure that place for himself.

Mr. Morrice, without ceremony, attacked his fair

neighbour; he talked of her journey, and the prospects of gaiety which it opened to her view; but by these finding her unmoved, he changed his theme, and expatiated upon the delights of the spot she was quitting. Studious to recommend himself to her notice, and indifferent by what means, one moment he flippantly extolled the entertainments of the town; and the next, rapturously described the charms of the country. A word, a look sufficed to mark her approbation or dissent, which he no sooner discovered, than he slided into her opinion, with as much facility and satisfaction as if it had originally been his own.

Mr. Monckton, suppressing his chagrin, waited some time in expectation that when this young man saw he was standing, he would yield to him his chair: but the remark was not made, and the resignation was not thought of. The captain, too, regarding the lady as his natural property for the morning, perceived with indignation by whom he was supplanted; while the company in general, saw with much surprize, the place they had severally forborne to occupy from respect to their host, thus familiarly seized upon by the man who, in the whole room, had the least claim, either from age or rank,* to consult nothing but his own inclination.

Mr. Monckton, however, when he found that delicacy and good manners had no weight with his guest, thought it most expedient to allow them none with himself; and therefore, disguising his displeasure under an appearance of facetiousness, he called out, "Come, Morrice, you that love Christmas sports, what say you to the game of move-all?"*

"I like it of all things!" answered Morrice, and starting from his chair, he skipped to another.

"So should I too," cried Mr. Monckton, instantly taking his place, "were I to remove from any seat but this."

Morrice, though he felt himself outwitted, was the first to laugh, and seemed as happy in the change as Mr. Monckton himself.

Mr. Monckton now, addressing himself to Cecilia, said, "We are going to lose you, and you seem concerned at leaving us; yet, in a very few months you will forget Bury, forget its inhabitants, and forget its environs."

"If you think so," answered Cecilia, "must I not thence
infer that Bury, its inhabitants, and its environs, will in a
very few months forget me?"

"Ay, ay, and so much the better!" said Lady Margaret,
muttering between her teeth, "so much the better!"

"I am sorry you think so, madam," cried Cecilia,
colouring at her ill-breeding.

"You will find," said Mr. Monckton, affecting the same
ignorance of her meaning that Cecilia really felt, "as you
mix with the world, you will find that Lady Margaret has
but expressed what by almost every body is thought: to
neglect old friends, and to court new acquaintance, though
perhaps not yet avowedly delivered as a precept from
parents to children, is nevertheless so universally recommended by example, that those who act differently, incur
general censure for affecting singularity."

"It is happy then, for me," answered Cecilia, "that
neither my actions nor myself will be sufficiently known to
attract public observation."

"You intend, then, madam," said Mr. Belfield, "in
defiance of these maxims of the world, to be guided by the
light of your own understanding."

"And such," returned Mr. Monckton, "at first setting
out in life, is the intention of every one. The closet reasoner
is always refined in his sentiments, and always confident in
his virtue; but when he mixes with the world, when he thinks
less and acts more, he soon finds the necessity of
accomodating himself to such customs as are already
received, and of pursuing quietly the track that is already
marked out."

"But not," exclaimed Mr. Belfield, "if he has the least
grain of spirit! the beaten track will be the last that a man
of parts will deign to tread,

> For common rules were ne'er design'd
> Directors of a noble mind."*

"A pernicious maxim! a most pernicious maxim!" cried
the old gentleman, who sat frowning in a corner of the
room.

"Deviations from common rules," said Mr. Monckton, without taking any notice of this interruption, "when they proceed from genius, are not merely pardonable, but admirable; and you, Belfield, have a peculiar right to plead their merits; but so little genius as there is in the world, you must surely grant that pleas of this sort are very rarely to be urged."

"And why rarely," cried Belfield, "but because your general rules, your appropriated customs, your settled forms, are but so many absurd arrangements to impede not merely the progress of genius, but the use of understanding? If man dared act for himself, if neither worldly views, contracted prejudices, eternal precepts, nor compulsive examples, swayed his better reason and impelled his conduct, how noble indeed would he be! *how infinite in faculties! in apprehension how like a God!*"†*

"All this," answered Mr. Monckton, "is but the doctrine of a lively imagination, that looks upon impossibilities simply as difficulties, and upon difficulties as mere invitations to victory. But experience teaches another lesson; experience shews that the opposition of an individual to a community is always dangerous in the operation, and seldom successful in the event;—never, indeed, without a concurrence strange as desirable, of fortunate circumstances with great abilities."

"And why is this," returned Belfield, "but because the attempt is so seldom made? The pitiful prevalence of general conformity extirpates genius, and murders originality; man is brought up, not as if he were "the noblest work of God,"* but as a mere ductile machine of human formation: he is early taught that he must neither consult his understanding, nor pursue his inclinations, lest, unhappily for his commerce with the world, his understanding should be averse to fools, and provoke him to despise them; and his inclinations to the tyranny of perpetual restraint, and give him courage to abjure it."

"I am ready enough to allow," answered Mr. Monckton, "that an excentric genius, such, for example, as yours, may

†Hamlet.

murmur at the tediousnèss of complying with the customs of
the world, and wish, unconfined, and at large, to range
through life without any settled plan or prudential
restriction; but would you, therefore, grant the same licence
to every one? would you wish to see the world peopled with
defiers of order, and contemners of established forms? and
not merely excuse the irregularities resulting from
uncommon parts, but encourage those, also, to lead, who
without blundering cannot even follow?''

"I would have *all* men," replied Belfield, "whether
philosophers or ideots, act for themselves. Every one would
then appear what he is; enterprize would be encouraged,
and imitation abolished; genius would feel its superiority,
and folly its insignificance; and then, and then only, should
we cease to be surfeited with that eternal sameness of
manner and appearance which at present runs through all
ranks of men.''

"Petrifying dull work this, *mon ami!*" said the captain, in
a whisper to Morrice, "*de grace*, start some new game."

"With all my heart," answered he; and then, suddenly
jumping up, exclaimed, "A hare! a hare!''

"Where?—where?—which way?'' and all the gentlemen
arose, and ran to different windows, except the master of the
house, the object of whose pursuit was already near him.

Morrice, with much pretended earnestness, flew from
window to window, to trace footsteps upon the turf which he
knew had not printed it: yet, never inattentive to his own
interest, when he perceived in the midst of the combustion
he had raised, that Lady Margaret was incensed at the noise
it produced, he artfully gave over his search, and seating
himself in a chair next to her, eagerly offered to assist her
with cakes, chocolate, or whatever the table afforded.

He had, however, effectually broken up the conversation;
and breakfast being over, Mr. Harrel ordered his chaise,
and Cecilia arose to take leave.

And now not without some difficulty could Mr. Monckton
disguise the uneasy fears which her departure occasioned
him. Taking her hand, "I suppose," he said, "you will not
permit an old friend to visit you in town, lest the sight of him

should prove a disagreeable memorial of the time you will soon regret having wasted in the country?"

"Why will you say this, Mr. Monckton?" cried Cecilia; "I am sure you cannot think it."

"These profound studiers of mankind, madam," said Belfield, "are mighty sorry champions for constancy or friendship. They wage war with all expectations but of depravity, and grant no quarter even to the purest designs, where they think there will be any temptation to deviate from them."

"Temptation," said Mr. Monckton, "is very easy of resistance in theory; but if you reflect upon the great change of situation Miss Beverley will experience, upon the new scenes she will see, the new acquaintance she must make, and the new connections she may form, you will not wonder at the anxiety of a friend for her welfare."

"But I presume," cried Belfield, with a laugh, "Miss Beverley does not mean to convey her person to town, and leave her understanding locked up, with other natural curiosities, in the country? Why, therefore, may not the same discernment regulate her adoption of new acquaintance, and choice of new connections, that guided her selection of old ones? Do you suppose that because she is to take leave of you, she is to take leave of herself?"

"Where fortune smiles upon youth and beauty," answered Mr. Monckton, "do you think it nothing that their fair possessor should make a sudden transition of situation from the quietness of a retired life in the country, to the gaiety of a splendid town residence?"

"Where fortune *frowns* upon youth and beauty," returned Belfield, "they may not irrationally excite commiseration; but where nature and chance unite their forces to bless the same object, what room there may be for alarm or lamentation I confess I cannot divine."

"What!" cried Mr. Monckton, with some emotion, "are there not sharpers, fortune-hunters, sycophants, wretches of all sorts and denominations, who watch the approach of the rich and unwary, feed upon their inexperience, and prey upon their property?"

"Come, come," cried Mr. Harrel, "it is time I should hasten my fair ward away, if this is your method of describing the place she is going to live in."

"Is it possible," cried the Captain, advancing to Cecilia, "that this lady has never yet tried the town?" and then, lowering his voice, and smiling languishingly in her face, he added "Can any thing so divinely handsome have been immured in the country? Ah! *quelle honte!* do you make it a principle to be so cruel?"

Cecilia, thinking such a compliment merited not any other notice than a slight bow, turned to Lady Margaret, and said "Should your ladyship be in town this winter, may I expect the honour of hearing where I may wait upon you?"

"I don't know whether I shall go or not;" answered the old lady, with her usual ungraciousness.

Cecilia would now have hastened away, but Mr. Monckton, stopping her, again expressed* his fears of the consequences of her journey; "Be upon your guard," he cried, "with all new acquaintance; judge nobody from appearances; form no friendship rashly; take time to look about you, and remember you can make no alteration in your way of life, without greater probability of faring worse, than chance of faring better. Keep therefore as you are, and the more you see of others, the more you will rejoice that you neither resemble nor are connected with them."

"This from you, Mr. Monckton!" cried Belfield, "what is become of your conformity system? I thought all the world was to be alike, or only so much the worse for any variation?"

"I spoke," said Mr. Monckton, "of the world in general, not of this lady in particular; and who that knows, who that sees her, would not wish it were possible she might continue in every respect exactly and unalterably what she is at present?"

"I find," said Cecilia, "you are determined that flattery at least, should I meet with it, shall owe no pernicious effects to its novelty."

"Well, Miss Beverley," cried Mr. Harrel, "will you now venture to accompany me to town? Or has Mr. Monckton frightened you from proceeding any farther?"

"If," replied Cecilia, "I felt no more sorrow in quitting my friends, than I feel terror in venturing to London, with how light a heart should I make the journey!"

"Brava!" cried Belfield, "I am happy to find the discourse of Mr. Monckton has not intimidated you, nor prevailed upon you to deplore your condition in having the accumulated misery of being young, fair and affluent."

"Alas! poor thing!" exclaimed the old gentleman who sat in the corner, fixing his eyes upon Cecilia with an expression of mingled grief and pity.

Cecilia started, but no one else paid him any attention.

The usual ceremonies of leave-taking now followed, and the Captain, with most obsequious reverence, advanced to conduct Cecilia to the carriage; but in the midst of the dumb eloquence of his bows and smiles,* Mr. Morrice, affecting not to perceive his design, skipped gaily between them, and, without any previous formality, seized the hand of Cecilia himself; failing not, however, to temper the freedom of his action by a look of respect the most profound.

The Captain shrugged and retired. But Mr. Monckton, enraged at his assurance, and determined it should nothing avail him, exclaimed "Why how now, Morrice, do you take away the privilege of my house?"

"True, true," answered Morrice, "you members of parliament have an undoubted right to be tenacious of your privileges."* Then, bowing with a look of veneration to Cecilia, he resigned her hand with an air of as much happiness as he had taken it.

Mr. Monckton, in leading her to the chaise, again begged permission to wait upon her in town: Mr. Harrel took the hint, and entreated him to consider his house as his own; and Cecilia, gratefully thanking him for his solicitude in her welfare, added "And I hope, sir, you will honour me with your counsel and admonitions with respect to my future conduct, whenever you have the goodness to let me see you."

This was precisely his wish. He begged, in return, that she would treat him with confidence, and then suffered the chaise to drive off.

CHAPTER III

An Arrival

AS soon as they lost sight of the house, Cecilia expressed her surprise at the behaviour of the old gentleman who sat in the corner, whose general silence, seclusion from the company, and absence of mind, had strongly excited her curiosity.

Mr. Harrel could give her very little satisfaction: he told her that he had twice or thrice met him in public places, where every body remarked the singularity of his manners and appearance, but that he had never discoursed with any one to whom he seemed known; and that he was as much surprised as herself in seeing so strange a character at the house of Mr. Monckton.

The conversation then turned upon the family they had just quitted, and Cecilia warmly declared the good opinion she had of Mr. Monckton, the obligations she owed to him for the interest which, from her childhood, he had always taken in her affairs; and her hopes of reaping much instruction from the friendship of a man who had so extensive a knowledge of the world.

Mr. Harrel professed himself well satisfied that she should have such a consellor; for though but little acquainted with him, he knew he was a man of fortune and fashion, and well esteemed in the world. They mutually compassionated his unhappy situation in domestic life, and Cecilia innocently expressed her concern at the dislike Lady Margaret seemed to have taken to her; a dislike which Mr. Harrel naturally enough* imputed to her youth and beauty, yet without suspecting any cause more cogent than a general jealousy of attractions of which she had herself so long outlived the possession.

As their journey drew near to its conclusion, all the uneasy and disagreeable sensations which in the bosom of Cecilia had accompanied its commencement, gave way to the expectation of quick approaching happiness in again meeting her favourite young friend.

Mrs. Harrel had in childhood been her playmate, and in youth her school-fellow; a similarity of disposition with respect to sweetness of temper, had early rendered them dear to each other, though the resemblance extended no farther, Mrs. Harrel having no pretensions to the wit or understanding of her friend; but she was amiable and obliging, and therefore sufficiently deserving affection, though neither blazing with attractions which laid claim to admiration, nor endowed with those superior qualities which mingle respect in the love they inspire.

From the time of her marriage, which was near three years, she had entirely quitted Suffolk, and had had no intercourse with Cecilia but by letter. She was now just returned from Violet Bank,* the name given by Mr. Harrel to a villa about twelve miles from London, where with a large party of company she had spent the Christmas holidays.

Their meeting was tender and affectionate; the sensibility of Cecilia's heart flowed from her eyes, and the gladness of Mrs. Harrel's dimpled her cheeks.

As soon as their mutual salutations, expressions of kindness, and general enquiries had been made, Mrs. Harrel begged to lead her to the drawing-room, "where," she added, "you will see some of my friends, who are impatient to be presented to you."

"I could have wished," said Cecilia, "after so long an absence, to have passed this first evening alone with you."

"They are all people who particularly desired to see you," she answered, "and I had them by way of entertaining you, as I was afraid you would be out of spirits at leaving Bury."

Cecilia, finding the kindness of her intentions, forbore any further expostulation, and quietly followed her to the drawing-room. But as the door was opened, she was struck with amazement upon finding that the apartment, which was spacious, lighted with brilliancy, and decorated with magnificence, was more than half filled with company, every one of which was dressed with gaiety and profusion.

Cecilia, who from the word friends, expected to have seen a small and private party, selected for the purpose of social converse, started involuntarily at the sight before her, and had hardly courage to proceed.

Mrs. Harrel, however, took her hand and introduced her to the whole company, who were all severally named to her; a ceremonial which though not merely agreeable but even necessary to those who live in the gay world, in order to obviate distressing mistakes, or unfortunate implications in discourse, would by Cecilia have been·willingly dispensed with, since to her their names were as new as their persons, and since knowing nothing of their histories, parties or connections, she could to nothing allude: it therefore served but to heighten her colour and increase her embarrassment.

A native dignity of mind, however, which had early taught her to distinguish modesty from bashfulness, enabled her in a short time to conquer her surprise, and recover her composure. She entreated Mrs. Harrel to apologize for her appearance, and being seated between two young ladies, endeavoured to seem reconciled to it herself.

Nor was this very difficult; for while her dress, which she had not changed since her journey, joined to the novelty of her face, attracted general observation, the report of her fortune, which had preceded her entrance, secured to her general respect. She soon found, too, that a company was not necessarily formidable because full dressed, that familiarity could be united with magnificence, and that though to her, every one seemed attired to walk in a procession, or to grace a drawing-room, no formality was assumed, and no solemnity was affected: every one was without restraint, even rank obtained but little distinction; ease was the general plan, and entertainment the general pursuit.

Cecilia, though new to London, which city the ill health of her uncle had hitherto prevented her seeing, was yet no stranger to company; she had passed her time in retirement, but not in obscurity, since for some years past she had presided at the table of the Dean, who was visited by the first people of the county in which he lived: and notwithstanding his parties, which were frequent, though small, and elegant, though private, had not prepared her for the splendour or the diversity of a London assembly, they yet, by initiating her in the practical rules of good breeding, had taught her to subdue the timid fears of total inexperience, and to repress the bashful feelings of shame-faced awkwardness; fears and feelings which rather call for compassion than admiration, and which, except in extreme youth, serve but to degrade the modesty they indicate.

She regarded, therefore, the two young ladies between whom she was seated, rather with a wish of addressing, than a shyness of being attacked by them; but the elder, Miss Larolles, was earnestly engaged in discourse with a gentleman, and the younger, Miss Leeson, totally discouraged her, by the invariable silence and gravity, with which from time to time she met her eyes.

Uninterrupted, therefore, except by occasional speeches from Mr. and Mrs. Harrel, she spent the first part of the evening merely in surveying the company.

Nor was the company dilatory in returning her notice, since from the time of her entrance into the room, she had been the object of general regard.

The ladies took an exact inventory of her dress, and internally settled how differently they would have been attired if blest with equal affluence.

The men disputed among themselves whether or not she was painted; and one of them offering boldly that she *rouged well*,* a debate ensued, which ended in a bet, and the decision was mutually agreed to depend upon the colour of her cheeks by the beginning of April, when, if unfaded by bad hours and continual dissipation, they wore the same bright bloom with which they were now glowing, her champion acknowledged that his wager would be lost.

In about half an hour the gentleman with whom Miss Larolles had been talking, left the room, and then that young lady, turning suddenly to Cecilia, exclaimed "How odd Mr. Meadows is! Do you know he says he shan't be well enough to go to Lady Nyland's assembly! How ridiculous! as if that could hurt him."

Cecilia, surprised at an attack so little ceremonious, lent her a civil, but silent attention.

"You shall be there, shan't you?" she added.

"No, ma'am, I have not the honour of being at all known to her ladyship."

"O there's nothing in that," returned she, "for Mrs. Harrel can acquaint her you are here, and then, you know, she'll send you a ticket, and then you can go."

"A ticket?" repeated Cecilia, "does Lady Nyland only admit her company with tickets?"

"O lord," cried Miss Larolles, laughing immoderately, "don't you know what I mean? Why a ticket is only a visiting card, with a name upon it; but we all call them tickets now."

Cecilia thanked her for the information, and then Miss Larolles enquired how many miles she had travelled since morning?

"Seventy-three," answered Cecilia, "which I hope will plead my apology for being so little dressed."

"O, you're vastly well," returned the other, "and for my part, I never think about dress. But only conceive what happened to me last year! Do you know I came to town the twentieth of March! was not that horrid provoking?"

"Perhaps so," said Cecilia, "but I am sure I cannot tell why."

"Not tell why?" repeated Miss Larolles, "why don't you know it was the very night of the grand private masquerade at Lord Dariens? I would not have missed it for the whole universe. I never travelled in such an agony in my life: we did not get to town till monstrous late, and then do you know I had neither a ticket nor a habit! Only conceive what a distress! well, I sent to every creature I knew for a ticket, but they all said there was not one to be had; so I was just like a mad creature——but about ten or eleven o'clock, a young lady of my particular acquaintance, by the greatest good luck in the world happened to be taken suddenly ill; so she sent me her ticket,—was not that delightful?"

"For *her*, extremely!" said Cecilia, laughing.

"Well," she continued, "then I was almost out of my wits

with joy; and I went about, and got one of the sweetest dresses you ever saw. If you'll call upon me some morning, I'll shew it you.''

Cecilia, not prepared for an invitation so abrupt, bowed without speaking, and Miss Larolles, too happy in talking herself to be offended at the silence of another, continued her narration.

''Well, but now comes the vilest part of the business; do you know, when every thing else was ready, I could not get my hair-dresser! I sent all over the town,—he was no where to be found; I thought I should have died with vexation; I assure you I cried so that if I had not gone in a mask, I should have been ashamed to be seen. And so, after all this monstrous fatigue, I was forced to have my hair dressed by my own maid, quite in a common way; was not it cruelly mortifying?''

''Why yes,'' answered Cecilia, ''I should think it was almost sufficient to make you regret the illness of the young lady who sent you her ticket.''

They were now interrupted by Mrs. Harrel, who advanced to them followed by a young man of a serious aspect and modest demeanour, and said, ''I am happy to see you both so well engaged; but my brother has been reproaching me with presenting every body to Miss Beverley but himself.''

''I cannot hope,'' said Mr. Arnott, ''that I have any place in the recollection of Miss Beverley, but long as I have been absent from Suffolk, and unfortunate as I was in not seeing her during my last visit there, I am yet sure, even at this distance of time, grown and formed as she is, I should instantly have known her.''

''Amazing!'' cried an elderly gentleman, in a tone of irony, who was standing near them, ''for the face is a very common one!''

''I remember well,'' said Cecilia, ''that when you left Suffolk I thought I had lost my best friend.''

''Is that possible?'' cried Mr. Arnott, with a look of much delight.

''Yes, indeed, and not without reason, for in all disputes

you were my advocate; in all plays, my companion; and in all difficulties, my assistant."

"Madam," cried the same gentleman, "if you liked him because he was your advocate, companion, and assistant, pray like me too, for I am ready to become all three at once."

"You are very good," said Cecilia, laughing, "but at present I find no want of any defender."

"That's pity," he returned, "for Mr. Arnott seems to me very willing to act the same parts over again with you."

"But for that purpose he must return to the Days of his childhood."

"Ah, would to heaven it were possible!" cried Mr. Arnott, "for they were the happiest of my life."

"After such a confession," said his companion, "surely you will let him attempt to renew them? 'tis but taking a walk backwards, and though it is very early in life for Mr. Arnott to sigh for that retrograde motion, which, in the regular course of things, we shall all in our turns desire,* yet with such a motive as recovering Miss Beverley for a playfellow, who can wonder that he anticipates in youth the hopeless wishes of age?"

Here Miss Larolles, who was one of that numerous tribe of young ladies to whom all conversation is irksome in which they are not themselves engaged, quitted her place, of which Mr. Gosport, Cecilia's new acquaintance, immediately took possession.

"Is it utterly impossible," continued this gentleman, "that I should assist in procuring Mr. Arnott such a renovation? Is there no subaltern part I can perform to facilitate the project? for I will either *hide* or *seek* with any boy in the Parish; and for a *Q in the corner*,* there is none more celebrated."

"I have no doubt, Sir," answered Cecilia, "of your accomplishments; and I should be not a little entertained with the surprize of the company if you could persuade yourself to display them."

"And what," cried he, "could the company do half so well as to arise also, and join in the sport? it would but interrupt some tale of scandal, or some description of a *toûpée*.* Active wit, however despicable when compared with intellectual, is yet surely better than the insignificant click-clack of modish conversation," casting his eyes towards Miss Larolles, "or even the pensive dullness of affected silence," changing their direction towards Miss Leeson.

Cecilia, though surprized at an attack upon the society her friend had selected, by one who was admitted to make a part of it, felt its justice too strongly to be offended at its severity.

"I have often wished," he continued, "that when large parties are collected, as here, without any possible reason why they might not as well be separated, something could be proposed in which each person might innocently take a share: for surely after the first half hour, they can find little new to observe in the dress of their neighbours, or to display in their own; and with whatever seeming gaiety they may contrive to fill up the middle and end of the evening, by wire-drawing* the comments afforded by the beginning, they are yet so miserably fatigued, that if they have not four or five places to run to every night, they suffer nearly as much from weariness of their friends in company, as they would do from weariness of themselves in solitude."

Here, by the general breaking up of the party, the conversation was interrupted, and Mr. Gosport was obliged to make his exit; not much to the regret of Cecilia, who was impatient to be alone with Mrs. Harrel.

The rest of the evening, therefore, was spent much more to her satisfaction; it was devoted to friendship, to mutual enquiries, to kind congratulations, and endearing recollections; and though it was late when she retired, she retired with reluctance.

CHAPTER IV

A Sketch of High Life

EAGER to renew a conversation which had afforded her so much pleasure, Cecilia, neither sensible of fatigue from her change of hours nor her journey, arose with the light, and as soon as she was dressed, hastened to the breakfast apartment.

She had not, however, been more impatient to enter than she soon became to quit it; for though not much surprized to find herself there before her friend, her ardour for waiting her arrival was somewhat chilled, upon finding the fire but just lighted, the room cold, and the servants still employed in putting it in order.

At 10 o'clock she made another attempt: the room was then better prepared for her reception, but still it was empty. Again she was retiring, when the appearance of Mr. Arnott stopt her.

He expressed his surprize at her early rising, in a manner that marked the pleasure it gave to him; and then, returning to the conversation of the preceding evening, he expatiated with warmth and feeling upon the happiness of his boyish days, remembered every circumstance belonging to the plays in which they had formerly been companions, and dwelt upon every incident with a minuteness of delight that shewed his unwillingness ever to have done with the subject.

This discourse detained her till they were joined by Mrs. Harrel, and then another, more gay and more general succeeded to it.

During their breakfast, Miss Larolles was announced as a visitor to Cecilia, to whom she immediately advanced with the intimacy of an old acquaintance, taking her hand, and assuring her she could no longer defer the honour of waiting upon her.

Cecilia, much amazed at this warmth of civility from one to whom she was almost a stranger, received her compliment rather coldly; but Miss Larolles, without consulting her looks, or attending to her manner, proceeded to express the earnest desire she had long had to be known to her; to hope they should meet very often; to declare nothing could make her so happy; and to beg leave to recommend to her notice her own milliner.

"I assure you," she continued, "she has all Paris in her

disposal; the sweetest caps!* the most beautiful trimmings! and her ribbons are quite divine! It is the most dangerous thing you can conceive to go near her; I never trust myself in her room but I am sure to be ruined. If you please, I'll take you to her this morning.''

''If her acquaintance is so ruinous,'' said Cecilia, ''I think I had better avoid it.''

''O impossible! there's no such thing as living without her. To be sure she's shockingly dear, that I must own; but then who can wonder? She makes such sweet things, 'tis impossible to pay her too much for them.''

Mrs. Harrel now joining in the recommendation, the party was agreed upon, and accompanied by Mr. Arnott, the ladies proceeded to the house of the milliner.

Here the raptures of Miss Larolles were again excited: she viewed the finery displayed with delight inexpressible, enquired who were the intended possessors, heard their names with envy, and sighed with all the bitterness of mortification that she was unable to order home almost every thing she looked at.

Having finished their business here, they proceeded to various other dress manufacturers, in whose praises Miss Larolles was almost equally eloquent, and to appropriate whose goods she was almost equally earnest: and then, after attending this loquacious young lady to her father's house, Mrs. Harrel and Cecilia returned to their own.

Cecilia rejoiced at the separation, and congratulated herself that the rest of the day might be spent alone with her friend.

''Why no,'' said Mrs. Harrel, ''not absolutely alone, for I expect some company at night.''

''Company again to-night?''

''Nay, don't be frightened, for it will be a very small party; not more than fifteen or twenty in all.''

''Is that so small a party?'' said Cecilia, smiling; ''and how short a time since would you, as well as I, have reckoned it a large one!''

''O, you mean when I lived in the country,'' returned Mrs. Harrel; ''but what in the world could I know of parties or company then?''

"Not much, indeed," said Cecilia, "as my present ignorance shews."

They then parted to dress for dinner.

The company of this evening were again all strangers to Cecilia, except Miss Leeson, who was seated next to her, and whose frigid looks again compelled her to observe the same silence she so resolutely practised herself. Yet not the less was her internal surprise that a lady who seemed determined neither to give nor receive any entertainment, should repeatedly chuse to shew herself in a company with no part of which she associated.

Mr. Arnott, who contrived to occupy the seat on her other side, suffered not the silence with which her fair neighbour had infected her to spread any further: he talked, indeed, upon no new subject; and upon the old one, of their former sports and amusements, he had already exhausted all that was worth being mentioned; but not yet had he exhausted the pleasure he received from the theme; it seemed always fresh and always enchanting to him; it employed his thoughts, regaled his imagination, and enlivened his discourse. Cecilia in vain tried to change it for another; he quitted it only by compulsion, and returned to it with redoubled eagerness.

When the company was retired, and Mr. Arnott only remained with the ladies, Cecilia, with no little surprise, enquired for Mr. Harrel, observing that she had not seen him the whole day.

"Oh," cried his lady, "don't think of wondering at that, for it happens continually. He dines at home, indeed, in general, but otherwise I should see nothing of him at all."

"Indeed? why how does he fill up his time?"

"That I am sure I cannot tell, for he never consults me about it; but I suppose much in the same way that other people do."

"Ah Priscilla!" cried Cecilia, with some earnestness, "how little did I ever expect to see you so much a fine lady!"

"A fine lady?" repeated Mrs. Harrel, "why what is it I do? don't I live exactly like every body else that mixes at all with the world?"

"You, Miss Beverley," said Mr. Arnott in a low voice, "will I hope give to the world an example, not take one from it."

Soon after, they separated for the night.

The next morning, Cecilia took care to fill up her time more advantageously, than in wandering about the house in search of a companion she now expected not to find: she got together her books, arranged them to her fancy, and secured to herself for the future occupation of her leisure hours, the exhaustless fund of entertainment which reading, that richest, highest, and noblest source of intellectual enjoyment, perpetually affords.

While they were yet at breakfast, they were again visited by Miss Larolles. "I am come," cried she, eagerly, "to run away with you both to my Lord Belgrade's sale. All the world will be there; and we shall go in with tickets, and you have no notion how it will be crowded."

"What is to be sold there?" said Cecilia.

"O every thing you can conceive; house, stables, china, laces, horses, caps, every thing in the world."

"And do you intend to buy any thing?"

"Lord, no; but one likes to see the people's things."

Cecilia then begged they would excuse her attendance.

"O by no means," cried Miss Larolles, "you must go, I assure you; there'll be such a monstrous crowd as you never saw in your life. I dare say we shall be half squeezed to death."

"That," said Cecilia, "is an inducement which you must not expect will have much weight with a poor rustic just out of the country: it must require all the polish of a long residence in the metropolis to make it attractive."

"O but do go, for I assure you it will be the best sale we shall have this season. I can't imagine, Mrs. Harrel, what poor Lady Belgrade will do with herself; I hear the creditors have seized every thing; I really believe creditors are the cruelest set of people in the world! they have taken those beautiful buckles out of her shoes! Poor soul! I declare it will make my heart ache to see them put up. Its quite shocking, upon my word. I wonder who'll buy them. I assure you they were the prettiest fancied I ever saw. But come, if we don't go directly, there will be no getting in.''

Cecilia again desired to be excused accompanying them, adding that she wished to spend the day at home.

"At home, my dear?" cried Mrs. Harrel; "why we have been engaged to Mrs. Mears this month, and she begged me to prevail with you to be of the party. I expect she'll call, or send you a ticket, every moment."

"How unlucky for me," said Cecilia, "that you should happen to have so many engagements just at this time! I hope, at least, there will not be any for to-morrow."

"O yes; to-morrow we go to Mrs. Elton's."

"Again to-morrow? and how long is this to last?"

"O heaven knows; I'll shew you my catalogue."

She then produced a book which contained a list of engagements for more than three weeks. "And as these," she said, "are struck off, new ones are made; and so it is we go on till after the birth-day.''*

When this list had been examined and commented upon by Miss Larolles, and viewed and wondered at by Cecilia, it was restored to its place, and the two ladies went together to the auction, permiting Cecilia, at her repeated request, to return to her own apartment.

She returned, however, neither satisfied with the behaviour of her friend, nor pleased with her own situation: the sobriety of her education, as it had early instilled into her mind the pure dictates of religion, and strict principles of honour, had also taught her to regard continual dissipation as an introduction to vice, and unbounded extravagance as the harbinger of injustice. Long accustomed to see Mrs. Harrel in the same retirement in which she had hitherto lived herself, when books were their first amusement, and the society of each other was their chief happiness, the change she now perceived in her mind and manners equally concerned and surprised her. She found her insensible to friendship, indifferent to her husband, and negligent of all social felicity. Dress, company, parties of pleasure, and public places, seemed not merely to occupy all her time; but to gratify all her wishes. Cecilia, in whose heart glowed the warmest affections and most generous virtue, was cruelly depressed and mortified by this disappointment; yet she had the good sense to determine against upbraiding her, well aware that if reproach has any power over indifference, it is only that of changing it into aversion.

Mrs. Harrel, in truth, was innocent of heart, though dissipated in life; married very young, she had made an immediate transition from living in a private family and a country town, to becoming mistress of one of the most elegant houses in Portman-square, at the head* of a splendid fortune, and wife to a man whose own pursuits soon shewed her the little value he himself set upon domestic happiness. Immersed in the fashionable round of company and diversions, her understanding naturally weak, was easily dazzled by the brilliancy of her situation; greedily, therefore, sucking in air impregnated with luxury and extravagance, she had soon no pleasure but to vie with some rival in elegance, and no ambition but to exceed some superior in expence.

The Dean of —— in naming Mr. Harrel for one of the guardians of his neice, had no other view than that of indulging her wishes by allowing her to reside in the house of her friend: he had little personal knowledge of him, but was satisfied with the nomination, because acquainted with his family, fortune, and connections, all which persuaded him to believe without further enquiry, that it was more peculiarly proper for his neice than any other he could make.

In his choice of the other two trustees he had been more prudent; the first of these, the honourable Mr. Delvile, was a man of high birth and character; the second, Mr. Briggs, had spent his whole life in business, in which he had already amassed an immense fortune, and had still no greater pleasure than that of encreasing it. From the high honour,* therefore, of Mr. Delvile, he expected the most scrupulous watchfulness that his neice should in nothing be injured, and from the experience of Mr. Briggs in money matters, and his diligence in transacting business, he hoped for the most vigilant observance that her fortune, while under his care, should be turned to the best account. And thus, as far as he was able, he had equally consulted her pleasure, her security, and her pecuniary advantage.

Mrs. Harrel returned home only in time to dress for the rest of the day.

When Cecilia was summoned to dinner, she found, besides her host and hostess and Mr. Arnott, a gentleman she had not before seen, but who as soon as she entered the parlour, Mr. Harrel presented to her, saying at the same time he was one of the most intimate of his friends.

This gentleman, Sir Robert Floyer, was about thirty years of age; his face was neither remarkable for its beauty nor its ugliness, but sufficiently distinguished by its expression of invincible assurance; his person, too, though neither striking for its grace nor its deformity, attracted notice from the insolence of his deportment. His manners, haughty and supercilious, marked the high opinion he cherished of his own importance; and his air and address, at once bold and negligent, announced his happy perfection in the character at which he aimed, that of an accomplished man of the town.

The moment Cecilia appeared, she became the object of his attention, though neither with the look of admiration due to her beauty, nor yet with that of curiosity excited by her novelty, but with the scrutinizing observation of a man on the point of making a bargain, who views with fault-seeking eyes the property he means to cheapen.*

Cecilia, wholly unused to an examination so little ceremonious, shrunk abashed from his regards: but his conversation was not less displeasing to her than his looks; his principal subjects, which were horse-racing, losses at play, and disputes at gaming-tables, could afford her but little amusement, because she could not understand them; and the episodes with which they were occasionally interspersed, consisting chiefly of comparative strictures upon celebrated beauties, hints of impending bankruptcies, and witticisms upon recent divorces,* were yet more disagreeable to her, because more intelligible. Wearied therefore, with uninteresting anecdotes, and offended with injudicious subjects of pleasantry, she waited with impatience for the moment of retiring; but Mrs. Harrel, less eager, because better entertained, was in no haste to remove, and therefore she was compelled to remain quiet, till they were both obliged to arise, in order to fulfil their engagement with Mrs. Mears.

As they went together to the house of that lady, in Mrs. Harrel's vis-à-vis,* Cecilia, not doubting but their opinions concerning the Baronet would accord, instantly and openly declared her disapprobation of every thing he had uttered; but Mrs. Harrel, far from confirming her expectations, only said, "I am sorry you don't like him, for he is almost always with us."

"Do you like him, then, yourself?"

"Extremely; he is very entertaining and clever, and knows the world."

"How judiciously do you praise him!" cried Cecilia; "and how long might you deliberate before you could add another word to his panegyric!"

Mrs. Harrel, satisfied to commend, without even attempting to vindicate him, was soon content to change the subject; and Cecilia, though much concerned that the husband of her friend had made so disgraceful an election of a favourite, yet hoped that the lenity of Mrs. Harrel resulted from her desire to excuse his choice, not from her own approbation.

CHAPTER V

An Assembly

MRS. Mears, whose character was of that common sort which renders delineation superfluous, received them with the customary forms of good breeding.

Mrs. Harrel soon engaged herself at a card-table: and Cecilia, who declined playing, was seated next to Miss Leeson, who arose to return the courtesy she made in advancing to her, but that past, did not again even look at her.

Cecilia, though fond of conversation and formed for

society, was too diffident to attempt speaking where so little encouraged; they both, therefore, continued silent, till Sir Robert Floyer, Mr. Harrel, and Mr. Arnott entered the room together, and all at the same time advanced to Cecilia.

"What," cried Mr. Harrel, "don't you chuse to play, Miss Beverley?"

"I flatter myself," cried Mr. Arnott, "that Miss Beverley never plays at all, for then, in one thing, I shall have the honour to resemble her."

"Very seldom, indeed," answered Cecilia, "and consquently very ill."

"O, you must take a few lessons," said Mr. Harrel, "Sir Robert Floyer, I am sure, will be proud to instruct you."

Sir Robert who had placed himself opposite to her, and was staring full in her face, made a slight inclination of his head, and said "certainly."

"I should be a very unpromising pupil," returned Cecilia, "for I fear I should not only want diligence to improve, but desire."

"O, you will learn better things," said Mr. Harrel; "we have had you yet but three days amongst us,—in three months we shall see the difference."

"I hope not," cried Mr. Arnott, "I earnestly hope there will be none!"

Mr. Harrel now joined another party; and Mr. Arnott seeing no seat vacant near that of Cecilia, moved round to the back of her chair, where he patiently stood for the rest of the evening. But Sir Robert still kept his post, and still, without troubling himself to speak, kept his eyes fixed upon the same object.

Cecilia, offended by his boldness, looked a thousand ways to avoid him; but her embarrassment, by giving greater play to her features, served only to keep awake an attention which might otherwise have wearied. She was almost tempted to move her chair round and face Mr. Arnott, but though she wished to shew her disapprobation of the Baronet, she had not yet been reconciled by fashion to turning her back upon the company at large, for the indulgence of conversing with some particular person: a fashion which to unaccustomed observers seems rude and repulsive, but which, when once adopted, carries with it imperceptibly its own recommendation, in the ease, convenience and freedom it promotes.

Thus disagreeably stationed, she found but little assistance from the neighbourhood of Mr. Arnott, since even his own desire of conversing with her, was swallowed up by an anxious and involuntary impulse to watch the looks and motions of Sir Robert.

At length quite tired of sitting as if merely an object to be gazed at, she determined to attempt entering into conversation with Miss Leeson.

The difficulty, however, was not inconsiderable how to make the attack; she was unacquainted with her friends and connections, uninformed of her way of thinking, or her way of life, ignorant even of the sound of her voice, and chilled by the coldness of her aspect: yet, having no other alternative, she was more willing to encounter the forbidding looks of this lady, than to continue silently abashed under the scrutinizing eyes of Sir Robert.

After much deliberation with what subject to begin, she remembered that Miss Larolles had been present the first time they had met, and thought it probable they might be acquainted with each other; and therefore, bending forward, she ventured to enquire if she had lately seen that young lady?

Miss Leeson in a voice alike inexpressive of satisfaction or displeasure, quietly answered "No, ma'am."

Cecilia, discouraged by this conciseness, was a few minutes silent; but the perseverance of Sir Robert in staring at her, exciting her own in trying to avoid his eyes, she exerted herself so far as to add "Does Mrs. Mears expect Miss Larolles here this evening?"

Miss Leeson, without raising her head, gravely replied "I don't know, ma'am."

All was now to be done over again, and a new subject to be started, for she could suggest nothing further to ask concerning Miss Larolles.

Cecilia had seen little of life, but that little she had well

marked, and her observation had taught her, that among
fashionable people, public places seemed a never-failing
source of conversation and entertainment: upon this topic,
therefore, she hoped for better success; and as to those who
have spent more time in the country than in London, no
place of amusement is so interesting as a theatre, she opened
the subject she had so happily suggested, by an enquiry
whether any new play had lately come out?

Miss Leeson, with the same dryness, only answered
"Indeed I can't tell."

Another pause now followed, and the spirits of Cecilia
were considerably dampt; but happening accidentally to
recollect the name of Almack, she presently revived, and,
congratulating herself that she should now be able to speak
of a place too fashionable for disdain, she asked her, in a
manner somewhat more assured, if she was a subscriber to
his assemblies?

"Yes, ma'am."

"Do you go to them constantly?"

"No, ma'am."

Again they were both silent. And now, tired of finding the
ill success of each particular enquiry, she thought a more
general one might obtain an answer less laconic, and
therefore begged she would inform her what was the most
fashionable place of diversion for the present season?

This question, however, cost Miss Leeson no more
trouble than any which had preceded it, for she only replied
"Indeed I don't know."

Cecilia now began to sicken of her attempt, and for some
minutes to give it up as hopeless; but afterwards when she
reflected how frivolous were the questions she had asked, she
felt more inclined to pardon the answers she had received,
and in a short time to fancy she had mistaken contempt for
stupidity, and to grow less angry with Miss Leeson than
ashamed of herself.

This supposition excited her to make yet another trial of
her talents for conversation, and therefore, summoning all
the courage in her power, she modestly apologised for the
liberty she was taking, and then begged her permission to

enquire whether there was any thing new in the literary way that she thought worth recommending?

Miss Leeson now turned her eyes towards her, with a look that implied a doubt whether she had heard right; and when the attentive attitude of Cecilia confirmed her question, surprise for a few instants took place of insensibility, and with rather more spirit than she had yet shewn, she answered "Indeed I know nothing of the matter."

Cecilia was now utterly disconcerted; and half angry with herself, and wholly provoked with her sullen neighbour, she resolved to let nothing in future provoke her to a similar trial with so unpromising a subject.

She had not, however, much longer to endure the examination of Sir Robert, who being pretty well satisfied with staring, turned upon his heel, and was striding out of the room, when he was stopt by Mr. Gosport, who for some time had been watching him.

Mr. Gosport was a man of good parts, and keen satire: minute in his observations, and ironical in his expressions.

"So you don't play, Sir Robert?" he cried.

"What here? No, I am going to Brookes's."

"But how do you like Harrel's Ward? You have taken a pretty good survey of her."

"Why faith I don't know; but not much, I think; she's a devilish fine woman too; but she has no spirit, no life."

"Did you try her? Have you talked to her?"

"Not I, truly!"

"Nay, then how do you mean to judge of her?"

"O, faith, that's all over, now; one never thinks of talking to the women by way of trying them."

"What other method, then, have you adopted?"

"None."

"None? Why then how do you go on?"

"Why they talk to us. The women take all that trouble upon themselves now."

"And pray how long may you have commenced *fade macaroni?** For this is a part of your character with which I was not acquainted."

"O, hang it, 'tis not from *ton*; no, it's merely from

laziness. Who the d——l will fatigue himself with dancing attendance upon the women, when keeping them at a distance makes them dance attendance upon us?"

Then stalking from him to Mr. Harrel, he took him by the arm, and they left the room together.

Mr. Gosport now advanced to Cecilia, and addressing her so as not to be heard by Miss Leeson, said "I have been wishing to approach you, some time, but the fear that you are already overpowered by the loquacity of your fair neighbour makes me cautious of attempting to engage you."

"You mean," said Cecilia, "to laugh at *my* loquacity, and indeed its ill success has rendered it sufficiently ridiculous."

"Are you, then, yet to learn," cried he, "that there are certain young ladies who make it a rule never to speak but to their own cronies? Of this class is Miss Leeson, and till you get into her particular Coterie, you must never expect to hear from her a word of two syllables. The TON misses, as they are called, who now infest the town, are in two divisions, the SUPERCILIOUS, and the VOLUBLE. The SUPERCILIOUS, like Miss Leeson, are silent, scornful, languid, and affected, and disdain all converse but with those of their own set: the VOLUBLE, like Miss Larolles, are flirting, communicative, restless, and familiar, and attack without the smallest ceremony, every one they think worthy their notice. But this they have in common, that at home they think of nothing but dress, abroad, of nothing but admiration, and that every where they hold in supreme contempt all but themselves."

"Probably, then," said Cecilia, "I have passed to night, for one of the VOLUBLES; however, all the advantage has been with the SUPERCILIOUS, for I have suffered a total repulse."

"Are you sure, however, you have not talked too well for her?"

"O, a child of five years old ought to have been whipt for not talking better!"

"But it is not capacity alone you are to consult when you talk with misses of the TON; were their understandings only to be considered, they would indeed be wonderfully easy of

access! in order therefore, to render their commerce somewhat difficult, they will only be pleased by an observance
of their humours: which are ever most various and most
exuberant where the intellects are weakest and least
cultivated. I have, however, a receipt which I have found
infallible for engaging the attention of young ladies of
whatsoever character or denomination.''

"O, then," cried Cecilia, "pray favour me with it, for I
have here an admirable opportunity to try its efficacy."

"I will give it you," he answered, "with full directions.
When you meet with a young lady who seems resolutely
determined not to speak, or who, if compelled by a direct
question to make some answer, drily gives a brief affirmative,
or coldly a laconic negative——"

"A case in point!" interrupted Cecilia.

"Well, thus circumstanced," he continued, "the remedy I
have to propose consists of three topics of discourse."

"Pray what are they?"

"Dress, public places, and love."

Cecilia, half surprised and half diverted, waited a fuller
explanation without giving any interruption.

"These three topics," he continued, "are to answer three
purposes, since there are no less than three causes from which
the silence of young ladies may proceed: sorrow, affectation,
and stupidity."

"Do you, then," cried Cecilia, "give nothing at all to
modesty?"

"I give much to it," he answered, "as an excuse, nay
almost as an equivalent for wit; but for that sullen silence
which resists all encouragement, modesty is a mere pretence,
not a cause."

"You must, however, be somewhat more explicit, if you
mean that I should benefit from your instructions."

"Well then," he answered, "I will briefly enumerate the
three causes, with directions for the three methods of cure. To
begin with sorrow. The taciturnity which really results from
that is attended with an incurable absence of mind, and a total
unconsciousness of the observation which it excites; upon this
occasion, public places may sometimes be tried in vain, and
even dress may fail; but love——"

"Are you sure, then," said Cecilia, with a laugh, "that sorrow has but that one source?"

"By no means," answered he, "for perhaps papa may have been angry, or mama may have been cross; a milliner may have sent a wrong pompoon,* or a chaperon to an assembly may have been taken ill;——"

"Bitter subjects of affliction, indeed! And are these all you allow us?"

"Nay, I speak but of young ladies of fashion, and what of greater importance can befall them? If, therefore, the grief of the fair patient proceeds from papa, mama, or the chaperon, then the mention of public places, those endless incentives of displeasure between the old and the young, will draw forth her complaints, and her complaints will bring their own cure, for those who lament find speedy consolation: if the milliner has occasioned the calamity, the discussion of dress will have the same effect; should both these medicines fail, love, as I said before, will be found infallible, for you will then have investigated every subject of uneasiness which a youthful female in high life can experience."

"They are greatly obliged to you," cried Cecilia, bowing, "for granting them motives of sorrow so honourable, and I thank you in the name of the whole sex."

"You, madam," said he, returning her bow, "are I hope an exception in the happiest way, that of having no sorrow at all. I come, now, to the silence of affectation, which is presently discernable by the roving of the eye round the room to see if it is heeded, by the sedulous care to avoid an accidental smile, and by the variety of disconsolate attitudes exhibited to the beholders. This species of silence has almost without exception its origin in that babyish vanity which is always gratified by exciting attention, without ever perceiving that it provokes contempt. In these cases, as nature is wholly out of the question, and the mind is guarded against its own feelings, dress and public places are almost certain of failing, but here again love is sure to vanquish; as soon as it is named, attention becomes involuntary, and in a short time a struggling simper discomposes the arrangement of the features, and then the business is presently over, for the young lady is either supporting some system, or opposing some proposition, before she is well aware that she has been cheated out of her sad silence at all.''

"So much," said Cecilia, "for sorrow and for affectation. Proceed next to stupidity; for that, in all probability, I shall most frequently encounter.''

"That always must be heavy work," returned he, "yet the road is plain, though it is all up hill. Love, here, may be talked of without exciting any emotion, or provoking any reply, and dress may be dilated upon without producing any other effect than that of attracting a vacant stare; but public places are indubitably certain of success. Dull and heavy characters, incapable of animating from wit or from reason, because unable to keep pace with them, and void of all internal sources of entertainment, require the stimulation of shew, glare, noise and bustle to interest or awaken them. Talk to them of such subjects and they adore you; no matter whether you paint to them joy or horror, let there but be action, and they are content; a battle has charms for them equal to a coronation, and a funeral amuses them as much as a wedding.''

"I am much obliged to you," said Cecilia, smiling, "for these instructions; yet I must confess I know not how upon the present occasion to make use of them: public places I have already tried, but tried in vain; dress I dare not mention, as I have not yet learned its technical terms,——''

"Well but," interrupted he, "be not desperate; you have yet the third topic unessayed.''

"O that," returned she laughing, "I leave to you!''

"Pardon me," cried he, "love is a source of loquacity only with yourselves: when it is started by men, young ladies dwindle into mere listeners. *Simpering* listeners, I confess; but it is only with one another that you will discuss its merits.''

At this time they were interrupted by the approach of Miss Larolles, who tripping towards Cecilia, exclaimed "Lord how glad I am to see you! So you would not go to the auction? Well, you had a prodigious loss, I assure you. All the wardrobe was sold, and all Lady Belgrade's trinkets. I never saw such a collection of sweet things in my life. I was ready to cry that I could not bid for half an hundred of them. I declare I was kept in an agony the whole morning. I would not but have been there for the world. Poor Lady Belgrade! you really can't conceive how I was shocked for her. All her beautiful things sold for almost nothing. I assure you if you had seen how they went you would have lost all patience. It's a thousand pities you were not there."

"On the contrary," said Cecilia, "I think I had a very fortunate escape, for the loss of patience without the acquisition of the trinkets, would have been rather mortifying."

"Yes," said Mr. Gosport; "but when you have lived some time longer in this commercial city, you will find the exchange of patience for mortification the most common and constant traffic among it's inhabitants."

"Pray have you been here long?" cried Miss Larolles, "for I have been to twenty places, wondering I did not meet with you before. But whereabouts is Mrs. Mears? O, I see her now; I'm sure there's no mistaking her; I could know her by that old red gown half a mile off. Did you ever see such a frightful thing in your life? And it's never off her back. I believe she sleeps in it. I am sure I have seen her in nothing else all winter. It quite tires one's eye. She's a monstrous shocking dresser. But do you know, I have met with the most provoking thing in the world this evening? I declare it has made me quite sick. I was never in such a passion in my life. You can conceive nothing like it."

"Like what?" cried Cecilia, laughing, "your passion, or your provocation?"

"Why I'll tell you what it was, and then you shall judge if it was not quite past endurance. You must know I commissioned a particular friend of mine, Miss Moffat, to buy me a trimming when she went to Paris; well, she sent it me over about a month ago by Mr. Meadows, and it's the sweetest thing you ever saw in your life; but I would not make it up, because there was not a creature in town, so I thought to bring it out quite new in about a week's time, for you know any thing does till after Christmas. Well, to night at Lady Jane Dranet's, who should I meet but Miss Moffat! She had been in town some days, but so monstrously engaged I could never find her at home. Well, I was quite delighted to see her, for you must know she's a prodigious favourite with me, so I ran up to her in a great hurry to shake hands, and what do you think was the first thing that struck my eyes? Why just such a trimming as my own, upon a nasty odious gown, and half dirty! Can you conceive any thing so distressing? I could have cried with pleasure."

"Why so?" said Cecilia; "If her trimming is dirty, yours will look the more delicate."

"O lord, but it's making it seem quite an old thing! half the town will get something like it. And I quite ruined myself to buy it. I declare I don't think any thing was ever half so mortifying. It distressed me so I could hardly speak to her. If she had stayed a month or two longer I should not have minded it, but it was the cruellest thing in the world to come over just now. I wish the Custom-house-officers* had kept all her cloaths till summer."

"The wish is tender, indeed," said Cecilia, "for a *particular friend*."

Mrs. Mears now rising from the card-table, Miss Larolles tript away to pay her compliments to her.

"Here, at least," cried Cecilia, "no receipt seems requisite for the cure of silence! I would have Miss Larolles be the constant companion of Miss Leeson: they could not but agree admirably, since that SUPERCILIOUS young lady seems determined never to speak, and the VOLUBLE Miss Larolles never to be silent. Were each to borrow something of the other, how greatly would both be the better!"

"The composition would still be a sorry one," answered Mr. Gosport, "for I believe they are equally weak, and equally ignorant; the only difference is, that one, though silly, is quick, the other, though deliberate is stupid. Upon a short acquaintance, that heaviness which leaves to others the whole weight of discourse, and whole search of entertainment, is the most fatiguing, but, upon a longer intimacy, even that is less irksome and less offensive, than the flippancy which hears nothing but itself."

Mrs. Harrel arose now to depart, and Cecilia, not more tired of the beginning of the evening than entertained with its conclusion, was handed to the carriage by Mr. Arnott.

CHAPTER VI

A Breakfast

THE next morning, during breakfast, a servant acquainted Cecilia that a young gentleman was in the hall, who begged to speak with her. She desired he might be admitted; and Mrs. Harrel, laughing, asked if she ought not to quit the room; while Mr. Arnott, with even more than his usual gravity, directed his eye towards the door to watch who should enter.

Neither of them, however, received any satisfaction when it was opened, for the gentleman who made his appearance was unknown to both: but great was the amazement of Cecilia, though little her emotion, when she saw Mr. Morrice!

He came forward with an air of the most profound respect for the company in general, and obsequiously advancing to Cecilia, made an earnest enquiry into her health after her journey, and hoped she had heard good news from her friends in the country.

Mrs. Harrel, naturally concluding both from his visit and behaviour, that he was an acquaintance of some intimacy, very civilly offered him a seat and some breakfast, which, very frankly, he accepted. But Mr. Arnott, who already felt the anxiety of a rising passion which was too full of veneration to be sanguine, looked at him with uneasiness, and waited his departure with impatience.

Cecilia began to imagine he had been commissioned to call upon her with some message from Mr. Monckton: for she knew not how to suppose that merely and accidentally having spent an hour or two in the same room with her, would authorize a visiting acquaintance. Mr. Morrice, however, had a facility the most happy of reconciling his

pretensions to his inclination; and therefore she soon found
that the pretence* she had suggested appeared to him
unnecessary. To lead, however, to the subject from which
she expected his excuse, she enquired how long he had left
Suffolk?

"But yesterday noon, ma'am," he answered, "or I
should certainly have taken the liberty to wait upon you
before."

Cecilia, who had only been perplexing herself to devise
some reason why he came at all, now looked at him with a
grave surprize, which would totally have abashed a man
whose courage had been less, or whose expectations had
been greater; but Mr. Morrice, though he hazarded every
danger upon the slightest chance of hope, knew too well the
weakness of his claims to be confident of success, and had
been too familiar with rebuffs to be much hurt by receiving
them. He might possibly have something to gain, but he
knew he had nothing to lose.

"I had the pleasure," he continued, "to leave all our
friends well, except poor lady Margaret, and she has had an
attack of the asthma; yet she would not have a physician,
though Mr. Monckton would fain have persuaded her:
however, I believe the old lady knows better things." And
he looked archly at Cecilia: but perceiving that the
insinuation gave her nothing but disgust, he changed his
tone, and added, "It is amazing how well they live together;
nobody would imagine the disparity in their years. Poor old
lady! Mr. Monckton will really have a great loss of her when
she dies."

"A loss of her!" repeated Mrs. Harrel, "I am sure she is
an exceeding ill-natured old woman. When I lived at Bury,
I was always frightened out of my wits at the sight of her."

"Why indeed, ma'am," said Morrice, "I must own
her appearance is rather against her: I had myself a
great aversion to her at first sight. But the house is
chearful,—very chearful: I like to spend a few days there
now and then of all things. Miss Bennet, too, is agreeable
enough, and ——."

"Miss Bennet agreeable!" cried Mrs. Harrel, "I think

she's the most odious creature I ever knew in my life; a nasty, spiteful old maid!''

"Why indeed, ma'am, as you say," answered Morrice, "she is not very young; and as to her temper, I confess I know very little about it; and Mr. Monckton is likely enough to try it, for he is pretty severe."

"Mr. Monckton," cried Cecilia, extremely provoked at hearing him censured by a man she thought highly honoured in being permitted to approach him, "whenever *I* have been his guest, has merited from me nothing but praise and gratitude."

"O," cried Morrice eagerly, "there is not a more worthy man in the world! he has so much wit, so much politeness! I don't know a more charming man any where than my friend Mr. Monckton."

Cecilia now perceiving that the opinions of her new acquaintance were as pliant as his bows, determined to pay him no further attention, and hoped by sitting silent to force from him the business of his visit, if any he had, or if, as she now suspected, he had none, to weary him into a retreat.

But this plan, though it would have succeeded with herself, failed with Mr. Morrice, who to a stock of good-humour that made him always ready to oblige others, added an equal portion of insensibility that hardened him against all indignity. Finding, therefore, that Cecilia, to whom his visit was intended, seemed already satisfied with its length, he prudently forbore to torment her; but perceiving that the lady of the house was more accessible, he quickly made a transfer of his attention, and addressed his discourse to her with as much pleasure as if his only view had been to see her, and as much ease as if he had known her all his life.

With Mrs. Harrel this conduct was not injudicious; she was pleased with his assiduity, amused with his vivacity, and sufficiently satisfied with his understanding. They conversed, therefore, upon pretty equal terms, and neither of them were yet tired, when they were interrupted by Mr. Harrel, who came into the room to ask if they had seen or heard any thing of Sir Robert Floyer?

"No," answered Mrs. Harrel, "nothing at all."

"I wish he was hanged," returned he, "for he has kept me waiting this hour. He made me promise not to ride out till he called, and now he'll stay till the morning is over."

"Pray where does he live, Sir?" cried Morrice, starting from his seat.

"In Cavendish-square, Sir," answered Mr. Harrel, looking at him with much surprise.

Not a word more said Morrice, but scampered out of the room.

"Pray who is this Genius?" cried Mr. Harrel, "and what has he run away for?"

"Upon my word I know nothing at all of him," said Mrs. Harrel; "he is a visitor of Miss Beverley's."

"And I, too," said Cecilia, "might almost equally disclaim all knowledge of him; for though I once saw, I never was introduced to him."

She then began a relation of her meeting him at Mr. Monckton's house, and had hardly concluded it, before again, and quite out of breath, he made his appearance.

"Sir Robert Floyer, Sir," said he to Mr. Harrel, "will be here in two minutes."

"I hope, Sir," said Mr. Harrel, "you have not given yourself the trouble of going to him?"

"No, Sir, it has given me nothing but pleasure; a run these cold mornings is the thing I like best."

"Sir, you are extremely good," said Mr. Harrel, "but I had not the least intention of your taking such a walk upon my account."

He then begged him to be seated, to rest himself, and to take some refreshment; which civilities he received without scruple.

"But, Miss Beverley," said Mr. Harrel, turning suddenly* to Cecilia, "you don't tell me what you think of my friend?"

"What friend, Sir?"

"Why, Sir Robert Floyer; I observed he never quitted you a moment while he stayed at Mrs. Mears."

"His stay, however, was too short," said Cecilia, "to allow me to form a fair opinion of him."

c.—5

"But perhaps," cried Morrice, "it was long enough to allow you to form a *foul* one.''*

Cecilia could not forbear laughing to hear the truth thus accidentally blundered out; but Mr. Harrel, looking very little pleased, said, "Surely you can find no fault with him? he is one of the most fashionable men I know.''

"My finding fault with him then," said Cecilia, "will only farther prove what I believe is already pretty evident, that I am yet a novice in the art of admiration.''

Mr. Arnott, animating at this speech, glided behind her chair, and said, "I knew you could not like him! I knew it from the turn of your mind;—I knew it even from your countenance!''

Soon after, Sir Robert Floyer arrived.

"You are a pretty fellow, a'n't you," cried Mr. Harrel, "to keep me waiting so long?''

"I could not come a moment sooner; I hardly expected to get here at all, for my horse has been so confounded resty* I could not tell how to get him along.''

"Do you come on horseback through the streets,* Sir Robert?'' asked Mrs. Harrel.

"Sometimes; when I am lazy. But what the d——l is the matter with him I don't know; he has started at every thing. I suspect there has been some foul play with him.''

"Is he at the door, Sir?'' cried Morrice.

"Yes," answered Sir Robert.

"Then I'll tell you what's the matter with him in a minute;'' and away again ran Morrice.

"What time did you get off last night Harrel?'' said Sir Robert.

"Not very early; but you were too much engaged to miss me. By the way," lowering his voice, "what do you think I lost?''

"I can't tell indeed, but I know what I gained: I have not had such a run of luck this winter.''

They then went up to a window to carry on their enquiries more privately.

At the words *what do you think I lost*, Cecilia, half starting, cast her eyes uneasily upon Mrs. Harrel, but perceived not the least change in her countenance. Mr. Arnott, however, seemed as little pleased as herself, and from a similar sensation looked anxiously at his sister.

Morrice now returning, called out, "He's had a fall, I assure you!"

"Curse him!" cried Sir Robert, "what shall I do now? he cost me the d——l and all of money, and I have not had him a twelvemonth. Can you lend me a horse for this morning, Harrel?"

"No, I have not one that will do for you. You must send to Astley."

"Who can I send? John* must take care of this."

"I'll go, Sir," cried Morrice, "if you'll give me the commission."

"By no means, Sir," said Sir Robert, "I can't think of giving you* such an office."

"It is the thing in the world I like best," answered he; "I understand horses, and had rather go to Astley's than any where."

The matter was now settled in a few minutes, and having received his directions, and an invitation to dinner, Morrice danced off, with an heart yet lighter than his heels.

"Why, Miss Beverley," said Mr. Harrel, "this friend of yours is the most obliging gentleman I ever met with; there was no avoiding asking him to dinner."

"Remember, however," said Cecilia, who was involuntarily diverted at the successful officiousness of her new acquaintance, "that if you receive him henceforth as your guest, he obtains admission through his own merits, and not through my interest."

At dinner, Morrice, who failed not to accept the invitation of Mr. Harrel, was the gayest, and indeed the happiest man in the company: the effort he had made to fasten himself upon Cecilia as an acquaintance, had not, it is true, from herself met with much encouragement; but he knew the chances were against him when he made the trial, and therefore the prospect of gaining admission into such a house as Mr. Harrel's, was not only sufficient to make amends for what scarcely amounted to a disappointment, but a subject of serious comfort from the credit of the connection, and of internal exultation at his own management and address.

In the evening, the ladies, as usual, went to a private assembly, and, as usual, were attended to it by Mr. Arnott. The other gentlemen had engagements elsewhere.

CHAPTER VII

A Project

SEVERAL days passed on nearly in the same manner; the mornings were all spent in gossipping, shopping and dressing, and the evenings were regularly appropriated to public places, or large parties of company.

Meanwhile Mr. Arnott lived almost entirely in Portman-square; he slept, indeed, at his own lodgings, but he boarded wholly with Mr. Harrel, whose house he never for a moment quitted till night, except to attend Cecilia and his sister in their visitings and rambles.

Mr. Arnott was a young man of unexceptionable character, and of a disposition mild, serious and benignant: his principles and blameless conduct obtained the universal esteem of the world, but his manners, which were rather too precise,* joined to an uncommon gravity of countenance and demeanour, made his society rather permitted as a duty, than sought as a pleasure.

The charms of Cecilia had forcibly, suddenly and deeply penetrated his heart; he only lived in her presence, away from her he hardly existed: the emotions she excited were rather those of adoration than of love, for he gazed upon her beauty till he thought her more than human, and hung upon her accents till all speech seemed impertinent to him but her own. Yet so small were his expectations of success, that not even to his sister did he hint at the situation of his heart: happy in an easy access to her, he contented himself with seeing, hearing and watching her, beyond which bounds he formed not any plan, and scarce indulged any hope.

Sir Robert Floyer, too, was a frequent visitor in Portman-

square, where he dined almost daily. Cecilia was chagrined
at seeing so much of him, and provoked to find herself
almost constantly the object of his unrestrained examination; she was, however, far more seriously concerned for
Mrs. Harrel, when she discovered that this favourite friend
of her husband was an unprincipled spendthrift, and an
extravagant gamester, for as he was the inseparable companion of Mr. Harrel, she dreaded the consequence both of
his influence and his example.

She saw, too, with an amazement that daily increased, the
fatigue, yet fascination of a life of pleasure: Mr. Harrel
seemed to consider his own house merely as an Hôtel, where
at any hour of the night he might disturb the family to claim
admittance, where letters and messages might be left for
him, where he dined when no other dinner was offered him,
and where, when he made an appointment, he was to be met
with. His lady, too, though more at home, was not therefore
more solitary; her acquaintance were numerous, expensive
and idle, and every moment not actually spent in company,
was scrupulously devoted to making arrangements for that
purpose.

In a short time Cecilia, who every day had hoped that the
next would afford her greater satisfaction, but who every day
found the present no better than the former, began to grow
weary of eternally running the same round, and to sicken at
the irksome repetition of unremitting yet uninteresting
dissipation. She saw nobody she wished to see, as she had
met with nobody for whom she could care; for though
sometimes those with whom she mixed appeared to be
amiable, she knew that their manners, like their persons,
were in their best array, and therefore she had too much
understanding to judge decisively of their characters. But
what chiefly damped her hopes of forming a friendship with
any of the new acquaintance to whom she was introduced,
was the observation she herself made how ill the coldness of
their hearts accorded with the warmth of their professions:
upon every first meeting, the civilities which were shewn
her, flattered her into believing she had excited a partiality
that a very little time would ripen into affection; the next

meeting commonly confirmed the expectation; but the third, and every future one, regularly destroyed it. She found that time added nothing to their fondness, nor intimacy to their sincerity; that the interest in her welfare which appeared to be taken at first sight, seldom, with whatever reason, encreased, and often without any abated; that the distinction she at first met with, was no effusion of kindness, but of curiosity, which is scarcely sooner gratified than satiated; and that those who lived always the life into which she had only lately been initiated, were as much harrassed with it as herself, though less spirited to relinquish, and more helpless to better it; and that they coveted nothing but what was new, because they had experienced the insufficiency of whatever was familiar.

She began now to regret the loss she sustained in quitting the neighbourhood, and being deprived of the conversation of Mr. Monckton, and yet more earnestly to miss the affection and sigh for the society of Mrs. Charlton, the lady with whom she had long and happily resided at Bury; for she was very soon compelled to give up all expectation of renewing the felicity of her earlier years, by being restored to the friendship of Mrs. Harrel, in whom she had mistaken the kindness of childish intimacy for the sincerity of chosen affection; and though she saw her credulous error with mortification and displeasure, she regretted it with tenderness and sorrow. "What, at last," cried she, "is human felicity, who has tasted, and where is it to be found? If I, who, to others, seem marked out for even a partial possession of it,—distinguished by fortune, caressed by the world, brought into the circle of high life, and surrounded with splendour, seek without finding it,* yet losing, scarce know how I miss it!"

Ashamed upon reflection to believe she was considered as an object of envy by others, while repining and discontented herself, she determined no longer to be the only one insensible to the blessings within her reach, but by projecting and adopting some plan of conduct, better suited to her taste and feelings than the frivolous insipidity of her present life, to make at once a more spirited and more worthy use of the affluence, freedom and power which she possessed.

A scheme of happiness at once rational and refined soon presented itself to her imagination. She purposed, for the basis of her plan, to become mistress of her own time, and with this view, to drop all idle and uninteresting acquaintance, who while they contribute neither to use nor pleasure, make so large a part of the community, that they may properly be called the underminers of existence: she could then shew some taste and discernment in her choice of friends, and she resolved to select such only as by their piety could elevate her mind, by their knowledge improve her understanding, or by their accomplishments and manners delight her affections. This regulation, if strictly adhered to, would soon relieve her from the fatigue of receiving many visitors, and therefore she might have all the leisure she could desire for the pursuit of her favourite studies, music and reading.

Having thus, from her own estimation of human perfection, culled whatever was noblest for her society, and from her own ideas of sedentary enjoyments, arranged the occupations of her hours of solitude, she felt fully satisfied with the portion of happiness which her scheme promised to herself, and began next to consider what was due from her to the world.

And not without trembling did she then look forward to the claims which the splendid income she was soon to possess would call upon her to discharge. A strong sense of DUTY, a fervent desire to ACT RIGHT, were the ruling characteristics of her mind: her affluence she therefore considered as a debt contracted with the poor, and her independence, as a tie upon her liberality to pay it with interest.

Many and various, then, soothing to her spirit and grateful to her sensibility, were the scenes which her fancy delineated; now she supported an orphan, now softened the sorrows of a widow, now snatched from iniquity the feeble trembler at poverty, and now rescued from shame the proud struggler with disgrace. The prospect at once exalted her

hopes, and enraptured her imagination; she regarded herself
as an agent of Charity, and already in idea anticipated the
rewards of a good and faithful delegate:* so animating are
the designs of disinterested benevolence! so pure is the bliss
of intellectual philanthropy!

Not immediately, however, could this plan be put in
execution; the society she meant to form could not be
selected in the house of another, where, though to some she
might shew a preference, there were none she could reject:
nor had she yet the power to indulge, according to the
munificence of her wishes, the extensive generosity she
projected: these purposes demanded an house of her own,
and the unlimited disposal of her fortune, neither of which
she could claim till she became of age. That period,
however, was only eight months distant, and she pleased
herself with the intention of meliorating her plan in the mean
time, and preparing to put it in practice.

But though, in common with all the race of still-expecting
man, she looked for that happiness in the time to come
which the present failed to afford, she had yet the spirit and
good sense to determine upon making every effort in her
power, to render her immediate way of life more useful and
contented.

Her first wish therefore, now, was to quit the house of Mr.
Harrel, where she neither met with entertainment nor
instruction, but was perpetually mortified by seeing the total
indifference of the friend in whose society she had hoped for
nothing but affection.

The will of her uncle, though it obliged her while under-
age to live with one of her guardians, left her at liberty to
chuse and to change amongst them according to her wishes
or convenience: she determined, therefore, to make a visit
herself to each of them, to observe their manners and way
of life, and then, to the best of her judgement, decide with
which she could be most contented: resolving, however, not
to hint at her intention till it was ripe for execution, and then
honestly to confess the reasons of her retreat.

She had acquainted them both of her journey to town the
morning after her arrival. She was almost an entire stranger

to each of them, as she had not seen Mr. Briggs since she was nine years old, nor Mr. Delvile within the time she could remember.

The very morning that she had settled her proceedings for the arrangement of this new plan, she intended to request the use of Mrs. Harrel's carriage, and to make, without delay, the visits preparatory to her removal: but when she entered the parlour upon a summons to breakfast, her eagerness to quit the house gave way, for the present, to the pleasure she felt at the sight of Mr. Monckton, who was just arrived from Suffolk.

She expressed her satisfaction in the most lively terms, and scrupled not to tell him she had not once been so much pleased since her journey to town, except at her first meeting with Mrs. Harrel.

Mr. Monckton, whose delight was infinitely superior to her own, and whose joy in seeing her was redoubled by the affectionate frankness of her reception, stifled the emotions to which her sight gave rise, and denying himself the solace of expressing his feelings, seemed much less charmed than herself at the meeting, and suffered no word nor look to escape him beyond what could be authorised by friendly civility.

He then renewed with Mrs. Harrel an acquaintance which had been formed before her marriage, but which she had dropt when her distance from Cecilia, upon whose account alone he had thought it worth cultivation, made it no longer of use to him. She afterwards introduced her brother to him; and a conversation very interesting to both ladies took place, concerning several families with which they had been formerly connected, as well as the neighbourhood at large in which they had lately dwelt.

Very little was the share taken by Mr. Arnott in these accounts and enquiries; the unaffected joy with which Cecilia had received Mr. Monckton, had struck him with a sensation of envy as involuntary as it was painful: he did not, indeed, suspect that gentleman's secret views; no reason for suspicion was obvious, and his penetration sunk not deeper than appearances; he knew, too, that he was married, and therefore no jealousy occurred to him; but still she had smiled upon him!——and he felt that to purchase for himself a smile of so much sweetness, he would have sacrificed almost all else that was valuable to him upon earth.

With an attention infinitely more accurate, Mr. Monckton had returned his observations. The uneasiness of his mind was apparent, and the anxious watchfulness of his eyes plainly manifested whence it arose. From a situation, indeed, which permitted an intercourse the most constant and unrestrained with such an object as Cecilia, nothing less could be expected, and therefore he considered his admiration as inevitable; all that remained to be discovered, was the reception it had met from his fair enslaver. Nor was he here long in doubt; he soon saw that she was not merely free from all passion herself, but had so little watched Mr. Arnott as to be unconscious she had inspired any.

Yet was his own serenity, though apparently unmoved, little less disturbed in secret than that of his rival; he did not think him a formidable candidate, but he dreaded the effects of intimacy, fearing she might first grow accustomed to his attentions, and then become pleased with them: he apprehended, also, the influence of his sister, and of Mr. Harrel in his favour; and though he had no difficulty to persuade himself that any offer he might now make would be rejected without hesitation, he knew too well the insidious properties of perseverance, to see him, without inquietude, situated so advantageously.

The morning was far advanced before he took leave, yet he found no opportunity of discoursing with Cecilia, though he impatiently desired to examine into the state of her mind, and to discover whether her London journey had added any fresh difficulties to the success of his long concerted scheme. But as Mrs. Harrel invited him to dinner, he hoped the afternoon would be more propitious to his wishes.

Cecilia, too, was eager to communicate to him her favourite project, and to receive his advice with respect to it's execution. She had long been used to his counsel, and she was now more than ever solicitous to obtain it, because she considered him as the only person in London who was interested in her welfare.

He saw, however no promise of better success when he made his appearance at dinner time, for not only Mr. Arnott was already arrived, but Sir Robert Floyer, and he found Cecilia so much the object of their mutual attention, that he had still less chance than in the morning of speaking to her unheard.

Yet was he not idle; the sight of Sir Robert gave abundant employment to his penetration, which was immediately at work, to discover the motive of his visit: but this, with all his sagacity, was not easily decided; for though the constant direction of his eyes towards Cecilia, proved, at least, that he was not insensible of her beauty, his carelessness whether or not she was hurt by his examination, the little pains he took to converse with her, and the invariable assurance and negligence of his manners, seemed strongly to demonstrate an indifference to the sentiments he inspired, totally incompatible with the solicitude of affection.

In Cecilia he had nothing to observe but what his knowledge of her character prepared him to expect, a shame no less indignant than modest at the freedom with which she saw herself surveyed.

Very little, therefore, was the satisfaction which this visit procured him, for soon after dinner the ladies retired; and as they had an early engagement for the evening, the gentlemen received no summons to their tea-table. But he contrived, before they quitted the room, to make an appointment for attending them the next morning to a rehearsal of a new serious Opera.*

He stayed not after their departure longer than decency required, for too much in earnest was his present pursuit, to fit him for such conversation as the house in Cecilia's absence could afford him.

CHAPTER VIII

*An Opera Rehearsal**

THE next day, between eleven and twelve o'clock, Mr.
Monckton was again in Portman-square; he found, as he
expected, both the ladies; and he found, as he feared, Mr.
Arnott prepared to be of their party. He had, however, but
little time to repine at this intrusion, before he was disturbed
by another, for, in a few minutes, they were joined by Sir
Robert Floyer, who also declared his intention of accompanying them to the Haymarket.

Mr. Monckton, to disguise his chagrin, pretended he was
in great haste to set off, lest they should be too late for the
overture: they were, therefore, quitting the breakfast room,
when they were stopt by the appearance of Mr. Morrice.

The surprise which the sight of him gave to Mr.
Monckton was extreme; he knew that he was unacquainted
with Mr. Harrel, for he remembered they were strangers to
each other when they lately met at his house; he concluded,
therefore, that Cecilia was the object of his visit, but he
could frame no conjecture under what pretence.

The easy terms upon which he seemed with all the family
by no means diminished his amazement; for when Mrs.
Harrel expressed some concern that she was obliged to go
out, he gaily begged her not to mind him, assuring her he
could not have stayed two minutes, and promising,
unasked, to call again the next day: and when she added,
"We would not hurry away so, only we are going to a
rehearsal of an Opera," he exclaimed with quickness, "A
rehearsal!—are you really? I have a great mind to go too!"

Then, perceiving Mr. Monckton, he bowed to him with
great respect, and enquired, with no little solemnity, how he
had left lady Margaret, hoped she was perfectly recovered
from her late indisposition, and asked sundry questions with
regard to her plan for the winter.

This discourse was ill constructed for rendering his

presence desirable to Mr. Monckton; he answered him very drily, and again pressed their departure.

"O," cried Morrice, "there's no occasion for such haste; the rehearsal does not begin till one."

"You are mistaken, Sir!" said Mr. Monckton; "it is to begin at twelve o'clock."

"O ay, very true," returned Morrice; "I had forgot the dances, and I suppose they are to be rehearsed first. Pray, Miss Beverley, did you ever see any dances rehearsed?"

"No, Sir."

"You'll be excessively entertained, then, I assure you. It's the most comical thing in the world to see those signores and signoras cutting capers in a morning. And the *figuranti** will divert you beyond measure; you never saw such a shabby set in your life: but the most amusing thing is to look in their faces, for all the time they are jumping and skipping about the stage as if they could not stand still for joy, they look as sedate and as dismal as if they were so many undertakers men."

"Not a word against dancing!" cried Sir Robert, "it's the only thing carries one to the Opera; and I am sure it's the only thing one minds at it."

The two ladies were then handed to Mrs. Harrel's *vis-à-vis*; and the gentlemen, joined without further ceremony by Mr. Morrice, followed them to the Haymarket.

The rehearsal was not begun, and Mrs. Harrel and Cecilia secured themselves a box upon the stage, from which the gentlemen of their party took care not to be very distant.

They were soon perceived by Mr. Gosport, who instantly entered into conversation with Cecilia. Miss Larolles, who with some other ladies came soon after into the next box, looked out to courtsie and nod, with her usual readiness, at Mrs. Harrel, but took not any notice of Cecilia, though she made the first advances.

"What's the matter now?" cried Mr. Gosport; "have you affronted your little prattling friend?"

"Not with my own knowledge," answered Cecilia; "perhaps she does not recollect me."

Just then Miss Larolles, tapping at the door, came in from

the next box to speak to Mrs. Harrel; with whom she stood chatting and laughing some minutes, without seeming to perceive that Cecilia was of her party.

"Why what have you done to the poor girl?" whispered Mr. Gosport; "did you talk more than herself when you saw her last?"

"Would that have been possible?" cried Cecilia; "however, I still fancy she does not know me."

She then stood up, which making Miss Larolles involuntarily turn towards her, she again courtsied; a civility which that young lady scarce deigned to return, before, bridling with an air of resentment, she hastily looked another way, and then, nodding good-humouredly at Mrs. Harrel, hurried back to her party.

Cecilia, much amazed, said to Mr. Gosport, "See now how great was our presumption in supposing this young lady's loquacity always at our devotion!"

"Ah madam!" cried he, laughing, "there is no permanency, no consistency in the world! no, not even in the tongue of a VOLUBLE! and if that fails, upon what may we depend?"

"But seriously," said Cecilia, "I am sorry I have offended her, and the more because I so little know how, that I can offer her no apology."

"Will you appoint me your envoy? Shall I demand the cause of these hostilities?"

She thanked him, and he followed Miss Larolles; who was now addressing herself with great earnestness to Mr. Meadows, the gentleman with whom she was conversing when Cecilia first saw her in Portman-square. He stopt a moment to let her finish her speech, which, with no little spirit, she did in these words, "I never knew any thing like it in my life; but I sha'n't put up with such airs, I assure her!"

Mr. Meadows made not any other return to her harangue, but stretching himself with a languid smile and yawning: Mr. Gosport, therefore, seizing the moment of cessation, said, "Miss Larolles, I hear a strange report about you."

"Do you?" returned she, with quickness, "pray what is it? something monstrous impertinent, I dare say,—however, I assure you it i'n't true."

"Your assurance," cried he, "carries conviction indisputable, for the report was that you had left off talking."

"O, was that all!" cried she, disappointed, "I thought it had been something about Mr. Sawyer, for I declare I have been plagued so about him, I am quite sick of his name."

"And for my part, I never heard it! so fear nothing from me upon his account."

"Lord, Mr. Gosport, how can you say so? I am sure you must know about the festino* that night, for it was all over the town in a moment."

"What festino?"

"Well, only conceive how provoking!—why, I know nothing else was talked of for a month!"

"You are most formidably stout* this morning! it is not two minutes since I saw you fling the gauntlet at Miss Beverley, and yet you are already prepared for another antagonist."

"O as to Miss Beverley, I must really beg you not to mention her; she has behaved so impertinently, that I don't intend ever to speak to her again."

"Why, what has she done?"

"O she's been so rude you've no notion. I'll tell you how it was. You must know I met her at Mrs. Harrel's the day she came to town, and the very next morning I waited on her myself,* for I would not send a ticket, because I really wished to be civil to her; well, the day after, she never came near me, though I called upon her again; however, I did not take any notice of that; but when the third day came, and I found she had not even sent me a ticket, I thought it monstrous ill bred indeed; and now there has past more than a week, and yet she has never called: so I suppose she don't like me; so I shall drop her acquaintance."

Mr. Gosport, satisfied now with the subject of her complaint, returned to Cecilia, and informed her of the heavy charge which was brought against her.

"I am glad, at least, to know my crime," said she, "for otherwise I should certainly have sinned on in ignorance, as I must confess I never thought of returning her visits: but even if I had, I should not have supposed I had yet lost much time."

"I beg your pardon there," said Mrs. Harrel; "a first visit ought to be returned always by the third day."

"Then have I an unanswerable excuse," said Cecilia, "for I remember that on the third day I saw her at your house."

"O that's nothing at all to the purpose; you should have waited upon her, or sent her a ticket, just the same as if you had not seen her."

The overture was now begun, and Cecilia declined any further conversation. This was the first Opera she had ever heard, yet she was not wholly a stranger to Italian compositions, having assiduously studied music from a natural love of the art, attended all the best concerts her neighbourhood afforded, and regularly received from London the works of the best masters. But the little skill she had thus gained, served rather to increase than to lessen the surprise with which she heard the present performance,—a surprize of which the discovery of her own ignorance made not the least part. Unconscious from the little she had acquired how much was to be learnt, she was astonished to find the inadequate power of written music to convey any idea of vocal abilities: with just knowledge enough, therefore, to understand something of the difficulties, and feel much of the merit, she gave to the whole Opera an avidity of attention almost painful from its own eagerness.

But both the surprize and the pleasure which she received from the performance in general, were faint, cold, and languid, compared to the strength of those emotions when excited by Signore Pacchierotti* in particular; and though not half the excellencies of that superior singer were necessary either to amaze or charm her unaccustomed ears, though the refinement of his taste and masterly originality of his genius, to be praised as they deserved, called for the judgment and knowledge of professors, yet a natural love of music in some measure supplied the place of cultivation, and what she could neither explain nor understand, she could feel and enjoy.

The opera was Artaserse; and the pleasure she received from the music was much augmented by her previous acquaintance with that interesting drama;* yet, as to all noviciates in science, whatever is least complicated is most pleasing, she found herself by nothing so deeply impressed, as by the plaintive and beautiful simplicity with which Pacchierotti uttered the affecting repetition of *sono innocente!** his voice, always either sweet or impassioned, delivered those words in a tone of softness, pathos, and sensibility, that struck her with a sensation not more new than delightful.

But though she was, perhaps, the only person thus astonished, she was by no means the only one enraptured; for notwithstanding she was too earnestly engaged to remark the company in general, she could not avoid taking notice of an old gentleman who stood by one of the side scenes, against which he lent his head in a manner that concealed his face, with an evident design to be wholly absorbed in listening: and during the songs of Pacchierotti he sighed so deeply that Cecilia, struck by his uncommon sensibility to the power of music, involuntarily watched him, whenever her mind was sufficiently at liberty to attend to any emotions but its own.

As soon as the rehearsal was over, the gentlemen of Mrs. Harrel's party crowded before her box; and Cecilia then perceived that the person whose musical enthusiasm had excited her curiosity, was the same old gentleman whose extraordinary behaviour had so much surprized her at the house of Mr. Monckton. Her desire to obtain some information concerning him again reviving, she was beginning to make fresh enquiries, when she was interrupted by the approach of Captain Aresby.

That gentleman, advancing to her with a smile of the extremest self-complacency, after hoping, in a low voice, he had the honour of seeing her well, exclaimed, "How wretchedly empty is the town! petrifying to a degree! I believe you do not find yourself at present *obsedé* by too much company?"

"*At present*, I believe the contrary!" cried Mr. Gosport.

"Really!" said the captain, unsuspicious of his sneer, "I protest I have hardly seen a soul. Have you tried the Pantheon yet, ma'am?"

"No, Sir."

"Nor I; I don't know whether people go there this year. It is not a favourite *spectacle** with me; that sitting to hear the music is a horrid bore. Have you done the Festino the honour to look in there yet?"

"No, Sir."

"Permit me, then, to have the honour to beg you will try it."

"O, ay, true," cried Mrs. Harrel; "I have really used you very ill about that; I should have got you in for a subscriber: but Lord, I have done nothing for you yet, and you never put me in mind. There's the ancient music, and Abel's concert;—as to the opera, we may have a box between us;—but there's the ladies concert* we must try for; and there's—O Lord, fifty other places we must think of!"

"Oh times of folly and dissipation!" exclaimed a voice at some distance; "Oh mignons* of idleness and luxury! What next will ye invent for the perdition of your time! How yet further will ye proceed in the annihilation of virtue!"

Every body stared; but Mrs. Harrel cooly said, "Dear, it's only the man-hater!"

"The man-hater?" repeated Cecilia, who found that the speech was made by the object of her former curiosity; "is that the name by which he is known?"

"He is known by fifty names," said Mr. Monckton; "his friends call him the *moralist*; the young ladies, the *crazy-man*; the macaronies, the *bore*; in short, he is called by any and every name but his own."

"He is a most petrifying wretch, I assure you," said the captain; "I am *obsedé* by him *partout*; if I had known he had been so near, I should certainly have said nothing."

"That you have done so well," cried Mr. Gosport, "that

if you had known it the whole time, you could have done it no better.''

The captain, who had not heard this speech, which was rather made at him than to him, continued his address to Cecilia; "Give me leave to have the honour of hoping you intend to honour our select masquerade at the Pantheon with your presence. We shall have but 500 tickets, and the subscription will only be three guineas and a half.''

"Oh objects of penury and want!'' again exclaimed the incognito; "Oh vassals of famine and distress! Come and listen to this wantonness of wealth! Come, naked and breadless as ye are, and learn how that money is consumed which to you might bring raiment and food!''

"That strange wretch,'' said the captain, "ought really to be confined; I have had the honour to be *degouté* by him so often, that I think him quite obnoxious. I make it quite* a principle to seal up my lips the moment I perceive him.''

"Where is it, then,'' said Cecilia, "that you have so often met him?''

"O,'' answered the captain, "*partout*; there is no greater bore about town. But the time I found him most petrifying was once when I happened to have the honour of dancing with a very young lady, who was but just come from a boarding-school, and whose friends had done me the honour to fix upon me upon the principle of first bringing her out: and while I was doing *mon possible* for killing the time, he came up, and in his particular manner, told her I had no meaning in any thing I said! I must own I never felt more tempted to be *enragé* with a person in years, in my life.''

Mr. Arnott now brought the ladies word that their carriage was ready, and they quitted their box: but as Cecilia had never before seen the interior parts of a theatre, Mr. Monckton, hoping while they loitered to have an opportunity of talking with her, asked Morrice why he did not *shew the lyons?** Morrice, always happy in being employed, declared it was *just the thing he liked best*, and begged permission to do the honours to Mrs. Harrel, who, ever eager in the search of amusement, willingly accepted his offer.

They all, therefore, marched upon the stage, their own party now being the only one that remained.

"We shall make a triumphal entry here," cried Sir Robert Floyer; "the very tread of the stage half tempts me to turn actor."

"You are a rare man," said Mr. Gosport, "if, at your time of life, that is a turn not already taken."

"My time of life!" repeated he; "what do you mean by that? do you take me for an old man!"

"No, Sir, but I take you to be past childhood, and consequently to have served your apprenticeship to the actors you have mixed with on the great stage of the world, and, for some years at least, to have set up for yourself."

"Come," cried Morrice, "let's have a little spouting; 'twill make us warm."

"Yes," said Sir Robert, "if we spout to an animating object. If Miss Beverley will be Juliet, I am Romeo at her service."

At this moment the incognito, quitting the corner in which he had planted himself, came suddenly forward, and standing before the whole group, cast upon Cecilia a look of much compassion, and called out, "Poor simple victim! hast thou already so many pursuers? yet seest not that thou art marked for sacrifice! yet knowest not that thou art destined for prey!"

Cecilia, extremely struck by this extraordinary address, stopt short and looked much disturbed: which, when he perceived, he added, "Let the danger, not the warning affect you! discard the sycophants that surround you, seek the virtuous, relieve the poor, and save yourself from the impending destruction of unfeeling prosperity!"

Having uttered these words with vehemence and authority, he sternly passed them, and disappeared.

Cecilia, too much astonished for speech, stood for some time immoveable, revolving in her mind various conjectures upon the meaning of an exhortation so strange and so urgent.

Nor was the rest of the company much less discomposed: Sir Robert, Mr. Monckton and Mr. Arnott, each conscious of their own particular plans, were each apprehensive that the warning pointed at himself: Mr. Gosport was offended at being included in the general appellation of sycophants; Mrs. Harrel was provoked at being interrupted in her ramble; and Captain Aresby, sickening at the very sight of him, retreated the moment he came forth.

"For heaven's sake," cried Cecilia, when somewhat recovered from her consternation, "who can this be, and what can he mean? You, Mr. Monckton, must surely know something of him; it was at your house I first saw him."

"Indeed," answered Mr. Monckton, "I knew almost nothing of him then, and I am but little better informed now. Belfield picked him up somewhere, and desired to bring him to my house: he called him by the name of Albany: * I found him a most extraordinary character, and Belfield, who is a worshipper of originality, was very fond of him."

"He's a devilish crabbed old fellow," cried Sir Robert, "and if he goes on much longer at this confounded rate, he stands a very fair chance of getting his ears cropt."*

"He is a man of the most singular conduct I have ever met with," said Mr. Gosport; "he seems to hold mankind in abhorrence, yet he is never a moment alone, and at the same time that he intrudes himself into all parties, he associates with none: he is commonly a stern and silent observer of all that passes, or when he speaks, it is but to utter some sentence of rigid morality, or some bitterness of indignant reproof."

The carriage was now again announced, and Mr. Monckton taking Cecilia's hand, while Mr. Morrice secured to himself the honour of Mrs. Harrel's, Sir Robert and Mr. Gosport made their bows and departed. But though they had now quitted the stage, and arrived at the head of a small stair case by which they were to descend out of the theatre, Mr. Monckton, finding all his tormentors retired, except Mr. Arnott, whom he hoped to elude, could not resist making one more attempt for a few moments conversation with Cecilia; and therefore, again applying to Morrice, he called out, "I don't think you have shewn the ladies any of the contrivances behind the scenes?"

"True," cried Morrice, "no more I have; suppose we go back?"

"I shall like it vastly," said Mrs. Harrel; and back they returned.

Mr. Monckton now soon found an opportunity to say to Cecilia, "Miss Beverley, what I foresaw has exactly come to pass; you are surrounded by selfish designers, by interested, double-minded people, who have nothing at heart but your fortune, and whose mercenary views, if you are not guarded against them—"

Here a loud scream from Mrs. Harrel interrupted his speech; Cecilia, much alarmed, turned from him to enquire the cause, and Mr. Monckton was obliged to follow her example: but his mortification was almost intolerable when he saw that lady in a violent fit of laughter, and found her scream was only occasioned by seeing Mr. Morrice, in his diligence to do the honours, pull upon his own head one of the side scenes!*

There was now no possibility of proposing any farther delay; but Mr. Monckton, in attending the ladies to their carriage, was obliged to have recourse to his utmost discretion and forbearance, in order to check his desire of reprimanding Morrice for his blundering officiousness.

Dressing, dining with company at home, and then going out with company abroad, filled up, as usual, the rest of the day.

CHAPTER IX

A Supplication

THE next morning Cecilia, at the repeated remonstrances of Mrs. Harrel, consented to call upon Miss Larolles. She felt the impracticability of beginning at present the alteration in her way of life she had projected, and therefore thought it most expedient to assume no singularity till her independency should enable her to support it with consistency; yet greater than ever was her internal eagerness to better satisfy her inclination and her conscience in the disposition of her time, and the distribution of her wealth, since she had heard the emphatic charge of her unknown Mentor.*

Mrs. Harrel declined accompanying her in this visit, because she had appointed a surveyor to bring a plan for the inspection of Mr. Harrel and herself, of a small temporary building,* to be erected at Violet-Bank, for the purpose of performing plays in private the ensuing Easter.

When the street door was opened for her to get into the carriage, she was struck with the appearance of an elderly woman who was standing at some distance, and seemed shivering with cold, and who, as she descended the steps, joined her hands in an act of supplication, and advanced nearer to the carriage.

Cecilia stopt to look at her: her dress, though parsimonious, was too neat for a beggar, and she considered a moment what she could offer her. The poor woman continued to move forward, but with a slowness of pace that indicated extreme weakness; and, as she approached and raised her head, she exhibited a countenance so wretched, and a complection so sickly, that Cecilia was impressed with horror at the sight.

With her hands still joined, and a voice that seemed fearful of its own sound, "Oh madam," she cried, "that you would but hear me!"

"Hear you!" repeated Cecilia, hastily feeling for her purse, "most certainly; and tell me how I shall assist you?"

"Heaven bless you for speaking so kindly, madam!" cried the woman, with a voice more assured: "I was sadly afraid you would be angry, but I saw the carriage at the door, and I thought I would try; for I could be no worse; and distress, madam, makes very bold."

"Angry!" said Cecilia, taking a crown from her purse, "no, indeed!—who could see such wretchedness, and feel any thing but pity!"

"Oh madam," returned the poor woman, "I could almost cry to hear you talk so, though I never thought to cry again, since I left it off for my poor Billy!"

"Have you, then, lost a son?"

"Yes, madam; but he was a great deal too good to live, so I have quite left off grieving for him now."

"Come in, good woman," said Cecilia, "it is too cold to stand here, and you seem half starved* already: come in, and let me have some talk with you."

She then gave orders that the carriage should be driven round the square till she was ready, and making the woman follow her into a parlour, desired to know what she should do for her; changing, while she spoke, from a movement of encreasing compassion, the crown which she held in her hand for double that sum.*

"You can do every thing, madam," she answered, "if you will but plead for us to his honour: he little thinks of our distress, because he has been afflicted with none himself, and I would not be so troublesome to him, but indeed, indeed, madam, we are quite pinched for want!"

Cecilia, struck with the words *he little thinks of our distress, because he has been afflicted with none himself*, felt again ashamed of the smallness of her intended donation, and taking from her purse another half guinea, said "will this assist you? Will a guinea be sufficient to you for the present?"

"I humbly thank you, madam," said the woman, curtsying low, "shall I give you a receipt?"

"A receipt?" cried Cecilia, with emotion, "for what? Alas, our accounts are by no means balanced! but I shall do more for you if I find you as deserving an object as you seem to be."

"You are very good, madam; but I only meant a receipt in part of payment."

"Payment for what? I don't understand you."

"Did his honour never tell you, madam, of our account?"

"What account?"

"Our bill, madam, for work done to the new Temple* at Violet-Bank: it was the last great work my poor husband was able to do, for it was there he met with his misfortune."

"What bill? What misfortune?" cried Cecilia; "What had your husband to do at Violet-Bank?"

"He was the carpenter, madam. I thought you might have seen poor Hill the carpenter there."

"No, I never was there myself. Perhaps you mistake me for Mrs. Harrel."

"Why sure, madam, a'n't you his honour's lady?"

"No. But tell me, what is this bill?"

"'Tis a bill, madam, for very hard work, for work, madam, which I am sure will cost my husband his life; and though I have been after his honour night and day to get it, and sent him letters and petitions with an account of our misfortunes, I have never received so much as a shilling! and now the servants won't even let me wait in the hall to speak to him. O madam! you who seem so good, plead to his honour in our behalf! tell him my poor husband cannot live! tell him my children are starving! and tell him my poor Billy, that used to help to keep us, is dead, and that all the work I can do by myself is not enough to maintain us!"

"Good heaven!" cried Cecilia, extremely moved, "is it then your own money for which you sue thus humbly?"

"Yes, madam, for my own just and honest money, as his honour knows, and will tell you himself."

"Impossible!" cried Cecilia, "he cannot know it; but I will take care he shall soon be informed of it. How much is the bill?"

"Two-and-twenty-pounds, madam."

"What, no more?"

"Ah madam, you gentlefolks little think how much that is to poor people! A hard working family, like mine, madam, with the help of 20*l*. will go on for a long while quite in paradise."

"Poor worthy woman!" cried Cecilia, whose eyes were filled with tears of compassion, "if 20*l*. will place you in paradise, and that 20*l*. only your just right, it is hard, indeed, that you should be kept without it; especially when your debtors are too affluent to miss it. Stay here a few moments, and I will bring you the money immediately."

Away she flew, and returned to the breakfast room, but found there only Mr. Arnott, who told her that Mr. Harrel was in the library, with his sister and some gentlemen. Cecilia briefly related her business, and begged he would

C.—6

inform Mr. Harrel she wished to speak to him directly. Mr. Arnott shook his head, but obeyed.

They returned together, and immediately.

"Miss Beverley," cried Mr. Harrel, gaily, "I am glad you are not gone, for we want much to consult with you, Will you come up stairs?"

"Presently," answered she; "but first I must speak to you about a poor woman with whom I have accidentally been talking, who has begged me to intercede with you to pay a little debt that she thinks you have forgotten, but that probably you have never heard mentioned."

"A debt?" cried he, with an immediate change of countenance, "to whom?"

"Her name, I think, is Hill; she is wife to the carpenter you employed about a new temple at Violet-Bank."

"O what—what that woman?—Well, well, I'll see she shall be paid. Come, let us go to the library."

"What, with my commission so ill executed? I promised to petition for her to have the money directly."

"Pho, pho, there's no such hurry; I don't know what I have done with her bill."

"I'll run and get another."

"O upon no account! She may send another in two or three days. She deserves to wait a twelvemonth for her impertinence in troubling you at all about it."

"That was entirely accidental: but indeed you must give me leave to perform my promise and plead for her. It must be almost the same to you whether you pay such a trifle as 20l. now, or a month hence, and to this poor woman, the difference seems little short of life or death, for she tells me her husband is dying, and her children are* half famished, and though she looks an object of the cruellest want and distress herself, she appears to be their only support."

"O," cried Mr. Harrel, laughing, "what a dismal tale has she been telling you! no doubt she saw you were fresh from the country! But if you give credit to all the farragos of these trumpery impostors, you will never have a moment to yourself, nor a guinea in your purse."

"This woman," answered Cecilia, "cannot be an

impostor, she carries marks but too evident and too dreadful in her countenance of the sufferings which she relates.''

"O," returned he, "when you know the town better, you will soon see through tricks of this sort; a sick husband and five small children are complaints so stale now, that they serve no other purpose in the world but to make a joke."

"Those, however, who can laugh at them must have notions of merriment very different to mine. And this poor woman, whose cause I have ventured to undertake, had she no family at all, must still and indisputably be an object of pity herself, for she is so weak she can hardly crawl, and so pallid, that she seems already half dead."

"All imposition, depend upon it! The moment she is out of your sight, her complaints will vanish."

"Nay, sir," cried Cecilia, a little impatiently, "there is no reason to suspect such deceit, since she does not come hither as a beggar, however well the state of beggary may accord with her poverty: she only sollicits the payment of a bill, and if in that there is any fraud, nothing can be so easy as detection."

Mr. Harrel bit his lips at this speech, and for some instants looked much disturbed; but soon recovering himself, he negligently said "Pray how did she get at you?"

"I met her at the street door. But tell me, is not her bill a just one?"

"I cannot say; I have never had time to look at it."

"But you know who the woman is, and that her husband worked for you, and therefore that in all probability it is right,—do you not?"

"Yes, yes, I know who the woman is well enough; she has taken care of that, for she has pestered me every day these nine months."

Cecilia was struck dumb by this speech: hitherto she had supposed that the dissipation of his life kept him ignorant of his own injustice; but when she found he was so well informed of it, yet, with such total indifference, could suffer a poor woman to claim a just debt every day for nine months together, she was shocked and astonished beyond measure. They were both some time silent, and then Mr. Harrel, yawning and stretching out his arms, indolently asked "Pray why does not the man come himself?"

"Did I not tell you," answered Cecilia, staring at so absent a question, "that he was very ill, and unable even to work?"

"Well, when he is better," added he, moving towards the door, "he may call, and I will talk to him."

Cecilia, all amazement at this unfeeling behaviour, turned involuntarily to Mr. Arnott, with a countenance that appealed for his assistance; but Mr. Arnott hung his head, ashamed to meet her eyes, and abruptly left the room.

Mean time Mr. Harrel, half turning back, though without looking Cecilia in the face, carelessly said, "Well, won't you come?"

"No, sir," answered she, coldly.

He then returned to the library, leaving her equally displeased, surprised and disconcerted at the conversation which had just passed between them. "Good heaven," cried she to herself, "what strange, what cruel insensibility! to suffer a wretched family to starve, from an obstinate determination to assert that they can live! to distress the poor by retaining the recompence for which alone they labour, and which at last they must have, merely from indolence, forgetfulness, or insolence! O how little did my uncle know, how little did I imagine to what a guardian I was intrusted!" She now felt ashamed even to return to the poor woman, though she resolved to do all in her power to soften her disappointment, and relieve her distress.

But before she had quitted the room, one of the servants came to tell her that his master begged the honor of her company up stairs. "Perhaps he relents!" thought she; and pleased with the hope, readily obeyed the summons.

She found him, his lady, Sir Robert Floyer, and two other gentlemen, all earnestly engaged in an argument over a large table, which was covered with plans and elevations of small buildings.

Mr. Harrel immediately addressed her with an air of vivacity and said "You are very good for coming; we can settle nothing without your advice: pray look at these different plans for our theatre, and tell us which is the best."

Cecilia advanced not a step: the sight of plans for new edifices when the workmen were yet unpaid for old ones; the cruel wantonness of raising fresh fabrics of expensive luxury, while those so lately built had brought their neglected labourers to ruin, excited an indignation she scarce thought right to repress: while the easy sprightliness of the director of these revels, to whom but the moment before she had represented the oppression of which they made him guilty, filled her with aversion and disgust: and, recollecting the charge given her by the stranger at the Opera rehearsal, she resolved to speed her departure to another house, internally repeating "Yes, I *will* save myself from *the impending destruction of unfeeling prosperity!*"*

Mrs. Harrel, surprised at her silence and extreme gravity, enquired if she was not well, and why she had put off her visit to Miss Larolles? And Sir Robert Floyer, turning suddenly to look at her, said "Do you begin to feel the London air already?"

Cecilia endeavoured to recover her serenity, and answer these questions in her usual manner; but she persisted in declining to give any opinion at all about the plans, and, after slightly looking at them, left the room.

Mr. Harrel, who knew better how to account for her behaviour than he thought proper to declare, saw with concern that she was more seriously displeased, than he had believed an occurrence which he had regarded as wholly unimportant, could have made her: and therefore, desirous that she should be appeased, he followed her out of the library, and said "Miss Beverley, will to-morrow be soon enough for your *Protegée?*"

"O yes, no doubt!" answered she, most agreeably surprised by the question.

"Well, then, will you take the trouble to bid her come to me in the morning?"

Delighted at this unexpected commission, she thanked him with smiles for the office; and as she hastened down stairs to chear the poor expectant with the welcome intelligence, she framed a thousand excuses for the part he had hitherto acted, and without any difficulty, persuaded herself he began to see the faults of his conduct, and to meditate a reformation.

She was received by the poor creature she so warmly wished to serve with a countenance already so much enlivened, that she fancied Mr. Harrel had himself anticipated her intended information: this, however, she found was not the case, for as soon as she heard his message, she shook her head, and said "Ah, madam, his honour always says to-morrow! but I can better bear to be disappointed now, so I'll grumble no more; for indeed, madam, I have been blest enough to-day to comfort me for every thing in the world, if I could but keep from thinking of poor Billy! I could bear all the rest, madam, but whenever my other troubles go off, that comes back to me so much the harder!''

"There, indeed, I can afford you no relief," said Cecilia, "but you must try to think less of him, and more of your husband and children who are now alive. To-morrow you will receive your money, and that, I hope, will raise your spirits. And pray let your husband have a physician, to tell you how to nurse and manage him; I will give you one fee for him now, and if he should want further advice, don't fear to let me know."

Cecilia had again taken out her purse, but Mrs. Hill, clasping her hands, called out "Oh madam no! I don't come here to fleece such goodness! but blessed be the hour that brought me here to-day, and if my poor Billy was alive, he should help me to thank you!''

She then told her that she was now quite rich, for while she was gone, a gentleman had come into the room, who had given her five guineas.

Cecilia, by her description, soon found this gentleman was Mr. Arnott, and a charity so sympathetic with her own, failed not to raise him greatly in her favour. But as her benevolence was a stranger to that parade which is only liberal from emulation, when she found more money not immediately wanted, she put up her purse, and charging Mrs. Hill to enquire for her the next morning when she came to be paid, bid her hasten back to her sick husband.

And then, again ordering the carriage to the door, she set off upon her visit to Miss Larolles, with a heart happy in the good already done, and happier still in the hope of doing more.

Miss Larolles was out, and she returned home; for she was too sanguine in her expectations from Mr. Harrel, to have any desire of seeking her other guardians. The rest of the day she was more than usually civil to him, with a view to mark her approbation of his good intentions; while Mr. Arnott, gratified by meeting the smiles he so much valued, thought his five guineas amply repaid, independently of the real pleasure which he took in doing good.

CHAPTER X

A Provocation

THE next morning, when breakfast was over, Cecilia waited with much impatience to hear some tidings of the poor carpenter's wife; but though Mr. Harrel, who had always that meal in his own room, came into his lady's at his usual hour, to see what was going forward, he did not mention her name. She therefore went into the hall herself, to enquire among the servants if Mrs. Hill was yet come?

Yes, they answered, and had seen their master, and was gone.

She then returned to the breakfast room, where her eagerness to procure some information detained her, though the entrance of Sir Robert Floyer made her wish to retire. But she was wholly at a loss, whether to impute to general forgetfulness, or to the failure of performing his promise, the silence of Mr. Harrel upon the subject of her petition.

In a few minutes they were visited by Mr. Morrice, who said he called to acquaint the ladies that the next morning there was to be a rehearsal of a very grand new dance at the Opera-House, where, though admission was difficult, if it was agreeable to them to go, he would undertake to introduce them.

Mrs. Harrel happened to be engaged, and therefore

declined the offer. He then turned to Cecilia, and said, "Well, ma'am, when did you see our friend Monckton?"

"Not since the rehearsal, Sir."

"He is a mighty agreeable fellow," he continued, "and his house in the country is charming. One is as easy at it as at home. Were you ever there, Sir Robert?"

"Not I, truly," replied Sir Robert; "what should I go for?—to see an old woman with never a tooth in her head sitting at the top of the table! Faith I'd go an hundred miles a day for a month never to see such a sight again."

"O but you don't know how well she does the honours," said Morrice; "and for my part, except just at meal times, I always contrive to keep out of her way."

"I wonder when she intends to die," said Mr. Harrel.

"She's been a long time about it," cried Sir Robert; "but those tough old cats last for ever. We all thought she was going when Monckton married her; however, if he had not managed like a driveler, he might have broke her heart nine years ago."

"I am sure I wish he had," cried Mrs. Harrel, "for she's an odious creature, and used always to make me afraid of her."

"But an old woman," answered Sir Robert, "is a person who has no sense of decency; if once she takes to living, the devil himself can't get rid of her."

"I dare say," cried Morrice, "she'll pop off before long in one of those fits of the asthma. I assure you sometimes you may hear her wheeze a mile off."

"She'll go never the sooner for that," said Sir Robert, "for I have got an old aunt of my own, who has been puffing and blowing as if she was at her last gasp ever since I can remember; and for all that, only yesterday, when I asked her doctor when she'd give up the ghost, he told me she might live these dozen years."

Cecilia was by no means sorry to have this brutal conversation interrupted by the entrance of a servant with a letter for her. She was immediately retiring to read it; but upon the petition of Mr. Monckton, who just then came into the room, she only went to a window. The letter was as follows:

                    To
                Miss,
        at his Honour Squire Harrel's,
                    These.
Honoured Madam,

  THIS with my humble duty. His Honour has given me
nothing. But I would not be troublesome, having wherewithal to wait, so conclude,
                Honoured Madam,
            Your dutiful servant to command,
                    till death,

                            M. HILL.

  The vexation with which Cecilia read this letter was
visible to the whole company; and while Mr. Arnott looked
at her with a wish of enquiry he did not dare express, and
Mr. Monckton, under an appearance of inattention,
concealed the most anxious curiosity, Mr. Morrice alone
had courage to interrogate her; and, pertly advancing, said,
"He is a happy man who writ that letter, ma'am, for I am
sure you have not read it with indifference."

  "Were I the writer," said Mr. Arnott, tenderly, "I am
sure I should reckon myself far otherwise, for Miss Beverley
seems to have read it with uneasiness."

  "However, I have read it," answered she, "I assure you
it is not from *any man*."

  "Oh pray, Miss Beverley," cried Sir Robert, coming
forward, "are you any better to-day?"

  "No, Sir, for I have not been ill."

  "A little vapoured,* I thought, yesterday; perhaps you
want exercise."

  "I wish the ladies would put themselves under my care,"
cried Morrice, "and take a turn round the park."

  "I don't doubt you, Sir," said Mr. Monckton,
contemptuously, "and, but for the check of modesty,
probably there is not a man here who would not wish the
same."

  "I could propose a much better scheme than that," said
Sir Robert; "what if you all walk to Harley-street, and give

me your notions of a house I am about there? what say you,
Mrs. Harrel?"

"O, I shall like it vastly."

"Done," cried Mr. Harrel; "'tis an excellent motion."

"Come then," said Sir Robert, "let's be off. Miss
Beverley, I hope you have a good warm cloak?"

"I must beg you to excuse my attending you, Sir."

Mr. Monckton, who had heard this proposal with the
utmost dread of its success, revived at the calm steadiness
with which it was declined. Mr. and Mrs. Harrel both teized
Cecilia to consent; but the haughty Baronet, evidently more
offended than hurt by her refusal, pressed the matter no
further: either with her or the rest of the party, and the
scheme was dropt entirely.

Mr. Monckton failed not to remark this circumstance,
which confirmed his suspicions, that though the proposal
seemed made by chance, its design* was nothing else than
to obtain Cecilia's opinion concerning his house. But while
this somewhat alarmed him, the unabated insolence of his
carriage, and the confident defiance of his pride, still more
surprized him; and notwithstanding all he observed of
Cecilia, seemed to promise nothing but dislike; he could
draw no other inference from his behaviour, than that if he
admired, he also concluded himself sure of her.

This was not a pleasant conjecture, however little weight
he allowed to it; and he resolved, by outstaying all the
company, to have a few minutes private discourse with her
upon the subject.

In about half an hour, Sir Robert and Mr. Harrel went
out together: Mr. Monckton still persevered in keeping his
ground, and tried, though already weary, to keep up a
general conversation; but what moved at once his wonder
and his indignation was the assurance of Morrice, who
seemed not only bent upon staying as long as himself, but
determined, by rattling away, to make his own
entertainment.

At length a servant came in to tell Mrs. Harrel that a
stranger, who was waiting in the house-keeper's room,
begged to speak with her upon very particular business.

"O I know," cried she, "'tis that odious John Groot: do pray, brother, try to get rid of him for me, for he comes to teize me about his bill, and I never know what to say to him."

Mr. Arnott went immediately, and Mr. Monckton could scarce refrain from going too, that he might entreat John Groot by no means to be satisfied without seeing Mrs. Harrel herself: John Groot, however, wanted not his entreaties, as the servant soon returned to summon his lady to the conference.

But though Mr. Monckton now seemed near the completion of his purpose, Morrice still remained; his vexation at this circumstance soon grew intolerable; to see himself upon the point of receiving the recompence of his perseverance, by the fortunate removal of all the obstacles in its way, and then to have it held from him by a young fellow he so much despised, and who had no entrance into the house but through his own boldness, and no inducement to stay in it but from his own impertinence, mortified him so insufferably, that it was with difficulty he even forbore affronting him. Nor would he have scrupled a moment desiring him to leave the room, had he not prudently determined to guard with the utmost sedulity against raising any suspicions of his passion for Cecilia.

He arose, however, and was moving towards her, with intention to occupy a part of a sofa on which she was seated, when Morrice, who was standing at the back of it, with a sudden spring which made the whole room shake, jumpt over, and sunk plump into the vacant place himself, calling out at the same time, "Come, come, what have you married men to do with young ladies? I shall seize this post for myself."

The rage of Mr. Monckton at this feat, and still more at the words *married men*, almost exceeded endurance; he stopt short, and looking at him with a fierceness that overpowered his discretion, was blurting out with, "Sir, you are an—— *impudent fellow*;" but checking himself when he got half way, concluded with, "a very facetious gentleman!"

Morrice, who wished nothing so little as disobliging Mr. Monckton, and whose behaviour was merely the result of levity and a want of early education, no sooner perceived his displeasure, than rising with yet more agility than he had seated himself, he resumed the obsequiousness of which an uncommon flow of spirits had robbed him, and guessing no other subject for his anger than the disturbance he had made, he bowed almost to the ground, first to him, and afterwards to Cecilia, most respectfully begging pardon of them both for his frolic, and protesting he had no notion he should have made such a noise!

Mrs. Harrel and Mr. Arnott now hastening back, enquired what had been the matter? Morrice, ashamed of his exploit, and frightened by the looks of Mr. Monckton, made an apology with the utmost humility, and hurried away: and Mr. Monckton, hopeless of any better fortune, soon did the same, gnawn with a cruel discontent which he did not dare avow, and longing to revenge himself upon Morrice, even by personal chastisement.

CHAPTER XI

A Narration

THE moment Cecilia was at liberty, she sent her own servant to examine into the real situation of the carpenter and his family, and to desire his wife would call upon her as soon as she was at leisure. The account which he brought back encreased her concern for the injuries of these poor people, and determined her not to rest satisfied till she saw them redressed. He informed her that they lived in a small lodging up two pair of stairs; that there were five children, all girls, the three eldest of whom were hard at work with their mother in matting chair-bottoms, and the fourth, though a mere child, was nursing the youngest; while the poor carpenter himself was confined to his bed, in consequence of a fall from a ladder while working at Violet-Bank, by which he was covered with wounds and contusions, and an object of misery and pain.

As soon as Mrs. Hill came, Cecilia sent for her into her

own room, where she received her with the most compassionate tenderness, and desired to know when Mr. Harrel talked of paying her?

"To-morrow, madam," she answered, shaking her head, "that is always his honour's speech: but I shall bear it while I can. However, though I dare not tell his honour, something bad will come of it, if I am not paid soon."

"Do you mean, then, to apply to the law?"

"I must not tell you, madam; but to be sure we have thought of it many a sad time and often; but still while we could rub on, we thought it best not to make enemies: but, indeed, madam, his honour was so hard-hearted this morning, that if I was not afraid you would be angry, I could not tell how to bear it; for when I told him I had no help now, for I had lost my Billy, he had the heart to say, so much the better, there's one the less of you."

"But what," cried Cecilia, extremely shocked by this unfeeling speech, "is the reason he gives for disappointing you so often?"

"He says, madam, that none of the other workmen are paid yet; and that, to be sure, is very true; but then they can all better afford to wait than we can, for we were the poorest of all, madam, and have been misfortunate from the beginning: and his honour would never have employed us, only he had run up such a bill with Mr. Wright, that he would not undertake any thing more till he was paid. We were told from the first we should not get our money; but we were willing to hope for the best, for we had nothing to do, and were hard run, and had never had the offer of so good a job before; and we had a great family to keep, and many losses, and so much illness!——Oh madam! if you did but know what the poor go through!"

This speech opened to Cecilia a new view of life; that a young man could appear so gay and happy, yet be guilty of such injustice and inhumanity, that he could take pride in works which not even money had made his own, and live with undiminished splendor, when his credit itself began to fail, seemed to her incongruities so irrational, that hitherto she had supposed them impossible.

She then enquired, if her husband had yet had any physician?

"Yes, madam, I humbly thank your goodness," she answered; "but I am not the poorer for that, for the gentleman was so kind he would take nothing."

"And does he give you any hopes? what does he say?"

"He says he must die, madam! but I knew that before."

"Poor woman! and what will you do then?"

"The same, madam, as I did when I lost my Billy, work on the harder!"

"Good heaven, how severe a lot! but tell me, why is it you seem to love your Billy so much better than the rest of your children?"

"Because, madam, he was the only boy that ever I had; he was seventeen years old, madam, and as tall and as pretty a lad! and so good, that he never cost me a wet eye till I lost him. He worked with his father, and all the folks used to say he was the better workman of the two."

"And what was the occasion of his death?"

"A consumption, madam, that wasted him quite to nothing: and he was ill a long time, and cost us a deal of money, for we spared neither for wine nor any thing, that we thought would but comfort him; and we loved him so we never grudged it. But he died, madam! and if it had not been for very hard work, the loss of him would quite have broke my heart."

"Try, however, to think less of him," said Cecilia; "and depend upon my speaking again for you to Mr. Harrel. You shall certainly have your money; take care, therefore, of your own health, and go home and give comfort to your sick husband."

"Oh madam," cried the poor woman, tears streaming down her cheeks, "you don't know how touching it is to hear gentlefolks talk so kindly! And I have been used to nothing but roughness from his honour! But what I most fear, madam, is that when my husband is gone, he will be harder to deal with than ever; for a widow, madam, is always hard to be righted; and I don't expect to hold out long myself, for sickness and sorrow wear fast: and then, when we are both gone, who is to help our poor children?"

"*I* will!" cried the generous Cecilia; "I am able, and I am willing; you shall not find all the rich hard-hearted, and I will try to make you some amends for the unkindness you have suffered."*

The poor woman, overcome by a promise so unexpected, burst into a passionate fit of tears, and sobbed out her thanks with a violence of emotion that frightened Cecilia almost as much as it melted her. She endeavoured, by reiterated assurances of assistance, to appease her, and solemnly pledged her own honour that she should certainly be paid the following Saturday, which was only three days distant.

Mrs. Hill, when a little calmer, dried her eyes, and humbly begging her to forgive a transport which she could not restrain, most gratefully thanked her for the engagement into which she had entered, protesting that she would not be *troublesome to her goodness* as long as she could help it; "And I believe," she continued, "that if his honour will but pay me time enough for the burial, I can make shift with what I have till then. But when my poor Billy died, we were sadly off indeed, for we could not bear but bury him prettily, because it was the last we could do for him: but we could hardly scrape up enough for it, and yet we all went without our dinners to help forward, except the little one of all. But that did not much matter, for we had no great heart for eating."

"I cannot bear this!" cried Cecilia; "you must tell me no more of your Billy; but go home, and chear your spirits, and do every thing in your power to save your husband."

"I will, madam," answered the woman, "and his dying prayers shall bless you! and all my children shall bless you, and every night they shall pray for you. And oh!"—again bursting into tears, "that* Billy was but alive to pray for you too!"

Cecilia kindly endeavoured to soothe her, but the poor creature, no longer able to suppress the violence of her awakened sorrows, cried out, "I must go, madam, and pray for you at home, for now I have once begun crying again, I don't know how to have done!" and hurried away.

Cecilia determined to make once more an effort with Mr.

Harrel for the payment of the bill, and if that, in two days, did not succeed, to take up money for the discharge of it herself, and rest all her security for reimbursement upon the shame with which such a proceeding must overwhelm him. Offended, however, by the repulse she had already received from him, and disgusted by all she had heard of his unfeeling negligence, she knew not how to address him, and resolved upon applying again to Mr. Arnott, who was already acquainted with the affair, for advice and assistance.

Mr. Arnott, though extremely gratified that she consulted him, betrayed by his looks an hopelessness of success that damped all her expectations. He promised, however, to speak to Mr. Harrel upon the subject, but the promise was evidently given to oblige the fair mediatrix, without any hope of advantage to the cause.

The next morning Mrs. Hill again came, and again without payment was dismissed.

Mr. Arnott then, at the request of Cecilia, followed Mr. Harrel into his room, to enquire into the reason of this breach of promise; they continued some time together, and when he returned to Cecilia, he told her, that his brother had assured him he would give orders to Davison, his gentleman, to let her have the money the next day.

The pleasure with which she would have heard this intelligence was much checked by the grave and cold manner in which it was communicated: she waited, therefore, with more impatience than confidence for the result of this fresh assurance.

The next morning, however, was the same as the last; Mrs. Hill came, saw Davison, and was sent away.

Cecilia, to whom she related her grievances, then flew to Mr. Arnott, and entreated him to enquire at least of Davison why the woman had again been disappointed.

Mr. Arnott obeyed her, and brought for answer, that Davison had received no orders from his master.

"I entreat you then," cried she, with mingled eagerness and vexation, "to go, for the last time, to Mr. Harrel. I am sorry to impose upon you an office so disagreeable, but I am sure you compassionate these poor people, and will serve them now with your interest, as you have already done with your purse. I only wish to know if there has been any mistake, or if these delays are merely to sicken me of petitioning."

Mr. Arnott, with a repugnance to the request which he could as ill conceal as his admiration of the zealous requester, again forced himself to follow Mr. Harrel. His stay was not long, and Cecilia at his return perceived that he was hurt and disconcerted. As soon as they were alone together, she begged to know what had passed? "Nothing," answered he, "that will give you any pleasure. When I entreated my brother to come to the point, he said it was his intention to pay all his workmen together, for that if he paid any one singly, all the rest would be dissatisfied."

"And why," said Cecilia, "should he not pay them at once? There can be no more comparison in the value of the money to him and to them, than, to speak with truth, there is in his and in their right to it."

"But, madam, the bills for the new house itself are none of them settled, and he says that the moment he is known to discharge an account for the Temple, he shall not have any rest for the clamours it will raise among the workmen who were employed about the house."

"How infinitely strange!" exclaimed Cecilia; "will he not, then, pay any body?"

"Next quarter, he says, he shall pay them all, but, at present, he has a particular call for his money."

Cecilia would not trust herself to make any comments upon such an avowal, but thanking Mr. Arnott for the trouble which he had taken, she determined, without any further application, to desire Mr. Harrel to advance her 20*l.* the next morning, and satisfy the carpenter herself, be the risk what it might.

The following day, therefore, which was the Saturday when payment was promised, she begged an audience of Mr. Harrel; which he immediately granted; but, before she could make her demand, he said to her, with an air of the utmost gaiety and good-humour, "Well, Miss Beverley, how fares it with your *protegée?* I hope, at length, she is contented. But I must beg you would charge her to keep her own counsel, as otherwise she will draw me into a scrape I shall not thank her for."

"Have you, then, paid her?" cried Cecilia, with much amazement.

"Yes; I promised you I would, you know."

This intelligence equally delighted and astonished her; she repeatedly thanked him for his attention to her petition, and, eager to communicate her success to Mr. Arnott, she hastened to find him. "Now," cried she, "I shall torment you no more with painful commissions; the Hills, at last, are paid!"

"From you, madam," answered he gravely, "no commissions could be painful."

"Well but," said Cecilia, somewhat disappointed, "you don't seem glad of this?"

"Yes," answered he, with a forced smile, "I am very glad to see you so."

"But how was it brought about? did Mr. Harrel relent? or did you attack him again?"

The hesitation of his answer convinced her there was some mystery in the transaction; she began to apprehend she had been deceived, and hastily quitting the room, sent for Mrs. Hill: but the moment the poor woman appeared, she was satisfied of the contrary, for, almost frantic with joy and gratitude, she immediately flung herself upon her knees, to thank her benefactress for having *seen her righted*.

Cecilia then gave her some general advice, promised to continue her friend, and offered her assistance in getting her husband into an hospital:* but she told her he had already been in one many months, where he had been pronounced incurable, and therefore was* desirous to spend his last days in his own lodgings.

"Well," said Cecilia, "make them as easy to him as you can, and come to me next week, and I will try to put you in a better way of living."

She then, still greatly perplexed about Mr. Arnott, sought him again, and, after various questions and conjectures, at length brought him to confess he had himself lent his brother the sum with which the Hills had been paid.

Struck with his generosity, she poured forth thanks and praises so grateful to his ears, that she soon gave him a recompense which he would have thought cheaply purchased by half his fortune.

BOOK II

CHAPTER I

A Man of Wealth

THE meanness with which Mr. Harrel had assumed the credit, as well as accepted the assistance of Mr. Arnott, encreased the disgust he had already excited in Cecilia, and hastened her resolution of quitting his house: and therefore, without waiting any longer for the advice of Mr. Monckton, she resolved to go instantly to her other guardians, and see what better prospects their habitations might offer.

For this purpose, she borrowed one of the carriages, and gave orders to be driven into the city, to the house of Mr. Briggs.

She told her name, and was shewn, by a little shabby foot-boy, into a parlour.

Here she waited, with tolerable patience, for half an hour, but then, imagining the boy had forgotten to tell his master she was in the house, she thought it expedient to make some enquiry.

No bell, however, could she find, and therefore she went into the passage in search of the foot-boy; but, as she was proceeding to the head of the kitchen stairs, she was startled by hearing a man's voice from the upper part of the house, exclaiming , in a furious passion, "Dare say you've* filched it for a dish-clout!"*

She called out, however, "Are any of Mr. Briggs's servants below?"

"Anan!"* answered the boy, who came to the foot of the stairs, with a knife in one hand, and an old shoe, upon the sole of which he was sharpening it, in the other, "Does any one call?"

"Yes," said Cecilia, "I do; for I could not find the bell."

"O, we have no bell in the parlour," returned the boy, "master always knocks with his stick."

"I am afraid Mr. Briggs is too busy to see me, and if so, I will come another time."

"No, ma'am," said the boy, "master's only looking over his things from the wash."

"Will you tell him, then, that I am waiting?"

"I has, ma'am; but master misses his shaving-rag, and he says he won't come to the Mogul* till he's found it." And then he went on with sharpening his knife.

This little circumstance was at least sufficient to satisfy Cecilia that if she fixed her abode with Mr. Briggs, she should not have much uneasiness to fear from the sight of extravagance and profusion.

She returned to the parlour, and after waiting another half hour, Mr. Briggs made his appearance.

Mr. Briggs was a short, thick, sturdy man, with very small keen black eyes, a square face, a dark complection, and a snub nose. His constant dress, both in winter and summer, was a snuff-colour suit* of cloaths, blue and white speckled worsted stockings, a plain skirt, and a bob wig. He was seldom without a stick in his hand, which he usually held to his forehead when not speaking.

This bob wig,* however, to the no small amazement of Cecilia, he now brought into the room upon the fore finger of his left hand, while, with his right, he was smoothing the curls; and his head, in defiance of the coldness of the weather, was bald and uncovered.

"Well," cried he, as he entered, "did you think should not come?"

"I was very willing, sir, to wait your leisure."

"Ay, ay, knew you had not much to do. Been looking for my shaving-rag. Going out of town; never use such a thing at home, paper does as well. Warrant master Harrel never heard of such a thing; ever see him comb his own wig? Warrant he don't know how! never trust mine out of my hands, the boy would tear off half the hair; all one to master Harrel, I suppose. Well, which is the warmer man, that's all? Will he cast an account* with me?"

Cecilia, at a loss what to say to this singular exordium, began an apology for not waiting upon him sooner.

"Ay, ay," cried he, "always gadding, no getting sight of you. Live a fine life! A pretty guardian master Harrel! and where's t'other? where's old Don Puffabout?"

"If you mean Mr. Delvile, sir, I have not yet seen him."

"Thought so. No matter, as well not. Only tell you he's a German Duke, or a Spanish Don Ferdinand.* Well you've me! poorly off else. A couple of ignoramusses! don't know when to buy nor when to sell. No doing business with either of them. We met once or twice; all to no purpose; only heard Don Vampus* count his old Grandees; how will that get interest for money? Then comes Master Harrel,——twenty bows to a word,—looks at a watch,—about as big as a six-pence,*—poor raw ninny!—a couple of rare guardians! Well you've me, I say; mind that!"

Cecilia was wholly unable to devise any answer to these effusions of contempt and anger; and therefore his harangue lasted without interruption, till he had exhausted all his subjects of complaint, and emptied his mind of ill-will; and then, settling his wig, he drew a chair near her, and twinkling his little black eyes in her face, his rage subsided into the most perfect good humour; and, after peering at her some time with a look of much approbation, he said, with an arch nod, "Well, my duck, got ever a sweet-heart yet?"

Cecilia laughed, and said "No."

"Ah, little rogue, don't believe you! all a fib! better speak out: come, fit I should know; a'n't you my own ward? to be sure almost of age, but not quite, so what's that to me?"

She then, more seriously, assured him she had no intelligence of that sort to communicate.

"Well, when you have tell, that's all. Warrant sparks* enough hankering. I'll give you some advice. Take care of sharpers; don't trust shoe-buckles, nothing but Bristol stones!* tricks in all things. A fine gentleman sharp as another man. Never give your heart to a gold topped cane, nothing but brass gilt over.* Cheats every where: fleece you in a year; wont leave you a groat. But one way to be safe,——bring 'em all to me."

Cecilia thanked him for his caution, and promised not to forget his advice.

"That's the way," he continued, "bring 'em to me. Won't be bamboozled. Know their tricks. Shew 'em the odds on't. Ask for the rent-roll,—see how they'll look! stare like stuck pigs!* got no such thing."

"Certainly, sir, that will be an excellent method of trial."

"Ay, ay, know the way! soon find if they are above par. Be sure don't mind gold waistcoats; nothing but tinsel, all shew and no substance; better leave the matter to me; take care of you myself; know where to find one will do."

She again thanked him; and, being fully satisfied with this specimen of his conversation, and unambitious of any further counsel from him, she arose to depart.

"Well," repeated he, nodding at her with a look of much kindness, "leave it to me, I say; I'll get you a careful husband, so take no thought about the matter."

Cecilia, half laughing, begged he would not give himself much trouble, and assured him she was not in any haste.

"All the better," said he, "good girl; no fear for you: look out myself; warrant I'll find one. Not very easy, neither; hard times! men scarce! wars and tumults! stocks low! women chargeable!*——but don't fear; do our best; get you off soon."

She then returned to her carriage; full of reflection upon the scene in which she had just been engaged, and upon the strangeness of hastening from one house to avoid a vice the very want of which seemed to render another insupportable! but she now found that though luxury was more baneful in it's consequences, it was less disgustful in it's progress than avarice; yet, insuperably averse to both, and almost equally desirous to fly from the unjust extravagance of Mr. Harrel, as from the comfortless and unnecessary parsimony of Mr. Briggs, she proceeded instantly to St. James's-Square, convinced that her third guardian, unless exactly resembling one of the others, must inevitably be preferable to both.

CHAPTER II

A Man of Family

THE house of Mr. Delvile was grand and spacious, fitted up not with modern taste, but with the magnificence of former times; the servants were all veterans, gorgeous in their liveries, and profoundly respectful in their manners; every thing had an air of state, but of a state so gloomy, that while it inspired awe, it repressed pleasure.

Cecilia sent in her name and was admitted without difficulty, and was then ushered with great pomp through sundry apartments, and rows of servants, before she came into the presence of Mr. Delvile.

He received her with an air of haughty affability which, to a spirit open and liberal as that of Cecilia, could not fail being extremely offensive: but too much occupied with the care of his own importance to penetrate into the feelings of another, he attributed the uneasiness which his reception occasioned, to the over-awing predominance of superior rank and consequence.

He ordered a servant to bring her a chair, while he only half rose from his own upon her entering into the room; then, waving his hand and bowing, with a motion that desired her to be seated, he said "I am very happy, Miss Beverley, that you have found me alone; you would rarely have had the same good fortune. At this time of day I am generally in a crowd. People of large connections have not much leisure in London, especially if they see a little after their own affairs, and if their estates, like mine, are dispersed in various parts of the kingdom. However, I am glad it happened so. And I am glad, too, that you have done me the favour of calling without waiting till I sent, which I really would have done as soon as I heard of your arrival, but that the multiplicity of my engagements allowed me no respite."

A display of importance so ostentatious made Cecilia

already half repent her visit, satisfied that the hope in which she had planned it would be fruitless.

Mr. Delvile, still imputing to embarrassment, an inquietude of countenance that proceeded merely from disappointment, imagined her veneration was every moment encreasing; and therefore, pitying a timidity which both gratified and softened him, and equally pleased with himself for inspiring, and with her for feeling it, he abated more and more of his greatness, till he became, at length, so infinitely condescending, with intention to give her courage, that he totally depressed her with mortification and chagrin.

After some general enquiries concerning her way of life, he told her that he hoped she was contented with her situation at the Harrels, adding "If you have any thing to complain of, remember to whom you may appeal." He then asked if she had seen Mr. Briggs?

"Yes, sir, I am this moment come from his house."

"I am sorry for it; his house cannot be a proper one for the reception of a young lady. When the Dean made application that I would be one of your guardians, I instantly sent him a refusal, as is my custom upon all such occasions, which indeed occur to me with a frequency extremely importunate: but the Dean was a man for whom I had really a regard, and therefore, when I found my refusal had affected him, I suffered myself to be prevailed upon to indulge him, contrary not only to my general rule, but to my inclination."

Here he stopt, as if to receive some compliment, but Cecilia, very little disposed to pay him any, went no farther than an inclination of the head.

"I knew not, however," he continued, "at the time I was induced to give my consent, with whom I was to be associated; nor could I have imagined the Dean so little conversant with the distinctions of the world, as to disgrace me with inferior co-adjutors: but the moment I learnt the state of the affair, I insisted upon withdrawing both my name and countenance."

Here again he paused; not in expectation of an answer from Cecilia, but merely to give her time to marvel in what manner he had at last been melted.

"The Dean," he resumed, "was then very ill; my displeasure, I believe, hurt him. I was sorry for it; he was a worthy man, and had not meant to offend me; in the end, I accepted his apology, and was even persuaded to accept the office. You have a right, therefore, to consider yourself as *personally* my ward, and though I do not think proper to mix much with your other guardians, I shall always be ready to serve and advise you, and much pleased to see you."

"You do me honour, sir;" said Cecilia, extremely wearied of such graciousness, and rising to be gone.

"Pray sit still," said he, with a smile; "I have not many engagements for this morning. You must give me some account how you pass your time. Are you much out? The Harrels, I am told, live at a great expence. What is their establishment?"

"I don't exactly know, sir."

"They are decent sort of people, I believe; are they not?"

"I hope so, sir!"

"And they have a tolerable acquaintance, I believe: I am told so; for I know nothing of them."

"They have, at least, a very numerous one, sir."

"Well, my dear," said he, taking her hand, "now you have once ventured to come, don't be apprehensive of repeating your visits: I must introduce you to Mrs. Delvile; I am sure she will be happy to shew you any kindness. Come, therefore, when you please, and without scruple. I would call upon you myself, but am fearful of being embarrassed by the people with whom you live."

He then rang his bell, and with the same ceremonies which had attended her admittance, she was conducted back to her carriage.

And here died away all hope of putting into execution, during her minority, the plan of which the formation had given her so much pleasure. She found that her present situation, however wide of her wishes, was by no means the most disagreeable in which she could be placed; she was tired, indeed, of dissipation, and shocked at the sight of unfeeling extravagance; but notwithstanding the houses of each of her other guardians were exempt from these particular vices, she saw not any prospect of happiness with either of them; vulgarity seemed leagued with avarice to drive her from the mansion of Mr. Briggs, and haughtiness with ostentation to exclude her from that of Mr. Delvile.

She came back, therefore, to Portman-Square, disappointed in her hopes, and sick both of those whom she quitted, and of those to whom she was returning; but in going to her own apartment Mrs. Harrel, eagerly stopping her, begged she would come into the drawing-room, where she promised her a most agreeable surprise.

Cecilia, for an instant, imagined that some old acquaintance was just arrived out of the country; but, upon her entrance, she saw only Mr. Harrel and some workmen, and found that the agreeable surprise was to proceed from the sight of an elegant Awning, prepared for one of the inner apartments, to be fixed over a long desert-table, which was to be ornamented with various devices of cut glass.

"Did you ever see any thing so beautiful in your life?" cried Mrs. Harrel; "and when the table is covered with the coloured ices,* and those sort of things, it will be as beautiful again. We shall have it ready for Tuesday se'nnight.*

"I understood you were engaged to go to the Masquerade?"

"So we shall; only we intend to see masks at home first."

"I have some thoughts," said Mr. Harrel, leading the way to another small room, "of running up a flight of steps, and a little light gallery here, and so making a little Orchestra.* What would such a thing come to, Mr. Tomkins?"

"O, a trifle, sir," answered Mr. Tomkins, "a mere nothing."

"Well, then, give orders for it, and let it be done directly. I don't care how slight it is, but pray let it be very elegant. Won't it be a great addition, Miss Beverley?"

'Indeed, sir, I don't think it seems to be very necessary;" said Cecilia, who wished much to take that moment for reminding him of the debt he had contracted with Mr. Arnott.

"Lord, Miss Beverley is so grave!" cried Mrs. Harrel; "nothing of this sort gives her any pleasure."

"She has indeed," answered Cecilia, trying to smile, "not much taste for the pleasure of being always surrounded by workmen."

And, as soon as she was able, she retired to her room, feeling, both on the part of Mr. Arnott and the Hills, a resentment at the injustice of Mr. Harrel, which fixed her in the resolution of breaking through that facility of compliance, which had hitherto confined her disapprobation to her own breast, and venturing, henceforward, to mark the opinion she entertained of his conduct, by consulting nothing but reason and principle in her own.

Her first effort towards this change was made immediately, in begging to be excused from accompanying Mrs. Harrel to a large card assembly that evening.

Mrs. Harrel, extremely surprised, asked a thousand times the reason of her refusal, imagining it to proceed from some very extraordinary cause; nor was she, without the utmost difficulty, persuaded at last that she merely meant to pass one evening by herself.

But the next day, when the refusal was repeated, she was still more incredulous; it seemed to her impossible that any one who had the power to be encircled with company, could by choice spend a second afternoon alone: and she was so urgent in her request to be entrusted with the secret, that Cecilia found no way left to appease her, but by frankly confessing she was weary of eternal visiting, and sick of living always in a crowd.

"Suppose, then," cried she, "I send for Miss Larolles to come and sit with you?"

Cecilia, not without laughing, declined this proposal, assuring her that no such assistant was necessary for her entertainment: yet it was not till after a long contention that she was able to convince her there would be no cruelty in leaving her by herself.

The following day, however, her trouble diminished; for Mrs. Harrel, ceasing to be surprised, thought little more of the matter, and forebore any earnestness of solicitation: and, from that time, she suffered her to follow her own humour with very little opposition. Cecilia was much concerned to find her so unmoved; and not less disappointed at the indifference of Mr. Harrel, who, being seldom of the same parties with his lady, and seeing her too rarely either to communicate or hear any domestic occurrences, far from being struck, as she had hoped, with the new way in which she passed her time, was scarce sensible of the change, and interfered not upon the subject.

Sir Robert Floyer, who continued to see her when he dined in Portman-Square, often enquired what she did with herself in an evening; but never obtaining any satisfactory answer, he concluded her engagements were with people to whom he was a stranger.

Poor Mr. Arnott felt the cruellest disappointment in being deprived of the happiness of attending her in her evening's expeditions, when, whether he conversed with her or not, he was sure of the indulgence of seeing and hearing her.

But the greatest sufferer from this new regulation was Mr. Monckton, who, unable any longer to endure the mortifications of which his morning visits to Portman-Square had been productive, determined not to trust his temper with such provocations in future, but rather to take his chance of meeting with her elsewhere: for which purpose, he assiduously frequented all public places, and sought acquaintance with every family and every person he believed to be known to the Harrels: but his patience was unrewarded, and his diligence unsuccessful; he met with her no where, and, while he continued his search, fancied every evil power was at work to lead him whither he was sure never to find her.

Mean while Cecilia passed her time greatly to her own satisfaction. Her first care was to assist and comfort the Hills. She went herself to their lodgings, ordered and paid for whatever the physician prescribed to the sick man, gave clothes to the children, and money and various necessaries to the wife. She found that the poor carpenter was not likely to languish much longer, and therefore, for the present, only thought of alleviating his sufferings, by procuring him such indulgencies as were authorised by his physician, and enabling his family to abate so much of their labour as was requisite for obtaining time to nurse and attend him: but she meant, as soon as the last duties should be paid to him, to assist his survivors in attempting to follow some better and more profitable business.

Her next solicitude was to furnish herself with a well-chosen collection of books; and this employment, which to a lover of literature, young and ardent in it's pursuit, is perhaps the mind's first luxury, proved a source of entertainment so fertile and delightful that it left her nothing to wish.

She confined not her acquisitions to the limits of her present power, but, as she was laying in a stock for future as well as immediate advantage, she was restrained by no expence from gratifying her taste and her inclination. She had now entered the last year of her minority, and therefore had not any doubt that her guardians would permit her to take up whatever sum she should require for such a purpose.

And thus, in the exercise of charity, the search of knowledge, and the enjoyment of quiet, serenely in innocent philosophy passed the hours of Cecilia.

CHAPTER III

A Masquerade

THE first check this tranquility received was upon the day of the masquerade, the preparations for which have been already mentioned. The whole house was then in commotion from various arrangments and improvements which were planned for almost every apartment that was to be opened for the reception of masks. Cecilia herself, however little pleased with the attendant circumstance of wantonly accumulating unnecessary debts, was not the least animated of the party: she was a stranger to every diversion of this sort, and from the novelty of the scene, hoped for uncommon satisfaction.

At noon Mrs. Harrel sent for her to consult upon a new scheme which occurred to Mr. Harrel, of fixing in fantastic forms some coloured lamps in the drawing room.

While they were all discoursing this matter over, one of the servants, who had two or three times whispered some message to Mr. Harrel, and then retired, said, in a voice not too low to be heard by Cecilia, "Indeed, Sir, I can't get him away."

"He's an insolent scoundrel," answered Mr. Harrel; "however, if I must speak to him, I must;" and went out of the room.

Mrs. Harrel still continued to exercise her fancy upon this new project, calling both upon Mr. Arnott and Cecilia to admire her taste and contrivance; till they were all interrupted by the loudness of a voice from below stairs, which frequently repeated, "Sir, I can wait no longer! I have been put off till I can be put off no more!"

Startled by this, Mrs. Harrel ceased her employment, and they all stood still and silent. They then heard Mr. Harrel with much softness answer, "Good Mr. Rawlins have a little patience; I shall receive a large sum of money to-morrow, or next day, and you may then depend upon being paid."

"Sir," cried the man, "you have so often told me the same, that it goes just for nothing: I have had a right to it a long time, and I have a bill to make up that can't be waited for any longer."

"Certainly, Mr. Rawlins," replied Mr. Harrel, with still increasing gentleness, "and certainly you shall have it: nobody means to dispute your right; I only beg you to wait a day, or two days at furthest, and you may then depend upon being paid. And you shall not be the worse for obliging me; I will never employ any body else, and I shall have occasion for you very soon, as I intend to make some alterations at Violet-Bank that will be very considerable."

"Sir," said the man, still louder, "it is of no use your employing me, if I can never get my money: All my workmen must be paid whether I am or no; and so, if I must needs speak to a lawyer, why there's no help for it."

"Did you ever hear any thing so impertinent?" exclaimed Mrs. Harrel; "I am sure Mr. Harrel will be very much to blame, if ever he lets that man do any thing more for him."

Just then Mr. Harrel appeared, and, with an air of

affected unconcern, said, "Here's the most insolent rascal of a mason below stairs I ever met with in my life; he has come upon me, quite unexpectedly, with a bill of 400*l*. and won't leave the house without the money. Brother Arnott, I wish you would do me the favour to speak to the fellow, for I could not bear to stay with him any longer."

"Do you wish me to give him a draught for the money upon my own banker?"

"That would be vastly obliging," answered Mr. Harrel, "and I will give you my note for it directly. And so we shall get rid of this fellow at once: and he shall do nothing more for me as long as he lives. I will run up a new building at Violet-Bank next summer, if only to shew him what a job he has lost."

"Pay the man at once, there's a good brother," cried Mrs. Harrel, "and let's hear no more of him."

The two gentlemen then retired to another room, and Mrs. Harrel, after praising the extreme good-nature of her brother, of whom she was very fond, and declaring that the mason's impertinence had quite frightened her, again returned to her plan of new decorations.

Cecilia, amazed at this indifference to the state of her husband's affairs, began to think it was her own duty to talk with her upon the subject: and therefore, after a silence so marked that Mrs. Harrel enquired into its reason, she said, "Will you pardon me, my dear friend, if I own I am rather surprized to see you continue these preparations?"

"Lord, why?"

"Because any fresh unnecessary expences just now, till Mr. Harrel actually receives the money he talks of——"

"Why, my dear, the expence of such a thing as this is nothing; in Mr. Harrel's affairs I assure you it will not be at all felt. Besides, he expects money so soon, that it is just the same as if he had it already."

Cecilia, unwilling to be too officious, began then to express her admiration of the goodness and generosity of Mr. Arnott; taking frequent occasion, in the course of her praise, to insinuate that those only can be properly liberal, who are just and œconomical.

She had prepared no masquerade habit for this evening, as Mrs. Harrel, by whose direction she was guided, informed her it was not necessary for ladies to be masked at home, and said she should receive her company herself in a dress which she might wear upon any other occasion. Mr. Harrel, also, and Mr. Arnott made not any alteration in their appearance.

At about eight o'clock the business of the evening began; and before nine, there were so many masks that Cecilia wished she had herself made one of the number, as she was far more conspicuous in being almost the only female in a common dress, than any masquerade habit could have made her. The novelty of the scene, however, joined to the general air of gaiety diffused throughout the company, shortly lessened her embarrassment; and, after being somewhat familiarized to the abruptness with which the masks approached her, and the freedom with which they looked at or addressed her, the first confusion of her situation subsided, and in her curiosity to watch others, she ceased to observe how much she was watched herself.

Her expectations of entertainment were not only fulfilled but surpassed; the variety of dresses, the medley of characters, the quick succession of figures, and the ludicrous mixture of groupes, kept her attention unwearied: while the conceited efforts at wit, the total thoughtlessness of consistency, and the ridiculous incongruity of the language with the appearance, were incitements to surprise and diversion without end. Even the local cant of, *Do you know me? Who are you?* and *I know you*;* with the sly pointing of the finger, the arch nod of the head, and the pert squeak of the voice, though wearisome to those who frequent such assemblies, were, to her unhackneyed observation, additional subjects of amusement.

Soon after nine o'clock, every room was occupied, and the common crowd of regular masqueraders were dispersed through the various apartments. Dominos* of no character, and fancy-dresses of no meaning, made, as is usual at such meetings, the general herd of the company: for the rest, the men were Spaniards, chimney-sweepers, Turks, watchmen, conjurers, and old women; and the ladies, shepherdesses, orange girls, Circassians, gipseys, haymakers, and sultanas.*

Cecilia had, as yet, escaped any address beyond the customary enquiry of *Do you know me?* and a few passing compliments; but when the rooms filled, and the general crowd gave general courage, she was attacked in a manner more pointed and singular.

The very first mask who approached her, seemed to have nothing less in view than preventing the approach of every other: yet had he little reason to hope favour for himself, as the person he represented, of all others least alluring to the view, was the devil! He was black from head to foot, save that two red horns seemed to issue from his forehead; his face was so completely covered, that the sight only of his eyes was visible, his feet were cloven, and in his right hand he held a wand the colour of fire.

Waving this wand as he advanced towards Cecilia, he cleared a semi-circular space before her chair, thrice with the most profound reverence bowed to her, thrice turned himself around with sundry grimaces, and then fiercely planted himself at her side.

Cecilia was amused by his mummery, but felt no great delight in his guardianship, and, after a short time, arose, with intention to walk to another place; but the black gentleman, adroitly moving round her, held out his wand to obstruct her passage, and therefore, preferring captivity to resistance, she was again obliged to seat herself.

An Hotspur,* who just then made his appearance, was now strutting boldly towards her; but the devil, rushing furiously forwards, placed himself immediately between them. Hotspur, putting his arms a-kembo* with an air of defiance, gave a loud stamp with his right foot, and then ——marched into another room!

The victorious devil ostentatiously waved his wand, and returned to his station.

Mr. Arnott, who had never moved two yards from Cecilia, knowing her too well to suppose she received any pleasure from being thus distinguished, modestly advanced to offer his assistance in releasing her from confinement; but the devil, again describing a circle with his wand, gave him three such smart raps on the head that his hair was disordered, and his face covered with powder.* A general laugh succeeded, and Mr. Arnott, too diffident to brave raillery, or withstand shame, retired in confusion.

The black gentleman seemed now to have all authority in his own hands, and his wand was brandished with more ferocity than ever, no one again venturing to invade the domain he thought fit to appropriate for his own.

At length, however, a Don Quixote appeared, and every mask in the room was eager to point out to him the imprisonment of Cecilia.

This Don Quixote was accoutered with tolerable exactness according to the description of the admirable Cervantes;* his armour was rusty, his helmet was a barber's bason, his shield, a pewter dish, and his lance, an old sword fastened to a slim cane. His figure, tall and thin, was well adapted to the character he represented, and his mask, which depictured a lean and haggard face, worn with care, yet fiery with crazy passions, exhibited with propriety the most striking, the knight of the doleful countenance.

The complaints against the devil with which immediately and from all quarters he was assailed, he heard with the most solemn taciturnity: after which, making a motion for general silence, he stalked majestically towards Cecilia, but stopping short of the limits prescribed by her guard, he kissed his spear in token of allegiance, and then, slowly dropping upon one knee, began the following address:

"Most incomparable Princess!

THUS humbly prostrate at the feet of your divine and ineffable beauty, graciously permit the most pitiful of your servitors, Don Quixote De la Mancha, from your high and tender grace, to salute the fair boards, which sustain your corporeal machine."

Then, bending down his head, he kissed the floor; after which, raising himself upon his feet, he proceeded in his speech.

"Report, O most fair and unmatchable virgin! daringly affirmeth, that a certain discourteous person, who calleth himself the devil, even now, and in thwart of your fair inclinations, keepeth and detaineth your irradiant frame in hostile thraldom. Suffer then, magnanimous and undiscribable lady! that I, the most groveling of your unworthy vassals, do sift the fair truth out of this foul sieve, and, obsequiously bending to your divine attractions, conjure* your highness veritably to inform me, if that honourable chair which haply supports your terrestrial perfections, containeth the inimitable burthen with the free and legal consent of your celestial spirit?"

Here he ceased: and Cecilia, who laughed at this characteristic address,* though she had not courage to answer it, again made an effort to quit her place, but again by the wand of her black persecutor was prevented.

This little incident was answer sufficient for the valorous knight, who indignantly exclaimed,

"Sublime Lady!

I BESEECH but of your exquisite mercy to refrain mouldering the clay composition of my unworthy body to impalpable dust, by the refulgence of those bright stars vulgarly called eyes, till I have lawfully wreaked my vengeance upon this unobliging caitiff, for his most disloyal obstruction of your highnesses adorable pleasure."

Then, bowing low, he turned from her, and thus addressed his intended antagonist:

"Uncourtly Miscreant,

THE black garment which envellopeth thy most unpleasant person, seemeth even of the most ravishing whiteness, in compare of the black bile* which floateth within thy sable exterior. Behold, then, my gauntlet!* yet ere I deign to be the instrument of thy extirpation, O thou most mean and ignoble enemy! that the honour of Don Quixote de la Mancha may not be sullied by thy extinction, I do here confer upon thee the honour of knighthood, dubbing thee, by my own sword, Don Devil, knight of the horrible physiognomy."

He then attempted to strike his shoulder with his spear, but the black gentleman, adroitly eluding the blow, defended himself with his wand: a mock fight ensued, conducted on both sides with admirable dexterity; but Cecilia, less eager to view it than to become again a free agent, made her escape into another apartment; while the rest of the ladies, though they almost all screamed, jumped upon chairs and sofas to peep at the combat.

In conclusion, the wand of the knight of the horrible physiognomy, was broken against the shield of the knight of the doleful countenance; upon which Don Quixote called out *victoria!** the whole room ecchoed the sound; the unfortunate new knight retired abruptly into another apartment, and the conquering Don, seizing the fragments of the weapon of his vanquished enemy, went out in search of the lady for whose releasement he had fought: and the moment he found her, prostrating both himself and the trophies at her feet, he again pressed the floor with his lips, and then, slowly arising, repeated his reverences with added formality, and, without waiting her acknowledgments, gravely retired.

The moment he departed a Minerva, not stately nor austere, not marching in warlike majesty, but gay and airy,

Tripping on light fantastic toe,*

ran up to Cecilia, and squeaked out, "Do you know me?"

"Not," answered she, instantly recollecting Miss Larolles, "by your *appearance*, I own! but by your *voice*, I think I can guess you."

"I was monstrous sorry," returned the goddess, without understanding this distinction, "that I was not at home when you called upon me. Pray how do you like my dress? I assure you I think it's the prettiest here. But do you know there's the most shocking thing in the world happened in the next room? I really believe there's a common chimney-sweeper got in! I assure you its enough to frighten one to death, for every time he moves the soot smells so you can't think; quite real soot, I assure you! only conceive how nasty! I declare I wish with all my heart it would suffocate him!"

Here she was interrupted by the re-appearance of *Don Devil*;* who, looking around him, and perceiving that his antagonist was gone, again advanced to Cecilia: not, however, with the authority of his first approach, for with his wand he had lost much of his power; but to recompense himself for this disgrace, he had recourse to another method equally effectual for keeping his prey to himself, for he began a growling, so dismal and disagreeable, that while many of the ladies, and, among the first, the *Goddess of Wisdom and Courage*,* ran away to avoid him, the men all stood aloof to watch what next was to follow.

Cecilia now became seriously uneasy; for she was made an object of general attention, yet could neither speak nor be spoken to. She could suggest no motive for behaviour so whimsical, though she imagined the only person who could have the assurance to practice it was Sir Robert Floyer.

After some time spent thus disagreeably, a white domino, who for a few minutes had been a very attentive spectator, suddenly came forward, and exclaiming, "*I'll cross him though he blast me!*"* rushed upon the fiend, and grasping one of his horns, called out to a Harlequin* who stood near him, "Harlequin! do you fear to fight the devil?"

"Not I truly!" answered Harlequin, whose voice immediately betrayed young Morrice, and who, issuing from the crowd, whirled himself round before the black gentleman with yet more agility than he had himself done before Cecilia, giving him, from time to time, many smart blows on his shoulders, head and back with his wooden sword.

The rage of *Don Devil* at this attack seemed somewhat beyond what a masquerade character rendered necessary; he foamed at the mouth with resentment, and defended himself with so much vehemence, that he soon drove poor Harlequin into another room: but, when he would have returned to his prey, the genius of pantomime, curbed, but not subdued, at the instigation of the white domino returned to the charge, and by a perpetual rotation of attack and retreat, kept him in constant employment, pursuing him from room to room, and teazing him without cessation or mercy.

Mean time Cecilia, delighted at being released, hurried into a corner, where she hoped to breathe and look on in quiet; and the white domino, having exhorted Harlequin to torment the tormentor, and keep him at bay, followed her with congratulations upon her recovered freedom.

"It is you," answered she, "I ought to thank for it, which indeed I do most heartily. I was so tired of confinement, that my mind seemed almost as little at liberty as my person."

"Your persecutor, I presume," said the domino, "is known to you."

"I hope so," answered she, "because there is one man I suspect, and I should be sorry to find there was another equally disagreeable."

"O, depend upon it," cried he, "there are many who would be happy to confine you in the same manner; neither have you much cause for complaint; you have, doubtless, been the aggressor, and played this game yourself without mercy, for I read in your face the captivity of thousands: have you, then, any right to be offended at the spirit of retaliation which one, out of such numbers, has courage to exert in return?"

"I protest," cried Cecilia, "I took you for my defender! whence is it you are become my accuser?"

"From seeing the danger to which my incautious knight errantry has exposed me; I begin, indeed, to take you for a very mischievous sort of person, and I fear the poor devil from whom I rescued you will be amply revenged for his disgrace, by finding that the first use you make of your freedom is to doom your deliverer to bondage."

Here they were disturbed by the extreme loquacity of two opposite parties: and listening attentively, they heard from one side, "My angel! fairest of creatures! goddess of my heart!" uttered in accents of rapture; while from the other, the vociferation was so violent they could distinctly hear nothing.

The white domino satisfied his curiosity by going to both parties; and then, returning to Cecilia, said, "Can you conjecture who was making those soft speeches? a Shylock! his knife all the time in his hand, and his design, doubtless, to *cut as near the heart as possible!** while the loud cackling from the other side, is owing to the riotous merriment of a noisy Mentor!* when next I hear a disturbance, I shall expect to see some simpering Pythagoras stunned by his talkative disciples."*

"To own the truth," said Cecilia, "the almost universal neglect of the characters assumed by these masquers, has been the chief source of my entertainment this evening: for at a place of this sort, the next best thing to a character well supported, is a character ridiculously burlesqued."

"You cannot, then, have wanted amusement," returned the domino, "for among all the persons assembled in these apartments, I have seen only three who have seemed conscious that any change but that of dress was necessary to disguise them."

"And pray who are those?"

"A Don Quixote, a school-master, and your friend the devil."

"O call him not my friend," exclaimed Cecilia, "for indeed in or out of that garb he is particularly my aversion."

"*My* friend, then, I will call him," said the Domino, "for so, were he ten devils, I must think him, since I owe to him the honour of conversing with you. And, after all, to give him his due, to which, you know, he is even proverbially entitled,* he has shewn such abilities in the performance of his part, so much skill in the display of malice, and so much perseverance in the art of tormenting,* that I cannot but respect his ingenuity and capacity. And, indeed, if instead of an evil genius, he had represented a guardian angel, he could not have shewn a more refined taste in his choice of an object to hover about."

Just then they were approached by a young hay-maker, to whom the white domino called out "You look as gay and as brisk as if fresh from the hay-field after only half a day's work. Pray how is it you pretty lasses find employment for the winter?"

"How?" cried she, pertly, "why the same as for the summer!" And pleased with her own readiness at repartee, without feeling the ignorance it betrayed, she tript lightly on.

Immediately after, the school-master, mentioned by the white domino, advanced to Cecilia. His dress was merely a long wrapping gown of green stuff,* a pair of red slippers, and a woollen night-cap of the same colour; while, as the symbol of his profession, he held a rod* in his hand.

"Ah, fair lady," he cried, "how soothing were it to the austerity of my life, how softening to the rigidity of my manners, might I—without a *breaking out of bounds*￼* which I ought to be the first to discourage, and a "confusion to all order"* for which the school-boy should himself chastise his master, be permitted to cast at your feet this emblem of my authority! and to forget, in the softness of your conversation, all the roughness of discipline!"

"No, no," cried Cecilia, "I will not be answerable for such corruption of taste!"

"This repulse," answered he, "is just what I feared; for alas! under what pretence could a poor miserable country pedagogue* presume to approach you? Should I examine you in the dead languages,* would not your living accents charm from me all power of reproof? Could I look at you, and hear a false concord?* Should I doom you to water-gruel as a dunce, would not my subsequent remorse make me want it myself as a mad-man?* Were your fair hand spread out to me for correction, should I help applying my lips to it, instead of my rat-tan? If I ordered you to be *called up*,* should I ever remember to have you sent back? And if I commanded you to stand in a corner, how should I forbear following you thither myself?"

Cecilia, who had no difficulty in knowing this pretended school-master for Mr. Gosport, was readily beginning to propose conditions, for according him her favour, when their ears were assailed by a forced phthisical cough,* which they found proceeded from an apparent old woman, who was a young man in disguise, and whose hobbling gait, grunting voice, and most grievous asthmatic complaints, seemed greatly enjoyed and applauded by the company.

"How true is it, yet how inconsistent," cried the white domino, "that while we all desire to live long, we have all an horror of being old! The figure now passing is not meant to ridicule any particular person, nor to stigmatize any particular absurdity; its sole view is to expose to contempt and derision the general and natural infirmities of age! and the design is not more disgusting than impolitic; for why, while so carefully we guard from all approaches of death, should we close the only avenues to happiness in long life, respect and tenderness."

Cecilia, delighted both by the understanding and humanity of her new acquaintance, and pleased at being joined by Mr. Gosport, was beginning to be perfectly satisfied with her situation, when, creeping softly towards her, she again perceived the black gentleman.

"Ah!" cried she, with some vexation, "here comes my old tormentor! screen me from him if possible, or he will again make me his prisoner."

"Fear not," cried the white domino, "he is an evil spirit, and we will surely lay him. If one spell fails, we must try another."

Cecilia then perceiving Mr. Arnott, begged he would also assist in barricading her from the fiend who so obstinately pursued her.

Mr. Arnott most gratefully acceded to the proposal; and the white domino, who acted as commanding officer, assigned to each his station: he desired Cecilia would keep quietly to her seat, appointed the school-master to be her guard on the left, took possession himself of the opposite post, and ordered Mr. Arnott to stand centinal in front.

This arrangement being settled, the guards of the right and left wings instantly secured their places; but while Mr. Arnott was considering whether it were better to face the besieged, or the enemy, the arch-foe rushed suddenly before him, and laid himself down at the feet of Cecilia.

Mr. Arnott, extremely disconcerted, began a serious expostulation upon the ill-breeding of this behaviour; but the devil, resting all excuse upon supporting his character, only answered by growling.

The white domino seemed to hesitate for a moment in what manner to conduct himself, and with a quickness that marked his chagrin, said to Cecilia, "You told me you knew him,—has he any right to follow you?"

"If he thinks he has," answered she, a little alarmed by his question, "this is no time to dispute it."

And then, to avoid any hazard of altercation, she discreetly forebore making further complaints, preferring any persecution to seriously remonstrating with a man of so much insolence as the Baronet.

The school-master, laughing at the whole transaction, only said "And pray, madam, after playing the devil with all mankind, what right have you to complain that one man plays the devil with you?"

"We shall, at least, fortify you," said the white domino, "from any other assailant: no three-headed Cerberus* could protect you more effectually: but you will not, therefore, fancy yourself in the lower regions, for, if I mistake not, the torment of *three guardians* is nothing new to you."

"And how," said Cecilia, surprised, "should you know of my three guardians? I hope I am not quite encompassed with evil spirits!"

"No," answered he; "you will find me as inoffensive as the hue of the domino I wear;——and would I could add as insensible!"

"This black gentleman," said the school-master, "who, and very innocently, I was going to call your *black-guard*,* has as noble and fiend-like a disposition as I remember to have seen; for without even attempting to take any diversion himself, he seems gratified to his heart's content, in excluding from it the lady he serves."

"He does me an honour I could well dispense with," said Cecilia; "but I hope he has some secret satisfaction in his situation which pays him for its apparent inconvenience."

Here the black gentleman half raised himself, and attempted to take her hand; she started, and with much displeasure drew it back: he then growled, and again sunk prostrate.

"This is a fiend," said the school-master, "who to himself sayeth *Budge not!* let his conscience never so often say *budge!** Well, fair lady, your fortifications, however, may now be deemed impregnable, since I, with a flourish of my rod, can keep off the young by recollection of the past, and since the fiend, with a jut* of his foot, may keep off the old from dread of the future!''

Here a Turk, richly habited and resplendent with jewels, stalked towards Cecilia, and, having regarded her some time, called out "I have been looking hard about me the whole evening, and, faith, I have seen nothing handsome before!''

The moment he opened his mouth, his voice, to her utter astonishment, betrayed Sir Robert Floyer! "Mercy on me,'' cried she aloud, and pointing to the fiend, "who, then, can this possibly be?''

"Do you not know?'' cried the white domino.

"I thought I had known with certainty,'' answered she, "but I now find I was mistaken.''

"He is a happy man,'' said the school-master, sarcastically looking at the Turk, "who has removed your suspicions only by appearing in another character!''

"Why what the deuce, then,'' exclaimed the Turk, "have you taken that black dog there for *me?*''

Before this question could be answered, an offensive smell of soot, making every body look around the room, the chimney-sweeper already mentioned by Miss Larolles, was perceived to enter it. Every way he moved, a passage was cleared for him, as the company, with general disgust, retreated wherever he advanced. He was short, and seemed somewhat incommoded by his dress; he held his soot-bag over one arm, and his shovel under the other. As soon as he espied Cecilia, whose situation was such as to prevent her eluding him, he hooted aloud, and came stumping up to her; "Ah ha,'' he cried, "found at last;'' then, throwing down his shovel, he opened the mouth of his bag, and pointing waggishly to her head, said "Come, shall I pop you?—A good place for naughty girls;* in, I say, poke in!*——cram you up the chimney.''

And then he put forth his sooty hands to reach her cap.

Cecilia, though she instantly knew the dialect of her guardian Mr. Briggs, was not therefore the more willing to be so handled, and started back to save herself from his touch; the white domino also came forward, and spread out his arms as a defence to her, while the Devil, who was still before her, again began to growl.

"Ah ha!" cried the chimney-sweeper, laughing, "so did not know me? Poor duck! won't hurt you; don't be frightened; nothing but old guardian; all a joke!" And then, patting her cheek with his dirty hand, and nodding at her with much kindness, "Pretty dove," he added, "be of good heart! sha'n't be meddled with; come to see after you. Heard of your tricks; thought I'd catch you!—come o'purpose.—Poor duck! did not know me! ha! ha!—good joke enough!"

"What do you mean, you dirty dog," cried the Turk, "by touching that lady?"

"Won't tell!" answered he; "not your business. Got a good right. Who cares for pearls? Nothing but French beads."* Pointing with a sneer to his turban. Then, again addressing Cecilia; "Fine doings!" he continued, "Here's a place! never saw the like before! turn a man's noddle!—All goings out; no comings in; wax candles* in every room; servants thick as mushrooms! And where's the cash? Who's to pay the piper? Come to more than a guinea; warrant Master Harrel thinks that nothing!"

"A guinea?" contemptuously repeated the Turk, "and what do you suppose a guinea will do?"

"What! Why keep a whole family handsome a week;— never spend so much myself; no, nor half neither."

"Why then how the devil do you live? Do you beg?"

"Beg? Who should beg of? You?—Got any thing to give? Are warm?"

"Take the trouble to speak more respectfully, sir!" said the Turk, haughtily; "I see you are some low fellow, and I shall not put up with your impudence."

"Shall, shall! I say!" answered the chimney-sweeper sturdily; "Hark'ee, my duck," chucking Cecilia under the chin, "don't be cajoled, nick* that spark! never mind gold trappings; none of his own; all a take-in; hired for eighteen pence; not worth a groat. Never set your heart on a fine outside, nothing within. Bristol stones won't buy stock: only wants to chouse* you.''

''What do you mean by that, you little old scrub!'' cried the imperious Turk; ''would you provoke me to soil my fingers by pulling that beastly snub nose?'' For Mr. Briggs had saved himself any actual mask, by merely blacking his face with soot.

''Beastly snub nose!'' sputtered out the chimney-sweeper, in much wrath, ''good nose enough; don't want a better; good as another man's. Where's the harm on't?''

''How could this black-guard get in?'' cried the Turk, ''I believe he's a mere common chimney-sweeper out of the streets, for he's all over dirt and filth. I never saw such a dress at a masquerade before in my life.''

''All the better,'' returned the other; ''would not change. What do think it cost?''

''Cost? Why not a crown.''

''A crown? ha! ha!—a pot o'beer! Little Tom borrowed it; had it of our own sweep. Said 'twas for himself. I bid him a pint; rascal would not take less.''

''Did your late uncle,'' said the white domino, in a low voice to Cecilia, ''chuse for two of your guardians, Mr. Harrel and Mr. Briggs, to give you an early lesson upon the opposite errors of profusion and meanness?''

''My uncle?'' cried Cecilia, starting, ''were you acquainted with my uncle?''

''No,'' said he, ''for my happiness I knew him not.''

''You would have owed no loss of happiness to an acquaintance with him,'' said Cecilia, very seriously, ''for he was one who dispensed to his friends nothing but good.''

''Perhaps so,'' said the domino; ''but I fear I should have found the good he dispensed through his niece not quite unmixed with evil!''

''What's here?'' cried the chimney-sweeper, stumbling over the fiend, ''what's this black thing? Don't like it; looks like the devil. You sha'n't stay with it; carry you away; take care of you myself.''

He then offered Cecilia his hand; but the black gentleman, raising himself upon his knees before her, paid her, in dumb shew, the humblest devoirs, yet prevented her from removing.

"Ah ha!" cried the chimney-sweeper, significantly nodding his head, "smell a rat! a sweet-heart in disguise. No bamboozling! it won't do; a'n't so soon put upon. If you've got any thing to say, tell *me*, that's the way. Where's the cash? Got ever a *rentall?** Are warm? That's the point; are warm?"

The fiend, without returning any answer, continued his homage to Cecilia; at which the enraged chimney-sweeper exclaimed "Come, come with me! won't be imposed upon; an old fox,—understand trap!"*

He then again held out his hand, but Cecilia, pointing to the fiend, answered "How can I come, sir?"

"Shew you the way," cried he, "shovel him off." And taking his shovel, he very roughly set about removing him.

The fiend then began a yell so horrid,* that it disturbed the whole company; but the chimney-sweeper, only saying "Aye, aye, blacky, growl away blacky,—makes no odds,—" sturdily continued his work, and, as the fiend had no chance of resisting so coarse an antagonist without a serious struggle, he was presently compelled to change his ground.

"Warm work!" cried the victorious chimney sweeper, taking off his wig, and wiping his head with the sleeves of his dress, "pure warm work this!"

Cecilia, once again freed from her persecutor, instantly quitted her place, almost equally desirous to escape the haughty Turk, who was peculiarly her aversion, and the facetious chimney-sweeper, whose vicinity, either on account of his dress or his conversation, was by no means desirable. She was not, however, displeased that the white domino and the school-master still continued to attend her.

"Pray look," said the white domino, as they entered another apartment, "at that figure of Hope; is there any in the room half so expressive of despondency?"

"The reason, however," answered the school-master, "is obvious; that light and beautiful silver anchor* upon which she reclines, presents an occasion irresistible for an attitude of elegant dejection; and the assumed character is always given up, where an opportunity offers to display any beauty, or manifest any perfection in the dear proper person!''

"But why," said Cecilia, "should she assume the character of *Hope?* Could she not have been equally dejected, and equally elegant as Niobe,* or some tragedy queen?''

"But she does not assume the character," answered the school-master, "she does not even think of it: the dress is her object, and that alone fills up all her ideas. Enquire of almost any body in the room concerning the persons they seem to represent, and you will find their ignorance more gross than you can imagine; they have not once thought upon the subject; accident, or convenience, or caprice has alone directed their choice."

A tall and elegant youth now approached them, whose laurels and harp announced Apollo.* The white domino immediately enquired of him if the noise and turbulence of the company, had any chance of being stilled into silence and rapture, by the divine music of the inspired god?

"No," answered he, pointing to the room in which was erected the new gallery, and whence, as he spoke, issued the sound of an *hautboy,* "there is a flute playing there already."

"O for a Midas,"* cried the white domino, "to return to this leather-eared god the disgrace he received from him!"

They now proceeded to the apartment which had been lately fitted up for refreshments, and which was so full of company, that they entered it with difficulty. And here they were again joined by Minerva, who, taking Cecilia's hand, said "Lord how glad I am you've got away from that frightful black mask! I can't conceive who he is; nobody can find out; it's monstrous odd, but he has not spoke a word all night, and he makes such a shocking noise when people touch him, that I assure you it's enough to put one in a fright."

"And pray," cried the school-master, disguising his voice, "how camest thou to take the helmet of Minerva for a fool's cap?"

"Lord, I have not," cried she, innocently, "why the whole dress is Minerva's; don't you see?"

"My dear child," answered he, "thou couldst as well with that little figure pass for a Goliah,* as with that little wit for a Pallas."*

Their attention was now drawn from the goddess of wisdom to a mad Edgar, who so vehemently ran about the room calling out "Poor Tom's a cold!"* that, in a short time, he was obliged to take off his mask, from an effect, not very delicate, of the heat!

Soon after, a gentleman desiring some lemonade whose toga spoke the consular* dignity, though his broken English betrayed a native of France, the school-master followed him, and, with reverence the most profound began to address him in Latin; but, turning quick towards him, he gayly said *"Monsieur, j'ai l'honneur de representer Ciceron, le grand Ciceron, pere de sa patrie! mais quoique j'ai cet honneur là, je ne suis pas pedant!——mon dieu, Monsieur, je ne parle que le François dans la bonne compagnie!"* And, politely bowing, he went on.

Just then Cecilia, while looking about the room for Mrs. Harrel, felt herself suddenly pinched by the cheek, and hastily turning round, perceived again her friend the chimney-sweeper, who laughing, cried "Only me! don't be frightened. Have something to tell you;—had no luck!—got never a husband yet! can't find one! looked all over, too; sharp as a needle. Not one to be had! all catched up!"

"I am glad to hear it, sir," said Cecilia, somewhat vexed by observing the white domino attentively listening; "and I hope, therefore, you will give yourself no farther trouble."

"Pretty duck!" cried he, chucking her under the chin; "never mind, don't be cast down; get one at last. Leave it to me. Nothing under a plum;* won't take up with less. Good by, ducky, good by! must go home now,—begin to be nodding."

And then, repeating his kind caresses, he walked away.

"Do you think, then," said the white domino, "more highly of Mr. Briggs for discernment and taste than of any body?"

"I hope not!" answered she, "for low indeed should I then think of the rest of the world!"

"The commission with which he is charged," returned

the domino, "has then misled me; I imagined discernment and taste might be necessary ingredients for making such a choice as your approbation would sanctify; but perhaps his skill in guarding against any fraud or deduction in the stipulation he mentioned, may be all that is requisite for the execution of his trust."

"I understand very well," said Cecilia, a little hurt, "the severity of your meaning; and if Mr. Briggs had any commission but of his own suggestion, it would fill me with shame and confusion; but as that is not the case, those at least are sensations which it cannot give me."

"My meaning," cried the domino, with some earnestness, "should I express it seriously, would but prove to you the respect and admiration with which you have inspired me, and if indeed, as Mr. Briggs hinted, such a prize is to be purchased by riches, I know not, from what I have seen of its merit, any sum I should think adequate to its value."

"You are determined, I see," said Cecilia, smiling, "to make most liberal amends for your asperity."

A loud clack of tongues now interrupted their discourse; and the domino, at the desire of Cecilia, for whom he had procured a seat, went forward to enquire what was the matter. But scarce had he given up his place a moment, before, to her great mortification, it was occupied by the fiend.

Again, but with the same determined silence he had hitherto preserved, he made signs of obedience and homage, and her perplexity to conjecture who he could be, or what were his motives for this persecution, became the more urgent as they seemed the less likely to be satisfied. But the fiend, who was no other than Mr. Monckton, had every instant less and less* encouragement to make himself known: his plan had in nothing succeeded, and his provocation at its failure had caused him the bitterest disappointment; he had intended, in the character of a tormentor, not only to pursue and hover around her himself, but he had also hoped, in the same character, to have kept at a distance all other admirers: but the violence with which he had over-acted his part, by raising her disgust and the indignation of the company, rendered his views wholly abortive: while the consciousness of an extravagance for which, if discovered, he could assign no reason not liable to excite suspicions of his secret motives, reduced him to guarding a painful and most irksome silence the whole evening. And Cecilia, to whose unsuspicious mind the idea of Mr. Monckton had never occurred, added continually to the cruelty of his situation, by an undisguised abhorrence of* his assiduity, as well as by a manifest preference to the attendance of the white domino. All, therefore, that his disappointed scheme now left in his power, was to watch her motions, listen to her discourse, and inflict occasionally upon others some part of the chagrin with which he was tormented himself.

While they were in this situation, Harlequin, in consequence of being ridiculed by the Turk for want of agility, offered to jump over the new desert table, and desired to have a little space cleared to give room for his motions. It was in vain the people who distributed the refreshments, and who were placed at the other side of the table, expostulated upon the danger of the experiment; Morrice had a rage of enterprize untameable, and therefore, first taking a run, he attempted the leap.

The consequence was such as might naturally be expected; he could not accomplish his purpose, but, finding himself falling, imprudently caught hold of the lately erected Awning, and pulled it entirely upon his own head, and with it the new contrived lights, which in various forms were fixed to it, and which all came down together.

The mischief and confusion occasioned by this exploit were very alarming, and almost dangerous; those who were near the table suffered most by the crush, but splinters of the glass flew yet further; and as the room, which was small, had been only lighted up by lamps hanging from the Awning, it was now in total darkness, except close to the door, which was still illuminated from the adjoining apartments.

The clamour of Harlequin, who was covered with glass, papier machée,* lamps and oil, the screams of the ladies, the universal buz of tongues, and the struggle between the frighted crowd which was enclosed to get out, and the curious crowd from the other apartments to get in, occasioned a disturbance and tumult equally noisy and confused. But the most serious sufferer was the unfortunate fiend, who being nearer the table than Cecilia, was so pressed upon by the numbers which poured from it, that he found a separation unavoidable, and was unable, from the darkness and the throng, to discover whether she was still in the same place, or had made her escape into another.

She had, however, encountered the white domino, and, under his protection, was safely conveyed to a further part of the room. Her intention and desire were to quit it immediately, but at the remonstrance of her conductor, she consented to remain some time longer. "The conflict at the door," said he, "will quite overpower you. Stay here but a few minutes, and both parties will have struggled themselves tired, and you may then go without difficulty. Mean time, can you not by this faint light, suppose me one of your guardians, Mr. Briggs, for example, or, if he is too old for me, Mr. Harrel, and entrust yourself to my care?"

"You seem wonderfully well acquainted with my guardians," said Cecilia; "I cannot imagine how you have had your intelligence."

"Nor can I," answered the domino, "imagine how Mr. Briggs became so particularly your favourite as to be entrusted with powers to dispose of you."

"You are mistaken indeed; he is entrusted with no powers but such as his own fancy has suggested."

"But how has Mr. Delvile offended you, that with him only you seem to have no commerce or communication?"

"Mr. Delvile!" repeated Cecilia, still more surprised, "are you also acquainted with Mr. Delvile?"

"He is certainly a man of fashion," continued the domino, "and he is also a man of honour; surely, then, he would be more pleasant for confidence and consultation, than one whose only notion of happiness is money, whose only idea of excellence is avarice, and whose only conception of sense is distrust!"

Here a violent outcry again interrupted their conversation; but not till Cecilia had satisfied her doubts concerning the white domino, by conjecturing he was Mr. Belfield, who might easily at the house of Mr. Monckton have gathered the little circumstances of her situation to which he alluded, and whose size and figure exactly resembled those of her new acquaintance.

The author of the former disturbance was now the occasion of the present: the fiend, having vainly traversed the room in search of Cecilia, stumbled accidentally upon Harlequin, before he was freed from the relicks of his own mischief; and unable to resist the temptation of opportunity, and the impulse of revenge, he gave vent to the wrath so often excited by the blunders, forwardness, and tricks of Morrice, and inflicted upon him, with his own wooden sword, which he seized for that purpose, a chastisement the most serious and severe.

Poor Harlequin, unable to imagine any reason for this violent attack, and already cut with the glass, and bruised with the fall, spared not his lungs in making known his disapprobation of such treatment: but the fiend, regardless either of his complaints or his resistance, forbore not to belabour him till compelled by the entrance of people with lights. And then, after artfully playing sundry anticks under pretence of still supporting his character, with a motion too sudden for prevention, and too rapid for pursuit, he escaped out of the room, and hurrying down stairs, threw himself into an hackney chair,* which conveyed him to a place where he privately changed his dress before he returned home: bitterly repenting the experiment he had made, and conscious too late that had he appeared in a character he might have avowed, he could, without impropriety, have attended Cecilia the whole evening. But such is deservedly the frequent fate of cunning, which while it plots surprise and detection of others, commonly overshoots its mark, and ends in its own disgrace.

The introduction of the lights now making manifest the confusion which the frolic of Harlequin had occasioned, he was seized with such a dread of the resentment of Mr.

Harrel, that, forgetting blows, bruises and wounds, not one of which were so frightful to him as reproof, he made the last exhibition of his agility by an abrupt and hasty retreat.

He had, however, no reason for apprehension, since in every thing that regarded expence, Mr. Harrel had no feeling, and his lady had no thought.

The rooms now began to empty very fast, but among the few masks yet remaining, Cecilia again perceived Don Quixote; and while, in conjunction with the white domino, she was allowing him the praise of having supported his character with more uniform propriety than any other person in the assembly, she observed him taking off his mask for the convenience of drinking some lemonade, and, looking in his face, found he was no other than Mr. Belfield! Much astonished, and more than ever perplexed, she again turned to the white domino, who seeing in her countenance a surprise of which he knew not the reason, said, half laughing, "You think, perhaps, I shall never be gone? And indeed I am almost of the same opinion: but what can I do? Instead of growing weary by the length of my stay, my reluctance to shorten it encreases with its duration: and all the methods I take, whether by speaking to you or looking at you, with a view to be satiated, only double my eagerness for looking and listening again! I must go, however; and if I am happy, I may perhaps meet with you again,—— though, if I am wise, I shall never seek you more!"

And then, with the last stragglers that reluctantly disappeared, he made his exit; leaving Cecilia greatly pleased with his conversation and his manners, but extremely perplexed to account for his knowledge of her affairs and situation.

The school-master had already been gone some time.

She was now earnestly pressed by the Harrels and Sir Robert, who still remained, to send to a warehouse* for a dress, and accompany them to the Pantheon; but though she was not without some inclination to comply, in the hope of further prolonging the entertainment of an evening from which she had received much pleasure, she disliked the attendance of the Baronet, and felt averse to grant any request that he could make, and therefore she begged they would excuse her; and having waited to see their dresses, which were very superb, she retired to her own apartment.

A great variety of conjecture upon all that had passed, now, and till the moment that she sunk to rest, occupied her mind; the extraordinary persecution of the fiend excited at once her curiosity and amazement, while the knowledge of her affairs shewn by the white domino, surprised her not less, and interested her more.

CHAPTER IV

An Affray

THE next morning during breakfast, Cecilia was informed that a gentleman desired to speak with her. She begged permission of Mrs. Harrel to have him asked up stairs, and was not a little surprized when he proved to be the same old gentleman whose singular exclamations had so much struck her at Mr. Monckton's, and at the rehearsal of Artaserse.

Abruptly and with a stern aspect advancing to her, "You are rich," he cried; "are you therefore worthless?"

"I hope not!" answered she, in some consternation; while Mrs. Harrel, believing his intention was to rob them, ran precipitately to the bell, which she rang without ceasing till two or three servants hastened into the room: by which time, being less alarmed, she only made signs to them to stay, and stood quietly herself to wait what would follow.

The old man, without attending to her, continued his dialogue with Cecilia.

"Know you then," he said, "a blameless use of riches? such a use as not only in the broad glare of day shall shine resplendent, but in the darkness of midnight, and stillness of repose, shall give you reflections unimbittered, and slumbers unbroken? tell me, know you this use?"

"Not so well, perhaps," answered she, "as I ought; but I am very willing to learn better."

"Begin, then, while yet youth and inexperience, new to

the callousness of power and affluence, leave something good to work upon: yesterday you saw the extravagance of luxury and folly; to day look deeper, and see, and learn to pity, the misery of disease and penury.''

He then put into her hand a paper which contained a most affecting account of the misery to which a poor and wretched family had been reduced, by sickness, and various other misfortunes.

Cecilia, ''open as day to melting charity,''* having hastily perused it, took out her purse, and offering to him three guineas, said, ''You must direct me, Sir, what to give if this is insufficient.''

''Hast thou so much heart?'' cried he, with emotion, ''and has fortune, though it has cursed thee with the temptation of prosperity, not yet rooted from thy mind its native benevolence? I return in part thy liberal contribution; this,'' taking one guinea, ''doubles my expectations; I will not, by making thy charity distress thee, accelerate the fatal hour of hardness and degeneracy.''

He was then going; but Cecilia, following him, said, ''No, take it all! Who should assist the poor if I will not? Rich, without connections; powerful, without wants; upon whom have they any claim if not upon me?''

''True,'' cried he, receiving the rest, ''and wise as true. Give, therefore, whilst yet thou hast the heart to give, and make, in thy days of innocence and kindness, some interest with Heaven and the poor!''*

And then he disappeared.

''Why, my dear,'' cried Mrs. Harrel, ''what could induce you to give the man so much money? Don't you see he is crazy? I dare say he would have been just as well contented with sixpence.''

''I know not what he is,'' said Cecilia, ''but his manners are not more singular than his sentiments are affecting; and if he is actuated by charity to raise subscriptions for the indigent, he can surely apply to no one who ought so readily to contribute as myself.''

Mr. Harrel then came in, and his lady most eagerly told him the transaction.

"Scandalous!" he exclaimed; "why this is no better than being a house-breaker! Pray give orders never to admit him again. Three Guineas! I never heard so impudent a thing in my life! Indeed, Miss Beverley, you must be more discreet in future, you will else be ruined before you know where you are."

"Thus it is," said Cecilia, half smiling, "that we can all lecture one another! to-day you recommend œconomy* to me; yesterday I with difficulty forbore recommending it to you."

"Nay" answered he, "that was quite another matter; expence incurred in the common way of a man's living is quite another thing to an extortion of this sort."

"It is another thing indeed," said she, "but I know not that it is therefore a better."

Mr. Harrel made no answer: and Cecilia, privately moralizing upon the different estimates of expence and œconomy made by the dissipated and the charitable, soon retired to her own apartment, determined firmly to adhere to her lately adopted plan, and hoping, by the assistance of her new and very singular monitor, to extend her practice of doing good, by enlarging her knowledge of distress.

Objects are, however, never wanting for the exercise of benevolence; report soon published her liberality, and those who wished to believe it, failed not to enquire into its truth. She was soon at the head of a little band of pensioners, and, never satisfied with the generosity of her donations, found in a very short time, that the common allowance of her guardians was scarce adequate to the calls of her munificence.

And thus, in acts of goodness and charity, passed undisturbed another week of the life of Cecilia: but when the fervour of self-approbation lost its novelty, the pleasure with which her new plan was begun first subsided into tranquility, and then sunk into languor. To a heart formed for friendship and affection the charms of solitude are very short-lived; and though she had sickened of the turbulence of perpetual company, she now wearied of passing all her time by herself, and sighed for the comfort of society, and the relief of communication. But she saw with astonishment the difficulty with which this was to be obtained: the endless succession of diversions, the continual rotation of assemblies, the numerousness of splendid engagements, of which while every one complained, every one was proud to boast, so effectually impeded private meetings and friendly intercourse, that, which ever way she turned herself, all commerce seemed impracticable, but such as either led to dissipation, or accidentally flowed from it.

Yet finding the error into which her ardour of reformation had hurried her, and that a rigid seclusion from company was productive of a lassitude as little favourable to active virtue as dissipation itself, she resolved to soften her plan, and by mingling amusement with benevolence, to try, at least, to approach that golden mean, which, like the philosopher's stone,* always eludes our grasp, yet always invites our wishes.

For this purpose she desired to attend Mrs. Harrel to the next Opera that should be represented.

The following Saturday, therefore, she accompanied that lady and Mrs. Mears to the Haymarket, escorted by Mr. Arnott.

They were very late; the Opera was begun, and even in the lobby the crowd was so great that their passage was obstructed. Here they were presently accosted by Miss Larolles, who, running up to Cecilia and taking her hand, said, "Lord, you can't conceive how glad I am to see you! why, my dear creature, where have you hid yourself these twenty ages? You are quite in luck in coming to-night, I assure you; it's the best Opera we have had this season: there's such a monstrous crowd there's no stirring. We sha'n't get in this half hour. The coffee-room is quite full; only come and see; is it not delightful?"

This intimation was sufficient for Mrs. Harrel, whose love of the Opera was merely a love of company, fashion, and shew; and therefore to the coffee-room she readily led the way.

And here Cecilia found rather the appearance of a brilliant assembly of ladies and gentlemen, collected merely to see and to entertain one another, than of distinct and casual parties, mixing solely from necessity, and waiting only for room to enter a theatre.

The first person that addressed them was Captain Aresby, who, with his usual delicate languishment, smiled upon Cecilia, and softly whispering, "How divinely you look to night!" proceeded to pay his compliments to some other ladies.

"Do pray now," cried Miss Larolles, "observe Mr. Meadows! only just see where he has fixed himself!* in the very best place in the room, and keeping the fire from every body! I do assure you that's always his way, and it's monstrous provoking, for if one's ever so cold, he lollops so, that one's quite starved.* But you must know there's another thing he does that is quite as bad, for if he gets a seat, he never offers to move, if he sees one sinking with fatigue. And besides, if one is waiting for one's carriage two hours together, he makes it a rule never to stir a step to see for it. Only think how monstrous!"

"These are heavy complaints, indeed," said Cecilia, looking at him attentively; "I should have expected from his appearance a very different account of his gallantry, for he seems dressed with more studied elegance than any body here."

"O yes," cried Miss Larolles, "he is the sweetest dresser in the world; he has the most delightful taste you can conceive, nobody has half so good a fancy. I assure you it's a great thing to be spoke to by him: we are all of us quite angry when he won't take any notice of us."

"Is your anger," said Cecilia, laughing, "in honour of himself or of his coat?"

"Why, Lord, don't you know all this time that he is an *ennuyé?*

"I know, at least," answered Cecilia, "that he would soon make one of me."

"O but one is never affronted with an *ennuyé*, if he is ever so provoking, because one always knows what it means."

"Is he agreeable?"

"Why, to tell you the truth,—but pray now don't

mention it,—I think him most excessive disagreeable! He yawns in one's face every time one looks at him. I assure you sometimes I expect to see him fall asleep while I am talking to him, for he is so immensely absent he don't hear one half that one says; only conceive how horrid!"

"But why, then, do you encourage him? why do you take any notice of him?"

"O, every body does, I assure you, else I would not for the world; but he is so courted you have no idea. However, of all things let me advise you never to dance with him; I did once myself, and I declare I was quite distressed to death the whole time, for he was taken with such a fit of absence he knew nothing he was about, sometimes skipping and jumping with all the violence in the world, just as if he only danced for exercise, and sometimes standing quite still, or lolling against the wainscoat and gaping,* and taking no more notice of me than if he had never seen me in his life!"

The captain now, again advancing to Cecilia, said, "So you would not do us the honour to try the masquerade at the Pantheon? however, I hear you had a very brilliant spectacle at Mr. Harrel's. I was quite *au desespoir* that I could not get there. I did *mon possible*, but it was quite beyond me."

"We should have been very happy," said Mrs. Harrel, "to have seen you; I assure you we had some excellent masks."

"So I have heard *partout*, and I am reduced to despair that I could not have the honour of sliding in. But I was *accablé* with affairs all day. Nothing could be so mortifying."*

Cecilia now, growing very impatient to hear the Opera, begged to know if they might not make a trial to get into the pit?*

"I fear," said the captain, smiling as they passed him, without offering any assistance, "you will find it extreme petrifying; for my part, I confess I am not upon the principle of crowding."

The ladies, however, accompanied by Mr. Arnott, made the attempt, and soon found, according to the custom of report, that the difficulty, for the pleasure of talking of it, had been considerably exaggerated. They were separated, indeed, but their accommodation was tolerably good.

Cecilia was much vexed to find the first act of the Opera almost over; but she was soon still more dissatisfied when she discovered that she had no chance of hearing the little which remained: the place she had happened to find vacant was next to a party of young ladies, who were so earnestly engaged in their own discourse, that they listened not to a note of the Opera, and so infinitely diverted with their own witticisms, that their tittering and loquacity allowed no one in their vicinity to hear better than themselves. Cecilia tried in vain to confine her attention to the singers, she was distant from the stage, and to them she was near, and her fruitless attempts all ended in chagrin and impatience.

At length she resolved to make an effort for entertainment in another way, and since the expectations which brought her to the Opera were destroyed, to try by listening to her fair neighbours, whether those who occasioned her disappointment, could make her any amends.

For this purpose she turned to them wholly; yet was at first in no little perplexity to understand what was going forward, since so universal was the eagerness for talking, and so insurmountable the antipathy to listening, that every one seemed to have her wishes bounded by a continual utterance of words, without waiting for any answer, or scarce even desiring to be heard.

But when, somewhat more used to their dialect and manner, she began better to comprehend their discourse, wretchedly indeed did it supply to her the loss of the Opera. She heard nothing but descriptions of trimmings, and complaints of hair-dressers, hints of conquest that teemed with vanity, and histories of engagements which were inflated with exultation.

At the end of the act, by the crowding forward of the gentlemen to see the dance, Mrs. Harrel had an opportunity of making room for her by herself, and she had then some reason to expect hearing the rest of the Opera in peace, for the company before her, consisting entirely of young men, seemed, even during the dance, fearful of speaking, lest their attention should be drawn for a moment from the stage.

But to her infinite surprize, no sooner was the second act begun, than their attention ended! they turned from the performers to each other, and entered into a whispering, but gay conversation, which though not loud enough to disturb the audience in general, kept in the ears of their neighbours, a buzzing which interrupted all pleasure from the representation. Of this effect of their gaiety it seemed uncertain whether they were conscious, but very evident that they were totally careless.*

The desperate resource which she had tried during the first act, of seeking entertainment from the very conversation which prevented her enjoying it, was not now even in her power: for these gentlemen, though as negligent as the young ladies had been whom they disturbed, were much more cautious whom they instructed: their language was ambiguous, and their terms, to Cecilia, were unintelligible: their subjects, indeed, required some discretion, being nothing less than a ludicrous calculation of the age and duration of jointured* widows, and of the chances and expectations of unmarried young ladies.

But what more even than their talking provoked her, was finding that the moment the act was over, when she cared not if their vociferation had been incessant, one of them called out, "Come, be quiet, the dance is begun;" and then they were again all silent attention!

In the third act, however, she was more fortunate; the gentleman again changed their places, and they were succeeded by others who came to the Opera not to hear themselves but the performers: and as soon as she was permitted to listen, the voice of Pacchierotti took from her all desire to hear any thing but itself.

During the last dance she was discovered by Sir Robert Floyer, who sauntering down fop's alley,* stationed himself by her side, and whenever the *figurante* relieved the principal dancers, turned his eyes from the stage to her face, as better worth his notice, and equally destined for his amusement.

Mr. Monckton too, who for some time had seen and

watched her, now approached; he had observed with much satisfaction that her whole mind had been intent upon the performance, yet still the familiarity of Sir Robert Floyer's admiration disturbed and perplexed him; he determined, therefore, to make an effort to satisfy his doubts by examining into his intentions: and, taking him apart, before the dance was quite over, "Well," he said, "who is so handsome here as Harrel's ward?"

"Yes," answered he, calmly, "she is handsome, but I don't like her expression."

"No? why, what is the fault of it?"

"Proud, cursed proud. It is not the sort of woman I like. If one says a civil thing to her, she only wishes one at the devil for one's pains."

"O, you have tried her, then, have you? why you are not, in general, much given to say civil things."

"Yes, you know I said something of that sort to her once about Juliet, at the rehearsal. Was not you by?"

"What, then, was that all? and did you imagine one compliment would do your business with her?"

"O, hang it, who ever dreams of complimenting the women now? that's all at an end."

"You won't find she thinks so, though; for, as you well say, her pride is insufferable, and I, who have long known her, can assure you it does not diminish upon intimacy."

"Perhaps not,—but there's very pretty picking in 3000*l.* per annum! one would not think much of a little incumbrance upon such an estate."

"Are you quite sure the estate is so considerable? Report is mightily given to magnify."

"O, I have pretty good intelligence: though, after all, I don't know but I may be off; she'll take a confounded deal of time and trouble."

Monckton, too much a man of interest and of the world to cherish that delicacy which covets universal admiration for the object of it's fondness, then artfully enlarged upon the obstacles he already apprehended, and insinuated such others as he believed would be most likely to intimidate him. But his subtlety was lost upon the impenetrable Baronet, who possessed that hard insensibility which obstinately pursues its own course, deaf to what is said, and indifferent to what is thought.

Meanwhile the ladies were now making way to the coffee-room, though very slowly on account of the crowd; and just as they got near the lobby, Cecilia perceived Mr. Belfield, who, immediately making himself known to her, was offering his service to hand her out of the pit, when Sir Robert Floyer, not seeing or not heeding him, pressed forward, and said, "Will you let me have the honour, Miss Beverley, of taking care of you?"

Cecilia, to whom he grew daily more disagreeeble, coldly declined his assistance, while she readily accepted that which had first been offered her by Mr. Belfield.

The haughty Baronet, extremely nettled, forced his way on, and rudely stalking up to Mr. Belfield, motioned with his hand for room to pass him, and said, "Make way, Sir!"

"Make way for *me*, Sir!" cried Belfield, opposing him with one hand, while with the other he held Cecilia.

"You, Sir? and who are you, Sir?" demanded the Baronet, disdainfully.

"Of that, Sir, I shall give you an account whenever you please," answered Belfield, with equal scorn.

"What the devil do you mean, Sir?"

"Nothing very difficult to be understood," replied Belfield, and attempted to draw on Cecilia, who, much alarmed, was shrinking back.

Sir Robert then, swelling with rage, reproachfully turned to her, and said, "Will you suffer such an impertinent fellow* as that, Miss Beverley, to have the honour of taking your hand?"

Belfield, with great indignation, demanded what he meant by the term impertinent fellow; and Sir Robert, yet more insolently repeated it: Cecilia, extremely shocked, earnestly besought them both to be quiet; but Belfield, at the repetition of this insult, hastily let go her hand and put his own upon his sword, while Sir Robert, taking advantage of his situation in being a step higher than his antagonist, fiercely pushed him back, and descended into the lobby.

Belfield, enraged beyond endurance, instantly drew his
sword, and Sir Robert was preparing to follow his example,
when Cecilia, in an agony of fright, called out, "Good
Heaven! will nobody interfere?" And then a young man,
forcing his way through the crowd, exclaimed, "For shame,
for shame, gentlemen! is this a place for such violence!"

Belfield, endeavouring to recover himself, put up his
sword, and, though in a voice half choked with passion,
said, "I thank you, Sir! I was off my guard. I beg pardon
of the whole company."

Then, walking up to Sir Robert, he put into his hand a
card with his name and direction, saying, "With you, Sir,
I shall be happy to settle what apologies are necessary at
your first leisure;" and hurried away.

Sir Robert, exclaiming aloud that he should soon teach
him to whom he had been so impertinent, was immediately
going to follow him, when the affrighted Cecilia again called
out aloud, "Oh stop him!—good God! will nobody stop
him!"—

The rapidity with which this angry scene had passed had
filled her with amazement, and the evident resentment of the
Baronet upon her refusing his assistance, gave her an
immediate consciousness that she was herself the real cause
of the quarrel; while the manner in which he was preparing
to follow Mr. Belfield, convinced her of the desperate scene
which was likely to succeed; fear, therefore, overcoming
every other feeling, forced from her this exclamation before
she knew what she said.

The moment she had spoken, the young man who had
already interposed again rushed foward, and seizing Sir
Robert by the arm, warmly remonstrated against the
violence of his proceedings, and being presently seconded by
other gentlemen, almost compelled him to give up his
design.

Then, hastening to Cecilia, "Be not alarmed, madam,"
he cried, "all is over, and every body is safe."

Cecilia, finding herself thus addressed by a gentleman she
had never before seen, felt extremely ashamed of having
rendered her interest in the debate so apparent; she

courtsied to him in some confusion, and taking hold of Mrs. Harrel's arm, hurried her back into the pit, in order to quit a crowd, of which she now found herself the principal object.

Curiosity, however, was universally excited, and her retreat served but to inflame it: some of the ladies, and most of the gentlemen, upon various pretences, returned into the pit merely to look at her, and in a few minutes the report was current that the young lady who had been the occasion of the quarrel, was dying with love for Sir Robert Floyer.

Mr. Monckton, who had kept by her side during the whole affair, felt thunderstruck by the emotion she had shewn; Mr. Arnott too, who had never quitted her, wished himself exposed to the same danger as Sir Robert, so that he might be honoured with the same concern: but they were both too much the dupes of their own apprehensions and jealousy, to perceive that what they instantly imputed to fondness, proceeded simply from general humanity, accidentally united with the consciousness of being accessary to the quarrel.

The young stranger who had officiated as mediator between the disputants, in a few moments followed her with a glass of water, which he had brought from the coffee-room, begging her to drink it and compose herself.

Cecilia, though she declined his civility with more vexation than gratitude, perceived, as she raised her eyes to thank him, that her new friend was a young man very strikingly elegant in his address and appearance.

Miss Larolles next, who, with her party, came back into the pit, ran up to Cecilia, crying, "O my dear creature, what a monstrous shocking thing! You've no Idea how I am frightened; do you know I happened to be quite at the further end of the coffee-room when it began, and I could not get out to see what was the matter for ten ages; only conceive what a situation!"

"Would your fright, then, have been less," said Cecilia, "had you been nearer the danger?"

"O Lord no, for when I came within sight I was fifty times worse! I gave such a monstrous scream, that it quite made Mr. Meadows start. I dare say he'll tell me of it these hundred years: but really when I saw them draw their swords I thought I should have died; I was so amazingly surprized you've no notion."

Here she was interrupted by the re-appearance of the active stranger, who again advancing to Cecilia, said, "I am in doubt whether the efforts I make to revive will please or irritate you, but though you rejected the last cordial I ventured to present you, perhaps you will look with a more favourable eye towards that of which I am now the herald."

Cecilia then, casting her eyes around, saw that he was followed by Sir Robert Floyer. Full of displeasure both at this introduction and at his presence, she turned hastily to Mr. Arnott, and entreated him to enquire if the carriage was not yet ready.

Sir Robert, looking at her with all the exultation of new-raised vanity, said, with more softness than he had ever before addressed her, "Have you been frightened?"

"Every body, I believe was frightened," answered Cecilia, with an air of dignity intended to check his rising expectations.

"There was no sort of cause," answered he; "the fellow did not know whom he spoke to, that was all."

"Lord, Sir Robert," cried Miss Larolles, "how could you be so shocking as to draw your sword? you can't conceive how horrid it looked."

"Why I did not draw my sword," cried he, "I only had my hand on the hilt."

"Lord, did not you, indeed! well, every body said you did, and I'm sure I thought I saw five-and-twenty swords all at once. I thought one of you would be killed every moment. It was horrid disagreeable, I assure you."

Sir Robert was now called away by some gentlemen; and Mr. Monckton, earnest to be better informed of Cecilia's real sentiments, said, with affected concern, "At present this matter is merely ridiculous; I am sorry to think in how short a time it may become more important."

"Surely," cried Cecilia with quickness, "some of their friends will interfere! surely upon so trifling a subject they will not be so mad, so inexcusable, as to proceed to more serious resentment!''

''Which ever of them,'' said the stranger, ''is most honoured by this anxiety, will be mad indeed to risk a life so valued!''

''Cannot you, Mr. Monckton,'' continued Cecilia, too much alarmed to regard this insinuation, ''speak with Mr. Belfield? You are acquainted with him, I know; is it impossible you can follow him?''

''I will with pleasure do whatever you wish; but still if Sir Robert——''

''O, as to Sir Robert, Mr. Harrel, I am very sure, will undertake him; I will try to see him to-night myself, and entreat him to exert all his influence.''

''Ah, madam,'' cried the stranger, archly, and lowering his voice, ''those *French beads* and *Bristol stones** have not, I find, shone in vain!''

At these words Cecilia recognized her white domino acquaintance at the masquerade; she had before recollected his voice, but was too much perturbed to consider where or when she had heard it.

''If Mr. Briggs,'' continued he, ''does not speedily come forth with his plum friend,* before the glittering of swords and spears is joined to that of jewels, the glare will be so resplendent, that he will fear to come within the influence of its rays. Though, perhaps, he may only think the stronger the light, the better he shall see to count his guineas: for as

——in ten thousand pounds
Ten thousand charms are centred,*

in an hundred thousand, the charms may have such magic power, that he may defy the united efforts of tinsel and knight-errantry to deliver you from the golden spell.''

Here the captain, advancing to Cecilia, said, ''I have been looking for you in vain *partout*, but the crowd has been so *accablant* I was almost reduced to despair. Give me leave to hope you are now recovered from the *horreur* of this little *fracas?*''

Mr. Arnott then brought intelligence that the carriage was

ready. Cecilia, glad to be gone, instantly hastened to it; and, as she was conducted by Mr. Monckton, most earnestly entreated him to take an active part, in endeavouring to prevent the fatal consequences with which the quarrel seemed likely to terminate.

CHAPTER V

A Fashionable Friend

AS soon as they returned home, Cecilia begged Mrs. Harrel not to lose a moment before she tried to acquaint Mr. Harrel with the state of the affair. But that lady was too helpless to know in what manner to set about it; she could not tell where he was, she could not conjecture where he might be.

Cecilia then rang for his own man, and upon enquiry, heard that he was, in all probability, at Brookes's in St. James's-Street.

She then begged Mrs. Harrel would write to him.

Mrs. Harrel knew not what to say.

Cecilia therefore, equally quick in forming and executing her designs, wrote to him herself, and entreated that without losing an instant he would find out his friend Sir Robert Floyer, and endeavour to effect an accommodation between him and Mr. Belfield, with whom he had had a dispute at the Opera-house.

The man soon returned with an answer that Mr. Harrel would not fail to obey her commands.

She determined to sit up till he came home in order to learn the event of the negotiation. She considered herself as the efficient cause of the quarrel, yet scarce knew how or in what to blame herself; the behaviour of Sir Robert had always been offensive to her; she disliked his manners, and detested his boldness; and she had already shewn her intention to accept the assistance of Mr. Belfield before he had followed her with an offer of his own. She was uncertain, indeed, whether he had remarked what had passed, but she had reason to think that, so circumstanced, to have changed her purpose, would have been construed into an encouragement that might have authorised his future presumption of her favour. All she could find to regret with regard to herself, was wanting the presence of mind to have refused the civilities of both.

Mrs. Harrel, though really sorry at the state of the affair, regarded herself as so entirely unconcerned in it, that, easily wearied when out of company, she soon grew sleepy, and retired to her own room.

The anxious Cecilia, hoping every instant the return of Mr. Harrel, sat up by herself: but it was not till near four o'clock in the morning that he made his appearance.

"Well, sir," cried she, the moment she saw him, "I fear by your coming home so late you have had much trouble, but I hope it has been successful?"

Great, however, was her mortification when he answered that he had not even seen the Baronet, having been engaged himself in so particular a manner, that he could not possibly break from his party till past three o'clock, at which time he drove to the house of Sir Robert, but heard that he was not yet come home.

Cecilia, though much disgusted by such a specimen of insensibility towards a man whom he pretended to call his friend, would not leave him till he had promised to arise as soon as it was light, and make an effort to recover the time lost.

She was now no longer surprised either at the debts of Mr. Harrel, or at his *particular occasions** for money. She was convinced he spent half the night in gaming, and the consequences, however dreadful, were but natural. That Sir Robert Floyer also did the same was a matter of much less importance to her, but that the life of any man should through her means be endangered, disturbed her inexpressibly.

She went, however, to bed, but arose again at six o'clock, and dressed herself by candle light. In an hour's time she sent to enquire if Mr. Harrel was stirring, and hearing he was asleep, gave orders to have him called. Yet he did not rise till eight o'clock, nor could all her messages or expostulations drive him out of the house till nine.

He was scarcely gone before Mr. Monckton arrived, who now for the first time had the satisfaction of finding her alone.

"You are very good for coming so early," cried she; "have you seen Mr. Belfield? Have you had any conversation with him?"

Alarmed at her eagerness, and still more at seeing by her looks the sleepless night she had passed, he made at first no reply; and when, with encreasing impatience, she repeated her question, he only said, "Has Belfield ever visited you since he had the honour of meeting you at my house?"

"No, never."

"Have you seen him often in public?"

"No, I have never seen him at all but the evening Mrs. Harrel received masks, and last night at the Opera."

"Is it, then, for the safety of Sir Robert you are so extremely anxious?"

"It is for the safety of both; the cause of their quarrel was so trifling, that I cannot bear to think its consequence should be serious."

"But do you not wish better to one of them than to the other?"

"As a matter of justice I do, but not from any partiality: Sir Robert was undoubtedly the aggressor, and Mr. Belfield, though at first too fiery, was certainly ill used."

The candour of this speech recovered Mr. Monckton from his apprehensions; and, carefully observing her looks while he spoke, he gave her the following account.

That he had hastened to Belfield's lodgings the moment he left the Opera-house, and, after repeated denials, absolutely forced himself into his room, where he was quite alone, and in much agitation: he conversed with him for more than an hour upon the subject of the quarrel, but found he so warmly resented the personal insult given him by Sir Robert, that no remonstrance had any effect in making him alter his resolution of demanding satisfaction.

"And could you bring him to consent to no compromise before you left him?" cried Cecilia.

"No; for before I got to him—the challenge had been sent."

"The challenge! good heaven!—and do you know the event?"

"I called again this morning at his lodgings, but he was not returned home."

"And was it impossible to follow him? Were there no means to discover whither he was gone?"

"None; to elude all pursuit, he went out before any body in the house was stirring, and took his servant with him."

"Have you, then, been to Sir Robert?"

"I have been to Cavendish-Square, but there, it seems, he has not appeared all night; I traced him, through his servants, from the Opera to a gaming-house, where I found he had amused himself till this morning."

The uneasiness of Cecilia now encreased every moment; and Mr. Monckton, seeing he had no other chance of satisfying her, offered his service to go again in search of both the gentlemen, and endeavour to bring her better information. She accepted the proposal with gratitude, and he departed.

Soon after she was joined by Mr. Arnott, who, though seized with all the horrors of jealousy at sight of her apprehensions, was so desirous to relieve them, that without even making any merit of obliging her, he almost instantly set out upon the same errand that employed Mr. Monckton, and determined not to mention his design till he found whether it would enable him to bring her good tidings.

He was scarce gone when she was told that Mr. Delvile begged to have the honour of speaking to her. Surprised at this condescension, she desired he might immediately be admitted; but much was her surprise augmented, when, instead of seeing her ostentatious guardian, she again beheld her masquerade friend, the white domino.

He entreated her pardon for an intrusion neither authorised by acquaintance nor by business, though somewhat, he hoped, palliated, by his near connection with one who was privileged to take an interest in her affairs: and then, hastening to the motives which had occasioned his visit, "when I had the honour," he said, "of seeing you last night at the Opera-house, the dispute which had just happened between two gentlemen, seemed to give you an uneasiness which could not but be painful to all who observed it, and as among that number I was not the least moved, you will forgive, I hope, my eagerness to be the first to bring you intelligence that nothing fatal has happened, or is likely to happen."

"You do me, sir," said Cecilia, "much honour; and indeed you relieve me from a suspence extremely disagreeable. The accommodation, I suppose, was brought about this morning?"

"I find," answered he, smiling, "You now expect too much; but hope is never so elastic as when it springs from the ruins of terror."

"What then is the matter? Are they at last, not safe?"

"Yes, perfectly safe; but I cannot tell you they have never been in danger."

"Well, if it is now over I am contented: but you will very much oblige me, sir, if you will inform me what has passed."

"You oblige me, madam, by the honour of your commands. I saw but too much reason to apprehend that measures the most violent would follow the affray of last night; yet as I found that the quarrel had been accidental, and the offence unpremeditated, I thought it not absolutely impossible that an expeditious mediation might effect a compromise: at least it was worth trying; for though wrath slowly kindled or long nourished is sullen and intractable, the sudden anger that has not had time to impress the mind with a deep sense of injury, will, when gently managed, be sometimes appeased with the same quickness it is excited: I hoped, therefore, that some trifling concession from Sir Robert, as the aggressor,—"

"Ah sir!" cried Cecilia, "that, I fear, was not to be obtained!"

"Not by me, I must own," he answered; "but I was not willing to think of the difficulty, and therefore ventured to make the proposal: nor did I leave the Opera-house till I had used every possible argument to persuade Sir Robert an apology would neither stain his courage nor his reputation. But his spirit brooked not the humiliation.''

"Spirit!'' cried Cecilia, ''how mild a word! What, then, could poor Mr. Belfield resolve upon?''

"That, I believe, took him very little time to decide. I discovered, by means of a gentleman at the Opera who was acquainted with him, where he lived, and I waited upon him with an intention to offer my services towards settling the affair by arbitration: for since you call him *poor* Mr. Belfield, I think you will permit me, without offence to his antagonist, to own that his gallantry, though too impetuous for commendation, engaged me in his interest.''

"I hope you don't think,'' cried Cecilia, ''that an offence to his antagonist must necessarily be an offence to me?''

"Whatever I may have thought,'' answered he, looking at her with evident surprise, ''I certainly did not wish that a sympathy offensive and defensive* had been concluded between you. I could not, however, gain access to Mr. Belfield last night, but the affair dwelt upon my mind, and this morning I called at his lodging as soon as it was light.''

"How good you have been!'' cried Cecilia; ''your kind offices have not, I hope, all proved ineffectual!''

"So valorous a Don Quixote,'' returned he, laughing, ''certainly merited a faithful Esquire!* he was, however, gone out, and nobody knew whither. About half an hour ago I called upon him again; he was then just returned home.''

"Well, Sir?''

"I saw him; the affair was over; and in a short time he will be able, if you will allow him so much honour, to thank you for these enquiries.''

"He is then wounded?''

"He is a little hurt, but Sir Robert is perfectly safe. Belfield fired first, and missed; the Baronet was not so successless.''

"I am grieved to hear it, indeed! and where is the wound?''

"The ball entered his right side, and the moment he felt it, he fired his second pistol in the air. This I heard from his servant. He was brought home carefully and slowly; no surgeon* had been upon the spot, but one was called to him immediately. I stayed to enquire his opinion after the wound had been dressed: he told me he had extracted the ball, and assured me Mr. Belfield was not in any danger. Your alarm, madam, last night, which had always been present to me, then encouraged me to take the liberty of waiting upon you; for I concluded you could yet have had no certain intelligence, and thought it best to let the plain and simple fact out-run the probable exaggeration of rumour.''

Cecilia thanked him for his attention, and Mrs. Harrel then making her appearance, he arose and said ''Had my father known the honour I have had this morning of waiting upon Miss Beverley, I am sure I should have been charged with his compliments, and such a commission would somewhat have lessened the presumption of this visit; but I feared lest while I should be making interest for my credentials, the pretence of my embassy might be lost, and other couriers, less scrupulous, might obtain previous audiences, and anticipate my dispatches.''

He then took his leave.

''This white domino, at last then,'' said Cecilia, ''is the son of Mr. Delvile! and thence the knowledge of my situation which gave me so much surprise:—a son how infinitely unlike his father!''

''Yes,'' said Mrs. Harrel, ''and as unlike his mother too, for I assure you she is more proud and haughty even than the old gentleman. I hate the very sight of her, for she keeps every body in such awe that there's nothing but restraint in her presence. But the son is a very pretty young man, and much admired; though I have only seen him in public, for none of the family visit here.''

Mr. Monckton, who now soon returned, was not a little surprised to find that all the intelligence he meant to communicate was already known: and not the more pleased to hear that the white domino, to whom before he owed no good will, had thus officiously preceded him.

Mr. Arnott, who also came just after him, had been so little satisfied with the result of his enquiries, that from the fear of encreasing Cecilia's uneasiness,* he determined not to make known whither he had been; but he soon found his forbearance was of no avail, as she was already acquainted with the duel and its consequences. Yet his unremitting desire to oblige her urged him twice in the course of the same day to again call at Mr. Belfield's lodgings, in order to bring her thence fresh and unsolicited intelligence.

Before breakfast was quite over, Miss Larolles, out of breath with eagerness, came to tell the news of the duel, in her way to *church*, as it was Sunday morning!* and soon after Mrs. Mears, who also was followed by other ladies, brought the same account, which by all was addressed to Cecilia, with expressions of concern that convinced her, to her infinite vexation, she was generally regarded as the person chiefly interested in the accident.

Mr. Harrel did not return till late, but then seemed in very high spirits: "Miss Beverley," he cried, "I bring you news that will repay all your fright; Sir Robert is not only safe, but is come off conqueror."

"I am very sorry, Sir," answered Cecilia, extremely provoked to be thus congratulated, "that any body conquered, or any body was vanquished."

"There is no need for sorrow," cried Mr. Harrel, "or for any thing but joy, for he has not killed his man; the victory, therefore, will neither cost him a flight nor a trial. To-day he means to wait upon you, and lay his laurels at your feet."

"He means, then, to take very fruitless trouble," said Cecilia, "for I have not any ambition to be so honoured."

"Ah, Miss Beverley," returned he, laughing, "this won't do now! it might have passed a little while ago, but it won't do now, I promise you!"

Cecilia, though much displeased by this accusation, found that disclaiming it only excited further raillery, and therefore prevailed upon herself to give him a quiet hearing, and scarce any reply.

At dinner, when Sir Robert arrived, the dislike she had originally taken to him, encreased already into disgust by his behaviour the preceding evening, was now fixed into the strongest aversion by the horror she conceived of his fierceness, and the indignation she felt excited by his arrogance. He seemed, from the success of this duel, to think himself raised to the highest pinnacle of human glory; triumph sat exulting on his brow; he looked down on whoever he deigned to look at all, and shewed that he thought his notice an honour, however imperious the manner in which it was accorded.

Upon Cecilia, however, he cast an eye of more complacency; he now believed her subdued, and his vanity revelled in the belief: her anxiety had so thoroughly satisfied him of her love, that she had hardly the power left to undeceive him; her silence he only attributed to admiration, her coldness to fear, and her reserve to shame.

Sickened by insolence so undisguised and unauthorised, and incensed at the triumph of his successful brutality, Cecilia with páin kept her seat, and with vexation reflected upon the necessity she was under of passing so large a portion of her time in company to which she was so extremely averse.

After dinner, when Mrs. Harrel was talking of her party for the evening, of which Cecilia declined making one, Sir Robert, with a sort of proud humility, that half feared rejection, and half proclaimed an indifference to meeting it, said "I don't much care for going further myself, if Miss Beverley will give me the honour of taking my tea with her."

Cecilia, regarding him with much surprise, answered that she had letters to write into the country, which would confine her to her own room for the rest of the evening. The Baronet, looking at his watch, instantly cried "Faith, that is very fortunate, for I have just recollected an engagement at the other end of the town which had slipt my memory."

Soon after they were all gone, Cecilia received a note from Mrs. Delvile, begging the favour of her company the next morning to breakfast. She readily accepted the invitation, though she was by no means prepared, by the character she had heard of her, to expect much pleasure from an acquaintance with that lady.

CHAPTER VI

A Family Party

CECILIA the next morning, between nine and ten o'clock, went to St. James'-square; she found nobody immediately ready to receive her, but in a short time was waited upon by Mr. Delvile.

After the usual salutations, "Miss Beverley," he said, "I have given express orders to my people, that I may not be interrupted while I have the pleasure of passing some minutes in conversation with you before you are presented to Mrs. Delvile."

And then, with an air of solemnity, he led her to a seat, and having himself taken possession of another, continued his speech.

"I have received information, from authority which I cannot doubt, that the indiscretion of certain of your admirers last Saturday at the Opera-house, occasioned a disturbance which to a young woman of delicacy I should imagine must be very alarming: now as I consider myself concerned in your fame and welfare from regarding you as my ward, I think it is incumbent upon me to make enquiries into such of your affairs as become public; for I should feel in some measure disgraced myself, should it appear to the world, while you are under my guardianship, that there was any want of propriety in the direction of your conduct."

Cecilia, not much flattered by this address, gravely answered that she fancied the affair had been misrepresented to him.

"I am not much addicted," he replied, "to give ear to any thing lightly; you must therefore permit me to enquire into the merits of the cause, and then to draw my own inferences. And let me, at the same time, assure you there is no other young lady who has any right to expect such an attention from me. I must begin by begging you to inform me upon what grounds the two gentlemen in question, for such, by courtesy, I presume they are called, thought themselves entitled publicly to dispute your favour?"

"My favour, Sir!" cried Cecilia, much amazed.

"My dear," said he, with a complacency meant to give her courage, "I know the question is difficult for a young lady to answer; but be not abashed, I should be sorry to distress you, and mean to the utmost of my power to save your blushes. Do not, therefore, fear me; consider me as your guardian, and assure yourself I am perfectly well disposed to consider you as my ward. Acquaint me, then, freely, what are the pretensions of these gentlemen?"

"To me, Sir, they have, I believe, no pretensions at all."

"I see you are shy," returned he, with encreasing gentleness, "I see you cannot be easy with me; and when I consider how little you are accustomed to me, I do not wonder. But pray take courage; I think it necessary to inform myself of your affairs, and therefore I beg you will speak to me with freedom."

Cecilia, more and more mortified by this humiliating condescension, again assured him he had been misinformed, and was again, though discredited, praised for her modesty, when, to her great relief, they were interrupted by the entrance of her friend the *white domino*.

"Mortimer," said Mr. Delvile, "I understand you have already had the pleasure of seeing this young lady?"

"Yes, Sir," he answered, "I have more than once had that happiness, but I have never had the honour of being introduced to her."

"Miss Beverley, then," said the father, "I must present to you Mr. Mortimer Delvile, my son; and, Mortimer, in Miss Beverley I desire you will remember that you respect a ward of your father's."

"I will not, Sir," answered he, "forget an injunction my own inclinations had already out-run."

Mortimer Delvile was tall and finely formed, his features, though not handsome, were full of expression, and a noble openness of manners and address spoke the elegance of his education, and the liberality of his mind.

When this introduction was over, a more general

conversation took place, till Mr. Delvile, suddenly rising, said to Cecilia, "You will pardon me, Miss Beverley, if I leave you for a few minutes; one of my tenants sets out to-morrow morning for my estate in the North, and he has been two hours waiting to speak with me. But if my son is not particularly engaged, I am sure he will be so good as to do the honours* of the house till his mother is ready to receive you."

And then, graciously waving his hand, he quitted the room.

"My father," cried young Delvile, "has left me an office which, could I execute it as perfectly as I shall willingly, would be performed without a fault."

"I am very sorry," said Cecilia, "that I have so much mistaken your hour of breakfast; but let me not be any restraint upon you, I shall find a book, or a news-paper, or something to fill up the time till Mrs. Delvile honours me with a summons."

"You can only be a restraint upon me," answered he, "by commanding me from your presence. I breakfasted long ago, and am now just come from Mr. Belfield. I had the pleasure, this morning, of being admitted into his room."

"And how, Sir, did you find him?"

"Not so well, I fear, as he thinks himself; but he was in high spirits, and surrounded by his friends, whom he was entertaining with all the gaiety of a man in full health, and entirely at his ease; though I perceived, by the frequent changes of his countenance, signs of pain and indisposition, that made me, however pleased with his conversation, think it necessary to shorten my own visit, and to hint to those who were near me the propriety of leaving him quiet."

"Did you see his surgeon, Sir?"

"No; but he told me he should only have one dressing more of his wound, and then get rid of the whole business by running into the country."

"Were you acquainted with him, Sir, before this accident?"

"No, not at all; but the little I have seen of him has strongly interested me in his favour: at Mr. Harrel's masquerade, where I first met with him, I was extremely entertained by his humour,—though there, perhaps, as I had also the honour of first seeing Miss Beverley, I might be too happy to feel much difficulty in being pleased. And even at the Opera he had the advantage of finding me in the same favourable disposition, as I had long distinguished you before I had taken any notice of him. I must, however, confess I did not think his anger that evening quite without provocation,—but I beg your pardon, I may perhaps be mistaken, and you, who know the whole affair, must undoubtedly be better able to account for what happened.''

Here he fixed his eyes upon Cecilia, with a look of curiosity that seemed eager to penetrate into her sentiments of the two antagonists.

''No, certainly,'' she answered, ''he had all the provocation that ill-breeding could give him.''

''And do you, madam,'' cried he, with much surprize, ''judge of this matter with such severity?''

''No, not with severity, simply with candour.''*

''With candour? alas, then, poor Sir Robert! Severity were not half so bad a sign for him!''

A servant now came in, to acquaint Cecilia that Mrs. Delvile waited breakfast for her.

This summons was immediately followed by the re-entrance of Mr. Delvile, who, taking her hand, said he would himself present her to his lady, and with much graciousness assured her of a kind reception.

The ceremonies preceding this interview, added to the character she had already heard of Mrs. Delvile, made Cecilia heartily wish it over; but, assuming all the courage in her power, she determined to support herself with a spirit that should struggle against the ostentatious superiority she was prepared to expect.

She found her seated upon a sofa, from which, however, she arose at her approach; but the moment Cecilia beheld her, all the unfavourable impressions with which she came into her presence immediately vanished, and that respect which the formalities of her introduction had failed to inspire, her air, figure, and countenance instantaneously excited.

She was not more than fifty years of age; her complection, though faded, kept the traces of its former loveliness, her eyes, though they had lost their youthful fire, retained a lustre that evinced their primeval brilliancy, and the fine symmetry of her features, still uninjured by the siege of time, not only indicated the perfection of her juvenile beauty, but still laid claim to admiration in every beholder.

Her carriage was lofty and commanding; but the dignity to which high birth and conscious superiority gave rise, was so judiciously regulated by good sense, and so happily blended with politeness, that though the world at large envied or hated her, the few for whom she had herself any regard, she was infallibly certain to captivate.

The surprise and admiration with which Cecilia at the first glance was struck proved reciprocal: Mrs. Delvile, though prepared for youth and beauty, expected not to see a countenance so intelligent, nor manners so well formed as those of Cecilia: thus mutually astonished and mutually pleased, their first salutations were accompanied by looks so flattering to both, that each saw in the other, an immediate prepossession in her favour, and from the moment that they met, they seemed instinctively impelled to admire.

"I have promised Miss Beverley, madam," said Mr. Delvile to his lady, "that you would give her a kind reception; and I need not remind you that my promises are always held sacred."

"But I hope you have not also promised," cried she, with quickness, "that I should give *you* a kind reception, for I feel at this very moment extremely inclined to quarrel with you."

"Why so, madam?"

"For not bringing us together sooner; for now I have seen her, I already look back with regret to the time I have lost without the pleasure of knowing her."

"What a claim is this," cried young Delvile, "upon the benevolence of Miss Beverley! for if she has not now the indulgence by frequent and diligent visits to make some reparation, she must consider herself as responsible for the dissention she will occasion."

"If peace depends upon my visits," answered Cecilia, "it may immediately be proclaimed; were it to be procured only by my absence, I know not if I should so readily agree to the conditions."

"I must request of you, madam," said Mr. Delvile, "that when my son and I retire, you will bestow half an hour upon this young lady, in making enquiries concerning the disturbance last Saturday at the Opera-House. I have not, myself, so much time to spare, as I have several appointments for this morning; but I am sure you will not object to the office, as I know you to be equally anxious with myself, that the minority of Miss Beverley should pass without reproach."

"Not only her minority, but her maturity," cried young Delvile, warmly, "and not only her maturity, but her decline of life will pass, I hope, not merely without reproach, but with fame and applause!"

"I hope so too;" replied Mr. Delvile: "I wish her well through every stage of her life, but for her minority alone it is my business to do more than wish. For that, I feel my own honour and my own credit concerned; my honour, as I gave it to the Dean that I would superintend her conduct, and my credit, as the world is acquainted with the claim she has to my protection."

"I will not make any enquiries," said Mrs. Delvile, turning to Cecilia with a sweetness that recompensed her for the haughtiness of her guardian, "till I have had some opportunity of convincing Miss Beverley, that my regard for her merits they should be answered."*

"You see, Miss Beverley," said Mr. Delvile, "how little reason you had to be afraid of us; Mrs. Delvile is as much disposed in your favour as myself, and as desirous to be of service to you. Endeavour, therefore, to cast off this timidity, and to make yourself easy. You must come to us often; use will do more towards removing your fears, than all the encouragement we can give you."

"But what are the fears," cried Mrs. Delvile, "that Miss Beverley can have to remove? unless, indeed, she apprehends her visits will make us encroachers, and that the more we are favoured with her presence, the less we shall bear her absence.''

"Pray, son," said Mr. Delvile, "what was the name of the person who was Sir Robert Floyer's opponent? I have again forgotten it."

"Belfield, Sir."

"True; it is a name I am perfectly unacquainted with: however, he may possibly be a very good sort of man; but certainly his opposing himself to Sir Robert Floyer, a man of some family, a gentleman, rich, and allied to some people of distinction, was a rather strange circumstance: I mean not, however, to prejudge the case; I will hear it fairly stated; and am* the more disposed to be cautious in what I pronounce, because I am persuaded Miss Beverley has too much sense to let my advice be thrown away upon her."

"I hope so, Sir; but with respect to the disturbance at the Opera, I know not that I have the least occasion to trouble you."

"If your measures," said he, very gravely, "are already taken, the Dean your uncle prevailed upon me to accept a very useless office; but if any thing is yet undecided, it will not, perhaps, be amiss that I should be consulted. Mean time, I will only recommend to you to consider that Mr. Belfield is a person whose name nobody has heard, and that a connection with Sir Robert Floyer would certainly be very honourable for you."

"Indeed, Sir," said Cecilia, "here is some great mistake; neither of these gentlemen, I believe, think of me at all."

"They have taken, then," cried young Delvile with a laugh, "a very extraordinary method to prove their indifference!"

"The affairs of Sir Robert Floyer," continued Mr. Delvile, "are indeed, I am informed, in some disorder; but he has a noble estate, and your fortune would soon clear all its incumbrances. Such an alliance, therefore, would be mutually advantageous: but what would result from a union with such a person as Mr. Belfield? he is of no family, though in that, perhaps, you would not be very scrupulous; but neither has he any money; what, then, recommends him?''

"To me, Sir, nothing!" answered Cecilia.

"And to me," cried young Delvile, "almost every thing! he has wit, spirit, and understanding, talents to create admiration, and qualities, I believe, to engage esteem!"

"You speak warmly," said Mrs. Delvile; "but if such is his character, he merits your earnestness. What is it you know of him?"

"Not enough, perhaps," answered he, "to coolly justify my praise; but he is one of those whose first appearance takes the mind by surprise, and leaves the judgment to make afterwards such terms as it can. Will you, madam, when he is recovered, permit me to introduce him to you?"

"Certainly," said she, smiling; "but have a care your recommendation does not disgrace your discernment."

"This warmth of disposition, Mortimer," cried Mr. Delvile, "produces nothing but difficulties and trouble: you neglect the connections I point out, and which a little attention might render serviceable as well as honourable, and run precipitately into forming such as can do you no good among people of rank, and are not only profitless in themselves, but generally lead you into expence and inconvenience. You are now of an age to correct this rashness: think, therefore, better of your own consequence, than thus idly to degrade yourself by forming friendships with every shewy adventurer* that comes in your way."

"I know not, Sir," answered he, "how Mr. Belfield deserves to be called an adventurer: he is not, indeed, rich; but he is in a profession where parts such as his seldom fail to acquire riches, however, as to me his wealth can be of no consequence, why should my regard to him wait for it? if he is a young man of worth and honour——"

"Mortimer," interrupted Mr. Delvile, "whatever he is, we know he is not a man of rank, and whatever he may be, we know he cannot become a man of family, and consequently for Mortimer Delvile he is no companion. If you can render him any service, I shall commend your so doing; it becomes your birth, it becomes your station in life to assist individuals, and promote the general good: but never in your zeal for others forget what is due to yourself, and to the ancient and honourable house from which you are sprung."

"But can we entertain Miss Beverley with nothing better than family lectures?" cried Mrs. Delvile.

"It is for me," said young Delvile, rising, "to beg pardon of Miss Beverley for having occasioned them; but when she is so good as to honour us with her company again, I hope I shall have more discretion."

He then left the room; and Mr. Delvile also rising to go, said, "My dear, I commit you to very kind hands; Mrs. Delvile, I am sure, will be happy to hear your story; speak to her, therefore, without reserve. And pray don't imagine that I make you over to her from any slight; on the contrary, I admire and commend your modesty very much; but my time is extremely precious, and I cannot devote so much of it to an explanation as your diffidence requires."

And then, to the great joy of Cecilia, he retired; leaving her much in doubt whether his haughtiness or his condescension humbled her most.

"These men," said Mrs. Delvile, "can never comprehend the pain of a delicate female mind upon entering into explanations of this sort: I understand it, however, too well to inflict it. We will, therefore, have no explanations at all till we are better acquainted, and then if you will venture to favour me with any confidence, my best advice, and, should any be in my power, my best services shall be at your command."

"You do me, madam, much honour," answered Cecilia, "but I must assure you I have no explanation to give."

"Well, well, at present," returned Mrs. Delvile, "I am content to hear that answer, as I have acquired no right to any other: but hereafter I shall hope for more openness: it is promised me by your countenance, and I mean to claim the promise by my friendship."

"Your friendship will both honour and delight me, and whatever are your enquiries, I shall always be proud to answer them; but indeed, with regard to this affair——"

"My dear Miss Beverley," interrupted Mrs. Delvile, with a look of arch incredulity, "men seldom risk their lives

where an escape is without hope of recompence. But we will
not now say a word more upon the subject. I hope you will
often favour me with your company, and by the frequency
of your visits, make us both forget the shortness of our
acquaintance.''

Cecilia, finding her resistance only gave birth to fresh
suspicion, now yielded, satisfied that a very little time must
unavoidably clear up the truth. But her visit was not
therefore shortened; the sudden partiality with which the
figure and countenance of Mrs. Delvile had impressed her,
was quickly ripened into esteem by the charms of her
conversation: she found her sensible, well bred, and high
spirited, gifted by nature with superior talents, and polished
by education and study with all the elegant embellishments
of cultivation. She saw in her, indeed, some portion of the
pride she had been taught to expect, but it was so much
softened by elegance, and so well tempered with kindness,
that it elevated her character, without rendering her
manners offensive.

With such a woman, subjects of discourse could never be
wanting, nor fertility of powers to make them entertaining:
and so much was Cecilia delighted with her visit, that
though her carriage was announced at twelve o'clock, she
reluctantly concluded it at two; and in taking her leave,
gladly accepted an invitation to dine with her new friend
three days after; who, equally pleased with her young guest,
promised before that time to return her visit.

CHAPTER VII

An Examination

CECILIA found Mrs. Harrel eagerly waiting to hear some
account how she had passed the morning, and fully
persuaded that she would leave the Delviles with a
determination never more, but by necessity, to see them: she
was, therefore, not only surprised but disappointed, when
instead of fulfilling her expectations, she assured her that she

had been delighted with Mrs. Delvile, whose engaging qualities amply recompensed her for the arrogance of her husband; that her visit had no fault but that of being too short, and that she had already appointed an early day for repeating it.

Mrs. Harrel was evidently hurt by this praise, and Cecilia, who perceived among all her guardians a powerful disposition to hatred and jealousy, soon dropt the subject: though so much had she been charmed with Mrs. Delvile, that a scheme of removal once more occurred to her, notwithstanding her dislike of her stately guardian.

At dinner, as usual, they were joined by Sir Robert Floyer, who grew more and more assiduous in his attendance, but who, this day, contrary to his general custom of remaining with the gentlemen, made his exit before the ladies left the table; and as soon as he was gone, Mr. Harrel desired a private conference with Cecilia.

They went together to the drawing-room, where, after a flourishing preface upon the merits of Sir Robert Floyer, he formally acquainted her that he was commissioned by that gentleman, to make her a tender of his hand and fortune.*

Cecilia, who had not much reason to be surprised at this overture, desired him to tell the Baronet, she was obliged to him for the honour he intended her, at the same time that she absolutely declined receiving it.

Mr. Harrel, laughing, told her this answer was very well for a beginning, though it would by no means serve beyond the first day of the declaration; but when Cecilia assured him she should firmly adhere to it, he remonstrated with equal surprise and discontent upon the reasons of her refusal. She thought it sufficient to tell him that Sir Robert did not please her, but, with much raillery,* he denied the assertion credit, assuring her that he was universally admired by the ladies, that she could not possibly receive a more honourable offer, and that he was reckoned by every body the finest gentleman about the town. His fortune, he added, was equally unexceptionable with his figure and his rank in life; all the world, he was certain, would approve the connexion, and the settlement made upon her should be dictated by herself.*

Cecilia begged him to be satisfied with an answer which she never could change, and to spare her the enumeration of particular objections, since Sir Robert was wholly and in every respect disagreeable to her.

"What, then," cried he, "could make you so frightened for him at the Opera-house? There has been but one opinion about town ever since of your prepossession in his favour."

"I am extremely concerned to hear it; my fright was but the effect of surprise, and belonged not more to Sir Robert than to Mr. Belfield."

He told her that nobody else thought the same, that her marriage with the Baronet was universally expected, and, in conclusion, notwithstanding her earnest desire that he would instantly and explicitly inform Sir Robert of her determination, he repeatedly refused to give him any final answer till she had taken more time for consideration.

Cecilia was extremely displeased at this irksome importunity, and still more chagrined to find her incautious emotion at the Opera-house, had given rise to suspicions of her harbouring a partiality for a man whom every day she more heartily disliked.

While she was deliberating in what manner she could clear up this mistake, which, after she was left alone, occupied all her thoughts, she was interrupted by the entrance of Mr. Monckton, whose joy in meeting her at length by herself exceeded not her own, for charmed as he was that he could now examine into the state of her affairs, she was not less delighted that she could make them known to him.

After mutual expressions, guarded, however, on the part of Mr. Monckton, though unreserved on that of Cecilia, of their satisfaction in being again able to converse as in former times, he asked if she would permit him, as the privilege of their long acquaintance, to speak to her with sincerity.

She assured him he could not more oblige her.

"Let me, then," said he, "enquire if yet that ardent confidence in your own steadiness, which so much disdained my fears that the change of your residence might produce a change in your sentiments, is still as unshaken as when we parted in Suffolk? Or whether experience, that foe to unpractised refinement, has already taught you the fallibility of theory?''

"When I assure you," replied Cecilia, "that your enquiry gives me no pain, I think I have sufficiently answered it, for were I conscious of any alteration, it could not but embarrass and distress me. Very far, however, from finding myself in the danger with which you threatened me, of *forgetting Bury, its inhabitants and its environs*,* I think with pleasure of little else, since London, instead of bewitching, has greatly disappointed me.''

"How so?" cried Mr. Monckton, much delighted.

"Not," answered she, "in itself, not in its magnificence, nor in its diversions, which seem to be inexhaustible; but these, though copious as instruments of pleasure, are very shallow as sources of happiness: the disappointment, therefore, comes nearer home, and springs not from London, but from my own situation.''

"Is that, then, disagreeable to you?"

"You shall yourself judge, when I have told you that from the time of my quitting your house till this very moment, when I have again the happiness of talking with you, I have never once had any conversation, society or intercourse, in which friendship or affection have had any share, or my mind has had the least interest.''

She then entered into a detail of her way of life, told him how little suited to her taste was the unbounded dissipation of the Harrels, and feelingly expatiated upon the disappointment she had received from the alteration in the manners and conduct of her young friend. "In her," she continued, "had I found the companion I came prepared to meet, the companion from whom I had so lately parted, and in whose society I expected to find consolation for the loss of yours and of Mrs. Charlton's, I should have complained of nothing; the very places that now tire, might then have entertained me, and all that now passes for unmeaning dissipation, might then have* worn the appearance of variety and pleasure. But where the mind is wholly without interest, every thing is languid and insipid; and accustomed as I have long been to think friendship the first of human blessings, and social converse the greatest of human enjoyments, how ever can I reconcile myself to a state of careless indifference, to making acquaintance without any concern either for preserving or esteeming them, and to going on from day to day in an eager search of amusement, with no companion for the hours of retirement, and no view beyond that of passing the present moment in apparent gaiety and thoughtlessness?''

Mr. Monckton, who heard these complaints with secret rapture, far from seeking to soften or remove, used his utmost endeavours to strengthen and encrease them, by artfully retracing her former way of life, and pointing out with added censures the change in it she had been lately compelled to make: ''a change,'' he continued, ''which though ruinous of your time, and detrimental to your happiness, use will, I fear, familiarize, and familiarity render pleasant.''

''These suspicions, Sir,'' said Cecilia, ''mortify me greatly; and why, when far from finding me pleased, you hear nothing but repining, should you still continue to harbour them?''

''Because your trial has yet been too short to prove your firmness, and because there is nothing to which time cannot contentedly accustom us.''

''I feel not much fear,'' said Cecilia, ''of standing such a test as might fully satisfy you; but nevertheless, not to be too presumptuous, I have by no means exposed myself to all the dangers which you think surround me, for of late I have spent almost every evening at home and by myself.''

This intelligence was to Mr. Monckton a surprise the most agreeable he could receive. Her distaste for the amusements which were offered her greatly relieved his fears of her forming any alarming connection, and the discovery that while so anxiously he had sought her every where in public, she had quietly passed her time by her own fire-side, not only re-assured him for the present, but gave him information where he might meet with her in future.

He then talked of the duel, and solicitously led her to

speak open* of Sir Robert Floyer; and here, too, his satisfaction was entire; he found her dislike of him such as his knowledge of her disposition made him expect, and she wholly removed his suspicions concerning her anxiety about the quarrel, by explaining to him her apprehensions of having occasioned it herself, from accepting the civility of Mr. Belfield, at the very moment she shewed her aversion to receiving that of Sir Robert.*

Neither did her confidence rest here; she acquainted him with the conversation she had just had with Mr. Harrel, and begged his advice in what manner she might secure herself from further importunity.

Mr. Monckton had now a new subject for his discernment. Every thing had confirmed to him the passion which Mr. Arnott had conceived for Cecilia, and he had therefore concluded the interest of the Harrels would be all in his favour: other ideas now struck him; he found that Mr. Arnott was given up for Sir Robert, and he determined carefully to watch the motions both of the Baronet and her young guardian, in order to discover the nature of their plans and connexion. Mean time, convinced by her unaffected aversion to the proposals she had received, that she was at present in no danger from the league he suspected, he merely advised her to persevere in manifesting a calm repugnance to their solicitations, which could not fail, before long, to dishearten them both.

"But Sir," cried Cecilia, "I now fear this man as much as I dislike him, for his late fierceness and brutality, though they have encreased my disgust, make me dread to shew it. I am impatient, therefore, to have done with him, and to see him no more. And for this purpose, I wish to quit the house of Mr. Harrel, where he has access at his pleasure."

"You can wish nothing more judiciously," cried he; "would you, then, return into the country?"

"That is not yet in my power; I am obliged to reside with one of my guardians. To day I have seen Mrs. Delvile, and—"

"Mrs. Delvile?" interrupted Mr. Monckton, in a voice of

astonishment, "Surely you do not think of removing into that family?"

"What can I do so well? Mrs. Delvile is a charming woman, and her conversation would afford me more entertainment and instruction in a single day, than under this roof I should obtain in a twelvemonth."

"Are you serious? Do you really think of making such a change?"

"I really wish it, but I know not yet if it is practicable: on Thursday, however, I am to dine with her, and then, if it is in my power, I will hint to her my desire."

"And can Miss Beverley possibly wish," cried Mr. Monckton with earnestness, "to reside in such a house? Is not Mr. Devile the most ostentatious, haughty, and self-sufficient of men? Is not his wife the proudest of women? And is not the whole family odious to all the world?"

"You amaze me!" cried Cecilia; "surely that cannot be their general character? Mr. Delvile, indeed, deserves all the censure he can meet for his wearisome parade of superiority; but his lady by no means merits to be included in the same reproach. I have spent this whole morning with her, and though I waited upon her with a strong prejudice in her disfavour, I observed in her no pride that exceeded the bounds of propriety and native dignity."

"Have you often been at the house? Do you know the son, too?"

"I have seen him three or four times."

"And what do you think of him?"

"I hardly know enough of him to judge fairly."

"But what does he seem to you! Do you not perceive in him already all the arrogance, all the contemptuous insolence of his father?"

"O no! far from it indeed; his mind seems to be liberal and noble, open to impressions of merit, and eager to honour and promote it."

"You are much deceived; you have been reading your own mind, and thought you had read his: I would advise you sedulously to avoid the whole family; you will find all intercourse with them irksome and comfortless: such as the father appears at once, the wife and the son will, in a few more meetings, appear also. They are descended from the same stock, and inherit the same self-complacency. Mr. Delvile married his cousin, and each of them instigates the other to believe that all birth and rank would be at an end in the world, if their own superb family had not a promise of support from their hopeful Mortimer. Should you precipitately settle yourself in their house, you would very soon be totally weighed down by their united insolence.''

Cecilia again and warmly attempted to defend them; but Mr. Monckton was so positive in his assertions, and so significant in his insinuations to their discredit, that she was at length persuaded she had judged too hastily, and, after thanking him for his counsel, promised not to take any measures towards a removal without his advice.

This was all he desired; and now, enlivened by finding that his influence with her was unimpaired, and that her heart was yet her own, he ceased his exhortations, and turned the discourse to subjects more gay and general, judiciously cautious neither by tedious admonitions to disgust, nor by fretful solicitude to alarm her. He did not quit her till the evening was far advanced, and then, in returning to his own house, felt all his anxieties and disappointments recompensed by the comfort this long and satisfactory conversation had afforded him. While Cecilia, charmed with having spent the morning with her new acquaintance, and the evening with her old friend, retired to rest better pleased with the disposal of her time than she had yet been since her journey from Suffolk.

CHAPTER VIII

A Tête à Tête

THE two following days had neither event nor disturbance, except some little vexation occasioned by the behaviour of Sir Robert Floyer, who still appeared not to entertain any doubt of the success of his addresses. This impertinent confidence she could only attribute to the officious encouragement of Mr. Harrel, and therefore she determined rather to seek than to avoid an explanation with him. But she had, in the mean time, the satisfaction of hearing from Mr. Arnott, who, ever eager to oblige her, was frequent in his enquiries, that Mr. Belfield was almost entirely recovered.

On Thursday, according to her appointment, she again went to St. James'-Square, and being shewn into the drawing-room till dinner was ready, found there only young Mr. Delvile.

After some general conversation, he asked her how lately she had had any news of Mr. Belfield?

"This morning," she answered, "when I had the pleasure of hearing he was quite recovered. Have you seen him again, Sir?"

"Yes, madam, twice."

"And did you think him almost well?"

"I thought," answered he, with some hesitation, "and I think still, that your enquiries ought to be his cure."

"O," cried Cecilia, "I hope he has far better medicines: but I am afraid I have been misinformed, for I see you do not think him better."

"You must not, however," replied he, "blame those messengers whose artifice has only had your satisfaction in view; nor should I be so malignant as to blast their designs, if I did not fear that Mr. Belfield's actual safety may be endangered by your continued deception."

"What deception, Sir? I don't at all understand you. How is his safety endangered?"

"Ah madam!" said he smiling, "what danger indeed is there that any man would not risk to give birth to such solicitude! Mr. Belfield however, I believe is in none from which a command of yours cannot rescue him."

"Then were I an hard-hearted damsel indeed not to issue it! but if my commands are so medicinal, pray instruct me how to administer them."

"You must order him to give up, for the present, his plan of going into the country, where he can have no assistance, and where his wound must be dressed only by a common servant, and to remain quietly in town till his surgeon pronounces that he may travel without any hazard.''

"But is he, seriously, so mad as to intend leaving town without the consent of his surgeon?''

"Nothing less than such an intention could have induced me to undeceive you with respect to his recovery. But indeed I am no friend to those artifices which purchase present relief by future misery: I venture, therefore, to speak to you the simple truth, that by a timely exertion of your influence you may prevent further evil.''

"I know not, Sir," said Cecilia, with the utmost surprise, "why you should suppose I have any such influence; nor can I imagine that any deception has been practiced.''

"Is it possible," answered he, "I may have been too much alarmed; but in such a case as this, no information ought to be depended upon but that of his surgeon. You, madam, may probably know his opinion?''

"Me?—No, indeed! I never saw his surgeon; I know not even who he is.''

"I purpose calling upon him to-morrow morning; will Miss Beverley permit me afterwards the honour of communicating to her what may pass?''

"I thank you, Sir," said she, colouring very high; "but my impatience is by no means so great as to occasion my giving you that trouble.''

Delvile, perceiving her change of countenance, instantly, and with much respect, entreated her pardon for the proposal; which, however, she had no sooner granted, than he said very archly "Why indeed you have not much right to be angry, since it was your own frankness that excited mine. And thus, you find, like most other culprits, I am ready to cast the blame of the offence upon the offended. I feel, however, an irresistible propensity to do service to Mr. Belfield;—shall I sin quite beyond forgiveness if I venture to tell you how I found him situated this morning?''

"No, certainly,—if you wish it, I can have no objection.''

"I found him, then, surrounded by a set of gay young men, who, by way of keeping up his spirits, made him laugh and talk without ceasing: he assured me himself that he was perfectly well, and intended to gallop out of town to-morrow morning; though, when I shook hands with him at parting, I was both shocked and alarmed to feel by the burning heat of the skin,* that far from discarding his surgeon, he ought rather to call in a physician.''*

"I am very much concerned to hear this account," said Cecilia; "but I do not well understand what you mean should on my part follow it?"

"That," answered he, bowing, with a look of mock gravity, "I pretend not to settle! In stating the case I have satisfied my conscience, and if in hearing it you can pardon the liberty I have taken, I shall as much honour the openness of your character, as I admire that of your countenance."

Cecilia now, to her no little astonishment, found she had the same mistake to clear up at present concerning Mr. Belfield, that only three days before she had explained with respect to the Baronet. But she had no time to speak further upon the subject, as the entrance of Mrs. Delvile put an end to their discourse.

That lady received her with the most distinguishing kindness; apologised for not sooner waiting upon her, and repeatedly declared that nothing but indisposition should have prevented her returning the favour of her first visit.

They were soon after summoned to dinner. Mr. Delvile, to the infinite joy of Cecilia, was out.

The day was spent greatly to her satisfaction. There was no interruption from visitors, she was tormented by the discussion of no disagreeable subjects, the duel was not mentioned, the antagonists were not hinted at, she was teized with no self-sufficient encouragement, and wearied with no mortifying affability; the conversation at once was lively and rational, and though general, was rendered interesting, by a reciprocation of good-will and pleasure in the conversers.

The favourable opinion she had conceived both of the mother and the son this long visit served to confirm: in Mrs. Delvile she found strong sense, quick parts, and high breeding; in Mortimer, sincerity and vivacity joined with softness and elegance; and in both there seemed the most liberal admiration of talents, with an openness of heart that disdained all disguise. Greatly pleased with their manners, and struck with all that was apparent in their characters, she much regretted the prejudice of Mr. Monckton, which now, with the promise she had given him, was all that opposed her making an immediate effort towards a change in her abode.

She did not take her leave till eleven o'clock,* when Mrs. Delvile, after repeatedly thanking her for her visit, said she would not so much encroach upon her good nature as to request another till she had waited upon her in return; but added, that she meant very speedily to pay that debt, in order to enable herself, by friendly and frequent meetings, to enter upon the confidential commission with which her guardian had entrusted her.

Cecilia was pleased with the delicacy which gave rise to this forbearance, yet having in fact nothing either to relate or conceal, she was rather sorry than glad at the delay of an explanation, since she found the whole family was in an error with respect to the situation of her affairs.

END OF THE FIRST VOLUME.

softness and elegance; and in both there seemed the most liberal admiration of talents, with an openness of heart that disdained all disguise. Greatly pleased with their manners, and struck with all that was apparent in their characters, she much regretted the prejudice of Mr. Monckton, which now, with the promise she had given him, was all that opposed her making an immediate effort towards a change in her abode.

She did not take her leave till eleven o'clock, when Mrs. Delvile, after repeatedly thanking her for her visit, said she would not so much encroach upon her good nature as to request another till she had waited upon her in return; but added, that she meant very speedily to pay that debt, in order to enable herself, by friendly and frequent meetings, to enter upon the confidential commission with which her guardian had entrusted her.

Cecilia was pleased with the delicacy which gave rise to this forbearance, yet having in fact nothing either to relate or conceal, she was rather sorry than glad at the delay of an explanation, since she found the whole family was in an error with respect to the situation of her affairs.

END OF THE FIRST VOLUME.

VOLUME II

BOOK III

CHAPTER I

An Application

CECILIA, upon her return home, heard with some surprise that Mr. and Mrs. Harrel were by themselves in the drawing room; and, while she was upon the stairs, Mrs. Harrel ran out, calling eagerly, "Is that my brother?"

Before she could make an answer, Mr. Harrel, in the same impatient tone, exclaimed, "Is it Mr. Arnott?"

"No;" said Cecilia, "did you expect him so late?"

"Expect him? Yes," answered Mr. Harrel, "I have expected him the whole evening, and cannot conceive what he has done with himself."

"'Tis abominably provoking," said Mrs. Harrel, "that he should be out of the way just now when he is wanted. However, I dare say to-morrow will do as well."

"I don't know that," cried Mr. Harrel; "Reeves is such a wretch that I am sure he will give me all the trouble in his power."

Here Mr. Arnott entered; and Mrs. Harrel called out "O brother, we have been distressed for you cruelly; we have had a man here who has plagued Mr. Harrel to death, and we wanted you sadly to speak to him."

"I should have been very glad," said Mr. Arnott, "to have been of any use, and perhaps it is not yet too late; who is the man?"

"O," cried Mr. Harrel, carelessly, "only a fellow from that rascally taylor who has been so troublesome to me lately. He has had the impudence, because I did not pay him the moment he was pleased to want his money, to put the bill into the hands of one Reeves, a griping attorney,* who has been here this evening, and thought proper to talk to me

pretty freely. I can tell the gentleman I shall not easily forget
his impertinence! however, I really wish mean time I could
get rid of him.''

"How much is the bill, Sir?'' said Mr. Arnott.

"Why its rather a round* sum; but I don't know how it
is, one's bills mount up before one is aware: those fellows
charge such confounded sums for tape and buckram;* I
hardly know what I have had of him, and yet he has run me
up a bill of between three and four hundred pound.''

Here there was a general silence; till Mrs. Harrel said
"Brother, can't you be so good as to lend us the money? Mr.
Harrel says he can pay it again very soon.''

"O yes, very soon,'' said Mr. Harrel, "for I shall receive
a great deal of money in a little time; I only want to stop this
fellow's mouth for the present.''

"Suppose I go and talk with him?'' said Mr. Arnott.

"O, he's a brute, a stock!''* cried Mr. Harrel, "nothing
but the money will satisfy him: he will hear no reason; one
might as well talk to a stone.''

Mr. Arnott now looked extremely distressed; but upon his
sister's warmly pressing him not to lose any time, he gently
said, "If this person will but wait a week or two, I should
be extremely glad, for really just now I cannot take up so
much money, without such particular loss and inconvenience, that I hardly know how to do it:— but yet, if he
will not be appeased, he must certainly have it.''

"Appeased?'' cried Mr. Harrel, "you might as well
appease the sea in a storm! he is hard as iron.''

Mr. Arnott then, forcing a smile, though evidently in
much uneasiness, said he would not fail to raise the money
the next morning, and was taking his leave, when Cecilia,
shocked that such tenderness and good-nature should be
thus grossly imposed upon, hastily begged to speak with
Mrs. Harrel, and taking her into another room, said, "I
beseech you, my dear friend, let not your worthy brother
suffer by his generosity; permit me in the present exigence
to assist Mr. Harrel: my having such a sum advanced can
be of no consequence; but I should grieve indeed that your
brother, who so nobly understands the use of money, should

take it up at any particular disadvantage."

"You are vastly kind," said Mrs. Harrel, "and I will run and speak to them about it: but which ever of you lends the money, Mr. Harrel has assured me he shall pay it very soon."

She then returned with the proposition. Mr. Arnott strongly opposed it, but Mr. Harrel seemed rather to prefer it, yet spoke so confidently of his speedy payment, that he appeared to think it a matter of little importance from which he accepted it. A generous contest ensued between Mr. Arnott and Cecilia, but as she was very earnest, she at length prevailed, and settled to go herself the next morning into the city, in order to have the money advanced by Mr. Briggs, who had the management of her fortune entirely to himself, her other guardians never interfering in the executive part of her affairs.

This arranged, they all retired.

And then, with encreasing astonishment, Cecilia reflected upon the ruinous levity of Mr. Harrel, and the blind security of his wife; she saw in their situation danger the most alarming, and in the behaviour of Mr. Harrel selfishness the most inexcusable; such glaring injustice to his creditors, such utter insensibility to his friends, took from her all wish of assisting him, though the indignant compassion with which she saw the easy generosity of Mr. Arnott so frequently abused, had now, for his sake merely, induced her to relieve him.

She resolved, however, as soon as the present difficulty was surmounted, to make another attempt to open the eyes of Mrs. Harrel to the evils which so apparently threatened her, and press her to exert all her influence with her husband, by means both of example and advice, to retrench his expences before it should be absolutely too late to save him from ruin.

She determined also at the same time that she applied for the money requisite for this debt, to take up enough for discharging her own bill at the booksellers, and putting in execution her plan of assisting the Hills.

The next morning she arose early, and attended by her

servant, set out for the house of Mr. Briggs, purposing, as the weather was clear and frosty, to walk through Oxford Road, and then put herself into a chair; and hoping to return to Mr. Harrel's by the usual hour of breakfast.

She had not proceeded far, before she saw a mob gathering, and the windows of almost all the houses filling with spectators. She desired her servant to enquire what this meant, and was informed that the people were assembling to see some malefactors pass by in their way to Tyburn.

Alarmed at this intelligence from the fear of meeting the unhappy criminals, she hastily turned down the next street, but found that also filling with people who were running to the scene she was trying to avoid: encircled thus every way, she applied to a maid servant who was standing at the door of a large house, and begged leave to step in till the mob* was gone by. The maid immediately consented, and she waited here while she sent her man for a chair.

He soon arrived with one; but just as she returned to the street door, a gentleman, who was hastily entering the house, standing back to let her pass, suddenly exclaimed, "Miss Beverley!" and looking at him, she perceived young Delvile.

"I cannot stop an instant," cried she, running down the steps, "lest the crowd should prevent the chair from going on."

"Will you not first," said he, handing her in, "tell me what news you have heard?"

"News?" repeated she, "No, I have heard none!"

"You will only, then, laugh at me for those officious offers you did so well to reject?"

"I know not what offers you mean!"

"They were indeed superfluous, and therefore I wonder not you have forgotten them. Shall I tell the chairmen whither to go?"

"To Mr. Briggs. But I cannot imagine what you mean."

"To Mr. Briggs!" repeated he, "O live for ever French beads and Bristol stones!* fresh offers may perhaps be made there, impertinent, officious, and useless as mine!"

He then told her servant the direction, and, making his bow, went into the house she had just quitted.

Cecilia, extremely amazed by this short, but unintelligible conversation, would again have called upon him to explain his meaning, but found the crowd encreasing so fast that she could not venture to detain the chair, which with difficulty made its way to the adjoining streets: but her surprize at what had passed so entirely occupied her, that when she stopt at the house of Mr. Briggs, she had almost forgotten what had brought her thither.

The foot-boy, who came to the door, told her that his master was at home, but not well.

She desired he might be acquainted that she wished to speak to him upon business, and would wait upon him again at any hour when he thought he should be able to see her.

The boy returned with an answer that she might call again the next week.

Cecilia, knowing that so long a delay would destroy all the kindness of her intention, determined to write to him for the money, and therefore went into the parlour, and desired to have pen and ink.

The boy, after making her wait some time in a room without any fire, brought her a pen and a little ink in a broken tea cup, saying "Master begs you won't spirt it about, for he's got no more; and all our blacking's as good as gone."

"Blacking?"* repeated Cecilia.

"Yes, Miss; when Master's shoes are blacked, we commonly gets a little drap* of fresh ink."

Cecilia promised to be careful, but desired him to fetch her a sheet of paper.

"Law, Miss," cried the boy, with a grin, "I dare say master'd as soon give you a bit of his nose! howsever, I'll go ax."

In a few minutes he again returned, and brought in his hand a slate and a black lead pencil;* "Miss," cried he, "Master says how you may write upon this, for he supposes you've no great matters to say."

Cecilia, much astonished at this extreme parsimony,

was obliged to consent, but as the point of the pencil was very blunt, desired the boy to get her a knife that she might cut it. He obeyed, but said "Pray Miss, take care it ben't known, for master don't do such a thing once in a year, and if he know'd I'd got you the knife, he'd go nigh to give me a good polt* of the head."

Cecilia then wrote upon the slate her desire to be informed in what manner she should send him her receipt for 600*l.* which she begged to have instantly advanced.

The boy came back grinning, and holding up his hands, and said, "Miss, there's a fine piece of work up stairs! Master's in a peck of troubles;* but he says how he'll come down, if you'll stay till he's got his things on."

"Does he keep his bed, then? I hope I have not made him rise?"

"No, Miss, he don't keep his bed, only he must get ready, for he wears no great matters of cloaths when he's alone. You are to know, Miss," lowering his voice, "that that day as he went abroad with our sweep's cloaths on, he comed home in sich* a pickle you never see! I believe somebody'd knocked him in the kennel;* so does Moll; but don't you say as I teld you! He's been special bad ever since. Moll and I was as glad as could be, because he's so plaguy sharp; for, to let you know, Miss, he's so near,* it's partly a wonder how he lives at all: and yet he's worth a power of money, too."

"Well, well," said Cecilia, not very desirous to encourage his forwardness, "if I want any thing, I'll call for you."

The boy, however, glad to tell his tale, went on.

"Our Moll won't stay with him above a week longer, Miss, because she says how she can't get nothing to eat, but just some old stinking salt meat, that's stayed in the butcher's shop so long, it would make a horse sick to look at it. But Moll's pretty nice;* howsever, Miss, to let you know, we don't get a good meal so often as once a quarter! why this last week we ha'n't had nothing at all but some dry musty red herrings; so you may think, Miss, we're kept pretty sharp!*

He was now interrupted by hearing Mr. Briggs coming

down the stairs, upon which, abruptly breaking off his complaints, he held up his finger to his nose in token of secrecy, and ran hastily into the kitchen.

The appearance of Mr. Briggs was by no means rendered more attractive by illness and negligence of dress. He had on a flannel gown and night cap; his black beard, of many days growth, was long and grim, and upon his nose and one of his cheeks was a large patch of brown paper,* which, as he entered the room, he held on with both his hands.

Cecilia made many apologies for having disturbed him, and some civil enquiries concerning his health.

"Ay, ay," cried he, pettishly, "bad enough: all along of that trumpery* masquerade; wish I had not gone! Fool for my pains."

"When were you taken ill, Sir?"

"Met with an accident; got a fall, broke my head,* like to have lost my wig. Wish the masquerade at old Nick! thought it would cost nothing, or would not have gone. Warrant sha'n't get me so soon to another!"

"Did you fall in going home, Sir?"

"Ay, ay, plump in the kennel; could hardly get out of it; felt myself a going, was afraid to tear my cloaths, knew the rascal would make me pay for them, so by holding up the old sack, come bolt on my face! off pops my wig; could not tell what to do; all as dark as pitch!"

"Did not you call for help?"

"Nobody by but scrubs,* knew they would not help for nothing. Scrawled* out as I could, groped about for my wig, found it at last, all soused* in the mud; stuck to my head like Turner's cerate."*

"I hope, then, you got into an hackney coach?"

"What for? to make things worse? was not bad enough, hay?—must pay two shillings beside?"

"But how did you find yourself when you got home, Sir?"

"How? why wet as muck; my head all bumps, my cheek all cut, my nose big as two! forced to wear a plaister; half ruined in vinegar.* Got a great cold; put me in a fever; never been well since."

"But have you had no advice, Sir? should not you send for a physician?"

"What to do, hay? fill me with jallop?* can get it myself, can't I? Had one once; was taken very bad, thought should have popt off; began to flinch, sent for the doctor, proved nothing but a cheat! cost me a guinea, gave it at fourth visit, and he never came again!—warrant won't have no more!"

Then perceiving upon the table some dust from the black lead pencil,* "What's here?" cried he, angrily, "who's been cutting the pencil? wish they were hanged; suppose its the boy; deserves to be horse-whipped: give him a good banging."

Cecilia immediately cleared him, by acknowledging she had herself been the culprit.

"Ay, ay," cried he, "thought as much all the time! guessed how it was; nothing but ruin and waste; sending for money, nobody knows why; wanting 600*l.*—what to do? throw it in the dirt? Never heard the like! Sha'n't have it, promise you that," nodding his head, "shan't have no such thing!"

"Sha'n't have it?" cried Cecilia, much surprised, "why not, Sir?"

"Keep it for your husband; get you one soon: won't have no juggling. Don't be in a hurry; one in my eye."

Cecilia then began a very earnest expostulation, assuring him she really wanted the money, for an occasion which would not admit of delay.

Her remonstrances, however, he wholly disregarded, telling her that girls knew nothing of the value of money, and ought not to be trusted with it; that he would not hear of such extravagance, and was resolved not to advance her a penny.

Cecilia was both provoked and confounded by a refusal so unexpected, and as she thought herself bound in honour to Mr. Harrel not to make known the motive of her urgency, she was for some time totally silenced: till recollecting her account with the bookseller, she determined to rest her plea upon that, persuaded that he could not, at least, deny her money to pay her own bills.

He heard her, however, with the utmost contempt; "Books?" he cried, "what do you want with books? do no good; all lost time; words get no cash."

She informed him his admonitions were now too late, as she had already received them, and must therefore necessarily pay for them.

"No, no," cried he, "send 'em back, that's best; keep no such rubbish, won't turn to account; do better without 'em."

"That, Sir, will be impossible, for I have had them some time, and cannot expect the bookseller to take them again."

"Must, must," cried he, "can't help himself; glad to have 'em too. Are but a minor, can't be made pay a farthing."*

Cecilia with much indignation heard such fraud recommended, and told him she could by no means consent to follow his advice. But she soon found, to her utter amazement, that he steadily refused to give her any other, or to bestow the slightest attention upon her expostulations, sturdily saying that her uncle had left her a noble estate, and he would take care to see it put in proper hands, by getting her a good and careful husband.

"I have no intention, no wish, Sir," cried she, "to break into the income or estate left me by my uncle; on the contrary, I hold them sacred, and think myself bound in conscience never to live beyond them: but the 10,000*l.* bequeathed me by my Father, I regard as more peculiarly my own property, and therefore think myself at liberty to dispose of it as I please."

"What," cried he, in a rage, "make it over to a scrubby bookseller! give it up for an old pot-hook?* no, no, won't suffer it; sha'n't be, sha'n't be, I say! if you want some books, go to Moorfields, pick up enough at an old stall; get 'em at two-pence a-piece; dear enough, too."

Cecilia for some time hoped he was merely indulging his strange and sordid humour by an opposition that was only intended to teize her; but she soon found herself extremely mistaken: he was immoveable in obstinacy, as he was incorrigible in avarice; he neither troubled himself with enquiries nor reasoning, but was contented with refusing her as a child might be refused, by peremptorily telling her she did not know what she wanted, and therefore should not have what she asked.

And with this answer, after all that she could urge, she was compelled to leave the house, as he complained that his brown paper plaister wanted fresh dipping in vinegar, and he could stay talking no longer.

The disgust with which this behaviour filled her, was doubled by the shame and concern of returning to the Harrels with her promise unperformed; she deliberated upon every method that occurred to her of still endeavouring to serve them, but could suggest nothing, except trying to prevail upon Mr. Delvile to interfere in her favour. She liked not, indeed, the office of solicitation to so haughty a man, but, having no other expedient, her repugnance gave way to her generosity, and she ordered the chairmen to carry her to St. James's Square.

CHAPTER II

A Perplexity

AND here, at the door of his Father's house, and just ascending the steps, she perceived young Delvile.

"Again!" cried he, handing her out of the chair, "surely some good genius is at work for me this morning!"

She told him she should not have called so early, now she was acquainted with the late hours of Mrs. Delvile, but that she merely meant to speak with his Father, for two minutes, upon business.

He attended her up stairs; and finding she was in haste, went himself with her message to Mr. Delvile: and soon returned with an answer that he would wait upon her presently.

The strange speeches he had made to her when they first

met in the morning now recurring to her memory, she determined to have them explained, and in order to lead to the subject, mentioned the disagreeable situation in which he had found her, while she was standing up to avoid the sight of the condemned malefactors.

"Indeed?" cried he, in a tone of voice somewhat incredulous, "and was that the purpose for which you stood up?"

"Certainly, Sir;—what other could I have?"

"None, surely!" said he, smiling, "but the accident was singularly opportune."

"Opportune?" cried Cecilia, staring, "how opportune? this is the second time in the same morning that I am not able to understand you!"

"How *should* you understand what is so little intelligible?"

"I see you have some meaning which I cannot fathom, why, else, should it be so extraordinary that I should endeavour to avoid a mob? or how could it be opportune that I should happen to meet with one?"

He laughed at first without making any answer; but perceiving she looked at him with impatience, he half gayly, half reproachfully, said, "Whence is it that young ladies, even such whose principles are most strict, seem universally, in those affairs where their affections are concerned, to think hypocrisy necessary, and deceit amiable? and hold it graceful to disavow to-day, what they may perhaps mean publicly to acknowledge to-morrow?"

Cecilia, who heard these questions with unfeigned astonishment, looked at him with the utmost eagerness for an explanation.

"Do you so much wonder," he continued, "that I should have hoped in Miss Beverley to have seen some deviation from such rules? and have expected more openness and candour in a young lady who has given so noble a proof of the liberality of her mind and understanding?"

"You amaze me beyond measure!" cried she, "what rules, what candour, what liberality, do you mean?"

"Must I speak yet more plainly? and if I do, will you bear to hear me?"

"Indeed I should be extremely glad if you would give me leave to understand you."

"And may I tell you what has charmed me, as well as what I have presumed to wonder at?"

"You may tell me any thing, if you will but be less mysterious."

"Forgive then the frankness you invite, and let me acknowledge to you how greatly I honour the nobleness of your conduct. Surrounded as you are by the opulent and the splendid, unshackled by dependance, unrestrained by authority, blest by nature with all that is attractive, by situation with all that is desirable,—to slight the rich, and disregard the powerful, for the purer pleasure of raising oppressed merit, and giving to desert that wealth in which alone it seemed deficient—how can a spirit so liberal be sufficiently admired, or a choice of so much dignity be too highly extolled?"

"I find," cried Cecilia, "I must forbear any further enquiry, for the more I hear, the less I understand."

"Pardon me, then," cried he, "if here I return to my first question: whence is it that a young lady who can think so nobly, and act so disinterestedly, should not be uniformly great, simple in truth, and unaffected in sincerity? Why should she be thus guarded, where frankness would do her so much honour? Why blush in owning what all others may blush in envying?"

"Indeed you perplex me intolerably;" cried Cecilia, with some vexation, "Why, Sir, will you not be more explicit?"

"And why, Madam," returned he, with a laugh, "would you tempt me to be more impertinent? have I not said strange things already?"

"Strange indeed," cried she, "for not one of them can I comprehend!"

"Pardon, then," cried he, "and forget them all! I scarce know myself what urged me to say them, but I began inadvertently, without intending to go on, and I have proceeded involuntarily, without knowing how to stop. The fault, however, is ultimately your own, for the sight of you creates an insurmountable desire to converse with you, and

your conversation a propensity equally incorrigible to take
some interest in your welfare.''

He would then have changed the discourse, and Cecilia,
ashamed of pressing him further, was for some time silent;
but when one of the servants came to inform her that his
master meant to wait upon her directly, her unwillingness to
leave the matter in suspense induced her, somewhat
abruptly, to say, ''Perhaps, Sir, you are thinking of Mr.
Belfield?''

''A happy conjecture!'' cried he, ''but so wild a one I
cannot but marvel how it should occur to you!''

''Well, Sir,'' said she, ''I must acknowledge I now
understand your meaning; but with respect to what has
given rise to it, I am as much a stranger as ever.''

The entrance of Mr. Delville here closed the conversation.

He began with his usual ostentatious apologies, declaring
he had so many people to attend, so many complaints to
hear, and so many grievances to redress, that it was
impossible for him to wait upon her sooner, and not without
difficulty that he waited upon her now.

Mean time his son almost immediately retired: and
Cecilia, instead of listening to this harangue, was only
disturbing herself with conjectures upon what had just
passed. She saw that young Delvile concluded she was
absolutely engaged to Mr. Belfield, and though she was
better pleased that any suspicion should fall there than upon
Sir Robert Floyer, she was yet both provoked and concerned
to be suspected at all. An attack so earnest from almost any
other person could hardly have failed being very offensive to
her, but in the manners of young Delvile good breeding was
so happily blended with frankness, that his freedom seemed
merely to result from the openness of his disposition, and
even in its very act pleaded its own excuse.

Her reverie was at length interrupted by Mr. Delvile's
desiring to know in what he could serve her.

She told him she had present occasion for 600*l.* and hoped
he would not object to her taking up that sum.

''Six hundred pounds,'' said he, after some deliberation,
''is rather an extraordinary demand for a young lady in your

situation; your allowance is considerable, you have yet no
house, no equipage, no establishment;* your expences, I
should imagine, cannot be very great—"

He stopt, and seemed weighing her request.

Cecilia, shocked at appearing extravagant, yet too
generous to mention Mr. Harrel, had again recourse to her
bookseller's bill, which she told him she was anxious to
discharge.

"A bookseller's bill?" cried he; "and do you want 600*l*.
for a bookseller's bill?"

"No, Sir," said she, stammering, "no,—not all for
that,—I have some other—I have a particular
occasion——"

"But what bill at all," cried he, with much surprise, "can
a young lady have with a bookseller? The Spectator, Tatler
and Guardian,* would make library sufficient for any female
in the kingdom, nor do I think it like a gentlewoman to have
more. Besides, if you ally yourself in such a manner as I shall
approve and recommend, you will, in all probability, find
already collected more books than there can ever be any
possible occasion for you to look into.* And let me counsel
you to remember that a lady, whether so called from birth
or only from fortune, should never degrade herself by being
put on a level with writers, and such sort of people."

Cecilia thanked him for his advice, but confessed that
upon the present occasion it came too late, as the books were
now actually in her own possession.

"And have you taken," cried he, "such a measure as this
without consulting me? I thought I had assured you my
opinion was always at your service when you were in any
dilemma."

"Yes, Sir," answered Cecilia; "but I knew how much
you were occupied, and wished to avoid taking up your
time."

"I cannot blame your modesty," he replied, "and
therefore, as you have contracted the debt, you are, in
honour, bound to pay it. Mr. Briggs, however, has the
entire management of your fortune, my many avocations
obliging me to decline so laborious a trust; apply, therefore,

to him, and, as things are situated, I will make no opposition to your demand."

"I have already, Sir," said Cecilia, "spoke to Mr. Briggs, but——"

"You went to him first, then?" interrupted Mr. Delvile, with a look of much displeasure.

"I was unwilling, Sir, to trouble you till I found it unavoidable." She then acquainted him with Mr. Briggs's refusal, and entreated he would do her the favour to intercede in her behalf, that the money might no longer be denied her.

Every word she spoke his pride seemed rising to resent, and when she had done, after regarding her some time with apparent indignation, he said, "*I* intercede! *I* become an agent!"

Cecilia, amazed to find him thus violently irritated, made a very earnest apology for her request; but without paying her any attention, he walked up and down the room, exclaiming, "an agent! and to Mr. Briggs!—This is an affront I could never have expected! why did I degrade myself by accepting this humiliating office? I ought to have known better!" Then, turning to Cecilia, "Child," he added, "for whom is it you take me, and for what?"

Cecilia again, though affronted in her turn, began some protestations of respect; but haughtily interrupting her, he said, "If of me, and of my rank in life you judge by Mr. Briggs or by Mr. Harrel, I may be subject to proposals such as these every day; suffer me, therefore, for your better information, to hint to you, that the head of an ancient and honourable house, is apt to think himself somewhat superior to people but just rising from dust and obscurity."

Thunderstruck by this imperious reproof, she could attempt no further vindication; but when he observed her consternation, he was somewhat appeased, and hoping he had now impressed her with a proper sense of his dignity, he more gently said, "You did not, I believe, intend to insult me."

"Good Heaven, Sir; no!" cried Cecilia, "nothing was

more distant from my thoughts: if my expressions have been faulty, it has been wholly from ignorance."

"Well, well, we will think then no more of it."

She then said she would no longer detain him, and, without daring to again mention her petition, she wished him good morning.

He suffered her to go, yet, as she left the room, graciously said, "Think no more of my displeasure, for it is over: I see you were not aware of the extraordinary thing you proposed. I am sorry I cannot possibly assist you; on any other occasion you may depend upon my services; but you know Mr. Briggs, you have seen him yourself,—judge, then how a man of any fashion is to accommodate himself with such a person!"

Cecilia concurred, and, courtsying, took her leave.

"Ah!" thought she, in her way home, "how happy is it for me that I followed the advice of Mr. Monckton! else I had surely made interest to become an inmate of that house, and then indeed, as he wisely foresaw, I should inevitably have been overwhelmed by this pompous insolence! no family, however amiable, could make amends for such a master of it."*

CHAPTER III

An Admonition

THE Harrels and Mr. Arnott waited the return of Cecilia with the utmost impatience; she told them with much concern the failure of her embassy, which Mr. Harrel heard with visible resentment and discontent, while Mr. Arnott, entreating him not to think of it, again made an offer of his services, and declared he would disregard all personal inconvenience for the pleasure of making him and his sister easy.

Cecilia was much mortified that she had not the power to act the same part, and asked Mr. Harrel whether he believed his own influence with Mr. Briggs would be more successful.

"No, no," answered he, "the old curmudgeon would but the rather refuse. I know his reason, and therefore am sure all pleas will be vain. He has dealings in the alley,* and I dare say games with your money as if it were his own. There is, indeed, one way——but I do not think you would like it——though I protest I hardly know why not——however, 'tis as well let alone."

Cecilia insisted upon hearing what he meant, and, after some hesitation, he hinted that there were means by which, with very little inconvenience, she might borrow the money.

Cecilia, with that horror natural to all unpractised minds at the first idea of contracting a voluntary debt, started at this suggestion, and seemed very ill disposed to listen to it. Mr. Harrel, perceiving her repugnance, turned to Mr. Arnott, and said, "Well, my good brother, I hardly know how to suffer you to sell out at such a loss, but yet, my present necessity is so urgent——"

"Don't mention it," cried Mr. Arnott, "I am very sorry I let you know it; be certain, however, that while I have any thing, it is yours and my sister's."

The two gentlemen were then retiring together; but Cecilia, shocked for Mr. Arnott, though unmoved by Mr. Harrel, stopt them to enquire what was the way by which it was meant she could borrow the money?

Mr. Harrel seemed averse to answer, but she would not be refused; and then he mentioned a Jew, of whose honesty he had made undoubted trial, and who, as she was so near being of age, would accept very trifling interest for whatever she should like to take up.

The heart of Cecilia recoiled at the very mention of a *Jew*, and *taking up money upon interest;** but, impelled strongly by her own generosity to emulate that of Mr. Arnott, she agreed, after some hesitation, to have recourse to this method.

Mr. Harrel then made some faint denials, and Mr. Arnott protested he had a thousand times rather sell out at any discount, than consent to her taking such a measure; but, when her first reluctance was conquered, all that he urged served but to shew his worthiness in a stronger light, and only encreased her desire of saving him from such repeated imposition.

Her total ignorance in what manner to transact this business, made her next put it wholly into the hands of Mr. Harrel, whom she begged to take up 600*l.* upon such terms as he thought equitable, and to which, whatever they might be, she would sign her name.

He seemed somewhat surprised at the sum, but without any question or objection undertook the commission: and Cecilia would not lessen it, because unwilling to do more for the security of the luxurious Mr. Harrel, than for the distresses of the laborious Hills.

Nothing could be more speedy than the execution of this affair, Mr. Harrel was diligent and expert, the whole was settled that morning, and, giving to the Jew her bond for the payment at the interest he required, she put into the hands of Mr. Harrel 350*l.* for which he gave his receipt, and she kept the rest for her own purposes.

She intended the morning after this transaction to settle her account with the bookseller. When she went into the parlour to breakfast, she was somewhat surprised to see Mr. Harrel seated there, in earnest discourse with his wife. Fearful of interrupting a tête à tête so uncommon, she would have retired, but Mr. Harrel, calling after her, said "O pray come in! I am only telling Priscilla a piece of my usual ill luck. You must know I happen to be in immediate want of 200*l.* though only for three or four days, and I sent to order honest old Aaron to come hither directly with the money, but it so happens that he went out of town the moment he had done with us yesterday, and will not be back again this week. Now I don't believe there is another Jew in the kingdom who will let me have money upon the same terms: they are such notorious rascals, that I hate the very thought of employing them."

Cecilia, who could not but understand what this meant, was too much displeased both by his extravagance and his indelicacy, to feel at all inclined to change the destination of the money she had just received; and therefore coolly agreed that it was unfortunate, but added nothing more.

"O, it is provoking indeed," cried he, "for the extra-interest I must pay one of those extortioners is absolutely so much money thrown away."

Cecilia, still without noticing these hints, began her breakfast. Mr. Harrel then said he would take his tea with them: and, while he was buttering some dry toast, exclaimed, as if from sudden recollection, "O Lord, now I think of it, I believe, Miss Beverley, you can lend me this money yourself for a day or two. The moment old Aaron comes to town, I will pay you."

Cecilia, whose generosity, however extensive, was neither thoughtless nor indiscriminate, found something so repulsive in this gross procedure, that instead of assenting to his request with her usual alacrity, she answered very gravely that the money she had just received was already appropriated to a particular purpose, and she knew not how to defer making use of it.

Mr. Harrel was extremely chagrined by this reply, which was by no means what he expected; but, tossing down a dish of tea, he began humming an air, and soon recovered his usual unconcern.

In a few minutes, ringing his bell, he desired a servant to go to Mr. Zackery, and inform him that he wanted to speak with him immediately.

"And now," said he, with a look in which vexation seemed struggling with carelessness, "the thing is done! I don't like, indeed, to get into such hands, for 'tis hard ever to get out of them when once one begins,—and hitherto I have kept pretty clear. But there's no help for it—Mr. Arnott cannot just now assist me—and so the thing must take its course. Priscilla, why do you look so grave?"

"I am thinking how unlucky it is my Brother should happen to be unable to lend you this money."

"O, don't think about it; I shall get rid of the man very soon I dare say*—I hope so, at least——I am sure I mean it."

Cecilia now grew a little disturbed; she looked at Mrs. Harrel, who seemed also uneasy, and then, with some hesitation, said "Have you really never, Sir, employed this man before?"

"Never in my life: never any but old Aaron. I dread the whole race; I have a sort of superstitious notion that if once I get into their clutches, I shall never be my own man again; and that induced me to beg your assistance. However, 'tis no great matter."

She then began to waver; she feared there might be future mischief as well as present inconvenience, in his applying to new usurers, and knowing she had now the power to prevent him, thought herself half cruel in refusing to exert it. She wished to consult Mr. Monckton, but found it necessary to take her measures immediately, as the Jew was already sent for, and must in a few moments be either employed or discarded.

Much perplext how to act, between a desire of doing good, and a fear of encouraging evil, she weighed each side hastily, but while still uncertain which ought to preponderate, her kindness for Mrs. Harrel interfered, and, in the hope of rescuing her husband from further bad practices, she said she would postpone her own business for the few days he mentioned, rather than see him compelled to open any new account with so dangerous a set of men.

He thanked her in his usual negligent manner, and accepting the 200*l.* gave her his receipt for it, and a promise she should be paid in a week.

Mrs. Harrel, however, seemed more grateful, and with many embraces spoke her sense of this friendly good nature. Cecilia, happy from believing she had revived in her some spark of sensibility, determined to avail herself of so favourable a symptom, and enter at once upon the disagreeable task she had set herself, of representing to her the danger of her present situation.

As soon, therefore, as breakfast was done, and Mr. Arnott, who came in before it was over, was gone, with a view to excite her attention by raising her curiosity, she begged the favour of a private conference in her own room, upon matters of some importance.

She began with hoping that the friendship in which they

had so long lived would make her pardon the liberty she was
going to take, and which nothing less than their former
intimacy, joined to strong apprehensions for her future
welfare, could authorise; "But oh Priscilla!" she continued,
"with open eyes to see your danger, yet not warn you of it,
would be a reserve treacherous in a friend, and cruel even
in a fellow-creature."

"What danger?" cried Mrs. Harrel, much alarmed, "do
you think me ill? do I look consumptive?"

"Yes, consumptive indeed!" said Cecilia, "but not, I
hope, in your constitution."

And then, with all the tenderness in her power, she came
to the point, and conjured her without delay to retrench her
expences, and change her thoughtless way of life for one
more considerate and domestic.

Mrs. Harrel, with much simplicity, assured her *she did
nothing but what every body else did*, and that it was quite
impossible for her to *appear in the world* in any other manner.

"But how are you to appear hereafter?" cried Cecilia, "if
now you live beyond your income, you must consider that
in time your income by such depredations will be
exhausted."

"But I declare to you," answered Mrs. Harrel, "I never
run in debt for more than half a year, for as soon as I receive
my own money, I generally pay it away every shilling: and
so borrow what I want till pay day comes round again."

"And that," said Cecilia, "seems a method expressly
devised for keeping you eternally comfortless: pardon me,
however, for speaking so openly, but I fear Mr. Harrel
himself must be even still less attentive and accurate in his
affairs, or he could not so frequently be embarrassed. And
what is to be the result? look but, my dear Priscilla, a little
forward, and you will tremble at the prospect before you!"

Mrs. Harrel seemed frightened at this speech, and begged
to know what she would have them do?

Cecilia then, with equal wisdom and friendliness,
proposed a general reform in the houshold, the public and
private expences of both: she advised that a strict
examination might be made into the state of their affairs,

that all their bills should be called in, and faithfully paid, and that an entire new plan of life should be adopted, according to the situation of their fortune and income when cleared of all incumbrances.

"Lord, my dear!" exclaimed Mrs. Harrel, with a look of astonishment, "why Mr. Harrel would no more do all this than fly! If I was only to make such a proposal, I dare say he would laugh in my face."

"And why?"

"Why!—why because it would seem such an odd thing— it's what nobody thinks of—though I am sure I am very much obliged to you for mentioning it.—Shall we go down stairs? I think I heard somebody come in."

"No matter who comes in," said Cecilia, "reflect for a moment upon my proposal, and, at least, if you disapprove it, suggest something more eligible."

"O, it's a very good proposal, that I agree," said Mrs. Harrel, looking very weary, "but only the thing is it's quite impossible."

"Why so? why is it impossible?"

"Why because—dear, I don't know—but I am sure it is."

"But what is your reason? What makes you sure of it?"

"Lord, I can't tell—but I know it is—because—I am very certain it is."

Argument such as this, though extremely fatiguing to the understanding of Cecilia, had yet no power to *blunt her purpose*:* she warmly expostulated against the weakness of her defence, strongly represented the imprudence of her conduct, and exhorted her by every tie of justice, honour and discretion to set about a reformation.

"Why what can I do?" cried Mrs. Harrel, impatiently, "one must live a little like other people. You would not have me be stared at, I suppose; and I am sure I don't know what I do that every body else does not do too."

"But were it not better," said Cecilia, with more energy, "to think less of *other people*, and more of *yourself*? to consult your own fortune, and your own situation in life, instead of being blindly guided by those of *other people*? If, indeed, *other people* would be responsible for your losses, for the diminution of your wealth, and for the disorder of your affairs, then might you rationally make their way of life the example of yours: but you cannot flatter yourself such will be the case; you know better; your losses, your diminished fortune, your embarrassed circumstances will be all your own! pitied, perhaps, by some, but blamed by more, and assisted by none!"

"Good Lord, Miss Beverley!" cried Mrs. Harrel, starting, "you talk just as if we were ruined!"

"I mean not that," replied Cecilia, "but I would fain, by pointing out your danger, prevail with you to prevent in time so dreadful a catastrophe."

Mrs. Harrel, more affronted than alarmed, heard this answer with much displeasure, and after a sullen hesitation, peevishly said, "I must own I don't take it very kind of you to say such frightful things to me; I am sure we only live like the rest of the world, and I don't see why a man of Mr. Harrel's fortune should live any worse. As to his having now and then a little debt or two, it is nothing but what every body else has. You only think it so odd, because you a'n't used to it: but you are quite mistaken if you suppose he does not mean to pay, for he told me this morning that as soon as ever he receives his rents, he intends to discharge every bill he has in the world."

"I am very glad to hear it," answered Cecilia, "and I heartily wish he may have the resolution to adhere to his purpose. I feared you would think me impertinent, but you do worse in believing me unkind: friendship and good-will could alone have induced me to hazard what I have said to you. I must, however, have done; though I cannot forbear adding that I hope what has already passed will sometimes recur to you."

They then separated; Mrs. Harrel half angry at remonstrances she thought only censorious,* and Cecilia offended at her pettishness and folly, though grieved at her blindness.

She was soon, however, recompensed for this vexation by a visit from Mrs. Delvile, who, finding her alone, sat with her some time, and by her spirit, understanding and elegance, dissipated all her chagrin.

From another circumstance, also, she received much pleasure, though a little perplexity; Mr. Arnott brought her word that Mr. Belfield, almost quite well, had actually left his lodgings, and was gone into the country.

She now half suspected that the account of his illness given her by young Delvile, was merely the effect of his curiosity to discover her sentiments of him; yet when she considered how foreign to his character appeared every species of artifice, she exculpated him from the design, and concluded that the impatient spirit of Belfield had hurried him away, when really unfit for travelling. She had no means, however, to hear more of him now he had quitted the town, and therefore, though uneasy, she was compelled to be patient.

In the evening she had again a visit from Mr. Monckton, who, though he was now acquainted how much she was at home, had the forbearance to avoid making frequent use of that knowledge, that his attendance might escape observation.

Cecilia, as usual, spoke to him of all her affairs with the utmost openness; and as her mind was now chiefly occupied by her apprehensions for the Harrels, she communicated to him the extravagance of which they were guilty, and hinted at the distress that from time to time it occasioned; but the assistance she had afforded them her own delicacy prevented her mentioning.

Mr. Monckton scrupled not from this account instantly to pronounce Harrel a *ruined man*; and thinking Cecilia, from her connection with him, in much danger of being involved in his future difficulties, he most earnestly exhorted her to suffer no inducement to prevail with her to advance him any money, confidently affirming she would have little chance of being ever repaid.

Cecilia listened to this charge with much alarm, but readily promised future circumspection. She confessed to him the conference she had had in the morning with Mrs. Harrel, and after lamenting her determined neglect of her affairs, she added, "I cannot but own that my esteem for her, even more than my affection, has lessened almost every day since I have been in her house; but this morning, when

I ventured to speak to her with earnestness, I found her powers of reasoning so weak, and her infatuation to luxury and expence so strong, that I have ever since felt ashamed of my own want of discernment in having formerly selected her for my friend.''

"When you gave her that title," said Mr. Monckton, "you had little choice in your power; her sweetness and good-nature attracted you; childhood is never troubled with foresight, and youth is seldom difficult: she was lively and pleasing, you were generous and affectionate; your acquaintance with her was formed while you were yet too young to know your own worth, your fondness of her grew from habit, and before the inferiority of her parts had weakened your regard, by offending your judgment, her early marriage separated you from her entirely. But now you meet again the scene is altered; three years of absence spent in the cultivation of an understanding naturally of the first order, by encreasing your wisdom, has made you more fastidious; while the same time spent by her in mere idleness and shew, has hurt her disposition, without adding to her knowledge, and robbed her of her natural excellencies, without enriching her with acquired ones. You see her now with impartiality, for you see her almost as a stranger, and all those deficiences which retirement and inexperience had formerly concealed, her vanity, and her superficial acquaintance with the world, have now rendered glaring. But folly weakens all bands; remember, therefore, if you would form a solid friendship, to consult not only the heart but the head, not only the temper, but the understanding.''

"Well, then," said Cecilia, "at least it must be confessed I have judiciously chosen *you*!''

"You have, indeed, done me the highest honour,'' he answered.

They then talked of Belfield, and Mr. Monckton confirmed the account of Mr. Arnott, that he had left London in good health. After which, he enquired if she had seen any thing more of the Delviles?

"Yes,'' said Cecilia, "Mrs. Delvile called upon me this

morning. She is a delightful woman; I am sorry you know her not enough to do her justice."

"Is she civil to you?"

"Civil? she is all kindness!"

"Then depend upon it she has something in view: whenever that is not the case, she is all insolence. And Mr. Delvile,—pray what do you think of him?"

"O, I think him insufferable! and I cannot sufficiently thank you for that timely caution which prevented my change of habitation. I would not live under the same roof with him for the world!"

"Well, and do you not now begin also to see the son properly?"

"Properly? I don't understand you."

"Why as the very son of such parents, haughty and impertinent."

"No, indeed; he has not the smallest resemblance of his father, and if he resembles his mother, it is only what every one must wish who impartially sees her."

"You know not that family. But how, indeed, should you, when they are in a combination to prevent your getting that knowledge? They have all their designs upon you, and if you are not carefully upon your guard, you will be the dupe to them."

"What can you possibly mean?"

"Nothing but what every body else must immediately see; they have a great share of pride, and a small one of wealth; you seem by fortune to be flung in their way, and doubtless they mean not to neglect so inviting an opportunity of repairing their estates."

"Indeed you are mistaken; I am certain they have no such intention: on the contrary, they all even teazingly persist in thinking me already engaged elsewhere."

She then gave him a history of their several suspicions. "The impertinence of report," she added, "has so much convinced them that Sir Robert Floyer and Mr. Belfield fought merely as rivals, that I can only clear myself of partiality for one of them, to have it instantly concluded I feel it for the other. And, far from seeming hurt that I

appear to be disposed of, Mr. Delvile openly seconds the
pretensions of Sir Robert, and his son officiously persuades
me that I am already Mr. Belfield's.''

"Tricks, nothing but tricks to discover your real
situation."

He then gave her some general cautions to be upon her
guard against their artifices, and changing the subject, talked,
for the rest of his visit, upon matters of general entertainment.

CHAPTER IV

An Evasion

CECILIA now for about a fortnight passed her time without
incident: the Harrels continued their accustomed dissipation,
Sir Robert Floyer, without even seeking a private conference,
persevered in his attentions, and Mr. Arnott, though still
silent and humble, seemed only to live by the pleasure of
beholding her. She spent two whole days with Mrs. Delvile,
both of which served to confirm her admiration of that lady
and of her son; and she joined the parties of the Harrels, or
stayed quietly at home, according to her spirits and inclinations: while she was visited by Mr. Monckton often enough to
satisfy him with her proceedings, yet too seldom to betray
either to herself or to the world any suspicion of his designs.

Her 200*l*. however, which was to have been returned at
the end of the first week, though a fortnight was now
elapsed, had not even been mentioned: she began to grow
very impatient, but not knowing what course to pursue, and
wanting courage to remind Mr. Harrel of his promise, she
still waited the performance of it without speaking.

At this time, preparations were making in the family for
removing to Violet-bank to spend the Easter holidays: but
Cecilia, who was too much grieved at such perpetual
encrease of unnecessary expences to have any enjoyment in
new prospects of entertainment, had at present some
business of her own which gave her full employment.

The poor carpenter, whose family she had taken under

her protection, was just dead, and, as soon as the last duties
had been paid him, she sent for his widow, and after trying
to console her for the loss she had suffered, assured her she
was immediately ready to fulfil the engagement into which
she had entered, of assisting her to undertake some better
method of procuring a livelihood; and therefore desired to
know in what manner she could serve her, and what she
thought herself able to do.

The good woman, pouring forth thanks and praises
innumerable, answered that she had a Cousin, who had
offered, for a certain premium, to take her into partnership
in a small haberdasher's shop. "But then, madam," continued she, "it's quite morally impossible I should raise such
a sum, or else, to be sure, such a shop as that, now I am
grown so poorly, would be quite a heaven upon earth to me:
for my strength, madam, is almost all gone away, and when I
do any hard work, it's quite a piteous sight to see me, for I am
all in a tremble after it, just as if I had an ague,* and yet all the
time my hands, madam, will be burning like a coal!"

"You have indeed been overworked," said Cecilia, "and
it is high time your feeble frame should have some rest.
What is the sum your cousin demands?"

"O madam, more than I should be able to get together in
all my life! for earn what I will, it goes as fast as it comes,
because there's many mouths, and small pay, and two of the
little ones that can't help at all;—and there's no Billy,
madam, to work for us now!"

"But tell me, what is the sum?"

"Sixty pound, madam."

"You shall have it!" cried the generous Cecilia, "if the
situation will make you happy, I will give it you myself."

The poor woman wept her thanks, and was long before
she could sufficiently compose herself to answer the further
questions of Cecilia, who next enquired what could be done
with the children? Mrs. Hill, however, hitherto hopeless of
such a provision for herself, had for them formed no plan.
She told her, therefore, to go to her cousin, and consult upon
this subject, as well as to make preparations for her own
removal.

The arrangement of this business now became her favourite occupation. She went herself to the shop, which was a very small one in Fetter-lane, and spoke with Mrs. Roberts, the cousin; who agreed to take the eldest girl, now sixteen years of age, by way of helper; but said she had room for no other: however, upon Cecilia's offering to raise the premium, she consented that the two little children should also live in the house, where they might be under the care of their mother and sister.

There were still two others to be disposed of; but as no immediate method of providing for them occurred to Cecilia, she determined, for the present, to place them in some cheap school, where they might be taught plain work,* which could not but prove a useful qualification for whatever sort of business they might hereafter attempt.

Her plan was to bestow upon Mrs. Hill and her children 100*l.* by way of putting them all into a decent way of living; and then, from time to time, to make them such small presents as their future exigencies or changes of situation might require.

Now, therefore, payment from Mr. Harrel became immediately necessary, for she had only 50*l.* of the 600*l.* she had taken up in her own possession, and her customary allowance was already so appropriated that she could make from it no considerable deduction.

There is something in the sight of laborious indigence so affecting and so respectable, that it renders dissipation peculiarly contemptible, and doubles the odium of extravagance: every time Cecilia saw this poor family, her aversion to the conduct and the principles of Mr. Harrel encreased, while her delicacy of shocking or shaming him diminished, and she soon acquired for them what she had failed to acquire for herself, the spirit and resolution to claim her debt.

One morning, therefore, as he was quitting the breakfast-room, she hastily arose, and following, begged to have a moment's discourse with him. They went together to the library, and after some apologies, and much hesitation, she told him she fancied he had forgotten the 200*l.* which she had lent him.

"The 200*l.*" cried he: "O, ay, true!—I protest it had escaped me. Well, but you don't want it immediately?"

"Indeed I do, if you can conveniently spare it."

"O yes, certainly!—without the least doubt!—Though now I think of it—its extremely unlucky, but really just at this time—why did not you put me in mind of it before?"

"I hoped you would have remembered it yourself."

"I could have paid you two days ago extremely well—however, you shall certainly have it very soon, that you may depend upon, and a day or two can make no great difference to you."

He then wished her good morning, and left her.

Cecilia, very much provoked, regretted that she had ever lent it at all, and determined for the future strictly to follow the advice of Mr. Monckton in trusting him no more.

Two or three days passed on, but still no notice was taken either of the payment or of the debt. She then resolved to renew her application, and be more serious and more urgent with him; but she found, to her utter surprise, this was not in her power, and that though she lived under the same roof with him, she had no opportunity to enforce her claim. Mr. Harrel, whenever she desired to speak with him, protested he was so much hurried he had not a moment to spare: and even when, tired of his excuses, she pursued him out of the room, he only quickened his speed, smiling, however, and bowing, and calling out "I am vastly sorry, but I am so late now I cannot stop an instant; however, as soon as I come back, I shall be wholly at your command."

When he came back, however, Sir Robert Floyer, or some other gentleman, was sure to be with him, and the difficulties of obtaining an audience were sure to be encreased. And by this method, which he constantly practised, of avoiding any private conversation, he frustrated all her schemes of remonstrating upon his delay, since her resentment, however great, could never urge her to the indelicacy of dunning him* in presence of a third person.

She was now much perplext herself how to put into execution her plan for the Hills: she knew it would be as vain to apply for money to Mr. Briggs, as for payment to Mr.

Harrel. Her word, however, had been given, and her word she held sacred: she resolved, therefore, for the present, to bestow upon them the 50*l*. she still retained, and, if the rest should be necessary before she became of age, to spare it, however inconveniently, from her private allowance, which, by the will of her uncle, was 500*l*. a year, 250*l*. of which Mr. Harrel received for her board and accommodations.

Having settled this matter in her own mind, she went to the lodgings of Mrs. Hill, in order to conclude the affair. She found her and all her children, except the youngest, hard at work, and their honest industry so much strengthened her compassion, that her wishes for serving them grew every instant more liberal.

Mrs. Hill readily undertook to make her cousin accept half the premium for the present, which would suffice to fix her, with three of her children, in the shop: Cecilia then went with her to Fetter-lane, and there, drawing up herself an agreement for their entering into partnership, she made each of them sign it and take a copy, and kept a third in her own possession: after which, she gave a promissory note to Mrs. Roberts for the rest of the money.

She presented Mrs. Hill, also, with 10*l*. to clothe them all decently, and enable her to send two of the children to school; and assured her that she would herself pay for their board and instruction, till she should be established in her business, and have power to save money for that purpose.

She then put herself into a chair to return home, followed by the prayers and blessings of the whole family.

CHAPTER V

An Adventure

NEVER had the heart of Cecilia felt so light, so gay, so glowing as after the transaction of this affair: her life had never appeared to her so important, nor her wealth so valuable. To see five helpless children provided for by herself, rescued from the extremes of penury and wretchedness, and put in a way to become useful to society, and comfortable to themselves; to behold their feeble mother, snatched from the hardship of that labour which, overpowering her strength, had almost destroyed her existence, now placed in a situation where a competent maintenance might be earned without fatigue, and the remnant of her days pass in easy employment—to view such sights, and have power to say "*These deeds are mine!*"* what, to a disposition fraught with tenderness and benevolence, could give purer self-applause, or more exquisite satisfaction?

Such were the pleasures which regaled the reflections of Cecilia when, in her way home, having got out of her chair to walk through the upper part of Oxford Street, she was suddenly met by the old gentleman whose emphatical addresses to her had so much excited her astonishment.

He was passing quick on, but stopping the moment he perceived her, he sternly called out "Are you proud? are you callous? are you hard of heart so soon?"

"Put me, if you please, to some trial!" cried Cecilia, with the virtuous courage of a self-acquitting conscience.

"I already have!" returned he, indignantly, "and already I have found you faulty!"

"I am sorry to hear it," said the amazed Cecilia, "but at least I hope you will tell me in what?"

"You refused me admittance," he answered, "yet I was your friend, yet I was willing to prolong the term of your genuine tranquility! I pointed out to you a method of preserving peace with your own soul; I came to you in behalf of the poor, and instructed you how to merit their prayers; you heard me, you were susceptible, you complied! I meant to have repeated the lesson, to have tuned your whole heart to compassion, and to have taught you the sad duties of sympathising humanity. For this purpose I called again, but again I was not admitted! Short was the period of my absence, yet long enough for the completion of your downfall!"

"Good heaven," cried Cecilia, "how dreadful is this language! when have you called, Sir? I never heard you had been at the house. Far from refusing you admittance, I wished to see you."

"Indeed?" cried he, with some softness, "and are you, in truth, not proud? not callous? not hard of heart? Follow me, then, and visit the humble and the poor, follow me, and give comfort to the fallen and dejected!"

At this invitation, however desirous to do good, Cecilia started; the strangeness of the inviter, his flightiness, his authoritative manner, and the uncertainty whither or to whom he might carry her, made her fearful of proceeding: yet a benevolent curiosity to see as well as serve the objects of his recommendation, joined to the eagerness of youthful integrity to clear her own character from the aspersion of hard-heartedness, soon conquered her irresolution, and, making a sign to her servant to keep near her, she followed as her conductor led.

He went on silently and solemnly till he came to Swallow-street, then turning into it, he stopt at a small and mean-looking house, knocked at the door, and without asking any question of the man who opened it, beckoned her to come after him, and hastened up some narrow winding stairs.

Cecilia again hesitated; but when she recollected that this old man, though little known, was frequently seen, and though with few people acquainted, was by many personally recognized, she thought it impossible he could mean her any injury. She ordered her servant, however, to come in, and bid him keep walking up and down the stairs till she returned to him. And then she obeyed the directions of her guide.

He proceeded till he came to the second floor, then, again beckoning her to follow him, he opened a door, and entered a small and very meanly furnished apartment.

And here, to her infinite astonishment, she perceived, employed in washing some china, a very lovely young woman, genteely dressed, and appearing hardly seventeen years of age.

The moment they came in, with evident marks of confusion, she instantly gave over her work, hastily putting the bason she was washing upon the table, and endeavouring to hide the towel with which she was wiping it behind her chair.

The old gentleman, advancing to her with quickness, said, "How is he now? Is he better? will he live?"

"Heaven forbid he should not!" answered the young woman with emotion, "but, indeed, he is no better!"

"Look here," said he, pointing to Cecilia, "I have brought you one who has power to serve you, and to relieve your distress: one who is rolling in affluence, a stranger to ill, a novice in the world;—unskilled in the miseries she is yet to endure, unconscious of the depravity into which she is to sink! receive her benefactions while yet she is untainted, satisfied that while she aids you, she is blessing herself!"

The young woman, blushing and abashed, said, "You are very good to me, Sir, but there is no occasion—there is no need—I have not any necessity—I am far from being so very much in want.—"

"Poor simple soul!" interrupted the old man, "and art thou ashamed of poverty? Guard, guard thyself from other shames, and the wealthiest may envy thee! Tell here thy story, plainly, roundly, truly; abate nothing of thy indigence, repress nothing of her liberality. The Poor not impoverished by their own Guilt, are Equals of the Affluent, not enriched by their own Virtue. Come, then, and let me present ye to each other! young as ye both are, with many years and many sorrows to encounter, lighten the burthen of each other's cares, by the heart-soothing exchange of gratitude for beneficence!"

He then took a hand of each, and joining them between his own, "*You*," he continued, "who though rich, are not hardened, and *you*, who though poor, are not debased, why should ye not love, why should ye not cherish each other? The afflictions of life are tedious, its joys are evanescent; ye are now both young, and, with little to enjoy, will find much to suffer. Ye are both, too, I believe, innocent—Oh could ye always remain so!——Cherubs were ye then, and the sons of men might worship you!"

He stopt, checked by his own rising emotion; but soon resuming his usual austerity, "Such, however," he continued, "is not the condition of humanity; in pity, therefore, to the evils impending over both, be kind to each other! I leave you together, and to your mutual tenderness I recommend you!"

Then, turning particularly to Cecilia, "Disdain not," he said, "to console the depressed; look upon her without scorn, converse with her without contempt: like you, she is an orphan, though not like you, an heiress;—like her, you are fatherless, though not like her friendless! If she is awaited by the temptations of adversity, you, also, are surrounded by the corruptions of prosperity. Your fall is most probable, her's most excusable;—commiserate *her* therefore now,—by and by she may commiserate *you*!"

And with these words he left the room.

A total silence for some time succeeded his departure: Cecilia found it difficult to recover from the surprise into which she had been thrown sufficiently for speech: in following her extraordinary director, her imagination had painted to her a scene such as she had so lately quitted, and prepared her to behold some family in distress, some helpless creature in sickness, or some children in want; but of these to see none, to meet but one person, and that one fair, young, and delicate,—an introduction so singular to an object so unthought of, deprived her of all power but that of shewing her amazement.

Mean while the young woman looked scarcely less surprised, and infinitely more embarrassed. She surveyed her apartment with vexation, and her guest with confusion; she had listened to the exhortation of the old man with visible uneasiness, and now he was gone, seemed overwhelmed with shame and chagrin.

Cecilia, who in observing these emotions felt both her curiosity and her compassion encrease, pressed her hand as she parted with it, and, when a little recovered, said, "You must think this a strange intrusion; but the gentleman who brought me hither is perhaps so well known to you, as to make his singularities plead with you their own apology."

"No, indeed, madam," she answered, bashfully, "he is very little known to me; but he is very good, and very desirous to do me service:—not but what I believe he thinks me much worse off than I really am, for, I assure you, madam, whatever he has said, I am not ill off at all—hardly."

The various doubts to her disadvantage which had at first,

from her uncommon situation, arisen in the mind of Cecilia, this anxiety to disguise, not display her distress, considerably removed, since it cleared her of all suspicion of seeking by artifice and imposition to play upon her feelings.

With a gentleness, therefore, the most soothing, she replied, "I should by no means have broken in upon you thus unexpectedly, if I had not concluded my conductor had some right to bring me. However, since we are actually met, let us remember his injunctions, and endeavour not to part till, by a mutual exchange of good-will, each has added a friend to the other."

"You are condescending indeed, madam," answered the young woman, with an air the most humble, "looking as you look, to talk of a friend when you come to such a place as this! up two pair of stairs!* no furniture! no servant! every thing in such disorder!—indeed I wonder at Mr. Albany! he should not——but he thinks every body's affairs may be made public, and does not care what he tells, nor who hears him;—he knows not the pain he gives, nor the mischief he may do."

"I am very much concerned," cried Cecilia, more and more surprised at all she heard, "to find I have been thus instrumental to distressing you. I was ignorant whither I was coming, and followed him, believe me, neither from curiosity nor inclination, but simply because I knew not how to refuse him. He is gone, however, and I will therefore relieve you by going too: but permit me to leave behind me a small testimony that the intention of my coming was not mere impertinence."

She then took out her purse; but the young woman, starting back with a look of resentful mortification, exclaimed, "No, madam! you are quite mistaken; pray put up your purse; I am no beggar! Mr. Albany has misrepresented me, if he has told you I am."

Cecilia, mortified in her turn at this unexpected rejection of an offer she had thought herself invited to make, stood some moments silent; and then said, "I am far from meaning to offend you, and I sincerely beg your pardon if I have misunderstood the charge just now given to me."

"I have nothing to pardon, madam," said she, more calmly, "except, indeed, to Mr. Albany; and to him, 'tis of no use to be angry, for he minds not what I say! he is very good, but he is very strange, for he thinks the whole world made to live in common, and that every one who is poor should ask, and every one who is rich should give: he does not know that there are many who would rather starve."

"And are you," said Cecilia, half-smiling, "of that number?"

"No, indeed, madam! I have not so much greatness of mind. But those to whom I belong have more fortitude and higher spirit. I wish I could imitate them!"

Struck with the candour and simplicity of this speech, Cecilia now felt a warm desire to serve her, and taking her hand, said, "Forgive me, but though I see you wish me gone, I know not how to leave you: recollect, therefore, the charge that has been given to us both, and if you refuse my assistance one way, point out to me in what other I may offer it."

"You are very kind, madam," she answered, "and I dare say you are very good; I am sure you look so, at least. But I want nothing; I do very well, and I have hopes of doing better. Mr. Albany is too impatient. He knows, indeed, that I am not extremely rich, but he is much to blame if he supposes me therefore an object of charity, and thinks me so mean as to receive money from a stranger."

"I am truly sorry," cried Cecilia, "for the error I have committed, but you must suffer me to make my peace with you before we part: yet, till I am better known to you, I am fearful of proposing terms. Perhaps you will permit me to leave you my direction, and do me the favour to call upon me yourself?"

"O no, madam! I have a sick relation whom I cannot leave: and indeed, if he were well, he would not like to have me make an acquaintance while I am in this place."

"I hope you are not his only nurse? I am sure you do not look able to bear such fatigue. Has he a physician? Is he properly attended?"

"No, madam; he has no physician, and no attendance at all!"

"And is it possible that in such a situation you can refuse
to be assisted? Surely you should accept some help for him,
if not for yourself."

"But what will that signify when, if I do, he will not make
use of it? and when he had a thousand and a thousand times
rather die, than let any one know he is in want?"

"Take it, then, unknown to him; serve him without
acquainting him you serve him. Surely you would not suffer
him to perish without aid?"

"Heaven forbid! But what can I do? I am under his
command, madam, not he under mine!"

"Is he your father?——Pardon my question, but your
youth seems much to want such a protector."

"No, madam, I have no father! I was happier when I had!
He is my brother."

"And what is his illness?"

"A fever."

"A fever, and without a physician! Are you sure, too, it
is not infectious?"

"O yes, too sure!"

"Too sure? how so?"

"Because I know too well the occasion of it!"

"And what is the occasion?" cried Cecilia, again taking
her hand, "pray trust me; indeed you shall not repent your
confidence. Your reserve hitherto has only raised you in my
esteem, but do not carry it so far as to mortify me by a total
rejection of my good offices."

"Ah madam!" said the young woman, sighing, "you
ought to be good, I am sure, for you will draw all out of me
by such kindness as this! the occasion was a neglected
wound, never properly healed."

"A wound? is he in the army?"

"No,—he was shot through the side in a duel."

"In a duel?" exclaimed Cecilia, "pray what is his
name?"

"O that I must not tell you! his name is a great secret
now, while he is in this poor place, for I know he had almost
rather never see the light again than have it known."

"Surely, surely," cried Cecilia, with much emotion, "he

cannot——I hope he cannot be Mr. Belfield?"

"Ah Heaven!" cried the young woman, screaming, "do you then know him?"

Here, in mutual astonishment, they looked at each other.

"You are then," said Cecilia, "the sister of Mr. Belfield! And Mr. Belfield is thus sick, his wound is not yet healed,— and he is without any help!"*

"And who, madam, are *you*?" cried she, "and how is it you know him?"

"My name is Beverley."

"Ah!" exclaimed she again, "I fear I have done nothing but mischief! I know very well who you are now, madam, but if my brother discovers that I have betrayed him, he will take it very unkind, and perhaps never forgive me."

"Be not alarmed," cried Cecilia; "rest assured he shall never know it. Is he not now in the country?"

"No, madam, he is now in the very next room."

"But what is become of the surgeon who used to attend him, and why does he not still visit him?"

"It is in vain, now, to hide any thing from you; my brother deceived him, and said he was going out of town merely to get rid of him."

"And what could induce him to act so strangely?"

"A reason which you, madam, I hope, will never know, Poverty!—he would not run up a bill he could not pay."

"Good Heaven!—But what can be done for him? He must not be suffered to linger thus; we must contrive some method of relieving and assisting him, whether he will consent or not."

"I fear that will not be possible. One of his friends has already found him out, and has written him the kindest letter! but he would not answer it, and would not see him, and was only fretted and angry."

"Well," said Cecilia, "I will not keep you longer, lest he should be alarmed by your absence. To-morrow morning, with your leave, I will call upon you again, and then, I hope, you will permit me to make some effort to assist you."

"If it only depended upon me, madam," she answered, "now I have the honour to know who you are, I believe I should not make much scruple, for I was not brought up to notions so high as my brother. Ah! happy had it been for him, for me, for all his family, if he had not had them neither!''

Cecilia then repeated her expressions of comfort and kindness, and took her leave.

This little adventure gave her infinite concern; all the horror which the duel had originally occasioned her, again returned; she accused herself with much bitterness for having brought it on; and finding that Mr. Belfield was so cruelly a sufferer both in his health and his affairs, she thought it incumbent upon her to relieve him to the utmost of her ability.

His sister, too, had extremely interested her; her youth, and the uncommon artlessness of her conversation, added to her melancholy situation, and the loveliness of her person, excited in her a desire to serve, and an inclination to love her; and she determined, if she found her as deserving as she seemed engaging, not only assist her at present, but, if her distresses continued, to receive her into her own house in future.

Again she regretted the undue detention of her 200*l*. What she now had to spare was extremely inadequate to what she now wished to bestow, and she looked forward to the conclusion of her minority with encreasing eagerness. The generous and elegant plan of life she then intended to pursue, daily gained ground in her imagination, and credit in her opinion.

CHAPTER VI

A Man of Genius

THE next morning, as soon as breakfast was over, Cecilia went in a chair to Swallow-street; she enquired for Miss Belfield, and was told to go up stairs: but what was her amazement to meet, just coming out of the room into which she was entering, young Delvile!

They both started, and Cecilia, from the seeming strangeness of her situation, felt a confusion with which she had hitherto been unacquainted. But Delvile, presently recovering from his surprise, said to her, with an expressive smile, "How good is Miss Beverley thus to visit the sick! and how much better might I have had the pleasure of seeing Mr. Belfield, had I but, by prescience, known her design, and deferred my own enquiries till he had been revived by hers!"

And then, bowing and wishing her good morning, he glided past her.

Cecilia, notwithstanding the openness and purity of her intentions, was so much disconcerted by this unexpected meeting, and pointed speech, that she had not the presence of mind to call him back and clear herself: and the various interrogatories and railleries which had already passed between them upon the subject of Mr. Belfield, made her suppose that what he had formerly suspected he would now think confirmed, and conclude that all her assertions of indifference, proceeded merely from that readiness at hypocrisy upon particular subjects, of which he had openly accused her whole Sex.

This circumstance and this apprehension took from her for a while all interest in the errand upon which she came; but the benevolence of her heart soon brought it back, when, upon going into the room, she saw her new favourite in tears.

"What is the matter?" cried she, tenderly; "no new affliction I hope has happened? Your brother is not worse?"

"No, madam, he is much the same; I was not then crying for him."

"For what then? tell me, acquaint me with your sorrows, and assure yourself you tell them to a friend."

"I was crying, madam, to find so much goodness in the world, when I thought there was so little! to find I have some chance of being again happy, when I thought I was miserable for ever! Two whole years have I spent in nothing but unhappiness, and I thought there was nothing else to be had; but yesterday, madam, brought me *you*, with every

promise of nobleness and protection; and to-day, a friend of
my brother's has behaved so generously, that even my
brother has listened to him, and almost consented to be
obliged to him!''

"And have you already known so much sorrow," said
Cecilia, "that this little dawn of prosperity should wholly
overpower your spirits? Gentle, amiable girl! may the future
recompence you for the past, and may Mr. Albany's kind
wishes be fulfilled in the reciprocation of our comfort and
affection!''

They then entered into a conversation which the
sweetness of Cecilia, and the gratitude of Miss Belfield, soon
rendered interesting, friendly and unreserved: and in a very
short time, whatever was essential in the story or situation
of the latter was fully communicated. She gave, however, a
charge the most earnest, that her brother should never be
acquainted with the confidence she had made.

Her father, who had been dead only two years, was a
linen-draper* in the city; he had six daughters, of whom
herself was the youngest, and only one son. This son, Mr
Belfield, was alike the darling of his father, mother, and
sisters: he was brought up at Eaton,* no expence was spared
in his education, nothing was denied that could make him
happy. With an excellent understanding he had uncommon
quickness of parts, and his progress in his studies was rapid
and honourable: his father, though he always meant him for
his successor in his business, heard of his improvement with
rapture, often saying, "My boy will be the ornament of the
city, he will be the best scholar in any shop in London.''

He was soon, however, taught another lesson; when, at
the age of sixteen, he returned home, and was placed in the
shop, instead of applying his talents, as his father had
expected, to trade, he both despised and abhorred the name
of it; when serious, treating it with contempt, when gay,
with derision.

He was seized, also, with a most ardent desire to finish his
education, like those of his school-fellows who left Eaton at
the same time, at one of the Universities;* and, after many
difficulties, this petition, at the intercession of his mother,

was granted, old Mr. Belfield telling him he hoped a little more learning would give him a little more sense, and that when he became a *finished student*, he would not only know the true value of business, but understand how to get money, and make a bargain, better than any man whatsoever within Temple-Bar.*

These expectations, equally short-sighted, were also equally fallacious with the former; the son again returned, and returned, as his father had hoped, a *finished student;* but, far from being more tractable, or better disposed for application to trade, his aversion to it now was more stubborn, and his opposition more hardy than ever. The young men of fashion with whom he had formed friendships at school, or at the university, and with whom, from the indulgence of his father, he was always able to vie in expence, and from the indulgence of Nature to excel in capacity, earnestly sought the continuance of his acquaintance, and courted and coveted the pleasure of his conversation: but though he was now totally disqualified for any other society, he lost all delight in their favour from the fear they should discover his abode, and sedulously endeavoured to avoid even occasionally meeting them, lest any of his family should at the same time approach him: for of his family, though wealthy, worthy and independent, he was now so utterly ashamed, that the mortification the most cruel he could receive, was to be asked his address, or told he should be visited.

Tired, at length, of evading the enquiries made by some, and forcing faint laughs at the detection made by others, he privately took a lodging at the West end of the town, to which he thence forward directed all his friends, and where, under various pretences, he contrived to spend the greatest part of his time.

In all his expensive deceits and frolics, his mother was his never-failing confident and assistant; for when she heard that the companions of her son were men of fashion, some born to titles, others destined to high stations, she concluded he was in the certain road to honour and profit, and frequently distressed herself, without ever repining, in order to enable him to preserve upon equal terms, connections which she believed so conducive to his future grandeur.

In this wild and unsettled manner he passed some time, struggling incessantly against the authority of his father, privately abetted by his mother, and constantly aided and admired by his sisters: till, sick of so desultory a way of life, he entered himself a volunteer in the army.

How soon he grew tired of this change has already been related,[†] as well as his reconciliation with his father, and his becoming a student at the Temple: for the father now grew as weary of opposing, as the young man of being opposed.

Here, for two or three years, he lived in happiness uninterrupted; he extended his acquaintance among the great, by whom he was no sooner known than caressed and admired, and he frequently visited his family, which, though he blushed to own in public, he affectionately loved in private. His profession, indeed, was but little in his thoughts, successive engagements occupying almost all his hours. Delighted with the favour of the world, and charmed to find his presence seemed the signal for entertainment, he soon forgot the uncertainty of his fortune, and the inferiority of his rank; the law grew more and more fatiguing, pleasure became more and more alluring, and, by degrees, he had not a day unappropriated to some party or amusement; voluntarily consigning the few leisure moments his gay circle afforded him, to the indulgence of his fancy in some hasty compositions in verse, which were handed about in manuscript, and which contributed to keep him in fashion.

Such was his situation at the death of his father; a new scene was then opened to him, and for some time he hesitated what course to pursue.

Old Mr. Belfield, though he lived in great affluence, left not behind him any considerable fortune, after the portions of his daughters,[*] to each of whom he bequeathed 2000*l*. had been deducted from it. But his stock in trade was great, and his business was prosperous and lucrative.

[†]See p. 12. Vol. I.

His son, however, did not merely want application and fortitude to become his successor, but skill and knowledge; his deliberation, therefore, was hasty, and his revolution improvident; he determined to continue at the Temple himself, while the shop, which he could by no means afford to relinquish, should be kept up by another name, and the business of it be transacted by an agent; hoping thus to secure and enjoy its emoluments, without either the trouble or the humiliation of attendance.

But this scheme, like most others that have their basis in vanity, ended in nothing but mortification and disappointment: the shop which under old Mr. Belfield had been flourishing and successful, and enriched himself and all his family, could now scarce support the expences of an individual. Without a master, without that diligent attention to its prosperity which the interest of possession alone can give, and the authority of a principal alone can enforce, it quicky lost its fame for the excellence of its goods, and soon after its customers from the report of its declension. The produce,* therefore, diminished every month; he was surprised, he was provoked; he was convinced he was cheated, and that his affairs were neglected; but though he threatened from time to time to enquire into the real state of the business, and investigate the cause of its decay, he felt himself inadequate to the task; and now first lamented that early contempt of trade, which by preventing him* acquiring some knowledge of it while he had youth and opportunity, made him now ignorant what redress to seek, though certain of imposition and injury.

But yet, however disturbed by alarming suggestions in his hours of retirement, no alteration was made in the general course of his life; he was still the darling of his friends, and the leader in all parties, and still, though his income was lessened, his expences encreased.

Such were his circumstances at the time Cecilia first saw him at the house of Mr. Monckton: from which, two days after her arrival in town, he was himself summoned, by an information that his agent had suddenly left the kingdom.

The fatal consequence of this fraudulent elopement was immediate bankrupcy.

His spirits, however, did not yet fail him; as he had never been the nominal master of the shop, he escaped all dishonour from its ruin, and was satisfied to consign what remained to the mercy of the creditors, so that his own name should not appear in the Gazette.*

Three of his sisters were already extremely well married to reputable tradesmen; the two elder of those who were yet single were settled with two of those who were married, and Henrietta, the youngest, resided with her mother, who had a comfortable annuity,* and a small house at Padington.

Bereft thus through vanity and imprudence of all the long labours of his father, he was now compelled to think seriously of some actual method of maintenance; since his mother, though willing to sacrifice to him even the nourishment which sustained her, could do for him but little, and that little he had too much justice to accept. The law, even to the most diligent and successful, is extremely slow of profit, and whatever, from his connections and abilities might be hoped hereafter, at present required an expence which he was no longer able to support.

It remained then to try his influence with his friends among the great and the powerful.

His canvass* proved extremely honourable; every one promised something, and all seemed delighted to have an opportunity of serving him.

Pleased with finding the world so much better than report had made it, he now saw the conclusion of his difficulties in the prospect of a place at court.*

Belfield, with half the penetration with which he was gifted, would have seen in any other man the delusive idleness of expectations no better founded; but though discernment teaches us the folly of others, experience singly can teach us our own! he flattered himself that his friends had been more wisely selected than the friends of those who in similar circumstances had been beguiled, and he suspected not the fraud of his vanity, till he found his invitations daily slacken, and that his time was at his own command.

All his hopes now rested upon one friend and patron, Mr. Floyer, an uncle of Sir Robert Floyer, a man of power in the royal houshold, with whom he had lived in great intimacy, and who at this period had the disposal of a place which he solicited. The only obstacle that seemed in his way was from Sir Robert himself, who warmly exerted his interest in favour of a friend of his own. Mr. Floyer, however, assured Belfield of the preference, and only begged his patience till he could find some opportunity of appeasing his nephew.

And this was the state of his affairs at the time of his quarrel at the Opera-house. Already declared opponents of each other, Sir Robert felt double wrath that for *him* Cecilia should reject his civilities; while Belfield, suspecting he presumed upon his known dependence on his uncle to affront him, felt also double indignation at the haughtiness of his behaviour. And thus, slight as seemed to the world the cause of their contest, each had private motives of animosity that served to stimulate revenge.

The very day after this duel, Mr. Floyer wrote him word that he was now obliged in common decency to take the part of his nephew, and therefore had already given the place to the friend he had recommended.

This was the termination of his hopes, and the signal of his ruin! To the pain of his wound he became insensible, from the superior pain of this unexpected miscarriage; yet his pride still enabled him to disguise his distress, and to see all the friends whom this accident induced to seek him, while from the sprightliness he forced in order to conceal his anguish, he appeared to them more lively and more entertaining than ever.

But these efforts, when left to himself and to nature, only sunk him the deeper in sadness; he found an immediate change in his way of life was necessary, yet could not brook to make it in sight of those with whom he had so long lived in all the brilliancy of equality. A high principle of honour which still, in the midst of his gay career, had remained uncorrupted, had scrupulously guarded him from running in debt, and therefore, though of little possessed, that little was strictly his own. He now published that he was going out of town for the benefit of purer air, discharged his surgeon, took a gay leave of his friends, and trusting no one with his secret but his servant, was privately conveyed to mean and cheap lodgings in Swallow-street.

Here, shut up from every human being he had formerly known, he purposed to remain till he grew better, and then again to seek his fortune in the army.

His present situation, however, was little calculated to contribute to his recovery; the dismission of the surgeon, the precipitation of his removal, the inconveniencies of his lodgings, and the unseasonable deprivation of long customary indulgencies, were unavoidable delays of his amendment; while the mortification of his present disgrace, and the bitterness of his late disappointment, preyed incessantly upon his mind, robbed him of rest, heightened his fever, and reduced him by degrees to a state so low and dangerous, that his servant, alarmed for his life, secretly acquainted his mother with his illness and retreat.

The mother, almost distracted by this intelligence, instantly, with her daughter, flew to his lodgings. She wished to have taken him immediately to her house at Padington, but he had suffered so much from his first removal, that he would not consent to another. She would then have called in a physician, but he refused even to see one; and she had too long given way to all his desires and opinions, to have now the force of mind for exerting the requisite authority of issuing her orders without consulting him.

She begged, she pleaded, indeed, and Henrietta joined in her entreaties; but sickness and vexation had not rendered him tame, though they had made him sullen: he resisted their prayers, and commonly silenced them by assurances that their opposition to the plan he had determined to pursue, only inflamed his fever, and retarded his recovery.

The motive of an obduracy so cruel to his friends was the fear of a detection which he thought not merely prejudicial to his affairs, but dishonourable to his character: for, without betraying any symptom of his distress, he had taken a general leave of his acquaintance upon pretence of going out of town, and he could ill endure to make a discovery which would at once proclaim his degradation and his deceit.

Mr. Albany had accidentally broken in upon him, by mistaking his room for that of another sick person in the same house, to whom his visit had been intended; but as he knew and reverenced that old gentleman, he did not much repine at his intrusion.

He was not so easy when the same discovery was made by young Delvile, who, chancing to meet his servant in the street, enquired concerning his master's health, and surprising from him its real state, followed him home; where, soon certain of the change in his affairs by the change of his habitation, he wrote him a letter, in which, after apologizing for his freedom, he warmly declared that nothing could make him so happy as being favoured with his commands, if, either through himself or his friends, he could be so fortunate as to do him any service.

Belfield, deeply mortified at this detection of his situation, returned only a verbal answer of cold thanks, and desired he would not speak of his being in town, as he was not well enough to be seen.

This reply gave almost equal mortification to young Delvile, who continued, however, to call at the door with enquiries how he went on, though he made no further attempt to see him.

Belfield, softened at length by the kindness of this conduct, determined to admit him; and he was just come from paying his first visit, when he was met by Cecilia upon the stairs.

His stay with him had been short, and he had taken no notice either of his change of abode, or his pretence of going into the country; he had talked to him only in general terms, and upon general subjects, till he arose to depart, and then he re-urged his offers of service with so much openness and warmth, that Belfield, affected by his earnestness, promised he would soon see him again, and intimated to his delighted mother and sister, that he would frankly consult with him upon his affairs.

Such was the tale which, with various minuter circumstances, Miss Belfield communicated to Cecilia. "My mother," she added, "who never quits him, knows that you are here, madam, for she heard me talking with somebody yesterday, and she made me tell her all that had passed, and that you said you would come again this morning."

Cecilia returned many acknowledgments for this artless and unreserved communication, but could not, when it was over, forbear enquiring by what early misery she had already, though so very young, spent *two years in nothing but unhappiness?**

"Because," she answered, "when my poor father died all our family separated, and I left every body to go and live with my mother at Padington; and I was never a favourite with my mother—no more, indeed, was any body but my brother, for she thinks all the rest of the world only made for his sake.* So she used to deny both herself and me almost common necessaries, in order to save up money to make him presents: though, if he had known how it was done, he would only have been angry instead of taking them. However, I should have regarded nothing that had but been for his benefit, for I loved him a great deal more than my own convenience; but sums that would distress us for months to save up, would by him be spent in a day, and then thought of no more! Nor was that all——O no! I had much greater uneasiness to suffer; for I was informed by one of my brothers-in-law how ill every thing went, and that certain ruin would come to my poor brother from the treachery of his agent; and the thought of this was always preying upon my mind, for I did not dare tell it my mother, for fear it should put her out of humour, for, sometimes, she is not very patient; and it mattered little what any of us said to my brother, for he was too gay and too confident to believe his danger."

"Well but," said Cecilia, "I hope, now, all will go better; if your brother will consent to see a physician——"

"Ah, madam! that is the thing I fear he never will do, because of being seen in these bad lodgings. I would kneel whole days to prevail with him, but he is unused to controul, and knows not how to submit to it; and he has lived so long among the great, that he forgets he was not born as high as themselves. Oh that he had never quitted his own family! If he had not been spoilt by ambition, he had the best heart and sweetest disposition in the world. But living always with his superiors, taught him to disdain his own relations, and be ashamed of us all; and yet now, in the hour of his distress——who else comes to help him?"

Cecilia then enquired if she wanted not assistance for herself and her mother, observing that they did not seem to have all the conveniences to which they were entitled.

"Why indeed, madam," she replied, with an ingenuous smile, "when you first came here I was a little like my brother, for I was sadly ashamed to let you see how ill we lived! but now you know the worst, so I shall fret about it no more."

"But this cannot be your usual way of life; I fear the misfortunes of Mr. Belfield have spread a ruin wider than his own."

"No indeed; he took care from the first not to involve us in his hazards, for he is very generous, madam, and very noble in all his notions, and could behave to us all no better about money matters than he has ever done. But from the moment we came to this dismal place, and saw his distress, and that he was sunk* so low who used always to be higher than any of us, we had a sad scene indeed! My poor mother, whose whole delight was to think that he lived like a nobleman, and who always flattered herself that he would rise to be as great as the company he kept, was so distracted with her disappointment, that she would not listen to reason, but immediately discharged both our servants, said she and I should do all the work ourselves, hired this poor room for us to live in, and sent to order a bill* to be put upon her house at Padington, for she said she would never return to it any more."

"But are you, then," cried Cecilia, "without any servant?"

"We have my brother's man, madam, and so he lights our fires, and takes away some of our litters; and there is not much else to be done, except sweeping the rooms, for we eat nothing but cold meat from the cook shops.''

"And how long is this to last?''

"Indeed I cannot tell; for the real truth is, my poor mother has almost lost her senses; and ever since our coming here, she has been so miserable and so complaining, that indeed, between her and my brother, I have almost lost mine too! For when she found all her hopes at an end, and that her darling son, instead of being rich and powerful, and surrounded by friends and admirers, all trying who should do the most for him, was shut up by himself in this poor little lodging, and instead of gaining more, had spent all he was worth at first, with not a creature to come near him, though ill, though confined, though keeping his bed!—Oh madam, had you seen my poor mother when she first cast her eyes upon him in that condition!—indeed you could never have forgotten it!''

"I wonder not at her disappointment,'' cried Cecilia; "with expectations so sanguine, and a son of so much merit, it might well indeed be bitter.''

"Yes, and besides the disappointment, she is now continually reproaching herself for always complying with his humours, and assisting him to appear better than the rest of his family, though my father never approved her doing so. But she thought herself so sure of his rising, that she believed we should all thank her for it in the end. And she always used to say that he was born to be a gentleman, and what a grievous thing it would be to have him made a tradesman.''

"I hope, at least, she has not the additional misery of seeing him ungrateful for her fondness, however injudicious it may have been?''

"O no! he does nothing but comfort and chear her! and indeed it is very good of him, for he has owned to me in private, that but for her encouragement, he could not have run the course he has run, for he should have been obliged to enter into business, whether he had liked it or not. But my poor mother knows this, though he will not tell it her, and therefore she says that unless he gets well, she will punish herself all the rest of her life, and never go back to her house, and never hire another servant, and never eat any thing but bread, nor drink any thing but water!"

"Poor unhappy woman!" cried Cecilia, "how dearly does she pay for her imprudent and short-sighted indulgence! but surely you are not also to suffer in the same manner?"

"No, madam, not by her fault, for she wants me to go and live with one of my sisters: but I would not quit her for the world; I should think myself wicked indeed to leave her now. Besides, I don't at all repine at the little hardships I go through at present, because my poor brother is in so much distress, that all we save may be really turned to account; but when we lived so hardly only to procure him luxuries he had no right to, I must own I used often to think it unfair, and if I had not loved him dearly, I should not have borne it so well, perhaps, as I ought."

Cecilia now began to think it high time to release her new acquaintance by quitting her, though she felt herself so much interested in her affairs, that every word she spoke gave her a desire to lengthen the conversation. She ardently wished to make her some present, but was restrained by the fear of offending, or of being again refused; she had, however, devised a private scheme for serving her more effectually than by the donation of a few guineas, and therefore, after earnestly begging to hear from her if she could possibly be of any use, she told her that she should not find her confidence misplaced, and promising again to see her soon, reluctantly departed.

CHAPTER VII

An Expedient

THE scheme now projected by Cecilia, was to acquaint the surgeon who had already attended Mr. Belfield with his present situation and address, and to desire him to continue his visits, for the payment of which she would herself be accountable.

The raillery of young Delvile, however, had taught her to fear the constructions of the world, and she therefore purposed to keep both the surgeon and Mr. Belfield ignorant to whom they were indebted. She was aware, indeed, that whatever might be her management, that high-spirited and unfortunate young man would be extremely hurt to find himself thus detected and pursued; but she thought his life too well worth preserving to let it be sacrificed to his pride, and her internal conviction of being herself the immediate cause of its present danger, gave to her an anxious and restless desire to be herself the means of extricating him from it.

Rupil, the name of the surgeon, she had already heard mentioned by Mr. Arnott, and in getting into her chair, she ordered Ralph, her man, to enquire where he lived.

"I know already where he lives, madam," answered Ralph, "for I saw his name over a door in Cavendish-street, Oxford-road; I took particular notice of it, because it was at the house where you stood up that day on account of the mob that was waiting to see the malefactors go to Tyburn."

This answer unravelled to Cecilia a mystery which had long perplext her; for the speeches of young Delvile when he had surprised her in that situation were now fully explained. In seeing her come out of the surgeon's house, he had naturally concluded she had only entered it to ask news of his patient, Mr. Belfield; her protestations of merely standing up to avoid the crowd, he had only laughed at; and his hints at her reserve and dissimulation, were meant but to reproach her for refusing his offer of procuring her intelligence, at the very time when, to all appearance, she anxiously, though clandestinely, sought it for herself.

This discovery, notwithstanding it relieved her from all suspence of his meaning, gave her much vexation: to be supposed to take an interest so ardent, yet so private, in the affairs of Mr. Belfield, might well authorise all suspicions of her partiality for him: and even if any doubt had yet remained, the unlucky meeting upon the stairs at his lodgings, would not fail to dispel it, and confirm the notion of her secret regard. She hoped, however, to have soon some opportunity of clearing up the mistake, and resolved in the mean time to be studiously cautious in avoiding all appearances that might strengthen it.

No caution, however, and no apprehension, could intimidate her active humanity from putting into immediate execution a plan in which she feared any delay might be fatal; and therefore the moment she got home, she wrote the following note to the surgeon.

"To —— RUPIL, Esq.

March 27, 1779.

A FRIEND of Mr. Belfield begs Mr. Rupil will immediately call upon that gentleman, who is in lodgings about the middle of Swallow-street, and insist upon visiting him till he is perfectly recovered. Mr. Rupil is entreated not to make known this request, nor to receive from Mr. Belfield any return for his attendance; but to attribute the discovery of his residence to accident, and to rest assured he shall be amply recompensed for his time and trouble by the friend who makes this application, and who is willing to give any security that Mr. Rupil shall think proper to mention, for the performance of this engagement."

Her next difficulty was in what manner to have this note conveyed; to send her own servant was inevitably betraying herself, to employ any other was risking a confidence that might be still more dangerous, and she could not trust to the penny-post,* as her proposal required an answer. After much deliberation, she at length determined to have recourse to Mrs. Hill, to whose services she was entitled, and upon whose fidelity she could rely.

The morning was already far advanced, but the Harrels dined late, and she would not lose a day where even an hour might be of importance. She went therefore immediately to Mrs. Hill, whom she found already removed into her new habitation in Fetter-lane, and equally busy and happy in the change of scene and of employment. She gave to her the note,* which she desired her to carry to Cavendish-street directly, and either to deliver it into Mr. Rupil's own hands, or to bring it back if he was out; but upon no

consideration to make known whence or from whom it
came.

She then went into the back part of the shop, which by
Mrs. Roberts was called the parlour, and amused herself
during the absence of her messenger, by playing with the
children.

Mrs. Hill at her return said she had found Mr. Rupil at
home, and as she refused to give the letter to the servant, she
had been taken into a room where he was talking with a
gentleman, to whom, as soon as he had read it, he said with
a laugh, "Why here's another person with the same
proposal as yours! however, I shall treat you both alike."
And then he wrote an answer, which he sealed up, and bid
her take care of. This answer was as follows:

"MR. RUPIL will certainly attend Mr. Belfield, whose
friends may be satisfied he will do all in his power to recover
him, without receiving any recompence but the pleasure of
serving a gentleman who is so much beloved."

Cecilia, charmed at this unhoped for success, was making
further enquiries into what had passed, when Mrs. Hill, in
a low voice, said, "There's the gentleman, madam, who was
with Mr. Rupil when I gave him the letter. I had a notion
he was dodging* me all the way I came, for I saw him just
behind me, turn which way I would."

Cecilia then looked—and perceived young Delvile! who,
after stopping a moment at the door, came into the shop,
and desired to be shewn some gloves, which, among other
things, were laid in the window.

Extremely disconcerted at the sight of him, she began now
almost to fancy there was some fatality attending her
acquaintance with him, since she was always sure of
meeting, when she had any reason to wish avoiding him.

As soon as he saw he was observed by her, he bowed with
the utmost respect: she coloured in returning the salutation,
and prepared, with no little vexation, for another attack,
and further raillery, similar to what she had already received
from him: but, as soon as he had made his purchase, he
bowed to her again, and, without speaking, left the shop.

A silence so unexpected at once astonished and disturbed her; she again desired to hear all that had passed at Mr. Rupil's, and from the relation gathered that Delvile had himself undertaken to be responsible for his attendance upon Mr. Belfield.

A liberality so like her own failed not to impress her with the most lively esteem: but this served rather to augment than lessen the pain with which she considered the clandestine appearance she thus repeatedly made to him. She had no doubt he had immediately concluded she was author of the application to the surgeon, and that he followed her messenger merely to ascertain the fact; while his silence when he had made the discovery, she could only attribute to his now believing that her regard for Mr. Belfield was too serious for raillery.

Doubly, however, she rejoiced at the generosity of Mr. Rupil, as it rendered wholly unnecessary her further interference: for she now saw with some alarm the danger to which benevolence itself, directed towards a youthful object, might expose her.

CHAPTER VIII

A Remonstrance

CECILIA returned home so late, that she was summoned to the dining parlour the moment she entered the house. Her morning dress, and her long absence, excited much curiosity in Mrs. Harrel, which a quick succession of questions evasively answered soon made general; and Sir Robert Floyer, turning to her with a look of surprise, said, "If you have such freaks as these, Miss Beverley, I must begin to enquire a little more into your proceedings."

"That, Sir," said Cecilia, very coldly, "would ill repay your trouble."

"When we get her to Violet Bank," cried Mr. Harrel, "we shall be able to keep a better watch over her."

"I hope so," answered Sir Robert; "though faith she has

been so demure, that I never supposed she did any thing but read sermons.* However, I find there's no going upon trust with women, any more than with money.''

"Ay, Sir Robert," cried Mrs. Harrel, "you know I always advised you not to be quite so easy, and I am sure I really think you deserve a little severity, for not being more afraid.''

"Afraid of what, madam?" cried the baronet; "of a young lady's walking out without me? Do you think I wish to be any restraint upon Miss Beverley's time in a morning, while I have the happiness of waiting upon her every afternoon?''

Cecilia was thunderstruck by this speech, which not only expressed an open avowal of his pretensions, but a confident security of his success. She was shocked that a man of such principles should even for a moment presume upon her favour, and irritated at the stubborness of Mr. Harrel in not acquainting him with her refusal.

His intimation of coming to the house for *the happiness of waiting upon her*, made her determine, without losing a moment, to seek herself an explanation with him: while the discovery that he was included in the Easter party, which various other concomitant causes had already rendered disagreeable to her, made her look forward to that purposed expedition with nothing but unwillingness and distaste.

But though her earnestness to conclude this affair made her now put herself voluntarily in the way of the baronet, she found her plan always counteracted by Mr. Harrel, who, with an officiousness too obvious to pass for chance, constantly stopt the progress of any discourse in which he did not himself bear a part. A more passionate admirer might not have been so easily defeated; but Sir Robert, too proud for solicitation, and too indolent for assiduity, was very soon checked, because very soon wearied.

The whole evening, therefore, to her infinite mortification, passed away without affording her any opportunity of making known to him his mistake.

Her next effort was to remonstrate with Mr. Harrel himself; but this scheme was not more easy of execution than the other, since Mr. Harrel, suspecting she meant again to dun him for her money, avoided all separate conversation with her so skilfully, that she could not find a moment to make him hear her.

She then resolved to apply to his lady; but here her success was not better: Mrs. Harrel, dreading another lecture upon œconomy, peevishly answered to her request of a conference, that she was not very well, and could not talk gravely.

Cecilia, justly offended with them all, had now no resource but in Mr. Monckton, whose counsel for effectually dismissing the baronet, she determined to solicit by the first opportunity.

The moment, therefore, that she next saw him, she acquainted him with the speeches of Sir Robert and the behaviour of Mr. Harrel.

There needed no rhetoric to point out to Mr. Monckton the danger of suffering such expectations, or the impropriety of her present situation: he was struck with both in a manner the most forcible, and spared not for warmth of expression to alarm her delicacy, or add to her displeasure. But chiefly he was exasperated against Mr. Harrel, assuring her there could be no doubt but that he had some particular interest in so strenuously and artfully supporting the pretensions of Sir Robert. Cecilia endeavoured to refute this opinion, which she regarded as proceeding rather from prejudice than justice; but when she mentioned that the baronet was invited to spend the Easter holidays at Violet Bank, he represented with such energy the consequent constructions of the world, as well as the unavoidable encouragement such intimacy would imply, that he terrified her into an earnest entreaty to suggest to her some way of deliverance.

"There is only one;" answered he, "you must peremptorily refuse to go to Violet Bank yourself. If, after what has passed, you are included in the same party with Sir Robert, you give a sanction yourself to the reports already circulated of your engagements with him: and the effect of such a sanction will be more serious than you can easily imagine, since the knowledge that a connection is believed in the world, frequently, if not generally, leads by imperceptible degrees to its real ratification.''

Cecilia, with the utmost alacrity, promised implicitly to follow his advice, whatever might be the opposition of Mr. Harrel. He quitted her, therefore, with unusual satisfaction, happy in his power over her mind, and anticipating with secret rapture the felicity he had in reserve from visiting her during the absence of the family.

As no private interview was necessary for making known her intention of giving up the Easter party, which was to take place in two days' time, she mentioned the next morning her design of spending the holidays in town, when Mr. Harrel sauntered into the breakfast room to give some commission to his lady.

At first he only laughed at her plan, gaily rallying her upon her love of solitude; but when he found it was serious, he very warmly opposed it, and called upon Mrs. Harrel to join in his expostulations. That lady complied, but in so faint a manner, that Cecilia soon saw she did not wish to prevail; and with a concern that cost her infinite pain, now finally perceived that not only all her former affection was subsided into indifference, but that, since she had endeavoured to abridge her amusements, she regarded her as a spy, and dreaded her as the censor of her conduct.

Mean while Mr. Arnott, who was present, though he interfered not in the debate, waited the event with anxiety; naturally hoping her objections arose from her dislike of Sir Robert, and secretly resolving to be guided himself by her motions.

Cecilia at length, tired of the importunities of Mr. Harrel, gravely said, that if he desired to hear the reasons which obliged her to refuse his request, she was ready to communicate them.

Mr. Harrel, after a little hesitation, accompanied her into another room.

She then declared her resolution not to live under the same roof with Sir Robert, and very openly expressed her vexation and displeasure, that he so evidently persisted in giving that gentleman encouragement.

"My dear Miss Beverley," answered he, carelessly, "when young ladies will not know their own minds, it is necessary some friend should tell it them: you were certainly very favourable to Sir Robert but a short time ago, and so, I dare say, you will be again, when you have seen more of him."

"You amaze me, Sir!" cried Cecilia: "when was I favourable to him? Has he not always and regularly been my aversion?"

"I fancy," answered Mr. Harrel, laughing, "you will not easily persuade him to think so; your behaviour at the Opera-house was ill calculated to give him that notion."

"My behaviour at the Opera-house, Sir, I have already explained to you; and if Sir Robert himself has any doubts, either from that circumstance or from any other, pardon me if I say they can only be attributed to your unwillingness to remove them. I entreat you, therefore, to trifle with him no longer, nor to subject me again to the freedom of implications extremely disagreeable to me."

"O fie, fie, Miss Beverley! after all that has passed, after his long expectations, and his constant attendance, you cannot for a moment think seriously of discarding him."

Cecilia, equally surprised and provoked by this speech, could not for a moment tell how to answer it; and Mr. Harrel, wilfully misinterpreting her silence, took her hand, and said, "Come, I am sure you have too much honour to make a fool of such a man as Sir Robert Floyer. There is not a woman in town who will not envy your choice, and I assure you there is not a man in England I would so soon recommend to you."

He would then have hurried her back to the next room; but, drawing away her hand with undisguised resentment, "No, Sir," she cried, "this must not pass! my positive rejection of Sir Robert the instant you communicated to me his proposals, you can neither have forgotten nor mistaken: and you must not wonder if I acknowledge myself extremely disobliged by your unaccountable perseverance in refusing to receive my answer."

"Young ladies who have been brought up in the

country," returned Mr. Harrel, with his usual negligence, "are always so high flown in their notions, it is difficult to deal with them; but as I am much better acquainted with the world than you can be, you must give me leave to tell you, that if, after all, you refuse Sir Robert, it will be using him very ill."

"Why will you say so, Sir?" cried Cecilia, "when it is utterly impossible you can have formed so preposterous an opinion. Pray hear me, however, finally, and pray tell Sir Robert——"

"No, no," interrupted he, with affected gaiety, "you shall manage it all your own way; I will have nothing to do with the quarrels of lovers."

And then, with a pretended laugh, he hastily left her.

Cecilia was so much incensed by this impracticable behaviour, that instead of returning to the family, she went directly to her own room. It was easy for her to see that Mr. Harrel was bent upon using every method he could devise, to entangle her into some engagement with Sir Robert, and though she could not imagine the meaning of such a scheme, the littleness of his behaviour excited her contempt, and the long-continued error of the baronet gave her the utmost uneasiness. She again determined to seek an explanation with him herself, and immovably to refuse joining the party to Violet Bank.

The following day, while the ladies and Mr. Arnott were at breakfast, Mr. Harrel came into the room to enquire if they should all be ready to set off for his villa by ten o'clock the next day. Mrs. Harrel and her brother answered in the affirmative; but Cecilia was silent, and he turned to her and repeated his question.

"Do you think me so capricious, Sir," said she, "that after telling you but yesterday I could not be of your party, I shall tell you to-day that I can?"

"Why you do not really mean to remain in town by yourself?" replied he, "you cannot suppose that will be an eligible plan for a young lady. On the contrary, it will be so very improper, that I think myself, as your Guardian, obliged to oppose it."

Amazed at this authoritative speech, Cecilia looked at him
with a mixture of mortification and anger; but knowing it
would be vain to resist his power if he was resolute to exert
it, she made not any answer.

"Besides," he continued, "I have a plan for some
alterations in the house during my absence; and I think your
room, in particular, will be much improved by them: but it
will be impossible to employ any workmen, if we do not all
quit the premises."

This determined persecution now seriously alarmed her;
she saw that Mr. Harrel would omit no expedient or
stratagem to encourage the addresses of Sir Robert, and
force her into his presence; and she began next to apprehend
that her connivance in his conduct might be presumed upon
by that gentleman: she resolved, therefore, as the last and
only effort in her power for avoiding him, to endeavour to
find an accommodation at the house of Mrs. Delvile, during
the excursion to Violet Bank: and if, when she returned to
Portman-square, the baronet still persevered in his
attendance, to entreat her friend Mr. Monckton would take
upon himself the charge of undeceiving him.

CHAPTER IX

A Victory

AS not a moment was now to be lost, Cecilia had no sooner
suggested this scheme, than she hastened to St. James's
Square, to try its practicability.

She found Mrs. Delvile alone, and still at breakfast.

After the first compliments were over, while she was
considering in what manner to introduce her proposal, Mrs.
Delvile herself led to the subject, by saying "I am very sorry
to hear we are so soon to lose you; but I hope Mr. Harrel
does not intend to make any long stay at his villa; for if he
does, I shall be half tempted to come and run away with you
from him."

"And that," said Cecilia, delighted with this opening,

"would be an honour I am *more* than half tempted to desire."

"Why indeed your leaving London at this time," continued Mrs. Delvile, "is, for me, particularly unfortunate, as, if I could now be favoured with your visits, I should doubly value them; for Mr. Delvile is gone to spend the holydays at the Duke of Derwent's, whither I was not well enough to accompany him; my son has his own engagements, and there are so few people I can bear to see, that I shall live almost entirely alone."

"If I," cried Cecilia, "in such a situation might hope to be admitted, how gladly for that happiness would I exchange my expedition to Violet-bank!"

"You are very good, and very amiable," said Mrs. Delvile, "and your society would, indeed, give me infinite satisfaction. Yet I am no enemy to solitude; on the contrary, company is commonly burthensome to me; I find few who have any power to give me entertainment, and even of those few, the chief part have in their manners, situation, or characters, an unfortunate *something*, that generally renders a near connection with them inconvenient or disagreeable. There are, indeed, so many draw-backs to regard and intimacy, from pride, from propriety, and various other collateral causes, that rarely as we meet with people of brilliant parts, there is almost ever some objection to our desire of meeting them again. Yet to live wholly alone is chearless and depressing; and with you, at least," taking Cecilia's hand, "I find not one single obstacle to oppose to a thousand inducements, which invite me to form a friendship that I can only hope may be as lasting, as I am sure it will be pleasant."

Cecilia expressed her sense of this partiality in the warmest terms; and Mrs. Devile, soon discovering by her manner that she took not any delight in her intended visit to Violet-Bank, began next to question her whether it would be possible for her to give it up.

She instantly answered in the affirmative.

"And would you really be so obliging," cried Mrs. Delvile, with some surprise, "as to bestow upon me the time you had destined for this gay excursion?"

"Most willingly," answered Cecilia, "if you are so good as to wish it."

"But can you also—for you must by no means remain alone in Portman Square,—manage to live entirely in my house till Mr. Harrel's return?"

To this proposal, which was what she most desired, Cecilia gave a glad assent; and Mrs. Delvile, extremely pleased with her compliance, promised to have an apartment prepared for her immediately.

She then hastened home, to announce her new plan.

This she took occasion to do when the family was assembled at dinner. The surprize with which she was heard was very general: Sir Robert seemed at a loss what conclusion to draw from her information; Mr. Arnott was half elated with pleasure, and half depressed with apprehension; Mrs. Harrel wondered, without any other sensation; and Mr. Harrel himself was evidently the most concerned of the party.

Every effort of persuasion and importunity he now essayed to prevail upon her to give up this scheme, and still accompany them to the villa; but she coolly answered that her engagement with Mrs. Delvile was decided, and she had appointed to wait upon her the next morning.

When her resolution was found so steady, a general ill humour took place of surprise: Sir Robert now had the air of a man who thought himself affronted; Mr. Arnott was wretched from a thousand uncertainties; Mrs. Harrel, indeed, was still the most indifferent; but Mr. Harrel could hardly repress his disappointment and anger.

Cecilia, however, was all gaiety and pleasure: in removing only from the house of one guardian to another, she knew she could not be opposed; and the flattering readiness with which Mrs. Delvile had anticipated her request, without enquiring into her motives, had relieved her from a situation which now grew extremely distressing, without giving to her the pain of making complaints of Mr. Harrel. The absence of Mr. Delvile contributed to her happiness, and she much rejoiced in having now the prospect of a speedy opportunity to explain to his son, whatever had appeared mysterious in her conduct respecting Mr. Belfield. If she had any thing to regret, it was merely the impossibility, at this time, of waiting for the counsel of Mr. Monckton.

The next morning, while the family was in the midst of preparation for departure, she took leave of Mrs. Harrel, who faintly lamented the loss of her company, and then hastily made her compliments to Mr. Harrel and Mr. Arnott, and putting herself into a chair, was conveyed to her new habitation.

Mrs. Delvile received her with the most distinguished politeness; she conducted her to the apartment which had been prepared for her, led her to the library, which she desired her to make use of as her own, and gave her the most obliging charges to remember that she was in a house of which she had the command.

Young Delvile did not make his appearance till dinner time. Cecilia, from recollecting the strange situations in which she had lately been seen by him, blushed extremely when she first met his eyes; but finding him gay and easy, general in his conversation, and undesigning in his looks, she soon recovered from her embarrassment, and passed the rest of the day without restraint or uneasiness.

Every hour she spent with Mrs. Delvile, contributed to raise in her esteem the mind and understanding of that lady. She found, indeed, that it was not for nothing she was accused of pride, but she found at the same time so many excellent qualities, so much true dignity of mind, and so noble a spirit of liberality, that however great was the respect she seemed to demand, it was always inferior to what she felt inclined to pay.

Nor was young Delvile less rapid in the progress he made in her favour; his character, upon every opportunity of shewing it, rose in her opinion, and his disposition and manners had a mingled sweetness and vivacity that rendered his society attractive, and his conversation spirited.

Here, therefore, Cecilia experienced that happiness she so long had coveted in vain: her life was neither public nor private, her amusements were neither dissipated nor retired; the company she saw were either people of high rank or strong parts, and their visits were neither frequent nor long. The situation she quitted gave a zest to that into which she entered, for she was now no longer shocked by extravagance or levity, no longer tormented with addresses which disgusted her, nor mortified by the ingratitude of the friend she had endeavoured to serve. All was smooth and serene, yet lively and interesting.

Her plan, however, of clearing to young Delvile his mistakes concerning Belfield, she could not put in execution; for he now never led to the subject, though he was frequently alone with her, nor seemed at all desirous to renew his former raillery, or repeat his enquiries. She wondered at this change in him, but chose rather to wait the revival of his own curiosity, than to distress or perplex herself by contriving methods of explanation.

Situated thus happily, she had now one only anxiety, which was to know whether, and in what manner, Mr. Belfield had received his surgeon, as well as the actual state of his own and his sister's affairs: but the fear of again encountering young Delvile in suspicious circumstances, deterred her at present from going to their house. Yet her natural benevolence, which partial convenience never lulled to sleep, impressing her with an apprehension that her services might be wanted, she was induced to write to Miss Belfield, though she forbore to visit her.

Her letter was short, but kind and to the purpose: she apologized for her officiousness, desired to know if her brother was better, and entreated her, in terms the most delicate, to acquaint her if yet she would accept from her any assistance.

She sent this letter by her servant, who, after waiting a considerable time, brought her the following answer.

To Miss BEVERLEY

Ah madam! your goodness quite melts me! we want nothing, however, yet, though I fear we shall not say so much longer. But though I hope I shall never forget myself so as to be proud and impertinent, I will rather struggle with any hardship than beg, for I will not disoblige my poor

brother by any fault that I can help, especially now he is
fallen so low. But, thank heaven, his wound has at last been
dressed, for the surgeon has found him out, and he attends
him for nothing; though my brother is willing to part with
every thing he is worth in the world, rather than owe that
obligation to him: yet I often wonder why he hates so to be
obliged, for when he was rich himself he was always doing
something to oblige other people. But I fear the surgeon
thinks him very bad! for he won't speak to us when we follow
him down stairs.

I am sadly ashamed to send this bad writing, but I dare
not ask my brother for any help, because he would only be
angry that I wrote any thing about him at all; but indeed I
have seen too little good come of pride to think of imitating
it; and as I have not his genius, I am sure there is no need
I should have his defects: ill, therefore, as I write, you,
madam, who have so much goodness and gentleness, would
forgive it, I believe, if it was worse, almost. And though we
are not in need of your kind offers, it is a great comfort to
me to think there is a lady in the world that, if we come to
be quite destitute, and if the proud heart of my poor
unhappy brother should be quite broke down, will look upon
our distress with pity, and generously help us from quite
sinking under it. I remain,

> Madam,
> with the most humble respect,
> your ever most obliged
> humble servant,
> HENRIETTA BELFIELD.

Cecilia, much moved by the simplicity of this letter,
determined that her very first visit from Portman-Square
should be to its fair and innocent writer. And having now
an assurance that she was in no immediate distress, and that
her brother was actually under Mr. Rupil's care, she
dismissed from her mind the only subject of uneasiness that
at present had endeavoured to disturb it, and gave herself
wholly up to the delightful serenity of unallayed happiness.
Few are the days of felicity unmixed* which we

acknowledge while we experience, though many are those we deplore, when by sorrow taught their value, and by misfortune, their loss. Time with Cecilia now glided on with such rapidity, that before she thought the morning half over, the evening was closed, and ere she was sensible the first week was past, the second was departed for ever. More and more pleased with the inmates of her new habitation, she found in the abilities of Mrs. Delvile sources inexhaustible of entertainment, and in the disposition and sentiments of her son something so concordant to her own, that almost every word he spoke shewed the sympathy of their minds, and almost every look which caught her eyes was a reciprocation of intelligence. Her heart, deeply wounded of late by unexpected indifference, and undeserved mortification, was now, perhaps, more than usually susceptible of those penetrating and exquisite pleasures which friendship and kindness possess the highest powers of bestowing. Easy, gay, and airy, she only rose to happiness, and only retired to rest; and not merely heightened was her present enjoyment by her past disappointment, but, carrying her retrospection to her earliest remembrance, she still found her actual situation more peculiarly adapted to her taste and temper, than any she had hitherto at any time experienced.

The very morning that the destined fortnight was elapsed, she received a note from Mrs. Harrel, with information of her arrival in town, and an entreaty that she would return to Portman-Square.

Cecilia, who, thus happy, had forgot to mark the progress of time, was now all amazement to find the term of her absence so soon past. She thought of going back with the utmost reluctance, and of quitting her new abode with the most lively regret. The representations of Mr. Monckton daily lost their force, and notwithstanding her dislike of Mr. Delvile, she had no wish so earnest as that of being settled in his family for the rest of her minority.

To effect this was her next thought; yet she knew not how to make the proposal, but from the uncommon partiality of

Mrs. Delvile, she hoped, with a very little encouragement, she would lead to it herself.

Here, however, she was disappointed; Mrs. Delvile, when she heard of the summons from the Harrels, expressed her sorrow at losing her in terms of the most flattering regret, yet seemed to think the parting indispensable, and dropt not the most distant hint of attempting to prevent it.

Cecilia, vexed and disconcerted, then made arrangements for her departure, which she fixed for the next morning.

The rest of this day, unlike every other which for the last fortnight had preceded it, was passed with little appearance, and no reality of satisfaction: Mrs. Delvile was evidently concerned, her son openly avowed his chagrin, and Cecilia felt the utmost mortification; yet, though every one was discontented, no effort was made towards obtaining any delay.

The next morning during breakfast, Mrs. Delvile very elegantly thanked her for granting to her so much of her time, and earnestly begged to see her in future whenever she could be spared from her other friends; protesting she was now so accustomed to her society, that she should require both long and frequent visits to soften the separation. This request was very eagerly seconded by young Delvile, who warmly spoke his satisfaction that his mother had found so charming a friend, and unaffectedly joined in her entreaties that the intimacy might be still more closely cemented.

Cecilia had no great difficulty in according her compliance to those demands, of which the kindness and cordiality somewhat lessened her disturbance at the parting.

When Mrs. Harrel's carriage arrived, Mrs. Delvile took a most affectionate leave of her, and her son attended her to the coach.

In her way down stairs, he stopt her for a few moments, and in some confusion said "I wish much to apologize to Miss Beverley, before her departure, for the very gross mistake of which I have been guilty. I know not if it is possible she can pardon me, and I hardly know myself by what perversity and blindness I persisted so long in my error."

"O," cried Cecilia, much rejoiced at this voluntary

explanation, "if you are but convinced you were really in an error, I have nothing more to wish. Appearances, indeed, were so strangely against me, that I ought not, perhaps, to wonder they deceived you."

"This is being candid indeed," answered he, again leading her on: "and in truth, though your anxiety was obvious, its cause was obscure, and where any thing is left to conjecture, opinion interferes, and the judgment is easily warped. My own partiality, however, for Mr. Belfield, will I hope plead my excuse, as from that, and not from any prejudice against the Baronet, my mistake arose: on the contrary, so highly I respect your taste and your discernment, that your approbation, when known, can scarcely fail of securing mine."

Great as was the astonishment of Cecilia at the conclusion of this speech; she was at the coach door before she could make any answer: but Delvile, perceiving her surprise, added, while he handed her in, "Is it possible——but no, it is *not* possible I should be again mistaken. I forbore to speak at all, till I had information by which I could not be misled."

"I know not in what unaccountable obscurity," cried Cecilia, "I, or my affairs, may be involved, but I perceive that the cloud which I had hoped was dissipated, is thicker and more impenetrable than ever."

Delvile then bowed to her with a look that accused her of insincerity, and the carriage drove away.

Teazed by these eternal mistakes, and provoked to find that though the object of her supposed partiality was so frequently changed, the notion of her positive engagement with one of the duelists was invariable, she resolved with all the speed in her power, to commission Mr. Monckton to wait upon Sir Robert Floyer, and in her own name give a formal rejection to his proposals, and desire him thenceforward to make known, by every opportunity, their total independance of each other: for sick of debating with Mr. Harrel, and detesting all intercourse with Sir Robert, she now dropt her design of seeking an explanation herself.

She was received by Mrs. Harrel with the same coldness with which she had parted from her. That lady appeared now to have some uneasiness upon her mind, and Cecilia endeavoured to draw from her its cause; but far from seeking any alleviation in friendship, she studiously avoided her, seeming pained by her conversation, and reproached by her sight. Cecilia perceived this encreasing roserve with much concern, but with more indignation, conscious that her good offices had merited a better reception, and angry to find that her advice had not merely failed of success, but even exposed her to aversion.

Mr. Harrel, on the contrary, behaved to her with unusual civility, seemed eager to oblige her, and desirous to render his house more agreeable to her than ever. But in this he did not prosper; for Cecilia, immediately upon her return, looking in her apartment for the projected alterations, and finding none had been made, was so disgusted by such a detection of duplicity, that he sunk yet lower than before in her opinion, and she repined at the necessity she was under of any longer continuing his guest.

The joy of Mr. Arnott at again seeing her, was visible and sincere; and not a little was it encreased by finding that Cecilia, who sought not more to avoid Mr. Harrel and Sir Robert, than she was herself avoided by Mrs. Harrel, talked with pleasure to nobody else in the house, and scarcely attempted to conceal that he was the only one of the family who possessed any portion of her esteem.

Even Sir Robert appeared now to have formed a design of paying her rather more respect than he had hitherto thought necessary; but the violence he did himself was so evident, and his imperious nature seemed so repugnant to the task, that his insolence, breaking forth by starts, and checked only by compulsion, was but the more conspicuous from his inadequate efforts to disguise it.

BOOK IV

CHAPTER I

A Complaint

AS Cecilia now found herself cleared, at least, of all suspicions of harbouring too tender a regard for Mr. Belfield, her objections to visiting his sister were removed, and the morning after her return to Mr. Harrel's, she went in a chair to Swallow-street.

She sent her servant up stairs to enquire if she might be admitted, and was immediately taken into the room where she had twice before been received.

In a few minutes Miss Belfield, softly opening and shutting the door of the next apartment, made her appearance. She looked thin and pale, but much gratified by the sight of Cecilia. "Ah madam!" she cried, "you are good indeed not to forget us! and you can little think how it chears and consoles me, that such a lady as you can condescend to be kind to me. It is quite the only pleasure that I have now in the whole world."

"I grieve that you have no greater;" cried Cecilia, "you seem much fatigued and harrassed. How is your brother? I fear you neglect your own health, by too much attention to his."

"No, indeed, madam; my mother does every thing for him herself, and hardly suffers any body else to go near him."

"What, then, makes you so melancholy?" said Cecilia, taking her hand; "you do not look well; your anxiety, I am sure, is too much for your strength."

"How should I look well, madam," answered she, "living as I live? however, I will not talk of myself, but of my brother,—O he is so ill! indeed I am sadly, sadly afraid he will never be well again!"

"What does his surgeon say? you are too tender, and too much frightened to be any judge."

"It is not that I think myself he will die of his wound, for Mr. Rupil says the wound is almost nothing; but he is in a constant fever, and so thin, and so weak, that indeed it is almost impossible he should recover!"

"You are too apprehensive," said Cecilia, "you know not what effect the country air may have upon him; there are many, many expedients that with so young a man may yet be successful."

"O no, the country air can do nothing for him! for I will not deceive you, madam, for that would be doubly a fault when I am so ready in blaming other people for wearing false appearances: besides, you are so good and so gentle, that it quite composes me to talk with you. So I will honestly speak the truth, and the whole truth at once; my poor brother is lost—O I fear for ever lost!—all by his own unhappy pride! he forgets his father was a tradesman, he is ashamed of all his family, and his whole desire is to live among the grandest people, as if he belonged to no other. And now that he can no longer do that, he takes the disappointment so to heart that he cannot get the better of it; and he told me this morning that he wished he was dead, for he did not know why he should live only to see his own ruin! But when he saw how I cried at his saying so, he was very sorry indeed, for he has always been the kindest brother in the world, when he has been away from the great folks who have spoilt him: but why, said he, Henrietta, why would you have me live, when instead of raising you and my poor mother into an higher station, I am sunk so low, that I only help to consume your own poor pittances to support me in my disgrace!"

"I am sorry indeed," said Cecilia, "to find he has so deep a sense of the failure of his expectations: but how happens it that *you* are so much wiser? Young and inexperienced as you are, and early as you must have been accustomed, from your mother as well as from Mr. Belfield, to far other doctrine, the clearness of your judgment, and the justness of your remarks, astonish as much as they charm me."

"Ah madam! brought up as I have been brought up, there is little wonder I should see the danger of an high education, let me be ever so ignorant of every thing else; for I, and all my sisters, have been the sufferers the whole time: and while we were kept backward, that he might be brought forward, while we were denied comforts, that he might have luxuries, how could we help seeing the evil of so much vanity, and wishing we had all been brought up according to our proper station? instead of living in continual inconvenience, and having one part of a family struggling with distress, only to let another part of it appear in a way he had no right to!"

"How rationally," said Cecilia, "have you considered this subject! and how much do I honour you for the affection you retain for your brother, notwithstanding the wrongs you have suffered to promote his elevation!"

"Indeed he deserves it; take but from him that one fault, pride, and I believe he has not another: and humoured and darling child as from his infancy he has always been, who at that can wonder, or be angry?"

"And has he still no plan, no scheme for his future destination?"

"No, madam, none at all; and that it is makes him so miserable, and being so miserable makes him so ill, for Mr. Rupil says that with such uneasiness upon his mind, he can never, in his present low state, get well. O it is melancholy to see how he is altered! and how he has lost all his fine spirits! he that used to be the life of us all!—And now he hardly ever speaks a word, or if he does, he says something so sorrowful that it cuts us to the soul! But yesterday, when my mother and I thought he was asleep, he lifted up his head, and looked at us both with the tears in his eyes, which almost broke our hearts to see, and then, in a low voice, he said 'what a lingering illness is this! Ah, my dear mother, you and poor Henrietta ought to wish it quicker over! for should I recover, my life, hereafter, will but linger like this illness.' And afterwards he called out 'what on earth is to become of me? I shall never have health for the army, nor interest, nor means; what am I to do? subsist in the very prime of my life upon the bounty of a widowed mother!

or, with such an education, such connections as mine, enter at last into some mean and sordid business?' ''

"It seems, then," said Cecilia, "he now less wants a physician than a friend."

"He has a friend, madam, a noble friend, would he but accept his services; but he never sees him without suffering fresh vexation, and his fever encreases after every visit he pays him."

"Well," cried Cecilia, rising, "I find we shall not have an easy task to manage him; but keep up your spirits, and assure yourself he shall not be lost, if it be possible to save him."

She then, though with much fearfulness of offending, once more made an offer of her purse. Miss Belfield no longer started at the proposal; yet, gratefully thanking her, said she was not in any immediate distress, and did not dare risk the displeasure of her brother, unless driven to it by severer necessity. Cecilia, however, drew from her a promise that she would apply to her in any sudden difficulty, and charged her never to think herself without a banker while her direction was known to her.

She then bid her adieu, and returned home; meditating the whole way upon some plan of employment and advantage for Mr. Belfield, which by clearing his prospects, might revive his spirits, and facilitate his recovery: for since his mind was so evidently the seat of his disease, she saw that unless she could do more for him, she had yet done nothing.

Her meditation, however, turned to no account; she could suggest nothing, for she was ignorant what was eligible to suggest. The stations and employments of men she only knew by occasionally hearing that such were their professions, and such their situations in life; but with the means and gradations by which they arose to them she was wholly unacquainted.

Mr. Monckton, her constant resource in all cases of difficulty, immediately occurred to her as her most able counsellor, and she determined by the first opportunity to consult with him upon the subject, certain of advice the most judicious from his experience, and knowledge of the world.

But though she rested upon him her serious expectations of assistance, another idea entered her mind not less pleasant, though less promising of utility: this was to mention her views to young Delvile. He was already, she knew, well informed of the distress of Mr. Belfield, and she hoped, by openly asking his opinion, to confirm to him her freedom from any engagement with that gentleman, and convince him, at the same time, by her application to himself, that she was equally clear of any tie with the Baronet.

CHAPTER II

A Sympathy

THE next day Cecilia had appointed to spend in St. James's Square; and she knew by experience that in its course, she should in all probability find some opportunity of speaking with Delvile alone.

This accordingly happened; for in the evening Mrs. Delvile quitted the room for a few moments to answer a letter. Cecilia then, left with her son, said, after a little hesitation, "Will you not think me very strange if I should take the liberty to consult you upon some business?"

"I already think you very strange," answered he; "so strange that I know not any one who at all resembles you. But what is this consultation in which you will permit me to have a voice?"

"You are acquainted, I believe, with the distress of Mr. Belfield?"

"I am; and I think his situation the most melancholy that can be imagined. I pity him with my whole soul, and nothing would give me greater joy than an opportunity of serving him."

"He is, indeed, much to be compassionated," returned Cecilia; "and if something is not speedily done for him, I fear he will be utterly lost. The agitation of his mind baffles all the power of medicine, and till that is relieved, his health can never be restored. His spirit, probably always too high for his rank in life, now struggles against every attack of sickness and of poverty, in preference to yielding to his fate, and applying to his friends for their interest and assistance. I mean not to vindicate his obduracy, yet I wish it were possible it could be surmounted. Indeed I dread to think what may become of him! feeling at present nothing but wretchedness and pain, looking forward in future to nothing but ruin and despair!''

''There is no man,'' cried young Delvile, with emotion, ''who might not rather envy than pity sufferings which give rise to such compassion!''

''Pecuniary assistance he will not accept,'' she continued, ''and, indeed, his mind is superior to receiving consolation from such temporary relief; I wish him, therefore, to be put into some way of life by which his own talents, which have long enough amused the world, may at length become serviceable to himself. Do you think, Sir, this is possible?''

''How do I rejoice,'' cried Delvile, colouring with pleasure while he spoke, ''in this flattering concurrence of our opinions! see, madam,'' taking from his pocket a letter, ''how I have been this very morning occupied, in endeavouring to procure for Mr. Belfield some employment by which his education might be rendered useful, and his parts redound to his own credit and advantage.''

He then broke the seal, and put into her hand a letter to a nobleman, whose son was soon going abroad, strongly recommending Belfield to him in capacity of a tutor.*

A sympathy of sentiment so striking impressed them at the same moment with surprise and esteem; Delvile earnestly regarded her with eyes of speaking admiration, while the occasion of his notice rendered it too pleasant to distress her, and filled her with an inward satisfaction which brightened her whole countenance.

She had only time, in a manner that strongly marked her approbation, to return the letter, before Mrs. Delvile again made her appearance.

During the rest of the evening but little was said; Cecilia

was not talkative, and young Delvile was so absent, that three times his mother reminded him of an engagement to meet his father, who that night was expected at the Duke of Derwent's house in town, before he heard that she spoke to him, and three times more before, when he had heard, he obeyed.

Cecilia, when she came back to Mr. Harrel's, found the house full of company. She went into the drawing-room, but did not remain there long: she was grave and thoughtful, she wished to be alone, and by the earliest opportunity, stole away to her own apartment.

Her mind was now occupied by new ideas, and her fancy was busied in the delineation of new prospects. She had been struck from her first meeting young Delvile with an involuntary admiration of his manners and conversation; she had found upon every succeeding interview something further to approve, and felt for him a rising partiality which made her always see him with pleasure, and never part from him without a wish to see him again. Yet, as she was not of that inflammable nature which is always ready to take fire, as her passions were under the controul of her reason, and she suffered not her affections to triumph over her principles, she started at her danger the moment she perceived it, and instantly determined to give no weak encouragement to a prepossession which neither time nor intimacy had justified. She denied herself the deluding satisfaction of dwelling upon the supposition of his worth, was unusually assiduous to occupy all her time, that her heart might have less leisure for imagination; and had she found that his character degenerated from the promise of his appearance, the well regulated purity of her mind would soon have enabled her to have driven him wholly from her thoughts.

Such was her situation when the circumstances of her affairs occasioned her becoming an inmate of his house; and here she grew less guarded, because less clear-sighted to the danger of negligence, for the frequency of their conversation allowed her little time to consider their effects. If at first she had been pleased with his deportment and elegance, upon

intimacy she was charmed with his disposition and his
behaviour; she found him manly, generous, open-hearted
and amiable, fond of literature, delighting in knowledge,
kind in his temper, and spirited in his actions.

Qualities such as these, when recommended by high
birth, a striking figure, and polished manners, formed but
a dangerous companion for a young woman, who, without
the guard of any former prepossession, was so fervent an
admirer of excellence as Cecilia. Her heart made no
resistance, for the attack was too gentle and too gradual to
alarm her vigilance, and therefore, though always sensible of
the pleasure she received from his society, it was not till she
returned to Portman-Square, after having lived under the
same roof with him for a fortnight, that she was conscious
her happiness was no longer in her own power.

Mr. Harrel's house, which had never pleased her, now
became utterly disgustful; she was wearied and
uncomfortable, yet, willing to attribute her uneasiness to
any other than the true cause, she fancied the house itself
was changed, and that all its inhabitants and visitors were
more than usually disagreeable: but this idle error was of
short duration, the moment of self-conviction was at hand,
and when Delvile presented her the letter he had written for
Mr. Belfield, it flashed in her eyes!

This detection of the altered state of her mind opened to
her views and her hopes a scene entirely new, for neither the
exertion of the most active benevolence, nor the steady
course of the most virtuous conduct, sufficed any longer to
wholly engage her thoughts, or constitute her felicity; she
had purposes that came nearer home, and cares that
threatened to absorb in themselves that heart and those
faculties which hitherto had only seemed animated for the
service of others.

Yet this loss of mental freedom gave her not much
uneasiness, since the choice of her heart, though
involuntary, was approved by her principles, and confirmed
by her judgment. Young Delvile's situation in life was just
what she wished, more elevated than her own, yet not so
exalted as to humble her with a sense of inferiority; his

connections were honourable, his mother appeared to her the first of women, his character and disposition seemed formed to make her happy, and her own fortune was so large, that to the state of his she was indifferent.

Delighted with so flattering a union of inclination with propriety, she now began to cherish the partiality she at first had repressed, and thinking the future deṣtination of her life already settled, looked forward with grateful joy to the prospect of ending her days with the man she thought most worthy to be entrusted with the disposal of her fortune.

She had not, indeed, any certainty that the regard of young Delvile was reciprocal, but she had every reason to believe he greatly admired her, and to suspect that his mistaken notion of her prior engagement, first with Mr. Belfield, and afterwards with Sir Robert Floyer, made him at present check those sentiments in her favour which, when that error was removed, she hoped to see encouraged.

Her purpose, therefore, was quietly to wait an explanation, which she rather wished retarded than forwarded, that her leisure and opportunity might be more for investigating his character, and saving herself from repentance.

CHAPTER III

A Conflict

THE day following this happy intellectual arrangement, Cecilia was visited by Mr. Monckton. That gentleman, who had enquired for her immediately after the Harrels went to their villa, and who had flattered himself with reaping much advantage from their absence, by frequent meetings and confidential discourses, suffered the severest mortification when he found that her stay in town rendered her not the less inaccessible to him, since he had no personal acquaintance with the Delviles, and could not venture to present himself at their house.

He was now received by her with more than usual

pleasure; the time had seemed long to her since she had conversed with him, and she was eager to ask his counsel and assistance in her affairs. She related to him the motives which had induced her to go to St. James' Square, and the incorrigible obstinacy with which Mr. Harrel still continued to encourage the addresses of Sir Robert Floyer; she earnestly entreated him to become her agent in a business to which she was unequal, by expostulating in her cause with Mr. Harrel, and by calling upon Sir Robert himself to insist upon his foregoing his unauthorised pretensions.

Mr. Monckton listened eagerly to her account and request, and when she had finished, assured her he would deliberate upon each circumstance of the affair, and then maturely weigh every method he could devise, to extricate her from an embarrassment which now grew far too serious to be safely neglected.

"I will not, however," continued he, "either act or give my opinion without further enquiry, as I am confident there is a mystery in this business which lies deeper than we can at present fathom. Mr. Harrel has doubtless purposes of his own to answer by this pretended zeal for Sir Robert; nor is it difficult to conjecture what they may be. Friendship, in a man of his light cast, is a mere cover, a mere name, to conceal a connection which has its basis solely in the licentious convenience of borrowing money, going to the same gaming house, and mutually communicating and boasting their mutual vices and intrigues, while, all the time, their regard for each other is equally hollow with their regard for truth and integrity."

He then cautioned her to be extremely careful with respect to any money transactions with Mr. Harrel, whose splendid extravagance he assured her was universally known to exceed his fortune.

The countenance of Cecilia during this exhortation was testimony sufficient to the penetrating eyes of Mr. Monckton that his advice came not too soon: a suspicion of the real state of the case speedily occurred to him, and he questioned her minutely upon the subject. She endeavoured to avoid making him any answer, but his discernment was too keen for her inartificial evasion,* and he very soon gathered all the particulars of her transactions with Mr. Harrel.

He was less alarmed at the sum she had lent him, which was rather within his expectations, than at the method she had been induced to take to procure it. He represented to her in the strongest manner the danger of imposition, nay of ruin, from the extortions and the craft of money-lenders; and he charged her upon no consideration to be tempted or persuaded again to have recourse to such perilous expedients.

She promised the most attentive observance of his advice: and then told him the acquaintance she had made with Miss Belfield, and her sorrow for the situation of her brother; though, satisfied for the present with the plan of young Delvile, she now gave up her design of soliciting his counsel.

In the midst of this conversation, a note was delivered to her from Mr. Delvile senior, acquainting her with his return to town, and begging the favour of her to call in St. James's Square the next morning, as he wished to speak to her upon some business of importance.

The eager manner in which Cecilia accepted this invitation, and her repeated and earnest exclamation of wonder at what Mr. Delvile could have to say, past not unnoticed by Mr. Monckton; he instantly turned the discourse from the Belfields, the Harrels, and the Baronet, to enquire how she had spent her time during her visit in St. James' Square, and what was her opinion of the family after her late opportunities of intimacy?

Cecilia answered that she had yet seen nothing more of Mr. Delvile, who had been absent the whole time, but with equal readiness and pleasure she replied to all his questions concerning his lady, expatiating with warmth and fervour upon her many rare and estimable qualities.

But when the same interrogatories were transferred to the son, she spoke no longer with the same ease, nor with her usual promptitude of sincerity; she was embarrassed, her answers were short, and she endeavoured to hasten from the subject.

Mr. Monckton remarked this change with the most apprehensive quickness, but, forcing a smile, "Have you yet," he said, "observed the family compact in which those people are bound to besiege you, and draw you into their snares?"

"No, indeed," cried Cecilia, much hurt by the question, "I am sure no such compact has been formed; and I am sure, too, that if you knew them better, you would yourself be the first to admire and do them justice."

"My dear Miss Beverley," cried he, "I know them already; I do not, indeed, visit them, but I am perfectly acquainted with their characters, which have been drawn to me by those who are most closely connected with them, and who have had opportunities of inspection which I hope will never fall to your share, since I am satisfied the trial would pain, though the proof would convince you."

"What then have you heard of them?" cried Cecilia, with much earnestness: "it is, at least, not possible any ill can be said of Mrs. Delvile."

"I beg your pardon," returned he, "Mrs. Delvile is not nearer perfection than the rest of her family, she has only more art in disguising her foibles; because, tho' she is the daughter of pride, she is the slave of interest."

"I see you have been greatly misinformed," said Cecilia warmly; "Mrs. Delvile is the noblest of women! she may, indeed, from her very exaltation, have enemies, but they are the enemies of envy, not of resentment, enemies raised by superior merit, not excited by injury or provocation!"

"You will know her better hereafter," said Mr. Monckton calmly, "I only hope your knowledge will not be purchased by the sacrifice of your happiness."

"And what knowledge of her, Sir," cried Cecilia, starting, "can have power to put my happiness in any danger?"

"I will tell you," answered he, "with all the openness you have a claim to from my regard, and then leave to time to shew if I am mistaken. The Delvile family, notwithstanding its ostentatious magnificence, I can solemnly assure you, is poor in every branch, alike lineal and collateral."

"But is it therefore the less estimable?"

"Yes, because the more rapacious. And while they count on each side Dukes, Earls and Barons in their genealogy, the very wealth with which, through your means, they project the support of their insolence, and which they will grasp with all the greediness of avarice, they will think honoured by being employed in their service, while the instrument, all amiable as she is, by which they attain it, will be constantly held down as the disgrace of their alliance."

Cecilia, stung to the soul by this speech, rose from her chair, unwilling to answer it, yet unable to conceal how much it shocked her. Mr. Monckton, perceiving her emotion, followed her, and taking her hand, said "I would not give this warning to one I thought too weak to profit from it; but as I am well informed of the use that is meant to be made of your fortune, and the abuse that will follow of yourself, I think it right to prepare you for their artifices, which merely to point out may render abortive."

Cecilia, too much disturbed to thank him, drew back her hand, and continued silent. Mr. Monckton, reading through her displeasure the state of her affections, saw with terror the greatness of the danger which threatened him. He found, however, that the present was no time for enforcing objections, and perceiving he had already gone too far, though he was by no means disposed to recant, he thought it most prudent to retreat, and let her meditate upon his exhortation while its impression was yet strong in her mind.

He would now, therefore, have taken leave; but Cecilia, endeavouring to recollect herself, and fully persuaded that however he had shocked her, he had only her interest in view, stopt him, saying "You think me, perhaps, ungrateful, but believe me I am not; I must, however, acknowledge that your censure of Mrs. Delvile hurts me extremely. Indeed I cannot doubt her worthiness, I must still, therefore, plead for her, and I hope the time may come when you will allow I have not pleaded unjustly."

"Justly or unjustly," answered Mr. Monckton, "I am at least sure you can never plead vainly. I give up, therefore, to your opinion my attack of Mrs. Delvile, and am willing from your commendations to suppose her the best of the race. Nay, I will even own that perhaps Mr. Delvile himself, as well as his lady, might pass through life and give but little offence, had they only themselves to think of, and no son to stimulate their arrogance.''

''Is the son, then,'' said Cecilia faintly, ''so much the most culpable?''

''The son, I believe,'' answered he, ''is at least the chief incentive to insolence and ostentation in the parents, since it is for his sake they covet with such avidity honours and riches, since they plume themselves upon regarding him as the support of their name and family, and since their pride in him even surpasses their pride in their lineage and themselves.''

''Ah!'' thought Cecilia, ''and of such a son who could help being proud!''

''Their purpose, therefore,'' he continued, ''is to secure through his means your fortune, which they will no sooner obtain, than, to my certain knowledge, they mean instantly, and most unmercifully, to employ it in repairing all their dilapidated estates.''

And then he quitted the subject; and, with that guarded warmth which accompanied all his expressions, told her he would carefully watch for her honour and welfare, and, repeating his promise of endeavouring to discover the tie by which Mr. Harrel seemed bound to the Baronet, he left her—a prey himself to an anxiety yet more severe than that with which he had filled her! He now saw all his long cherished hopes in danger of final destruction, and suddenly cast upon the brink of a precipice, where, while he struggled to protect them from falling, his eyes were dazzled by beholding them totter.

Mean while Cecilia, disturbed from the calm of soft serenity to which she had yielded every avenue of her soul, now looked forward with distrust and uneasiness, even to the completion of the views which but a few minutes before had comprised all her notions of felicity. The alliance which so lately had seemed wholly unexceptionable, now appeared teeming with objections, and threatening with difficulties.

The representations of Mr. Monckton had cruelly mortified her; well acquainted with his knowledge of the world, and wholly unsuspicious of his selfish motives, she gave to his assertions involuntary credit, and even while she attempted to combat them, they made upon her mind an impression scarce ever to be erased.

Full, therefore, of doubt and inquietude, she passed the night in discomfort and irresolution, now determining to give way to her feelings, and now to be wholly governed by the counsel of Mr. Monckton.

CHAPTER IV

An Expectation

IN this disposition of mind Cecilia the next morning obeyed the summons of Mr. Delvile, and for the first time went to St. James' Square in a humour to look for evil instead of good, and meanness instead of nobleness.

She was shewn into an apartment where she found Mr. Delvile alone, and was received by him, as usual, with the most stately solemnity.

When she was seated, "I have given you, Miss Beverley," said he, "the trouble of calling, in order to discuss with you the internal state of your affairs; a duty which, at this juncture, I hold to be incumbent upon my character. The delicacy due to your sex would certainly have induced me to wait upon you myself for this purpose, but for the reasons I have already hinted to you, of fearing the people with whom you live might think it necessary to return my visit. Persons of low origin are commonly in those matters the most forward. Not, however, that I would prejudice you against them; though, for myself, it is fit I remember that a general and indiscriminate acquaintance, by levelling all ranks, does injury to the rites of society."

Ah! thought Cecilia, how infallible is Mr. Monckton! and how inevitably, in a family of which Mr. Delvile is the head, should I be cruelly *held down, as the disgrace of their alliance!*

"I have applied," continued he, "to Mrs. Delvile, to know if the communication which I had recommended to you, and to which she had promised her attention, had yet passed; but I am informed you have not spoken to her upon the subject."

"I had nothing, Sir, to communicate," answered Cecilia, "and I had hoped, as Mrs. Delvile made no enquiries, she was satisfied she had nothing to hear."

"With respect to enquiries," said Mr. Delvile, "I fear you are not sufficiently aware of the distance between a lady of Mrs. Delvile's rank, both by birth and alliance, and such a young woman as Mrs. Harrel, whose ancestors, but a short time since, were mere Suffolk farmers. But I beg your pardon;——I mean not any reflection upon yours: I have always heard they were very worthy people. And a farmer is certainly a very respectable person. Your father, I think, no more than the Dean your uncle, did nothing in that way himself?"

"No, Sir," said Cecilia, drily, and much provoked by this contemptuous courtesy.

"I have always been told he was a very good sort of man: I knew none of the family myself, but the Dean. His connections with the Bishop of ——, my relation, put him often in my way. Though his naming me for one of his trustees, I must own, was rather extraordinary: but I mean not to hurt you; on the contrary, I should be much concerned to give you any uneasiness."

Again Mr. Monckton arose in the mind of Cecilia, and again she acknowledged the truth of his strictures; and though she much wondered in what an harrangue so pompous was to end, her disgust so far conquered her curiosity, that without hearing it, she wished herself away.

"To return," said he, "to my purpose. The present period of your life is such as to render advice particularly seasonable; I am sorry, therefore, as I before said, you have not disclosed your situation to Mrs. Delvile. A young lady on the point of making an establishment, and with many engagements in her power, is extremely liable to be mistaken in her judgment, and therefore should solicit instruction from those who are able to acquaint her what connection would be most to her advantage. One thing, however, I am happy to commend, the young man who was wounded in the duel——I cannot recollect his name——is, I hear, totally out of the question."

What next? thought Cecilia; though still she gave him no interruption, for the haughtiness of his manner was repulsive to reply.

"My design, therefore, is to speak to you of Sir Robert Floyer. When I had last the pleasure of addressing you upon this subject, you may probably remember my voice was in his favour; but I then regarded him merely as the rival of an inconsiderable young man, to rescue you from whom he appeared an eligible person. The affair is now altered, that young man is thought of no more, and another rival comes forward, to whom Sir Robert is as inconsiderable as the first rival was to Sir Robert."

Cecilia started at this information, livelier sensations stimulated her curiosity, and surmises in which she was most deeply interested quickened her attention.

"This rival," proceeded he, "I should imagine no young lady would a moment hesitate in electing; he is every way the superior of Sir Robert except in fortune, and the deficiencies of that the splendour of your own may amply supply."

The deepest crimson now tinged the cheeks of Cecilia; the prophecy of Mr. Monckton seemed immediately fulfilling, and she trembled with a rising conflict between her approbation of the offer, and her dread of its consequences.

"I know not, indeed," continued he, "in what estimation you may have been accustomed to hold rank and connection, nor whether you are impressed with a proper sense of their superiority and value; for early prejudices are not easily rooted out, and those who have lived chiefly with monied people, regard even birth itself as unimportant when compared with wealth."

The colour which first glowed in the cheeks of Cecilia from expectation, now rose yet higher from resentment:

she thought herself already insulted by a prelude so ostentatious and humiliating to the proposals which were to follow; and she angrily determined, with whatever pain to her heart, to assert her own dignity by refusing them at once, too well satisfied by what she now saw of the present, that Mr. Monckton had been just in his prediction of the future.

"Your rejection, therefore," continued he, "of this honourable offer, may perhaps have been merely the consequence of the principles in which you have been educated.—"

"Rejection?" interrupted Cecilia, amazed, "what rejection, Sir?"

"Have you not refused the proposals of my Lord Ernolf for his son?"

"Lord Ernolf? never! nor have I ever seen either his Lordship or his son but in public."

"That," replied Mr. Delvile, "is little to the purpose; where the connexion is a proper one, a young lady of delicacy has only to accede to it. But though this rejection came not immediately from yourself, it had doubtless your concurrence."

"It had not, Sir, even my knowledge."

"Your alliance then with Sir Robert Floyer is probably nearer a conclusion than I had imagined, for otherwise Mr. Harrel would not, without consulting you, have given the Earl so determinate an answer."

"No, Sir," said Cecilia, impatiently, "my alliance with him was never more distant, nor do I mean it should ever approach more near."

She was now little disposed for further conversation. Her heroic design of refusing young Delvile by no means reconciled her to the discovery she now made that he had not meant to address her; and though she was provoked and fretted at this new proof that Mr. Harrel scrupled neither assertions nor actions to make her engagement with Sir Robert credited, her disappointment in finding that Mr. Delvile, instead of pleading the cause of his son, was exerting his interest for another person, affected her so much more nearly, that notwithstanding he still continued his parading harangue, she scarcely knew even the subject of his discourse, and seized the first opportunity of a cessation to rise and take her leave.

He asked her if she would not call upon Mrs. Delvile; but desirous to be alone, she declined the invitation; he then charged her to proceed no further with Sir Robert till he had made some enquiries concerning Lord Ernolf, and graciously promising his protection and counsel, suffered her to depart.

Cecilia now perceived she might plan her rejections, or study her dignity at her leisure, for neither Mr. Delvile nor his son seemed in any haste to put her fortitude to the proof. With regard, therefore, to their plots and intentions, Mr. Monckton she found was wrong, but with respect to their conduct and sentiments, she had every reason to believe him right: and though her heart refused to rejoice in escaping a trial of its strength, her judgment was so well convinced that his painting was from the life, that she determined to conquer her partiality for young Delvile, since she looked forward to nothing but mortification in a connexion with his family.*

CHAPTER V

An Agitation

WITH this intention, and every faculty of her mind absorbed in reflecting upon the reasons which gave rise to it, she returned to Portman-square.

As her chair was carried into the hall, she observed, with some alarm, a look of consternation among the servants, and an appearance of confusion in the whole house. She was proceeding to her own room, intending to enquire of her maid if any evil had happened, when she was crossed upon the stairs by Mr. Harrel, who passed her with an air so wild and perturbed, that he hardly seemed to know her.

Frightened and amazed, she stopt short, irresolute which

way to go; but, hastily returning, he beckoned her to follow him.

She obeyed, and he led her to the library. He then shut the door, and abruptly seizing her hand, called out, "Miss Beverley, I am ruined!—I am undone!—I am blasted for ever!"

"I hope not, Sir!" said Cecilia, extremely terrified, "I hope not! Where is Mrs. Harrel?"

"O I know not! I know not!" cried he, in a frantic manner, "but I have not seen her,—I cannot see her,—I hope I shall never see her more!—"

"O fie! fie!" said Cecilia, "let me call her, I beg; you should consult with her in this distress, and seek comfort from her affection."

"From her affection?" repeated he, fiercely, "from her hatred you mean! do you not know that she, too, is ruined? Oh past redemption ruined!—and yet that I should hesitate, that I should a moment hesitate, to conclude the whole business at once!"

"How dreadful!" cried Cecilia, "what horrible thing has happened?"

"I have undone Priscilla!" cried he, "I have blasted my credit! I have destroyed—no, not yet quite destroyed myself!"

"O yet nor ever!" cried Cecilia, whose agitation now almost equalled his own, "be not so desperate, I conjure you! speak to me more intelligibly,—what does all this mean? How has it come to pass?"

"My debts!—my creditors!—one way only," striking his hand upon his forehead, "is left for me!"

"Do not say so, Sir!" said Cecilia, "you shall find many ways; pray have courage! pray speak calmly; and if you will but be more prudent, will but, in future, better regulate your affairs, I will myself undertake——"

She stopt; checked in the full career of her overflowing compassion, by a sense of the worthlessness of its object; and by the remembrance of the injunctions of Mr. Monckton.

"What will you undertake?" cried he, eagerly, "I know you are an angel!—tell me, what will you undertake?"

"I will,—" said Cecilia, hesitating, "I will speak to Mr. Monckton,—I will consult——"

"You may as well consult with every cursed creditor in the house!" interrupted he; "but do so, if you please; my disgrace must perforce reach him soon, and a short anticipation is not worth begging off."

"Are your creditors then actually in the house?"

"O yes, yes! and therefore it is high time I should be out of it!—Did you not see them?—Do they not line the hall?—They threaten me with three executions before night!—three executions unless I satisfy their immediate demands!—"

"And to what do their demands amount?"

"I know not!—I dare not ask!—to some thousand pounds, perhaps,—and I have not, at this minute, forty guineas in the house!"

"Nay, then," cried Cecilia, retreating, "I can indeed do nothing! if their demands are so high, I *ought* to do nothing."

She would then have quitted him, not more shocked at his situation, than indignant at the wilful extravagance which had occasioned it.

"Stay," cried he, "and hear me!" then, lowering his voice, "seek out," he continued, "your unfortunate friend,—go to the poor ruined Priscilla,—prepare her for tidings of horror! and do not, though you renounce Me, do not abandon Her!"

Then, fiercely passing her, he was himself leaving the room; but Cecilia, alarmed by the fury of his manner, called out, "What is it you mean? what tidings of horror? whither are you going?"

"To hell!" cried he, and rushed out of the apartment.

Cecilia screamed aloud, and conjuring him to hear her, ran after him; he paid her no regard, but, flying faster than she had power to pursue, reached his own dressing-room, shut himself into it with violence, and just as she arrived at the door, turned the key, and bolted it.

Her terror was now inexpressible; she believed him in the very act of suicide,* and her refusal of assistance seemed the signal for the deed: her whole fortune, at that moment, was valueless and unimportant to her, compared with the preservation of a fellow-creature: she called out with all the vehemence of agony to beg he would open the door, and eagerly promised by all that was sacred to do every thing in her power to save him.

As these words he opened it; his face was totally without colour, and he grasped a razor* in his hand.

"You have stopt me," said he, in a voice scarce audible, "at the very moment I had gathered courage for the blow: but if indeed you will assist me, I will shut this up,—if not, I will steep it in my blood!"

"I will! I will!" cried Cecilia, "I will do every thing you desire!"

"And quickly?"

"Immediately."

"Before my disgrace is known? and while all may yet be hushed up?"

"Yes, yes! all—any—every thing you wish!"

"Swear, then!"

Here Cecilia drew back; her recollection returned as her terror abated, and her repugnance to entering into an engagement for she knew not what, with a man whose actions she condemned, and whose principles she abhorred, made all her fright now give way to indignation, and, after a short pause, she angrily answered, "No, Sir, I will not swear!—but yet, all that is reasonable, all that is friendly——"

"Hear *me* swear, then!" interrupted he, furiously, "which at this moment I do, by every thing eternal, and by every thing infernal, that I will not outlive the seizure of my property, and that the moment I am informed there is an execution in my house, shall be the last of my existence!"

"What cruelty! what compulsion! what impiety!" cried Cecilia: "give me, however, that horrible instrument, and prescribe to me what conditions you please."

A noise was now heard below stairs, at which Cecilia, who had not dared call for help lest she should quicken his desperation, was secretly beginning to rejoice, when, starting at the sound, he exclaimed, "I believe you are too late!—the ruffians have already seized my house!" then, endeavouring to force her out of the room, "Go," he cried, "to my wife;—I want to be alone!"

"Oh give me first," cried she, "that weapon, and I will take what oath you please!"

"No, no!—go,—leave me,—" cried he, almost breathless with emotion, "I must not now be trifled with."

"I do not trifle! indeed I do not!" cried Cecilia, holding by his arm: "try, put me to the proof!"

"Swear, solemnly swear, to empty my house of these creditors this moment!"

"I *do* swear," cried she, with energy, "and Heaven prosper me as I am sincere!"

"I see, I see you are an angel!" cried he, rapturously, "and as such I worship and adore you! O you have restored me to life, and rescued me from perdition!"

"Give me, then, that fatal instrument!"

"That instrument," returned he, "is nothing, since so many others are in my power; but you have now taken from me all desire of using them. Go, then, and stop those wretches from coming to me,—send immediately for the Jew!—he will advance what money you please,—my man knows where to find him;—consult with Mr. Arnott,—speak a word of comfort to Priscilla,—but do nothing, nothing at all, till you have cleared my house of those cursed scoundrels!"

Cecilia, whose heart sunk within her at the solemn promise she had given, the mention of the Jew, and the arduous task she had undertaken, quitted him without reply, and was going to her own room, to compose her hurried spirits, and consider what steps she had to take, when hearing the noise in the hall grow louder, she stopt to listen, and catching some words that greatly alarmed her, went half way down stairs, when she was met by Davison, Mr. Harrel's man, of whom she enquired into the occasion of the disturbance.

He answered that he must go immediately to his master, for the bailiffs were coming into the house.

"Let him not know it if you value his life!" cried she, with new terror. "Where is Mr. Arnott? call him to me,—

beg him to come this moment;—I will wait for him here."

The man flew to obey her; and Cecilia, finding she had time neither for deliberation nor regret, and dreading lest Mr. Harrel, by hearing of the arrival of the bailiffs, should relapse into despair, determined to call to her aid all the courage, prudence, and judgment she possessed, and, since to act she was compelled, endeavour with her best ability, to save his credit, and retrieve his affairs.

The moment Mr. Arnott came, she ordered Davison to hasten to his master, and watch his motions.

Then, addressing Mr. Arnott, "Will you, Sir," she said, "go and tell those people that if they will instantly quit the house, every thing shall be settled, and Mr. Harrel will satisfy their demands?"

"Ah madam!" cried Mr. Arnott, mournfully, "and how? he has no means to pay them, and I have none—without ruin to myself,—to help him!"

"Send them but away," said Cecilia, "and I will myself be your security that your promise shall not be disgraced."

"Alas, madam," cried he, "what are you doing? well as I wish to Mr. Harrel, miserable as I am for my unfortunate sister, I yet cannot bear that such goodness, such beneficence should be injured!"

Cecilia, however, persisted, and with evident reluctance he obeyed her.

While she waited his return, Davison came from Mr. Harrel, who had ordered him to run instantly for the Jew.

Good Heaven, thought Cecilia, that a man so wretchedly selfish and worldly, should dare, with all his guilt upon his head,

To rush unlicenced on eternity![†] [*]

Mr. Arnott was more than half an hour with the people; and when, at last, he returned, his countenance immediately proclaimed the ill success of his errand. The creditors, he said, declared they had so frequently been deceived, that

[†] Mason's Elfrida.

they would not dismiss the bailiffs, or retire themselves, without actual payment.

"Tell them, then, Sir," said Cecilia, "to send me their accounts, and, if it be possible, I will discharge them directly."

Mr. Arnott's eyes were filled with tears at this declaration, and he protested, be the consequence to himself what it might, he would pay away every shilling he was worth, rather than witness such injustice.

"No," cried Cecilia, exerting more spirit, that she might shock him less, "I did not save Mr. Harrel, to destroy so much better a man! you have suffered but too much oppression already; the present evil is mine; and from me, at least, none I hope will ever spread to Mr. Arnott."

Mr. Arnott could not bear this; he was struck with grief, with admiration, and with gratitude, and finding his tears now refused to be restrained, he went to execute her commission in silent dejection.

The dejection, however, was encreased, though his tears were dispersed, when he returned; "Oh madam!" he cried, "all your efforts, generous as they are, will be of no avail! the bills even now in the house amount to more than 7000*l*.!"

Cecilia, amazed and confounded, started and clasped her hands, calling out, "What must I do! to what have I bound myself! and how can I answer to my conscience,—to my successors, such a disposal, such an abuse of so large a part of my fortune!"

Mr. Arnott could make no answer; and they stood looking at each other in silent irresolution, till Davison brought intelligence that the Jew was already come, and waited to speak with her.

"And what can I say to him?" cried she, more and more agitated; "I understand nothing of usury; how am I to deal with him?"

Mr. Arnott then confessed that he should himself have instantly been bail for his brother,* but that his fortune, originally not large, was now so much impaired by the many debts which from time to time he had paid for him, that as he hoped some day to have a family of his own, he dared not run a risk by which he might be utterly ruined, and the less, as his sister had at Violet Bank been prevailed upon to give up her settlement.*

This account, which explained the late uneasiness of Mrs. Harrel, still encreased the distress of Cecilia; and every moment she obtained for reflection, augmented her reluctance to parting with so large a sum of money for so worthless an object, and added strength to her resentment for the unjustifiable menaces which had extorted from her such a promise. Yet not an instant would she listen to Mr. Arnott's offer of fulfilling her engagement, and charged him, as he considered her own self-esteem worth her keeping, not to urge to her a proposal so ungenerous and selfish.

Davison now came again to hasten her, and said that the Jew was with his master, and they both impatiently expected her.

Cecilia, half distracted with her uncertainty how to act, changed colour at this message, and exclaimed "Oh Mr. Arnott, run I beseech you for Mr. Monckton! bring him hither directly,—if any body can save me it is him; but if I go back to Mr. Harrel, I know it will be all over!"

"Certainly," said Mr. Arnott, "I will run to him this moment."

"Yet no!—stop!—" cried the trembling Cecilia, "he can now do me no good,—his counsel will arrive too late to serve me,—it cannot call back the oath I have given! it cannot, compulsory* as it was, make me break it, and not be miserable for ever!"

This idea sufficed to determine her; and the apprehension of self-reproach, should the threat of Mr. Harrel be put in execution, was more insupportable to her blameless and upright mind, than any loss or diminution which her fortune could sustain.

Slowly however, with tardy and unwilling steps, her judgment repugnant, and her spirit repining, she obeyed the summons of Mr. Harrel, who, impatient of her delay, came forward to meet her.

"Miss Beverley," he cried, "there is not a moment to be lost; this good man will bring you any sum of money, upon a proper consideration, that you will command; but if he is not immediately commissioned, and these cursed fellows are not got out of my house, the affair will be blown,——and what will follow," added he, lowering his voice, "I will not again frighten you by repeating, though I shall never recant."

Cecilia turned from him in horror; and with a faltering voice and heavy heart, entreated Mr. Arnott to settle for her with the Jew.

Large as was the sum, she was so near being of age, and her security was so good, that the transaction was soon finished: 7500*l.* was received of the Jew, Mr. Harrel gave Cecilia his bond for the payment, the creditors were satisfied, the bailiffs were dismissed, and the house was soon restored to its customary appearance of splendid gaiety.

Mrs. Harrel, who during this scene had shut herself up in her own room to weep and lament, now flew to Cecilia, and in a transport of joy and gratitude, thanked her upon her knees for thus preserving her from utter ruin: the gentle Mr. Arnott seemed uncertain whether most to grieve or rejoice; and Mr. Harrel repeatedly protested she should have the sole guidance of his future conduct.

This promise, the hope of his amendment, and the joy she had expanded, somewhat revived the spirits of Cecilia; who, however, deeply affected by what had passed, hastened from them all to her own room.

She had now parted with 8050*l.* to Mr. Harrel, without any security when or how it was to be paid; and that ardour of benevolence which taught her to value her riches merely as they enabled her to do good and generous actions, was here of no avail to console or reward her, for her gift was compelled, and its receiver was all but detested. "How much better," cried she, "would this have been bestowed upon the amiable Miss Belfield! or upon her noble-minded, though proud-spirited brother! and how much less a sum would have made the virtuous and industrious Hills easy and happy for life! but here, to become the tool of the extravagance I abhor! to be made responsible for the luxury I condemn! to be liberal in opposition to my principles, and lavish in defiance of my judgment!—Oh that my much-deceived Uncle had better known to what dangerous hands he committed me! and that my weak and unhappy friend had met with a worthier protector of her virtue and safety!''

As soon, however, as she recovered from the first shock of her reflections, she turned her thoughts from herself to the formation of some plan that might, at least, render her donation of serious and lasting use. The signal service she had just done them gave her at present an ascendency over the Harrels, which she hoped, if immediately exerted, might prevent the return of so calamitous a scene, by engaging them both to an immediate change of conduct. But unequal herself to contriving expedients for this purpose that might not easily be controverted, she determined to send the next morning a petition to Mr. Monckton to call upon her, reveal to him the whole transaction, and entreat him to suggest to her what, with most probability of success, she might offer to their consideration.

While this was passing in her mind, on the evening of the day in which she had so dearly purchased the right of giving counsel, she was summoned to tea.

She found Mr. Harrel and his lady engaged in earnest discourse; as soon as she appeared, the former said, ''My dear Miss Beverley, after the extraordinary kindness you have shown me this morning, you will not, I am sure, deny me one trifling favour which I mean to ask this evening.''

''No,'' said Mrs. Harrel, ''that I am sure she will not, when she knows that our future appearance in the world depends upon her granting it.''

''I hope, then,'' said Cecilia, ''I shall not wish to refuse it.''

''It is nothing in the world,'' said Mr. Harrel, ''but to go with us to-night to the Pantheon.''

Cecilia was struck with the utmost indignation at this proposal; that the man who in the morning had an execution in his house, should languish in the evening for the amusement of a public place,—that he who but a few hours before was plunging uncalled into eternity, should, while the intended instrument of death was yet scarce cold from the grasp of his hand, deliberately court a return of his distress, by instantly recurring to the methods which had involved him in it, irritated and shocked her beyond even a wish of disguising her displeasure, and therefore, after an expressive silence, she gave a cold, but absolute denial.

"I see," said Mr. Harrel, somewhat confused, "you do not understand the motives of our request. The unfortunate affair of this morning is very likely to spread presently all over the town; the only refutation that can be given to it, is by our all appearing in public before any body knows whether to believe it or not."

"Do, my dearest friend," cried his lady, "oblige me by your compliance; indeed our whole reputation depends upon it. I made an engagement yesterday to go with Mrs. Mears, and if I disappoint her, every body will be guessing the reason."

"At least," answered Cecilia, "*my* going can answer no purpose to you: pray, therefore, do not ask me; I am ill disposed for such sort of amusement, and have by no means your opinion of its necessity."

"But if we do not *all* go," said Mr. Harrel, "we do almost nothing: you are known to live with us, and your appearance at this critical time is important to our credit. If this misfortune gets wind, the consequence is that every dirty tradesman in town to whom I owe a shilling, will be forming the same cursed combination those scoundrels formed this morning, of coming in a body, and waiting for their money, or else bringing an execution into my house. The only way to silence report is by putting a good face upon the matter at once, and shewing ourselves to the world as if nothing had happened. Favour us, therefore, to-night with your company, which is really important to us, or ten to one,* but in another fortnight, I shall be just in the same scrape."

Cecilia, however incensed at this intelligence that his debts were still so numerous, felt now as much alarmed at the mention of an execution, as if she was in actual danger of ruin herself. Terrified, therefore, though not convinced, she yielded to their persuasions, and consented to accompany them.

They soon after separated to make some alteration in their dress, and then, calling in their way for Mrs. Mears, they proceeded to the Pantheon.

CHAPTER VI

A Man of the Ton

AT the door of the Pantheon they were joined by Mr. Arnott and Sir Robert Floyer, whom Cecilia now saw with added aversion: they entered the great room during the second act of the Concert, to which as no one of the party but herself had any desire to listen, no sort of attention was paid; the ladies entertaining themselves as if no Orchestra* was in the room, and the gentlemen, with an equal disregard to it, struggling for a place by the fire, about which they continued hovering till the music was over.

Soon after they were seated, Mr. Meadows, sauntering towards them, whispered something to Mrs. Mears, who, immediately rising, introduced him to Cecilia; after which, the place next to her being vacant, he cast himself upon it, and lolling as much at his ease as his situation would permit, began something like a conversation with her.

"Have you been long in town, ma'am?"

"No, Sir."

"This is not your first winter?"

"Of being in town, it is."

"Then you have something new to see; O charming! how I envy you!—Are you pleased with the Pantheon?"

"Very much; I have seen no building at all equal to it."

"You have not been abroad. Travelling is the ruin of all happiness! There's no looking at a building here after seeing Italy."

"Does all happiness, then, depend upon the sight of buildings?" said Cecilia, when, turning towards her companion, she perceived him yawning, with such evident inattention to her answer, that not chusing to interrupt his reverie, she turned her head another way.

For some minutes he took no notice of this; and then, as if suddenly recollecting himself, he called out hastily "I beg your pardon, ma'am, you were saying something?"

"No, Sir, nothing worth repeating."

"O pray don't punish me so severely as not to let me hear it!"

Cecilia, though merely not to seem offended at his negligence, was then again beginning an answer, when, looking at him as she spoke, she perceived that he was biting his nails with so absent an air, that he appeared not to know he had asked any question. She therefore broke off, and left him to his cogitation.

Sometime after he addressed her again, saying "Don't you find this place extremely tiresome, ma'am?"

"Yes, Sir," said she, half laughing, "it is, indeed, not very entertaining!"

"Nothing is entertaining," answered he, "for two minutes together. Things are so little different one from another, that there is no making pleasure out of any thing. We go the same dull round for ever; nothing new, no variety! all the same thing over again! Are you fond of public places, ma'am?"

"Yes, Sir, *soberly*, as Lady Grace says."*

"Then I envy you extremely, for you have some amusement always in your power. How desirable that is!"

"And have you not the same resources?"

"O no! I am tired to death! tired of every thing! I would give the universe for a disposition less difficult to please. Yet, after all, what is there to give pleasure? When one has seen one thing, one has seen every thing. O, 'tis heavy work! Don't you find it so ma'am?"

This speech was ended with so violent a fit of yawning, that Cecilia would not trouble herself to answer it: but her silence, as before, passed wholly unnoticed, exciting neither question nor comment.

A long pause now succeeded, which he broke at last, by saying, as he writhed himself about upon his seat, "These

forms* would be much more agreeable if there were backs
to them. 'Tis intolerable to be forced to sit like a school-boy.
The first study of life is ease. There is, indeed, no other
study that pays the trouble of attainment. Don't you think
so, ma'am?''

"But may not even that," said Cecilia, "by so much
study, become labour?''

"I am vastly happy you think so."

"Sir?"

"I beg your pardon, ma'am, but I thought you said——I
really beg your pardon, but I was thinking of something
else.''

"You did very right, Sir," said Cecilia, laughing, "for
what I said by no means merited any attention.''

"Will you do me the favour to repeat it?" cried he, taking
out his glass* to examine some lady at a distance.

"O no," said Cecilia, "that would be trying your
patience too severely.''

"These glasses shew one nothing but defects," said he; "I
am sorry they were ever invented. They are the ruin of all
beauty; no complexion can stand them. I believe that solo
will never be over! I hate a solo; it sinks, it depresses me
intolerably.''

"You will presently, Sir," said Cecilia, looking at the bill
of the concert, "have a full piece; and that, I hope, will
revive you.''

"A full piece! oh insupportable! it stuns, it fatigues, it
overpowers me beyond endurance! no taste in it, no
delicacy, no room for the smallest feeling.''

"Perhaps, then, you are only fond of singing?''

"I should be, if I could hear it; but we are now so
miserably off in voices, that I hardly ever attempt to listen
to a song, without fancying myself deaf from the feebleness
of the performers. I hate every thing that requires attention.
Nothing gives pleasure that does not force its own way.''

"You only, then, like loud voices, and great powers?''

"O worse and worse!——no, nothing is so disgusting to
me. All my amazement is that these people think it worth
while to give Concerts at all; one is sick to death of music.''

"Nay," cried Cecilia, "if it gives no pleasure, at least it takes none away; for, far from being any impediment to conversation, I think every body talks more during the performance than between the acts. And what is there better you could substitute in its place?"

Cecilia, receiving no answer to this question, again looked round to see if she had been heard; when she observed her new acquaintance, with a very thoughtful air, had turned from her to fix his eyes upon the statue of Britannia.

Very soon after, he hastily arose, and seeming entirely to forget that he had spoke* to her, very abruptly walked away.

Mr. Gosport, who was advancing to Cecilia, and had watched part of this scene, stopt him as he was retreating, and said "Why Meadows, how's this? are you caught at last?"

"O worn to death! worn to a thread!" cried he, stretching himself, and yawning; "I have been talking with a young lady to entertain her! O such heavy work! I would not go through it again for millions!"

"What, have you talked yourself out of breath?"

"No; but the effort! the effort!—O, it has unhinged me for a fortnight!—Entertaining a young lady!—one had better be a galley-slave at once!"

"Well but, did she not pay your toils? She is surely a sweet creature."

"Nothing can pay one for such insufferable exertion! though she's well enough, too,—better than the common run,—but shy, quite too shy; no drawing her out."

"I thought that was to your taste. You commonly hate much volubility. How have I heard you bemoan yourself when attacked by Miss Larolles!"

"Larolles? O distraction! She talks me into a fever in two minutes. But so it is for ever! nothing but extremes to be met with! common girls are too forward, this lady is too reserved——always some fault! always some drawback! nothing ever perfect!"

"Nay, nay," cried Mr. Gosport, "you do not know her; she is perfect enough in all conscience."

"Better not know her, then," answered he, again

yawning, "for she cannot be pleasing. Nothing perfect is natural;—I hate every thing out of nature."

He then strolled on, and Mr. Gosport approached Cecilia.

"I have been wishing," cried he, "to address you this half hour, but as you were engaged with Mr. Meadows, I did not dare advance."

"O, I see your malice!" cried Cecilia; "you were determined to add weight to the value of your company, by making me fully sensible where the balance would preponderate."

"Nay, if you do not admire Mr. Meadows," cried he, "you must not even whisper it to the winds."

"Is he, then, so very admirable?"

"O, he is now in the very height of fashionable favour: his dress is a model, his manners are imitated, his attention is courted, and his notice is envied."

"Are you not laughing?"

"No, indeed; his privileges are much more extensive than I have mentioned: his decision fixes the exact limits between what is vulgar and what is elegant, his praise gives reputation, and a word from him in public confers fashion!"

"And by what wonderful powers has he acquired such influence?"

"By nothing but a happy art in catching the reigning foibles of the times, and carrying them to an extreme yet more absurd than any one had done before him. Ceremony, he found, was already exploded for ease, he, therefore, exploded ease for indolence; devotion to the fair sex, had given way to a more equal and rational intercourse, which, to push still farther, he presently exchanged for rudeness; joviality, too, was already banished for philosophical indifference, and that, therefore, he discarded, for weariness and disgust."

"And is it possible that qualities such as these should recommend him to favour and admiration?"

"Very possible, for qualities such as these constitute the present taste of the times. A man of the *Ton*, who would now be conspicuous in the gay world, must invariably be insipid, negligent, and selfish."

"Admirable requisites!" cried Cecilia; "and Mr. Meadows, I acknowledge, seems to have attained them all."

"He must never," continued Mr. Gosport, "confess the least pleasure from any thing, a total apathy being the chief ingredient of his character; he must, upon no account, sustain a conversation with any spirit, lest he should appear, to his utter disgrace, interested in what is said: and when he is quite tired of his existence, from a total vacuity of ideas, he must affect a look of absence, and pretend, on the sudden, to be wholly lost in thought."

"I would not wish," said Cecilia, laughing, "a more amiable companion!"

"If he is asked his opinion of any lady," he continued, "he must commonly answer by a grimace; and if he is seated next to one, he must take the utmost pains to shew by his listlessness, yawning and inattention, that he is sick of his situation; for what he holds of all things to be most gothic,* is gallantry to the women. To avoid this is, indeed, the principal solicitude of his life. If he sees a lady in distress for her carriage, he is to enquire of her what is the matter, and then, with a shrug, wish her well through her fatigues, wink at some byestander, and walk away. If he is in a room where there is a crowd of company, and a scarcity of seats, he must early ensure one of the best in the place, be blind to all looks of fatigue, and deaf to all hints of assistance, and seeming totally to forget himself, lounge at his ease, and appear an unconscious spectator of what is going forward. If he is at a ball where there are more women than men, he must decline dancing at all, though it should happen to be his favourite amusement, and smiling as he passes the disengaged young ladies, wonder to see them sit still, and perhaps ask them the reason!"

"A most alluring character indeed!" cried Cecilia; "and pray how long have these been the accomplishments of a fine gentleman?"

"I am but an indifferent chronologer of the modes,"* he answered, "but I know it has been long enough to raise just expectations that some new folly will be started soon, by which the present race of INSENSIBLISTS may be driven out. Mr. Meadows is now at the head of this sect, as Miss Larolles is of the VOLUBLE, and Miss Leeson of the SUPERCILIOUS.* But this way comes another, who, though in a different manner, labours with the same view, and aspires at the same reward, which stimulate the ambition of this happy *Triplet*,* that of exciting wonder by peculiarity, and envy by wonder."

This description announced Capt. Aresby; who, advancing from the fire-place, told Cecilia how much he rejoiced in seeing her, said he had been *reduced to despair* by so long missing that honour, and that he had feared she *made it a principle* to avoid coming in public, having sought her in vain *partout*.

He then smiled, and strolled on to another party.

"And pray of what sect," said Cecilia, "is this gentleman?"

"Of the sect of JARGONISTS,"* answered Mr. Gosport; "he has not an ambition beyond paying a passing compliment, nor a word to make use of that he has not picked up at public places. Yet this dearth of language, however you may despise it, is not merely owing to a narrow capacity: foppery and conceit have their share in the limitation, for though his phrases are almost always ridiculous or misapplied, they are selected with much study, and introduced with infinite pains."*

"Poor man!" cried Cecilia, "is it possible it can cost him any trouble to render himself so completely absurd?"

"Yes; but not more than it costs his neighbours to keep him in countenance. Miss Leeson, since she has presided over the sect of the SUPERCILIOUS, spends at least half her life in wishing the annihilation of the other half; for as she must only speak in her own Coterie, she is compelled to be frequently silent, and therefore, having nothing to think of, she is commonly gnawn with self-denial, and soured with want of amusement: Miss Larolles, indeed, is better off, for in talking faster than she thinks, she has but followed the natural bent of her disposition: as to this poor JARGONIST, he has, I must own, rather a hard task, from the continual restraint of speaking only out of his own

Liliputian vocabulary,* and denying himself the relief of ever uttering one word by the call of occasion: but what hardship is that, compared with what is borne by Mr. Meadows? who, since he commenced INSENSIBLIST, has never once dared to be pleased, nor ventured for a moment to look in good humour!"

"Surely, then," said Cecilia, "in a short time, the punishment of this affectation will bring its cure."

"No; for the trick grows into habit, and habit is a second nature. A secret idea of fame makes his forbearance of happiness supportable to him: for he has now the self-satisfaction of considering himself raised to that highest pinnacle of fashionable refinement which is built upon apathy and scorn, and from which, proclaiming himself superior to all possibility of enjoyment, he views the whole world with contempt! holding neither beauty, virtue, wealth nor power of importance sufficient to kindle the smallest emotion!"

"O that they could all round listen to you!" cried Cecilia; "they would soon, I think, sicken of their folly, if they heard it thus admirably exposed."

"No; they would but triumph that it had obtained them so much notice!—But pray do you see that gentleman, or don't you chuse to know him, who has been bowing to you this half hour?"

"Where?" cried Cecilia, and, looking round, perceived Mr. Morrice; who, upon her returning his salutation, instantly approached her, though he had never ventured to shew himself at Mr. Harrel's, since his unfortunate accident on the evening of the masquerade.

Entirely casting aside the easy familiarity at which he had latterly arrived, he enquired after her health with the most fearful diffidence, and then, bowing profoundly, was modestly retiring; when Mrs. Harrel, perceiving him, smiled with so much good-humour, that he gathered courage to return and address her, and found her, to his infinite delight, as obliging and civil as ever.

The Concert was now over; the ladies arose, and the gentlemen joined them. Morrice, at sight of Mr. Harrel, was again shrinking; but Mr. Harrel, immediately shaking hands with him, enquired what had kept him so long from Portman-Square? Morrice then, finding, to his great surprise, that no one had thought more of the mischief but himself who had committed it, joyously discarded his timidity, and became as sprightly as before his mortification.

A motion was now made for going to the tea-room; and as they walked on, Cecilia, in looking up to examine the building, saw in one of the galleries young Delvile, and almost at the same time caught his eye.

Scarcely now did a moment elapse before he joined her. The sight of him, strongly reviving in her mind the painful contrariety of opinion with which she had lately thought of him, the sentiments so much in his favour which but a few days before she had encouraged, and which it was only that morning she had endeavoured to crush, made her meet him with a kind of melancholy that almost induced her to lament he was amiable, and repine that she knew none like him.

His appearance, mean time, was far different; he seemed enchanted at the sight of her, he flew eagerly to meet her, and his eyes sparkled with pleasure as he approached her; a pleasure neither moderate nor disguised, but lively, unrestrained, and expressive.

Cecilia, whose plans since she had last seen him had twice varied, who first had looked forward to being united with him for ever, and afterwards had determined to avoid with him even a common acquaintance, could not, while these thoughts were all recurring to her memory, receive much delight from observing his gaiety, or feel at all gratified by his unembarrassed manners. The openness of his attentions, and the frankness of his admiration, which hitherto had charmed her as marks of the sincerity of his character, now shocked her as proofs of the indifference of his heart, which feeling for her a mere common regard, that affected neither his spirits nor his peace, he manifested without scruple, since it was not accompanied with even a wish beyond the present hour.

She now, too, recollected that such had always been his conduct, one single and singular moment excepted, when,

as he gave to her his letter for Mr. Belfield, he seemed struck
as she was herself by the extraordinary co-incidence of their
ideas and proceedings: that emotion, however, she now
regarded as casual and transitory, and seeing him so much
happier than herself, she felt ashamed of her delusion, and
angry at her easy captivation.

Reflections such as these, though they added fresh
motives to her resolution of giving up all thoughts of his
alliance, were yet so humiliating, that they robbed her of all
power of receiving pleasure from what was passing, and
made her forget that the place she was in was even intended
for a place of entertainment.

Young Delvile, after painting in lively colours the loss his
house had sustained by her quitting it, and dwelling with
equal force upon the regret of his mother and his own, asked
in a low voice if she would do him so much honour as to
introduce him to Mr. Harrel; "As the son," added he, of
a brother guardian, I think I have a kind of claim to his
acquaintance."

Cecilia could not refuse, though as the request was likely
to occasion more frequent meetings, she persuaded herself
she was unwilling to comply. The ceremony therefore past,
and was again repeated with Mrs. Harrel, who, though she
had several times seen him, had never been formally made
known to him.

The Harrels were both of them much pleased at this mark
of civility in a young man whose family had prepared them
rather to expect his scorn, and expressed their wishes that he
would drink his tea in their party; he accepted their
invitation with alacrity, and turning to Cecilia, said "Have
I not skilfully timed my introduction? But though you have
done me this honour with Mr. and Mrs. Harrel, I must not
yet, I presume, entreat you to extend it to a certain happy
gentleman of this company;" glancing his eyes towards Sir
Robert Floyer.

"No, Sir," answered she, with quickness, "yet, nor
ever!"

They were now at the door leading down stairs to the tea-
room. Cecilia saw that Sir Robert, who had hitherto been

engaged with some gentlemen, seemed to be seeking her; and the remembrance of the quarrel which had followed her refusal of his assistance at the Opera-house, obliged her to determine, should he offer it again, to accept it: but the same brutality which forced this intention, contributed to render it repugnant to her, and she resolved if possible to avoid him, by hurrying down stairs before he reached her. She made, therefore, a sudden attempt to slip through the crowd, and as she was light and active, she easily succeeded; but though her hasty motion separated her from the rest of her party, Delvile, who was earnestly looking at her, to discover her meaning in the disclaiming speech she made about Sir Robert, saw into her design, but suffered her not to go alone; he contrived in a moment to follow and join her, while she was stopping at the foot of the stairs for Mrs. Harrel.

"Why what a little thief you are," cried he, "to run away from us thus! what do you think Sir Robert will say? I saw him looking for you at the very instant of your flight."

"Then you saw at the same time," said Cecilia, "the reason of it."

"Will you give me leave," cried he, laughing, "to repeat this to my Lord Ernolf?"

"You may repeat it, Sir, if you please," said Cecilia, piqued that he had not rather thought of himself than of Lord Ernolf, "to the whole Pantheon."

"And if I should," cried he, "half of it, at least, would thank me; and to obtain the applause of so noble an assembly, what would it signify that Sir Robert should cut my throat?"

"I believe," said Cecilia, deeply mortified by a raillery that shewed so little interest in her avowal of indifference, "you are determined to make me as sick of that man's name, as I am of his conversation."

"And is it possible," exclaimed Delvile, in a tone of surprise, "that such can be your opinion, and yet, situated as you are, the whole world at your command, and all mankind at your devotion——but I am answering you seriously, when you are only speaking by rule."

"What rule, Sir?"

"That which young ladies, upon certain occasions, always prescribe themselves."

Here they were interrupted by the arrival of the rest of the company; though not before Cecilia had received some little consolation for her displeasure, by finding that young Delvile still supposed she was engaged, and flattering herself his language would be different were he informed of the contrary.

Morrice now undertook to procure them a table for tea, which, as the room was very full, was not easily done; and while they were waiting his success, Miss Larolles, who from the stairs had perceived Cecilia, came running up to her, and taking her hand, called out "Lord, my dear creature, who'd have thought of seeing you here? I was never so surprised in my life! I really thought you was gone into a convent,* it's so extreme long since I've seen you. But of all things in the world, why was you not at Lady Nyland's last assembly? I thought of asking Mr. Harrel fifty times why you did not come, but it always went out of my head. You've no notion how excessively I was disappointed."

"You are very obliging," said Cecilia laughing, "but I hope, since you so often forgot it, the disappointment did much lessen your entertainment."*

"O Lord no! I was never so happy in my life. There was such a crowd, you could not move a finger. Every body in the world was there. You've no idea how delightful it was. I thought verily I should have fainted with the heat."

"That was delightful indeed! And how long did you stay?"

"Why we danced till three in the morning. We began with Cotillons, and finished with country dances. It was the most elegant thing you ever saw in your life; every thing quite in a style. I was so monstrously fatigued, I could hardly get through the last dance. I really thought I should have dropt down dead. Only conceive dancing five hours in such a monstrous crowd! I assure you when I got home my feet were all blisters. You have no idea how they smarted."

"And whence comes it," cried young Delvile, "that *you* partake so little of these delights?"

"Because I fear," answered Cecilia, "I came too late into the school of fashion to be a ductile pupil."

"Do you know," continued Miss Larolles, "Mr. Meadows has not spoke one word to me all the evening! Though I am sure he saw me, for I sat at the outside on purpose* to speak to a person or two, that I knew would be strolling about; for if one sits on the inside, there's no speaking to a creature, you know, so I never do it at the Opera, nor in the boxes at Ranelagh, nor any where. It's the shockingest thing you can conceive to be made sit in the middle of those forms; one might as well be at home, for nobody can speak to one."

"But you don't seem to have had much better success," said Cecilia, "in keeping at the outside."

"O yes I have, for I got a little chat with two or three people as they were passing, for, you know, when one sits there, they can't help saying something; though I assure you all the men are so excessively odd they don't care whether they speak to one or no. As to Mr. Meadows, he's really enough to provoke one to death. I suppose he's in one of his absent fits. However, I assure you I think it's extreme impertinent of him, and so I shall tell Mr. Sawyer, for I know he'll make a point of telling him of it again."

"I rather think," said Cecilia, "the best would be to return the compliment in kind, and when he next recollects you, appear to have forgotten him."

"O Lord, that's a very good notion! so I will, I declare. But you can't conceive how glad I am the Concert's over; for I assure you, though I sat as near the fire as possible, I was so extreme cold you've no idea, for Mr. Meadows never would let me have the least peep at it. I declare I believe he does it on purpose to plague one, for he grows worse and worse every day. You can't think how I hate him!"

"Not easily, I believe indeed!" said Cecilia, archly.

"O do but look!" resumed the fair VOLUBLE, "if there is not Mrs. Mears in her old red gown again! I begin to think she'll never have another. I wish she was to have an execution in her house, if it was only to get rid of it! I am so fatigued with the sight of it you can't conceive."

Mr. Morrice now brought intelligence that he had secured one side of a table which would very well accommodate the ladies; and that the other side was only occupied by one gentleman, who, as he was not drinking tea himself, would doubtless give up his place when the party appeared.

Miss Larolles then ran back to her own set, and the rest followed Mr. Morrice: Mrs. Harrel, Mrs. Mears and Cecilia took their places. The gentleman opposite to them proved to be Mr. Meadows: Morrice, therefore, was much deceived in his expectations, for, far from giving up his place, he had flung himself all along upon the form in such a lounging posture, while he rested one arm upon the table, that, not contented with merely keeping his own seat, he filled up a space meant for three.

Mr. Harrel had already walked off to another party: Delvile stood aloof for some minutes, expecting Sir Robert Floyer would station himself behind Cecilia; but Sir Robert, who would scarce have thought such a condescension due to a princess, disdained any appearance of assiduity, even while he made it his care to publish his pretensions: and therefore, finding no accommodation to please him, he stalked towards some gentlemen in another part of the room. Delvile then took the post he had neglected, and Mr. Arnott, who had not had courage to make any effort in his own favour, modestly stood near him. Cecilia contrived to make room for Mr. Gosport next to herself, and Morrice was sufficiently happy in being allowed to call the waiters, superintend the provisions, and serve the whole party.

The task of making tea fell upon Cecilia, who being somewhat incommoded by the vicinity of her neighbours, Mrs. Mears called out to Mr. Meadows "Do pray, Sir, be so good as to make room for one of us at your side."

Mr. Meadows, who was indolently picking his teeth, and examining them with a tooth pick case glass,* did not, at first, seem to hear her; and when she repeated her request, he only looked at her, and said "umph?"

"Now really, Mr. Meadows," said she, "when you see any ladies in such distress, I wonder how you can forbear helping them."

"In distress, are you?" cried he, with a vacant smile, "pray what's the matter?"

"Don't you see? we are so crowded we can hardly sit."

"Can't you?" cried he, "upon my honour it's very shameful that these people don't contrive some seats more convenient."

"Yes," said Mrs. Mears; "but if you would be so kind as to let somebody else sit by you we should not want any contrivance."

Here Mr. Meadows was seized with a furious fit of yawning, which as much diverted Cecilia and Mr. Gosport, as it offended Mrs. Mears, who with great displeasure added, "Indeed, Mr. Meadows, it's very strange that you never hear what's said to you."

"I beg your pardon," said he, "were you speaking to me?" and again began picking his teeth.

Morrice, eager to contrast his civility with the inattention of Mr. Meadows, now flew round to the other side of the table, and calling out "let *me* help you, Miss Beverley, I can make tea better than any body," he lent over that part of the form which Mr. Meadows had occupied with one of his feet, in order to pour it out himself: but Mr. Meadows, by an unfortunate removal of his foot, bringing him forwarder than he was prepared to go, the tea pot and its contents were overturned immediately opposite to Cecilia.

Young Delvile, who saw the impending evil, from an impetuous impulse to prevent her suffering by it, hastily drew her back, and bending down before her, secured her preservation by receiving himself the mischief with which she was threatened.

Mrs. Mears and Mrs. Harrel vacated their seats in a moment, and Mr. Gosport and Mr. Arnott assisted in clearing the table, and removing Cecilia, who was very slightly hurt, and at once surprised, ashamed and pleased at the manner in which she had been saved.

Young Delvile, though a sufferer from his gallantry, the hot water having penetrated through his coat to his arm and shoulder, was at first insensible to his situation, from an apprehension that Cecilia had not wholly escaped; and his enquiries were so eager and so anxious, made with a look of such solicitude, and a voice of such alarm, that, equally astonished and gratified, she secretly blest the accident which had given birth to his uneasiness, however she grieved for its consequence to himself.

But no sooner was he satisfied of her safety, than he felt himself obliged to retire; yet attributing to inconvenience what was really the effect of pain, he hurried away with an appearance of sport, saying, "There is something, I must own, rather *unknightly* in quitting the field for a wet jacket, but the company, I hope, will only give me credit for flying away to Ranelagh. So

> Like a brave general after being beat,
> I'll exult and rejoice in a prudent retreat.[†] [*]

He then hastened to his carriage: and poor Morrice, frightened and confounded at the disaster he had occasioned, sneaked after him, with much less ceremony. While Mr. Meadows, wholly unconcerned by the distress and confusion around him, sat quietly picking his teeth, and looking on, during the whole transaction, with an unmeaning stare, that made it doubtful whether he had even perceived it.

Order being now soon restored, the ladies finished their tea, and went up stairs. Cecilia, to whom the late accident had afforded much new and interesting matter for reflection, wished immediately to have returned home, but she was not the leader of the party, and therefore could not make the proposal.

They then strolled through all the apartments, and having walked about till the fashionable time of retiring, they were joined by Sir Robert Floyer, and proceeded to the little room near the entrance to the great one, in order to wait for their carriages.

Here Cecilia again met Miss Larolles, who came to make various remarks, and infinite ridicule, upon sundry unfashionable or uncostly articles in the dresses of the

[†] Smart.

surrounding company; as well as to complain, with no little resentment, that Mr. Meadows was again standing before the fire!

Captain Aresby also advanced, to tell her he was quite *abattu* by having so long lost sight of her, to hope she *would make a renounce* of mortifying the world by discarding it, and to protest he had waited for his carriage till he was actually upon the point of being *acablé*.

In the midst of this *jargon*, to which the fulness of Cecilia's mind hardly permitted her to listen, there suddenly appeared at the door of the apartment, Mr. Albany, who, with his usual austerity of countenance, stopt to look round upon the company.

"Do you see," cried Mr. Gosport to Cecilia, "who approaches? your poor *sycophants** will again be taken to task, and I, for one, tremble at the coming storm!"

"O Lord," cried Miss Larolles, "I wish I was safe in my chair! that man always frightens me out of my senses. You've no notion what disagreeable things he says to one. I assure you I've no doubt but he's crazy; and I'm always in the shockingest fright in the world for fear he should be taken with a fit while I'm near him."

"It is really a petrifying thing," said the Captain, "that one can go to no *spectacle* without the *horreur* of being *obsedé* by that person! if he comes this way, I shall certainly make a renounce, and retire."

"Why so?" said Sir Robert, "what the d—l do you mind him for?"

"O he is the greatest bore in nature!" cried the Captain, "and I always do *mon possible* to avoid him; for he breaks out into such barbarous phrases, that I find myself *degouté* with him in a moment."

"O, I assure you," said Miss Larolles, "he attacks one sometimes in a manner you've no idea. One day he came up to me all of a sudden, and asked me what good I thought I did by dressing so much? Only conceive how shocking!"

"O, I have had the *horreur* of questions of that sort from him *sans fin*," said the Captain; "once he took the liberty to ask me, what service I was of to the world! and another time, he desired me to inform him whether I had ever made any poor person pray for me! and, in short, he has so frequently inconvenienced me by his impertinences, that he really bores me to a degree."

"That's just the thing that makes him hunt you down," said Sir Robert; "if he were to ask me questions for a month together, I should never trouble myself to move a muscle."

"The matter of his discourse," said Mr. Gosport, "is not more singular than the manner, for without any seeming effort or consciousness, he runs into blank verse perpetually. I have made much enquiry about him, but all I am able to learn, is that he was certainly confined, at one part of his life, in a private mad-house:* and though now, from not being mischievous, he is set at liberty, his looks, language, and whole behaviour, announce the former injury of his intellects."

"O Lord," cried Miss Larolles, half-screaming, "what shocking notions you put in one's head! I declare I dare say I sha'n't get safe home for him, for I assure you I believe he's taken a spite to me! and all because one day, before I knew of his odd ways, I happened to fall a laughing at his going about in that old coat. Do you know it put him quite in a passion! only conceive how ill-natured!"

"O he has distressed me," exclaimed the Captain, with a shrug, "*partout!* and found so much fault with every thing I have done, that I should really be glad to have the honour to cut,* for the moment he comes up to me, I know what I have to expect!"

"But I must tell you," cried Miss Larolles, "how monstrously he put me in a fright one evening when I was talking with Miss Moffat. Do you know, he came up to us, and asked what we were saying! and because we could not think in a minute of something to answer him, he said he supposed we were only talking some scandal, and so we had better go home, and employ ourselves in working for the poor!* only think how horrid! and after that, he was so excessive impertinent in his remarks, there was quite no bearing him. I assure you he cut me up so you've no notion."

Here Mr. Albany advanced; and every body but Sir Robert moved out of the way.

Fixing his eyes upon Cecilia, with an expression *more in sorrow than in anger*,* after contemplating her some time in silence, he exclaimed, "Ah lovely, but perishable flower! how long will that ingenuous countenance, wearing, because wanting no disguise, look responsive of the whiteness of the region within? How long will that air of innocence irradiate your whole appearance? unspoilt by prosperity, unperverted by power! pure in the midst of surrounding depravity! unsullied in the tainted air of infectious perdition!"

The confusion of Cecilia at this public address, which drew upon her the eyes and attention of all the company, was inexpressible; she arose from her seat, covered with blushes, and saying, "I fancy the carriage must be ready," pressed forward to quit the room, followed by Sir Robert, who answered, "No, no, they'll call it when it comes up. Arnott, will you go and see where it is?"

Cecilia stopt, but whispered Mrs. Harrel to stand near her.

"And whither," cried Albany indignantly, "whither wouldst thou go? Art thou already disdainful of my precepts? and canst thou not one short moment spare from the tumultuous folly which encircles thee? Many and many are the hours thou mayst spend with such as these; the world, alas! is full of them; weary not then, so soon, of an old man that would admonish thee,—he cannot call upon thee long, for soon he will be called upon himself!"

This solemn exhortation extremely distressed her; and fearing to still further offend him by making another effort to escape, she answered in a low voice, "I will not only hear, but thank you for your precepts, if you will forbear to give them before so many witnesses."

"Whence," cried he sternly, "these vain and superficial distinctions? Do you not dance in public? What renders you more conspicuous? Do you not dress to be admired, and walk to be observed? Why then this fantastical scruple, unjustified by reason, unsupported by analogy? Is folly only to be published? Is vanity alone to be exhibited? Oh slaves of senseless contradiction! Oh feeble followers of yet feebler prejudice! daring to be wicked, yet fearing to be wise; dauntless in levity, yet shrinking from the name of virtue!''

The latter part of this speech, during which he turned with energy to the whole company, raised such a general alarm, that all the ladies hastily quitted the room, and all the gentlemen endeavoured to enter it, equally curious to see the man who made the oration, and the lady to whom it was addressed. Cecilia, therefore, found her situation unsupportable; "I must go," she cried, "whether there is a carriage or not! pray, Mrs. Harrel, let us go!"

Sir Robert then offered to take her hand, which she was extremely ready to give him; but while the crowd made their passage difficult, Albany, following and stopping her, said, "What is it you fear? a miserable old man, worn out by the sorrows of that experience from which he offers you counsel? What, too, is it you trust? a libertine wretch, coveting nothing but your wealth, for the gift of which he will repay you by the perversion of your principles!"

"What the d—l do you mean by that?" cried the Baronet.

"To shew," answered he, austerely, "the inconsistency of false delicacy; to shew how those who are too timid for truth, can fearless meet licentiousness."

"For Heaven's sake, Sir," cried Cecilia, "say no more to me now! call upon me in Portman-square when you please,—reprove me in whatever you think me blameable, I shall be grateful for your instructions, and bettered, perhaps, by your care;—but lessons and notice thus public can do me nothing but injury."

"How happy," cried he, "were no other injury near thee! spotless were then the hour of thy danger, bright, fair and refulgent thy passage to security! the Good would receive thee with praise, the Guilty would supplicate thy prayers, the Poor would follow thee with blessings, and Children would be taught by thy example!"

He then quitted her, every body making way as he moved, and proceeded into the great room. Mrs. Harrel's carriage being also announced at the same time, Cecilia lost not an instant in hastening away.

Sir Robert, as he conducted her, disdainfully laughed at the adventure, which the general licence allowed to Mr. Albany prevented his resenting, and which therefore he scorned to appear moved at.

Mrs. Harrel could talk of nothing else, neither was Cecilia disposed to change the subject, for the remains of insanity which seemed to hang upon him were affecting without being alarming, and her desire to know more of him grew every instant stronger.

This desire, however, outlived not the conversation to which it gave rise; when she returned to her own room, no vestige of it remained upon her mind, which a nearer concern and deeper interest wholly occupied.

The behaviour of young Delvile had pained, pleased, and disturbed her; his activity to save her from mischief might proceed merely from gallantry or good nature; upon that, therefore, she dwelt little: but his eagerness, his anxiety, his insensibility to himself, were more than good breeding could claim, and seemed to spring from a motive less artificial.

She now, therefore, believed that her partiality was returned; and this belief had power to shake all her resolves, and enfeeble all her objections. The arrogance of Mr. Delvile lessened in her reflections, the admonitions of Mr. Monckton abated in their influence. With the first she considered that though connected she need not live, and for the second, though she acknowledged the excellence of his judgment, she concluded him wholly ignorant of her sentiments of Delvile; which she imagined, when once revealed, would make every obstacle to the alliance seem trifling, when put in competition with mutual esteem and affection.

CHAPTER VII

A Reproof

THE attention of Cecilia to her own affairs, did not make her forgetful of those of the Harrels: and the morning after the busy day which was last recorded, as soon as she quitted the breakfast-room, she began a note to Mr. Monckton, but was interrupted with information that he was already in the house.

She went to him immediately, and had the satisfaction of finding him alone: but desirous as she was to relate to him the transactions of the preceding day, there was in his countenance a gravity so unusual, that her impatience was involuntarily checked, and she waited first to hear if he had himself any thing to communicate.

He kept her not long in suspense; "Miss Beverley," he said, "I bring you intelligence which though I know you will be very sorry to hear, it is absolutely necessary should be told you immediately: you may otherwise, from however laudable motives, be drawn into some action which you may repent for life."

"What now!" cried Cecilia, much alarmed.

"All that I suspected," said he, "and more than I hinted to you, is true; Mr. Harrel is a ruined man! he is not worth a groat, and he is in debt beyond what he ever possessed."

Cecilia made no answer: she knew but too fatally the desperate state of his affairs, yet that *his debts were more than he had ever possessed*, she had not thought possible.

"My enquiries," continued he, "have been among principals, and such as would not dare deceive me. I hastened, therefore, to you, that this timely notice might enforce the injunctions I gave you when I had the pleasure of seeing you last, and prevent a misjudging generosity from leading you into any injury of your own fortune, for a man who is past all relief from it, and who cannot be saved, even though you were to be destroyed for his sake."

"You are very good," said Cecilia, "but your counsel is now too late!" She then briefly acquainted him with what passed, and with how large a sum she had parted.

He heard her with rage, amazement, and horror: and after inveighing against Mr. Harrel in the bitterest terms, he said, "But why, before you signed your name to so base an imposition, could you not send for me?"

"I wished, I meant to have done it," cried she, "but I

thought the time past when you could help me; how, indeed, could you have saved me? my word was given, given with an oath the most solemn, and the first I have ever taken in my life."

"An oath so forced," answered he, "the most delicate conscience would have absolved you from performing. You have, indeed, been grossly imposed upon, and pardon me if I add unaccountably to blame. Was it not obvious that relief so circumstanced must be temporary? If his ruin had been any thing less than certain, what tradesmen would have been insolent?* You have therefore deprived yourself of the power of doing good to a worthier object, merely to grant a longer date to extravagance and villainy."

"Yet how," cried Cecilia, deeply touched by this reproof, "how could I do otherwise? Could I see a man in the agonies of despair, hear him first darkly hint his own destruction, and afterwards behold him almost in the very act of suicide, the instrument of self-murder in his desperate hand—and yet, though he put his life in my power, though he told me I could preserve him, and told me he had no other reliance or resource, could I leave him to his dreadful despondence, refuse my assisting hand to raise him from perdition,* and, to save what, after all, I am well able to spare, suffer a fellow-creature, who flung himself upon my mercy, to offer up his last accounts with an action blacker than any which had preceded it?—No, I cannot repent what I have done, though I lament, indeed, that the object was not more deserving."

"Your representation," said Mr. Monckton, "like every thing else that I ever heard you utter, breathes nothing but benevolence and goodness: but your pity has been abused, and your understanding imposed upon. Mr. Harrel had no intention to destroy himself; the whole was an infamous trick, which, had not your generosity been too well known, would never have been played."

"I cannot think quite so ill of him," said Cecilia, "nor for the world would I have risked my own future reproaches by trusting to such a suspicion, which, had it proved wrong, and had Mr. Harrel, upon my refusal, committed the fatal deed, would have made his murder upon my own conscience rest for ever! surely the experiment would have been too hazardous, when the consequence had all my future peace in its power.''

"It is impossible not to revere your scruples," said Mr. Monckton, "even while I consider them as causeless; for causeless they undoubtedly were: the man who could act so atrocious a part, who could so scandalously pillage a young lady who was his guest and his ward, take advantage of her temper for the plunder of her fortune, and extort her compliance by the basest and most dishonourable arts, meant only to terrify her into compliance, for he can be nothing less than a downright and thorough scoundrel, capable of every species of mean villainy.''

He then protested he would at least acquaint her other guardians with what had passed, whose business it would be to enquire if there was any chance of redress.

Cecilia, however, had not much trouble in combating this proposal; for though her objections, which were merely those of punctilious honour and delicacy, weighed nothing with a man who regarded them as absurdities, yet his own apprehensions of appearing too officious in her affairs, forced him, after a little deliberation, to give up the design.

"Besides," said Cecilia, "as I have his bond for what I have parted with, I have, at least, no right to complain, unless, after he receives his rents, he refuses to pay me.''

"His bonds! his rents!" exclaimed Mr. Monckton, "what is a man's bond who is not worth a guinea? and what are his rents, when all he ever owned must be sold before they are due, and when he will not himself receive a penny from the sale, as he has neither land, house, nor possession of any sort that is not mortgaged?''

"Nay, then," said Cecilia, "if so, it is indeed all over! I am sorry, I am grieved!—but it is past, and nothing, therefore, remains, but that I try to forget I ever was richer!''

"This is very youthful philosophy," said Mr. Monckton; "but it will not lessen your regret hereafter, when the value of money is better known to you.''

"If I shall dearly buy my experience," said Cecilia, "let me be the more attentive to making good use of it; and, since my loss seems irremediable to myself, let me at least endeavour to secure its utility to Mr. Harrel."

She then told him her wish to propose to that gentleman some scheme of reformation, while yesterday's events were yet recent in his mind: but Mr. Monckton, who had hardly patience to hear her, exclaimed, "He is a wretch, and deserves the full force of the disgrace he is courting. What is now most necessary is to guard you from his further machinations, for you may else be involved in ruin as deep as his own. He now knows the way to frighten you, and he will not fail to put it in practice."

"No, Sir," answered Cecilia, "he would vainly apply to me in future: I cannot repent that I ventured not yesterday to brave his menaces, but too little is the comfort I feel from what I have bestowed, to suffer any consideration to make me part with more."

"Your resolution," answered he, "will be as feeble as your generosity will be potent: depend nothing upon yourself, but instantly quit his house. You will else be made responsible for every debt that he contracts, and whatever may be his difficulties hereafter, he will know that to extricate himself from them, he has but to talk of dying, and to shew you a sword or a pistol."

"If so, then," said Cecilia, looking down while she spoke, "I suppose I must again go to Mr. Delvile's."

This was by no means the purpose of Mr. Monckton, who saw not more danger to her fortune with one of her guardians, than to her person with the other. He ventured, therefore, to recommend to her a residence with Mr. Briggs, well knowing that his house would be a security against her seeing any man equal to himself, and hoping that under his roof he might again be as unrivalled in her opinion and esteem, as he formerly was in the country.

But here the opposition of Cecilia was too earnest for any hope that it might be surmounted; for, added to her dislike of Mr. Briggs, her repugnance to such an habitation was

strongly, though silently encreased, by her secret inclination
to return to St. James's-square.

"I mention not Mr. Briggs as an eligible host," said Mr.
Monckton, after listening to her objections, "but merely as
one more proper for you than Mr. Delvile, with whom your
fixing at present would be but ill thought of in the world."

"Ill thought of, Sir? Why so?"

"Because he has a son; for whose sake alone it would be
universally concluded you changed your abode: and to give
any pretence for such a report, would by no means accord
with the usual delicacy of your conduct."

Cecilia was confounded by this speech: the truth of the
charge she felt, and the probability of the censure she did not
dare dispute.

He then gave her a thousand exhortations to beware of the
schemes and artifices of Mr. Harrel, which he foresaw would
be innumerable. He told her, too, that with respect to Sir
Robert Floyer, he thought she had better suffer the report to
subside of itself, which in time it must necessarily do, than
give to it so much consequence as to send a message to the
Baronet, from which he might pretend to infer that hitherto
she had been wavering, or she would have sent to him
sooner.

But the real motive of this advice was, that as he found Sir
Robert by no means to be dreaded, he hoped the report, if
generally circulated and credited, might keep off other
pretenders, and intimidate or deceive young Delvile.

The purport for which Cecilia had wished this conference
was, however, wholly unanswered; Mr. Monckton, enraged
by the conduct of Mr. Harrel, refused to talk of his affairs,
and could only mention him with detestation: but Cecilia,
less severe in her judgment, and more tender in her heart,
would not yet give up the hope of an amendment she so
anxiously wished; and having now no other person to whom
she could apply, determined to consult with Mr. Arnott,
whose affection for his sister would give him a zeal in the
affair that might somewhat supply the place of superior
abilities.

There was, indeed, no time to be lost in making the

projected attempt, for no sooner was the immediate danger
of suffering removed, than the alarm wore away, and the
penitence was forgotten; every thing went on as usual, no
new regulations were made, no expences abated, no
pleasures forborn, not a thought of hereafter admitted; and
ruinous and terrible as had been the preceding storm, no
trace of it was visible in the serenity of the present calm.

An occasion of discussion with Mr. Arnott very speedily
offered. Mr. Harrel said he had observed in the looks of his
friends at the Pantheon much surprise at the sight of him,
and declared he should take yet another measure for removing
all suspicion. This was to give a splendid entertainment at
his own house to all his acquaintance, to which he meant to
invite every body of any consequence he had ever seen, and
almost every body he had ever heard of, in his life.

Levity so unfeeling, and a spirit of extravagance so
irreclaimable, were hopeless prognostics; yet Cecilia would
not desist from her design. She therefore took the earliest
opportunity of speaking with Mr. Arnott upon the subject,
when she openly expressed her uneasiness at the state of his
brother's affairs, and warmly acknowledged her displeasure
at his dissipated way of life.

Mr. Arnott soon shewed that example was all he wanted
to declare the same sentiments. He owned he had long
disapproved the conduct of Mr. Harrel, and trembled at the
situation of his sister. They then considered what it was
possible to propose that might retrieve their affairs, and
concluded that entirely to quit London for some years, was
the only chance that remained of saving them from absolute
destruction.

Mr. Arnott, therefore, though fearfully, and averse to the
task, told his sister their mutual advice. She thanked him,
said she was much obliged to him, and would certainly
consider his proposal, and mention it to Mr. Harrel.—
Parties of pleasure, however, intervened, and the promise
was neglected.

Cecilia then again spoke herself. Mrs. Harrel, much
softened by her late acts of kindness, was no longer offended
by her interference, but contented herself with confessing

that she quite hated the country, and could only bear to live in it in summer time. And when Cecilia very earnestly expostulated on the weakness of such an objection to a step absolutely necessary for her future safety and happiness, she said, *she could do no worse than that if already ruined*, and therefore that she thought *it would be very hard to expect from her such a sacrifice before-hand*.*

It was in vain Cecilia remonstrated: Mrs. Harrel's love of pleasure was stronger than her understanding, and therefore, though she listened to her with patience, she concluded with the same answer she had begun.

Cecilia then, though almost heartless,* resolved upon talking with Mr. Harrel himself: and therefore, taking an opportunity which he had not time to elude, she ingenuously told him her opinion of his danger, and of the manner in which it might be avoided.

He paid unusual attention to her advice, but said she was much mistaken with respect to his affairs, which he believed he should now very speedily retrieve, as he had had the preceding night an uncommon *run of luck*,* and flattered himself with being able very shortly to pay all his debts, and begin the world again upon a new score.

This open confession of gaming was but a new shock to Cecilia, who scrupled not to represent to him the uncertainty of so hazardous a reliance, and the inevitable evils of so destructive a practice.

She made not, however, the least impression upon his mind; he assured her he doubted not giving her shortly a good account of himself, and that living in the country was a resource of desperation which need not be anticipated.

Cecilia, though grieved and provoked by their mutual folly and blindness, could proceed no further: advice and admonition she spared not, but authority she had none to use. She regretted her ineffectual attempt to Mr. Arnott, who was yet more cruelly afflicted at it; but though they conversed upon the subject by every opportunity, they were equally unable to relate any success from their efforts, or to devise any plan more likely to ensure it.

CHAPTER VIII

A Mistake

MEAN time young Delvile failed not to honour Cecilia's introduction of him to Mr. Harrel, by waiting upon that gentleman as soon as the ill effects of his accident at the Pantheon permitted him to leave his own house. Mr. Harrel, though just going out when he called, was desirous of being upon good terms with his family, and therefore took him up stairs to present him to his lady, and invited him to tea and cards the next evening.

Cecilia, who was with Mrs. Harrel, did not see him without emotion; which was not much lessened by the task of thanking him for his assistance at the Pantheon, and enquiring how he had himself fared. No sign, however, of emotion appeared in return, either when he first addressed, or afterwards answered her: the look of solicitude with which she had been so much struck when they last parted was no longer discernable, and the voice of sensibility which had removed all her doubts, was no longer to be heard. His general ease, and natural gaiety were again unruffled, and though he had never seemed really indifferent to her, there was not the least appearance of any added partiality.

Cecilia felt an involuntary mortification as she observed this change: yet, upon reflection, she still attributed his whole behaviour to his mistake with respect to her situation, and therefore was but the more gratified by the preference he occasionally betrayed.

The invitation for the next evening was accepted, and Cecilia, for once, felt no repugnance to joining the company. Young Delvile again was in excellent spirits; but though his chief pleasure was evidently derived from conversing with her, she had the vexation to observe that he seemed to think her the undoubted property of the Baronet, always retreating when he approached, and as careful, when next her, to yield his place if he advanced, as, when he was distant, to guard it from all others.

But when Sir Robert was employed at cards, all scruples ceasing, he neglected not to engross her almost wholly. He was eager to speak to her of the affairs of Mr. Belfield, which he told her wore now a better aspect. The letter, indeed, of recommendation which he had shewn to her, had failed, as the nobleman to whom it was written had already entered into an engagement for his son; but he had made application elsewhere which he believed would be successful, and he had communicated his proceedings to Mr. Belfield, whose spirits he hoped would recover by this prospect of employment and advantage. "It is, however, but too true," he added, "that I have rather obtained his consent to the steps I am taking, than his approbation of them: nor do I believe, had I previously consulted him, I should have had even that. Disappointed in his higher views, his spirit is broken, and he is heartless and hopeless, scarce condescending to accept relief, from the bitter remembrance that he expected preferment. Time, however, will blunt this acute sensibility, and reflection will make him blush at this unreasonable delicacy. But we must patiently sooth him till he is more himself, or while we mean to serve, we shall only torment him. Sickness, sorrow, and poverty have all fallen heavily upon him, and they have all fallen at once: we must not, therefore, wonder to find him intractable, when his mind is as much depressed, as his body is enervated."

Cecilia, to whom his candour and generosity always gave fresh delight, strengthened his opinions by her concurrence, and confirmed his designs by the interest which she took in them.

From this time he found almost daily some occasion for calling in Portman-Square. The application of Cecilia in favour of Mr. Belfield gave him a right to communicate to her all his proceedings concerning him; and he had some letter* to shew, some new scheme to propose, some refusal to lament, or some hope to rejoice over, almost perpetually: or even when these failed, Cecilia had a cold, which he came to enquire after, or Mrs. Harrel gave him an invitation, which rendered any excuse unnecessary. But though his intimacy with Cecilia was encreased, though his admiration of her was conspicuous, and his fondness for her society seemed to grow with the enjoyment of it, he yet never manifested any doubt of her engagement with the Baronet, nor betrayed either intention or desire to supplant him. Cecilia, however, repined not much at the mistake, since she thought it might be instrumental to procuring her a more impartial acquaintance with his character, than she could rationally expect, if, as she hoped, the explanation of his error should make him seek her good opinion with more study and design.

To satisfy herself not only concerning the brother but the sister, she again visited Miss Belfield, and had the pleasure of finding her in better spirits, and hearing that the *noble friend** of her brother, whom she had already mentioned, and whom Cecilia had before suspected to be young Delvile, had now pointed out to him a method of conduct by which his affairs might be decently retrieved, and himself creditably employed. Miss Belfield spoke of the plan with the highest satisfaction; yet she acknowledged that her mother was extremely discontented with it, and that her brother himself was rather led by shame than inclination to its adoption. Yet he was evidently easier in his mind, though far from happy, and already so much better, that Mr. Rupil said he would very soon be able to leave his room.

Such was the quiet and contented situation of Cecilia, when one evening, which was destined for company at home, while she was alone in the drawing-room, which Mrs. Harrel had just left to answer a note, Sir Robert Floyer accidentally came up stairs before the other gentlemen.

"Ha!" cried he, the moment he saw her, "at last have I the good fortune to meet with you alone! this, indeed, is a favour I thought I was always to be denied."

He was then approaching her; but Cecilia, who shrunk involuntary* at the sight of him, was retreating hastily to quit the room, when suddenly recollecting that no better opportunity might ever offer for a final explanation with him, she irresolutely stopt; and Sir Robert, immediately following, took her hand, and pressing it to his lips as she endeavoured to withdraw it, exclaimed "You are a most charming creature!" when the door was opened, and young Delvile at the same moment was announced and appeared.

Cecilia, colouring violently, and extremely chagrined, hastily disengaged herself from his hold. Delvile seemed uncertain whether he ought not to retire, which Sir Robert perceiving, bowed to him with an air of mingled triumph and vexation, and said "Sir your most obedient!"

The doubt, however, in which every one appeared of what was next to be done, was immediately removed by the return of Mrs. Harrel, and the arrival at almost the same moment of more company.

The rest of the evening was spent, on the part of Cecilia, most painfully: the explanation she had planned had ended in worse than nothing, for by suffering the Baronet to detain her, she had rather shewn a disposition to oblige, than any intention to discard him; and the situation in which she had been surprised by young Delvile, was the last to clear the suspicions she so little wished him to harbour: while, on his part, the accident seemed to occasion no other alteration than that of rendering him more than usually assiduous to give way to Sir Robert whenever he approached her.

Nor was Sir Robert slack in taking advantage of this attention: he was highly in spirits, talked to her with more than common freedom, and wore the whole evening an air of exulting satisfaction.

Cecilia, provoked by this presumption, hurt by the behaviour of young Delvile, and mortified by the whole affair, determined to leave this mistake no longer in the power of accident, but to apply immediately to Mr. Delvile senior, and desire him, as her guardian, to wait upon Sir Robert himself, and acquaint him that his perseverance in pursuing her was both useless and offensive: and by this method she hoped at once to disentangle herself for ever from the Baronet, and to discover more fully the sentiments of young Delvile: for the provocation she had just endured, robbed her of all patience for waiting the advice of Mr. Monckton.

CHAPTER IX

An Explanation

THE following morning, therefore, Cecilia went early to St. James's Square: and, after the usual ceremonies of messages and long waiting, she was shewn into an apartment where she found Mr. Delvile and his son.

She rejoiced to see them together, and determined to make known to them both the purport of her visit: and therefore, after some apologies and a little hesitation, she told Mr. Delvile, that encouraged by his offers of serving her, she had taken the liberty to call upon him with a view to entreat his assistance.

Young Delvile, immediately arising, would have quitted the room; but Cecilia, assuring him she rather desired what she had to say should be known than kept secret, begged that he would not disturb himself.

Delvile, pleased with this permission to hear her, and curious to know what would follow, very readily returned to his seat.

"I should by no means," she continued, "have thought of proclaiming even to the most intimate of my friends, the partiality which Sir Robert Floyer has been pleased to shew me, had he left to me the choice of publishing or concealing it: but, on the contrary, his own behaviour seems intended not merely to display it, but to insinuate that it meets with my approbation. Mr. Harrel, also, urged by too much warmth of friendship, has encouraged this belief; nor, indeed, do I know at present where the mistake stops, nor what it is report has not scrupled to affirm. But I think I ought no longer to neglect it, and therefore I have presumed to solicit your advice in what manner I may most effectually contradict it."

The extreme surprise of young Delvile at this speech was not more evident than pleasant to Cecilia, to whom it accounted for all that had perplext her in his conduct, while it animated every expectation she wished to encourage.

"The behaviour of Mr. Harrel," answered Mr. Delvile, "has by no means been such as to lead me to forget that his father was the son of a steward* of Mr. Grant, who lived in the neighbourhood of my friend and relation the Duke of Derwent: nor can I sufficiently congratulate myself that I have always declined acting with him. The late Dean, indeed, never committed so strange an impropriety as that of nominating Mr. Harrel and Mr. Briggs coadjutors with Mr. Delvile. The impropriety, however, though extremely offensive to me, has never obliterated from my mind the esteem I bore the Dean: nor can I possibly give a greater proof of it than the readiness I have always shewn to offer my counsel and instruction to his neice. Mr. Harrel, therefore, ought certainly to have desired Sir Robert Floyer to acquaint me with his proposals before he gave to him any answer."

"Undoubtedly, Sir," said Cecilia, willing to shorten this parading harangue, "but as he neglected that intention,* will you think me too impertinent should I entreat the favour of you to speak with Sir Robert yourself, and explain to him the total inefficacy of his pursuit, since my determination against him is unalterable?"

Here the conference was interrupted by the entrance of a servant who said something to Mr. Delvile, which occasioned his apologizing to Cecilia for leaving her for a few moments, and ostentatiously assuring her that no business, however important, should prevent his thinking of her affairs, or detain him from returning to her as soon as possible.

The astonishment of young Delvile at the strength of her last expression kept him silent some time after his father left the room; and then, with a countenance that still marked his amazement, he said "Is it possible, Miss Beverley, that I should twice have been thus egregiously deceived? or rather, that the whole town, and even the most intimate of your friends, should so unaccountably have persisted in a mistake."

"For the town," answered Cecilia, "I know not how it can have had any concern in so small a matter; but for my intimate friends, I have too few to make it probable they should ever have been so strangely misinformed."

"Pardon me," cried he, "it was from one who ought to know, that I had myself the intelligence."

"I intreat you, then," said Cecilia, "to acquaint me who it was?"

"Mr. Harrel himself; who communicated it to a lady in my hearing, and at a public place."

Cecilia cast up her eyes in wonder and indignation at a proof so incontrovertible of his falsehood, but made not any answer.

"Even yet," continued he, "I can scarcely feel undeceived; your engagement seemed so positive, your connexion so irretrievable,—so,—so *fixed*, I mean,—" He hesitated, a little embarrassed; but then suddenly exclaimed, "Yet whence, if to *neither* favourable, if indifferent alike to Sir Robert and to Belfield, whence that animated apprehension for their safety at the Opera-house? whence that never to be forgotten *oh stop him! good God! will nobody stop him!**—Words of anxiety so tender! and sounds that still vibrate in my ear!"

Cecilia, struck with amazement in her turn at the strength of his own expressions,* blushed, and for a few minutes hesitated how to answer him: but then, to leave nothing that related to so disagreeable a report in any doubt, she resolved to tell him ingenuously the circumstances that had occasioned her alarm: and therefore, though with some pain to her modesty, she confessed her fears that she had herself provoked the affront, though her only view had been to discountenance Sir Robert, without meaning to shew any distinction to Mr. Belfield.

Delvile, who seemed charmed with the candour of this explanation, said, when she had finished it, "You are then at liberty?——Ah madam!—how many may rue so dangerous a discovery!"

"Could you think," said Cecilia, endeavouring to speak with her usual ease, "that Sir Robert Floyer would be found so irresistible?"

"Oh no!" cried he, "far otherwise; a thousand times I have wondered at his happiness; a thousand times, when I have looked at you, and listened to you, I have thought it impossible!—yet my authority seemed indisputable. And how was I to discredit what was not uttered as a conjecture, but asserted as a fact? asserted, too, by the guardian with whom you lived? and not hinted as a secret, but affirmed as a point settled?"

"Yet surely," said Cecilia, "you have heard me make use of expressions that could not but lead you to suppose there was some mistake, whatever might be the authority which had won your belief."

"No," answered he, "I never supposed any mistake, though sometimes I thought you repented your engagement. I concluded, indeed, you had been unwarily drawn in, and I have even, at times, been tempted to acknowledge my suspicions to you, state your independence, and exhort you——as a *friend*, exhort you—to use it with spirit, and, if you were shackled unwillingly, incautiously, or unworthily, to break the chains by which you were confined, and restore to yourself that freedom of choice upon the use of which all your happiness must ultimately depend. But I doubted if this were honourable to the Baronet,—and what, indeed, was my right to such a liberty? none that every man might not be proud of, a wish to do honour to myself, under the officious pretence of serving the most amiable of women."

"Mr. Harrel," said Cecilia, "has been so strangely bigotted to his friend, that in his eagerness to manifest his regard for him, he seems to, have forgotten every other consideration; he would not, else, have spread so widely a report that could so ill stand enquiry."

"If Sir Robert," returned he, "is himself deceived while he deceives others, who can forbear to pity him? for my own part, instead of repining that hitherto I have been mistaken, ought I not rather to bless an error that may have been my preservative from danger?"

Cecilia, distressed in what manner to support her part in the conversation, began now to wish the return of Mr. Delvile; and, not knowing what else to say, she expressed her surprise at his long absence.

"It is not, indeed, well timed," said young Delvile, "just now,—at the moment when—" he stopt, and presently exclaiming "Oh dangerous interval!" he arose from his seat in manifest disorder.

Cecilia arose too, and hastily ringing the bell, said "Mr. Delvile I am sure is detained, and therefore I will order my chair, and call another time."

"Do I frighten you away?" said he, assuming an appearance more placid.

"No," answered she, "but I would not hasten Mr. Delvile."

A servant then came, and said the chair was ready.

She would immediately have followed him, but young Delvile again speaking, she stopt a moment to hear him. "I fear," said he, with much hesitation, "I have strangely exposed myself——and that you cannot—but the extreme astonishment—" he stopt again, in the utmost confusion, and then adding "you will permit me to attend you to the chair," he handed her down stairs, and in quitting her, bowed without saying a word more.

Cecilia, who was almost wholly indifferent to every part of the explanation but that which had actually passed, was now in a state of felicity more delightful than any she had ever experienced. She had not a doubt remaining of her influence over the mind of young Delvile, and the surprise which had made him rather betray than express his regard, was infinitely more flattering and satisfactory to her than any formal or direct declaration. She had now convinced him she was disengaged, and in return, though without seeming to intend it, he had convinced her of the deep interest which he took in the discovery. His perturbation, the words which escaped him, and his evident struggle to say no more, were proofs just such as she wished to receive of his partial admiration, since while they satisfied her heart, they also soothed her pride, by shewing a diffidence of success which assured her that her own secret was still sacred, and that no weakness or inadvertency on her part had robbed her of the power of mingling dignity with the frankness with which she meant to receive his addresses. All, therefore, that now employed her care, was to keep off any indissoluble engagement till each should be better known to the other.

For this reserve, however, she had less immediate occasion than she expected; she saw no more of young Delvile that day; neither did he appear the next. The third she fully expected him,—but still he came not. And while she wondered at an absence so uncommon, she received a note from Lord Ernolf, to beg permission to wait upon her for two minutes, at any time she would appoint.

She readily sent word that she should be at home for the rest of the day, as she wished much for an opportunity of immediately finishing every affair but one, and setting her mind at liberty to think only of that which she desired should prosper.

Lord Ernolf was with her in half an hour. She found him sensible and well bred, extremely desirous to promote her alliance with his son, and apparently as much pleased with herself as with her fortune. He acquainted her that he had addressed himself to Mr. Harrel long since, but had been informed that she was actually engaged to Sir Robert Floyer: he should, therefore, have forborn taking up any part of her time, had he not, the preceding day, while on a visit at Mr. Delvile's, been assured that Mr. Harrel was mistaken, and that she had not yet declared for any body. He hoped, therefore, that she would allow his son the honour of waiting upon her, and permit him to talk with Mr. Briggs, who he understood was her acting guardian, upon such matters as ought to be speedily adjusted.

Cecilia thanked him for the honour he intended her, and confirmed the truth of the account he had heard in St. James's-square, but at the same time told him she must decline receiving any visits from his lordship's son, and intreated him to take no measure towards the promotion of an affair which never could succeed.

He seemed much concerned at her answer, and endeavoured for some time to soften her, but found her so steady, though civil in her refusal, that he was obliged, however unwillingly, to give up his attempt.

Cecilia, when he was gone, reflected with much vexation on the readiness of the Delviles to encourage his visit; she considered, however, that the intelligence he had heard might possibly be gathered in general conversation; but she blamed herself that she had not led to some enquiry what part of the family he had seen, and who was present when the information was given him.

Mean while she found that neither coldness, distance, nor aversion were sufficient to repress Sir Robert Floyer, who continued to persecute her with as much confidence of success as could have arisen from the utmost encouragement. She again, though with much difficulty, contrived to speak with Mr. Harrel upon the subject, and openly accused him of spreading a report abroad, as well as countenancing an expectation at home, that had neither truth nor justice to support them.

Mr. Harrel, with his usual levity and carelessness, laughed at the charge, but denied any belief in her displeasure, and affected to think she was merely playing the coquet, while Sir Robert was not the less her decided choice.

Provoked and wearied, Cecilia resolved no longer to depend upon any body but herself for the management of her own affairs, and therefore, to conclude the business without any possibility of further cavilling, she wrote the following note to Sir Robert herself.

To SIR ROBERT FLOYER, Bart.

MISS BEVERLEY presents her compliments to Sir Robert Floyer, and as she has some reason to fear Mr. Harrel did not explicitly acquaint him with her answer to the commission with which he was entrusted, she thinks it necessary, in order to obviate any possible mis-understanding, to take this method of returning him thanks for the honour of his good opinion, but of begging at the same time that he would not lose a moment upon her account, as her thanks are all she can now, or ever, offer in return.

Portman-square,
    May 11th, 1779.

To this note Cecilia received no answer: but she had the pleasure to observe that Sir Robert forbore his usual visit on the day she sent it, and, though he appeared again the day following, he never spoke to her, and seemed sullen and out of humour.

Yet still young Delvile came not, and still, as her surprise encreased, her tranquility was diminished. She could form no excuse for his delay, nor conjecture any reason for his absence. Every motive seemed to favour his seeking, and not one his shunning her: the explanation which had so lately passed had informed him he had no rival to fear, and the manner in which he had heard it assured her the information was not indifferent to him; why, then, so assiduous in his visits when he thought her engaged, and so slack in all attendance when he knew she was at liberty?

CHAPTER X

A Murmuring

UNABLE to relieve herself from this perplexity, Cecilia, to divert her chagrin, again visited Miss Belfield. She had then the pleasure to hear that her brother was much recovered, and had been able, the preceding day, to take an airing, which he had borne so well that Mr. Rupil had charged him to use the same exercise every morning.

"And will he?" said Cecilia.

"No, madam, I am sadly afraid not," she answered, "for coach hire is very expensive, and we are willing, now, to save all we can in order to help fitting him out for going abroad."

Cecilia then earnestly entreated her to accept some assistance; but she assured her she did not dare without the consent of her mother, which, however, she undertook to obtain.

The next day, when Cecilia called to hear her success, Mrs. Belfield, who hitherto had kept out of sight, made her appearance. She found her, alike in person, manners and conversation, a coarse and ordinary woman, not more unlike her son in talents and acquired accomplishments, than dissimilar to her daughter in softness and natural delicacy.

The moment Cecilia was seated, she began, without waiting for any ceremony, or requiring any solicitation, abruptly to talk of her affairs, and repiningly to relate her misfortunes.

"I find, madam," she said, "you have been so kind as to visit my daughter Henny a great many times, but as I have no time for company, I have always kept out of the way, having other things to do than sit still to talk. I have had a sad time of it here, ma'am, with my poor son's illness, having no conveniences about me, and much ado to make him mind me; for he's all for having his own way, poor dear soul, and I'm sure I don't know who could contradict him, for it's what I never had the heart to do. But then, ma'am, what is to come of it? You see how bad things go! for though I have got a very good income, it won't do for every thing. And if it was as much again, I should want to save it all now. For here my poor son, you see, is reduced all in a minute, as one may say, from being one of the first gentlemen in the town, to a mere poor object, without a farthing in the world!"

"He is, however, I hope now much better in his health?" said Cecilia.

"Yes, madam, thank heaven, for if he was worse, those might tell of it that would, for I'm sure I should never live to hear of it. He has been the best son in the world, madam, and used nothing but the best company, for I spared neither pains nor cost to bring him up genteely, and I believe there's not a nobleman in the land that looks more the gentleman. However, there's come no good of it, for though his acquaintances was all among the first quality, he never received the value of a penny from the best of them. So I have no great need to be proud. But I meant for the best, though I have often enough wished I had not meddled in the matter, but left him to be brought up in the shop, as his father was before him."

"His present plan, however," said Cecilia, "will I hope make you ample amends both for your sufferings and your tenderness."

"What, madam, when he's going to leave me, and settle in foreign parts? If you was a mother yourself, madam, you would not think that such good amends."

"Settle?" said Cecilia, "No, he only goes for a year or two."

"That's more than I can say, madam, or any body else; and nobody knows what may happen in that time. And how I shall keep myself up* when he's beyond seas, I am sure I don't know, for he has always been the pride of my life, and every penny I saved for him, I thought to have been paid in pounds."

"You will still have your daughter, and she seems so amiable, that I am sure you can want no consolation she will not endeavour to give you."

"But what is a daughter, madam, to such a son as mine? a son that I thought to have seen living like a prince, and sending his own coach for me to dine with him! And now he's going to be taken away from me, and nobody knows if I shall live till he comes back. But I may thank myself, for if I had but been content to see him brought up in the shop——yet all the world would have cried shame upon it, for when he was quite a child in arms, the people used all to say he was born to be a gentleman, and would live to make many a fine lady's heart ache."

"If he can but make *your* heart easy," said Cecilia, smiling, "we will not grieve that the fine ladies should escape the prophecy."

"O, ma'am, I don't mean by that to say he has been over gay among the ladies, for it's a thing I never heard of him; and I dare say if any lady was to take a fancy to him, she'd find there was not a modester young man in the world. But you must needs think what a hardship it is to me to have him turn out so unlucky, after all I have done for him, when I thought to have seen him at the top of the tree, as one may say!"

"He will yet, I hope," said Cecilia, "make you rejoice in

all your kindness to him: his health is already returning, and his affairs wear again a more prosperous aspect."

"But do you suppose, ma'am, that having him sent two or three hundred miles away from me, with some young master to take care of, is the way to make up to me what I have gone through for him? why I used to deny myself every thing in the world, in order to save money to buy him smart cloaths, and let him go to the Opera, and Ranelagh, and such sort of places, that he might keep himself in fortune's way! and now you see the end of it! here he is, in a little shabby room up two pair of stairs, with not one of the great folks coming near him, to see if he's so much as dead or alive."

"I do not wonder," said Cecilia, "that you resent their shewing so little gratitude for the pleasure and entertainment they have formerly received from him: but comfort yourself that it will at least secure you from any similar disappointment, as Mr. Belfield will, in future, be guarded from forming such precarious expectations."

"But what good will that do me, ma'am, for all the money he has been throwing after them all this while? do you think I would have scraped it up for him, and gone without every thing in the world, to see it all end in this manner? why he might as well have been brought up the commonest journeyman,* for any comfort I shall have of him at this rate. And suppose he should be drowned in going beyond seas? what am I to do then?"

"You must not," said Cecilia, "indulge such fears; I doubt not but your son will return well, and return all that you wish."

"Nobody knows that, ma'am; and the only way to be certain is for him not to go at all; and I'm surprised, ma'am, you can wish him to make such a journey to nobody knows where, with nothing but a young master that he must as good as teach his A.B.C. all the way they go!"

"Certainly," said Cecilia, amazed at this accusation, "I should not wish him to go abroad, if any thing more eligible could be done by his remaining in England: but as no prospect of that sort seems before him, you must endeavour to reconcile yourself to parting with him."

"Yes, but how am I to do that, when I don't know if ever I shall see him again? Who could have thought of his living so among the great folks, and then coming to want! I'm sure I thought they'd have provided for him like a son of their own, for he used to go about to all the public places just as they did themselves. Day after day I used to be counting for when he would come to tell me he'd got a place at court, or something of that sort, for I never could tell what it would be: and then the next news I heard, was that he was shut up in this poor bit of place,* with nobody troubling their heads about him! however, I'll never be persuaded but he might have done better, if he would but have spoke a good word for himself, or else have let me done it for him: instead of which, he never would so much as let me see any of his grand friends, though I would not have made the least scruple in the world to have asked them for any thing he had a mind to."

Cecilia again endeavoured to give her comfort; but finding her only satisfaction was to express her discontent, she arose to take leave. But, turning first to Miss Belfield, contrived to make a private enquiry whether she might repeat her offer of assistance. A downcast and dejected look answering in the affirmative, she put into her hand a ten pound bank note, and wishing them good morning, hurried out of the room.

Miss Belfield was running after her, but stopt by her mother, who called out, "What is it?—How much is it?— Let me look at it!"—And then, following Cecilia herself, she thanked her aloud all the way down stairs for her *genteelness*,* assuring her she would not fail making it known to her son.

Cecilia at this declaration turned back, and exhorted her by no means to mention it; after which she got into her chair, and returned home; pitying Miss Belfield for the unjust partiality shewn to her brother, and excusing the proud shame he had manifested of his relations, from the vulgarity and selfishness of her who was at the head of them.

Almost a fortnight had now elapsed since her explanation with young Delvile, yet not once had he been in Portman-square, though in the fortnight which had preceded, scarce

a day had passed which had not afforded him some pretence
for calling there.

At length a note arrived from Mrs. Delvile. It contained
the most flattering reproaches for her long absence, and a
pressing invitation that she would dine and spend the next
day with her.

Cecilia, who had merely denied herself the pleasure of this
visit from an apprehension of seeming too desirous of
keeping up the connexion, now, from the same sense of
propriety, determined upon making it, wishing equally to
avoid all appearance of consciousness, either by seeking or
avoiding the intimacy of the family.

Not a little was her anxiety to know in what manner
young Delvile would receive her, whether he would be grave
or gay, agitated, as during their last conversation, or easy,
as in the meetings which had preceded it.

She found Mrs. Delvile, however, alone; and, extremely
kind to her, yet much surprised, and half displeased, that
she had so long been absent. Cecilia, though somewhat
distressed what excuses to offer, was happy to find herself so
highly in favour, and not very reluctant to promise more
frequent visits in future.

They were then summoned to dinner; but still no young
Delvile was visible: they were joined only by his father, and
she found that no one else was expected.

Her astonishment now was greater than ever, and she
could account by no possible conjecture for a conduct so
extraordinary. Hitherto, whenever she had visited in St.
James's-square by appointment, the air with which he had
received her, constantly announced that he had impatiently
waited her arrival; he had given up other engagements to
stay with her, he had openly expressed his hopes that she
would never be long absent, and seemed to take a pleasure
in her society to which every other was inferior. And now,
how striking the difference! he forbore all visits at the house
where she resided, he even flew from his own when he knew
she was approaching it!

Nor was this the only vexation of which this day was
productive; Mr. Delvile, when the servants were withdrawn

after dinner, expressed some concern that he had been called from her during their last conversation, and added that he would take the present opportunity to talk with her upon some matters of importance.

He then began the usual parading prelude, which, upon all occasions, he thought necessary, in order to enhance the value of his interposition, remind her of her inferiority, and impress her with a deeper sense of the honour which his guardianship conferred upon her: after which, he proceeded to make a formal enquiry whether she had positively dismissed Sir Robert Floyer?

She assured him she had.

"I understood my Lord Ernolf," said he, "that you had totally discouraged the addresses of his son?"

"Yes, Sir," answered Cecilia, "for I never mean to receive them."

"Have you, then, any other engagement?"

"No, Sir," cried she, colouring between shame and displeasure, "none at all."

"This is a very extraordinary circumstance!" replied he: "the son of an earl to be rejected by a young woman of no family, and yet no reason assigned for it!"

This contemptuous speech so cruelly shocked Cecilia, that though he continued to harangue her for a great part of the afternoon, she only answered him when compelled by some question, and was so evidently discomposed, that Mrs. Delvile, who perceived her uneasiness with much concern, redoubled her civilities and caresses, and used every method in her power to oblige and enliven her.

Cecilia was not ungrateful for her care, and shewed her sense of it by added respect and attention; but her mind was disturbed, and she quitted the house as soon as she was able.

Mr. Delvile's speech, from her previous knowledge of the extreme haughtiness of his character, would not have occasioned her the smallest emotion, had it merely related to him or to herself: but as it concerned Lord Ernolf, she regarded it as also concerning his son, and she found that, far from trying to promote the union Mr. Monckton had told her he had planned, he did not seem even to think of it, but, on the contrary, proposed and seconded with all his interest another alliance.

This, added to the behaviour of young Delvile, made her suspect that some engagement was in agitation on his own part, and that while she thought him so sedulous only to avoid her, he was simply occupied in seeking another. This painful suggestion, which every thing seemed to confirm, again overset all her schemes, and destroyed all her visionary happiness. Yet how to reconcile it with what had passed at their last meeting she knew not; she had then every reason to believe that his heart was in her power, and that courage, or an opportunity more seasonable, was all he wanted to make known his devotion to her; why, then, shun if he loved her? why, if he loved her not, seem so perturbed at the explanation of her independance?

A very little time, however, she hoped would unravel this mystery; in two days, the entertainment which Mr. Harrel had planned, to deceive the world by an appearance of affluence to which he had lost all title, was to take place; young Delvile, in common with every other person who had ever been seen at the house, had early received an invitation, which he had readily promised to accept some time before the conversation that seemed the period of their acquaintance had passed. Should he, after being so long engaged, fail to keep his appointment, she could no longer have any doubt of the justice of her conjecture; should he, on the contrary, again appear, from his behaviour and his looks she might perhaps be able to gather why he had so long been absent.

END OF THE SECOND VOLUME

VOLUME III

BOOK V

CHAPTER I

*A Rout**

THE day at length arrived of which the evening and the entrance of company were, for the first time, as eagerly wished by Cecilia as by her dissipated host and hostess. No expence and no pains had been spared to render this long projected entertainment splendid and elegant; it was to begin with a concert, which was to be followed by a ball, and succeeded by a supper.

Cecilia, though unusually anxious about her own affairs, was not so engrossed by them as to behold with indifference a scene of such unjustifiable extravagance; it contributed to render her thoughtful and uneasy, and to deprive her of all mental power of participating in the gaiety of the assembly. Mr. Arnott was yet more deeply affected by the mad folly of the scheme, and received from the whole evening no other satisfaction than that which a look of sympathetic concern from Cecilia occasionally afforded him.

Till nine o'clock no company appeared, except Sir Robert Floyer, who stayed from dinner time, and Mr. Morrice, who having received an invitation for the evening, was so much delighted with the permission to again enter the house, that he made use of it between six and seven o'clock, and before the family had left the dining parlour. He apologized with the utmost humility to Cecilia for the unfortunate accident at the Pantheon; but as to her it had been productive of nothing but pleasure, by exciting in young Delvile the most flattering alarm for her safety, she found no great difficulty in according him her pardon.

Among those who came in the first crowd was Mr.

Monckton, who, had he been equally unconscious of sinister views, would in following his own inclination, have been as early in his attendance as Mr. Morrice; but who, to obviate all suspicious remarks, conformed to the fashionable tardiness of the times.

Cecilia's chief apprehension for the evening was that Sir Robert Floyer would ask her to dance with him, which she could not refuse without sitting still during the ball, nor accept, after the reports she knew to be spread, without seeming to give a public sanction to them. To Mr. Monckton therefore, innocently considering him as a married man and her old friend, she frankly told her distress, adding, by way of excuse for the hint, that the partners were to be changed every two dances.

Mr. Monckton, though his principal study was carefully to avoid all public gallantry or assiduity towards Cecilia, had not the forbearance to resist this intimation, and therefore she had the pleasure of telling Sir Robert, when he asked the honour of her hand for the two first dances, that she was already engaged.

She then expected that he would immediately secure her for the two following; but, to her great joy, he was so much piqued by the evident pleasure with which she announced her engagement, that he proudly walked away without adding another word.

Much satisfied with this arrangement, and not without hopes that, if she was at liberty when he arrived, she might be applied to by young Delvile, she now endeavoured to procure herself a place in the music room.

This, with some difficulty, she effected; but though there was an excellent concert, in which several capital performers played and sung, she found it impossible to hear a note, as she chanced to be seated just by Miss Leeson, and two other young ladies, who were paying one another compliments upon their dress and their looks, settling to dance in the same cotillon, guessing who would begin the minuets, and wondering there were not more gentlemen. Yet, in the midst of this unmeaning conversation, of which she remarked that Miss Leeson bore the principal part, not one of them failed, from time to time, to exclaim with great rapture "*What sweet music!—*" "*Oh how charming!*" "*Did you ever hear any thing so delightful?—*"

"Ah," said Cecilia to Mr. Gosport, who now approached her, "but for your explanatory observations, how much would the sudden loquacity of this *supercilious* lady, whom I had imagined all but dumb, have perplext me!"

"Those who are most silent to strangers," answered Mr. Gosport, "commonly talk most fluently to their intimates, for they are deeply in arrears, and eager to pay off their debts. Miss Leeson now is in her proper set, and therefore appears in her natural character: and the poor girl's joy in being able to utter all the nothings she has painfully hoarded while separated from her coterie, gives to her now the wild transport of a bird just let loose from a cage. I rejoice to see the little creature at liberty, for what can be so melancholy as a forced appearance of thinking, where there are no materials for such an occupation?"

Soon after, Miss Larolles, who was laughing immoderately, contrived to crowd herself into their party, calling out to them, "O you have had the greatest loss in the world! if you had but been in the next room just now!— there's the drollest figure there you can conceive: enough to frighten one to look at him." And presently she added "O Lord, if you stoop a little this way, you may see him!"

Then followed a general tittering, accompanied with exclamations of "Lord, what a fright!" "It's enough to kill one with laughing to look at him!" "Did you ever see such a horrid creature in your life?" And soon after, one of them screamed out "O Lord, see!—he's grinning at Miss Beverley!"

Cecilia then turned her head towards the door, and there, to her own as well as her neighbours amazement, she perceived Mr. Briggs! who, in order to look about him at his ease, was standing upon a chair, from which, having singled her out, he was regarding her with a facetious smirk, which, when it caught her eye, was converted into a familiar nod.

She returned his salutation, but was not much charmed to observe, that presently descending from his exalted post, which had moved the wonder and risibility of all the company, he made a motion to approach her; for which purpose, regardless of either ladies or gentlemen in his way, he sturdily pushed forward, with the same unconcerned hardiness he would have forced himself through a crowd in the street; and taking not the smallest notice of their frowns, supplications that he would stand still, and exclamations of "Pray, Sir!"—"Lord, how troublesome!" and "Sir, I do assure you here's no room!" he fairly and adroitly elbowed them from him till he reached her seat: and then, with a waggish grin, he looked round, to shew he had got the better, and to see whom he had discomposed.

When he had enjoyed this triumph, he turned to Cecilia, and chucking her under the chin, said "Well, my little duck, how goes it? got to you at last; squeezed my way; would not be nicked; warrant I'll mob with the best of them! Look here! all in a heat!—hot as the dog-days."*

And then, to the utter consternation of the company, he took off his wig to wipe his head! which occasioned such universal horrour, that all who were near the door escaped into other apartments, while those who were too much enclosed for flight, with one accord turned away their heads.

Captain Aresby, being applied to by some of the ladies to remonstrate upon this unexampled behaviour, advanced to him, and said, "I am quite *abimé*, Sir, to incommode you, but the commands of the ladies are insuperable. Give me leave, Sir, to entreat that you would put on your wig."

"My wig?" cried he, "ay, ay, shall in a moment, only want to wipe my head first."

"I am quite *assommé*, Sir," returned the Captain, "to disturb you, but I must really hint you don't comprehend me: the ladies are extremely inconvenienced by these sort of sights, and we make it a principle they should never be *accablées* with them."

"Anan!" cried Mr. Briggs, staring.

"I say, Sir," replied the Captain, "the ladies are quite *au desespoir* that you will not cover your head."

"What for?" cried he, "what's the matter with my head?

ne'er a man here got a better! very good stuff in it: won't change it with ne'er a one of you!"

And then, half unconscious of the offence he had given, and half angry at the rebuke he had received, he leisurely compleated his design, and again put on his wig, settling it to his face with as much composure as if he had performed the operation in his own dressing-room.

The Captain, having gained his point, walked away, making, however, various grimaces of disgust, and whispering from side to side "he's the most petrifying fellow I ever was *obsedé* by!"

Mr. Briggs then, with much derision, and sundry distortions of countenance, listened to an Italian song; after which, he bustled back to the outer apartment, in search of Cecilia, who, ashamed of seeming a party in the disturbance he had excited, had taken the opportunity of his dispute with the Captain, to run into the next room; where, however, he presently found her, while she was giving an account to Mr. Gosport of her connexion with him, to which Morrice, ever curious and eager to know what was going forward, was also listening.

"Ah, little chick!" cried he, "got to you again! soon out-jostle those jemmy* sparks! But where's the supper? see nothing of the supper! Time to go to bed,—suppose there is none; all a take-in; nothing but a little piping."

"Supper, Sir?" cried Cecilia; "the Concert is not over yet. Was supper mentioned in your card of invitation?"

"Ay, to be sure, should not have come else. Don't visit often; always costs money. Wish I had not come now; wore a hole in my shoe; hardly a crack in it before."

"Why you did not walk, Sir?"

"Did, did; why not? Might as well have stayed away though; daubed my best coat, like to have spoilt it."

"So much the better for the taylors, Sir," said Morrice, pertly, "for then you must have another."

"Another! what for? ha'n't had this seven years; just as good as new."

"I hope," said Cecilia, "you had not another fall?"

"Worse, worse; like to have lost my bundle."

"What bundle, Sir?"

"Best coat and waistcoat; brought 'em in my hand-kerchief, purpose to save them. When will Master Harrel do as much?"

"But had you no apprehensions, Sir," said Mr. Gosport drily, "that the handkerchief would be the sooner worn out for having a knot tied in it?"

"Took care of that, tied it slack. Met an unlucky boy; little dog gave it a pluck; knot slipt; coat and waistcoat popt out."

"But what became of the boy, Sir?" cried Morrice, "I hope he got off?"

"Could not run for laughing; caught him in a minute; gave him something to laugh for; drubbed him soundly."

"O poor fellow!" cried Morrice with a loud hallow,* "I am really sorry for him. But pray, Sir, what became of your best coat and waistcoat while you gave him this drubbing? did you leave them in the dirt?"

"No, Mr. Nincompoop," answered Briggs angrily, "I put them on a stall."

"That was a perilous expedient, Sir," said Mr. Gosport, "and I should fear might be attended with ill consequences, for the owner of the stall would be apt to expect some little *douçeur*. How did you manage, Sir?"

"Bought a halfpenny worth of apples. Serve for supper to-morrow night."

"But how, Sir, did you get your cloaths dried, or cleaned?"

"Went to an alehouse; cost me half a pint."

"And pray, Sir," cried Morrice, "where, at last, did you make your toilette?"

"Sha'n't tell, sha'n't tell; ask no more questions. What signifies where a man slips on a coat and waistcoat?"

"Why, Sir, this will prove an expensive expedition to you," said Mr. Gosport, very gravely; "Have you cast up what it may cost you?"

"More than it's worth, more than it's worth," answered he pettishly; "ha'n't laid out so much in pleasure these five years."

"Ha! ha!" cried Morrice, hallowing aloud, "why it can't be more than sixpence in all!"

"Sixpence?" repeated he scornfully, "if you don't know the value of sixpence, you'll never be worth fivepence three farthings. How do think got rich, hay?—by wearing fine coats, and frizzling my pate?* No, no; Master Harrel for that! ask him if he'll cast an account with me!—never knew a man worth a penny with such a coat as that on."

Morrice again laughed, and again Mr. Briggs reproved him; and Cecilia, taking advantage of the squabble, stole back to the music-room.

Here, in a few minutes, Mrs. Panton, a lady who frequently visited at the house, approached Cecilia, followed by a gentleman, whom she had never before seen, but who was so evidently charmed with her, that he had looked at no other object since his entrance into the house.

Mrs. Panton, presenting him to her by the name of Mr. Marriot, told her he had begged her intercession for the honour of her hand in the two first dances: and the moment she answered that she was already engaged, the same request was made for the two following. Cecilia had then no excuse, and was therefore obliged to accept him.

The hope she had entertained in the early part of the evening, was already almost wholly extinguished; Delvile appeared not! though her eye watched the entrance of every new visitor, and her vexation made her believe that he alone, of all the town, was absent.

When the Concert was over, the company joined promiscuously for chat and refreshments before the ball; and Mr. Gosport advanced to Cecilia, to relate a ridiculous dispute which had just passed between Mr. Briggs and Morrice.

"You, Mr. Gosport," said Cecilia, "who seem to make the *minutiæ* of absurd characters your study, can explain to me, perhaps, why Mr. Briggs seems to have as much pleasure in proclaiming his meanness, as in boasting his wealth?"

"Because," answered Mr. Gosport, "he knows them, in his own affairs, to be so nearly allied, that but for practising the one, he had never possessed the other; ignorant, therefore, of all discrimination,——except, indeed, of pounds, shillings and pence!—he supposes them necessarily inseparable, because with him they were united. What you, however, call meanness, he thinks wisdom, and recollects, therefore, not with shame but with triumph, the various little arts and subterfuges by which his coffers have been filled."

Here Lord Ernolf, concluding Cecilia still disengaged from seeing her only discourse with Mr. Gosport and Mr. Monckton, one of whom was old enough to be her father, and the other was a *married man*,* advanced, and presenting to her Lord Derford, his son, a youth not yet of age, solicited for him the honour of her hand as his partner.

Cecilia, having a double excuse, easily declined this proposal; Lord Ernolf, however, was too earnest to be repulsed, and told her he should again try his interest when her two present engagements were fulfilled. Hopeless, now, of young Delvile, she heard this intimation with indifference; and was accompanying Mr. Monckton into the ball-room, when Miss Larolles, flying towards her with an air of infinite eagerness, caught her hand, and said in a whisper "pray let me wish you joy!"

"Certainly!" said Cecilia, "but pray let me ask you of what?"

"O Lord, now," answered she, "I am sure you know what I mean; but you must know I have a prodigious monstrous great favour to beg of you: now pray don't refuse me; I assure you if you do, I shall be so mortified you've no notion."

"Well, what is it?"

"Nothing but to let me be one of your bride maids. I assure you I shall take it as the greatest favour in the world."

"My bride maid!" cried Cecilia; "but do you not think the bridegroom himself will be rather offended to find a bridemaid appointed, before he is even thought of?"

"O pray, now," cried she, "don't be ill-natured, for if you are, you've no idea how I shall be disappointed. Only conceive what happened to me three weeks ago! you must know I was invited to Miss Clinton's wedding, and so I made up a new dress on purpose, in a very particular sort of shape, quite of my own invention, and it had the sweetest effect you can conceive; well, and when the time came, do you know her mother happened to die! Never any thing was so excessive unlucky, for now she won't be married this half year, and my dress will be quite old and yellow; for its all white, and the most beautiful thing you ever saw in your life."

"Upon my word you are very obliging!" cried Cecilia laughing; "and pray do you make interest regularly round with all your female acquaintance to be married upon this occasion, or am I the only one you think this distress will work upon?"

"Now how excessive teazing!" cried Miss Larolles, "when you know so well what I mean, and when all the town knows as well as myself."

Cecilia then seriously enquired whether she had really any meaning at all.

"Lord yes," answered she, "you know I mean about Sir Robert Floyer: for I'm told you've quite refused Lord Derford."

"And are you also told that I have accepted Sir Robert Floyer?"

"O dear yes!—the jewels are bought, and the equipages are built; it's quite a settled thing, I know very well."

Cecilia then very gravely began an attempt to undeceive her; but the dancing beginning also at the same time, she stayed not to hear her, hurrying, with a beating heart, to the place of action. Mr. Monckton and his fair partner then followed, mutually exclaiming against Mr. Harrel's impenetrable conduct; of which Cecilia, however, in a short time ceased wholly to think, for as soon as the first cotillon was over, she perceived young Delvile just walking into the room.

Surprise, pleasure and confusion assailed her all at once; she had entirely given up her expectation of seeing him, and an absence so determined had led her to conclude he had pursuits which ought to make her join in wishing it lengthened; but now he appeared, that conclusion, with the fears that gave rise to it, vanished; and she regretted nothing but the unfortunate succession of engagements which would prevent her dancing with him at all, and probably keep off all conversation with him till supper time.

She soon, however, perceived a change in his air and behaviour that extremely astonished her: he looked grave and thoughtful, saluted her at a distance, shewed no sign of any intention to approach her, regarded the dancing and dancers as a public spectacle in which he had no chance of personal interest, and seemed wholly altered, not merely with respect to her, but to himself, as his former eagerness for her society was not more abated than her former general gaiety.*

She had no time, however, for comments, as she was presently called to the second cotillon; but the confused and unpleasant ideas which, without waiting for time or reflection, crowded upon her imagination on observing his behaviour, were not more depressing to herself, than obvious to her partner; Mr. Monckton by the change in her countenance first perceived the entrance of young Delvile, and by her apparent emotion and uneasiness, readily penetrated into the state of her mind; he was confirmed that her affections were engaged; he saw, too, that she was doubtful with what return.

The grief with which he made the first discovery, was somewhat lessened by the hopes he conceived from the second; yet the evening was to him as painful as to Cecilia, since he now knew that whatever prosperity might ultimately attend his address and assiduity, her heart was not her own to bestow; and that even were he sure of young Delvile's indifference, and actually at liberty to make proposals for himself, the time of being first in her esteem was at an end, and the long earned good opinion which he had hoped would have ripened into affection, might now be wholly undermined by the sudden impression of a lively stranger, without trouble to himself, and perhaps without pleasure!

Reflections such as these wholly embittered the delight

he had promised himself from dancing with her, and took from him all power to combat the anxiety with which she was seized; when the second cotillon, therefore, was over, instead of following her to a seat, or taking the privilege of his present situation to converse with her, the jealousy rising in his breast robbed him of all satisfaction, and gave to him no other desire than to judge its justice by watching her motions at a distance.

Mean while Cecilia, inattentive whether he accompanied or quitted her, proceeded to the first vacant seat. Young Delvile was standing near it, and, in a short time, but rather as if he could not avoid than as if he wished it, he came to enquire how she did.

The simplest question, in the then situation of her mind, was sufficient to confuse her, and though she answered, she hardly knew what he had asked. A minute's recollection, however, restored an apparent composure, and she talked to him of Mrs. Delvile, with her usual partial regard for that lady, and with an earnest endeavour to seem unconscious of any alteration in his behaviour.

Yet, to him, even this trifling and general conversation was evidently painful, and he looked relieved by the approach of Sir Robert Floyer, who soon after joined them.

At this time a young lady who was sitting by Cecilia, called to a servant who was passing, for a glass of lemonade: Cecilia desired he would bring her one also; but Delvile, not sorry to break off the discourse, said he would himself be her cup-bearer, and for that purpose went away.

A moment after, the servant returned with some lemonade to Cecilia's neighbour, and Sir Robert, taking a glass from him, brought it to Cecilia at the very instant young Delvile came with another.

"I think I am before-hand with you, Sir," said the insolent Baronet.

"No, Sir," answered young Delvile, "I think we were both in together: Miss Beverley, however, is steward of the race,* and we must submit to her decision."

"Well, madam," cried Sir Robert, "here we stand, waiting your pleasure. Which is to be the happy man!"

"Each, I hope," answered Cecilia, with admirable presence of mind, "since I expect no less than that you will both do me the honour of drinking my health."

This little contrivance, which saved her alike from shewing favour or giving offence, could not but be applauded by both parties: and while they obeyed her orders, she took a third glass herself from the servant.

While this was passing, Mr. Briggs, again perceiving her, stumpt hastily towards her, calling out "Ah ha! my duck! what's that? got something nice? Come here, my lad, taste it myself."

He then took a glass, but having only put it to his mouth, made a wry face, and returned it, saying "Bad! bad! poor punch indeed!—not a drop of rum* in it!"

"So much the better, Sir," cried Morrice, who diverted himself by following him, "for then you see the master of the house spares in something, and you said he spared in nothing."

"Don't spare in fools!" returned Mr. Briggs, "keeps them in plenty."

"No, Sir, nor in any out of the way characters," answered Morrice.

"So much the worse," cried Briggs, "so much the worse! Eat him out of house and home; won't leave him a rag to his back, nor a penny in his pocket. Never mind 'em, my little duck; mind none of your guardians but me: t'other two a'n't worth a rush."*

Cecilia, somewhat ashamed of this speech, looked towards young Delvile, in whom it occasioned the first smile she had seen that evening.

"Been looking about for you!" continued Briggs, nodding sagaciously; "believe I've found one will do. Guess what I mean;—100,000l.—hay?—what say to that? any thing better at the west end of the town?"*

"100,000l.!" cried Morrice, "and pray, Sir, who may this be?"

"Not you, Mr. jackanapes!* sure of that. An't quite positive he'll have you, neither. Think he will, though."

"Pray, Sir, what age is he?" cried the never daunted Morrice.

"Why about—let's see—don't know, never heard,—what signifies?"

"But, Sir, he's an old man, I suppose, by being so rich?"

"Old? no, no such thing; about my own standing."

"What, Sir, and do you propose him for an husband to Miss Beverley?"

"Why not? know ever a one warmer? think Master Harrel will get her a better? or t'other old Don, in the grand square?"

"If you please, Sir," cried Cecilia hastily, "we will talk of this matter another time."

"No, pray," cried young Delvile, who could not forbear laughing, "let it be discussed now."

"Hate 'em," continued Mr. Briggs, "hate 'em both! one spending more than he's worth, cheated and over-reached by fools, running into gaol to please a parcel of knaves: t'other counting nothing but uncles and grandfathers, dealing out fine names instead of cash, casting up* more cousins than guineas—"

Again Cecilia endeavoured to silence him, but, only chucking her under the chin, he went on, "Ay, ay, my little duck, never mind 'em; one of 'em i'n't worth a penny, and t'other has nothing in his pockets but lists of the defunct. What good will come of that? would not give twopence a dozen for 'em! A poor set of grandees, with nothing but a tie-wig* for their portions!"

Cecilia, unable to bear this harangue in the presence of young Delvile, who, however, laughed it off with a very good grace, arose with an intention to retreat, which being perceived by Sir Robert Floyer, who had attended to this dialogue with haughty contempt, he came forward, and said "now then, madam, may I have the honour of your hand?"

"No, Sir," answered Cecilia, "I am engaged."

"Engaged again?" cried he, with the air of a man who thought himself much injured.

"Glad of it, glad of it!" said Mr. Briggs; "served very right! have nothing to say to him, my chick!"

"Why not, Sir?" cried Sir Robert, with an imperious look.

"Sha'n't have her, sha'n't have her! can tell you that; won't consent; know you of old."

"And what do you know of me, pray Sir?"

"No good, no good; nothing to say to you; found fault with my nose! ha'n't forgot it."

At this moment Mr. Marriot came to claim his partner, who very willing to quit this scene of wrangling and vulgarity, immediately attended him.

Miss Larolles, again flying up to her, said "O my dear, we are all expiring to know who that creature is! I never saw such a horrid fright in my life!"

Cecilia was beginning to satisfy her, but some more young ladies coming up to join in the request, she endeavoured to pass on; "O but", cried Miss Larolles, detaining her, "do pray stop, for I've something to tell you that's so monstrous you've no idea. Do you know Mr. Meadows has not danced at all! and he's been standing with Mr. Sawyer, and looking on all the time, and whispering and laughing so you've no notion. However, I assure you, I'm excessive glad he did not ask me, for all I have been sitting still all this time, for I had a great deal rather sit still, I assure you: only I'm sorry I put on this dress, for any thing would have done just to look on in that stupid manner."

Here Mr. Meadows sauntered towards them; and all the young ladies began playing with their fans, and turning their heads another way, to disguise the expectations which his approach awakened; and Miss Larolles, in a hasty whisper to Cecilia, cried, "Pray don't take any notice of what I said, for if he should happen to ask me, I can't well refuse him, you know, for if I do, he'll be so excessive affronted you can't think."

Mr. Meadows then, mixing in the little group, began, with sundry grimaces, to exclaim "how intollerably hot it is! there's no such thing as breathing. How can any body think of dancing! I am amazed Mr. Harrel has not a ventilator* in this room. Don't you think it would be a great improvement?"

This speech, though particularly addressed to no one, received immediately an assenting answer from all the young ladies.

Then, turning to Miss Larolles, "Don't you dance?" he said.

"Me?" cried she, embarrassed, "yes, I believe so,—really I don't know,—I a'n't quite determined."

"O, do dance!" cried he, stretching himself and yawning, "it always gives me spirits to see you."

Then, turning suddenly to Cecilia, without any previous ceremony of renewing his acquaintance, either by speaking or bowing, he abruptly said "Do you love dancing, ma'am?"

"Yes, Sir, extremely well."

"I am very glad to hear it. You have one thing, then, to soften existence."

"Do you dislike it yourself?"

"What dancing? Oh dreadful! how it was ever adopted in a civilized country I cannot find out; 'tis certainly a Barbarian exercise, and of savage origin. Don't you think so, Miss Larolles?"

"Lord no," cried Miss Larolles, "I assure you I like it better than any thing; I know nothing so delightful, I declare I dare say I could not live without it; I should be so stupid you can't conceive."

"Why I remember," said Mr. Marriot, "when Mr. Meadows was always dancing himself. Have you forgot, Sir, when you used to wish the night would last for ever, that you might dance without ceasing?"

Mr. Meadows, who was now intently surveying a painting that was over the chimney-piece, seemed not to hear this question, but presently called out "I am amazed Mr. Harrel can suffer such a picture as this to be in his house. I hate a portrait, 'tis so wearisome looking at a thing that is doing nothing!"

"Do you like historical pictures, Sir, any better?"

"O no, I detest them! views of battles, murders, and death! Shocking! shocking!—I shrink from them with horror!"

"Perhaps you are fond of landscapes?"

"By no means! Green trees and fat cows! what do they tell one? I hate every thing that is insipid."

"Your toleration, then," said Cecilia, "will not be very extensive."

"No," said he, yawning, "one can tolerate nothing! one's patience is wholly exhausted by the total tediousness of every thing one sees, and every body one talks with. Don't you find it so, ma'am?"

"*Sometimes!*" said Cecilia, rather archly.

"You are right, ma'am, extremely right; one does not know what in the world to do with one's self. At home, one is killed with meditation, abroad, one is overpowered by ceremony; no possibility of finding ease or comfort. You never go into public, I think, ma'am?"

"Why not to be much *marked*, I find!" said Cecilia, laughing.

"O, I beg your pardon! I believe I saw you one evening at Almack's: I really beg your pardon, but I had quite forgot it."

"Lord, Mr. Meadows," said Miss Larolles, "don't you know you are meaning the Pantheon? only conceive how you forget things!"

"The Pantheon, was it? I never know one of those places from another. I heartily wish they were all abolished; I hate public places. 'Tis terrible to be under the same roof with a set of people who would care nothing if they saw one expiring!"

"You are, at least, then, fond of the society of your friends?"

"O no! to be worn out by seeing always the same faces!— one is sick to death of friends; nothing makes one so melancholy."

Cecilia now went to join the dancers, and Mr. Meadows, turning to Miss Larolles, said "Pray don't let me keep you from dancing; I am afraid you'll lose your place."

"No," cried she, bridling, "I sha'n't dance at all."

"How cruel!" cried he, yawning, "when you know how it exhilarates me to see you! Don't you think this room is very close? I must go and try another atmosphere,——But I hope you will relent, and dance?''

And then, stretching his arms as if half asleep, he sauntered into the next room, where he flung himself upon a sofa till the ball was over.

The new partner of Cecilia, who was a wealthy, but very simple young man, used his utmost efforts to entertain and oblige her, and, flattered by the warmth of his own desire, he fancied that he succeeded; though, in a state of such suspence and anxiety, a man of brighter talents had failed.

At the end of the two dances, Lord Ernolf again attempted to engage her for his son, but she now excused herself from dancing any more, and sat quietly as a spectatress till the rest of the company gave over. Mr. Marriot, however, would not quit her, and she was compelled to support with him a trifling conversation, which, though irksome to herself, to him, who had not *seen her in her happier hour*,* was delightful.

She expected every instant to be again joined by young Delvile, but the expectation was disappointed; he came not; she concluded he was in another apartment; the company was summoned to supper, she then thought it impossible to miss him; but, after waiting and looking for him in vain, she found he had already left the house.

The rest of the evening she scarce knew what passed, for she attended to nothing; Mr. Monckton might watch, and Mr. Briggs might exhort her, Sir Robert might display his insolence, or Mr. Marriot his gallantry,—all was equally indifferent, and equally unheeded, and before half the company left the house, she retired to her own room.

She spent the night in the utmost disturbance; the occurrences of the evening with respect to young Delvile she looked upon as decisive: if his absence had chagrined her, his presence had still more shocked her, since, while she was left to conjecture, though she had fears she had hopes, and though all she saw was gloomy, all she expected was pleasant; but they had now met, and those expectations proved fallacious. She knew not, indeed, how to account for the strangeness of his conduct; but in seeing it was strange, she was convinced it was unfavourable: he had evidently avoided her while it was in his power, and when, at last, he was obliged to meet her, he was formal, distant, and reserved.

The more she recollected and dwelt upon the difference of his behaviour in their preceding meeting, the more angry as well as amazed she became at the change, and tho' she still concluded the pursuit of some other object occasioned it, she could find no excuse for his fickleness if that pursuit was recent, nor for his caprice if it was anterior.

CHAPTER II

A Broad Hint

THE next day Cecilia, to drive Delvile a little from her thoughts, which she now no longer wished him to occupy, again made a visit to Miss Belfield, whose society afforded her more consolation than any other she could procure.

She found her employed in packing up, and preparing to remove to another lodging, for her brother, she said, was so much better, that he did not think it right to continue in so disgraceful a situation.

She talked with her accustomed openness of her affairs, and the interest which Cecilia involuntarily took in them, contributed to lessen her vexation in thinking of her own. "The generous friend of my brother," said she, "who, though but a new acquaintance to him, has courted him in all his sorrows, when every body else forsook him, has brought him at last into a better way of thinking. He says there is a gentleman whose son is soon going abroad, who he is almost sure will like my brother vastly, and in another week, he is to be introduced to him. And so, if my mother can but reconcile herself to parting with him, perhaps we may all do well again."

"Your mother," said Cecilia, "when he is gone, will better know the value of the blessing she has left in her daughter."

"O no, madam, no; she is wrapt up in him, and cares

nothing for all the world besides. It was always so, and we have all of us been used to it. But we have had a sad scene since you were so kind as to come last; for when she told him what you had done, he was almost out of his senses with anger that we had acquainted you with his distress, and he said it was publishing his misery, and undoing whatever his friend or himself could do, for it was making him ashamed to appear in the world, even when his affairs might be better. But I told him again and again that you had as much sweetness as goodness, and instead of hurting his reputation, would do him nothing but credit.''

"I am sorry," said Cecilia, "Mrs. Belfield mentioned the circumstance at all; it would have been better, for many reasons, that he should not have heard of it."

"She hoped it would please him," answered Miss Belfield, "however, he made us both promise we would take no such step in future, for he said *we* were not reduced to so much indigence, whatever he was: and that as to our accepting money from other people, that we might save up our own for him, it would be answering no purpose, for he should think himself a monster to make use of it."

"And what said your mother?"

"Why she gave him a great many promises that she would never vex him about it again; and indeed, much as I know we are obliged to you, madam, and gratefully as I am sure I would lay down my life to serve you, I am very glad in this case that my brother has found it out. For though I so much wish him to do something for himself, and not to be so proud, and live in a manner he has no right to do, I think, for all that, that it is a great disgrace to my poor father's honest memory, to have us turn beggars after his death, when he left us all so well provided for, if we had but known how to be satisfied."

"There is a natural rectitude in your heart," said Cecilia, "that the ablest casuists could not mend."*

She then enquired whither they were removing, and Miss Belfield told her to Portland-street, Oxford Road, where they were to have two apartments up two pair of stairs, and the use of a very good parlour, in which her brother might see his friends. "And this," added she, "is a luxury for which nobody can blame him, because if he has not the appearance of a decent home, no gentleman will employ him."

The Padington house, she said, was already let, and her mother was determined not to hire another, but still to live as penuriously as possible, in order, notwithstanding his remonstrances, to save all she could of her income for her son.

Here the conversation was interrupted by the entrance of Mrs. Belfield, who very familiarly said she came to tell Cecilia they were *all in the wrong box** in letting her son know of the 10*l.* Bank note, "for," continued she, "he has a pride that would grace a duke, and he thinks nothing of his hardships, so long as nobody knows of them. So another time we must manage things better, and when we do him any good, not let him know a word of the matter. We'll settle it all among ourselves, and one day or other he'll be glad enough to thank us."

Cecilia, who saw Miss Belfield colour with shame at the freedom of this hint, now arose to depart: but Mrs. Belfield begged her not to go so soon, and pressed her with such urgency to again sit down, that she was obliged to comply.

She then began a warm commendation of her son, lavishly praising all his good qualities, and exalting even his defects, concluding with saying "But, ma'am, for all he's such a complete gentleman, and for all he's made so much of, he was so diffident, I could not get him to call and thank you for the present you made him, though, when he went his last airing, I almost knelt to him to do it. But, with all his merit, he wants as much encouragement as a lady, for I can tell you it is not a little will do for him."

Cecilia, amazed at this extraordinary speech, looked from the mother to the daughter in order to discover it's meaning, which, however, was soon rendered plainer by what followed.

"But pray now, ma'am, don't think him the more un-grateful for his shyness, for young ladies so high in the world as you are, must go pretty good lengths before a young man will get courage to speak to them. And though I have told my son over and over that the ladies never like a man the worse for being a little bold, he's so much down in the mouth* that it has no effect upon him. But it all comes of his being brought up at the university, for that makes him think he knows better than I can tell him. And so, to be sure, he does. However, for all that, it is a hard thing upon a mother to find all she says goes just for nothing. But I hope you'll excuse him, ma'am, for it's nothing in the world but his over-modesty.''

Cecilia now stared with a look of so much astonishment and displeasure, that Mrs. Belfield, suspecting she had gone rather too far, added ''I beg you won't take what I've said amiss, ma'am, for we mothers of families are more used to speak out than maiden ladies. And I should not have said so much, but only I was afraid you would misconstrue my son's backwardness, and so that he might be flung out of your favour at last, and all for nothing but having too much respect for you.''

''O dear mother!'' cried Miss Belfield, whose face was the colour of scarlet, ''pray!''—

''What's the matter now?'' cried Mrs. Belfield; ''you are as shy as your brother; and if we are all to be so, when are we to come to an understanding?''

''Not immediately, I believe indeed,'' said Cecilia, rising, ''but that we may not plunge deeper in our mistakes, I will for the present take my leave.''

''No, ma'am,'' cried Mrs. Belfield, stopping her, ''pray don't go yet, for I've got a great many things I want to talk to you about. In the first place, ma'am, pray what is your opinion of this scheme for sending my son abroad into foreign parts? I don't know what you may think of it, but as to me, it half drives me out of my senses to have him taken away from me at last in that unnatural manner. And I'm sure, ma'am, if you would only put in a word against it, I dare say he would give it up without a demur.''

''Me?'' cried Cecilia, disengaging herself from her hold, ''No, madam, you must apply to those friends who better understand his affairs, and who would have a deeper interest in detaining him.''

"Lack a day!'' cried Mrs. Belfield, with scarcely smothered vexation, ''how hard it is to make these grand young ladies come to reason! As to my son's other friends, what good will it do for him to mind what they say? who can expect him to give up his journey, without knowing what amends he shall get for it?''

''You must settle this matter with him at your leisure,'' said Cecilia, ''I cannot now stay another moment.''

Mrs. Belfield, again finding she had been too precipitate, tried to draw back, saying ''Pray, ma'am, don't let what I have mentioned go against my son in your good opinion, for he knows no more of it than the furthest person in the world, as my daughter can testify: for as to shyness, he's just as shy as a lady himself; so what good he ever got at the University, as to the matter of making his fortune, it's what I never could discover. However, I dare say he knows best; though when all comes to all, if I was to speak my mind, I think he's made but a poor hand of it.''*

Cecilia, who only through compassion to the blushing Henrietta forbore repressing this forwardness more seriously, merely answered Mrs. Belfield by wishing her good morning: but, while she was taking a kinder leave of her timid daughter, the mother added ''As to the present, ma'am, you was so kind to make us, Henny can witness for me every penny of it shall go to my son.''

''I rather meant it,'' said Cecilia, ''for your daughter; but if it is of use to any body, my purpose is sufficiently answered.''

Mrs. Belfield again pressed her to sit down, but she would not again listen to her, coldly saying ''I am sorry you troubled Mr. Belfield with any mention of what passed between his sister and me, but should you speak of it again, I beg you will explain to him that he had no concern in that little transaction, which belonged wholly to ourselves.''

She then hastened down stairs, followed, however, by Mrs. Belfield, making awkward excuses for what she had said, intermixed with frequent hints that she knew all the time she was in the right.

This little incident, which convinced Cecilia Mrs. Belfield was firmly persuaded she was in love with her son, gave her much uneasiness; she feared the son himself might entertain the same notion, and thought it most probable the daughter also had imbibed it, though but for the forward vulgarity of the sanguine mother, their opinions might long have remained concealed. Her benevolence towards them, notwithstanding its purity, must now therefore cease to be exerted: nor could she even visit Miss Belfield, since prudence, and a regard for her own character, seemed immediately to prohibit all commerce with the family.

"And thus difficult," cried she, "is the blameless use of riches, though all who want them, think nothing so easy as their disposal! This family I have so much wished to serve, I may at last only have injured, since the disappointment of their higher expectations, may render all smaller benefits contemptible. And thus this unfortunate misconstruction of my good offices, robs them of a useful assistant, and deprives me at the same time of an amiable companion."

As soon as she returned home, she had a letter put into her hand which came from Mr. Marriot, whose servant had twice called for an answer in the short time she had been absent.

This letter contained a most passionate avowal of the impression she had made on his heart the preceding evening, and an angry complaint that Mr. Harrel had refused to hear his proposals. He entreated her permission to wait upon her for only five minutes, and concluded with the most fervent professions of respect and admiration.

The precipitancy of this declaration served merely to confirm the opinion she had already conceived of the weakness of his understanding: but the obstinacy of Mr. Harrel irritated and distressed her; though weary of expostulating with so hopeless a subject, whom neither reason nor gratitude could turn from his own purposes, she was obliged to submit to his management, and was well content, in the present instance, to affirm his decree.

She therefore wrote a concise answer to her new admirer, in the usual form of civil rejection.

CHAPTER III

An Accommodation

CECILIA was informed the next morning that a young woman begged to speak with her, and upon sending for her up stairs, she saw, to her great surprise, Miss Belfield.

She came in fear and trembling, sent, she said, by her mother, to entreat her pardon for what had passed the preceding day; "But I know, madam," she added, "you cannot pardon it, and therefore all that I mean to do is to clear my brother from any share in what was said, for indeed he has too much sense to harbour any such presumption; and to thank you with a most grateful heart for all the goodness you have shewn us."

And then, modestly courtsying, she would have returned home; but Cecilia, much touched by her gentleness, took her hand, and kindly reviving her by assurances of esteem, entreated that she would lengthen her stay.

"How good is this, madam," said she, "after having so much reason to think so ill of me and of all of us! I tried all in my power to undeceive my mother, or at least to keep her quiet; but she was so much persuaded she was right, that she never would listen to me, and always said, did I suppose it was for *me* you condescended to come so often?"

"Yes," answered Cecilia, "most undoubtedly; had I not known you, however well I might have wished your brother, I should certainly not have visited at his house. But I am very happy to hear the mistake had spread no further."

"No indeed, madam, I never once thought of it; and as to my brother, when my mother only hinted it to him, he was quite angry. But though I don't mean to vindicate what has happened, you will not, I hope, be displeased if I say my mother is much more pardonable than she seems to be, for the same mistake she made with you, she would have been as apt to have made with a princess; it was not, therefore, from any want of respect, but merely from thinking my brother might marry as high as he pleased, and believing no lady would refuse him, if he would but have the courage to speak.''

Cecilia assured her she would think no more of the error, but told her that to avoid its renewal, she must decline calling upon her again till her brother was gone. She begged therefore to see her in Portman-square whenever she had leisure, repeatedly assuring her of her good opinion and regard, and of the pleasure with which she should seize every opportunity of shewing them.

Delighted by a reception so kind, Miss Belfield remained with her all the morning; and when at last she was obliged to leave her, she was but too happy in being solicited to repeat her visit.

She suffered one day only to elapse before she shewed her readiness to accept the friendship that was offered her; and Cecilia, much pleased by this eagerness, redoubled her efforts to oblige and to serve her.

From this time, hardly a day passed in which she did not call in Portman-square, where nothing in her reception was omitted that could contribute to her contentment. Cecilia was glad to employ her mind in any way that related not to Delvile, whom she now earnestly endeavoured to think of no more, denying herself even the pleasure of talking of him with Miss Belfield, by the name of *her brother's noble friend.**

During this time she devised various methods, all too delicate to give even the shadow of offence, for making both useful and ornamental presents to her new favourite, with whom she grew daily more satisfied, and to whom she purposed hereafter offering a residence in her own house.

The trial of intimacy, so difficult to the ablest to stand, and from which even the most faultless are so rarely acquitted, Miss Belfield sustained with honour. Cecilia found her artless, ingenuous, and affectionate; her understanding was good, though no pains had been taken to improve it; her disposition though ardent was soft, and her mind seemed informed by intuitive integrity.

She communicated to Cecilia all the affairs of her family, disguising from her neither distress nor meanness, and seeking to palliate nothing but the grosser parts of the character of her mother. She seemed equally ready to make known to her even the most chosen secrets of her own bosom, for that such she had was evident, from a frequent appearance of absence and uneasiness which she took but little trouble to conceal. Cecilia, however, trusted not herself, in the present critical situation of her own mind, with any enquiries that might lead to a subject she was conscious she ought not to dwell upon: a short time, she hoped, would totally remove her suspence; but as she had much less reason to expect good than evil, she made it her immediate study to prepare for the worst, and therefore carefully avoided all discourse that by nourishing her tenderness, might weaken her resolution.

While thus, in friendly conversation and virtuous forbearance, passed gravely, but not unhappily, the time of Cecilia, the rest of the house was very differently employed: feasting, revelling, amusements of all sorts were pursued with more eagerness than ever, and the alarm which so lately threatened their destruction, seemed now merely to heighten the avidity with which they were sought. Yet never was the disunion of happiness and diversion more striking and obvious; Mr. Harrel, in spite of his natural levity, was seized from time to time with fits of horror that embittered his gayest moments, and cast a cloud upon all his enjoyments. Always an enemy to solitude, he now found it wholly insupportable, and ran into company of any sort, less from a hope of finding entertainment, than from a dread of spending half an hour by himself.

Cecilia, who saw that his rapacity for pleasure encreased with his uneasiness, once more ventured to speak with his lady upon the subject of reformation; counselling her to take advantage of his present apparent discontent, which shewed at least some sensibility of his situation, in order to point out to him the necessity of an immediate inspection into his affairs, which, with a total change in his way of life, was her only chance for snatching him from the dismal despondency into which he was sinking.

Mrs. Harrel declared herself unequal to following this advice, and said that her whole study was to find Mr. Harrel amusement, for he was grown so ill-humoured and petulant she quite feared being alone with him.

The house therefore now was more crowded than ever, and nothing but dissipation was thought of. Among those who upon this plan were courted to it, the foremost was Mr. Morrice, who, from a peculiar talent of uniting servility of conduct with gaiety of speech, made himself at once so agreeable and useful in the family, that in a short time they fancied it impossible to live without him. And Morrice, though his first view in obtaining admittance had been the cultivation of his acquaintance with Cecilia, was perfectly satisfied with the turn that matters had taken, since his utmost vanity had never led him to entertain any matrimonial hopes with her, and he thought his fortune as likely to profit from the civility of her friends as of herself. For Morrice, however flighty and wild, had always at heart the study of his own interest; and though from a giddy forwardness of disposition he often gave offence, his meaning and his serious attention was not the less directed to the advancement of his own affairs: he formed no connection from which he hoped not some benefit, and he considered the acquaintance and friendship of his superiors in no other light than that of procuring him sooner or later recommendations to new clients.*

Sir Robert Floyer also was more frequent than ever in his visits, and Mr. Harrel, notwithstanding the remonstrances of Cecilia, contrived every possible opportunity of giving him access to her. Mrs. Harrel herself, though hitherto neutral, now pleaded his cause with earnestness; and Mr. Arnott, who had been her former refuge from this persecution, grew so serious and so tender in his devoirs, that unable any longer to doubt the sentiments she had inspired, she was compelled even with him to be guarded and distant.

She now with daily concern looked back to the sacrifice she had made to the worthless and ungrateful Mr. Harrel, and was sometimes tempted to immediately chuse another guardian, and leave his house for ever: yet the delicacy of her disposition was averse to any step that might publicly expose him, and her early regard for his wife would not suffer her to put it in execution.

These circumstances contributed strongly to encrease her intimacy with Miss Belfield; she now never saw Mrs. Delvile, whom alone she preferred to her, and from the troublesome assiduity of Sir Robert, scarce ever met Mr. Monckton but in his presence: she found, therefore, no resource against teazing and vexation, but what was afforded her by the conversation of the amiable Henrietta.

CHAPTER IV

A Detection

A FORTNIGHT had now elapsed in which Cecilia had had no sort of communication with the Delviles, whom equally from pride and from prudence she forbore to seek herself, when one morning, while she was sitting with Miss Belfield, her maid told her* that young Mr. Delvile was in the drawing-room, and begged the honour of seeing her for a few moments.

Cecilia, though she started and changed colour with surprize at this message, was unconscious she did either, from the yet greater surprize she received by the behaviour of Miss Belfield, who hastily arising, exclaimed "Good God, Mr. Delvile!——do you know Mr. Delvile, madam?—does Mr. Delvile visit at this house?"

"Sometimes; not often," answered Cecilia; "but why?"

"I don't know,—nothing, madam,—I only asked by accident, I believe,—but it's very—it's extremely—I did not know—" and colouring violently, she again sat down.

An apprehension the most painful now took possession of Cecilia, and absorbed in thought, she continued for some minutes silent and immoveable.

From this state she was awakened by her maid, who asked if she chose to have her gloves.*

Cecilia, taking them from her without speaking, left the room, and not daring to stop for enquiry or consideration, hastened down stairs; but when she entered the apartment where young Delvile was waiting for her, all utterance seemed denied her, and she courtsied without saying a word.

Struck with the look and uncommon manner of her entrance, he became in a moment as much disturbed as herself, pouring forth a thousand unnecessary and embarrassed apologies for his visit, and so totally forgetting even the reason why he made it, that he had taken his leave and was departing before he recollected it. He then turned back, forcing a laugh at his own absence of mind, and told her he had only called to acquaint her, that the commands with which she had honoured him were now obeyed, and, he hoped, to her satisfaction.

Cecilia, who knew not she had ever given him any, waited his further explanation; and he then informed her he had that very morning introduced Mr. Belfield to the Earl of Vannelt, who had already heard him very advantageously spoken of by some gentlemen to whom he had been known at the University, and who was so much pleased with him upon this first interview, that he meant, after a few enquiries, which could not but turn out to his credit, to commit his eldest son to his trust in making the tour of Europe.

Cecilia thanked him for her share in the trouble he had taken in this transaction; and then asked if Mrs. Delvile continued well.

"Yes," answered he, with a smile half reproachful, "as well as one who having ever hoped your favour, can easily be after finding that hope disappointed. But much as she has taught her son, there is one lesson she might perhaps learn from him;—to fly, not seek, those dangerous indulgences of which the deprivation is the loss of peace!"

He then bowed, and made his exit.

This unexpected reproof, and the yet more unexpected compliment that accompanied it, in both which *more seemed meant than met the ear*,* encreased the perturbation into which Cecilia had already been thrown. It occurred to her that under the sanction of his mother's name, he had taken an opportunity of making an apology for his own conduct; yet why avoiding her society, if to that he alluded, should be *flying a dangerous indulgence*, she could not understand, since he had so little reason to fear any repulse in continuing to seek it.

Sorry, however, for the abrupt manner in which she had left Miss Belfield, she lost not a moment in hastening back to her; but when she came into the room, she found her employed in looking out of the window, her eye following some object with such earnestness of attention, that she perceived not her return.

Cecilia, who could not doubt the motive of her curiosity, had no great difficulty in forbearing to offer her any interruption. She drew her head back in a few minutes, and casting it upwards, with her hands clasped, softly whispered, "Heaven ever shield and bless him! and O may he never feel such pain as I do!"

She then again looked out, but soon drawing herself in, said, in the same soft accents, "Oh why art thou gone! sweetest and noblest of men! why might I not see thee longer, when, under heaven, there is no other blessing I wish for!"

A sigh which at these words escaped Cecilia made her start and turn towards the door; the deepest blushes overspread the cheeks of both as their eyes met each other, and while Miss Belfield trembled in every limb at the discovery* she had made, Cecilia herself was hardly able to stand.

A painful and most embarrassed silence succeeded, which was only broken by Miss Belfield's bursting into tears.

Cecilia, extremely moved, forgot for a moment her own interest in what was passing, and tenderly approaching, embraced her with the utmost kindness: but still she spoke not, fearing to make any enquiry, from dreading to hear any explanation.

Miss Belfield, soothed by her softness, clung about her, and hiding her face in her arms, sobbed out "Ah madam!

who ought to be unhappy if befriended by you! if I could
help it, I would love nobody else in almost the whole world.
But you must let me leave you now, and to-morrow I will
tell you every thing."

Cecilia, who had no wish for making any opposition,
embraced her again, and suffered her quietly to depart.

Her own mind was now in a state of the utmost confusion.
The rectitude of her heart and the soundness of her
judgment had hitherto guarded her both from error and
blame, and, except during her recent suspence, had
preserved her tranquility inviolate: but her commerce with
the world had been small and confined, and her actions had
had little reference but to herself. The case was now altered;
and she was suddenly in a conjuncture of all others the most
delicate, that of accidentally discovering a rival in a
favourite friend.

The fondness she had conceived for Miss Belfield, and the
sincerity of her intentions as well as promises to serve her,
made the detection of this secret peculiarly cruel: she had
lately felt no pleasure but in her society, and looked forward
to much future comfort from the continuance of her regard,
and from their constantly living together: but now this was
no longer even to be desired, since the utter annihilation of
the wishes of both, by young Delvile's being disposed of to
a third person, could alone render eligible their dwelling
under the same roof.

Her pity, however, for Miss Belfield was almost wholly
unallayed by jealousy; she harboured not any suspicion that
she was loved by young Delvile, whose aspiring spirit led her
infinitely more to fear some higher rival, than to believe he
bestowed even a thought upon the poor Henrietta: but still
she wished with the utmost ardour to know the length of
their acquaintance, how often they had met, when they had
conversed, what notice he had taken of her, and how so
dangerous a preference had invaded her heart.

But though this curiosity was both natural and powerful,
her principal concern was the arrangement of her own
conduct: the next day Miss Belfield was to tell her every
thing by a voluntary promise; but she doubted if she had any

right to accept such a confidence. Miss Belfield, she was sure, knew not she was interested in the tale, since she had not even imagined that Delvile was known to her. She might hope, therefore, not only for advice but assistance, and fancy that while she reposed her secret in the bosom of a friend, she secured herself her best offices and best wishes for ever.

Would she obtain them? no; the most romantic generosity would revolt from such a demand, for however precarious was her own chance with young Delvile, Miss Belfield she was sure could not have any: neither her birth nor education fitted her for his rank in life, and even were both unexceptionable, the smallness of her fortune, as Mr. Monckton had instructed her, would be an obstacle insurmountable.

Would it not be a kind of treachery to gather from her every thing, yet aid her in nothing? to take advantage of her unsuspicious openness in order to learn all that related to one whom she yet hoped would belong ultimately to herself, and gratify an interested curiosity at the expence of a candour not more simple than amiable? "No," cried Cecilia, "arts that I could never forgive, I never will practice; this sweet, but unhappy girl shall tell me nothing: betrayed already by the tenderness of her own heart, she shall at least suffer no further from any duplicity in mine. If, indeed, Mr. Delvile, as I suspect, is engaged elsewhere, I will make this gentle Henrietta the object of my future solicitude: the sympathy of our situations will not then divide but unite us, and I will take her to my bosom, hear all her sorrows, and calm her troubled spirit by participating in her sensibility. But if, on the contrary, this mystery ends more happily for myself, if Mr. Delvile has now no other engagement, and hereafter clears his conduct to my satisfaction, I will not be accessory to loading her future recollection with the shame of a confidence she then cannot but repent, nor with an injury to her delicacy that may wound it for ever."

She determined, therefore, carefully to avoid the subject for the present, since she could offer no advice for which she might not, hereafter, be suspected of selfish motives;

but yet, from a real regard to the tender-hearted girl, to give all the tacit discouragement that was in her power, to a passion which she firmly believed would be productive of nothing but misery.

Once, from the frankness natural to her disposition, she thought not merely of receiving but returning her confidence: her better judgment, however, soon led her from so hazardous a plan, which could only have exposed them both to a romantic humiliation, by which, in the end, their mutual expectations might prove sources of mutual distrust.

When Miss Belfield, therefore, the next morning, her air unusually timid, and her whole face covered with blushes, made her visit, Cecilia, not seeming to notice her confusion, told her she was very sorry she was obliged to go out herself, and contrived, under various pretences, to keep her maid in the room. Miss Belfield, supposing this to be accidental, rejoiced in her imaginary reprieve, and soon recovered her usual chearfulness: and Cecilia, who really meant to call upon Mrs. Delvile, borrowed Mrs. Harrel's carriage, and set down her artless young friend at her new lodgings in Portland-street, before she proceeded to St. James's-square, talking the whole time upon matters of utter indifference.

CHAPTER V

A Sarcasm

THE reproach which Cecilia had received from young Delvile in the name of his mother, determined her upon making this visit; for though, in her present uncertainty, she wished only to see that family when sought by themselves, she was yet desirous to avoid all appearance of singularity, lest any suspicions should be raised of her sentiments.

Mrs. Delvile received her with a cold civility that chilled and afflicted her: she found her seriously offended by her long absence, and now for the first time perceived that haughtiness of character which hitherto she had thought only given to her by the calumny of envy; for though her displeasure was undisguised, she deigned not to make any reproaches, evidently shewing that her disappointment in the loss of her society, was embittered by a proud regret for the kindness she believed she had thrown away. But though she scrupulously forbore the smallest complaint, she failed not from time to time to cast out reflections upon fickleness and caprice the most satirical and pointed.

Cecilia, who could not possibly avow the motives of her behaviour, ventured not to offer any apology for her apparent negligence; but, hitherto accustomèd to the most distinguished kindness, a change to so much bitterness shocked and overpowered her, and she sat almost wholly silent, and hardly able to look up.

Lady Honoria Pemberton, a daughter of the Duke of Derwent, now came into the room, and afforded her some relief by the sprightliness of her conversation. This young lady, who was a relation of the Delviles, and of a character the most airy and unthinking, ran on during her whole visit in a vein of fashionable scandal, with a levity that the censures of Mrs. Delvile, though by no means spared, had no power to controll: and, after having completely ransacked the topics of the day, she turned suddenly to Cecilia, with whom during her residence in St. James's-square she had made some acquaintance, and said, "So I hear, Miss Beverley, that after half the town has given you to Sir Robert Floyer, and the other half to my Lord Derford, you intend, without regarding one side or the other, to disappoint them both, and give yourself to Mr. Marriot."

"Me? no, indeed," answered Cecilia, "your ladyship has been much misinformed."

"I hope so," said Mrs. Delvile, "for Mr. Marriot, by all I ever heard of him, seems to have but one recommendation, and that the last Miss Beverley ought to value, a good estate."

Cecilia, secretly delighted by a speech which she could not resist flattering herself had reference to her son, now a little revived, and endeavoured to bear some part in the conversation.

"Every body one meets," cried Lady Honoria, "disposes

of Miss Beverley to some new person; yet the common opinion is that Sir Robert Floyer will be the man. But upon my word, for my own part, I cannot conjecture how she will manage among them, for Mr. Marriot declares he's determined he won't be refused, and Sir Robert vows that he'll never give her up. So we none of us know how it will end: but I am vastly glad she keeps them so long in suspence."

"If there is any suspence," said Cecilia, "I am at least sure it must be wilful. But why should your ladyship rejoice in it?"

"O, because it helps to torment them, and keeps something going forward. Besides, we are all looking in the news-papers every day, to see when they'll fight another duel for you."

"Another?" cried Cecilia; "indeed they have never yet fought any for me."

"O, I beg your pardon," answered her ladyship, "Sir Robert, you know, fought one for you in the beginning of the winter, with that Irish fortune hunter* who affronted you at the Opera."

"Irish fortune-hunter?" repeated Cecilia, "how strangely has that quarrel been misrepresented! In the first place, I never was affronted at the Opera at all, and in the second, if your Ladyship means Mr. Belfield, I question if he ever was in Ireland in his life."

"Well," cried Lady Honoria, "he might come from Scotland, for ought I know, but somewhere he certainly came from; and they tell me he is wounded terribly, and Sir Robert has had all his things packed up this month, that in case he should die, he may go abroad in a moment.

"And pray where, Lady Honoria," cried Mrs. Delvile, "do you contrive to pick up all this rattle?"*

"O, I don't know; every body tells me something, so I put it all together as well as I can. But I could acquaint you with a stranger piece of news than any you have heard yet."

"And what is that?"

"O, if I let you know it, you'll tell your son."

"No indeed," said Mrs. Delvile laughing, "I shall probably forget it myself."

She then made some further difficulty, and Cecilia, uncertain if she was meant to be a party in the communication, strolled to a window; where, however, as Lady Honoria did not lower her voice, she heard her say "Why you must know I am told he keeps a mistress somewhere in Oxford-Road. They say she's mighty pretty; I should like vastly to see her."

The consternation of Cecilia at this intelligence would certainly have betrayed all she so much wished to conceal, had not her fortunate removal to the window guarded her from observation. She kept her post, fearing to look round, but was much pleased when Mrs. Delvile, with great indignation answered "I am sorry, Lady Honoria, you can find any amusement in listening to such idle scandal, which those who tell will never respect you for hearing. In times less daring in slander, the character of Mortimer would have proved to him a shield from all injurious aspersions; yet who shall wonder he could not escape, and who shall contemn the inventors of calumny, if Lady Honoria Pemberton condescends to be entertained with it?"

"Dear Mrs. Delvile," cried Lady Honoria, giddily, "you take me too seriously."

"And dear Lady Honoria," said Mrs. Delvile, "I would it were possible to make you take yourself seriously; for could you once see with clearness and precision how much you lower your own dignity, while you stoop to depreciate that of others, the very subjects that now make your diversion, would then, far more properly, move your resentment."

"Ay but, dear madam," cried Lady Honoria, "if that were the case, I should be quite perfect, and then you and I should never quarrel, and I don't know what we should do for conversation."

And with these words, hastily shaking hands with her, she took leave.

"Such conversation," said Mrs. Delvile when she was gone, "as results from the mixture of fruitless admonition with incorrigible levity, would be indeed *more honoured in the breach than the observance.* * But levity is so much the fashionable characteristic of the present age, that a gay young girl who, like Lady Honoria Pemberton, rules the friends by whom she ought to be ruled, had little chance of escaping it."

"She seems so open, however, to reproof," said Cecilia, "that I should hope in a short time she may also be open to conviction."

"No," answered Mrs. Delvile, "I have no hope of her at all. I once took much pains with her; but I soon found that the easiness with which she hears of her faults, is only another effect of the levity with which she commits them. But if the young are never tired of erring in conduct, neither are the older in erring in judgment; the fallibility of *mine* I have indeed very lately experienced."

Cecilia, who strongly felt the poignancy of this sarcasm, and whose constant and unaffected value of Mrs. Delvile by no means deserved it, was again silenced, and again most cruelly depressed: nor could she secretly forbear repining that at the very moment she found herself threatened with a necessity of foregoing the society of her new favourite, Miss Belfield, the woman in the whole world whom she most wished to have for her friend, from an unhappy mistake was ready to relinquish her. Grieved to be thus fallen in her esteem, and shocked that she could offer no justification, after a short and thoughtful pause, she gravely arose to take leave.

Mrs. Delvile then told her that if she had any business to transact with Mr. Delvile, she advised her to acquaint him with it soon, as the whole family left town in a few days.

This was a new and severe blow to Cecilia, who sorrowfully repeated "In a few days, madam?"

"Yes," answered Mrs. Delvile, "I hope you intend to be much concerned?"

"Ah madam!" cried Cecilia, who could no longer preserve her quietness, "if you knew but half the respect I bear you, but half the sincerity with which I value and revere you, all protestations would be useless, for all accusations would be over!"

Mrs. Delvile, at once surprised and softened by the warmth of this declaration, instantly took her hand, and said "They shall now, and for ever be over, if it pains you to hear them. I concluded that what I said would be a matter of indifference to you, or all my displeasure would immediately have been satisfied, when once I had intimated that your absence had excited it."

"That I have excited it at all," answered Cecilia, "gives me indeed the severest uneasiness; but believe me, madam, however unfortunately appearances may be against me, I have always had the highest sense of the kindness with which you have honoured me, and never has there been the smallest abatement in the veneration, gratitude and affection I have inviolably borne you."

"You see, then," said Mrs. Delvile with a smile, "that where reproof takes any effect, it is not received with that easiness you were just now admiring: on the contrary, where a concession is made without pain, it is also made without meaning, for it is not in human nature to project any amendment without a secret repugnance. That here, however, you should differ from Lady Honoria Pemberton, who can wonder, when you are superior to all comparison with her in every thing?"

"Will you then," said Cecilia, "accept my apology, and forgive me?"

"I will do more," said Mrs. Delvile laughing, "I will forgive you *without* an apology; for the truth is I have heard none! But come," continued she, perceiving Cecilia much abashed by this comment, "I will enquire no more about the matter; I am glad to receive my young friend again, and even half ashamed, deserving as she is, to say *how* glad!"

She then embraced her affectionately, and owned she had been more mortified by her fancied desertion than she had been willing to own even to herself, repeatedly assuring her that for many years she had not made any aquaintance she so much wished to cultivate, nor enjoyed any society from which she had derived so much pleasure.

Cecilia, whose eyes glistened with modest joy, while her heart beat quick with revived expectation, in listening to an

effusion of praise so infinitely grateful to her, found little
difficulty in returning her friendly professions, and, in a few
minutes, was not merely reconciled, but more firmly united
with her than ever.

Mrs. Delvile insisted upon keeping her to dinner, and
Cecilia, but too happy in her earnestness, readily agreed to
send Mrs. Harrel an excuse.

Neither of the Mr. Delviles spent the day at home, and
nothing, therefore, disturbed or interrupted those glowing
and delightful sensations which spring from a cordial
renewal of friendship and kindness. The report, indeed, of
Lady Honoria Pemberton gave her some uneasiness, yet the
flighty character of that lady, and Mrs. Delvile's reply to it,
soon made her drive it from her mind.

She returned home early in the evening, as other company
was expected, and she had not changed her dress since the
morning; but she first made a promise to see Mrs. Delvile
some part of every day during the short time that she meant
to remain in town.

CHAPTER VI

A Surmise

THE next morning opened with another scene; Mrs. Harrel
ran into Cecilia's room before breakfast, and acquainted her
that Mr. Harrel had not been at home all night.

The consternation with which she heard this account she
instantly endeavoured to dissipate, in order to soften the
apprehension with which it was communicated: Mrs.
Harrel, however, was extremely uneasy, and sent all the
town over to make enquiries, but without receiving any
intelligence.

Cecilia, unwilling to leave her in a state of such alarm,
wrote an excuse to Mrs. Delvile, that she might continue
with her till some information was procured. A subject also
of such immediate concern, was sufficient apology for
avoiding any particular conversation with Miss Belfield,

who called as usual, about noon, and whose susceptible heart was much affected by the evident disturbance in which she found Cecilia.

The whole day passed, and no news arrived: but, greatly to her astonishment, Mrs. Harrel in the evening prepared for going to an assembly! yet declaring at the same time it was extremely disagreeable to her, only she was afraid, if she stayed away, every body would suppose something was the matter.

"Who then at last, thought Cecilia, are half so much the slaves of the world as the gay and the dissipated? Those who work for hire, have at least their hours of rest, those who labour for subsistence, are at liberty when subsistence is procured; but those who toil to please the vain and the idle, undertake a task which can never be finished, however scrupulously all private peace, and all internal comfort, may be sacrificed in reality to the folly of saving appearances!"

Losing, however, the motive for which she had given up her own engagement, she now sent for her chair, in order to spend an hour or two with Mrs. Delvile.

The servants, as they conducted her up stairs, said they would call their lady; and in entering the drawing-room she saw, reading and alone, young Delvile.

He seemed much surprised, but received her with the utmost respect, apologizing for the absence of his mother, whom he said had understood she was not to see her till the next day, and had left him to write letters now, that she might then be at liberty.

Cecilia in return made excuses for her seeming inconsistency; after which, for some time, all conversation dropt.

The silence was at length broken by young Delvile's saying "Mr. Belfield's merit has not been thrown away upon Lord Vannelt; he has heard an excellent character of him from all his former acquaintance, and is now fitting up an apartment for him in his own house till his son begins his tour."

Cecilia said she was very happy in hearing such intelligence; and then again they were both silent.

"You have seen," said young Delvile, after this second pause, "Mr. Belfield's sister?"

Cecilia, not without changing colour, answered "Yes, Sir."

"She is very amiable," he continued, "too amiable, indeed, for her situation, since her relations, her brother alone excepted, are all utterly unworthy of her."

He stopt; but Cecilia made no answer, and he presently added "Perhaps you do not think her amiable?——you may have seen more of her, and know something to her disadvantage?"

"O no!" cried Cecilia, with a forced alacrity, "but only I was thinking that——did you say you knew all her relations?"

"No," he answered, "but when I have been with Mr. Belfield, some of them have called upon him."

Again they were both silent; and then Cecilia, ashamed of her apparent backwardness to give praise, compelled herself to say, "Miss Belfield is indeed a very sweet girl, and I wish—" she stopt, not well knowing herself what she meant to add.

"I have been greatly pleased," said he, after waiting some time to hear if she would finish her speech, "by being informed of your goodness to her, and I think she seems equally to require and to deserve it. I doubt not you will extend it to her when she is deprived of her brother, for then will be the time that by doing her most service, it will reflect on yourself most honour."

Cecilia, confounded by this recommendation, faintly answered "Certainly,——whatever is in my power,—I shall be very glad—"

And just then Mrs. Delvile made her appearance, and during the mutual apologies that followed, her son left the room. Cecilia, glad of any pretence to leave it also, insisted upon giving no interruption to Mrs. Delvile's letter writing, and having promised to spend all the next day with her, hurried back to her chair.

The reflections that followed her thither were by no means the most soothing: she began now to apprehend that the pity she had bestowed upon Miss Belfield, Miss Belfield in a short time might bestow upon her: at any other time, his recommendation would merely have served to confirm her opinion of his benevolence, but in her present state of anxiety and uncertainty, every thing gave birth to conjecture, and had power to alarm her. He had behaved to her of late with the strangest coldness and distance,——his praise of Henrietta had been ready and animated,—Henrietta she knew adored him, and she knew not with what reason,—but an involuntary suspicion arose in her mind, that the partiality she had herself once excited, was now transferred to that little dreaded, but not less dangerous rival.

Yet, if such was the case, what was to become either of the pride or the interest of his family? Would his relations ever pardon an alliance stimulated neither by rank nor riches? would Mr. Delvile, who hardly ever spoke but to the high-born, without seeming to think his dignity somewhat injured, deign to receive for a daughter in law the child of a citizen* and tradesman? would Mrs. Delvile herself, little less elevated in her notions, though infinitely softer in her manners, ever condescend to acknowledge her? Cecilia's own birth and connections, superior as they were to those of Miss Belfield, were even openly disdained by Mr. Delvile, and all her expectations of being received into his family were founded upon the largeness of her fortune, in favour of which the brevity of her genealogy might perhaps pass unnoticed. But what was the chance of Miss Belfield, who neither had ancestors to boast, nor wealth to allure?

This thought, however, awakened all the generosity of her soul; "If, cried she, the advantages I possess are merely those of riches, how little should I be flattered by any appearance of preference! and how ill can I judge with what sincerity it may be offered! happier in that case is the lowly Henrietta, who to poverty may attribute neglect, but who can only be sought and caressed from motives of purest regard. She loves Mr. Delvile, loves him with the most artless affection;—perhaps, too, he loves her in return,—why else his solicitude to know my opinion of her, and why so sudden his alarm when he thought it unfavourable? Perhaps he means to marry her, and to sacrifice to her innocence and her attractions all plans of ambition, and all views of aggrandizement:—thrice happy Henrietta, if such is thy prospect of felicity! to have inspired a passion so disinterested, may humble the most insolent of thy superiors, and teach even the wealthiest to envy thee!"*

CHAPTER VII

A Bold Stroke

WHEN Cecilia returned home, she heard with much concern that no tidings of Mr. Harrel had yet been obtained. His lady, who did not stay out late, was now very seriously frightened, and entreated Cecilia to sit up with her till some news could be procured: she sent also for her brother, and they all three, in trembling expectation of what was to ensue, passed the whole night in watching.

At six o'clock in the morning, Mr. Arnott besought his sister and Cecilia to take some rest, promising to go out himself to every place where Mr. Harrel was known to resort, and not to return without bringing some account of him.

Mrs. Harrel, whose feelings were not very acute, finding the persuasions of her brother were seconded by her own fatigue, consented to follow his advice, and desired him to begin his search immediately.

A few moments after he was gone, while Mrs. Harrel and Cecilia were upon the stairs, they were startled by a violent knocking at the door: Cecilia, prepared for some calamity, hurried her friend back to the drawing room, and then flying out of it again to enquire who entered, saw to her equal surprize and relief, Mr. Harrel himself.

She ran back with the welcome information, and he instantly followed her: Mrs. Harrel eagerly told him of her fright, and Cecilia expressed her pleasure at his return: but the satisfaction of neither was of long duration.

He came into the room with a look of fierceness the most terrifying, his hat on, and his arms folded. He made no answer to what they said, but pushed back the door with his foot, and flung himself upon a sofa.

Cecilia would now have withdrawn, but Mrs. Harrel caught her hand to prevent her. They continued some minutes in this situation, and then Mr. Harrel, suddenly rising, called out "Have you any thing to pack up?"

"Pack up?" repeated Mrs. Harrel, "Lord bless me, for what?"

"I am going abroad;" he answered, "I shall set off to-morrow."

"Abroad?" cried she, bursting into tears, "I am sure I hope not!"

"Hope nothing!" returned he, in a voice of rage; and then, with a dreadful oath, he ordered her to leave him and pack up.

Mrs. Harrel, wholly unused to such treatment, was frightened into violent hysterics; of which, however, he took no notice, but swearing at her for *a fool who had been the cause of his ruin*, he left the room.

Cecilia, though she instantly rang the bell, and hastened to her assistance, was so much shocked by this unexpected brutality, that she scarcely knew how to act, or what to order. Mrs. Harrel, however, soon recovered, and Cecilia accompanied her to her own apartment, where she stayed, and endeavoured to sooth her till Mr. Arnott returned.

The terrible state in which Mr. Harrel had at last come home was immediately communicated to him, and his sister entreated him to use all his influence that the scheme for going abroad might be deferred, at least, if not wholly given up.

Fearfully he went on the embassy, but speedily, and with a look wholly dismayed, he returned. Mr. Harrel, he said, told him that he had contracted a larger debt of honour than he had any means to raise, and as he could not appear till it was paid, he was obliged to quit the kingdom without delay.

"Oh brother!" cried Mrs. Harrel, "and can you suffer us to go?"

"Alas, my dear sister," answered he, "what can I do to prevent it? and who, if I too am ruined, will in future help you?"

Mrs. Harrel then wept bitterly, nor could the gentle Mr. Arnott, forbear, while he tried to comfort her, mixing his own tears with those of his beloved sister; but Cecilia, whose reason was stronger, and whose justice was offended, felt other sensations: and leaving Mrs. Harrel to the care of her brother, whose tenderness she infinitely compassionated, she retreated into her own room. Not, however, to rest; the dreadful situation of the family made her forget she wanted it, but to deliberate upon what course she ought herself to pursue.

She determined without any hesitation against accompanying them in their flight, as the irreparable injury she was convinced she had already done her fortune, was more than sufficient to satisfy the most romantic ideas of friendship and humanity: but her own place of abode must now immediately be changed, and her choice rested only between Mr. Delvile and Mr. Briggs.

Important as were the obstacles which opposed her residence at Mr. Delvile's, all that belonged to inclination and to happiness encouraged it: while with respect to Mr. Briggs, though the objections were lighter, there was not a single allurement. Yet whenever the suspicion recurred to her that Miss Belfield was beloved by young Delvile, she resolved at all events to avoid him: but when better hopes intervened, and represented that his enquiries were probably accidental, the wish of being finally acquainted with his sentiments, made nothing so desirable as an intercourse more frequent.

Such still was her irresolution, when she received a message from Mr. Arnott to entreat the honour of seeing her. She immediately went down stairs, and found him in the utmost distress; "O Miss Beverley," he cried, "what can I do for my sister! what can I possibly devise to relieve her affliction!"

"Indeed I know not!" said Cecilia, "but the utter impracticability of preparing her for this blow, obviously as it has long been impending, makes it now fall so heavily I wish much to assist her,—but a debt so unjustifiably contracted—"

"O madam," interrupted he, "imagine not I sent to you with so treacherous a view as to involve you in our misery; far too unworthily has your generosity already been abused. I only wish to consult with you what I can do for my sister."

Cecilia, after some little consideration, proposed that Mrs. Harrel should still be left in England, and under their joint care.

"Alas!" cried he, "I have already made that proposal, but Mr. Harrel will not go without her, though his whole behaviour is so totally altered, that I fear to trust her with him."

"Who is there, then, that has more weight with him?" said Cecilia, "shall we send for Sir Robert Floyer to second our request?"

To this Mr. Arnott assented, forgetting in his apprehension of losing his sister, the pain he should suffer from the interference of his rival.

The Baronet presently arrived, and Cecilia, not chusing to apply to him herself, left him with Mr. Arnott, and waited for intelligence in the library.

In about an hour after, Mrs. Harrel ran into the room, her tears dried up, and out of breath with joy, and called out "My dearest friend, my fate is now all in your hands, and I am sure you will not refuse to make me happy."

"What is it I can do for you?" cried Cecilia, dreading some impracticable proposal; "ask me not, I beseech you, what I cannot perform!"

"No, no," answered she, "what I ask requires nothing but good nature; Sir Robert Floyer has been begging Mr. Harrel to leave me behind, and he has promised to comply, upon condition you will hasten your marriage, and take me into your own house."

"My marriage!" cried the astonished Cecilia.

Here they were joined by Mr. Harrel himself, who repeated the same offer.

"You both amaze and shock me!" cried Cecilia, "what is it you mean, and why do you talk to me so wildly?"

"Miss Beverley," cried Mr. Harrel, "it is high time now to give up this reserve, and trifle no longer with a gentleman so unexceptionable as Sir Robert Floyer. The whole town has long acknowledged him as your husband, and you are every where regarded as his bride; a little frankness, therefore, in accepting him, will not only bind him to you for ever, but do credit to the generosity of your character."

At that moment Sir Robert himself burst into the room, and seizing one of her hands, while both of them were uplifted in mute amazement, he pressed it to his lips, poured forth a volley of such compliments as he had never before prevailed with himself to utter, and confidently entreated her to complete his long-attended happiness without the cruelty of further delay.

Cecilia, almost petrified by the excess of her surprise, at an attack so violent, so bold, and apparently so sanguine, was for some time scarce able to speak or to defend herself; but when Sir Robert, presuming on her silence, said she had made him the happiest of men, she indignantly drew back her hand, and with a look of displeasure that required little explanation, would have walked out of the room: when Mr. Harrel, in a tone of bitterness and disappointment, called out "Is this lady-like tyranny then never to end?" And Sir Robert, impatiently following her, said "And is my suspence to endure for ever? After so many months attendance—"

"This, indeed, is something too much," said Cecilia, turning back. "You have been kept, Sir, in no suspense; the whole tenor of my conduct has uniformly declared the same disapprobation I at present avow, and which my letter, at least, must have put beyond all doubt."

"Harrel," exclaimed Sir Robert, "did not you tell me—"

"Pho, pho," cried Harrel, "what signifies calling upon me? I never saw in Miss Beverley any disapprobation beyond what it is customary for young ladies of a sentimental turn to shew; and every body knows that where a gentleman is allowed to pay his devoirs for any length of time, no lady intends to use him very severely."

"And can you, Mr. Harrel," said Cecilia, "after such conversations as have passed between us, persevere in this wilful misapprehension? But it is vain* to debate where all reasoning is disregarded, or to make any protestations where even rejection is received as a favour."

And then, with an air of disdain, she insisted upon passing them, and went to her own room.

Mrs. Harrel, however, still followed, and clinging round her, still supplicated her pity and compliance.

"What infatuation is this!" cried Cecilia, "is it possible that you, too, can suppose I ever mean to accept Sir Robert?"

"To be sure I do," answered she, "for Mr. Harrel has told me a thousand times, that however you played the prude, you would be his at last."

Cecilia, though doubly irritated against Mr. Harrel, was now appeased with his lady, whose mistake, however ill-founded, offered an excuse for her behaviour: but she assured her in the strongest terms that her repugnance to the Baronet was unalterable, yet told her she might claim from her every good office that was not wholly unreasonable.

These were words of slender comfort to Mrs. Harrel, who well knew that her wishes and reason had but little affinity, and she soon, therefore, left the room.

Cecilia then resolved to go instantly to Mrs. Delvile, acquaint her with the necessity of her removal, and make her decision whither, according to the manner in which her intelligence should be received.

She sent, therefore, to order a chair, and was already in the hall, when she was stopt by the entrance of Mr. Monckton, who, addressing her with a look of haste and earnestness, said, "I will not ask whither you are going so early, or upon what errand, for I must beg a moment's audience, be your business what it may."

Cecilia then accompanied him to the deserted breakfast-room, which none but the servants had this morning entered, and there, grasping her hand, he said "Miss Beverley, you must fly this house directly! it is the region of disorder and licentiousness, and unfit to contain you."

She assured him she was that moment preparing to quit it, but begged he would explain himself.

"I have taken care," he answered, "for some time past, to be well informed of all the proceedings of Mr. Harrel; and the intelligence I procured this morning is of the most alarming nature. I find he spent the night before the last entirely at a gaming table, where, intoxicated by a run of good luck, he passed the whole of the next day in rioting with his profligate intimates, and last night, returning again to his favourite amusement, he not only lost all he had gained, but much more than he could pay. Doubt not, therefore, but you will be called upon to assist him: he still considers you as his resource in times of danger, and while he knows you are under his roof, he will always believe himself secure."

"Every thing indeed conspires," said Cecilia, more shocked than surprised at this account, "to make it necessary I should quit his house: yet I do not think he has at present any further expectations from me, as he came into the room this morning not merely without speaking to me, but behaved with a brutality to Mrs. Harrel that he must be certain would give me disgust. It shewed me, indeed, a new part of his character, for ill as I have long thought of him, I did not suspect he could be guilty of such unmanly cruelty."

"The character of a gamester," said Mr. Monckton, "depends solely upon his luck; his disposition varies with every throw of the dice, and he is airy, gay and good humoured, or sour, morose, and savage, neither from nature nor from principle, but wholly by the caprice of chance."

Cecilia then related to him the scene in which she had just been engaged with Sir Robert Floyer.

"This," cried he, "is a *manœuvre* I have been some time expecting: but Mr. Harrel, though artful and selfish, is by no means deep. The plan he had formed would have succeeded with some women, and he therefore concluded it would with all. So many of your sex have been subdued by perseverance, and so many have been conquered by boldness, that he supposed when he united two such powerful besiegers in the person of a Baronet, he should vanquish all obstacles. By assuring you that the world thought the marriage already settled, he hoped to surprise you into believing there was no help for it, and by the suddenness and vehemence of the attack, to frighten and hurry you into compliance. His own wife, he knew, might have been managed thus with ease, and so, probably, might his sister, and his mother, and his cousin, for in love matters, or what are so called, women in general are readily duped. He discerned not the superiority of your understanding to tricks so shallow and impertinent, nor the firmness of your mind in maintaining its own independence. No doubt but he was amply to have been rewarded for his assistance, and probably had you this morning been propitious, the Baronet in return was to have cleared him from his present difficulty."

"Even in my own mind," said Cecilia, "I can no longer defend him, for he could never have been so eager to promote the interest of Sir Robert, in the present terrible situation of his own affairs, had he not been stimulated by some secret motives. His schemes and his artifices, however, will now be utterly lost upon me, since your warning and advice, aided by my own suffering experience of the inutility of all I can do for him, will effectually guard me from all his future attempts."

"Rest no security upon yourself," said Mr. Monckton, "since you have no knowledge of the many tricks and inventions by which you may yet be plundered. Perhaps he may beg permission to reside in your house in Suffolk, or desire an annuity for his wife, or chuse to receive your first rents when you come of age; and whatever he may fix upon, his dagger and his bowl* will not fail to procure him. A heart so liberal as yours can only be guarded by flight. You were going, you said, when I came,—and whither?"

"To—to St. James's-square," answered she, with a deep blush.

"Indeed!—is young Delvile, then, going abroad?"

"Abroad?—no,—I believe not."

"Nay, I only imagined it from your chusing to reside in his house."

"I do not chuse it," cried Cecilia, with quickness, "but is not any thing preferable to dwelling with Mr. Briggs?"

"Certainly," said Mr. Monckton coolly, "nor should I have supposed he had any chance with you, had I not hitherto observed that your convenience has always been sacrificed to your sense of propriety."

Cecilia, touched by praise so full of censure, and earnest to vindicate her delicacy, after an internal struggle, which Mr. Monckton was too subtle to interrupt, protested she would go instantly to Mr. Briggs, and see if it were possible to be settled in his house, before she made any attempt to fix herself elsewhere.

"And when?" said Mr. Monckton.

"I don't know," answered she, with some hesitation, "perhaps this afternoon."

"Why not this morning?"

"I can go out no where this morning; I must stay with Mrs. Harrel."

"You thought otherwise when I came, you were then content to leave her."

Cecilia's alacrity, however, for changing her abode, was now at an end, and she would fain have been left quietly to re-consider her plans: but Mr. Monckton urged so strongly the danger of her lengthened stay in the house of so designing a man as Mr. Harrel, that he prevailed with her to quit it without delay, and had himself the satisfaction of handing her to her chair.

CHAPTER VIII

A Miser's Mansion

MR. BRIGGS was at home, and Cecilia instantly and briefly informed him that it was inconvenient for her to live any longer at Mr. Harrel's, and that if she could be accommodated at his house, she should be glad to reside with him during the rest of her minority.

"Shall, shall," cried he, extremely pleased, "take you with all my heart. Warrant master Harrel's made a good penny of you. Not a bit the better for dressing so fine; many a rogue in a gold lace hat."

Cecilia begged to know what apartments he could spare for her.

"Take you up stairs," cried he, "shew you a place for a queen."

He then led her up stairs, and took her to a room entirely dark, and so close for want of air that she could hardly breathe in it. She retreated to the landing-place till he had opened the shutters, and then saw an apartment the most forlorn she had ever beheld, containing no other furniture than a ragged stuff bed, two worn-out rush-bottomed chairs, an old wooden box, and a bit of broken glass which was fastened to the wall by two bent nails.

"See here, my little chick," cried he, "every thing ready! and a box for your gimcracks into the bargain."

"You don't mean this place for me, Sir!" cried Cecilia, staring.

"Do, do;" cried he, "a deal nicer by and by. Only wants a little furbishing: soon put to rights. Never sweep a room out of use; only wears out brooms for nothing."

"But, Sir, can I not have an apartment on the first floor?"

"No, no, something else to do with it; belongs to the club; secrets in all things!* Make this do well enough. Come again next week; wear quite a new face. Nothing wanting but a table; pick you up one at a broker's."*

"But I am obliged, Sir, to leave Mr. Harrel's house directly."

"Well, well, make shift without a table at first; no great matter if you ha'n't one at all, nothing particular to do with it. Want another blanket, though. Know where to get one; a very good broker hard by. Understand how to deal with him! A close dog, but warm."*

"I have also two servants, Sir," said Cecilia.

"Won't have 'em! Sha'n't come! Eat me out of house and home."

"Whatever they eat, Sir," answered she, "will be wholly at my expence, as will everything else that belongs to them."

"Better get rid of them: hate servants; all a pack of rogues: think of nothing but stuffing and guttling."*

Then opening another door, "see here," he cried, "my own room just by; snug as a church!"

Cecilia, following him into it, lost a great part of her surprise at the praise he had lavished upon that which he destined for herself, by perceiving that his own was yet more scantily furnished, having nothing in it but a miserable bed without any curtains,* and a large chest, which, while it contained his clothes, sufficed both for table and chair.

"What are doing here?" cried he angrily, to a maid who was making the bed, "can't you take more care? beat out all the feathers, see! two on the ground; nothing but waste and extravagance! never mind how soon a man's ruined. Come to want, you slut, see that, come to want!"

"I can never want more than I do here," said the girl, "so that's one comfort."

Cecilia now began to repent she had made known the purport of her· visit, for she found it would be utterly impossible to accommodate either her mind or her person to a residence such as was here to be obtained: and she only wished Mr. Monckton had been present, that he might himself be convinced of the impracticability of his scheme. Her whole business, therefore, now, was to retract her offer, and escape from the house.

"I see, Sir," said she, when he turned from his servant, "that I cannot be received here without inconvenience, and therefore I will make some new arrangement in my plan."

"No, no," cried he, "like to have you, 'tis but fair, all in our turn; won't be choused; Master Harrel's had his share.* Sorry could not get you that sweet-heart! would not bite; soon find out another; never fret."

"But there are so many things with which I cannot possibly dispense," said Cecilia, "that I am certain my removing hither would occasion you far more trouble than you at present foresee.''

''No, no; get all in order soon: go about myself; know how to bid; understand trap; always go shabby; no making a bargain in a good coat. Look sharp at the goods; say they won't do; come away; send somebody else for 'em. Never go twice myself; nothing got cheap if one seems to have a hankering.''

''But I am sure it is not possible,'' said Cecilia, hurrying down stairs, ''that my room, and one for each of my servants, should be ready in time.''

''Yes, yes,'' cried he, following her, ''ready in a trice. Make a little shift at first; double the blanket till we get another; lie with the maid a night or two; never stand for a trifle.''*

And, when she was seated in her chair, the whole time disclaiming her intention of returning, he only pinched her cheek with a facetious smirk, and said ''By, by, little duck; come again soon. Warrant I'll have the room ready. Sha'n't half know it again; make it as smart as a carrot.''*

And then she left the house; fully satisfied that no one could blame her refusing to inhabit it, and much less chagrined than she was willing to suppose herself, in finding she had now no resource but in the Delviles.

Yet, in her serious reflections, she could not but think herself strangely unfortunate that the guardian with whom alone it seemed proper for her to reside, should by parsimony, vulgarity, and meanness, render riches contemptible, prosperity unavailing, and œconomy odious: and that the choice of her uncle should thus unhappily have fallen upon the lowest and most wretched of misers, in a city abounding with opulence, hospitality, and splendour, and of which the principal inhabitants, long eminent for their wealth and their probity, were now almost universally rising in elegance and liberality.

CHAPTER IX

A Declaration

CECILIA's next progress, therefore, was to St. James's-square, whither she went in the utmost anxiety, from her uncertainty of the reception with which her proposal would meet.

The servants informed her that Mr. and Mrs. Delvile were at breakfast, and that the Duke of Derwent and his two daughters were with them.

Before such witnesses to relate the reasons of her leaving the Harrels was impossible; and from such a party to send for Mrs. Delvile, would, by her stately guardian, be deemed an indecorum unpardonable. She was obliged, therefore, to return to Portman-square in order to open her cause in a letter to Mrs. Delvile.

Mr. Arnott, flying instantly to meet her, called out "O madam, what alarm has your absence occasioned! My sister believed she should see you no more, Mr. Harrel feared a premature discovery of his purposed retreat, and we have all been under the cruelest apprehensions lest you meant not to come back."

"I am sorry I spoke not with you before I went out," said Cecilia, accompanying him to the library, "but I thought you were all too much occupied to miss me. I have been, indeed, preparing for a removal, but I meant not to leave your sister without bidding her adieu, nor, indeed, to quit any part of the family with so little ceremony. Is Mr. Harrel still firm to his last plan?"

"I fear so! I have tried what is possible to dissuade him, and my poor sister has wept without ceasing. Indeed, if she will take no consolation, I believe I shall do what she pleases, for I cannot bear the sight of her in such distress."

"You are too generous, and too good!" said Cecilia, "and I know not how, while flying from danger myself, to forbear counselling you to avoid it also."

"Ah madam!" cried he, "the greatest danger for *me* is what I have now no power to run from!"

Cecilia, though she could not but understand him, felt not the less his friend for knowing him the humblest of her admirers; and as she saw the threatening ruin to which his too great tenderness exposed him, she kindly said "Mr. Arnott, I will speak to you without reserve. It is not difficult to see that the destruction which awaits Mr. Harrel, is ready also to ensnare his brother-in-law: but let not that blindness to the future which we have so often lamented for him, hereafter be lamented for yourself. Till his present connexions are broken, and his way of living is changed, nothing can be done for him, and whatever you were to advance, would merely be sunk at the gaming table. Reserve, therefore, your liberality till it may indeed be of service to him, for believe me, at present, his mind is as much injured as his fortune."

"And is it possible, madam," said Mr. Arnott, in an accent of surprize and delight, "that you can deign to be interested in what may become of *me!* and that *my* sharing or escaping the ruin of this house is not wholly indifferent to you?"

"Certainly not," answered Cecilia; "as the brother of my earliest friend, I can never be insensible to your welfare."

"Ah madam!" cried he, "as her brother!——Oh that there were any other tie!——"

"Think a little," said Cecilia, preparing to quit the room, "of what I have mentioned, and, for your sister's sake, be firm now, if you would be kind hereafter."

"I will be any and every thing," cried he, "that Miss Beverley will command."

Cecilia, fearful of any misinterpretation, then came back, and gravely said, "No, Sir, be ruled only by your own judgment: or, should my advice have any weight with you, remember it is given from the most disinterested motives, and with no other view than that of securing your power to be of service to your sister."

"For that sister's sake, then, have the goodness to hear my situation, and honour me with further directions."

"You will make me fear to speak," said Cecilia, "if you give so much consequence to my opinion. I have seen, however, nothing in your conduct I have ever wished changed, except too little attention to your own interest and affairs."

"Ah!" cried he, "with what rapture should I hear those words, could I but imagine ——"

"Come, come," said Cecilia, smiling, "no digression! you called me back to talk of your sister; if you change your subject, perhaps you may lose your auditor."

"I would not, madam, for the world encroach upon your goodness; the favour I have found has indeed always exceeded my expectations, as it has always surpassed my desert: yet has it never blinded me to my own unworthiness. Do not, then, fear to indulge me with your conversation; I shall draw from it no inference but of pity, and though pity from Miss Beverley is the sweetest balm to my heart, it shall never seduce me to the encouragement of higher hopes."

Cecilia had long had reason to expect such a declaration, yet she heard it with unaffected concern, and looking at him with the utmost gentleness, said "Mr. Arnott, your regard does me honour, and, were it somewhat more rational, would give me pleasure; take, then, from it what is more than I wish or merit, and, while you preserve the rest, be assured it will be faithfully returned."

"Your rejection is so mild," cried he, "that I, who had no hope of acceptance, find relief in having at last told my sufferings. Could I but continue to see you every day, and to be blest with your conversation, I think I should be happy, and I am sure I should be grateful."

"You are already," answered she, shaking her head, and moving towards the door, "infringing the conditions upon which our friendship is to be founded."

"Do not go, madam," he cried, "till I have done what you have just promised to permit, acquainted you with my situation, and been honoured with your advice. I must own to you, then, that 5000*l.* which I had in the stocks, as well as a considerable sum in a banker's hands, I have parted with, as I now find for ever: but I have no heart for refusal, nor

would my sister at this moment be thus distressed, but that
I have nothing more to give without I cut down my trees,
or sell some farm, since all I was worth, except my landed
property, is already gone. What, therefore, I can now do to
save Mr. Harrel from this desperate expedition I know
not.''

"I am sorry," said Cecilia, "to speak with severity of one
so nearly connected with you, yet, suffer me to ask, why
should he be saved from it at all? and what is there he can
at present do better? Has not he long been threatened with
every evil that is now arrived? have we not both warned
him, and have not the clamours of his creditors assailed
him? yet what has been the consequence? he has not
submitted to the smallest change in his way of life, he has not
denied himself a single indulgence, nor spared any expence,
nor thought of any reformation. Luxury has followed
luxury, and he has only grown fonder of extravagance, as
extravagance has become more dangerous. Till the present
storm, therefore, blows over, leave him to his fate, and when
a calm succeeds, I will myself, for the sake of Priscilla, aid
you to save what is possible of the wreck."

"All you say, madam, is as wise as it is good, and now
I am acquainted with your opinion, I will wholly new model
myself upon it, and grow as steady against all attacks as
hitherto I have been yielding."

Cecilia was then retiring; but again detaining her, he said
"You spoke, madam, of a removal, and indeed it is high
time you should quit this scene: yet I hope you intend not
to go till to-morrow, as Mr. Harrel has declared your
leaving him sooner will be his destruction."

"Heaven forbid," said Cecilia, "for I mean to be gone
with all the speed in my power."

"Mr. Harrel," answered he, "did not explain himself;
but I believe he apprehends your deserting his house at this
critical time, will raise a suspicion of his own design of going
abroad, and make his creditors interfere to prevent him."

"To what a wretched state," cried Cecilia, "has he
reduced himself! I will not, however, be the voluntary
instrument of his disgrace; and if you think my stay is so

material to his security, I will continue here till to-morrow morning.''

Mr. Arnott almost wept his thanks for this concession, and Cecilia, happy in making it to him, instead of Mr. Harrel; then went to her own room, and wrote the following letter to Mrs. Delvile.

To the Hon. Mrs. DELVILE, St. James's-square.

Dear Madam,

Portman-square, June 12.

I AM willing to hope you have been rather surprised that I have not sooner availed myself of the permission with which you yesterday honoured me of spending this whole day with you, but, unfortunately for myself, I am prevented waiting upon you even for any part of it. Do not, however, think me now ungrateful if I stay away, nor to-morrow impertinent, if I venture to enquire whether that apartment which you had once the goodness to appropriate to my use, may then again be spared for me! The accidents which have prompted this strange request will, I trust, be sufficient apology for the liberty I take in making it, when I have the honour to see you, and acquaint you what they are. I am, with the utmost respect,

Dear Madam,

your most obedient

humble servant,

CECILIA BEVERLEY.

She would not have been thus concise, had not the caution of Mr. Arnott made her fear, in the present perilous situation of affairs, to trust the secret of Mr. Harrel to paper. The following answer was returned her from Mrs. Delvile.

To Miss BEVERLEY, Portman-square.

THE accidents you mention are not, I hope, of a very serious nature, since I shall find difficulty insurmountable in trying to lament them, if they are productive of a lengthened visit from my dear Miss Beverley to her

Faithful humble servant,

AUGUSTA DELVILE.

Cecilia, charmed with this note, could now no longer forbear looking forward to brighter prospects, flattering herself that once under the roof of Mrs. Delvile, she must necessarily be happy, let the engagements or behaviour of her son be what they might.

CHAPTER X

A Gamester's Conscience

FROM this soothing prospect, Cecilia was presently disturbed by Mrs. Harrel's maid, who came to entreat she would hasten to her lady, whom she feared was going into fits.

Cecilia flew to her immediately, and found her in the most violent affliction. She used every kind effort in her power to quiet and console her, but it was not without the utmost difficulty she could sob out the cause of this fresh sorrow, which indeed was not trifling. Mr. Harrel, she said, had told her he could not possibly raise money even for his travelling expences, without risking a discovery of his project, and being seized by his creditors: he had therefore charged her, *through her brother or her friend*, to procure for him 3000*l*. as less would not suffice to maintain them while abroad, and he knew no method by which he could have any remittances without danger. And, when she hesitated in her compliance, he furiously accused her of having brought on all this distress by her negligence and want of management, and declared that if she did not get the money, she would only be served as she merited by starving in a foreign gaol, which he swore would be the fate of them both.

The horror and indignation with which Cecilia heard this account were unspeakable. She saw evidently that she was again to be played upon by terror and distress, and the cautions and opinions of Mr. Monckton no longer appeared overstrained; *one year's income** was already demanded, the annuity and the country house might next be required: she rejoiced, however, that thus wisely forewarned, she was not liable to surprise, and she determined, be their entreaties or representations what they might, to be immovably steady in her purpose of leaving them the next morning.

Yet she could not but grieve at suffering the whole burthen of this clamorous imposition to fall upon the soft-hearted Mr. Arnott, whose inability to resist solicitation made him so unequal to sustaining its weight: but when Mrs. Harrel was again able to go on with her account, she heard, to her infinite surprise, that all application to her brother had proved fruitless. "He will not hear me," continued Mrs. Harrel, "and he never was deaf to me before! so now I have lost my only and last resource, my brother himself gives me up, and there is no one else upon earth who will assist me!"

"With pleasure, with readiness, with joy," cried Cecilia, "should you find assistance from me, were it to you alone it were given; but to supply fewel for the very fire that is consuming you—no, no, my whole heart is hardened against gaming and gamesters, and neither now or ever will I suffer any consideration to soften me in their favour."

Mrs. Harrel only answered by tears and lamentations; and Cecilia, whose justice shut not out compassion, having now declared her purposed firmness, again attempted to sooth her, entreating her not to give way to such immoderate grief, since better prospects might arise from the very gloom now before her, and a short time spent in solitude and œconomy, might enable her to return to her native land with recovered happiness.

"No, I shall never return!" cried she, weeping, "I shall die, I shall break my heart before I have been banished a month! Oh Miss Beverley, how happy are you! able to stay where you please,—rich,—rolling in wealth which you do not want,—of which had we but *one* year's income only, all this misery would be over, and we might stay in our dear, dear country!"

Cecilia, struck by a hint that so nearly bordered upon reproach, and offended by seeing the impossibility of ever doing enough, while any thing remained to be done, forbore not without difficulty enquiring what next was expected from her, and whether any part of her fortune might be guarded, without giving room for some censure! but the deep affliction of Mrs. Harrel soon removed her resentment, and scarcely thinking her, while in a state of such wretchedness, answerable for what she said, after a little recollection, she mildly replied "As affluence is all comparative, you may at present think I have more than my share: but the time is only this moment past, when your own situation seemed as subject to the envy of others as mine may be now. My future destiny is yet undetermined, and the occasion I may have for my fortune is unknown to myself; but whether I possess it in peace or in turbulence, whether it proves to me a blessing or an injury, so long as I can call it my own, I shall always remember with alacrity the claim upon that and upon me which early friendship has so justly given Mrs. Harrel. Yet permit me, at the same time, to add, that I do not hold myself so entirely independent as you may probably suppose me. I have not, it is true, any Relations to call me to account, but respect for their memory supplies the place of their authority, and I cannot, in the distribution of the fortune which has devolved to me, forbear sometimes considering how they would have wished it should be spent, and always remembering that what was acquired by industry and labour, should never be dissipated in idleness and vanity. Forgive me for thus speaking to the point; you will not find me less friendly to yourself, for this frankness with respect to your situation."

Tears were again the only answer of Mrs. Harrel; yet Cecilia, who pitied the weakness of her mind, stayed by her with the most patient kindness till the servants announced dinner. She then declared she would not go down stairs: but Cecilia so strongly represented the danger of awakening suspicion in the servants, that she at last prevailed with her to make her appearance.

Mr. Harrel was already in the parlour, and enquiring for Mr. Arnott, but was told by the servants he had sent word he had another engagement. Sir Robert Floyer also kept away, and, for the first time since her arrival in town, Cecilia dined with no other company than the master and mistress of the house.

Mrs. Harrel could eat nothing; Cecilia, merely to avoid creating surprise in the servants, forbore following her example; but Mr. Harrel eat much as usual, talked all dinner-time, was extremely civil to Cecilia, and discovered not by his manners the least alteration in his affairs.

When the servants were gone, he desired his wife to step for a moment with him into the library. They soon returned, and then Mr. Harrel, after walking in a disordered manner about the room, rang the bell, and ordered his hat and cane, and as he took them, said "If this fails—" and, stopping short, without speaking to his wife, or even bowing to Cecilia, he hastily went out of the house.

Mrs. Harrel told Cecilia that he had merely called her to know the event of her two petitions, and had heard her double failure in total silence. Whither he was now gone it was not easy to conjecture, nor what was the new resource which he still seemed to think worth trying; but the manner of his quitting the house, and the threat implied by *if this fails*, contributed not to lessen the grief of Mrs. Harrel, and gave to Cecilia herself the utmost alarm.

They continued together till tea-time, the servants having been ordered to admit no company. Mr. Harrel himself then returned, and returned, to the amazement of Cecilia, accompanied by Mr. Marriot.

He presented that young man to both the ladies as a gentleman whose acquaintance and friendship he was very desirous to cultivate. Mrs. Harrel, too much absorbed in her own affairs to care about any other, saw his entrance with a momentary surprise, and then thought of it no more: but it was not so with Cecilia, whose better understanding led her to deeper reflection.

Even the visits of Mr. Marriot but a few weeks since Mr. Harrel had prohibited, yet he now introduced him into his house with particular distinction; he came back too himself in admirable spirits, enlivened in his countenance, and restored to his good humour. A change so extraordinary both in conduct and disposition, convinced her that some change no less extraordinary of circumstance must previously have happened: what that might be it was not possible for her to divine, but the lessons she had received from Mr. Monckton led her to suspicions of the darkest kind.

Every part of his behaviour served still further to confirm them; he was civil even to excess to Mr. Marriot; he gave orders aloud not to be at home to Sir Robert Floyer; he made his court to Cecilia with unusual assiduity, and he took every method in his power to procure opportunity to her admirer of addressing and approaching her.

The young man, who seemed *enamoured even to madness*,* could scarce refrain not merely from prostration to the object of his passion, but to Mr. Harrel himself for permitting him to see her. Cecilia, who not without some concern perceived a fondness so fruitless, and who knew not by what arts or with what views Mr. Harrel might think proper to encourage it, determined to take all the means that were in her own power towards giving it immediate control. She behaved, therefore, with the utmost reserve, and the moment tea was over, though earnestly entreated to remain with them, she retired to her own room, without making any other apology than coldly saying she could not stay.

In about an hour Mrs. Harrel ran up stairs to her.

"Oh Miss Beverley," she cried, "a little respite is now granted me! Mr. Harrel says he shall stay another day; he says, too, one single thousand pound would now make him a new man."

Cecilia returned no answer; she conjectured some new deceit was in agitation to raise money, and she feared Mr. Marriot was the next dupe to be played upon.

Mrs. Harrel, therefore, with a look of the utmost disappointment, left her, saying she would send for her brother, and once more try if he had yet any remaining regard for her.

Cecilia rested quiet till eleven o'clock, when she was summoned to supper: she found Mr. Marriot still the only guest, and that Mr. Arnott made not his appearance.

She now resolved to publish her resolution of going the next morning to St. James's-square. As soon, therefore, as the servants withdrew, she enquired of Mr. Harrel if he had any commands with Mr. or Mrs. Delvile, as she should see them the next morning, and purposed to spend some time with them.

Mr. Harrel, with a look of much alarm, asked if she meant the whole day.

Many days, she answered, and probably some months.

Mrs. Harrel exclaimed her surprise aloud, and Mr. Harrel looked aghast: while his new young friend cast upon him a glance of reproach and resentment, which fully convinced Cecilia he imagined he had procured himself a title to an easiness of intercourse and frequency of meeting which this intelligence destroyed.

Cecilia, thinking after all that had passed, no other ceremony on her part was necessary but that of simply speaking her intention, then arose and returned to her own room.

She acquainted her maid that she was going to make a visit to Mrs. Delvile, and gave her directions about packing up her clothes, and sending for a man in the morning to take care of her books.

This employment was soon interrupted by the entrance of Mrs. Harrel, who desiring to speak with her alone, when the maid was gone, said "O Miss Beverley, can you indeed be so barbarous as to leave me?"

"I entreat you, Mrs. Harrel," answered Cecilia, "to save both yourself and me any further discussions. I have delayed this removal very long, and I can now delay it no longer."

Mrs. Harrel then flung herself upon a chair in the bitterest sorrow, declaring she was utterly undone; that Mr. Harrel had declared he could not stay even an hour in England if she was not in his house; that he had already had a violent quarrel with Mr. Marriot upon the subject; and that her brother, though she had sent him the most earnest entreaties, would not come near her.

Cecilia, tired of vain attempts to offer comfort, now urged the warmest expostulations against her opposition, strongly representing the real necessity of her going abroad, and the unpardonable weakness of wishing to continue such a life as she now led, adding debt to debt, and hoarding distress upon distress.

Mrs. Harrel then, though rather from compulsion than conviction, declared she would agree to go, if she had not a dread of ill usage; but Mr. Harrel, she said, had behaved to her with the utmost brutality, calling her the cause of his ruin, and threatening that if she procured not this thousand pound before the ensuing evening, she should be treated as she deserved for her extravagance and folly.

"Does he think, then," said Cecilia with the utmost indignation, "that I am to be frightened through your fears into what compliances he pleases?"

"O no," cried Mrs. Harrel, "no; his expectations are all from my brother. He surely thought that when I supplicated and pleaded to him, he would do what I wished, for so he always did formerly, and so once again I am sure he would do now, could I but make him come to me, and tell him how I am used, and tell him that if Mr. Harrel takes me abroad in this humour, I verily think in his rage he will half murder me."

Cecilia, who well knew she was herself the real cause of Mr. Arnott's resistance, now felt her resolution waver, internally reproaching herself with the sufferings of his sister; alarmed, however, for her own constancy, she earnestly besought Mrs. Harrel to go and compose herself for the night, and promised to deliberate what could be done for her before morning.

Mrs. Harrel complied; but scarce was her own rest more broken than that of Cecilia, who, though extremely fatigued with a whole night's watching, was so perturbed in her mind she could not close her eyes. Mrs. Harrel was her earliest, and had once been her dearest friend; she had deprived her by her own advice of her customary refuge in her brother; to refuse, therefore, assistance to her seemed cruelty, though to deny it to Mr. Harrel was justice: she endeavoured, therefore, to make a compromise between her judgment and compassion, by resolving that though she would grant nothing further to Mr. Harrel while he remained in London, she would contribute from time to time both to his necessities and comfort, when once he was established elsewhere upon some plan of prudence and œconomy.

CHAPTER XI

A Persecution

THE next morning by five o'clock Mrs. Harrel came into Cecilia's room to know the result of her deliberation; and Cecilia, with that graceful readiness which accompanied all her kind offices, instantly assured her the thousand pound should be her own, if she would consent to seek some quiet retreat, and receive it in small sums, of fifty or one hundred pounds at a time, which should be carefully transmitted, and which, by being delivered to herself, might secure better treatment from Mr. Harrel, and be a motive to revive his care and affection.

She flew, much delighted, with this proposal to her husband; but presently, and with a dejected look, returning, said Mr. Harrel protested he could not possibly set out without first receiving the money. "I shall go myself, therefore," said she, "to my brother after breakfast, for he will not, I see, unkind as he is grown, come to me; and if I do not succeed with him, I believe I shall never come back!"

To this Cecilia, offended and disappointed, answered "I am sorry for Mr. Arnott, but for myself I have done!"

Mrs. Harrel then left her, and she arose to make immediate preparations for her removal to St. James's-square, whither, with all the speed in her power, she sent her books, her trunks, and all that belonged to her.

When she was summoned down stairs, she found, for the first time, Mr. Harrel breakfasting at the same table with his wife: they seemed mutually out of humour and comfortless, nothing hardly was spoken, and little was swallowed: Mr. Harrel, however, was civil, but his wife was totally silent, and Cecilia the whole time was planning how to take her leave.

When the tea things were removed, Mr. Harrel said "You have not, I hope, Miss Beverley, quite determined upon this strange scheme?"

"Indeed I have, Sir," she answered, "and already I have sent my clothes."

At this information he seemed thunderstruck; but, after somewhat recovering, said with much bitterness "Well, madam, at least may I request you will stay here till the evening?"

"No, Sir," answered she coolly, "I am going instantly."

"And will you not," said he, with yet greater asperity, "amuse yourself first with seeing bailiffs take possession of my house, and your friend Priscilla follow me to Jail?"

"Good God, Mr. Harrel!" exclaimed Cecilia, with uplifted hands, "is this a question, is this behaviour I have merited!"

"O no, !" cried he with quickness, "should I once think that way——" then rising and striking his forehead, he walked about the room.

Mrs. Harrel arose too, and weeping violently went away.

"Will you at least," said Cecilia, when she was gone, "till your affairs are settled, leave Priscilla with me? When I go into my own house, she shall accompany me, and mean time Mr. Arnott's I am sure will gladly be open to her."

"No, no," answered he, "she deserves no such indulgence; she has not any reason to complain, she has been as negligent, as profuse, as expensive as myself; she has practised neither œconomy nor self-denial, she has neither thought of me nor my affairs, nor is she now afflicted at any thing but the loss of that affluence she has done her best towards diminishing."

"All recrimination," said Cecilia, "were vain, or what might not Mrs. Harrel urge in return! but let us not enlarge upon so ungrateful a subject, the wisest and the happiest scheme now were mutually and kindly to console each other."

"Consolation and kindness," cried he, with abruptness, "are out of the question. I have ordered a post chaise* to be here at night, and if till then you will stay, I will promise to release you without further petition: if not, eternal destruction be my portion if I *live* to see the scene which your removal will occasion!"

"My removal!" cried Cecilia, shuddering, "good heaven, and how can my removal be of such dreadful consequence?"

"Ask me not," cried he, fiercely, "questions or reasons now; the crisis is at hand, and you will soon, happen what may, know all: mean time what I have said is a fact, and immutable: and you must hasten my end, or give me a chance for avoiding it, as you think fit. I scarce care at this instant which way you decide: remember, however, all I ask of you is to defer your departure; what else I have to hope is from Mr. Arnott."

He then left the room.

Cecilia now was again a coward! In vain she called to her support the advice, the prophesies, the cautions of Mr. Monckton, in vain she recollected the impositions she had already seen practised, for neither the warnings of her counsellor, nor the lessons of her own experience, were proofs against the terrors which threats so desperate inspired: and though more than once she determined to fly at all events from a tyranny he had so little right to usurp, the mere remembrance of the words *if you stay not till night I will not live*, robbed her of all courage; and however long she had prepared herself for this very attack, when the moment arrived, its power over her mind was too strong for resistance.

While this conflict between fear and resolution was still undecided, her servant brought her the following letter from Mr. Arnott.

To Miss BEVERLEY, Portman-square.

June 13th, 1779.

Madam,

Determined to obey those commands which you had the goodness to honour me with, I have absented myself from town till Mr. Harrel is settled; for though I am as sensible of your wisdom as of your beauty, I find myself too weak to bear the distress of my unhappy sister, and therefore I run from the sight, nor shall any letter or message follow me, unless it comes from Miss Beverley herself, lest she should in future refuse the only favour I dare presume to solicit, that of sometimes deigning to honour with her directions

The most humble
and devoted of her servants,
J. ARNOTT.

In the midst of her apprehensions for herself and her own interest, Cecilia could not forbear rejoicing that Mr. Arnott, at least, had escaped the present storm: yet she was certain it would fall the more heavily upon herself, and dreaded the sight of Mrs. Harrel after the shock which this flight would occasion.

Her expectations were but too quickly fulfilled: Mrs. Harrel in a short time after rushed wildly into the room, calling out "My brother is gone! he has left me for ever! Oh save me, Miss Beverley, save me from abuse and insult!" And she wept with so much violence she could utter nothing more.

Cecilia, quite tortured by this persecution, faintly asked what she could do for her?

"Send," cried she "to my brother, and beseech him not to abandon me! send to him, and conjure him to advance this thousand pound!—the chaise is already ordered,—Mr. Harrel is fixed upon going,—yet he says without that money we must both starve in a strange land,—O send to my cruel brother! he has left word that nothing must follow him that does not come from you."

"For the world, then," cried Cecilia, "would I not baffle his discretion! indeed you must submit to your fate, indeed Mrs. Harrel you must endeavour to bear it better."

Mrs. Harrel, shedding a flood of tears, declared she would try to follow her advice, but again besought her in the utmost agony to send after her brother, protesting she did not think even her life would be safe in making so long a journey with Mr. Harrel in his present state of mind: his character, she said, was totally changed, his gaiety, good humour and sprightliness were turned into roughness and moroseness, and, since his great losses at play, he was grown so fierce and furious, that to oppose him even in a trifle, rendered him quite outrageous in passion.

Cecilia, though truly concerned, and almost melted, yet refused to interfere with Mr. Arnott, and even thought it but justice to acknowledge she had advised his retreat.

"And can you have been so cruel?" cried Mrs. Harrel, with still encreasing violence of sorrow, "to rob me of my only friend, to deprive me of my Brother's affection, at the very time I am forced out of the kingdom, with a husband who is ready to murder me, and who says he hates the sight of me, and all because I cannot get him this fatal, fatal money!—O Miss Beverley, how could I have thought to have had such an office* from you?"

Cecilia was beginning a justification, when a message came from Mr. Harrel, desiring to see his wife immediately.

Mrs. Harrel, in great terror, cast herself at Cecilia's feet, and clinging to her knees, called out "I dare not go to him! I dare not go to him! he wants to know my success, and when he hears my brother is run away, I am sure he will kill me!—Oh Miss Beverley, how could you send him away? how could you be so inhuman as to leave me to the rage of Mr. Harrel?"

Cecilia, distressed and trembling herself, conjured her to rise and be consoled; but Mrs. Harrel, weak and frightened, could only weep and supplicate; "I don't ask you," she cried, "to give me the money yourself, but only to send for my brother, that he may protect me, and beg Mr. Harrel not to treat me so cruelly,—consider but what a long, long journey I am going to make! consider how often you used to say you would love me for ever! consider you have robbed me of the tenderest brother in the world!—Oh Miss Beverley, send for him back, or be a sister to me yourself, and let not your poor Priscilla leave her native land without help or pity?"

Cecilia, wholly overcome, now knelt too, and embracing her with tears, said "Oh Priscilla, plead and reproach no more! what you wish shall be yours,—I will send for your brother,—I will do what you please!"

"Now you are my friend indeed!" cried Mrs. Harrel, "let me but *see* my brother, and his heart will yield to my distress, and he will soften Mr. Harrel by giving his unhappy sister this parting bounty."

Cecilia then took a pen in her hand to write to Mr. Arnott; but struck almost in the same moment with a notion of treachery in calling him from a retreat which her own counsel had made him seek, professedly to expose him to a supplication which from his present situation might lead him to ruin, she hastily flung it from her, and exclaimed "No, excellent Mr. Arnott, I will not so unworthily betray you!"

"And can you, Miss Beverley, can you at last," cried Mrs. Harrel, "be so barbarous as to retract?"

"No, my poor Priscilla," answered Cecilia, "I cannot so cruelly disappoint you; my pity shall however make no sufferer but myself,—I cannot send for Mr. Arnott,—from me you must have the money, and may it answer the purpose for which it is given, and restore to you the tenderness of your husband, and the peace of your own heart!"

Priscilla, scarce waiting to thank her, flew with this intelligence to Mr. Harrel; who with the same impetuosity, scarce waiting to say he was glad of it, ran himself to bring the Jew from whom the money was to be procured. Every thing was soon settled, Cecilia had no time for retracting, and repentance they had not the delicacy to regard: again, therefore, she signed her name for paying the principal and interest of another 1000*l.* within ten days after she was of age: and having taken the money, she accompanied Mr. and Mrs. Harrel into another room. Presenting it then with an affecting solemnity to Mrs. Harrel, "accept, Priscilla," she cried, this irrefragable mark of the sincerity of my friendship: but suffer me at the same time to tell you, it is the last to so considerable an amount I ever mean to offer; receive it, therefore, with kindness, but use it with discretion."

She then embraced her, and eager now to avoid acknowledgement, as before she had been to escape importunities, she left them together.

The soothing recompense of succouring benevolence, followed not this gift, nor made amends for this loss: perplexity and uneasiness, regret and resentment, accompanied the donation, and rested upon her mind; she feared she had done wrong; she was certain Mr. Monkton would blame her; he knew not the persecution she suffered, nor would he make any allowance for the threats which alarmed, or the intreaties which melted her.

Far other had been her feelings at the generosity she exerted for the Hills; no doubts then tormented her, and no repentance embittered her beneficence. Their worth was without suspicion, and their misfortunes were not of their own seeking; the post in which they had been stationed they had never deserted, and the poverty into which they had sunk was accidental and unavoidable.

But here, every evil had been wantonly incurred by vanity and licentiousness, and shamelessly followed by injustice and fraud: the disturbance of her mind only increased by reflection, for when the rights of the creditors with their injuries occurred to her, she enquired of herself by what title or equity, she had so liberally assisted Mr. Harrel in eluding their claims, and flying the punishment which the law would inflict.

Startled by this consideration, she most severely reproached herself for a compliance of which she had so lightly weighed the consequences, and thought with the utmost dismay, that while she had flattered herself she was merely indulging the dictates of humanity, she might perhaps be accused by the world as an abettor of guile and injustice.

"And yet," she continued, "whom can I essentially have injured but myself? would his creditors have been benefitted by my refusal? had I braved the execution of his dreadful threat, and quitted his house before I was wrought upon to assist him, would his suicide have lessened their losses, or secured their demands? even if he had no intention but to intimidate me, who will be wronged by my enabling him to go abroad, or who would be better paid were he seized and confined? All that remains of his shattered fortune may still be claimed, though I have saved him from a lingering imprisonment, desperate for himself and his wife, and useless for those he has plundered."

And thus, now soothed by the purity of her intentions, and now uneasy from the rectitude of her principles, she alternately rejoiced and repined at what she had done.

At dinner Mr. Harrel was all civility and good humour. He warmly thanked Cecilia for the kindness she had shewn him, and gaily added, "You should be absolved from all the mischief you may do for a twelvemonth to come, in reward for the preservation from mischief which you have this day effected."

"The preservation," said Cecilia, "will I hope be for many days. But tell me, sir, exactly, at what time I may acquaint Mrs. Delvile I shall wait upon her?"

"Perhaps," he answered, "by eight o'clock; perhaps by nine; you will not mind half an hour?"

"Certainly not;" she answered, unwilling by disputing about a trifle to diminish his satisfaction in her assistance. She wrote, therefore, another note to Mrs. Delvile, desiring she would not expect her till near ten o'clock, and promising to account and apologize for these seeming caprices when she had the honour of seeing her.

The rest of the afternoon she spent wholly in exhorting Mrs. Harrel to shew more fortitude, and conjuring her to study nothing while abroad but œconomy, prudence and housewifry: a lesson how hard for the thoughtless and negligent Priscilla! she heard the advice with repugnance, and only answered it with helpless complaints that she knew not how to spend less money than she had always done.

After tea, Mr. Harrel, still in high spirits, went out, entreating Cecilia to stay with Priscilla till his return, which he promised should be early.

Nine o'clock, however, came, and he did not appear; Cecilia then grew anxious to keep her appointment with Mrs. Delvile; but ten o'clock also came, and still Mr. Harrel was absent.

She then determined to wait no longer, and rang her bell for her servant and chair: but when Mrs. Harrel desired to be informed the moment that Mr. Harrel returned, the man said he had been come home more than half an hour.

Much surprised, she enquired where he was.

"In his own room, madam, and gave orders not to be disturbed."

Cecilia, who was not much pleased at this account, was easily persuaded to stay a few minutes longer; and, fearing some new evil, she was going to send him a message, by way of knowing how he was employed, when he came himself into the room.

"Well, ladies," he cried in a hurrying manner, "who is for Vauxhall?"

"Vauxhall!" repeated Mrs. Harrel, while Cecilia, staring, perceived in his face a look of perturbation that extremely alarmed her.

"Come, come," he cried, "we have no time to lose. A hackney coach will serve us; we won't wait for our own."

"Have you then given up going abroad?" said Mrs. Harrel.

"No, no; where can we go from half so well? let us live while we live! I have ordered a chaise to be in waiting there. Come, let's be gone."

"First," said Cecilia, "let me wish you both good night."

"Will you not go with me?" cried Mrs. Harrel, "how can I go to Vauxhall alone?"

"You are not alone," answered she; "but if I go, how am I to return?"

"She shall return with you," cried Mr. Harrel, "if you desire it; you shall return together."

Mrs. Harrel, starting up in rapture, called out "Oh Mr. Harrel, will you indeed leave me in England?"

"Yes," answered he reproachfully, "if you will make a better friend than you have made a wife, and if Miss Beverley is content to take charge of you."

"What can all this mean?" exclaimed Cecilia, "is it possible you can be serious? Are you really going yourself, and will you suffer Mrs. Harrel to remain?"

"I am," he answered, "and I will."

Then ringing the bell, he ordered a hackney coach.

Mrs. Harrel was scarce able to breathe for extacy, nor Cecilia for amazement: while Mr. Harrel, attending to neither of them, walked for some time silently about the room.

"But how," cried Cecilia at last, "can I possibly go? Mrs. Delvile must already be astonished at my delay, and if I disappoint her again she will hardly receive me."

"O make not any difficulties", cried Mrs. Harrel in an agony; "if Mr. Harrel will let me stay, sure you will not be so cruel as to oppose him?"

"But why," said Cecilia, "should either of us go to Vauxhall? surely that is no place for a parting so melancholy."

A servant then came in, and said the hackney coach was at the door.

Mrs. Harrel, starting at the sound, called out, "come, what do we wait for? if we go not immediately, we may be prevented."

Cecilia then again wished them good night, protesting she could fail Mrs. Delvile no longer.

Mrs. Harrel, half wild at this refusal, conjured her in the most frantic manner, to give way, exclaiming, "Oh cruel! cruel! to deny me this last request! I will kneel to you day and night," sinking upon the ground before her, "and I will serve you as the humblest of your slaves, if you will but be kind in this last instance, and save me from banishment and misery!"

"Oh rise, Mrs. Harrel," cried Cecilia, ashamed of her prostration, and shocked by her vehemence, "rise and let me rest!—it is painful to me to refuse, but to comply for ever in defiance of my judgment—Oh Mrs. Harrel, I know no longer what is kind or what is cruel, nor have I known for some time past right from wrong, nor good from evil!"

"Come," cried Mr. Harrel impetuously, "I wait not another minute!"

"Leave her then with me!" said Cecilia, "I will perform my promise, Mr. Arnott will I am sure hold his to be sacred, she shall now go with him, she shall hereafter come to me,—leave her but behind, and depend upon our care."

"No, no," cried he, with quickness, "I must take care of her myself. I shall not carry her abroad with me, but the only legacy I can leave her, is a warning which I hope she will remember for ever. *You*, however, need not go."

"What," cried Mrs. Harrel, "leave me at Vauxhall, and yet leave me alone?"

"What of that?" cried he with fierceness, "do you not desire to be left? have you any regard for me? or for any thing upon earth but yourself! cease these vain clamours, and come, I insist upon it, this moment."

And then, with a violent oath, he declared he would be detained no longer, and approached in great rage to seize her; Mrs. Harrel shrieked aloud, and the terrified Cecilia exclaimed, "If indeed you are to part to night, part not thus dreadfully!—rise, Mrs. Harrel, and comply!—be reconciled, be kind to her, Mr. Harrel!—and I will go with her myself,— we will all go together!"

"And why," cried Mr. Harrel, more gently yet with the utmost emotion, "why should *you* go!—*you* want no warning! *you* need no terror!—better far had you fly us, and my wife when I am set out may find you."

Mrs. Harrel, however, suffered her not to recede; and Cecilia, though half distracted by the scenes of horror and perplexity in which she was perpetually engaged, ordered her servant to acquaint Mrs. Delvile she was again compelled to defer waiting upon her.

Mr. Harrel then hurried them both into the coach, which he directed to Vauxhall.

"Pray write to me when you are landed," said Mrs. Harrel, who now released from her personal apprehensions, began to feel some for her husband.

He made not any answer. She then asked to what part of France he meant to go: but still he did not reply: and when she urged him by a third question, he told her in a rage to torment him no more.

During the rest of the ride not another word was said; Mrs. Harrel wept, her husband guarded a gloomy silence, and Cecilia most unpleasantly passed her time between anxious suspicions of some new scheme, and a terrified wonder in what all these transactions would terminate.

CHAPTER XII

A Man of Business

WHEN they entered Vauxhall, Mr. Harrel endeavoured to dismiss his moroseness, and affecting his usual gaiety, struggled to recover his spirits; but the effort was vain, he could neither talk nor look like himself, and though from time to time he resumed his air of wonted levity, he could not support it, but drooped and hung his head in evident despondency.

He made them take several turns in the midst of the company, and walked so fast that they could hardly keep pace with him, as if he hoped by exercise to restore his vivacity; but every attempt failed, he sunk and grew sadder, and muttering between his teeth "this is not to be borne!" he hastily called to a waiter to bring him a bottle of champagne.

Of this he drank glass after glass, notwithstanding Cecilia, as Mrs. Harrel had not courage to speak, entreated him to forbear. He seemed, however, not to hear her; but when he had drunk what he thought necessary to revive him, he conveyed them into an unfrequented part of the garden, and as soon as they were out of sight of all but a few stragglers, he suddenly stopt, and, in great agitation, said, "my chaise will soon be ready, and I shall take of you a long farewell!—all my affairs are unpropitious to my speedy return;—the wine is now mounting into my head, and perhaps I may not be able to say much by and by. I fear I have been cruel to you, Priscilla, and I begin to wish I had spared you this parting scene; yet let it not be banished your remembrance, but think of it when you are tempted to such mad folly as has ruined us."

Mrs. Harrel wept too much tc make any answer; and turning from her to Cecilia, "Oh Madam," he cried, "to *you*, indeed, I dare not speak! I have used you most unworthily, but I pay for it all! I ask you not to pity or forgive me, I know it is impossible you should do either.''

"No," cried the softened Cecilia, "it is not impossible, I do both at this moment, and I hope—"

"Do not hope," interrupted he, "be not so angelic, for I cannot bear it! benevolence like yours should have fallen into worthier hands. But come, let us return to the company. My head grows giddy, but my heart is still heavy; I must make them more fit companions for each other.''

He would then have hurried them back; but Cecilia, endeavouring to stop him, said "You do not mean, I hope, to call for more wine?"

"Why not?" cried he, with affected spirit, "what, shall we not be merry before we part? Yes, we will all be merry, for if we are not, how shall we part at all?—Oh not without a struggle!—" Then, stopping, he paused a moment, and casting off the mask of levity, said in accents the most solemn "I commit this packet to *you*," giving a sealed parcel to Cecilia; "had I written it later, its contents had been kinder to my wife, for now the hour of separation approaches, ill will and resentment subside. Poor Priscilla!—I am sorry—but you will succour her, I am sure you will,—Oh had I known you myself before this infatuation—bright pattern of all goodness!—but I was devoted,—a ruined wretch before ever you entered my house; unworthy to be saved, unworthy that virtues such as yours should dwell under the same roof with me! But come,—come now, or my resolution will waver, and I shall not go at last.''

"But what is this packet?" cried Cecilia, "and why do you give it to me?"

"No matter, no matter, you will know by and by;—the chaise waits, and I must gather courage to be gone.''

He then pressed forward, answering neither to remonstrance nor intreaty from his frightened companions.

The moment they returned to the covered walk, they were met by Mr. Marriot; Mr. Harrel, starting, endeavoured to pass him; but when he approached, and said "you have sent, Sir, no answer to my letter!" he stopt, and in a tone of forced politeness, said, "No, Sir, but I shall answer it to-morrow, and to-night I hope you will do me the honour of supping with me."

Mr. Marriot, looking openly at Cecilia as his inducement, though evidently regarding himself as an injured man, hesitated a moment, yet accepted the invitation.

"To supper?" cried Mrs. Harrel, "what here?"

"To supper?" repeated Cecilia, "and how are we to get home?"

"Think not of that these two hours," answered he; "come, let us look for a box."

Cecilia then grew quite urgent with him to give up a scheme which must keep them so late, and Mrs. Harrel repeatedly exclaimed "Indeed people will think it very odd to see us here without any party:" but he heeded them not, and perceiving at some distance Mr. Morrice, he called out to him to find them a box; for the evening was very pleasant, and the gardens were so much crowded that no accommodation was unseized.

"Sir," cried Morrice, with his usual readiness, "I'll get you one if I turn out ten old Aldermen sucking custards."*

Just after he was gone, a fat, sleek, vulgar-looking man, dressed in a bright purple coat, with a deep red waistcoat, and a wig bulging far from his head with small round curls, while his plump face and person announced plenty and good living, and an air of defiance spoke the fullness of his purse, strutted boldly up to Mr. Harrel, and accosting him in a manner that shewed some diffidence of his reception, but none of his right, said "Sir your humble servant." And made a bow first to him, and then to the ladies.

"Sir yours," replied Mr. Harrel scornfully, and without touching his hat he walked quick on.

His fat acquaintance, who seemed but little disposed to be offended with impunity, instantly replaced his hat on his head, and with a look that implied *I'll fit you for this!** put his hands to his sides, and following him, said "Sir, I must make bold to beg the favour of exchanging a few words with you."

"Ay, Sir," answered Mr. Harrel, "come to me to-morrow, and you shall exchange as many as you please."

"Nothing like the time present, Sir," answered the man; "as for to-morrow, I believe it intends to come no more; for I have heard of it any time these three years. I mean no reflections, Sir, but let every man have his right. That's what I say, and that's my notion of things."

Mr. Harrel, with a violent execration, asked what he meant by dunning him at such a place as Vauxhall?

"One place, Sir," he replied, "is as good as another place; for so as what one does is good, 'tis no matter for where it may be. A *man of business* never wants a counter if he can meet with a joint-stool.* For my part, I'm all for a clear conscience, and no bills without receipts to them."

"And if you were all for broken bones," cried Mr. Harrel, angrily, "I would oblige you with them without delay."

"Sir," cried the man, equally provoked, "this is talking quite out of character, for as to broken bones, there's ne'er a person in all England, gentle nor simple, can say he's a right to break mine, for I'm not a person of that sort, but a man of as good property as another man; and there's ne'er a customer I have in the world that's more his own man than myself."

"Lord bless me, Mr. Hobson," cried Mrs. Harrel, "don't follow us in this manner! If we meet any of our acquaintance they'll think us half crazy."

"Ma'am," answered Mr. Hobson, again taking off his hat, "if I'm treated with proper respect, no man will behave more generous than myself; but if I'm affronted, all I can say is, it may go harder with some folks than they think for."

Here a little mean-looking man, very thin, and almost bent double with perpetual cringing, came up to Mr. Hobson, and pulling him by the sleeve, whispered, yet loud enough to be heard, "It's surprizeable to me, Mr. Hobson, you can behave so out of the way! For my part, perhaps I've as much my due as another person, but I dares to say I shall have it when it's convenient, and I'd scorn for to mislest* a gentleman when he's taking his pleasure."

"Lord bless me," cried Mrs. Harrel, "what shall we do now? here's all Mr. Harrel's creditors coming upon us!"

"Do?" cried Mr. Harrel, re-assuming an air of gaiety, "why give them all a supper, to be sure. Come, gentlemen, will you favour me with your company to supper?"

"Sir," answered Mr. Hobson, somewhat softened by this unexpected invitation, "I've supped this hour and more, and had my glass too, for I'm as willing to spend my money as another man; only what I say is this, I don't chuse to be cheated, for that's losing one's substance, and getting no credit; however, as to drinking another glass, or such a matter as that, I'll do it with all the pleasure in life."

"And as to me," said the other man, whose name was Simkins, and whose head almost touched the ground by the profoundness of his reverence, "I can't upon no account think of taking the liberty; but if I may just stand without, I'll make bold to go so far as just for to drink my humble duty to the ladies in a cup of cyder."

"Are you mad, Mr. Harrel, are you mad!" cried his wife, "to think of asking such people as these to supper? what will every body say? suppose any of our acquaintance should see us? I am sure I shall die with shame."

"Mad!" repeated he, "no, not mad but merry. O ho, Mr. Morrice, why have you been so long? what have you done for us?"

"Why Sir," answered Morrice, returning with a look somewhat less elated than he had set out, "the gardens are so full, there is not a box to be had: but I hope we shall get one for all that; for I observed one of the best boxes in the garden, just to the right there, with nobody in it but that gentleman who made me spill the tea-pot at the Pantheon. So I made an apology, and told him the case; but he only said humph? and hay? so then I told it all over again, but he served me just the same, for he never seems to hear what one says till one's just done, and then he begins to recollect one's speaking to him; however, though I repeated it all over and over again, I could get nothing from him but just that humph? and hay? but he is so remarkably absent, that I dare

say if we all go and sit down round him, he won't know a
word of the matter."

"Won't he?" cried Mr. Harrel, "have at him, then!"

And he followed Mr. Morrice, though Cecilia, who now
half suspected that all was to end in a mere idle frolic,
warmly joined her remonstrances to those of Mrs. Harrel,
which were made with the utmost, but with fruitless
earnestness.

Mr. Meadows, who was seated in the middle of the box,
was lolloping upon the table with his customary ease, and
picking his teeth with his usual inattention to all about him.
The intrusion, however, of so large a party, seemed to
threaten his insensibility with unavoidable disturbance;
though imagining they meant but to look in at the box, and
pass on, he made not at their first approach any alteration
in his attitude or employment.

"See, ladies," cried the officious Morrice, "I told you
there was room; and I am sure this gentleman will be very
happy to make way for you, if it's only out of good-nature
to the waiters, as he is neither eating nor drinking, nor doing
any thing at all. So if you two ladies will go in at that side,
Mr. Harrel and that other gentleman," pointing to Mr.
Marriot, "may go to the other, and then I'll sit by the ladies
here, and those other two gentlemen——"

Here Mr. Meadows, raising himself from his reclining
posture, and staring Morrice in the face, gravely said,
"What's all this, Sir!"

Morrice, who expected to have arranged the whole party
without a question, and who understood so little of modish
airs as to suspect neither affectation nor trick in the absence
of mind and indolence of manners which he observed in Mr.
Meadows, was utterly amazed by this interrogatory, and
staring himself in return, said, "Sir, you seemed so
thoughtful—I did not think—I did not suppose you would
have taken any notice of just a person or two coming into the
box."

"Did not you, Sir?" said Mr. Meadows very coldly,
"why then now you do, perhaps you'll be so obliging as to
let me have my own box to myself."

And then again he returned to his favourite position.

"Certainly, Sir," said Morrice, bowing; "I am sure I did not mean to disturb you: for you seemed so lost in thought, that I'm sure I did not much believe you would have seen us."

"Why Sir," said Mr. Hobson, strutting forward, "if I may speak my opinion, I should think, as you happen to be quite alone, a little agreeable company would be no such bad thing. At least that's my notion."

"And if I might take the liberty," said the smooth tongued Mr. Simkins, "for to put in a word, I should think the best way would be, if the gentleman has no peticklar objection, for me just to stand somewhere hereabouts, and so, when he's had what he's a mind to, be ready for to pop in at one side, as he comes out at the t'other; for if one does not look pretty 'cute* such a full night as this, a box is whipt away before one knows where one is."

"No, no, no," cried Mrs. Harrel impatiently, "let us neither sup in this box nor in any other; let us go away entirely."

"Indeed we must! indeed we ought!" cried Cecilia; "it is utterly improper we should stay; pray let us be gone immediately."

Mr. Harrel paid not the least regard to these requests; but Mr. Meadows, who could no longer seem unconscious of what passed, did himself so much violence as to arise, and ask if the ladies would be seated.

"I said so!" cried Morrice triumphantly, "I was sure there was no gentleman but would be happy to accommodate two such ladies!"

The ladies, however, far from happy in being so accommodated, again tried their utmost influence in persuading Mr. Harrel to give up this scheme; but he would not hear them, he insisted upon their going into the box, and, extending the privilege which Mr. Meadows had given, he invited without ceremony the whole party to follow.

Mr. Meadows, though he seemed to think this a very extraordinary encroachment, had already made such an effort from his general languor in the repulse he had given to Morrice, that he could exert himself no further; but after looking around him with mingled vacancy and contempt, he again seated himself, and suffered Morrice to do the honours without more opposition.

Morrice, but too happy in the office, placed Cecilia next to Mr. Meadows, and would have made Mr. Marriot her other neighbour, but she insisted upon not being parted from Mrs. Harrel, and therefore, as he chose to sit also by that lady himself, Mr. Marriot was obliged to follow Mr. Harrel to the other side of the box: Mr. Hobson, without further invitation, placed himself comfortably in one of the corners, and Mr. Simkins, who stood modestly for some time in another, finding the further encouragement for which he waited was not likely to arrive, dropt quietly into his seat without it.

Supper was now ordered, and while it was preparing Mr. Harrel sat totally silent; but Mr. Meadows thought proper to force himself to talk with Cecilia, though she could well have dispensed with such an exertion of his politeness.

"Do you like this place, ma'am?"

"Indeed I hardly know,—I never was here before."

"No wonder! the only surprise is that any body can come to it at all. To see a set of people walking after nothing! strolling about without view or object! 'tis strange! don't you think so, ma'am?"

"Yes,——I believe so," said Cecilia, scarce hearing him.

"O it gives me the vapours, the horrors," cried he, "to see what poor creatures we all are! taking pleasure even from the privation of it! forcing ourselves into exercise and toil, when we might at least have the indulgence of sitting still and reposing!"

"Lord, Sir," cried Morrice, "don't you like walking?"

"Walking?" cried he, "I know nothing so humiliating: to see a rational being in such mechanical motion! with no knowledge upon what principles he proceeds, but plodding on, one foot before another, without even any consciousness which is first, or how either—"

"Sir," interrupted Mr. Hobson, "I hope you won't take it amiss if I make bold to tell my opinion, for my way is this, let every man speak his maxim! But what I say as to this matter, is this, if a man must always be stopping to consider what foot he is standing upon, he had need have little to do, being the right does as well as the left, and the left as well as the right. And that, Sir, I think is a fair argument.''

Mr. Meadows deigned no other answer to this speech than a look of contempt.

''I fancy, Sir,'' said Morrice, ''you are fond of riding, for all your good horsemen like nothing else.''

''Riding!'' exclaimed Mr. Meadows, ''Oh barbarous! Wrestling and boxing are polite arts to it! trusting to the discretion of an animal less intellectual than ourselves! a sudden spring may break all our limbs, a stumble may fracture our sculls! And what is the inducement? to get melted with heat, killed with fatigue, and covered with dust! miserable infatuation!—Do you love riding, ma'am?''

''Yes, very well, Sir.''

''I am glad to hear it,'' cried he, with a vacant smile; ''you are quite right; I am entirely of your opinion.''

Mr. Simkins now, with a look of much perplexity, yet rising and bowing, said ''I don't mean, Sir, to be so rude as to put in my oar, but if I did not take you wrong, I'm sure just now I thought you seemed for to make no great 'count of riding, and yet now, all of the sudden, one would think you was a speaking up for it!''

''Why Sir,'' cried Morrice, ''if you neither like riding nor walking, you can have no pleasure at all but only in sitting.''

''Sitting!'' repeated Mr. Meadows, with a yawn, ''O worse and worse! it dispirits me to death! it robs me of all fire and life! it weakens circulation, and destroys elasticity.''

''Pray then, Sir,'' said Morrice, ''do you like any better to stand?''

''To stand? O intolerable! the most unmeaning thing in the world! one had better be made a mummy!''

''Why then, pray Sir,'' said Mr. Hobson, ''let me ask the favour of you to tell us what it is you *do* like?''

Mr. Meadows, though he stared him full in the face, began picking his teeth without making any answer.

''You see, Mr. Hobson,'' said Mr. Simkins, ''the

gentleman has no mind for to tell you; but if I may take the liberty just to put in, I think if he neither likes walking, nor riding, nor sitting, nor standing, I take it he likes nothing.''

"Well, Sir,'' said Morrice, "but here comes supper, and I hope you will like that. Pray Sir, may I help you to a bit of this ham?''

Mr. Meadows, not seeming to hear him, suddenly, and with an air of extreme weariness, arose, and without speaking to any body, abruptly made his way out of the box.

Mr. Harrel now, starting from the gloomy reverie into which he had sunk, undertook to do the honours of the table, insisting with much violence upon helping every body, calling for more provisions, and struggling to appear in high spirits and good humour.

In a few minutes Captain Aresby, who was passing by the box, stopt to make his compliments to Mrs. Harrel and Cecilia.

"What a concourse!'' he cried, casting up his eyes with an expression of half-dying fatigue, "are you not *accablé?* for my part, I hardly respire. I have really hardly ever had the honour of being so *obsedé* before.''

"We can make very good room, Sir,'' said Morrice, "if you chuse to come in.''

"Yes,'' said Mr. Simkins, obsequiously standing up, "I am sure the gentleman will be very welcome to take my place, for I did not mean for to sit down, only just to look agreeable.''

"By no means, Sir,'' answered the Captain: "I shall be quite *au desespoir* if I derange any body.''

"Sir,'' said Mr. Hobson, "I don't offer you my place, because I take it for granted if you had a mind to come in, you would not stand upon ceremony; for what I say is, let every man speak his mind, and then we shall all know how to conduct ourselves. That's my way, and let any man tell me a better!''

The Captain, after looking at him with a surprise not wholly unmixt with horror, turned from him without making any answer, and said to Cecilia, "And how long, ma'am, have you tried this petrifying place?''

"An hour,—two hours, I believe," she answered.

"Really? and nobody here! *assez de monde*, but nobody here! a blank *partout!*"

"Sir," said Mr. Simkins, getting out of the box that he might bow with more facility, "I humbly crave pardon for the liberty, but if I understood right, you said something of a blank?* pray, Sir, if I may be so free, has there been any thing of the nature of a lottery, or a raffle, in the garden? or the like of that?"

"Sir!" said the Captain, regarding him from head to foot, "I am quite *assommé* that I cannot comprehend your allusion."

"Sir, I ask pardon," said the man, bowing still lower, "I only thought if in case it should not be above half a crown, or such a matter as that, I might perhaps stretch a point once in a way."

The Captain, more and more amazed, stared at him again, but not thinking it necessary to take any further notice of him, he enquired of Cecilia if she meant to stay late.

"I hope not," she replied, "I have already stayed later than I wished to do."

"Really!" said he, with an unmeaning smile, "Well, that is as horrid a thing as I have the *malheur* to know. For my part, I make it a principle not to stay long in these semi-barbarous places, for after a certain time, they bore me to that degree I am quite *abîmé*. I shall, however, do *mon possible* to have the honour of seeing you again."

And then, with a smile of yet greater insipidity, he protested he was *reduced to despair* in leaving her, and walked on.

"Pray, ma'am, if I may be so bold," said Mr. Hobson, "what countryman may that gentleman be?"

"An Englishman, I suppose, Sir," said Cecilia.

"An Englishman, ma'am!" said Mr. Hobson, "why I could not understand one word in ten that came out of his mouth."

"Why indeed," said Mr. Simkins, "he has a mighty peticklar way of speaking, for I'm sure I thought I could have sworn he said something of a blank, or to that amount, but I could make nothing of it when I come to ask him about it."

"Let every man speak to be understood," cried Mr. Hobson, "that's my notion of things: for as to all those fine words that nobody can make out, I hold them to be of no use. Suppose a man was to talk in that manner when he's doing business, what would be the upshot? who'd understand what he meant? Well, that's the proof; what i'n't fit for business, i'n't of no value: that's my way of judging, and that's what I go upon."

"He said some other things," rejoined Mr. Simkins, "that I could not make out very clear, only I had no mind to ask any more questions, for fear of his answering me something I should not understand: but as well as I could make it out, I thought I heard him say there was nobody here! what he could mean by that, I can't pretend for to guess, for I'm sure the garden is so stock full, that if there was to come many more, I don't know where they could cram 'em."

"I took notice of it at the time," said Mr. Hobson, "for it i'n't many things are lost upon me; and, to tell you the truth, I thought he had been making pretty free with his bottle, by his seeing no better."

"Bottle!" cried Mr. Harrel, "a most excellent hint, Mr. Hobson! come! let us all make free with the bottle!"

He then called for more wine, and insisted that every body should pledge him. Mr. Marriot and Mr. Morrice made not any objection, and Mr. Hobson and Mr. Simkins consented with much delight.

Mr. Harrel now grew extremely unruly, the wine he had already drunk being thus powerfully aided; and his next project was to make his wife and Cecilia follow his example. Cecilia, more incensed than ever to see no preparation made for his departure, and all possible pains taken to unfit him for setting out, refused him with equal firmness and displeasure, and lamented, with the bitterest self-reproaches, the consent which had been forced from her to be present at a scene of such disorder: but Mrs. Harrel would have opposed him in vain, had not his attention been called off to another object. This was Sir Robert Floyer, who perceiving the party at some distance, no sooner observed Mr. Marriot in such company, than advancing to the box with an air of rage and defiance, he told Mr. Harrel he had something to say to him.

"Ay," cried Harrel, "say to me? and so have I to say to you! Come amongst us and be merry! Here, make room, make way! Sit close, my friends!"

Sir Robert, who now saw he was in no situation to be reasoned with, stood for a moment silent; and then, looking round the box, and observing Messrs. Hobson and Simkins, he exclaimed aloud "Why what queer party have you got into? who the d—l have you picked up here?"

Mr. Hobson, who, to the importance of lately acquired wealth, now added the courage of newly drunk Champaigne, stoutly kept his ground, without seeming at all conscious he was included in this interrogation; but Mr. Simkins, who had still his way to make in the world, and whose habitual servility would have resisted a larger draught, was easily intimidated; he again, therefore stood up, and with the most cringing respect offered the Baronet his place: who, taking neither of the offer nor offerer the smallest notice, still stood opposite to Mr. Harrel, waiting for some explanation.

Mr. Harrel, however, who now grew really incapable of giving any, only repeated his invitation that he would make one among them.

"One among you?" cried he, angrily, and pointing to Mr. Hobson, "why you don't fancy I'll sit down with a bricklayer?"

"A bricklayer?" said Mr. Harrel, "ay, sure, and a hosier too; sit down, Mr. Simkins, keep your place, man!"

Mr. Simkins most thankfully bowed; but Mr. Hobson, who could no longer avoid feeling the personality of this reflection, boldly answered, "Sir, you may sit down with a worse man any day in the week! I have done nothing I'm ashamed of, and no man can say to me why did you so? I don't tell you, Sir, what I'm worth; no one has a right to ask; I only say three times five is fifteen! that's all."

"Why what the d—l, you impudent fellow," cried the haughty Baronet, "you don't presume to mutter, do you?"

"Sir," answered Mr. Hobson, very hotly, "I sha'n't put up with abuse from no man! I've got a fair character in the world, and wherewithal to live by my own liking. And what I have is my own, and all I say is let every one say the same, for that's the way to fear no man, and face the d—l."

"What do you mean by that, fellow?" cried Sir Robert.

"Fellow, Sir! this is talking no how. Do you think a man of substance, that's got above the world, is to be treated like a little scrubby* apprentice? Let every man have his own, that's always my way of thinking; and this I can say for myself, I have as good a right to shew my head where I please as ever a member of parliament in all England: and I wish every body here could say as much."

Sir Robert, fury starting into his eyes, was beginning an answer; but Mrs. Harrel with terror, and Cecilia with dignity, calling upon them both to forbear, the Baronet desired Morrice to relinquish his place to him, and seating himself next to Mrs. Harrel, gave over the contest.

Mean-while Mr. Simkins, hoping to ingratiate himself with the company, advanced to Mr. Hobson, already cooled by finding himself unanswered, and reproachfully said "Mr. Hobson, if I may make so free, I must needs be bold to say I am quite ashamed of you! a person of your standing and credit for to talk so disrespectful! as if a gentleman had not a right to take a little pleasure, because he just happens to owe you a little matters of money: fie, fie, Mr. Hobson! I did not expect you to behave so despiseable!"

"Despiseable!" answered Mr. Hobson, "I'd scorn as much to do any thing despiseable as yourself, or any thing misbecoming of a gentleman; and as to coming to such a place as this may be, why I have no objection to it. All I stand to is this, let every man have his due; for as to taking a little pleasure, here I am, as one may say, doing the same myself; but where's the harm of that? who's a right to call a man to account that's clear of the world? Not that I mean to boast, nor nothing like it, but, as I said before, five times five is fifteen;*—that's my calculation."

Mr. Harrel, who, during this debate, had still continued drinking, regardless of all opposition from his wife and Cecilia, now grew more and more turbulent: he insisted that Mr. Simkins should return to his seat, ordered him another bumper of champagne, and saying he had not half company enough to raise his spirits, desired Morrice to go and invite more.

Morrice, always ready to promote a frolic, most chearfully consented; but when Cecilia, in a low voice, supplicated him to bring no one back, with still more readiness he made signs that he understood and would obey her.

Mr. Harrel then began to sing, and in so noisy and riotous a manner, that nobody approached the box without stopping to stare at him; and those who were new to such scenes, not contented with merely looking in, stationed themselves at some distance before it, to observe what was passing, and to contemplate with envy and admiration an appearance of mirth and enjoyment which they attributed to happiness and pleasure!

Mrs. Harrel, shocked to be seen in such mixed company, grew every instant more restless and miserable; and Cecilia, half distracted to think how they were to get home, had passed* all her time in making secret vows that if once again she was delivered from Mr. Harrel she would never see him more.

Sir Robert Floyer perceiving their mutual uneasiness, proposed to escort them home himself; and Cecilia, notwithstanding her aversion to him, was listening to the scheme, when Mr. Marriot, who had been evidently provoked and disconcerted since the junction of the Baronet, suspecting what was passing, offered his services also, and in a tone of voice that did not promise a very quiet acquiescence in a refusal.

Cecilia, who, too easily, in their looks, saw all the eagerness of rivalry, now dreaded the consequence of her decision, and therefore declined the assistance of either: but her distress was unspeakable, as there was not one person in the party to whose care she could commit herself, though the behaviour of Mr. Harrel, which every moment grew more disorderly, rendered the necessity of quitting him urgent and uncontroulable.

When Morrice returned, stopping in the midst of his loud and violent singing, he vehemently demanded what company he had brought him?

"None at all, Sir," answered Morrice, looking significantly at Cecilia; "I have really been so unlucky as not to meet with any body who had a mind to come."

"Why then," answered he, starting up, "I will seek some for myself." "O no, pray, Mr. Harrel, bring nobody else," cried his wife. "Hear us in pity," cried Cecilia, "and distress us no further." "Distress you?" cried he, with quickness, "what shall I not bring you those pretty girls? Yes, one more glass, and I will teach you to welcome them."

And he poured out another bumper.

"This is so insupportable!" cried Cecilia, rising, "and I can remain here no longer."

"This is cruel indeed," cried Mrs. Harrel, bursting into tears; "did you only bring me here to insult me?"

"No!" cried he, suddenly embracing her, "by this parting kiss!" then wildly jumping upon his seat, he leapt over the table, and was out of sight in an instant.

Amazement seized all who remained; Mrs. Harrel and Cecilia, indeed, doubted not but he was actually gone to the chaise he had ordered; but the manner of his departure affrighted them, and his preceding behaviour had made them cease to expect it: Mrs. Harrel, leaning upon Cecilia, continued to weep, while she, confounded and alarmed, scarce knew whether she should stay and console her, or fly after Mr. Harrel, who she feared had incapacitated himself from finding his chaise, by the very method he had taken to gather courage for seeking it.

This, however, was but the apprehension of a moment; another and a far more horrible one drove it from her imagination: for scarcely had Mr. Harrel quitted the box and their sight, before their ears were suddenly struck with the report of a pistol.

Mrs. Harrel gave a loud scream, which was involuntarily echoed by Cecilia: every body arose, some with officious zeal to serve the ladies, and others to hasten to the spot whence the dreadful sound proceeded.

Sir Robert Floyer again offered his services in conducting
them home; but they could listen to no such proposal:
Cecilia, with difficulty refrained from rushing out herself to
discover what was passing; but her dread of being followed
by Mrs. Harrel prevented her; they both, therefore, waited,
expecting every instant some intelligence, as all but the
Baronet and Mr. Marriot were now gone to seek it.

Nobody, however, returned; and their terrors encreased
every moment: Mrs. Harrel wanted to run out herself, but
Cecilia, conjuring her to keep still, begged Mr. Marriot to
bring them some account. Mr. Marriot, like the messengers
who had preceded him, came not back: an instant seemed
an age, and Sir Robert Floyer was also entreated to procure
information.

Mrs. Harrel and Cecilia were now left to themselves, and
their horror was too great for speech or motion: they stood
close to each other, listening to every sound and receiving
every possible addition to their alarm, by the general
confusion which they observed in the gardens, in which,
though both gentlemen and waiters were running to and fro,
not a creature was walking, and all amusement seemed
forgotten.

From this dreadful state they were at length removed,
though not relieved, by the sight of a waiter, who, as he was
passing shewed himself almost covered with blood! Mrs.
Harrel vehemently called after him, demanding whence it
came? "From the gentleman, ma'am," answered he in
haste, "that has shot himself," and then ran on.

Mrs. Harrel uttered a piercing scream, and sunk on the
ground; for Cecilia, shuddering with horror, lost all her own
strength, and could no longer lend her any support.

So great at this time was the general confusion of the
place, that for some minutes their particular distress was
unknown, and their situation unnoticed; till at length an
elderly gentleman came up to the box, and humanely offered
his assistance.

Cecilia, pointing to her unfortunate friend, who had not
fallen into a fainting fit, but merely from weakness and
terror, accepted his help in raising her. She was lifted up,

however, without the smallest effort on her own part, and was only kept upon her seat by being held there by the stranger, for Cecilia, whose whole frame was shaking, tried in vain to sustain her.

This gentleman, from the violence of their distress, began now to suspect its motive, and addressing himself to Cecilia, said, "I am afraid, madam, this unfortunate gentleman was some Relation to you?"

Neither of them spoke, but their silence was sufficiently expressive.

"It is pity, madam," he continued, "that some friend can't order him out of the crowd, and have him kept quiet till a surgeon can be brought."

"A surgeon!" exclaimed Cecilia, recovering from one surprize by the effect of another, "is it then possible he may be saved?"

And without waiting to have her question answered, she ran out of the box herself, flying wildly about the garden, and calling for help as she flew, till she found the house by the entrance; and then, going up to the bar, "Is a surgeon sent for?" she exclaimed, "let a surgeon be fetched instantly!" "A surgeon, ma'am," she was answered, "is not the gentleman dead?" "No, no, no!" she cried; "he must be brought in; let some careful people go and bring him in." Nor would she quit the bar, till two or three waiters were called, and received her orders. And then, eager to see them executed herself, she ran, fearless of being alone, and without thought of being lost, towards the fatal spot whither the crowd guided her. She could not, indeed, have been more secure from insult or molestation if surrounded by twenty guards; for the scene of desperation and horror which many had witnessed, and of which all had heard the signal, engrossed the universal attention, and took, even from the most idle and licentious, all spirit for gallantry and amusement.

Here, while making vain attempts to penetrate through the multitude, that she might see and herself judge the actual situation of Mr. Harrel, and give, if yet there was room for hope, such orders as would best conduce to his safety and

recovery, she was met by Mr. Marriot, who entreated her
not to press forward to a sight which he had found too
shocking for himself, and insisted upon protecting her
through the crowd.

"If he is alive," cried she, refusing his aid, "and if there
is any chance he may be saved, no sight shall be too shocking
to deter me from seeing him properly attended."

"All attendance," answered he, "will be in vain: he is not
indeed, yet dead, but his recovery is impossible. There is a
surgeon with him already; one who happened to be in the
gardens, and he told me himself that the wound was
inevitably mortal."

Cecilia, though greatly disappointed, still determined to
make way to him, that she might herself enquire if, in his
last moments, there was any thing he wished to communicate, or desired to have done: but, as she struggled to
proceed, she was next met and stopt by Sir Robert Floyer,
who, forcing her back, acquainted her that all was over!

The shock with which she received this account, though
unmixed with any tenderness of regret, and resulting merely
from general humanity, was yet so violent as almost to
overpower her. Mr. Harrel, indeed, had forfeited all right to
her esteem, and the unfeeling selfishness of his whole
behaviour had long provoked her resentment and excited
her disgust; yet a catastrophe so dreadful, and from which
she had herself made such efforts to rescue him, filled her
with so much horror, that, turning extremely sick, she was
obliged to be supported to the nearest box, and stop there
for hartshorn* and water.

A few minutes, however, sufficed to divest her of all care
for herself, in the concern with which she recollected the
situation of Mrs. Harrel; she hastened, therefore, back to
her, attended by the Baronet and Mr. Marriot, and found
her still leaning upon the stranger, and weeping aloud.

The fatal news had already reached her; and though all
affection between Mr. Harrel and herself had mutually
subsided from the first two or three months of their
marriage, a conclusion so horrible to all connection between
them could not be heard without sorrow and distress. Her

temper, too, naturally soft, retained not resentment, and Mr. Harrel, now separated from her for ever, was only remembered as the Mr. Harrel who first won her heart.

Neither pains nor tenderness were spared on the part of Cecilia to console her; who finding her utterly incapable either of acting or directing for herself, and knowing her at all times to be extremely helpless, now summoned to her own aid all the strength of mind she possessed, and determined upon this melancholy occasion, both to think and act for her widowed friend to the utmost stretch of her abilities and power.

As soon, therefore, as the first effusions of her grief were over, she prevailed with her to go to the house, where she was humanely offered the use of a quiet room till she should be better able to set off for town.

Cecilia, having seen her thus safely lodged, begged Mr. Marriot to stay with her, and then, accompanied by the Baronet, returned herself to the bar, and desiring the footman who had attended them to be called, sent him instantly to his late master, and proceeded next with great presence of mind, to inquire further into the particulars of what had passed, and to consult upon what was immediately to be done with the deceased: for she thought it neither decent nor right to leave to chance or to strangers the last duties which could be paid him.

He had lingered, she found, about a quarter of an hour, but in a condition too dreadful for description, quite speechless, and, by all that could be judged, out of his senses; yet so distorted with pain, and wounded so desperately beyond any power of relief, that the surgeon, who every instant expected his death, said it would not be merely useless but inhuman, to remove him till he had breathed his last. He died, therefore, in the arms of this gentleman and a waiter.

"A waiter!" cried Cecilia, reproachfully looking at Sir Robert, "and was there no friend who for the few poor moments that remained had patience to support him!"

"Where would be the good," said Sir Robert, "of supporting a man in his last agonies?"

This unfeeling speech she attempted not to answer, but, suffering neither her dislike to him, nor her scruples for herself, to interfere with the present occasion, she desired to have his advice what was now best to be done.

Undertaker's men must immediately, he said, be sent for, to remove the body.

She then gave orders for that purpose, which were instantly executed.

Whither the body was to go was the next question: Cecilia wished the removal to be directly to the town-house, but Sir Robert told her it must be carried to the nearest undertaker's, and kept there till it could be conveyed to town in a coffin.

For this, also, in the name of Mrs. Harrel, she gave directions. And then addressing herself to Sir Robert, "You will now Sir, I hope, she said, return to the fatal spot, and watch by your late unfortunate friend till the proper people arrive to take charge of him?"

"And what good will that do?" cried he; "had I not better watch by you?"

"It will do good," answered she, with some severity, "to decency and to humanity, and surely you cannot refuse to see who is with him, and in what situation he lies, and whether he has met, from the strangers with whom he was left, the tenderness and care which his friends ought to have paid him."

"Will you promise, then," he answered, "not to go away till I come back? for I have no great ambition to sacrifice the living for the dead."

"I will promise nothing, Sir," said she, shocked at his callous insensibility; "but if you refuse this last poor office, I must apply elsewhere; and firmly I believe there is no other I can ask who will a moment hesitate in complying."

She then went back to Mrs. Harrel, leaving, however, an impression upon the mind of Sir Robert, that made him no longer dare dispute her commands.

Her next solicitude was how they should return to town; they had no equipage of their own, and the only servant who came with them was employed in performing the last duties for his deceased master. Her first intention was to order a hackney coach, but the deplorable state of Mrs. Harrel made it almost impossible she could take the sole care of her, and the lateness of the night, and their distance from home, gave her a dread invincible to going so far without some guard or assistant. Mr. Marriot earnestly desired to have the honour of conveying them to Portman-square in his own carriage, and notwithstanding there were many objections to such a proposal, the humanity of his behaviour upon the present occasion, and the evident veneration which accompanied his passion, joined to her encreasing aversion to the Baronet, from whom she could not endure to receive the smallest obligation, determined her, after much perplexity and hesitation, to accept his offer.

She begged him, therefore, to immediately order his coach, and, happy to obey her, he went out with that design; but, instantly coming back, told her, in a low voice, that they must wait some time longer, as the Undertaker's people were then entering the garden, and if they stayed not till the removal had taken place, Mrs. Harrel might be shocked with the sight of some of the men, or perhaps even meet the dead body.

Cecilia, thanking him for this considerate precaution, readily agreed to defer setting out; devoting, mean time, all her attention to Mrs. Harrel, whose sorrow, though violent, forbad not consolation. But before the garden was cleared, and the carriage ordered, Sir Robert returned; saying to Cecilia, with an air of parading obedience which seemed to claim some applause, "Miss Beverley, your commands have been executed."

Cecilia made not any answer, and he presently added "Whenever you chuse to go I will order up my coach."

"*My* coach, Sir," said Mr. Marriot, "will be ordered when the ladies are ready, and I hope to have the honour myself of conducting them to town."

"No, Sir," cried the Baronet, "that can never be; my long acquaintance with Mrs. Harrel gives me a prior right to attend her, and I can by no means suffer any other person to rob me of it."

"I have nothing," said Mr. Marriot, "to say to that, Sir, but Miss Beverley herself has done me the honour to consent to make use of my carriage."

"Miss Beverley, I think," said Sir Robert, extremely piqued, "can never have sent me out of the way in order to execute her own commands, merely to deprive me of the pleasure of attending her and Mrs. Harrel home."

Cecilia, somewhat alarmed, now sought to lessen the favour of her decision, though she adhered to it without wavering.

"My intention," said she, "was not to confer, but to receive an obligation; and I had hoped, while Mr. Marriot assisted us, Sir Robert would be far more humanely employed in taking charge of what we cannot superintend, and yet are infinitely more anxious should not be neglected."

"That," said Sir Robert, "is all done; and I hope, therefore, after sending me upon such an errand, you don't mean to refuse me the pleasure of seeing you to town?"

"Sir Robert," said Cecilia, greatly displeased, "I cannot argue with you now; I have already settled my plan, and I am not at leisure to re-consider it."

Sir Robert bit his lips for a moment in angry silence; but not enduring to lose the victory to a young rival he despised, he presently said, "If I must talk no more about it to you, madam, I must at least beg leave to talk of it to this gentleman, and take the liberty to represent to him—"

Cecilia now, dreading how his speech might be answered, prevented its being finished, and with an air of the most spirited dignity, said, "Is it possible, sir, that at a time such as this, you should not be wholly indifferent to a matter so frivolous? little indeed will be the pleasure which our society can afford! your dispute however, has given it some importance, and therefore Mr. Marriot must accept my thanks for his civility, and excuse me for retracting my consent."

Supplications and remonstrances were, however, still poured upon her from both, and the danger, the impossibility that two ladies could go to town alone, in a hackney coach, and without even a servant, at near four o'clock in the morning, they mutually urged, vehemently entreating that she would run no such hazard.

Cecilia was far other than insensible to these representations: the danger, indeed, appeared to her so formidable, that her inclination the whole time opposed her refusal; yet her repugnance to giving way to the overbearing Baronet, and her fear of his resentment if she listened to Mr. Marriot, forced her to be steady, since she saw that her preference would prove the signal of a quarrel.

Inattentive, therefore, to their joint persecution, she again deliberated by what possible method she could get home in safety; but unable to devise any, she at last resolved to make enquiries of the people in the bar, who had been extremely humane and civil, whether they could assist or counsel her. She therefore desired the two gentlemen to take care of Mrs. Harrel, to which neither dared dissent, as both could not refuse, and hastily arising, went out of the room: but great indeed was her surprize when, as she was walking up to the bar, she was addressed by young Delvile!

Approaching her with that air of gravity and distance which of late he had assumed in her presence, he was beginning some speech about his mother; but the instant the sound of his voice reached Cecilia, she joyfully clasped her hands, and eagerly exclaimed, "Mr. Delvile!—O now we are safe!—this is fortunate indeed!"

"Safe, Madam," cried he astonished, "yes I hope so!— has any thing endangered your safety?"

"O no matter for danger," cried she, "we will now trust ourselves with you, and I am sure you will protect us."

Protect you! repeated he again, and with warmth, "yes, while I live!—but what is the matter?—why are you so pale?—are you ill?—are you frightened?—what is the matter?"

And losing all coldness and reserve, with the utmost earnestness he begged her to explain herself.

"Do you not know," cried she, "what has happened? can you be here and not have heard it?"

"Heard what?" cried he, "I am but this moment arrived:

my mother grew uneasy that she did not see you, she sent to your house, and was told that you were not returned from Vauxhall; some other circumstances also alarmed her, and therefore, late as it was, I came hither myself. The instant I entered this place, I saw you here. This is all my history; tell me now yours. Where is your party? where are Mr. and Mrs. Harrel?—Why are you alone?"

"O ask not!" cried she, "I cannot tell you!—take us but under your care, and you will soon know all."

She then hurried from him, and returning to Mrs. Harrel, said she had now a conveyance at once safe and proper, and begged her to rise and come away.

The gentlemen, however, rose first, each of them declaring he would himself attend them.

"No," said Cecilia, steadily, "that trouble will now be superfluous: Mrs. Delvile herself has sent for me, and her son is now waiting till we join him."

Amazement and disappointment at this intelligence were visible in the faces of them both: Cecilia waited not a single question, but finding she was unable to support Mrs. Harrel, who rather suffered herself to be carried than led, she entrusted her between them, and ran forward to enquire of Delvile if his carriage was ready.

She found him with a look of horror that told the tale he had been hearing, listening to one of the waiters: the moment she appeared, he flew to her, and with the utmost emotion exclaimed, "Amiable Miss Beverley! what a dreadful scene have you witnessed! what a cruel task have you nobly performed! such spirit with such softness! so much presence of mind with such feeling!—but you are all excellence! human nature can rise no higher! I believe indeed you are its most perfect ornament!"

Praise such as this, so unexpected, and delivered with such energy, Cecilia heard not without pleasure, even at a moment when her whole mind was occupied by matters foreign to its peculiar interests. She made, however, her enquiry about the carriage, and he told her that he had come in a hackney coach, which was waiting for him at the door.

Mrs. Harrel was now brought in, and little was the

recompence her assistants received for their aid, when they saw Cecilia so contentedly engaged with young Delvile, whose eyes were rivetted on her face, with an expression of the most lively admiration: Each, however, then quitted the other, and hastened to the fair mourner; no time was now lost, Mrs. Harrel was supported to the coach, Cecilia followed her, and Delvile, jumping in after them, ordered the man to drive to Portman-square.

Sir Robert and Mr. Marriot, confounded though enraged, saw their departure in passive silence: the right of attendance they had so tenaciously denied to each other, here admitted not of dispute: Delvile upon this occasion, appeared as the representative of his father, and his authority seemed the authority of a guardian. Their only consolation was that neither had yielded to the other, and all spirit of altercation or revenge was sunk in their mutual mortification. At the petition of the waiters, from sullen but proud emulation, they paid the expences of the night, and then throwing themselves into their carriages, returned to their respective houses.

CHAPTER XIII

A Solution

DURING the ride to town, not merely Cecilia, but Delvile himself attended wholly to Mrs. Harrel, whose grief as it became less violent, was more easy to be soothed.

The distress of this eventful night was however not yet over; when they came to Portman-square, Delvile eagerly called to the coachman not to drive up to the house, and anxiously begged Cecilia and Mrs. Harrel to sit still, while he went out himself to make some enquiries. They were surprised at the request, yet immediately consented; but before he had quitted them, Davison, who was watching their return, came up to them with information that an execution was then in the house.

Fresh misery was now opened for Mrs. Harrel, and fresh

horror and perplexity for Cecilia: she had no longer, however, the whole weight either of thought or of conduct upon herself; Delvile in her cares took the most animated interest, and beseeching her to wait a moment and appease her friend, he went himself into the house to learn the state of the affair.

He returned in a few minutes, and seemed in no haste to communicate what he had heard, but entreated them both to go immediately to St. James's-square.

Cecilia felt extremely fearful of offending his father by the introduction of Mrs. Harrel: yet she had nothing better to propose, and therefore, after a short and distressed argument, she complied.

Delvile then told her that the alarm of his mother, at which he had already hinted, proceeded from a rumour of this very misfortune, to which, though they knew not whether they might give credit, was owing the anxiety which at so late an hour, had induced him to go to Vauxhall in search of her.

They gained admittance without any disturbance, as the servant of young Delvile had been ordered to sit up for his master. Cecilia much disliked thus taking possession of the house in the night-time, though Delvile, solicitous to relieve her, desired she would not waste a thought upon the subject, and making his servant shew her the room which had been prepared for her reception, he begged her to compose her spirits, and to comfort her friend, and promised to acquaint his father and mother when they arose with what had happened, that she might be saved all pain from surprise or curiosity when they met.

This service she thankfully accepted, for she dreaded, after the liberty she had taken, to encounter the pride of Mr. Delvile without some previous apology, and she feared still more to see his lady without the same preparation, as her frequent breach of appointment might reasonably have offended her, and as her displeasure would affect her more deeply.

It was now near six o'clock, yet the hours seemed as long as they were melancholy till the family arose. They settled to remain quiet till some message was sent to them, but before any arrived, Mrs. Harrel, who was seated upon the bed, wearied by fatigue and sorrow, cried herself to sleep like a child.

Cecilia rejoiced in seeing this reprieve from affliction, though her keener sensations unfitted her from partaking of it; much indeed was the uneasiness which kept her awake; the care of Mrs. Harrel seemed to devolve upon herself, the reception she might meet from the Delviles was uncertain, and the horrible adventures of the night, refused for a moment to quit her remembrance.

At ten o'clock, a message was brought from Mrs. Delvile, to know whether they were ready for breakfast.

Mrs. Harrel was still asleep, but Cecilia carried her own answer by hastening down stairs.

In her way she was met by young Delvile, whose air upon first approaching her spoke him again prepared to address her with the most distant gravity: but almost the moment he looked at her, he forgot his purpose; her paleness, the heaviness of her eyes, and the fatigue of long watching betrayed by her whole face, again surprised him into all the tenderness of anxiety, and he enquired after her health not as a compliment of civility, but as a question in which his whole heart was most deeply interested.

Cecilia thanked him for his attention to her friend the night before, and then proceeded to his mother.

Mrs. Delvile, coming forward to meet her, removed at once all her fears of displeasure, and banished all necessity of apology, by instantly embracing her, and warmly exclaiming "Charming Miss Beverley! how shall I ever tell you half the admiration with which I have heard of your conduct! The exertion of so much fortitude at a juncture when a weaker mind would have been overpowered by terror, and a heart less under the dominion of well-regulated principles, would have sought only its own relief by flying from distress and confusion, shews such *propriety of mind** as can only result from the union of good sense with virtue. You are indeed a noble creature! I thought so from the moment I beheld you; I shall think so, I hope, to the last that I live!"

Cecilia, penetrated with joy and gratitude, felt in that instant the amplest recompense for all that she had suffered, and for all that she had lost. Such praise from Mrs. Delvile was alone sufficient to make her happy; but when she considered whence it sprung, and that the circumstances with which she was so much struck, must have been related to her by her son, her delight was augmented to an emotion the most pleasing she could experience, from seeing how high she was held in the esteem of those who were highest in her own.

Mrs. Delvile then, with the utmost cordiality, began to talk of her affairs, saving her the pain of proposing the change of habitation that now seemed unavoidable, by an immediate invitation to her house, which she made with as much delicacy as if Mr. Harrel's had still been open to her, and choice, not necessity, had directed her removal. The whole family, she told her, went into the country in two days, and she hoped that a new scene, with quietness and early hours, would restore both the bloom and sprightliness which her late cares and restlessness had injured. And though she very seriously lamented the rash action of Mr. Harrel, she much rejoiced in the acquisition which her own house and happiness would receive from her society.

She next discussed the situation of her widowed friend, and Cecilia produced the packet which had been entrusted to her by her late husband. Mrs. Delvile advised her to open it in the presence of Mr. Arnott, and begged her to send for any other of her friends she might wish to see or consult, and to claim freely from herself whatever advice or assistance she could bestow.

And then, without waiting for Mr. Delvile, she suffered her to swallow a hasty breakfast, and return to Mrs. Harrel, whom she had desired the servants to attend, as she concluded that in her present situation she would not chuse to make her appearance.

Cecilia, lightened now from all her own cares, more pleased than ever with Mrs. Delvile, and enchanted that at last she was settled under her roof, went back with as much ability as inclination to give comfort to Mrs. Harrel. She found her but just awaking, and scarce yet conscious where she was, or why not in her own house.

As her powers of recollection returned, she was soothed with the softest compassion by Cecilia, who in pursuance of Mrs. Delvile's advice, sent her servant in search of Mr. Arnott, and in consequence of her permission, wrote a note of invitation to Mr. Monckton.

Mr. Arnott, who was already in town, soon arrived: his own man, whom he had left to watch the motions of Mr. Harrel, having early in the morning rode to the place of his retreat, with the melancholy tidings of the suicide and execution.

Cecilia instantly went down stairs to him. The meeting was extremely painful to them both. Mr. Arnott severely blamed himself for his flight, believing it had hastened the fatal blow, which some further sacrifices might perhaps have eluded: and Cecilia half repented the advice she had given him, though the failure of her own efforts proved the situation of Mr. Harrel too desperate for remedy.

He then made the tenderest enquiries about his sister, and entreated her to communicate to him the minutest particulars of the dreadful transaction: after which, she produced the packet, but neither of them had the courage to break the seal; and concluding the contents would be no less than his last will, they determined some third person should be present when they opened it. Cecilia wished much for Mr. Monckton, but as his being immediately found was uncertain, and the packet might consist of orders which ought not to be delayed, she proposed, for the sake of expedition, to call in Mr. Delvile.

Mr. Arnott readily agreed, and she sent to beg a moment's audience with that gentleman.

She was desired to walk into the breakfast-room, where he was sitting with his lady and his son.

Not such was now her reception as when she entered that apartment before; Mr. Delvile looked displeased and out of humour, and, making her a stiff bow, while his son brought her a chair, coldly said, "If you are hurried, Miss Beverley, I will attend you directly; if not, I will finish my breakfast, as I shall have but little time the rest of the morning, from the concourse of people upon business, who will crowd upon me till dinner, most of whom will be extremely distressed if I leave town without contriving to see them.''

"There is not the least occasion, Sir,'' answered Cecilia, "that I should trouble you to quit the room: I merely came to beg you would have the goodness to be present while Mr. Arnott opens a small packet which was last night put into my hands by Mr. Harrel.''

"And has Mr. Arnott,'' answered he, somewhat sternly, "thought proper to send me such a request?''

"No, Sir,'' said Cecilia, "the request is mine; and if, as I now fear, it is impertinent, I must entreat you to forget it.''

"As far as relates merely to yourself,'' returned Mr. Delvile, "it is another matter; but certainly Mr. Arnott, can have no possible claim upon my time or attention; and I think it rather extraordinary, that a young man with whom I have no sort of connection or commerce, and whose very name is almost unknown to me, should suppose a person in my stile of life so little occupied as to be wholly at his command.''

"He had no such idea, Sir,'' said Cecilia greatly disconcerted; "the honour of your presence is merely solicited by myself, and simply from the apprehension that some directions may be contained in the papers which, perhaps, ought immediately to be executed.''

"I am not, I repeat,'' said Mr. Delvile, more mildly, "displeased at your part of this transaction; your want of experience and knowledge of the world makes you not at all aware of the consequences which may follow my compliance: the papers you speak of may perhaps be of great importance, and hereafter the first witnesses to their being read may be publickly called upon. You know not the trouble such an affair may occasion, but Mr. Arnott ought to be better informed.''

Cecilia, making another apology for the error which she had committed, was in no small confusion, quitting the room; but Mr. Delvile, perfectly appeased by seeing her distress, stopt her, to say, with much graciousness, "For your sake, Miss Beverley, I am sorry I cannot act in this business; but you see how I am situated! overpowered with affairs of my own, and people who can do nothing without my orders. Besides, should there hereafter be any investigation into the matter, my name might, perhaps, be mentioned, and it would be superfluous to say how ill I should think it used by being brought into such company."

Cecilia then left the room, secretly vowing that no possible exigence should in future tempt her to apply for assistance to Mr. Delvile, which, however ostentatiously offered, was constantly with-held when claimed.

She was beginning to communicate to Mr. Arnott her ill success, when young Delvile, with an air of eagerness, followed her into the room. "Pardon me," he cried, "for this intrusion,—but, tell me, is it impossible that in this affair I can represent my father? may not the office you meant for him, devolve upon me? remember how near we are to each other, and honour me for once with supposing us the same!"

Ah who, or what, thought Cecilia, can be so different? She thanked him, with much sweetness, for his offer, but declined accepting it, saying "I will not, now I know the inconveniencies of my request, be so selfish as even to suffer it should be granted."

"You must not deny me," cried he; "where is the packet? why should you lose a moment?"

"Rather ask," answered she, "why I should permit *you* to lose a moment in a matter that does not concern you? and to risk, perhaps, the loss of many moments hereafter, from a too incautious politeness." "And what can I risk," cried he, "half so precious as your smallest satisfaction? do you suppose I can flatter myself with a possibility of contributing to it, and yet have the resolution to refuse myself so much pleasure? no, no, the heroic times are over, and self-denial is no longer in fashion!"

"You are very good," said Cecilia; "but indeed after what has passed—"

"No matter for what has passed," interrupted he, "we are now to think of what is to come. I know you too well to doubt your impatience in the execution of a commission which circumstances have rendered sacred; and should any thing either be done or omitted contrary to the directions in your packet, will you not be apt, blameless as you are, to disturb yourself with a thousand fears that you took not proper methods for the discharge of your trust?''

There was something in this earnestness so like his former behaviour, and so far removed from his late reserve, that Cecilia, who perceived it with a pleasure she could hardly disguise, now opposed him no longer, but took up the packet, and broke the seal.

And then, to her no small amazement, instead of the expected will, she found a roll of enormous bills, and a collection of letters from various creditors, threatening the utmost severity of the law if their demands were longer unanswered.

Upon a slip of paper which held these together, was written, in Mr. Harrel's hand.

To be all paid to-night with a BULLET.

Next appeared two letters of another sort; the first of which was from Sir Robert Floyer, and in these words:

SIR,

As all prospects are now over of the alliance, I hope you will excuse my reminding you of the affair at Brookes's of last Christmas. I have the honour to be,

SIR, your's,

R. FLOYER.

The other was from Mr. Marriot.

SIR,

Though I should think 2000*l.* nothing for the smallest hope, I must take the liberty to say I think it a great deal for only ten minutes: you can't have forgot, Sir, the terms of our agreement, but as I find you cannot keep to them, I must beg to be off also on my side, and I am persuaded you are too much a man of honour to take advantage of my over-eagerness in parting with my money without better security.

I am, SIR,

Your most humble servant,

A. MARRIOT.

What a scene of fraud, double-dealing, and iniquity was here laid open! Cecilia, who at first meant to read every thing aloud, found the attempt utterly vain, for so much was she shocked, that she could hardly read on to herself.

Last of all appeared a paper in Mr. Harrel's own hand-writing, containing these words.

For Mrs. HARREL, Miss BEVERLEY, and
Mr. ARNOTT.

I can struggle no longer, the last blow must now be struck! another day robs me of my house and my liberty, and blasts me by the fatal discovery of my double attempts.

This is what I have wished; wholly to be freed, or ruined past all resource, and driven to the long-projected remedy.

A burthen has my existence been these two years, gay as I have appeared; not a night have I gone to bed, but heated and inflamed from a gaming table; not a morning have I awaked, but to be soured with a dun!*

I would not lead such a life again, if the slave who works hardest at the oar would change with me.

Had I a son, I would bequeath him a plough; I should then leave him happier than my parents left me.

Idleness has been my destruction; the want of something to do led me into all evil.

A good wife perhaps might have saved me,—mine, I thank her! tried not. Disengaged from me and my affairs, her own pleasures and amusements have occupied her solely. Dreadful will be the catastrophe she will see to-night; let her bring it home, and live better!

If any pity is felt for me, it will be where I have least deserved it! Mr. Arnott—Miss Beverley! it will come from you!

To bring myself to this final resolution, hard, I confess, have been my conflicts: it is not that I have feared death, no,

I have long wished it, for shame and dread have embittered my days; but something there is within me that causes a deeper horror,—that asks my preparation for another world! that demands my authority for quitting this!—what may hereafter—O terrible!—Pray for me, generous Miss Beverley!——kind, gentle Mr. Arnott, pray for me!—

———————————

Wretch as Mr. Harrel appeared, without religion, principle, or honour, this incoherent letter, evidently written in the desperate moment of determined suicide, very much affected both Cecilia and Mr. Arnott, and in spite either of abhorrence or resentment, they mutually shed tears over the address to themselves.

Delvile, to whom every part of the affair was new, could only consider these papers as so many specimens of guilt and infamy; he read them, therefore, with astonishment and detestation, and openly congratulated Cecilia upon having escaped the double snares that were spread for her.

While this was passing, Mr. Monckton arrived; who felt but little satisfaction from beholding the lady of his heart in confidential discourse with two of his rivals, one of whom had long attacked her by the dangerous flattery of perseverance, and the other, without any attack, had an influence yet more powerful.

Delvile, having performed the office for which he came, concluded, upon the entrance of Mr. Monckton, that Cecilia had nothing further to wish from him; for her long acquaintance with that gentleman, his being a *married man*, and her neighbour in the country, were circumstances well known to him: he merely, therefore, enquired if she would honour him with any commands, and upon her assuring him she had none, he quietly withdrew.

This was no little relief to Mr. Monckton, into whose hands Cecilia then put the fatal packet: and while he was reading it, at the desire of Mr. Arnott, she went up stairs to prepare Mrs. Harrel for his admission.

Mrs. Harrel, unused to solitude, and as eager for company when unhappy to console, as when easy to divert her, consented to receive him with pleasure: they both wept at the meeting, and Cecilia, after some words of general comfort, left them together.

She had then a very long and circumstantial conversation with Mr. Monckton, who explained whatever had appeared dark in the writings left by Mr. Harrel, and who came to her before he saw them, with full knowledge of what they contained.

Mr. Harrel had contracted with Sir Robert Floyer a large debt of honour before the arrival in town of Cecilia; and having no power to discharge it, he promised that the prize he expected in his ward should fall to his share, upon condition that the debt was cancelled.

Nothing was thought more easy than to arrange this business, for the Baronet was always to be in her way, and the report of the intended alliance was to keep off all other pretenders. Several times, however, her coldness made him think the matter hopeless; and when he received her letter, he would have given up the whole affair: but Mr. Harrel, well knowing his inability to satisfy the claims that would follow such a defection, constantly persuaded him the reserve was affected, and that his own pride and want of assiduity occasioned all her discouragement.

But while thus, by amusing the Baronet with false hopes, he kept off his demands, those of others were not less clamorous: his debts encreased, his power of paying them diminished; he grew sour and desperate, and in one night lost 3000*l.* beyond what he could produce, or offer any security for.

This, as he said, was *what he wished*;* and now he was, for the present, to extricate himself by doubling stakes and winning, or to force himself into suicide by doubling such a loss. For though, with tolerable ease, he could forget accounts innumerable with his tradesmen, one neglected *debt of honour* rendered his existence insupportable!

For this last great effort, his difficulty was to raise the 3000*l.* already due, without which the proposal could not be made: and, after various artifices and attempts, he at length contrived a meeting with Mr. Marriot, intreated him to lend him 2000*l.* for only two days, and offered his warmest services in his favour with Cecilia.

The rash and impassioned young man, deceived by his accounts into believing that his ward was wholly at his disposal, readily advanced the money, without any other condition than that of leave to visit freely at his house, to the exclusion of Sir Robert Floyer. "The other 1000*l.*", continued Mr. Monckton, "I know not how he obtained, but he certainly had three. You, I hope, were not so unguarded——"

"Ah, Mr. Monckton," said Cecilia, "blame me not too severely! the attacks that were made,—the necessity of otherwise betraying the worthy and half ruined Mr. Arnott—"

"O fie!" cried he, "to suffer *your* understanding to be lulled asleep, because the weak-minded Mr. Arnott's could not be kept awake! I thought, after such cautions from me, and such experience of your own, you could not again have been thus duped."

"I thought so too," answered she, "but yet when the trial came on,—indeed you know not how I was persecuted."

"Yet you see," returned he, "the utter inutility of the attempt; you see, and I told you beforehand, that nothing could save him."

"True; but had I been firmer in refusal, I might not so well have known it; I might then have upbraided myself with supposing that my compliance would have rescued him."

"You have indeed," cried Mr. Monckton, "fallen into most worthless hands, and the Dean was much to blame for naming so lightly a guardian to a fortune such as yours."

"Pardon me," cried Cecilia, "he never entrusted him with my fortune, he committed it wholly to Mr. Briggs."

"But if he knew not the various subterfuges by which such a caution might be baffled, he ought to have taken advice of those who were better informed. Mr. Briggs, too! what a wretch! mean, low, vulgar, sordid!—the whole city of London, I believe, could not produce such another! how unaccountable to make you the ward of a man whose house you cannot enter without disgust!"

"His house," cried Cecilia, "my uncle never wished me to enter; he believed, and he was right, that my fortune would be safe in his hands; but for myself, he concluded I should always reside at Mr. Harrel's."

"But does not the city at this time," said Mr. Monckton, "abound in families where, while your fortune was in security, you might yourself have lived with propriety? Nothing requires circumspection so minute as the choice of a guardian to a girl of large fortune, and in general one thing only is attended to, an appearance of property. Morals, integrity, character, are either not thought of, or investigated so superficially, that the enquiry were as well wholly omitted."

He then continued his relation.

Mr. Harrel hastened with his 3000l. to the gaming table; one throw of the dice settled the business, he lost, and ought immediately to have doubled the sum. That, however, was never more likely to be in his power; he knew it; he knew, too, the joint claims of Cecilia's deceived admirers, and that his house was again threatened with executions from various quarters:—he went home, loaded his pistols, and took the methods already related to work himself into courage for the deed.

The means by which Mr. Monckton had procured these particulars were many and various, and not all such as he could avow: since in the course of his researches, he had tampered with servants and waiters, and scrupled at no methods that led but to discovery.

Nor did his intelligence stop here; he had often, he said, wondered at the patience of Mr. Harrel's creditors, but now even that was cleared up by a fresh proof of infamy: he had been himself at the house in Portman-square, where he was informed that Mr. Harrel had kept them quiet, by repeated assurances that his ward, in a short time, meant to lend him money for discharging them all.

Cecilia saw now but too clearly the reason her stay in his house was so important to him; and wondered less at his vehemence upon that subject, though she detested it more.

"Oh how little," cried she, "are the gay and the

dissipated to be known upon a short acquaintance! expensive, indeed, and thoughtless and luxurious he appeared to me immediately; but fraudulent, base, designing, capable of every pernicious art of treachery and duplicity,—such, indeed, I expected not to find him, his very flightiness and levity seemed incompatible with such hypocrisy."

"His flightiness," said Mr. Monckton, "proceeded not from gaiety of heart, it was merely the effect of effort; and his spirits were as mechanical as his taste for diversion. He had not strong parts, nor were his vices the result of his passions; had œconomy been as much in fashion as extravagance, he would have been equally eager to practice it; he was a mere time-server, he struggled but to be *something*, and having neither talents nor sentiment to know *what*, he looked around him for any pursuit, and seeing distinction was more easily attained in the road to ruin than in any other, he galloped along it, thoughtless of being thrown when he came to the bottom, and sufficiently gratified in shewing his horsemanship by the way."

And now, all that he had either to hear or to communicate upon this subject being told, he enquired, with a face strongly expressive of his disapprobation, why he found her at Mr. Delvile's, and what had become of her resolution to avoid his house?

Cecilia, who, in the hurry of her mind and her affairs, had wholly forgotten that such a resolution had been taken, blushed at the question, and could not, at first, recollect what had urged her to break it: but when he proceeded to mention Mr. Briggs, she was no longer distressed; she gave a circumstantial account of her visit to him, related the mean misery in which he lived, and told him the impracticability of her residing in such a house.

Mr. Monckton could now in decency make no further opposition, however painful and reluctant was his acquiescence: yet before he quitted her, he gave himself the consolation of considerably obliging her, and softened his chagrin by the sweetness of her acknowledgments.

He enquired how much money in all she had now taken

up of the Jew; and hearing it was 9050*l.* he represented to her the additional loss she must suffer by paying an exorbitant interest* for so large a sum, and the almost certainty with which she might be assured of very gross imposition: he expatiated, also, upon the injury which her character might receive in the world, were it known that she used such methods to procure money, since the circumstances which had been her inducement would probably either be unnoticed or misrepresented: and when he had awakened in her much uneasiness and regret upon this subject, he offered to pay the Jew without delay, clear her wholly from his power, and quietly receive the money when she came of age from herself.

A proposal so truly friendly made her look upon the regard of Mr. Monckton in a higher and nobler point of view than her utmost esteem and reverence had hitherto placed it: yet she declined at first accepting the offer, from an apprehension it might occasion him inconvenience; but when he assured her he had a yet larger sum lying at present useless in a Banker's hands, and promised to receive the same interest for his money he should be paid from the funds,* she joyfully listened to him; and it was settled that they should send for the Jew, take his discharge, and utterly dismiss him.

Mr. Monckton, however, fearful of appearing too officious in her affairs, wished not to have his part in the transaction published, and advised Cecilia not to reveal the matter to the Delviles. But great as was his ascendant over her mind, her aversion to mystery and hypocrisy were still greater; she would not, therefore, give him this promise, though her own desire to wait some seasonable opportunity for disclosing it, made her content that their meeting with the Jew should be at the house of Mrs. Roberts in Fetter-lane, at twelve o'clock the next morning; where she might also see Mrs. Hill and her children before she left town.

They now parted, Cecilia charmed more than ever with her friend, whose kindness, as she suspected not his motives, seemed to spring from the most disinterested generosity.

That, however, was the smallest feature in the character

of Mr. Monckton, who was entirely a man of the world, shrewd, penetrating, attentive to his interest, and watchful of every advantage to improve it. In the service he now did Cecilia, he was gratified by giving her pleasure, but that was by no means his only gratification: he still hoped her fortune would one day be his own, he was glad to transact any business with her, and happy in making her owe to him an obligation: but his principal inducement was yet stronger: he saw with much alarm the facility of her liberality; and he feared while she continued in correspondence with the Jew, that the easiness with which she could raise money would be a motive with her to continue the practice whenever she was softened by distress, or subdued by entreaty: but he hoped, by totally concluding the negociation, the temptation would be removed: and that the hazard and incovenience of renewing it, would strengthen her aversion to such an expedient, till, between difficulties and disuse, that dangerous resource would be thought of no more.

Cecilia then returned to Mrs. Harrel, whom she found as she had left, weeping in the arms of her brother. They consulted upon what was best to be done, and agreed that she ought instantly to leave town; for which purpose a chaise was ordered directly. They settled also that Mr. Arnott, when he had conveyed her to his country house, which was in Suffolk, should hasten back to superintend the funeral, and see if any thing could be saved from the creditors for his sister.

Yet this plan, till Cecilia was summoned to dinner, they had not the resolution to put in practice. They were then obliged to be gone, and their parting was very melancholy. Mrs. Harrel wept immoderately, and Mr. Arnott felt a concern too tender for avowal, though too sincere for concealment. Cecilia, however glad to change her situation, was extremely depressed by their sorrow, and entreated to have frequent accounts of their proceedings, warmly repeating her offers of service, and protestations of faithful regard.

She accompanied them to the chaise, and then went to the dining parlour, where she found Mr. and Mrs. Delvile, but saw nothing more of their son the whole day.

The next morning after breakfast, Mrs. Delvile set out upon some leave-taking visits, and Cecilia went in a chair to Fetter-lane: here, already waiting for her, she met the punctual Mr. Monckton, and the disappointed Jew, who most unwillingly was paid off, and relinquished his bonds; and who found in the severe and crafty Mr. Monckton, another sort of man to deal with than the necessitous and heedless Mr. Harrel.

As soon as he was dismissed, other bonds were drawn and signed, the old ones were destroyed; and Cecilia, to her infinite satisfaction, had no creditor but Mr. Monckton. Her bookseller, indeed, was still unpaid, but her debt with him was public, and gave her not any uneasiness.

She now, with the warmest expressions of gratitude, took leave of Mr. Monckton, who suffered the most painful struggles in repressing the various apprehensions to which the parting, and her establishment at the Delviles gave rise.

She then enquired briefly into the affairs of Mrs. Hill, and having heard a satisfactory account of them, returned to St. James's-square.

BOOK VI

CHAPTER I

A Debate

IT was still early, and Mrs. Delvile was not expected till late. Cecilia, therefore, determined to make a visit to Miss Belfield, to whom she had been denied during the late disorders at Mr. Harrel's, and whom she could not endure to mortify by quitting town without seeing, since whatever were her doubts about Delvile, of her she had none.

To Portland-street, therefore, she ordered her chair, deliberating as she went whether it were better to adhere to the reserve she had hitherto maintained, or to satisfy her perplexity at once by an investigation into the truth. And still were these scruples undecided, when, looking in at the windows as she passed them to the door of the house, she perceived Miss Belfield standing in the parlour with a letter in her hand which she was fervently pressing to her lips.

Struck by this sight, a thousand painful conjectures occurred to her, all representing that the letter was from Delvile, and all explaining to his dishonour the mystery of his late conduct. And far were her suspicions from diminishing, when, upon being shewn into the parlour, Miss Belfield, trembling with her eagerness to hide it, hastily forced the letter into her pocket.*

Cecilia, surprised, dismayed, alarmed, stopt involuntarily at the door; but Miss Belfield, having secured what was so evidently precious to her, advanced, though not without blushing, and taking her hand, said "How good this is of you, madam, to come to me! when I did not know where to find you, and when I was almost afraid I should have found you no more!"

She then told her, that the first news she had heard the preceding morning, was the violent death of Mr. Harrel, which had been related to her, with all its circumstances, by the landlord of their lodgings, who was himself one of his principal creditors, and had immediately been at Portman-square to put in his claims; where he had learnt that all the family had quitted the house, which was entirely occupied by bailiffs. "And I was so sorry," she continued, "that *you* should meet with any hardships, and not know where to go, and have another home to seek, when I am sure the commonest beggar would never want an habitation, if you had one in your power to give him!—But how sad and melancholy you look! I am afraid this bad action of Mr. Harrel has made you quite unhappy? Ah madam! you are too good for this guilty world! your own compassion and benevolence will not suffer you to rest in it!"

Cecilia, touched by this tender mistake of her present uneasiness, embraced her, and with much kindness, answered, "No, sweet Henrietta! it is *you* who are good, who are innocent, who are guileless!—*you*, too, I hope are happy!"

"And are not you, madam?" cried Henrietta, fondly returning her caresses. "Oh if you are not, who will ever deserve to be! I think I should rather be unhappy myself, than see you so; at least I am sure I ought, for the whole world may be the better for your welfare, and as to me,—who would care what became of me!"

"Ah Henrietta!" cried Cecilia, "do you speak sincerely? do you indeed think yourself so little valued?"

"Why I don't say," answered she, "but that I hope there are some who think a little kindly of me, for if I had not that hope, I should wish to break my heart and die! but what is that to the love and reverence so many have for you?"

"Suppose," said Cecilia, with a forced smile, "I should put *your* love and reverence to the proof? do you think they would stand it?"

"O yes, indeed I do! and I have wished a thousand and a thousand times that I could but shew you my affection, and let you see that I did not love you because you were a great lady, and high in the world, and full of power to do me service, but because you were so good and so kind, so gentle to the unfortunate, and so sweet to every body!"

"Hold, hold," cried Cecilia, "and let me try if indeed, fairly and truly, you will answer what I mean to ask."

"O yes," cried she warmly, "if it is the dearest secret I have in the world! there is nothing I will not tell you; I will open my whole heart to you, and I shall be proud to think you will let me trust you,—for I am sure if you did not care a little for me, you would not take such a trouble."

"You are indeed a sweet creature!" said Cecilia, hesitating whether or not to take advantage of her frankness, "and every time I see you, I love you better. For the world would I not injure you,—and perhaps your confidence—I know not, indeed, if it is fair or right to exact it—" she stopt, extremely perplext, and while Henrietta waited her further enquiries, they were interrupted by the entrance of Mrs. Belfield.

"Sure, Child," cried she, to her daughter, "you might have let me know before now who was here, when you knew so well how much I wished an opportunity to see the young lady myself: but here you come down upon pretence to see your brother, and then stay away all the morning, doing nobody knows what."

Then, turning to Cecilia, "Ma'am," she continued, "I have been in the greatest concern in the world for the little accident that happened when I saw you before; for to be sure I thought, and indeed nobody will persuade me to the contrary, that it was rather an odd thing for such a young lady as you to come so often after Henny, without so much as thinking of any other reason; especially when, to be sure, there's no more comparison between her and my son, than between any thing in the world; however, if it is so, it is so, and I mean to say no more about it, and to be sure he's as contented to think so as if he was as mere an insignificant animal as could be."

"This matter, madam," said Cecilia, "has so long been settled, that I am sorry you should trouble yourself to think of it again."

"O, ma'am, I only mention it by the way of making the proper apology, for as to taking any other notice of it, I have quite left it off; though to be sure what I think I think; but as to my son, he has so got the upper hand of me, that it all goes for nothing, and I might just as well sing to him. Not that I mean to find fault with him neither; so pray, ma'am, don't let what I say be to his prejudice, for I believe all the time, there's nobody like him, neither at this end of the town nor the other; for as to the other, he has more the look of a lord, by half, than of a shopman, and the reason's plain, for that's the sort of company he's always kept, as I dare say a lady such as you must have seen long ago. But for all that, there's some little matters that we mothers fancy we can see into as well as our children; however, if they don't think so, why it answers no purpose to dispute; for as to a better son, to be sure there never was one, and that, as I always say, is the best sign I know for making a good husband.''

During this discourse, Henrietta was in the utmost confusion, dreading lest the grossness of her mother should again send off Cecilia in anger: but Cecilia, who perceived her uneasiness, and who was more charmed with her character than ever, from the simplicity of her sincerity, determined to save her that pain, by quietly* hearing her harangue, and then quietly departing: though she was much provoked to find from the complaining hints every instant thrown out, that Mrs. Belfield was still internally convinced her son's obstinate bashfulness was the only obstacle to his chusing whom he pleased: and that though she no longer dared speak her opinion with openness, she was fully persuaded Cecilia was at his service.

''And for that reason,'' continued Mrs. Belfield, ''to be sure any lady that knew her own true advantage, could do nothing better than to take the recommendation of a mother, who must naturally know more of her own children's disposition than can be expected from a stranger: and as to such a son as mine, perhaps there a'n't two such in the world, for he's had a gentleman's education, and turn him which way he will, he'll see never a handsomer person than his own; though, poor dear love, he was always of the thinnest. But the misfortunes he's had to struggle with would make nobody fatter.''

Here she was interrupted, and Cecilia not a little

surprised, by the entrance of Mr. Hobson and Mr.
Simkins.

"Ladies," cried Mr. Hobson, whom she soon found was
Mrs. Belfield's landlord: "I would not go up stairs without
just stopping to let you know a little how the world
goes."

Then perceiving and recollecting Cecilia, he exclaimed "I
am proud to see you again, ma'am,—Miss, I believe I
should say, for I take it you are too young a lady to be
entered into matrimony yet."

"Matrimony?" cried Mr. Simkins, "no, to be sure, Mr.
Hobson, how can you be so out of the way? the young lady
looks more like to* a Miss from a boarding-school, if I might
take the liberty for to say so."

"Ay, more's the pity," cried Mrs. Belfield, "for as to
young ladies waiting and waiting, I don't see the great good
of it; especially if a proper match offers; for as to a good
husband, I think no lady should be above accepting him, if
he's modest and well-behaved, and has been brought up
with a genteel education."

"Why as to that, ma'am," said Mr. Simkins, "it's
anotherguess* matter, for as to the lady's having a proper
spouse, if I may be so free, I think as it's no bad thing."

Cecilia now, taking Henrietta's hand, was wishing her
good morning; but hearing Mr. Hobson say he was just
come from Portman-square, her curiosity was excited, and
she stayed a little longer.

"Sad work, ma'am," said he; "who'd have thought Mr.
Harrel asked us all to supper for the mere purpose of such
a thing as that! just to serve for a blind, as one may say. But
when a man's conscience is foul, what I say is it's ten to one
but he makes away with himself. Let every man keep clear
of the world,* that's my notion, and then he will be in no
such hurry to get out of it."

"Why indeed, ma'am," said Mr. Simkins, advancing
with many bows to Cecilia, "humbly craving pardon for the
liberty, I can't pretend for to say I think Mr. Harrel did
quite the honourable thing by us; for as to his making us
drink all that Champagne, and the like, it was a sheer take

in, so that if I was to speak my mind, I can't say as I esteem it much of a favour.''

"Well," said Mrs. Belfield, "nothing's to me so surprising as a person's being his own executioner, for as to me, if I was to die for it fifty times, I don't think I could do it."

"So here," resumed Mr. Hobson, "we're all defrauded of our dues! nobody's able to get his own, let him have worked for it ever so hard. Sad doings in the square, Miss! all at sixes and sevens; for my part I came off from Vauxhall as soon as the thing had happened, hoping to get the start of the others, or else I should have been proud to wait upon you, ladies, with the particulars: but a man of business never stands upon ceremony, for when money's at stake, that's out of the question. However, I was too late, for the house was seized before ever I could get nigh it."

"I hope, ma'am, if I may be so free," said Mr. Simkins, again profoundly bowing, "that you and the other lady did not take it much amiss my not coming back to you, for it was not out of no disrespect, but only I got so squeezed in by the ladies and gentlemen that was a looking on, that I could not make my way out, do what I could. But by what I see, I must needs say if one's never in* such genteel company, people are always rather of the rudest when one's in a crowd, for if one begs and prays never so, there's no making 'em conformable."

"Pray," said Cecilia, "is it likely any thing will remain for Mrs. Harrel?"

"Remain, ma'am?" repeated Mr. Hobson, "yes, a matter of a hundred bills without a receipt to 'em!* To be sure, ma'am, I don't want to affront you, that was his intimate acquaintance, more especially as you've done nothing disrespectful by me, which is more than I can say for Mrs. Harrel, who seemed downright ashamed of me, and of Mr. Simkins too, though all things considered, 'twould have been as well for her not to have been quite so high.* But of that in its proper season!"

"Fie, Mr. Hobson fie," cried the supple Mr. Simkins, "how can you be so hard? for my share, I must needs own

I think the poor lady's to be pitied; for it must have been but a molloncholy sight to her, to see her spouse cut off so in the flower of his youth, as one may say: and you ought to scorn to take exceptions at a lady's proudness when she's in so much trouble. To be sure, I can't say myself as she was over-complaisant to make us welcome; but I hope I am above being so unpitiful as for to owe her a grudge for it now she's so down in the mouth."

"Let every body be civil!" cried Mr. Hobson, "that's my notion; and then I shall be as much above being unpitiful as any body else."

"Mrs. Harrel," said Cecilia, "was then too unhappy, and is now, surely, too unfortunate, to make it possible any resentment should be harboured against her."

"You speak, ma'am, like a lady of sense," returned Mr. Hobson, "and, indeed, that's the character I hear of you; but for all that, ma'am, every body's willing to stand up for their own friends, for which reason, ma'am, to be sure you'll be making the best of it, both for the Relict, and the late gentleman himself; but, ma'am, if I was to make bold to speak my mind in a fair manner, what I should say would be this: a man here to go shooting himself with all his debts unpaid, is a mere piece of scandal, ma'am! I beg pardon, but what I say is, the truth's the truth, and I can't call it by no other nomination."

Cecilia now, finding she had not any chance of pacifying him, rang for her servant and chair.

Mr. Simkins then, affecting to lower his voice, said reproachfully to his friend "Indeed, Mr. Hobson, to speak ingenusly, I must needs say I don't think it over and above pelite in you to be so hard upon the young lady's acquaintance that was, now he's defunct. To be sure I can't pretend for to deny but he behaved rather comical;* for not paying of nobody, nor so much as making one a little compliment, or the like, though he made no bones of taking all one's goods, and always chused to have the prime of every thing, why it's what I can't pretend to stand up for. But that's neither here nor there, for if he had behaved as bad again, poor Miss could not tell how to help it; and I

dares to say she had no more hand in it than nobody at
all.''

''No, to be sure,'' cried Mrs. Belfield, ''what should she
have to do with it? do you suppose a young lady of her
fortune would want to take advantage of a person in trade!
I am sure it would be both a shame and a sin if she did, for
if she has not money enough, I wonder who has. And for my
part, I think when a young lady has such a fine fortune as
that, the only thing she has to do, is to be thinking of making
a good use of it, by dividing it, as one may say, with a good
husband. For as to keeping it all for herself, I dare say she's
a lady of too much generosity; and as to only marrying
somebody that's got as much of his own, why it is not half
so much a favour: and if the young lady would take my
advice, she'd marry for love, for as to lucre,* she's enough
in all conscience.''

''As to all that,'' said Mr. Hobson, ''it makes no
alteration in my argument; I am speaking to the purpose,
and not for the matter of complaisance: and therefore I'm
bold to say Mr. Harrel's action had nothing of the
gentleman in it. A man has a right to his own life, you'll tell
me; but what of that? that's no argument at all, for it does
not give him a bit the more right to my property; and a
man's running in debt, and spending other people's
substances, for no reason in the world but just because he
can blow out his own brains when he's done,—though its a
thing neither lawful nor religious to do,—why it's acting
quite out of character, and a great hardship to trade into the
bargain.''

''I heartily wish it had been otherwise,'' said Cecilia;
''but I still hope, if any thing can be done for Mrs. Harrel,
you will not object to such a proposal.''

''Ma'am, as I said before,'' returned Mr. Hobson, ''I see
you're a lady of sense, and for that I honour you: but as to
any thing being done, it's what I call a distinct thing. What's
mine is mine, and what's another man's is his; that's my
way of arguing; but then if he takes what's mine, where's the
law to hinder my taking what's his? This is what I call
talking to the purpose. Now as to a man's cutting his throat,

or the like of that, for blowing out his own brains may be called the self-same thing, what are his creditors the better for that? nothing at all, but so much the worse: it's a false notion to respect it, for there's no respect in it; it's contrary to law, and a prejudice against religion.''

"I agree entirely in your opinion," said Cecilia, "but still Mrs. Harrel——" "I know your argument, ma'am," interrupted Mr. Hobson; "Mrs. Harrel i'n't the worse for her husband's being shot through the head, because she was no accessory to the same, and for that reason, it's a hardship she should lose all her substance; this, ma'am, is what I say, speaking to your side of the argument. But now, ma'am, please to take notice what I argue upon the reply; what have we creditors to do with a man's family? Suppose I am a cabinet-maker? When I send in my chairs, do I ask who is to sit upon them? No; it's all one to me whether it's the gentleman's progeny or his friends, I must be paid for the chairs the same, use them who may. That's the law, ma'am, and no man need be ashamed to abide by it.''

The truth of this speech palliating it's sententious absurdity, made Cecilia give up her faint attempt to soften him; and her chair being ready, she arose to take leave.

"Lack-a-day, ma'am," cried Mrs. Belfield, "I hope you won't go yet, for I expect my son home soon, and I've a heap of things to talk to you about besides, only Mr. Hobson having so much to say stopt my mouth. But I should take it as a great favour, ma'am, if you would come some afternoon and drink a dish of tea with me, for then we should have time to say all our say. And I'm sure, ma'am, if you would only let one of your footmen just take a run to let me know when you'd come, my son would be very proud to give you the meeting; and the servants can't have much else to do at your house, for where there's such a heap of 'em, they commonly think of nothing all day long but standing and gaping at one another.''

"I am going out of town to-morrow," said Cecilia, coldly, "and therefore cannot have the pleasure of calling upon Miss Belfield again.''

She then slightly courtsied, and left the room.

The gentle Henrietta, her eyes swimming in tears, followed her to her chair; but she followed her not alone, Mrs. Belfield also attended, repining very loudly at the unlucky absence of her son: and the cringing Mr. Simkins, creeping after her and bowing, said in a low voice, "I humbly crave pardon, ma'am, for the liberty, but I hope you won't think as I have any share in Mr. Hobson's behaving so rude, for I must needs say, I don't think it over genteel in no shape." And Mr. Hobson himself, bent upon having one more sentence heard, called out, even after she was seated in her chair. "All I say ma'am, is this; let every man be honest; that's what I argue, and that's my notion of things."

Cecilia still reached home before Mrs. Delvile; but most uneasy were her sensations, and most unquiet was her heart: the letter she had seen in the hands of Henrietta seemed to corroborate all her former suspicions, since if it came not from one infinitely dear to her she would not have shewn such fondness for it, and if that one was not dear to her in secret, she would not have concealed it.

Where then was the hope that any but Delvile could have written it? *in secret* she could not cherish *two*, and that Delvile was cherished most fondly, the artlessness of her character unfitted her for disguising.

And why should he write to her? what was his pretence? That he loved her she could now less than ever believe, since his late conduct to herself, though perplexing and inconsistent, evinced at least a partiality incompatible with a passion for another. What then, could she infer, but that he had seduced her affections, and ruined her peace, for the idle and cruel gratification of temporary vanity?

"And if such," cried she, "is the depravity of this accomplished hypocrite, if such is the littleness of soul that a manner so noble disguises, shall he next, urged, perhaps, rather by prudence than preference, make *me* the object of his pursuit, and the food of his vain-glory? And shall *I*, warned and instructed as I am, be as easy a prey, and as wretched a dupe? No, I will be better satisfied with his conduct, before I venture to trust him, and since I am richer than Henrietta and less likely to be deserted, when won, I will be more on my guard to know why I am addressed, and vindicate the rights of innocence, if I find she has been thus deluded, by forgetting his talents in his treachery, and renouncing him for ever!"

Such were the reflections and surmises that dampt all the long-sought pleasure of her change of residence, and made her habitation in St. James's Square no happier than it had been at Mr. Harrel's!

She dined again with only Mr. and Mrs. Delvile, and did not see their son all day; which, in her present uncertainty what to think of him, was an absence she scarcely regretted.

When the servants retired, Mr. Delvile told her that he had that morning received two visits upon her account, both from admirers, who each pretended to having had leave to wait upon her from Mr. Harrel.

He then named Sir Robert Floyer and Mr. Marriot.

"I believe, indeed," said Cecilia, "that neither of them were treated perfectly well; to me, however, their own behaviour has by no means been strictly honourable. I have always, when referred to, been very explicit; and what other methods they were pleased to take, I cannot wonder should fail."

"I told them," said Mr. Delvile, "that, since you were now under my roof, I could not refuse to receive their proposals, especially as there would be no impropriety in your alliance with either of them: but I told them, at the same time, that I could by no means think of pressing their suit, as that was an office which, however well it might do for Mr. Harrel, would be totally improper and unbecoming for me."

"Certainly;" said Cecilia, "and permit me, Sir, to entreat that, should they again apply to you, they may be wholly discouraged from repeating their visits, and assured that far from having trifled with them hitherto, the resolutions I have declared will never be varied."

"I am happy," said Mrs. Delvile, "to see so much spirit and discernment where arts of all sorts will be practised to ensnare and delude. Fortune and independance were never so securely lodged as in Miss Beverley, and I doubt not but her choice, whenever it is decided, will reflect as much honour upon her heart, as her difficulty in making it does upon her understanding."

Mr. Delvile then enquired whether she had fixed upon any person to chuse as a guardian in the place of Mr. Harrel. No, she said, nor should she, unless it were absolutely necessary.

"I believe, indeed," said Mrs. Delvile, "your affairs will not much miss him! Since I have heard of the excess of his extravagance, I have extremely rejoiced in the uncommon prudence and sagacity of his fair ward, who, in such dangerous hands, with less penetration and sound sense, might have been drawn into a thousand difficulties, and perhaps defrauded of half her fortune."

Cecilia received but little joy from this most unseasonable compliment, which, with many of the same sort that were frequently, though accidentally, made, intimidated her from the confession she had planned: and finding nothing but censure was likely to follow the discovery, she at length determined to give it up wholly, unless any connection should take place which might render necessary it's avowal. Yet something she could not but murmur, that an action so detrimental to her own interest, and which, at the time, appeared indispensable to her benevolence, should now be considered as a mark of such folly and imprudence that she did not dare own it.

CHAPTER II

A Railing

THE next morning the family purposed setting off as soon as breakfast was over: young Delvile, however, waited not so long; the fineness of the weather tempted him, he said, to travel on horseback, and therefore he had risen very early, and was already gone. Cecilia could not but wonder, yet did not repine.

Just as breakfast was over, and Mr. and Mrs. Delvile and
Cecilia were preparing to depart, to their no little surprise,
the door was opened, and, out of breath with haste and with
heat, in stumpt Mr. Briggs! "So," cried he, to Cecilia,
"what's all this? hay?—where are going?—a coach at the
door! horses to every wheel! Servants fine as lords! what's in
the wind now? think to chouse me out of my belongings?"

"I thought, Sir," said Cecilia, who instantly understood
him, though Mr. and Mrs. Delvile stared at him in utter
astonishment, "I had explained before I left you that I
should not return."

"Did n't, did n't!" answered he, angrily; "waited for you
three days, dressed a breast o' mutton o' purpose; got in a
lobster, and two crabs; all spoilt by keeping; stink already;
weather quite muggy, forced to souse 'em in vinegar; one
expence brings on another; never begin the like agen."

"I am very sorry, indeed," said Cecilia, much
disconcerted, "if there has been any mistake through my
neglect; but I had hoped I was understood, and I have been
so much occupied——"

"Ay, ay," interrupted he, "fine work! rare doings! a
merry Vauxhalling, with pistols at all your noddles! thought
as much! thought he'd tip the perch; saw he was n't stanch;
knew he'd go by his company,—a set of jackanapes! all
blacklegs!* nobody warm among 'em: fellows with a
month's good living upon their backs, and not sixpence for
the hangman in their pockets!"

Mrs. Delvile now, with a look of arch congratulation at
Cecilia as the object of this agreeable visit, finding it not
likely to be immediately concluded, returned to her chair:
but Mr. Delvile, leaning sternly upon his cane, moved not
from the spot where he stood at his entrance, but surveyed
him from head to foot, with the most astonished contempt
at his undaunted vulgarity.

"Well I'd all your cash myself; seized that, else!—run out
the constable* for you, next, and made you blow out your
brains for company. Mind what I say, never give your mind
to a gold lace hat! many a-one wears it don't know five
farthings from twopence. A good man always wears a bob

wig;* make that your rule. Ever see Master Harrel wear
such a thing? No, I'll warrant! better if he had; kept his head
on his own shoulders. And now, pray, how does he cut up?*
what has he left behind him? a *twey*-case,* I suppose, and a
bit of a hat won't go on a man's head!''

Cecilia, perceiving, with great confusion, that Mr.
Delvile, though evidently provoked by this intrusion, would
not deign to speak, that Mr. Briggs might be regarded as
belonging wholly to herself, hastily said ''I will not, Sir, as
your time is precious, detain you here, but, as soon as it is
in my power, I will wait upon you in the city.''

Mr. Briggs, however, without listening to her, thought
proper to continue his harangue.

''Invited me once to his house; sent me a card, half of it
printed like a book! t'other half a scrawl could not read;
pretended to give a supper; all a mere bam;* went without
my dinner, and got nothing to eat; all glass and shew;
victuals painted all manner o' colours; lighted up like a
pastry-cook on twelfth-day;* wanted something solid, and
got a great lump of sweetmeat;* found it as cold as a stone,
all froze in my mouth like ice; made me jump again, and
brought the tears in my eyes; forced to spit it out; believe it
was nothing but a snow-ball, just set up for shew, and
covered over with a little sugar. Pretty way to spend money!
Stuffing, and piping, and hopping!* never could rest till
every farthing was gone; nothing left but his own fool's pate,
and even that he could not hold together.''

''At present, Sir,'' said Cecilia, ''we are all going out of
town; the carriage is waiting at the door, and therefore——''

''No such thing,'' cried he; ''Sha'n't go; come for you
myself; take you to my own house. Got every thing ready,
been to the broker's, bought a nice blanket, hardly a brack*
in it. Pick up a table soon; one in my eye.''

''I am sorry you have so totally mistaken me, Sir; for I am
now going into the country with Mr. and Mrs. Delvile.''

''Won't consent, won't consent! what will you go there
for? hear of nothing but dead dukes; as well visit an old
tomb.''

Here Mr. Delvile, who felt himself insulted in a manner

he could least support, after looking at him very
disdainfully, turned to Cecilia, and said "Miss Beverley, if
this person wishes for a longer conference with you, I am
sorry you did not appoint a more seasonable hour for your
interview."

"Ay, ay," cried the impenetrable Mr. Briggs; "want to
hurry her off! see that! But 'twon't do; a'n't to be nicked;
chuse to come in for my thirds;* won't be gulled,* shan't
have more than your share."

"Sir!" cried Mr. Delvile, with a look meant to be nothing
less than petrific.*

"What!" cried he, with an arch leer; "all above it, hay?
warrant your Spanish Don never thinks of such a thing!
don't believe 'em my duck! great cry and little wool;* no
more of the ready than other folks; mere puff and go one."*

"This is language, Sir," said Mr. Delvile, "so utterly
incomprehensible, that I presume you do not even intend it
should be understood: otherwise, I should very little scruple
to inform you, that no man of the name of Delvile brooks
the smallest insinuation of dishonour."

"Don't he?" returned Mr. Briggs, with a grin; "why how
will he help it? will the old grandees jump out of their graves
to frighten us?"

"What old grandees, Sir? to whom are you pleased to
allude?"

"Why all them old grandfathers and aunts you brag of;
a set of poor souls you won't let rest in their coffins; mere
clay and dirt! fine things to be proud of! a parcel of old
mouldy rubbish quite departed this life! raking up bones and
dust, nobody knows for what! ought to be ashamed; who
cares for dead carcases? nothing but carion. My little Tom's
worth forty of 'em."

"I can so ill make out, Miss Beverley," said the
astonished Mr. Delvile, "what this person is pleased to dive
at, that I cannot pretend to enter into any sort of
conversation with him; you will therefore be so good as to
let me know when he has finished his discourse, and you are
at leisure to set off."

And then, with a very stately air, he was quitting the

room; but was soon stopt, upon Mr. Briggs' calling out "Ay, ay, Don Duke, poke in the old charnel houses by yourself, none of your defunct for me! did n't care if they were all hung in a string. Who's the better for 'em?"

"Pray, Sir," cried Mr. Delvile, turning round, "to whom were you pleased to address that speech?"

"To one Don Puffendorff,"* replied Mr. Briggs; "know ever such a person, hay?"

"Don who? Sir!" said Mr. Delvile, stalking nearer to him, "I must trouble you to say that name over again."

"Suppose don't chuse it? how then?"

"I am to blame," said Mr. Delvile, scornfully waving his hand with a repulsive motion, "to suffer myself to be irritated so unworthily; and I am sorry, in my own house, to be compelled to hint that the sooner I have it to myself, the better I shall be contented with it."

"Ay, ay, want to get me off; want to have her to yourself! won't be so soon choused; who's the better man? hay? which do you think is warmest? and all got by myself; obliged to never a grandee for a penny; what do you say to that? will you cast an account with me?"

"Very extraordinary this!" cried Mr. Delvile; "the most extraordinary circumstance of the kind I ever met with! a person to enter my house in order to talk in this incomprehensible manner! a person, too, I hardly know by sight!"

"Never mind, old Don," cried Briggs, with a facetious nod, "Know me better another time!"

"Old who, Sir!—what!"

"Come to a fair reckoning," continued Mr. Briggs; "suppose you were in my case, and had never a farthing but of your own getting; where would you be then? What would become of your fine coach and horses? you might stump your feet off before you'd ever get into one. Where would be all this fine* crockery work for your breakfast? you might pop your head under a pump, or drink out of your own paw. What would you do for that fine jemmy tye? Where would you get a gold head to your stick? You might dig long enough in them cold vaults before any of your old grandfathers would pop out to give you one."

Mr. Delvile, feeling more enraged than he thought suited* his dignity, restrained himself from making any further answer, but going up to the bell, rang it with great violence.

"And as to ringing a bell," continued Mr. Briggs, "you'd never know what it was in your life, unless could make interest to be a dust-man."*

"A dust-man!"—repeated Mr. Delvile, unable to command his silence longer, "I protest—" and biting his lips, he stopt short.

"Ay, love it, don't you? suits your taste; why not one dust as well as another? Dust in a cart good as dust of a charnel-house; don't smell half so bad."

A servant now entering, Mr. Delvile called out "Is every thing ready?"

"Yes, Sir."

He then begged Mrs. Delvile to go into the coach, and telling Cecilia to follow when at leisure, left the room.

"I will come immediately, Sir," said Cecilia; "Mr. Briggs, I am sorry to leave you, and much concerned you have had this trouble; but I can detain Mr. Delvile no longer."

And then away she ran, notwithstanding he repeatedly charged her to stay. He followed them, however, to the coach, with bitter revilings that every body was to make more of his ward than himself, and with the most virulent complaints of his losses from the blanket, the breast of mutton, the crabs and the lobster!

Nothing, however, more was said to him; Cecilia, as if she had not heard him, only bowed her head, and the coach driving off, they soon lost sight of him.

This incident by no means rendered the journey pleasant, or Mr. Delvile gracious: his own dignity, that constant object of his thoughts and his cares, had received a wound from this attack which he had not the sense to despise; and the vulgarity and impudence of Mr. Briggs, which ought to have made his familiarity and boldness equally contemptible and ridiculous, served only with a man whose pride out-run his understanding, to render them doubly mortifying and

stinging. He could talk, therefore, of nothing the whole way
that they went, but the extreme impropriety of which the
Dean of —— had been guilty, in exposing him to scenes and
situations so much beneath his Rank, by leaguing him with
a *person* so coarse and disgraceful.

They slept one night upon the road, and arrived the next
day at Delvile Castle.*

CHAPTER III

An Antique Mansion

DELVILE Castle was situated in a large and woody park,
and surrounded by a moat. A draw-bridge which fronted
the entrance was every night, by order of Mr. Delvile, with
the same care as if still necessary for the preservation of
the family, regularly drawn up. Some fortifications still
remained entire, and vestiges were every where to be traced
of more; no taste was shewn in the disposition of the
grounds, no openings were contrived through the wood for
distant views or beautiful objects:* the mansion-house was
ancient, large and magnificent, but constructed with as little
attention to convenience and comfort, as to airiness and
elegance; it was dark, heavy and monastic, equally in want
of repair and of improvement. The grandeur of its former
inhabitants was every where visible, but the decay into
which it was falling rendered such remains mere objects for
meditation and melancholy; while the evident struggle to
support some appearance of its ancient dignity, made the
dwelling and all in it's vicinity wear an aspect of constraint
and austerity. Festivity, joy and pleasure, seemed foreign to
the purposes of it's construction; silence, solemnity and
contemplation were adapted to it only.

Mrs. Delvile, however, took all possible care to make the
apartments and situation of Cecilia commodious and
pleasant, and to banish by her kindness and animation the
gloom and formality which her mansion inspired. Nor were
her efforts ungratefully received; Cecilia, charmed by every

mark of attention from a woman she so highly admired, returned her solicitude by encreasing affection, and repaid all her care by the revival of her spirits. She was happy, indeed, to have quitted the disorderly house of Mr. Harrel, where terror, so continually awakened, was only to be lulled by the grossest imposition; and though her mind, depressed by what was passed, and in suspence with what was to come, was by no means in a state for uninterrupted enjoyment, yet to find herself placed, at last, without effort or impropriety, in the very mansion she had so long considered as her road to happiness, rendered her, notwithstanding her remaining sources of inquietude, more contented than she had yet felt herself since her departure from Suffolk.

Even the imperious Mr. Delvile was more supportable here than in London: secure in his own castle, he looked around him with a pride of power and of possession which softened while it swelled him. His superiority was undisputed, his will was without controul. He was not, as in the great capital of the kingdom, surrounded by competitors; no rivalry disturbed his peace, no equality mortified his greatness; all he saw were either vassals of his power, or guests bending to his pleasure; he abated therefore, considerably, the stern gloom of his haughtiness, and soothed his proud mind by the courtesy of condescension.

Little, however, was the opportunity Cecilia found, for evincing that spirit and forbearance she had planned in relation to Delvile; he breakfasted by himself every morning, rode or walked out alone till driven home by the heat of the day, and spent the rest of his time till dinner in his own study. When he then appeared, his conversation was always general, and his attention not more engaged by Cecilia than by his mother. Left by them with his father, sometimes he appeared again at tea-time, but more commonly he rode* or strolled out to some neighbouring family, and it was always uncertain whether he was again seen before dinner the next day.

By this conduct, reserve on her part was rendered totally unnecessary; she could give no discouragement where she met with no assiduity; she had no occasion to fly where she was never pursued.

Strange, however, she thought such behaviour, and utterly impossible to be the effect of accident; his desire to avoid her seemed scrupulous and pointed, and however to the world it might wear the appearance of chance, to her watchful anxiety a thousand circumstances marked it for design. She found that his friends at home had never seen so little of him, complaints were continually made of his frequent absences, and much surprise was expressed at his new manner of life, and what might be the occupations which so strangely engrossed his time.

Had her heart not interfered in this matter, she might now have been perfectly at rest, since she was spared the renunciation she had projected, and since, without either mental exertion or personal trouble, the affair seemed totally dropt, and Delvile, far from manifesting any design of conquest, shunned all occasions of gallantry, and sedulously avoided even common conversation with her. If he saw her preparing to walk out in an evening, he was certain to stay at home; if his mother was with her, and invited him to join them, he was sure to be ready with some other engagement; and if by accident he met her in the park, he merely stopt to speak of the weather, bowed, and hurried on.

How to reconcile a coldness so extraordinary with a fervour so animated as that which he had lately shewn, was indeed not easy; sometimes she fancied he had entangled not only the poor Henrietta but himself, at other times she believed him merely capricious; but that he studied to avoid her she was convinced invariably, and such a conviction was alone sufficient to determine her upon forwarding his purpose. And, when her first surprise was over, and first chagrin abated, her own pride came to her aid, and she resolved to use every method in her power to conquer a partiality so ungratefully bestowed. She rejoiced that in no instance she had ever betrayed it, and she saw that his own behaviour prevented all suspicion of it in the family. Yet, in the midst of her mortification and displeasure, she found some consolation in seeing that those mercenary views of

which she had once been led to accuse him, were farthest
from his thoughts, and that whatever was the state of his
mind, she had no artifice to apprehend, nor design to guard
against. All therefore that remained was to imitate his
example, be civil and formal, shun all interviews that were
not public, and decline all discourse but what good breeding
occasionally made necessary.

By these means their meetings became more rare than
ever, and of shorter duration, for if one by any accident was
detained, the other retired; till, by their mutual diligence,
they soon only saw each other at dinner: and though neither
of them knew the motives or the intentions of the other, the
best concerted agreement could not more effectually have
separated them.

This task to Cecilia was at first extremely painful; but
time and constancy of mind soon lessened its difficulty. She
amused herself with walking and reading, she commissioned
Mr. Monckton to send her a Piano Forte of Merlin's,* she
was fond of fine work,* and she found in the conversation
of Mrs. Delvile a never-failing resource against languor and
sadness. Leaving therefore to himself her mysterious son,
she wisely resolved to find other employment for her
thoughts, than conjectures with which she could not be
satisfied, and doubts that might never be explained.

Very few families visited at the castle, and fewer still had
their visits returned. The arrogance of Mr. Delvile had
offended all the neighbouring gentry, who could easily be
better entertained than by receiving instructions of their own
inferiority, which however readily they might allow, was by
no means so pleasant a subject as to recompense them for
hearing no other. And if Mr. Delvile was shunned through
hatred, his lady no less was avoided through fear; high-
spirited and fastidious, she was easily wearied and disgusted,
she bore neither with frailty nor folly—those two principal
ingredients in human nature! She required, to obtain her
favour, the union of virtue and abilities with elegance, which
meeting but rarely, she was rarely disposed to be pleased;
and disdaining to conceal either contempt or aversion, she
inspired in return nothing but dread or resentment: making

thus, by a want of that lenity which is the *milk of human kindness*,* and the bond of society, enemies the most numerous and illiberal by those very talents which, more *meekly borne*,* would have rendered her not merely admired, but adored!

In proportion, however, as she was thus at war with the world in general, the chosen few who were honoured with her favour, she loved with a zeal all her own; her heart, liberal, open, and but too daringly sincere, was fervent in affection, and enthusiastic in admiration; the friends who were dear to her, she was devoted to serve, she magnified their virtues till she thought them of an higher race of beings, she inflamed her generosity with ideas of what she owed to them, till her life seemed too small a sacrifice to be refused for their service.

Such was the love which already she felt for Cecilia; her countenance had struck, her manners had charmed her, her understanding was displayed by the quick intelligence of her eyes, and every action and every notion spoke her mind the seat of elegance. In secret she sometimes regretted that she was not higher born, but that regret always vanished when she saw and conversed with her.

Her own youth had been passed in all the severity of affliction; she had been married to Mr. Delvile by her relations, without any consultation of her heart or her will. Her strong mind disdained useless complaints, yet her discontent, however private, was deep. Ardent in her disposition, and naturally violent in her passions, her feelings were extremely acute, and to curb them by reason and principle had been the chief and hard study of her life. The effort had calmed, though it had not made her happy. To love Mr. Delvile she felt was impossible; proud without merit, and imperious without capacity, she saw with bitterness the inferiority of his faculties, and she found in his temper no qualities to endear or attract: yet she respected his birth and his family, of which her own was a branch, and whatever was her misery from the connection, she steadily behaved to him with the strictest propriety.

Her son, however, when she was blessed with his

presence, had a power over her mind that mitigated all her sorrows, and almost lulled even her wishes to sleep: she rather idolised than loved him, yet her fondness flowed not from relationship, but from his worth and his character, his talents and his disposition. She saw in him, indeed, all her own virtues and excellencies, with a toleration for the imperfections of others to which she was wholly a stranger. Whatever was great or good she expected him to perform; occasion alone she thought wanting to manifest him the first of human beings.

Nor here was Mr. Delvile himself less sanguine in his hopes: his son was not only the first object of his affection, but the chief idol of his pride, and he did not merely cherish but reverence him as his successor, the only support of his ancient name and family, without whose life and health the whole race would be extinct. He consulted him in all his affairs, never mentioned him but with distinction, and expected the whole world to bow down before him.

Delvile in his behaviour to his father imitated the conduct of his mother, who opposed him in nothing when his pleasure was made known, but who forbore to enquire into his opinion except in cases of necessity. Their minds, indeed, were totally dissimilar; and Delvile well knew that if he submitted to his directions, he must demand such respect as the world would refuse with indignation, and scarcely speak to a man whose genealogy was not known to him.

But though duty and gratitude were the only ties that bound him to his father, he loved his mother not merely with filial affection, but with the purest esteem and highest reverence; he knew, too, that while without him her existence would be a burthen, her tenderness was no effusion of weak partiality, but founded on the strongest assurances of his worth; and however to maternal indulgence its origin might be owing, the rectitude of his own conduct could alone save it from diminution.

Such was the house in which Cecilia was now settled, and with which she lived almost to the exclusion of the sight of any other; for though she had now been three weeks at the castle, she had only at church seen any family but the Delviles.

Nor did any thing in the course of that time occur to her, but the reception of a melancholy letter from Mrs. Harrel, filled with complaints of her retirement and misery; and another from Mr. Arnott, with an account of the funeral, the difficulties he had had to encounter with the creditors, who had even seized the dead body,* and the numerous expences in which he had been involved, by petitions he could not withstand, from the meaner and more clamorous of those whom his late brother-in-law had left unpaid. He concluded with a pathetic prayer for her happiness, and a declaration that his own was lost for ever, since now he was even deprived of her sight. Cecilia wrote an affectionate answer to Mrs. Harrel, promising, when fully at liberty, that she would herself fetch her to her own house in Suffolk: but she could only send her compliments to Mr. Arnott, though her compassion urged a kinder message; as she feared even a shadow of encouragement to so serious, yet hopeless a passion.

CHAPTER IV

A Rattle

AT this time, the house was much enlivened by a visit from Lady Honoria Pemberton, who came to spend a month with Mrs. Delvile.

Cecilia had now but little leisure, for Lady Honoria would hardly rest a moment away from her; she insisted upon walking with her, sitting with her, working with her, and singing with her; whatever she did, she chose to do also; wherever she went, she was bent upon accompanying her; and Mrs. Delvile, who wished her well, though she had no patience with her foibles, encouraged this intimacy from the hope it might do her service.

It was not, however, that Lady Honoria had conceived any regard for Cecilia; on the contrary, had she been told she should see her no more, she would have heard it with the same composure as if she had been told she should meet with her daily: she had no motive for pursuing her but that she had nothing else to do, and no fondness for her society but what resulted from aversion to solitude.

Lady Honoria had received a fashionable education, in which her proficiency had been equal to what fashion made requisite; she sung a little, played the harpsichord a little, painted a little, worked a little, and danced a great deal. She had quick parts and high spirits, though her mind was uncultivated, and she was totally void of judgment or discretion: she was careless of giving offence, and indifferent to all that was thought of her; the delight of her life was to create wonder by her rattle, and whether that wonder was to her advantage or discredit, she did not for a moment trouble herself to consider.

A character of so much levity with so little heart had no great chance of raising esteem or regard in Cecilia, who at almost any other period of her life would have been wearied of her importunate attendance; but at present, the unsettled state of her own mind made her glad to give it any employment, and the sprightliness of Lady Honoria served therefore to amuse her. Yet she could not forbear being hurt by finding that the behaviour of Delvile was so exactly the same to them both, that any common observer would with difficulty have pronounced which he preferred.

One morning about a week after her ladyship's arrival at the castle, she came running into Cecilia's room, saying she had very good news for her.

"A charming opening!" cried Cecilia, "pray tell it me."

"Why my Lord Derford is coming!"

"O what a melancholy dearth of incident," cried Cecilia, "if this is your best intelligence!"

"Why it's better than nothing: better than going to sleep over a family-party; and I vow I have sometimes such difficulty to keep awake, that I am frightened to death lest I should be taken with a sudden nap, and affront them all. Now pray speak the truth without squeamishness, don't you find it very terrible?"

"No, I find nothing very terrible with Mrs. Delvile."

"O, I like Mrs. Delvile, too, of all things, for I believe

she's the cleverest woman in the world; but then I know she does not like me, so there's no being very fond of her. Besides, really, if I admired her as much again, I should be dreadfully tired of seeing nothing else. She never stirs out, you know, and has no company at home, which is an extremely tiresome plan, for it only serves to make us all doubly sick of one another; though you must know it's one great reason why my father likes I should come; for he has some very old-fashioned notions, though I take a great deal of pains to make him get the better of them. But I am always excessively rejoiced when the visit has been paid, for I am obliged to come every year. I don't mean *now*, indeed, because your being here makes it vastly more tolerable."

'You do me much honour," said Cecilia, laughing.

"But really, when my Lord Derford comes, it can't possibly be quite so bad, for at least there will be something else to look at; and you must know my eyes tire extremely of always seeing the same objects. And we can ask him, too, for a little news, and that will put Mrs. Delvile in a passion, which will help to give us a little spirit: though I know we shall not get the smallest intelligence from him, for he knows nothing in the world that's going forward. And, indeed, that's no great matter, for if he did, he would not know how to tell it, he's so excessively silly. However, I shall ask him all sort of things, for the less he can answer, the more it will plague him; and I like to plague a fool amazingly, because he can never plague one again.—Though really I ought to beg your pardon, for he is one of your admirers."

"O pray make no stranger of me! you have my free consent to say whatever you please of him."

"I assure you, then, I like my old Lord Ernolf the best of the two, for he has a thousand times more sense than his son, and upon my word I don't think he is much uglier. But I wonder vastly you would not marry him, for all that, for you might have done exactly what you pleased with him, which, all together, would have been no inconvenient circumstance."

"When I want a pupil," answered Cecilia, "I shall think that an admirable recommendation: but were I to marry, I would rather find a tutor, of the two."

"I am sure I should not," cried lady Honoria, carelessly, "for one has enough to do with tutors before hand, and the best thing I know of marrying is to get rid of them. I fancy you think so too, only it's a pretty speech to make. Oh how my sister Euphrasia would adore you!—Pray are you always as grave as you are now?"

"No,—yes,—indeed I hardly know."

"I fancy it's this dismal place that hurts your spirits. I remember when I saw you in St. James's-square I thought you very lively. But really these thick walls are enough to inspire the vapours if one never had them before."

'I don't think they have had a very bad effect upon your ladyship!"

"O yes they have; if Euphrasia was here she would hardly know me. And the extreme want of taste and entertainment in all the family is quite melancholy: for even if by chance one has the good fortune to hear any intelligence, Mrs. Delvile will hardly let it be repeated, for fear it should happen to be untrue, as if that could possibly signify! I am sure I had as lieve the things were false as not, for they tell as well one way as the other, if she would but have patience to hear them. But she's extremely severe, you know, as almost all those very clever women are; so that she keeps a kind of restraint upon me whether I will or no. However, that's nothing compared to her *caro sposo*,* for he is utterly insufferable; so solemn, and so dull! so stately and so tiresome! Mortimer, too, gets worse and worse; O 'tis a sad tribe! I dare say he will soon grow quite as horrible as his father. Don' you think so?"

"Why indeed,—no,——I don't think there's much resemblance," said Cecilia, with some hesitation.

"He is the most altered creature," continued her ladyship, "I ever saw in my life. Once I thought him the most agreeable young man in the world: but if you observe, that's all over now, and he is getting just as stupid and dismal as the rest of them. I wish you had been here last summer; I assure you, you would quite have fallen in love with him."

"Should I?" said Cecilia, with a conscious smile.

"Yes, for he was quite delightful; all spirit and gaiety; but now, if it was not for you, I really think I should pretend to lose my way, and instead of going over that old draw-bridge, throw myself into the moat. I wish Euphrasia was here. It's just the right place for her. She'll fancy herself in a monastry as soon as she comes, and nothing will make her half so happy, for she is always wishing to be a Nun, poor little simpleton."

"Is there any chance that Lady Euphrasia may come?"

"Oh no, she can't at present, because it would not be proper: but I mean if ever she is married to Mortimer."

"Married to him!" repeated Cecilia, in the utmost consternation.

"I believe, my dear," cried Lady Honoria, looking at her very archly, "you intend to be married to him yourself?"

"Me? no, indeed!"

"You look very guilty, though," cried she laughing, "and indeed when you came hither, every body said that the whole affair was arranged."

"For shame, Lady Honoria!" said Cecilia, again changing colour, "I am sure this must be your own fancy,—invention,—"

"No, I assure you; I heard it at several places; and every body said how charmingly your fortune would build up all these old fortifications: but some people said they knew Mr. Harrel had sold you to Mr. Marriot, and that if you married Mortimer, there would be a law-suit that would take away half your estate; and others said you had promised your hand to Sir Robert Floyer, and repented when you heard of his mortgages, and he gave it out every where that he would fight any man that pretended to you; and then again some said that you were all the time privately married to Mr. Arnott, but did not dare own it, because he was so afraid of fighting with Sir Robert."

"O Lady Honoria!" cried Cecilia, half laughing, "what wild inventions are these! and all I hope, your own?"

"No, indeed, they were current over the whole town. But don't take any notice of what I told you about Euphrasia, for perhaps, it may never happen."

"Perhaps," said Cecilia, reviving by believing it all fiction, "it has never been in agitation?"

"O yes; it is negociating at this very moment, I believe, among the higher powers; only Mr. Delvile does not yet know whether Euphrasia has fortune enough for what he wants."

Ah, thought Cecilia, how do I rejoice that my independent situation exempts me from being disposed of for life, by thus being set up to sale!

"They thought of me, once, for Mortimer," continued Lady Honoria, "but I'm vastly glad that's over, for I never should have survived being shut up in this place; it's much fitter for Euphrasia. To tell you the truth, I believe they could not make out money enough; but Euphrasia has a fortune of her own, besides what we shall have together, for Grandmama left her every thing that was in her own power."

"Is Lady Euphrasia your elder sister?"

"O no, poor little thing, she's two years younger. Grandmama brought her up, and she has seen nothing at all of the world, for she has never been presented yet, so she is not *come out*,* you know: but she's to come out next year. However, she once saw Mortimer, but she did not like him at all."

"Not like him!" cried Cecilia, greatly surprised.

"No, she thought him too gay,—Oh dear, I wish she could see him now! I am sure I hope she would find him sad enough! she is the most formal little grave thing you ever beheld: she'll preach to you sometimes for half an hour together. Grandmama taught her nothing in the world but to say her prayers, so that almost every other word you say, she thinks is quite wicked."

The conversation was now interrupted by their separating to dress for dinner. It left Cecilia in much perplexity; she knew not what wholly to credit, or wholly to disbelieve; but her chief concern arose from the unfortunate change of countenance which Lady Honoria had been so quick in observing.

The next time she was alone with Mrs. Delvile, "Miss

Beverley," she said "has your little rattling tormentor acquainted you who is coming?"

"Lord Derford, do you mean, ma'am?"

"Yes, with his father; shall you dislike to see them?"

"Not if, as I hope, they come merely to wait upon you and Mr. Delvile."

"Mr. Delvile and myself," answered she smiling, "will certainly have the honour of *receiving* them."

"Lord Ernolf," said Cecilia, "can never suppose his visit will make any change in me; I have been very explicit with him, and he seemed equally rational and well bred in forbearing any importunity upon the subject."

"It has however been much believed in town," said Mrs. Delvile, "that you were strangely shackled by Mr. Harrel, and therefore his lordship may probably hope that a change in your situation may be followed by a change in his favour."

"I shall be sorry if he does," said Cecilia, "for he will then find himself much deceived."

"You are right, very right," cried Mrs. Delvile, "to be difficult in your choice, and to take time for looking around you before you make any. I have forborn all questions upon this subject, lest you should find any reluctance in answering them; but I am now too deeply interested in your welfare to be contented in total ignorance of your designs: will you, then, suffer me to make a few enquiries?"

Cecilia gave a ready, but blushing assent.

"Tell me, then, of the many admirers who have graced your train, which there is you have distinguished with any intention of future preference?"

"Not one, madam!"

"And, out of so many, is there not one that, hereafter, you mean to distinguish?"

"Ah madam!" cried Cecilia, shaking her head, "many as they may seem, I have little reason to be proud of them; there is one only who, had my fortune been smaller, would, I believe, ever have thought of me, and there is *one* only, who, were it now diminished, would ever think of me more."

"This sincerity," cried Mrs. Delvile, "is just what I expected from you. There is, then, *one?*"

"I believe there is,—and the worthy Mr. Arnott is the man; I am much indeed deceived, if his partiality for me is not truly disinterested, and I almost wish—"

"What, my love?"

"That I could return it more gratefully!"

"And do you not?"

"No!—I cannot! I esteem him, I have the truest regard for his character, and were I now by any fatal necessity, compelled to belong to any one of those who have been pleased to address me, I should not hesitate a moment in shewing him my gratitude; but yet, for some time at least, such a proof of it would render me very miserable."

"You may perhaps think so now," returned Mrs. Delvile; "but with sentiments so strongly in his favour, you will probably be led hereafter to pity——and accept him."

"No, indeed, madam; I pretend not, I own, to open my whole heart to you;—I know not that you would have patience, for so uninteresting a detail; but though there are some things I venture not to mention, there is nothing, believe me, in which I will deceive you."

"I *do* believe you," cried Mrs. Delvile, embracing her; "and the more readily because, not merely among your avowed admirers, but among the whole race of men, I scarce know one to whom I should think you worthily consigned!"

Ah! thought Cecilia, that scarce! who may it mean to except?

"To shew you," she continued, "that I will deserve your confidence in future, I will refrain from distressing you by any further questions at present: you will not, I think, act materially without consulting me, and for your thoughts—it were tyranny, not friendship, to investigate them more narrowly."

Cecilia's gratitude for this delicacy, would instantly have induced her to tell every secret of her soul, had she not apprehended such a confession would have seemed soliciting her interest and assistance, in the only affair in which she would have disdained even to receive them.

She thanked her, therefore, for her kindness, and the conversation was dropt; she much wished to have known whether these enquiries sprung simply from friendly curiosity, or whether she was desirous from any nearer motive to be satisfied with respect to her freedom or engagements. This, however, she had no method of discovering, and was therefore compelled to wait quietly till time should make it clear.

CHAPTER V

A Storm

ONE evening about this time, which was the latter end of July, Lady Honoria and Cecilia deferred walking out till very late, and then found it so pleasant, that they had strolled into the Park two miles from the house, when they were met by young Delvile; who, however, only reminded them how far they had to return, and walked on.

"He grows quite intolerable!" cried Lady Honoria, when he was gone; "it's really a melancholy thing to see a young man behave so like an old Monk. I dare say in another week he won't take off his hat to us; and, in about a fortnight, I suppose he'll shut himself up in one of those little round towers, and shave his head, and live upon roots, and howl if any body comes near him. I really half wonder he does not think it too dissipated to let Fidel run after him so. A thousand to one but he shoots him some day for giving a sudden bark when he's in one of these gloomy fits. Something, however, must certainly be the matter with him. Perhaps he is in love."

"Can nothing be the matter with him but that?" cried Cecilia.

"Nay, I don't know; but I am sure if he is, his Mistress has not much occasion to be jealous of you or me, for never, I think, were two poor Damsels so neglected!"

The utmost art of malice could not have furnished a speech more truly mortifying to Cecilia than this thoughtless

and accidental sally of Lady Honoria's: particularly,
however, upon her guard, from the raillery she had already
endured, she answered, with apparent indifference, "he is
meditating, perhaps, upon Lady Euphrasia."

"O no," cried Lady Honoria, "for he did not take any
notice of her when he saw her; I am sure if he marries her,
it will only be because he cannot help it."

"Poor Lady Euphrasia!"

"O no, not at all; he'll make her two or three fine
speeches, and then she'll be perfectly contented: especially
if he looks as dismally at her as he does at us! and that
probably he will do the more readily for not liking to look
at her at all. But she's such a romantic little thing, she'll
never suspect him."

Here they were somewhat alarmed by a sudden darkness
in the air, which was presently succeeded by a thunder
storm; they instantly turned back, and began running home,
when a violent shower of rain obliged them to take shelter
under a large tree; where in two minutes they were joined
by Delvile, who came to offer his assistance in hurrying them
home; and finding the thunder and lightening continue,
begged them to move on, in defiance of the rain, as their
present situation exposed them to more danger than a wet
hat and cloak, which might be changed in a moment.

Cecilia readily assented; but Lady Honoria, extremely
frightened, protested she would not stir till the storm was
over. It was in vain he represented her mistake in supposing
herself in a place of security; she clung to the tree, screamed
at every flash of lightening, and all her gay spirits were lost
in her apprehensions.

Delvile then earnestly proposed to Cecilia conducting her
home by herself, and returning again to Lady Honoria; but
she thought it wrong to quit her companion, and hardly
right to accept his assistance separately. They waited,
therefore, some time all together; but the storm encreasing
with great violence, the thunder growing louder, and the
lightning becoming stronger, Delvile grew impatient even
to anger at Lady Honoria's resistance, and warmly
expostulated upon its folly and danger. But the present* was

no season for lessons in philosophy; prejudices she had never been taught to surmount made her think herself in a place of safety, and she was now too much terrified to give argument fair play.

Finding her thus impracticable, Delvile eagerly said to Cecilia, "Come then, Miss Beverley, let us wait no longer; I will see you home, and then return to Lady Honoria."

"By no means," cried she, "my life is not more precious than either of yours, and therefore it may run the same risk."

"It is more precious," cried he with vehemence, "than the air I breathe!" and seizing her hand, he drew it under his arm, and, without waiting her consent, almost forced her away with him, saying as they ran, "How could a thousand Lady Honorias recompence the world for the loss of one Miss Beverley? we may, indeed, find many thousand such as Lady Honoria, but such as Miss Beverley—where shall we ever find another?"

Cecilia, surprised, yet gratified, could not speak, for the speed with which they ran almost took away her breath; and before they were near home, slackening her pace, and panting, she confessed her strength was exhausted, and that she could go so fast no further.

"Let us then stop and rest," cried he; "but why will you not lean upon me? surely this is no time for scruples, and for idle and unnecessary scruples, Miss Beverley can never find a time."

Cecilia then, urged equally by shame at his speech and by weakness from fatigue, leant upon his arm; but she soon repented her condescension; for Delvile, with an emotion he seemed to find wholly irrepressible, passionately exclaimed "sweet lovely burthen! O why not thus for ever!"

The strength of Cecilia was now instantly restored, and she hastily withdrew from his hold; he suffered her to disengage herself, but said in a faultering voice, "pardon me, Cecilia!—Madam!—Miss Beverley,* I mean!——"

Cecilia, without making any answer, walked on by herself, as quick a pace as she was able; and Delvile, not venturing to oppose her, silently followed.

They had gone but a few steps, before there came a violent shower of hail; and the wind, which was very high, being immediately in their faces, Cecilia was so pelted and incommoded, that she was frequently obliged to stop, in defiance of her utmost efforts to force herself forward. Delvile then approaching her, proposed that she should again stand under a tree, as the thunder and lightening for the present seemed over, and wait there till the fury of the hail was past: and Cecilia, though never before so little disposed to oblige him, was so much distressed by the violence of the wind and hail, that she was forced to comply.

Every instant now seemed an age; yet neither hail nor wind abated: mean time they were both silent, and both, though with different feelings, equally comfortless.

Delvile, however, who took care to place himself on the side whence the wind blew hardest, perceived, in spite of his endeavours to save her, some hail-stones lodged upon her thin summer cloak: he then took off his own hat, and, though he ventured not to let it touch her, held it in such a manner as to shelter her better.

Cecilia now could no longer be either silent or unmoved, but turning to him with much emotion, said, "Why will you do this, Mr. Delvile?"

"What would I *not* do," answered he, "to obtain forgiveness from Miss Beverley?"

"Well, well,—pray put on your hat."

"Do you command it?"

"No, certainly!—but I wish it."

"Ah!" cried he, instantly putting it on, "whose are the commands that would have half the weight with your wishes?"

And then, after another pause, he added, "do you forgive me?"

Cecilia, ashamed of the cause of their dissention, and softened by the seriousness of his manner, answered very readily, "yes, yes,—why will you make me remember such nonsense?"

"All sweetness," cried he warmly, and snatching her hand, "is Miss Beverley!—O that I had power—that it were not utterly impossible—that the cruelty of my situation——"

"I find," cried she, greatly agitated, and forcibly drawing away her hand, "you will teach me, for another time, the folly of fearing bad weather!"

And she hurried from beneath the tree; and Delvile perceiving one of the servants approach with an Umbrella, went forward to take it from him, and directed him to hasten instantly to Lady Honoria.

Then returning to Cecilia, he would have held it over her head, but with an air of displeasure, she took it into her own hand.

"Will you not let me carry it for you?" he cried.

"No, Sir, there is not any occasion."

They then proceeded silently on.

The storm was now soon over; but it grew very dark, and as they had quitted the path while they ran, in order to get home by a shorter cut, the walk was so bad from the height of the grass, and the unevenness of the ground, that Cecilia had the utmost difficulty to make her way; yet she resolutely refused any assistance from Delvile, who walked anxiously by her side, and seemed equally fearful upon his own account and upon hers, to trust himself with being importunate.

At length they came to a place which Cecilia in vain tried to pass; Delvile then grew more urgent to help her; firm, however, in declining all aid, she preferred going a considerable way round to another part of the park which led to the house. Delvile, angry as well as mortified, proposed to assist her no more, but followed without saying a word.

Cecilia, though she felt not all the resentment she displayed, still thought it necessary to support it, as she was much provoked with the perpetual inconsistency of his behaviour, and deemed it wholly improper to suffer, without discouragement, occasional sallies of tenderness from one who, in his general conduct, behaved with the most scrupulous reserve.

They now arrived at the castle; but entering by a back way, came to a small and narrow passage which obstructed the entrance of the umbrella: Delvile once more, and almost involuntarily, offered to help her; but, letting down the spring, she coldly said she had no further use for it.

He then went forward to open a small gate which led by another long passage into the hall: but hearing the servants advance, he held it for an instant in his hand, while, in a tone of voice the most dejected, he said "I am grieved to find you thus offended; but were it possible you could know half the wretchedness of my heart, the generosity of your own would make you regret this severity!" and then, opening the gate, he bowed, and went another way.

Cecilia was now in the midst of servants; but so much shocked and astonished by the unexpected speech of Delvile, which instantly changed all her anger into sorrow, that she scarce knew what they said to her, nor what she replied; though they all with one voice enquired what was become of Lady Honoria, and which way they should run to seek her.

Mrs. Delvile then came also, and she was obliged to recollect herself. She immediately proposed her going to bed, and drinking white wine whey* to prevent taking cold: cold, indeed, she feared not; yet she agreed to the proposal, for she was confounded and dismayed by what had passed, and utterly unable to hold any conversation.

Her perplexity and distress were, however, all attributed to fatigue and fright; and Mrs. Delvile, having assisted in hurrying her to bed, went to perform the same office for Lady Honoria, who arrived at that time.

Left at length by herself, she revolved in her mind the adventure of the evening, and the whole behaviour of Delvile since first she was acquainted with him. That he loved her with tenderness, with fondness loved her, seemed no longer to admit of any doubt, for however distant and cold he appeared, when acting with circumspection and design, the moment he was off his guard from surprise, terror, accident of any sort, the moment that he was betrayed into acting from nature and inclination, he was constantly certain to discover a regard the most animated and flattering.

This regard, however, was not more evident than his

desire to conceal and to conquer it: he seemed to dread even her sight, and to have imposed upon himself the most rigid forbearance of all conversation or intercourse with her.

Whence could this arise? what strange and unfathomable cause could render necessary a conduct so mysterious? he knew not, indeed, that she herself wished it changed, but he could not be ignorant that his chance with almost any woman would at least be worth trying.

Was the obstacle which thus discouraged him the condition imposed by her uncle's will of giving her own name to the man she married? this she herself thought was an unpleasant circumstance, but yet so common for an heiress,* that it could hardly out-weigh the many advantages of such a connection.

Henrietta again occurred to her; the letter she had seen in her hands was still unexplained: yet her entire conviction that Henrietta was not loved by him, joined to a certainty that affection alone could ever make him think of her, lessened upon this subject her suspicions every moment.

Lady Euphrasia Pemberton, at last, rested most upon her mind, and she thought it probable some actual treaty was negociating with the Duke of Derwent.

Mrs. Delvile she had every reason to believe was her friend, though she was scrupulously delicate in avoiding either raillery or observation upon the subject of her son, whom she rarely mentioned, and never but upon occasions in which Cecilia could have no possible interest.

The Father, therefore, notwithstanding all Mr. Monckton had represented to the contrary, appeared to be the real obstacle; his pride might readily object to her birth, which though not contemptible, was merely decent, and which, if traced beyond her grandfather, lost all title even to that epithet.

"If this, however," she cried, "is at last his situation, how much have I been to blame in censuring his conduct! for while to me he has appeared capricious, he has, in fact, acted wholly from necessity: if his father insists upon his forming another connection, has he not been honourable, prudent and just, in flying an object that made him think of disobedience, and endeavouring to keep her ignorant of a partiality it is his duty to curb?

All, therefore, that remained for her to do or to resolve, was to guard her own secret with more assiduous care than ever, and since she found that their union was by himself thought impossible, to keep from his knowledge that the regret was not all his own.

CHAPTER VI

A Mystery

FOR two days, in consequence of violent colds caught during the storm, Lady Honoria Pemberton and Cecilia were confined to their rooms. Cecilia, glad by solitude and reflection to compose her spirits and settle her plan of conduct, would willingly have still prolonged her retirement, but the abatement of her cold affording her no pretence, she was obliged on the third day to make her appearance.

Lady Honoria, though less recovered, as she had been more a sufferer, was impatient of any restraint, and would take no denial to quitting her room at the same time; at dinner, therefore, all the family met as usual.

Mr. Delvile, with his accustomed solemnity of civility, made various enquiries and congratulations upon their danger and their security, carefully in both, addressing himself first to Lady Honoria, and then with more stateliness in his kindness, to Cecilia. His lady, who had frequently visited them both, had nothing new to hear.

Delvile did not come in till they were all seated, when, hastily saying he was glad to see both the ladies so well again, he instantly employed himself in carving, with the agitation of a man who feared trusting himself to sit idle.

Little, however, as he said, Cecilia was much struck by the melancholy tone of his voice, and the moment she raised her eyes, she observed that his countenance was equally sad.

"Mortimer," cried Mr. Delvile, "I am sure you are not well; I cannot imagine why you will not have some advice."

"Were I to send for a physician, Sir," cried Delvile, with affected cheerfulness, "he would find it much more difficult to imagine what advice to give me."

"Permit me however, Mr. Mortimer," cried Lady Honoria, "to return you my humble thanks for the honour of your assistance in the thunder storm! I am afraid you made yourself ill by attending *me!*"

"Your ladyship," returned Delvile, colouring very high, yet pretending to laugh; "made so great a coward of me, that I ran away from shame at my own inferiority of courage."

"Were you, then, with Lady Honoria during the storm?" cried Mrs. Delvile.

"No, Madam!" cried Lady Honoria very quick; "but he was so good as to *leave* me during the storm."

"Mortimer," said Mr. Delvile, "is this possible?"

"O Lady Honoria was such a Heroine," answered Delvile, "that she wholly disdained receiving any assistance; her valour was so much more undaunted than mine, that she ventured to brave the lightning under an oak tree!"

"Now, dear Mrs. Delvile," exclaimed Lady Honoria, "think what a simpleton he would have made of me! he wanted to persuade me that in the open air I should be less exposed to danger than under the shelter of a thick tree!"

"Lady Honoria," replied Mrs. Delvile, with a sarcastic smile, "the next tale of scandal you oblige me to hear, I will insist for your punishment that you shall read one of Mr. Newbury's little books! there are twenty of them* that will explain this matter to you, and such reading will at least employ your time as usefully as such tales!"

"Well, ma'am," said Lady Honoria, "I don't know whether you are laughing at me or not, but really I concluded Mr. Mortimer only chose to amuse himself in a tête à tête with Miss Beverley."

"He was not with Miss Beverley," cried Mrs. Delvile with quickness; "she was alone,—I saw her myself the moment she came in."

"Yes, ma'am,—but not then,—he was gone;"—said Cecilia, endeavouring, but not very successfully, to speak with composure.

"I had the honour," cried Delvile, making, with equal success, the same attempt, "to wait upon Miss Beverley to the little gate; and I was then returning to Lady Honoria when I met her ladyship just coming in."

"Very extraordinary, Mortimer," said Mr. Delvile, staring, "to attend Lady Honoria the last!"

"Don't be angry in earnest, Sir," cried Lady Honoria, gayly, "for I did not mean to turn tell-tale."

Here the subject was dropt: greatly to the joy both of Delvile and Cecilia, who mutually exerted themselves in talking upon what next was started, in order to prevent its being recurred to again.

That fear, however, over, Delvile said little more; sadness hung heavily on his mind; he was absent, disturbed, uneasy; yet he endeavoured no longer to avoid Cecilia; on the contrary, when she arose to quit the room, he looked evidently disappointed.

The ladies' colds kept them at home all the evening, and Delvile, for the first time since their arrival at the castle, joined them at tea: nor when it was over, did he as usual retire; he loitered, pretended to be caught by a new pamphlet,* and looked as anxiously eager to speak with Cecilia, as he had hitherto appeared to shun her.

With new emotion and fresh distress Cecilia perceived this change; what he might have to say she could not conjecture, but all that foreran his communication convinced her it was nothing she could wish; and much as she had desired some explanation of his designs, when the long-expected moment seemed arriving, prognostications the most cruel of the event, repressed her impatience, and deadened her curiosity. She earnestly lamented her unfortunate residence in his house, where the adoration of every inhabitant, from his father to the lowest servant, had impressed her with the strongest belief of his general worthiness, and greatly, though imperceptibly, encreased her regard for him, since she had now not a doubt remaining but that some cruel, some fatal obstacle, prohibited their union.

To collect fortitude to hear it with composure, was now her whole study; but though, when alone, she thought any discovery preferable to suspence, all her courage failed her when Delvile appeared, and if she could not detain Lady Honoria, she involuntarily followed her.

Thus passed four or five days; during which the health of Delvile seemed to suffer with his mind, and though he refused to acknowledge he was ill, it was evident to every body that he was far from well.

Mr. Delvile frequently urged him to consent to have some advice; but he always revived, though with forced and transitory spirits, at the mention of a physician, and the proposal ended in nothing.

Mrs. Delvile, too, at length grew alarmed; her enquiries were more penetrating and pointed, but they were not more successful; every attack of this sort was followed by immediate gaiety, which, however constrained, served, for the time, to change the subject. Mrs. Delvile, however, was not soon to be deceived; she watched her son incessantly, and seemed to feel an inquietude scarce less than his own.

Cecilia's distress was now augmented every moment, and the difficulty to conceal it grew every hour more painful; she felt herself the cause of the dejection of the son, and that thought made her feel guilty in the presence of the mother; the explanation she expected threatened her with new misery, and the courage to endure it she tried in vain to acquire; her heart was most cruelly oppressed, apprehension and suspence never left it for an instant; rest abandoned her at night, and chearfulness by day.

At this time the two lords, Ernolf and Derford, arrived; and Cecilia, who at first had lamented their design, now rejoiced in their presence, since they divided the attention of Mrs. Delvile, which she began to fear was not wholly directed to her son, and since they saved her from having the whole force of Lady Honoria's high spirits and gay rattle to herself.

Their immediate observations upon the ill looks of

c.—23

Delvile, startled both Cecilia and the mother even more than their own fears, which they had hoped were rather the result of apprehension than of reason. Cecilia now severely reproached herself with having deferred the conference he was evidently seeking, not doubting but she had contributed to his indisposition by denying him the relief he might expect from concluding the affair.

Melancholy as was this idea, it was yet a motive to overpower her reluctance, and determine her no longer to shun what it seemed necessary to endure.

Deep reasoners, however, when they are also nice casuists, frequently resolve with a tardiness which renders their resolutions of no effect: this was the case with Cecilia; the same morning that she came down stairs prepared to meet with firmness the blow which she believed awaited her, Delvile, who, since the arrival of the two lords, had always appeared at the general breakfast, acknowledged in answer to his mother's earnest enquiries, that he had a cold and head-ache: and had he, at the same time, acknowledged a pleurisy* and fever, the alarm instantly spread in the family could not have been greater; Mr. Delvile, furiously ringing the bell, ordered a man and horse to go that moment to Dr. Lyster, the physician to the family, and not to return without him if he was himself alive; and Mrs. Delvile, not less distressed, though more quiet, fixed her eyes upon her son, with an expression of anxiety that shewed her whole happiness was bound in his recovery.

Delvile endeavoured to laugh away their fears, assuring them he should be well the next day, and representing in ridiculous terms the perplexity of Dr. Lyster to contrive some prescription for him.

Cecilia's behaviour, guided by prudence and modesty, was steady and composed; she believed his illness and his uneasiness were the same, and she hoped the resolution she had taken would bring relief to them both: while the terrors of Mr. and Mrs. Delvile seemed so greatly beyond the occasion, that her own were rather lessened than encreased by them.

Dr. Lyster soon arrived; he was a humane and excellent physician, and a man of sound judgment.

Delvile, gayly shaking hands with him, said "I believe, Dr. Lyster, you little expected to meet a patient, who, were he as skilful, would be as able to do business as yourself."

"What, with such a hand as this?" cried the Doctor; "come, come, you must not teach me my own profession. When I attend a patient, I come to tell how he is myself, not to be told."

"He is, then ill!" cried Mrs. Delvile; "oh Mortimer, why have you thus deceived us!"

"What is his disorder?" cried Mr. Delvile; "let us call in more help; who shall we send for, doctor?"

And again he rang the bell.

"What now?" said Dr. Lyster, coolly; "must a man be dying if he is not in perfect health? we want nobody else; I hope I can prescribe for a cold without demanding a consultation?"

"But are you sure it is merely a cold?" cried Mr. Delvile; "may not some dreadful malady——"

"Pray, Sir, have patience," interrupted the doctor; "Mr. Mortimer and I will have some discourse together presently; meantime, let us all sit down, and behave like Christians: I never talk of my art before company. 'Tis hard you won't let me be a gentleman at large for two minutes!"

Lady Honoria and Cecilia would then have risen, but neither Dr. Lyster nor Delvile would permit them to go; and a conversation tolerably lively took place, after which, the party in general separating, the doctor accompanied Delvile to his own apartment.

Cecilia then went up stairs, where she most impatiently waited some intelligence: none, however, arriving, in about half an hour she returned to the parlour; she found it empty, but was soon joined by Lady Honoria and Lord Ernolf.

Lady Honoria, happy in having something going forward, and not much concerning herself whether it were good or evil, was as eager to communicate what she had gathered, as Cecilia was to hear it.

"Well, my dear," she cried, "so I don't find at last but that all this prodigious illness will be laid to your account."

"To my account?" cried Cecilia, "how is that possible?"

"Why this tender chicken caught cold in the storm last week, and not being put to bed by its mama, and nursed with white-wine whey, the poor thing has got a fever."

"He is a fine young man," said Lord Ernolf; "I should be sorry any harm happened to him."

"He *was* a fine young man, my Lord," cried Lady Honoria, "but he is grown intolerably stupid lately; however, it's all the fault of his father and mother. Was ever any thing half so ridiculous as their behaviour this morning? it was with the utmost difficulty I forbore laughing in their faces: and really, I believe if I was to meet with such an unfortunate accident with Mr. Delvile, it would turn him to marble at once! indeed he is little better now, but such an affront as that would never let him move from the spot where he received it."

"I forgive him, however," returned Lord Ernolf, "for his anxiety about his son, since he is the last of so ancient a family."

"That is his great misfortune, my lord," answered Lady Honoria, "because it is the very reason they make such a puppet of him. If there were but a few more little masters to dandle and fondle, I'll answer for it this precious Mortimer would soon be left to himself: and then, really, I believe he would be a good tolerable sort of young man. Don't you think he would, Miss Beverley?"

"O yes!" said Cecilia, "I believe—I think so!"

"Nay, nay, I did not ask if you thought him tolerable *now*, so no need to be frightened."

Here they were interrupted by the entrance of Dr. Lyster.

"Well, Sir," cried Lady Honoria, "and when am I to go into mourning for my cousin Mortimer?"

"Why very soon," answered he, "unless you take better care of him. He has confessed to me that after being out in the storm last Wednesday, he sat in his wet cloaths all the evening."

"Dear," cried Lady Honoria, "and what would that do to him? I have no notion of a man's always wanting a cambric handkerchief about his throat."*

"Perhaps your ladyship had rather make him apply it to

his eyes?'' cried the doctor: "however, sitting inactive in wet cloaths would destroy a stouter man than Mr. Delvile; but he *forgot* it, he says! which of you two young ladies could not have given as good reason?"

"Your most obedient," said Lady Honoria; "and why should not a lady give as good a reason as a gentleman?"

"I don't know," answered he, drily, "but from want of practice, I believe."

"O worse and worse!" cried Lady Honoria; "you shall never be my physician; if I was to be attended by you, you'd make me sick instead of well."

"All the better," answered he, "for then I must have the honour of attending you till I made you well instead of sick." And with a good-humoured smile, he left them; and Lord Derford, at the same time, coming into the room, Cecilia contrived to stroll out into the park.

The account to which she had been listening redoubled her uneasiness; she was conscious that whatever was the indisposition of Delvile, and whether it was mental or bodily, she was herself its occasion: through her he had been negligent, she had rendered him forgetful, and in consulting her own fears in preference to his peace, she had avoided an explanation, though he had vigilantly sought one. *She knew not*, he told her *half the wretchedness of his heart.**—Alas! thought she, he little conjectures the state of mine!

Lady Honoria suffered her not to be long alone; in about half an hour she ran after her, gayly calling out, "O Miss Beverley, you have lost the delightfullest diversion in the world! I have just had the most ridiculous scene with my Lord Derford that you ever heard in your life! I asked him what put it in his head to be in love with you,—and he had the simplicity to answer, quite seriously, his father!"

"He was very right," said Cecilia, "if the desire of uniting two estates is to be denominated being in love; for that, most certainly, was put into his head by his father."

"O but you have not heard half. I told him, then, that, as a friend, in confidence I must acquaint him, I believed you intended to marry Mortimer—"

"Good heaven, Lady Honoria!"

"O, you shall hear the reason; because, as I assured him, it was proper he should immediately call him to account."*

"Are you mad, Lady Honoria?"

"For you know," said I, "Miss Beverley has had one duel fought for her already, and a lady who has once had that compliment paid her, always expects it from every new admirer; and I really believe your not observing that form is the true cause of her coldness to you."

"Is it possible you can have talked so wildly?"

"Yes, and what is much better, he believed every word I said!"

"Much better?—No, indeed, it is much worse! and if, in fact, he is so uncommonly weak, I shall really be but a little indebted to your ladyship for giving him such notions."

"O I would not but have done it for the world! for I never laughed so immoderately in my life. He began assuring me he was not afraid, for he said he had practised fencing more than any thing: so I made him promise to send a challenge to Mortimer as soon as he is well enough to come down again: for Dr. Lyster has ordered him to keep to his room."

Cecilia, smothering her concern for this last piece of intelligence by pretending to feel it merely for the former, expostulated with Lady Honoria upon so mischievous a frolic, and earnestly entreated her to go back and contradict it all.

"No, no, not for the world!" cried she; "he has not the least spirit, and I dare say he would not fight to save the whole nation from destruction; but I'll make him believe that it's necessary, in order to give him something to think of, for really his poor head is so vacant, that I am sure if one might but play upon it with sticks, it would sound just like a drum."

Cecilia, finding it vain to combat with her fantasies, was at length obliged to submit.

The rest of the day she passed very unpleasantly; Delvile appeared not; his father was restless and disturbed, and his mother, though attentive to her guests, and, for their sakes rallying her spirits, was visibly ill disposed to think or to talk but of her son.

One diversion, however, Cecilia found for herself; Delvile had a favourite spaniel, which, when he walked followed him, and when he rode, ran by his horse; this dog, who was not admitted into the house, she now took under her own care; and spent almost the whole day out of doors, chiefly for the satisfaction of making him her companion.

The next morning, when Dr. Lyster came again, she kept in the way, in order to hear his opinion; and was sitting with Lady Honoria in the parlour, when he entered it to write a prescription.

Mrs. Delvile, in a few moments, followed him, and with a face and voice of the tenderest maternal apprehensions, said "Doctor, one thing entrust me with immediately; I can neither bear imposition nor suspence;—you know what I would say!—tell me if I have any thing to fear, that my preparations may be adequate!"

"Nothing, I believe, in the world."

"You believe!" repeated Mrs. Delvile, starting; "Oh doctor!"

"Why you would not have me say I am *certain*, would you? these are no times for Popery and infallibility; however, I assure you I think him perfectly safe. He has done a foolish and idle trick, but no man is wise always. We must get rid of his fever, and then if his cold remains, with any cough, he may make a little excursion to Bristol."*

"To Bristol! nay then,—I understand you too well!"

"No, no, you don't understand me at all; I don't send him to Bristol because he is in a bad way, but merely because I mean to put him in a good one."

"Let him, then, go immediately; why should he encrease the danger by waiting a moment? I will order—"

"Hold, hold! I know what to order myself! 'Tis a strange thing people will always teach me my own duty! why should I make a man travel such weather as this in a fever? do you think I want to confine him in a mad-house, or be confined in one myself?"

"Certainly you know best—but still if there is any danger—"

"No, no, there is not! only we don't chuse there should

be any. And how will he entertain himself better than by going to Bristol? I send him merely on a jaunt of pleasure; and I am sure he will be safer there than shut up in a house with two such young ladies as these."

And then he made off. Mrs. Delvile, too anxious for conversation, left the room, and Cecilia, too conscious for silence, forced herself into discourse with Lady Honoria.

Three days she passed in this uncertainty what she had to expect; blaming those fears which had deferred an explanation, and tormented by Lady Honoria, whose raillery and levity now grew very unseasonable. Fidel, the favourite spaniel, was almost her only consolation, and she pleased herself not inconsiderably by making a friend of the faithful animal.*

CHAPTER VII

An Anecdote

ON the fourth day the house wore a better aspect; Delvile's fever was gone, and Dr. Lyster permitted him to leave his room: a cough, however, remained, and his journey to Bristol was settled to take place in three days. Cecilia, knowing he was now expected down stairs, hastened out of the parlour the moment she had finished her breakfast; for affected by his illness, and hurt at the approaching separation, she dreaded the first meeting, and wished to fortify her mind for bearing it with propriety.

In a very few minutes, Lady Honoria, running after her, entreated that she would come down; "for Mortimer," she cried, "is in the parlour, and the poor child is made so much of by its papa and mama, that I wish they don't half kill him by their ridiculous fondness. It is amazing to me he is so patient with them, for if they·teized me half as much, I should be ready to jump up and shake them. But I wish you would come down, for I assure you it's a comical scene."

"Your ladyship is soon diverted! but what is there so comical in the anxiety of parents for an only son?"

"Lord, they don't care a straw for him all the time! it's merely that he may live to keep up this old castle, which I hope in my heart he will pull down the moment they are dead! But do pray come; it will really give you spirits to see them all. The father keeps ringing the bell to order half a hundred pair of boots for him, and all the great coats in the county; and the mother sits and looks as if a hearse and mourning coach were already coming over the draw-bridge: but the most diverting object among them is my Lord Derford! O, it is really too entertaining to see him! there he sits, thinking the whole time of his challenge! I intend to employ him all this afternoon in practising to shoot at a mark."

And then again she pressed her to join the group, and Cecilia, fearing her opposition might seem strange, consented.

Delvile arose at her entrance, and, with tolerable steadiness she congratulated him on his recovery: and then, taking her usual seat, employed herself in embroidering a screen.* She joined too, occasionally, in the conversation, and observed, not without surprise, that Delvile seemed much less dejected than before his confinement.

Soon after, he ordered his horse, and, accompanied by Lord Derford, rode out. Mr. Delvile then took Lord Ernolf to shew him some intended improvements in another part of the castle, and Lady Honoria walked away in search of any entertainment she could find.

Mrs. Delvile, in better spirits than she had been for many days, sent for her own work, and sitting by Cecilia, conversed with her again as in former times; mixing instruction with entertainment, and general satire with particular kindness, in a manner at once so lively and so flattering, that Cecilia herself reviving, found but little difficulty in bearing her part in the conversation.

And thus, with some gaiety, and tolerable ease, was spent the greatest part of the morning; but just as they were talking of changing their dress for dinner, Lady Honoria with an air of the utmost exultation, came flying into the room. "Well, ma'am," she cried, "I have some news now

that I *must* tell you, because it will make you believe me
another time: though I know it will put you in a passion."

"That's sweetly designed, at least!" said Mrs. Delvile,
laughing; "however, I'll trust you, for my passions will not,
just now, be irritated by straws."

"Why, ma'am, don't you remember I told you when you
were in town that Mr. Mortimer kept a mistress—"

"Yes!" cried Mrs. Delvile, disdainfully, "and you may
remember, Lady Honoria, I told you——"

"O, you would not believe a word of it! but it's all true,
I assure you! and now he has brought her down here; he sent
for her about three weeks ago, and he has boarded her at a
cottage, about half a mile from the Park-gate."

Cecilia, to whom Henrietta Belfield was instantly present,
changed colour repeatedly, and turned so extremely sick,
she could with difficulty keep her seat. She forced herself,
however, to continue her work, though she knew so little
what she was about, that she put her needle in and out of
the same place without ceasing.

Mean-while Mrs. Delvile, with a countenance of the
utmost indignation, exclaimed "Lady Honoria, if you think
a tale of scandal such as this reflects no disgrace upon its
relater, you must pardon me for entreating you to find an
auditor more of the same opinion than myself."

"Nay, ma'am, since you are so angry, I'll tell you the
whole affair, for this is but half of it. He has a child here,
too,——I vow I long to see it!—and he is so fond of it that
he spends half his time in nursing it;—and that, I suppose,
is the thing that takes him out so much; and I fancy, too,
that's what has made him grow so grave, for may be he
thinks it would not be pretty to be very frisky, now he's a
papa."

Not only Cecilia, but Mrs. Delvile herself was now
overpowered, and she sat for some time wholly silent and
confounded; Lady Honoria then, turning to Cecilia
exclaimed, "Bless me, Miss Beverley, what are you about!
why that flower is the most ridiculous thing I ever saw! you
have spoilt your whole work."

Cecilia, in the utmost confusion, though pretending to

laugh, then began to unpick it; and Mrs. Delvile, recovering, more calmly, though not less angrily, said "And has this tale the honour of being invented solely by your ladyship, or had it any other assistant?"

"O no, I assure you, it's no invention of mine; I had it from very good authority upon my word. But only look at Miss Beverley! would not one think I had said that she had a child herself? She looks as pale as death. My dear, I am sure you can't be well?"

"I beg your pardon," cried Cecilia, forcing a smile, though extremely provoked with her; "I never was better."

And then, with the hope of appearing unconcerned, she raised her head; but meeting the eyes of Mrs. Delvile fixed upon her face with a look of penetrating observation, abashed and guilty, she again dropt it, and resumed her work.

"Well, my dear," said Lady Honoria, "I am sure there is no occasion to send for Dr. Lyster to *you*, for you recover yourself in a moment: you have the finest colour now I ever saw: has not she, Mrs. Delvile? did you ever see any body blush so becomingly?"

"I wish, Lady Honoria," said Mrs. Delvile, with severity, "it were possible to see *you* blush!"

"O but I never do! not but what it's pretty enough too; but I don't know how it is, it never happens. Now Euphrasia can blush from morning to night. I can't think how she contrives it. Miss Beverley, too, plays at it vastly well; she's red and white, and white and red half a dozen times in a minute. Especially," looking at her archly, and lowering her voice, "if you talk to her of Mortimer!"

"No, indeed! no such thing!" cried Cecilia with some resentment, and again looking up; but glancing her eyes towards Mrs. Delvile, and again meeting hers, filled with the strongest expression of enquiring solicitude, unable to sustain their inquisition, and shocked to find herself thus watchfully observed, she returned in hasty confusion to her employment.

"Well, my dear," cried Lady Honoria, again, "but what are you about now? do you intend to unpick the whole screen?"

"How can she tell what she is doing," said Mrs. Delvile, with quickness, "if you torment her thus incessantly? I will take you away from her, that she may have a little peace. You shall do me the honour to attend my toilette, and acquaint me with some further particulars of this extraordinary discovery."

Mrs. Delvile then left the room, but Lady Honoria, before she followed her, said in a low voice "Pity me, Miss Beverley, if you have the least good-nature! I am now going to hear a lecture of two hours long!"

Cecilia, left to herself, was in a perturbation almost insupportable: Delvile's mysterious conduct seemed the result of some entanglement of vice; Henrietta Belfield, the artless Henrietta Belfield, she feared had been abused, and her own ill-fated partiality, which now more than ever she wished unknown even to herself, was evidently betrayed where most the dignity of her mind made her desire it to be concealed!

In this state of shame, regret and resentment, which made her forget to change her dress, or her place, she was suddenly surprised by Delvile.

Starting and colouring, she busied herself with collecting her work, that she might hurry out of the room. Delvile, though silent himself, endeavoured to assist her; but when she would have gone, he attempted to stop her, saying "Miss Beverley, for three minutes only."

"No, Sir," cried she, indignantly, "not for an instant!" and leaving him utterly astonished, she hastened to her own apartment.

She was then sorry she had been so precipitate; nothing had been clearly proved against him; no authority was so likely to be fallacious as that of Lady Honoria; neither was he under any engagement to herself that could give her any right to manifest such displeasure. These reflections, however, came too late, and the quick feelings of her agitated mind were too rapid to wait the dictates of cool reason.

At dinner she attended wholly to Lord Ernolf, whose assiduous politeness, profitting by the humour, saved her the painful effort of forcing conversation, or the guilty consciousness of giving way to silence, and enabled her to preserve her general tenor between taciturnity and loquaciousness. Mrs. Delvile she did not once dare look at; but her son, she saw, seemed greatly hurt; yet it was proudly, not sorrowfully, and therefore she saw it with less uneasiness.

During the rest of the day, which was passed in general society, Mrs. Delvile, though much occupied, frequently leaving the room, and sending for Lady Honoria, was more soft, kind and gentle with Cecilia than ever, looking at her with the utmost tenderness, often taking her hand, and speaking to her with even unusual sweetness. Cecilia with mingled sadness and pleasure observed this encreasing regard, which she could not but attribute to the discovery made through Lady Honoria's mischievous intelligence, and which, while it rejoiced her with the belief of her approbation, added fresh force to her regret in considering it was fruitless. Delvile, mean-time, evidently offended himself, conversed only with the gentlemen, and went very early into his own room.

When they were all retiring, Mrs. Delvile, following Cecilia, dismissed her maid to talk with her alone.

"I am not, I hope, often," she cried, "solicitous or importunate to speak about my son: his character, I believe, wants no vindication; clear and unsullied, it has always been its own support: yet the aspersion cast upon it this morning by Lady Honoria, I think myself bound to explain, not partially as his mother, but simply as his friend."

Cecilia, who knew not whither such an explanation might lead, nor wherefore it was made, heard this opening with much emotion, but gave neither to that nor to what followed any interruption.

Mrs. Delvile then continued: she had taken the trouble, she said, to sift the whole affair, in order to shame Lady Honoria by a pointed conviction of what she had invented, and to trace from the foundation the circumstances whence her surmises or report had sprung.

Delvile, it seems, about a fortnight before the present

time, in one of his morning walks, had observed a gipsey*
sitting by the side of the high road, who seemed extremely
ill, and who had a very beautiful child tied to her back.

Struck with the baby, he stopt to enquire to whom it
belonged; to herself, she said, and begged his charity with
the most pitiable cries of distress; telling him that she was
travelling to join some of her fraternity, who were in a body
near Bath, but was so ill with an ague and fever that she
feared she should die on the road.

Delvile desired her to go to the next cottage, and promised
to pay for her board there till she was better. He then spoke
to the man and his wife who owned it to take them in, who,
glad to oblige his Honour, instantly consented, and he had
since called twice to see in what manner they went on.

"How simple, continued Mrs. Delvile, is a matter of fact
in itself, and how complex when embellished! This tale has
been told by the cottagers to our servants; it has travelled,
probably gaining something from every mouth, to Lady
Honoria's maid, and, having reached her ladyship, was
swelled in a moment into all we heard! I think, however,
that, for some time at least, her levity will be rather less
daring. I have not, in this affair, at all spared her; I made
her hear from Mortimer himself the little story as it
happened; I then carried her to the cottage, where we had
the whole matter confirmed; and I afterwards insisted upon
being told myself by her maid all she had related to her lady,
that she might thus be unanswerably convicted of inventing
whatever she omitted. I have occasioned her some confusion, and, for the moment, a little resentment; but she is
so volatile that neither will last; and though, with regard to
my own family, I may perhaps have rendered her more
cautious, I fear, with regard to the world in general, she is
utterly incorrigible, because it has neither pleasure nor
advantage to offer, that can compensate for the deprivation
of relating one staring* story, or ridiculous anecdote.

And then, wishing her good night, she added, "I make
not any apology for this detail, which you owe not, believe
me, to a mother's folly, but, if I know myself at all, to a love
of truth and justice. Mortimer, independent of all connection

with me, cannot but to every body appear of a character which may be deemed even exemplary; calumny, therefore, falling upon such a subject, injures not only himself but society, since it weakens all confidence in virtue, and strengthens the scepticism of depravity."

She then left her.

"Ah! thought Cecilia, to me, at least, this solicitude for his fame needs no apology! humane and generous Delvile! never, again, will I a moment doubt your worthiness!" And then, cherishing that darling idea, she forgot all her cares and apprehensions, her quarrel, her suspicions, and the approaching separation, and, recompensed for every thing by this refutation of his guilt, she hastened to bed, and composed herself to rest.

CHAPTER VIII

A Conference

EARLY the next morning Cecilia had a visit from Lady Honoria, who came to tell her story her own way, and laugh at the anxiety of Mrs. Delvile, and the trouble she had taken; "for, after all, continued she, what did the whole matter signify? and how could I possibly help the mistake? when I heard of his paying for a woman's board, what was so natural as to suppose she must be his mistress? especially as there was a child in the case. O how I wish you had been with us! you never saw such a ridiculous sight in your life; away we went in the chaise full drive* to the cottage, frightening all the people almost into fits; out came the poor woman, away ran the poor man,—both of them thought the end of the world at hand! The gipsey was best off, for she went to her old business, and began begging. I assure you, I believe she would be very pretty if she was not so ill, and so I dare say Mortimer thought too, or I fancy he would not have taken such care of her."

"Fie; fie, Lady Honoria! will nothing bring conviction to you?"

"Nay, you know, there's no harm in that, for why should not pretty people live as well as ugly ones? There's no occasion to leave nothing in the world but frights. I looked hard at the baby, to see if it was like Mortimer, but I could not make it out; those young things are like nothing. I tried if it would talk, for I wanted sadly to make it call Mrs. Delvile grandmama; however, the little urchin could say nothing to be understood. O what a rage would Mrs. Delvile have been in! I suppose this whole castle would hardly have been thought heavy enough to crush such an insolent brat, though it were to have fallen upon it all at a blow!"

Thus rattled this light-hearted lady till the family was assembled to breakfast; and then Cecilia, softened towards Delvile by newly-excited admiration, as well as by the absence which would separate them the following day, intended, by every little courteous office in her power, to make her peace with him before his departure: but she observed, with much chagrin, that Mrs. Delvile never ceased to watch her, which, added to an air of pride in the coldness of Delvile, that he had never before assumed, discouraged her from making the attempt, and compelled her to seem quiet and unconcerned.

As soon as breakfast was over, the gentlemen all rode or walked out; and when the ladies were by themselves, Lady Honoria suddenly exclaimed, "Mrs. Delvile, I can't imagine for what reason you send Mr. Mortimer to Bristol."

"For a reason, Lady Honoria, that with all your wildness, I should be very sorry you should know better by experience."

"Why then, ma'am, had we not better make a party, and all go? Miss Beverley, should you like to join it? I am afraid it would be vastly disagreeable to you."

Cecilia, now again was *red and white, and white and red a dozen times in a minute*;* and Mrs. Delvile, rising and taking her hand, expressively said, "Miss Beverley, you have a thousand times too much sensibility for this mad-cap of a companion. I believe I shall punish her by taking you away from her all this morning; will you come and sit with me in the dressing room?"

Cecilia assented without daring to look at her, and followed in trembling, up stairs. Something of importance, she fancied, would ensue, her secret she saw was revealed, and therefore she could form no conjecture but that Delvile would be the subject of the discourse: yet whether to explain his behaviour, or plead his cause, whether to express her separate approbation, or communicate some intelligence from himself, she had neither time, opportunity nor clue to unravel. All that was undoubted seemed the affection of Mrs. Delvile, all that, on her own part, could be resolved, was to suppress her partiality till she knew if it might properly be avowed.

Mrs. Delvile, who saw her perturbation, led immediately to subjects of indifference, and talked upon them so long, and with so much ease, that Cecilia, recovering her composure, began to think she had been mistaken, and that nothing was intended but a tranquil conversation.

As soon, however, as she had quieted her apprehensions, she sat silent herself, with a look that Cecilia easily construed into thoughtful perplexity in what manner she should introduce what she meant to communicate.

This pause was succeeded by her speaking of Lady Honoria; "how wild, how careless, how incorrigible she is! she lost her mother early; and the Duke, who idolizes her, and who, marrying very late, is already an old man, she rules entirely; with him, and a supple governess, who has neither courage to oppose her, nor heart to wish well but to her own interest, she has lived almost wholly. Lately, indeed, she has come more into the world, but without even a desire of improvement, and with no view and no thought but to gratify her idle humour by laughing at whatever goes forward."

"She certainly neither wants parts nor discernment," said Cecilia; "and, when my mind is not occupied by other matters, I find her conversation entertaining and agreeable."

"Yes," said Mrs. Delvile, "but that light sort of wit which attacks, with equal alacrity, what is serious or what is gay, is twenty times offensive, to once that it is exhilarating; since it shews that while its only aim is self-diversion, it has the most insolent negligence with respect to any pain it gives to others. The rank of Lady Honoria, though it has not rendered her proud, nor even made her conscious she has any dignity to support, has yet given her a saucy indifference whom she pleases or hurts, that borders upon what in a woman is of all things the most odious, a daring defiance of the world and its opinions.''

Cecilia, never less disposed to enter upon her defence, made but little answer; and, soon after, Mrs. Delvile added, ''I heartily wish she were properly established; and yet, according to the pernicious manners and maxims of the present age, she is perhaps more secure from misconduct while single, than she will be when married. Her father, I fear, will leave her too much to herself, and in that case I scarce know what may become of her; she has neither judgement nor principle to direct her choice, and therefore, in all probability, the same whim which one day will guide it, will the next lead her to repent it.''

Again they were both silent; and then Mrs. Delvile, gravely, yet with energy exclaimed, ''How few are there, how very few, who marry at once upon principles rational, and feelings pleasant! interest and inclination are eternally at strife, and where either is wholly sacrificed, the other is inadequate to happiness. Yet how rarely do they divide the attention! the young are rash, and the aged are mercenary; their deliberations are never in concert, their views are scarce ever blended; one vanquishes, and the other submits; neither party temporizes, and commonly each is unhappy.''

''The time,'' she continued, ''is now arrived when reflections of this sort cannot too seriously occupy me; the errors I have observed in others, I would fain avoid committing; yet such is the blindness of self-love, that perhaps, even at the moment I censure them, I am falling, without consciousness, into the same! nothing, however, shall through negligence be wrong; for where is the son who merits care and attention, if Mortimer from his parents deserves not to meet them?''

The expectations of Cecilia were now again awakened,

and awakened with fresh terrors lest Mrs. Delvile, from compassion, meant to offer her services; vigorously, therefore, she determined to exert herself, and rather give up Mortimer and all thoughts of him for-ever, than submit to receive assistance in persuading him to the union.

"Mr. Delvile," she continued, "is most earnest and impatient that some alliance should take place without further delay; and for myself, could I see him with propriety and with happiness disposed of, what a weight of anxiety would be removed from my heart!"

Cecilia now made an effort to speak, attempting to say "Certainly, it is a matter of great consequence;" but so low was her voice, and so confused her manner, that Mrs. Delvile, though attentively listening, heard not a word. She forbore, however, to make her repeat what she said, and went on herself as if speaking in answer.

"Not only his own, but the peace of his whole family will depend upon his election, since he is the last of his race. This castle and estate, and another in the north, were entailed upon him by the late Lord Delvile, his grandfather, who, disobliged by his eldest son, the present lord, left every thing he had power to dispose of to his second son, Mr. Delvile, and at his death, to his grandson, Mortimer. And even the present lord, though always at variance with his brother, is fond of his nephew, and has declared him his heir. I, also, have one sister, who is rich, who has no children, and who has made the same declaration. Yet though with such high expectations, he must not connect himself imprudently; for his paternal estate wants repair, and he is well entitled with a wife to expect what it requires."

Most true! thought Cecilia, yet ashamed of her recent failure, she applied herself to her work, and would not again try to speak.

"He is amiable, accomplished, well educated, and well born; far may we look, and not meet with his equal; no woman need disdain, and few women would refuse him."

Cecilia blushed her concurrence; yet could well at that moment have spared hearing the eulogy.

"Yet how difficult," she continued, "to find a proper

alliance! there are many who have some recommendations, but who is there wholly unexceptionable?''

This question seemed unanswerable; nor could Cecilia devise what it meant.

"Girls of high family have but seldom large fortunes, since the heads of their house commonly require their whole wealth for the support of their own dignity; while on the other hand, girls of large fortune are frequently ignorant, insolent, or low born; kept up by their friends lest they should fall a prey to adventurers, they have no acquaintance with the world, and little enlargement from education; their instructions are limited to a few merely youthful accomplishments; the first notion they imbibe is of their own importance, the first lesson they are taught is the value of riches, and even from their cradles, their little minds are narrowed, and their self-sufficiency is excited, by cautions to beware of fortune-hunters, and assurances that the whole world will be at their feet. Among such should we seek a companion for Mortimer? surely not. Formed for domestic happiness, and delighting in elegant society, his mind would disdain an alliance in which its affections had no share.''

Cecilia colouring and trembling, thought now the moment of her trial was approaching, and half mortified and half frightened prepared herself to sustain it with firmness.

"I venture, therefore, my dear Miss Beverley, to speak to you upon this subject as a friend who will have patience to hear my perplexities; you see upon what they hang,—where the birth is such as Mortimer Delvile may claim, the fortune generally fails; and where the fortune is adequate to his expectations, the birth yet more frequently would disgrace us.''

Cecilia, astonished by this speech, and quite off her guard from momentary surprize, involuntarily raised her head to look at Mrs. Delvile, in whose countenance she observed the most anxious concern, though her manner of speaking had seemed placid and composed.

"Once,'' she continued, without appearing to remark the emotion of her auditor, "Mr. Delvile thought of uniting him with his cousin Lady Honoria; but he never could endure the proposal; and who shall blame his repugnance? her sister, indeed, Lady Euphrasia, is much preferable, her education has been better, and her fortune is much more considerable. At present, however, Mortimer seems greatly averse to her, and who has a right to be difficult, if we deny it to him?''

Wonder, uncertainty, expectation and suspence now all attacked Cecilia, and all harrassed her with redoubled violence; why she was called to this conference she knew not; the approbation she had thought so certain, she doubted, and the proposal of assistance she had apprehended, she ceased to think would be offered: some fearful mystery, some cruel obscurity, still clouded all her prospects, and not merely obstructed her view of the future, but made what was immediately before her gloomy and indistinct.

The state of her mind seemed read by Mrs. Delvile, who examined her with eyes of such penetrating keenness, that they rather made discoveries than enquiries. She was silent some time, and looked irresolute, how to proceed; but at length, she arose, and taking Cecilia by the hand, who almost drew it back from her dread of what would follow, she said "I will torment you no more, my sweet young friend, with perplexities which you cannot relieve: this only I will say, and then drop the subject for ever: when my solicitude for Mortimer is removed, and he is established to the satisfaction of us all, no care will remain in the heart of his mother, half so fervent, so anxious and so sincere as the disposal of my amiable Cecilia, for whose welfare and happiness my wishes are even maternal."

She then kissed her glowing cheek, and perceiving her almost stupified with astonishment, spared her any effort to speak, by hastily leaving her in possession of her room.

Undeceived in her expectations and chilled in her hopes, the heart of Cecilia no longer struggled to sustain its dignity, or conceal its tenderness; the conflict was at an end, Mrs. Delvile had been open, though her son was mysterious; but, in removing her doubts, she had bereft her of her peace. She now found her own mistake in building upon her approbation; she saw nothing was less in her intentions, and that even when most ardent in affectionate regard, she separated her interest from that of her son as if their union was a matter of utter impossibility. "Yet why," cried Cecilia, "oh why is it deemed so! that she loves me, she is ever eager to proclaim, that my fortune would be peculiarly useful, she makes not a secret, and that I, at least, should start no insuperable objections, she has, alas! but too obviously discovered! Has she doubts of her son?—no, she has too much discernment; the father, then, the haughty, impracticable father, has destined him for some woman of rank, and will listen to no other alliance."

This notion somewhat soothed her in the disappointment she suffered; yet to know herself betrayed to Mrs. Delvile, and to see no other consequence ensue but that of exciting a tender compassion, which led her to discourage, from benevolence, hopes too high to be indulged, was a mortification so severe, that it caused her a deeper depression of spirits than any occurrence of her life had yet occasioned. "What Henrietta Belfield is to me," she cried, "I am to Mrs. Delvile! but what in her is amiable and artless, in me is disgraceful and unworthy. And this is the situation which so long I have desired! This is the change of habitation which I thought would make me so happy! oh who can chuse, who can judge for himself? who can point out the road to his own felicity, or decide upon the spot where his peace will be ensured!" Still, however, she had something to do, some spirit to exert, and some fortitude to manifest: Mortimer, she was certain, suspected not his own power; his mother, she knew, was both too good and too wise to reveal it to him, and she determined, by caution and firmness upon his leave-taking and departure, to retrieve, if possible, that credit with Mrs. Delvile, which she feared her betrayed susceptibility had weakened.

As soon, therefore, as she recovered from her consternation, she quitted Mrs. Delvile's apartment, and seeking Lady Honoria herself, determined not to spend even a moment alone, till Mortimer was gone; lest the sadness of her reflections should overpower her resolution, and give a melancholy to her air and manner which he might attribute, with but too much justice, to concern upon his own account.

CHAPTER IX

An Attack

AT dinner, with the assistance of Lord Ernolf, who was most happy to give it, Cecilia seemed tolerably easy. Lord Derford, too, encouraged by his father, endeavoured to engage some share of her attention; but he totally failed; her mind was superior to little arts of coquetry, and her pride had too much dignity to evaporate in pique; she determined, therefore, at this time, as at all others, to be consistent in shewing him he had no chance of her favour.

At tea, when they were again assembled, Mortimer's journey was the only subject of discourse, and it was agreed that he should set out very early in the morning, and, as the weather was extremely hot, not travel at all in the middle of the day.

Lady Honoria then, in a whisper to Cecilia, said, "I suppose, Miss Beverley, you will rise with the lark to-morrow morning? for your health, I mean. Early rising, you know, is vastly good for you."

Cecilia, affecting not to understand her, said she should rise, she supposed, at her usual time.

"I'll tell Mortimer, however," returned her ladyship, "to look up at your window before he goes off; for if he will play Romeo, you, I dare say, will play Juliet, and this old castle is quite the thing for the musty family of the Capulets: I dare say Shakespear thought of it when he wrote of them."

"Say to him what you please for yourself," cried Cecilia, "but let me entreat you to say nothing for me."

"And my Lord Derford, continued she, will make an excessive pretty Paris, for he is vastly in love, though he has got nothing to say; but what shall we do for a Mercutio? we may find 500 whining Romeos to one gay and charming Mercutio. Besides, Mrs. Delvile, to do her justice, is really too good for the old Nurse, though Mr. Delvile himself may serve for all the Capulets and all the Montagues at once, for he has pride enough for both their houses, and twenty more

besides. By the way, if I don't take care, I shall have this
Romeo run away before I have made my little dainty
country Paris pick a quarrel with him."*

She then walked up to one of the windows, and motioning
Lord Derford to follow her, Cecilia heard her say to him,
"Well, my lord, have you writ your letter? and have you
sent it? Miss Beverley, I assure you, will be charmed beyond
measure by such a piece of gallantry."

"No, ma'am," answered the simple young lord, "I have
not sent it yet, for I have only writ a foul copy."

"O my lord," cried she, "that is the very thing you ought
to send! a foul copy of a challenge is always better than a fair
one, for it looks written with more agitation. I am vastly glad
you mentioned that."

Cecilia then, rising and joining them, said, "What
mischief is Lady Honoria about now? we must all be upon
our guards, my lord, for she has a spirit of diversion that will
not spare us."

"Pray why do you interfere?" cried Lady Honoria, and
then, in a lower voice, she added, "what do you apprehend?
do you suppose Mortimer cannot manage such a poor little
ideot as this?"

"I don't suppose any thing about the matter!"

"Well, then, don't interrupt my operations. Lord
Derford, Miss Beverley has been whispering me, that if you
put this scheme in execution, she shall find you, ever after,
irresistible."

"Lord Derford, I hope," said Cecilia, laughing, "is too
well acquainted with your ladyship to be in any danger of
credulity."

"Vastly well!" cried she, "I see you are determined to
provoke me, so if you spoil my schemes, I will spoil yours,
and tell a certain gentleman your tender terrors for his
safety."

Cecilia now, extremely alarmed, most earnestly entreated
her to be quiet; but the discovery of her fright only excited
her ladyship's laughter, and, with a look the most
mischievously wicked, she called out "Pray Mr. Mortimer,
come hither!"

Mortimer instantly obeyed; and Cecilia at the same moment would with pleasure have endured almost any punishment to have been twenty miles off.

"I have something," continued her ladyship, "of the utmost consequence to communicate to you. We have been settling an admirable plan for you; will you promise to be guided by us if I tell it you?"

"O certainly!" cried he; "to doubt that would disgrace us all round."

"Well, then,—Miss Beverley, have you any objection to my proceeding?"

"None at all!" answered Cecilia, who had the understanding to know that the greatest excitement to ridicule is opposition.

"Well, then, I must tell you," she continued, "it is the advice of us all, that as soon as you come to the possession of your estate, you make some capital alterations in this antient castle."

Cecilia, greatly relieved, could with gratitude have embraced her: and Mortimer, very certain that such rattle was all her own, promised the utmost submission to her orders, and begged her further directions, declaring that he could not, at least, desire a fairer architect.

"What we mean," said she, "may be effected with the utmost ease; it is only to take out these old windows, and fix some thick iron grates in their place, and so turn the castle into a gaol for the county."

Mortimer laughed heartily at this proposition; but his father, unfortunately hearing it, sternly advanced, and with great austerity said, "If I thought my son capable of putting such an insult upon his ancestors, whatever may be the value I feel for him, I would banish him my presence for ever."

"Dear sir," cried Lady Honoria, "how would his ancestors ever know it?"

"How?—why—that is a very extraordinary question, Lady Honoria!"

"Besides, sir, I dare say the sheriff, or the mayor and corporation,* or some of those sort of people, would give him money enough, for the use of it, to run him up a mighty pretty neat little box somewhere near Richmond."*

"A box!" exclaimed he indignantly; "a neat little box for the heir of an estate such as this!"

"I only mean," cried she, giddily, "that he might have some place a little more pleasant to live in, for really that old moat and draw-bridge are enough to vapour him to death; I cannot for my life imagine any use they are of: unless, indeed, to frighten away the deer, for nothing else offers to come over. But, if you were to turn the house into a gaol—"

"A gaol?" cried Mr. Delvile, still more angrily, "your ladyship must pardon me if I entreat you not to mention that word again when you are pleased to speak of Delvile castle."

"Dear sir, why not?"

"Because it is a term that, in itself, from a young lady, has a sound peculiarly improper; and which, applied to any gentleman's antient family seat,—a thing, lady Honoria, always respectable, however lightly spoken of!—has an effect the least agreeable that can be devised: for it implies an idea either that the family, or the mansion, is going into decay."

"Well, sir, you know, with regard to the mansion, it is certainly very true, for all that other side, by the old tower, looks as if it would fall upon one's head every time one is forced to pass it."

"I protest, Lady Honoria," said Mr. Delvile, "that old tower, of which you are pleased to speak so slightingly, is the most honourable testimony to the antiquity of the castle of any now remaining, and I would not part with it for all the new boxes, as you style them, in the kingdom."

"I am sure I am very glad of it, sir, for I dare say nobody would give even one of them for it."

"Pardon me, Lady Honoria, you are greatly mistaken; they would give a thousand; such a thing, belonging to a man from his own ancestors, is invaluable."

"Why, dear sir, what in the world could they do with it? unless, indeed, they were to let some man paint it for an opera scene."

"A worthy use indeed!" cried Mr. Delvile, more and more affronted: "and pray does your ladyship talk thus to my Lord Duke?"

"O yes; and he never minds it at all."

"It were strange if he did!" cried Mrs. Delvile; "my only astonishment is that any body can be found who *does* mind it."

"Why now, Mrs. Delvile," she answered, "pray be sincere; can you possibly think this gothic ugly old place at all comparable to any of the new villas about town?"

"Gothic ugly old place!" repeated Mr. Delvile, in utter amazement at her dauntless flightiness; "your ladyship really does my humble dwelling too much honour!"

"Lord, I beg a thousand pardons!" cried she, "I really did not think of what I was saying. Come, dear Miss Beverley, and walk out with me, for I am too much shocked to stay a moment longer."

And then, taking Cecilia by the arm, she hurried her into the park, through a door which led thither from the parlour.

"For heaven's sake, Lady Honoria," said Cecilia, "could you find no better entertainment for Mr. Delvile than ridiculing his own house?"

"O," cried she, laughing, "did you never hear us quarrel before? why when I was here last summer, I used to affront him ten times a day."

"And was that a regular ceremony?"

"No, really, I did not do it purposely; but it so happened; either by talking of the castle, or the tower, or the draw-bridge, or the fortifications; or wishing they were all employed to fill up that odious moat; or something of that sort; for you know a small matter will put him out of humour."

"And do you call it so small a matter to wish a man's whole habitation annihilated?"

"Lord, I don't wish any thing about it! I only say so to provoke him."

"And what strange pleasure can that give you?"

"O the greatest in the world! I take much delight in seeing any body in a passion. It makes them look so excessively ugly!"

"And is that the way you like *every* body should look, Lady Honoria?"

"O my dear, if you mean *me*, I never was in a passion twice in my life: for as soon as ever I have provoked the people, I always run away. But sometimes I am in a dreadful fright lest they should see me laugh, for they make such horrid grimaces it is hardly possible to look at them. When my father has been angry with me, I have sometimes been obliged to pretend I was crying, by way of excuse for putting my handkerchief to my face: for really he looks so excessively hideous, you would suppose he was making mouths, like the children, merely to frighten one."

"Amazing!" exclaimed Cecilia, "your ladyship can, indeed, never want diversion, to find it in the anger of your father. But does it give you no other sensation? are you not afraid?"

"O never! what can he do to me, you know? he can only storm a little, and swear a little, for he always swears when he is angry; and perhaps order me to my own room; and ten to one but that happens to be the very thing I want; for we never quarrel but when we are alone, and then it's so dull, I am always wishing to run away."

"And can you take no other method of leaving him?"

"Why I think none so easily: and it can do him no harm, you know; I often tell him, when we make friends, that if it were not for a postilion and his daughter, he would be quite out of practice in scolding and swearing: for whenever he is upon the road he does nothing else: though why he is in such a hurry, nobody can divine, for go whither he will he has nothing to do."

Thus ran on this flighty lady, happy in high animal spirits, and careless who was otherwise, till, at some distance, they perceived Lord Derford, who was approaching to join them.

"Miss Beverley," cried she, "here comes your adorer: I shall therefore only walk on till we arrive at that large oak, and then make him prostrate himself at your feet, and leave you together."

"Your ladyship is extremely good! but I am glad to be apprized of your intention, as it will enable me to save you that trouble."

She then turned quick back, and passing Lord Derford, who still walked on towards Lady Honoria, she returned to the house; but, upon entering the parlour, found all the company dispersed, Delvile alone excepted, who was walking about the room, with his tablets* in his hand, in which he had been writing.

From a mixture of shame and surprize, Cecilia, at the sight of him, was involuntarily retreating; but, hastening to the door, he called out in a reproachful tone, "Will you not even enter the same room with me?"

"O yes," cried she, returning; "I was only afraid I disturbed you."

"No, madam," answered he, gravely; "you are the only person who could *not* disturb me, since my employment was making memorandums for a letter to yourself: with which, however, I did not desire to importune you, but that you have denied me the honour of even a five minutes audience."

Cecilia, in the utmost confusion at this attack, knew not whether to stand still or proceed; but, as he presently continued his speech, she found she had no choice but to stay.

"I should be sorry to quit this place, especially as the length of my absence is extremely uncertain, while I have the unhappiness to be under your displeasure, without making some little attempt to apologize for the behaviour which incurred it. Must I, then, finish my letter, or will you at last deign to hear me?"

"My displeasure, sir," said Cecilia "died with its occasion; I beg, therefore, that it may rest no longer in your remembrance."

"I meant not, madam, to infer,* that the subject or indeed that the object merited your deliberate attention; I simply wish to explain what may have appeared mysterious in my conduct, and for what may have seemed still more censurable, to beg your pardon."

Cecilia now, recovered from her first apprehensions, and calmed, because piqued, by the calmness with which he spoke himself, made no opposition to his request, but suffering him to shut both the door leading into the garden, and that which led into the hall, she seated herself at one of the windows, determined to listen with intrepidity to this long expected explanation.

The preparations, however, which he made to obviate being overheard, added to the steadiness with which Cecilia waited his further proceedings, soon robbed him of the courage with which he began the assault, and evidently gave him a wish of retreating himself.

At length, after much hesitation, he said "This indulgence, madam, deserves my most grateful acknowledgements; it is, indeed, what I had little right, and still less reason, after the severity I have met with from you, to expect."

And here, at the very mention of severity, his courage, called upon by his pride, instantly returned, and he went on with the same spirit he had begun.

"That severity, however, I mean not to lament; on the contrary, in a situation such as mine, it was perhaps the first blessing I could receive; I have found from it, indeed, more advantage and relief than from all that philosophy, reflection or fortitude could offer. It has shewn me the vanity of bewailing the barrier, placed by fate to my wishes, since it has shewn me that another, less inevitable, but equally insuperable, would have opposed them. I have determined, therefore, after a struggle I must confess the most painful, to deny myself the dangerous solace of your society, and endeavour, by joining dissipation to reason, to forget the too great pleasure which hitherto it has afforded me."

"Easy, Sir," cried Cecilia, "will be your task: I can only wish the re-establishment of your health may be found no more difficult."

"Ah, madam," cried he, with a reproachful smile, " *he jests at scars who never felt a wound!** —but this is a strain in which I have no right to talk, and I will neither offend your delicacy, nor my own integrity, by endeavouring to work upon the generosity of your disposition in order to excite your compassion. Not such was the motive with which I begged this audience; but merely a desire, before I tear myself away, to open to you my heart, without palliation or reserve."

He paused a few moments; and Cecilia finding her suspicions just that this interview was meant to be final, considered that her trial, however severe, would be short, and called forth all her resolution to sustain it with spirit.

"Long before I had the honour of your acquaintance," he continued, "your character and your accomplishments were known to me: Mr. Biddulph of Suffolk, who was my first friend at Oxford, and with whom my intimacy is still undiminished, was early sensible of your excellencies: we corresponded, and his letters were filled with your praises. He confessed to me, that his admiration had been unfortunate:—alas! I might now make the same confession to him!"

Mr. Biddulph, among many of the neighbouring gentlemen, had made proposals to the Dean for Cecilia, which, at her desire, were rejected.

"When Mr. Harrel saw masks* in Portman-square, my curiosity to behold a lady so adored, and so cruel, led me thither; your dress made you easily distinguished.—Ah Miss Beverley! I venture not to mention what I then felt for my friend! I will only say that something which I felt for myself, warned me instantly to avoid you, since the clause in your uncle's will was already well known to me."

Now, then, at last, thought Cecilia, all perplexity is over!—the change of name is the obstacle; he inherits all the pride of his family,—and therefore to that family will I unrepining leave him!

"This warning," he continued, "I should not have disregarded, had I not, at the Opera, been deceived into a belief you were engaged; I then wished no longer to shun you; bound in honour to forbear all efforts at supplanting a man, to whom I thought you almost united, I considered you already as married, and eagerly as I sought your society, I sought it not with more pleasure than innocence. Yet even then, to be candid, I found in myself a restlessness about your affairs that kept me in eternal perturbation: but I flattered myself it was mere curiosity, and only excited by the perpetual change of opinion to which occasion gave rise, concerning which was the happy man."

"I am sorry," said Cecilia, coolly, "there was any such mistake."

"I will not, madam, fatigue you," he returned, "by tracing the progress of my unfortunate admiration; I will endeavour to be more brief, for I see you are already wearied." He stopt a moment, hoping for some little encouragement; but Cecilia, in no humour to give it, assumed an air of unconcern, and sat wholly quiet.

"I knew not," he then went on, with a look of extreme mortification, "the warmth with which I honoured your virtues, till you deigned to plead to me for Mr. Belfield,—but let me not recollect the feelings of that moment!—yet were they nothing,—cold, languid, lifeless to what I afterwards experienced, when you undeceived me finally with respect to your situation, and informed me the report concerning Sir Robert Floyer was equally erroneous with that which concerned Belfield! O what was the agitation of my whole soul at that instant!—to know you disengaged,—to see you before me,—by the disorder of my whole frame to discover the mistake I had cherished—"

Cecilia then, half rising, yet again seating herself, looked extremely impatient to be gone.

"Pardon me, madam," he cried; "I will have done, and trace my feelings and my sufferings no longer, but hasten, for my own sake as well as yours, to the reason why I have spoken at all. From the hour that my ill-destined passion was fully known to myself, I weighed all the consequences of indulging it, and found, added to the extreme hazard of success, an impropriety even in the attempt. *My* honour in the honour of my family is bound; what to that would seem wrong, in me would be unjustifiable: yet where inducements so numerous were opposed by one single objection!—where virtue, beauty, education and family were all unexceptionable,—Oh cruel clause! barbarous and repulsive clause! that forbids my aspiring to the first of women, but by an action that with my own family would degrade me for ever!"

He stopt, overpowered by his own emotion, and Cecilia arose. "I see, madam," he cried, "your eagerness to be gone, and however at this moment I may lament it, I shall recollect it hereafter with advantage. But to conclude: I determined to avoid you, and, by avoiding, to endeavour to forget you: I determined, also, that no human being, and yourself least of all, should know, should even suspect the situation of my mind: and though upon various occasions, my prudence and forbearance have suddenly yielded to surprise and to passion, the surrender has been short, and almost, I believe, unnoticed.

"This silence and this avoidance I sustained with decent constancy, till during the storm, in an ill-fated moment, I saw, or thought I saw you in some danger, and then, all caution off guard, all resolution surprised, every passion awake, and tenderness triumphant——"

"Why, Sir," cried Cecilia, angrily, "and for what purpose all this?"

"Alas, I know not!" said he, with a deep sigh, "I thought myself better qualified for this conference, and meant to be firm and concise. I have told my story ill, but as your own understanding will point out the cause, your own benevolence will perhaps urge some excuse.

"Too certain, since that unfortunate accident, that all disguise was vain, and convinced by your displeasure of the impropriety of which I had been guilty, I determined, as the only apology I could offer, to open to you my whole heart, and then fly you perhaps for ever.

"This, madam, incoherently indeed, yet with sincerity, I have now done: my sufferings and my conflicts I do not mention, for I dare not! O were I to paint to you the bitter struggles of a mind all at war with itself,—Duty, spirit, and fortitude, combating love, happiness and inclination,—each conquering alternately, and alternately each vanquished,—I could endure it no longer, I resolved by one effort to finish the strife, and to undergo an instant of even exquisite torture, in preference to a continuance of such lingering misery!"

"The restoration of your health, Sir, and since you fancy it has been injured, of your happiness," said Cecilia, "will, I hope, be as speedy, as I doubt not they are certain."

"*Since I fancy it has been injured*!" repeated he; "what a phrase, after an avowal such as mine! But why should I wish to convince you of my sincerity, when to you it cannot be more indifferent, than to myself it is unfortunate! I have now only to entreat your pardon for the robbery I have committed upon your time, and to repeat my acknowledgments that you have endeavoured to hear me with patience."

"If you honour me, Sir, with some portion of your esteem," said the offended Cecilia, "these acknowledgements, perhaps, should be mine; suppose them, however made, for I have a letter to write, and can therefore stay no longer."

"Nor do I presume, madam," cried he proudly, "to detain you: hitherto you may frequently have thought me mysterious, sometimes strange and capricious, and perhaps almost always, unmeaning; to clear myself from these imputations, by a candid confession of the motives which have governed me, is all that I wished. Once, also—I hope but once,—you thought me impertinent,—there, indeed, I less dare vindicate myself—"

"There is no occasion, Sir," interrupted she, walking towards the door, "for further vindication in any thing; I am perfectly satisfied, and if my good wishes are worth your acceptance, assure yourself you possess them."

"Barbarous, and insulting!" cried he, half to himself; and then, with a quick motion hastening to open the door for her, "Go, madam," he added, almost breathless with conflicting emotions, "go, and be your happiness unalterable as your inflexibility!"

Cecilia was turning back to answer this reproach, but the sight of Lady Honoria, who was entering at the other door, deterred her, and she went on.

When she came to her own room, she walked about it some time in a state so unsettled, between anger and disappointment, sorrow and pride, that she scarce knew to which emotion to give way, and felt almost bursting with each.

"The dye, she cried, is at last thrown; and this affair is concluded for ever! Delvile himself is content to relinquish

me; no father has commanded, no mother has interfered, he
has required no admonition, full well enabled to act for
himself by the powerful instigation of hereditary arrogance!
Yet my family, he says,—unexpected condescension! my
family and every other circumstance is unexceptionable;
how feeble, then, is that regard which yields to one only
objection! how potent that haughtiness which to nothing will
give way! Well, let him keep his name! since so wonderous
its properties, so all-sufficient its preservation, what vanity,
what presumption in me, to suppose myself an equivalent
for its loss!''

Thus, deeply offended, her spirits were supported by
resentment, and not only while in company, but when
alone, she found herself scarce averse to the approaching
separation, and enabled to endure it without repining.

CHAPTER X

A Retreat

THE next morning Cecilia arose late, not only to avoid the
raillery of Lady Honoria, but to escape seeing the departure
of Delvile; she knew that the spirit with which she had left
him, made him, at present, think her wholly insensible, and
she was at least happy to be spared the mortification of a
discovery, since she found him thus content, without even
solicitation, to resign her.

Before she was dressed, Lady Honoria ran into her room,
''A new scheme of politics!'' she cried; ''our great statesman
intends to leave us: he can't trust his baby out of his sight,
so he is going to nurse him while upon the road himself.
Poor pretty dear Mortimer! what a puppet do they make of
him! I have a vast inclination to get a pap-boat* myself, and
make him a present of it.''

Cecilia then enquired further particulars, and heard that
Mr. Delvile purposed accompanying his son to Bristol,
whose journey, therefore, was postponed for a few hours to
give time for new preparations.

Mr. Delvile, who, upon this occasion, thought himself overwhelmed with business, because, before his departure, he had some directions to give to his domestics, chose to breakfast in his own apartment: Mrs. Delvile, also, wishing for some private conversation with her son, invited him to partake of her's in her dressing-room, sending an apology to her guests, and begging they would order their breakfasts when they pleased.

Mr. Delvile, scrupulous in ceremony, had made sundry apologies to Lord Ernolf for leaving him; but his real anxiety for his son overpowering his artificial character, the excuses he gave to that nobleman were such as could not possibly offend; and the views of his lordship himself in his visit, being nothing interrupted, so long as Cecilia continued at the castle, he readily engaged, as a proof that he was not affronted, to remain with Mrs. Delvile till his return.

Cecilia, therefore, had her breakfast with the two lords and Lady Honoria; and when it was over, Lord Ernolf proposed to his son riding the first stage* with the two Mr. Delviles on horseback. This was agreed upon, and they left the room: and then Lady Honoria, full of frolic and gaiety, seized one of the napkins, and protested she would send it to Mortimer for a *slabbering-bib*: she therefore made it up in a parcel, and wrote upon the inside of the paper with which she envelloped it, "A *pin-a-fore* for Master Mortimer Delvile, lest he should daub his pappy when he is feeding him." Eager to have this properly conveyed, she then ran out, to give it in charge to her own man, who was to present him with it as he got into the chaise.

She had but just quitted the room, when the door of it was again opened, and by Mortimer himself, booted, and equipped for his journey.

"Miss Beverley here! and alone!" cried he, with a look, and in a voice, which shewed that all the pride of the preceding evening was sunk into the deepest dejection; "and does she not fly as I approach her? can she patiently bear in her sight one so strange, so fiery, so inconsistent? But she is too wise to resent the ravings of a madman;—and who, under the influence of a passion at once hopeless and violent, can boast, but at intervals, full possession of his reason!"

Cecilia, utterly astonished by a gentleness so humble, looked at him in silent surprise; he advanced to her mournfully, and added, "I am ashamed, indeed, of the bitterness of spirit with which I last night provoked your displeasure, when I should have supplicated your lenity: but though I was prepared for your coldness, I could not endure it, and though your indifference was almost friendly, it made me little less than frantic; so strangely may justice be blinded by passion, and every faculty of reason be warped by selfishness!"

"You have no apology to make, Sir," cried Cecilia, "since, believe me, I require none."

"You may well," returned he, half-smiling, "dispense with my apologies, since under the sanction of that word, I obtained your hearing yesterday. But, believe me, you will now find me far more reasonable; a whole night's reflections——reflections which no repose interrupted!—have brought me to my senses. Even lunatics, you know, have lucid moments!"

"Do you intend, Sir, to set off soon?"

"I believe so; I wait only for my father. But why is Miss Beverley so impatient? I shall not soon *return*; that, at least, is certain, and, for a few instants delay, may surely offer some palliation;——See! if I am not ready to again accuse you of severity!—I must run, I find, or all my boasted reformation will end but in fresh offence, fresh disgrace, and fresh contrition! Adieu, madam!—and may all prosperity attend you! That will be ever my darling wish, however long my absence, however distant the climates* which may part us!" He was then hurrying away, but Cecilia, from an impulse of surprise too sudden to be restrained, exclaimed, "The climates?—do you, then, mean to leave England?"

"Yes," cried he, with quickness, "for why should I remain in it? a few weeks only could I fill up in any tour so near home, and hither in a few weeks to return would be folly and madness: in an absence so brief, what thought but that of the approaching meeting would occupy me? and what, at that meeting, should I feel, but joy the most dangerous, and delight which I dare not think of!—every conflict renewed, every struggle re-felt, again all this scene would require to be acted, again I must tear myself away, and every tumultuous passion now beating in my heart would be revived, and, if possible, be revived with added misery!—No!—neither my temper nor my constitution will endure such another shock, one parting shall suffice, and the fortitude with which I will lengthen my self-exile, shall atone to myself for the weakness which makes it requisite!''

And then, with a vehemence that seemed fearful of the smallest delay, he was again, and yet more hastily going, when Cecilia, with much emotion, called out, ''Two moments, Sir!''

''Two thousand! two million!'' cried he, impetuously, and returning, with a look of the most earnest surprise, he added, ''What is it Miss Beverley will condescend to command?''

''Nothing,'' cried she, recovering her presence of mind, ''but to beg you will by no means, upon my account, quit your country and your friends, since another asylum can be found for myself, and since I would much sooner part from Mrs. Delvile, greatly and sincerely as I reverence her, than be instrumental to robbing her, even for a month, of her son.''

''Generous and humane is the consideration,'' cried he; ''but who half so generous, so humane as Miss Beverley? so soft to all others, so noble in herself? Can my mother have a wish, when I leave her with you? No; she is sensible of your worth, she adores you, almost as I adore you myself! you are now under her protection, you seem, indeed, born for each other; let me not, then, deprive her of so honourable a charge:——Oh, why must he, who sees in such colours the excellencies of both, who admires with such fervour the perfections you unite, be torn with this violence from the objects he reveres, even though half his life he would sacrifice, to spend in their society what remained!''——

''Well, then, Sir,'' said Cecilia, who now felt her courage decline, and the softness of sorrow steal fast upon her spirits, ''if you will not give up your scheme, let me no longer detain you.''

''Will you not wish me a good journey?''

"Yes,—very sincerely."

"And will you pardon the unguarded errors which have offended you?"

"I will think of them, Sir, no more."

"Farewell, then, most amiable of women, and may every blessing you deserve light on your head! I leave to you my mother, certain of your sympathetic affection for a character so resembling your own. When *you*, madam, leave her, may the happy successor in your favour—" He paused, his voice faultered, Cecilia, too, turned away from him, and, uttering a deep sigh, he caught her hand, and pressing it to his lips, exclaimed, "O great be your felicity, in whatever way you receive it!—pure as your virtues, and warm as your benevolence!—Oh too lovely Miss Beverley!—why, why must I quit you!"

Cecilia, though she trusted not her voice to reprove him, forced away her hand, and then, in the utmost perturbation, he rushed out of the room.

This scene for Cecilia, was the most unfortunate that could have happened; the gentleness of Delvile was alone sufficient to melt her, since her pride had no subsistence when not fed by his own; and while his mildness had blunted her displeasure, his anguish had penetrated her heart. Lost in thought and in sadness, she continued fixed to her seat; and looking at the door through which he had passed, as if, with himself, he had shut out all for which she existed.

This pensive dejection was not long uninterrupted; Lady Honoria came running back, with intelligence, in what manner she had disposed of her napkin, and Cecilia in listening, endeavoured to find some diversion; but her ladyship, though volatile not undiscerning, soon perceived that her attention was constrained, and looking at her with much archness, said "I believe, my dear, I must find another napkin for *you!* not, however, for your *mouth*, but for your *eyes!* Has Mortimer been in to take leave of you?"

"Take leave of me?——No,—is he gone?"

"O no, Pappy has a world of business to settle first; he won't be ready these two hours. But don't look so sorrowful, for I'll run and bring Mortimer to console you."

Away she flew, and Cecilia, who had no power to prevent her, finding her spirits unequal either to another parting, or to the raillery of Lady Honoria, should Mortimer, for his own sake, avoid it, took refuge in flight, and seizing an umbrella, escaped into the Park; where, to perplex any pursuers, instead of chusing her usual walk, she directed her steps to a thick and unfrequented wood, and never rested till she was more than two miles from the house. Fidel, however, who now always accompanied her, ran by her side, and, when she thought herself sufficiently distant and private to be safe, she sat down under a tree, and caressing her faithful favourite, soothed her own tenderness by lamenting that *he* had lost his master; and, having now no part to act, and no dignity to support, no observation to fear, and no inference to guard against, she gave vent to her long smothered emotions, by weeping without caution or restraint.

She had met with an object whose character answered all her wishes for him with whom she should entrust her fortune, and whose turn of mind, so similar to her own, promised her the highest domestic felicity: to this object her affections had involuntarily bent, they were seconded by esteem, and unchecked by any suspicion of impropriety in her choice: she had found too, in return, that his heart was all her own: her birth, indeed, was inferior, but it was not disgraceful; her disposition, education and temper seemed equal to his fondest wishes: yet, at the very time when their union appeared most likely, when they mixed with the same society, and dwelt under the same roof, when the father to one, was the guardian to the other, and interest seemed to invite their alliance even more than affection, the young man himself, without counsel or command, could tear himself from her presence by an effort all his own, forbear to seek her heart, and almost charge her not to grant it, and determining upon voluntary exile, quit his country and his connections with no view, and for no reason, but merely that he might avoid the sight of her he loved!

Though the motive for this conduct was now no longer unknown to her, she neither thought it satisfactory nor necessary; yet, while she censured his flight, she bewailed his loss, and though his inducement was repugnant to her opinion, his command over his passions she admired and applauded.

CHAPTER XI

A Worry

CECILIA continued in this private spot, happy at least to be alone, till she was summoned by the dinner bell to return home.

As soon as she entered the parlour, where every body was assembled before her, she observed, by the countenance of Mrs. Delvile, that she had passed the morning as sadly as herself.

"Miss Beverley," cried Lady Honoria, before she was seated, "I insist upon your taking my place to-day."

"Why so, madam?"

"Because I cannot suffer you to sit by a window with such a terrible cold."

"Your ladyship is very good, but indeed I have not any cold at all."

"O my dear, I must beg your pardon there; your eyes are quite blood-shot; Mrs. Delvile, Lord Ernolf, are not her eyes quite red?—Lord, and so I protest are her cheeks! now do pray look in the glass, I assure you you will hardly know yourself."

Mrs. Delvile, who regarded her with the utmost kindness, affected to understand Lady Honoria's speech literally, both to lessen her apparent confusion, and the suspicious surmises of Lord Ernolf; she therefore said, "you have indeed a bad cold, my love; but shade your eyes with your hat, and after dinner you shall bathe them in rose water,* which will soon take off the inflammation."

Cecilia, perceiving her intention, for which she felt the utmost gratitude, no longer denied her cold, nor refused the offer of Lady Honoria: who, delighting in mischief, whencesoever it proceeded, presently added, "This cold is a judgment upon you for leaving me alone all this morning; but I suppose you chose a tête à tête with your favourite, without the intrusion of any third person."

Here every body stared, and Cecilia very seriously declared she had been quite alone.

"Is it possible you can so forget yourself?" cried Lady Honoria; "had you not your dearly beloved with you?"

Cecilia, who now comprehended that she meant Fidel, coloured more deeply then ever, but attempted to laugh, and began eating her dinner.

"Here seems some matter of much intricacy," cried Lord Ernolf, "but, to me, wholly unintelligible."

"And to me also," cried Mrs. Delvile, "but I am content to let it remain so; for the mysteries of Lady Honoria are so frequent, that they deaden curiosity."

"Dear madam, that is very unnatural," cried Lady Honoria, "for I am sure you must long to know who I mean."

"*I* do, at least," said Lord Ernolf.

"Why then, my lord, you must know, Miss Beverley has two companions, and I am one, and Fidel is the other; but Fidel was with her all this morning, and she would not admit me to the conference. I suppose she had something private to say to him of his master's journey."

"What rattle is this?" cried Mrs. Delvile; "Fidel is gone with my son, is he not?" turning to the servants.

"No, madam, Mr. Mortimer did not enquire for him."

"That's very strange," said she, "I never knew him quit home without him before."

"Dear ma'am, if he had taken him," cried Lady Honoria, "what could poor Miss Beverley have done? for she has no friend here but him and me, and really he's so much the greater favourite, that it is well if I do not poison him some day for very spite."

Cecilia had no resource but in forcing a laugh, and Mrs. Delvile, who evidently felt for her, contrived soon to change the subject: yet not before Lord Ernolf, with infinite chargrin, was certain by all that passed of the hopeless* state of affairs for his son.

The rest of the day, and every hour of the two days following, Cecilia passed in the most comfortless constraint, fearful of being a moment alone, lest the heaviness of her heart should seek relief in tears, which consolation, melancholy as it was, she found too dangerous for indulgence: yet the gaiety of Lady Honoria lost all power of entertainment, and even the kindness of Mrs. Delvile, now she imputed it to compassion, gave her more mortification than pleasure.

On the third day, letters arrived from Bristol: but they brought with them nothing of comfort, for though Mortimer wrote gaily, his father sent word that his fever seemed threatening to return.

Mrs. Delvile was now in the extremest anxiety; and the task of Cecilia in appearing chearful and unconcerned, became more and more difficult to perform. Lord Ernolf's efforts to oblige her grew as hopeless to himself, as they were irksome to her; and Lady Honoria alone, of the whole house, could either find or make the smallest diversion. But while Lord Derford remained, she had still an object for ridicule, and while Cecilia could colour and be confused, she had still a subject for mischief.

Thus passed a week, during which the news from Bristol being every day less and less pleasant, Mrs. Delvile shewed an earnest desire to make a journey thither herself, and proposed, half laughing and half seriously, that the whole party should accompany her.

Lady Honoria's time, however, was already expired, and her father intended to send for her in a few days.

Mrs. Delvile, who knew that such a charge would occupy all her time, willingly deferred setting out till her ladyship should be gone, but wrote word to Bristol that she should shortly be there, attended by the two lords, who insisted upon escorting her.

Cecilia now was in a state of the utmost distress; her stay at the castle she knew kept Delvile at a distance; to accompany his mother to Bristol, was forcing herself into his sight, which equally from prudence and pride she wished to avoid; and even Mrs. Delvile evidently desired her absence, since whenever the journey was talked of, she preferably addressed herself to any one else who was present.

All she could devise to relieve herself from a situation so painful, was begging permission to make a visit without delay to her old friend Mrs. Charlton in Suffolk.

This resolution taken, she put it into immediate execution, and seeking Mrs. Delvile, enquired if she might venture to make a petition to her?

"Undoubtedly," answered she; "but let it not be very disagreeable, since I feel already that I can refuse you nothing."

"I have an old friend, ma'am," she then cried, speaking fast, and in much haste to have done, "who I have not for many months seen, and, as *my* health does not require a Bristol journey,—if you would honour me with mentioning my request to Mr. Delvile, I think I might take the present opportunity of making Mrs. Charlton a visit."

Mrs. Delvile looked at her some time without speaking, and then, fervently embracing her, "sweet Cecilia!" she cried, "yes, you are all that I thought you! good, wise, discreet, tender, and noble at once!—how to part with you, indeed, I know not,—but you shall do as you please, for that I am sure will be right, and therefore I will make no opposition."

Cecilia blushed and thanked her, yet saw but too plainly that all the motives of her scheme were clearly comprehended. She hastened, therefore, to write to Mrs. Charlton, and prepare* for her reception.

Mr. Delvile, though with his usual formality, sent his permission: and Mortimer at the same time, begged his mother would bring with her Fidel,* whom he had unluckily forgotten.

Lady Honoria, who was present when Mrs. Delvile mentioned this commission, said in a whisper to Cecilia, "Miss Beverley, don't let him go."

"Why not?"

"O, you had a great deal better take him slyly into Suffolk."

"I would as soon," answered Cecilia, "take with me the

·side-board of plate,* for I should scarcely think it more a robbery.''

"O, I beg your pardon, I am sure they might all take such a theft for an honour; and if I was going to Bristol, I would bid Mortimer send him to you immediately. However, if you wish it, I will write to him. He's my cousin, you know, so there will be no great impropriety in it.''

Cecilia thanked her for so courteous an offer, but entreated that she might by no means draw her into such a condescension.

She then made immediate preparations for her journey into Suffolk, which she saw gave equal surprize and chagrin to Lord Ernolf, upon whose affairs Mrs. Delvile herself now desired to speak with her.

"Tell me, Miss Beverley," she cried, "briefly and positively your opinion of Lord Derford?''

"I think of him so little, madam," she answered, "that I cannot say of him much; he appears, however, to be inoffensive; but, indeed, were I never to see him again, he is one of those I should forget I had ever seen at all.''

"That is so exactly the case with myself also," cried Mrs. Delvile, "that to plead for him, I find utterly impossible, though my Lord Ernolf has strongly requested me: but to press such an alliance, I should think an indignity to your understanding.''

Cecilia was much gratified by this speech; but she soon after added, "There is one reason, indeed, which would render such a connection desirable, though that is only one.''

"What is it, madam?''

"His title.''

"And why so? I am sure I have no ambition of that sort.''

"No, my love," said Mrs. Delvile, smiling, "I mean not by way of gratification to *your* pride, but to *his*; since a title, by taking place of a family name, would obviate the *only* objection that *any* man could form to an alliance with Miss Beverley.''*

Cecilia, who too well understood her, suppressed a sigh, and changed the subject of conversation.

One day was sufficient for all the preparations she required, and, as she meant to set out very early the next morning, she took leave of Lady Honoria, and the Lords Ernolf and Derford, when they separated for the night; but Mrs. Delvile followed her to her room.

She expressed her concern at losing her in the warmest and most flattering terms, yet said nothing of her coming back, nor of the length of her stay; she desired, however, to hear from her frequently, and assured her that out of her own immediate family, there was nobody in the world she so tenderly valued.

She continued with her till it grew so late that they were almost necessarily parted: and then rising, to be gone, "See," she cried, "with what reluctance I quit you! no interest but so dear a one as that which calls me away, should induce me, with my own consent, to bear your absence scarcely an hour: but the world is full of mortifications, and to endure, or to sink under them, makes all the distinction between the noble or the weak-minded. To *you* this may be said with safety; to most young women it would pass for a reflection."

"You are very good," said Cecilia, smothering the emotions to which this speech gave rise, "and if indeed you honour me with an opinion so flattering, I will endeavour, if it is possibly in my power, not to forfeit it."

"Ah, my love!" cried Mrs. Delvile warmly, "if upon my opinion of *you* alone depended our residence with each other, when should we ever part, and how live a moment asunder? But what title have I to monopolize two such blessings? the mother of Mortimer Delvile should at nothing repine; the mother of Cecilia Beverley had alone equal reason to be proud."

"You are determined, madam," said Cecilia, forcing a smile, "that I *shall* be worthy, by giving me the sweetest of motives, that of deserving such praise." And then, in a faint voice, she desired her respects to Mr. Delvile, and added, "you will find, I hope, every body at Bristol better than you expect."

"I hope so," returned she; "and that you too, will find

your Mrs. Charlton well, happy, and good as you left her: but suffer her not to drive *me* from your remembrance, and never fancy that because she has known you longer, she loves you more; my acquaintance with you, though short, has been critical, and she must hear from you a world of anecdotes, before she can have reason to love you as much.''

"Ah, madam," cried Cecilia, tears starting into her eyes, "let us part now!——where will be that strength of mind you expect from me, if I listen to you any longer!"

"You are right, my love," answered Mrs. Delvile, "since all tenderness enfeebles fortitude." Then affectionately embracing her, "Adieu," she cried, "sweetest Cecilia, amiable and most excellent creature, adieu!—you carry with you my highest approbation, my love, my esteem, my fondest wishes!—and shall I—yes, generous girl! I *will* add my warmest gratitude!"

This last word she spoke almost in a whisper, again kissed her, and hastened out of the room.

Cecilia, surprised and affected, gratified and depressed, remained almost motionless, and could not, for a great length of time, either ring for her maid, or persuade herself to go to rest. She saw throughout the whole behaviour of Mrs. Delvile, a warmth of regard which, though strongly opposed by family pride, made her almost miserable to promote the very union she thought necessary to discountenance; she saw, too, that it was with the utmost difficulty she preserved the steadiness of her opposition, and that she had a conflict perpetual with herself, to forbear openly acknowledging the contrariety of her wishes, and the perplexity of her distress; but chiefly she was struck with her expressive use of the word gratitude. "Wherefore should she be grateful," thought Cecilia, "what have I done, or had power to do? infinitely, indeed, is she deceived, if she supposes that her son has acted by my directions; my influence with him is nothing, and he could not be more his own master, were he utterly indifferent to me. To conceal my own disappointment has been all I have attempted; and perhaps she may think of me thus highly, from supposing that the firmness of her son is owing to my caution and reserve: ah, she knows him not!——were my heart at this moment laid open to him,—were all its weakness, its partiality, its ill-fated admiration displayed, he would but double his vigilance to avoid and forget me, and find the task all the easier by his abatement of esteem. Oh strange infatuation of unconquerable prejudice! his very life will he sacrifice in preference to his name, and while the conflict of his mind threatens to level him with the dust, he disdains to unite himself where one wish is unsatisfied!''

These reflections, and the uncertainty if she should ever in Delvile castle sleep again, disturbed her the whole night, and made all calling in the morning unnecessary: She arose at five o'clock, dressed herself with the utmost heaviness of heart, and in going through a long gallery which led to the stair-case, as she passed the door of Mortimer's chamber, the thought of his ill health, his intended long journey, and the probability that she might never see him more, so deeply impressed and saddened her, that scarcely could she force herself to proceed, without stopping to weep and to pray for him; she was surrounded, however, by servants, and compelled therefore to hasten to the chaise; she flung herself in, and, leaning back, drew her hat over her eyes, and thought, as the carriage drove off, her last hope of earthly happiness extinguished.

END OF THE THIRD VOLUME.

VOLUME IV

BOOK VII

CHAPTER I

A Renovation

CECILIA was accompanied by her maid in the chaise, and her own servant and one of Mrs. Delvile's attended her on horseback.

The quietness of her dejection was soon interrupted by a loud cry among the men of "home! home! home!" She then looked out of one of the windows, and perceived Fidel, running after the carriage, and barking at the servants, who were all endeavouring to send him back.

Touched by this proof of the animal's gratitude for her attention to him, and conscious she had herself occasioned his master's leaving him, the scheme of Lady Honoria occurred to her, and she almost wished to put it in execution, but this was the thought of a moment, and motioning him with her hand to go back, she desired Mrs. Delvile's man to return with him immediately, and commit him to the care of somebody in the castle.

This little incident, however trifling, was the most important of her journey, for she arrived at the house of Mrs. Charlton without meeting any other.

The sight of that lady gave her a sensation of pleasure to which she had long been a stranger, pleasure pure, unmixed, unaffected and unrestrained: it revived all her early affection, and with it, something resembling at least her early tranquility: again she was in the house where it had once been undisturbed, again she enjoyed the society which was once all she had wished, and again saw the same scene, the same faces, and same prospects she had beheld while her heart was all devoted to her friends.

Mrs. Charlton, though old and infirm, preserved an understanding, which, whenever unbiassed by her affections, was sure to direct her unerringly; but the extreme softness of her temper frequently misled her judgment, by making it, at the pleasure either of misfortune or of artifice, always yield to compassion, and pliant to entreaty. Where her counsel and opinion were demanded, they were certain to reflect honour on her capacity and discernment; but where her assistance or her pity were supplicated, her purse and her tears were immediately bestowed, and in her zeal to alleviate distress she forgot if the object were deserving her solicitude, and stopt not to consider propriety or discretion, if happiness, however momentary, were in her power to grant.

This generous foible was, however, kept somewhat in subjection by the watchfulness of two grand-daughters, who, fearing the injury they might themselves receive from it, failed not to point out both its inconvenience and its danger.

These ladies were daughters of a deceased and only son of Mrs. Charlton; they were single, and lived with their grandmother, whose fortune, which was considerable, they expected to share between them, and they waited with eagerness for the moment of appropriation; narrow-minded and rapacious, they wished to monopolize whatever she possessed, and thought themselves aggrieved by her smallest donations. Their chief employment was to keep from her all objects of distress, and in this though they could not succeed, they at least confined her liberality to such as resembled themselves; since neither the spirited could brook, nor the delicate support the checks and rebuffs from the grand-daughters, which followed the gifts of Mrs. Charlton. Cecilia, of all her acquaintance, was the only one whose intimacy they encouraged, for they knew her fortune made her superior to any mercenary views, and they received from her themselves more civilities than they paid.

Mrs. Charlton loved Cecilia with an excess of fondness, that not only took place of the love she bore her other friends, but to which even her regard for the Miss Charltons was inferior and feeble. Cecilia when a child had reverenced her as a mother, and, grateful for her tenderness and care, had afterwards cherished her as a friend. The revival of this early connection delighted them both, it was balm to the wounded mind of Cecilia, it was renovation to the existence of Mrs. Charlton.

Early the next morning she wrote a card to Mr. Monckton and Lady Margaret, acquainting them with her return into Suffolk, and desiring to know when she might pay her respects to her Ladyship. She received from the old lady a verbal answer, *when she pleased*, but Mr. Monckton came instantly himself to Mrs. Charlton's.

His astonishment, his rapture at this unexpected incident were almost boundless; he thought it a sudden turn of fortune in his own favour, and concluded, now she had escaped the danger of Delvile Castle, the road was short and certain that led to his own security.

Her satisfaction in the meeting was as sincere, though not so animated as his own: but this similarity in their feelings was of short duration, for when he enquired into what had passed at the castle, with the reasons of her quitting it, the pain she felt in giving even a cursory and evasive account, was opposed on his part by the warmest delight in hearing it: he could not obtain from her the particulars of what had happened, but the reluctance with which she spoke, the air of mortification with which she heard his questions, and the evident displeasure which was mingled in her chagrin, when he forced her to mention Delvile, were all proofs the most indisputable and satisfactory, that they had either parted without any explanation, or with one by which Cecilia had been hurt and offended.

He now readily concluded that since the fiery trial he had most apprehended was over, and she had quitted in anger the asylum she had sought in extacy, Delvile himself did not covet the alliance, which, since they were separated, was never likely to take place. He had therefore little difficulty in promising all success to himself.

She was once more upon the spot where she had regarded him as the first of men, he knew that during her absence no one had settled in the neighbourhood who had any pretensions to dispute with him that pre-eminence, he should again have access to her, at pleasure, and so sanguine grew his hopes, that he almost began to rejoice even in the partiality to Delvile that had hitherto been his terror, from believing it would give her for a time, that sullen distaste of all other connections, to which those who at once are delicate and fervent are commonly led by early disappointment. His whole solicitude therefore now was to preserve her esteem, to seek her confidence, and to regain whatever by absence might be lost of the ascendant over her mind which her respect for his knowledge and capacity had for many years given him. Fortune at this time seemed to prosper all his views, and, by a stroke the most sudden and unexpected, to render more rational his hopes and his plans than he had himself been able to effect by the utmost craft of worldly wisdom.

The day following Cecilia, in Mrs. Charlton's chaise, waited upon Lady Margaret. She was received by Miss Bennet, her companion, with the most fawning courtesy; but when conducted to the lady of the house, she saw herself so evidently unwelcome, that she even regretted the civility which had prompted her visit.

She found with her nobody but Mr. Morrice, who was the only young man that could persuade himself to endure her company in the absence of her husband, but who, in common with most young men who are assiduous in their attendance upon old ladies, doubted not but he ensured himself a handsome legacy for his trouble.

Almost the first speech which her ladyship made, was "So you are not married yet, I find; if Mr. Monckton had been a real friend, he would have taken care to have seen for some establishment for you."

"I was by no means," cried Cecilia, with spirit, "either in so much haste or distress as to require from Mr. Monckton any such exertion of his friendship."

"Ma'am," cried Morrice, "what a terrible night we had of it at Vauxhall! poor Harrel! I was really excessively sorry for him. I had not courage to see you or Mrs. Harrel after it. But as soon as I heard you were in St. James's-Square,

I tried to wait upon you; for really going to Mr. Harrel's again would have been quite too dismal. I would rather have run a mile by the side of a race-horse.''

"There is no occasion for any apology," said Cecilia, "for I was very little disposed either to see or think of visitors."

"So I thought, ma'am;" answered he, with quickness, "and really that made me the less alert in finding you out. However, ma'am, next winter I shall be excessively happy to make up for the deficiency; besides, I shall be much obliged to you to introduce me to Mr. Delvile, for I have a great desire to be acquainted with him."

Mr. Delvile, thought Cecilia, would be but too proud* to hear it! However, she merely answered that she had no present prospect of spending any time at Mr. Delvile's next winter.

"True, ma'am, true," cried he, "now I recollect, you become your own mistress between this and then; and so I suppose you will naturally chuse a house of your own, which will be much more eligible."

"I don't think that," said Lady Margaret, "I never saw any thing eligible come of young women's having houses of their own; she will do a much better thing to marry, and have some proper person to take care of her."

"Nothing more right, ma'am!" returned he; "a young lady in a house by herself must be subject to a thousand dangers. What sort of place, ma'am, has Mr. Delvile got in the country? I hear he has a good deal of ground there, and a large house."

"It is an old castle, Sir, and situated in a park."

"That must be terribly forlorn: I dare say, ma'am, you were very happy to return into Suffolk."

"I did not find it forlorn; I was very well satisfied with it."

"Why, indeed, upon second thoughts, I don't much wonder; an old castle in a large park must make a very romàntic appearance; something noble in it, I dare say."

"Aye," cried Lady Margaret, "they said you were to become mistress of it, and marry Mr. Delvile's son: and I cannot, for my own part, see any objection to it."

"I am told of so many strange reports," said Cecilia, "and all, to myself so unaccountable, that I begin now to hear of them without much wonder."

"That's a charming young man, I believe," said Morrice; "I had the pleasure once or twice of meeting him at poor Harrel's, and he seemed mighty agreeable. Is not he so, ma'am?"

"Yes,—I believe so."

"Nay, I don't mean to speak of him as any thing very extraordinary," cried Morrice, imagining her hesitation proceeded from dislike, "I merely meant as the world goes,—in a common sort of way."

Here they were joined by Mr. Monckton and some gentlemen who were on a visit at his house; for his anxiety was not of a sort to lead him to solitude, nor his disposition to make him deny himself any kind of enjoyment which he had power to attain. A general conversation ensued, which lasted till Cecilia ended her visit; Mr. Monckton then took her hand to lead her to the chaise, but told her, in their way out, of some alterations in his grounds, which he desired to shew her: his view of detaining her was to gather what she thought of her reception, and whether she had yet any suspicions of the jealousy of Lady Margaret; well knowing, from the delicacy of her character, that if once she became acquainted with it, she would scrupulously avoid all intercourse with him, from the fear of encreasing her uneasiness.

He began, therefore, with talking of the pleasure which Lady Margaret took in the plantations, and of his hope that Cecilia would often favour her by visiting them, without waiting to have her visits returned, as she was entitled by her infirmities to particular indulgencies. He was continuing in this strain, receiving from Cecilia hardly any answer; when suddenly from behind a thick laurel bush, jumpt up Mr. Morrice; who had run out of the house by a shorter cut, and planted himself there to surprise them.

"So ho!" cried he with a loud laugh, "I have caught you! This will be a fine anecdote for Lady Margaret; I vow I'll tell her."

Mr. Monckton, never off his guard, readily answered "Aye, prithee do, Morrice; but don't omit to relate also what we said of yourself."

"Of me?" cried he, with some eagerness; "why you never mentioned me."

"O that won't pass, I assure you; we shall tell another tale at table by and by; and bring the old proverb of the ill luck of listeners* upon you in its full force."

"Well, I'll be hanged if I know what you mean!"

"Why you won't pretend you did not hear Miss Beverley say you were the truest Ouran Outang, or man-monkey,* she ever knew?"

"No, indeed, that I did not!"

"No?—Nor how much she admired your dexterity in escaping being horse-whipt three times a day for your incurable impudence?"

"Not a word on't! Horse-whipt!——Miss Beverley, pray did you say any such thing?"

"Ay," cried Monckton, again, "and not only horse-whipt, but horse-ponded, for she thought when one had heated, the other might cool you; and then you might be fitted again for your native woods, for she insists upon it you was brought from Africa, and are not yet half tamed."

"O lord!" cried Morrice, amazed, "I should not have suspected Miss Beverley would have talked so!"

"And do you suspect she did now?" cried Cecilia.

"Pho, pho," cried Monckton, coolly, "why he heard it himself the whole time! and so shall all our party by and bye, if I can but remember to mention it."

Cecilia then returned to the chaise, leaving Mr. Monckton to settle the matter with his credulous guest as he pleased; for supposing he was merely gratifying a love of sport, or taking this method of checking the general forwardness of the young man, she forebore any interference that might mar his intention.

But Mr. Monckton loved not to be rallied concerning Cecilia, though he was indifferent to all that could be said to him of any other woman; he meant, therefore, to intimidate Morrice from renewing the subject; and he succeeded to his wish; poor Morrice, whose watching and whose speech were the mere blunders of chance, made without the slightest suspicion of Mr. Monckton's designs, now apprehended some scheme to render himself ridiculous, and though he did not believe Cecilia had made use of such expressions, he fancied Mr. Monckton meant to turn the laugh against him, and determined, therefore, to say nothing that might remind him of what had passed.

Mr. Monckton had at this time admitted him to his house merely from an expectation of finding more amusement in his blundering and giddiness, than he was capable, during his anxiety concerning Cecilia, of receiving from conversation of an higher sort.

The character of Morrice was, indeed, particularly adapted for the entertainment of a large house in the country; eager for sport, and always ready for enterprize; willing to oblige, yet tormented with no delicacy about offending; the first to promote mischief for any other, and the last to be offended when exposed to it himself; gay, thoughtless, and volatile,—a happy composition of levity and good-humour.

Cecilia, however, in quitting the house, determined not to visit it again very speedily; for she was extremely disgusted with Lady Margaret, though she suspected no particular motives of enmity, against which she was guarded alike by her own unsuspicious innocence, and by an high esteem of Mr. Monckton, which she firmly believed he returned with equal honesty of undesigning friendship.

Her next excursion was to visit Mrs. Harrel; she found that unhappy lady a prey to all the misery of unoccupied solitude: torn from whatever had, to her, made existence seem valuable, her mind was as listless as her person was inactive, and she was at a loss how to employ even a moment of the day: she had now neither a party to form, nor an entertainment to plan, company to arrange, nor dress to consider; and these, with visits and public places, had filled all her time since her marriage, which, as it had happened* very early in her life, had merely taken place of girlish amusements, masters and governesses.

This helplessness of insipidity, however, though naturally the effect of a mind devoid of all genuine resources, was dignified by herself with the appellation of sorrow: nor was this merely a screen to the world; unused to investigate her feelings or examine her heart, the general compassion she met for the loss of her husband, persuaded her that indeed she lamented his destiny; though had no change in her life been caused by his suicide, she would scarcely, when the first shock was over, have thought of it again.

She received Cecilia with great pleasure; and with still greater, heard the renewal of her promises to fit up a room for her in her house, as soon as she came of age; a period which now was hardly a month distant.

Far greater, however, as well as infinitely purer, was the joy which her presence bestowed upon Mr. Arnott; she saw it herself with a sensation of regret, not only at the constant passion which occasioned it, but even at her own inability to participate in or reward it: for with him an alliance would meet with no opposition; his character was amiable, his situation in life unexceptionable: he loved her with the tenderest affection, and no pride, she well knew, would interfere to overpower it; yet, in return, to grant him her love, she felt as utterly impossible as to refuse him her esteem: and the superior attractions of Delvile, of which neither displeasure nor mortification could rob him, shut up her heart, for the present, more firmly than ever, as Mr. Monckton had well imagined, to all other assailants.

Yet she by no means weakly gave way to repining or regret: her suspence was at an end, her hopes and her fears were subsided into certainty; Delvile, in quitting her, had acquainted her that he left her for ever, and even, though not, indeed, with much steadiness, had prayed for her happiness in union with some other; she held it therefore as essential to her character as to her peace, to manifest equal fortitude in subduing her partiality; she forebore to hint to Mrs. Charlton what had passed, that the subject might never be started; allowed herself no time for dangerous recollection; strolled in her old walks, and renewed her old acquaintance, and by a vigorous exertion of active wisdom, doubted not compleating, before long, the subjection of her unfortunate tenderness. Nor was her task so difficult as she had feared; resolution, in such cases, may act the office of time, and anticipate by reason and self-denial, what that, much less nobly, effects through forgetfulness and inconstancy.

CHAPTER II

A Visit

ONE week only, however, had yet tried the perseverance of Cecilia, when, while she was working with Mrs. Charlton in her dressing-room, her maid hastily entered it, and with a smile that seemed announcing welcome news, said, "Lord, ma'am, here's Fidel!" and, at the same moment, she was followed by the dog, who jumpt upon Cecilia in a transport of delight.

"Good heaven," cried she, all amazement, "who has brought him? whence does he come?"

"A country man brought him, ma'am; but he only put him in, and would not stay a minute."

"But whom did he enquire for?—who saw him?—what did he say?"

"He saw Ralph, ma'am."

Ralph, then, was instantly called: and these questions being repeated, he said, "Ma'am, it was a man I never saw before; but he only bid me take care to deliver the dog into your own hands, and said you would have a letter about him soon, and then went away: I wanted him to stay till I came up stairs, but he was off at once."

Cecilia, quite confounded by this account, could make neither comment nor answer; but, as soon as the servants had left the room, Mrs. Charlton entreated to know to whom the dog had belonged, convinced by her extreme agitation, that something interesting and uncommon must relate to him.

This was no time for disguise; astonishment and confusion bereft Cecilia of all power to attempt it; and, after a very few evasions, she briefly communicated her situation with respect to Delvile, his leaving her, his motives, and his mother's evident concurrence: for these were all so connected with her knowledge of Fidel, that she led to them unavoidably in telling what she knew of him.

Very little penetration was requisite, to gather from her manner all that was united* in her narrative of her own feelings and disappointment in the course of this affair: and Mrs. Charlton, who had hitherto believed the whole world at her disposal, and that she continued single from no reason but her own difficulty of choice, was utterly amazed to find that any man existed who could withstand the united allurements of so much beauty, sweetness, and fortune. She felt herself sometimes inclined to hate, and at other times to pity him; yet concluded that her own extreme coldness was the real cause of his flight, and warmly blamed a reserve which had thus ruined her happiness.

Cecilia was in the extremest perplexity and distress to conjecture the meaning of so unaccountable a present, and so strange a message. Delvile, she knew, had desired the dog might follow him to Bristol; his mother, always pleased to oblige him, would now less than ever neglect any opportunity; she could not, therefore, doubt that she had sent or taken him thither, and thence, according to all appearances, he must now come. But was it likely Delvile would take such a liberty? Was it probable, when so lately he had almost exhorted her to forget him, he would even wish to present her with such a remembrance of himself? And what was the letter she was bid to expect? Whence and from whom was it to come?

All was inexplicable! the only thing she could surmise, with any semblance of probability, was that the whole was some frolic of Lady Honoria Pemberton, who had persuaded Delvile to send her the dog, and perhaps assured him she had herself requested to have him.

Provoked by this suggestion, her first thought was instantly having him conveyed to the castle; but uncertain what the whole affair meant, and hoping some explanation in the letter she was promised, she determined to wait till it came, or at least till she heard from Mrs. Delvile, before she took any measures herself in the business. Mutual accounts of their safe arrivals at Bristol and in Suffolk, had already passed between them, and she expected very soon to have further intelligence: though she was now, by the whole behaviour of Mrs. Delvile, convinced she wished not again to have her an inmate of her house, and that the rest of her minority might pass, without opposition, in the house of Mrs. Charlton.

Day after day, however, passed, and yet she heard nothing more; a week, a fortnight elapsed, and still no letter came. She now concluded the promise was a deception, and repented that she had waited a moment with any such expectation. Her peace, during this time, was greatly disturbed; this present made her fear she was thought meanly of by Mr. Delvile; the silence of his mother gave her apprehensions for his health, and her own irresolution how to act, kept her in perpetual inquietude. She tried in vain to behave as if this incident had not happened; her mind was uneasy, and the same actions produced not the same effects; when she now worked or read, the sight of Fidel by her side distracted her attention; when she walked, it was the same, for Fidel always followed her; and though, in visiting her old acquaintance, she forbore to let him accompany her, she was secretly planning the whole time the contents of some letter, which she expected to meet with, on returning to Mrs. Charlton's.

Those gentlemen in the country who, during the life-time of the Dean, had paid their addresses to Cecilia, again waited upon her at Mrs. Charlton's, and renewed their proposals. They had now, however, still less chance of success, and their dismission was brief and decisive.

Among these came Mr. Biddulph; and to him Cecilia was involuntarily most civil, because she knew him to be the friend of Delvile. Yet his conversation encreased the uneasiness of her suspence; for after speaking of the family in general which she had left, he enquired more particularly concerning Delvile, and then added, "I am, indeed, greatly grieved to find, by all the accounts I receive of him, that he is now in a very bad state of health."

This speech gave her fresh subject for apprehension; and in proportion as the silence of Mrs. Delvile grew more alarming, her regard for her favourite Fidel became more partial. The affectionate animal seemed to mourn the loss of his master, and while sometimes she indulged herself in fancifully telling him her fears, she imagined she read in his countenance the faithfullest sympathy.

One week of her minority was now all that remained, and she was soon wholly occupied in preparations for coming of age. She purposed taking possession of a large house that had belonged to her uncle, which was situated only three miles from that of Mrs. Charlton; and she employed herself in giving orders for fitting it up, and in hearing complaints, and promising indulgencies, to various of her tenants.

At this time, while she was at breakfast one morning, a letter arrived from Mrs. Delvile. She apologised for not writing sooner, but added that various family occurrences, which had robbed her of all leisure, might easily be imagined, when she acquainted her that Mortimer had determined upon again going abroad. . . . . . They were all, she said, returned to Delvile-Castle, but mentioned nothing either of the health of her son, or of her own regret, and filled up the rest of her letter with general news, and expressions of kindness: though, in a postscript, was inserted, "We have lost our poor Fidel."

Cecilia was still meditating upon this letter, by which her perplexity how to act was rather encreased than diminished, when, to her great surprise, Lady Honoria Pemberton was announced. She hastily begged one of the Miss Charltons to convey Fidel out of sight, from a dread of her raillery, should she, at last, be unconcerned in the transaction, and then went to receive her.

Lady Honoria, who was with her governess, gave a brief history of her quitting Delvile-Castle, and said she was now going with her father to visit a noble family in Norfolk:* but she had obtained his permission to leave him at the inn where they had slept, in order to make a short excursion to Bury, for the pleasure of seeing Miss Beverley.

"And therefore," she continued, "I can stay but half an hour; so you must give me some account of yourself as fast as possible."

"What account does your ladyship require?"

"Why, who you live with here, and who are your companions, and what you do with yourself."

"Why, I live with Mrs. Charlton; and for companions, I have at least a score; here are her two grand-daughters, and Mrs. and Miss ——"

"Pho, pho," interrupted Lady Honoria, "but I don't mean such hum-drum companions as those; you'll tell me next, I suppose, of the parson, and his wife and three daughters, with all their cousins and aunts: I hate those sort of people. What I desire to hear of is, who are your particular favourites; and whether you take long walks here, as you used to do at the Castle, and who you have to accompany you?" And then, looking at her very archly, she added, "A pretty little dog, now, I should think, would be vastly agreeable in such a place as this.—Ah, Miss Beverley! you have not left off that trick of colouring, I see!"

"If I colour now," said Cecilia, fully convinced of the justness of her suspicions, "I think it must be for your ladyship, not myself; for, if I am not much mistaken, either in person, or by proxy, a blush from Lady Honoria Pemberton would not, just now, be wholly out of season."

"Lord," cried she, "how like that is to a speech of Mrs. Delvile's! She has taught you exactly her manner of talking. But do you know I am informed you have got Fidel with you here? O fie, Miss Beverley! What will papa and mamma say, when they find you have taken away poor little master's play-thing?"

"And O fie, Lady Honoria! what shall *I* say, when I find you guilty of this mischievous frolic! I must beg, however, since you have gone thus far, that you will proceed a little farther, and send back the dog to the person from whom you received him."

"No, not I! manage him all your own way: if you chuse

to accept dogs from gentlemen, you know, it is your affair, and not mine."

"If you really will not return him yourself, you must at least pardon me should you hear that *I* do in your ladyship's name."

Lady Honoria for some time only laughed and rallied, without coming to any explanation; but when she had exhausted all the sport she could make, she frankly owned that she had herself ordered the dog to be privately stolen, and then sent a man with him to Mrs. Charlton's.

"But you know," she continued, "I really owed you a spite for being so ill-natured as to run away after sending me to call Mortimer to comfort and take leave of you."

"Do you dream, Lady Honoria? when did I send you?"

"Why you know you looked as if you wished it, and that was the same thing. But really it made me appear excessively silly, when I had forced him to come back with me, and told him you were waiting for him,—to see nothing of you at all, and not be able to find or trace you. He took it all for my own invention."

"And was it *not* your own invention?"

"Why that's nothing to the purpose; I wanted him to believe you sent me, for I knew else he would not come."

"Your ladyship was a great deal too good!"

"Why now suppose I had brought you together, what possible harm could have happened from it? It would merely have given each of you some notion of a fever and ague; for first you would both have been hot, and then you would both have been cold, and then you would both have turned red, and then you would both have turned white, and then you would both have pretended to simper at the trick; and then there would have been an end of it."

"This is a very easy way of settling it all," cried Cecilia laughing; "however, you must be content to abide by your own theft, for you cannot in conscience expect I should take it upon myself."

"You are terribly ungrateful, I see," said her ladyship, "for all the trouble and contrivance and expence I have been at merely to oblige you, while the whole time, poor

Mortimer, I dare say, has had his sweet Pet advertised in all
the news-papers, and cried in every market-town* in the
kingdom. By the way, if you do send him back, I would
advise you to let your man demand the reward that has been
offered for him, which may serve in part of payment for his
travelling expences.''

Cecilia could only shake her head, and recollect Mrs.
Delvile's expression, that her levity was incorrigible.

"O if you had seen," she continued, "how sheepish
Mortimer looked when I told him you were dying to see him
before he set off! he coloured so!—just as you do now!—but
I think you're vastly alike.''

"I fear, then," cried Cecilia, not very angry at this
speech, "there is but little chance your ladyship should like
either of us.''

"O yes, I do! I like odd people of all things.''

"Odd people? and in what are we so very odd?''

"O, in a thousand things. You're so good, you know, and
so grave, and so squeamish.''

"Squeamish? how?''

"Why, you know, you never laugh at the old folks, and
never fly at your servants, nor smoke* people before their
faces, and are so civil to all the old *fograms*,* you would make
one imagine you liked nobody so well. By the way, I could
do no good with my little Lord Derford; he pretended to find
out I was only laughing at him, and so he minded nothing
I told him. I dare say, however, his father made the
detection, for I am sure he had not wit enough to discover
it himself.''

Cecilia then, very seriously began to entreat that she
would return the dog herself, and confess her frolic, remonstrating in strong terms upon the mischievous tendency and
consequences of such inconsiderate slights.

"Well," cried she, rising, "this is all vastly true; but I
have no time to hear any more of it just now; besides, it's
only forestalling my next lecture from Mrs. Delvile, for you
talk so much alike, that it is really very perplexing to me to
remember which is which.''

She then hurried away, protesting she had already

outstayed her father's patience, and declaring the delay of another minute would occasion half a dozen expresses to know whether she was gone towards Scotland or Flanders.*

This visit, however, was both pleasant and consolatory to Cecilia; who was now relieved from her suspence, and revived in her spirits by the intelligence that Delvile had no share in sending her a present, which, from him, would have been humiliating and impertinent. She regretted, indeed, that she had not instantly returned it to the castle, which she was now convinced was the measure she ought to have pursued; but to make all possible reparation, she determined that her own servant should set out with him* the next morning to Bristol, and take a letter to Mrs. Delvile to explain what had happened, since to conceal it from any delicacy to Lady Honoria, would be to expose herself to suspicions the most mortifying, for which that gay and careless young lady would never thank her.

She gave orders, therefore, to her servant to get ready for the journey.

When she communicated these little transactions to Mrs. Charlton, that kind-hearted old lady, who knew her fondness for Fidel, advised her not yet to part with him, but merely to acquaint Mrs. Delvile where he was, and what Lady Honoria had done, and, by leaving to herself the care of settling his restoration, to give her, at least, an opportunity of offering him to her acceptance.

Cecilia, however, would listen to no such proposal; she saw the firmness of Delvile in his resolution to avoid her, and knew that policy, as well as propriety, made it necessary she should part with what she could only retain to remind her of one whom she now most wished to forget.

CHAPTER III

An Incident

THE spirits of Cecilia, however, internally failed her: she considered her separation from Delvile to be now, in all probability, for life, since she saw that no struggle either of interest, inclination, or health, could bend him from his purpose; his mother, too, seemed to regard his name and his existence as equally valuable, and the scruples of his father she was certain would be still more insurmountable. Her own pride, excited by theirs, made her, indeed, with more anger than sorrow,* see this general consent to abandon her; but pride and anger both failed when she considered the situation of his health; sorrow, there, took the lead, and admitted no partner: it represented him to her not only as lost to herself, but to the world; and so sad grew her reflections, and so heavy her heart, that, to avoid from Mrs. Charlton observations which pained her, she stole into a summer-house in the garden* the moment she had done tea, declining any companion but her affectionate Fidel.

Her tenderness and her sorrow found here a romantic consolation, in complaining to him of the absence of his master, his voluntary exile, and her fears for his health: calling upon him to participate in her sorrow, and lamenting that even this little relief would soon be denied her; and that in losing Fidel no vestige of Mortimer, but in her own breast, would remain; "Go, then, dear Fidel," she cried, "carry back to your master all that nourishes his remembrance! Bid him not love you the less for having some time belonged to Cecilia; but never may his proud heart be fed with the vain glory, of knowing how fondly for his sake she has cherished you! Go, dear Fidel, guard him by night, and follow him by day; serve him with zeal, and love him with fidelity;—oh that his health were invincible as his pride!—there, alone, is he vulnerable——"

Here Fidel, with a loud barking, suddenly sprang away from her, and, as she turned her eyes towards the door to see what had thus startled him, she beheld standing there, as if immoveable, young Delvile himself!

Her astonishment at this sight almost bereft her of her understanding; it appeared to her super-natural, and she rather believed it was his ghost than himself. Fixed in mute wonder, she stood still though terrified, her eyes almost bursting from their sockets to be satisfied if what they saw was real.

Delvile, too, was some time speechless; he looked not at her, indeed, with any doubt of her existence, but as if what he had heard was to him as amazing as to her what she saw. At length, however, tormented by the dog, who jumpt up to him, licked his hands, and by his rapturous joy forced himself into notice, he was moved to return his caresses, saying, "Yes, *dear Fidel!** you have a claim indeed to my attention, and with the fondest gratitude will I cherish you ever!"

At the sound of his voice, Cecilia again began to breathe; and Delvile having quieted the dog, now entered the summer-house, saying, as he advanced, "Is this possible!— am I not in a dream?—Good God! is it indeed possible!"

The consternation of doubt and astonishment which had seized every faculty of Cecilia, now changed into certainty that Delvile indeed was present, all her recollection returned as she listened to this question, and the wild rambling of fancy with which she had incautiously indulged her sorrow, rushing suddenly upon her mind, she felt herself wholly overpowered by consciouness and shame, and sunk, almost fainting, upon a window-seat.

Delvile instantly flew to her, penetrated with gratitude, and filled with wonder and delight, which, however internally combated by sensations less pleasant, were too potent for controul, and he poured forth at her feet the most passionate acknowledgments.

Cecilia, surprised, affected, and trembling with a thousand emotions, endeavoured to break from him and rise; but, eagerly detaining her, "No, loveliest Miss Beverley," he cried, "not thus must we now part! this moment only have I discovered what a treasure I was leaving; and, but for Fidel, I had quitted it in ignorance for ever."

"Indeed," cried Cecilia, in the extremest agitation, "indeed you may believe me Fidel is here quite by accident.—Lady Honoria took him away,—I knew nothing of the matter,—she stole him, she sent him, she did every thing herself."

"O kind Lady Honoria!," cried Delvile, more and more delighted, "how shall I ever thank her!—And did she also tell you to caress and to cherish him?—to talk to him of his master——"

"O heaven!" interrupted Cecilia, in an agony of mortification and shame, "to what has my unguarded folly reduced me!" Then again endeavouring to break from him, "Leave me, Mr. Delvile," she cried, "leave me, or let me pass!—never can I see you more!—never bear you again in my sight!"

"Come, *dear Fidel!*" cried he, still detaining her, "come and plead for your master! come and ask in his name who *now* has a proud heart, whose pride *now* is invincible!"

"Oh go!" cried Cecilia, looking away from him while she spoke, "repeat not those hateful words, if you wish me not to detest myself eternally!"

"Ever-lovely Miss Beverley," cried he, more seriously, "why this resentment? why all this causeless distress? Has not *my* heart long since been known to you? have you not witnessed its sufferings, and been assured of its tenderness? why, then, this untimely reserve? this unabating coldness? Oh why try to rob me of the felicity you have inadvertently given me! and to sour the happiness of a moment that recompenses such exquisite misery!"

"Oh Mr. Delvile!" cried she, impatiently, though half softened, "was this honourable or right? to steal upon me thus privately—to listen to me thus secretly——"

"You blame me," cried he, "too soon; your own friend, Mrs. Charlton, permitted me to come hither in search of you;—then, indeed, when I heard the sound of your voice—when I heard that voice talk of *Fidel*—of his master——"

"Oh stop, stop!" cried she; "I cannot support the recollection! there is no punishment, indeed, which my own indiscretion does not merit,—but I shall have sufficient in the bitterness of self-reproach!"

"Why will you talk thus, my beloved Miss Beverley? what have you done,—what, let me ask, have *I* done, that such infinite disgrace and depression should follow this little sensibility to a passion so fervent? Does it not render you more dear to me than ever? does it not add new life, new vigour, to the devotion by which I am bound to you?''

"No, no," cried the mortified Cecilia, who from the moment she found herself betrayed, believed herself to be lost, "far other is the effect it will have! and the same mad folly by which I am ruined in my own esteem, will ruin me in yours!—I cannot endure to think of it!— why will you persist in detaining me?—You have filled me with anguish and mortification,—you have taught me the bitterest of lessons, that of hating and contemning myself!''

"Good heaven," cried he, much hurt, "what strange apprehensions thus terrify you? are you with me less safe than with yourself? is it my honour you doubt? is it my integrity you fear? Surely I cannot be so little known to you; and to make protestations now, would but give a new alarm to a delicacy already too agitated.—Else would I tell you that more sacred than my life will I hold what I have heard, that the words just now graven on my heart, shall remain there to eternity unseen; and that higher than ever, not only in my love, but my esteem, is the beautiful speaker.—''

"Ah no!" cried Cecilia, with a sigh, "that, at least, is impossible, for lower than ever is she sunk from deserving it!''

"No," cried he, with fervour, "she is raised, she is exalted! I find her more excellent and perfect than I had even dared believe her; I discover new virtues in the spring of every action; I see what I took for indifference, was dignity; I perceive what I imagined the most rigid insensibility, was nobleness, was propriety, was true greatness of mind!''

Cecilia was somewhat appeased by this speech; and, after a little hesitation, she said, with a half smile, "Must I thank you for this good-nature in seeking to reconcile me with myself?—or shall I quarrel with you for flattery, in giving me praise you can so little think I merit?''

"Ah!" cried he, "were I to praise as I think of you! were my language permitted to accord with my opinion of your worth, you would not then simply call me a flatterer, you would tell me I was an idolator, and fear at least for my principles, if not for my understanding."

"I shall have but little right, however," said Cecilia, again rising, "to arraign your understanding while I act as if bereft of my own. Now, at least, let me pass; indeed you will greatly displease me by any further opposition."

"Will you suffer me, then, to see you early to-morrow morning?"

"No, Sir; nor the next morning, nor the morning after that! This meeting has been wrong, another would be worse; in this I have accusation enough for folly;—in another the charge would be far more heavy."

"Does Miss Beverley, then," cried he gravely, "think me capable of desiring to see her for mere selfish gratification? of intending to trifle either with her time or her feelings? no; the conference I desire will be important and decisive. This night I shall devote solely to deliberation; to-morrow shall be given to action. Without some thinking I dare venture at no plan;—I presume not to communicate to you the various interests that divide me, but the result of them all I can take no denial to your hearing."

Cecilia, who felt when thus stated the justice of his request, now opposed it no longer, but insisted upon his instantly departing.

"True," cried he, "I must go!—the longer I stay, the more I am fascinated, and the weaker are those reasoning powers of which I now want the strongest exertion." He then repeated his professions of eternal regard, besought her not to regret the happiness she had given him, and after disobeying her injunctions of going till she was seriously displeased, he only stayed to obtain her pardon, and permission to be early the next morning, and then, though still slowly and reluctantly, he left her.

Scarce was Cecilia again alone, but the whole of what had passed seemed a vision of her imagination. That Delvile should be at Bury, that he should visit her at Mrs. Charlton's, surprise her by herself, and discover her most secret thoughts, appeared so strange and so incredible, that, occupied rather by wonder than thinking, she continued almost motionless in the place where he had left her, till

Mrs. Charlton sent to request that she would return to the house. She then enquired if any body was with her, and being answered in the negative, obeyed the summons.

Mrs. Charlton, with a smile of much meaning, hoped she had had a pleasant walk: but Cecilia seriously remonstrated on the dangerous imprudence she had committed in suffering her to be so unguardedly surprised. Mrs. Charlton, however, more anxious for her future and solid happiness, than for her present apprehensions and delicacy, repented not the step she had taken; and when she gathered from Cecilia the substance of what had past, unmindful of the expostulations which accompanied it, she thought with exultation that the sudden meeting she had permitted, would now, by making known to each their mutual affection, determine them to defer no longer a union upon which their mutual peace of mind so much depended. And Cecilia, finding she had been thus betrayed designedly, not inadvertently, could hardly reproach her zeal, though she lamented its indiscretion.

She then asked by what means he had obtained admission, and made himself known; and heard that he had enquired at the door for Miss Beverley, and, having sent in his name, was shewn into the parlour, where Mrs. Charlton, much pleased with his appearance, had suddenly conceived the little plan which she had executed, of contriving a surprise for Cecilia, from which she rationally expected the very consequences that ensued, though the immediate means she had not conjectured.

The account was still unsatisfactory to Cecilia, who could frame to herself no possible reason for a visit so extra-ordinary, and so totally inconsistent with his declarations and resolutions.

This, however, was a matter of but little moment, compared with the other subjects to which the interview had given rise; Delvile, upon whom so long, though secretly, her dearest hopes of happiness had rested, was now become acquainted with his power, and knew himself the master of her destiny; he had quitted her avowedly to decide what it should be, since his present subject of deliberation included her fate in his own: the next morning he was to call, and acquaint her with his decree, not doubting her concurrence which ever way he resolved.

A subjection so undue, and which she could not but consider as disgraceful, both shocked and afflicted her; and the reflection that the man who of all men she preferred, was acquainted with her preference, yet hesitated whether to accept or abandon her, mortified and provoked her, alternately, occupied her thoughts the whole night, and kept her from peace and from rest.

CHAPTER IV

A Proposition

EARLY the next morning, Delvile again made his appearance. Cecilia, who was at breakfast with Mrs. and Miss Charltons, received him with the most painful confusion, and he was evidently himself in a state of the utmost perturbation. Mrs. Charlton made a pretence almost immediately for sending away both her grand-daughters, and then, without taking the trouble of devising one for herself, arose and followed them, though Cecilia made sundry signs of solicitation that she would stay.

Finding herself now alone with him, she hastily, and without knowing what she said, cried, "How is Mrs. Delvile, Sir? Is she still at Bristol?"

"At Bristol? no; have you never heard she is returned to Delvile-Castle?"

"O, true!—I meant Delvile-Castle,—but I hope she found some benefit from the waters?"

"She had not, I believe, any occasion to try them."

Cecilia, ashamed of these two following mistakes, coloured high, but ventured not again to speak: and Delvile, who seemed big with something he feared to utter, arose, and walked for a few instants about the room; after which, exclaiming aloud "How vain is every plan which passes the present hour!" He advanced to Cecilia, who pretended to be looking at some work, and, seating himself next her, "when we parted yesterday," he cried, "I presumed to say one night alone should be given to deliberation,—and to-day, this very day to action!—but I forgot that though in deliberating I had only myself to consult, in acting I was not so independent; and that when my own doubts were satisfied, and my own resolutions taken, other doubts and other resolutions must be considered, by which my purposed proceedings might be retarded, might perhaps be wholly prevented!"

He paused, but Cecilia, unable to conjecture to what he was leading, made not any answer.

"Upon you, madam," he continued, "all that is good or evil of my future life, as far as relates to its happiness or misery, will, from this very hour, almost solely depend: yet much as I rely upon your goodness, and superior as I know you to trifling or affectation, what I now come to propose— to petition—to entreat—I cannot summon courage to mention, from a dread of alarming you!"

What next, thought Cecilia, trembling at this introduction, is preparing for me! does he mean to ask *me* to solicit Mrs. Delvile's consent! or from myself must he receive commands that we should never meet more!

"Is Miss Beverley," cried he, "determined not to speak to me? Is she bent upon silence only to intimidate me? Indeed if she knew how greatly I respect her, she would honour me with more confidence."

"When, Sir," cried she, "do you mean to make your tour?"

"Never!" cried he, with fervour, "unless banished by *you*, never!—no, loveliest Miss Beverley, I can now quit you no more! Fortune, beauty, worth and sweetness I had power to relinquish, and severe as was the task, I compelled myself to perform it,—but when to these I find joined so attractive a softness,—a pity for my sufferings so unexpectedly gentle——no! sweetest Miss Beverley, I can quit you no more!" And then, seizing her hand, with yet greater energy, he went on, "I here," he cried, "offer you my vows, I here own you sole arbitress of my fate! I give you not merely the possession of my heart,—that, indeed, I had no power to with-hold from you,—but I give you the direction of my conduct, I entreat you to become my counsellor and guide. Will Miss Beverley accept such an office? Will she deign to listen to such a prayer?"

"Yes," cried Cecilia, involuntarily delighted to find that such was the result of his night's deliberation, "I am most ready to give you my counsel; which I now do,—that you set off for the continent to-morrow morning."

"O how malicious!" cried he, half laughing, "yet not so immediately do I even request your counsel; something must first be done to qualify you for giving it: penetration, skill and understanding, however amply you possess them, are not sufficient to fit you for the charge; something still more is requisite, you must be invested with fuller powers, you must have a right less disputable, and a title, that not alone, inclination, not even judgment alone must sanctify, —but which law must enforce, and rites the most solemn support!"

"I think, then," said Cecilia, deeply blushing, "I must be content to forbear giving any counsel at all, if the qualifications for it are so difficult of acquirement."

"Resent not my presumption," cried he, "my beloved Miss Beverley, but let the severity of my recent sufferings palliate my present temerity; for where affliction has been deep and serious, causeless and unnecessary misery will find little encouragement; and mine has been serious indeed! Sweetly, then, permit me, in proportion to its bitterness, to rejoice in the soft reverse which now flatters me with its approach."

Cecilia, abashed and uneasy, uncertain of what was to follow, and unwilling to speak till more assured, paused, and then abruptly exclaimed "I am afraid Mrs. Charlton is waiting for me," and would have hurried away: but Delvile, almost forcibly preventing her, compelled her to stay; and, after a short conversation, on his side the most impassioned, and on hers the most confused, obtained from her, what, indeed, after the surprise of the preceding evening she could but ill deny, a frank confirmation of his power over her heart, and an ingenuous, though reluctant acknowledgment, how long he had possessed it.

This confession, made, as affairs now stood, wholly in opposition to her judgement, was torn from her by an impetuous urgency which she had not presence of mind to resist, and with which Delvile, when particularly animated, had long been accustomed to overpower all opposition. The joy with which he heard it, though but little mixed with wonder, was as violent as the eagerness with which he had sought it; yet it was not of long duration, a sudden, and most painful recollection presently quelled it, and even in the midst of his rapturous acknowledgements, seemed to strike him to the heart.

Cecilia, soon perceiving both in his countenance and manner an alteration that shocked her, bitterly repented an avowal she could never recall, and looked aghast with expectation and dread.

Delvile, who with quickness saw a change of expression in her of which in himself he was unconscious, exclaimed, with much emotion "Oh how transient is human felicity! How rapidly fly those rare and exquisite moments in which it is perfect! Ah! sweetest Miss Beverley, what words shall I find to soften what I have now to reveal! to tell you that, after goodness, candour, generosity such as yours, a request, a supplication remains yet to be uttered that banishes me, if refused, from your presence for ever!"

Cecilia, extremely dismayed, desired to know what it was: an evident dread of offending her kept him some time from proceeding, but at length, after repeatedly expressing his fears of her disapprobation, and a repugnance even on his own part to the very measure he was obliged to urge, he acknowledged that all his hopes of being ever united to her, rested upon obtaining her consent to an immediate and secret marriage.

Cecilia, thunderstruck by this declaration remained for a few instants too much confounded to speak; but when he was beginning an explanatory apology, she started up, and glowing with indignation, said, "I had flattered myself, Sir, that both my character and my conduct, independent of my situation in life, would have exempted me at all times from a proposal which I shall ever think myself degraded by having heard."

And then she was again going, but Delvile still preventing her, said "I knew too well how much you would be alarmed, and such was my dread of your displeasure that it had power even to embitter the happiness I sought with so much earnestness, and to render your condescension insufficient to ensure it. Yet wonder not at my scheme; wild as it may appear, it is the result of deliberation, and censurable as it may seem, it springs not from unworthy motives."

"Whatever may be your motives with respect to yourself, Sir," said Cecilia, "with respect to me they must certainly be disgraceful; I will not, therefore, listen to them."

"You wrong me cruelly," cried he, with warmth, "and a moment's reflection must tell you that however distinct may be our honour or our disgrace in every other instance, in that by which we should be united, they must inevitably be the same: and far sooner would I voluntarily relinquish you, than be myself accessary to tainting that delicacy of which the unsullied purity has been the chief source of my admiration."

"Why, then," cried Cecilia, reproachfully, "have you mentioned to me such a project?"

"Circumstances the most singular, and necessity the most unavoidable," he answered, "should alone have ever tempted me to form it. No longer ago than yesterday morning, I believed myself incapable of even wishing it; but extraordinary situations call for extraordinary resolutions, and in private as well as public life, palliate, at least, extraordinary actions. Alas! the proposal which so much offends you is my final resource! it is the sole barrier between myself and perpetual misery!—the only expedient in my power to save me from eternally parting with you!—for I am now cruelly compelled to confess, that my family, I am certain, will never consent to our union!"

"Neither, then, Sir," cried Cecilia, with great spirit, "will I! The disdain I may meet with I pretend not to retort, but wilfully to encounter, were meanly to deserve it. I will enter into no family in opposition to its wishes, I will consent to no alliance that may expose me to indignity. Nothing is so contagious as contempt!—The example of your friends might work powerfully upon yourself, and who shall dare assure me you would not catch the infection?"

"*I* dare assure you!" cried he; "hasty you may perhaps think me, and somewhat impetuous I cannot deny myself; but believe me not of so wretched a character as to be capable, in any affair of moment, of fickleness or caprice."

"But what, Sir, is my security to the contrary? Have you not this moment avowed that but yesterday you held in abhorrence the very plan that to-day you propose? And may you not to-morrow resume again the same opinion?"

"Cruel Miss Beverley! how unjust is this inference! If yesterday I disapproved what to-day I recommend, a little recollection must surely tell you why: and that not my opinion, but my situation is changed."

The conscious Cecilia here turned away her head; too certain he alluded to the discovery of her partiality.

"Have you not yourself," he continued, "witnessed the steadiness of my mind? Have you not beheld me fly, when I had power to pursue, and avoid, when I had opportunity to seek you? After witnessing my constancy upon such trying occasions, is it equitable, is it right to suspect me of wavering?"

"But what," cried she, "was the constancy which brought you into Suffolk?—When all occasion was over for our meeting any more, when you told me you were going abroad, and took leave of me for-ever,—where, then, was your steadiness in this unnecessary journey?"

"Have a care," cried he, half smiling, and taking a letter from his pocket, "have a care, upon this point, how you provoke me to shew my justification!"

"Ah!" cried Cecilia, blushing, " 'tis some trick of Lady Honoria!"

"No, upon my honour. The authority is less doubtful: I believe I should hardly else have regarded it."

Cecilia, much alarmed, held out her hand for the letter; and looking first at the end was much astonished to see the name of Biddulph. She then cast her eye over the beginning, and when she saw her own name, read the following paragraph.

"Miss Beverley, as you doubtless know, is returned into Suffolk; every body here saw her with the utmost surprise; from the moment I had heard of her residence in Delvile-Castle, I had given her up for lost: but, upon her unexpected appearance among us again, I was weak enough once more to make trial of her heart. I soon found, however, that the pain of a second rejection *you* might have spared me, and that though she had quitted Delvile-Castle, she had not for nothing entered it: at the sound of your name, she blushes; at the mention of your illness, she turns pale; and the dog you have given her, which I recollected immediately, is her darling companion. Oh happy Delvile! yet so lovely a conquest you abandon.——"

Cecilia could read no more; the letter dropt from her hand: to find herself thus by her own emotions betrayed, made her instantly conclude she was universally discovered: and turning sick at the supposition, all her spirit forsook her, and she burst into tears.

"Good heaven," cried Delvile, extremely shocked, "what has thus affected you? Can the jealous surmises of an apprehensive rival——"

"Do not talk to me," interrupted she, impatiently, "and do not detain me,—I am extremely disturbed,——I wish to be alone,—I beg, I even entreat you would leave me."

"I will go, I will obey you in every thing!" cried he, eagerly, "tell me but when I may return, and when you will suffer me to explain to you all the motives of my proposal?"

"Never, never!" cried she, with earnestness, "I am sufficiently lowered already, but never will I intrude myself into a family that disdains me!"

"Disdains? No, you are revered in it! who could disdain you! That fatal clause alone——"

"Well, well, pray leave me; indeed I cannot hear you; I

am unfit for argument, and all reasoning now is nothing less than cruelty."

"I am gone," cried he, "this moment! I would not even wish to take advantage of your agitation in order to work upon your sensibility. My desire is not to surprize, but to reconcile you to my plan. What is it I seek in Miss Beverley? An Heiress? No, as such she has seen I could resist her; nor yet the light trifler of a spring or two, neglected when no longer a novelty; no, no!—it is a companion for ever, it is a solace for every care, it is a bosom friend through every period of life that I seek in Miss Beverley! Her esteem, therefore, to me is as precious as her affection, for how can I hope her friendship in the winter of my days, if their brighter and gayer season is darkened by doubts of my integrity? All shall be clear and explicit; no latent cause of uneasiness shall disturb our future quiet: we will now be sincere, that hereafter we may be easy; and sweetly in unclouded felicity, time shall glide away imperceptibly, and we will make an interest with each other in the gaiety of youth, to bear with the infirmities of age, and alleviate them by kindness and sympathy. And then shall my soothing Cecilia—"

"O say no more!" interrupted she, softened in her own despite by a plan so consonant to her wishes, "what language is this! how improper for you to use, or me to hear!"

She then very earnestly insisted upon his going; and after a thousand times taking leave and returning, promising obedience, yet pursuing his own way, he at length said if she would consent to receive a letter from him, he would endeavour to commit what he had to communicate to paper, since their mutual agitation made him unable to explain himself with clearness, and rather hurt his cause than assisted it, by leaving all his arguments unfinished and obscure.

Another dispute now arose; Cecilia protesting she would receive no letter, and hear nothing upon the subject; and Delvile impetuously declaring he would submit to no award without being first heard. At length he conquered, and at length he departed.

Cecilia then felt her whole heart sink within her at the unhappiness of her situation. She considered herself now condemned to refuse Delvile herself, as the only condition upon which he even solicited her favour, neither the strictness of her principles, nor the delicacy of her mind, would suffer her to accept. Her displeasure at the proposal had been wholly unaffected, and she regarded it as an injury to her character ever to have received it; yet that Delvile's pride of heart should give way to his passion, that he should love her with so much fondness as to relinquish for her the ambitious schemes of his family, and even that darling name which so lately seemed annexed to his existence, were circumstances to which she was not insensible, and proofs of tenderness and regard which she had thought incompatible with the general spirit of his disposition. Yet however by these she was gratified, she resolved never to comply with so humiliating a measure, but to wait the consent of his friends, or renounce him for ever.*

CHAPTER V

A Letter

AS soon as Mrs. Charlton was acquainted with the departure of young Delvile, she returned to Cecilia, impatient to be informed what had passed. The narration she heard both hurt and astonished her; that Cecilia, the Heiress of such a fortune, the possessor of so much beauty, descended of a worthy family, and formed and educated to grace a noble one, should be rejected by people to whom her wealth would be most useful, and only in secret have their alliance proposed to her, she deemed an indignity that called for nothing but resentment, and approved and enforced the resolution of her young friend to resist all solicitations which Mr. and Mrs. Delvile did not second themselves.

About two hours after Delvile was gone, his letter arrived. Cecilia opened it with trepidation, and read as follows.

To Miss Beverley.

September 20, 1779.

What could be the apprehensions, the suspicions of Miss Beverley when so earnestly she prohibited my writing? From a temper so unguarded as mine could she fear any subtlety of doctrine? Is my character so little known to her that she can think me capable of craft or duplicity? Had I even the desire, I have neither the address nor the patience to practise them; no, loveliest Miss Beverley, though sometimes by vehemence I may incautiously offend, by sophistry, believe me, I never shall injure: my ambition, as I have told you, is to convince, not beguile, and my arguments shall be simple as my professions shall be sincere.

Yet how again may I venture to mention a proposal which so lately almost before you had heard you rejected? Suffer me, however, to assure you it resulted neither from insensibility to your delicacy, nor to my own duty; I made it, on the contrary, with that reluctance and timidity which were given me by an apprehension that both seemed to be offended by it:—but alas! already I have said what with grief I must repeat, I have no resource, no alternative, between receiving the honour of your hand in secret or foregoing you for-ever.

You will wonder, you may well wonder at such a declaration; and again that severe renunciation with which you wounded me, will tremble on your lips,—Oh there let it stop! nor let the air again be agitated with sounds so discordant!

In that cruel and heart-breaking moment when I tore myself from you at Delvile-Castle, I confessed to you the reason of my flight, and I determined to see you no more. I named not to you, then, my family, the potency of my own objections against daring to solicit your favour rendering their's immaterial: my own are now wholly removed,—— but their's remain in full force.

My father, descended of a race which though decaying in wealth, is unsubdued in pride, considers himself as the guardian of the honour of his house, to which he holds the name of his ancestors inseparably annexed: my mother, born of the same family, and bred to the same ideas, has strengthened this opinion by giving it the sanction of her own.

Such being their sentiments, you will not, madam, be surprised that their only son, the sole inheritor of their fortune, and sole object of their expectations, should early have admitted the same. Indeed almost the first lesson I was taught was that of reverencing the family from which I am descended, and the name to which I am born. I was bid consider myself as its only remaining support, and sedulously instructed neither to act nor think but with a view to its aggrandizement and dignity.

Thus, unchecked by ourselves, and uncontrouled by the world, this haughty self-importance acquired by time a strength, and by mutual encouragement a firmness, which Miss Beverley alone could possibly, I believe, have shaken! What, therefore, was my secret alarm, when first I was conscious of the force of her attractions, and found my mind wholly occupied with admiration of her excellencies! All that pride could demand, and all to which ambition could aspire, all that happiness could covet, or the most scrupulous delicacy exact, in her I found united; and while my heart was enslaved by her charms, my understanding exulted in its fetters.——Yet to forfeit my name, to give up for-ever a family which upon me rested its latest expectations,—— Honour, I thought forbad it, propriety and manly spirit revolted at the sacrifice. The renunciation of my birth-right seemed a desertion of the post in which I was stationed: I forebore, therefore, even in my wishes, to solicit your favour, and vigorously determined to fly you as dangerous to my peace, because unattainable without dishonour.

Such was the intended regulation of my conduct at the time I received Biddulph's letter; in three days I was to leave England; my father, with much persuasion, had consented to my departure; my mother, who penetrated into my motives, had never opposed it: but how great was the change wrought upon my mind by reading that letter! my steadiness forsook me, my resolution wavered; yet I thought him deceived, and attributed his suspicions to jealousy: but still, Fidel I knew was missing—and to hear he was your darling companion——was it possible to quit England in a state of such uncertainty? to be harrassed in distant climates with conjectures I might then never satisfy? No; I told my friends I must visit Biddulph before I left the kingdom, and promising to return to them in three or four days, I hastily set out for Suffolk, and rested not till I arrived at Mrs. Charlton's.

What a scene there awaited me! to behold the loved mistress of my heart, the opposed, yet resistless object of my fondest admiration, caressing an animal she knew to be mine, mourning over him his master's ill health, and sweetly recommending to him fidelity,——Ah! forgive the retrospection, I will dwell on it no longer. Little, indeed, had I imagined with what softness the dignity of Miss Beverley was blended, though always conscious that her virtues, her attractions, and her excellencies, would reflect lustre upon the highest station to which human grandeur could raise her, and would still be more exalted than her rank, though that were the most eminent upon earth.—And had there been a thousand, and ten thousand obstacles to oppose my addressing her, vigourously and undauntedly would I have combated with them all, in preference to yielding to this single objection!

Let not the frankness of this declaration irritate you, but rather let it serve to convince you of the sincerity of what follows: various as are the calamities of life which may render me miserable, YOU only, among even its chosen felicities, have power to make me happy. Fame, honours, wealth, ambition, were insufficient without you; all chance of internal peace, and every softer hope is now centered in your favour, and to lose you, from whatever cause, ensures me wretchedness unmitigated.

With respect therefore to myself, the die is finally cast, and the conflict between bosom felicity and family pride is deliberately over. This name which so vainly I have cherished and so painfully supported, I now find inadequate to recompense me for the sacrifice which its preservation requires. I part with it, I own, with regret that the surrender is necessary; yet is it* rather an imaginary than an actual evil, and though a deep wound to pride, no offence to morality.

Thus have I laid open to you my whole heart, confessed my perplexities, acknowledged my vain-glory, and exposed with equal sincerity the sources of my doubts, and the motives of my decision: but now, indeed, how to proceed I know not; the difficulties which are yet to encounter I fear to enumerate, and the petition I have to urge I have scarce courage to mention.

My family, mistaking ambition for honour, and rank for dignity, have long planned a splendid connection for me, to which though my invariable repugnance has stopt any advances, their wishes and their views immovably adhere. I am but too certain they will now listen to no other. I dread, therefore, to make a trial where I despair of success, I know not how to risk a prayer with those who may silence me by a command.

In a situation so desperate, what then remains? Must I make an application with a certainty of rejection, and then mock all authority by acting in defiance of it? Or, harder task yet! relinquish my dearest hopes when no longer persuaded of their impropriety? Ah! sweetest Miss Beverley, end the struggle at once! My happiness, my peace, are wholly in your power, for the moment of our union secures them for life.

It may seem to you strange that I should thus purpose to brave the friends whom I venture not to entreat; but from my knowledge of their characters and sentiments I am certain I have no other resource. Their favourite principles were too early imbibed to be now at this late season eradicated. Slaves that we all are to habits, and dupes to appearances, jealous guardians of our pride, to which our comfort is sacrificed, and even our virtue made subservient, what conviction can be offered by reason, to notions that exist but by prejudice? They have been cherished too long for rhetorick to remove them, they can only be expelled by all-powerful Necessity. Life is, indeed, too brief, and success too precarious, to trust, in any case where happiness is concerned, the extirpation of deep-rooted and darling opinions, to the slow-working influence of argument and disquisition.

Yet bigotted as they are to rank and family, they adore Miss Beverley, and though their consent to the forfeiture of their name might for-ever be denied, when once they beheld her the head and ornament of their house, her elegance and accomplishments joined to the splendour of her fortune, would speedily make them forget the plans which now wholly absorb them. Their sense of honour is in nothing inferior to their sense of high birth; your condescension, therefore, would be felt by them in its fullest force, and though, during their first surprize, they might be irritated against their son, they would make it the study of their lives that the lady who for him had done so much, should never, through their means, repine for herself.

With regard to settlements, the privacy of our union would not affect them: one Confident we must unavoidably trust, and I would deposit in the hands of whatever person you would name, a bond by which I would engage myself to settle both your fortune and my own, according to the arbitration of our mutual friends.

The time for secrecy though painful would be short, and even from the altar, if you desired it, I would hasten to Delvile-Castle. Not one of my friends should you see till they waited upon you themselves to solicit your presence at their house, till our residence elsewhere was fixed.

Oh loveliest Cecilia, from a dream of a happiness so sweet awaken me not! from a plan of felicity so attractive turn not away! If one part of it is unpleasant, reject not therefore all; and since without some drawback no earthly bliss is attainable, do not, by a refinement too scrupulous for the short period of our existence, deny yourself that delight which your benevolence will afford you, in snatching from the pangs of unavailing regret and misery, the gratefullest of men in the

humblest and most devoted

of your servants,

Mortimer Delvile.

Cecilia read and re-read this letter, but with a perturbation of mind that made her little able to weigh its contents. Paragraph by paragraph her sentiments varied, and her determination was changed: the earnestness of his supplication now softened her into compliance, the acknowledged pride of his family now irritated her into

resentment, and the confession of his own regret now
sickened her into despondence. She meant in an immediate
answer to have written a final dismission; but though proof
against his entreaties, because not convinced by his
arguments, there was something in the conclusion of his
letter that staggered her resolution.

Those scruples and that refinement against which he
warned her, she herself thought might be overstrained, and
to gratify unnecessary punctilio, the short period of existence
be rendered causelessly unhappy. He had truly said that
their union would be no offence to morality, and with
respect merely to pride, why should that be spared? He
knew he possessed her heart, she had long been certain of
his, her character had early gained the affection of his
mother, and the essential service which an income such as
her's must do the family, would soon be felt too powerfully
to make her connection with it regretted.

These reflections were so pleasant she knew not how to
discard them; and the consciousness that her secret was
betrayed not only to himself, but to Mr. Biddulph, Lord
Ernolf, Lady Honoria Pemberton, and Mrs. Delvile, gave
them additional force, by making it probable she was yet
more widely suspected.

But still her delicacy and her principles revolted against a
conduct of which the secrecy seemed to imply the
impropriety. "How shall I meet Mrs. Delvile," cried she,
"after an action so clandestine? How, after praise such as
she has bestowed upon me, bear the severity of her eye,
when she thinks I have seduced from her the obedience of
her son! A son who is the sole solace and first hope of her
existence, whose virtues make all her happiness, and whose
filial piety is her only glory!—And well may she glory in a
son such as Delvile! Nobly has he exerted himself in
situations the most difficult, his family and his ideas of
honour he has preferred to his peace and health, he has
fulfilled with spirit and integrity the various, the conflicting
duties of life. Even now, perhaps, in his present application,
he may merely think himself bound by knowing me no
longer free, and his generous sensibility to the weakness he

has discovered, without any of the conviction to which he pretends, may have occasioned this proposal!''

A suggestion so mortifying again changed her determination; and the tears of Henrietta Belfield, with the letter which she had surprized in her hand recurring to her memory, all her thoughts turned once more upon rejecting him for-ever.

In this fluctuating state of mind she found writing impracticable; while uncertain what to wish, to decide was impossible. She desdained coquetry, she was superior to trifling, the candour and openness of Delvile had merited all her sincerity, and therefore while any doubt remained, with herself, she held it unworthy her character to tell him she had none.

Mrs. Charlton, upon reading the letter, became again the advocate of Delvile; the frankness with which he had stated his difficultes assured her of his probity, and by explaining his former conduct, satisfied her with the rectitude of his future intentions. ''Do not, therefore, my dear child,'' cried she, ''become the parent of your own misery by refusing him; he deserves you alike from his principles and his affection, and the task would both be long and melancholy to disengage him from your heart. I see not, however, the least occasion for the disgrace of a private marriage; I know not any family to which you would not be an honour, and those who feel not your merit, are little worth pleasing. Let Mr. Delvile, therefore, apply openly to his friends, and if they refuse their consent, be their prejudices their reward. You are freed from all obligations where caprice only can raise objections, and you may then, in the face of the world, vindicate your choice.''

The wishes of Cecilia accorded with this advice, though the general tenour of Delvile's letter gave her little reason to expect he would follow it.

CHAPTER VI

A Discussion

THE day past away, and Cecilia had yet written no answer; the evening came,* and her resolution was still unfixed.

Delvile, at length, was again announced; and though she dreaded trusting herself to his entreaties, the necessity of hastening some decision deterred her from refusing to see him.

Mrs. Charlton was with her when he entered the room; he attempted at first some general conversation, though the anxiety of his mind was strongly pictured upon his face. Cecilia endeavoured also to talk upon common topics, though her evident embarrassment spoke the absence of her thoughts.

Delvile at length, unable any longer to bear suspence, turned to Mrs. Charlton, and said, "You are probably acquainted, madam, with the purport of the letter I had the honour of sending to Miss Beverley this morning?"

"Yes, Sir," answered the old lady, "and you need desire little more than that her opinion of it may be as favourable as mine."

Delvile bowed and thanked her; and looking at Cecilia, to whom he ventured not to speak, he perceived in her countenance a mixture of dejection and confusion, that told him whatever might be her opinion, it had by no means encreased her happiness.

"But why, Sir," said Mrs. Charlton, "should you be thus sure of the disapprobation of your friends? had you not better hear what they have to say?"

"I *know*, madam, what they have to say," returned he; "for their language and their principles have been invariable from my birth: to apply to them, therefore, for a concession which I am certain they will not grant, were only a cruel device to lay all my misery to their account."

"And if they are so perverse, they deserve from you nothing better," said Mrs. Charlton; "speak to them, however; you will then have done your duty; and if they are obstinately unjust, you will have acquired a right to act for yourself."

"To mock their authority," answered Delvile, "would be more offensive than to oppose it: to solicit their approbation, and then act in defiance of it, might justly provoke their indignation.—No; if at last I am reduced to appeal to them, by their decision I must abide."

To this Mrs. Charlton could make no answer, and in a few minutes she left the room.

"And is such, also," said Delvile, "the opinion of Miss Beverley? has she doomed me to be wretched, and does she wish that doom to be signed by my nearest friends!"

"If your friends, Sir," said Cecilia, "are so undoubtedly inflexible, it were madness, upon any plan, to risk their displeasure."

"To entreaty," he answered, "they will be inflexible, but not to forgiveness. My father, though haughty, dearly, even passionately loves me; my mother, though high-spirited, is just, noble, and generous. She is, indeed, the most exalted of women, and her power over my mind I am unaccustomed to resist. Miss Beverley alone seems born to be her daughter——"

"No, no," interrupted Cecilia, "as her daughter she rejects me!"

"She loves, she adores you!" cried he, warmly; "and were I not certain she feels your excellencies as they ought to be felt, my veneration for you *both* should even yet spare you my present supplication. But you would become, I am certain, the first blessing of her life; in you she would behold all the felicity of her son,—his restoration to health, to his country, to his friends!"

"O Sir," cried Cecilia, with emotion, "how deep a trench of real misery do you sink, in order to raise this pile* of fancied happiness! But I will not be responsible for your offending such a mother; scarcely can you honour her yourself more than I do; and I here declare most solemnly——"

"O stop!" interrupted Delvile, "and resolve not till you have heard me. Would you, were she no more, were my father also no more, would you yet persist in refusing me?"

"Why should you ask me?" said Cecilia, blushing; "you would then be your own agent, and perhaps——"

She hesitated, and Delvile vehemently exclaimed, "Oh make me not a monster! force me not to desire the death of the very beings by whom I live! weaken not the bonds of affection by which they are endeared to me, and compel me not to wish them no more as the sole barriers to my happiness!''

''Heaven forbid!'' cried Cecilia; ''could I believe you so impious, I should suffer little indeed in desiring your eternal absence.''

''Why then only upon their extinction must I rest my hope of your favour?''

Cecilia, staggered and distressed by this question, could make no answer. Delvile, perceiving her embarrassment, redoubled his urgency; and before she had power to recollect herself, she had almost consented to his plan, when Henrietta Belfield rushing into her memory, she hastily exclaimed, ''One doubt there is, which I know not how to mention, but ought to have cleared up;—you are acquainted with—you remember Miss Belfield?''

''Certainly; but what of Miss Belfield that can raise a doubt in the mind of Miss Beverley?''

Cecilia coloured, and was silent.

''Is it possible,'' continued he, ''you could ever for an instant suppose—but I cannot even name a supposition so foreign to all possibility.''

''She is surely very amiable?''

''Yes,'' answered he, ''she is innocent, gentle, and engaging; and I heartily wish she were in a better situation.''

''Did you ever occasionally, or by any accident, correspond with her?''

''Never in my life.''

''And were not your visits to the brother *sometimes*——''

''Have a care,'' interrupted he, laughing, ''lest I reverse the question, and ask if your visits to the sister were not *sometimes* for the brother! But what does this mean? Could Miss Beverley imagine that *after* knowing her, the charms of Miss Belfield could put me in any danger?''

Cecilia, bound in delicacy and friendship not to betray the tender and trusting Henrietta, and internally satisfied of his innocence by his frankness, evaded any answer, and would now have done with the subject; but Delvile, eager wholly to exculpate himself, though by no means displeased at an enquiry which shewed so much interest in his affections, continued his explanation.

"Miss Belfield has, I grant, an attraction in the simplicity of her manners which charms by its singularity: her heart, too, seems all purity, and her temper all softness. I have not, you find, been blind to her merit; on the contrary, I have both admired and pitied her. But far indeed is she removed from all chance of rivalry in my heart! A character such as hers for a while is irresistably alluring; but when its novelty is over, simplicity uninformed becomes wearisome, and softness without dignity is too indiscriminate to give delight. We sigh for entertainment, when cloyed by mere sweetness; and heavily drags on the load of life when the companion of our social hours wants spirit, intelligence, and cultivation. With Miss Beverley all these——"

"Talk not of all these," cried Cecilia, "when one single obstacle has power to render them valueless."

"But now," cried he, "that obstacle is surmounted."

"Surmounted only for a moment! for even in your letter this morning you confess the regret with which it fills you."

"And why should I deceive you? Why pretend to think with pleasure, or even with indifference, of an obstacle which has had thus long the power to make me miserable? But where is happiness without allay? Is perfect bliss the condition of humanity? Oh if we refuse to taste it till in its last state of refinement, how shall the cup of evil be ever from our lips?"

"How indeed?" said Cecilia, with a sigh; "the regret, I believe, will remain eternally upon your mind, and she, perhaps, who should cause, might soon be taught to partake of it."

"O Miss Beverley! how have I merited this severity? Did I make my proposals lightly? Did I suffer my eagerness to conquer my reason? Have I not, on the contrary, been steady and considerate? neither biassed by passion nor betrayed by tenderness?"

"And yet in what," said Cecilia, "consists this boasted steadiness? I perceived it indeed, at Delvile-Castle, but here——"

"The pride of heart which supported me there," cried he, "will support me no longer; what sustained my firmness, but your apparent severity? What enabled me to fly you, but your invariable coldness? The rigour with which I trampled upon my feelings I thought fortitude and spirit,—but I knew not then the pitying sympathy of Cecilia!"

"O that you knew it not yet!" cried she, blushing; "before that fatal accident you thought of me, I believe, in a manner far more honourable."

"Impossible! differently, I thought of you, but never better, never so well as now. I then represented you all lovely in beauty, all perfect in goodness and virtue; but it was virtue in its highest majesty, not, as now, blended with the softest sensibility."

"Alas!" said Cecilia, "how the portrait is faded!"

"No, it is but more from the life: it is the sublimity of an angel, mingled with all that is attractive in woman. But who is the friend we may venture to trust? To whom may I give my bond? And from whom may I receive a treasure which for the rest of my life will constitute all its felicity?"

"Where can I," cried Cecilia, "find a friend, who, in this critical moment will instruct me how to act!"

"You will find one," answered he, "in your own bosom: ask but yourself this plain question; will any virtue be offended by your honouring me with your hand?"

"Yes; duty will be offended, since it is contrary to the will of your parents."

"But is there no time for emancipation? Am not I of an age to chuse for myself the partner of my life? Will not you in a few days be the uncontrolled mistress of your actions? Are we not both independant? Your ample fortune all your own, and the estates of my father so entailed they must unavoidably be mine?"

"And are these," said Cecilia, "considerations to set us free from our duty?"

"No, but they are circumstances to relieve us from slavery. Let me not offend you if I am still more explicit. When no law, human or divine, can be injured by our union, when one motive of pride is all that can be opposed to a thousand motives of convenience and happiness, why should we *both* be made unhappy, merely lest that pride should lose its gratification?"

This question, which so often and so angrily she had revolved in her own mind, again silenced her; and Delvile, with the eagerness of approaching success, redoubled his solicitations.

"Be mine," he cried, "sweetest Cecilia, and all will go well. To refer me to my friends is, effectually, to banish me for-ever. Spare me, then, the unavailing task; and save me from the resistless entreaties of a mother, whose every desire I have held sacred, whose wish has been my law, and whose commands I have implicitly, invariably obeyed! Oh generously save me from the dreadful alternative of wounding her maternal heart by a peremptory refusal, or of torturing my own with pangs to which it is unequal by an extorted obedience!"

"Alas!" cried Cecilia, "how utterly impossible I can relieve you!"

"And why? once mine, irrevocably mine——"

"No, that would but irritate,—and irritate past hope of pardon."

"Indeed you are mistaken: to your merit they are far from insensible, and your fortune is just what they wish. Trust me, therefore, when I assure you that their displeasure, which both respect and justice will guard them from ever shewing *you*, will soon die wholly away. I speak not merely from my hopes; in judging my own friends, I consider human nature in general. Inevitable evils are ever best supported. It is suspence, it is hope that make the food of misery; certainty is always endured, because known to be past amendment, and felt to give defiance to struggling."

"And can you," cried Cecilia, "with reasoning so desperate be satisfied?"

"In a situation so extraordinary as ours," answered he, "there is no other. The voice of the world at large will be all in our favour. Our union neither injures our fortunes, nor taints our morality: with the character of each other is satisfied, and both must be alike exculpated from mercenary views of interest, or romantic contempt of poverty; what right have we, then, to repine at an objection which, however potent, is single? Surely none. Oh if wholly unchecked were the happiness I now have in view, if no foul storm sometimes lowered over the prospect, and for a moment obscured its brightness, how could my heart find room for joy so superlative? The whole world might rise against me as the first man in it who had nothing left to wish!''

Cecilia, whose own hopes aided this reasoning, found not much to oppose to it; and with little more of entreaty, and still less of argument, Delvile at length obtained her consent to his plan. Fearfully, indeed, and with unfeigned reluctance she gave it, but it was the only alternative with a separation for-ever, to which she held not the necessity adequate to the pain.

The thanks of Delvile were as vehement as had been his entreaties, which yet, however, were not at an end; the concession she had made was imperfect, unless its performance were immediate, and he now endeavoured to prevail with her to be his before the expiration of a week.

Here, however, his task ceased to be difficult; Cecilia, as ingenuous by nature as she was honourable from principle, having once brought her mind to consent to his proposal, sought not by studied difficulties to enhance the value of her compliance: the great point resolved upon, she held all else of too little importance for a contest.

Mrs. Charlton was now called in, and acquainted with the result of their conference. Her approbation by no means followed the scheme of privacy; yet she was too much rejoiced in seeing her young friend near the period of her long suspence and uneasiness, to oppose any plan which might forward their termination.

Delvile then again begged to know what male confident might be entrusted with their project.

Mr. Monckton immediately occurred to Cecilia, though the certainty of his ill-will to the cause made all application to him disagreeable: but his long and steady friendship for her, his readiness to counsel and assist her, and the promises she had occasionally made, not to act without his advice, all concurred to persuade her that in a matter of such importance, she owed to him her confidence, and should be culpable to proceed without it. Upon him, therefore, she fixed; yet finding in herself a repugnance insuperable to acquainting him with her situation, she agreed that Delvile, who instantly proposed to be her messenger, should open to him the affair, and prepare him for their meeting.

Delvile then, rapid in thought and fertile in expedients, with a celerity and vigour which bore down all objections, arranged the whole conduct of the business. To avoid suspicion, he determined instantly to quit her, and, as soon as he had executed his commission with Mr. Monckton, to hasten to London, that the necessary preparations for their marriage might be made, with dispatch and secrecy. He purposed, also, to find out Mr. Belfield, that he might draw up the bond with which he meant to entrust Mr. Monckton. This measure Cecilia would have opposed, but he refused to listen to her. Mrs. Charlton herself, though her age and infirmities had long confined her to her own house, gratified Cecilia upon this critical occasion with consenting to accompany her to the altar. Mr. Monckton was depended upon for giving her away, and a church in London was the place appointed for the performance of the ceremony. In three days the principal difficulties to the union would be removed by Cecilia's coming of age,* and in five days it was agreed they should actually meet in town. The moment they were married Delvile promised to set off for the Castle, while in another chaise, Cecilia returned to Mrs. Charlton's.

This settled, he conjured her to be punctual, and earnestly recommending himself to her fidelity and affection, he bid her adieu.

CHAPTER VII

A Retrospection

LEFT now to herself, sensations unfelt before filled the heart of Cecilia. All that had passed for a while appeared a dream; her ideas were indistinct, her memory was confused, her faculties seemed all out of order, and she had but an imperfect consciousness either of the transaction in which she had just been engaged, or of the promise she had bound herself to fulfil: even truth from imagination she scarcely could separate, all was darkness and doubt, inquietude and disorder!

But when at length her recollection more clearly returned, and her situation appeared to her such as it really was, divested alike of false terrors or delusive expectations, she found herself still further removed from tranquility.

Hitherto, though no stranger to sorrow, which the sickness and early loss of her friends had first taught her to feel, and which the subsequent anxiety of her own heart had since instructed her to bear, she had yet invariably possessed the consolation of self-approving reflections: but the step she was now about to take, all her principles opposed; it terrified her as undutiful, it shocked her as clandestine, and scarce was Delvile out of sight, before she regretted her consent to it as the loss of her self-esteem, and believed, even if a reconciliation took place, the remembrance of a wilful fault would still follow her, blemish in her own eyes the character she had hoped to support, and be a constant allay to her happiness, by telling her how unworthily she had obtained it.

Where frailty has never been voluntary, nor error stubborn, where the pride of early integrity is unsubdued, and the first purity of innocence is inviolate, how fearfully delicate, how "tremblingly alive,"* is the conscience of man! strange, that what in its first state is so tender, can in its last become so callous!

Compared with the general lot of human misery, Cecilia had suffered nothing; but compared with the exaltation of ideal happiness, she had suffered much; willingly, however, would she again have borne all that had distressed her, experienced the same painful suspence, endured the same melancholy parting, and gone through the same cruel task of combating inclination with reason, to have relieved her virtuous mind from the new-born and intolerable terror of conscientious reproaches.

The equity of her notions permitted her not from the earnestness of Delvile's entreaties to draw any palliation for her consent to his proposal; she was conscious that but for her own too great facility those entreaties would have been ineffectual, since she well knew how little from any other of her admirers they would have availed.

But chiefly her affliction and repentance hung upon Mrs. Delvile, whom she loved, reverenced and honoured, whom she dreaded to offend, and whom she well knew expected from her even exemplary virtue. Her praises, her partiality, her confidence in her character, which hitherto had been her pride, she now only recollected with shame and with sadness. The terror of the first interview never ceased to be present to her; she shrunk even in imagination from her wrath-darting eye, she felt stung by pointed satire, and subdued by cold contempt.

Yet to disappoint Delvile so late, by forfeiting a promise so positively accorded; to trifle with a man who to her had been uniformly candid, to waver when her word was engaged, and retract when he thought himself secure,— honour, justice and shame told her the time was now past.

"And yet is not this," cried she, "placing nominal before actual evil? Is it not studying appearance at the expence of reality? If agreeing to wrong is criminal, is not performing it worse? If repentance for ill actions calls for mercy, has not repentance for ill intentions a yet higher claim?—And what reproaches from Delvile can be so bitter as my own? What separation, what sorrow, what possible calamity can hang upon my mind with such heaviness, as the sense of committing voluntary evil?"

This thought so much affected her, that, conquering all regret either for Delvile or herself, she resolved to write to him instantly, and acquaint him of the alteration in her sentiments.

This, however, after having so deeply engaged herself, was by no means easy; and many letters were begun, but not one of them was finished, when a sudden recollection obliged her to give over the attempt,—for she knew not whither to direct to him.

In the haste with which their plan had been formed and settled, it had never once occurred to them that any occasion for writing was likely to happen. Delvile, indeed, knew that her address would still be the same; and with regard to his own, as his journey to London was to be secret, he purposed not having any fixed habitation. On the day of their marriage, and not before, they had appointed to meet at the house of Mrs. Roberts, in Fetter-Lane, whence they were instantly to proceed to the church.

She might still, indeed, enclose a letter for him in one to Mrs. Hill, to be delivered to him on the destined morning when he called to claim her; but to fail him at the last moment, when Mr. Belfield would have drawn up the bond, when a licence was procured, the clergyman waiting to perform the ceremony, and Delvile without a suspicion but that the next moment would unite them for ever, seemed extending prudence into treachery, and power into tyranny. Delvile had done nothing to merit such treatment, he had practised no deceit, he had been guilty of no perfidy, he had opened to her his whole heart, and after shewing it without any disguise, the option had been all her own to accept or refuse him.

A ray of joy now broke its way through the gloom of her apprehensions. "Ah!" cried she, "I have not, then, any means to recede! an unprovoked breach of promise at the very moment destined for its performance, would but vary the mode of acting wrong, without approaching nearer to acting right!"

This idea for a while not merely calmed but delighted her; to be the wife of Delvile seemed now a matter of necessity, and she soothed herself with believing that to struggle against it were vain.

The next morning during breakfast Mr. Monckton arrived.

Not greater, though winged with joy, had been the expedition of Delvile to open to him his plan, than was his own, though only goaded by desperation, to make some effort with Cecilia for rendering it abortive. Nor could all his self-denial, the command which he held over his passions, nor the rigour with which his feelings were made subservient to his interest, in this sudden hour of trial, avail to preserve his equanimity. The refinements of hypocrisy, and the arts of insinuation, offered advantages too distant, and exacted attentions too subtle, for a moment so alarming; those arts and those attentions he had already for many years practised, with an address the most masterly, and a diligence the most indefatigable: success had of late seemed to follow his toils; the encreasing infirmities of his wife, the disappointment and retirement of Cecilia, uniting to promise him a conclusion equally speedy and happy; when now, by a sudden and unexpected stroke, the sweet solace of his future cares, the long-projected recompence of his past sufferings, was to be snatched from him for-ever, and by one who, compared with himself, was but the acquaintance of a day.

Almost wholly off his guard from the surprise and horror of this apprehension, he entered the room with such an air of haste and perturbation, that Mrs. Charlton and her grand-daughters demanded what was the matter.

"I am come," he answered abruptly, yet endeavouring to recollect himself, "to speak with Miss Beverley upon business of some importance."

"My dear, then," said Mrs. Charlton, "you had better go with Mr. Monckton into your dressing-room."*

Cecilia, deeply blushing, arose and led the way: slowly, however, she proceeded, though urged by Mr. Monckton to make speed. Certain of his disapprobation, and but doubtfully relieved from her own, she dreaded a conference which on his side, she foresaw, would be all exhortation and reproof, and on hers all timidity and shame.

"Good God," cried he, "Miss Beverley, what is this you have done? bound yourself to marry a man who despises, who scorns, who refuses to own you!"

Shocked by this opening, she started, but could make no answer.

"See you not," he continued, "the indignity which is offered you? Does the loose, the flimsy veil with which it is covered, hide it from your understanding, or disguise it from your delicacy?"

"I thought not,—I meant not," said she, more and more

confounded, "to submit to any indignity, though my pride, in an exigence so peculiar, may give way, for a while, to convenience."

"To convenience?" repeated he, "to contempt, to derision, to insolence!"—

"O Mr. Monckton!" interrupted Cecilia, "make not use of such expressions! they are too cruel for me to hear, and if I thought they were just, would make me miserable for life!"

"You are deceived, grossly deceived," replied he, "if you doubt their truth for a moment: they are not, indeed, even decently concealed from you; they are glaring as the day, and wilful blindness can alone obscure them."

"I am sorry, Sir," said Cecilia, whose confusion, at a charge so rough, began now to give way to anger, "if this is your opinion; and I am sorry, too, for the liberty I have taken in troubling you upon such a subject."

An apology so full of displeasure instantly taught Mr. Monckton the error he was committing, and checking, therefore, the violence of those emotions to which his sudden and desperate disappointment gave rise, and which betrayed him into reproaches so unskilful, he endeavoured to recover his accustomed equanimity, and assuming an air of friendly openness, said, "Let me not offend you, my dear Miss Beverley, by a freedom which results merely from a solicitude to serve you, and which the length and intimacy of our acquaintance had, I hoped, long since authorised. I know not how to see you on the brink of destruction without speaking, yet, if you are averse to my sincerity, I will curb it, and have done."

"No, do not have done," cried she, much softened; "your sincerity does me nothing but honour, and hitherto, I am sure, it has done me nothing but good. Perhaps I deserve your utmost censure; I feared it, indeed, before you came, and ought, therefore, to have better prepared myself for meeting with it."

This speech completed Mr. Monckton's self-victory; it shewed him not only the impropriety of his turbulence, but gave him room to hope that a mildness more crafty would have better success.

"You cannot but be certain," he answered, "that my zeal proceeds wholly from a desire to be of use to you: my knowledge of the world might possibly, I thought, assist your inexperience, and the disinterestedness of my regard, might enable me to see and to point out the dangers to which you are exposed, from artifice and duplicity in those who have other purposes to answer than what simply belong to your welfare."

"Neither artifice nor duplicity," cried Cecilia, jealous for the honour of Delvile, "have been practised against me. Argument, and not persuasion, determined me, and if I have done wrong—those who prompted me have erred as unwittingly as myself."

"You are too generous to perceive the difference, or you would find nothing less alike. If, however, my plainness will not offend you, before it is quite too late, I will point out to you a few of the evils,—for there are some I cannot even mention, which at this instant do not merely threaten, but await you."

Cecilia started at this terrifying offer, and afraid to accept, yet ashamed to refuse it, hung back irresolute.

"I see," said Mr. Monckton, after a pause of some continuance, "your determination admits no appeal. The consequence must, indeed, be all your own, but I am greatly grieved to find how little you are aware of its seriousness. Hereafter you will wish, perhaps, that the friend of your earliest youth had been permitted to advise you; at present you only think him officious and impertinent, and therefore he can do nothing you will be so likely to approve as quitting you. I wish you, then, greater happiness than seems prepared to follow you, and a counsellor more prosperous in offering his assistance."

He would then have taken his leave: but Cecilia called out, "Oh, Mr. Monckton! do you then give me up?"

"Not unless you wish it."

"Alas, I know not what to wish! except, indeed, the restoration of that security from self-blame, which till yesterday, even in the midst of disappointment, quieted and consoled me."

"Are you, then, sensible you have gone wrong, yet resolute not to turn back?"

"Could I tell, could I see," cried she, with energy, "which way I *ought* to turn, not a moment would I hesitate how to act! my heart should have no power, my happiness no choice,—I would recover my own esteem by any sacrifice that could be made!"

"What, then, can possibly be your doubt? To be as you were yesterday what is wanting but your own inclination?"

"Every thing is wanting; right, honour, firmness, all by which the just are bound, and all which the conscientious hold sacred!"

"These scruples are merely romantic; your own good sense, had it fairer play, would contemn them; but it is warped at present by prejudice and prepossession."

"No, indeed!" cried she, colouring at the charge, "I may have entered too precipitately into an engagement I ought to have avoided, but it is weakness of judgment, not of heart, that disables me from retrieving my error."

"Yet you will neither hear whither it may lead you, nor which way you may escape from it?"

"Yes, Sir," cried she, trembling, "I am now ready to hear both."

"Briefly, then, I will tell you. It will lead you into a family of which every individual will disdain you; it will make you inmate of an house of which no other inmate will associate with you; you will be insulted as an inferior, and reproached as an intruder; your birth will be a subject of ridicule, and your whole race only named with derision: and while the elders of the proud castle treat you with open contempt, the man for whom you suffer will not dare to support you."

"Impossible! impossible!" cried Cecilia, with the most angry emotion; "this whole representation is exaggerated, and the latter part is utterly without foundation."

"The latter part," said Mr. Monckton, "is of all other least disputable: the man who now dares not own, will then never venture to defend you. On the contrary, to make peace for himself, he will be the first to neglect you. The ruined estates of his ancestors will be repaired by your fortune, while the name which you carry into his family will be constantly resented as an injury; you will thus be plundered though you are scorned, and told to consider yourself honoured that they condescend to make use of you! nor here rests the evil of a forced connection with so much arrogance,—even your children, should you have any, will be educated to despise you!"

"Dreadful and horrible!" cried Cecilia;—"I can hear no more,—Oh, Mr. Monckton, what a prospect have you opened to my view!"

"Fly from it, then, while it is yet in your power,—when two paths are before you, chuse not that which leads to destruction; send instantly after Delvile, and tell him you have* recovered your senses."

"I would long since have sent,—I wanted not a representation such as this,—but I know not how to direct to him, nor whither he is gone."

"All art and baseness to prevent your recantation!"

"No, Sir, no," cried she, with quickness; "whatever may be the truth of your painting in general, all that concerns——"

Ashamed of the vindication she intended, which yet in her own mind was firm and animated, she stopt, and left the sentence unfinished.

"In what place were you to meet?" said Mr. Monckton; "you can at least send to him there."

"We were only to have met," answered she, in much confusion, "at the last moment,—and that would be too late—it would be too——I could not, without some previous notice, break a promise which I gave without any restriction."

"Is this your only objection?"

"It is: but it is one which I cannot conquer."

"Then you would give up this ill-boding connection, but from notions of delicacy with regard to the time?"

"Indeed I meant it, before you came."

"*I*, then, will obviate this objection: give me but the commission, either verbally or in writing, and I will undertake to find him out, and deliver it before night."

Cecilia, little expecting this offer, turned extremely pale, and after pausing some moments, said in a faultering voice, "What, then, Sir, is your advice, in what manner——"

"I will say to him all that is necessary; trust the matter with me."

"No,—he deserves, at least, an apology from myself,—though how to make it—"

She stopt, she hesitated, she went out of the room for pen and ink, she returned without them, and the agitation of her mind every instant encreasing, she begged him, in a faint voice, to excuse her while she consulted with Mrs. Charlton, and promising to wait upon him again, was hurrying away.

Mr. Monckton, however, saw too great danger in so much emotion to trust her out of his sight: he told her, therefore, that she would only encrease her perplexity, without reaping any advantage, by an application to Mrs. Charlton, and that* if she was really sincere in wishing to recede, there was not a moment to be lost, and Delvile should immediately be pursued.

Cecilia, sensible of the truth of this speech, and once more recollecting the unaffected earnestness with which but an hour or two before, she had herself desired to renounce this engagement, now summoned her utmost courage to her aid, and, after a short, but painful struggle, determined to act consistently with her professions and her character, and, by one great and final effort, to conclude all her doubts, and try to silence even her regret, by completing the triumph of fortitude over inclination.

She called, therefore, for pen and ink, and without venturing herself from the room, wrote the following letter.

TO MORTIMER DELVILE, Esq.

Accuse me not of caprice, and pardon my irresolution, when you find me shrinking with terror from the promise I have made, and no longer either able or willing to perform it. The reproaches of your family I should very ill endure; but the reproaches of my own heart for an action I can neither approve nor defend, would be still more oppressive.

With such a weight upon the mind length of life would be
burthensome; with a sensation of guilt early death would be
terrific! These being my notions of the engagement into
which we have entered, you cannot wonder, and you have
still less reason to repine, that I dare not fulfil it. Alas! where
would be your chance of happiness with one who in the very
act of becoming yours would forfeit her own!

I blush at this tardy recantation, and I grieve at the
disappointment it may occasion you: but I have yielded to
the exhortations of an inward monitor, who is never to be
neglected with impunity. Consult him yourself; and I shall
need no other advocate.

Adieu, and may all felicity attend you! if to hear of the
almost total privation of mine, will mitigate the resentment
with which you will probably read this letter, it may be
mitigated but too easily! Yet my consent to a clandestine
action shall never be repeated; and though I confess to you
I am not happy, I solemnly declare my resolution is
unalterable. A little reflection will tell you I am right, though
a great deal of lenity may scarce suffice to make you pardon
my being right no sooner.

C.B.

This letter, which with trembling haste, resulting from a
fear of her own steadiness, she folded and sealed, Mr.
Monckton, from the same apprehension, yet more eagerly
received, and scarce waiting to bid her good morning,
mounted his horse, and pursued his way to London.

Cecilia returned to Mrs. Charlton to acquaint her with
what had passed: and notwithstanding the sorrow she felt in
apparently injuring the man whom, in the whole world she
most wished to oblige, she yet found a satisfaction in the
sacrifice she had made, that recompensed her for much of
her sufferings, and soothed her into something like
tranquility; the true power of virtue she had scarce
experienced before, for she found it a resource against the
cruellest dejection, and a supporter in the bitterest
disappointment.

CHAPTER VIII

An Embarrassment

THE day passed on without any intelligence; the next day, also, passed in the same manner, and on the third, which was her birth-day, Cecilia became of age.

The preparations which had long been making among her tenants to celebrate this event, Cecilia appeared to take some share, and endeavoured to find some pleasure in. She gave a public dinner to all who were willing to partake of it, she promised redress to those who complained of hard usage, she pardoned many debts, and distributed money, food, and cloathing to the poor. These benevolent occupations made time seem less heavy, and while they freed her from solitude, diverted her suspense. She still, however, continued at the house of Mrs. Charlton, the workmen having disappointed her in finishing her own.

But, in defiance of her utmost exertion, towards the evening of this day the uneasiness of her uncertainty grew almost intolerable. The next morning she had promised Delvile to set out for London, and he expected the morning after to claim her for his wife; yet Mr. Monckton neither sent nor came, and she knew not if her letter was delivered, or if still he was unprepared for the disappointment by which he was awaited. A secret regret for the unhappiness she must occasion him, which silently yet powerfully reproached her, stole fast upon her mind, and poisoned its tranquility; for though her opinion was invariable in holding his proposal to be wrong, she thought too highly of his character to believe he would have made it but from a mistaken notion it was right. She painted him, therefore, to herself, as glowing with indignation, accusing her of inconsistency, and perhaps suspecting her of coquetry, and imputing her change of conduct to motives the most trifling and narrow, till with resentment and disdain, he drove her wholly from his thoughts.

In a few minutes, however, the picture was reversed; Delvile no more appeared storming nor unreasonable; his face wore an aspect of sorrow, and his brow was clouded with disappointment: he forebore to reproach her, but the look which her imagination delineated was more piercing than words of severest import.

These images pursued and tormented her, drew tears from her eyes, and loaded her heart with anguish. Yet, when she recollected that her conduct had had in view an higher motive than pleasing Delvile, she felt that it ought to offer her an higher satisfaction: she tried, therefore, to revive her spirits, by reflecting upon her integrity, and refused all indulgence to this enervating sadness, beyond what the weakness of human nature demands, as some relief to its sufferings upon every fresh attack of misery.

A conduct such as this was the best antidote against affliction, whose arrows are never with so little difficulty repelled, as when they light upon a conscience which no self-reproach has laid bare to their malignancy.

Before six o'clock the next morning, her maid came to her bedside with the following letter, which she told her had been brought by an express.

TO MISS BEVERLEY.

May this letter, with one only from Delvile-Castle, be the last that *Miss Beverley* may ever receive!

Yet sweet to me as is that hope, I write in the utmost uneasiness; I have just heard that a gentleman, whom, by the description that is given of him, I imagine is Mr. Monckton, has been in search of me with a letter which he was anxious to deliver immediately.

Perhaps this letter is from Miss Beverley, perhaps it contains directions which ought instantly to be followed: could I divine what they are, with what eagerness would I study to anticipate their execution! It will not, I hope, be too late to receive them on Saturday, when her power over my actions will be confirmed, and when every wish she will communicate, shall be gratefully, joyfully, and with delight fulfilled.

I have sought Belfield in vain; he has left Lord Vannelt, and no one knows whither he is gone. I have been obliged, therefore, to trust a stranger to draw up the bond; but he is a man of good character, and the time of secresy will be too short to put his discretion in much danger. To-morrow, Friday, I shall spend solely in endeavouring to discover Mr. Monckton; I have leisure sufficient for the search, since so prosperous has been my diligence, that *every thing is prepared!*

I have seen some lodgings in Pall-Mall, which I think are commodious and will suit you: send a servant, therefore, before you to secure them. If upon your arrival I should venture to meet you there, be not, I beseech you, offended or alarmed; I shall take every possible precaution neither to be known nor seen, and I will stay with you only three minutes. The messenger who carries this is ignorant from whom it comes, for I fear his repeating my name among your servants, and he could scarce return to me with an answer before you will yourself be in town. Yes, loveliest Cecilia! at the very moment you receive this letter, the chaise will, I flatter myself, be at the door, which is to bring to me a treasure that will enrich every future hour of my life! And oh as to me it will be exhaustless, may but its sweet dispenser experience some share of the happiness she bestows, and then what, save her own purity, will be so perfect, so unsullied, as the felicity of her

                                                          M. D?

The perturbation of Cecilia upon reading this letter was unspeakable: Mr. Monckton, she found, had been wholly unsuccessful, all her heroism had answered no purpose, and the transacton was as backward as before she had exerted it.

She was now, therefore, called upon to think and act entirely for herself. Her opinion was still the same, nor did her resolution waver, yet how to put it in execution she could not discern.

To write to him was impossible, since she was ignorant where he was to be found; to disappoint him at the last moment she could not resolve, since such a conduct appeared to her unfeeling and unjustifiable: for a few instants she thought of having him waited for at night in London, with a letter; but the danger of entrusting any one with such a commission, and the uncertainty of finding him, should he disguise himself, made the success of this scheme too precarious for trial.

One expedient alone occurred to her, which, though she felt to be hazardous, she believed was without an alternative: this was no other than hastening to London herself, consenting to the interview he had proposed in Pall-Mall, and then, by strongly stating her objections, and confessing the grief they occasioned her, to pique at once his generosity and his pride upon releasing her himself from the engagement into which he had entered.

She had no time to deliberate; her plan, therefore, was decided almost as soon as formed, and every moment being precious, she was obliged to awaken Mrs. Charlton, and communicate to her at once the letter from Delvile, and the new resolution she had taken.

Mrs. Charlton, having no object in view but the happiness of her young friend, with a facility that looked not for objections, and scarce saw them when presented, agreed to the expedition, and kindly consented to accompany her to London; for Cecilia, however concerned to hurry and fatigue her, was too anxious for the sanction of her presence to hesitate in soliciting it.

A chaise, therefore, was ordered; and with post-horses for speed,* and two servants on horseback, the moment Mrs. Charlton was ready, they set out on their journey.

Scarce had they proceeded two miles on their way, when they were met by Mr. Monckton, who was hastening to their house.

Amazed and alarmed at a sight so unexpected, he stopt the chaise to enquire whither they was going.*

Cecilia, without answering, asked if her letter had yet been received?

"I could not," said Mr. Monckton, "deliver it to a man who was not to be found: I was this moment coming to acquaint how vainly I had sought him; but still that your journey is unnecessary unless voluntary, since I have left it at the house where you told me you should meet to-morrow morning, and where he must then unavoidably receive it.''

"Indeed, Sir," cried Cecilia, "to-morrow morning will be too late,—in conscience, in justice, and even in decency too late! I *must*, therefore, go to town; yet I go not, believe me, in opposition to your injunctions, but to enable myself, without treachery or dishonour, to fulfil them."

Mr. Monckton, aghast and confounded, made not any answer, till Cecilia gave orders to the postilion to drive on: he then hastily called to stop him, and began the warmest expostulations; but Cecilia, firm when she believed herself right, though wavering when fearful she was wrong, told him it was now too late to change her plan, and repeating her orders to the postilion, left him to his own reflections: grieved herself to reject his counsel, yet too intently occupied by her own affairs and designs, to think long of any other.

CHAPTER IX

A Torment

AT —— they stopt for dinner; Mrs. Charlton being too much fatigued to go on without some rest, though the haste of Cecilia to meet Delvile time enough for new arranging their affairs, made her regret every moment that was spent upon the road.

Their meal was not long, and they were returning to their chaise, when they were suddenly encountered by Mr. Morrice, who was just alighted from his horse.

He congratulated himself upon the happiness of meeting them with the air of a man who nothing doubted that happiness being mutual; then hastening to speak of the Grove, "I could hardly," he cried, "get away; my friend Monckton won't know what to do without me, for Lady Margaret, poor old soul, is in a shocking bad way indeed; there's hardly any staying in the room with her; her breathing is just like the grunting of a hog. She can't possibly last long, for she's quite upon her last legs, and tumbles about so when she walks alone, one would swear she was drunk."

"If you take infirmity," said Mrs. Charlton, who was now helped into the chaise, "for intoxication, you must suppose no old person sober."

"Vastly well said, ma'am," cried he; "I really forgot your being an old lady yourself, or I should not have made the observation. However, as to poor Lady Margaret, she may do as well as ever by and bye, for she has an excellent constitution, and I suppose she has been hardly any better than she is now these forty years, for I remember when I was quite a boy hearing her called a limping old puddle."*

"Well, we'll discuss this matter, if you please," said Cecilia, "some other time." And ordered the postilion to drive on. But before they came to their next stage, Morrice having changed his horse, joined them, and rode on by their side, begging them to observe what haste he had made on purpose to have the pleasure of escorting them.

This forwardness was very offensive to Mrs. Charlton, whose years and character had long procured her more deference and respect: but Cecilia, anxious only to hasten her journey, was indifferent to every thing, save what retarded it.

At the same Inn they both again changed horses, and he still continued riding with them, and occasionally talking, till they were within twenty miles of London, when a disturbance upon the road exciting his curiosity, he hastily rode away from them to enquire into its cause.

Upon coming up to the place whence it proceeded, they saw a party of gentleman on horseback surrounding a chaise which had been just overturned; and while the confusion in the road obliged the postilion to stop, Cecilia heard a lady's voice exclaiming, "I declare I dare say I am killed!" and instantly recollecting Miss Larolles, the fear of discovery and delay made her desire the man to drive on with all speed. He was preparing to obey her, but Morrice, gallopping after them, called out "Miss Beverley, one of the ladies that has been overturned, is an acquaintance of yours. I used to see her with you at Mrs. Harrel's."

"Did you?" said Cecilia, much disconcerted, "I hope she is not hurt?"

"No, not at all; but the lady with her is bruised to death; won't you come and see her?"

"I am too much in haste at present,—and I can do them no good; but Mrs. Charlton I am sure will spare her servant, if he can be of any use."

"O but the young lady wants to speak to you; she is coming up to the chaise as fast as ever she can."

"And how should she know me?" cried Cecilia, with much surprise; "I am sure she could not see me."

"O, I told her," answered Morrice, with a nod of self-approbation for what he had done, "I told her it was you, for I knew I could soon overtake you."

Displeasure at this officiousness was unavailing, for looking out of the window, she perceived Miss Larolles, followed by half her party, not three paces from the chaise."

"O my dear creature," she called out, "what a terrible accident! I assure you I am so monstrously frightened you've no idea. It's the luckiest thing in the world that you were going this way. Never any thing happened so excessively provoking; you've no notion what a fall we've had. It's horrid shocking, I assure you. How have you been all this time? You can't conceive how glad I am to see you."

"And to which will Miss Beverley answer first," cried a voice which announced Mr. Gosport, "the joy or the sorrow? For so adroitly are they blended, that a common auditor could with difficulty decide whether condolence, or congratulation should have the precedency."

"How can you be so excessive horrid," cried Miss Larolles, to talk of congratulation, when one's in such a shocking panic that one does not know if one's dead or alive!"

"Dead, then, for any wager," returned he, "if we may judge by* your stillness."

"I desire, now, you won't begin joking," cried she, "for I assure you it's an excessive serious affair. I was never so rejoiced in my life as when I found I was not killed. I've been so squeezed you've no notion. I thought for a full hour I had broke both my arms."

"And my heart at the same time," said Mr. Gosport; "I hope you did not imagine that the least fragile of the three?"

"All our hearts, give me leave to add," said Captain Aresby—just then advancing, "all our hearts must have been *abimés*, by the indisposition of Miss Larolles, had not their doom been fortunately revoked by the sight of Miss Beverley."

"Well, this is excessive odd," cried Miss Larolles, "that every body should run away so from poor Mrs. Mears; she'll be so affronted you've no idea. I thought, Captain Aresby, you would have stayed to take care of her."

"I'll run and see how she is myself," cried Morrice, and away he gallopped.

"Really, ma'am," said the Captain, "I am quite *au desespoir* to have failed in any of my devoirs;* but I make it a principle to be a mere looker on upon these occasions, lest I should be so unhappy as to commit any *faux pas* by too much *empressement*."

"An admirable caution!" said Mr. Gosport, "and, to so ardent a temper, a necessary check!"

Cecilia, whom the surprise and vexation of so unseasonable a meeting, when she particularly wished to have escaped all notice, had hitherto kept in painful silence, began now to recover some presence of mind; and making her compliments to Miss Larolles and Mr. Gosport, with a slight bow to the Captain, she apologized for hurrying away, but told them she had an engagement in London which could not be deferred, and was then giving orders to the postilion to drive on, when Morrice returning full speed, called out "The poor lady's so bad she is not able to stir a step; she can't put a foot to the ground, and she says she's quite black and blue; so I told her I was sure Miss Beverley would not refuse to make room for her in her chaise, till the other can be put to rights; and she says she shall take it as a great favour. Here, postilion, a little more to the right! come, ladies and gentlemen, get out of the way."

This impertinence, however extraordinary, Cecilia could not oppose; for Mrs. Charlton, ever compassionate and complying where there was any appearance of distress,

instantly seconded the proposal: the chaise, therefore, was
turned back, and she was obliged to offer a place in it to
Mrs. Mears, who, though more frightened than hurt,
readily accepted it, notwithstanding, to make way for her
without incommoding Mrs. Charlton, she was forced to get
out herself.*

She failed not, however, to desire that all possible
expedition might be used, in refitting the other chaise for
their reception; and all the gentlemen but one, dismounted
their horses, in order to assist, or seem to assist in getting it
ready.

This only* unconcerned spectator in the midst of the
apparent general bustle, was Mr. Meadows; who viewed all
that passed without troubling himself to interfere, and with
an air of the most evident carelessness whether matters went
well or went ill.

Miss Larolles, now returning to the scene of action,
suddenly screamed out, "O dear, where's my little dog! I
never thought of him, I declare! I love him better than any
thing in the world. I would not have him hurt for an
hundred thousand pounds. Lord, where is he?"

"Crushed or suffocated in the overturn, no doubt," said
Mr. Gosport; "but as you must have been his executioner,
what softer death could he die? If you will yourself inflict the
punishment, I will submit to the same fate."

"Lord, how you love to plague one!" cried she: and then
enquired among the servants what was become of her
dog. The poor little animal, forgotten by its mistress, and
disregarded by all others, was now discovered by its yelping;
and soon found to have been the most material sufferer by
the overturn, one of its fore legs being broken.

Could screams or lamentations, reproaches to the servants,
or complaints against the Destinies, have abated his pain,
or made a callus of the fracture, but short would have
been the duration of his misery; for neither words were
saved, nor lungs were spared, the very air was rent with
cries, and all present were upbraided as if accomplices in the
disaster.

The postilion, at length, interrupted this vociferation with news that the chaise was again fit for use; and Cecilia, eager to be gone, finding him little regarded, repeated what he said to Miss Larolles.

"The chaise?" cried she, "why you don't suppose I'll ever get into that horrid chaise any more? I do assure you I would not upon any account."

"Not get into it?" said Cecilia, "for what purpose, then, have we all waited till it was ready?"

"O, I declare I would not go in it for forty thousand worlds. I would rather walk to an inn, if it's a hundred and fifty miles off."

"But as it happens," said Mr. Gosport, "to be only seven miles, I fancy you will condescend to ride."

"Seven miles! Lord how shocking! you frighten me so you have no idea. Poor Mrs. Mears! She'll have to go quite alone. I dare say the chaise will be down fifty times by the way. Ten to one but she breaks her neck! only conceive how horrid! I assure you I am excessive glad I am out of it."

"Very friendly, indeed!" said Mr. Gosport. "Mrs. Mears, then, may break her bones at her leisure!"

Mrs. Mears, however, when applied to, professed an equal aversion to the carriage in which she had been so unfortunate, and declared she would rather walk than return to it, though one of her ancles was already so swelled that she could hardly stand.

"Why then the best way, ladies," cried Morrice, with the look of a man happy in vanquishing all difficulties, "will be for Mrs. Charlton, and that poor lady with the bruises, to go together in that sound chaise, and then for us gentlemen to escort this young lady and Miss Beverley on foot, till we all come to the next inn. Miss Beverley, I know, is an excellent walker, for I have heard Mr. Monckton say so."

Cecilia, though in the utmost consternation at a proposal, which must so long retard a journey she had so many reasons to wish hastened, knew not how either in decency or humanity to oppose it: and the fear of raising suspicion, from a consciousness how much there was to suspect, forced her to curb her impatience, and reduced her even to repeat the offer which Morrice had made, though she could scarce look at him for anger at his unseasonable forwardness.

No voice dissenting, the troop began to be formed. The foot consisted of the two young ladies and Mr. Gosport, who alighted to walk with Cecilia; the cavalry, of Mr. Meadows, the Captain, and Morrice, who walked their horses a foot pace, while the rest of the party rode on with the chaise, as attendants upon Mrs. Mears.

Just before they set off, Mr. Meadows, riding negligently up to the carriage, exerted himself so far as to say to Mrs. Mears, "Are you hurt, ma'am?" and, at the same instant, seeming to recollect Cecilia, he turned about, and yawning while he touched his hat, said, "O, how d'ye do, ma'am?" and then, without waiting an answer to either of his questions, flapped it over his eyes, and joined the cavalcade, though without appearing to have any consciousness that he belonged to it.

Cecilia would most gladly have used the rejected chaise herself, but could not make such a proposal to Mrs. Charlton, who was past the age and the courage for even any appearance of enterprize. Upon enquiry, however, she had the satisfaction to hear that the distance to the next stage was but two miles, though multiplied to seven by the malice of Mr. Gosport.

Miss Larolles carried her little dog in her arms, declaring she would never more trust him a moment away from her. She acquainted Cecilia that she had been for some time upon a visit to Mrs. Mears, who, with the rest of the party, had taken her to see —— house and gardens, where they had made an early dinner, from which they were just returning home when the chaise broke down.

She then proceeded, with her usual volubility, to relate the little nothings that had passed since the winter, flying from subject to subject, with no meaning but to be heard, and no wish but to talk, ever rapid in speech, though minute in detail. This loquacity met not with any interruption, save now and then a sarcastic remark from Mr. Gosport; for Cecilia was too much occupied by her own affairs, to answer or listen to such uninteresting discourse.

Her silence, however, was at length forcibly broken; Mr. Gosport, taking advantage of the first moment Miss Larolles stopt for breath, said, "Pray what carries you to town, Miss Beverley, at this time of the year?"

Cecilia, whose thoughts had been wholly employed upon what would pass at her approaching meeting with Delvile, was so entirely unprepared for this question, that she could make to it no manner of answer, till Mr. Gosport, in a tone of some surprise, repeated it, and then, not without hesitation, she said,* "I have some business, Sir, in London,— pray how long have you been in the country?"

"Business, have you?" cried he, struck by her evasion; "and pray what can you and business have in common?"

"More than you may imagine," answered she, with greater steadiness; "and perhaps before long I may even have enough to teach me the enjoyment of leisure."

"Why you don't pretend to play my Lady Notable, and become your own steward?"*

"And what can I do better?"

"What? Why seek one ready made to take the trouble off your hands. There are such creatures to be found, I promise you: beasts of burthen, who will freely undertake the management of your estate, for no other reward than the trifling one of possessing it. Can you no where meet with such an animal?"

"I don't know," answered she, laughing, "I have not been looking out."

"And have none such made application to you?"

"Why no,—I believe not."

"Fie, fie! no register-office keeper* has been pestered with more claimants. You know they assault you by dozens."

"You must pardon me, indeed, I know not any such thing."

"You know, then, why they do not, and that is much the same."

"I may conjecture why, at least: the place, I suppose, is not worth the service."

"No, no; the place, they conclude, is already seized, and the fee-simple* of the estate is the heart of the owner. Is it not so?"

"The heart of the owner," answered she, a little

confused, "may, indeed, be simple, but not, perhaps, so easily seized as you imagine."

"Have you, then, wisely saved it from a storm, by a generous surrender? you have been, indeed, in an excellent school for the study both of attack and defence; Delvile-Castle is a fortress which, even in ruins, proves its strength by its antiquity: and it teaches, also, an admirable lesson, by displaying the dangerous, the infallible power of time, which defies all might, and undermines all strength; which breaks down every barrier, and shews nothing endurable but itself." Then looking at her with an arch earnestness, "I think," he added, "You made a long visit there; did this observation never occur to you? did you never perceive, never *feel*, rather, the insidious properties of time?"

"Yes, certainly," answered she, alarmed at the very mention of Delvile-Castle, yet affecting to understand literally what was said metaphorically, "the havock of time upon the place could not fail striking me."

"And was its havock," said he, yet more archly, "merely external? is all within safe? sound and firm? and did the length of your residence shew its power by no new mischief?"

"Doubtless, not," answered she, with the same pretended ignorance, "the place is not in so desperate a condition as to exhibit any visible marks of decay in the course of three or four months."

"And, do you not know," cried he, "that the place to which I allude may receive a mischief in as many minutes which double the number of years cannot rectify? The internal parts of a building are not less vulnerable to accident than its outside; and though the evil may more easily be concealed, it will with greater difficulty be remedied. Many a fair structure have I seen, which, like that now before me," (looking with much significance at Cecilia,) "has to the eye seemed perfect in all its parts, and unhurt either by time or casualty, while within, some lurking evil, some latent injury, has secretly worked its way into the very *heart* of the edifice, where it has consumed its strength, and laid waste its powers, till, sinking deeper and deeper, it has sapped its very foundation, before the superstructure has exhibited any token of danger. Is such an accident among the things you hold to be possible?"

"Your language," said she, colouring very high, "is so florid, that I must own it renders your meaning rather obscure."

"Shall I illustrate it by an example? Suppose, during your abode in Delvile-Castle,——"

"No, no," interrupted she, with involuntary quickness, "why should I trouble you to make illustrations?"

"O pray, my dear creature," cried Miss Larolles, "how is Mrs. Harrel? I was never so sorry for any body in my life. I quite forgot to ask after her."

"Ay, poor Harrel!" cried Morrice, "he was a great loss to his friends. I had just begun to have a regard for him: we were growing extremely intimate. Poor fellow! he really gave most excellent dinners."

"Harrel?" suddenly exclaimed Mr. Meadows, who seemed just then to first hear what was going forward, "who was he?"

"O, as good-natured a fellow as ever I knew in my life," answered Morrice; "he was never out of humour: he was drinking and singing and dancing to the very last moment. Don't you remember him, Sir, that night at Vauxhall?"

Mr. Meadows made not any answer, but rode languidly on.

Morrice, ever more flippant than sagacious, called out, "I really believe the gentleman's deaf! he won't so much as say *umph*, and *hay*, now; but I'll give him such a hallow in his ears, as shall make him hear me whether he will or no. Sir! I say!" bawling aloud, "have you forgot that night at Vauxhall?"

Mr. Meadows, starting at being thus shouted at, looked towards Morrice with some surprise, and said, "Were you so obliging, Sir, as to speak to me?"

"Lord, yes, Sir," said Morrice, amazed; "I thought you had asked something about Mr. Harrel, so I just made an answer to it;—that's all."

"Sir you are very good," returned he, slightly bowing,

and then looking another way, as if thoroughly satisfied with
what had passed.

"But I say, Sir," resumed Morrice, "don't you
remember how Mr. Harrel——"

"Mr. who, Sir?"

"Mr. Harrel, Sir; was not you just now asking me who
he was?"

"O, ay, true," cried Meadows, in a tone of extreme
weariness, "I am much obliged to you. Pray give my
respects to him." And, touching his hat,* he was riding
away; but the astonished Morrice called out, "Your respects
to him? why lord! Sir, don't you know he's dead?"

"Dead?—who, Sir?"

"Why Mr. Harrel, Sir."

"Harrel?—O, very true," cried Meadows, with a face of
sudden recollection; "he shot himself, I think, or was
knocked down, or something of that sort. I remember it
perfectly."

"O pray," cried Miss Larolles, "don't let's talk about it,
it's the cruellest thing I ever knew in my life. I assure you
I was so shocked, I thought I should never have got the
better of it. I remember the next night at Ranelagh I could
talk of nothing else. I dare say I told it to 500 people. I assure
you I was tired to death; only conceive how distressing!"

"An excellent method," cried Mr. Gosport, "to drive it
out of your own head, by driving it into the heads of your
neighbours! But were you not afraid, by such an ebullition
of pathos, to burst as many hearts as you had auditors?"

"O I assure you," cried she, "every body was so
excessive shocked you've no notion; one heard of nothing
else; all the world was raving mad about it."

"Really yes," cried the Captain; "the subject was *obsedé*
upon one *partout*. There was scarce any breathing for it: it
poured from all directions; I must confess I was *aneanti* with
it to a degree."

"But the most shocking thing in nature," cried Miss
Larolles, "was going to the sale. I never missed a single
day.* One used to meet the whole world there, and every
body was so sorry you can't conceive. It was quite horrid.

I assure you I never suffered so much before; it made me so unhappy you can't imagine."

"That I am most ready to grant," said Mr. Gosport, "be the powers of imagination ever so excentric."

"Sir Robert Floyer and Mr. Marriot," continued Miss Larolles, "have behaved so ill you've no idea, for they have done nothing ever since but say how monstrously Mr. Harrel had cheated them, and how they lost such immense sums by him;—only conceive how ill-natured!"

"And they complain," cried Morrice, "that old Mr. Delvile used them worse; for that when they had been defrauded of all that money on purpose to pay their addresses to Miss Beverley, he would never let them see her, but all of a sudden took her off into the country, on purpose to marry her to his own son."

The cheeks of Cecilia now glowed with the deepest blushes; but finding by a general silence that she was expected to make some answer, she said, with what unconcern she could assume, "They were very much mistaken; Mr. Delvile had no such view."

"Indeed?" cried Mr. Gosport, again perceiving her change of countenance; "and is it possible you have actually escaped a siege, while every body concluded you taken by assault? Pray where is young Delvile at present?"

"I don't—I can't tell, Sir."

"Is it long since you have seen him?"

"It is two months," answered she, with yet more hesitation, "since I was at Delvile-Castle."

"O, but," cried Morrice, "did not you see him while he was in Suffolk? I believe, indeed, he is there now, for it was only yesterday I heard of his coming down, by a gentleman who called upon Lady Margaret, and told us he had seen a stranger, a day or two ago, at Mrs. Charlton's door, and when he asked who he was, they told him his name was Delvile, and said he was on a visit at Mr. Biddulph's."

Cecilia was quite confounded by this speech; to have it known that Delvile had visited her, was in itself alarming, but to have her own equivocation thus glaringly exposed, was infinitely more dangerous. The just suspicions to which it must give rise filled her with dread, and the palpable evasion in which she had been discovered, overwhelmed her with confusion.

"So you had forgotten," said Mr. Gosport, looking at her with much archness, "that you had seen him *within* the two months? but no wonder; for where is the lady who having so many admirers, can be at the trouble to remember which of them she saw last? or who, being so accustomed to adulation, can hold it worth while to enquire whence it comes? A thousand Mr. Delviles are to Miss Beverley but as one; used from them all to the same tale, she regards them not individually as lovers, but collectively as men; and to gather, even from herself, which she is most inclined to favour, she must probably desire, like Portia in the Merchant of Venice, that their names may be run over one by one, before she can distinctly tell which is which."*

The gallant gaiety of this speech was some relief to Cecilia, who was beginning a laughing reply, when Morrice called out, "That man looks as if he was upon the scout."* And, raising her eyes, she perceived a man on horseback, who, though much muffled up, his hat flapped,* and a handkerchief held to his mouth and chin, she instantly, by his air and figure, recognized to be Delvile.

In much consternation at this sight, she forgot what she meant to say, and dropping her eyes, walked silently on. Mr. Gosport, attentive to her motions, looked from her to the horseman, and after a short examination, said, "I think I have seen that man before; have *you*, Miss Beverley?"

"Me?—no,"—answered she, "I believe not,—I hardly, indeed, see him now."

"*I* have, I am pretty sure," said Morrice; "and if I could see his face, I dare say I should recollect him."

"He seems very willing to know if he can recollect any of *us*," said Mr. Gosport, "and, if I am not mistaken, he sees much better than he is seen."

He was now come up to them, and though a glance sufficed to discover the object of his search, the sight of the party with which she was surrounded made him not dare

stop or speak to her, and therefore, clapping spurs to his
horse, he galloped past them.

"See," cried Morrice, looking after him, "how he turns
round to examine us! I wonder who he is."

"Perhaps some highwayman!" cried Miss Larolles; "I
assure you I am in a prodigious fright: I should hate to be
robbed so you can't think."

"I was going to make much the same conjecture," said
Mr. Gosport, "and, if I am not greatly deceived, that man
is a robber of no common sort. What think you, Miss
Beverley, can you discern a thief in disguise?"

"No, indeed; I pretend to no such extraordinary
knowledge."

"That's true; for all that you pretend is extraordinary
ignorance."

"I have a good mind," said Morrice, "to ride after him,
and see what he is about."

"What for?" exclaimed Cecilia, greatly alarmed; "there
can certainly be no occasion!"

"No, pray don't," cried Miss Larolles, "for I assure you
if he should come back to rob us, I should die upon the spot.
Nothing could be so disagreeable; I should scream so,
you've no idea."

Morrice then gave up the proposal, and they walked
quietly on; but Cecilia was extremely disturbed by this
accident; she readily conjectured that, impatient for her
arrival, Delvile had ridden that way, to see what had
retarded her, and she was sensible that nothing could be so
desirable as an immediate explanation of the motive of her
journey. Such a meeting, therefore, had she been alone, was
just what she could have wished, though, thus unluckily
encompassed, it only added to her anxiety.

Involuntarily, however, she quickened her pace, through
her eagerness to be relieved from so troublesome a party: but
Miss Larolles, who was in no such haste, protested she could
not keep up with her; saying, "You don't consider that I
have got this sweet little dog to carry, and he is such a
shocking plague to me you've no notion. Only conceive
what a weight he is!"

"Pray, ma'am," cried Morrice, "let me take him for you; I'll be very careful of him, I promise you; and you need not be afraid to trust me, for I understand more about dogs than about any thing."

Miss Larolles, after many fond caresses, being really weary, consented, and Morrice placed the little animal before him on horseback: but while this matter was adjusting, and Miss Larolles was giving directions how she would have it held, Morrice exclaimed, "Look, Look! that man is coming back! He is certainly watching us. There! now he's going off again!—I suppose he saw me remarking him."

"I dare say he's laying in wait to rob us," said Miss Larolles; "so when we turn off the high road, to go to Mrs. Mears, I suppose he'll come galloping after us. It's excessive horrid, I assure you."

"'Tis a petrifying thing," said the captain, "that one must always be *degouté* by some wretched being or other of this sort; but pray be not deranged, I will ride after him, if you please, and do *mon possible* to get rid of him."

"Indeed I wish you would," answered Miss Larolles, "for I assure you he has put such shocking notions into my head, it's quite disagreeable."

"I shall make it a principle," said the captain, "to have the honour of obeying you." And was riding off, when Cecilia, in great agitation, called out "Why should you go, Sir?—he is not in our way,—pray let him alone,—for what purpose should you pursue him?"

"I hope," said Mr. Gosport, "for the purpose of making him join our company, to some part of which I fancy he would be no very intolerable addition."

This speech again silenced Cecilia, who perceived, with the utmost confusion, that both Delvile and herself were undoubtedly suspected by Mr. Gosport, if not already actually betrayed to him. She was obliged, therefore, to let the matter take its course, though quite sick with apprehension lest a full discovery should follow the projected pursuit.

The Captain, who wanted not courage, however deeply in vanity and affectation he had buried common sense, stood suspended, upon the request of Cecilia, that he would not go, and, with a shrug of distress, said, "Give me leave to own I am *parfaitment* in a state the most *accablant* in the world: nothing could give me greater pleasure than to profit of the occasion to accommodate either of these ladies; but as they proceed upon different principles, I am *indecidé* to a degree which way to turn myself!"

"Put it to the vote, then," said Morrice; "the two ladies have both spoke; now, then, for the gentlemen. Come, Sir," to Mr. Gosport, "what say you?"

"O, fetch the culprit back, by all means," answered he; "and then let us all insist upon his opening his cause, by telling us in what he has offended us; for there is no part of his business, I believe, with which we are less acquainted."

"Well," said Morrice, "I'm for asking him a few questions too; so is the Captain; so every body has spoke but you, Sir," addressing himself to Mr. Meadows, "So now, Sir, let's hear your opinion."

Mr. Meadows, appearing wholly inattentive, rode on. "Why, Sir! I say!" cried Morris, louder, "we are all waiting for your vote. Pray what is the gentleman's name? it's duced hard to make him hear one."

"His name is Meadows," said Miss Larolles, in a low voice, "and I assure you sometimes he won't hear people by the hour together. He's so excessive absent you've no notion. One day he made me so mad, that I could not help crying; and Mr. Sawyer was standing by the whole time! and I assure you I believe he laughed at me. Only conceive how distressing!"

"May be," said Morrice, "its out of bashfulness: perhaps he thinks we shall cut him up."*

"Bashfulness," repeated Miss Larolles; "Lord, you don't conceive the thing at all. Why he's at the very head of the *ton*. There's nothing in the world so fashionable as taking no notice of things, and never seeing people, and saying nothing at all, and never hearing a word, and not knowing one's own acquaintance. All the *ton* people do so,* and I assure you as to Mr. Meadows, he's so excessively courted by every body, that if he does but say a syllable, he thinks it such an immense favour, you've no idea."

This account, however little alluring in itself, of his celebrity, was yet sufficient to make Morrice covet his further acquaintance: for Morrice was ever attentive to turn his pleasure to his profit, and never negligent of his interest, but when ignorant how to pursue it. He returned, therefore, to the charge, though by no means with the same freedom he had begun it, and lowering his voice to a tone of respect and submission, he said, "Pray, Sir, may we take the liberty to ask your advice, whether we shall go on, or take a turn back?"

Mr. Meadows made not any answer; but when Morrice was going to repeat his question, without appearing even to know that he was near him, he abruptly said to Miss Larolles, "Pray what is become of Mrs. Mears? I don't see her amongst us."

"Lord, Mr. Meadows," exclaimed she, "how can you be so odd? Don't you remember she went on in a chaise to the inn?"

"O, ay, true," cried he; "I protest I had quite forgot it; I beg your pardon, indeed. Yes, I recollect now,—she fell off her horse."

"Her horse! Why you know she was in her chaise."

"Her chaise, was it?—ay, true, so it was. Poor thing!—I am glad she was not hurt."

"Not hurt? Why she's so excessively bruised, she can't stir a step. Only conceive what a memory you've got!"

"I am most extremely sorry for her indeed," cried he, again stretching himself and yawning; "poor soul!—I hope she won't die. Do you think she will!"

"Die!" repeated Miss Larolles, with a scream, "Lord, how shocking! You are really enough to frighten one to hear you."

"But Sir," said Morrice, "I wish you would be so kind as to give us your vote; the man will else be gone so far, we sha'n't be able to overtake him.—Though I do really believe that is the very fellow coming back to peep at us again!"

"I am *ennuyé* to a degree," cried the Captain; "he is certainly set upon us as a spy, and I must really beg leave to enquire of him upon what principle he incommodes us."—And instantly he rode after him.

"And so will I too," cried Morrice, following.

Miss Larolles screamed after him to give her first her little dog; but with a school-boy's eagerness to be foremost, he gallopped on without heeding her.

The uneasiness of Cecilia now encreased every moment; the discovery of Delvile seemed unavoidable, and his impatient and indiscreet watchfulness must have rendered the motives of his disguise but too glaring. All she had left to hope was arriving at the inn before the detection was announced, and at least saving herself the cruel mortification of hearing the raillery which would follow it.

Even this, however, was not allowed her; Miss Larolles, whom she had no means to quit, hardly stirred another step, from her anxiety for her dog, and the earnestness of her curiosity about the stranger. She loitered, stopt now to talk, and now to listen, and was scarce moved a yard from the spot where she had been left, when the Captain and Morrice returned.

"We could not for our lives overtake the fellow," said Morrice; "he was well mounted, I promise you, and I'll warrant he knows what he's about, for he turned off so short at a place where there were two narrow lanes, that we could not make out which way he went."

Cecilia, relieved and delighted by this unexpected escape, now recovered her composure, and was content to saunter on without repining.

"But though we could not seize his person," said the Captain, "we have debarrassed ourselves *tout à fait* from his pursuit; I hope, therefore, Miss Larolles will make a revoke of her apprehensions."

The answer to this was nothing but a loud scream, with an exclamation, "Lord, where's my dog?"

"Your dog!" cried Morrice, looking aghast, "good stars! I never thought of him!"

"How excessive barbarous!" cried Miss Larolles, "you've killed him, I dare say. Only think how shocking! I had rather have seen any body served so in the world. I shall never forgive it, I assure you."

"Lord, ma'am," said Morrice, "How can you suppose I've killed him? Poor, pretty creature, I'm sure I liked him prodigiously. I can't think for my life where he can be: but I have a notion he must have dropt down some where while I happened to be on the full gallop. I'll go look him, however, for we went at such a rate that I never missed him.''

Away again rode Morrice.

''I am *abimé* to the greatest degree,'' said the Captain, ''that the poor little sweet fellow should be lost: if I had thought him in any danger, I would have made it a principle to have had a regard to his person myself. Will you give me leave, ma'am, to have the honour of seeking him *partout?*''

''O, I wish you would with all my heart; for I assure you if I don't find him, I shall think it so excessive distressing you can't conceive.''

The Captain touched his hat, and was gone.

These repeated impediments almost robbed Cecilia of all patience; yet her total inability of resistance obliged her to submit, and compelled her to go, stop, or turn, according to their own motions.

''Now if Mr. Meadows had the least good-nature in the world,'' said Miss Larolles, ''he would offer to help us; but he's so excessive odd, that I believe if we were all of us to fall down and break our necks, he would be so absent he would hardly take the trouble to ask us how we did.''

''Why in so desperate a case,'' said Mr. Gosport, ''the trouble would be rather superfluous. However, don't repine that one of the cavaliers stays with us by way of guard, lest your friend the spy should take take us by surprize while our troop is dispersed.''

''O Lord,'' cried Miss Larolles, ''now you put it in my head, I dare say that wretch has got my dog! only think how horrid!''

''I saw plainly,'' said Mr. Gosport, looking significantly at Cecilia, ''that he was feloniously inclined, though I must confess I took him not for a dog-stealer.''

Miss Larolles then, running up to Mr. Meadows, called out, ''I have a prodigious immense favour to ask of you, Mr. Meadows.''

''Ma'am!'' cried Mr. Meadows, with his usual start.

"It's only to know, whether if that horrid creature should come back, you could not just ride up to him and shoot him, before he gets to us? Now will you promise me to do it?"

"You are vastly good," said he, with a vacant smile; "what a charming evening! Do you love the country?"

"Yes, vastly; only I'm so monstrously tired, I can hardly stir a step. Do *you* like it?"

"The country? O no! I detest it! Dusty hedges, and chirping sparrows! 'Tis amazing to me any body can exist upon such terms."

"I assure you," cried Miss Larolles, "I'm quite of your opinion. I hate the country so you've no notion. I wish with all my heart it was all under ground. I declare, when I first go into it for the summer, I cry so you can't think. I like nothing but London.—Don't you?"

"London!" repeated Mr. Meadows, "O melancholy! the sink of all vice and depravity. Streets without light! Houses without air! Neighbourhood without society! Talkers without listeners!—'Tis astonishing any rational being can endure to be so miserably immured."

"Lord, Mr. Meadows," cried she, angrily, "I believe you would have one live no where!"

"True, very true, ma'am," said he, yawning, "one really lives no where; one does but vegetate, and wish it all at an end. Don't you find it so, ma'am?"

"Me? no indeed; I assure you I like living of all things. Whenever I'm ill, I'm in such a fright you've no idea. I always think I'm going to die, and it puts me so out of spirits you can't think. Does not it you, too?"

Here Mr. Meadows, looking another way, began to whistle.

"Lord," cried Miss Larolles, "how exessive distressing! to ask one questions, and then never hear what one answers!"

Here the Captain returned alone; and Miss Larolles, flying to meet him, demanded where was her dog?

"I have the *malheur* to assure you," answered he, "that I never was more *aneanti* in my life! the pretty little fellow has broke another leg!"

Miss Larolles, in a passion of grief, then declared she was certain that Morrice had maimed him thus on purpose, and desired to know where the vile wretch was?

"He was so much discomposed at the incident," replied the Captain, "that he rode instantly another way. I took up the pretty fellow therefore myself, and have done *mon possible* not to derange him."

The unfortunate little animal was then delivered to Miss Larolles; and after much lamentation, they at length continued their walk, and, without further adventure, arrived at the inn.

BOOK VIII

CHAPTER I

An Interruption

BUT here, instead of finding, as she expected, Mrs.
Charlton and fresh horses in readiness, Cecilia saw neither
chaise nor preparation; Mrs. Charlton was quietly seated in
a parlour, and drinking tea with Mrs. Mears.

Vexed and disappointed, she ordered horses immediately
to the chaise, and entreated Mrs. Charlton to lose no more
time. But the various delays which had already retarded
them, had made it now so late that it was impossible to get
into London by day-light, and Mrs Charlton not having
courage to be upon the road after dark, had settled to sleep
at the inn, and purposed not to proceed till the next
morning.

Half distracted at this new difficulty, Cecilia begged to
speak with her alone, and then represented in the most
earnest manner, the absolute necessity there was for her
being in London that night: "Every thing," said she,
"depends upon it, and the whole purpose of my journey will
otherwise be lost, for Mr. Delvile will else think himself
extremely ill used, and to make him reparation, I may be
compelled to submit to almost whatever terms he shall
propose."

Mrs. Charlton, kind and yielding, withstood not this
entreaty, which Cecilia made with infinite pain to herself,
from the reluctance she felt to pursuing her own interest and
inclination in opposition to those of her worthy old friend:
but as she was now circumstanced, she considered the
immediate prosecution of her journey as her only resource
against first irritating Delvile by an abrupt disappointment,
and appeasing him next by a concession which would make
that disappointment end in nothing.

The chaise was soon ready, and Mrs. Charlton and

Cecilia were rising to take leave of the company, when a man and horse gallopped full speed into the inn-yard, and in less than a minute, Morrice bounced into the room.

"Ladies and gentlemen," cried he, quite out of breath with haste, "I have got some news for you! I've just found out who that person is that has been watching us."

Cecilia, starting at this most unwelcome intelligence, would now have run into the chaise without hearing him proceed; but Mrs. Charlton, who knew neither whom nor what he meant, involuntarily stopt, and Cecilia, whose arm she leant upon, was compelled to stay.

Every one else eagerly desired to know who he was.

"Why I'll tell you," said he, "how I found him out. I was thinking in my own mind what I could possibly do to make amends for that unlucky accident about the dog, and just then I spied the very man that had made me drop him; so I thought at least I'd find out who he was. I rode up to him so quick that he could not get away from me, though I saw plainly it was the thing he meant. But still he kept himself muffled up, just as he did before. Not so snug, thought I, my friend, I shall have you yet! It's a fine evening, Sir, says I; but he took no notice: so then I came more to the point; Sir, says I, I think I have had the pleasure of seeing you, though I quite forget where. Still he made no answer: if you have no objection, Sir, says I, I shall be glad to ride with you, for the night's coming on, and we have neither of us a servant. But then, without a word speaking, he rode on the quicker. However, I jogged by his side, as fast as he, and said, Pray, Sir, did you know any thing of that company you were looking at so hard just now? And at this he could hold out no longer; he turned to me in a most fierce passion, and said pray, Sir, don't be troublesome. And then he got off; for when I found by his voice who he was, I let him alone."

Cecilia, who could bear to hear no more, again hastened Mrs. Charlton, who now moved on; but Morrice, stepping between them both and the door, said "Now do pray, Miss Beverley, guess who it was."

"No indeed, I cannot," said she, in the utmost confusion,

"nor have I any time to hear. Come, dear madam, we shall be very late indeed."

"O but I *must* tell you before you go;—why it was young Mr. Delvile! the same that I saw with you one night at the Pantheon, and that I used to meet last spring at Mr. Harrel's."

"Mr. Delvile!" repeated every one; "very strange he should not speak."

"Pray, ma'am," continued Morrice, "is it not the same gentleman that was at Mr. Biddulph's?"

Cecilia, half dead with shame and vexation, stammered out "No, no,——I believe not,—I can't tell;—I have not a moment to spare."

And then, at last, got* Mrs. Charlton out of the room, and into the chaise. But thither, before she could drive off, she was followed by Mr. Gosport, who gravely came to offer his advice that she would immediately lodge an information at the Public Office in Bow-Street,* that a very suspicious looking man had been observed loitering in those parts, who appeared to harbour most dangerous designs against her person and property.

Cecilia was too much confounded to rally or reply, and Mr. Gosport returned to his party with his speech unanswered.

The rest of the journey was without any new casualty, for late as it was, they escaped being robbed: but neither robbers nor new casualties were wanting to make it unpleasant to Cecilia; the incidents which had already happened sufficed for that purpose; and the consciousness of being so generally betrayed, added to the delay of her recantation, prepared her for nothing but mortifications to herself, and conflicts with Delvile the most bitter and severe.

It was near ten o'clock before they arrived in Pall-Mall. The house to which Delvile had given directions was easily found, and the servant sent forward had prepared the people of it for their reception.

In the cruellest anxiety and trepidation, Cecilia then counted every moment till Delvile came. She planned an apology for her conduct with all the address of which she was mistress, and determined to bear his disappointment and indignation with firmness: yet the part she had to act was both hard and artificial; she sighed to have it over, and repined she must have it at all.

The instant there was a knock at the door, she flew out upon the stairs to listen; and hearing his well-known voice enquiring for the ladies who had just taken the lodgings, she ran back to Mrs. Charlton, saying, "Ah, madam, assist me I entreat! for now must I merit, or forfeit your esteem for-ever!"

"Can you pardon," cried Delvile, as he entered the room, "an intrusion which was not *in our bond*?* But how could I wait till to-morrow, when I knew you were in town to-night?"

He then made his compliments to Mrs. Charlton, and, after enquiring how she had borne her journey, turned again to Cecilia, whose uneasy sensations he saw but too plainly in her countenance: "Are you angry," cried he, anxiously, "that I have ventured to come hither to night?"

"No," answered she, struggling with all her feelings for composure; "what we wish is easily excused; and I am glad to see you to night, because otherwise——"

She hesitated; and Delvile, little imagining why, thanked her in the warmest terms for her condescension. He then related how he had been tormented by Morrice, enquired why Mr. Monckton had not accompanied her, and what could possibly have induced her to make her journey so late, or, with so large a party, to be walking upon the high road instead of hastening to London.

"I wonder not," answered she, more steadily, "at your surprise, though I have now no time to lessen it. You have never, I find, received my letter?"

"No," cried he, much struck by her manner; "was it to forbid our meeting till to-morrow?"

"To-morrow!" she repeated expressively, "no; it was to forbid——"

Here the door was suddenly opened, and Morrice burst into the room.

The dismay and astonishment of Delvile at sight of him

could only be equalled by the confusion and consternation of Cecilia; but Morrice, perceiving neither, abruptly called out "Miss Beverley, I quite beg your pardon for coming so late, but you must know——" then stopping short upon seeing Delvile, "Good lord," he exclaimed, "if here is not our *gentleman spy!* Why, Sir, you have not spared the spur! I left you galloping off quite another way."

"However that may be, Sir," cried Delvile, equally enraged at the interruption and the observation, "you did not, I presume, wait upon Miss Beverley to talk of *me?*"

"No, Sir," answered he, lightly, "for I had told her all about you at the inn. Did not I, Miss Beverley? Did not I tell you I was sure it was Mr. Delvile that was dodging us about so? Though I believe, Sir, you thought I had not found you out?"

"And pray, young man," said Mrs. Charlton, much offended by this familiar intrusion, "how did you find *us* out?"

"Why, ma'am, by the luckiest accident in the world! Just as I was riding into town, I met the returned chaise that brought you; and I knew the postilion very well, as I go that road pretty often: so, by the merest chance in the world, I saw him by the light of the moon. And then he told me where he had set you down."

"And pray, Sir," again asked Mrs. Charlton, "what was your reason for making the enquiry?"

"Why, ma'am, I had a little favour to ask of Miss Beverley, that made me think I would take the liberty to call."

"And was this time of night, Sir," she returned, "the only one you could chuse for that purpose?"

"Why, ma'am, I'll tell you how that was; I did not mean to have called till to-morrow morning; but as I was willing to know if the postilion had given me a right direction, I knocked one soft little knock at the door, thinking you might be gone to bed after your journey, merely to ask if it was the right house; but when the servant told me there was a gentleman with you already, I thought there would be no harm in just stepping for a moment up stairs."

"And what, Sir," said Cecilia, whom mingled shame and vexation had hitherto kept silent, "is your business with me?"

"Why, ma'am, I only just called to give you a direction to a most excellent dog-doctor, as we call him, that lives at the corner of——"

"A dog-doctor, Sir?" repeated Cecilia, "and what have I to do with any such direction?"

"Why you must know, ma'am, I have been in the greatest concern imaginable about that accident which happened to me with the poor little dog, and so——"

"What little dog, Sir?" cried Delvile, who now began to conclude he was not sober, "do you know what you are talking of?"

"Yes, Sir, for it was that very little dog you made me drop out of my arms, by which means he broke his other leg."

"*I* made you drop him?" cried Delvile, angrily, "I believe, Sir, you had much better call some other time; it does not appear to me that you are in a proper situation for remaining here at present."

"Sir, I shall be gone in an instant," answered Morrice; "I merely wanted to beg the favour of Miss Beverley to tell that young lady that owned the dog, that if she will carry him to this man, I am sure he will make a cure of him."

"Come, Sir," said Delvile, convinced now of his inebriety, "if you please we will walk away together."

"I don't mean to take *you* away, Sir," said Morrice, looking very significantly, "for I suppose you have not rode so hard to go so soon; but as to me, I'll only write the direction, and be off."

Delvile, amazed and irritated at so many following specimens of ignorant assurance, would not, in his present eagerness, have scrupled turning him out of the house, had he not thought it imprudent, upon such an occasion, to quarrel with him, and improper, at so late an hour, to be left behind: he therefore only, while he was writing the direction, told Cecilia, in a low voice, that he would get rid of him and return in an instant.

They then went together; leaving Cecilia in an agony of

distress surpassing all she had hitherto experienced. "Ah, Mrs. Charlton," she cried, "what refuge have I now from ridicule, or perhaps disgrace! Mr. Delvile has been detected watching me in disguise! he has been discovered at this late hour meeting me in private! The story will reach his family with all the hyperbole of exaggeration;——how will his noble mother disdain me! how cruelly shall I sink before the severity of her eye!"

Mrs. Charlton tried to comfort her, but the effort was vain, and she spent her time in the bitterest repining till eleven o'clock. Delvile's not returning then added wonder to her sadness, and the impropriety of his returning at all so late, grew every instant more glaring.

At last, though in great disturbance, and evidently much ruffled in his temper, he came: "I feared," he cried, "I had passed the time for admittance, and the torture I have suffered from being detained has almost driven me wild. I have been in misery to see you again,——your looks, your manner,—the letter you talk of,—all have filled me with alarm; and though I know not what it is, I have to dread, I find it impossible to rest a moment without some explanation. Tell me, then, why you seem thus strange and thus depressed? Tell me what that letter was to forbid? Tell me any thing, and every thing, but that you repent your condescension."

"That letter," said Cecilia, "would have explained to you all. I scarce know how to communicate its contents: yet I hope you will hear with patience what I acknowledge I have resolved upon only from necessity. That letter was to tell you that to-morrow we must not meet;—it was to prepare you, indeed, for our meeting, perhaps, never more!"

"Gracious heaven!" exclaimed he, starting, "what is it you mean?"

"That I have made a promise too rash to be kept; that you must pardon me if, late as it is, I retract, since I am convinced it was wrong, and must be wretched in performing it."

Confounded and dismayed, for a moment he continued silent, and then passionately called out, "Who has been with you to defame me in your opinion? Who has barbarously wronged my character since I left you last Monday? Mr. Monckton received me coldly,—has he injured me in your esteem? Tell, tell me but to whom I owe this change, that my vindication, if it restores not your favour, may at least make you cease to blush that once I was honoured with some share of it!''

''It wants not to be restored,'' said Cecilia, with much softness, ''since it has never been alienated. Be satisfied that I think of you as I thought when we last parted, and generously forbear to reproach me, when I assure you I am actuated by principles which you ought not to disapprove.''

''And are you then, unchanged?'' cried he, more gently, ''and is your esteem for me still——''

''I thought it justice to say so once,'' cried she, hastily interrupting him, ''but exact from me nothing more. It is too late for us now to talk any longer; to-morrow you may find my letter at Mrs. Roberts's and that, short as it is, contains my resolution and its cause.''

''Never,'' cried he vehemently, ''can I quit you without knowing it! I would not linger till to-morrow in this suspense to be master of the universe!''

''I have told it you, Sir, already: whatever is clandestine carries a consciousness of evil, and so repugnant do I find it to my disposition and opinions, that till you give me back the promise I so unworthily made, I must be a stranger to peace, because at war with my own actions and myself.''

''Recover, then, your peace,'' cried Delvile, with much emotion, ''for I here acquit you of all promise!—to fetter, to compel you, were too inhuman to afford me any happiness. Yet hear me, dispassionately hear me, and deliberate a moment before you resolve upon my exile. Your scruples I am not now going to combat, I grieve that they are so powerful, but I have no new arguments with which to oppose them; all I have to say, is, that it is now too late for a retreat to satisfy them.''

''True, Sir, and far too true! yet is it always best to do right, however tardily; always better to repent, than to grow callous in wrong.''

"Suffer not, however, your delicacy for my family to make you forget what is due to yourself as well as to me: the fear of shocking you led me just now to conceal what a greater fear now urges me to mention. The honour I have had in view is already known to many, and in a very short time there are none will be ignorant of it. That impudent young man, Morrice, had the effrontery to rally me upon my passion for you, and though I reproved him with great asperity, he followed me into a coffee-house, whither I went merely to avoid him. There I forced myself to stay, till I saw him engaged with a news-paper, and then, through various private streets and alleys, I returned hither; but judge my indignation, when the moment I knocked at the door, I perceived him again at my side!"

"Did he, then, see you come in?"

"I angrily demanded what he meant by thus pursuing me; he very submissively begged my pardon, and said he had had a notion I should come back, and had therefore only followed me to see if he was right! I hesitated for an instant whether to chastise, or confide in him, but believing a few hours would make his impertinence immaterial, I did neither,—the door opened, and I came in."

He stopt; but Cecilia was too much shocked to answer him.

"Now, then," said he, "weigh your objections against the consequences which must follow. It is discovered I attended you in town; it will be presumed I had your permission for such attendance: to separate, therefore, now, will be to no purpose with respect to that delicacy which makes you wish it. It will be food for conjecture, for enquiry, for wonder, almost while both our names are remembered, and while to me it will bring the keenest misery in the severity of my disappointment, it will cast over your own conduct a veil of mystery and obscurity wholly subversive of that unclouded openness, that fair, transparent ingenousness, by which it has hitherto been distinguished."

"Alas, then," said she, "how dreadfully have I erred, that whatever path I now take must lead me wrong!"

"You overwhelm me with grief," cried Delvile, "by

finding you thus distressed, when I had hoped—Oh cruel
Cecilia! how different to this did I hope to have met you!—
all your doubts settled, all your fears removed, your mind
perfectly composed, and ready, unreluctantly, to ratify the
promise with so much sweetness accorded me!—where now
are those hopes!——where now——''

"Why will you not begone?" cried Cecilia, uneasily,
"indeed it is too late to stay."

"Tell me first," cried he, with great energy, "and let good
Mrs. Charlton speak too,—ought not every objection to our
union, however potent, to give way, without further hesitation,
to the certainty that our intending it must become public? Who
that hears of our meeting in London, at such a season, in
such circumstances, and at such hours, ——"

"And why," cried Cecilia, angrily, "do you mention
them, and yet stay?"

"I *must* speak now," answered he with quickness, "or lose
for-ever all that is dear to me, and add to the misery of that
loss, the heart-piercing reflection of having injured her whom
of all the world I most love, most value, and most revere!"

"And how injured?" cried Cecilia, half alarmed and half
displeased; "Surely I must strangely have lived to fear now
the voice of calumny?"

"If any one has ever," returned he, "so lived as to dare
defy it, Miss Beverley is she: but though safe by the
established purity of your character from calumny, there are
other, and scarce less invidious attacks, from which no one
is exempt, and of which the refinement, the sensibility of
your mind, will render you but the more susceptible:
ridicule has shafts, and impertinence has arrows, which
though against innocence they may be levelled in vain, have
always the power of wounding tranquility."

Struck with a truth which she could not controvert,
Cecilia sighed deeply, but spoke not.

"Mr. Delvile is right;" said Mrs. Charlton, "and though
your plan, my dear Cecilia, was certainly virtuous and
proper, when you set out from Bury, the purpose of your
journey must now be made so public, that it will no longer
be judicious nor rational."

Delvile poured forth his warmest thanks for this friendly interposition, and then, strengthened by such an advocate, re-urged all his arguments with redoubled hope and spirit.

Cecilia, disturbed, uncertain, comfortless, could frame her mind to no resolution; she walked about the room, deliberated,—determined,—wavered and deliberated again. Delvile then grew more urgent, and represented so strongly the various mortifications which must follow so tardy a renunciation of their intentions, that, terrified and perplexed, and fearing the breach of their union would now be more injurious to her than its ratification, she ceased all opposition to his arguments, and uttered no words but of solicitation that he would leave her.

"I will," cried he, "I will begone this very moment. Tell me but first you will think of what I have said, and refer me not to your letter, but deign yourself to pronounce my doom, when you have considered if it may not be softened."

To this she tacitly consented; and elated with fresh rising hope, he recommended his cause to the patronage of Mrs. Charlton, and then, taking leave of Cecilia, "I go," he said, "though I have yet a thousand things to propose and to supplicate, and though still in a suspense that my temper knows ill how to endure; but I should rather be rendered miserable than happy, in merely overpowering your reason by entreaty. I leave you, therefore, to your own reflections; yet remember,——and refuse not to remember with some compunction, that all chance, all possibility of earthly happiness for *me* depends upon your decision."

He then tore himself away.

Cecilia, shocked at the fatigue she had occasioned her good old friend, now compelled her to go to rest, and dedicated the remaining part of the night to uninterrupted deliberation.

It seemed once more in her power to be mistress of her destiny; but the very liberty of choice she had so much coveted, now attained appeared the most heavy of calamities; since, uncertain even what she ought to do, she rather wished to be drawn than to lead, rather desired to be guided than to guide. She was to be responsible not only to the world but to herself for the whole of this momentous transaction, and the terror of leaving either dissatisfied, made independence burthensome, and unlimited power a grievance.

The happiness or misery which awaited her resolution were but secondary considerations in the present state of her mind; her consent to a clandestine action she lamented as an eternal blot to her character, and the undoubted publication of that consent as equally injurious to her fame. Neither retracting nor fulfilling her engagement could now retrieve what was past, and in the bitterness of regret for the error she had committed, she thought happiness unattainable for the remainder of her life.

In this gloomy despondence passed the night, her eyes never closed, her determination never formed. Morning, however, came, and upon something to fix was indes-pensable.

She now, therefore, finally employed herself in briefly comparing the good with the evil of giving Delvile wholly up, or becoming his for-ever.

In accepting him, she was exposed to all the displeasure of his relations, and, which affected her most, to the indignant severity of his mother: but not another obstacle could be found that seemed of any weight to oppose him.

In refusing him she was liable to the derision of the world, to sneers from strangers, and remonstrances from her friends, to becoming a topic for ridicule, if not for slander, and an object of curiosity if not of contempt.

The ills, therefore, that threatened her marriage, though most afflicting, were least disgraceful, and those which awaited its breach, if less serious, were more mortifying.

At length, after weighing every circumstance as well as her perturbed spirits would permit, she concluded that so late to reject him must bring misery without any alleviation, while accepting him, though followed by wrath and reproach, left some opening for future hope, and some prospect of better days.

To fulfil, therefore, her engagement was her final resolution.

wild with delight, as he had before been with apprehension, and poured forth his acknowledgements with so much fervour of gratitude, that she imperceptibly grew reconciled to herself, and before she missed her dejection, participated in his content.

She quitted him as soon as she had power, to acquaint

CHAPTER II

An Event

SCARCE less unhappy in her decision than in her uncertainty, and every way dissatisfied with her situation, her views and herself, Cecilia was still so distressed and uncomfortable, when Delvile called the next morning, that he could not discover what her determination had been, and fearfully enquired his doom with hardly any hope of finding favour.

But Cecilia was above affectation, and a stranger to art. "I would not, Sir," she said, "keep you an instant in suspense, when I am no longer in suspense myself. I may have appeared trifling, but I have been nothing less, and you would readily exculpate me of caprice, if half the distress of my irresolution was known to you. Even now, when I hesitate no more, my mind is so ill at ease, that I could neither wonder nor be displeased should you hesitate in your turn."

"You hesitate no more?" cried he, almost breathless at the sound of those words, "and is it possible——Oh my Cecilia!—is it possible your resolution is in my favour?"

"Alas!" cried she, "how little is your reason to rejoice! a dejected and melancholy gift is all you can receive!"

"Ere I take it, then," cried he, in a voice that spoke joy, pain, and fear all at once in commotion, "tell me if your reluctance has its origin in *me*, that I may rather even yet relinquish you, than merely owe your hand to the selfishness of persecution?"

"Your pride," said she, half smiling, "has some right to be alarmed, though I meant not to alarm it. No! it is with myself only I am at variance, with my own weakness and want of judgement that I quarrel,——in *you* I have all the reliance that the highest opinion of your honour and integrity can give me."

This was enough for the warm heart of Delvile, not only to restore peace, but to awaken rapture. He was almost as wild with delight, as he had before been with apprehension, and poured forth his acknowledgements with so much fervour of gratitude, that Cecilia imperceptibly grew reconciled to herself, and before she missed her dejection, participated in his contentment.

She quitted him as soon as she had power, to acquaint Mrs. Charlton with what had passed, and assist in preparing her to accompany them to the altar; while Delvile flew to his new acquaintance, Mr. Singleton, the lawyer, to request him to supply the place of Mr. Monckton in giving her away.

All was now hastened with the utmost expedition, and to avoid observation, they agreed to meet at the church; their desire of secresy, however potent, never urging them to wish the ceremony should be performed in a place less awful.

When the chairs, however, came, which were to carry the two ladies thither, Cecilia trembled and hung back. The greatness of her undertaking, the hazard of all her future happiness, the disgraceful secresy of her conduct, the expected reproaches of Mrs. Delvile, and the boldness and indelicacy of the step she was about to take, all so forcibly struck, and so painfully wounded her, that the moment she was summoned to set out, she again lost her resolution, and regretting the hour that ever Delvile was known to her, she sunk into a chair, and gave up her whole soul to anguish and sorrow.

The good Mrs. Charlton tried in vain to console her; a sudden horror against herself had now seized her spirits, which, exhausted by long struggles, could rally no more.

In this situation she was at length surprised by Delvile, whose uneasy astonishment that she had failed in her appointment, was only to be equalled by that with which he was struck at the sight of her tears. He demanded the cause with the utmost tenderness and apprehension; Cecilia for some time could not speak, and then, with a deep sigh "Ah!" she cried, "Mr. Delvile! how weak are we all when unsupported by our own esteem! how feeble, how inconsistent, how changeable, when our courage has any foundation but duty!"

Delvile, much relieved by finding her sadness sprung not from any new affliction, gently reproached her breach of promise, and earnestly entreated her to repair it. "The clergyman," cried he, "is waiting; I have left him with Mr. Singleton in the vestry; no new objections have started, and no new obstacles have intervened; why, then, torment ourselves with discussing again the old ones, which we have already considered till every possible argument upon them is exhausted? Tranquilize, I conjure you, your agitated spirits, and if the truest tenderness, the most animated esteem, and the gratefullest admiration, can soften your future cares, and ensure your future peace, every anniversary of this day will recompense my Cecilia for every pang she now suffers!"

Cecilia, half soothed and half ashamed, finding she had in fact nothing new to say or to object, compelled herself to rise, and, penetrated by his solicitations, endeavoured to compose her mind, and promised to follow him.

He would not trust her, however, from his sight, but seizing the very instant of her renewed consent, he dismissed the chairs, and ordering a hackney-coach, preferred any risk to that of her again wavering, and insisted upon accompanying her in it himself.

Cecilia had now scarce time to breathe, before she found herself at the porch of —— church. Delvile hurried her out of the carriage, and then offered his arm to Mrs. Charlton. Not a word was spoken by any of the party till they went into the vestry, where Delvile ordered Cecilia a glass of water, and having hastily made his compliments to the clergyman, gave her hand to Mr. Singleton, who led her to the altar.

The ceremony was now begun; and Cecilia, finding herself past all power of retracting, soon called her thoughts from wishing it, and turned her whole attention to the awful service; to which though she listened with reverence, her full satisfaction in the object of her vows, made her listen without terror. But when the priest came to that solemn adjuration, *If any man can shew any just cause why they may not lawfully be joined together*, a conscious tear stole into her eye, and a sigh escaped from Delvile that went to her heart:

but, when the priest concluded the exhortation with *let him now speak, or else hereafter for-ever hold his peace*, a female voice at some distance, called out in shrill accents, "I do!"

The ceremony was instantly stopt. The astonished priest immediately shut up the book to regard the intended bride and bridegroom; Delvile started with amazement to see whence the sound proceeded; and Cecilia, aghast, and struck with horror, faintly shriekt, and caught hold of Mrs. Charlton.

The consternation was general, and general was the silence, though all of one accord turned round towards the place whence the voice issued: a female form at the same moment was seen rushing from a pew, who glided out of the church with the quickness of lightning.

Not a word was yet uttered, every one seeming rooted to the spot on which he stood, and regarding in mute wonder the place this form had crossed.

Delvile at length exclaimed "What can this mean?"

"Did you not know the woman, Sir?" said the clergyman.

"No, Sir, I did not even see her."

"Nor you, madam?" said he, addressing Cecilia.

"No, Sir," she answered, in a voice that scarce articulated the two syllables, and changing colour so frequently, that Delvile, apprehensive she would faint, flew to her, calling out "Let *me* support you!"

She turned from him hastily, and still holding by Mrs. Charlton, moved away from the altar.

"Whither," cried Delvile, fearfully following her, "whither are you going?"

She made not any answer; but still, though tottering as much from emotion as Mrs. Charlton from infirmity, she walked on.

"Why did you stop the ceremony, Sir?" cried Delvile, impatiently speaking to the clergyman.

"No ceremony, Sir," he returned, "could proceed with such an interruption."

"It has been wholly accidental," cried he, "for we neither of us know the woman, who could not have any right or authority for the prohibition." Then yet more anxiously, pursuing Cecilia, "why," he continued, "do you thus move off?—Why leave the ceremony unfinished?——Mrs. Charlton, what is it you are about?—Cecilia, I beseech you return, and let the service go on!"

Cecilia, making a motion with her hand to forbid his following her, still silently proceeded, though drawing along with equal difficulty Mrs. Charlton and herself.

"This is insupportable!" cried Delvile, with vehemence, "turn, I conjure you!—my Cecilia!—my wife!—why is it you thus abandon me?——Turn, I implore you, and receive my eternal vows!—Mrs. Charlton, bring her back,—Cecilia, you *must* not go!—"

He now attempted to take her hand, but shrinking from his touch, in an emphatic but low voice, she said "Yes, Sir, I must!—an interdiction such as this!—for the world could I not brave it!"

She then made an effort to somewhat quicken her pace.

"Where," cried Delvile, half frantic, "where is this infamous woman? This wretch who has thus wantonly destroyed me!"

And he rushed out of the church in pursuit of her.

The clergyman and Mr. Singleton, who had hitherto been wondering spectators, came now to offer their assistance to Cecilia. She declined any help for herself, but gladly accepted their services for Mrs. Charlton, who, thunderstruck by all that had past, seemed almost robbed of her faculties. Mr. Singleton proposed calling a hackney coach, she consented, and they stopt for it at the church porch.

The clergyman now began to enquire of the pew-opener,* what she knew of the woman, who she was, and how she had got into the church? She knew of her, she answered, nothing, but that she had come in to early prayers, and she supposed she had hid herself in a pew when they were over, as she had thought the church entirely empty.

An hackney coach now drew up, and while the gentlemen were assisting Mrs. Charlton into it, Delvile returned.

"I have pursued and enquired," cried he, "in vain, I can neither discover nor hear of her.—But what is all this?

Whither are you going?—What does this coach do here?——
Mrs. Charlton, why do you get into it?—Cecilia, what are
you doing?''

Cecilia turned away from him in silence. The shock she had
received, took from her all power of speech, while amazement
and terror deprived her even of relief from tears. She believed
Delvile to blame, though she knew not in what, but the obscurity
of her fears served only to render them more dreadful.

She was now getting into the coach herself, but Delvile,
who could neither brook her displeasure, nor endure her
departure, forcibly caught her hand, and called out "You
are *mine*, you are my *wife!*—I will part with you no more,
and go withersoever you will, I will follow and claim you!''

"Stop me not!'' cried she, impatiently though faintly, "I
am sick, I am ill already,——if you detain me any longer,
I shall be unable to support myself!''

"Oh then rest on *me!*'' cried he, still holding her; "rest
but upon me till the ceremony is over!——you will drive me
to despair and to madness if you leave me in this barbarous
manner!''

A crowd now began to gather, and the words bride and
bridegroom reached the ears of Cecilia; who half dead with
shame, with fear, and with distress, hastily said "You are
determined to make me miserable!'' and snatching away her
hand, which Delvile at those words could no longer hold, she
threw herself into the carriage.

Delvile, however, jumped in after her, and with an air of
authority ordered the coachman to Pall-Mall, and then drew
up the glasses,* with a look of fierceness at the mob.

Cecilia had neither spirits nor power to resist him; yet,
offended by his violence, and shocked to be thus publickly
pursued by him, her looks spoke a resentment far more
mortifying than any verbal reproach.

"Inhuman Cecilia!'' cried he, passionately, "to desert me
at the very altar!—to cast me off at the instant the most
sacred rites were uniting us!——and then thus to look at
me!—to treat me with this disdain at a time of such
distraction!—to scorn me thus injuriously at the moment
you unjustly abandon me!——''

"To how dreadful a scene," said Cecilia, recovering from her consternation, "have you exposed me! to what shame, what indignity, what irreparable disgrace!"

"Oh heaven!" cried he with horror, "if any crime, any offence of mine has occasioned this fatal blow, the whole world holds not a wretch so culpable as myself, nor one who will sooner allow the justice of your rigour! my veneration for you has ever equalled my affection, and could I think it was through *me* you have suffered any indignity, I should soon abhor myself as you seem to abhor me. But what is it I have done? How have I thus incensed you? By what action, by what guilt, have I incurred this displeasure?"

"Whence," cried she, "came that voice which still vibrates in my ear? The prohibition could not be on *my* account, since none to whom I am known have either right or interest in even wishing it."

"What an inference is this! over *me*, then, do you conclude this woman had any power?"

Here they stopt at the lodgings. Delvile handed both the ladies out. Cecilia, eager to avoid his importunities, and dreadfully disturbed, hastily past him, and ran up stairs; but Mrs. Charlton refused not his arm, on which she lent till they reached the drawing-room.

Cecilia then rang the bell for her servant, and gave orders that a post-chaise might be sent for immediately.

Delvile now felt offended in his turn; but suppressing his vehemence, he gravely and quietly said "Determined as you are to leave me, indifferent to my peace, and incredulous of my word, deign, at least, before we part, to be more explicit in your accusation, and tell me if indeed it is possible you can suspect that the wretch who broke off the ceremony, had ever from me received provocation for such an action?"

"I know not what to suspect," said Cecilia, "where every thing is thus involved in obscurity; but I must own I should have some difficulty to think those words the effect of chance, or to credit that their speaker was concealed without design."

"You are right, then, madam," cried he, resentfully, "to discard me! to treat me with contempt, to banish me without repugnance, since I see you believe me capable of duplicity, and imagine I am better informed in this affair than I appear to be. You have said I shall make you miserable,—no, madam, no! your happiness and misery depend not upon one you hold so worthless!"

"On whatever they depend," said Cecilia, "I am too little at ease for discussion. I would no more be daring than superstitious, but none of our proceedings have prospered, and since their privacy has always been contrary both to my judgment and my principles, I know not how to repine at a failure I cannot think unmerited. Mrs. Charlton, our chaise is coming; you will be ready, I hope, to set off in it directly?"

Delvile, too angry to trust himself to speak, now walked about the room, and endeavoured to calm himself; but so little was his success, that though silent till the chaise was announced, when he heard that dreaded sound, and saw Cecilia steady in her purpose of departing, he was so much shocked and afflicted, that, clasping his hands in a transport of passion and grief, he exclaimed "This, then, Cecilia, is your faith! this is the felicity you bid me hope! this is the recompense of my sufferings, and the performance of your engagement!"

Cecilia, struck by these reproaches, turned back; but while she hesitated how to answer them, he went on. "You are insensible to my misery and impenetrable to my entreaties; a secret enemy has had power to make me odious in your sight, though for her enmity I can assign no cause, though even her existence was this morning unknown to me! Ever ready to abandon, and most willing to condemn me, you have more confidence in a vague conjecture, than in all you have observed of the whole tenour of my character. Without knowing why, you are disposed to believe me criminal, without deigning to say wherefore, you are eager to banish me your presence. Yet scarce could a conscious-ness of guilt itself, wound me so forcibly, so keenly, as your suspecting I am guilty!"

"Again, then," cried Cecilia, "shall I subject myself to a scene of such disgrace and horror? No, never!——The punishment of my error shall at least secure its reformation. Yet if I merit your reproaches, I deserve not your regard; cease, therefore, to profess any for me, or make them no more.''

"Shew but to them," cried he, "the smallest sensibility, shew but for me the most distant concern, and I will try to bear my disappointment without murmuring, and submit to your decrees as to those from which there is no appeal: but to wound without deigning even to look at what you destroy,—to shoot at random those arrows that are pointed with poison,—to see them fasten on the heart, and corrode its vital functions, yet look on without compunction, or turn away with cold disdain,—Oh where is the candour I thought lodged in Cecilia! where the justice, the equity, I believed a part of herself!''

"After all that has past," said Cecilia, sensibly touched by his distress, "I expected not these complaints, nor that, from me, any assurances would be wanted; yet, if it will quiet your mind, if it will better reconcile you to our separation——''

"Oh fatal prelude!" interrupted he, "what on earth can quiet my mind that leads to our separation?—Give to me no condescension with any such view,—preserve your indifference, persevere in your coldness, triumph still in your power of inspiring those feelings you can never return, —all, every thing is more supportable than to talk of our separation!''

"Yet how," cried she, "parted, torn asunder as we have been, how is it now to be avoided?''

"Trust in my honour! Shew me but the confidence which I will venture to say I deserve, and then will that union no longer be impeded, which in future, I am certain, will never be repented!''

"Good heaven, what a request! faith so implicit would be frenzy.''

"You doubt, then, my integrity? You suspect——''

"Indeed I do not; yet in a case of such importance, what ought to guide me but my own reason, my own conscience, my own sense of right? Pain me not, therefore, with reproaches, distress me no more with entreaties, when I solemnly declare that no earthly consideration shall ever again make me promise you my hand, while the terror of Mrs. Delvile's displeasure has possession of my heart. And now adieu."

"You give me, then, up?"

"Be patient, I beseech you; and attempt not to follow me; 'tis a step I cannot permit."

"Not follow you? And who has power to prevent me?"

"*I* have, Sir, if to incur my endless resentment is of any consequence to you."

She then, with an air of determined steadiness, moved on; Mrs. Charlton, assisted by the servants, being already upon the stairs.

"O tyranny!" cried he, "what submission is it you exact!—May I not even enquire into the dreadful mystery of this morning?"

"Yes, certainly."

"And may I not acquaint you with it, should it be discovered?"

"I shall not be sorry to hear it. Adieu."

She was now half way down the stairs; when, losing all forbearance, he hastily flew after her, and endeavouring to stop her, called out, "If you do not hate and detest me,—if I am not loathsome and abhorrent to you, O quit me not thus insensibly!—Cecilia! my beloved Cecilia!—speak to me, at least, one word of less severity! Look at me once more, and tell me we part not for-ever!"

Cecilia then turned round, and while a starting tear shewed her sympathetic distress, said, "Why will you thus oppress me with entreaties I ought not to gratify?—Have I not accompanied you to the altar,—and can you doubt what I have thought of you?"

"*Have* thought?—Oh Cecilia!—is it then all over?"

"Pray suffer me to go quietly, and fear not I shall go too happily! Suppress your own feelings, rather than seek to awaken mine. Alas! there is little occasion!——Oh Mr. Delvile! were our connexion opposed by no duty, and repugnant to no friends, were it attended by no impropriety, and carried on with no necessity of disguise,——you would not thus charge me with indifference, you would not suspect me of insensibility,—Oh no! the choice of my heart would then be its glory, and all I now blush to feel, I should openly and with pride acknowledge!''

She then hurried to the chaise, Delvile pursuing her with thanks and blessings, and gratefully assuring her, as he handed her into it, that he would obey all her injunctions, and not even attempt to see her, till he could bring her some intelligence concerning the morning's transaction.

The chaise then drove off.

CHAPTER III

A Consternation

THE journey was melancholy and tedious: Mrs. Charlton, extremely fatigued by the unusual hurry and exercise both of mind and body which she had lately gone through, was obliged to travel very slowly, and to lie upon the road.*
Cecilia, however, was in no haste to proceed: she was going to no one she wished to see, she was wholly without expectation of meeting with any thing that could give her pleasure. The unfortunate expedition in which she had been engaged, left her now nothing but regret, and only promised her in future sorrow and mortification.

Mrs. Charlton, after her return home, still continued ill, and Cecilia, who constantly attended her, had the additional affliction of imputing her indisposition to herself. Every thing she thought conspired to punish the error she had committed; her proceedings were discovered, though her motives were unknown; the Delvile family could not fail to hear of her enterprize, and while they attributed it to her temerity, they would exult in its failure: but chiefly hung upon her mind the unaccountable prohibition of her marriage. Whence that could proceed she was wholly without ability to divine, yet her surmizes were not more fruitless than various. At one moment she imagined it some frolic of Morrice, at another some perfidy of Monckton, and at another an idle and unmeaning trick of some stranger to them all. But none of these suppositions carried with them any air of probability; Morrice, even if he had watched their motions and pursued them to the church, which his inquisitive impertinence made by no means impossible, could yet hardly have had either time or oppportunity to engage any woman in so extraordinary an undertaking; Mr. Monckton, however averse to the connection, she considered as a man of too much honour to break it off in a manner so alarming and disgraceful; and mischief so wanton in any stranger, seemed to require a share of unfeeling effrontery, which could fall to the lot of so few as to make this suggestion unnatural and incredible.

Sometimes she imagined that Delvile might formerly have been affianced to some woman, who, having accidentally discovered his intentions, took this desperate method of rendering them abortive: but this was a short-lived thought, and speedily gave way to her esteem for his general character, and her confidence in the firmness of his probity.

All, therefore, was dark and mysterious; conjecture was baffled, and meditation was useless. Her opinions were unfixed, and her heart was miserable; she could only be steady in believing Delvile as unhappy as herself, and only find consolation in believing him, also, as blameless.

Three days passed thus, without incident or intelligence; her time wholly occupied in attending Mrs. Charlton; her thoughts all engrossed upon her own situation: but upon the fourth day she was informed that a lady was in the parlour, who desired to speak with her.

She presently went down stairs,—and, upon entering the room, perceived Mrs. Delvile!

Seized with astonishment and fear, she stopt short, and, looking aghast, held by the door, robbed of all power to receive so unexpected and unwelcome a visitor, by an internal sensation of guilt, mingled with a dread of discovery and reproach.

Mrs. Delvile, addressing her with the coldest politeness, said, "I fear I have surprised you; I am sorry I had not time to acquaint you of my intention to wait upon you."

Cecilia then, moving from the door, faintly answered, "I cannot, madam, but be honoured by your notice, whenever you are pleased to confer it."

They then sat down; Mrs. Delvile preserving an air the most formal and distant, and Cecilia half sinking with apprehensive dismay.

After a short and ill-boding silence, "I mean not," said Mrs. Delvile, "to embarrass or distress you; I will not, therefore, keep you in suspense of the purport of my visit. I come not to make enquiries, I come not to put your sincerity to any trial, nor to torture your delicacy; I dispense with all explanation, for I have not one doubt to solve: I *know* what has passed, I *know* that my son loves you."

Not all her secret alarm, nor all the perturbation of her fears, had taught Cecilia to expect so direct an attack, nor enabled her to bear the shock of it with any composure: she could not speak, she could not look at Mrs. Delvile; she arose, and walked to the window, without knowing what she was doing.

Here, however, her distress was not likely to diminish; for the first sight she saw was Fidel, who barked, and jumped up at the window to lick her hands.

"Good God! Fidel here!" exclaimed Mrs. Delvile, amazed.

Cecilia, totally overpowered, covered her glowing face with both her hands, and sunk into a chair.

Mrs. Delvile for a few minutes was silent; and then, following her, said, 'Imagine not I am making any discovery, nor suspect me of any design to develop your sentiments. That Mortimer could love in vain I never believed; that Miss Beverley, possessing so much merit, could be blind to it in another, I never thought possible. I mean not, therefore, to solicit any account or explanation, but merely to beg your patience while I talk to you myself, and your permission to speak to you with openness and truth."

Cecilia, though relieved by this calmness from all apprehension of reproach, found in her manner a coldness that convinced her of the loss of her affection, and in the introduction to her business a solemnity that assured her what she should decree would be unalterable. She uncovered her face to shew her respectful attention, but she could not raise it up, and could not utter a word.

Mrs. Delvile then seated herself next her, and gravely continued her discourse.

"Miss Beverley, however little acquainted with the state of our family affairs, can scarcely have been uninformed that a fortune such as hers seems almost all that family can desire; nor can she have failed to observe, that her merit and accomplishments have no where been more felt and admired: the choice therefore of Mortimer she could not doubt would have our sanction, and when she honoured his proposals with her favour, she might naturally conclude she gave happiness and pleasure to all his friends."

Cecilia, superior to accepting a palliation of which she felt herself undeserving, now lifted up her head, and forcing herself to speak, said "No, madam, I will not deceive you, for I have never been deceived myself: I presumed not to expect your approbation,—though in missing it I have for ever lost my own!"

"Has Mortimer, then," cried she with eagerness, "been strictly honourable? has he neither beguiled nor betrayed you?"

"No, madam," said she, blushing, "I have nothing to reproach him with."

"Then he is indeed my son!" cried Mrs. Delvile, with emotion; "had he been treacherous to you, while disobedient to us, I had indisputably renounced him."

Cecilia, who now seemed the only culprit, felt herself in a state of humiliation not to be borne; she collected, therefore, all her courage, and said, "I have cleared Mr. Delvile; permit me, madam, now, to say something for myself."

"Certainly; you cannot oblige me more than by speaking without disguise."

"It is not in the hope of regaining your good opinion,— that, I see, is lost!—but merely—"

"No, not lost," said Mrs. Delvile, "but if once it was yet

higher, the fault was my own, in indulging an expectation of perfection to which human nature is perhaps unequal.''

Ah, then, thought Cecilia, all is over! the contempt I so much feared is incurred, and though it may be softened, it can never be removed!

"Speak, then, and with sincerity," she continued, "all you wish me to hear, and then grant me your attention in return to the purpose of my present journey.''

"I have little, madam," answered the depressed Cecilia, "to say; you tell me you already know all that has past; I will not, therefore, pretend to take any merit from revealing it: I will only add, that my consent to this transaction has made me miserable almost from the moment I gave it; that I meant and wished to retract as soon as reflection pointed out to me my error, and that circumstances the most perverse, not blindness to propriety, nor stubborness in wrong, led me to make, at last, that fatal attempt, of which the recollection, to my last hour, must fill me with regret and shame.''

"I wonder not," said Mrs. Delvile, "that in a situation where delicacy was so much less requisite than courage, Miss Beverley should feel herself distressed and unhappy. A mind such as hers could never err with impunity; and it is solely from a certainty of her innate sense of right, that I venture to wait upon her now, and that I have any hope to influence *her* upon whose influence alone our whole family must in future depend. Shall I now proceed, or is there any thing you wish to say first?''

"No, madam, nothing.''

"Hear me, then, I beg of you, with no pre-determination to disregard me, but with an equitable resolution to attend to reason, and a candour that leaves an opening to conviction. Not easy, indeed, is such a task, to a mind pre-occupied with an intention to be guided by the dictates of inclination,——''

"You wrong me, indeed, madam!" interrupted Cecilia, greatly hurt, "my mind harbours no such intention, it has no desire but to be guided by duty, it is wretched with a consciousness of having failed in it! I pine, I sicken to recover my own good opinion; I should then no longer feel unworthy of yours; and whether or not I might be able to regain it, I should at least lose this cruel depression that now sinks me in your presence!"

"To regain it," said Mrs. Delvile, "were to exercise but half your power, which at this moment enables you, if such is your wish, to make me think of you more highly than one human being ever thought of another. Do you condescend to hold this worth your while?"

Cecilia started at the question; her heart beat quick with struggling passions; she saw the sacrifice which was to be required, and her pride, her affronted pride, arose high to anticipate the rejection; but the design was combated by her affections, which opposed the indignant rashness, and told her that one hasty speech might separate her from Delvile for ever. When this painful conflict was over, of which Mrs. Delvile patiently waited the issue, she answered, with much hesitation, "To regain your good opinion, madam, greatly, truly as I value it,—is what I now scarcely dare hope."

"Say not so," cried she, "since, if you hope, you cannot miss it. I purpose to point out to you the means to recover it, and to tell you how greatly I shall think myself your debtor if you refuse not to employ them."

She stopt; but Cecilia hung back; fearful of her own strength, she dared venture at no professions; yet, how either to support, or dispute her compliance, she dreaded to think.

"I come to you, then," Mrs. Delvile solemnly resumed, "in the name of Mr. Delvile, and in the name of our whole family; a family as ancient as it is honourable, as honourable as it is ancient. Consider me as its representative, and hear in me its common voice, common opinion, and common address.

"My son, the supporter of our house, the sole guardian of its name, and the heir of our united fortunes, has selected you, we know, for the lady of his choice, and so fondly has fixed upon you his affections, that he is ready to relinquish us all in preference to subduing them. To yourself alone, then, can we apply, and I come to you——"

"O hold, madam, hold!" interrupted Cecilia, whose courage now revived from resentment, "I know what you would say; you come to tell me of your disdain; you come to reproach my presumption, and to kill me with your contempt! There is little occasion for such a step; I am depressed, I am self-condemned already: spare me, therefore, this insupportable humiliation, wound me not with your scorn, oppress me not with your superiority! I aim at no competition, I attempt no vindication, I acknowledge my own littleness as readily as you can despise it, and nothing but indignity could urge me to defend it!"

"Believe me," said Mrs. Delvile, "I meant not to hurt or offend you, and I am sorry if I have appeared to you either arrogant or assuming. The peculiar and perilous situation of my family has perhaps betrayed me into offensive expressions, and made me guilty myself of an ostentation which in others has often disgusted me. Ill, indeed, can we any of us bear the test of experiment, when tried upon those subjects which call forth our particular propensities. We may strive to be disinterested, we may struggle to be impartial, but self will still predominate, still shew us the imperfection of our natures, and the narrowness of our souls. Yet acquit me, I beg, of any intentional insolence, and imagine not that in speaking highly of my own family, I mean to depreciate yours: on the contrary, I know it to be respectable, I know, too, that were it the lowest in the kingdom, the first might envy it that it gave birth to such a daughter."

Cecilia, somewhat soothed by this speech, begged her pardon for having interrupted her, and she proceeded.

"To your family, then, I assure you, whatever may be the pride of our own, *you* being its offspring, we would not object. With your merit we are all well acquainted, your character has our highest esteem, and your fortune exceeds even our most sanguine desires. Strange at once and afflicting! that not all these requisites for the satisfaction of prudence, nor all these allurements for the gratification of happiness, can suffice to fulfil or to silence the claims of either! There are yet other demands to which we must attend, demands which ancestry and blood call upon us aloud to ratify! Such claimants are not to be neglected with impunity; they assert their rights with the authority of prescription, they forbid us alike either to bend to inclination, or stoop to interest, and from generation to generation their injuries will call out for redress, should their noble and long unsullied name be voluntarily consigned to oblivion!"

Cecilia, extremely struck by these words, scarce wondered, since so strong and so established were her opinions, that the obstacle to her marriage, though but one, should be considered as insuperable.

"Not, therefore, to *your* name are we averse," she continued, "but simply to our own more partial. To sink that, indeed, in *any* other, were base and unworthy:—what, then, must be the shock of my disappointment, should Mortimer Delvile, the darling of my hopes, the last survivor of his house, in whose birth I rejoiced as the promise of its support, in whose accomplishments I gloried, as the revival of its lustre,—should *he*, should *my* son be the first to abandon it! to give up the name he seemed born to make live, and to cause in effect its utter annihilation!—Oh how should I know my son when an alien to his family! how bear to think I had cherished in my bosom the betrayer of its dearest interests, the destroyer of its very existence!"

Cecilia, scarce more afflicted than offended, now hastily answered, "Not for me, madam, shall he commit this crime, not on *my* account shall he be reprobated by his family! Think of him, therefore, no more, with any reference to me, for I would not be the cause of unworthiness or guilt in him to be mistress of the universe!"

"Nobly said!" cried Mrs. Delvile, her eyes sparkling with joy, and her cheeks glowing with pleasure, "now again do I know Miss Beverley! now again see the refined, the excellent young woman, whose virtues taught me to expect the renunciation even of her own happiness, when found to be incompatible with her duty!"

Cecilia now trembled and turned pale; she scarce knew herself what she had said, but, she found by Mrs. Delvile's construction of her words, they had been regarded as her final relinquishing of her son. She ardently wished to quit the room before she was called upon to confirm the sentence, but she had not courage to make the effort, nor to rise, speak, or move.

"I grieve, indeed," continued Mrs. Delvile, whose coldness and austerity were changed into mildness and compassion, "at the necessity I have been under to draw from you a concurrence so painful: but no other resource was in my power. My influence with Mortimer, whatever it may be, I have not any right to try, without obtaining your previous consent, since I regard him myself as bound to you in honour, and only to be released by your own virtuous desire. I will leave you, however, for my presence, I see, is oppressive to you. Farewell; and when you *can* forgive me, I think you *will*."

"I have nothing, madam," said Cecilia, coldly, "to forgive; you have only asserted your own dignity, and I have nobody to blame but myself, for having given you occasion."

'Alas," cried Mrs. Delvile, "if worth and nobleness of soul on your part, if esteem and tenderest affection on mine, were all which that dignity which offends you requires, how should I crave the blessing of such a daughter! how rejoice in joining my son to excellence so like his own, and ensuring his happiness while I stimulated his virtue!"

"Do not talk to me of affection, madam," said Cecilia, turning away from her; "whatever you had for me is past,—even your esteem is gone,—you may pity me, indeed, but your pity is mixed with contempt, and I am not so abject as to find comfort from exciting it."

"O little," cried Mrs. Delvile, looking at her with the utmost tenderness, "little do you see the state of my heart, for never have you appeared to me so worthy as at this moment! In tearing you from my son, I partake all the wretchedness I give, but your own sense of duty must something plead for the strictness with which I act up to mine."

She then moved towards the door.

"Is your carriage, madam," said Cecilia, struggling to disguise her inward anguish under an appearance of sullenness, "in waiting?"

Mrs. Delvile then came back, and holding out her hand, while her eyes glistened with tears, said, "To part from you thus frigidly, while my heart so warmly admires you, is almost more than I can endure. Oh gentlest Cecilia! condemn not a mother who is impelled to this severity, who performing what she holds to be her duty, thinks the office her bitterest misfortune, who foresees in the rage of her husband, and the resistance of her son, all the misery of domestic contention, and who can only secure the honour of her family by destroying its peace!—You will not, then, give me your hand?—"

Cecilia, who had affected not to see that she waited for it, now coldly put it out, distantly courtesying, and seeking to preserve her steadiness by avoiding to speak. Mrs. Delvile took it, and as she repeated her adieu, affectionately pressed it to her lips; Cecilia, starting, and breathing short, from encreasing yet smothered agitation, called out "Why, why this condescension?—pray,—I entreat you, madam!—"

"Heaven bless you, my love!" said Mrs. Delvile, dropping a tear upon the hand she still held, "heaven bless you, and restore the tranquillity you so nobly deserve!"

"Ah madam!" cried Cecilia, vainly striving to repress any longer the tears which now forced their way down her cheeks, "why will you break my heart with this kindness! why will you still compel me to love,—when now I almost wish to hate you!—"

"No, hate me not," said Mrs. Delvile, kissing from her cheeks the tears that watered them, "hate me not, sweetest Cecilia, though in wounding your gentle bosom, I am almost detestable to myself. Even the cruel scene which awaits me with my son will not more deeply afflict me. But adieu,—I must now prepare for him!"

She then left the room: but Cecilia, whose pride had no power to resist this tenderness, ran hastily after her, saying "Shall I not see you again, madam?"

"You shall yourself decide," answered she, "if my coming will not give you more pain than pleasure, I will wait upon you whenever you please."

Cecilia sighed and paused; she knew not what to desire,

yet rather wished any thing to be done, than quietly to sit down to uninterrupted reflection.

"Shall I postpone quitting this place," continued Mrs. Delvile, "till to-morrow morning, and will you admit me this afternoon, should I call upon you again?"

"I should be sorry," said she, still hesitating, "to detain you,—"

"You will rejoice me," cried Mrs. Delvile, "by bearing me in your sight."

And she then went into her carriage.

Cecilia, unfitted to attend her old friend, and unequal to the task of explaining to her the cruel scene in which she had just been engaged, then hastened to her own apartment. Her hitherto stifled emotions broke forth in tears and repinings: her fate was finally determined, and its determination was not more unhappy than humiliating; she was openly rejected by the family whose alliance she was known to wish; she was compelled to refuse the man of her choice, though satisfied his affections were her own. A misery so peculiar she found hard to support, and almost bursting with conflicting passions, her heart alternately swelled from offended pride, and sunk from disappointed tenderness.

CHAPTER IV

A Perturbation

CECILIA was still in this tempestuous state, when a message was brought her that a gentleman was below stairs, who begged to have the honour of seeing her. She concluded he was Delvile, and the thought of meeting him merely to communicate what must so bitterly afflict him, redoubled her distress, and she went down in an agony of perturbation and sorrow.

He met her at the door, where, before he could speak, "Mr. Delvile," she cried, in a hurrying manner, "why will you come? Why will you thus insist upon seeing me, in defiance of every obstacle, and in contempt of my prohibition?"

"Good heavens," cried he, amazed, "whence this reproach? Did you not permit me to wait upon you with the result of my enquiries? Had I not your consent—but why do you look thus disturbed?—Your eyes are red,—you have been weeping.—Oh my Cecilia! have *I* any share in your sorrow?—Those tears, which never flow weakly, tell me, have they——has *one* of them been shed upon my account?"

"And what," cried she, "has been the result of your enquiries?—Speak quick, for I wish to know,——and in another instant I must be gone."

"How strange," cried the astonished Delvile, "is this language! how strange are these looks! What new has come to pass? Has any fresh calamity happened? Is there yet some evil which I do not expect?"

"Why will you not answer first?" cried she; "When *I* have spoken, you will perhaps be less willing."

"You terrify, you shock, you amaze me! What dreadful blow awaits me? For what horror are you preparing me?— That which I have just experienced, and which tore you from me even at the foot of the altar, still remains inexplicable, still continues to be involved in darkness and mystery, for the wretch who separated us I have never been able to discover."

"Have you procured, then, no intelligence?"

"No, none; though since we parted I have never rested a moment."

"Make, then, no further enquiry, for now all explanation would be useless. That we *were* parted, we know, though *why* we cannot tell: but that again we shall ever meet——"

She stopt; her streaming eyes cast upwards, and a deep sigh bursting from her heart.

"Oh what," cried Delvile, endeavouring to take her hand, which she hastily withdrew from him, "what does this mean? loveliest, dearest Cecilia, my betrothed, my affianced wife! why flow those tears which agony only can wring from you? Why refuse me that hand which so lately was the pledge of your faith? Am I not the same Delvile to whom so few days since you gave it? Why will you not open to him your heart? Why thus distrust his honour, and repulse his tenderness? Oh why, giving him such exquisite misery, refuse him the smallest consolation?"

"What consolation," cried the weeping Cecilia, "can I give? Alas! it is not, perhaps, *you* who most want it!——"

Here the door was opened by one of the Miss Charltons, who came into the room with a message from her grandmother, requesting to see Cecilia. Cecilia, ashamed of being thus surprised with Delvile, and in tears, waited not either to make any excuse to him, or any answer to Miss Charlton, but instantly hurried out of the room;—not, however, to her old friend, whom now less than ever she could meet, but to her own apartment, where a very short indulgence of grief was succeeded by the severest examination of her own conduct.

A retrospection of this sort rarely brings much subject of exultation, when made with the rigid sincerity of secret impartiality: so much stronger is our reason than our virtue, so much higher our sense of duty than our performance!

All she had done she now repented, all she had said she disapproved; her conduct, seldom equal to her notions of right, was now infinitely below them, and the reproaches of her judgement made her forget for a while the afflictions which had misled it.

The sorrow to which she had openly given way in the presence of Delvile, though their total separation but the moment before had been finally decreed, she considered as a weak effusion of tenderness, injurious to delicacy, and censurable by propriety. "His power over my heart," cried she, "it were now, indeed, too late to conceal, but his power over my understanding it is time to cancel. I am not to be his,—my own voice has ratified the renunciation, and since I made it to his mother, it must never, without her consent, be invalidated. Honour, therefore, to her, and regard for myself, equally command me to fly him, till I cease to be thus affected by his sight."

When Delvile, therefore, sent up an entreaty that he might be again admitted into her presence, she returned for answer that she was not well, and could not see any body.

He then left the house, and, in a few minutes, she received the following note from him.

To Miss BEVERLEY.

YOU drive me from you, Cecilia, tortured with suspense, and distracted with apprehension,—you drive me from you, certain of my misery, yet leaving me to bear it as I may! I would call you unfeeling, but that I saw you were unhappy; I would reproach you with tyranny, but that your eyes when you quitted me were swolen with weeping! I go, therefore, I obey the harsh mandate, since my absence is your desire, and I will shut myself up at Biddulph's till I receive your commands. Yet disdain not to reflect that every instant will seem endless, while Cecilia must appear to me unjust, or wound my very soul by the recollection of her in sorrow.

MORTIMER DELVILE.

The mixture of fondness and resentment with which this letter was dictated, marked so strongly the sufferings and disordered state of the writer, that all the softness of Cecilia returned when she perused it, and left her not a wish but to lessen his inquietude, by assurances of unalterable regard: yet she determined not to trust herself in his sight, certain they could only meet to grieve over each other, and conscious that a participation of sorrow would but prove a reciprocation of tenderness. Calling, therefore, upon her duty to resist her inclination, she resolved to commit the whole affair to the will of Mrs. Delvile, to whom, though under no promise, she now considered herself responsible. Desirous, however, to shorten the period of Delvile's uncertainty, she would not wait till the time she had appointed to see his mother, but wrote the following note to hasten their meeting.

To the Hon. Mrs. DELVILE.

Madam,

Your son is now at Bury; shall I acquaint him of your arrival? or will you announce it yourself? Inform me of your desire, and I will endeavour to fulfil it. As my own Agent I

regard myself no longer; if, as yours, I can give pleasure, or
be of service, I shall gladly receive your commands. I have
the honour to be,

> Madam,
>> Your most obedient servant,

>> CECILIA BEVERLEY.

When she had sent off this letter, her heart was more at
ease, because reconciled with her conscience: she had
sacrificed the son, she had resigned herself to the mother; it
now only remained to heal her wounded pride, by suffering
the sacrifice with dignity, and to recover her tranquility in
virtue, by making the resignation without repining.

Her reflections, too, growing clearer as the mist of passion
was dispersed, she recollected with confusion her cold and
sullen behaviour to Mrs. Delvile. That lady had but done
what she had believed was her duty, and that duty was no
more than she had been taught to expect from her. In the
beginning of her visit, and while doubtful of its success,
she had indeed, been austere, but the moment victory
appeared in view, she became tender, affectionate and
gentle. Her justice, therefore, condemned the resentment to
which she had given way, and she fortified her mind for the
interview which was to follow, by an earnest desire to make
reparation both to Mrs. Delvile and herself for that which
was past.

In this resolution she was not a little strengthened, by
seriously considering with herself the great abatement to all
her possible happiness, which must have been made by the
humilating circumstances of forcing herself into a family
which held all connection with her as disgraceful. She
desired not to be the wife even of Delvile upon such terms,
for the more she esteemed and admired him, the more
anxious she became for his honour, and the less could she
endure being regarded herself as the occasion of its
diminution.

Now, therefore, her plan of conduct settled, with calmer

spirits, though a heavy heart, she attended upon Mrs. Charlton; but fearing to lose the steadiness she had just acquired before it should be called upon, if she trusted herself to relate the decision which had been made, she besought her for the present to dispense with the account, and then forced herself into conversation upon less interesting subjects.

This prudence had its proper effect,. and with tolerable tranquility she heard Mrs. Delvile again announced, and waited upon her in the parlour with an air of composure.

Not so did Mrs. Delvile receive her; she was all eagerness and emotion; she flew to her the moment she appeared, and throwing her arms around her, warmly exclaimed "Oh charming girl! Saver of our family! preserver of our honour! How poor are words to express my admiration! how inadequate are thanks in return for such obligations as I owe you!"

"You owe me none, madam," said Cecilia, suppressing a sigh; "on *my* side will be all the obligation, if you can pardon the petulance of my behaviour this morning."

"Call not by so harsh a name," answered Mrs. Delvile, "the keenness of a sensibility by which you have yourself alone been the sufferer. You have had a trial the most severe, and however able to sustain, it was impossible you should not feel it. That you should give up *any* man whose friends solicit not your alliance, your mind is too delicate to make wonderful; but your generosity in submitting, unasked, the arrangement of that resignation to those for whose interest it is made, and your high sense of honour in holding yourself accountable to *me*, though under no tie, and bound by no promise, mark a greatness of mind which calls for reverence rather than thanks, and which I never can praise half so much as I admire."

Cecilia, who received this applause but as a confirmation of her rejection, thanked her only by courtsying; and Mrs. Delvile, having seated herself next her, continued her speech.

"My son, you have the goodness to tell me, is here,— have you seen him?"

"Yes, madam," answered she, blushing, "but hardly for a moment."

"And he knows not of my arrival?"

"No,——I believe he certainly does not."

"Sad, then, is the trial which awaits him, and heavy for me the office I must perform! Do you expect to see him again?"

"No,—yes,—perhaps——indeed I hardly—"

She stammered, and Mrs. Delvile, taking her hand, said "Tell me, Miss Beverley, *why* should you see him again?"

Cecilia was thunderstruck by this question, and, colouring yet more deeply, looked down, but could not answer.

"Consider," continued Mrs. Delvile, "the *purpose* of any further meeting; your union is impossible, you have nobly consented to relinquish all thoughts of it: why then tear your own heart, and torture his, by an intercourse which seems nothing but an ill-judged invitation to fruitless and unavailing sorrow?"

Cecilia was still silent; the truth of the expostulation her reason acknowledged, but to assent to its consequence her whole heart refused.

"The ungenerous triumph of little female vanity," said Mrs. Delvile, "is far, I am sure, from your mind, of which the enlargement and liberality will rather find consolation from lessening than from imbittering his sufferings. Speak to me, then, and tell me, honestly, judiciously, candidly tell me,——will it not be wiser and more right, to avoid rather than seek an object which can only give birth to regret? an interview which can excite no sensations but of misery and sadness?"

Cecilia then turned pale, she endeavoured to speak, but could not; she wished to comply,—yet to think she had seen him for the last time, to remember how abruptly she had parted from him, and to fear she had treated him unkindly;——these were obstacles which opposed her concurrence, though both judgment and propriety demanded it.

"Can you, then," said Mrs. Delvile, after a pause, "can

you wish to see Mortimer merely to behold his grief? Can you desire he should see you, only to sharpen his affliction at your loss?"

"O no!" cried Cecilia, to whom this reproof restored speech and resolution, "I am not so despicable, I am not, I hope, so unworthy!—I will be ruled by you wholly; I will commit to you every thing;—yet *once*, perhaps,—no more!——"

"Ah, my dear Miss Beverley! to meet confessedly for *once*,—what were that but planting a dagger in the heart of Mortimer? What were it but infusing poison into your own?"

"If you think so, madam," said she, "I had better——I will certainly—" she sighed, stammered, and stopt.

"Hear me," cried Mrs. Delvile, "and rather let me try to convince than persuade you. Were there any possibility, by argument, by reflection, or even by accident, to remove the obstacles to our connection, then would it be well to meet, for then might discussion turn to account, and an interchange of sentiments be productive of some happy expedient: but here—"

She hesitated, and Cecilia, shocked and ashamed, turned away her face, and cried "I know, madam, what you would say,—here all is over! and therefore——"

"Yet suffer me," interrupted she, "to be explicit, since we speak upon this matter now for the last time. Here, then I say, where not ONE doubt remains, where ALL is finally, though not happily decided, what can an interview produce? Mischief of every sort, pain, horror, and repining! To Mortimer you may think it would be kind, and grant it to his prayers, as an alleviation of his misery; mistaken notion! nothing could so greatly augment it. All his passions would be raised, all his prudence would be extinguished, his soul would be torn with resentment and regret, and force, only, would part him from you, when previously he knew that parting was to be eternal. To yourself——"

"Talk not, madam, of *me*," cried the unhappy Cecilia, "what you say of your son is sufficient, and I will yield——"

"Yet hear me," proceeded she, "and believe me not so

unjust as to consider him alone; you, also, would be an equal, though a less stormy sufferer. You fancy, at this moment, that once more to meet him would soothe your uneasiness, and that to take of him a farewell, would soften the pain of the separation: how false such reasoning! how dangerous such consolation! acquainted ere you meet that you were to meet him no more, your heart would be all softness and grief, and at the very moment when tenderness should be banished from your intercourse, it would bear down all opposition of judgment, spirit, and dignity: you would hang upon every word, because every word would seem the last, every look, every expression would be rivetted in your memory, and his image in this parting distress would be painted upon your mind, in colours that would eat into its peace, and perhaps never be erased."

"Enough, enough," said Cecilia, "I will not see him,—— I will not even desire it!"

"Is this compliance or conviction? Is what I have said true, or only terrifying?"

"Both, both! I believe, indeed, the conflict would have overpowered me.—I see you are right,—and I thank you, madam, for saving me from a scene I might so cruelly have rued."

"Oh Daughter of my mind!" cried Mrs. Delvile, rising and embracing her, "noble, generous, yet gentle Cecilia! what tie, what connection, could make you more dear to me? Who is there like you? Who half so excellent? So open to reason, so ingenuous in error! so rational! so just! so feeling, yet so wise!"

"You are very good," said Cecilia, with a forced serenity, "and I am thankful that your resentment for the past obstructs not your lenity for the present."

"Alas, my love, how shall I resent the past, when I ought myself to have foreseen this calamity! and I *should* have foreseen it, had I not been informed you were engaged, and upon your engagement built our security. Else had I been more alarmed, for my own admiration would have bid me look forward to my son's. You were just, indeed, the woman he had least chance to resist, you were precisely the character to seize his very soul. To a softness the most fatally alluring, you join a dignity which rescues from their own contempt even the most humble of your admirers. You seem born to have all the world wish your exaltation, and no part of it murmur at your superiority. Were any obstacle but this insuperable one in the way, should nobles, nay, should princes offer their daughters to my election, I would reject without murmuring the most magnificent proposals, and take in triumph to my heart my son's nobler choice!"

"Oh madam," cried Cecilia, "talk not to me thus!——speak not such flattering words!—ah, rather scorn and upbraid me, tell me you despise my character, my family and my connections,—load, load me with contempt, but do not thus torture me with approbation!"

"Pardon me, sweetest girl, if I have awakened those emotions you so wisely seek to subdue. May my son but emulate your example, and my pride in his virtue shall be the solace of my affliction for his misfortunes."

She then tenderly embraced her, and abruptly took her leave.

Cecilia had now acted her part, and acted it to her own satisfaction; but the curtain dropt when Mrs. Delvile left the house, nature resumed her rights, and the sorrow of her heart was no longer disguised or repressed. Some faint ray of hope had till now broke through the gloomiest cloud of her misery, and secretly flattered her that its dispersion was possible, through distant: but that ray was extinct, that hope was no more; she had solemnly promised to banish Delvile her sight, and his mother had absolutely declared that even the subject had been discussed for the last time.

Mrs. Charlton, impatient of some explanation of the morning's transactions, soon sent again to beg Cecilia would come to her. Cecilia reluctantly obeyed, for she feared encreasing her indisposition by the intelligence she had to communicate; she struggled, therefore, to appear to her with tolerable calmness, and in briefly relating what had passed, forbore to mingle with the narrative her own feelings and unhappiness.

Mrs. Charlton heard the account with the utmost concern; she accused Mrs. Delvile of severity, and even of cruelty; she lamented the strange accident by which the marriage ceremony had been stopt, and regretted that it had not again been begun, as the only means to have rendered ineffectual the present fatal interposition.

But the grief of Cecilia, however violent, induced her not to join in this regret: she mourned only the obstacle which had occasioned the separation, and not the incident which had merely interrupted the ceremony: convinced, by the conversations in which she had just been engaged, of Mrs. Delvile's inflexibility, she rather rejoiced than repined that she had put it to no nearer trial: sorrow was all she felt; for her mind was too liberal to harbour resentment against a conduct which she saw was dictated by a sense of right; and too ductile and too affectionate to remain unmoved by the personal kindness which had softened the rejection, and the many marks of esteem and regard which had shewn her it was lamented, though considered as indispensable.

How and by whom this affair had been betrayed to Mrs. Delvile she knew not; but the discovery was nothing less than surprising, since, by various unfortunate accidents, it was known to so many, and since, in the horror and confusion of the mysterious prohibition to the marriage, neither Delvile nor herself had thought of even attempting to give any caution to the witnesses of that scene, not to make it known: an attempt, however, which must almost necessarily have been unavailing, as the incident was too extraordinary and too singular to have any chance of suppression.

During this conversation, one of the servants came to inform Cecilia, that a man was below to enquire if there was no answer to the note he had brought in the forenoon.

Cecilia, greatly distressed, knew not upon what to resolve; that the patience of Delvile should be exhausted, she did not, indeed, wonder, and to relieve his anxiety was now almost her only wish; she would therefore instantly have written to him, confessed her sympathy in his sufferings, and besought him to endure with fortitude an evil which was no longer to be withstood: but she was uncertain whether he was yet

acquainted with the journey of his mother to Bury, and
having agreed to commit to her the whole management of
the affair, she feared it would be dishonourable to take any
step in it without her concurrence. She returned, therefore,
a message that she had yet no answer ready.

In a very few minutes Delvile called himself, and sent up
an earnest request for permission to see her.

Here, at least, she had no perplexity; an interview she had
given her positive word to refuse, and therefore, without a
moment's hesitation, she bid the servant inform him she was
particularly engaged, and sorry it was not in her power to
see any company.

In the greatest perturbation he left the house, and
immediately wrote to her the following lines.

To Miss BEVERLEY.

I entreat you to see me! if only for an instant, I entreat,
I implore you to see me! Mrs. Charlton may be present,
——all the world, if you wish it, may be present,—but deny
me not admission, I supplicate, I conjure you!

I will call in an hour; in that time you may have finished
your present engagement. I will otherwise wait longer, and
call again. You will not, I think, turn me from your door,
and, till I have seen you, I can only live in its vicinity.

M.D.

The man who brought this note, waited not for any answer.

Cecilia read it in an agony of mind inexpressible: she saw,
by its style, how much Delvile was irritated, and her
knowledge of his temper made her certain his irritation
proceeded from believing himself ill-used. She ardently
wished to appease and to quiet him, and regretted the
necessity of appearing obdurate and unfeeling, even more,
at that moment, than the separation itself. To a mind
priding in its purity, and animated in its affections, few
sensations can excite keener misery, than those by which an
apprehension is raised of being thought worthless or
ungrateful by the objects of our chosen regard. To be
deprived of their society is less bitter, to be robbed of our
own tranquillity by any other means, is less afflicting.

Yet to this it was necessary to submit, or incur the only penalty which, to such a mind, would be more severe, self-reproach: she had promised to be governed by Mrs. Delvile, she had nothing, therefore, to do but obey her.

Yet *to turn*, as he expressed himself, *from the door*, a man who, but for an incident the most incomprehensible, would now have been sole master of herself and her actions, seemed so unkind and so tyrannical, that she could not endure to be within hearing of his repulse: she begged, therefore, the use of Mrs. Charlton's carriage, and determined to make a visit to Mrs. Harrel till Delvile and his mother had wholly quitted Bury. She was not, indeed, quite satisfied in going to the house of Mr. Arnott, but she had no time to weigh objections, and knew not any other place to which still greater might not be started.

She wrote a short letter to Mrs. Delvile, acquainting her with her purpose, and its reason, and repeating her assurances that she would be guided by her implicitly; and then, embracing Mrs. Charlton, whom she left to the care of her grand-daughters, she got into a chaise, accompanied only by her maid, and one man and horse, and ordered the postilion to drive to Mr. Arnott's.*

CHAPTER V

A Cottage

THE evening was already far advanced, and before she arrived at the end of her little journey it was quite dark. When they came within a mile of Mr. Arnott's house, the postilion, in turning too suddenly from the turnpike to the cross-road, overset the carriage. The accident, however, occasioned no other mischief than delaying their proceeding, and Cecilia and her maid were helped out of the chaise unhurt. The servants, assisted by a man who was walking upon the road, began lifting it up; and Cecilia, too busy within to be attentive to what passed without, disregarded what went forward, till she heard her footman call for help.

She then hastily advanced to enquire what was the matter, and found that the passenger who had lent his aid, had, by working in the dark, unfortunately slipped his foot under one of the wheels, and so much hurt it, that without great pain he could not put it to the ground.

Cecilia immediately desired that the sufferer might be carried to his own home in the chaise, while she and the maid walked on to Mr. Arnott's, attended by her servant on horseback.

This little incident proved of singular service to her upon first entering the house; Mrs. Harrel was at supper with her brother, and hearing the voice of Cecilia in the hall, hastened with the extremest surprise to enquire what had occasioned so late a visit; followed by Mr. Arnott, whose amazement was accompanied with a thousand other sensations too powerful for speech. Cecilia, unprepared with any excuse, instantly related the adventure she had met with on the road, which quieted their curiosity, by turning their attention to her personal safety. They ordered a room to be prepared for her, entreated her to go to rest with all speed, and postpone any further account till the next day. With this request she most gladly complied, happy to be spared the embarrassment of enquiry, and rejoiced to be relieved from the fatigue of conversation.

Her night was restless and miserable: to know how Delvile would bear her flight was never a moment from her thoughts, and to hear whether he would obey or oppose his mother was her incessant wish. She was fixt, however, to be faithful in refusing to see him, and at least to suffer nothing new from her own enterprize or fault.

Early in the morning Mrs. Harrel came to see her. She was eager to learn why, after invitations repeatedly refused, she was thus suddenly arrived without any; and she was still more eager to talk of herself, and relate the weary life she led thus shut up in the country, and confined to the society of her brother.

Cecilia evaded giving any immediate answer to her questions, and Mrs. Harrel, happy in an opportunity to rehearse her own complaints, soon forgot that she had asked any, and, in a very short time, was perfectly, though imperceptibly, contented to be herself the only subject upon which they conversed.

But not such was the selfishness of Mr. Arnott; and Cecilia, when she went down to breakfast, perceived with the utmost concern that he had passed a night as sleepless as her own. A visit so sudden, so unexpected, and so unaccountable, from an object that no discouragement could make him think of with indifference, had been a subject to him of conjecture and wonder that had revived all the hopes and the fears* which had lately, though still unextinguished, lain dormant. The enquiries, however, which his sister had given up, he ventured not to renew, and thought himself but too happy in her presence, whatever might be the cause of her visit.

He perceived, however, immediately, the sadness that hung upon her mind, and his own was redoubled by the sight: Mrs. Harrel, also, saw that she looked ill, but attributed it to the fatigue and fright of the preceding evening, well knowing that a similar accident would have made her ill herself, or fancy that she was so.

During breakfast, Cecilia sent for the postilion, to enquire of him how the man had fared, whose good-natured assitance in their distress had been so unfortunate to himself. He answered that he had turned out to be a day labourer,* who lived about half a mile off. And then, partly to gratify her own humanity, and partly to find any other employment for herself and friends than uninteresting conversation, she proposed that they should all walk to the poor man's habitation, and offer him some amends for the injury he had received. This was readily assented to, and the postilion directed them whither to go.

The place was a cottage, situated upon a common; they entered it without ceremony, and found a clean looking woman at work.

Cecilia enquired for her husband, and was told that he was gone out to day-labour.

"I am very glad to hear it," returned she; "I hope then he has got the better of the accident he met with last night?"

"It was not him, madam," said the woman, "met with the accident, it was John;—there he is, working in the garden."

To the garden then they* all went, and saw him upon the ground, weeding.

The moment they approached he arose, and, without speaking, began to limp, for he could hardly walk, away.

"I am sorry, master," said Cecilia, "that you are so much hurt. Have you had any thing put to your foot?"

The man made no answer, but still turned away from her; a glance, however, of his eye, which the next instant he fixed upon the ground, startled her; she moved round to look at him again,—and perceived Mr. Belfield!

"Good God!" she exclaimed; but seeing him still retreat, she recollected in a moment how little he would be obliged to her for betraying him, and, suffering him to go on, turned back to her party, and led the way again into the house.

As soon as the first emotion of her surprise was over, she enquired how long *John* had belonged to this cottage, and what was his way of life.

The woman answered he had only been with them a week, and that he went* out to day-labour with her husband.

Cecilia then, finding their stay kept him from his employment, and willing to save him the distress of being seen by Mr. Arnott or Mrs. Harrel, proposed their returning home. She grieved most sincerely at beholding in so melancholy an occupation a young man of such talents and abilities; she wished much to assist him, and began considering by what means it might be done, when, as they were walking from the cottage, a voice at some distance called out "Madam! Miss Beverley!" and, looking round, to her utter amazement she saw Belfield endeavouring to follow her.

She instantly stopt, and he advanced, his hat in his hand, and his whole air indicating he sought not to be disguised.

Surprised at this sudden change of behaviour, she then stept forward to meet him, accompanied by her friends: but when they came up to each other, she checked her desire of speaking, to leave him fully at liberty to make himself known, or keep concealed.

He bowed with a look of assumed gaiety and ease, but the deep scarlet that tinged his whole face manifested his internal confusion; and in a voice that attempted to sound lively, though its tremulous accents betrayed uneasiness and distress, he exclaimed, with a forced smile, "Is it possible Miss Beverley can deign to notice a poor miserable day-labourer such as I am? how will she be justified in the beau monde, when even the sight of such a wretch ought to fill her with horror? Henceforth let hystericks be blown to the winds, and let nerves be discarded from the female vocabulary, since a lady so young and fair can stand this shock without hartshorn or fainting!"

"I am happy," answered Cecilia, "to find your spirits so good; yet my own, I must confess, are not raised by seeing you in this strange situation."

"My spirits!" cried he, with an air of defiance, "never were they better, never so good as at this moment. Strange as seems my situation, it is all that I wish; I have found out, at last, the true secret of happiness! that secret which so long I pursued in vain, but which always eluded my grasp, till the instant of despair arrived, when, slackening my pace, I gave it up as a phantom. Go from me, I cried, I will be cheated no more! thou airy bubble! thou fleeting shadow! I will live no longer in thy sight, since thy beams dazzle without warming me! Mankind seems only composed as matter for thy experiments, and I will quit the whole race, that thy delusions may be presented to me no more!"

This romantic flight, which startled even Cecilia, though acquainted with his character, gave to Mrs. Harrel and Mr. Arnott the utmost surprize; his appearance, and the account they had just heard of him, having by no means prepared them for such sentiments or such language.

"Is then this great secret of happiness," said Cecilia, "nothing, at last, but total seclusion from the world?"

"No, madam," answered he, "it is Labour with Independence."

Cecilia now wished much to ask some explanation of his affairs, but was doubtful whether he would gratify her before Mrs. Harrel and Mr. Arnott, and hurt to keep him standing, though he leant upon a stick; she told him, therefore, she would at present detain him no longer, but endeavour again to see him before she quitted her friends.

Mr. Arnott then interfered, and desired his sister would entreat Miss Beverley to invite whom she pleased to his house.

Cecilia thanked him, and instantly asked Belfield to call upon her in the afternoon.

"No, madam, no," cried he, "I have done with visits and society! I will not so soon break through a system with much difficulty formed, when all my future tranquility depends upon adhering to it. The worthlessness of mankind has disgusted me with the world, and my resolution in quitting it shall be immoveable as its baseness."

"I must not venture then," said Cecilia, "to enquire—"

"Enquire, madam," interrupted he with quickness, "what you please: there is nothing I will not answer to you,—to this lady, to this gentleman, to any and to every body. What can I wish to conceal, where I have nothing to gain or to lose? When first, indeed, I saw you, I involuntarily shrunk; a weak shame for a moment seized me, I felt fallen and debased, and I wished to avoid you: but a little recollection brought me back to my senses. And where, cried I, is the disgrace of exercising for my subsistence the strength with which I am endued? and why should I blush to lead the life which uncorrupted Nature first prescribed to man?"

"Well, then," said Cecilia, more and more interested to hear him, "if you will not visit us, will you at least permit us to return with you to some place where you can be seated?"

"I will with pleasure," cried he, "go to any place where you may be seated yourselves; but for me, I have ceased to regard accommodation or inconvenience."

They then all went back to the cottage, which was now empty, the woman being out at work.

"Will you then, Sir," said Cecilia, "give me leave to enquire whether Lord Vannelt is acquainted with your retirement, and if it will not much surprize and disappoint him?"

"Lord Vannelt," cried he, haughtily, "has no right to be surprised. I would have quitted *his* house, if no other, not even this cottage, had a roof to afford me shelter!"

"I am sorry, indeed, to hear it," said Cecilia; "I had hoped he would have known your value, and merited your regard."

"Ill-usage," answered he, "is as hard to relate as to be endured. There is commonly something pitiful in a complaint; and though oppression in a general sense provokes the wrath of mankind, the investigation of its minuter circumstances excites nothing but derision. Those who give the offence, by the worthy few may be hated, but those who receive it, by the world at large will be despised. Conscious of this, I disdained making any appeal; myself the only sufferer, I had a right to be the only judge, and, shaking off the base trammels of interest and subjection, I quitted the house in silent indignation, not chusing to remonstrate, where I desired not to be reconciled."

"And was there no mode of life," said Cecilia, "to adopt, but living with Lord Vannelt, or giving up the whole world?"

"I weighed every thing maturely," answered he, "before I made my determination, and I found it so much the most eligible, that I am certain I can never repent it. I had friends who would with pleasure have presented me to some other nobleman; but my whole heart revolted against leading that kind of life, and I would not, therefore, idly rove from one great man to another, adding ill-will to disgrace, and pursuing hope in defiance of common sense; no; when I quitted Lord Vannelt, I resolved to give up patronage for ever.

"I retired to private lodgings to deliberate what next could be done. I had lived in many ways, I had been unfortunate or imprudent in all. The law I had tried, but its rudiments were tedious and disgusting; the army, too, but there found my mind more fatigued with indolence, than my body with action; general dissipation had then its turn, but the expence to which it led was ruinous, and self-reproach baffled pleasure while I pursued it; I have even—yes, there are few things I have left untried,—I have even,—for why now disguise it?—"

He stopt and coloured, but in a quicker voice presently proceeded.

"Trade, also, has had its share in my experiments; for that, in truth, I was originally destined,—but my education had ill suited me to such a destination, and the trader's first maxim I reversed, in lavishing when I ought to have accumulated.

"What, then, remained for me? to run over again the same irksome round I had not patience, and to attempt any thing new I was unqualified: money I had none; my friends I could bear to burthen no longer; a fortnight I lingered in wretched irresolution,—a simple accident at the end of it happily settled me; I was walking, one morning, in Hyde Park, forming a thousand plans for my future life, but quarrelling with them all; when a gentleman met me on horseback, from whom, at my Lord Vannelt's, I had received particular civilities; I looked another way not to be seen by him, and the change in my dress since I left his Lordship's made me easily pass unnoticed. He had rode on, however, but a few yards, before, by some accident or mismanagement, he had a fall from his horse. Forgetting all my caution, I flew instantly to his assistance; he was bruised, but not otherwise hurt; I helpt him up, and he leant upon my arm; in my haste of enquiring how he had fared, I called him by his name. He knew me, but looked suprised at my appearance; he was speaking to me, however, with kindness, when seeing some gentlemen of his acquaintance galloping up to him, he hastily disengaged himself from me, and instantly beginning to recount to them what had happened, he sedulously looked another way, and joining his new companions, walked off without taking further notice of me. For a moment I was almost tempted to trouble him to come back; but a little recollection told me how ill he deserved my resentment, and bid me transfer it for the future from the pitiful individual to the worthless community.

"Here finished my deliberation; the disgust to the world which I had already conceived, this little incident confirmed;

I saw it was only made for the great and the rich;—poor, therefore, and low, what had I to do in it? I determined to quit it for ever, and to end every disappointment, by crushing every hope.

"I wrote to Lord Vannelt to send my trunks to my mother; I wrote to my mother that I was well, and would soon let her hear more: I then paid off my lodgings, and "shaking the dust from my feet,"* bid a long adieu to London; and committing my route to chance, strole* on into the country, without knowing or caring which way.

"My first thought was simply to seek retirement, and to depend for my future repose upon nothing but a total seclusion from society: but my slow method of travelling gave me time for reflection, and reflection soon shewed me the error of this notion.

"Guilt, cried I, may, indeed, be avoided by solitude; but will misery? will regret? will deep dejection of mind? no; they will follow more assiduously than ever; for what is there to oppose them, where neither business occupies the time, nor hope the imagination? where the past has left nothing but resentment, and the future opens only to a dismal, uninteresting void? No stranger to life, I knew human nature could not exist on such terms; still less a stranger to books, I respected the voice of wisdom and experience in the first of moralists, and most enlightened of men,†* and reading the letter of Cowley, I saw the vanity and absurdity of *panting after solitude*.‡*

"I sought not, therefore, a cell;* but, since I purposed to live for myself, I determined for myself also to think. Servility of imitation has ever been as much my scorn as servility of dependence; I resolved, therefore, to strike out something new, and no more to retire as every other man had retired, than to linger in the world as every other man had lingered.

"The result of all you now see. I found out this cottage, and took up my abode in it. I am here out of the way of all society, yet avoid the great evil of retreat, *having nothing to*

† Dr. JOHNSON.
‡ Life of Cowley, p. 34.

do.* I am constantly, not capriciously employed, and the exercise which benefits my health imperceptibly raises my spirits in despight of adversity. I am removed from all temptation. I have scarce even the power to do wrong; I have no object for ambition, for repining I have no time:—I have found out, I repeat, the true secret of happiness, Labour with Independence.''

He stopt; and Cecilia, who had listened to this narrative with a mixture of compassion, admiration and censure, was too much struck with its singularity to be readily able to answer it. Her curiosity to hear him had sprung wholly from her desire to assist him, and she had expected from his story to gather some hint upon which her services might be offered. But none had occurred; he professed himself fully satisfied with his situation; and though reason and probability contradicted the profession, she could not venture to dispute it with any delicacy or prudence.

She thanked him, therefore, for his relation, with many apologies for the trouble she had given him, and added, ''I must not express my concern for misfortunes which you seem to regard as conducive to your contentment, nor remonstrate at the step you have taken, since you have been led to it by choice, not necessity: but yet, you must pardon me if I cannot help hoping I shall some time see you happier, according to the common, however vulgar ideas of the rest of the world.''

''No, never, never! I am sick of mankind, not from theory, but experience; and the precautions I have taken against mental fatigue, will secure me from repentance, or any desire of change; for it is not the active, but the indolent who weary; it is not the temperate, but the pampered who are capricious.''

''Is your sister, Sir, acquainted with this change in your fortune and opinions?''

''Poor girl, no! She and her unhappy mother have borne but too long with my enterprizes and misfortunes. Even yet they would sacrifice whatever they possess to enable me to play once more the game so often lost; but I will not abuse their affection, nor suffer them again to be slaves to my caprices, nor dupes to their own delusive expectations. I have sent them word I am happy; I have not yet told them how or where. I fear much the affliction of their disappointment, and, for a while, shall conceal from them my situation, which they would fancy was disgraceful, and grieve at as cruel."

"And is it *not* cruel?" said Cecilia, "is labour indeed so sweet? and can you seriously derive happiness from what all others consider as misery?"

"Not sweet," answered he, "in itself; but sweet, most sweet and salutary in its effects. When I work, I forget all the world; my projects for the future, my disappointments from the past. Mental fatigue is overpowered by personal; I toil till I require rest, and that rest which nature, not luxury demands, leads not to idle meditation, but to sound, heavy, necessary sleep. I awake the next morning to the same thought-exiling business, work again till my powers are exhausted, and am relieved again at night by the same health-recruiting insensibility."

"And if this," cried Cecilia, "is the life of happiness, why have we so many complaints of the sufferings of the poor, and why so eternally do we hear of their hardship and distress?"

"They have known no other life. They are strangers, therefore, to the felicity of their lot. Had they mingled in the world, fed high their fancy with hope, and looked forward with expectation of enjoyment; had they been courted by the great, and offered with profusion adulation for their abilities, yet, even when starving, been offered nothing else!—had they seen an attentive circle wait all its entertainment from their powers, yet found themselves forgotten as soon as out of sight, and perceived themselves avoided when no longer buffoons!—Oh had they known and felt provocations such as these, how gladly would their resentful spirits turn from the whole unfeeling race, and how would they respect that noble and manly labour, which at once disentangles them from such subjugating snares, and enables them to fly the ingratitude they abhor! Without the contrast of vice, virtue unloved may be lovely; without the experience of misery, happiness is simply a dull privation of evil."

"And are you so content," cried Cecilia, "with your present situation, as even to think it offers you reparation for your past sufferings?"

"Content!" repeated he with energy, "O more than content, I am proud of my present situation! I glory in shewing to the world, I glory still more in shewing to myself, that those whom I cannot but despise I will not scruple to defy, and that where I have been treated unworthily, I will scorn to be obliged."

"But will you pardon me," said Cecilia, "should I ask again, why in quitting Lord Vannelt, you concluded no one else worthy a trial?"

"Because it was less my Lord Vannelt, madam, than my own situation, that disgusted me: for though I liked not his behaviour, I found him a man too generally esteemed to flatter myself better usage would await me in merely changing my abode, while my station was the same. I believe, indeed, he never meant to offend me; but I was offended the more that he should think me an object to receive indignity without knowing it. To have had this pointed out to him, would have been at once mortifying and vain; for delicacy, like taste, can only partially be taught, and will always be superficial and erring where it is not innate. Those wrongs, which though too trifling to resent, are too humiliating to be borne, speech can convey no idea of; the soul must feel, or the understanding can never comprehend them."

"But surely," said Cecilia, "though people of refinement are rare, they yet exist; why, then, remove yourself from the possibility of meeting with them?"

"Must I run about the nation," cried he, "proclaiming my distress, and describing my temper? telling the world that though dependent I demand respect as well as assistance; and publishing to mankind, that though poor I will accept no gifts if offered with contumely? Who will listen to such an account? who will care for my misfortunes, but as they may humble me to his service? who will hear my mortifications, but to say I deserve them? what has the world to do with my feelings and peculiarities? I know it too well to think calamity will soften it; I need no new lessons to instruct me that to conquer affliction is more wise than to relate it.''

''Unfortunate as you have been,'' said Cecilia, ''I cannot wonder at your asperity; but yet, it is surely no more than justice to acknowledge, that hard-heartedness to distress is by no means the fault of the present times: on the contrary, it is scarce sooner made known, then every one is ready to contribute to its relief.''

''And how contribute?'' cried he, ''by a paltry donation of money? Yes, the man whose only want is a few guineas, may, indeed, obtain them; but he who asks kindness and protection, whose oppressed spirit calls for consolation even more than his ruined fortune for repair, how is his struggling soul, if superior to his fate, to brook the ostentation of patronage, and the insolence of condescension? Yes, yes, the world will save the poor beggar who is starving; but the fallen wretch, who will not cringe for his support, may consume in his own wretchedness without pity and without help!''

Cecilia now saw that the wound his sensibility had received was too painful for argument, and too recent immediately to be healed. She forbore, therefore, to detain him any longer, but expressing her best wishes, without venturing to hint at her services, she arose, and they all took their leave;—Belfield hastening, as they went, to return to the garden, where, looking over the hedge as they passed, they saw him employed again in weeding, with the eagerness of a man who pursues his favourite occupation.

Cecilia half forgot her own anxieties and sadness, in the concern which she felt for this unfortunate and extraordinary young man. She wished much to devise some means for drawing him from a life of such hardship and obscurity; but what to a man thus ''jealous in honour,''* thus scrupulous in delicacy, could she propose, without more risk of offence, than probability of obliging? His account had, indeed, convinced her how much he stood in need of assistance, but it had shewn her no less how fastidious he would be in receiving it.

Nor was she wholly without fear that an earnest solicitude to serve him, his youth, talents, and striking manners considered, might occasion even in himself a misconstruction of her motives, such as she already had given birth to in his forward and partial mother.

The present, therefore, all circumstances weighed, seemed no season for her liberality, which she yet resolved to exert the first moment it was un-opposed by propriety.

CHAPTER VI

A Contest

THE rest of the day was passed in discussing this adventure; but in the evening, Cecilia's interest in it was all sunk, by the reception of the following letter from Mrs. Delvile.

To Miss BEVERLEY.

I grieve to interrupt the tranquillity of a retirement so judiciously chosen, and I lament the necessity of again calling to trial the virtue of which the exertion, though so captivating, is so painful; but alas, my excellent young friend, we came not hither to enjoy, but to suffer; and happy only are those whose sufferings have neither by folly been sought, nor by guilt been merited, but arising merely from the imperfection of humanity, have been resisted with fortitude, or endured with patience.

I am informed of your virtuous steadiness, which corresponds with my expectations, while it excites my respect. All further conflict I had hoped to have saved you; and to the triumph of your goodness I had trusted for the recovery of your peace: but Mortimer has disappointed me, and our work is still unfinished.

He avers that he is solemnly engaged to you, and in pleading to me his honour, he silences both expostulation and authority. From your own words alone will he acknowledge his dismission; and notwithstanding my reluctance to impose upon you this task, I cannot silence or quiet him without making the request.

For a purpose such as this, can you, then, admit us? Can you bear with your own lips to confirm the irrevocable decision? You will feel, I am sure, for the unfortunate Mortimer, and it was earnestly my desire to spare you the sight of his affliction; yet such is my confidence in your prudence, that since I find him bent upon seeing you, I am not without hope, that from witnessing the greatness of your mind, the interview may rather calm than inflame him.

This proposal you will take into consideration, and if you are able, upon such terms, to again meet my son, we will wait upon you together, where and when you will appoint; but if the gentleness of your nature will make the effort too severe for you, scruple not to decline it, for Mortimer, when he knows your pleasure, will submit to it as he ought.

Adieu, most amiable and but too lovely Cecilia; whatever you determine, be sure of my concurrence, for nobly have you earned, and ever must you retain, the esteem, the affection, and the gratitude of

AUGUSTA DELVILE.

"Alas," cried Cecilia, "when shall I be at rest? when cease to be persecuted by new conflicts! Oh why must I so often, so cruelly, though so reluctantly, reject and reprove the man who of all men I wish to accept and to please!"

But yet, though repining at this hard necessity, she hesitated not a moment in complying with Mrs. Delvile's request, and immediately sent an answer that she would meet her the next morning at Mrs. Charlton's.

She then returned to the parlour, and apologized to Mrs. Harrel and Mr. Arnott for the abruptness of her visit, and the suddenness of her departure. Mr. Arnott heard her in silent dejection; and Mrs. Harrel used all the persuasion in her power to prevail with her to stay, her presence being some relief to her solitude: but finding it ineffectual, she earnestly pressed her to hasten her entrance into her own house, that their absence might be shortened, and their meeting more sprightly.

Cecilia passed the night in planning her behaviour for the next day; she found how much was expected from her by Mrs. Delvile, who had even exhorted her to decline the interview if doubtful of her own strength. Delvile's firmness in insisting the refusal should come directly from herself, surprised, gratified and perplexed her in turn; she had imagined, that from the moment of the discovery, he would implicitly have submitted to the award of a parent at once so reverenced and so beloved, and how he had summoned courage to contend with her she could not conjecture: yet that courage and that contention astonished not more than they soothed her, since, from her knowledge of his filial tenderness, she considered them as the most indubitable proofs she had yet received of the fervour and constancy of his regard for her. But would he, when she had ratified the decision of his mother, forbear all further struggle, and for ever yield up all pretensions to her? this was the point upon which her uncertainty turned, and the ruling subject of her thoughts and meditation.

To be steady, however, herself, be his conduct what it might, was invariably her intention, and was all her ambition: yet earnestly she wished the meeting over, for she dreaded to see the sorrow of Delvile, and she dreaded still more the susceptibility of her own heart.

The next morning, to her great concern, Mr. Arnott was waiting in the hall when she came down stairs, and so much grieved at her departure, that he handed her to the chaise without being able to speak to her, and hardly heard her thanks and compliments but by recollection after she was gone.

She arrived at Mrs. Charlton's very early, and found her old friend in the same state she had left her. She communicated to her the purpose of her return, and begged she would keep her grand daughters up stairs, that the conference in the parlour might be uninterrupted and unheard.

She then made a forced and hasty breakfast, and went down to be ready to receive them. They came not till eleven o'clock, and the time of her waiting was passed in agonies of expectation.

At length they were announced, and at length they entered the room.

Cecilia, with her utmost efforts for courage, could hardly stand to receive them. They came in together, but Mrs. Delvile, advancing before her son, and endeavouring so to stand as to intercept his view of her, with the hope that in a few instants her emotion would be less visible, said, in the most soothing accents, "What honour Miss Beverley does us by permitting this visit! I should have been sorry to have left Suffolk without the satisfaction of again seeing you; and my son, sensible of the high respect he owes you, was most unwilling to be gone, before he had paid you his devoirs."

Cecilia courtsied; but depressed by the cruel task which awaited her, had no power to speak; and Mrs. Delvile, finding she still trembled, made her sit down, and drew a chair next to her.

Mean while Delvile, with an emotion far more violent, because wholly unrestrained, waited impatiently till the ceremonial of the reception was over, and then, approaching Cecilia, in a voice of perturbation and resentment, said, "In this presence, at least, I hope I may be heard; though my letters have been unanswered, my visits refused, though inexorably you have flown me—"

"Mortimer," interrupted Mrs. Delvile, "forget not that what I have told you is irrevocable; you now meet Miss Beverley for no other purpose than to give and to receive a mutual release of all tie or engagement with each other."

"Pardon me, madam," cried he, "this is a condition to which I have never assented. I come not to release, but to claim her! I am hers, and hers wholly! I protest it in the face of the world! The time, therefore, is now past for the sacrifice which you demand, since scarce are you more my mother, than I consider her as my wife."

Cecilia, amazed at this dauntless declaration, now almost lost her fear in her surprise; while Mrs. Delvile, with an air calm though displeased, answered, "This is not a point to be at present discussed, and I had hoped you knew better what was due to your auditors. I only consented to this interview as a mark of your respect for Miss Beverley, to whom in propriety it belongs to break off this unfortunate connexion."

Cecilia, who at this call could not longer be silent, now gathered fortitude to say, "Whatever tie or obligation may be supposed to depend upon me, I have already relinquished; and I am now ready to declare——"

"That you wholly give me up?" interrupted Delvile, "is that what you would say?—Oh how have I offended you? how have I merited a displeasure that can draw upon me such a sentence?—Answer, speak to me, Cecilia, what is it I have done?"

"Nothing, Sir," said Cecilia, confounded at this language in the presence of his mother, "you have done nothing,—but yet—"

"Yet what?—have you conceived to me an aversion? has any dreadful and horrible antipathy succeeded to your esteem?—tell, tell me without disguise, do you hate, do you abhor me?"

Cecilia sighed, and turned away her head; and Mrs. Delvile indignantly exclaimed, "What madness and absurdity! I scarce know you under the influence of such irrational violence. Why will you interrupt Miss Beverley in the only speech you ought to hear from her? Why, at once, oppress her, and irritate me, by words of more passion than reason? Go on, charming girl, finish what so wisely, so judiciously you were beginning, and then you shall be released from this turbulent persecution."

"No madam, she must not go on!" cried Delvile, "if she does not utterly abhor me, I will not *suffer* her to go on;—Pardon, pardon me, Cecilia, but your too exquisite delicacy is betraying not only my happiness, but your own. Once more, therefore, I conjure you to hear me, and then if, deliberately and unbiassed, you renounce me, I will never more distress you by resisting your decree."

Cecilia, abashed and changing colour, was silent, and he proceeded.

"All that has past between us, the vows I have offered you of faith, constancy and affection, the consent I obtained from you to be legally mine, the bond of settlement I have had drawn up, and the high honour you conferred upon me in suffering me to lead you to the altar,—all these particulars are already known to so many, that the least reflection must convince you they will soon be concealed from none: tell me, then, if your own fame pleads not for me, and if the scruples which lead you to refuse, by taking another direction, will not, with much more propriety, urge, nay enjoin you to accept me?—You hesitate at least,—O Miss Beverley! I see in that hesitation——"

"Nothing, nothing!" cried she, hastily, and checking her rising irresolution; "there is nothing for you to see, but that every way I now turn I have rendered myself miserable!"

"Mortimer," said Mrs. Delvile, seized with terror as she penetrated into the mental yielding of Cecilia, "you have now spoken to Miss Beverley; and unwilling as I am to obtrude upon her our difference of sentiment, it is necessary, since she has heard you, that I, also, should claim her attention."

"First let her speak!" cried Delvile, who in her apparent wavering built new hopes, "first let her answer what she has already deigned to listen to."

"No, first let her hear!" cried Mrs. Delvile, "for so only can she judge what answer will reflect upon her most honour."

Then, solemnly turning to Cecilia, she continued: "You see here, Miss Beverley, a young man who passionately adores you, and who forgets in his adoration friends, family, and connections, the opinions in which he has been educated, the honour of his house, his own former views, and all his primitive sense of duty, both public and private!—A passion built on such a defalcation* of principle renders him unworthy your acceptance; and not more ignoble for him would be a union which would blot his name from the injured stock whence he sprung, than indelicate for you, who upon such terms ought to despise him."

"Heavens, madam," exclaimed Delvile, "what a speech!"

c.—31

"O never," cried Cecilia, rising, "may I hear such another! Indeed, madam, there is no occasion to probe me so deeply, for I would not now enter your family, for all that the whole world could offer me!"

"At length, then, madam," cried Delvile, turning reproachfully to his mother, "are you satisfied? is your purpose now answered? and is the dagger you have transfixed in my heart sunk deep enough to appease you?"

"O could I draw it out," cried Mrs. Delvile, "and leave upon it no stain of ignominy, with what joy should my own bosom receive it, to heal the wound I have most compulsatorily inflicted!—Were this excellent young creature portionless, I would not hesitate in giving my consent; every claim of interest would be overbalanced by her virtues, and I would not grieve to see you poor, where so conscious you were happy; but here to concede, would annihilate every hope with which hitherto I have looked up to my son."

"Let us now, then, madam," said Cecilia, "break up this conference. I have spoken, I have heard, the decree is past, and therefore,—"

"You are indeed an angel!" cried Mrs. Delvile, rising and embracing her; "and never can I reproach my son with what has past, when I consider for what an object the sacrifice was planned. *You* cannot be unhappy, you have purchased peace by the exercise of virtue, and the close of every day will bring to you a reward, in the sweets of a self-approving mind.—But we will part, since you think it right; I do wrong to occasion any delay."

"No, we will *not* part!" cried Delvile, with encreasing vehemence; "if you force me, madam, from her, you will drive me to distraction! What is there in this world that can offer me a recompense? And what can pride even to the proudest afford as an equivalent? Her perfections you acknowledge, her greatness of mind is like your own; she has generously given me her heart,—Oh sacred and fascinating charge! Shall I, after such a deposite, consent to an eternal separation? Repeal, repeal your sentence, my Cecilia! let us live to ourselves and our consciences, and leave the vain prejudices of the world to those who can be paid by them for the loss of all besides!''

''Is this conflict, then,'' said Mrs. Delvile, ''to last forever? Oh end it, Mortimer, finish it, and make me happy! she is just, and will forgive you, she is noble-minded, and will honour you. Fly, then, at this critical moment, for in flight alone is your safety; and then will your father see the son of his hopes, and then shall the fond blessings of your idolizing mother soothe all your affliction, and soften all your regret!''

''Oh madam!'' cried Delvile, ''for mercy, for humanity, forbear this cruel supplication!''

''Nay, more than supplication, you have my commands; commands you have never yet disputed, and misery, ten-fold misery, will follow their disobedience. Hear me, Mortimer, for I speak prophetically; I know your heart, I know it to be formed for rectitude and duty, or destined by their neglect to repentance and horror.''

Delvile, struck by these words, turned suddenly from them both, and in gloomy despondence walked to the other end of the room. Mrs. Delvile perceived the moment of her power, and determined to pursue the blow: taking, therefore, the hand of Cecilia, while her eyes sparkled with the animation of reviving hope, ''See,'' she cried, pointing to her son, ''see if I am deceived! can he bear even the suggestion of future contrition? Think you when it falls upon him, he will support it better? No; he will sink under it. And you, pure as you are of mind, and stedfast in principle, what would your chance be of happiness with a man who never erring till he knew you, could never look at you without regret, be his fondness what it might?''

''Oh madam,'' cried the greatly shocked Cecilia, ''let him, then, see me no more!—take, take him all to yourself! forgive, console him! I will not have the misery of involving him in repentance, nor of incurring the reproaches of the mother he so much reverences!''

''Exalted creature!'' cried Mrs. Delvile; ''tenderness such as this would confer honour upon a monarch.'' Then, calling out exultingly to her son, ''See,'' she added, ''how great* a woman can act, when stimulated by generosity, and a just sense of duty! Follow then, at least, the example you ought to have led, and deserve my esteem and love, or be content to forego them.''

''And can I only deserve them,'' said Delvile, in a tone of the deepest anguish, ''by a compliance to which not merely my happiness, but my reason must be sacrificed? What honour do I injure that is not factitious? What evil threatens our union, that is not imaginary? In the general commerce of the world it may be right to yield to its prejudices, but in matters of serious importance, it is weakness to be shackled by scruples so frivolous, and it is cowardly to be governed by the customs we condemn. Religion and the laws of our country should then alone be consulted, and where those are neither opposed nor infringed, we should hold ourselves superior to all other considerations.''

''Mistaken notions!'' said Mrs. Delvile; ''and how long do you flatter yourself this independant happiness would endure? How long could you live contented by mere self-gratification, in defiance of the censure of mankind, the renunciation of your family, and the curses of your father?''

''The curses of my father!'' repeated he, starting and shuddering, ''O no, he could never be so barbarous!''

''He could,'' said she, steadily, ''nor do I doubt but he would. If now, however, you are affected by the prospect of his disclaiming you, think but what you will feel when first forbid to appear before either of us! and think of your remorse for involving Miss Beverley in such disgrace!''

''O speak not such words!'' cried he, with agonizing earnestness, ''to disgrace her,——to be banished by you, ——present not, I conjure you, such scenes to my imagination!''

''Yet would they be unavoidable,'' continued she; ''nor have I said to you all; blinded as you now are by passion, your nobler feelings are only obscured, not extirpated; think, then, how they will all rise in revenge of your insulted dignity, when your name becomes a stranger to your ears, and you are first saluted by one so meanly adopted!—''

''Hold, hold, madam,'' interrupted he, ''this is more than I can bear!''

"Heavens!" still continued she, disregarding his entreaty, "what in the universe can pay you for that first moment of indignity! Think of it well ere you proceed, and anticipate your sensations, lest the shock should wholly overcome you. How will the blood of your wronged ancestors rise into your guilty cheeks, and how will your heart throb with secret shame and reproach, when wished joy upon your marriage by the name of *Mr. Beverley!*"

Delvile, stung to the soul, attempted not any answer, but walked about the room in the utmost disorder of mind. Cecilia would have retired, but feared irritating him to some extravagance; and Mrs. Delvile, looking after him, added "For myself, I would still see, for I should pity your wife, ——but NEVER would I behold my son when sunk into an object of compassion!"

"It shall not be!" cried he, in a transport of rage; "cease, cease to distract me!—be content, madam,——you have conquered!"

"Then you are my son!" cried she, rapturously embracing him; "now I know again my Mortimer! now I see the fair promise of his upright youth, and the flattering completion of my maternal expectations!"

Cecilia, finding all thus concluded, desired nothing so much as to congratulate them on their reconciliation; but having only said "Let *me*, too,—" her voice failed her, she stopt short, and hoping she had been unheard, would have glided out of the room.

But Delvile, penetrated and tortured, yet delighted at this sensibility, broke from his mother, and seizing her hand, exclaimed, "Oh Miss Beverley, if *you* are not happy——"

"I am! I am!" cried she, with quickness; 'let me pass,— and think no more of me."

"That voice,—those looks,—" cried he, still holding her, "they speak not serenity!—Oh if I have injured your peace,—if that heart, which, pure as angels, deserves to be as sacred from sorrow, through my means, or for my sake, suffers any diminution of tranquility—"

"None, none!" interrupted she, with precipitation.

"I know well," cried he, "your greatness of soul; and if

this dreadful sacrifice gives lasting torture only to myself,—if of *your* returning happiness I could be assured,—I would struggle to bear it."

"You *may* be assured of it," cried she, with reviving dignity, "I have no right to expect escaping all calamity, but while I share the common lot, I will submit to it without repining."

"Heaven then bless, and hovering angels watch you!" cried he, and letting go her hand, he ran hastily out of the room.

"Oh Virtue, how bright is thy triumph!" exclaimed Mrs. Delvile, flying up to Cecilia, and folding her in her arms; "Noble, incomparable young creature! I knew not that so much worth was compatible with human frailty!"

But the heroism of Cecilia, in losing its object, lost its force; she sighed, she could not speak, tears gushed into her eyes, and kissing Mrs. Delvile's hand with a look that shewed her inability to converse with her, she hastened, though scarce able to support herself, away, with intention to shut herself up in her own apartment: and Mrs. Delvile, who perceived that her utmost fortitude was exhausted, opposed not her going, and wisely forebore to encrease her emotion, by following her even with her blessings.

But when she came into the hall, she started, and could proceed no further; for there she beheld Delvile, who in too great agony to be seen, had stopt to recover some composure before he quitted the house.

At the first sound of an opening door, he was hastily escaping; but perceiving Cecilia, and discerning her situation, he more hastily turned back, saying, "Is it possible?—To *me* were you coming?"

She shook her head, and made a motion with her hand to say no, and would then have gone on.

"You are weeping!" cried he, "you are pale!——Oh Miss Beverley! is this your happiness!"

"I am very well,—" cried she, not knowing what she answered, "I am quite well,—pray go,—I am very——" her words died away inarticulated.

"Oh what a voice is that!" exclaimed he, "it pierces my very soul!"

Mrs. Delvile now came to the parlour door, and looked aghast at the situation in which she saw them: Cecilia again moved on, and reached the stairs, but tottered, and was obliged to cling to the banisters.

"O suffer me to support you," cried he; "you are not able to stand,—whither is it you would go?"

"Any where,—I don't know,—" answered she, in faltering accents, "but if you would leave me, I should be well."

And, turning from him, she walked again towards the parlour, finding by her shaking frame, the impossibility of getting unaided up the stairs.

"Give me your hand, my love," said Mrs. Delvile, cruelly alarmed by this return; and the moment they re-entered the parlour, she said impatiently to her son, "Mortimer, why are you not gone?"

He heard her not, however; his whole attention was upon Cecilia, who, sinking into a chair, hid her face against Mrs. Delvile: but, reviving in a few moments, and blushing at the weakness she had betrayed, she raised her head, and, with an assumed serenity, said, 'I am better,—much better,——I was rather sick,—but it is over; and now, if you will excuse me, I will go to my own room."

She then arose, but her knees trembled, and her head was giddy, and again seating herself, she forced a faint smile, and said, "Perhaps I had better keep quiet."

"Can I bear this!" cried Delvile, "no, it shakes all my resolution!——loveliest and most beloved Cecilia! forgive my rash declaration, which I here retract and forswear, and which no false pride, no worthless vanity shall again surprise from me!——raise, then, your eyes—"

"Hot-headed young man!" interrupted Mrs. Delvile, with an air of haughty displeasure, "if you cannot be rational, at least be silent. Miss Beverley, we will both leave him."

Shame, and her own earnestness, now restored some strength to Cecilia, who read with terror in the looks of Mrs. Delvile the passions with which she was agitated, and instantly obeyed her by rising; but her son, who inherited a portion of her own spirit, rushed between then both and the door, and exclaimed "Stay, madam, stay! I cannot let you go: I see your intention, I see your dreadful purpose; you will work upon the feelings of Miss Beverley, you will extort from her a promise to see me no more!"

"Oppose not my passing!" cried Mrs. Delvile, whose voice, face and manner, spoke the encreasing disturbance of her soul; "I have but too long talked to you in vain; I must now take some better method for the security of the honour of my family."

This moment appeared to Delvile decisive; and casting off in desperation all timidity and restraint, he suddenly sprang forward, and snatching the hand of Cecilia from his mother, he exclaimed, "I cannot, I will not give her up!— nor now, madam, nor ever!—I protest it most solemnly! I affirm it by my best hopes! I swear it by all that I hold sacred!"

Grief and horror next to frenzy at a disappointment thus unexpected, and thus peremptory, rose in the face of Mrs. Delvile, who, striking her hand upon her forehead, cried "My brain is on fire!" and rushed out of the room.

Cecilia had now no difficulty to disengage herself from Delvile, who, shocked at the exclamation, and confounded by the sudden departure of his mother, hastened eagerly to pursue her: she had only flown into the next parlour; but, upon following her thither, what was his dread and his alarm, when he saw her extended upon the floor, her face, hands and neck all covered with blood! "Great Heaven!" he exclaimed, prostrating himself by her side, "what is it you have done!—where are you wounded?—what direful curse have you denounced against your son?"

Not able to speak, she angrily shook her head, and indignantly made a motion with her hand, that commanded him from her sight.

Cecilia, who had followed, though half dead with terror, had yet the presence of mind to ring the bell. A servant came immediately; and Delvile, starting up from his mother, ordered him to fetch the first surgeon or physician he could find.

The alarm now brought the rest of the servants into the

room, and Mrs. Delvile suffered herself to be raised from the ground, and seated in a chair; she was still silent, but shewed a disgust to any assistance from her son, that made him deliver her into the hands of the servants, while, in speechless agony, he only looked on and watched her.

Neither did Cecilia, though forgetting her own sorrow, and no longer sensible of personal weakness, venture to approach her: uncertain what had happened, she yet considered herself as the ultimate cause of this dreadful scene, and feared to risk the effect of the smallest additional emotion.

The servant returned with a surgeon in a few minutes: Cecilia, unable to wait and hear what he would say, glided hastily out of the room; and Delvile, in still greater agitation, followed her quick into the next parlour; but having eagerly advanced to speak to her, he turned precipitately about, and hurrying into the hall, walked in hasty steps up and down it, without courage to enquire what was passing.

At length the surgeon came out: Delvile flew to him, and stopt him, but could ask no question. His countenance, however, rendered words unnecessary; the surgeon understood him, and said, "The lady will do very well; she has burst a blood vessel, but I think it will be of no consequence. She must be kept quiet and easy, and upon no account suffered to talk, or to use any exertion."

Delvile now let him go, and flew himself into a corner to return thanks to heaven that the evil, however great, was less than he had at first apprehended. He then went into the parlour to Cecilia, eagerly calling out, "Heaven be praised, my mother has not voluntarily cursed me!"

"O now then," cried Cecilia, "once more make her bless you! the violence of her agitation has already almost destroyed her, and her frame is too weak for this struggle of contending passions;—go to her, then, and calm the tumult of her spirits, by acquiescing wholly in her will, and being to her again the son she thinks she has lost!"

"Alas!" said he, in a tone of the deepest dejection; "I have been preparing myself for that purpose, and waited but your commands to finally determine me."

"Let us both go to her instantly," said Cecilia; "the least delay may be fatal."

She now led the way, and approaching Mrs. Delvile, who, faint and weak, was seated upon an arm chair, and resting her head upon the shoulder of a maid servant, said, "Lean, dearest madam, upon *me*, and speak not, but hear us!"

She then took the place of the maid, and desired her and the other servants to go out of the room. Delvile advanced, but his mother's eye, recovering, at his sight, its wonted fire, darted upon him a glance of such displeasure, that, shuddering with the apprehension of inflaming again those passions which threatened her destruction, he hastily sunk on one knee, and abruptly exclaimed, "Look at me with less abhorrence, for I come but to resign myself to your will."

"Mine, also," cried Cecilia, "that will shall be; you need not speak it, we know it, and here solemnly we promise that we will separate for ever."

"Revive, then, my mother," said Delvile, "rely upon our plighted honours, and think only of your health, for your son will never more offend you."

Mrs. Delvile, much surprised, and strongly affected, held out her hand to him, with a look of mingled compassion and obligation, and dropping her head upon the bosom of Cecilia, who with her other arm she pressed towards her, she burst into an agony of tears.

"Go, go, Sir!" said Cecilia, cruelly alarmed, "you have said all that is necessary; leave Mrs. Delvile now, and she will be more composed."

Delvile instantly obeyed, and then his mother, whose mouth still continued to fill with blood, though it gushed not from her with the violence it had begun, was prevailed upon by the prayers of Cecilia to consent to be conveyed into her room; and, as her immediate removal to another house might be dangerous, she complied also, though very reluctantly, with her urgent entreaties, that she would take entire possession of it till the next day.

This point gained, Cecilia left her, to communicate what had past to Mrs. Charlton; but was told by one of the servants, that Mr. Delvile begged first to speak with her in the next room.

She hesitated for a moment whether to grant this request; but recollecting it was right to acquaint him with his mother's intention of staying all night, she went to him.

"How indulgent you are," cried he, in a melancholy voice as she opened the door; "I am now going post* to Dr. Lyster, whom I shall entreat to come hither instantly; but I am fearful of again disturbing my mother; and must therefore rely upon you to acquaint her what is become of me."

"Most certainly; I have begged her to remain here to night, and I hope I shall prevail with her to continue with me till Dr. Lyster's arrival; after which she will, doubtless, be guided either in staying longer, or removing elsewhere, by his advice."

"You are all goodness," said he, with a deep sigh; "and how I shall support—but I mean not to return hither, at least not to this house,—unless, indeed, Dr. Lyster's account should be alarming. I leave my mother, therefore, to your kindness, and only hope, only entreat, that your own health,—your own peace of mind—neither by attendance upon her—by anxiety—by pity for her son—"

He stopt, and seemed gasping for breath; Cecilia turned from him to hide her emotion, and he proceeded with a rapidity of speech that shewed his terror of continuing with her any longer, and his struggle with himself to be gone: "The promise you have made in both our names to my mother, I shall hold myself bound to observe. I see, indeed, that her reason or her life would fall the sacrifice of further opposition: of myself, therefore, it is no longer time to think.—I take of you no leave—I cannot! yet I would fain tell you the high reverence—but it is better to say nothing—"

"Much better," cried Cecilia, with a forced and faint smile; "lose not, therefore, an instant, but hasten to this good Dr. Lyster."

"I will;" answered he, going to the door; but there, stopping and turning round, "one thing I should yet," he added, "wish to say,—I have been impetuous, violent, unreasonable,—with shame and with regret I recollect how impetuous, and how unreasonable: I have persecuted, where I ought in silence to have submitted; I have reproached, where I ought in candour to have approved; and in the vehemence with which I have pursued you, I have censured that very dignity of conduct which has been the basis of my admiration, my esteem, my devotion! but never can I forget, and never without fresh wonder remember, the sweetness with which you have borne with me, even when most I offended you. For this impatience, this violence, this inconsistency, I now most sincerely beg your pardon; and if, before I go, you could so far condescend as to pronounce my forgiveness, with a lighter heart, I think, I should quit you.''

"Do not talk of forgiveness," said Cecilia, "you have never offended me; I always knew—always was sure—always imputed—" she stopt, unable to proceed.

Deeply penetrated by her apparent distress, he with difficulty restrained himself from falling at her feet; but after a moment's pause and recollection, he said, "I understand the generous indulgence you have shewn me, an indulgence I shall ever revere, and ever grieve to have abused. I ask you not to remember me,—far, far happier do I wish you than such a remembrance could make you; but I will pain the humanity of your disposition no longer. You will tell my mother—but no matter!—Heaven preserve you, my angelic Cecilia!—Miss Beverley, I mean,—Heaven guide, protect, and bless you! And should I see you no more, should this be the last sad moment——"

He paused, but presently recovering himself, added, "May I hear, at least, of your tranquillity, for that alone can have any chance to quiet or repress the anguish I feel here!"

He then abruptly retreated, and ran out of the house.

Cecilia for a while remained almost stupified with sorrow; she forgot Mrs. Delvile, she forgot Mrs. Charlton, she forgot her own design of apologizing to one, or assisting the other: she continued in the posture in which he had left her, quite without motion, and almost without sensibility.

CHAPTER VII

A Message

FROM this lethargy of sadness Cecilia was soon, however, awakened by the return of the surgeon; who had brought with him a physician to consult upon Mrs. Delvile's situation. Terror for the mother once more drove the son from her thoughts, and she waited with the most apprehensive impatience to hear the result of the consultation. The physician declined giving any positive opinion, but, having written a prescription, only repeated the injunction of the surgeon, that she should be kept extremely quiet, and on no account be suffered to talk.

Cecilia, though shocked and frightened at the occasion, was yet by no means sorry at an order which thus precluded all conversation; unfitted for it by her own misery, she was glad to be relieved from all necessity of imposing upon herself the irksome task of finding subjects for discourse to which she was wholly indifferent, while obliged with sedulity to avoid those by which alone her mind was occupied.

The worthy Mrs. Charlton heard the events of the morning with the utmost concern, but charged her granddaughters to assist her young friend in doing the honours of her house to Mrs. Delvile, while she ordered another apartment to be prepared for Cecilia, to whom she administered all the consolation her friendly zeal could suggest.

Cecilia, however unhappy, had too just a way of thinking to indulge in selfish grief, where occasion called her to action for the benefit of others: scarce a moment, therefore now did she allow to sorrow and herself, but assiduously bestowed the whole of her time upon her two sick friends, dividing her attention according to their own desire or convenience, without consulting or regarding any choice of her own. Choice, indeed, she had none; she loved Mrs. Charlton, she revered Mrs. Delvile; the warmest wish with which her heart glowed, was the recovery of both, but too deep was her affliction to receive pleasure from either.

Two days passed thus, during which the constancy of her attendance, which at another time would have fatigued her, proved the only relief she was capable of receiving. Mrs. Delvile was evidently affected by her vigilant tenderness, but seemed equally desirous with herself to make use of the prohibition to speech as an excuse for uninterrupted silence. She enquired not even after her son, though the eagerness of her look towards the door whenever it was opened, shewed either a hope, or an apprehension that he might enter. Cecilia wished to tell her whither he was gone, but dreaded trusting her voice with his name; and their silence, after a while, seemed so much by mutual consent, that she had soon as little courage as she had inclination to break it.

The arrival of Dr. Lyster gave her much satisfaction, for upon him rested her hopes of Mrs. Delvile's re-establishment. He sent for her down stairs, to enquire whether he was expected; and hearing that he was not, desired her to announce him, as the smallest emotion might do mischief.

She returned up stairs, and after a short preparation, said, "Your favourite Dr. Lyster, madam, is come, and I shall be much the happier for having you under his care."

"Dr. Lyster?" cried she, "who sent for him?"

"I believe—I fancy—Mr. Delvile fetched him."

"My son?—is he here, then?"

"No,—he went, the moment he left you, for Dr. Lyster,—and Dr. Lyster is come by himself."

"Does he write to you?"

"No, indeed!—he writes not—he comes not—dearest madam be satisfied, he will do neither to *me* ever more!"

"Exemplary young man!" cried she, in a voice hardly audible, "how great is his loss!—unhappy Mortimer!—ill-fated, and ill-rewarded!"

She sighed, and said no more; but this short conversation, the only one which had passed between them since her illness, agitated her so much, that Dr. Lyster, who now came up stairs, found her in a state of trembling and weakness that both alarmed and surprised him. Cecilia, glad of an opportunity to be gone, left the room, and sent, by Dr. Lyster's desire, for the physician and surgeon who had already attended.

After they had been some time with their patient, they retired to a consultation, and when it was over, Dr. Lyster waited upon Cecilia in the parlour, and assured her he had no apprehension of danger for Mrs. Delvile, "Though, for another week, he added, I would have her continue *your* patient, as she is not yet fit to be removed. But pray mind that she is kept quiet; let nobody go near her, not even her own son. By the way he is waiting for me at the inn, so I'll just speak again to his mother, and be gone."

Cecilia was well pleased by this accidental information, to learn both the anxiety of Delvile for his mother, and the steadiness of his forbearance for himself. When Dr. Lyster came down stairs again, "I shall stay," he said, "till to-morrow, but I hope she will be able in another week to get to Bristol. In the mean time I shall leave her, I see, with an excellent nurse. But, my good young lady, in your care of her, don't neglect yourself; I am not quite pleased with your looks, though it is but an old fashioned speech to tell you so.—What have you been doing to yourself?"

"Nothing;" said she, a little embarrassed; "but had you not better have some tea?"

"Why yes, I think I had;—but what shall I do with my young man?"

Cecilia understood the hint, but coloured, and made no answer.

"He is waiting for me," he continued, "at the inn; however, I never yet knew the young man I would prefer to a young woman, so if you will give me some tea here, I shall certainly jilt him."

Cecilia instantly rang the bell, and ordered tea.

"Well now," said he, "remember the sin of this breach of appointment lies wholly at your door. I shall tell him you laid violent hands on me; and if that is not enough to excuse me, I shall desire he will try whether he could be more of a stoic with you himself."

"I think I must *un*order the tea," said she, with what gaiety she could assume, "if I am to be responsible for any mischief from your drinking it."

"No, no, you shan't be off now; but pray would it be quite out of rule for you to send and ask him to come to us?"

"Why I believe—I think—" said she, stammering, "it's very likely he may be engaged."

"Well, well, I don't mean to propose any violent incongruity. You must excuse my blundering; I understand but little of the *etiquette* of young ladies. 'Tis a science too intricate to be learned without more study than we plodding men of business can well spare time for. However, when I have done *writing* prescriptions, I will set about *reading* them, provided you will be my instructress."

Cecilia, though ashamed of a charge in which prudery and affectation were implied, was compelled to submit to it, as either to send for Delvile, or explain her objections, was equally impossible. The Miss Charltons, therefore, joined them, and they went to tea.

Just as they had done, a note was delivered to Dr. Lyster; "See here," cried he, when he had read it, "what a fine thing it is to be a *young* man! Why now, Mr. Mortimer understands as much of all this *etiquette* as you ladies do yourselves; for he only writes a note even to ask how his mother does."

He then put it into Cecilia's hand.

To Dr. LYSTER.

TELL me, my dear Sir, how you have found my mother? I am uneasy at your long stay, and engaged with my friend Biddulph, or I should have followed you in person.

M. D.

"So you see," continued the doctor, "I need not do pennance for engaging myself to *you*, when this young gentleman can find such good entertainment for himself."

Cecilia, who well knew the honourable motive of Delvile's

engagement, with difficulty forbore speaking in his vindication. Dr. Lyster immediately began an answer, but before
he had finished it, called out, "Now as I am told you are a
very good young woman, I think you can do no less than
assist me to punish this gay spark, for playing the *macaroni*,
when he ought to visit his sick mother."

Cecilia, much hurt for Delvile, and much confused for
herself, looked abashed, but knew not what to answer.

"My scheme," continued the doctor, "is to tell him, that
as he has found one engagement for tea, he may find another
for supper; but that as to me, I am better disposed of, for
you insist upon keeping me to yourself. Come, what says
etiquette? may I treat myself with this puff?"*

"Certainly," said Cecilia, endeavouring to look pleased,
"if you will favour us with your company, Miss Charltons
and myself will think the *puffing* should rather be ours than
yours."

"That, then," said the doctor, "will not answer my
purpose, for I mean the puff to be my own, or how do I
punish him? So, suppose I tell him I shall not only sup with
three young ladies, but be invited to a tête à tête with one
of them into the bargain?"

The young ladies only laughed, and the Dr. finished his
note, and sent it away; and then, turning gayly to Cecilia,
"Come," he said, "why don't you give me this invitation?
surely you don't mean to make me guilty of perjury?"

Cecilia, but little disposed for pleasantry, would gladly now
have dropt the subject; but Dr. Lyster, turning to the Miss
Charltons, said, "Young ladies, I call you both to witness if
this is not very bad usage: this young woman has connived at
my writing a downright falsehood, and all the time took me in
to believe it was a truth. The only way I can think of to cure her
of such frolics, is for both of you to leave us together, and so
make her keep her word whether she will or no."

The Miss Charltons took the hint, and went away; while
Cecilia, who had not at all suspected he meant seriously to
speak with her, remained extremely perplexed to think what
he had to say.

"Mrs. Delvile," cried he, continuing the same air of easy

good humour, "though I allowed her not to speak to me
above twenty words, took up near ten of them to tell me that
you had behaved to her like an angel. Why so she ought,
cried I; what else was she sent for here to look so like one?
I charged her, therefore, to take all that as a thing of course;
and to prove that I really think what I say, I am now going
to make a trial of you, that, if you are any thing less, will
induce you to order some of your men to drive me into the
street. The truth is, I have had a little commission given me,
which in the first place I know not how to introduce, and
which, in the second, as far as I can judge, appears to be
absolutely superfluous."

Cecilia now felt uneasy and alarmed, and begged him to
explain himself. He then dropt the levity with which he
had begun the discourse, and after a grave, yet gentle
preparation, expressive of his unwillingness to distress her,
and his firm persuasion of her uncommon worthiness, he
acquainted her that he was no stranger to her situation with
respect to the Delvile family.

"Good God!" cried she, blushing and much amazed;
"and who—"

"I knew it," said he, "from the moment I attended Mr.
Mortimer in his illness at Delvile-Castle. He could not
conceal from me that the seat of his disorder was his mind;
and I could not know that, without readily conjecturing the
cause, when I saw who was his father's guest, and when I
knew what was his father's character. He found he was
betrayed to me, and upon my advising a journey, he
understood me properly. His openness to counsel, and the
manly firmness with which he behaved in quitting you,
made me hope the danger was blown over. But last week,
when I was at the Castle, where I have for some time
attended Mr. Delvile, who has had a severe fit of the gout,
I found him in an agitation of spirits that made me
apprehend it would be thrown into his stomach.* I desired
Mrs. Delvile to use her influence to calm him; but she was
herself in still greater emotion, and acquainting me she was
obliged to leave him, desired I would spend with him every
moment in my power. I have therefore almost lived at the

Castle during her absence, and, in the course of our many conversations, he has acknowledged to me the uneasiness under which he laboured, from the intelligence concerning his son, which he had just received.''

Cecilia wished here to enquire *how* received, and from whom, but had not the courage, and therefore he proceeded.

''I was still with the father when Mr. Mortimer arrived post at my house to fetch me hither. I was sent for home; he informed me of his errand without disguise, for he knew I was well acquainted with the original secret whence all the evil arose. I told him my distress in what manner to leave his father; and he was extremely shocked himself when acquainted with his situation. We agreed that it would be vain to conceal from him the indisposition of Mrs. Delvile, which the delay of her return, and a thousand other accidents, might in some unfortunate way make known to him. He commissioned me, therefore, to break it to him, that he might consent to my journey, and at the same time to quiet his own mind, by assuring him all he had apprehended was wholly at an end.''

He stopt, and looked to see how Cecilia bore these words.

''It *is* all at an end, Sir;'' said she, with firmness; ''but I have not yet heard your commission; what, and from whom is that?''

''I am thoroughly satisfied it is unnecessary;'' he answered, ''since the young man can but submit, and you can but give him up.''

''But still, if there is a message, it is fit I should hear it.''

''If you chuse it, so it is. I told Mr. Delvile whither I was coming, and I repeated to him his son's assurances. He was relieved, but not satisfied; he would not see him, and gave me for him a prohibition of extreme severity,——and to *you* he bid me say——''

''From *him*, then, is my message?'' cried Cecilia, half frightened, and much disappointed.

''Yes,'' said he, understanding her immediately, ''for the son, after giving me his first account, had the wisdom and forbearance not once to mention you.''

"I am very glad," said she, with a mixture of admiration and regret, "to hear it. But, what, Sir, said Mr. Delvile?"

"He bid me tell you that either *he*, or *you* must see his son never more."

"It was indeed unnecessary," cried she, colouring with resentment, "to send me such a message. I meant not to see him again, he meant not to desire it. I return him, however, no answer, and I will make him no promise; to Mrs. Delvile alone I hold myself bound; to him, send what messages he may, I shall always hold myself free. But believe me, Dr. Lyster, if with his name, his son had inherited his character, his desire of our separation would be feeble, and trifling, compared with my own!"

"I am sorry, my good young lady," said he, "to have given you this disturbance; yet I admire your spirit, and doubt not but it will enable you to forget any little disappointment you may have suffered. And what, after all, have you to regret? Mortimer Delvile is, indeed, a young man that any woman might wish to attach; but every woman cannot have him, and you, of all women, have least reason to repine in missing him, for scarcely is there another man you may not chuse or reject at your pleasure."

Little as was the consolation Cecilia could draw from this speech, she was sensible it became not her situation to make complaints, and therefore, to end the conversation, she proposed calling in the Miss Charltons.

"No, no," said he, "I must step up again to Mrs. Delvile, and then be-gone. To-morrow morning I shall but call to see how she is, and leave some directions, and set off. Mr. Mortimer Delvile accompanies me back: but he means to return hither in a week, in order to travel with his mother to Bristol. Mean time, I purpose to bring about a reconciliation between him and his father, whose prejudices are more intractable than any man's I ever met with."

"It will be strange indeed," said Cecilia, "should a reconciliation *now* be difficult!"

"True; but it is long since he was young himself, and the softer affections he never was acquainted with, and only regards them in his son as derogatory to his whole race.

However, if there were not some few such men, there would hardly be a family in the kingdom that could count a great grand-father. I am not, I must own, of his humour myself, but I think it rather peculiarly stranger, than peculiarly worse than most other peoples; and how, for example, was that of *your* uncle a whit the better? He was just as fond of *his* name, as if, like Mr. Delvile, he could trace it from the time of the Saxons."

Cecilia strongly felt the truth of this observation, but not chusing to discuss it, made not any answer, and Dr. Lyster, after a few good-natured apologies, both for his friends the Delviles and himself, went up stairs.

"What continual disturbance," cried she, when left alone, "keeps me thus for-ever from rest! no sooner is one wound closed, but another is opened; mortification constantly succeeds distress, and when my heart is spared, my pride is attacked, that not a moment of tranquility may ever be allowed me! Had the lowest of women won the affections of Mr. Delvile, could his father with less delicacy or less decency have acquainted her with his inflexible disapprobation? To send with so little ceremony a message so contemptuous and so peremptory!—but perhaps it is better, for had he, too, like Mrs. Delvile, joined kindness with rejection, I might still more keenly have felt the perverseness of my destiny."

CHAPTER VIII

A Parting

THE next morning Dr. Lyster called early, and having visited Mrs. Delvile, and again met the two gentlemen of the faculty in whose care she was to remain, he took his leave. But not without contriving first to speak a few words to Cecilia in private, in which he charged her to be careful of her health, and re-animate her spirits. "Don't suppose," said he, "that because I am a friend of the Delvile family, I am either blind to your merits, or to their foibles, far from it; but then why should they interfere with one another? Let them keep their prejudices, which, though different, are not worse than their neighbours, and do you retain your excellencies, and draw from them the happiness which they ought to give you. People reason and refine themselves into a thousand miseries, by chusing to settle that they can only be contented one way; whereas, there are fifty ways, if they would but look about them, that would commonly do as well.''

''I believe, indeed, you are right,'' answered Cecilia, ''and I thank you for the admonition; I will do what I can towards studying your scheme of philosophy, and it is always one step to amendment, to be convinced that we want it.''

''You are a sensible and charming girl,'' said Dr. Lyster, ''and Mr. Delvile, should he find a daughter-in-law descended in a right line from Egbert, first king of all England,* won't be so well off as if he had satisfied himself with you. However, the old gentleman has a fair right, after all, to be pleased his own way, and let us blame him how we will, we shall find, upon sifting, it is for no other reason but because his humour happens to clash with our own.''

''That, indeed,'' said Cecilia, smiling, ''is a truth incontrovertible! and a truth to which, for the future, I will endeavour to give more weight. But will you permit me now to ask one question?—Can you tell me from whom, how, or when the intelligence which has caused all this disturbance——''

She hesitated, but, comprehending her readily, he answered ''How they got at it, I never heard, for I never thought it worth while to enquire, as it is so generally known, that nobody I meet with seems ignorant of it.''

This was another, and a cruel shock to Cecilia, and Dr. Lyster, perceiving it, again attempted to comfort her. ''That the affair is somewhat spread,'' said he, ''is now not to be helped, and therefore little worth thinking of; every body will agree that the choice of both does honour to both, and nobody need be ashamed to be successor to either, whenever the course of things leads Mr. Mortimer and yourself to

make another election. He wisely intends to go abroad, and
will not return till he is his own man again. And as to you,
my good young lady, what, after a short time given to
vexation, need interrupt your happiness? You have the
whole world before you, with youth, fortune, talents, beauty
and independence; drive, therefore, from your head this
unlucky affair, and remember there can hardly be a family
in the kingdom, this one excepted, that will not rejoice in a
connection with you.''

He then good-humouredly shook hands with her, and
went into his chaise.

Cecilia, though not slow in remarking the ease and
philosophy with which every one can argue upon the
calamities, and moralize upon the misconduct of others, had
still the candour and good sense to see that there was reason
in what he urged, and to resolve upon making the best use
in her power of the hints for consolation she might draw
from his discourse.

During the following week, she devoted herself almost
wholly to Mrs. Delvile, sharing with the maid, whom she
had brought with her from the Castle, the fatigue of nursing
her, and leaving to the Miss Charltons the chief care of their
grand-mother. For Mrs. Delvile appeared every hour more
sensible of her attention, and more desirous of her presence,
and though neither of them spoke, each was endeared to the
other by the tender offices of friendship which were paid and
received.

When this week was expired, Dr. Lyster was prevailed
upon to return again to Bury, in order to travel himself with
Mrs. Delvile to Bristol. ''Well,'' cried he, taking Cecilia by
the first opportunity aside, ''how are you? Have you studied
my scheme of philosophy, as you promised me?''

''O yes,'' said she, ''and made, I flatter myself, no little
proficiency.''

''You are a good girl,'' cried he, ''a very extraordinary
girl! I am sure you are; and upon my honour I pity poor
Mortimer with all my soul! But he is a noble young fellow,
and behaves with a courage and spirit that does me good to
behold. To have obtained you, he would have moved heaven

and earth, but finding you out of his reach, he submits to his fate like a man."

Cecilia's eyes glistened at this speech; "Yes," said she, "he long since said 'tis suspence, 'tis hope, that make the misery of life,*—for there the Passions have all power, and Reason has none. But when evils are irremediable, and we have neither resources to plan, nor castle-building* to delude us, we find time for the cultivation of philosophy, and flatter ourselves, perhaps, that we have found inclination!"

"Why you have considered this matter very deeply," said he; "but I must not have you give way to these serious reflections. Thought, after all, has a cruel spite against happiness; I would have you, therefore, keep as much as you conveniently can, out of its company. Run about and divert yourself, 'tis all you have for it. The true art of happiness in this most whimsical world, seems nothing more nor less than this—Let those who have leisure, find employment, and those who have business, find leisure."

He then told her that Mr. Delvile senior was much better, and no longer confined to his room: and that he had had the pleasure of seeing an entire reconciliation take place between him and his son, of whom he was more fond and more proud than any other father in the universe.

"Think of him, however, my dear young lady," he continued, "no more, for the matter I see is desperate: you must pardon my being a little officious, when I confess to you I could not help proposing to the old gentleman an expedient of my own; for as I could not drive you out of my head, I employed myself in thinking what might be done by way of accommodation. Now my scheme was really a very good one, only when people are prejudiced, all reasoning is thrown away upon them. I proposed sinking *both* your names, since they are so at variance with one another, and so adopting a third, by means of a title.* But Mr. Delvile angrily declared, that though such a scheme might do very well for the needy Lord Ernolf, a Peer of twenty years, his own noble ancestors should never, by his consent, forfeit a name which so many centuries had rendered honourable. His son Mortimer, he added, must inevitably inherit the title of his grandfather, his uncle being old and unmarried; but yet he would rather see him a beggar, than lose his dearest hope that *Delvile*, Lord *Delvile*, would descend, both name and title, from generation to generation unsullied and uninterrupted.''*

"I am sorry, indeed," said Cecilia, "that such a proposal was made, and I earnestly entreat that none of any sort may be repeated."

"Well, well," said he, "I would not for the world do any mischief, but who would not have supposed such a proposal would have done good?"

"Mr. Mortimer," he then added, "is to meet us at ———— for he would not, he said, come again to this place, upon such terms as he was here last week, for the whole worth of the king's dominions."

The carriage was now ready, and Mrs. Delvile was prepared to depart. Cecilia approached to take leave of her, but Dr. Lyster following, said "No talking! no thanking! no compliments of any sort! I shall carry off my Patient without permitting one civil speech, and for all the rudeness I make her guilty of, I am willing to be responsible."

Cecilia would then have retreated, but Mrs. Delvile, holding out both her hands, said "To every thing else, Dr. Lyster, I am content to submit; but were I to die while uttering the words, I cannot leave this inestimable creature without first saying how much I love her, how I honour, and how I thank her! without entreating her to be careful of her health, and conjuring her to compleat the greatness of her conduct, by not suffering her spirits to sink from the exertion of her virtue. And now my love, God bless you!"

She then embraced her, and went on; Cecilia, at a motion of Dr. Lyster's, forbearing to follow her.

"And thus," cried she, when they were gone, "thus ends all my connection with this family! which it seems as if I was only to have known for the purpose of affording a new proof of the insufficiency of situation to constitute happiness. Who looks not upon mine as the perfection of human felicity? ————And so, perhaps, it is, for it may be that Felicity and Humanity are never permitted to come nearer."

And thus, in philosophic sadness, by reasoning upon the universality of misery, she restrained, at least, all violence of sorrow, though her spirits were dejected, and her heart was heavy.

But the next day brought with it some comfort that a little lightened her sadness; Mrs. Charlton, almost wholly recovered, was able to go down stairs, and Cecilia had at least the satisfaction of seeing an happy conclusion to an illness of which, with the utmost concern and regret, she considered herself as the cause. She attended her with the most unremitting assiduity, and being really very thankful, endeavoured to appear happy, and flattered herself that, by continual effort, the appearance in a short time would become reality.

Mrs. Charlton retired early, and Cecilia accompanied her up stairs: and while she was with her, was informed that Mr. Monckton was in the parlour.

The various, afflicting, and uncommon scenes in which she had been engaged since she last saw him, had almost wholly driven him from her remembrance, or when at any time he recurred to it, it was only to attribute the discontinuance of his visits to the offence she had given him, in refusing to follow his advice by relinquishing her London expedition.

Full, therefore, of the mortifying transactions which had passed since their parting, and fearful of his enquiries into disgraces he had nearly foretold, she heard him announced with chagrin, and waited upon him in the most painful confusion.

Far different were the feelings of Mr. Monckton; he read in her countenance the dejection of disappointment, which impressed upon his heart the vivacity of hope: her evident shame was to him secret triumph, her ill-concealed sorrow revived all his expectations.

She hastily began a conversation by mentioning her debt to him, and apologising for not paying it the moment she was of age. He knew but too well how her time had been occupied, and assured her the delay was wholly immaterial.

He then led to an enquiry into the present situation of her

affairs; but unable to endure a disquisition, which could only be productive of censure and mortification, she hastily stopt it, exclaiming, "Ask me not, I entreat you, Sir, any detail of what has passed,——the event has brought me sufferings that may well make blame dispensed with;—I acknowledge all your wisdom, I am sensible of my own error, but the affair is wholly dropt, and the unhappy connexion I was forming is broken off for-ever!"

Little now was Mr. Monckton's effort in repressing his further curiosity, and he started other subjects with readiness, gaiety and address. He mentioned Mrs. Charlton, for whom he had not the smallest regard; he talked to her of Mrs. Harrel, whose very existence was indifferent to him; and he spoke of their common acquaintance in the country, for not one of whom he would have grieved, if assured of meeting no more. His powers of conversation were enlivened by his hopes; and his exhilarated spirits made all subjects seem happy to him. A weight was removed from his mind which had nearly borne down even his remotest hopes; the object of his eager pursuit seemed still within his reach, and the rival into whose power he had so lately almost beheld her delivered, was totally renounced, and no longer to be dreaded. A revolution such as this, raised expectations more sanguine than ever; and in quitting the house, he exultingly considered himself released from every obstacle to his views—till, just as he arrived home, he recollected his wife!

CHAPTER IX

A Tale

A WEEK passed, during which Cecilia, however sad, spent her time as usual with the family, denying to herself all voluntary indulgence of grief, and forbearing to seek consolation from solitude, or relief from tears. She never named Delvile, she begged Mrs. Charlton never to mention him; she called to her aid the account she had received from

Dr. Lyster of his firmness, and endeavoured, by an emulous ambition, to fortify her mind from the weakness of depression and regret.

This week, a week of struggle with all her feelings, was just elapsed, when she received by the post the following letter from Mrs. Delvile.

To Miss BEVERLEY.

Bristol, Oct. 21.

MY sweet young friend will not, I hope, be sorry to hear of my safe arrival at this place: to me every account of her health and welfare, will ever be the intelligence I shall most covet to receive. Yet I mean not to ask for it in return; to chance I will trust for information, and I only write now to say I shall write no more.

Too much for thanks is what I owe you, and what I think of you is beyond all power of expression. Do not, then, wish me ill, ill as I have seemed to merit of you, for my own heart is almost broken by the tyranny I have been compelled to practice upon yours.

And now let me bid a long adieu to you, my admirable Cecilia; you shall not be tormented with a useless correspondence, which can only awaken painful recollections, or give rise to yet more painful new anxieties. Fervently will I pray for the restoration of your happiness, to which nothing can so greatly contribute as that wise, that uniform command, so feminine, yet so dignified, you maintain over your passions; which often I have admired, though never so feelingly as at this conscious moment! when my own health is the sacrifice of emotions most fatally unrestrained.

Send to me no answer, even if you have the sweetness to wish it; every new proof of the generosity of your nature is to me but a new wound. Forget us, therefore, wholly,—alas! you have only known us for sorrow!—forget us, dear and invaluable Cecilia! though ever, as you have nobly deserved, must you be fondly and gratefully remembered by

AUGUSTA DELVILE.

The attempted philosophy, and laboured resignation of Cecilia, this letter destroyed: the struggle was over, the apathy was at an end, and she burst into an agony of tears, which finding the vent they had long sought, now flowed unchecked down her cheeks, sad monitors of the weakness of reason opposed to the anguish of sorrow!

A letter at once so caressing, yet so absolute, forced its way to her heart, in spite of the fortitude she had flattered herself was its guard. In giving up Delvile she was satisfied of the propriety of seeing him no more, and convinced that even to talk of him would be folly and imprudence; but to be told that for the future they must remain strangers to the existence of each other—there seemed in this a hardship, a rigour, that was insupportable.

"Oh what," cried she, "is human nature! in its best state how imperfect! that a woman such as this, so noble in character, so elevated in sentiment, with heroism to sacrifice to her sense of duty the happiness of a son, whom with joy she would die to serve, can herself be thus governed by prejudice, thus enslaved, thus subdued by opinion!" Yet never, even when miserable, unjust or irrational; her grief was unmixed with anger, and her tears streamed not from resentment, but affliction. The situation of Mrs. Delvile, however different, she considered to be as wretched as her own. She read, therefore, with sadness, but not bitterness, her farewell, and received not with disdain, but with gratitude, her sympathy. Yet though her indignation was not irritated, her sufferings were doubled, by a farewell so kind, yet so despotic, a sympathy so affectionate, yet so hopeless.

In this first indulgence of grief which she had granted to her disappointment, she was soon interrupted by a summons down stairs to a gentleman.

Unfit and unwilling to be seen, she begged that he might leave his name, and appoint a time for calling again.

Her maid brought for answer, that he believed his name was unknown to her, and desired to see her now, unless she was employed in some matter of moment.

She then put up her letter, and went into the parlour; and there, to her infinite amazement, beheld Mr. Albany.

"How little, Sir," she cried, "did I expect this pleasure."

"This pleasure," repeated he, "do you call it?—what strange abuse of words! what causeless trifling with honesty! is language of no purpose but to wound the ear with untruths? is the gift of speech only granted us to pervert the use of understanding? I can give you no pleasure, I have no power to give it any one; you can give none to me—the whole world could not invest you with the means!"

"Well, Sir," said Cecilia, who had little spirit to defend herself, "I will not vindicate the expression, but of this I will unfeignedly assure you, I am at least as glad to see you just now, as I should be to see any body."

"Your eyes," cried he, "are red, your voice is inarticulate;—young, rich, and attractive, the world at your feet; that world yet untried, and its falsehood unknown, how have you thus found means to anticipate misery? which way have you uncovered the cauldron of human woes? Fatal and early anticipation! that cover once removed, can never be replaced; those woes, those boiling woes, will pour out upon you continually, and only when your heart ceases to beat, will their ebullition cease to torture you!"

"Alas!" cried Cecilia, shuddering, "how cruel, yet how true!"

"Why went you," cried he, "to the cauldron? it came not to you. Misery seeks not man, but man misery. He walks out in the sun, but stops not for a cloud; confident, he pursues his way, till the storm which, gathering, he might have avoided, bursts over his devoted head. Scared and amazed, he repents his temerity; he calls, but it is then too late; he runs, but it is thunder which follows him! Such is the presumption of man, such at once is the arrogance and shallowness of his nature! And thou, simple and blind! hast thou, too, followed whither Fancy has led thee, unheeding that thy career was too vehement for tranquility, nor missing that lovely companion of youth's early innocence, till, adventurous and unthinking, thou hast lost her for ever!"

In the present weak state of Cecilia's spirits, this attack was too much for her; and the tears she had just, and with difficulty restrained, again forced their way down her cheeks, as she answered, "It is but too true,—I have lost her for ever!"

"Poor thing," said he, while the rigour of his countenance was softened into the gentlest commiseration, "so young!—looking, too, so innocent!—'tis hard!—And is nothing left thee? no small remaining hope, to cheat, humanely cheat thy yet not wholly extinguished credulity?"

Cecilia wept without answering.

"Let me not," said he, "waste my compassion upon nothing; compassion is with me no effusion of affectation; tell me, then, if thou deservest it, or if thy misfortunes are imaginary, and thy grief is factitious?"

"Factitious," repeated she, "Good heaven!"

"Answer me, then, these questions, in which I shall comprise the only calamities for which sorrow has no controul, or none from human motives. Tell me, then, have you lost by death the friend of your bosom?"

"No!"

"Is your fortune dissipated by extravagance, and your power of relieving the distressed at an end?"

"No; the power and the will are I hope equally undiminished."

"O then, unhappy girl! have you been guilty of some vice, and hangs remorse thus heavy on your conscience?"

"No, no; thank heaven, to that misery, at least, I am a stranger!"

His countenance now again resumed its severity, and, in the sternest manner, "Whence then," he said, "these tears? and what is this caprice you dignify with the name of sorrow?—strange wantonness of indolence and luxury! perverse repining of ungrateful plenitude!—oh hadst thou known what *I* have suffered!—"

"Could I lessen what you have suffered," said Cecilia, "I should sincerely rejoice; but heavy indeed must be your affliction, if mine in its comparison deserves to be styled caprice!"

"Caprice!" repeated he, " 'tis joy! 'tis extacy compared with mine!—Thou hast not in licentiousness wasted thy inheritance! thou hast not by remorse barred each avenue to enjoyment! nor yet has the cold grave seized the beloved of thy soul!''

''Neither,'' said Cecilia, ''I hope, are the evils you have yourself sustained so irremediable?''

''Yes, I have borne them all!—*have* borne? I bear them still; I shall bear them while I breathe! I may rue them, perhaps, yet longer.''

''Good God!'' cried Cecilia, shrinking, ''what a world is this! how full of woe and wickedness!''

''Yet thou, too, canst complain,'' cried he, ''though happy in life's only blessing, Innocence! thou, too, canst murmur, tho' stranger to death's only terror, Sin! Oh yet if thy sorrow is unpolluted with guilt, be regardless of all else, and rejoice in thy destiny!''

''But who,'' cried she, deeply sighing, ''shall teach me such a lesson of joy, when all within rises to oppose it?''

''I,'' cried he, ''will teach it thee, for I will tell thee my own sad story. Then wilt thou find how much happier is thy lot, then wilt thou raise thy head in thankful triumph.''

''O no! triumph comes not so lightly! yet if you will venture to trust me with some account of yourself, I shall be glad to hear it, and much obliged by the communication.''

''I will,'' he answered, ''whatever I may suffer: to awaken thee from this dream of fancied sorrow, I will open all my wounds, and thou shalt probe them with fresh shame.''

''No, indeed,'' cried Cecilia with quickness, ''I will not hear you, if the relation will be so painful.''

''Upon *me* this humanity is lost,'' said he, ''since punishment and penitence alone give me comfort. I will tell thee, therefore, my crimes, that thou mayst know thy own felicity, lest, ignorant it means nothing but innocence, thou shouldst lose it, unconscious of its value. Listen then to me, and learn what Misery is! Guilt is alone the basis of lasting unhappiness;—Guilt is the basis of mine, and therefore I am a wretch for ever!''

Cecilia would again have declined hearing him, but he refused to be spared: and as her curiosity had long been excited to know something of his history, and the motives of his extraordinary conduct, she was glad to have it satisfied, and gave him the utmost attention.

"I will not speak to you of my family," said he; "historical accuracy would little answer to either of us. I am a native of the West Indies,* and I was early sent hither to be educated. While I was yet at the University, I saw, I adored, and I pursued the fairest flower that ever put forth its sweet buds, the softest heart that ever was broken by ill-usage! She was poor and unprotected, the daughter of a villager; she was untaught and unpretending, the child of simplicity! But fifteen summers had she bloomed, and her heart was an easy conquest; yet, once made mine, it resisted all allurement to infidelity. My fellow students attacked her; she was assaulted by all the arts of seduction; flattery, bribery, supplication, all were employed, yet all failed; she was wholly my own; and with sincerity so attractive, I determined to marry her in defiance of all worldly objections.

"The sudden death of my father called me hastily to Jamaica; I feared leaving this treasure unguarded, yet in decency could neither marry nor take her directly; I pledged my faith, therefore, to return to her, as soon as I had settled my affairs, and I left to a bosom friend the inspection of her conduct in my absence.

"To leave her was madness,—to trust in man was madness,—Oh hateful race! how has the world been abhorrent to me since that time! I have loathed the light of the sun, I have shrunk from the commerce of my fellow-creatures; the voice of man I have detested, his sight I have abominated!—but oh, more than all should I be abominated myself!

"When I came to my fortune, intoxicated with sudden power, I forgot this fair blossom, I revelled in licentiousness and vice, and left it exposed and forlorn. Riot succeeded riot, till a fever, incurred by my own intemperance, first gave me time to think. Then was she revenged, for then first remorse was my portion: her image was brought back to my mind with frantic fondness, and bitterest contrition. The moment I recovered, I returned to England; I flew to claim her,—but she was lost! no one knew whither she was gone; the wretch I had trusted pretended to know least of all; yet, after a furious search, I traced her to a cottage, where he had concealed her himself!

"When she saw me, she screamed and would have flown; I stopt her, and told her I came faithfully and honourably to make her my wife;—her own faith and honour, though sullied, were not extinguished, for she instantly acknowledged the fatal tale of her undoing!

"Did I recompense this ingenuousness? this unexampled, this beautiful sacrifice to intuitive integrity? Yes! with my curses!—I loaded her with execrations, I reviled her in language the most opprobrious, I insulted her even for her confession! I invoked all evil upon her from the bottom of my heart!—She knelt at my feet, she implored my forgiveness and compassion, she wept with the bitterness of despair,——and yet I spurned her from me!—Spurned?—let me not hide my shame! I barbarously struck her!——nor single was the blow!—it was doubled, it was reiterated!—Oh wretch, unyielding and unpitying! where shall hereafter be clemency for thee!—So fair a form! so young a culprit! so infamously seduced! so humbly penitent!

"In this miserable condition, helpless and deplorable, mangled by these savage hands, and reviled by this inhuman tongue, I left her, in search of the villain who had destroyed her: but, cowardly as treacherous, he had absconded. Repenting my fury, I hastened to her again; the fierceness of my cruelty shamed me when I grew calmer, the softness of her sorrow melted me upon recollection: I returned, therefore, to soothe her,—but again she was gone! terrified with expectation of insult, she hid herself from all my enquiries. I wandered in search of her two long years to no purpose, regardless of my affairs, and of all things but that pursuit. At length, I thought I saw her—in London, alone, and walking in the streets at midnight,——I fearfully followed her,—and followed her into an house of infamy!

"The wretches by whom she was surrounded were noisy and drinking, they heeded me little,——but she saw and knew me at once! She did not speak, nor did I,—but in two moments she fainted and fell.

"Yet did I not help her; the people took their own

measures to recover her, and when she was again able to stand, would have removed her to another apartment.

"I then went forward, and forcing them away from her with all the strength of desperation, I turned to the unhappy sinner, who to chance only seemed to leave what became of her, and cried, From this scene of vice and horror let me yet rescue you! you look still unfit for such society, trust yourself, therefore, to me. I seized her hand, I drew, I almost dragged her away. She trembled, she could scarce totter, but neither consented nor refused, neither shed a tear, nor spoke a word, and her countenance presented a picture of affright, amazement and horror.

"I took her to a house in the country, each of us silent the whole way. I gave her an apartment and a female attendant, and ordered for her every convenience I could suggest. I stayed myself in the same house, but distracted with remorse for the guilt and ruin into which I had terrified her, I could not bear her sight.

"In a few days her maid assured me the life she led must destroy her; that she would taste nothing but bread and water, never spoke, and never slept.

"Alarmed by this account, I flew into her apartment; pride and resentment gave way to pity and fondness, and I besought her to take comfort. I spoke, however, to a statue, she replied not, nor seemed to hear me. I then humbled myself to her as in the days of her innocence and first power, supplicating her notice, entreating even her commiseration! all was to no purpose; she neither received nor repulsed me, and was alike inattentive to exhortation and to prayer.

"Whole hours did I spend at her feet, vowing never to arise till she spoke to me,—all, all, in vain! she seemed deaf, mute, insensible, her face unmoved, a settled despair fixed in her eyes,—those eyes that had never looked at me but with dove-like softness and compliance!—She sat constantly in one chair, she never changed her dress, no persuasions could prevail with her to lie down, and at meals she just swallowed so much dry bread as might save her from dying for want of food.

"What was the distraction of my soul, to find her bent

upon this course to her last hour!——quick came that hour, but never will it be forgotten! rapidly it was gone, but eternally it will be remembered!

"When she felt herself expiring, she acknowledged she had made a vow, upon entering the house, to live speechless and motionless, as a pennance for her offences!

"I kept her loved corpse till my own senses failed me,—it was then only torn from me,—and I have lost all recollection of three years of my existence!"

Cecilia shuddered at this hint, yet was not surprised by it; Mr. Gosport had acquainted her he had been formerly confined;* and his flightiness, wildness, florid language, and extraordinary way of life, had long led her to suspect his reason had been impaired.

"The scene to which my memory first leads me back," he continued, "is visiting her grave; solemnly upon it I returned her vow, though not by one of equal severity. To her poor remains did I pledge myself, that the day should never pass in which I would receive nourishment, nor the night come in which I would take rest, till I had done, or zealously attempted to do, some service to a fellow-creature.

"For this purpose have I wandered from city to city, from the town to the country, and from the rich to the poor. I go into every house where I can gain admittance, I admonish all who will hear me, I shame even those who will not. I seek the distressed where-ever they are hid, I follow the prosperous to beg a mite to serve them. I look for the Dissipated in public, where, amidst their licentiousness, I check them; I pursue the Unhappy in private, where I counsel and endeavour to assist them. My own power is small; my relations, during my sufferings, limiting me to an annuity; but there is no one I scruple to solicit, and by zeal I supply ability.

"Oh life of hardship and pennance! laborious, toilsome, and restless! but I have merited no better, and I will not repine at it; I have vowed that I will endure it, and I will not be forsworn.

"One indulgence alone from time to time I allow myself,—'tis Music! which has power to delight me even to rapture! it quiets all anxiety, it carries me out of myself, I forget through it every calamity, even the bitterest anguish.

"Now then, that thou hast heard me, tell me, hast *thou* cause of sorrow?"

"Alas," cried Cecilia, "this indeed is a Picture of Misery to make *my* lot seem all happiness!"

"Art thou thus open to conviction?" cried he, mildly; "and dost thou not fly the voice of truth! for truth and reproof are one."

"No, I would rather seek it; I feel myself wretched, however inadequate may be the cause; I wish to be more resigned, and if you can instruct me how, I shall thankfully attend to you."

"Oh yet uncorrupted creature!" cried he, "with joy will I be thy monitor,—joy long untasted! Many have I wished to serve, all hitherto, have rejected my offices; too honest to flatter them, they had not the fortitude to listen to me; too low to advance them, they had not the virtue to bear with me. You alone have I yet found pure enough not to fear inspection, and good enough to wish to be better. Yet words alone will not content me; I must also have deeds. Nor will your purse, however readily opened, suffice, you must give to me also your time and your thoughts; for money sent by others, to others only will afford relief; to lighten your own cares, you must distribute it yourself."

"You shall find me," said she, "a docile pupil, and most glad to be instructed how my existence may be useful."

"Happy then," cried he, "was the hour that brought me to this county; yet not in search of you did I come, but of the mutable and ill-fated Belfield. Erring, yet ingenious young man! what a lesson to the vanity of talents, to the gaiety, the brilliancy of wit, is the sight of that green fallen plant! not sapless by age, nor withered by disease, but destroyed by want of pruning, and bending, breaking by its own luxuriance!"

"And where, Sir, is he now?"

"Labouring wilfully in the field, with those who labour compulsatorily; such are we all by nature, discontented, perverse, and changeable; though all have not courage to appear so, and few, like Belfield, are worth watching when they do. He told me he was happy; I knew it could not be: but his employment was inoffensive, and I left him without reproach. In this neighbourhood I heard of you, and found your name was coupled with praise. I came to see if you deserved it; I have seen, and am satisfied."

"You are not, then, very difficult, for I have yet done nothing. How are we to begin these operations you propose? You have awakened me by them to an expectation of pleasure, which nothing else, I believe, could just now have given me."

"We will work," cried he, "together, till not a woe shall remain upon your mind. The blessings of the fatherless, the prayers of little children, shall heal all your wounds with balm of sweetest fragrance. When sad, they shall chear, when complaining, they shall soothe you. We will go to their roofless houses, and see them repaired; we will exclude from their dwellings the inclemency of the weather; we will clothe them from cold, we will rescue them from hunger. The cries of distress shall be changed to notes of joy: your heart shall be enraptured, mine, too, shall revive—oh whither am I wandering? I am painting an Elysium! and while I idly speak, some fainting object dies for want of succour! Farewell; I will fly to the abodes of wretchedness, and come to you tomorrow to render them the abodes of happiness."

He then went away.

This singular visit was for Cecilia most fortunately timed: it almost surprised her out of her peculiar grief, by the view which it opened to her of general calamity; wild, flighty and imaginative as were his language and his counsels, their morality was striking, and their benevolence was affecting. Taught by him to compare her state with that of at least half her species, she began more candidly to weigh what was left with what was withdrawn, and found the balance in her favour. The plan he had presented to her of good works was consonant to her character and inclinations; and the active charity in which he proposed to engage her, re-animated her fallen hopes, though to far different subjects from those which had depressed them. Any scheme of worldly happiness would have sickened and disgusted her; but her mind was just in the situation to be impressed with elevated piety, and to adopt any design in which virtue humoured melancholy.

CHAPTER X

A Shock

CECILIA passed the rest of the day in fanciful projects of beneficence; she determined to wander with her romantic new ally whither-so-ever he would lead her, and to spare neither fortune, time, nor trouble, in seeking and relieving the distressed. Not all her attempted philosophy had calmed her mind like this plan; in merely refusing indulgence to grief, she had only locked it up in her heart, where eternally struggling for vent, she was almost overpowered by restraining it; but now her affliction had no longer her whole faculties to itself; the hope of doing good, the pleasure of easing pain, the intention of devoting her time to the service of the unhappy, once more delighted her imagination,—that source of promissory enjoyment, which though often obstructed, is never, in youth, exhausted.

She would not give Mrs. Charlton the unnecessary pain of hearing the letter with which she had been so much affected, but she told her of the visit of Albany, and pleased her with the account of their scheme.

At night, with less sadness than usual, she retired to rest. In her sleep she bestowed riches, and poured plenty upon the land; she humbled the oppressor, she exalted the oppressed;* slaves were raised to dignities, captives restored to liberty; beggars saw smiling abundance, and wretchedness was banished the world. From a cloud in which she was supported by angels,* Cecilia beheld these wonders; and while enjoying the glorious illusion, she was awakened by her maid, with news that Mrs. Charlton was dying!

She started up, and, undressed, was running to her

apartment,—when the maid, calling to stop her, confessed she was already dead!

She had made her exit in the night, but the time was not exactly known; her own maid, who slept in the room with her, going early to her bedside to enquire how she did, found her cold and motionless, and could only conclude that a paralytic stroke had taken her off.

Happily and in good time had Cecilia been somewhat recruited by one night of refreshing slumbers and flattering dreams, for the shock she now received promised her not soon another.

She lost in Mrs. Charlton a friend, whom nearly from her infancy she had considered as a mother, and by whom she had been cherished with tenderness almost unequalled. She was not a woman of bright parts, or much cultivation, but her heart was excellent, and her disposition was amiable. Cecilia had known her longer than her memory could look back, though the earliest circumstances she could trace were kindnesses received from her. Since she had entered into life, and found the difficulty of the part she had to act, to this worthy old lady alone had she unbosomed her secret cares. Though little assisted by her counsel, she was always certain of her sympathy; and while her own superior judgment directed her conduct, she had the relief of communicating her schemes, and weighing her perplexities, with a friend to whom nothing that concerned her was indifferent, and whose greatest wish and chief pleasure was the enjoyment of her conversation.

If left to herself, in the present period of her life, Mrs. Charlton had certainly not been the friend of her choice. The delicacy of her mind, and the refinement of her ideas, had now rendered her fastidious, and she would have looked out for elegancies and talents to which Mrs. Charlton had no pretensions: but those who live in the country have little power of selection; confined to a small circle, they must be content with what it offers; and however they may idolize extraordinary merit when they meet with it, they must not regard it as essential to friendship, for in their circumscribed rotation, whatever may be their discontent, they can make but little change.

Such had been the situation to which Mrs. Charlton and Mrs. Harrel owed the friendship of Cecilia. Greatly their superior in understanding and intelligence, had the candidates for her favour been more numerous, the election had not fallen upon either of them. But she became known to both before discrimination made her difficult, and when her enlightened mind discerned their deficiences, they had already an interest in her affections, which made her see them with lenity: and though sometimes, perhaps, conscious she should not have chosen them from many, she adhered to them with sincerity, and would have changed them for none.

Mrs. Harrel, however, too weak for similar sentiments, forgot her when out of sight, and by the time they met again, was insensible to every thing but shew and dissipation. Cecilia, shocked and surprised, first grieved from disappointed affection, and then lost that affection in angry contempt. But her fondness for Mrs. Charlton had never known abatement, as the kindness which had excited it had never known allay. She had loved her first from childish gratitude; but that love, strengthened and confirmed by confidential intercourse, was now as sincere and affectionate as if it had originated from sympathetic admiration. Her loss, therefore, was felt with the utmost severity, and neither seeing nor knowing any means of replacing it, she considered it as irreparable, and mourned it with bitterness.

When the first surprize of this cruel stroke was somewhat lessened, she sent an express to Mr. Monckton with the news, and entreated to see him immediately. He came without delay, and she begged his counsel what step she ought herself to take in consequence of this event. Her own house was still unprepared for her; she had of late neglected to hasten the workmen, and almost forgotten her intention of entering it. It was necessary, however, to change her abode immediately; she was no longer in the house of Mrs. Charlton, but of her grand-daughters and co-heiresses, each of whom she disliked, and upon neither of whom she had any claim.

Mr. Monckton then, with the quickness of a man who

utters a thought at the very moment of its projection, mentioned a scheme upon which during his whole ride he had been ruminating; which was that she would instantly remove to his house, and remain there till settled to her satisfaction.

Cecilia objected her little right of surprising Lady Margaret; but, without waiting to discuss it, lest new objections should arise, he quitted her, to fetch himself from her ladyship an invitation he meant to insist upon her sending.

Cecilia, though heartily disliking this plan, knew not at present what better to adopt, and thought any thing preferable to going again to Mrs. Harrel, since that only could be done by feeding the anxiety of Mr. Arnott.

Mr. Monckton soon returned with a message of his own fabrication; for his lady, though obliged to receive whom he pleased, took care to guard inviolate the independence of speech, sullenly persevering in refusing to say any thing, or perversely saying only what he least wished to hear.

Cecilia then took a hasty leave of Miss Charltons,* who, little affected by what they had lost, and eager to examine what they had gained, parted from her gladly, and, with a heavy heart and weeping eyes, borrowed for the last time the carriage of her late worthy old friend, and for-ever quitting her hospitable house, sorrowfully set out for the Grove.

END OF THE FOURTH VOLUME.

VOLUME V

BOOK IX

CHAPTER I

A Cogitation

LADY Margaret Monckton received Cecilia with the most
gloomy coldness: she apologised for the liberty she had taken
in making use of her ladyship's house, but, meeting no
return of civility, she withdrew to the room which had been
prepared for her, and resolved as much as possible to keep
out of her sight.

It now became necessary without further delay to settle
her plan of life, and fix her place of residence. The
foreboding looks of Lady Margaret made her hasten her
resolves, which otherwise would for a while have given way
to grief for her recent misfortune.

She sent for the surveyor who had the superintendance of
her estates, to enquire how soon her own house would be fit for
her reception; and heard there was yet work for near two
months.

This answer made her very uncomfortable. To continue
two months under the roof with Lady Margaret was a penance
she could not enjoin herself, nor was she at all sure Lady
Margaret would submit to it any better: she determined,
therefore, to release herself from the conscious burthen of
being an unwelcome visitor, by boarding with some creditable
family at Bury, and devoting the two months in which she was
to be kept from her house, to a general arrangement of her
affairs, and a final settling with her guardians.

For these purposes it would be necessary she should go to
London: but with whom, or in what manner, she could not
decide. She desired, therefore, another conference with Mr.
Monckton, who met her in the parlour.

She then communicated to him her schemes; and begged his counsel in her perplexities.

He was delighted at the application, and extremely well pleased with her design of boarding at Bury, well knowing, he could then watch and visit her at his pleasure, and have far more comfort in her society than even in his own house, where all the vigilance with which he observed her, was short of that with which he was himself observed by Lady Margaret. He endeavoured, however, to dissuade her from going to town, but her eagerness to pay the large sum she owed him, was now too great to be conquered. Of age, her fortune wholly in her power, and all attendance upon Mrs. Charlton at an end, she had no longer any excuse for having a debt in the world, and would suffer no persuasion to make her begin her career in life, with a negligence in settling her accounts which she had so often censured in others. To go to London therefore she was fixed, and all that she desired was his advice concerning the journey.

He then told her that in order to settle with her guardians, she must write to them in form, to demand an account of the sums that had been expended during her minority, and announce her intention for the future to take the management of her fortune into her own hands.

She immediately followed his directions, and consented to remain at the Grove till their answers arrived.

Being now, therefore, unavoidably fixed for some time at the house, she thought it proper and decent to attempt softening Lady Margaret in her favour. She exerted all her powers to please and to oblige her; but the exertion was necessarily vain, not only from the disposition, but the situation of her ladyship, since every effort made for this conciliatory purpose, rendered her doubly amiable in the eyes of her husband, and consequently to herself more odious than ever. Her jealousy, already but too well founded, received every hour the poisonous nourishment of fresh conviction, which so much soured and exasperated a temper naturally harsh, that her malignity and ill-humour grew daily more acrimonious. Nor would she have contented herself with displaying this irascibility by general moroseness, had not the same suspicious watchfulness which discovered to her the passion of her husband, served equally to make manifest the indifference and innocence of Cecilia; to reproach her therefore, she had not any pretence, though her knowledge how much she had to dread her, past current in her mind for sufficient reason to hate her. The Angry and the Violent use little discrimination; whom they like, they inquire not if they approve; but whoever, no matter how unwittingly, stands in their way, they scruple not to ill use, and conclude they may laudably detest.

Cecilia, though much disgusted, gave not over her attempt, which she considered but as her due while she continued in her house. Her general character, also, for peevishness and haughty ill-breeding, skilfully, from time to time, displayed, and artfully repined at by Mr. Monckton, still kept her from suspecting any peculiar animosity to herself, and made her impute all that passed to the mere rancour of ill-humour. She confined herself, however, as much as possible to her own apartment, where her sorrow for Mrs. Charlton almost hourly encreased, by the comparison she was forced upon making of her house with the Grove.

That worthy old lady left her grand-daughters her co-heiresses and sole executrixes. She bequeathed from them nothing considerable, though she left some donations for the poor, and several of her friends were remembered by small legacies. Among them Cecilia had her picture, and favourite trinkets, with a paragraph in her will, that as there was no one she so much loved, had her fortune been less splendid, she should have shared with her grand-daughters whatever she had to bestow.

Cecilia was much affected by this last and solemn remembrance. She more than ever coveted to be alone, that she might grieve undisturbed, and she lamented without ceasing the fatigue and the illness which, in so late a period, as it proved, of her life, she had herself been the means of occasioning to her.

Mr. Monckton had too much prudence to interrupt this desire of solitude, which indeed cost him little pain, as he considered her least in danger when alone. She received in about a week answers from both her guardians. Mr. Delvile's letter was closely to the purpose, without a word but of business, and couched in the haughtiest terms. As he had never, he said, acted, he had no accounts to send in; but as he was going to town in a few days, he would see her for a moment in the presence of Mr. Briggs, that a joint release might be signed, to prevent any future application to him.

Cecilia much lamented there was any necessity for her seeing him at all, and looked forward to the interview as the greatest mortification she could suffer.

Mr. Briggs, though still more concise, was far kinder in his language: but he advised her to defer her scheme of taking the money into her own hands, assuring her she would be cheated, and had better leave it to him.

When she communicated these epistles to Mr. Monckton, he failed not to read, with an emphasis, by which his arrogant meaning was still more arrogantly enforced, the letter of Mr. Delvile aloud. Nor was he sparing in comments that might render it yet more offensive. Cecilia neither concurred in what he said, nor opposed it, but contented herself, when he was silent, with producing the other letter.

Mr. Monckton read not this with more favour. He openly attacked the character of Briggs, as covetous, rapacious, and over-reaching, and warned her by no means to abide by his counsel, without first taking the opinion of some disinterested person. He then stated the various arts which might be practised upon her inexperience, enumerated the dangers to which her ignorance of business exposed her, and annotated upon the cheats, double dealings, and tricks of stock jobbing,* to which he assured her Mr. Briggs owed all he was worth, till, perplexed and confounded, she declared herself at a loss how to proceed, and earnestly regretted that she could not have his counsel upon the spot.

This was his aim: to draw the wish from her, drew all suspicion of selfish views from himself: and he told her that he considered her present situation as so critical, the future confusion or regularity of her money transactions seeming to depend upon it, that he would endeavour to arrange his affairs for meeting her in London.

Cecilia gave him many thanks for the kind intention, and determined to be totally guided by him in the disposal and direction of her fortune.

Mean time he had now another part to act; he saw that with Cecilia nothing more remained to be done, and that, harbouring not a doubt of his motives, she thought his design in her favour did her nothing but honour; but he had too much knowledge of the world to believe it would judge him in the same manner, and too much consciousness of duplicity to set its judgment at defiance. To parry, therefore, the conjectures which might follow his attending her, he had already prepared Lady Margaret to wish herself of the party: for however disagreeable to him was her presence and her company, he had no other means to be under the same roof with Cecilia.

Miss Bennet, the wretched tool of his various schemes, and the mean sycophant of his lady, had been employed by him to work upon her jealousy, by secretly informing her of his intention to go to town, at the same time that Cecilia went thither to meet her guardians. She pretended to have learned this intelligence by accident, and to communicate it from respectful regard; and advised her to go to London herself at the same time, that she might see into his designs, and be some check upon his pleasure.

The encreasing infirmities of Lady Margaret made this counsel by no means palatable: but Miss Bennet, following the artful instructions which she received, put in her way so strong a motive, by assuring her how little her company was wished, that in the madness of her spite she determined upon the journey. And little heeding how she tormented herself while she had any view of tormenting Mr. Monckton, she was led on by her false confident to invite Cecilia to her town house.

Mr. Monckton, in whom by long practice, artifice was almost nature, well knowing his wife's perverseness, affected to look much disconcerted at the proposal; while Cecilia, by no means thinking it necessary to extend her compliance to such a punishment, instantly made an apology, and declined the invitation.

Lady Margaret, little versed in civility, and unused to the arts of persuasion, could not, even for a favourite project, prevail upon herself to use entreaty, and therefore, thinking her scheme defeated, looked gloomily disappointed, and said nothing more.

Mr. Monckton saw with delight how much this difficulty inflamed her, though the moment he could speak alone with Cecilia he made it his care to remove it.

He represented to her that, however privately she might live, she was too young to be in London lodgings by herself, and gave an hint which she could not but understand, that in going or in staying with only servants, suspicions might soon be raised, that the plan and motive of her journey were different to those given out.

She knew* he meant to insinuate that it would be conjectured she designed to meet Delvile, and though colouring, vext and provoked at the suggestion, the idea was sufficient to frighten her into his plan.

In a few days, therefore, the matter was wholly arranged, Mr. Monckton, by his skill and address, leading every one whither he pleased, while, by the artful coolness of his manner, he appeared but to follow himself. He set out the day before, though earnestly wishing to accompany them, but having as yet in no single instance gone to town in the same carriage with Lady Margaret, he dared trust neither the neighbourhood nor the servants with so dangerous a subject for their comments.

Cecilia, compelled thus to travel with only her Ladyship and Miss Bennet, had a journey the most disagreeable, and determined, if possible, to stay in London but two days. She had already fixed upon a house in which she could board at Bury when she returned, and there she meant quietly to reside till she could enter her own.

Lady Margaret herself, exhilarated by a notion of having outwitted her husband, was in unusual good spirits, and almost in good humour. The idea of thwarting his designs, and being in the way of his entertainment, gave to her a delight she had seldom received from any thing; and the belief that this was effected by the superiority of her cunning, doubled her contentment, and raised it to exultation. She owed him, indeed, much provocation and uneasiness, and was happy in this opportunity of paying her arrears.

Mean while that consummate master in every species of hypocrisy, indulged her in this notion, by the air of dissatisfaction with which he left the house. It was not that she meant by her presence to obviate any impropriety: early and long acquainted with the character of Cecilia, she well knew, that during her life the passion of her husband must be confined to his own breast: but conscious of his aversion to herself, which she resented with the bitterest ill-will, and knowing how little, at any time, he desired her company, she consoled herself for her inability to give pleasure by the power she possessed of giving pain, and bore with the fatigue of a journey disagreeable and inconvenient to her, with no other view than the hope of breaking into his plan of avoiding her. Little imagining that the whole time she was forwarding his favourite pursuit, and only acting the part which he had appointed her to perform.

CHAPTER II

A Surprize

LADY Margaret's town house was in Soho Square; and scarcely had Cecilia entered it, before her desire to speed her departure, made her send a note to each of her guardians, acquainting them of her arrival, and begging, if possible, to see them the next day.

She had soon the two following answers:

To Miss CECILIA BEVERLEY.

These. *

November 8, 1779.

Miss,
Received yours of the same date; can't come to-morrow. Will, Wednesday the 10th.

Am, &c.

JNº BRIGGS.

Miss Cecilia Beverley.

c.—33

To Miss BEVERLEY.

Mr. Delvile has too many affairs of importance upon his hands, to make any appointment till he has deliberated how to arrange them. Mr. Delvile will acquaint Miss Beverley when it shall be in his power to see her.

St. James's-Square, Nov. 8.

These characteristic letters, which at another time might have diverted Cecilia, now merely served to torment her. She was eager to quit town, she was more eager to have her meeting with Mr. Delvile over, who, oppressive to her even when he meant to be kind, she foresaw, now he was in wrath, would be imperious even to rudeness. Desirous, however, to make one interview suffice for both, and to settle whatever business might remain unfinished by letters, she again wrote to Mr. Briggs, whom she had not spirits to encounter without absolute necessity, and informing him of Mr. Delvile's delay, begged he would not trouble himself to call till he heard from her again.

Two days passed without any message from them; they were spent chiefly alone, and very uncomfortably, Mr. Monckton being content to see little of her, while he knew she saw nothing of any body else. On the third morning, weary of her own thoughts, weary of Lady Margaret's ill-humoured looks, and still more weary of Miss Bennet's parasitical conversation, she determined, for a little relief to the heaviness of her mind, to go to her bookseller, and look over and order into the country such new publications as seemed to promise her any pleasure.

She sent therefore, for a chair, and glad to have devised for herself any amusement, set out in it immediately.

Upon entering the shop, she saw the Bookseller* engaged in close conference with a man meanly dressed, and much muffled up, who seemed talking to him with uncommon earnestness, and just as she was approaching, said, "To terms I am indifferent, for writing is no labour to me; on the contrary, it is the first delight of my life, and therefore, and not for dirty pelf, I wish to make it my profession."

The speech struck Cecilia, but the voice struck her more,

it was Belfield's! and her amazement was so great, that she stopt short to look at him, without heeding a man who attended her, and desired to know her commands.

The bookseller now perceiving her, came forward, and Belfield, turning to see who interrupted them, started as if a spectre had crossed his eyes, flapped his hat over his face, and hastily went out of the shop.

Cecilia checking her inclination to speak to him, from observing his eagerness to escape her, soon recollected her own errand, and employed herself in looking over new books.

Her surprize, however, at a change so sudden in the condition of this young man, and at a declaration of a passion for writing, so opposite to all the sentiments which he had professed at their late meeting in the cottage, awakened in her a strong curiosity to be informed of his situation; and after putting aside some books which she desired to have packed up for her, she asked if the gentleman who had just left the shop, and who, she found by what he had said, was an Author, had written any thing that was published with his name?

"No, ma'am," answered the Bookseller, "nothing of any consequence; he is known, however, to have written several things that have appeared as anonymous; and I fancy, now, soon, we shall see something considerable from him."

"He is about some great work, then?"

"Why no, not exactly that, perhaps, at present; we must feel our way, with some little smart *jeu d'esprit* before we undertake a great work. But he is a very great genius, and I doubt not will produce something extraordinary."

"Whatever he produces," said Cecilia, "as I have now chanced to see him, I shall be glad you will, at any time, send to me."

"Certainly, ma'am; but it must be among other things, for he does not chuse, just now, to be known: and it is a rule in our business never to tell people's names when they desire to be secret. He is a little out of cash, just now, as you may suppose by his appearance, so instead of buying books, he comes to sell them. However, he has taken a very good road to bring himself home again, for we pay very handsomely for things of any merit, especially if they deal smartly in a few touches of the times.''

Cecilia chose not to risk any further questions, lest her knowledge of him should be suspected, but got into her chair, and returned to Lady Margaret's.

The sight of Belfield reminded her not only of himself; the gentle Henrietta again took her place in her memory, whence her various distresses and suspences had of late driven from it everybody but Delvile, and those whom Delvile brought into it. But her regard for that amiable girl, though sunk in the busy scenes of her calamitous uncertainties, was only sunk in her own bosom, and ready, upon their removal, to revive with fresh vigour. She was now indeed more unhappy than even in the period of her forgetfulness, yet her mind was no longer filled with the restless turbulence of hope, which still more than despondency unfitted it for thinking of others.

This remembrance thus awakened, awakened also a desire of renewing the connection so long neglected. All scruples concerning Delvile had now lost their foundation, since the doubts from which they arose were both explained and removed: she was certain alike of his indifference to Henrietta, and his separation from herself; she knew that nothing was to be feared from painful or offensive rivalry, and she resolved, therefore, to lose no time in seeking the first pleasure to which since her disappointment she had voluntarily looked forward.

Early in the evening, she told Lady Margaret she was going out for an hour or two, and sending again for a chair, was carried to Portland-Street.

She enquired for Miss Belfield, and was shewn into a parlour, where she found her drinking tea with her mother, and Mr. Hobson, their landlord.

Henrietta almost screamed at her sight, from a sudden impulse of joy and surprize, and, running up to her, flung her arms round her neck, and embraced her with the most rapturous emotion: but then, drawing back with a look of timidity and shame, she bashfully apologized for her freedom, saying, "Indeed, dearest Miss Beverley, it is no want of respect, but I am so very glad to see you it makes me quite forget myself!''

Cecilia, charmed at a reception so ingenuously affectionate, soon satisfied her doubting diffidence by the warmest thanks that she had preserved so much regard for her, and by doubling the kindness with which she returned her caresses.

''Mercy on me, madam,'' cried Mrs. Belfield, who during this time had been busily employed in sweeping the hearth, wiping some slops upon the table, and smoothing her handkerchief and apron, ''why the girl's enough to smother you. Henny, how can you be so troublesome? I never saw you behave in this way before.''

''Miss Beverley, madam,'' said Henrietta, again retreating, ''is so kind as to pardon me, and I was so much surprised at seeing her, that I hardly knew what I was about.''

''The young ladies, ma'am,'' said Mr. Hobson, ''have a mighty way of saluting* one another till such time as they get husbands: and then I'll warrant you they can meet without any salutation at all. That's my remark, at least, and what I've seen of the world has set me upon making it.''

This speech led Cecilia to check, however artless, the tenderness of her fervent young friend, whom she was much teized by meeting in such company, but who seemed not to dare understand the frequent looks which she gave her expressive of a wish to be alone with her.

''Come, ladies,'' continued the facetious Mr. Hobson, ''what if we were all to sit down, and have a good dish of tea? and suppose, Mrs. Belfield, you was to order us a fresh round of toast and butter? do you think the young ladies here would have any objection? and what if we were to have a little more water in the tea-kettle? not forgetting a little more tea in the tea-pot. What I say is this, let us all be comfortable; that's my notion of things.''

''And a very good notion too,'' said Mrs. Belfield, ''for you who* have nothing to vex you. Ah, ma'am, you have heard, I suppose, about my son? gone off! nobody knows where! left that lord's house, where he might have lived like a king, and gone out into the wide world nobody knows for what!''

"Indeed?" said Cecilia, who from seeing him in London concluded he was again with his family, "and has he not acquainted you where he is?"

"No, ma'am, no," cried Mrs. Belfield, "he's never once told me where he is gone, nor let me know the least about the matter, for if I did I would not taste a dish of tea again for a twelvemonth till I saw him get back again to that lord's! and I believe in my heart there's never such another in the three kingdoms,* for he has sent here after him I dare say a score of times. And no wonder, for I will take upon me to say he won't find his fellow in a hurry, Lord as he is."

"As to his being a Lord," said Mr. Hobson, "I am one of them that lay no great stress upon that, unless he has got a good long purse of his own, and then, to be sure, a Lord's no bad thing. But as to the matter of saying Lord such a one, how d'ye do? and Lord such a one, what do you want? and such sort of compliments, why in my mind, it's a mere nothing, in comparison of a good income. As to your son, ma'am, he did not go the right way to work. He should have begun with business, and gone into pleasure afterwards: and if he had but done that, I'll be bold to say we might have had him at this very minute drinking tea with us over this fire-side."

"My son, Sir," said Mrs. Belfield, rather angrily, "was another sort of a person than a person of business: he always despised it from a child, and come of it what may, I am sure he was born to be a gentleman."

"As to his despising business," said Mr. Hobson, very contemptuously, "why so much the worse, for business is no such despiseable thing. And if he had been brought up behind a counter, instead of dangling after these same Lords, why he might have had a house of his own over his head, and been as good a man as myself."

"A house over his head?" said Mrs. Belfield, "why he might have had what he would, and have done what he would, if he had but followed my advice, and put himself a little forward. I have told him a hundred times to ask some of those great people he lived amongst for a place at court, for I know they've so many they hardly know what to do with them, and it was always my design from the beginning that he should be something of a great man; but I never could persuade him, though, for any thing I know, as I have often told him, if he had but had a little courage he might have been an Ambassador by this time. And now, all of a sudden, to be gone nobody knows where!''—

"I am sorry, indeed,'' said Cecilia, who knew not whether most to pity or wonder at her blind folly; "but I doubt not you will hear of him soon.''

"As to being an Ambassador, ma'am'' said Mr. Hobson, "it's talking quite out of character. Those sort of great people keep things of that kind for their own poor relations and cousins. What I say is this; a man's best way is to take care of himself. The more those great people see you want them, the less they like your company. Let every man be brought up to business, and then when he's made his fortune, he may walk with his hat on.* Why now there was your friend, ma'am,'' turning to Cecilia, "that shot out his brains without paying any body a souse; pray how was that being more genteel than standing behind a counter, and not owing a shilling?''

"Do you think a young lady,'' cried Mrs. Belfield warmly, "can bear to hear of such a thing as standing behind a counter? I am sure if my son had ever done it, I should not expect any lady would so much as look at him. And yet, though I say it, she might look a good while, and not see many such persons, let her look where she pleased. And then he has such a winning manner into the bargain, that I believe in my heart there's never a lady in the land could say no to him. And yet he has such a prodigious shyness, I never could make him own he had so much as asked the question. And what lady can begin first?''

"Why no,'' said Mr. Hobson, "that would be out of character another way. Now my notion is this; let every man be agreeable! and then he may ask what lady he pleases. And when he's a mind of a lady, he should look upon a frown or two as nothing; for the ladies frown in courtship as a thing of course; it's just like a man's swearing at a coachman; why he's not a bit more in a passion, only he thinks he sha'n't be minded without it.''

"Well, for my part," said Mrs. Belfield, "I am sure if I was a young lady, and most especially if I was a young lady of fortune, and all that, I should like a modest young gentleman, such as my son, for example, better by half than a bold swearing young fellow, that would make a point to have me whether I would or no."

"Ha! Ha! Ha!" cried Mr. Hobson; "but the young ladies are not of that way of thinking; they are all for a little life and spirit. Don't I say right, young ladies?"

Cecilia, who could not but perceive that these speeches was* levelled at herself, felt offended and tired; and finding she had no chance of any private conversation with Henrietta, arose to take leave: but while she stopped in* the passage to enquire when she could see her alone, a footman knocked at the door, who, having asked if Mr. Belfield lodged there, and been answered in the affirmative, begged to know whether Miss Beverley was then in the house?

Cecilia, much surprised, went forward, and told him who she was.

"I have been, madam," said he, "with a messsage to you at Mr. Monckton's, in Soho-Square: but nobody knew where you was; and Mr. Monckton came out and spoke to me himself, and said that all he could suppose was that you might be at this house. So he directed me to come here."

"And from whom, Sir, is your message?"

"From the honourable Mr. Delvile, madam, in St. James's-Square. He desires to know if you shall be at home on Saturday morning, the day after to-morrow, and whether you can appoint Mr. Briggs to meet him by twelve o'clock exactly, as he sha'n't be able to stay above three minutes."

Cecilia gave an answer as cold as the message; that she would be in Soho-Square at the time he mentioned, and acquaint Mr. Briggs of his intention.

The footman then went away; and Henrietta told her, that if she could call some morning she might perhaps contrive to be alone with her, and added, "indeed I wish much to see you, if you could possibly do me so great an honour; for I am very miserable, and have nobody to tell so! Ah, Miss Beverley! you that have so many friends, and that deserve as many again, you little know what a hard thing it is to have none!—but my brother's strange disappearing has half broke our hearts!"

Cecilia was beginning a consolatory speech, in which she meant to give her private assurances of his health and safety, when she was interrupted by Mr. Albany, who came suddenly into the passage.

Henrietta received him with a look of pleasure, and enquired why he had so long been absent; but, surprised by the sight of Cecilia, he exclaimed, without answering her, "why didst thou fail me? why appoint me to a place thou wert quitting thyself?—thou thing of fair professions! thou inveigler of esteem! thou vain, delusive promiser of pleasure!"

"You condemn me too hastily," said Cecilia; "if I failed in my promise, it was not owing to caprice or insincerity, but to a real and bitter misfortune which incapacitated me from keeping it. I shall soon, however,—nay, I am already at your disposal, if you have any commands for me."

"I have always," answered he, "commands for the rich, for I have always compassion for the poor."

"Come to me, then, at Mr. Monckton's in Soho-Square," cried she, and hastened into her chair, impatient to end a conference which she saw excited the wonder of the servants, and which also now drew out from the parlour Mr. Hobson and Mrs. Belfield. She then kissed her hand to Henrietta, and ordered the chairmen to carry her home.

It had not been without difficulty that she had restrained herself from mentioning what she knew of Belfield, when she found his mother and sister in a state of such painful uncertainty concerning him. But her utter ignorance of his plans, joined to her undoubted knowledge of his wish of concealment, made her fear doing mischief by officiousness, and think it wiser not to betray what she had seen of him, till better informed of his own views and intentions. Yet, willing to shorten a suspense so uneasy to them, she determined to entreat Mr. Monckton would endeavour to find him out, and acquaint him with their anxiety.

That gentleman, when she returned to his house, was in a

state of mind by no means enviable. Missing her at tea, he had asked Miss Bennet where she was, and hearing she had not left word, he could scarce conceal his chagrin. Knowing, however, how few were her acquaintances in town, he soon concluded she was with Miss Belfield, but, not satisfied with sending Mr. Delvile's messenger after her, he privately employed one in whom he trusted for himself, to make enquiries at the house without saying whence he came.

But though this man was returned, and he knew her safety, he still felt alarmed; he had flattered himself, from the length of time in which she had now done nothing without consulting him, she would scarce even think of any action without his previous concurrence. And he had hoped, by a little longer use, to make his counsel become necessary, which he knew to be a very short step from rendering it absolute.

Nor was he well pleased to perceive, by this voluntary excursion, a struggle to cast off her sadness, and a wish to procure herself entertainment: it was not that he desired her misery, but he was earnest that all relief from it should spring from himself: and though far from displeased that Delvile should lose his sovereignty over her thoughts, he was yet of opinion that, till his own liberty was restored, he had less to apprehend from grief indulged, than grief allayed; one could but lead her to repining retirement, the other might guide her to a consolatory rival.

He well knew, however, it was as essential to his cause to disguise his disappointments as his expectations, and, certain that by pleasing alone he had any chance of acquiring power, he cleared up when Cecilia returned, who as unconscious of feeling, as of owing any subjection to him, preserved uncontrolled the right of acting for herself, however desirous and glad of occasional instruction.

She had told him where she had been, and related her meeting Belfield, and the unhappiness of his friends, and hinted her wish that he could be informed what they suffered. Mr. Monckton, eager to oblige her, went instantly in search of him, and returning to supper, told her he had traced him through the Bookseller, who had not the dexterity to parry his artful enquiries, and had actually appointed him to breakfast in Soho-Square the next morning.

He had found him, he said, writing, but in high spirits and good humour. He had resisted, for a while, his invitation on account of his dress, all his clothes but the very coat which he had on being packed up and at his mother's: but, when laughed at by Mr. Monckton for still retaining some foppery, he gayly protested what remained of it should be extinguished; and acknowledging that his shame was no part of his philosophy, declared he would throw it wholly aside, and, in spite of his degradation, renew his visits at his house.

"I would not tell him," Mr. Monckton continued, "of the anxiety of his family; I thought it would come more powerfully from yourself, who, having seen, can better enforce it."

Cecilia was very thankful for this compliance with her request, and anticipated the pleasure she hoped soon to give Henrietta, by the restoration of a brother so much loved and so regretted.

She sent, mean time, to Mr. Briggs the message she had received from Mr. Delvile, and had the satisfaction of an answer that he would observe the appointment.

CHAPTER III

A Confabulation

THE next morning, while the family was* at breakfast, Belfield, according to his promise, made his visit.

A high colour overspread his face as he entered the room, resulting from a sensation of grief at his fallen fortune, and shame at his altered appearance, which though he endeavoured to cover under an air of gaiety and unconcern, gave an awkwardness to his manners, and a visible distress to his countenance: Mr. Monckton received him with pleasure, and Cecilia, who saw the conflict of his philosophy with his pride, dressed her features once more in smiles, which however faint and heartless, shewed her desire to re-assure him. Miss Bennet, as usual when not called upon by the master or lady of the house, sat as a cypher; and Lady Margaret, always disagreeable and repulsive to the friends of her husband, though she was not now more than commonly ungracious, struck the quick-feeling and irritable Belfield, to wear an air of rude superiority meant to reproach him with his disgrace.

This notion, which strongly affected him, made him, for one instant, hesitate whether he should remain another in the same room with her: but the friendliness of Mr. Monckton, and the gentleness and good breeding of Cecilia, seemed so studious to make amends for her moroseness, that he checked his too ready indignation, and took his seat at the table. Yet was it some time before he could recover even the assumed vivacity which this suspected insult had robbed him of, sufficiently to enter into conversation with any appearance of ease or pleasure. But, after a while, soothed by the attentions of Cecilia and Mr. Monckton, his uneasiness wore off, and the native spirit and liveliness of his character broke forth with their accustomed energy.

"This good company, I hope," said he, addressing himself, however, only to Cecilia, "will not so much *mistake the thing** as to criticise my dress of this morning; since it is perfectly according to rule, and to rule established from time immemorial: but lest any of you should so much err as to fancy shabby what is only characteristic, I must endeavour to be beforehand with the malice of conjecture, and have the honour to inform you, that I am enlisted in the Grub-Street regiment, of the third story,* and under the tattered banner of scribbling volunteers! a race which, if it boasts not the courage of heroes, at least equals them in enmity. This coat, therefore, is merely the uniform of my corps, and you will all, I hope, respect it as emblematical of wit and erudition."

"We must at least respect you," said Cecilia, "who thus gaily can sport with it."

"Ah, madam!" said he, more seriously, "it is not from you I ought to look for respect! I must appear to you the most unsteady and coward-hearted of beings. But lately I blushed to see you from poverty, though more worthily employed than when I had been seen by you in affluence; that shame vanished, another equally narrow took its place, and yesterday I blushed again that you detected me in a new pursuit, though I had only quitted my former one from a conviction it was ill chosen. There seems in human nature a worthlessness not to be conquered! yet I will struggle with it to the last, and either die in the attempt, or dare seem that which I am, without adding to the miseries of life, the sting, the envenomed sting of dastardly false shame!''

''Your language is wonderfully altered within this twelvemonth,'' said Mr. Monckton; ''the *worthlessness of human nature!* the *miseries of life!* this from you! so lately the champion of human nature, and the panegyrist of human life!''

''Soured by personal disappointment,'' answered he, ''I may perhaps speak with too much acrimony; yet, ultimately, my opinions have not much changed. Happiness is given to us with more liberality than we are willing to confess; it is judgment only that is dealt us sparingly, and of that we have so little, that when felicity is before us, we turn to the right or left, or when at the right or left, we proceed strait forward. It has been so with me; I have sought it at a distance, amidst difficulty and danger, when all that I could wish had been immediately within my grasp.''

''It must be owned,'' said Mr. Monckton, ''after what you have suffered from this world you were wont to defend, there is little reason to wonder at some change in your opinion.''

''Yet whatever have been my sufferings,'' he answered, ''I have generally been involved in them by my own rashness or caprice. My last enterprise especially, from which my expectations were highest, was the most ill judged of any. I considered not how little my way of life had fitted me for the experiment I was making, how irreparably I was enervated by long sedentary habits, and how insufficient for bodily strength was mental resolution. We may fight against partial prejudices, and by spirit and fortitude we may

overcome them; but it will not do to war with the general
tenor of education. We may blame, despise, regret as we
please, but customs long established, and habits long
indulged, assume an empire despotic, though their power is
but prescriptive. Opposing them is vain; Nature herself,
when forced aside, is not more elastic in her rebound.''

"Will you not then," said Cecilia, "since your
experiment has failed, return again to your family, and to
the plan of life you formerly settled?''

"You speak of them together," said he, with a smile, "as
if you thought them inseparable; and indeed my own
apprehension they would be deemed so, has made me thus
fear to see my friends, since I love not resistance, yet cannot
again attempt the plan of life they would have me pursue.
I have given up my cottage, but my independence is as dear
to me as ever; and all that I have gathered from experience,
is to maintain it by those employments for which my
education has fitted me, instead of seeking it injudiciously by
the very road for which it has unqualified me.''

"And what is this independence," cried Mr. Monckton,
"which has thus bewitched your imagination? a mere idle
dream of romance and enthusiasm; without existence in
nature, without possibility in life. In uncivilised countries,
or in lawless times, independence, for a while, may perhaps
stalk abroad; but in a regular government, 'tis only the
vision of a heated brain; one part of a community must
inevitably hang upon another, and 'tis a farce to call either
independent, when to break the chain by which they are
linked would prove destruction to both. The soldier wants
not the officer more than the officer the soldier, nor the
tenant the landlord, more than the landlord the tenant. The
rich owe their distinction, their luxuries, to the poor, as
much as the poor owe their rewards, their necessaries, to the
rich.''

"Man treated as an Automaton," answered Belfield,
"and considered merely with respect to his bodily
operations, may indeed be called dependent, since the food
by which he lives, or, rather, without which he dies, cannot
wholly be cultivated and prepared by his own hands: but

considered in a nobler sense, he deserves not the degrading epithet; speak of him, then, as a being of feeling and understanding, with pride to alarm, with nerves to tremble, with honour to satisfy, and with a soul to be immortal!—as such, may he not claim the freedom of his own thoughts? may not that claim be extended to the liberty of speaking, and the power of being governed by them? and when thoughts, words, and actions are exempt from controul, will you brand him with dependency merely because the Grazier feeds his meat, and the Baker kneeds his bread?''

''But who is there in the whole world,'' said Mr. Monckton, ''extensive as it is, and dissimilar as are its inhabitants, that can pretend to assert, his thoughts, words, and actions, are exempt from controul? even where interest, which you so much disdain, interferes not,—though where that is I confess I cannot tell!—are we not kept silent where we wish to reprove by the fear of offending? and made speak where we wish to be silent by the desire of obliging? do we not bow to the scoundrel as low as to the man of honour? are we not by mere forms kept standing when tired? made give place to those we despise? and smiles to those we hate? or if we refuse these attentions, are we not regarded as savages, and shut out of society?''

''All these,'' answered Belfield, ''are so merely matters of ceremony, that the concession can neither cost pain to the proud, nor give pleasure to the vain. The bow is to the coat, the attention is to the rank, and the fear of offending ought to extend to all mankind. Homage such as this infringes not our sincerity, since it is as much a matter of course as the dress that we wear, and has as little reason to flatter a man as the shadow which follows him. I no more, therefore, hold him deceitful for not opposing this pantomimical parade, than I hold him to be dependent for eating corn he has not sown.''

''Where, then, do you draw the line? and what is the boundary beyond which your independence must not step?''

''I hold that man,'' cried he, with energy, ''to be independent, who treats the Great as the Little, and the Little as the Great, who neither exults in riches nor blushes in poverty, who owes no man a groat,* and who spends not a shilling he has not earned."

"You will not, indeed, then, have a very numerous acquaintance, if this is the description of those with whom you purpose to associate! but is it possible you imagine you can live by such notions? why the Carthusian in his monastery, who is at least removed from temptation, is not mortified so severely* as a man of spirit living in the world, who would prescribe himself such rules."

"Not merely have I prescribed," returned Belfield, "I have already put them in practice; and far from finding any pennance, I never before found happiness. I have now adopted, though poor, the very plan of life I should have elected if rich; my pleasure, therefore, is become my business, and my business my pleasure."

"And is this plan," cried Monckton, "nothing more than turning Knight-errant to the Booksellers?"

"'Tis a Knight-errantry," answered Belfield, laughing, "which, however ludicrous it may seem to you, requires more soul and more brains than any other. Our giants may, indeed, be only windmills,* but they must be attacked with as much spirit, and conquered with as much bravery, as any fort or any town, in time of war should be demolished; and though the siege, I must confess, may be of less national utility, the asssailants of the quill have their honour as much at heart as the assailants of the sword."

"I suppose then," said Monckton, archly, "if a man wants a biting lampoon, or an handsome panegyric, some news-paper scandal, or a sonnet for a lady—"

"No, no," interrupted Belfield eagerly, "if you imagine me a hireling scribbler for the purposes of defamation or of flattery, you as little know my situation as my character. My subjects shall be my own, and my satire shall be general. I would as much disdain to be personal with an anonymous pen, as to attack an unarmed man in the dark with a dagger I had kept concealed."

A reply of rallying incredulity was rising to the lips of Mr. Monckton, when reading in the looks of Cecilia an entire approbation of this sentiment, he checked his desire of ridicule, and exclaimed, "spoken like a man of honour, and one whose works may profit the world!"

"From my earliest youth to the present hour," continued Belfield, "literature has been the favourite object of my pursuit, my recreation in leisure, and my hope in employment. My propensity to it, indeed, has been so ungovernable, that I may properly call it the source of my several miscarriages throughout life. It was the bar to my preferment, for it gave me a distaste to other studies; it was the cause of my unsteadiness in all my undertakings, because to all I preferred it. It has sunk me to distress, it has involved me in difficulties; it has brought me to the brink of ruin by making me neglect the means of living, yet never, till now, did I discern it might itself be my support."

"I am heartily glad, Sir," said Cecilia, "your various enterprizes and struggles have at length ended in a project which promises you so much satisfaction. But you will surely suffer your sister and your mother to partake of it? for who is there that your prosperity will make so happy?"

"You do them infinite honour, madam, by taking any interest in their affairs; but to own to you the truth, what to me appears prosperity, will to them wear another aspect. They have looked forward to my elevation with expectations the most improbable, and thought every thing within my grasp, with a simplicity incredible. But though their hopes were absurd, I am pained by their disappointment, and I have not courage to meet their tears, which I am sure will not be spared when they see me."

"'Tis from tenderness, then," said Cecilia, half smiling, "that you are cruel, and from affection to your friends that you make them believe you have forgotten them?"

There was a delicacy in this reproach exactly suited to work upon Belfield, who feeling it with quickness, started up, and cried, "I believe I am wrong!—I will go to them this moment!"

Cecilia felt eager to second the generous impulse; but Mr. Monckton, laughing at his impetuosity, insisted he should first finish his breakfast.

"Your friends," said Cecilia, "can have no mortification

so hard to bear as your voluntary absence; and if they see but that you are happy, they will soon be reconciled to whatever situation you may chuse."

"Happy!" repeated he, with animation, "Oh I am in Paradise! I am come from a region in the first rude state of nature, to civilization and refinement! the life I led at the cottage was the life of a savage; no intercourse with society, no consolation from books; my mind locked up, every source dried of intellectual delight, and no enjoyment in my power but from sleep and from food. Weary of an existence which thus levelled me with a brute, I grew ashamed of the approximation, and listening to the remonstrance of my understanding, I gave up the precipitate plan, to pursue one more consonant to reason. I came to town, hired a room, and sent for pen, ink and paper: what I have written are trifles, but the Bookseller has not rejected them. I was settled, therefore, in a moment, and comparing my new occupation with that I had just quitted, I seemed exalted on the sudden from a mere creature of instinct, to a rational and intelligent being. But when first I* opened a book, after so long an abstinence from all mental nourishment,—Oh it was rapture! no half-famished beggar regaled suddenly with food, ever seized on his repast with more hungry avidity."

"Let fortune turn which way it will," cried Monckton, "you may defy all its malice, while possessed of a spirit of enjoyment which nothing can subdue!"

"But were you not, Sir," said Cecilia, "as great an enthusiast the other day for your cottage, and for labour?"

"I was, madam; but there my philosophy was erroneous: in my ardour to fly from meanness and from dependence, I thought in labour and retirement I should find freedom and happiness; but I forgot that my body was not seasoned for such work, and considered not that a mind which had once been opened by knowledge, could ill endure the contraction of dark and perpetual ignorance. The approach, however, of winter, brought me acquainted with my mistake. It grew cold, it grew bleak; little guarded against the inclemency of the weather, I felt its severity in every limb, and missed a thousand indulgencies which in possession I had never valued. To rise at break of day, chill, freezing, and comfortless! no sun abroad, no fire at home! to go out in all weather to work, that work rough, coarse and laborious!—unused to such hardships, I found I could not bear them, and, however unwillingly, was compelled to relinquish the attempt."

Breakfast now being over, he again arose to take leave.

"You are going, then, Sir," said Cecilia, "immediately to your friends?"

"No, madam," answered he hesitating, "not just this moment; to-morrow morning perhaps,—but it is now late, and I have business for the rest of the day."

"Ah, Mr. Monckton!" cried Cecilia, "what mischief have you done by occasioning this delay!"

"This goodness, madam," said Belfield, "my sister can never sufficiently acknowledge. But I will own, that though, just now, in a warm moment, I felt eager to present myself to her and my mother, I rather wish, now I am cooler, to be saved the pain of telling them in person my situation. I mean, therefore, first to write to them."

"You will not fail, then, to see them to-morrow?"

"Certainly—I think not."

"Nay, but certainly you *must* not, for I shall call upon them to-day, and assure them they may expect you. Can I soften your talk of writing by giving them any message from you?"

"Ah, madam, have a care!" cried he; "this condescension to a poor author may be more dangerous than you have any suspicion! and before you have power to help yourself, you may see your name prefixed to the Dedication of some trumpery pamphlet!"*

"I will run," cried she, "all risks; remember, therefore, you will be responsible for the performance of my promise."

"I will be sure," answered he, "not to forget what reflects so much honour upon myself."

Cecilia was satisfied by this assent, and he then went away.

"A strange flighty character!" cried Mr. Monckton, "yet of uncommon capacity, and full of genius. Were he less imaginative, wild and eccentric, he has abilities for any station, and might fix and distinguish himself almost where-ever he pleased.''

''I knew not,'' said Cecilia, ''the full worth of steadiness and prudence till I knew this young man; for he has every thing else; talents the most striking, a love of virtue the most elevated, and manners the most pleasing; yet wanting steadiness and prudence, he can neither act with consistency nor prosper with continuance.''

''He is well enough,'' said Lady Margaret, who had heard the whole argument in sullen taciturnity, ''he is well enough, I say; and there comes no good from young women's being so difficult.''

Cecilia, offended by a speech which implied a rude desire to dispose of her, went up stairs to her own room; and Mr. Monckton, always enraged when young men and Cecilia were alluded to in the same sentence, retired to his library.

She then ordered a chair, and went to Portland-Street, to fulfil what she had offered to Belfield, and to revive his mother and sister by the pleasure of the promised interview.

She found them together: and her intelligence being of equal consequence to both, she did not now repine at the presence of Mrs. Belfield. She made her communication with the most cautious attention to their characters, softening the ill she had to relate with respect to Belfield's present way of living, by endeavouring to awaken affection and joy from the prospect of the approaching meeting. She counselled them as much as possible to restrain their chagrin at his misfortunes, which he would but construe into reproach of his ill management; and she represented that when once he was restored to his family, he might almost imperceptibly be led into some less wild and more profitable scheme of business.

When she had told all she thought proper to relate, kindly interspersing her account with the best advice and best comfort she could suggest, she made an end of her visit; for the affliction of Mrs. Belfield upon hearing the actual situation of her son, was so clamorous and unappeasable, that, little wondering at Belfield's want of courage to encounter it, and having no opportunity in such a storm to console the soft Henrietta, whose tears flowed abundantly that her brother should thus be fallen, she only promised before she left town to see her again, and beseeching Mrs. Belfield to moderate her concern, was glad to leave the house, where her presence had no power to quiet their distress.

She passed the rest of the day in sad reflections upon the meeting she was herself* to have the next morning with Mr. Delvile. She wished ardently to know whether his son was gone abroad, and whether Mrs. Delvile was recovered, whose health, in her own letter, was mentioned in terms the most melancholy:* yet neither of these enquiries could she even think of making, since reasonably, without them, apprehensive of some reproach.*

CHAPTER IV

A Wrangling

MR. Monckton, the next day, as soon as breakfast was over, went out, to avoid showing, even to Cecilia, the anxiety he felt concerning the regulation of her fortune, and arrangement of her affairs. He strongly, however, advised her not to mention her large debt, which, though contracted in the innocence of the purest benevolence, would incur nothing but reproof and disapprobation, from all who only heard of it, when they heard of its inutility.

At eleven o'clock, though an hour before the time appointed, while Cecilia was sitting in Lady Margaret's dressing-room, "with sad civility and an aching head,"* she was summoned to Mr. Briggs in the parlour.

He immediately began reproaching her with having eloped from him, in the summer, and with the various expences she had caused him from useless purchases and spoilt provisions. He then complained of Mr. Delvile, whom he charged with defrauding him of his dues; but observing in the midst of his railing her dejection of countenance, he suddenly broke off, and looking at her with some concern, said, "what's the matter, Ducky? a'n't well? look as if you could not help it."

"O yes," cried Cecilia, "I thank you, Sir, I am very well."

"What do look so blank for, then?" said he, "hay? what are fretting for?—crossed in love?—lost your sweet-heart?"

"No, no, no," cried she, with quickness.

"Never mind, my chick, never mind," said he, pinching her cheek, with resumed good humour, "more to be had; if one won't snap,* another will; put me in a passion by going off from me with that old grandee, or would have got one long ago. Hate that old Don; used me very ill; wish I could trounce him. Thinks more of a fusty old parchment than the price of stocks. Fit for nothing but to be stuck upon an old monument for a Death's head."*

He then told her that her accounts were all made out, and he was ready at any time to produce them; he approved much of her finishing wholly with the *old Don*, who had been a mere cypher in the executorship; but he advised her not to think of taking her money into her own hands, as he was willing to keep the charge of it himself till she was married.

Cecilia, thanking him for the offer, said she meant now to make her acknowledgments for all the trouble he had already taken, but by no means purposed to give him any more.

He debated the matter with her warmly, told her she had no chance to save herself from knaves and cheats, but by trusting to nobody but himself, and informing her what interest he had already made of her money, enquired how she would set about getting more?

Cecilia, though prejudiced against him by Mr. Monckton, knew not how to combat his arguments; yet conscious that scarce any part of the money to which he alluded was in fact her own, she could not yield to them. He was, however, so stubborn and so difficult to deal with, that she at length let him talk without troubling herself to answer, and privately determined to beg Mr. Monckton would fight her battle.

She was not, therefore, displeased by his interruption,

though very much surprised by the sight of his person, when, in the midst of Mr. Briggs's oratory, Mr. Hobson entered the parlour.

"I ask pardon, ma'am," cried he, "if I intrude; but I made free to call upon the account of two ladies that are acquaintances of yours, that are quite, as one may say, at their wit's ends."

"What is the matter with them, Sir?"

"Why, ma'am, no great matter, but mothers are soon frightened, and when once they are upon the fret, one may as well talk to the boards!* they know no more of reasoning and arguing, than they do of a shop ledger! however, my maxim is this; every body in their way; one has no more right to expect courageousness from a lady in them cases, than one has from a child in arms; for what I say is, they have not the proper use of their heads, which makes it very excusable."

"But what has occasioned any alarm? nothing, I hope, is the matter with Miss Belfield?"

"No, ma'am; thank God, the young lady enjoys her health very well: but she is taking on just in the same way as her mamma, as what can be more natural? Example, ma'am, is apt to be catching, and one lady's crying makes another think she must do the same, for a little thing serves for a lady's tears, being they can cry at any time: but a man is quite of another nature, let him but have a good conscience, and be clear of the world, and I'll engage he'll not wash his face without soap! that's what I say!"

"Will, will!" cried Mr. Briggs, "do it myself! never use soap; nothing but waste; take a little sand; does as well."

"Let every man have his own proposal;" answered Hobson; "for my part, I take every morning a large bowl of water, and souse my whole head in it; and then when I've rubbed it dry, on goes my wig, and I am quite fresh and agreeable: and then I take a walk in Tottenham Court Road as far as the Tabernacle,* or thereabouts, and snuff in a little fresh country air, and then I come back, with a good wholesome appetite, and in a fine breathing heat, asking the young lady's pardon; and I enjoy my pot of fresh tea, and

my round of hot toast and butter, with as good a relish as
if I was a Prince.''

"Pot of fresh tea,'' cried Briggs, "bring a man to ruin;
toast and butter! never suffer it in my house. Breakfast on
water-gruel, sooner done; fills one up* in a second. Give it
my servants; can't eat much of it, bob* 'em there!'' nodding
significantly.

"Water-gruel!'' exclaimed Mr. Hobson, "why I could
not get it down if I might have the world for it! it would
make me quite sick, asking the young lady's pardon, by
reason I should always think I was preparing for the small-
pox.* My notion is quite of another nature; the first thing
I do is to have a good fire; for what I say is this, if a man
is cold in his fingers, it's odds if ever he gets warm in his
purse! ha! ha! *warm*, you take me, Sir? I mean a pun.
Though I ought to ask pardon, for I suppose the young lady
don't know what I am a saying.''

"I should indeed be better pleased, Sir,'' said Cecilia, "to
hear what you have to say about Miss Belfield.''

"Why, ma'am, the thing is this; we have been expecting
the young 'Squire, as I call him, all the morning, and he has
never come; so Mrs. Belfield, not knowing where to send
after him, was of opinion he might be here, knowing your
kindness to him, and that.''

"You make the enquiry at the wrong place, Sir,'' said
Cecilia, much provoked by the implication it conveyed; "if
Mr. Belfield is in this house, you must seek him with Mr.
Monckton.''

"You take no offence, I hope, ma'am, at my just asking
of the question? for Mrs. Belfield crying, and being in that
dilemma, I thought I could do no less than oblige her by
coming to see if the young gentleman was here.''

"What's this? what's this?'' cried Mr. Briggs eagerly;
"who are talking of? hay?—who do mean? is this the sweet
heart? eh, Duck?''

"No, no, Sir,'' cried Cecilia.

"No tricks! won't be bit!* who is it? will know; tell me,
I say!''

"*I'll* tell you, Sir,'' cried Mr. Hobson; "it's a very

handsome young gentleman, with as fine a person, and as genteel a way of behaviour, and withal, as pretty a manner of dressing himself, and that, as any lady need desire. He has no great head for business, as I am told, but the ladies don't stand much upon that topic, being they know nothing of it themselves."

"Has he got the ready?" cried Mr. Briggs, impatiently; "can cast an account? that's the point; can come down handsomely? eh?"

"Why as to that, Sir, I'm not bound to speak to a gentleman's private affairs. What's my own, is my own, and what is another person's, is another person's; that's my way of arguing, and that's what I call talking to the purpose."

"Dare say he's a rogue! don't have him, chick. Bet a wager i'n't worth two shillings; and that will go for powder and pomatum; hate a plaistered pate; commonly a numscull: love a good bob jerom."*

"Why this is talking quite wide of the mark," said Mr. Hobson, "to suppose a young lady of fortunes would marry a man with a bob jerom. What I say is, let every body follow their nature; that's the way to be comfortable; and then if they pay every one his own, who's a right to call 'em to account, whether they wear a bob jerom, or a pig-tail down to the calves of their legs?"*

"Ay, ay," cried Briggs, sneeringly, "or whether they stuff their gullets with hot rounds of toast and butter."

"And what if they do, Sir?" returned Hobson, a little angrily; "when a man's got above the world, where's the harm of living a little genteel? as to a round of toast and butter, and a few oysters, fresh opened, by way of a damper* before dinner, no man need be ashamed of them, provided he pays as he goes: and as to living upon water-gruel, and scrubbing one's flesh with sand, one might as well be a galley-slave at once. You don't understand life, Sir, I see that."

"Do! do!" cried Briggs, speaking through his shut teeth; "you're out there! oysters!—come to ruin, tell you! bring you to jail!"

"To jail, Sir?" exclaimed Hobson, "this is talking quite

ungenteel! let every man be civil; that's what *I* say, for that's
the way to make every thing agreeable: but as to telling a
man he'll go to jail, and that, it's tantamount to affronting
him."

A rap at the street-door gave now a new relief to Cecilia,
who began to grow very apprehensive lest the delight of
spending money, thus warmly contested with that of
hoarding it, should give rise to a quarrel, which, between
two such sturdy champions for their own opinions, might
lead to a conclusion rather more rough and violent than she
desired to witness: but when the parlour-door opened,
instead of Mr. Delvile, whom she now fully expected, Mr.
Albany made his entrance.

This was rather distressing, as her real business with her
guardians made it proper her conference with them should
be undisturbed: and Albany was not a man with whom a
hint that she was engaged could be risked: but she had
made no preparation to guard against interruption, as her
little acquaintance in London had prevented her expecting
any visitors.

He advanced with a solemn air to Cecilia, and, looking as
if hardly determined whether to speak with severity or
gentleness, said, "once more I come to prove thy sincerity;
now wilt thou go with me where sorrow calls thee? sorrow
thy charity can mitigate?"

"I am very much concerned," she answered, "but indeed
at present it is utterly impossible."

"Again," cried he, with a look at once stern and disappointed, "again thou failest me? what wanton trifling! why
shouldst thou thus elate a worn-out mind, only to make it
feel its lingering credulity? or why, teaching me to think I
had found an angel, so unkindly undeceive me?"

"Indeed," said Cecilia, much affected by this reproof, "if
you knew how heavy a loss I had personally suffered—"

"I do know it," cried he, "and I grieved for thee when
I heard it. Thou hast lost a faithful old friend, a loss which
with every setting sun thou may'st mourn, for the rising sun
will never repair it! but was that a reason for shunning the
duties of humanity? was the sight of death a motive for

neglecting the claims of benevolence? ought it not rather to
have hastened your fulfilling them? and should not your own
suffering experience of the brevity of life, have taught you
the vanity of all things but preparing for its end?''

"Perhaps so, but my grief at that time made me think
only of myself."

"And of what else dost thou think now?"

"Most probably of the same person still!" said she, half
smiling, "but yet believe me, I have real business to
transact."

"Frivolous, unmeaning, ever-ready excuses! what business is so important as the relief of a fellow-creature?''

"I shall not, I hope, there," answered she, with alacrity,
"be backward; but at least for this morning I must beg to
make you my Almoner."

She then took out her purse.

Mr. Briggs and Mr. Hobson, whose quarrel had been
suspended by the appearance of a third person, and who had
stood during this short dialogue in silent amazement, having
first lost their anger in their mutual consternation, now lost
their consternation in their mutual displeasure: Mr. Hobson
felt offended to hear business spoken of slightly, and Mr.
Briggs felt enraged at the sight of Cecilia's ready purse.
Neither of them, however, knew which way to interfere, the
stern gravity of Albany, joined to a language too lofty for
their comprehension, intimidating them both. They took,
however, the relief of communing with one another, and
Mr. Hobson said in a whisper "This, you must know, is, I
am told, a very particular old gentleman; quite what I call
a genius. He comes often to my house, to see my lodger Miss
Henny Belfield, though I never happened to light upon him
myself, except once in the passage: but what I hear of him
is this; he makes a practice, as one may say, of going about
into people's houses, to do nothing but find fault."

"Shan't get into mine!" returned Briggs; "promise him
that! don't half like him; be bound he's an old sharper."

Cecilia, mean time, enquired what he desired to have.

Half a guinea, he answered.

"Will that do?"

"For those who have nothing," said he, "it is much. Hereafter, you may assist them again. Go but and see their distresses, and you will wish to give them every thing."

Mr. Briggs now, when actually between her fingers he saw the half guinea, could contain no longer; he twitched the sleeve of her gown, and pinching her arm, with a look of painful eagerness, said in a whisper "Don't give it! don't let him have it! chouse him, chouse him! nothing but an old bite!"

"Pardon me, Sir," said Cecilia, in a low voice, "his character is very well known to me." And then, disengaging her arm from him, she presented her little offering.

At this sight, Mr. Briggs was almost outrageous, and losing in his wrath, all fear of the stranger, he burst forth with fury into the following outcries, "Be ruined! see it plainly; be fleeced! be stript! be robbed! won't have a gown to your back! won't have a shoe to your foot! won't have a rag in the world! be a beggar in the street! come to the parish! rot in a jail?—half a guinea at a time!—enough to break the Great Mogul!"*

"Inhuman spirit of selfish parsimony!" exclaimed Albany, "repinest thou at this loan, given from thousands to those who have worse than nothing? who pay to day in hunger for bread they borrowed yesterday from pity? who to save themselves from the deadly pangs of famine, solicit but what the rich know not when they possess, and miss not when they give?"

"Anan!" cried Briggs; recovering his temper from the perplexity of his understanding, at a discourse to which his ears were wholly unaccustomed, "what d'ye say?"

"If to thyself distress may cry in vain," continued Albany, "if thy own heart resists the suppliant's prayer, callous to entreaty, and hardened in the world, suffer, at least, a creature yet untainted, who melts at sorrow, and who glows with charity, to pay from her vast wealth a generous tax of thankfulness, that fate has not reversed her doom, and those whom she relieves, relieve not her!"

"Anan!" was again all the wondering Mr. Briggs could say.

"Pray, ma'am," said Mr. Hobson to Cecilia, "if its no offence, was the Gentleman ever a player?"

"I fancy not, indeed!"

"I ask pardon, then, ma'am; I mean no harm; but my notion was the gentleman might be speaking something by heart."

"Is it but on the stage, humanity exists?" cried Albany, indignantly; "Oh thither hasten, then, ye monopolizers of plenty! ye selfish, unfeeling engrossers of wealth, which ye dissipate without enjoying, and of abundance, which ye waste while ye refuse to distribute! thither, thither haste, if there humanity exists!"

"As to engrossing,"* said Mr. Hobson, happy to hear at last a word with which he was familiar, "it's what I never approved myself. My maxim is this; if a man makes a fair penny, without any underhand dealings, why he has as much a title to enjoy his pleasure as the Chief Justice, or the Lord Chancellor:* and its odds but he's as happy as a greater man. Though what I hold to be best of all, is a clear conscience, with a neat income of 2 or 3000 a year.* That's my notion; and I don't think it's a bad one."

"Weak policy of short-sighted ignorance!" cried Albany, "to wish for what, if used, brings care, and if neglected, remorse! have you not now beyond what nature craves? why then still sigh for more?"

"Why?" cried Mr. Briggs, who by dint of deep attention began now better to comprehend him, "why to buy in, to be sure! ever hear of stocks, eh? know any thing of money?"

"Still to make more and more," cried Albany, "and wherefore? to spend in vice and idleness, or hoard in chearless misery! not to give succour to the wretched, not to support the falling; all is for self, however little wanted, all goes to added stores, or added luxury; no fellow-creature served, nor even one beggar relieved!"

"Glad of it!" cried Briggs, "glad of it; would not have 'em relieved; don't like 'em; hate a beggar; ought to be all whipt; live upon spunging."

"Why as to a beggar, I must needs say," cried Mr. Hobson, "I am by no means an approver of that mode of proceeding; being I take 'em all for cheats: for what I say is this, what a man earns, he earns, and it's no man's business to enquire what he spends, for a free-born Englishman is his own master by the nature of the law, and as to his being a subject, why a Duke is no more, nor a Judge, nor the Lord High Chancellor, and the like of those; which makes it tantamount to nothing, being he is answerable to nobody by the right of Magna Charta:* except in cases of treason, felony, and that. But as to a beggar, it's quite another thing; he comes and asks me for money; but what has he to shew for it? what does he bring me in exchange? why a long story that he i'n't worth a penny! what's that to me? nothing at all. Let every man have his own; that's my way of arguing.''

''Ungentle mortals!'' cried Albany, ''in wealth exulting; even* in inhumanity! think you these wretched outcasts have less sensibility than yourselves? think you, in cold and hunger, they lose those feelings which even in voluptuous prosperity from time to time disturb you? you say they are all cheats? 'tis but the niggard cant* of avarice, to lure away remorse from obduracy. Think you the naked wanderer begs from choice? give him your wealth and try.''

''Give him a whip!'' cried Briggs, ''sha'n't have a souse!* send him to Bridewell!* nothing but a pauper; hate 'em; hate 'em all! full of tricks; break their own legs, put out their arms, cut off their fingers, snap their own ancles,—all for what? to get at the chink!* to chouse us of cash! ought to be well flogged; have 'em all sent to the Thames;* worse than the Convicts.''

''Poor subterfuge of callous cruelty! you cheat yourselves, to shun the fraud of others! and yet, how better do you use the wealth so guarded? what nobler purpose can it answer to you, than even a chance to snatch some wretch from sinking? think less how *much* ye save, and more for *what*; and then consider how thy full coffers may hereafter make reparation, for the empty catalogue of thy virtues.''

''Anan!'' said Mr. Briggs, again lost in perplexity and wonder.

''Oh yet,'' continued Albany, turning towards Cecilia,

"preach not here the hardness which ye practice; rather amend yourselves than corrupt her; and give with liberality what ye ought to receive with gratitude!"

"This is not my doctrine," cried Hobson; "I am not a near man, neither, but as to giving at that rate, it's quite out of character. I have as good a right to my own savings, as to my own gettings; and what I say is this, who'll give to *me*? let me see that, and it's quite another thing: and begin who will, I'll be bound to go on with him, pound for pound, or pence for pence. But as to giving to them beggars, it's what I don't approve; I pay the poor's rate,* and that's what I call charity enough for any man. But for the matter of living well, and spending one's money handsomely, and having one's comforts about one, why it's a thing of another nature, and I can say this for myself, and that is, I never grudged myself any thing in my life. I always made myself agreeable, and lived on the best. That's my way."

"Bad way too," cried Briggs, "never get on with it, never see beyond your nose; won't be worth a plum while your head wags!" then, taking Cecilia apart, "hark'ee, my duck," he added, pointing to Albany, "who is that Mr. Bounce,* eh? what is he?"

"I have known him but a short time, Sir; but I think of him very highly."

"Is he a *good** man? that's the point, is he a *good* man?"

"Indeed he appears to me uncommonly benevolent and charitable."

"But that i'n't the thing; is he *warm?* that's the point, is he *warm?*"

"If you mean *passionate*," said Cecilia, "I believe the energy of his manner is merely to enforce what he says."

"Don't take me, don't take me,"* cried he, impatiently; "can come down with the ready, that's the matter; can chink the little gold boys?* eh?"

"Why I rather fear not by his appearance; but I know nothing of his affairs."

"What does come for? eh? come a courting?"

"Mercy on me, no!"

"What for then? only a spunging?"

"No, indeed. He seems to have no wish but to assist and plead for others."

"All fudge! think he i'n't touched?* ay, ay; nothing but a trick! only to get at the chink: see he's as poor as a rat, talks of nothing but giving money; a bad sign! if he'd got any, would not do it. Wanted to make us come down; warrant thought to bam us all! out there! a'n't so soon gulled."

A knock at the street-door gave now a new interruption, and Mr. Delvile at length appeared.

Cecilia, whom his sight could not fail to disconcert, felt doubly distressed by the unnecessary presence of Albany and Hobson; she regretted the absence of Mr. Monckton, who could easily have taken them away; for though without scruple she could herself have acquainted Mr. Hobson she had business, she dreaded offending Albany, whose esteem she was ambitious of obtaining.

Mr. Delvile entered the room with an air stately and erect; he took off his hat, but deigned not to make the smallest inclination of his head, nor offered any excuse to Mr. Briggs for being past the hour of his appointment: but having advanced a few paces, without looking either to the right or left, said, "as I have never acted, my coming may not, perhaps, be essential; but as my name is in the Dean's Will, and I have once or twice met the other executors mentioned in it, I think it a duty I owe to my own heirs to prevent any possible future enquiry or trouble to them."

This speech was directly addressed to no one, though meant to be attended to by every one, and seemed proudly uttered as a mere apology to himself for not having declined the meeting.

Cecilia, though she recovered from her confusion by the help of her aversion to this self-sufficiency, made not any answer. Albany retired to a corner of the room; Mr. Hobson began to believe it was time for him to depart; and Mr. Briggs thinking only of the quarrel in which he had separated with Mr. Delvile in the summer, stood swelling with venom, which he longed for an opportunity to spit out.

Mr. Delvile, who regarded this silence as the effect of his awe-inspiring presence, became rather more complacent; but casting his eyes round the room, and perceiving the two strangers, he was visibly surprised, and looking at Cecilia for some explanation, seemed to stand suspended from the purpose of his visit till he heard one.

Cecilia, earnest to have the business concluded, turned to Mr. Briggs, and said, "Sir, here is pen and ink: are you to write, or am I? or what is to be done?"

"No, no," said he, with a sneer, "give it t'other; all in our turn; don't come before his Grace the Right Honourable Mr. Vampus."

"Before whom, Sir?" said Mr. Delvile, reddening.

"Before my Lord Don Pedigree," answered Briggs, with a spiteful grin, "know him? eh? ever hear of such a person?"

Mr. Delvile coloured still deeper, but turning contemptuously from him, disdained making any reply.

Mr. Briggs, who now regarded him as a defeated man, said exultingly to Mr. Hobson, "what do stand* here for?—hay?—fall o' your marrowbones;* don't see 'Squire High and Mighty?"

"As to falling on my marrowbones," answered Mr. Hobson, "it's what I shall do to no man, except he was the King himself, or the like of that, and going to make me Chancellor of the Exchequer, or Commissioner of Excise.* Not that I mean the gentleman any offence; but a man's a man, and for one man to worship another is quite out of law."

"Must, must!" cried Briggs, "tell all his old grand-dads* else: keeps 'em in a roll; locks 'em in a closet; says his prayers to 'em; can't live without 'em: likes 'em better than cash!—wish had 'em here! pop 'em all in the sink!"*

"If your intention, Sir," cried Mr. Delvile, fiercely, "is only to insult me, I am prepared for what measures I shall take. I declined seeing you in my own house, that I might not be under the same restraint as when it was my unfortunate lot to meet you last."

"Who cares?" cried Briggs, with an air of defiance, "what

can do, eh? poke me into a family vault? bind me o' top of an old monument? tie me to a stinking carcase? make a corpse of me, and call it one of your famous cousins?—''

''For heaven's sake, Mr. Briggs,'' interrupted Cecilia, who saw that Mr. Delvile, trembling with passion, scarce refrained lifting up his stick, ''be appeased, and let us finish our business!''

Albany now, hearing in Cecilia's voice the alarm with which she was seized, came forward and exclaimed, ''whence this unmeaning dissention? to what purpose this irritating abuse? Oh vain and foolish! live ye so happily, last ye so long, that time and peace may thus be trifled with?''

''There, there!'' cried Briggs, holding up his finger at Mr. Delvile, ''have it now! got old Mr. Bounce upon you! give you enough of it; promise you that!''

''Restrain,'' continued Albany, ''this idle wrath; and if ye have ardent passions, employ them to nobler uses; let them stimulate acts of virtue, let them animate deeds of beneficence! Oh waste not spirits that may urge you to good, lead you to honour, warm you to charity, in poor and angry words, in unfriendly, unmanly debate!''

Mr. Delvile, who from the approach of Albany, had given him his whole attention, was struck with astonishment at this address, and almost petrified with wonder at his language and exhortations.

''Why I must own,'' said Mr. Hobson, ''as to this matter I am much of the same mind myself; for quarreling's a thing I don't uphold; being it advances one no way; for what I say is this, if a man gets the better, he's only where he was before, and if he gets worsted, why it's odds but the laugh's against him: so, if I may make bold to give my verdict, I would have one of these gentlemen take the other by the hand, and so put an end to bad words. That's my maxim, and that's what I call being agreeable.''

Mr. Delvile, at the words *one of these gentlemen take the other by the hand*, looked scornfully upon Mr. Hobson, with a frown that expressed his highest indignation, at being thus familiarly coupled with Mr. Briggs. And then, turning from him to Cecilia, haughtily said, ''Are these two persons,'' pointing towards Albany and Hobson, "waiting here to be witnesses to any transaction?"

"No, Sir, no," cried Hobson, "I don't mean to intrude, I am going directly. So you can give me no insight, ma'am," addressing Cecilia, "as to where I might light upon Mr. Belfield?"

"Me? no!" cried she, much provoked by observing that Mr. Delvile suddenly looked at her.

"Well, ma'am, well, I mean no harm: only I hold it that the right way to hear of a young gentleman, is to ask for him of a young lady: that's my maxim. Come, Sir," to Mr. Briggs, "you and I had like to have fallen out, but what I say is this; let no man bear malice; that's my way: so I hope we part without ill blood?"

"Ay, ay;" said Mr. Briggs, giving him a nod.

"Well, then," added Hobson, "I hope the good-will may go round, and that not only you and I, but these two good old gentlemen will also lend a hand."

Mr. Delvile now was at a loss which way to turn for very rage; but after looking at every one with a face flaming with ire,* he said to Cecilia, "If you have collected together these persons for the purpose of affronting me, I must beg you to remember I am not one to be affronted with impunity!"

Cecilia, half frightened, was beginning an answer that disclaimed any such intention, when Albany, with the most indignant energy, called out, "Oh pride of heart, with littleness of soul! check this vile arrogance, too vain for man, and spare to others some part of that lenity thou nourishest for thyself, or justly bestow on thyself that contempt thou nourishest for others!"

And with these words he sternly left the house.

The thunderstruck Mr. Delvile began now to fancy that all the demons of torment were designedly let loose upon him, and his surprise and resentment operated so powerfully that it was only in broken sentences he could express either. "Very extraordinary!—a new method of conduct!—liberties to which I am not much used!—impertinences I shall not hastily forget,—treatment that would scarce be pardonable to a person wholly unknown!—"

"Why indeed, Sir," said Hobson, "I can't but say it was rather a cut up;* but the old gentleman is what one may call a genius, which makes it a little excusable; for he does things all his own way, and I am told it's the same thing who he speaks to, so he can but find fault, and that."

"Sir," interrupted the still more highly offended Mr. Delvile, "what *you* may be told is extremely immaterial to *me*; and I must take the liberty to hint to you, a conversation of this easy kind is not what I am much in practice in hearing."

"Sir, I ask pardon," said Hobson, "I meant nothing but what was agreeable; however, I have done, and I wish you good day. Your humble servant, ma'am, and I hope, Sir," to Mr. Briggs, "you won't begin bad words again?"

"No, no," said Briggs, "ready to make up; all at end;* only don't much like *Spain*, that's all!" winking significantly, "nor a'n't over fond of a *skeleton!*"

Mr. Hobson now retired; and Mr. Delvile and Mr. Briggs, being both wearied and both in haste to have done, settled in about five minutes all for which they met, after passing more than an hour in agreeing what that was.

Mr. Briggs then, saying he had an engagement upon business, declined settling his own accounts till another time, but promised to see Cecilia again soon, and added, "be sure take care of that old Mr. Bounce! cracked in the noddle; see that with half an eye! better not trust him! break out some day:* do you a mischief!"

He then went away: but while the parlour-door was still open, to the no little surprise of Cecilia, the servant announced Mr. Belfield. He hardly entered the room, and his countenance spoke haste and eagerness. "I have this moment, madam," he said, "been informed a complaint has been lodged* against me here, and I could not rest till I had the honour of assuring you, that though I have been rather dilatory, I have not neglected my appointment, nor has the condescension of your interference been thrown away."

He then bowed, shut the door, and ran off. Cecilia, though happy to understand by this speech that he was actually restored to his family, was sorry at these repeated intrusions in the presence of Mr. Delvile, who was now the only one that remained.

She expected every instant that he would ring for his chair, which he kept in waiting; but, after a pause of some continuance, to her equal surprise and disturbance, he made the following speech. "As it is probable I am now for the last time alone with you, ma'am, and as it is certain we shall meet no more upon business, I cannot, in justice to my own character, and to the respect I retain for the memory of the Dean, your uncle, take a final leave of the office with which he was pleased to invest me, without first fulfilling my own ideas of the duty it requires from me, by giving you some counsel relating to your future establishment."

This was not a preface much to enliven Cecilia; it prepared her for such speeches as she was least willing to hear, and gave to her the mixt and painful sensation of spirits depressed, with pride alarmed.

"My numerous engagements," he continued, "and the appropriation of my time, already settled, to their various claims, must make me brief in what I have to represent, and somewhat, perhaps, abrupt in coming to the purpose. But that you will excuse."

Cecilia disdained to humour this arrogance by any compliments or concessions: she was silent, therefore; and when they were both seated, he went on.

"You are now at a time of life when it is natural for young women to wish for some connection: and the largeness of your fortune will remove from you such difficulties as prove bars to the pretensions, in this expensive age, of those who possess not such advantages. It would have been some pleasure to me, while I yet considered you as my Ward, to have seen you properly disposed of: but as that time is past, I can only give you some general advice, which you may follow or neglect as you think fit. By giving it, I shall satisfy myself; for the rest, I am not responsible."

He paused; but Cecilia felt less and less inclination to make use of the opportunity by speaking in her turn.

"Yet though, as I just now hinted, young women of

large fortunes may have little trouble in finding themselves establishments, they ought not, therefore, to trifle when proper ones are in their power, nor to suppose themselves equal to any they may chance to desire.''

Cecilia coloured high at this pointed reprehension; but feeling her disgust every moment encrease, determined to sustain herself with dignity, and at least not suffer* him to perceive the triumph of his ostentation and rudeness.

''The proposals,'' he continued ''of the Earl of Ernolf had always my approbation; it was certainly an ill-judged thing to neglect such an opportunity of being honourably settled. The clause of the name was, to *him*, immaterial; since his own name half a century ago was unheard of, and since he is himself only known by his title.* He is still, however, I have authority to acquaint you, perfectly well disposed to renew his application to you.''

''I am sorry, Sir,'' said Cecilia coldly, ''to hear it.''

''You have, perhaps, some other better offer in view?''

''No, Sir,'' cried she, with spirit, ''nor even in desire.''

''Am I, then, to infer that some inferior offer has more chance of your approbation?''

''There is no reason, Sir, to infer any thing; I am content with my actual situation, and have, at present, neither prospect nor intention of changing it.''

''I perceive, but without surprise, your unwillingness to discuss the subject; nor do I mean to press it: I shall merely offer to your consideration one caution, and then relieve you from my presence. Young women of ample fortunes, who are early independent, are sometimes apt to presume they may do every thing with impunity; but they are mistaken; they are as liable to censure as those who are wholly unprovided for.''

''I hope, Sir,'' said Cecilia, staring, ''this at least is a caution rather drawn from my situation than my behaviour?''

''I mean not, ma'am, narrowly to go into, or investigate the subject; what I have said you may make your own use of; I have only to observe further, that when young women, at your time of life, are at all negligent of so nice a thing as reputation, they commonly live to repent it."

He then arose to go, but Cecilia, not more offended than amazed, said, "I must beg, Sir, you will explain yourself!"

"Certainly this matter," he answered, "must be immaterial to *me*: yet, as I have once been your guardian by the nomination of the Dean your uncle, I cannot forbear making an effort towards preventing any indiscretion: and frequent visits to a young man——"

"Good God! Sir," interrupted Cecilia, "what is it you mean?"

"It can certainly, as I said before, be nothing to *me*, though I should be glad to see you in better hands: but I cannot suppose you have been led to take such steps without some serious plan; and I would advise you, without loss of time, to think better of what you are about."

"Should I think, Sir, to eternity," cried Cecilia, "I could never conjecture what you mean!"

"You may not chuse," said he, proudly, "to understand me; but I have done. If it had been in my power to have interfered in your service with my Lord Derford, notwithstanding my reluctance to being involved in any fresh employment, I should have made a point of not refusing it: but this young man is nobody,—a very imprudent connection—"

"What young man, Sir?"

"Nay, *I* know nothing of him! it is by no means likely I should: but as I had already been informed of your attention to him, the corroborating incidents of my servant's following you to his house, his friend's seeking him at yours, and his own waiting upon you this morning; were not well calculated to make me withdraw my credence to it."

"Is it, then, Mr. Belfield, Sir, concerning whom you draw these inferences, from circumstances the most accidental and unmeaning?"

"It is by no means my practice," cried he, haughtily, and with evident marks of high displeasure at this speech, "to believe any thing lightly, or without even unquestionable authority; what once, therefore, I have credited, I do not often find erroneous. Mistake not, however, what I have said into supposing I have any objection to your marrying; on the contrary, it had been for the honour of my family had you been married a year ago: I should not then have suffered the degradation of seeing a son of the first expectations in the kingdom upon the point of renouncing his birth, nor a woman of the first distinction ruined in her health, and broken for ever in her constitution.''

The emotions of Cecilia at this speech were too powerful for concealment; her colour varied, now reddening with indignation, now turning pale with apprehension; she arose, she trembled and sat down, she arose again, but not knowing what to say or what to do, again sat down.

Mr. Delvile then, making a stiff bow, wished her good morning.

''Go not so, Sir!'' cried she, in faltering accents; ''let me at least convince you of the mistake with regard to Mr. Belfield—''

''My mistakes, ma'am,'' said he, with a contemptuous smile, ''are perhaps not easily convicted: and I may possibly labour under others that would give you no less trouble: it may therefore be better to avoid any further disquisition.''

''No, not better,'' answered she, again recovering her courage from this fresh provocation; ''I fear no disquisition; on the contrary, it is my interest to solicit one.''

''This intrepidity in a young woman,'' said he, ironically, ''is certainly very commendable; and doubtless, as you are your own mistress, your having run out great part of your fortune, is nothing beyond what you have a right to do.''

''Me!'' cried Cecilia, astonished, ''run out great part of my fortune!''

''Perhaps that is another *mistake!* I have not often been so unfortunate; and you are not, then, in debt?''

''In debt, Sir?''

''Nay, I have no intention to enquire into your affairs. Good morning to you, ma'am.''

''I beg, I entreat, Sir, that you will stop!—make me, at least, understand what you mean, whether you deign to hear my justification or not.''

''O, I am mistaken, it seems! misinformed, deceived; and

you have neither spent more than you have received, nor taken up money of Jews? your minority has been clear of debts? and your fortune, now you are of age, will be free from incumbrances?''

Cecilia, who now began to understand him, eagerly answered, ''do you mean, Sir, the money which I took up last spring?''

''O no; by no means, I conceive the whole to be a *mistake!*''

And he went to the door.

''Hear me but a moment, Sir!'' cried she hastily, following him; ''since you know of that transaction, do not refuse to listen to its occasion; I took up the money for Mr. Harrel; it was all, and solely for him.''

''For Mr. Harrel, was it?'' said he, with an air of supercilious incredulity; ''that was rather an unlucky step. Your servant, ma'am.''

And he opened the door.

''You will not hear me, then? you will not credit me?'' cried she in the cruellest agitation.

''Some other time, ma'am; at present my avocations are too numerous to permit me.''

And again, stiffly bowing, he called to his servants, who were waiting in the hall, and put himself into his chair.

CHAPTER V

A Suspicion

CECILIA was now left in a state of perturbation that was hardly to be endured. The contempt with which she had been treated during the whole visit was nothing short of insult, but the accusations with which it was concluded did not more irritate than astonish her.

That some strange prejudice had been taken against her, even more than belonged to her connection with young Delvile, the message brought her by Dr. Lyster had given her reason to suppose: what that prejudice was she now knew, though how excited she was still ignorant; but she found Mr. Delvile had been informed she had taken up money of a Jew, without having heard it was for Mr. Harrel, and that he had been acquainted with her visits in Portland-Street, without seeming to know Mr. Belfield had a sister. Two charges such as these, so serious in their nature, and so destructive of her character, filled her with horror and consternation, and even somewhat served to palliate his illiberal and injurious behaviour.

But how reports thus false and thus disgraceful should be raised, and by what dark work of slander and malignity they had been spread, remained a doubt inexplicable. They could not, she was certain, be the mere rumour of chance, since in both the assertions there was some foundation of truth, however cruelly perverted, or basely over-charged.

This led her to consider how few people there were not only who had interest, but who had power to propagate such calumnies; even her acquaintance with the Belfields she remembered not ever mentioning, for she knew none of their friends, and none of her own knew them. How, then, should it be circulated, that she "visited often at the house?" how ever be invented that it was from her "attention to the young man?" Henrietta, she was sure, was too good and too innocent to be guilty of such perfidy; and the young man himself had always shewn a modesty and propriety that manifested his total freedom from the vanity of such a suspicion, and an elevation of sentiment that would have taught him to scorn the boast, even if he believed the partiality.

The mother, however, had neither been so modest nor so rational; she had openly avowed her opinion that Cecilia was in love with her son; and as that son, by never offering himself, had never been refused, her opinion had received no check of sufficient force, for a mind so gross and literal, to change it.

This part, therefore, of the charge she gave to Mrs. Belfield, whose officious and loquacious forwardness she concluded had induced her to narrate her suspicions, till, step by step, they had reached Mr. Delvile.

But though able, by the probability of this conjecture, to

account for the report concerning Belfield, the whole affair of the debt remained a difficulty not to be solved. Mr. Harrel, his wife, Mr. Arnott, the Jew and Mr. Monckton, were the only persons to whom the transaction was known; and though from five, a secret, in the course of so many months, might easily be supposed likely to transpire, those five were so particularly bound to silence, not only for her interest but their own, that it was not unreasonable to believe it as safe among them all, as if solely consigned to one. For herself, she had revealed it to no creature but Mr. Monckton; not even to Delvile; though, upon her consenting to marry him, he had an undoubted right to be acquainted with the true state of her affairs; but such had been the hurry, distress, confusion and irresolution of her mind at that period, that this whole circumstance had been driven from it entirely, and she had, since, frequently blamed herself for such want of recollection. Mr. Harrel, for a thousand reasons, she was certain had never named it; and had the communication come from his widow or from Mr. Arnott, the motives would have been related as well as the debt, and she had been spared the reproach of contracting it for purposes of her own extravagance. The Jew, indeed, was, to her, under no obligation of secrecy, but he had an obligation far more binding,—he was tied to himself.*

A suspicion now arose in her mind which made it thrill with horror; "good God!" she exclaimed, "can Mr. Monckton—"

She stopt, even to herself;—she checked the idea;—she drove it hastily from her;—she was certain it was false and cruel;—she hated herself for having started it.

"No," cried she, "he is my friend, the confirmed friend of many years, my well-wisher from childhood, my zealous counsellor and assistant almost from my birth to this hour:—such perfidy from him would not even be human!"

Yet still her perplexity was undiminished; the affair was undoubtedly known, and it only could be known by the treachery of some one entrusted with it: and however earnestly her generosity combated her rising suspicions, she could not wholly quell them; and Mr. Monckton's strange aversion to the Delviles, his earnestness to break off her connexion with them, occurred to her remembrance, and haunted her perforce with surmises to his disadvantage.

That gentleman, when he came home, found her in this comfortless and fluctuating state, endeavouring to form conjectures upon what had happened, yet unable to succeed, but by suggestions which one moment excited her abhorrence of him, and the next of herself.

He enquired, with his usual appearance of easy friendliness, into what had passed with her two guardians, and how she had settled her affairs. She answered without hesitation all his questions, but her manner was cold and reserved, though her communication was frank.

This was not unheeded by Mr. Monckton, who, after a short time, begged to know if any thing had disturbed her.

Cecilia ashamed of her doubts, though unable to get rid of them, then endeavoured to brighten up, and changed the subject to the difficulties she had had to encounter from the obstinacy of Mr. Briggs.

Mr. Monckton for a while humoured this evasion; but when, by her own exertion, her solemnity began to wear off, he repeated his interrogatory, and would not be satisfied without an answer.

Cecilia, earnest that surmises so injurious should be removed, then honestly, but without comments, related the scene which had just past between Mr. Delvile and herself.

No comments were, however, wanting to explain to Mr. Monckton the change of her behaviour: "I see," he cried hastily, "what you cannot but suspect; and I will go myself to Mr. Delvile, and insist upon his clearing me."

Cecilia, shocked to have thus betrayed what was passing within her, assured him his vindication required not such a step, and begged he would counsel her how to discover this treachery, without drawing from her concern at it a conclusion so offensive to himself.

He was evidently, however, and greatly disturbed; he declared his own wonder equal to her's how the affair had been betrayed, expressed the warmest indignation at the malevolent insinuations against her conduct, and lamented with mingled acrimony and grief, that there should exist even the possibility of casting the odium of such villainy upon himself.

Cecilia, distressed, perplexed, and ashamed at once, again endeavoured to appease him, and though a lurking doubt obstinately clung to her understanding, the purity of her own principles, and the softness of her heart, pleaded strongly for his innocence, and urged her to detest her suspicion, though to conquer it they were unequal.

"It is true," said he, with an air ingenuous though mortified, "I dislike the Delviles, and have always disliked them; they appear to me a jealous, vindictive, and insolent race, and I should have thought I betrayed the faithful regard I professed for you, had I concealed my opinion when I saw you in danger of forming an alliance with them; I spoke to you, therefore, with honest zeal, thoughtless of any enmity I might draw upon myself; but though it was an interference from which I hoped, by preventing the connection, to contribute to your happiness, it was not with a design to stop it at the expence of your character,—a design black, horrible and diabolical! a design which must be formed by a Dæmon, but which even a Dæmon could never, I think, execute!"

The candour of this speech, in which his aversion to the Delviles was openly acknowledged, and rationally justified, somewhat quieted the suspicions of Cecilia, which far more anxiously sought to be confuted than confirmed: she began, therefore, to conclude that some accident, inexplicable as unfortunate, had occasioned the partial discovery to Mr. Delvile, by which her own goodness proved the source of her defamation: and though something still hung upon her mind that destroyed that firm confidence she had hitherto felt in the friendship of Mr. Monckton, she held it utterly unjust to condemn him without proof, which she was not more unable to procure, than to satisfy herself with any reason why so perfidiously he should calumniate her.

Comfortless, however, and tormented with conjectures equally vague and afflicting, she could only clear him to be lost in perplexity, she could only accuse him to be penetrated with horror. She endeavoured to suspend her judgment till time should develop the mystery, and only for the present sought to finish her business and leave London.

She renewed, therefore, again, the subject of Mr. Briggs, and told him how vain had been her effort to settle with him. Mr. Monckton instantly offered his services in assisting her, and the next morning they went together to his house, where, after an obstinate battle, they gained a complete victory: Mr. Briggs gave up all his accounts, and, in a few days, by the active interference of Mr. Monckton, her affairs were wholly taken out of his hands. He stormed, and prophesied all ill to Cecilia, but it was not to any purpose; he was so disagreeable to her, by his manners, and so unintelligible to her in matters of business, that she was happy to have done with him; even though, upon inspecting his accounts, they were all found clear and exact, and his desire to retain his power over her fortune, proved to have no other motive than a love of money so potent, that to manage it, even for another, gave him a satisfaction he knew not how to relinquish.

Mr. Monckton, who, though a man of pleasure, under-stood business perfectly well, now instructed and directed her in making a general arrangement of her affairs. The estate which devolved to her from her uncle, and which was all in landed property, she continued to commit to the management of the steward who was employed in his life-time; and her own fortune from her father, which was all in the stocks, she now diminished to nothing by selling out to pay Mr. Monckton the principal and interest which she owed him, and by settling with her Bookseller.

While these matters were transacting, which, notwith-standing her eagerness to leave town, could not be brought into such a train as to permit her absence in less than a week, she passed her time chiefly alone. Her wishes all inclined her to bestow it upon Henrietta, but the late attack of Mr. Delvile had frightened her from keeping up that connection, since however carefully she might confine it to the daughter, Mrs. Belfield, she was certain, would impute it all to the son.

That attack rested upon her mind, in defiance of all her endeavours to banish it; the contempt with which it was made seemed intentionally offensive, as if he had been happy to derive from her supposed ill conduct, a right to triumph over as well as reject her. She concluded, also, that Delvile would be informed of these calumnies, yet she judged his generosity by her own, and was therefore convinced he would not credit them: but what chiefly at this time encreased her sadness and uneasiness, was the mention of Mrs. Delvile's broken constitution and ruined health. She had always preserved for that lady the most affectionate respect, and could not consider herself as the cause of her sufferings, without feeling the utmost concern, however conscious she had not wilfully occasioned them.

Nor was this scene the only one by which her efforts to forget this family were defeated; her watchful monitor, Albany, failed not again to claim her promise; and though Mr. Monckton earnestly exhorted her not to trust herself out with him, she preferred a little risk to the keenness of his reproaches, and the weather being good on the morning that he called, she consented to accompany him in his rambles: only charging her footman to follow where-ever they went, and not to fail enquiring for her if she stayed long out of his sight. These precautions were rather taken to satisfy Mr. Monckton than herself, who, having now procured intelligence of the former disorder of his intellects, was fearful of some extravagance, and apprehensive for her safety.

He took her to a miserable house in a court leading into Piccadilly, where, up three pair of stairs, was a wretched woman ill in bed, while a large family of children were playing in the room.

"See here," cried he, "what human nature can endure! look at that poor wretch, distracted with torture, yet lying in all this noise! unable to stir in her bed, yet without any assistant! suffering the pangs of acute disease, yet wanting the necessaries of life!"

Cecilia went up to the bed-side, and enquired more particularly into the situation of the invalid; but finding she could hardly speak from pain, she sent for the woman of the house, who kept a Green Grocer's shop on the ground floor, and desired her to hire a nurse for her sick lodger, to call all the children down stairs, and to send for an apothecary,* whose bill she promised to pay. She then gave her some money to get what necessaries might be wanted, and said she would come again in two days to see how they went on.

Albany, who listened to these directions with silent, yet eager attention, now clasped both his hands with a look of rapture, and exclaimed "Virtue yet lives,—and I have found her?"

Cecilia, proud of such praise, and ambitious to deserve it, chearfully said, "where, Sir, shall we go now?"

"Home," answered he with an aspect the most benign; "I will not wear out thy pity by rendering woe familiar to it."

Cecilia, though at this moment more disposed for acts of charity than for business or for pleasure, remembered that her fortune however large was not unlimited, and would not press any further bounty for objects she knew not, certain that occasions and claimants, far beyond her ability of answering, would but too frequently arise among those with whom she was more connected, she therefore yielded herself to his direction, and returned to Soho-Square.

Again, however, he failed not to call at the time she had appointed for re-visiting the invalid, to whom, with much gladness, he conducted her.

The poor woman, whose disease was a rheumatic fever, was already much better; she had been attended by an apothecary who had given her some alleviating medicine; she had a nurse at her bed-side, and the room being cleared of the children, she had had the refreshment of some sleep.

She was now able to raise her head, and make her acknowledgments to her benefactress; but not a little was the surprise of Cecilia, when, upon looking in her face, she said, "Ah, madam, I have seen you before!"

Cecilia, who had not the smallest recollection of her, in return desired to know "when, or where?"

"When you were going to be married, madam, I was the Pew-Opener at —— Church."

Cecilia started with secret horror, and involuntarily retreated from the bed; while Albany with a look of astonishment exclaimed, "Married!—why, then, is it unknown?"

"Ask me not!" cried she, hastily; "it is all a mistake."

"Poor thing!" cried he, "this, then, is the string thy nerves endure not to have touched! sooner will I expire than a breath of mine shall make it vibrate! Oh sacred be thy sorrow, for thou canst melt at that of the indigent!"

Cecilia then made a few general enquiries, and heard that the poor woman, who was a widow, had been obliged to give up her office, from the frequent attacks which she suffered of the rheumatism; that she had received much assistance both from the Rector and the Curate of —— Church, but her continual illness, with the largeness of her family, kept her distressed in spite of all help.

Cecilia promised to consider what she could do for her, and then giving her more money, returned to Lady Margaret's.

Albany, who found that the unfortunate recollection of the Pew-Opener had awakened in his young pupil a melancholy train of reflections, seemed now to compassionate the sadness which hitherto he had reproved, and walking silently by her side till she came to Soho-Square, said in accents of kindness, "Peace light upon thy head, and dissipate thy woes!" and left her.

"Ah when!" cried she to herself, "if thus they are to be revived for-ever!"

Mr. Monckton, who observed that something had greatly affected her, now expostulated warmly against Albany and his wild schemes; "You trifle with your own happiness," he cried, "by witnessing these scenes of distress, and you will trifle away your fortune upon projects you can never fulfil: the very air in those miserable houses is unwholesome for you to breathe; you will soon be infected with some of the diseases to which you so incautiously expose yourself, and while not half you give in charity will answer the purpose you wish, you will be plundered by cheats and sharpers till you have nothing left to bestow. You must be more considerate for yourself, and not thus governed by Albany, whose insanity is but partially cured, and whose projects are so boundless, that the whole capital of the East India Company* would not suffice to fulfil them.''

Cecilia, though she liked not the severity of this remonstrance, acknowledged there was some truth in it, and promised to be discreet, and take the reins into her own hands.

There remained for her, however, no other satisfaction; and the path which had thus been pointed out to her, grew more and more alluring every step. Her old friends, the poor Hills, now occurred to her memory, and she determined to see herself in what manner they went on.

The scene which this enquiry presented to her, was by no means calculated to strengthen Mr. Monckton's doctrine, for the prosperity in which she found this little family, amply rewarded the liberality she had shewn to it, and proved an irresistible encouragement to similar actions. Mrs. Hill wept for joy in recounting how well she succeeded, and Cecilia, delighted by the power of giving such pleasure, forgot all cautions and promises in the generosity which she displayed. She paid Mrs. Roberts the arrears that were due to her, she discharged all that was owing for the children who had been put to school, desired they might still be sent to it solely at her expence, and gave the mother a sum of money to be laid out in presents for them all.

To perform her promise with the Pew-Opener was however more difficult; her ill health, and the extreme youth of her children making her utterly helpless: but these were not considerations for Cecilia to desert her, but rather motives for regarding her as more peculiarly an object of charity. She found she had once been a clear-starcher, and was a tolerable plain work-woman;* she resolved, therefore, to send her into the country, where she hoped to be able to get her some business, and knew that at least, she could help her, if unsuccessful, and see that her children were brought up to useful employments. The woman herself was enchanted at the plan, and firmly persuaded the country air would restore her health. Cecilia told her only to wait till she was well enough to travel, and promised, in the mean time, to look out some little habitation for her. She then gave her money to pay her bills, and for her journey, and writing a full direction where she would hear of her at Bury, took leave of her till that time.

These magnificent donations and designs, being communicated to Albany, seemed a renovation to him of youth, spirit, and joy! while their effect upon Mr. Monckton resembled an annihilation of all three! to see money thus sported away, which he had long considered as his own, to behold those sums which he had destined for his pleasures, thus lavishly bestowed upon beggars, excited a rage he could with difficulty conceal, and an uneasiness he could hardly endure; and he languished, he sickened for the time, when he might put a period to such romantic proceedings.

Such were the only occupations which interrupted the solitude of Cecilia, except those which were given to her by actual business; and the moment her affairs were in so much forwardness that they could be managed by letters, she prepared for returning into the country. She acquainted Lady Margaret and Mr. Monckton with her design, and gave orders to her servants to be ready to set off the next day.

Mr. Monckton made not any opposition, and refused himself the satisfaction of accompanying her: and Lady Margaret, whose purpose was now answered, and who wished to be in the country herself, determined to follow her.

CHAPTER VI

A Disturbance

THIS matter being settled at breakfast, Cecilia, having but one day more to spend in London, knew not how to let it pass without taking leave of Henrietta, though she chose not again to expose herself to the forward insinuations of her mother; she sent her, therefore, a short note, begging to see her at Lady Margaret's, and acquainting her that the next day she was going out of town.

Henrietta returned the following answer.

To Miss BEVERLEY.

Madam,

My mother is gone to market, and I must not go out without her leave; I have run to the door at every knock this whole week in hopes you were coming, and my heart has jumpt at every coach that has gone through the street. Dearest lady, why did you tell me you would come? I should not have thought of such a great honour if you had not put it in my head. And now I have got the use of a room where I can often be alone for two or three hours together. And so I shall this morning, if it was possible my dear Miss Beverley could come. But I don't mean to be teasing, and I would not be impertinent or encroaching for the world; but only the thing is I have a great deal to say to you, and if you was not so rich a lady, and so much above me, I am sure I should love you better than any body in the whole world, almost; and now I dare say I shan't see you at all; for it rains very hard, and my mother, I know, will be sadly angry if I ask to go in a coach. O dear! I don't know what I can do! for it will half break my heart, if my dear Miss Beverley should go out of town, and I not see her!

I am, Madam,
with the greatest respectfulness,
your most humble servant,
HENRIETTA BELFIELD.

This artless remonstrance, joined to the intelligence that she could see her alone, made Cecilia instantly order a chair, and go herself to Portland-street: for she found by this letter there was much doubt if she could otherwise see her, and the earnestness of Henrietta made her now not endure to disappoint her. "She has much, cried she, to say to me, and I will no longer refuse to hear her; she shall unbosom to me her gentle heart, for we have now nothing to fear from each

other. She promises herself pleasure from the communication, and doubtless it must be some relief to her. Oh
were there any friendly bosom, in which I might myself
confide!—happier Henrietta! less fearful of thy pride, less
tenacious of thy dignity! thy sorrows at least seek the
consolation of sympathy,—mine, alas! fettered by prudence,
must fly it!''

She was shewn into the parlour, which she had the
pleasure to find empty; and, in an instant, the warm-hearted
Henrietta was in her arms. "This is sweet of you indeed,"
cried she, "for I did not know how to ask it, though it rains
so hard I could not have walked to you, and I don't know
what I should have done, if you had gone away and quite
forgot me.''

She then took her into the back parlour, which she said
they had lately hired, and, as it was made but little use of,
she had it almost entirely to herself.

There had passed a sad scene, she told her, at the meeting
with her brother, though now they were a little more
comfortable; yet, her mother, she was sure, would never be
at rest till he got into some higher way of life; "And, indeed,
I have some hopes," she continued, "that we shall be able
by and bye to do something better for him; for he has got
one friend in the world, yet, thank God, and such a noble
friend!—indeed I believe he can do whatever he pleases for
him,—that is I mean I believe if he was to ask any thing for
him, there's nobody would deny him. And this is what I
wanted to talk to you about.''——

Cecilia, who doubted not but she meant Delvile, scarce
knew how to press the subject, though she came with no
other view: Henrietta, however, too eager to want solicitation, went on.

"But the question is whether we shall be able to prevail
upon my brother to accept any thing, for he grows more and
more unwilling to be obliged, and the reason is, that being
poor, he is afraid, I believe, people should think he wants to
beg of them: though if they knew him as well as I do, they
would not long think that, for I am sure he would a great
deal rather be starved to death. But indeed, to say the

truth, I am afraid he has been sadly to blame in this affair, and quarrelled when there was no need to be affronted; for I have seen a gentleman who knows a great deal better than my brother what people should do, and he says he took every thing wrong that was done, all the time he was at Lord Vannelt's."

"And how does this gentleman know it?"

"O because he went himself to enquire about it; for he knows Lord Vannelt very well, and it was by his means my brother came acquainted with him. And this gentleman would not have wished my brother to be used ill any more than I should myself, so I am sure I may believe what he says. But my poor brother, not being a lord himself, thought every body meant to be rude to him, and because he knew he was poor, he suspected they all behaved disrespectfully to him. But this gentleman gave me his word that every body liked him and esteemed him, and if he would not have been so suspicious, they would all have done any thing for him in the world."

"You know this gentleman very well, then?"

"O no, madam!" she answered hastily, "I don't know him at all! he only comes here to see my brother; it would be very impertinent for me to call him an acquaintance of mine."

"Was it before your brother, then, he held this conversation with you?"

"O no, my brother would have been affronted with him, too, if he had! but he called here to enquire for him at the time when he was lost to us, and my mother quite went down upon her knees to him to beg him to go to Lord Vannelt's, and make excuses for him, if he had not behaved properly: but if my brother was to know this, he would hardly speak to her again! so when this gentleman came next, I begged him not to mention it, for my mother happened to be out, and so I saw him alone."

"And did he stay with you long?"

"No, ma'am, a very short time indeed; but I asked him questions all the while, and kept him as long as I could, that I might hear all he had to say about my brother."

"Have you never seen him since?"

"No, ma'am, not once! I suppose he does not know

my brother is come back to us. Perhaps when he does, he
will call.''

"Do you wish him to call?"

"Me?" cried she, blushing, "a little;—sometimes I
do;—for my brother's sake.''

"For your brother's sake! Ah my dear Henrietta!——but
tell me,—or *don't* tell me if you had rather not,—did I not
once see you kissing a letter? perhaps it was from this same
noble friend?''

"It was not a letter, madam," said she, looking down, "it
was only the cover of one to my brother.''

"The cover of a letter only!—and that to your brother!
——is it possible you could so much value it?''

"Ah madam! *You*, who are always used to the good and
the wise, who see no other sort of people but those in high
life, *you* can have no notion how they strike those that they
are new to!——but I who see them seldom, and who live
with people so very unlike them—Oh you cannot guess how
sweet to *me* is every thing that belongs to them! whatever has
but once been touched by their hands, I should like to lock
up, and keep for ever! though if I was used to them, as you
are, perhaps I might think less of them.''

Alas! thought Cecilia, who by *them* knew she only meant
him, little indeed would further intimacy protect you!

"We are all over-ready," continued Henrietta, "to blame
others, and that is the way I have been doing all this time
myself; but I don't blame my poor brother now for living so
with the great as I used to do, for now I have seen a little
more of the world, I don't wonder any longer at his
behaviour: for I know how it is, and I see that those who
have had good educations, and kept great company, and
mixed with the world,—O it is another thing!—they seem
quite a different species!—they are so gentle, so soft-
mannered! nothing comes from them but what is meant to
oblige! they seem as if they only lived to give pleasure to
other people, and as if they never thought at all of
themselves!''

"Ah Henrietta!" said Cecilia, shaking her head, "you
have caught the enthusiasm of your brother, though you

so long condemned it! Oh have a care lest, like him also, you find it as pernicious as it is alluring!''

"There is no danger for *me*, madam,'' answered she, "for the people I so much admire are quite out of my reach. I hardly ever even see them; and perhaps it may so happen I may see them no more!''

"The people?'' said Cecilia, smiling, "are there, then, many you so much distinguish?''

"Oh no indeed!'' cried she, eagerly, "there is only one! there *can* be—I mean there are only a few—'' she checked herself, and stopt.

"Whoever you admire,'' cried Cecilia, "your admiration cannot but honour: yet indulge it not too far, lest it should wander from your heart to your peace, and make you wretched for life.''

"Ah madam!—I see you know who is the particular person I was thinking of! but indeed you are quite mistaken if you suppose any thing bad of me!''

"Bad of you!'' cried Cecilia, embracing her, "I scarce think so well of any one!''

"But I mean, madam, if you think I forget he is so much above me. But indeed I never do; for I only admire him for his goodness to my brother, and never think of him at all, but just by way of comparing him, sometimes, to the other people that I see, because he makes me hate them so, that I wish I was never to see them again.''

"His acquaintance, then,'' said Cecilia, "has done you but an ill office, and happy it would be for you could you forget you had ever made it.''

"O, I shall never do that! for the more I think of him, the more I am out of humour with every body else! O Miss Beverley! we have a sad acquaintance indeed! I'm sure I don't wonder my brother was so ashamed of them. They are all so rude, and so free, and put one so out of countenance,—O how different is this person you are thinking of! he would not distress any body, or make one ashamed for all the world! *You* only are like him! always gentle, always obliging!——sometimes I think you must be his sister—once, too, I heard——but that was contradicted.''

A deep sigh escaped Cecilia at this speech; she guessed too well what she might have heard, and she knew too well how it might be contradicted.

"Surely, *you* cannot be unhappy, Miss Beverley!" said Henrietta, with a look of mingled surprise and concern.

"I have much, I own," cried Cecilia, assuming more chearfulness, "to be thankful for, and I endeavour not to forget it."

"O how often do I think," cried Henrietta, "that you, madam, are the happiest person in the world! with every thing at your own disposal,—with every body in love with you, with all the money that you can wish for, and so much sweetness that nobody can envy you it! with power to keep just what company you please, and every body proud to be one of the number!—Oh if I could chuse who I would be, I should sooner say Miss Beverley than any princess in the world!"

Ah, thought Cecilia, if such is my situation,—how cruel that by one dreadful blow all its happiness should be thrown away!

"Were I a rich lady, like you," continued Henrietta, "and quite in my own power, then, indeed, I might soon think of nothing but those people that I admire! and that makes me often wonder that *you*, madam, who are just such another as himself——but then, indeed, you may see so many of the same sort, that just this one may not so much strike you: and for that reason I hope with all my heart that he will never be married as long as he lives, for as he must take some lady in just such high life as his own, I should always be afraid that she would never love him as she ought to do!"

He need not now be single, thought Cecilia, were that all he had cause to apprehend!

"I often think," added Henrietta, "that the rich would be as much happier for marrying the poor, as the poor for marrying the rich, for then they would take somebody that would try to deserve their kindness, and now they only take those that know they have a right to it. Often and often have I thought so about this very gentleman! and sometimes when I have been in his company, and seen his civility and his sweetness, I have fancied I was rich and grand myself, and it has quite gone out of my head that I was nothing but poor Henrietta Belfield!''

"Did he, then,'' cried Cecilia a little alarmed, "ever seek to ingratiate himself into your favour?''

"No, never! but when treated with so much softness, 'tis hard always to remember ones meanness! You, madam, have no notion of that task: no more had I myself till lately, for I cared not who was high, nor who was low: but now, indeed, I must own I have sometimes wished myself richer! yet he assumes so little, that at other times, I have almost forgot all distance between us, and even thought——Oh foolish thought!——''

"Tell it, sweet Henrietta, however!''

"I will tell you, madam, every thing! for my heart has been bursting to open itself, and nobody have I dared trust. I have thought, then, I have sometimes thought,—my true affection, my faithful fondness, my glad obedience,—might make him, if he did but know them, happier in me than in a greater lady!''

"Indeed,'' cried Cecilia, extremely affected by this plaintive tenderness, "I believe it!—and were I him, I could not, I think, hesitate a moment in my choice!''

Henrietta now, hearing her mother coming in, made a sign to her to be silent; but Mrs. Belfield had not been an instant in the passage, before a thundering knocking at the street-door occasioned it to be instantly re-opened. A servant then enquired if Mrs. Belfield was at home, and being answered by herself in the affirmative, a chair was brought into the house.

But what was the astonishment of Cecilia, when, in another moment, she heard from the next parlour the voice of Mr. Delvile senior, saying, "Your servant, ma'am; Mrs. Belfield, I presume?''

There was no occasion, now, to make a sign to her of silence, for her own amazement was sufficient to deprive her of speech.

"Yes, Sir," answered Mrs. Belfield; "but I suppose, Sir, you are some gentleman to my son."

"No, madam," he returned, "my business is with yourself."

Cecilia now recovering from her surprise, determined to hasten unnoticed out of the house, well knowing that to be seen in it would be regarded as a confirmation of all that he had asserted. She whispered, therefore, to Henrietta, that she must instantly run away, but, upon softly opening the door leading to the passage, she found Mr. Delvile's chairmen, and a footman there in waiting.

She closed it again, irresolute what to do: but after a little deliberation, she concluded to out-stay him, as she was known to all his servants, who would not fail to mention seeing her; and a retreat so private was worse than any other risk. A chair was also in waiting for herself, but it was a hackney one, and she could not be known by it; and her footman she had fortunately dismissed, as he had business to transact for her journey next day.

Mean-while the thinness of the partition between the two parlours made her hearing every word that was said unavoidable.

"I am sure, Sir, I shall be very willing to oblige you," Mrs. Belfield answered; "but pray, Sir, what's your name?"

"My name, ma'am," he replied, in a rather elevated voice, "I am seldom obliged to announce myself; nor is there any present necessity I should make it known. It is sufficient I assure you, you are speaking to no very common person, and probably to one you will have little chance to meet with again."

"But how can I tell your business, Sir, if I don't so much as know your name?"

"My business, madam, I mean to tell myself; your affair is only to hear it. I have some questions, indeed, to ask, which I must trouble you to answer, but they will sufficiently explain themselves to prevent any difficulty upon your part. There is no need, therefore, of any introductory ceremonial."

"Well, Sir," said Mrs. Belfield, wholly insensible of this ambiguous greatness, "if you mean to make your name a secret."

"Few names, I believe, ma'am," cried he, haughtily, "have less the advantage of secrecy than mine! on the contrary, this is but one among a very few houses in this town to which my person would not immediately announce it. That, however, is immaterial; and you will be so good as to rest satisfied with my assurances, that the person with whom you are now conversing, will prove no disgrace to your character."

Mrs. Belfield, overpowered, though hardly knowing with what, only said *he was very welcome*, and begged him to sit down.

"Excuse me, ma'am," he answered, "My business is but of a moment, and my avocations are too many to suffer my infringing that time. You say you have a son; I have heard of him, also, somewhere before; pray will you give me leave to enquire——I don't mean to go deep into the matter,—but particular family occurrences make it essential for me to know,—whether there is not a young person of rather a capital fortune, to whom he is supposed to make proposals?"

"Lack-a-day, no, Sir!" answered Mrs. Belfield, to the infinite relief of Cecilia, who instantly concluded this question referred to herself.

"I beg your pardon, then; good morning to you ma'am," said Mr. Delvile, in a tone that spoke his disappointment; but added "And there is no such young person, you say, who favours his pretensions?"

"Dear Sir," cried she, "why there's nobody he'll so much as put the question to! there's a young lady at this very time, a great fortune, that has as much a mind to him, I tell him, as any man need desire to see; but there's no making him think it! though he has been brought up at the university, and knows more about all the things, or as much, as any body in the king's dominions."

"O, then," cried Mr. Delvile, in a voice of far more complacency, "it is not on the side of the young woman that the difficulty seems to rest?"

"Lord, no, Sir! he might have had her again and again only for asking! She came after him ever so often; but being brought up, as I said, at the university, he thought he knew better than me, and so my preaching was all as good as lost upon him."

The consternation of Cecilia at these speeches could by nothing be equalled but the shame of Henrietta, who, though she knew not to whom her mother made them, felt all the disgrace and the shock of them herself.

"I suppose, Sir," continued Mrs. Belfield, "you know my son?"

"No, ma'am; my acquaintance is——not very universal."

"Then, Sir, you are no judge how well he might make his own terms. And as to this young lady, she found him out, Sir, when not one of his own natural friends could tell where in the world he was gone! She was the first, Sir, to come and tell me news of him, though I was his own mother! Love, Sir, is prodigious for quickness! it can see, I sometimes think, through bricks and mortar. Yet all this would not do, he was so obstinate not to take the hint!"

Cecilia now felt so extremely provoked, she was upon the point of bursting in upon them to make her own vindication; but as her passions, though they tried her reason never conquered it, she restrained herself by considering that to issue forth from a room in that house, would do more towards strengthening what was thus boldly asserted, than all her protestations could have chance to destroy.

"And as to young ladies themselves," continued Mrs. Belfield, "they know no more how to make their minds known than a baby does: so I suppose he'll shilly shally* till somebody else will cry snap, and take her. It is but a little while ago that it was all the report she was to have young Mr. Delvile, one of her guardians' sons."

"I am sorry report was so impertinent," cried Mr. Delvile, with much displeasure; "young Mr. Delvile is not to be disposed of with so little ceremony; he knows better what is due to his family."

Cecilia here blushed from indignation, and Henrietta sighed from despondency.

"Lord, Sir," answered Mrs. Belfield, "what should his family do better? I never heard they were any so rich, and I dare say the old gentleman, being her guardian, took care to put his son enough in her way, however it came about that they did not make a match of it: for as to old Mr. Delvile, all the world says——"

"All the world takes a very great liberty," angrily interrupted Mr. Delvile, "in saying any thing about him: and you will excuse my informing you that a person of his rank and consideration, is not lightly to be mentioned upon every little occasion that occurs."

"Lord, Sir," cried Mrs. Belfield, somewhat surprised at this unexpected prohibition, "I don't care for my part if I never mention the old gentleman's name again! I never heard any good of him in my life, for they say he's as proud as Lucifer,* and nobody knows what it's of, for they say—"

"*They* say?" cried he, firing with rage, "and who are *they?* be so good as inform me that?"

"Lord, every body, Sir! it's his common character."

"Then every body is extremely indecent," speaking very loud, "to pay no more respect to one of the first families in England. It is a licentiousness that ought by no means to be suffered with impunity."

Here, the street-door being kept open by the servants in waiting, a new step was heard in the passage, which Henrietta immediately knowing, turned, with uplifted hands to Cecilia, and whispered, "How unlucky! it's my brother! I thought he would not have returned till night!"

"Surely he will not come in here?" re-whispered Cecilia.

But, at the same moment, he opened the door, and entered the room. He was immediately beginning an apology, and starting back, but Henrietta catching him by the arm, told him in a low voice, that she had made use of his room because she had thought him engaged for the day, but begged him to keep still and quiet, as the least noise would discover them.

Belfield then stopt; but the embarrassment of Cecilia was

extreme; to find herself in his room after the speeches she had heard from his mother, and to continue with him in it by connivance, when she knew she had been represented as quite at his service, distressed and provoked her immeasurably; and she felt very angry with Henrietta for not sooner informing her whose apartment she had borrowed. Yet now to remove, and to be seen, was not to be thought of; she kept, therefore, fixed to her seat, though changing colour every moment from the variety of her emotions.

During this painful interruption she lost Mrs. Belfield's next answer, and another speech or two from Mr. Delvile, to whose own passion and loudness was owing Belfield's entering his room unheard: but the next voice that called their attention was that of Mr. Hobson, who just then walked into the parlour.

"Why what's to do here?" cried he, facetiously, "nothing but chairs and livery servants! Why ma'am, what is this your rout day?* Sir your most humble servant. I ask pardon, but I did not know you at first. But come, suppose we were all to sit down? Sitting's as cheap as standing, and what I say is this; when a man's tired, it's more agreeable."

"Have you any thing further, ma'am," said Mr. Delvile, with great solemnity, "to communicate to me?"

"No, Sir," said Mrs. Belfield, rather angrily, "it's no business of mine to be communicating myself to a gentleman that I don't know the name of. Why, Mr. Hobson, how come you to know the gentleman?"

"To know *me!*" repeated Mr. Delvile, scornfully.

"Why I can't say much, ma'am," answered Mr. Hobson, "as to my knowing the gentleman, being I have been in his company but once; and what I say is, to know a person if one leaves but a quart in a hogshead, it's two pints too much.* That's my notion. But, Sir, that was but an ungain* business at 'Squire Monckton's t'other morning. Every body was no-how, as one may say. But, Sir, if I may be so free, pray what is your private opinion of that old gentleman that talked so much out of the way?"

"My private opinion, Sir?"

"Yes, Sir; I mean if its no secret, for as to a secret, I hold it's what no man has a right to enquire into, being of its own nature it's a thing not to be told. Now as to what I think myself, my doctrine is this; I am quite of the old gentleman's mind about some things, and about others I hold him to be quite wide of the mark. But as to talking in such a whisky frisky* manner that nobody can understand him, why it's tantamount to not talking at all, being he might as well hold his tongue. That's what *I* say. And then as to that other article, of abusing a person for not giving away all his lawful gains to every cripple in the streets, just because he happens to have but one leg, or one eye, or some such matter, why it's knowing nothing of business! it's what I call talking at random."

"When you have finished, Sir," said Mr. Delvile, "you will be so good to let me know."

"I don't mean to intrude, Sir; that's not my way, so if you are upon business——"

"What else, Sir, could you suppose brought me hither? However, I by no means purpose any discussion. I have only a few words more to say to this gentlewoman, and as my time is not wholly inconsequential, I should not be sorry to have an early opportunity of being heard."

"I shall leave you with the lady directly, Sir; for I know business better than to interrupt it: but seeing chairs in the entry, my notion was I should see ladies in the parlour, not much thinking of gentlemen's going about in that manner, being I never did it myself. But I have nothing to offer against that; let every man have his own way; that's what *I* say. Only just let me ask the lady before I go, what's the meaning of my seeing two chairs in the entry, and only a person for one in the parlour? The gentleman, I suppose, did not come in *both*; ha! ha! ha!"

"Why now you put me in mind," said Mrs. Belfield, "I saw a chair as soon as I come in; and I was just going to say who's here, when this gentleman's coming put it out of my head."

"Why this is what I call Hocus Pocus* work!" said Mr. Hobson; "but I shall make free to ask the chairman who they are waiting for."

Mrs. Belfield, however, anticipated him; for running into the passage, she angrily called out, "What do you do here, Misters? do you only come to be out of the rain? I'll* have no stand made of my entry,* I can tell you!"

"Why we are waiting for the lady," cried one of them.

"Waiting for a fiddlestick!" said Mrs. Belfield; "here's no lady here, nor no company; so if you think I'll have my entry filled up by two hulking fellows for nothing, I shall shew you the difference. One's dirt enough of one's own, without taking people out of the streets to help one. Who do you think's to clean after you?"

"That's no business of ours; the lady bid us wait," answered the man.

Cecilia at this dispute could with pleasure have cast herself out of the window to avoid being discovered; but all plan of escape was too late; Mrs. Belfield called aloud for her daughter, and then, returning to the front parlour, said, "I'll soon know if there's company come to my house without my knowing it!" and opened a door leading to the next room!

Cecilia, who had hitherto sat fixed to her chair, now hastily arose, but in a confusion too cruel for speech: Belfield, wondering even at his own situation, and equally concerned and surprised at her evident distress, had himself the feeling of a culprit, though without the least knowledge of any cause: and Henrietta, terrified at the prospect of her mother's anger, retreated as much as possible out of sight.

Such was the situation of the discovered, abashed, perplexed, and embarrassed! while that of the discoverers, far different, was bold, delighted, and triumphant!

"So!" cried Mrs. Belfield, "why here's Miss Beverley!—in my son's back room!" winking at Mr. Delvile.

"Why here's a lady, sure enough!" said Mr. Hobson, "and just where she should be, and that is with a gentleman. Ha! ha! that's the right way, according to my notion! that's the true maxim for living agreeable."

"I came to see Miss Belfield," cried Cecilia, endeavouring, but vainly, to speak with composure, "and she brought me into this room."

"I am but this moment," cried Belfield, with eagerness, "returned home; and unfortunately broke into the room, from total ignorance of the honour which Miss Beverley did my sister."

These speeches, though both literally true, sounded, in the circumstances which brought them out, so much as mere excuses, that while Mr. Delvile haughtily marked his incredulity by a motion of his chin, Mrs. Belfield continued winking at him most significantly, and Mr. Hobson, with still less ceremony, laughed aloud.

"I have nothing more, ma'am," said Mr. Delvile to Mrs. Belfield, "to enquire, for the few doubts with which I came to this house are now entirely satisfied. Good morning to you, ma'am."

"Give me leave, Sir," said Cecilia, advancing with more spirit, "to explain, in presence of those who can best testify my veracity, the real circumstances—"

"I would by no means occasion you such unnecessary trouble, ma'am," answered he, with an air at once exulting and pompous, "the situation in which I see you abundantly satisfies my curiosity, and saves me from the apprehension I was under of being again convicted of a *mistake!*"*

He then made her a stiff bow, and went to his chair.

Cecilia, colouring deeply at this contemptuous treatment, coldly took leave of Henrietta, and courtsying to Mrs. Belfield, hastened into the passage, to get into her own.

Henrietta was too much intimidated to speak, and Belfield was too delicate to follow her; Mr. Hobson only said "The young lady seems quite dashed;" but Mrs. Belfield pursued her with entreaties she would stay.

She was too angry, however, to make any answer but by a distant bow of the head, and left the house with a resolution little short of a vow never again to enter it.

Her reflections upon this unfortunate visit were bitter beyond measure; the situation in which she had been surprised,—clandestinely concealed with only Belfield and his sister,—joined to the positive assertions of her partiality for him made by his mother, could not, to Mr. Delvile, but appear marks irrefragable that his charge in his former conversation was rather mild than overstrained, and that the connection he had mentioned, for whatever motives denied, was incontestably formed.

The apparent conviction of this part of the accusation, might also authorise, to one but too happy in believing ill of her, an implicit faith in that which regarded her having run out her fortune. His determination not to hear her shewed the inflexibility of his character; and it was evident, notwithstanding his parading pretensions of wishing her welfare, that his inordinate pride was inflamed, at the very supposition he could be mistaken or deceived for a moment.

Even Delvile himself, if gone abroad, might now hear this account with exaggerations that would baffle all his confidence: his mother, too, greatly as she esteemed and loved her, might have the matter so represented as to stagger her good opinion;——these were thoughts the most afflicting she could harbour, though their probability was such that to banish them was impossible.

To apply again to Mr. Delvile to hear her vindication, was to subject herself to insolence, and almost to court indignity. She disdained even to write to him, since his behaviour called for resentment, not concession; and such an eagerness to be heard, in opposition to all discouragement, would be practising a meanness that would almost merit repulsion.

Her first inclination was to write to Mrs. Delvile, but what now, to her, was either her defence or accusation? She had solemnly renounced all further intercourse with her, she had declared against writing again, and prohibited her letters: and, therefore, after much fluctuation of opinion, her delicacy concurred with her judgment, to conclude it would be most proper, in a situation so intricate, to leave the matter to chance, and commit her character to time.

In the evening, while she was at tea with Lady Margaret and Miss Bennet, she was suddenly called out to speak to a young woman; and found, to her great surprise, she was no other than Henrietta.

"Ah madam!" she cried, "how angrily did you go away this morning! it has made me miserable ever since, and if you go out of town without forgiving me, I shall fret myself quite ill! my mother is gone out to tea, and I have run here all alone, and in the dark, and in the wet, to beg and pray you will forgive me, for else I don't know what I shall do!''

"Sweet, gentle girl!" cried Cecilia, affectionately embracing her, "if you had excited all the anger I am capable of feeling, such softness as this would banish it, and make me love you more than ever!"

Henrietta then said, in her excuse, that she had thought herself quite sure of her brother's absence, who almost always spent the whole day at the booksellers, as in writing himself he perpetually wanted to consult other authors, and had very few books at their lodgings: but she would not mention that the room was his, lest Cecilia should object to making use of it, and she knew she had no other chance of having the conversation with her she had so very long wished for. She then again begged her pardon, and hoped the behaviour of her mother would not induce her to give her up, as she was shocked at it beyond measure, and as her brother, she assured her, was as innocent of it as herself.

Cecilia heard her with pleasure, and felt for her an encreasing regard. The openness of her confidence in the morning had merited all her affection, and she gave her the warmest protestations of a friendship which she was certain would be lasting as her life.

Henrietta then, with a countenance that spoke the lightness of her heart, hastily took her leave, saying she did not dare be out longer, lest her mother should discover her excursion. Cecilia insisted, however, upon her going in a chair, which she ordered her servant to attend, and take care himself to discharge.

This visit, joined to the tender and unreserved conversation of the morning, gave Cecilia the strongest desire to invite her to her house in the country; but the terror of Mrs. Belfield's insinuations, added to the cruel interpretations she had to expect from Mr. Delvile, forbid her indulging this wish, though it was the only one that just now she could form.

CHAPTER VII

A Calm

CECILIA took leave over night* of the family, as she would not stay their rising in the morning: Mr. Monckton, though certain not to sleep when she was going, forbearing to mark his solicitude by quitting his apartment at any unusual hour. Lady Margaret parted from her with her accustomed ungraciousness, and Miss Bennet, because in her presence, in a manner scarce less displeasing.

The next morning, with only her servants, the moment it was light, she set out. Her journey was without incident or interruption, and she went immediately to the house of Mrs. Bayley, where she had settled to board till her own was finished.

Mrs. Bayley was a mere good sort of woman, who lived decently well with her servants, and tolerably well with her neighbours, upon a small annuity, which made her easy and comfortable, though by no means superior to such an addition to her little income as an occasional boarder might produce.

Here Cecilia continued a full month: which time had no other employment than what she voluntarily gave to herself by active deeds of benevolence.

At Christmas, to the no little joy of the neighbourhood, she took possession of her own house, which was situated about three miles from Bury.

The better sort of people were happy to see her thus settled amongst them, and the poorer, who by what they already had received, knew well what they still might* expect, regarded the day in which she fixed herself in her mansion, as a day to themselves of prosperity and triumph.

As she was no longer, as hitherto, repairing to a temporary habitation, which at pleasure she might quit, and to which, at a certain period, she could have no possible claim, but to a house which was her own for ever, or, at least, could solely by her* own choice be transferred, she determined, as much as was in her power, in quitting her desultory dwellings, to empty her mind of the transactions which had passed in them, and upon entering a house where she was permanently to reside, to make the expulsion of her past sorrows, the basis upon which to establish her future serenity.

And this, though a work of pain and difficulty, was not impracticable; her sensibility, indeed, was keen, and she had suffered from it the utmost torture; but her feelings were not more powerful than her understanding was strong, and her fortitude was equal to her trials. Her calamities had saddened, but not weakened her mind, and the words of Delvile in speaking of his mother occurred to her now with all the conviction of experience, that "evils inevitable are always best supported, because known to be past amendment, and felt to give defiance to struggling."†*

A plan by which so great a revolution was to be wrought in her mind, was not to be effected by any sudden effort of magnanimity, but by a regular and even tenour of courage mingled with prudence. Nothing, therefore, appeared to her so indispensable as constant employment, by which a variety of new images might force their way in her mind to supplant the old ones, and by which no time might be allowed for brooding over melancholy retrospections.

Her first effort, in this work of mental reformation, was to part with Fidel, whom hitherto she had almost involuntarily guarded, but whom she only could see to revive the most dangerous recollections. She sent him, therefore, to the castle, but without any message; Mrs. Delvile, she was sure, would require none to make her rejoice in his restoration.

Her next step was writing to Albany, who had given her his direction, to acquaint him she was now ready to put in practice their long concerted scheme. Albany instantly hastened to her, and joyfully accepted the office of becoming at once her Almoner and her Monitor. He made it his business to seek objects of distress, and always but too certain to find them, of conducting her himself to their

†See Vol. IV, p. 573.

habitations, and then leaving to her own liberality the assistance their several cases demanded: and, in the overflowing of his zeal upon these occasions, and the rapture of his heart in thus disposing, almost at his pleasure, of her noble fortune, he seemed, at times, to feel an extasy that, from its novelty and its excess, was almost too exquisite to be borne. He joined with the beggars in pouring blessings upon her head, he prayed for her with the poor, and he thanked her with the succoured.

The pew-opener and her children failed not to keep their appointment, and Cecilia presently contrived to settle them in her neighbourhood: where the poor woman, as she recovered her strength, soon got a little work, and all deficiencies in her power of maintaining herself were supplied by her generous patroness. The children, however, she ordered to be coarsely brought up, having no intention to provide for them but by helping them to common employments.

The promise, also, so long made to Mrs. Harrel of an apartment in her house, was now performed. That lady accepted it with the utmost alacrity, glad to make any change in her situation, which constant solitude had rendered wholly insupportable. Mr. Arnott accompanied her to the house, and spent one day there; but receiving from Cecilia, though extremely civil and sweet to him, no hint of any invitation for repeating his visit, he left it in sadness, and returned to his own in deep dejection. Cecilia saw with concern how he nourished his hopeless passion, but knew that to suffer his visits would almost authorise his feeding it; and while she pitied unaffectedly the unhappiness she occasioned, she resolved to double her own efforts towards avoiding similar wretchedness.

This action, however, was a point of honour, not of friendship, the time being long since past that the society of Mrs. Harrel could afford her any pleasure; but the promises she had so often made to Mr. Harrel in his distresses, though extorted from her merely by the terrors of the moment, still were promises, and, therefore, she held herself bound to fulfil them.

Yet far from finding comfort in this addition to her family, Mrs. Harrel proved to her nothing more than a trouble and an incumbrance; with no inherent resources, she was continually in search of occasional supplies; she fatigued Cecilia with wonder at the privacy of her life, and tormented her with proposals of parties and entertainments. She was eternally in amazement that with powers so large, she had wishes so confined, and was evidently disappointed that upon coming to so ample an estate, she lived, with respect to herself and her family, with no more magnificence or shew than if Heiress to only 500*l.* a year.

But Cecilia was determined to think and to live for herself, without regard to unmeaning wonder or selfish remonstrances; she had neither ambition for splendour, nor spirits for dissipation; the recent sorrow of her heart had deadened it for the present to all personal taste of happiness, and her only chance for regaining it, seemed through the medium of bestowing it upon others. She had seen, too, by Mr. Harrel, how wretchedly external brilliancy could cover inward woe, and she had learned at Delvile Castle to grow sick of parade and grandeur. Her equipage, therefore, was without glare, though not without elegance, her table was plain, though hospitably plentiful, her servants were for use, though too numerous to be for labour. The system of her œconomy, like that of her liberality, was formed by rules of reason, and her own ideas of right, and not by compliance with example, nor by emulation with the gentry in her neighbourhood.

But though thus deviating in her actions from the usual customs of the young and rich, she was peculiarly careful not to offend them by singularity of manners. When she mixed with them, she was easy, unaffected, and well bred, and though she saw them but seldom, her good humour and desire of obliging kept them always her friends. The plan she had early formed at Mrs. Harrel's she now studied daily to put in practice; but that part by which the useless or frivolous were to be excluded her house, she found could only be supported by driving from her half her acquaintance.

Another part, also, of that project she found still less easy
of adoption, which was solacing herself with the society of
the wise, good, and intelligent. Few answered this description, and those few were with difficulty attainable. Many
might with joy have sought out her liberal dwelling, but no
one had idly waited till the moment it was at her disposal.
All who possessed at once both talents and wealth, were so
generally courted they were rarely to be procured; and all
who to talents alone owed their consequence, demanded, if
worth acquiring, time and delicacy to be obtained. Fortune
she knew, however, was so often at war with Nature, that
she doubted not shortly meeting those who would gladly
avail themselves of her offered protection.

Yet, tired of the murmurs of Mrs. Harrel, she longed for
some relief from her society, and her desire daily grew
stronger to owe that relief to Henrietta Belfield. The more
she meditated upon this wish, the less unattainable it
appeared to her, till by frequently combating its difficulties,
she began to consider them imaginary: Mrs. Belfield, while
her son was actually with herself, might see she took not
Henrietta as his appendage; and Mr. Delvile, should he make
further enquiries, might hear that her real connection was
with the sister, since she received her in the country, where the
brother made no pretence to follow her. She considered, too,
how ill she should be rewarded in giving up Henrietta for Mr.
Delvile, who was already determined to think ill of her, and
whose prejudices no sacrifice would remove.

Having hesitated, therefore, some time between the desire
of present alleviation, and the fear of future mischief, the
consciousness of her own innocence at length vanquished all
dread of unjust censure, and she wrote an invitation to
Henrietta enclosed in a letter to her mother.

The answer of Henrietta expressed her rapture at the
proposal; and that of Mrs. Belfield made no objection but to
the expence.

Cecilia, therefore, sent her own maid to travel with her
into Suffolk, with proper directions to pay for the journey.

The gratitude of the delighted Henrietta at the meeting
was boundless; and her joy at so unexpected a mark of

favour made her half wild. Cecilia suffered it not to languish for want of kindness to support it; she took her to her bosom, became the soother of all her cares, and reposed in her, in return, every thought that led not to Delvile.

There, however, she was uniformly silent; solemnly and eternally parted from him, far from trusting the secret of her former connexion to Henrietta, the whole study of her life was to drive the remembrance of it from herself.

Henrietta now tasted a happiness to which as yet her whole life had been a stranger; she was suddenly removed from turbulent vulgarity to the enjoyment of calm elegance; and the gentleness of her disposition, instead of being tyrannically imposed upon, not only made her loved with affection, but treated with the most scrupulous delicacy. Cecilia had her share in all the comfort she bestowed; she had now a friend to oblige, and a companion to converse with. She communicated to her all her schemes, and made her the partner of her benevolent excursions; she found her disposition as amiable upon trial, as her looks and her manners her been engaging at first sight; and her constant presence and constant sweetness, imperceptibly revived her spirits, and gave a new interest to her existence.

Meantime Mr. Monckton, who returned in about a fortnight to the Grove, observed the encreasing influence of Albany with the most serious concern. The bounties of Cecilia, extensive, magnificent, unlimited, were the theme of every tongue, and though sometimes censured and sometimes admired, they were wondered at universally. He suffered her for a while to go on without remonstrance, hoping her enthusiasm would abate, as its novelty wore out: but finding that week following week was still distinguished by some fresh act of beneficence, he grew so alarmed and uneasy, he could restrain himself no longer. He spoke to her with warmth, he represented her conduct as highly dangerous in its consequence; he said she would but court impostors from every corner of the kingdom, called Albany a lunatic, whom she should rather avoid than obey; and insinuated that if a report was spread of her proceedings, a charity so prodigal, would excite such alarm, that no man would think even her large and splendid fortune, would ensure him from ruin in seeking her alliance.

Cecilia heard this exhortation without either terror or impatience, and answered it with the utmost steadiness. His influence over her mind was no longer uncontrolled, for though her suspicions were not strengthened, they had never been removed, and friendship has no foe so dangerous as distrust! She thanked him, however, for his zeal, but assured him his apprehensions were groundless, since though she acted from inclination, she acted not without thought. Her income was very large, and she was wholly without family or connection; to spend it merely upon herself would be something still worse than extravagance, it must result from wilfulness the most inexcusable, as her disposition was naturally averse to luxury and expence. She might save indeed, but for whom? not a creature had such a claim upon her; and with regard to herself, she was so provided for it would be unnecessary. She would never, she declared, run in debt even for a week, but while her estate was wholly clear, she would spend it without restriction.

To his hint of any future alliance, she only said that those who disapproved her conduct, would probably be those she should disapprove in her turn; should such an event however take place, the retrenching from that time all her present peculiar expences, would surely, in a clear 3000*l.* a-year, leave her rich enough for any man, without making it incumbent upon her at present, to deny herself the only pleasure she could taste, in bestowing that money which to her was superfluous, upon those who received it as the prolongation of their existence.

A firmness so deliberate in a system he so much dreaded, greatly shocked Mr. Monckton, though it intimidated him from opposing it; he saw she was too earnest, and too well satisfied she was right, to venture giving her disgust by controverting her arguments: the conversation, therefore, ended with new discontent to himself, and with an impression upon the mind of Cecilia, that though he was zealous and friendly, he was somewhat too worldly and suspicious.

She went on, therefore, as before, distributing with a

lavish hand all she could spare from her own household; careful of nothing but of guarding against imposition, which, though she sometimes unavoidably endured, her discernment, and the activity of her investigating diligence, saved her from suffering frequently. And the steadiness with which she repulsed those whom she detected in deceit, was a check upon tricks and fraud, though it could not wholly put a stop to them.

Money, to her, had long appeared worthless and valueless; it had failed to procure her the establishment for which she once flattered herself it seemed purposely designed; it had been disdained by the Delviles, for the sake of whose connection she had alone ever truly rejoiced in possessing it; and after such a conviction of its inefficacy to secure her happiness, she regarded it as of little importance to herself, and therefore thought it almost the due of those whose distresses gave it a consequence to which with her it was a stranger.

In this manner with Cecilia passed the first winter of her majority. She had sedulously filled it with occupations, and her occupations had proved fertile in keeping her mind from idleness, and in restoring it to chearfulness. Calls upon her attention so soothing, and avocations so various for her time, had answered the great purpose for which originally she had planned them, in almost forcing from her thoughts those sorrows which, if indulged, would have rested in them incessantly.

CHAPTER VIII

An Alarm

THE spring was now advancing, and the weather was remarkably fine; when one morning, while Cecilia was walking with Mrs. Harrel and Henrietta on the lawn before her house, to which the last dinner bell was just summoning them, to return, Mrs. Harrel looked round and stopt at sight of a gentleman galloping towards them, who in less than a

minute approached, and dismounting and leaving his horse
to his servant, struck them all at the same instant to be no
other than young Delvile!

A sight so unexpected, so unaccountable, so wonderful,
after an absence so long, and to which they were mutually
bound, almost wholly over-powered Cecilia from surprise
and a thousand other feelings, and she caught Mrs. Harrel
by the arm, not knowing what she did, as if for succour;
while Henrietta with scarce less, though much more glad
emotion, suddenly exclaimed, "'tis Mr. Delvile!" and
sprang forward to meet him.

He had reached them, and in a voice that spoke hurry and
perturbation, respectfully made his compliments to them all,
before Cecilia recovered even the use of her feet: but no sooner
were they restored to her, than she employed them with the
quickest motion in her power, still leaning upon Mrs. Harrel,
to hasten into the house. Her solemn promise to Mrs. Delvile
became uppermost in her thoughts, and her surprise was soon
succeeded by displeasure, that thus, without any preparation,
he forced her to break it by an interview she had no means to
prevent.

Just as they reached the entrance into the house, the
Butler came to tell Cecilia that dinner was upon the table.
Delvile then went up to her, and said, "May I wait upon
you for one instant before—or after you dine?"

"I am engaged, Sir," answered she, though hardly able
to speak, "for the whole day."

"You will not, I hope, refuse to hear me," cried he,
eagerly, "I cannot write what I have to say,——"

"There is no occasion that you should, Sir," interrupted
she, "since I should scarcely find time to read it."

She then courtsied, though without looking at him, and
went into the house; Delvile remaining in utter dismay, not
daring, however wishing, to follow her. But when Mrs.
Harrel, much surprised at behaviour so unusual from
Cecilia, approached him with some civil speeches, he
started, and wishing her good day, bowed, and remounted
his horse: pursued by the soft eyes of Henrietta till wholly
out of sight.

They then both followed Cecilia to the dining-parlour.

Had not Mrs. Harrel been of this small party, the dinner would have been served in vain; Cecilia, still trembling with emotion, bewildered with conjecture, angry with Delvile for thus surprising her, angry with herself for so severely receiving him, amazed what had tempted him to such a violation of their joint agreement, and irresolute as much what to wish as what to think, was little disposed for eating, and with difficulty compelled herself to do the honours of her table.

Henrietta, whom the sight of Delvile had at once delighted and disturbed, whom the behaviour of Cecilia had filled with wonder and consternation, and whom the evident inquietude and disappointment which that behaviour had given to Delvile, had struck with grief and terror, could not swallow even a morsel, but having cut her meat about her plate, gave it, untouched, to a servant.

Mrs. Harrel, however, though she had had her share in the surprise, had wholly escaped all other emotion; and only concluded in her own mind, that Cecilia could sometimes be out of humour and ill bred, as well as the rest of the world.

While the desert was serving, a note was brought to Henrietta, which a servant was waiting in great haste to have answered.

Henrietta, stranger to all forms of politeness, though by nature soft, obliging and delicate, opened it immediately; she started as she cast her eye over it, but blushed, sparkled, and looked enchanted, and hastily rising, without even a thought of any apology, ran out of the room to answer it.

Cecilia, whose quick eye, by a glance unavoidable, had seen the hand of Delvile, was filled with new amazement at the sight. As soon as the servants were gone, she begged Mrs. Harrel to excuse her, and went to her own apartment.

Here, in a few minutes, she was followed by Henrietta, whose countenance beamed with pleasure, and whose voice spoke tumultuous delight. "My dear, dear Miss Beverley!" she cried, "I have such a thing to tell you!—you would never guess it,—I don't know how to believe it myself,—but Mr. Delvile has written to me!—he has indeed! that note was from him.—I have been locking it up, for fear of accidents, but I'll run and fetch it, that you may see it yourself."

She then ran away; leaving Cecilia much perplexed, much uneasy for herself, and both grieved and alarmed for the too tender, too susceptible Henrietta, who was thus easily the sport of every airy and credulous hope.

"If I did not shew it you," cried Henrietta, running back in a moment, "you would never think it possible, for it is to make such a request—that it has frightened me almost out of my wits!"

Cecilia then read the note.

To Miss BELFIELD.

Mr. Delvile presents his compliments to Miss Belfield, and begs to be permitted to wait upon her for a few minutes, at any time in the afternoon she will be so good as to appoint.

"Only think," cried the rapturous Henrietta, "it was *me*, poor simple *me*, of all people, that he wanted so to speak with!—I am sure I thought a different thought when he went away! but do, dearest Miss Beverley, tell me this one thing, what do you think he can have to say to me?"

"Indeed," replied Cecilia, extremely embarrassed, "it is impossible for me to conjecture."

"If *you* can't, I am sure, then, it is no wonder *I* can't! and I have been thinking of a million of things in a minute. It can't be about any business, because I know nothing in the world of any business; and it can't be about my brother, because he would go to our house in town about him, and there he would see him himself; and it can't be about my dear Miss Beverley, because then he would have written the note to her: and it can't be about any body else, because I know nobody else of his acquaintance."

Thus went on the sanguine Henrietta, settling whom and what it could *not* be about, till she left but the one thing to which her wishes pointed that it *could* be about. Cecilia heard her with true compassion, certain that she was deceiving herself with imaginations the most pernicious; yet unable to know how to quell them, while in such doubt and darkness herself.

This conversation was soon interrupted, by a message that a gentleman in the parlour begged to speak with Miss Belfield.

"O dearest, dearest Miss Beverley!" cried Henrietta, with encreasing agitation, "what in the world shall I say to him, advise me, pray advise me, for I can't think of a single word!"

"Impossible, my dear Henrietta, unless I knew what he would say to you!"

"O but I can guess, I can guess!"—cried she, her cheeks glowing, while her whole frame shook, "and I sha'n't know what in the whole world to answer him! I know I shall behave like a fool,—I know I shall disgrace myself sadly!"

Cecilia, truly sorry Delvile should see her in such emotion, endeavoured earnestly to compose her, though never less tranquil herself. But she could not succeed, and she went down stairs with expectations of happiness almost too potent for her reason.

Not such were those of Cecilia; a dread of some new conflict took possession of her mind, that mind so long tortured with struggles, so lately restored to serenity!

Henrietta soon returned, but not the same Henrietta she went;—the glow, the hope, the flutter were all over; she looked pale and wan, but attempting, as she entered the room, to call up a smile, she failed, and burst into tears.

Cecilia threw her arms round her neck, and tried to console her; but, happy to hide her face in her bosom, she only gave the freer indulgence to her grief, and rather melted than comforted by her tenderness, sobbed aloud.

Cecilia too easily conjectured the disappointment she had met, to pain her by asking it; she forbore even to gratify her own curiosity by questions that could not but lead to her mortification, and suffering her therefore to* take her own time for what she had to communicate, she hung over her in silence with the most patient pity.

Henrietta was very sensible of this kindness, though she

knew not half its merit: but it was a long time before she could articulate, for sobbing, that *all* Mr. Delvile wanted, at last, was only to beg she would acquaint Miss Beverley, that he had done himself the honour of waiting upon her with a message from Mrs. Delvile.

"From Mrs. Delvile?" exclaimed Cecilia, all emotion in her turn, "good heaven! how much, then, have I been to blame? where is he now?—where can I send to him?—tell me, my sweet Henrietta, this instant!"

Oh madam!" cried Henrietta, bursting into a fresh flood of tears, "how foolish have I been to open my silly heart to you!—he is come to pay his addresses to you!—I am sure he is!——"

"No, no, no!" cried Cecilia, "indeed he is not!—but I must, I ought to see him,—where, my love, is he?"

"In the parlour,—waiting, for an answer.—"

Cecilia, who at any other time would have been provoked at such a delay in the delivery of a message so important, felt now nothing but concern for Henrietta, whom she hastily kissed, but instantly, however, quitted, and hurried to Delvile, with expectations almost equally sanguine as those her poor friend but the moment before had crushed.

"Oh now, thought she, if at last Mrs. Delvile herself has relented, with what joy will I give up all reserve, all disguise, and frankly avow the faithful affection of my heart!"

Delvile received her not with the eagerness with which he had first addressed her; he looked extremely disturbed, and, even after her entrance, undetermined how to begin.

She waited, however, his explanation in silence; and, after an irresolute pause, he said, with a gravity not wholly free from resentment, "I presumed, madam, to wait upon you from the permission of my mother; but I believe I have obtained it so late, that the influence I hoped from it is past!"

"I had no means, Sir," answered she, chearfully, "to know that you came from her: I should else have received her commands without any hesitation."

"I would thank you for the honour you do her, were it less pointedly exclusive. I have, however, no right of reproach! yet suffer me to ask, could you, madam, after such a parting, after a renunciation so absolute of all future claim upon you, which though extorted from me by duty, I was bound, having promised, to fulfil by principle,—could you imagine me so unsteady, so dishonourable, as to obtrude myself into your presence while that promise was still in force?"

"I find," cried Cecilia, in whom a secret hope every moment grew stronger, "I have been too hasty; I did indeed believe Mrs. Delvile would never authorise such a visit; but as you have so much surprised me, I have a right to your pardon for a little doubt."

"There spoke Miss Beverley!" cried Delvile, re-animating at this little apology, "the same, the unaltered Miss Beverley I hoped to find!—yet *is* she unaltered? am I not too precipitate? and is the tale I have heard about Belfield a dream? an error? a falsehood?"

"But that so quick a succession of quarrels," said Cecilia, half smiling, "would be endless perplexity, I, now, would be affronted that you can ask me such a question."

"Had I, indeed, *thought* it a question," cried he, "I would not have asked it: but never for a moment did I credit it, till the rigour of your repulse alarmed me. You have con-descended, now, to account for that, and I am therefore encouraged to make known to you the purpose of my ven-turing this visit. Yet not with confidence shall I speak if, scarce even with hope!—it is a purpose that is the offspring of despair,—"

"One thing, Sir," cried Cecilia, who now became frightened again, "let me say before you proceed; if your purpose has not the sanction of Mrs. Delvile, as well as your visit, I would gladly be excused hearing it, since I shall most certainly refuse it."

"I would mention nothing," answered he, "without her concurrence; she has given it me: and my father himself has permitted my present application."

"Good Heaven!" cried Cecilia, "is it possible!" clasping her hands together in the eagerness of her surprise and delight.

"*Is it possible!*" repeated Delvile, with a look of rapture;

"ah Miss Beverley!—once my own Cecilia!—do you, can you *wish* it possible?"

"No, no!" cried she, while pleasure and expectation sparkled in her eyes, "I wish nothing about it.—Yet tell me how it has happened,—I am *curious*," added she, smiling, "though not interested in it."

"What hope would this sweetness give me," cried he, "were my scheme almost any other than it is!—but you cannot,—no, it would be unreasonable,—it would be madness to expect your compliance!—it is next to madness even in me to wish it,—but how shall a man who is desperate be prudent and circumspect?"

"Spare, spare yourself," cried the ingenuous Cecilia, "this unnecessary pain!—you will find from me no unnecessary scruples."

"You know not what you say!—all noble as you are, the sacrifice I have to propose—"

"Speak it," cried she, "with confidence! speak it even with certainty of success! I will be wholly undisguised, and openly, honestly own to you, that no proposal, no sacrifice can be mentioned, to which I will not instantly agree, if first it has had the approbation of Mrs. Delvile."

Delvile's gratitude and thanks for a concession never before so voluntarily made to him, interrupted for a while, even his power of explaining himself. And now, for the first time, Cecilia's sincerity was chearful, since now, for the first time, it seemed opposed by no duty.

When still, therefore, he hesitated, she herself held out her hand to him, saying, "what must I do more? must I offer this pledge to you?"

"For my life would I not resign it!" cried he, delightedly receiving it; "but oh, how soon will you withdraw it, when the only terms upon which I can hold it, are those of making it sign from itself its natural right and inheritance?"

Cecilia, not comprehending him, only looked amazed, and he proceeded.

"Can you, for my sake, make such a sacrifice as this? can you for a man who for yours is not permitted to give up his name, give up yourself the fortune of your late uncle?

consent to such settlements as I can make upon you from my own? part with so splendid an income wholly and for-ever?— and with only your paternal 10,000*l.* condescend to become mine, as if your uncle had never existed, and you had been Heiress to no other wealth?''

This, indeed, was a stroke to Cecilia unequalled by any she had met, and more cruel than any she could have in reserve. At the proposal of parting with her uncle's fortune, which, desirable as it was, had as yet been only productive to her of misery, her heart, disinterested, and wholly careless of money, was prompt to accede to the condition; but at the mention of her paternal fortune, that fortune, of which, now, not the smallest vestige remained, horror seized all her faculties! she turned pale, she trembled, she involuntarily drew back her hand, and betrayed, by speechless agitation, the sudden agonies of her soul!

Delvile, struck by this evident dismay, instantly con-cluded his plan had disgusted her. He waited some minutes in anxious expectation of an answer, but finding her silence continue while her emotion encreased, the deepest crimson dyed his face, and unable to check his chagrin, though not daring to confess his disappointment, he suddenly quitted her, and walked, in much disorder, about the room. But soon recovering some composure, from the assistance of pride, ''Pardon, madam,'' he said, ''a trial such as no man can be vindicated in making. I have indulged a romantic whim, which your better judgment disapproves, and I receive but the mortification my presumption deserved.''

''You know not then,'' said Cecilia, in a faint voice, ''my inability to comply?''

''Your ability, or inability, I presume are elective?''

''Oh no!—my power is lost!—my fortune itself is gone!''

''Impossible! utterly impossible!'' cried he with vehemence.

''Oh that it were!—your father knows it but too well.''

''My father!''

''Did he, then, never hint it to you?''

''Oh distraction!'' cried Delvile, ''what horrible confirmation is coming!'' and again he walked away, as if wanting courage to hear her.

Cecilia was too much shocked to force upon him her explanation; but presently returning to her, he said *"you*, only, could have made this credible!''

"Had you, then, actually heard it?''

"Oh I had heard it as the most infamous of falsehoods! my heart swelled with indignation at so villainous a calumny, and had it not come from my father, my resentment at it had been inveterate!''

"Alas!'' cried Cecilia, "the fact is undeniable! yet the circumstances you may have heard with it, are I doubt not exaggerated.''

"Exaggerated indeed!'' he answered; " I was told you had been surprised concealed with Belfield in a back room, I was told that your parental fortune was totally exhausted, and that during your minority you had been a dealer with Jews! I was told all this by my father;—you may believe I had else not easily been made hear it!''

"Yet thus far,'' said she, "he told you but what is true; though——''

"True!'' interrupted Delvile, with a start almost frantic. "Oh never, then, was truth so scandalously wronged!—I denied the whole charge!—I disbelieved every syllable!—I pledged my own honour to prove every assertion false!''

"Generous Delvile!'' cried Cecilia, melting into tears, "this is what I expected from you! and, believe me, in *your* integrity my reliance had been similar!''

"Why does Miss Beverley weep?'' cried he, softened, and approaching her, "and why has she given me this alarm? these things must at least have been misrepresented, deign, then, to clear up a mystery in which suspense is torture!''

Cecilia, then, with what precision and clearness her agitation allowed her, related the whole history of her taking up the money of the Jew for Mr. Harrel, and told, without reserve, the reason of her trying to abscond from his father at Mrs. Belfield's. Delvile listened to her account with almost an agony of attention, now admiring her conduct; now resenting her ill usage; now compassionating her losses;

but though variously moved by different parts, receiving from the whole the delight he most coveted in the establishment of her innocence.

Thanks and applause the warmest, both accompanied and followed her narration; and then, at her request, he related in return the several incidents and circumstances to which he had owed the permission of this visit.

He had meant immediately to have gone abroad; but the indisposition of his mother made him unwilling to leave the kingdom till her health seemed in a situation less precarious. That time, however, came not; the Winter advanced, and she grew evidently worse. He gave over, therefore, his design till the next Spring, when, if she were able, it was her desire to try the South of France* for her recovery, whither he meant to conduct her.

But, during his attendance upon her, the plan he had just mentioned occurred to him, and he considered how much greater would be his chance of happiness in marrying Cecilia with scarce any fortune at all, than in marrying another with the largest. He was convinced she was far other than expensive, or a lover of shew, and soon flattered himself she might be prevailed upon to concur with him, that in living together, though comparatively upon little, they should mutually be happier than in living asunder upon much.

When he started this scheme to his mother, she heard it with mingled admiration of his disinterestedness, and regret at its occasion: yet the loftiness of her own mind, her high personal value for Cecilia, her anxiety to see her son finally settled while she lived, lest his disappointment should keep him single from a lasting disgust, joined to a dejection of spirits from an apprehension that her interference had been cruel, all favoured his scheme, and forbid her resistance. She had often protested, in their former conflicts, that had Cecilia been portionless, her objections had been less than to an estate so conditioned; and that to give to her son a woman so exalted in herself, she would have conquered the mere opposition of interest, though that of family honour she held invincible. Delvile now called upon her to remember those words, and ever strict in fidelity, she still promised to abide by them.

Ah! thought Cecilia, is virtue, then, as inconsistent as vice? and can the same character be thus high-souled, thus nobly disinterested with regard to riches, whose pride is so narrow and so insurmountable, with respect to family prejudice!

Yet such a sacrifice from Cecilia herself, whose income intitled her to settlements the most splendid, Mrs. Delvile thought scarcely to be solicited; but as her son was conscious he gave up in expectation no less than she would give up in possession, he resolved upon making the experiment, and felt an internal assurance of success.

This matter being finally settled with his mother, the harder task remained of vanquishing the father, by whom, and before whom the name of Cecilia was never mentioned, not even after his return from town, though loaded with imaginary charges against her. Mr. Delvile held it a diminution of his own in the honour of his son, to suppose he wanted still fresh motives for resigning her. He kept, therefore, to himself the ill opinion he brought down, as a resource in case of danger, but a resource he disdained to make use of, unless driven to it by absolute necessity.

But, at the new proposal of his son, the accusation held in reserve broke out; he called Cecilia a dabler with Jews, and said she had been so from the time of her uncle's death; he charged her with the grossest general extravagance, to which he added a most insidious attack upon her character, drawn from her visits at Belfield's of long standing, as well as the particular time when he had himself surprised her concealed with the young man in a back parlour: and he asserted, that most of the large sums she was continually taking up from her fortune, were lavished without scruple upon this dangerous and improper favourite.

Delvile had heard this accusation with a rage scarce restrained from violence; confident in her innocence, he boldly pronounced the whole a forgery, and demanded the author of such cruel defamation. Mr. Delvile, much offended, refused to name any authority, but consented, with an air of triumph, to abide by the effect of his own proposal, and gave him a supercilious promise no longer to oppose the marriage, if the terms he meant to offer to Miss Beverley, of renouncing her uncle's estate, and producing her father's fortune, were accepted.

"Oh little did I credit," said Delvile in conclusion, "that he knew indeed so well this last condition was impracticable! his assertions were without proof; I thought them prejudiced surmises; and I came in the full hope I should convict him of his error. My mother, too, who warmly and even angrily defended you, was as firmly satisfied as myself that the whole was a mistake, and that enquiry would prove your fortune as undiminished as your purity. How will she be shocked at the tale I have now to unfold! how irritated at your injuries from Harrel! how grieved that your own too great benevolence should be productive of such black aspersions upon your character!"

"I have been," cried Cecilia, "too facile and too unguarded; yet always, at the moment, I seemed but guided by common humanity. I have ever thought myself secure of more wealth than I could require, and regarded the want of money as an evil from which I was unavoidably exempted. My own fortune, therefore, appeared to me of small consequence, while the revenue of my uncle ensured me perpetual prosperity.—Oh had I foreseen this moment!—"

"Would you, then, have listened to my romantic proposal?"

"Would I have listened?——do you not see too plainly I could not have hesitated!"

"Oh yet, then, most generous of human beings, yet then be mine! By our own œconomy we will pay off our mortgages; by living a while abroad, we will clear all our estates; I will still keep the name to which my family is bigotted, and my gratitude for your compliance shall make you forget what you lose by it!"

"Speak not to me such words!" cried Cecilia, hastily rising; "your friends will not listen to them, neither, therefore, must I."

"My friends," cried he with energy, "are henceforth out

of the question: my father's concurrence with a proposal he *knew* you had not power to grant, was in fact a mere permission to insult you; for if, instead of dark charges, he had given any authority for your losses, I had myself spared you the shock you have so undeservedly received from hearing it.—But to consent to a plan which *could* not be accepted!—to make *me* a tool to offer indignity to Miss Beverley!——he has released me from his power by so erroneous an exertion of it, and my own honour has a claim to which his commands must give place. That honour binds me to Miss Beverley as forcibly as my admiration, and no voice but her own shall determine my future destiny."

"That voice, then," said Cecilia, "again refers you to your mother. Mr. Delvile, indeed, has not treated me kindly; and this last mock concession was unnecessary cruelty; but Mrs. Delvile merits my utmost respect, and I will listen to nothing which has not her previous sanction."

"But will her sanction be sufficient? and may I hope, in obtaining it, the security of yours?"

"When I have said I will hear nothing without it, may you not almost infer——I will refuse nothing with it!"

The acknowledgements he would now have poured forth, Cecilia would not hear, telling him, with some gaiety, they were yet unauthorized by Mrs. Delvile. She insisted upon his leaving her immediately, and never again returning, without his mother's express approbation. With regard to his father, she left him totally to his own inclination; she had received from him nothing but pride and incivility, and determined to shew publicly her superior respect for Mrs. Delvile, by whose discretion and decision she was content to abide.

"Will you not, then, from time to time," cried Delvile, "suffer me to consult with you?"

"No, no," answered she, "do not ask it! I have never been insincere with you, never but from motives not to be overcome, reserved even for a moment; I have told you I will put every thing into the power of Mrs. Delvile, but I will not, a second time risk my peace by any action unknown to her."

Delvile gratefully acknowledged her goodness, and

promised to require nothing more. He then obeyed her by taking leave, eager himself to put an end to this new uncertainty, and supplicating only that her good wishes might follow his enterprise.

And thus, again, was wholly broken the tranquility of Cecilia; new hopes, however faint, awakened all her affections, and strong fears, but too reasonable, interrupted her repose. Her destiny, once more, was as undecided as ever, and the expectations she had crushed, retook possession of her heart.

The suspicions she had conceived of Mr. Monckton again occurred to her; though unable to ascertain and unwilling to believe them, she tried to drive them from her thoughts. She lamented, however, with bitterness, her unfortunate connexion with Mr. Harrel, whose unworthy impositions upon her kindness of temper and generosity, now proved to her an evil far more serious and extensive, than in the midst of her repugnance to them she had ever apprehended.

CHAPTER IX

A Suspense

DELVILE had been gone but a short time, before Henrietta, her eyes still red, though no longer streaming, opened the parlour door, and asked if she might come in?

Cecilia wished to be alone, yet could not refuse her.

"Well, madam," cried she, with a forced smile, and constrained air of bravery, "did not I guess right?"

"In what?" said Cecilia, unwilling to understand her.

"In what I said would happen?—I am sure you know what I mean."

Cecilia, extremely embarrassed, made no answer; she much regretted the circumstances which had prevented an earlier communication, and was uncertain whether, now, it would prove most kind or most cruel to acquaint her with what was in agitation, which, should it terminate in nothing, was unnecessarily wounding her delicacy for the openness of her confidence, and which, however serviceable it might prove to her in the end, was in the means so rough and piercing she felt the utmost repugnance to the experiment.

"You think me, madam, too free," said Henrietta, "in asking such a question; and indeed your kindness has been so great, it may well make me forget myself: but if it does, I am sure I deserve you should send me home directly, and then there is not much fear I shall soon be brought to my senses!"

"No, my dear Henrietta, I can never think you too free, I have told you already every thing I thought you would have pleasure in hearing; whatever I have concealed, I have been fearful would only pain you."

"I have *deserved*, madam," said she, with spirit, "to be pained, for I have behaved with the folly of a baby. I am very angry with myself indeed! I was old enough to have known better,—and I ought to have been wise enough."

"You must then be angry with yourself, next," said Cecilia, anxious to re-encourage her, "for all the love that I bear you; since to your openness and frankness it was entirely owing."

"But there are some things that people should *not* be frank in; however, I am only come now to beg you will tell me, madam, when it is to be;—and don't think I ask out of nothing but curiosity, for I have a very great reason for it indeed."

"What be, my dear Henrietta?—you are very rapid in your ideas!"

"I will tell you, madam, what my reason is; I shall go away to my own home,—and so I would if it were ten times a worse home than it is!——just exactly the day before. Because afterwards I shall never like to look that gentleman in the face,—never, never!—for married ladies I know are not to be trusted!"

"Be not apprehensive; you have no occasion. Whatever may be my fate, I will never be so treacherous as to betray my beloved Henrietta to *any* body."

"May I ask you, madam, one question?"

"Certainly."

"Why did all this never happen before?"

"Indeed," cried Cecilia, much distressed, "I know not that it will happen now."

"Why what, dear madam, can hinder it?"

"A thousand, thousand things! nothing can be less secure."

"And then I am still as much puzzled as ever. I heard, a good while ago, and we all heard that it was to be; and I thought that it was no wonder, I am sure, for I used often to think it was just what was most likely; but afterwards we heard it was no such thing, and from that moment I always believed there had been nothing at all in it."

"I must speak to you, I find, with sincerity; my affairs have long been in strange perplexity: I have not known myself what to expect; one day has perpetually reversed the prospect of another, and my mind has been in a state of uncertainty and disorder, that has kept it—that still keeps it from comfort and from rest!"

"This surprises me indeed, madam! I thought *you* were all happiness! but I was sure you deserved it, and I thought you had it for that reward. And this has been the thing that has made me behave so wrong; for I took it into my head I might tell you every thing, because I concluded it could be nothing to you; for if great people loved one another, I always supposed they married directly; poor people, indeed, must stay till they are able to settle; but what in the whole world, thought I, if they like one another, should hinder such a rich lady as Miss Beverley from marrying such a rich gentleman at once?"

Cecilia now, finding there was no longer any chance for concealment, thought it better to give the poor Henrietta at least the gratification of unreserved confidence, which might somewhat sooth her uneasiness by proving her reliance in her faith. She frankly, therefore, confessed to her the whole of her situation. Henrietta wept at the recital with bitterness, thought Mr. Delvile a monster, and Mrs. Delvile herself scarce human; pitied Cecilia with unaffected tenderness, and wondered that the person could exist who had the heart to give grief to young Delvile! She thanked her most gratefully for reposing such trust in her; and Cecilia made use of this opportunity, to enforce the necessity of her struggling more seriously to recover her indifferency.

She promised she would not fail; and forbore steadily from that time to name Delvile any more: but the depression of her spirits shewed she had suffered a disappointment such as astonished even Cecilia. Though modest and humble, she had conceived hopes the most romantic, and though she denied, even to herself, any expectations from Delvile, she involuntarily nourished them with the most sanguine simplicity. To compose and to strengthen her became the whole business of Cecilia; who, during her present suspense, could find no other employment in which she could take any interest.

Mr. Monckton, to whom nothing was unknown that related to Cecilia, was soon informed of Delvile's visit, and hastened in the utmost alarm, to learn its event. She had now lost all the pleasure she had formerly derived from confiding in him, but though averse and confused, could not withstand his enquiries.

Unlike the tender Henrietta's was his disappointment at this relation, and his rage at such repeated trials was almost more than he could curb. He spared neither the Delviles for their insolence of mutability in rejecting or seeking her at their pleasure, nor herself for her easiness of submission in being thus the dupe of their caprices. The subject was difficult for Cecilia to dilate upon; she wished to clear, as he deserved, Delvile himself from any share in the censure, and she felt hurt and offended at the charge of her own improper readiness; yet shame and pride united in preventing much vindication of either, and she heard almost in silence what with pain she bore to hear at all.

He now saw, with inexpressible disturbance, that whatever was his power to make her uneasy, he had none to make her retract, and that the conditional promise she had given Delvile to be wholly governed by his mother, she was firm in regarding to be as sacred as one made at the altar.

Perceiving this, he dared trust his temper with no further debate; he assumed a momentary calmness for the purpose of taking leave of her, and with pretended good wishes for her happiness, whatever might be her determination, he stifled the reproaches with which his whole heart was swelling, and precipitately left her.

Cecilia, affected by his earnestness, yet perplexed in all her opinions, was glad to be relieved from useless exhortations, and not sorry, in her present uncertainty, that his visit was not repeated.

She neither saw nor heard from Delvile for a week, and augured nothing but evil from such delay. The following letter then came by the post.

To Miss BEVERLEY.

April 2d, 1780.

I must write without comments, for I dare not trust myself with making any; I must write without any beginning address, for I know not how you will permit me to address you.

I have lived a life of tumult since last compelled to leave you, and when it may subside, I am still in utter ignorance.

The affecting account of the losses you have suffered thro' your beneficence to the Harrels, and the explanatory one of the calumnies you have sustained from your kindness to the Belfields, I related with the plainness which alone I thought necessary to make them felt. I then told the high honour I had received, in meeting with no other repulse to my proposal, than was owing to an inability to accede to it; and informed my mother of the condescending powers with which you had invested her. In conclusion I mentioned my new scheme, and firmly, before I would listen to any opposition, I declared that though wholly to their decision I left the relinquishing my own name or your fortune, I was not only by your generosity more internally yours than ever, but that since again I had ventured, and with permission to apply to you, I should hold myself hence forward unalterably engaged to you.

And so I do, and so I shall! nor, after a renewal so public, will any prohibition but yours have force to keep me from throwing myself at your feet.

My father's answer I will not mention; I would I could forget it! his prejudices are irremediable, his resolutions are inflexible. Who or what has worked him into an animosity so irreclaimable, I cannot conjecture, nor will he tell; but something darkly mysterious has part in his wrath and his injustice.

My mother was much affected by your reference to herself. Words of the sweetest praise broke repeatedly from her; no other such woman, she said, existed; no other such instance could be found of fidelity so exalted! her son must have no heart but for low and mercenary selfishness, if, after a proof of regard so unexampled, he could bear to live without her! Oh how did such a sentence from lips so highly reverenced, animate, delight, confirm, and oblige me at once!

The displeasure of my father at this declaration was dreadful; his charges, always as improbable as injurious, now became too horrible for my ears; he disbelieved you had taken up the money for Harrel, he discredited that you visited the Belfields for Henrietta: passion not merely banished his justice, but clouded his reason, and I soon left the room, that at least I might not hear the aspersions he forbid me to answer.

I left not, however, your fame to a weak champion: my mother defended it with all the spirit of truth, and all the confidence of similar virtue! yet they parted without conviction, and so mutually irritated with each other, that they agreed to meet no more.

This was too terrible! and I instantly consolidated my resentment to my father, and my gratitude to my mother, into concessions and supplications to both; I could not, however, succeed; my mother was deeply offended, my father was sternly inexorable: nor here rests the evil of their dissention, for the violence of the conflict has occasioned a return more alarming than ever of the illness of my mother.

All her faith in her recovery is now built upon going abroad; she is earnest to set off immediately; but Dr. Lyster has advised her to make London in her way, and have a consultation of physicians before she departs.

To this she has agreed; and we are now upon the road thither.

Such is, at present, the melancholy state of my affairs. My mother *advised* me to write; forgive me, therefore, that I waited not something more decisive to say. I could prevail upon neither party to meet before the journey; nor could I draw from my father the base fabricator of the calumnies by which he has been thus abused.

Unhappily, I have nothing more to add: and whether intelligence, such as this, or total suspense, would be least irksome, I know not. If my mother bears her journey tolerably well, I have yet one more effort to make; and of that the success or the failure will be instantly communicated to Miss Beverley, by her eternally devoted, but half distracted

MORTIMER DELVILE.

Scarcely could Cecilia herself decide whether this comfortless letter or none at all were preferable. The implacability of Mr. Delvile was shocking, but his slandering her character was still more intolerable; yet the praises of the mother, and her generous vindication, joined to the invariable reliance of Delvile upon her innocence, conferred upon her an honour that offered some alleviation.

The mention of a fabricator again brought Mr. Monckton to her mind, and not all her unwillingness to think him capable of such treachery, could now root out her suspicions. Delvile's temper, however, she knew was too impetuous to be trusted with this conjecture, and her fear of committing injustice being thus seconded by prudence, she determined to keep to herself doubts that could not without danger be divulged.

She communicated briefly to Henrietta, who looked her earnest curiosity, the continuance of her suspense; and to her own fate Henrietta became somewhat more reconciled, when she saw that no station in life rendered happiness certain or permanent.

CHAPTER X

A Relation

ANOTHER week past still without any further intelligence. Cecilia was then summoned to the parlour, and to Delvile himself.

He looked hurried and anxious; yet the glow of his face, and the animation of his eyes, immediately declared he at least came not to take leave of her.

"Can you forgive," cried he, "the dismal and unsatisfactory letter I wrote you? I would not disobey you twice in the same manner, and I could not till now have written in any other."

"The consultation with the physicians, then," said Cecilia, "is over?"

"Alas, yes; and the result is most alarming; they all agree my mother is in a dangerous way, and they rather forbear to oppose, than advise her going abroad: but upon that she is earnestly bent, and intends to set out without delay. I shall return to her, therefore, with all speed, and mean not to take any rest till I have seen her."

Cecilia expressed with tenderness her sorrow for Mrs. Delvile: nor were her looks illiberal in including her son in her concern.

"I must hasten," he cried, "to the credentials by which I am authorised for coming, and I must hasten to prove if Miss Beverley has not flattered my mother in her appeal."

He then informed her that Mrs. Delvile, apprehensive for herself, and softened for him by the confession of her danger, which she had extorted from her physicians, had tenderly resolved upon making one final effort for his happiness, and ill and impatient as she was, upon deferring her journey to wait its effect.

Generously, therefore, giving up her own resentment, she wrote to Mr. Delvile in terms of peace and kindness, lamenting their late dissention, and ardently expressing her desire to be reconciled to him before she left England. She told him the uncertainty of her recovery which had been acknowledged by her physicians, who had declared a calmer mind was more essential to her than a purer air. She then added, that such serenity was only to be given her, by the removal of her anxiety at the comfortless state of her son. She begged him, therefore, to make known the author of Miss Beverley's defamation, assuring him, that upon enquiry, he would find her character and her fame as unsullied as his own; and strongly representing, that after the sacrifice to which she had consented, their son would be utterly dishonourable in thinking of any other connexion. She then to this reasoning joined the most earnest supplication, protesting, in her present disordered state of health, her life might pay the forfeiture of her continual uneasiness.

"I held out," she concluded, "while his personal dignity, and the honour of his name and family were endangered; but where interest alone is concerned, and that interest is combatted by the peace of his mind, and the delicacy of his word, my opposition is at an end. And though our extensive and well founded views for a splendid alliance are abolished, you will agree with me hereafter, upon a closer inspection, that the object for whom he relinquishes them, offers in herself the noblest reparation."

Cecilia felt gratified, humbled, animated and depressed at once by this letter, of which Delvile brought her a copy. "And what," cried she, "was the answer?"

"I cannot in decency," he replied, "speak my opinion of it; read it yourself,—and let me hear yours."

To the Honourable Mrs. DELVILE.

YOUR extraordinary letter, madam, has extremely surprised me. I had been willing to hope the affair over from the time my disapprobation of it was formally announced. I am sorry you are so much indisposed, but I cannot conclude your health would be restored by my acceding to a plan so derogatory to my house. I disapprove it upon every account, not only of the name and the fortune, but the lady herself. I have reasons more important than those I assign, but they are such as I am bound in honour not to mention. After such a declaration, nobody, I presume, will affront me by asking them. Her defence you have only from herself, her accusation I have received from authority less partial. I command, therefore, that my son, upon pain of my eternal displeasure, may never speak to me on the subject again, and I hope, madam, from you the same complaisance to my request. I cannot explain myself further, nor is it necessary; it is no news, I flatter myself, to Mortimer Delvile or his mother, that I do nothing without reason, and I believe nothing upon slight grounds.

A few cold compliments concerning her journey, and the re-establishment of her health, concluded the letter.

Cecilia, having read, hastily returned it, and indignantly said, "My opinion, Sir, upon this letter, must surely be yours; that we had done wiser, long since, to have spared your mother and ourselves, those vain and fruitless conflicts which we ought better to have foreseen were liable to such a conclusion. Now, at least, let them be ended, and let us not pursue disgrace wilfully, after suffering from it with so much rigour involuntarily."

"O no," cried Delvile, "rather let us now spurn it for ever! those conflicts must indeed be ended, but not by a separation still more bitter than all of them."

He then told her, that his mother, highly offended to observe by the extreme coldness of this letter, the rancour he still nourished for the contest preceding her leaving him, no longer now refused even her separate consent, for a measure which she thought her son absolutely engaged to take.

"Good heaven!" cried Cecilia, much amazed, "this from Mrs. Delvile!—a separate consent!—"

"She has always maintained," he answered, "an independent mind, always judged for herself, and refused all other arbitration: when so impetuously she parted us, my father's will happened to be her's, and thence their concurrence: my father, of a temper immoveable and stern, retains stubbonly the prejudices which once have taken possession of him; my mother, generous as fiery, and noble as proud, is open to conviction, and no sooner convinced, than ingenuous in acknowledging it: and thence their dissention. From my father I may hope forgiveness, but must never expect concession; from my mother I may hope all she ought to grant, for pardon but her vehemence,—and she has every great quality that can dignify human nature!''

Cecilia, whose affection and reverence for Mrs. Delvile were unfeigned, and who loved in her son this filial enthusiasm, readily concurred with him in praising her, and sincerely esteemed her the first among women.

''Now, then,'' cried he, with earnestness, ''now is the time when your generous admiration of her is put to the test; see what she writes to you;—she has left to me all explanation: but I insisted upon some credential, lest you should believe I only owed her concurrence to a happy dream.''

Cecilia in much trepidation took the letter, and hastily run it over.

To Miss BEVERLEY.

MISERY, my sweet young friend, has long been busy with us all; much have we owed to the clash of different interests, much to that rapacity which to enjoy any thing, demands every thing, and much to that general perverseness which labours to place happiness in what is with-held. Thus do we struggle on till we can struggle no longer; the felicity with which we trifle, at best is but temporary; and before reason and reflection shew its value, sickness and sorrow are commonly become stationary.

Be it yours, my love, and my son's, to profit by the experience, while you pity the errors, of the many who illustrate this truth. Your mutual partiality has been mutually unfortunate, and must always continue so for the interests of both: but how blind is it to wait, in our own peculiar lots, for that perfection of enjoyment we can all see wanting in the lot of others! My expectations for my son had ''outstepped the modesty of''* probability. I looked for rank and high birth, with the fortune of Cecilia, and Cecilia's rare character. Alas! a new constellation in the heavens might as rationally have been looked for!

My extravagance, however, has been all for his felicity, dearer to me than life,—dearer to me than all things but his own honour! Let us but save that, and then let wealth, ambition, interest, grandeur and pride, since they cannot constitute his happiness, be removed from destroying it. I will no longer play the tyrant that, weighing good and evil by my own feelings and opinions, insists upon his acting by the notions I have formed, whatever misery they may bring him by opposing all his own.

I leave the kingdom with little reason to expect I shall return to it; I leave it——Oh blindness of vanity and passion!—from the effect of that violence with which so lately I opposed what now I am content to advance! But the extraordinary resignation to which you have agreed, shews your heart so wholly my son's, and so even more than worthy the whole possession of his, that it reflects upon him an honour more bright and more alluring, than any the most illustrious other alliance could now confer.

I would fain see you ere I go, lest I should see you no more; fain ratify by word of mouth the consent that by word of mouth I so absolutely refused! I know not how to come to Suffolk,—is it not possible you can come to London? I am told you leave to me the arbitration of your fate,—in giving you to my son, I best shew my sense of such an honour.

Hasten then, my love, to town, that I may see you once more! wait no longer a concurrence thus unjustly with-held, but hasten, that I may bless the daughter I have so often wished to own! that I may entreat her forgiveness for all the pain I have occasioned her, and committing to her charge the future happiness of my son, fold to my maternal heart the two objects most dear to it!

Augusta Delvile.

Cecilia wept over this letter with tenderness, grief and alarm; but declared, had it even summoned her to follow her abroad, she could not, after reading it, have hesitated in complying.

"O now, then," cried Delvile, "let our long suspenses end! hear me with the candour my mother has already listened to me—be mine, my Cecilia, at once,—and force me not, by eternal scruples, to risk another separation."

"Good heaven, Sir!" cried Cecilia, starting, "in such a state as Mrs. Delvile thinks herself, would you have her journey delayed?"

"No, not a moment! I would but ensure you mine, and go with her all over the world!"

"Wild and impossible!—and what is to be done with Mr. Delvile?"

"It is on his account wholly I am thus earnestly precipitate. If I do not by an immediate marriage prevent his further interference, all I have already suffered may again be repeated, and some fresh contest with my mother may occasion another relapse."

Cecilia, who now understood him, ardently protested she would not listen for a moment to any clandestine expedient.

He besought her to be patient; and then anxiously represented to her their peculiar situations. All application to his father he was peremptorily forbid making, all efforts to remove his prejudices their impenetrable mystery prevented; a public marriage, therefore, with such obstacles, would almost irritate him to phrenzy, by its daring defiance of his prohibition and authority.

"Alas!" exclaimed Cecilia, "we can never do right but in parting!"

"Say it not," cried he, "I conjure you! we shall yet live, I hope, to prove the contrary."

"And can you, then," cried she, reproachfully, "Oh Mr. Delvile! can you again urge me to enter your family in secret?"

"I grieve, indeed," he answered, "that your goodness should so severely be tried; yet did you not condescend to commit the arbitration to my mother?"

"True; and I thought her approbation would secure my peace of mind; but how could I have expected Mrs.

Delvile's consent to such a scheme!''

"She has merely accorded it from a certainty there is no other resource. Believe me, therefore, my whole hope rests upon your present compliance. My father, I am certain, by his letter, will now hear neither petition nor defence; on the contrary, he will only enrage at the temerity of offering to confute him. But when he knows you are his daughter, *his* honour will then be concerned in yours, and it will be as much his desire to have it cleared, as it is now to have it censured.''

"Wait at least your return, and let us try what can be done with him.''

"Oh why,'' cried Delvile, with much earnesness, "must I linger out month after month in this wretched uncertainty! If I wait I am undone! my father, by the orders I must unavoidably leave, will discover the preparations making without his consent, and he will work upon you in my absence, and compel you to give me up!''

"Are you sure,'' said she, half smiling, "he would have so much power?''

"I am but too sure, that the least intimation, in his present irritable state of mind, reaching him of my intentions, would make him not scruple, in his fury, pronouncing some malediction upon my disobedience that *neither* of us, I must own, could tranquilly disregard.''

This was an argument that came home to Cecilia, whose deliberation upon it, though silent, was evidently not unfavourable.

He then told her that with respect to settlements, he would instantly have a bond drawn up, similar to that prepared for their former intended union, which should be properly signed and sealed, and by which he would engage himself to make, upon coming to his estate, the same settlement upon her that was made upon his mother.

"And as, instead of keeping up three houses,'' he continued, "in the manner my father does at present, I mean to put my whole estate *out to nurse,* * while we reside for a while abroad, or in the country, I doubt not but in a very few years we shall be as rich and as easy as we shall desire.''

He told her, also, of his well-founded expectations from the Relations already mentioned; which the concurrence of his mother with his marriage would thence forward secure to him.

He then, with more coherence, stated his plan at large. He purposed, without losing a moment, to return to London; he conjured her, in the name of his mother, to set out herself early the next day, that the following evening might be dedicated wholly to Mrs. Delvile: through her intercession he might then hope Cecilia's compliance, and every thing on the morning after should be prepared for their union. The long-desired ceremony over, he would instantly ride post to his father, and pay him, at least, the respect of being the first to communicate it. He would then attend his mother to the Continent, and leave the arrangement of every thing to his return. "Still, therefore, as a single man," he continued, "I mean to make the journey, and I shall take care, by the time I return, to have all things in readiness for claiming my sweet Bride. Tell me, then, now, if you can reasonably oppose this plan?"

"Indeed," said Cecilia, after some hesitation, "I cannot see the necessity of such violent precipitancy."

"Do you not try me too much," cried Delvile impatiently, "to talk *now* of precipitancy! after such painful waiting, such wearisome expectation! I ask you not to involve your own affairs in confusion by accompanying me abroad; sweet to me as would be such an indulgence, I would not make a run-away of you in the opinion of the world. All I wish is the secret certainty I cannot be robbed of you, that no cruel machinations may again work our separation, that you are mine, unalterably mine, beyond the power of caprice or ill fortune."

Cecilia made no answer; tortured with irresolution, she knew not upon what to determine.

"We might then, according to the favour or displeasure of my father, settle wholly abroad for the present, or occasionally visit him in England; my mother would be always and openly our friend.——Oh be firm, then, I conjure you, to the promise you have given her, and deign to be mine on the conditions she prescribes. She will be bound to you for ever by so generous a concession, and even her health may be restored by the cessation of her anxieties. With such a wife, such a mother, what will be wanting for *me!* Could I lament not being richer, I must be rapacious indeed!—Speak, then, my Cecilia! relieve me from the agony of this eternal uncertainty, and tell me your word is invariable as your honour, and tell me my mother gives not her sanction in vain!"

Cecilia sighed deeply, but, after some hesitation, said, "I little knew what I promised, nor know I now what to perform!—there must ever, I find, be some check to human happiness! yet, since upon these terms, Mrs. Delvile herself is content to wish me of her family—"

She stopt; but, urged earnestly by Delvile, added "I must not, I think, withdraw the powers with which I entrusted her."

Delvile, grateful and enchanted, now forgot his haste and his business, and lost every wish but to re-animate her spirits: she compelled him, however, to leave her, that his visit might less be wondered at, and sent by him a message to Mrs. Delvile, that, wholly relying upon her wisdom, she implicitly submitted to her decree.

CHAPTER XI

An Enterprise

CECILIA now had no time for after-thoughts or anxious repentance, since notwithstanding the hurry of her spirits, and the confusion of her mind, she had too much real business, to yield to pensive indulgence.

Averse to all falsehood, she invented none upon this occasion; she merely told her guests she was summoned to London upon an affair of importance; and though she saw their curiosity, not being at liberty to satisfy it with the truth, she attempted not to appease it by fiction, but quietly left it to its common fare, conjecture. She would gladly have made

Henrietta the companion of her journey, but Henrietta was the last to whom that journey could give pleasure. She only, therefore, took her maid in the chaise, and, attended by one servant on horseback, at six o'clock the next morning, she quitted her mansion, to enter into an engagement by which soon she was to resign it for ever.

Disinterested as she was, she considered her situation as peculiarly perverse, that from the time of her coming to a fortune which most others regarded as enviable, she had been a stranger to peace, a fruitless seeker of happiness, a dupe to the fraudulent, and a prey to the needy! the little comfort she had received, had been merely from dispensing it, and now only had she any chance of being happy herself, when upon the point of relinquishing what all others built their happiness upon obtaining!

These reflections only gave way to others still more disagreeable; she was now a second time engaged in a transaction she could not approve, and suffering the whole peace of her future life to hang upon an action dark, private and imprudent: an action by which the liberal kindness of her late uncle would be annulled, by which the father of her intended husband would be disobeyed, and which already, in a similar instance, had brought her to affliction and disgrace. These melancholy thoughts haunted her during the whole journey, and though the assurance of Mrs. Delvile's approbation was some relief to her uneasiness, she involuntarily prepared herself for meeting new mortifications, and was tormented with an apprehension that this second attempt made her merit them.

She drove immediately, by the previous direction of Delvile, to a lodging-house in Albemarle-Street, which he had taken care to have prepared for her reception. She then sent for a chair, and went to Mrs. Delvile's. Her being seen by the servants of that house was not very important, as their master was soon to be acquainted with the real motive of her journey.

She was shewn into a parlour, while Mrs. Delvile was informed of her arrival, and there flown to by Delvile with the most grateful eagerness. Yet she saw in his countenance that all was not well, and heard upon enquiry that his mother was considerably worse.

Extremely shocked by this intelligence, she already began to lament her unfortunate enterprise. Delvile struggled, by exerting his own spirits, to restore her's, but forced gaiety is never exhilarating; and, full of care and anxiety, he was ill able to appear sprightly and easy.

They were soon summoned up stairs into the apartment of Mrs. Delvile, who was lying upon a couch, pale, weak, and much altered. Delvile led the way, saying, "Here, madam, comes one whose sight will bring peace and pleasure to you!"

"This, indeed,' cried Mrs. Delvile, half rising and embracing her, "is the form in which they are most welcome to me! virtuous, noble Cecilia! what honour you do my son! with what joy, should I ever recover, shall I assist him in paying the gratitude he owes you!"

Cecilia, grieved at her situation, and affected by her kindness, could only answer with her tears; which, however, were not shed alone; for Delvile's eyes were full, as he passionately exclaimed, "This, this is the sight my heart has thus long desired! the wife of my choice taken to the bosom of the parent I revere! be yet but well, my beloved mother, and I will be thankful for every calamity that has led to so sweet a conclusion!"

"Content yourself, however, my son, with one of us," cried Mrs. Delvile, smiling; "and content yourself, if you can, though your hard lot should make that one this creature of full bloom, health, and youth! Ah, my love," added she, more seriously, and addressing the still weeping Cecilia, "should now Mortimer, in losing me, lose those cares by which alone, for some months past, my life has been rendered tolerable, how peaceably shall I resign him to one so able to recompense his filial patience and services!"

This was not a speech to stop the tears of Cecilia, though such warmth of approbation quieted her conscientious scruples. Delvile now earnestly interfered; he told her that his mother had been ordered not to talk or exert herself, and entreated her to be composed, and his mother to be silent.

"Be it *your* business, then," said Mrs. Delvile, more gaily, "to find us entertainment. We will promise to be very still if you will take that trouble upon yourself."

"I will not," answered he, "be rallied from my purpose; if I cannot entertain, it will be something to weary you, for that may incline you to take rest, which will be answering a better purpose."

"Mortimer," returned she, "is this the ingenuity of duty or of love? and which are you just now thinking of, my health, or a conversation uninterrupted with Miss Beverley?"

"Perhaps a little of both!" said he, chearfully, though colouring.

"But you rather meant it should pass," said Mrs. Delvile, "you were thinking only of me? I have always observed, that where one scheme answers two purposes, the ostensive is never the purpose most at heart."

"Why it is but common prudence," answered Delvile, "to feel our way a little before we mention what we most wish, and so cast the hazard of the refusal upon something rather less important."

"Admirably settled!" cried Mrs. Delvile: "so my rest is but to prove Miss Beverley's disturbance!—Well, it is only anticipating our future way of life, when her disturbance, in taking the management of you to herself, will of course prove my rest."

She then quietly reposed herself, and Delvile discoursed with Cecilia upon their future plans, hopes and actions.

He meant to set off from the church-door to Delvile Castle, to acquaint his father with his marriage, and then to return instantly to London: there he entreated Cecilia to stay with his mother, that, finding them both together, he might not exhaust her patience, by making his parting visit occasion another journey to Suffolk.

But here Cecilia resolutely opposed him; saying, her only chance to escape discovery, was going instantly to her own house; and representing so earnestly her desire that their marriage should be unknown till his return to England, upon a thousand motives of delicacy, propriety, and fearfulness, that the obligation he owed already to a compliance which he saw grew more and more reluctant, restrained him both in gratitude and pity from persecuting her further. Neither would she consent to seeing him in Suffolk; which could but delay his mother's journey, and expose her to unnecessary suspicions; she promised, however, to write to him often, and as, from his mother's weakness, he must travel very slowly, she took a plan of his route, and engaged that he should find a letter from her at every great town.

The bond which he had already had altered, he insisted upon leaving in her own custody, averse to applying to Mr. Monckton, whose behaviour to him had before given him disgust, and in whom Cecilia herself no longer wished to confide. He had again applied to the same lawyer, Mr. Singleton, to give her away; for though to his secrecy he had no tie, he had still less to any entire stranger. Mrs. Delvile was too ill to attend them to church, nor would Delvile have desired from her such absolute defiance of his father.

Cecilia now gave another sigh to her departed friend Mrs. Charlton, whose presence upon this awful occasion would else again have soothed and supported her. She had no female friend in whom she could rely; but feeling a repugnance invincible to being accompanied only by men, she accepted the attendance of Mrs. Delvile's own woman, who had lived many years in the family, and was high in the favour and confidence of her lady.

The arrangement of these and other articles, with occasional interruptions from Mrs. Delvile, fully employed the evening. Delvile would not trust again to meeting her at the church; but begged her to send out her servants between seven and eight o'clock in the morning, at which time he would himself call for her with a chair.

She went away early, that Mrs. Delvile might go to rest, and it was mutually agreed they should risk no meeting the next day. Delvile conjured them to part with firmness and chearfulness, and Cecilia, fearing her own emotion, would have retired without bidding her adieu. But Mrs. Delvile, calling after her, said, "Take with you my blessing!" and tenderly embracing her, added, "My son, as my chief nurse, claims a prescriptive right to govern me, but I will break from his control to tell my sweet Cecilia what ease and what delight she has already given to my mind! my best hope of recovery is founded on the pleasure I anticipate in witnessing your mutual happiness: but should my illness prove fatal, and that felicity be denied me, my greatest earthly care is already removed by the security I feel of Mortimer's future peace. Take with you, then, my blessing, for you are become one to me! long daughter of my affection, now wife of my darling son! love her, Mortimer, as she merits, and cherish her with tenderest gratitude!— banish, sweetest Cecilia, every apprehension that oppresses you, and receive in Mortimer Delvile a husband that will revere your virtues, and dignify your choice!"

She then embraced her again, and seeing that her heart was too full for speech, suffered her to go without making any answer. Delvile attended her to her chair, scarce less moved than herself, and found only opportunity to entreat her punctuality the next morning.

She had, indeed, no inclination to fail in her appointment, or risk the repetition of scenes so affecting, or situations so alarming. Mrs. Delvile's full approbation somewhat restored to her her own, but nothing could remove the fearful anxiety, which still privately tormented her with expectations of another disappointment.

The next morning she arose with the light, and calling all her courage to her aid, determined to consider this day as decisive of her destiny with regard to Delvile, and, rejoicing that at least all suspense would be over, to support herself with fortitude, be that destiny what it might.

At the appointed time she sent her maid to visit Mrs. Hill, and gave some errands to her man that carried him to a distant part of the town: but she charged them both to return to the lodgings by nine o'clock, at which hour she ordered a chaise for returning into the country.

Delvile, who was impatiently watching for their quitting the house, only waited till they were out of sight, to present himself at the door. He was shewn into a parlour, where she

instantly attended him; and being told that the clergyman,
Mr. Singleton, and Mrs. Delvile's woman, were already in
the church, she gave him her hand in silence, and he led her
to the chair.

The calmness of stifled hope had now taken place in
Cecilia of quick sensations and alarm. Occupied with a firm
belief she should never be the wife of Delvile, she only
waited, with a desperate sort of patience, to see when and
by whom she was next to be parted from him.

When they arrived near the church, Delvile stopt the
chair. He handed Cecilia out of it, and discharging the
chairmen, conducted her into the church. He was surprised
himself at her composure, but earnestly wishing it to last,
took care not to say to her a word that should make any
answer from her necessary.

He gave her, as before, to Mr. Singleton, secretly praying
that not, as before, she might be given him in vain: Mrs.
Delvile's woman attended her; the clergyman was ready,
and they all proceeded to the altar.

The ceremony was begun; Cecilia, rather mechanically
than with consciousness, appearing to listen to it: but at the
words, *If any man can shew any just cause why they may not
lawfully be joined together*, Delvile himself shook with terror,
lest some concealed person should again answer it, and
Cecilia, with a sort of steady dismay in her countenance,
cast her eyes round the church, with no other view than that
of seeing from what corner the prohibiter would start.

She looked, however, to no purpose; no prohibiter
appeared, the ceremony was performed without any
interruption, and she received the thanks of Delvile, and the
congratulations of the little set, before the idea which had so
strongly pre-occupied her imagination, was sufficiently
removed from it to satisfy her she was really married.

They then went to the vestry, where their business was not
long; and Delvile again put Cecilia into a chair, which again
he accompanied on foot.

Her sensibility now soon returned, though still attended
with strangeness and a sensation of incredulity. But the sight
of Delvile at her lodgings, contrary to their agreement,

wholly recovered her senses from the stupor which had dulled them. He came, however, but to acknowledge how highly she had obliged him, to see her himself restored to the animation natural to her character, and to give her a million of charges, resulting from anxiety and tenderness. And then, fearing the return of her servants, he quitted her, and set out for Delvile Castle.

The amazement of Cecilia was still unconquerable; to be actually united with Delvile! to be his with the full consent of his mother,—to have him her's, beyond the power of his father,—she could not reconcile it with possibility; she fancied it a dream,—but a dream from which she wished not to awake.

BOOK X

CHAPTER I

A Discovery

CECILIA's journey back to the country was as safe and free from interruption as her journey had been to town, and all that distinguished them was what passed in her own mind: the doubts, apprehensions, and desponding suspense which had accompanied her setting out, were now all removed, and certainty, ease, the expectation of happiness, and the cessation of all perplexity, had taken their place. She had nothing left to dread but the inflexibility of Mr. Delvile, and hardly any thing even to hope but the recovery of his lady.

Her friends at her return expressed their wonder at her expedition, but their wonder at what occasioned it, though still greater, met no satisfaction. Henrietta rejoiced in her sight, though her absence had been so short; and Cecilia, whose affection with her pity increased, intimated to her the event for which she wished her to prepare herself, and frankly acknowledged she had reason to expect it would soon take place.

Henrietta endeavoured with composure to receive this intelligence, and to return such a mark of confidence with chearful congratulations: but her fortitude was unequal to an effort so heroic, and her character was too simple to assume a greatness she felt not: she sighed and changed colour; and hastily quitted the room that she might sob aloud in another.

Warm-hearted, tender, and susceptible, her affections were all undisguised: struck with the elegance of Delvile, and enchanted by his services to her brother, she had lost to him her heart at first without missing it, and, when missed, without seeking to reclaim it. The hopelessness of such a passion she never considered, nor asked herself its end, or scarce suspected its aim; it was pleasant to her at the time,

and she looked not to the future, but fed it with visionary
schemes, and soothed it with voluntary fancies. Now she
knew all was over, she felt the folly she had committed, but
though sensibly and candidly angry at her own error, its
conviction offered nothing but sorrow to succeed it.

The felicity of Cecilia, whom she loved, admired and
revered, she wished with the genuine ardour of zealous
sincerity; but that Delvile, the very cause and sole subject*
of her own personal unhappiness, should himself constitute
that felicity, was too much for her spirits, and seemed to her
mortified mind too cruel in her destiny.

Cecilia, who in the very vehemence of her sorrow saw its
innocence, was too just and too noble to be offended by it,
or impute to the bad passions of envy or jealousy, the artless
regret of an untutored mind. To be penetrated too deeply
with the merit of Delvile, with her wanted no excuse, and
she grieved for her situation with but little mixture of blame,
and none of surprise. She redoubled her kindness and
caresses with the hope of consoling her, but ventured to trust
her no further, till reflection, and her natural good sense,
should better enable her to bear an explanation.

Nor was this friendly exertion any longer a hardship to
her; the sudden removal, in her own feelings and affairs, of
distress and expectation, had now so much lightened her
heart, that she could spare without repining, some portion
of its spirit to her dejected young friend.

But an incident happened two mornings after which called
back, and most unpleasantly, her attention to herself. She
was told that Mrs. Matt, the poor woman she had settled in
Bury, begged an audience, and upon sending for her up
stairs, and desiring to know what she could do for her,
"Nothing, madam, just now," she answered, "for I don't
come upon my own business, but to tell some news to you,
madam. You bid me never take notice of the wedding, that
was to be, and I'm sure I never opened my mouth about it
from that time to this; but I have found out who it was put
a stop to it, and so I come to tell you."

Cecilia, extremely amazed, eagerly desired her to go on.

"Why, madam, I don't know the gentlewoman's name

quite right yet, but I can tell you where she lives, for I knew her as soon as I set eyes on her, when I see her at church last Sunday, and I would have followed her home, but she went into a coach, and I could not walk fast enough; but I asked one of the footmen where she lived, and he said at the great house at the Grove: and perhaps, madam, you may know where that is: and then he told me her name, but that I can't just now think of."

"Good heaven!" cried Cecilia,——"it could not be Bennet?"

"Yes, ma'am, that's the very name; I know it again now I hear it."

Cecilia then hastily dismissed her, first desiring her not to mention the circumstance to any body.

Shocked and dismayed, she now saw, but saw with horror, the removal of all her doubts, and the explanation of all her difficulties, in the full and irrefragable discovery of the perfidy of her oldest friend and confidant.

Miss Bennet herself she regarded in the affair as a mere tool, which, though in effect it did the work, was innocent of its mischief, because powerless but in the hand of its employer.

"That employer," cried she, "must be Mr. Monckton! Mr. Monckton whom so long I have known, who so willingly has been my counsellor, so ably my instructor! in whose integrity I have confided, upon whose friendship I have relied! my succour in all emergencies, my guide in all perplexities!——Mr. *Monckton* thus dishonourably, thus barbarously to betray me! to turn against me the very confidence I had reposed in his regard for me! and make use of my own trust to furnish the means to injure me!"—

She was now wholly confirmed that he had wronged her with Mr. Delvile; she could not have two enemies so malignant without provocation, and he who so unfeelingly could dissolve a union at the very altar, could alone have the baseness to calumniate her so cruelly.

Evil thoughts thus awakened, stopt not merely upon facts; conjecture carried her further, and conjecture built upon probability. The officiousness of Morrice in pursuing her to

London, his visiting her when there, and his following and watching Delvile, she now reasonably concluded were actions directed by Mr. Monckton, whose house he had but just left, and whose orders, whatever they might be, she was almost certain he would obey. Availing himself, therefore, of the forwardness and suppleness which met in this young man, she doubted not but his intelligence had contributed to acquaint him with her proceedings.

The motive of such deep concerted and accumulated treachery was next to be sought: nor was the search long; one only could have tempted him to schemes so hazardous and costly; and, unsuspicious as she was, she now saw into his whole design.

Long accustomed to regard him as a safe and disinterested old friend, the respect with which, as a child, she had looked up to him, she had insensibly preserved when a woman. That respect had taught her to consider his notice as a favour, and far from suspiciously shunning, she had innocently courted it: and his readiness in advising and tutoring her, his frank and easy friendliness of behaviour, had kept his influence unimpaired, by preventing its secret purpose from being detected.

But now the whole mystery was revealed; his aversion to the Delviles, to which hitherto she had attributed all she disapproved in his behaviour, she was convinced must be inadequate to stimulate him to such lengths. That aversion itself was by this late surmise accounted for, and no sooner did it occur to her, than a thousand circumstances confirmed it.

The first among these was the evident ill will of Lady Margaret, which though she had constantly imputed to the general irascibility for which her character was notorious, she had often wondered to find impenetrable to all endeavours to please or soften her. His care of her fortune, his exhortations against her expences, his wish to make her live with Mr. Briggs, all contributed to point out the selfishness of his attentions, which in one instance rendered visible, became obvious in every other.

Yet various as were the incidents that now poured upon

her memory to his disgrace, not one among them took its rise from his behaviour to herself, which always had been scrupulously circumspect, or if for a moment unguarded, only at a season when her own distress or confusion had prevented her from perceiving it. This recollection almost staggered her suspicions; yet so absolute seemed the confirmation they received from every other, that her doubt was overpowered, and soon wholly extinguished.

She was yet ruminating upon this subject, when word was brought her that Mr. Monckton was in the parlour.

Mingled disgust and indignation made her shudder at his name, and without pausing a moment, she sent him word she was engaged, and could not possibly leave her room.

Astonished by such a dismission, he left the house in the utmost confusion. But Cecilia could not endure to see him, after a discovery of such hypocrisy and villainy.

She considered, however, that the matter could not rest here: he would demand an explanation, and perhaps, by his unparalleled address, again contrive to seem innocent, notwithstanding appearances were at present so much against him. Expecting, therefore, some artifice, and determined not to be duped by it, she sent again for the Pew-opener, to examine her more strictly.

The woman was out at work in a private family, and could not come till the evening: but, when further questioned, the description she gave of Miss Bennet was too exact to be disputed.

She then desired her to call again the next morning: and sent a servant to the Grove, with her compliments to Miss Bennet, and a request that she might send her carriage for her the next day, at any time she pleased, as she wished much to speak with her.

This message, she was aware, might create some suspicion, and put her upon her guard; but she thought, nevertheless, a sudden meeting with the Pew-opener, whom she meant abruptly to confront with her, would baffle the security of any previously settled scheme.

To a conviction such as this even Mr. Monckton must submit, and since he was lost to her as a friend, she might at least save herself the pain of keeping up his acquaintance.

CHAPTER II

An Interview

THE servant did not return till it was dark; and then, with a look of much dismay, said he had been able to meet with nobody who could either give or take a message; that the Grove was all in confusion, and the whole country in an uproar, for Mr. Monckton, just as he arrived, had been brought home dead!

Cecilia screamed with involuntary horror; a pang like remorse seized her mind, with the apprehension she had some share in this catastrophe, and innocent as she was either of his fall or his crimes, she no sooner heard he was no more, than she forgot he had offended her, and reproached herself with severity for the shame to which she meant to expose him the next morning.

Dreadfully disturbed by this horrible incident, she entreated Mrs. Harrel and Henrietta to sup by themselves, and going into her own room, determined to write the whole affair to Delvile, in a letter she should direct to be left at the post-office for him at Margate.*

And here strongly she felt the happiness of being actually his wife; she could now without reserve make him acquainted with all her affairs, and tell to the master of her heart every emotion that entered it.

While engaged in this office, the very action of which quieted her, a letter was brought her from Delvile himself. She received it with gratitude and opened it with joy; he had promised to write soon, but *so* soon she had thought impossible.

The reading took not much time; the letter contained but the following words:

To Miss BEVERLEY.

My CECILIA!

Be alone, I conjure you; dismiss every body, and admit me this moment!

Great was her astonishment at this note! no name to it,
no conclusion, the characters indistinct, the writing crooked,
the words so few, and those few scarce legible!

He desired to see her, and to see her alone; she could not
hesitate in her compliance,—but whom could she dismiss?—her servants, if ordered away, would but be curi-
ously upon the watch,—she could think of no expedient, she
was all hurry and amazement.

She asked if any one waited for an answer? The footman
said no; that the note was given in by somebody who did not
speak, and who ran out of sight the moment he had
delivered it.

She could not doubt this was Delvile himself,—Delvile
who should now be just returned from the castle to his
mother, and whom she had thought not even a letter would
reach if directed any where nearer than Margate!

All she could devise in obedience to him, was to go and
wait for him alone in her dressing-room, giving orders that
if any one called they might be immediately brought up to
her, as she expected somebody upon business, with whom
she must not be interrupted.

This was extremely disagreeable to her; yet, contrary as
it was to their agreement, she felt no inclination to reproach
Delvile; the abruptness of his note, the evident hand-shaking
with which it had been written, the strangeness of the
request in a situation such as theirs,—all concurred to assure
her he came not to her idly, and all led her to apprehend he
came to her with evil tidings.

What they might be, she had no time to conjecture; a
servant, in a few minutes, opened the dressing-room door,
and said "Ma'am, a gentleman;" and Delvile, abruptly
entering, shut it himself, in his eagerness to get rid of him.

At his sight, her prognostication of ill became stronger!
she went forward to meet him, and he advanced to her
smiling and in haste; but that smile did not well do its office;
it concealed not a pallid countenance, in which every feature
spoke horror; it disguised not an aching heart, which almost
visibly throbbed with intolerable emotion! Yet he addressed
her in terms of tenderness and peace; but his tremulous

voice counteracted his words, and spoke that all within was tumult and war!

Cecilia, amazed, affrighted, had no power to hasten an explanation, which, on his own part, he seemed unable, or fearful to begin. He talked to her of his happiness in again seeing her before he left the kingdom, entreated her to write to him continually, said the same thing two and three times in a breath, began with one subject, and seemed unconscious he wandered presently into another, and asked her questions innumerable about her health, journey, affairs, and ease of mind, without hearing from her any answer, or seeming to miss that she made none.

Cecilia grew dreadfully terrified; something strange and most alarming she was sure must have happened, but *what*, she had no means to know, nor courage, nor even words to enquire.

Delvile, at length, the first hurry of his spirits abating, became more coherent and considerate: and looking anxiously at her, said, "Why this silence, my Cecilia?"

"I know not!" said she, endeavouring to recover herself, "but your coming was unexpected; I was just writing to you at Margate."

"Write still, then; but direct to Ostend; I shall be quicker than the post; and I would not lose a letter—a line—a word from you, for all the world can offer me!"

"Quicker than the post?" cried Cecilia; "but how can Mrs. Delvile—" she stopt; not knowing what she might venture to ask.

"She is now on the road to Margate; I hope to be there to receive her. I mean but to bid you adieu, and be gone."

Cecilia made no answer; she was more and more astonished, more and more confounded.

"You are thoughtful?" said he, with tenderness; "are you unhappy?—sweetest Cecilia! most excellent of human creatures! if I have made you unhappy—and I must!—it is inevitable!—"

"Oh Delvile!" cried she, now assuming more courage, "why will you not speak to me openly?—something, I see, is wrong; may I not hear it? may I not tell you, at least, my concern that any thing has distressed you?"

"You are too good!" cried he; "to deserve you is not possible,—but to afflict you is inhuman!"

"Why so?" cried she, more chearfully; "must I not share the common lot? or expect the whole world to be new modelled, lest I should meet in it any thing but happiness?"

"There is not, indeed, much danger! Have you pen and ink here?"

She brought them to him immediately, with paper.

"You have been writing to me, you say?—I will begin a letter myself."

"To me?" cried she.

He made no answer, but took up the pen, and wrote a few words, and then, flinging it down, said "Fool!—— I could have done this without coming!"

"May I look at it?" said she; and, finding he made no opposition, advanced and read.

I fear to alarm you by rash precipitation,—I fear to alarm you by lingering suspense,—but all is not well—

"Fear nothing!" cried she, turning to him with the kindest earnestness; "tell me, whatever it may be!—Am I not your wife? bound by every tie divine and human to share in all your sorrows, if, unhappily, I cannot mitigate them!"

"Since you allow me," cried he, gratefully, "so sweet a claim, a claim to which all others yield, and which if you repent not giving me, will make all others nearly immaterial to me,—I will own to you that all, indeed, is not well! I have been hasty,—you will blame me; I deserve, indeed, to be blamed!—entrusted with your peace and happiness, to suffer rage, resentment, violence, to make me forego what I owed to such a deposite!—If your blame, however, stops short of repentance—but it cannot!"

"What, then," cried she with warmth, "must you have done? for there is not an action of which I believe you capable, there is not an event which I believe to be possible, that can ever make me repent belonging to you wholly!"

"Generous, condescending Cecilia!" cried he; "Words

such as these, hung there not upon me an evil the most
depressing, would be almost more than I could bear—would
make me too blest for mortality!"

"But words such as these," said she more gaily, "I might
long have coquetted ere I had spoken, had you not drawn
them from me by this alarm. Take, therefore, the good with
the ill, and remember, if all does not go right, you have now
a trusty friend, as willing to be the partner of your serious
as your happiest hours."

"Shew but as much firmness as you have shewn
sweetness," cried he, "and I will fear to tell you nothing."

She reiterated her assurances; they then both sat down,
and he began his account.

"Immediately from your lodgings I went where I had
ordered a chaise, and stopt only to change horses till I
reached Delvile Castle. My father saw me with surprise, and
received me with coldness. I was compelled by my situation
to be abrupt, and told him I came, before I accompanied my
mother abroad, to make him acquainted with an affair
which I thought myself bound in duty and respect to suffer
no one to communicate to him but myself. He then sternly
interrupted me, and declared in high terms, that if this affair
concerned *you*, he would not listen to it. I attempted to
remonstrate upon this injustice, when he passionately broke
forth into new and horrible charges against you, affirming
that he had them from authority as indisputable as ocular
demonstration. I was then certain of some foul play."—

"Foul play indeed!" cried Cecilia, who now knew but too
well by whom she had been injured. "Good heaven, how
have I been deceived, where most I have trusted!"

"I told him," continued Delvile, "some gross imposition
had been practiced upon him, and earnestly conjured him
no longer to conceal from me by whom. This, unfortunately,
encreased his rage; imposition, he said, was not so easily
played upon him, he left that for *me* who so readily was
duped; while for himself, he had only given credit to a man
of much consideration in Suffolk, who had known you from
a child, who had solemnly assured him he had repeatedly
endeavoured to reclaim you, who had rescued you from

the hands of Jews at his own hazard and loss, and who actually shewed him bonds acknowledging immense debts, which were signed with your own hand.''

''Horrible!'' exclaimed Cecilia, ''I believed not such guilt and perfidy possible!''

''I was scarce myself,'' resumed Delvile, ''while I heard him: I demanded even with fierceness his author, whom I scrupled not to execrate as he deserved; he coldly answered he was bound by an oath never to reveal him, nor should he repay his honourable attention to his family by a breach of his own word, were it even less formally engaged. I then lost all patience; to mention honour, I cried, was a farce, where such infamous calumnies were listened to;—but let me not shock you unnecessarily, you may readily conjecture what passed.''

''Ah me!'' cried Cecilia, ''you have then quarrelled with your father!''

''I have!'' said he; ''nor does he yet know I am married: in so much wrath there was no room for narration; I only pledged myself by all I held sacred, never to rest till I had cleared your fame, by the detection of this villainy, and then left him without further explanation.''

''Oh return, then, to him directly!'' cried Cecilia; ''he is your father, you are bound to bear with his displeasure; —alas! had you never known me, you had never incurred it!''

''Believe me,'' he answered, ''I am ill at ease under it: if you wish it, when you have heard me, I will go to him immediately; if not, I will write, and you shall yourself dictate what.''

Cecilia thanked him, and begged he would continue his account.

''My first step, when I left the Castle, was to send a letter to my mother, in which I entreated her to set out as soon as possible for Margate, as I was detained from her unavoidably, and was unwilling my delay should either retard our journey, or oblige her to travel faster. At Margate I hoped to be as soon as herself, if not before her.''

"And why," cried Cecilia, "did you not go to town as you had promised, and accompany her?"

"I had business another way. I came hither."

"Directly?"

"No;—but soon."

"Where did you go first?"

"My Cecilia, it is now you must summon your fortitude: I left my father without an explanation on *my* part;—but not till, in his rage of asserting his authority, he had unwarily named his informant."

"Well!"

"That informant—the most deceitful of men!—was your long pretended friend, Mr. Monckton!"

"So I feared!" said Cecilia, whose blood now ran cold through her veins with sudden and new apprehensions.

"I rode to the Grove, on hack-horses, and on a full gallop the whole way. I got to him early in the evening. I was shewn into his library. I told him my errand.— You look pale, my love? You are not well?—"

Cecilia, too sick for speech, leant her head upon a table. Delvile was going to call for help; but she put her hand upon his arm to stop him, and, perceiving she was only mentally affected, he rested, and endeavoured by every possible means to revive her.

After a while, she again raised her head, faintly saying, "I am sorry I interrupted you; but the conclusion I already know,—Mr. Monckton is dead!"

"Not dead," cried he; "dangerously, indeed, wounded, but thank heaven, not actually dead!"

"Not dead?" cried Cecilia, with recruited strength and spirits, "Oh then all yet may be well!—if he is not dead, he may recover!"

"He may; I hope he will!"

"Now, then," she cried, "tell me all: I can bear any intelligence but of death by human means."

"I meant not to have gone such lengths; far from it; I hold duels in abhorrence, as unjustifiable acts of violence, and savage devices of revenge. I have offended against my own conviction,—but, transported with passion at his infamous charges, I was not master of my reason; I accused him of his perfidy; he denied it; I told him I had it from my father, —he changed the subject to pour abuse upon him; I insisted on a recantation to clear you; he asked by what right? I fiercely answered, by a husband's! His countenance, then, explained at least the motives of his treachery,—he loves you himself! he had probably schemed to keep you free till his wife died, and then concluded his machinations would secure you his own. For this purpose, finding he was in danger of losing you, he was content even to blast your character, rather than suffer you to escape him! But the moment I acknowledged my marriage he grew more furious than myself; and, in short—for why relate the frenzies of rage? we walked out together; my travelling pistols* were already charged; I gave him his choice of them, and, the challenge being mine, for insolence joined with guilt had robbed me of all forbearance, he fired first, but missed me: I then demanded whether he would clear your fame? he called out "Fire! I will make no terms,"—I did fire,—and unfortunately aimed better! We had neither of us any second, all was the result of immediate passion; but I soon got people to him, and assisted in conveying him home. He was at first believed to be dead, and I was seized by his servants; but he afterwards shewed signs of life, and by sending for my friend Biddulph, I was released. Such is the melancholy transaction I came to relate to you, flattering myself it would something less shock you from me than from another: yet my own real concern for the affair, the repentance with which from the moment the wretch fell, I was struck in being his destroyer, and the sorrow, the remorse, rather, which I felt, in coming to wound you with such black, such fearful intelligence,—you to whom all I owe is peace and comfort!——these thoughts gave me so much disturbance, that, in fact, I knew less than any other how to prepare you for such a tale."

He stopt; but Cecilia could say nothing: to censure him now would both be cruel and vain; yet to pretend she was satisfied with his conduct, would be doing violence to her judgment and veracity. She saw, too, that his error had

sprung wholly from a generous ardor in her defence, and
that his confidence in her character, had resisted, without
wavering, every attack that menaced it. For this she felt
truly grateful; yet his quarrel with his father,—the danger of
his mother,—his necessary absence,—her own clandestine
situation,—and more than all, the threatened death of Mr.
Monckton by his hands, were circumstances so full of dread
and sadness, she knew not upon which to speak,—how to
offer him comfort,—how to assume a countenance that
looked able to receive any, or by what means to repress the
emotions which so many ways assailed her. Delvile, having
vainly waited some reply, then in a tone the most
melancholy, said, "If it is yet possible you can be sufficiently
interested in my fate to care what becomes of me, aid me
now with your counsel, or rather with your instructions; I
am scarce able to think for myself, and to be thought for by
you, would yet be a consolation that would give me spirit for
any thing."

Cecilia, starting from her reverie, repeated, "To care
what becomes of you? Oh Delvile!—make not my heart
bleed by words of such unkindness!"

"Forgive me," cried he, "I meant not a reproach; I
meant but to state my own consciousness how little I deserve
from you. You talked to me of going to my father? do you
still wish it?"

"I think so!" cried she; too much disturbed to know what
she said, yet fearing again to hurt him by making him wait
her answer.

"I will go then," said he, "without doubt: too happy to
be guided by you, which-ever way I steer. I have now,
indeed, much to tell him; but whatever may be his wrath,
there is little fear, at this time, that my own temper cannot
bear it! what next shall I do?"

"What next?" repeated she; "indeed I know not!"

"Shall I go immediately to Margate? or shall I first ride
hither?"

"If you please," said she much perturbed, and deeply
sighing.

"I please nothing but by your direction, to follow that is

my only chance of pleasure. Which, then, shall I do?—you will not, now, refuse to direct me?''

"No, certainly, not for the world!''

"Speak to me, then, my love, and tell me;—why are you thus silent?—is it painful to you to counsel me?''

"No, indeed!'' said she, putting her hand to her head, "I will speak to you in a few minutes.''

"Oh my Cecilia!'' cried he, looking at her with much alarm, "call back your recollection! you know not what you say, you take no interest in what you answer.''

"Indeed I do!'' said she, sighing deeply, and oppressed beyond the power of thinking, beyond any power but an internal consciousness of wretchedness.

"Sigh not so bitterly,'' cried he, "if you have any compassion! sigh not so bitterly,—I cannot bear to hear you!''

"I am very sorry indeed!'' said she, sighing again, and not seeming sensible she spoke.

"Good Heaven!'' cried he, rising, "distract me not with this horror!—speak not to me in such broken sentences!— Do you hear me, Cecilia?—why will you not answer me?''

She started and trembled, looked pale and affrighted, and putting both her hands upon her heart, said, "Oh yes!— but I have an oppression here,—a tightness, a fulness,—I have not room for breath!''

"Oh beloved of my heart!'' cried he, wildly casting himself at her feet, "kill me not with this terror!—call back your faculties,—awake from this dreadful insensibility! tell me at least you know me!—tell me I have not tortured you quite to madness!—sole darling of my affections! my own, my wedded Cecilia!—rescue me from this agony! it is more than I can support!——''

This energy of distress brought back her scattered senses, scarce more stunned by the shock of all this misery, than by the restraint of her feelings in struggling to conceal it. But these passionate exclamations restoring her sensibility, she burst into tears, which happily relieved her mind from the conflict with which it was labouring, and which, not thus effected, might have ended more fatally.

Never had Delvile more rejoiced in her smiles than now in these seasonable tears, which he regarded and blest as the preservers of her reason. They flowed long without any intermission, his soothing and tenderness but melting her to more sorrow: after a while, however, the return of her faculties, which at first seemed all consigned over to grief, was manifested by the returning strength of her mind: she blamed herself severely for the little fortitude she had shewn, but having now given vent to emotions too forcible to be wholly stifled, she assured him he might depend upon her better courage for the future, and entreated him to consider and settle his affairs.

Not speedily, however, could Delvile himself recover. The torture he had suffered in believing, though only for a few moments, that the terror he had given to Cecilia had affected her intellects, made even a deeper impression upon his imagination, than the scene of fury and death, which had occasioned that terror: and Cecilia, who now strained every nerve to repair by her firmness, the pain which by her weakness she had given him, was sooner in a condition for reasoning and deliberation than himself.

"Ah Delvile!" she cried, comprehending what passed within him, "do you allow nothing for surprize? and nothing for the hard conflict of endeavouring to suppress it? do you think me still as unfit to advise with, and as worthless, as feeble a counsellor, as during the first confusion of my mind?"

"Hurry not your tender spirits, I beseech you," cried he, "we have time enough; we will talk about business by and by."

"What time?" cried she, "what is it now o'clock?"

"Good Heaven!" cried he, looking at his watch, "already past ten! you must turn me out, my Cecilia, or calumny will still be busy, even though poor Monckton is quiet."

"I *will* turn you out," cried she, "I am indeed most earnest to have you gone. But tell me your plan, and which way you mean to go?"

"That," he answered, "you shall decide for me yourself:

whether to Delvile Castle, to finish one tale, and wholly communicate another, or to Margate, to hasten my mother abroad, before the news of this calamity reaches her."

"Go to Margate," cried she, eagerly, "set off this very moment! you can write to your father from Ostend. But continue, I conjure you, on the continent, till we see if this unhappy man lives, and enquire, of those who can judge, what must follow if he should not!"

"A trial," said he, "must follow, and it will go, I fear, but hardly with me! the challenge was mine; his servants can all witness I went to him, not he to me,—Oh my Cecilia! the rashness of which I have been guilty, is so opposite to my principles, and, all generous as is your silence, I know it so opposite to yours, that never, should his blood be on my hands, wretch as he was, never will my heart be quiet more!"

"He will live, he will live!" cried Cecilia, repressing her horror, "fear nothing, for he will live;—and as to his wound and his sufferings, his perfidy has deserved them. Go, then, to Margate; think only of Mrs. Devile, and save her, if possible, from hearing what has happened."

"I will go,—stay,—do which and whatever you bid me: but, should what I fear come to pass, should my mother continue ill, my father inflexible, should this wretched man die, and should England no longer be a country I shall love to dwell in,——could you, then, bear to own,—would you, then, consent to follow me?—"

"Could I?—am I not yours? may you not command me? tell me, then,—you have only to say,—shall I accompany you at once?"

Delvile, affected by her generosity, could scarce utter his thanks; yet he did not hesitate in denying to avail himself of it; "No, my Cecilia," he cried, "I am not so selfish. If we have not happier days, we will at least wait for more desperate necessity. With the uncertainty if I have not this man's life to answer for at the hazard of my own, to take my wife—my bride,—from the kingdom I must fly!—to make her a fugitive and an exile in the first publishing that she is mine! No, if I am not a destined alien for life I can never permit it. Nothing less, believe me, shall ever urge my consent to wound the chaste propriety of your character, by making you an eloper with a duelist.''

They then again consulted upon their future plans; and concluded that in the present disordered state of their affairs, it would be best not to acknowledge even to Mr. Delvile their mariage, to whom the news of the duel, and Mr. Monckton's danger, would be a blow so severe, that, to add to it any other might half distract him.

To the few people already acquainted with it, Delvile therefore determined to write from Ostend, re-urging his entreaties for their discretion and secresy. Cecilia promised every post to acquaint him how Mr. Monckton went on, and she then besought him to go instantly, that he might out-travel the ill news to his mother.

He complied, and took leave of her in the tenderest manner, conjuring her to support her spirits, and be careful of her health. "Happiness," said he, "is much in arrears with us, and though my violence may have frightened it away, your sweetness and gentleness will yet attract it back: all that for me is in store must be received at your hands,— what is offered in any other way, I shall only mistake for evil! droop not, therefore, my generous Cecilia, but in yourself preserve me!''

"I will not droop;'' said she; "you will find, I hope, you have not intrusted yourself in ill hands.''

"Peace then be with you, my love!—my comforting, my soul-reviving Cecilia! Peace, such as angels give, and such as may drive from your mind the remembrance of this bitter hour!''

He then tore himself away.

Cecilia, who to his blessings could almost, like the tender Belvidera, have exclaimed

O do not leave me!—stay with me and curse me!*

listened to his steps till she could hear them no longer, as if the remaining moments of her life were to be measured by them: but then, remembering the danger both to herself and him of his stay, she endeavoured to rejoice that he was gone, and, but that her mind was in no state for joy, was too rational not to have succeeded.

Grief and horror for what was past, apprehension and suspense for what was to come, so disordered her whole frame, so confused even her intellects, that when not all the assistance of fancy could persuade her she still heard the footsteps of Delvile, she went to the chair upon which he had been seated, and taking possession of it, sat with her arms crossed, silent, quiet, and erect, almost vacant of all thought, yet with a secret idea she was doing something right.

Here she continued till Henrietta came to wish her good night; whose surprise and concern at the strangeness of her look and attitude, once more recovered her. But terrified herself at this threatened wandering of her reason, and certain she must all night be a stranger to rest, she accepted the affectionate offer of the kind-hearted girl to stay with her, who was too much grieved for her grief to sleep any more than herself.

She told her not what had passed; that, she knew, would be fruitless affliction to her: but she was soothed by her gentleness, and her conversation was some security from the dangerous rambling of her ideas.

Henrietta herself found no little consolation in her own private sorrows, that she was able to give comfort to her beloved Miss Beverley, from whom she had received favours and kind offices innumerable. She quitted her not night nor day, and in the honest pride of a little power to shew the gratefulness of her heart, she felt a pleasure and self-consequence she had never before experienced.

by them; but then, remembering the danger both to herself and him of his stay, she endeavoured to rejoice that he was gone, and that that her state for joy, was too rational not to have succeeded.

Grief and horror for what was past, apprehension and suspense for what was to come, so disordered her whole

CHAPTER III

A Summons

CECILIA's earliest care, almost at break of day, was to send to the Grove; from thence she heard nothing but evil; Mr. Monckton was still alive, but with little or no hope of recovery, constantly delirious, and talking of Miss Beverley, and of her being married to young Delvile.

Cecilia, who knew well this, at least, was no delirium, though shocked that he talked of it, hoped his danger less than was apprehended.

The next day, however, more fatal news was brought her, though not from the quarter she expected it: Mr. Monckton, in one of his raving fits, had sent for Lady Margaret to his bed side, and used her almost inhumanly: he had railed at her age and infirmities with incredible fury, called her the cause of all his sufferings, and accused her as the immediate agent of Lucifer in his present wound and danger. Lady Margaret, whom neither jealousy nor malignity had cured of loving him, was dismayed and affrighted; and in hurrying out of the room upon his attempting, in his frenzy, to strike her, she dropt down dead in an apoplectic fit.

"Good Heaven! thought Cecilia, what an exemplary punishment has this man! he looses his hated wife at the very moment when her death could no long answer his purposes! Poor Lady Margaret! her life has been as bitter as her temper! married from a view of interest, ill used as a bar to happiness, and destroyed from the fruitless ravings of despair!"

She wrote all this intelligence to Ostend, whence she received a letter from Delvile, acquainting her he was detained from proceeding further by the weakness and illness of his mother, whose sufferings from sea-sickness* had almost put an end to her existence.

Thus passed a miserable week; Monckton still merely alive, Delvile detained at Ostend, and Cecilia tortured alike

by what was recently passed, actually present, and fearfully expected; when one morning she was told a gentleman upon business desired immediately to speak with
her.

She hastily obeyed the summons; the constant image of
her own mind, Delvile, being already present to her, and a
thousand wild conjectures upon what had brought him back,
rapidly occurring to her.

Her expectations, however, were ill answered, for she
found an entire stranger; an elderly man, of no pleasant
aspect or manners.

She desired to know his business.

"I presume, madam, you are the lady of this house?"
She bowed an assent.

"May I take the liberty, madam, to ask your name?"
"My name, sir?"

"You will do me a favour, madam, by telling it
me."

"Is it possible you are come hither without already
knowing it?"

"I know it only by common report, madam."

"Common report, sir, I believe is seldom wrong in a
matter where to be right is so easy."

"Have you any objection, madam, to telling me your
name?"

"No, sir; but your business can hardly be very important,
if you are yet to learn whom you are to address. It will be
time enough, therefore, for us to meet when you are
elsewhere satisfied in this point."

She would then have left the room.

"I beg, madam," cried the stranger, "you will have
patience; it is necessary, before I can open my business, that
I should hear your name from yourself."

"Well, sir," cried she with some hesitation, "you can
scarce have come to this house, without knowing that its
owner is Cecilia Beverley."

"That, madam, is your maiden name."

"My maiden name?" cried she, starting.

"Are you not married, madam?"

"Married, sir?" she repeated, while her cheeks were the colour of scarlet.

"It is, properly, therefore, madam, the name of your husband* that I mean to ask."

"And by what authority, sir," cried she, equally astonished and offended, "do you make these extraordinary enquiries?"

"I am deputed, madam, to wait upon you by Mr. Eggleston, the next heir to this estate, by your uncle's will, if you die without children,* or change your name when you marry. His authority of enquiry, madam, I presume you will allow, and he has vested it in me by a letter of attorney."

Cecilia's distress and confusion were now unspeakable; she knew not what to own or deny, she could not conjecture how she had been betrayed, and she had never made the smallest preparation against such an attack.

"Mr. Eggleston, madam," he continued, "has been pretty credibly informed that you are actually married: he is very desirous, therefore, to know what are your intentions, for your continuing to be called *Miss* Beverley, as if still single, leaves him quite in the dark: but, as he is so deeply concerned in the affair, he expects, as a lady of honour, you will deal with him without prevarication."

"This demand, sir," said Cecilia, stammering, "is so extremely——so—so little expected——"

"The way, madam, in these cases, is to keep pretty closely to the point; are you married or are you not?"

Cecilia, quite confounded, made no answer: to disavow her marriage, when thus formally called upon, was every way unjustifiable; to acknowledge it in her present situation, would involve her in difficulties innumerable.

"This is not, madam, a slight thing; Mr. Eggleston has a large family and a small fortune, and that, into the bargain, very much encumbered; it cannot, therefore, be expected that he will knowingly connive at cheating himself, by submitting to your being actually married, and still enjoying your estate though your husband does not take your name."

Cecilia, now, summoning more presence of mind, answered, "Mr. Eggleston, sir, has, at least, nothing to fear from imposition: those with whom he has, or may have any transactions in this affair, are not accustomed to practice it."

"I am far from meaning any offence, madam; my commission from Mr. Eggleston is simply this, to beg you will satisfy him upon what grounds you now evade the will of your late uncle, which, till cleared up, appears a point manifestly to his prejudice."

"Tell him, then, sir, that whatever he wishes to know shall be explained to him in about a week. At present I can give no other answer."

"Very well, madam; he will wait that time, I am sure, for he does not wish to put you to any inconvenience. But when he heard the gentleman was gone abroad without owning his marriage, he thought it high time to take some notice of the matter."

Cecilia, who by this speech found she was every way discovered, was again in the utmost confusion, and with much trepidation, said, "since you seem so well, sir, acquainted with this affair, I should be glad you would inform me by what means you came to the knowledge of it?"

"I heard it, madam, from Mr. Eggleston himself, who has long known it."

"Long, sir?—impossible! when it is not yet a fortnight—not ten days, or no more, that——"

She stopt, recollecting she was making a confession better deferred.

"That, madam," he answered, "may perhaps bear a little contention: for when this business comes to be settled, it will be very essential to be exact as to the time, even to the very hour; for a large income per annum, divides into a small one per diem; and if your husband keeps his own name, you must not only give up your uncle's inheritance from the time of relinquishing yours, but refund from the very day of your marriage."

"There is not the least doubt of it," answered she; "nor will the smallest difficulty be made."

"You will please, then, to recollect, madam, that this sum is every hour encreasing; and has been since last September, which made half a year accountable for last March. Since then there is now added——"*

"Good Heaven, sir," cried Cecilia, "what calculation are you making out? do you call last week last September?"

"No, madam; but I call last September the month in which you were married."

"You will find yourself, then, sir, extremely mistaken; and Mr. Eggleston is preparing himself for much dispointment, if he supposes me so long in arrears with him."

"Mr. Eggleston, madam, happens to be well informed of this transaction, as, if there is any dispute in it, you will find. He was your immediate successor in the house to which you went last September in Pall-Mall; the woman who kept it acquainted his servants that the last lady who hired it stayed with her but a day, and only came to town, she found, to be married: and hearing, upon enquiry, this lady was Miss Beverley, the servants, well knowing that their master was her conditional heir, told him the circumstance."

"You will find all this, sir, end in nothing."

"That, madam, as I said before, remains to be proved. If a young lady at eight o'clock in the morning, is seen,—and she was seen, going into a church with a young gentleman, and one female friend; and is afterwards observed to come out of it, followed by a clergyman and another person, supposed to have officiated as father,* and is seen get into a coach with same young gentleman, and same female friend, why the circumstances are pretty strong!——"

"They may seem so, sir; but all conclusions drawn from them will be erroneous. I was not married then, upon my honour!"

"We have little, madam, to do with professions; the circumstances are strong enough to bear a trial, and——"

"A trial!——"

"We have traced, madam, many witnesses able to stand

to divers particulars; and eight months share* of such an estate as this, is well worth a little trouble.''

''I am amazed, sir! surely Mr. Eggleston never desired you to make use of this language to me?''

''Mr. Eggleston, madam, has behaved very honourably; though he knew the whole affair so long ago, he was persuaded Mr. Delvile had private reasons for a short concealment; and expecting every day when they would be cleared up by his taking your name, he never interfered: but being now informed he set out last week for the continent, he has been advised by his friends to claim his rights.''

''That claim, sir, he need not fear will be satisfied; and without any occasion for threats of enquiries or law suits.''

''The truth, madam, is this; Mr. Eggleston is at present in a little difficulty about some money matters, which makes it a point with him of some consequence to have the affair settled speedily: unless you could conveniently compromise the matter, by advancing a particular sum, till it suits you to refund the whole that is due to him, and quit the premises.''

''Nothing, sir, is due to him! at least, nothing worth mentioning. I shall enter into no terms, for I have no compromise to make. As to the premises, I will quit them with all the expedition in my power.''

''You will do well, madam; for the truth is, it will not be convenient to him to wait much longer.''

He then went away.

''When, next,'' cried Cecilia, ''shall I again be weak, vain, blind enough to form any plan with a hope of secrecy? or enter, with *any* hope, into a clandestine scheme! betrayed by those I have trusted, discovered by those I have not thought of, exposed to the cruellest alarms, and defenceless from the most shocking attacks!——Such has been the life I have led since the moment I first consented to a private engagement!——Ah Delvile! your mother, in her tenderness, forgot her dignity, or she would not have concurred in an action which to such disgrace made me liable!''

CHAPTER IV

A Deliberation

IT was necessary, however, not to moralize, but to act; Cecilia had undertaken to give her answer in a week, and the artful attorney had drawn from her an acknowledgement of her situation, by which he might claim it yet sooner.

The law-suit with which she was threatened for the arrears of eight months, alarmed her not, though it shocked her, as she was certain she could prove her marriage so much later.

It was easy to perceive that this man had been sent with a view of working from her a confession, and terrifying from her some money; the confession, indeed, in conscience and honesty she could not wholly elude, but she had suffered too often by a facility in parting with money to be there easily duped.

Nothing, however, was more true, than that she now lived upon an estate of which she no longer was the owner, and that all she either spent or received was to be accounted for and returned, since by the will of her uncle, unless her husband took her name, her estate on the very day of her marriage was to be forfeited, and entered upon by the Egglestons. Delvile's plan and hope of secresy had made them little weigh this matter, though this premature discovery so unexpectedly exposed her to their power.

The first thought that occurred to her, was to send an express to Delvile, and desire his instructions how to proceed; but she dreaded his impetuosity of temper, and was almost certain that the instant he should hear she was in any uneasiness or perplexity, he would return to her at all hazards, even though Mr. Monckton were dead, and his mother herself dying. This step, therefore, she did not dare risk, preferring any personal hardship, to endangering the already precarious life of Mrs. Delvile, or to hastening her son home while Mr. Monckton was in so desperate a situation.

But though what to avoid was easy to settle, what to seek was difficult to devise. She had now no Mrs. Charlton to receive her, nor a creature in whom she could confide. To continue her present way of living was deeply involving Delvile in debt, a circumstance she had never considered, in the confusion and hurry attending all their plans and conversations, and a circumstance which, though to him it might have occurred, he could not in common delicacy mention.

Yet to have quitted her house, and retrenched her expences, would have raised suspicions that must have anticipated the discovery she so much wished to have delayed. That wish, by the present danger of its failure, was but more ardent; to have her affairs and situation become publicly known at the present period, she felt would half distract her.——Privately married, parted from her husband at the very moment of their union, a husband by whose hand the apparent friend of her earliest youth was all but killed, whose father had execrated the match, whose mother was now falling a sacrifice to the vehemence with which she had opposed it, and who himself, little short of an exile, knew not yet if, with personal safety, he might return to his native land!

To circumstances so dreadful, she had now the additional shock of being uncertain whether her own house might not be seized, before any other could be prepared for her reception!

Yet still whither to go, what to do, or what to resolve, she was wholly unable to determine; and after meditating almost to madness in the search of some plan or expedient, she was obliged to give over the attempt, and be satisfied with remaining quietly where she was, till she had better news from Delvile of his mother, or better news to send him of

Mr. Monckton, carefully, mean time, in all her letters avoiding to alarm him by any hint of her distress.

Yet was she not idle, either from despair or helplessness: she found her difficulties encreased, and she called forth more resolution to combat them: she animated herself by the promise she had made Delvile, and recovering from the sadness to which she had at first given way, she now exerted herself with vigour to perform it as she ought.

She began by making an immediate inspection into her affairs, and endeavouring, where expence seemed unnecessary, to lessen it. She gave Henrietta to understand she feared they must soon part; and so afflicted was the unhappy girl at the news, that she found it the most cruel office she had to execute. The same intimation she gave to Mrs. Harrel, who repined at it more openly, but with a selfishness so evident that it blunted the edge of pity. She then announced to Albany her inability to pursue, at present, their extensive schemes of benevolence; and though he instantly left her, to carry on his laborious plan elsewhere, the reverence she had now excited in him of her character, made him leave her with no sensation but of regret, and readily promise to return when her affairs were settled, or her mind more composed.

These little preparations, which were all she could make, with enquiries after Mr. Monckon, and writing to Delvile, sufficiently filled up her time, though her thoughts were by no means confined to them. Day after day passed, and Mr. Monckton continued to linger rather than live; the letters of Delvile, still only dated from Ostend, contained the most melancholy complaints of the illness of his mother; and the time advanced when her answer would be claimed by the attorney.

The thought of such another visit was almost intolerable; and within two days of the time that she expected it, she resolved to endeavour herself to prevail with Mr. Eggleston to wait longer.

Mr. Eggleston was a gentleman whom she knew little more than by sight; he was no relation to her family, nor had any connection with the Dean, but by being a cousin to a lady he had married, and who had left him no children. The dean had no particular regard for him, and had rather mentioned him in his will as the successor of Cecilia, in case she died unmarried or changed her name, as a mark that he approved of her doing neither, than as a matter he thought probable, if even possible, to turn out in his favour.

He was a man of a large family, the sons of which, who were extravagant and dissipated, had much impaired his fortune by prevailing with him to pay their debts, and much distressed him in his affairs by successfully teasing him for money.

Cecilia, acquainted with these circumstances, knew but too well with what avidity her estate would be seized by them, and how little the sons would endure delay, even if the father consented to it. Yet since the sacrifice to which she had agreed must soon make it indisputably their own, she determined to deal with them openly; and acknowledged, therefore, in her letter, her marriage without disguise, but begged their patience and secrecy, and promised, in a short time, the most honourable retribution and satisfaction.

She sent this letter by a man and horse, Mr. Eggleston's habitation being within fifteen miles of her own.

The answer was from his eldest son, who acquainted her that his father was very ill, and had put all his affairs into the hands of Mr. Carn, his attorney, who was a man of great credit, and would see justice done on all sides.

If this answer, which she broke open the instant she took it into her hand, was in itself a cruel disappointment to her, how was that disappointment embittered by shame and terror, when, upon again folding it up, she saw it was directed to Mrs. Mortimer Delvile!*

This was a decisive stroke; what they wrote to her, she was sure they would mention to all others; she saw they were too impatient for her estate to be moved by any representations to a delay, and that their eagerness to publish their right, took from them all consideration of what they might make her suffer. Mr. Eggleston, she found, permitted himself to be wholly governed by his son; his son was a needy and

profligate spendthrift, and by throwing the management of
the affair into the hands of an attorney, craftily meant to
shield himself from the future resentment of Delvile, to
whom, hereafter, he might affect, at his convenience, to
disapprove Mr. Carn's behaviour, while Mr. Carn was
always secure, by averring he only exerted himself for the
interest of his client.

The discerning Cecilia, though but little experienced in
business, and wholly unsuspicious by nature, yet saw into
this management, and doubted not these excuses were
already arranged. She had only, therefore, to save herself an
actual ejectment, by quitting a house in which she was
exposed to such a disgrace.

But still whither to go she knew not! One only attempt
seemed in her power for an honourable asylum, and that
was more irksomely painful to her than seeking shelter in the
meanest retreat: it was applying to Mr. Delvile senior.

The action of leaving her house, whether quietly or
forcibly, could not but instantly authenticate the reports
spread by the Egglestons of her marriage: to hope therefore
for secresy any longer would be folly, and Mr. Delvile's rage
at such intelligence might be still greater to hear it by chance
than from herself. She now lamented that Delvile had not at
once told the tale, but, little foreseeing such a discovery as
the present, they had mutually concluded to defer the
communication till his return.

Her own anger at the contemptuous ill treatment she had
repeatedly met from him, she was now content not merely
to suppress but to dismiss, since, as the wife of his son
without his consent, she considered herself no longer as
wholly innocent of incurring it. Yet, such was her dread of
his austerity and the arrogance of his reproaches, that, by
choice, she would have preferred an habitation with her own
pensioner, the pew-opener, to the grandest apartment in
Delvile Castle while he continued its lord.

In her present situation, however, her choice was little to
be consulted: the honour of Delvile was concerned in her
escaping even temporary disgrace, and nothing, she knew,
would so much gratify him, as any attention from her to his

father. She wrote to him, therefore, the following letter, which she sent by an express.

To the Hon. COMPTON DELVILE.

SIR,
                                        APRIL 29th, 1780.

I should not, even by letter, presume thus to force myself upon your remembrance, did I not think it a duty I now owe your son, both to risk and to bear the displeasure it may unhappily occasion. After such an acknowledgment, all other concession would be superfluous; and uncertain as I am if you will ever deign to own me, more words than are necessary would be merely impertinent.

It was the intention of your son, Sir, when he left the kingdom, to submit wholly to your arbitration, at his return, which should be resigned, his own name or my fortune: but his request for your decision, and his supplication for your forgiveness, are both, most unfortunately, prevented, by a premature and unforeseen discovery of our situation, which renders an immediate determination absolutely unavoidable.

At this distance from him, I cannot, in time, receive his directions upon the measures I have to take; pardon me then, Sir, if well knowing my reference to him will not be more implicit than his own to you, I venture, in the present important crisis of my affairs, to entreat those commands instantly, by which I am certain of being guided ultimately.

I would commend myself to your favour but that I dread exciting your resentment. I will detain you, therefore, only to add, that the father of Mr. Mortimer Devile, will ever meet the most profound respect from her who, without his permission, dares sign no name to the honour she now has in declaring herself

his most humble,
and most obedient servant.

Her mind was somewhat easier when this letter was written, because she thought it a duty, yet felt reluctance in performing it. She wished to have represented to him strongly the danger of Delvile's hearing her distress, but she knew so well his inordinate self-sufficiency, she feared a hint of that sort might be construed into an insult, and concluded her only chance that he would do any thing, was by leaving wholly to his own suggestions the weighing and settling what.

But though nothing was more uncertain than whether she should be received at Delvile Castle, nothing was more fixed than that she must quit her own house, since the pride of Mr. Delvile left not even a chance that his interest would conquer it. She deferred not, therefore, any longer making preparations for her removal, though wholly unsettled whither.

Her first, which was also her most painful task, was to acquaint Henrietta with her situation: she sent, therefore, to desire to speak with her, but the countenance of Henrietta shewed her communication would not surprise her.

"What is the matter with my dear Henrietta?" cried Cecilia; "who is it has already afflicted that kind heart which I am now compelled to afflict for myself?"

Henrietta, in whom anger appeared to be struggling with sorrow, answered, "No, madam, not afflicted for *you!* it would be strange if I were, thinking as I think!"

"I am glad," said Cecilia, calmly, "if you are not, for I would give to you, were it possible, nothing but pleasure and joy."

"Ah madam!" cried Henrietta, bursting into tears, "why will you say so when you don't care what becomes of me! when you are going to cast me off!—and when you will soon be too happy ever to think of me more!"

"If I am never happy till then," said Cecilia, "sad, indeed, will be my life! no, my gentlest friend, you will always have your share in my heart; and always, to me, would have been the welcomest guest in my house, but for those unhappy circumstances which make our separating inevitable."

"Yet you suffered me, madam, to hear from any body that you was married and going away; and all the common servants in the house knew it before me."

"I am amazed!" said Cecilia; "how and which way can they have heard it?"

"The man that went to Mr. Eggleston brought the first news of it, for he said all the servants there talked of nothing else, and that their master was to come and take possession here next Thursday."

Cecilia started at this most unwelcome intelligence; "Yet you envy me," she cried, "Henrietta, though I am forced from my house! though in quitting it, I am unprovided with any other, and though him for whom I relinquish it, is far off, without means of protecting, or power of returning to me!"

"But you are married to him, madam!" cried she, expressively.

"True, my love; but, also, I am parted from him!"

"Oh how differently," exclaimed Henrietta, "do the great think from the little! were *I* married,—and *so* married, I should want neither house, nor fine cloaths, nor riches, nor any thing;—I should not care where I lived,—every place would be paradise! I would walk to him barefoot if he were a thousand miles off, and I should mind nobody else in the world while I had him to take care of me!"

Ah Delvile! thought Cecilia, what powers of fascination are yours! should I be tempted to repine at what I have to bear, I will think of this heroick girl, and blush!

Mrs. Harrel now broke in upon them, eager to be informed of the truth or falsehood of the reports which were buzzed throughout the house. Cecilia briefly related to them both the state of her affairs, earnestly expressing her concern at the abrupt separation which must take place, and for which she had been unable to prepare them, as the circumstances which led to it had been wholly unforeseen by herself.

Mrs. Harrel listened to the account with much curiosity and surprize; but Henrietta wept incessantly in hearing it: the object of a passion ardent as it was romantic, lost to her

c.—39

past recovery; torn herself, probably for ever, from the best friend she had in the world; and obliged to return thus suddenly to an home she detested,—Henrietta possessed not the fortitude to hear evils such as these, which, to her inexperienced heart, appeared the severest that could be inflicted.

This conversation over, Cecilia sent for her Steward, and desired him, with the utmost expedition, to call in all her bills, and instantly to go round to her tenants within twenty miles, and gather in, from those who were able to pay, the arrears now due to her; charging him, however, upon no account, to be urgent with such as seemed distressed.

The bills she had to pay were collected without difficulty; she never owed much, and creditors are seldom hard of access; but the money she hoped to receive fell very short of her expectations, for the indulgence she had shewn to her tenants had ill prepared them for so sudden a demand.

CHAPTER V

A Decision

THIS business effectually occupied the present and following day; the third, Cecilia expected her answer from Delvile Castle, and the visit she so much dreaded from the attorney.

The answer arrived first.

To Miss BEVERLEY.

Madam,

As my son has never apprized me of the extraordinary step which your letter intimates, I am too unwilling to believe him capable of so far forgetting what he owes his family, to ratify any such intimation by interfering with my counsel or opinion.

I am, Madam, &c.

COMPTON DELVILE.

DELVILE-CASTLE,
May 1st, 1780.

Cecilia had little right to be surprised by this letter, and she had not a moment to comment upon it, before the attorney arrived.

"Well, madam," said the man, as he entered the parlour, "Mr. Eggleston has stayed your own time very patiently: he commissions me now to enquire if it is convenient to you to quit the premises."

"No, Sir, it is by no means convenient to me; and if Mr. Eggleston will wait some time longer, I shall be greatly obliged to him."

"No doubt, madam, but he will, upon proper considerations."

"What, Sir, do you call proper?"

"Upon your advancing to him, as I hinted before, an immediate particular sum from what must, by and bye, be legally restituted."

"If this is the condition of his courtesy, I will quit the house without giving him further trouble."

"Just as it suits you, madam. He will be glad to take possession to-morrow or next day."

"You did well, Sir, to commend his patience! I shall, however, merely discharge my servants, and settle my accounts, and be ready to make way for him."

"You will not take it amiss, madam, if I remind you that the account with Mr. Eggleston must be the first that is settled."

"If you mean the arrears of this last fortnight or three weeks, I believe I must desire him to wait Mr. Delvile's return, as I may otherwise myself be distressed for ready money."

"That, madam, is not likely, as it is well known you have

a fortune that was independent of your late uncle; and as to distress for ready money, it is a plea Mr. Eggleston can urge much more strongly.''

''This is being strangely hasty, Sir!—so short a time as it is since Mr. Eggleston could expect *any* part of this estate!''

''That, madam, is nothing to the purpose; from the moment it is his, he has as many wants for it as any other gentleman. He desired me, however, to accquaint you, that if you still chose an apartment in this house, till Mr. Delvile returns, you shall have one at your service.''

''To be a *guest* in this house, Sir,'' said Cecilia, drily, ''might perhaps seem strange to me; I will not, therefore, be so much in his way.''

Mr. Carn then informed her she might put her seal* upon whatever she meant hereafter to claim or dispute, and took his leave.

Cecilia now shut herself up in her own room, to meditate without interruption, before she would proceed to any action. She felt much inclination to send instantly for some lawyer; but when she considered her peculiar situation, the absence of her husband, the renunciation of his father, the loss of her fortune, and her ignorance upon the subject, she thought it better to rest quiet till Delvile's own fate, and own opinion could be known, than to involve herself in a lawsuit she was so little able to superintend.

In this cruel perplexity of her mind and her affairs, her first thought was to board again with Mrs. Bayley; but that was soon given up, for she felt a repugnance unconquerable to continuing in her native county, when deprived of her fortune, and cast out of her dwelling. Her situation, indeed, was singularly unhappy, since, by this unforeseen vicissitude of fortune, she was suddenly, from being an object of envy and admiration, sunk into distress, and threatened with disgrace; from being every where caressed, and by every voice praised, she blushed to be seen, and expected to be censured; and, from being generally regarded as an example of happiness, and a model of virtue, she was now in one moment to appear to the world, an outcast from her own house, yet received into no other! a bride, unclaimed by a husband! an HEIRESS, dispossessed of all wealth!

To be first acknowledged as *Mrs. Delvile* in a state so degrading, she could not endure; and to escape from it, one way alone remained, which was going instantly abroad.

Upon this, therefore, she finally determined: her former objections to such a step being now wholly, though unpleasantly removed, since she had neither estate nor affairs to demand her stay, and since all hopes of concealment were totally at an end. Her marriage, therefore, and its disgraceful consequences being published to the world, she resolved without delay to seek the only asylum which was proper for her, in the protection of the husband for whom she had given up every other.

She purposed, therefore, to go immediately and privately to London, whence she could best settle her route for the continent: where she hoped to arrive before the news of her distress reached Delvile, whom nothing, she was certain, but her own presence, could keep there for a moment after hearing it.

Thus decided, at length, in her plan, she proceeded to put it in execution with calmness and intrepidity; comforting herself that the conveniencies and indulgencies with which she was now parting, would soon be restored to her, and though not with equal power, with far more satisfaction. She told her steward her design of going the next morning to London, bid him pay instantly all her debts, and discharge all her servants, determining to keep no account open but that with Mr. Eggleston, which he had made so intricate by double and undue demands, that she thought it most prudent and safe to leave him wholly to Delvile.

She then packed up all her papers and letters, and ordered her maid to pack up her clothes.

She next put her own seal upon her cabinets, drawers, and many other things, and employed almost all her servants at once, in making complete inventories of what every room contained.

She advised Mrs. Harrel to send without delay for Mr. Arnott, and return to his house. She had first purposed to carry Henrietta home to her mother herself; but another scheme for her now occurred, from which she hoped much future advantage to the amiable and dejected girl.

She knew well, that deep as was at present her despondency, the removal of all possibility of hope, by her knowledge of Delvile's marriage, must awaken her before long from the delusive visions of her romantic fancy; Mr. Arnott himself was in a situation exactly similar, and the knowledge of the same event would probably be productive of the same effect. When Mrs. Harrel, therefore, began to repine at the solitude to which she was returning, Cecilia proposed to her the society of Henrietta, which, glad to catch at any thing that would break into her loneliness, she listened to with pleasure, and seconded by an invitation.

Henrietta, to whom all houses appeared preferable to her own home, joyfully accepted the offer, committing to Cecilia the communication of the change of her abode to Mrs. Belfield.

Cecilia, who in the known and tried honour of Mr. Arnott would unreluctantly have trusted a sister, was much pleased by this little arrangement, from which should no good ensue, no evil, at least, was probable. But she hoped, through the mutual pity their mutual melancholy might inspire, that their minds, already not dissimilar, would be softened in favour of each other, and that, in conclusion, each might be happy in receiving the consolation each could give, and a union would take place, in which their reciprocal disappointment might, in time, be nearly forgotten.

There was not, indeed, much promise of such an event in the countenance of Mr. Arnott, when, late at night, he came for his sister, nor in the unbounded sorrow of Henrietta, when the moment of leave-taking arrived. Mr. Arnott looked half dead with the shock his sister's intelligence had given him, and Henrietta's heart, torn asunder between friendship and love, was scarce able to bear a parting, which from Cecilia, she regarded as eternal, added to the consciousness it was occasioned by her going to join Delvile for life!

Cecilia, who both read and pitied these conflicting

emotions, was herself extremely hurt by this necessary separation. She tenderly loved Henrietta, she loved her even the more for the sympathy of their affections, which called forth the most forcible commiseration,—that which springs from fellow feeling!

"Farewell," she cried, "my Henrietta, be but happy as you are innocent, and be both as I love you, and nothing will your friends have to wish for you, or yourself to regret."

"I must always regret," cried the sobbing Henrietta, "that I cannot live with you for ever! I should regret it if I were queen of all the world, how much more then, when I am nothing and nobody! I do not wish *you* happy, madam, for I think happiness was made on purpose for you, and nobody else ever had it before; I only wish you health and long life, for the sake of those who will be made as happy as you,—for you will spoil them,—as you have spoilt me,—from being ever happy without you!"

Cecilia re-iterated her assurances of a most faithful regard, embraced Mrs. Harrel, spoke words of kindness to the drooping Mr. Arnott, and then parted with them all.

Having still many small matters to settle, and neither company nor appetite, she would eat no supper; but, in passing thro' the hall, in her way to her own room, she was much surprised to see all her domestics assembled in a body. She stopt to enquire their intention, when they eagerly pressed forward, humbly and earnestly entreating to know why they were discharged?

"For no reason in the world," cried Cecilia, "but because it is at present out of my power to keep you any longer."

"Dont part with *me*, madam, for that," cried one of them, "for I will serve you for nothing!"

"So will I!" cried another, "And I!" "And I!" was echoed by them all; while "no other such mistress is to be found!" "We can never bear any other place!" and "keep *me*, madam, at least!" was even clamorously urged by each of them.

Cecilia, distressed and flattered at once by their unwillingness to quit her, received this testimony of gratitude for the kind and liberal treatment they had received, with the warmest thanks both for their services and fidelity, and assured them that when again she was settled, all those who should be yet unprovided with places, should be preferred in her house before any other claimants.

Having, with difficulty, broken from them, she sent for her own man, Ralph, who had lived with her many years before the death of the Dean, and told him she meant still to continue him in her service. The man heard it with great delight, and promised to re-double his diligence to deserve her favour. She then communicated the same news to her maid, who had also resided with her some years, and by whom with the same, or more pleasure it was heard.

These and other regulations employed her almost all night; yet late and fatigued as she went to bed, she could not close her eyes: fearful something was left undone, she robbed herself of the short time she had allowed to rest, by incessant meditation upon what yet remained to be executed. She could recollect, however, one only thing that had escaped her vigilance, which was acquainting the pew-opener, and two or three other poor women who had weekly pensions from her, that they must, at least for the present, depend no longer upon her assistance.

Nothing indeed could be more painful to her than giving them such information, yet not to be speedy with it would double the barbarity of their disappointment. She even felt for these poor women, whose loss in her she knew would be irreparable, a compassion that drove from her mind almost every other subject, and determined her, in order to soften to them this misfortune, to communicate it herself, that she might prevent their from* sinking under it, by reviving them with hopes of her future assistance.

She had ordered at seven o'clock in the morning an hired chaise at the door, and she did not suffer it long to wait for her. She quitted her house with a heart full of care and anxiety, grieving at the necessity of making such a sacrifice, uncertain how it would turn out, and labouring under a thousand perplexities with respect to the measures she ought immediately to take. She passed, when she reached the hall, through a row of weeping domestics, not one of whom with dry eyes could see the house bereft of such a mistress. She spoke to them all with kindness, and as much as was in her power with chearfulness: but the tone of her voice gave them little reason to think the concern at this journey was all their own.

She ordered her chaise to drive round to the pew-opener's, and thence to the rest of her immediate dependents. She soon, however, regretted that she had given herself this task; the affliction of these poor pensioners was clamorous, was almost heart-breaking; they could live, they said, no longer, they were ruined for ever; they should soon be without bread to eat, and they might cry for help in vain, when their generous, their only benefactress was far away!

Cecilia made the kindest efforts to comfort and encourage them, assuring them the very moment her own affairs were arranged, she would remember them all, visit them herself, and contribute to their relief, with all the power she should have left. Nothing, however, could console them; they clung about her, almost took the horses from the chaise, and conjured her not to desert those who were solely cherished by her bounty!

Nor was this all she had to suffer; the news of her intention to quit the county was now reported throughout the neighbourhood, and had spread the utmost consternation among the poor in general, and the lower class of her own tenants in particular, and the road was soon lined with women and children, wringing their hands and crying. They followed her carriage with supplications that she would return to them, mixing blessings with their lamentations, and prayers for her happiness with the bitterest repinings at their own loss!

Cecilia was extremely affected; her liberal and ever-ready hand was every other instant involuntarily seeking her purse, which her many immediate expences, made her prudence as often check: and now first she felt the capital error she had committed, in living constantly to the utmost extent of her income, without ever preparing, though so able to have done it, against any unfortunate contingency.

When she escaped, at last, from receiving any longer this

painful tribute to her benevolence, she gave orders to her man to ride forward, and stop at the Grove, that a precise and minute account of Mr. Monckton, might be the last, as it was now become the most important, news she should hear in Suffolk. This he did, when to her equal surprise and delight, she heard that he was suddenly so much better, there were hopes of his recovery.

Intelligence so joyful made her amends for almost every thing; yet she hesitated not in her plan of going abroad, as she knew not where to be in England, and could not endure to hurry Delvile from his sick mother, by acquainting him with her helpless and distressed situation. But so revived were her spirits by these unexpected tidings, that a gleam of brightest hope once more danced before her eyes, and she felt herself invigorated with fresh courage and new strength, sufficient to support her through all hardships and fatigues.

Spirits and courage were indeed much wanted for the enterprize she had formed; but little used to travelling, and having never been out of England, she knew nothing of the route* but by a general knowledge of geography, which, though it could guide her east or west, could teach her nothing of foreign customs, the preparations necessary for the journey, the impositions she should guard against, nor the various dangers to which she might be exposed, from total ignorance of the country through which she had to pass.

Conscious of these deficiencies for such an undertaking, she deliberated without intermission how to obviate them. Yet sometimes, when to these hazards, those arising from her youth and sex were added, she was upon the point of relinquishing her scheme, as too perilous for execution, and resolving to continue privately in London till some change happened in her affairs.

But though to every thing she could suggest, doubts and difficulties arose, she had no friend to consult, nor could devise any means by which they might be terminated. Her maid was her only companion, and Ralph, who had spent almost his whole life in Suffolk, her only guard and attendant. To hire immediately some French servant, used to travelling in his own country, seemed the first step she had to take, and so essential, that no other appeared feasible till it was done. But where to hear of such a man she could not tell, and to take one not well recommended, would be exposing herself to frauds and dangers innumerable.

Yet so slow as Delvile travelled, from whom her last letter was still dated Ostend, she thought herself almost certain, could she once reach the continent, of overtaking him in his route within a day or two of her landing.

The earnest inclination with which this scheme was seconded, made her every moment less willing to forego it. It seemed the only harbour for her after the storm she had weathered, and the only refuge she could properly seek while thus houseless and helpless. Even were Delvile in England, he had no place at present to offer her, nor could any thing be proposed so unexceptionable as her living with Mrs. Delvile at Nice, till he knew his father's pleasure, and, in a separate journey home, had arranged his affairs either for her return, or her continuance abroad.

With what regret did she now look back to the time when, in a distress such as this, she should have applied for, and received the advice of Mr. Monckton as oracular! The loss of a counsellor so long, so implicitly relied upon, lost to her also, only by his own interested worthlessness, she felt almost daily, for almost daily some intricacy or embarrassment made her miss his assistance: and though glad, since she found him so undeserving, that she had escaped the snares he had spread for her, she grieved much that she knew no man of honest character and equal abilities, that would care for her sufficiently to supply his place in her confidence.

As she was situated at present, she could think only of Mr. Belfield to whom she could apply for any advice. Nor even to him was the application unexceptionable, the calumnies of Mr. Delvile senior making it disagreeable to her even to see him. But he was at once a man of the world and a man of honour; he was the friend of Mortimer, whose confidence in him was great, and his own behaviour had uniformly shewn a respect far removed from impertinence or vanity, and a mind superior to being led to them by the influence of his gross mother. She had, indeed, when she last quitted his house, determined never to re-enter it; but determinations hasty or violent, are rarely observed, because rarely practicable; she had promised Henrietta to inform Mrs. Belfield whither she was gone, and reconcile her to the absence she still hoped to make from home. She concluded, therefore to go to Portland-Street without delay, and enquire openly and at once whether, and when, she might speak with Mr. Belfield; resolving, if tormented again by any forward insinuations, to rectify all mistakes by acknowledging her marriage.

She gave directions accordingly to the post-boy and Ralph.

With respect to her own lodgings while in town, as money was no longer unimportant to her, she meant from the Belfields to go to the Hills, by whom she might be recommended to some reputable and cheap place. To the Belfields, however, though very late when she arrived in town, she went first, unwilling to lose a moment in promoting her scheme of going abroad.

She left her maid in the chaise, and sent Ralph on to Mrs. Hill, with directions to endeavour immediately to procure her a lodging.

CHAPTER VI

A Prating*

CECILIA was shewn into a parlour, where Mrs. Belfield was very earnestly discoursing with Mr. Hobson and Mr. Simkins; and Belfield himself, to her great satisfaction, was already there, and reading.

"Lack-a-day!" cried Mrs. Belfield, "if one does not always see the people one's talking of! Why it was but this morning, madam, I was saying to Mr. Hobson, I wonder, says I, a young lady of such fortunes as Miss Beverley should mope herself up so in the country! Don't you remember it, Mr. Hobson?"

"Yes, madam," answered Mr. Hobson, "but I think, for my part, the young lady's quite in the right to do as she's a mind; for that's what I call living agreeable: and if I was a young lady to-morrow, with such fine fortunes, and that, it's just what I should do myself: for what I say is this: where's the joy of having a little money, and being a little matter above the world, if one has not one's own will?"

"Ma'am," said Mr. Simkins, who had scarce yet raised his head from the profoundness of his bow upon Cecilia's entrance into the room, "if I may be so free, may I make bold just for to offer you this chair?"

"I called, madam," said Cecilia, seizing the first moment in her power to speak, "in order to acquaint you that your daughter, who is perfectly well, has made a little change in her situation, which she was anxious you should hear from myself."

"Ha! ha! stolen a match upon you, I warrant!" cried the facetious Mr. Hobson; "a good example for you, young lady; and if you take my advice, you won't be long before you follow it; for as to a lady, let her be worth never so much, she's a mere nobody, as one may say, till she can get herself a husband, being she knows nothing of business, and is made to pay for every thing through the nose."

"Fie, Mr. Hobson, fie!" said Mr. Simkins, "to talk so slighting of the ladies before their faces! what one says in a corner, is quite of another nature; but for to talk so rude in their company,—I thought you would scorn to do such a thing."

"Sir, I don't want to be rude no more than yourself," said Mr. Hobson; "for what I say is, rudeness is a thing that makes nobody agreeable; but I don't see because of that, why a man is not to speak his mind to a lady as well as to a gentleman, provided he does it in a complaisant fashion."

"Mr. Hobson," cried Mrs. Belfield, very impatiently, "you might as well let *me* speak, when the matter is all about my own daughter."

"I ask pardon, ma'am," said he, "I did not mean to stop you; for as to not letting a lady speak, once might as well tell a man in business not to look at the Daily Advertiser;* why, its morally impossible!''

"But sure, madam," cried Mrs. Belfield, "it's no such thing? You can't have got her off already?"

I would I had! thought Cecilia; who then explained her meaning; but in talking of Mrs. Harrel, avoided all mention of Mr. Arnott, well foreseeing that to hear such a man existed, and was in the same house with her daughter, would be sufficient authority to her sanguine expectations, for depending upon a union between them, and reporting it among her friends.

This circumstance being made clear, Cecilia added, "I could by no means have consented voluntarily to parting so soon with Miss Belfield, but that my own affairs call me at present out of the kingdom." And then, addressing herself to Belfield, she enquired if he could recommend to her a trusty foreign servant, who would be hired only for the time she was to spend abroad?

While Belfield was endeavouring to recollect some such person, Mr. Hobson eagerly called out "As to going abroad, madam, to be sure you're to do as you like, for that, as I say, is the soul of every thing; but else I can't say it's a thing I much approve; for my notion is this; here's a fine fortune, got as a man may say, out of the bowels of one's mother country, and this fine fortune, in default of male issue, is obliged to come to a female, the law making no proviso to the contrary.* Well, this female, going into a strange country, naturally takes with her this fortune, by reason it's the main article she has to depend upon; what's the upshot? why she gets pilfered by a set of sharpers that never saw England in their lives, and that never lose sight of her till she has not a sous in the world. But the hardship of the thing is this; when it's all gone, the lady can come back, but will the money come back?—No, you'll never see it again: now this is what I call being no true patriot."

"I am quite ashamed for to hear you talk so, Mr. Hobson!" cried Mr. Simkins, affecting to whisper; "to go for to take a person to task at this rate, is behaving quite unbearable; it's enough to make the young lady afraid to speak before you.''

"Why, Mr. Simkins," answered Mr. Hobson, "Truth is truth, whether one speaks it or not; and that, ma'am, I dare say, a young lady of your good sense knows as well as myself.''

"I think, madam," said Belfield, who waited their silence with great impatience, "that I know just such a man as you will require, and one upon whose honesty I believe you may rely.''

"That's more," said Mr. Hobson, "than I would take upon me to say for any *Englishman!* where you may meet with such a *Frenchman*, I won't be bold to say.''

"Why indeed," said Mr. Simkins, "if I might take the liberty for to put in, though I don't mean in no shape to go to contradicting the young gentleman, but if I was to make bold to speak my private opinion upon the head, I should be inclinable for to say, that as to putting a dependance upon the French, it's a thing quite dubious how it may turn out.''

"I take it as a great favour, ma'am," said Mrs. Belfield, "that you have been so complaisant as to make me this visit to-night, for I was almost afraid you would not have done me the favour any more; for, to be sure, when you was here last, things went a little unlucky: but I had no notion, for my part, who the old gentleman was till after he was gone, when Mr. Hobson told me it was old Mr. Delvile: though, sure enough, I thought it rather upon the extraordinary order, that he should come here into my parlour, and make such a secret of his name, on purpose to ask me questions about my own son.''

"Why I think, indeed, if I may be so free," said Mr. Simkins, "it was rather petickeler of the gentleman; for, to be sure, if he was so over curious to hear about your private concerns, the genteel thing, if I may take the liberty for to differ, would have been for him to say, ma'am, says he, I'm come to ask the favour of you just to let me a little into your son's goings on; and any thing, ma'am, you should take a fancy for to ask me upon the return, why I shall be very compliable, ma'am, says he, to giving of you satisfaction.''

"I dare say," answered Mrs. Belfield, "he would not have said so much if you'd have gone down on your knees to ask him. Why he was upon the very point of being quite in a passion because I only asked him his name! though what harm that could do him, I'm sure I never could guess. However, as he was so mighty inquisitive about my son, if I had but known who he was in time, I should have made no scruple in the world to ask him if he could not have spoke a few words for him to some of those great people that could have done him some good. But the thing that I believe put him so out of humour, was my being so unlucky as to say, before ever I knew who he was, that I had heard he was not over and above good-natured; for I saw he did not seem much to like it at the time."

"If he had done the generous thing," said Mr. Simkins, "it would have been for him to have made the proffer of his services of his own free-will; and it's rather supriseable to me he should never have thought of it; for what could be so natural as for him to say, I see, ma'am, says he, you've got a very likely young gentleman here, that's a little out of cash, says he, so I suppose, ma'am, says he, a place, or a pension,* or something in that shape of life, would be no bad compliment, says he."

"But no such good luck as that will come to my share," cried Mrs. Belfield, "I can tell you that, for every thing I want to do goes quite contrary. Who would not have thought such a son as mine, though I say it before his face, could not have made his fortune long ago, living as he did, among all the great folks, and dining at their table just like one of themselves? yet, for all that, you see they let him go on his own way, and think of him no more than of nobody! I'm sure they might be ashamed to shew their faces, and so I should tell them at once, if I could but get sight of them."

"I don't mean, ma'am," said Mr. Simkins, "for to be finding fault with what you say, for I would not be unpelite in no shape; but if I might be so free as for to differ a little bit, I must needs say I am rather for going to work in anotherguess sort of a manner; and if I was as you—"

"Mr. Simkins," interrupted Belfield, "we will settle this

matter another time." And then, turning to the wearied Cecilia, "The man, madam," he said, "whom I have done myself the honour to recommend to you, I can see to-morrow morning; may I then tell him to wait upon you?"

"I ask pardon for just putting in," cried Mr. Simkins, before Cecilia could answer, and again bowing down to the ground, "but I only mean to say I had no thought for to be impertinent, for as to what I was a going to remark, it was not of no consequence in the least."

"Its a great piece of luck, ma'am," said Mrs. Belfield, "that you should happen to come here, of a holiday! If my son had not been at home, I should have been ready to cry for a week: and you might come any day the year through but a Sunday, and not meet with him any more than if he had never a home to come to."

"If Mr. Belfield's home-visits are so periodical," said Cecilia, "it must be rather less, than more, difficult to meet with him."

"Why you know, ma'am," answered Mrs. Belfield, "to day is a red-letter day,* so that's the reason of it."

"A red-letter day?"

"Good lack, madam, why have not you heard that my son is turned book-keeper?"

Cecilia, much surprised, looked at Belfield, who, colouring very high, and apparently much provoked by his mother's loquacity, said, "Had Miss Beverley not heard it even now, madam, I should probably have lost with her no credit."

"You can surely lose none, Sir," answered Cecilia, "by an employment too little pleasant to have been undertaken from any but the most laudable motives."

"It is not, madam, the employment," said he, "for which I so much blush as for the person employed—for *myself!* In the beginning of the winter you left me just engaged in another business, a business with which I was madly delighted, and fully persuaded I should be enchanted for ever;—now, again, in the beginning of the summer,—you find me, already, in a new occupation!"

"I am sorry," said Cecilia, "but far indeed from

surprised, that you found yourself deceived by such
sanguine expectations.''

"Deceived!" cried he, with energy, "I was bewitched, I
was infatuated! common sense was estranged by the
seduction of a chimera; my understanding was in a ferment
from the ebullition of my imagination! But when this new
way of life lost its novelty,—novelty! that short-liv'd, but
exquisite bliss! no sooner caught than it vanishes, no sooner
tasted than it is gone! which charms but to fly, and comes
but to destroy what it leaves behind!—when that was lost,
reason, cool, heartless reason, took its place, and teaching
me to wonder at the frenzy of my folly, brought me back to
the tameness—the sadness of reality!''

"I am sure," cried Mrs. Belfield, "whatever it has
brought you back to, it has brought you back to no good! it's
a hard case, you must needs think, madam, to a mother, to
see a son that might do whatever he would, if he'd only set
about it, contenting himself with doing nothing but scribble
and scribe one day, and when he gets tired of that, thinking
of nothing better than casting up two and two!''

"Why, madam," said Mr. Hobson, "what I have seen of
the world is this; there's nothing methodizes a man but
business. If he's never so much upon the stilts,* that's
always a sure way to bring him down, by reason he soon
finds there's nothing to be got by rhodomontading.* Let
every man be his own carver;* but what I say is, them
gentlemen that are what one may call geniuses, commonly
think nothing of the main chance, till they get a tap on the
shoulder with a writ;* and a solid lad, that knows three
times five is fifteen, will get the better of them in the long
run. But as to arguing with gentlemen of that sort, where's
the good of it? You can never bring them to the point, say
what you will; all you can get from them, is a farrago
of fine words, that you can't understand without a
dictionary.''

"I am inclinable to think," said Mr. Simkins, "that the
young gentleman is rather of opinion to like pleasure better
than business; and, to be sure, it's very excusable of him,
because its more agreeabler. And I must needs say, if I may

be so free, I'm partly of the young gentleman's mind, for business is a deal more trouble."

"I hope, however," said Cecilia to Belfield, "your present situation is less irksome to you?"

"Any situation, madam, must be less irksome than that which I quitted: to write by rule, to compose by necessity, to make the understanding, nature's first gift, subservient to interest, that meanest offspring of art!—when weary, listless, spiritless, to rack the head for invention, the memory for images, and the fancy for ornament and allusion; and when the mind is wholly occupied by its own affections and affairs, to call forth all its faculties for foreign subjects, uninteresting discussions, or fictitious incidents!——Heavens! what a life of struggle between the head and the heart! how cruel, how unnatural a war between the intellects and the feelings!"

"As to these sort of things," said Mr. Hobson, "I can't say I am much versed in them, by reason they are things I never much studied; but if I was to speak my notion, it is this; the best way to thrive in the world is to get money; but how is it to be got? Why by business: for business is to money, what fine words are to a lady, a sure road to success. Now I don't mean by this to be censorious upon the ladies, being they have nothing else to go by, for as to examining if a man knows any thing of the world, and that, they have nothing whereby to judge, knowing nothing of it themselves. So that when they are taken in by rogues and sharpers, the fault is all in the law, for making no proviso against their having money in their own hands. Let every one be trusted according to their head-piece: and what I say is this: a lady in them cases is much to be pitied, for she is obligated to take a man upon his own credit, which is tantamount to no credit at all, being what man will speak an ill word of himself? you may as well expect a bad shilling to cry out don't take me! That's what I say, and that's my way of giving my vote."

Cecilia, quite tired of these interruptions, and impatient to be gone, now said to Belfield, "I should be much obliged to you, Sir, if you could send to me the man you speak of to-morrow morning. I wished, also, to consult you with

regard to the route I ought to take. My purpose is to go to
Nice, and as I am very desirous to travel expeditiously, you
may perhaps be able to instruct me what is the best method
for me to pursue.''

"Come, Mr. Hobson and Mr. Simkins," cried Mrs.
Belfield, with a look of much significance and delight,
"suppose you two and I was to walk into the next room?
There's no need for us to hear all the young lady may have
a mind to say.''

"She has nothing to say, madam," cried Cecilia, "that
the whole world may not hear. Neither is it my purpose to
talk, but to listen, if Mr. Belfield is at leisure to favour me
with his advice.''

"I must always be at leisure, and always be proud,
madam," Belfield began, when Hobson, interrupting him,
said, "I ask pardon, Sir, for intruding, but I only mean to
wish the young lady good night. As to interfering with
business, that's not my way, for it's not the right method,
by reason——''

"We will listen to your reason, Sir," cried Belfield,
"some other time; at present we will give you all credit for
it unheard.''

"Let every man speak his own maxim, Sir," cried
Hobson; "for that's what I call fair arguing: but as to one
person's speaking, and then making an answer for another
into the bargain, why it's going to work no-how; you may
as well talk to a counter, and think because you make a noise
upon it with your own hand, it gives you the reply.''

"Why, Mr. Hobson," cried Mrs. Belfield, "I am quite
ashamed of you for being so dull! don't you see my son has
something to say to the lady that you and I have no business
to be meddling with?''

"I'm sure, ma'am, for my part," said Mr. Simkins, "I'm
very agreeable to going away, for as to putting the young
lady to the blush, it's what I would not do in no shape.''

"I only mean," said Mr. Hobson, when he was
interrupted by Mrs. Belfield, who, out of all patience, now
turned him out of the room by the shoulders, and, pulling
Mr. Simkins after, followed herself, and shut the door,

though Cecilia, much provoked, desired she would stay, and declared repeatedly that all her business was public.

Belfield, who had looked ready to murder them all during this short scene, now approached Cecilia, and with an air of mingled spirit and respect, said, "I am much grieved, much confounded, madam, that your ears should be offended by speeches so improper to reach them; yet if it is possible I can have the honour of being of any use to you, in me, still, I hope, you feel you may confide. I am too distant from you in situation to give you reason to apprehend I can form any sinister views in serving you; and, permit me to add, I am too near you in mind, ever to give you the pain of bidding me remember that distance."

Cecilia then, extremely unwilling to shock a sensibility not more generous than jealous, determined to continue her enquiries, and, at the same time, to prevent any further misapprehension, by revealing her actual situation.

"I am sorry, Sir," she answered, "to have occasioned this disturbance; Mrs. Belfield, I find, is wholly unacquainted with the circumstance which now carries me abroad, or it would not have happened."—

Here a little noise in the passage interrupting her, she heard Mrs. Belfield, though in a low voice, say "Hush, Sir, hush! you must not come in just now; you've caught me, I confess, rather upon the listening order; but to tell you the truth, I did not know what might be going forward. However, there's no admittance now, I assure you, for my son's upon particular business with a lady, and Mr. Hobson and Mr. Simkins and I, have all been as good as turned out by them but just now."

Cecilia and Belfield, though they heard this speech with mutual indignation, had no time to mark or express it, as it was answered without in a voice at once loud and furious, "*You*, madam, may be content to listen here; pardon me if I am less humbly disposed!"

And the door was abruptly opened by young Delvile!

Cecilia, who half screamed from excess of astonishment, would scarcely, even by the presence of Belfield and his mother, have been restrained from flying to meet him, had his own aspect invited such a mark of tenderness; but far other was the case; when the door was open, he stopt short with a look half petrified, his feet seeming rooted to the spot upon which they stood.

"I declare I ask pardon, ma'am," cried Mrs. Belfield, "but the interruption was no fault of mine, for the gentleman would come in; and—"

"It is no interruption, madam;" cried Belfield, "Mr. Delvile does me nothing but honour."

"I thank you, Sir!" said Delvile, trying to recover and come forward, but trembling violently, and speaking with the most frigid coldness.

They were then, for a few instants, all silent; Cecilia, amazed by his arrival, still more amazed by his behaviour, feared to speak lest he meant not, as yet, to avow his marriage, and felt a thousand apprehensions that some new calamity had hurried him home: while Belfield was both hurt by his strangeness, and embarrassed for the sake of Cecilia; and his mother, though wondering at them all, was kept quiet by her son's looks.

Delvile then, struggling for an appearance of more ease, said, "I seem to have made a general confusion here:— pray, I beg"——

"None at all, Sir;" said Belfield, and offered a chair to Cecilia.

"No, Sir," she answered, in a voice scarce audible, "I was just going." And again rang the bell.

"I fear I hurry you, madam?" cried Delvile, whose whole frame was now shaking with uncontrollable emotion; "you are upon business—I ought to beg your pardon—my entrance, I believe, was unseasonable."——

"Sir!" cried she, looking aghast at this speech.

"I should have been rather surprised," he added, "to have met you here, so late,—so unexpectedly,—so deeply engaged—had I not happened to see your servant in the street, who told me the honour I should be likely to have by coming."

"Good God!—" exclaimed she, involuntarily; but, checking herself as well as she could, she courtsied to Mrs.

Belfield, unable to speak to her, and avoiding even to look at Belfield, who respectfully hung back, she hastened out of the room: accompanied by Mrs. Belfield, who again began the most voluble and vulgar apologies for the intrusion she had met with.

Delvile also, after a moment's pause, followed, saying, "Give me leave, madam, to see you to your carriage."

Cecilia then, notwithstanding Mrs. Belfield still kept talking, could no longer refrain saying, "Good heaven, what does all this mean?"

"Rather for *me* is that question," he answered, in such agitation he could not, though he meant it, assist her into the chaise, "for mine, I believe, is the greater surprise!"

"What surprise?" cried she, "explain, I conjure you!"

"By and bye I will," he answered; "go on postilion."

"Where, Sir?"

"Where you came from, I suppose."

"What, Sir, back to Rumford?"*

"Rumford!" exclaimed he, with encreasing disorder, "you came then from Suffolk hither?—from Suffolk to this very house?"

"Good heaven!" cried Cecilia, "come into the chaise, and let me speak and hear to be understood!"

"Who is that now in it?"

"My maid."

"Your maid?—and she waits for you thus at the door?"—

"What, what is it you mean?"

"Tell the man, madam, whither to go."

"I don't know myself—any where you please—do you order him."

"*I* order him!——you came not hither to receive orders from *me*!—where was it you had purposed to rest?"

"I don't know—I meant to go to Mrs. Hill's—I have no place taken."—

"No place taken!" repeated he, in a voice faultering between passion and grief; "you purposed, then, to stay here?—I have perhaps driven you away?"

"Here!" cried Cecilia, mingling, in her turn, indignation

with surprise, "gracious heaven! what is it you mean to doubt?"

"Nothing!" cried he, with emphasis, "I never *have* had, I never *will* have a doubt! I will *know*, I will have *conviction* for every thing! Postilion, drive to St. James's-square!—to Mr. Delvile's. There, madam, I will wait upon you."

"No! stay, postilion!" called out Cecilia, seized with terror inexpressible; "let me get out, let me speak with you at once!"

"It cannot be; I will follow you in a few minutes——drive on, postilion!"

"No, no!—I will not go—I dare not leave you—unkind Delvile!——what is it you suspect?"

"Cecilia," cried he, putting his hand upon the chaise-door, "I have ever believed you spotless as an angel! and, by heaven! I believe you so still, in spite of appearances—in defiance of every thing!——Now then be satisfied;—I will be with you very soon. Mean while, take this letter, I was just going to send to you.—Postilion, drive on, or be at your peril!"

The man waited no further orders, nor regarded the prohibition of Cecilia, who called out to him without ceasing; but he would not listen to her till he got to the end of the street; he then stopt, and she broke the seal of letter, and read, by the light of the lamps,* enough to let her know that Delvile had written it upon the road from Dover to London, to acquaint her his mother was now better, and had taken pity of his suspense and impatience, and insisted upon his coming privately to England, to satisfy himself fully about Mr. Monckton, communicate his marriage to his father, and give those orders towards preparing for its being made public, which his unhappy precipitation in leaving the kingdom had prevented.

This letter, which, though written but a few hours before she received it, was full of tenderness, gratitude, and anxiety for her happiness, instantly convinced her that his strange behaviour had been wholly the effect of a sudden impulse of jealousy; excited by so unexpectedly finding her in town, at the very house where his father had assured him she had an improper connexion, and alone, so suspiciously, with the young man affirmed to be her favourite. He knew nothing of the ejectment, nothing of any reason for her leaving Suffolk, every thing had the semblance of no motive but to indulge a private and criminal inclination.

These thoughts, which confusedly, yet forcibly, rushed upon her mind, brought with them at once an excuse for his conduct, and an alarm for his danger; "He must think," she cried, "I came to town only to meet Mr. Belfield!" then, opening the chaise-door herself, she jumpt out, and ran back into Portland-street, too impatient to argue with the postilion to return with her, and stopt not till she came to Mrs. Belfield's house.

She knocked at the door with violence; Mrs. Belfield came to it herself; "Where," cried she, hastily entering as she spoke, "are the gentlemen?"

"Lack-a-day! ma'am," answered Mrs. Belfield, "they are both gone out."

"Gone out?—where to?—which way?"

"I am sure I can't tell, ma'am, no more than you can; but I am sadly afraid they'll have a quarrel before they've done."

"Oh heaven!" cried Cecilia, who now doubted not a second duel, "tell me, shew me, which way they went?"

"Why, ma'am, to let you into the secret," answered Mrs. Belfield, "only I beg you'll take no notice of it to my son, but, seeing them so much out of sorts, I begged the favour of Mr. Simkins, as Mr. Hobson was gone out to his club, just to follow them, and see what they were after."

Cecilia was much rejoiced this caution had been taken, and determined to wait his return. She would have sent for the chaise to follow her; but Mrs. Belfield kept no servant, and the maid of the house was employed in preparing the supper.

When Mr. Simkins came back, she learnt, after various interruptions from Mrs. Belfield, and much delay from his own slowness and circumlocution, that he had pursued the two gentlemen to the * * * * coffee-house.

She hesitated not a moment in resolving to follow them:

she feared the failure of any commission, nor did she know whom to entrust with one: and the danger was too urgent for much deliberation. She begged, therefore, that Mr. Simkins would walk with her to the chaise; but hearing that the coffee-house was another way, she desired Mrs. Belfield to let the servant run and order it to Mrs. Roberts, in Fetter-lane, and then eagerly requested Mr. Simkins to accompany her on foot till they met with an hackney-coach.

They then set out, Mr. Simkins feeling proud and happy in being allowed to attend her, while Cecilia, glad of any protection, accepted his offer of continuing with her, even after she met with an hackney-coach.

When she arrived at the coffee-house, she ordered the coach-man to desire the master of it to come and speak with her.

He came, and she hastily called out, "Pray, are two gentlemen here?"

"Here are several gentlemen here, madam."

"Yes, yes—but are two upon any business—any particular business—"

"Two gentlemen, madam, came about half an hour ago, and asked for a room to themselves."

"And where are they now?—are they up stairs?——down stairs?——where are they?"

"One of them went away in about ten minutes, and the other soon after."

Bitterly chagrined and disappointed, she knew not what step to take next; but, after some consideration, concluded upon obeying Delvile's own directions, and proceeding to St. James's-square, where alone, now, she seemed to have any chance of meeting with him. Gladly, however, she still consented to be accompanied by Mr. Simkins, for her dread of being alone, at so late an hour, in an hackney-coach, was invincible. Whether Delvile himself had any authority for directing her to his father's, or whether, in the perturbation of his new-excited and agonizing sensations of jealousy, he had forgotten that any authority was necessary, she knew not; nor could she now interest herself in the doubt: a second scene, such as had so lately passed with Mr. Monckton, occupied all her thoughts: she knew the too great probability that the high spirit of Belfield would disdain making the explanation which Delvile in his present agitation might require, and the consequence of such a refusal must almost inevitably be fatal.

CHAPTER VII

A Pursuit

THE moment the porter came to the door, Cecilia eagerly called out from the coach, "Is Mr. Delvile here?"

"Yes, madam," he answered, "but I believe he is engaged."

"Oh no matter for any engagement!" cried she, "open the door,—I must speak to him this moment!"

"If you will please to step into the parlour, madam, I will tell his gentleman you are here; but he will be much displeased if he is disturbed without notice."

"Ah heaven!" exclaimed she, "what Mr. Delvile are you talking of?"

"My master, madam."

Cecilia, who had got out of the coach, now hastily returned to it, and was some time in too great agony to answer either the porter, who desired some message, or the coachman, who asked whither he was to drive. To see Mr. Delvile, unprotected by his son, and contrary to his orders, appeared to her insupportable; yet to what place could she go? where was she likely to meet with Delvile? how could he find her if she went to Mrs. Hill's? and in what other house could she at present claim admittance?

After a little recovering from this cruel shock, she ventured, though in a faultering voice, to enquire whether young Mr. Delvile had been there?

"Yes, madam," the porter answered; "we thought he was abroad, but he called just now, and asked if any lady had been at the house. He would not even stay to go up to my master, and we have not dared tell him of his arrival."

This a little revived her; to hear that he had actually

been enquiring for her, at least assured her of his safety from any immediate violence, and she began to hope she might now possibly meet with him time enough to explain all that had past in his absence, and occasioned her seemingly strange and suspicious situation at Belfield's. She compelled herself, therefore, to summon courage for seeing his father, since, as he had directed her to the house, she concluded he would return there to seek her, when he had wandered else where to no purpose.

She then, though with much timidity and reluctance, sent a message to Mr. Delvile to entreat a moment's audience.

An answer was brought her that he saw no company so late at night.

Losing now all dread of his reproaches, in her superior dread of missing Delvile, she called out earnestly to the man, "Tell him, Sir, I beseech him not to refuse me! tell him I have something to communicate that requires his immediate attention!"

The servant obeyed; but soon returning, said his master desired him to acquaint her he was engaged every moment he stayed in town, and must positively decline seeing her.

"Go to him again," cried the harrassed Cecilia, "assure him I come not from myself, but by the desire of one he most values: tell him I entreat but permission to wait an hour in his house, and that I have no other place in the world whither I can go!"

Mr. Delvile's own gentleman brought, with evident concern, the answer to this petition; which was, that while the Honourable Mr. Delvile was himself alive, he thought the desire of any other person concerning his house, was taking with him a very extraordinary liberty; and that he was now going to bed, and had given orders to his servants to carry him no more messages whatsoever, upon pain of instant dismission.

Cecilia now seemed totally destitute of all resource, and for a few dreadful minutes, gave herself up to utter despondency: nor, when she recovered her presence of mind, could she form any better plan than that of waiting in the coach to watch the return of Delvile.

She told the coachman, therefore, to drive to a corner of the square, begging Mr. Simkins to have patience, which he promised with much readiness, and endeavoured to give her comfort, by talking without cessation.

She waited here near half an hour. She then feared the disappointment of Delvile in not meeting her at first, had made him conclude she meant not to obey his directions, and had perhaps urged him to call again upon Belfield, whom he might fancy privy to her non-appearance. This was new horror to her, and she resolved at all risks to drive to Portland-street, and enquire if Belfield himself was returned home. Yet, lest they should mutually be pursuing each other all night, she stopt again at Mr. Delvile's, and left word with the porter, that if young Mr. Delvile should come home, he would hear of the person he was enquiring for at Mrs. Roberts's in Fetter-lane. To Belfield's she did not dare to direct him; and it was her intention, if there she procured no new intelligence, to leave the same message, and then go to Mrs. Roberts without further delay. To make such an arrangement with a servant who knew not her connection with his young master, was extremely repugnant to her; but the exigence was too urgent for scruples, and there was nothing to which she would not have consented, to prevent the fatal catastrophe she apprehended.

When she came to Belfield's, not daring to enter the house, she sent in Mr. Simkins, to desire that Mrs. Belfield would be so good as to step to the coach door.

"Is your son, madam," she cried, eagerly, "come home? and is any body with him?"

"No, ma'am; he has never once been across the threshold since that gentleman took him out; and I am half out of my wits to think——"

"Has that gentleman," interrupted Cecilia, "been here any more?"

"Yes, ma'am, that's what I was going to tell you; he came again just now, and said——"

"Just now?—good heaven!—and which way is he gone?"

"Why he is after no good, I am afraid, for he was in a great passion, and would hardly hear any thing I said."

"Pray, pray answer me quick!—where, which way did he go?"

"Why, he asked me if I knew whither my son was come from the * * coffee-house; why, says I, I'm sure I can't tell, for if it had not been for Mr. Simkins, I should not so much as have known he ever went to the * * coffee-house; however, I hope he a'n't come away, because if he is, poor Miss Beverley will have had all that trouble for nothing; for she's gone after him in a prodigious hurry; and upon my only saying that, he seemed quite beside himself, and said, if I don't meet with your son at the * * coffee-house myself, pray, when he comes in, tell him I shall be highly obliged to him to call there; and then he went away, in as great a pet as ever you saw."

Cecilia listened to this account with the utmost terror and misery; the suspicions of Delvile would now be aggravated, and the message he had left for Belfield, would by him be regarded as a defiance. Again, however, to the * * coffee-house she instantly ordered the coach, an immediate explanation from herself seeming the only possible chance for preventing the most horrible conclusion to this unfortunate and eventful evening.

She was still accompanied by Mr. Simkins, and, but that she attended to nothing he said, would not inconsiderably have been tormented by his conversation. She sent him immediately into the coffee-room, to enquire if either of the gentlemen were then in the house.

He returned to her with a waiter, who said, "One of them, madam, called again just now, but he only stopt to write a note, which he left to be given to the gentleman who came with him at first. He is but this moment gone, and I don't think he can be at the bottom of the street."

"Oh drive then, gallop after him!"—cried Cecilia; "coachman! go this moment!"

"My horses are tired," said the man, "they have been out all day, and they will gallop no further, if I don't stop and give them a drink."

Cecilia, too full both of hope and impatience for this delay, forced open the door herself, and without saying another word, jumped out of the carriage, with intention to run down the street; but the coachman immediately seizing her, protested she should not stir till he was paid.

In the utmost agony of mind at an hindrance by which she imagined Delvile would be lost to her perhaps for ever, she put her hand in her pocket, in order to give up her purse for her liberty; but Mr. Simkins, who was making a tiresome expostulation with the coachman, took it himself, and declaring he would not see the lady cheated, began a tedious calculation of his fare.

"O pay him any thing!" cried she, "and let us be gone! an instant's delay may be fatal!"

Mr. Simkins, too earnest to conquer the coachman to attend to her distress, continued his prolix harangue concerning a disputed shilling, appealing to some gathering spectators upon the justice of his cause; while his adversary, who was far from sober, still held Cecilia, saying the coach had been hired for the lady, and he would be paid by herself.

"Good God!" cried the agitated Cecilia,—"give him my purse at once!—give him every thing he desires!"—

The coachman, at this permission, encreased his demands, and Mr. Simkins, taking the number of his coach,* protested he would summons him to the Court of Conscience* the next morning. A gentleman, who then came out of the coffee-house, offered to assist the lady, but the coachman, who still held her arm, swore he would have his right.

"Let me go! let me pass!" cried she, with encreasing eagerness and emotion; "detain me at your peril!—release me this moment!—only let me run to the end of the street,—good God! good Heaven! detain me not for mercy!"

Mr. Simkins, humbly desiring her not to be in haste, began a formal apology for his conduct; but the inebriety of the coachman became evident; a mob was collecting; Cecilia, breathless with vehemence and terror, was encircled, yet struggled in vain to break away; and the stranger gentleman, protesting, with sundry compliments, he would himself take care of her, very freely seized her hand.

This moment, for the unhappy Cecilia, teemed with calamity; she was wholly overpowered; terror for Delvile, horror for herself, hurry, confusion, heat and fatigue, all assailing her at once, while all means of repelling them were denied her, the attack was too strong for her fears, feelings, and faculties, and her reason suddenly, yet totally failing her, she madly called out, "He will be gone! he will be gone! and I must follow him to Nice!"

The gentleman now retreated; but Mr. Simkins, who was talking to the mob, did not hear her; and the coachman, too much intoxicated to perceive her rising frenzy, persisted in detaining her.

"I am going to France!" cried she, still more wildly, "why do you stop me? he will die if I do not see him, he will bleed to death!"

The coachman, still unmoved, began to grow very abusive; but the stranger, touched by compassion, gave up his attempted gallantry, and Mr. Simkins, much astonished, entreated her not to be frightened: she was, however, in no condition to listen to him; with a strength hitherto unknown to her, she forcibly disengaged herself from her persecutors; yet her senses were wholly disordered; she forgot her situation, her intention, and herself; the single idea of Delvile's danger took sole possession of her brain, though all connection with its occasion was lost, and the moment she was released, she fervently clasped her hands, exclaiming, "I will yet heal his wound, even at the hazard of my life!" and springing forward, was almost instantly out of sight.

Mr. Simkins now, much alarmed, and earnestly calling after her, entered into a compromise with the coachman, that he might attend her; but the length of his negociation defeated its purpose, and before he was at liberty to follow her, all trace was lost by which he might have overtaken her. He stopt every passenger he met to make enquiries, but though they led him on some way, they led him on in vain; and, after a useless and ill-managed pursuit, he went quietly to his own home, determining to acquaint Mrs. Belfield with what had happened the next morning.

Mean while the frantic Cecilia escaped both pursuit and insult by the velocity of her own motion. She called aloud upon Delvile as she flew to the end of the street. No Delvile was there!—she turned the corner; yet saw nothing of him; she still went on, though unknowing whither, the distraction of her mind every instant growing greater, from the inflammation of fatigue, heat, and disappointment. She was spoken to repeatedly, she was even caught once or twice by her riding habit;* but she forced herself along by her own vehement rapidity, not hearing what was said, not heeding what was thought. Delvile, bleeding by the arm of Belfield, was the image before her eyes, and took such full possession of her senses, that still, as she ran on, she fancied it in view. She scarce touched the ground; she scarce felt her own motion; she seemed as if endued with supernatural speed, gliding from place to place, from street to street; with no consciousness of any plan, and following no other direction than that of darting forward where-ever there was most room, and turning back when she met with any obstruction; till quite spent and exhausted, she abruptly ran into a yet open shop, where, breathless and panting, she sunk upon the floor, and, with a look disconsolate and helpless, sat for some time without speaking.

The people of the house, concluding at first she was a woman of the town, were going roughly to turn her out; but soon seeing their mistake by the evident distraction of her air and manner, they enquired of some idle people who, late as it was, had followed her, if any of them knew who she was, or whence she came?

They could give no account of her, but supposed she was broke lose from Bedlam.*

Cecilia then, wildly starting up, exclaimed, "No, no—I am not mad,—I am going to Nice—to my husband."

"She's quite crazy," said the man of the house, who was a Pawn-Broker; "we had better get rid of her before she grows mischievous."

"She's somebody broke out from a private mad house, I

dare say," said a man who had followed her into the shop; "and if you were to take care of her a little while, ten to one but you'll get a reward for it."

"She's a gentlewoman, sure enough," said the mistress of the house, "because she's got such good things on."

And then, under pretence of trying to find some direction to her upon a letter, or paper, she insisted upon searching her pockets: here, however, she was disappointed in her expectations: her purse was in the custody of Mr. Simkins, but neither her terror nor distress had saved her from the daring dexterity of villainy, and her pockets, in the mob, had been rifled of whatever else they contained. The woman therefore hestitated some time whether to take charge of her or not: but being urged by the man who made the proposal, and who said they might depend upon seeing her soon advertised, as having escaped from her keepers, they ventured to undertake her.

Mean while she endeavoured again to get out, calling aloud upon Delvile to rescue her, but so wholly bereft of sense and recollection, she could give no account who she was, whence she came, or whither she wished to go.

They then carried her up stairs, and attempted to make her lie down upon a bed; but supposing she refused because it was not of straw, they desisted; and, taking away the candle, locked the door, and all went to rest.

In this miserable condition, alone and raving, she was left to pass the night! in the early part of it, she called upon Delvile without intermission, beseeching him to come to her defence in one moment, and deploring his death the next; but afterwards, her strength being wholly exhausted by these various exertions and fatigues, she threw herself upon the floor, and lay for some minutes quite still. Her head then began to grow cooler, as the fever into which terror and immoderate exercise had thrown her abated, and her memory recovered its functions.

This was, however, only a circumstance of horror to her: she found herself shut up in a place of confinement, without light, without knowledge where she was, and not a human being near her!

Yet the same returning reason which enabled her to take this view of her own situation, brought also to her mind that in which she had left Delvile;—under all the perturbation of new-kindled jealousy, just calling upon Belfield,—Belfield, tenacious of his honour even more than himself,—to satisfy doubts of which the very mention would be received as a challenge!

"Oh yet, oh yet," cried she, "let me fly and overtake them!—I may find them before morning, and to night it must surely have been too late for this work of death!"

She then arose to feel for the door, and succeeded; but it was locked, and no effort she could make enabled her to open it.

Her agony was unspeakable; she called out with violence upon the people of the house, conjured them to set her at liberty, offered any reward for their assistance, and threatened them with a prosecution if detained.

Nobody, however, came near her: some slept on notwithstanding all the disturbance she could make, and others, though awakened by her cries, concluded them the ravings of a mad woman, and listened not to what she said.

Her head was by no means in a condition to bear this violence of distress; every pulse was throbbing, every vein seemed bursting, her reason, so lately returned, could not bear the repetition of such a shock, and from supplicating for help with all the energy of feeling and understanding, she soon continued the cry from mere vehemence of distraction.

Thus dreadfully passed the night; and in the morning, when the woman of the house came to see after her, she found her raving with such frenzy, and desperation, that her conscience was perfectly at ease in the treatment she had given her, being now firmly satisfied she required the strictest confinement.

She still, however, tried to get away; talked of Delvile without cessation, said she should be too late to serve him, told the woman she desired but to prevent murder, and repeatedly called out, "Oh beloved of my heart! wait but a moment, and I will snatch thee from destruction!"

Mrs. Wyers, this woman, now sought no longer to draw

from her whence she came, or who she was, but heard her frantic exclamations without any emotion, contentedly concluding that her madness was incurable: and though she was in a high fever, refused all sustenance, and had every symptom of an alarming and dangerous malady, she was fully persuaded that her case was that of decided insanity, and had not any notion of temporary or accidental alienation of reason.

All she could think of by way of indulgence to her, was to bring her a quantity of straw, having heard that mad people were fond of it; and putting it in a heap in one corner of the room, she expected to see her eagerly fly to it.

Cecilia, however, distracted as she was, was eager for nothing but to escape, which was constantly her aim, alike when violent or when quiet. Mrs. Wyers, finding this, kept her closely confined, and the door always locked, whether absent or present.

CHAPTER VIII

An Encounter

Two whole days passed thus; no enquiries reached Mrs. Wyers, and she found in the news-papers no advertisement. Meanwhile Cecilia grew worse every moment, tasted neither drink nor food, raved incessantly, called out twenty times in a breath, "Where is he? which way is he gone?" and implored the woman by the most pathetic remonstrances, to save her unhappy Delvile, *dearer to her than life, more precious than peace or rest!*

At other times she talked of her marriage, of the displeasure of his family, and of her own remorse; entreated the woman not to betray her, and promised to spend the remnant of her days in the heaviness of sorrow and contrition.

Again her fancy roved, and Mr. Monckton took sole possession of it. She reproached him for his perfidy, she bewailed that he was massacred, she would not a moment out-live him, and wildly declared *her last remains should moulder in his hearse!* And thus, though naturally and commonly of a silent and quiet disposition, she was now not a moment still, for the irregular starts of a terrified and disordered imagination, were changed into the constant ravings of morbid delirium.

The woman, growing uneasy from her uncertainty of pay for her trouble, asked the advice of some of her friends what was proper for her to do; and they counselled her to put an advertisement into the papers herself the next morning.

The following, therefore, was drawn up and sent to the printer of the Daily Advertiser.*

MADNESS

Whereas a crazy young lady, tall, fair complexioned, with blue eyes and light hair, ran into the Three Blue Balls,* in——street, on Thursday night, the 2d instant, and has been kept there since out of charity. She was dressed in a riding habit. Whoever she belongs to is desired to send after her immediately. She has been treated with the utmost care and tenderness. She talks much of some person by the name of Delvile.

N.B. She had no money about her.

May, 1780.

This had but just been sent off, when Mr. Wyers, the man of the house, coming up stairs, said, "Now we shall have two of them, for here's the crazy old gentleman below, that says he has just heard in the neighbourhood of what has happened to us, and he desires to see the poor lady."

"It's as well let him come up, then," answered Mrs. Wyers, "for he goes to all sort of places and people, and ten to one but he'll bustle about till he finds out who she is."

Mr. Wyers then went down stairs to send him up.

He came instantly. It was Albany, who in his vagrant rambles, having heard an unknown mad lady was at this

pawn-broker's, came, with his customary eagerness to visit
and serve the unhappy, to see what could be done for her.

When he entered the room, she was sitting upon the bed,
her eyes earnestly fixed upon the window, from which she
was privately indulging a wish to make her escape. Her dress
was in much disorder, her fine hair was dishevelled, and the
feathers of her riding hat were broken and half falling down,
some shading her face, others reaching to her shoulder.*

"Poor lady!" cried Albany, approaching her, "how long
has she been in this state?"

She started at the sound at a new voice, she looked
round,—but what was the astonishment of Albany to see
who it was!—He stept back,—he came forward,—he
doubted his own senses,—he looked at her earnestly,—he
turned from her to look at the woman of the house,—he cast
his eyes round the room itself, and then, lifting up his hands,
"O sight of woe!" he cried, "the generous and good! the
kind reliever of distress! the benign sustainer of misery!——
is *This* Cecilia!"——

Cecilia, imperfectly recollecting, though not understanding him, sunk down at his feet, tremblingly called out,
"Oh, if he is yet to be saved, if already he is not
murdered,—go to him! fly after him! you will presently
overtake him, he is only in the next street, I left him there
myself, his sword drawn, and covered with human blood!"

"Sweet powers of kindness and compassion!" cried the
old man, "look upon this creature with pity! she who raised
the depressed, she who cheared the unhappy! she whose
liberal hand turned lamentations into joy! who never with a
tearless eye could hear the voice of sorrow!—is *This* she
herself!—can *This* be Cecilia!"

"O do not wait to talk!" cried she, "go to him now, or
you will never see him more! the hand of death is on him,—
cold, clay-cold is its touch! he is breathing his last—Oh
murdered Delvile! massacred husband of my heart! groan
not so piteously! fly to him, and weep over him!—fly to him
and pluck* the poniard from his wounded bosom!"

"Oh sounds of anguish and horror!" cried the melted
moralist, tears running quick down his rugged cheeks;

"melancholy indeed is this sight, humiliating to morality! such is human strength, such human felicity!——weak as our virtues, frail as our guilty natures!"

"Ah," cried she, more wildly, "no one will save me now! I am married, and no one will listen to me! ill were the auspices under which I gave my hand! Oh it was a work of darkness, unacceptable and offensive! it has been sealed, therefore, with blood, and to-morrow it will be signed with murder!"

"Poor distracted creature!" exclaimed he, "thy pangs I have felt, but thy innocence I have forfeited!—my own wounds bleed afresh,——my own brain threatens new frenzy."——

Then, starting up, "Good woman," he added, "kindly attend her,—I will seek out her friends, put her into bed, comfort, sooth, compose her.——I will come to you again, and as soon as I can."

He then hurried away.

"Oh hour of joy!" cried Cecilia, "he is gone to rescue him! oh blissful moment! he will yet be snatched from slaughter!"

The woman lost not an instant in obeying the orders she had received; she was put into bed, and nothing was neglected, as far as she had power and thought, to give a look of decency and attention to her accommodations.

He had not left them an hour, when Mary, the maid who had attended her from Suffolk, came to enquire for her lady. Albany, who was now wandering over the town in search of some of her friends, and who entered every house where he imagined she was known, had hastened to that of Mrs. Hill the first of any, as he was well acquainted with her obligations to Cecilia; there, Mary herself, by the directions which her lady had given Mrs. Belfield, had gone; and there, in the utmost astonishment and uneasiness, had continued till Albany brought news of her.

She was surprised and afflicted beyond measure, not only at the state of her mind, and her health, but to find her in a bed and an appartment so unsuitable to her rank of life, and so different to what she had ever been accustomed. She wept bitterly while she enquired at the bed-side how her lady did, but wept still more, when, without answering or seeming to know her, Cecilia started up, and called out, "I must be removed this moment! I must go to St. James's-square,—if I stay an instant longer, the passing-bell will toll, and then how shall I be in time for the funeral?"

Mary, alarmed and amazed, turned hastily from her to the woman of the house, who calmly said, the lady was only in a raving fit, and must not be minded.

Extremely frightened at this intelligence, she entreated her to be quiet and lie still. But Cecilia grew suddenly so violent, that force only could keep her from rising; and Mary, unused to dispute her commands, prepared to obey them.

Mrs. Wyers now in her turn opposed in vain; Cecilia was peremptory, and Mary became implicit, and, though not without much difficulty, she was again dressed in her riding habit. This operation over, she moved towards the door, the temporary strength of delirium giving her a hardiness that combated fever, illness, fatigue, and feebleness. Mary, however averse and fearful, assisted her, and Mrs. Wyers, compelled by the obedience of her own servant, went before them to order a chair.

Cecilia, however, felt her weakness when she attempted to move down stairs; her feet tottered, and her head became dizzy; she leaned it against Mary, who called aloud for more help, and made her sit down till it came. Her resolution, however, was not to be altered; a stubbornness, wholly foreign to her genuine character, now made her stern and positive; and Mary, who thought her submission indispensable, cried, but did not offer to oppose her.

Mr. and Mrs. Wyers both came up to assist in supporting her, and Mr. Wyers offered to carry her in his arms; but she would not consent; when she came to the bottom of the stairs, her head grew worse, she again lent it upon Mary, but Mr. Wyers was obliged to hold them both. She still, however, was firm in her determination, and was making another effort to proceed, when Delvile rushed hastily into the shop.

He had just encountered Albany; who, knowing his acquaintance, though ignorant of his marriage with Cecilia, had informed him where to seek her.

He was going to make enquiry if he was come to the right house, when he perceived her,——feeble, shaking, leaning upon one person, and half carried by another!——he started back, staggered, gasped for breath,——but finding they were proceeding, advanced with trepidation, furiously calling out, "Hold! stop!——what is it you are doing! Monsters of savage barbarity, are you murdering my wife?"

The well-known voice no sooner struck the ears of Cecilia, than instantly recollecting it, she screamed, and, in suddenly endeavouring to spring forward, fell to the ground.

Delvile had vehemently advanced to catch her in his arms and save her fall, which her unexpected quickness had prevented her attendants from doing; but the sight of her changed complection, and the wildness of her eyes and air, again made him start,——his blood froze through his veins, and he stood looking at her, cold and almost petrified.

Her own recollection of him seemed lost already; and exhausted by the fatigue she had gone through in dressing and coming down stairs, she remained still and quiet, forgetting her design of proceeding, and forming no new one for returning.

Mary, to whom, as to all her fellow servants, the marriage of Cecilia had been known, before she left the country, now desired from Delvile directions what was to be done.

Delvile, starting suddenly at this call from the deepest horror into the most desperate rage, fiercely exclaimed, "Inhuman wretches! unfeeling, execrable wretches, what is it you have done to her! how came she hither?——who brought her? who dragged her?——by what infamous usage has she been sunk into this state?"

"Indeed, sir, I don't know!" cried Mary.

"I assure you, sir," said Mrs. Wyers, "the lady——"

"Peace!" cried he, furiously, "I will not hear your falsehoods!—peace, and begone!"——

Then, casting himself upon the ground by her side, "Oh my Cecilia," he cried, "where hast thou been thus long?

how have I lost thee? what dreadful calamity has befallen thee?—answer me, my love! raise your sweet head and answer me!——oh speak!——say to me any thing; the bitterest words will be mercy to this silence?''——

Cecilia then, suddenly looking up, called out with great quickness, ''Who are you?''

''Who am I!'' cried he, amazed and affrighted.

''I should be glad you would go away,'' cried she, in a hurrying manner, ''for you are quite unknown to me.''

Delvile, unconscious of her insanity, and attributing to resentment this aversion and repulse, hastily moved from her, mournfully answering, ''Well indeed may you disclaim me, refuse all forgiveness, load me with hatred and reproach, and consign me to eternal anguish! I have merited severer punishment still; I have behaved like a monster, and I am abhorrent to myself!''

Cecilia now, half rising, and regarding him with mingled terror and anger, eagerly exclaimed, ''If you do not mean to mangle and destroy me, begone this instant.''

''To mangle you!'' repeated Delvile, shuddering, ''how horrible!—but I deserve it!*—look not, however, so terrified, and I will tear myself away from you. Suffer me but to assist in removing you from this place, and I will only watch you at a distance, and never see you more till you permit me to approach you.''

''Why, why,'' cried Cecilia, with a look of perplexity and impatience, ''will you not tell me your name, and where you come from?''

''Do you not know me?'' said he, struck with new horror; ''or do you only mean to kill me by the question?''

''Do you bring me any message from Mr. Monckton?''

''From Mr. Monckton?—no; but he lives and will recover.''

''I thought you had been Mr. Monckton yourself.''

''Too cruel, yet justly cruel Cecilia!—is then Delvile utterly renounced?—the guilty, the unhappy Delvile!—is he cast off for ever? have you driven him wholly from your heart? do you deny him even a place in your remembrance?''

''Is your name, then, Delvile?''

"O what is it you mean! is it me or my name you thus disown?"

"'Tis a name," cried she, sitting up, "I well remember to have heard, and once I loved it, and three times I called upon it in the dead of night. And when I was cold and wretched, I cherished it; and when I was abandoned and left alone, I repeated it and sung to it."

"All-gracious powers!" cried Delvile, "her reason is utterly gone!" And, hastily rising, he desperately added, "what is death to this blow?—Cecilia, I am content to part with thee!"

Mary now, and Mrs. Wyers, poured upon him eagerly an account of her illness, and insanity, her desire of removal, and their inability to control her.

Delvile, however, made no answer; he scarce heard them: the deepest despair took possession of his mind, and, rooted to the spot where he stood, he contemplated in dreadful stillness the fallen and altered object of his best hopes and affections; already in her faded cheeks and weakened frame, his agonizing terror read the quick impending destruction of all his earthly happiness! the sight was too much for his fortitude, and almost for his understanding; and when his woe became utterable, he wrung his hands, and groaning aloud, called out, "Art thou gone so soon! my wife! my Cecilia! have I lost thee already?"

Cecilia, with utter insensibility to what was passing, now suddenly, and with a rapid yet continued motion, turned her head from side to side, her eyes wildly glaring, yet apparently regarding nothing.

"Dreadful, dreadful!" exclaimed Delvile, "what a sight is this!" and turning from her to the people of the house, he angrily said, "why is she here upon the floor? could you not even allow her a bed? Who attends her? Who waits upon her? Why has nobody sent for help?—Don't answer me,—I will not hear you, fly this moment for a physician,—bring two, bring three—bring all you can find!"

Then, still looking from Cecilia, whose sight he could no longer support, he consulted with Mary whither she should be conveyed: and, as the night was far advanced, and no place was prepared for her elsewhere, they soon agreed that she could only be removed up stairs.

Delvile now attempted to carry her in his arms; but trembling and unsteady, he had not strength to sustain her; yet not enduring to behold the helplessness he could not assist, he conjured them to be careful and gentle, and, committing her to their trust, ran out himself for a physician.

Cecilia resisted them with her utmost power, imploring them not to bury her alive, and averring she had received intelligence they meant to entomb her with Mr. Monckton.

They put her, however, to bed, but her raving grew still more wild and incessant.

Delvile soon returned with a physician, but had not courage to attend him to her room. He waited for him at the foot of the stairs, where, hastily stopping him, "Well, sir," he cried, "is it not all over? is it not impossible she can live?"

"She is very ill, indeed, sir," he answered, "but I have given directions which perhaps——"

"*Perhaps!*" interrupted Delvile, shuddering; "do not stab me with such a word!"

"She is very delirious," he continued, "but as her fever is very high, that is not so material. If the orders I have given take effect, and the fever is got under, all the rest will be well of course."

He then went away; leaving Delvile as much thunder-struck by answers so alarming, as if he had consulted him in full hope, and without even suspicion of her danger.

The moment he recovered from this shock, he flew out of the house for more advice.

He returned and brought with him two physicians.

They confirmed the directions already given, but would pronounce nothing decisively of her situation.

Delvile, half mad with the acuteness of his misery, charged them all with want of skill, and wrote instantly into the country for Dr. Lyster.

He went out himself in search of a messenger to ride off express, though it was midnight, with his letter; and then, returning, he was hastening to her room, but, while yet at the door, hearing her still raving, his horror conquered his eagerness, and, hurrying down stairs, he spent the remnant of the long and seemingly endless night in the shop.

CHAPTER IX

A Tribute

MEAN-WHILE Cecilia went thro' very severe discipline,* sometimes strongly opposing it, at other times scarce sensible what was done to her.

The whole of the next day passed in much the same manner, neither did the next night bring any visible alteration. She had now nurses and attendants even more than sufficient, for Delvile had no relief but from calling in more help. His terror of again seeing her encreased with his forbearance; the interview which had already past had almost torn him asunder, and losing all courage for attempting to enter her room, he now spent almost all his time upon the stairs which led to it. Whenever she was still, he seated himself at her chamber door, where, if he could hear her breathe or move, a sudden hope of her recovery gave to him a momentary extasy that recompensed all his sufferings. But the instant she spoke, unable to bear the sound of so loved a voice uttering nothing but the incoherent ravings of lightheadedness, he hastened down stairs, and flying out of the house, walked in the neighbouring streets, till he could again gather courage to enquire or to listen how she went on.

The following morning, however, Dr. Lyster came, and every hope revived. He flew to embrace him, told him instantly his marriage with Cecilia, and besought him by some superior effort of his extraordinary abilities to save him the distraction of her loss.

"My good friend," cried the worthy Doctor, "what is this you ask of me? and how can this poor young lady herself want advice more than you do? Do you think these able physicians actually upon the spot, with all the experience of full practice in London to assist their skill, want a petty Doctor out the country to come and teach them what is right?"

"I have more reliance upon you," cried Delvile, "than upon the whole faculty; come, therefore, and prescribe for her,—take some new course"—

"Impossible, my good Sir, impossible! I must not lose my wits from vanity, because you have lost yours from affliction. I could not refuse to come to you when you wrote to me with such urgency, and I will now go and see the young lady, as a *friend*, with all my heart. I am sorry for you at my soul, Mr. Mortimer! She is a lovely young creature, and has an understanding, for her years and sex, unequalled."

"Never mention her to me!" cried the impatient Delvile, "I cannot bear it! Go up to her, dear Doctor, and if you want a consultation, send, if you please, for every physician in town."

Dr. Lyster desired only that those who had already* attended might be summoned; and then, giving up to his entreaties the accustomed ceremonial of waiting for them, he went to Cecilia.

Delvile did not dare accompany him; and so well was he acquainted with his plainness and sincerity, that though he expected his return with eagerness, he no sooner heard him upon the stairs, than fearing to know his opinion, he hastily snatched up his hat, and rushed vehemently out of the house to avoid him.

He continued to walk about the streets, till even the dread of ill news was less horrible to him than this voluntary suspense, and then he returned to the house.

He found Dr. Lyster in a small back parlour, which Mrs. Wyers, finding she should now be well paid, had appropriated for Delvile's use.

Delvile, putting his hand upon the Doctor's shoulder, said, "Well, my dear Doctor Lyster, *you*, still, I hope"—

"I would I could make you easy!" interrupted the Doctor; "yet, if you are rational, one comfort, at all events, I can give you; the crisis seems approaching, and either she will recover, or before to-morrow morning"——

"Don't go on, Sir!" cried Delvile, with mingled rage and horror, "I will not have her days limited! I sent not for you to give me such an account!"

And again he flew out of the house, leaving Dr. Lyster unaffectedly concerned for him, and too kind-hearted and too wise to be offended at the injustice of immoderate sorrow.

In a few minutes, however, from the effect rather of despair than philosophy, Delvile grew more composed, and waited upon Dr. Lyster to apologize for his behaviour. He received his hearty forgiveness, and prevailed upon him to continue in town till the whole was decided.

About noon, Cecilia, from the wildest rambling and most perpetual agitation, sunk suddenly into a state of such utter insensibility, that she appeared unconscious even of her existence; and but that she breathed, she might already have passed for being dead.

When Delvile heard this, he could no longer endure even his post upon the stairs; he spent his whole time in wandering about the streets, or stopping in Dr. Lyster's parlour to enquire if all was over.

That humane physician, not more alarmed at the danger of Cecilia, than grieved at the situation of Delvile, thought the present fearful crisis at least offered an opportunity of reconciling him with his father. He waited, therefore, upon that gentleman in St. James's-square, and openly informed him of the dangerous state of Cecilia, and the misery of his son.

Mr. Delvile, though he would gladly, to have annulled an alliance he held disgraceful to his family, have received intelligence that Cecilia was no more, was yet extremely disconcerted to hear of sufferings to which his own refusal of an asylum he was conscious had largely contributed; and after a haughty struggle between tenderness and wrath, he begged the advice of Dr. Lyster how his son might be drawn from such a scene.

Dr. Lyster, who well knew Delvile was too desperate to be tractable, proposed surprising him into an interview by their returning together: Mr. Delvile, however apprehensive and relenting, conceded most unwillingly to a measure he held beneath him, and, when he came to the shop, could scarce be persuaded to enter it.* Mortimer, at that time, was taking a solitary ramble; and Dr. Lyster, to complete the work he had begun of subduing the hard pride of his father, contrived, under pretence of waiting for him, to conduct him to the room of the invalide.*

Mr. Delvile, who knew not whither he was going, at first sight of the bed and the attendants, was hastily retreating; but the changed and livid face of Cecilia caught his eye, and, struck with sudden consternation, he involuntarily stopt.

"Look at the poor young lady!" cried Dr. Lyster; "can you wonder a sight such as this should make Mr. Mortimer forget every thing else?"

She was wholly insensible, but perfectly quiet; she seemed to distinguish nothing, and neither spoke nor moved.

Mr. Delvile regarded her with the utmost horror: the refuge he so implacably refused her on the night when her intellects were disordered, he would now gladly have offered at the expence of almost similar sufferings, to have relieved himself from those rising pangs which called him author of this scene of woe. His pride, his pomp, his ancient name, were now sunk in his estimation; and while he considered himself the destroyer of this unhappy young creature, he would have sacrificed them all to have called himself her protector. Little is the boast of insolence when it is analysed by the conscience! bitter is the agony of self-reproach, where misery follows hardness of heart! yet, when the first painful astonishment from her situation abated, the remorse she excited being far stronger than the pity, he gave an angry glance at Dr. Lyster for betraying him into such a sight, and hastily left the room.

Delvile, who was now* impatiently waiting to see Dr. Lyster in the little parlour, alarmed at the sound of a new step upon the stairs, came out to enquire who had been admitted. When he saw his father, he shrunk back; but Mr. Delvile, no longer supported by pride, and unable to recover from the shock he had just received, caught him in his arms, and said "Oh come home to me, my son! this is a place to destroy you!"

"Ah, Sir," cried Delvile, "think not of me now!—you must shew me no kindness; I am not in a state to bear it!" And, forcibly breaking from him, he hurried out of the house.

Mr. Delvile, all the father awakened in his bosom, saw his departure with more dread than anger; and returned himself to St. James's-square, tortured with parental fears, and stung by personal remorse, lamenting his own inflexibility, and pursued by the pale image of Cecilia.

She was still in this unconscious state, and apparently as free from suffering as from enjoyment, when a new voice was suddenly heard without, exclaiming, "Oh where is she? where is she? where is my dear Miss Beverley!" and Henrietta Belfield ran wildly into the room.

The advertisement in the news-papers had at once brought her to town, and directed her to the house: the mention that the lost lady *talked much of a person by the name of Delvile*, struck her instantly to mean Cecilia; the description corresponded with this idea, and the account of the dress confirmed it: Mr. Arnott, equally terrified with herself, had therefore lent her his chaise to learn the truth of this conjecture, and she had travelled all night.

Flying up to the bedside, "Who is this?" she cried, "this is not Miss Beverley?" and then screaming with unrestrained horror, "Oh mercy! mercy!" she called out, "yes, it is indeed! and nobody would know her!—her own mother would not think her her child!"

"You must come away, Miss Belfield," said Mary, "you must indeed,—the doctors all say my lady must not be disturbed."

"Who shall take me away?" cried she, angrily, "nobody Mary! not all the doctors in the world! Oh sweet Miss Beverley! I will lie down by your side,—I will never quit you while you live,—and I wish, I wish I could die to save your precious life!"

Then, leaning over her, and wringing her hands, "Oh I shall break my heart," she cried, "to see her in this condition! Is this the so happy Miss Beverley, that I thought every body born to give joy to? the Miss Beverley that seemed queen of the whole world! yet so good and so gentle, so kind to the meanest person! excusing every body's faults but her own, and telling them how they might mend, and trying to make them as good as herself!—Oh who would know her! who would know her! what have they done to you, my beloved Miss Beverley? how have they altered and disfigured you in this wicked and barbarous manner?''

In the midst of this simple yet pathetic testimony, to the worth and various excellencies of Cecilia, Dr. Lyster came into the room. The women all flocked around him, except Mary, to vindicate themselves from any share in permitting this new comer's entrance and behaviour; but Mary only told him who she was, and said, that if her lady was well enough to know her, there was nobody she was certain she would have been so glad to see.

"Young lady," said the doctor, "I would advise you to walk into another room till you are a little more composed."

"Every body, I find, is for hurrying me away;" cried the sobbing Henrietta, whose honest heart swelled with its own affectionate integrity; "but they might all save themselves the trouble, for go I will not!"

"This is very wrong," said the doctor, "and must not be suffered: do you call it friendship to come about a sick person in this manner?"

"Oh my Miss Beverley!" cried Henrietta, "do you hear how they all upbraid me? how they all want to force me away from you, and to hinder me even from looking at you! Speak for me, sweet lady! speak for me yourself! tell them the poor Henrietta will not do you any harm; tell them she only wishes just to sit by you, and to see you!——I will hold by this dear hand,—I will cling to it till the last minute; and you will not, I know you will not, give orders to have it taken away from me!"

Dr. Lyster, though his own good nature was much affected by this fond sorrow, now half angrily represented to her the impropriety of indulging it: but Henrietta, unused to disguise or repress her feelings, grew only the more violent, the more she was convinced of Cecilia's danger: "Oh look but at her," she exclaimed, "and take me from her if you can! see how her sweet eyes are fixed! look but what a change in her complexion!—She does not see me, she does not know me,—she does not hear me! her hand seems quite lifeless already, her face is all fallen away!—Oh that I had died twenty deaths before I had lived to see this sight!—poor wretched Henrietta, thou hast now no friend left in the world! thou mayst go and lie down in some corner, and no one will come and say to thee a word of comfort!"

"This must not be!" said Dr. Lyster, "you must take her away."

"You shall not!" cried she, desperately, "I will stay with her till she has breathed her last, and I will stay with her still longer! and if she was to speak to you at this moment, she would tell you that she chose it. She loved the poor Henrietta, and loved to have her near her; and when she was ill, and in much distress, she never once bid me leave her room. Is it not true, my sweet Miss Beverley? do you not know it to be true? Oh look not so dreadfully! turn to your unhappy Henrietta; sweetest, best of ladies! will you not speak to her once more? will you not say to her one single word?"

Dr. Lyster now grew very angry, and telling her such violence might have fatal consequences, frightened her into more order, and drew her away himself. He had then the kindness to go with her into another room, where, when her first vehemence was spent, his remonstrances and reasoning brought her to a sense of the danger she might occasion, and made her promise not to return to the room till she had gained strength to behave better.

When Dr. Lyster went again to Delvile, he found him greatly alarmed by his long stay; he communicated to him briefly what had passed, and counselled him to avoid encreasing his own grief by the sight of what was suffered by this unguarded and ardent girl. Delvile readily assented, for the weight of his own woe was too heavy to bear any addition.

Henrietta now, kept in order by Dr. Lyster, contented herself with only sitting upon the bed, without attempting to speak, and with no other employment than alternately looking at her sick friend, and covering her streaming eyes with her handkerchief; from time to time quitting the room wholly, for the relief of sobbing at liberty and aloud in another.

But, in the evening, while Delvile and Dr. Lyster were taking one of their melancholy rambles, a new scene was acted in the apartment of the still senseless Cecilia. Albany suddenly made his entrance into it, accompanied by three children, two girls and one boy, from the ages of four to six, neatly dressed, clean, and healthy.

"See here!" cried he, as he came in, "see here what I have brought you! raise, raise your languid head, and look this way! you think me rigid,—an enemy to pleasure, austere, harsh, and a forbidder of joy: look at this sight, and see the contrary! who shall bring you comfort, joy, pleasure, like this? three innocent children, clothed and fed by your bounty!"

Henrietta and Mary, who both knew him well, were but little surprised at any thing he said or did, and the nurses presumed not to interfere but by whispers.

Cecilia, however, observed nothing that passed; and Albany, somewhat astonished, approached nearer to the bed; "Wilt thou not speak?" he cried.

"She can't, Sir," said one of the women; "she has been speechless many hours."

The air of triumph with which he had entered the room was now changed into disappointment and consternation. For some minutes he thoughtfully and sorrowfully contemplated her, and then, with a deep sigh, said, "How will the poor rue this day!"

Then, turning to the children, who, awed by this scene, were quiet from terror, "Alas!" he said, "ye helpless babes, ye know not what you have lost: presumptuously we came; unheeded we must return! I brought you to be seen by your benefactress, but she is going where she will find many such."

He then led them away; but, suddenly coming back, "I may see her, perhaps, no more! shall I not, then, pray for her? Great and aweful is the change she is making; what are human revolutions, how pitiful, how insignificant, compared with it?—Come, little babies, come; with gifts has she often blessed *you*, with wishes bless *her!* Come, let us kneel round her bed; let us all pray for her together; lift up your innocent hands, and for all of you I will speak.''

He then made the children obey his injunctions, and having knelt himself, while Henrietta and Mary instantly did the same, ''Sweet flower!'' he cried, ''untimely cropt in years, yet in excellence mature! early decayed in misery, yet fragrant in innocence! Gentle be thy exit, for unsullied have been thy days; brief be thy pains, for few have been thy offences! Look at her sweet babes, and bear her in your remembrance; often will I visit you and revive the solemn scene. Look at her ye, also, who are nearer to your end— Ah! will you bear it like her!''

He paused; and the nurses and Mrs. Wyers, struck by this call, and moved by the general example, crept to the bed, and dropt on their knees, almost involuntarily.

''She departs,'' resumed Albany, ''the envy of the world! while yet no guilt had seized her soul, and no remorse had marred her peace. She was the hand-maid of charity, and pity dwelt in her bosom! her mouth was never opened but to give comfort; her footsteps were followed by blessings! Oh happy in purity, be thine the song of triumph!—softly shalt thou sink to temporary sleep,——sublimely shalt thou rise to life that wakes for ever!''

He then got up, took the children by their little hands, and went away.

CHAPTER X

A Termination

DR. Lyster and Delvile met them at the entrance into the house. Extremely alarmed lest Cecilia had received any disturbance, they both hastened up stairs, but Delvile proceeded only to the door. He stopt there and listened; but all was silent: the prayers of Albany had struck an awe into every one; and Dr. Lyster soon returned to tell him there was no alteration in his patient.

"And he has not disturbed her?" cried Delvile.

"No, not at all."

"I think, then," said he, advancing, though trembling, "I will yet see her once more."

"No, no, Mr. Mortimer," cried the doctor, "why should you give yourself so unnecessary a shock?"

"The shock," answered he, "is over!—tell me, however, is there any chance I may hurt *her?*"

"I believe not; I do not think, just now, she will perceive you."

"Well, then,—I may grieve, perhaps, hereafter, that once more—that one glance!"—He stopt, irresolute: the doctor would again have dissuaded him, but, after a little hesitation, he assured him he was prepared for the worst, and forced himself into the room.

When again, however, he beheld Cecilia,—senseless, speechless, motionless, her features void of all expression, her cheeks without colour, her eyes without meaning,—he shrunk from the sight, he leant upon Dr. Lyster, and almost groaned aloud.

The doctor would have conducted him out of the apartment; but, recovering from this first agony, he turned again to view her, and casting up his eyes, fervently ejaculated, "Oh merciful powers! Take, or destroy her! let her not linger thus, rather let me lose her for ever!—Oh far rather would I see her dead, than in this dreadful condition!"

Then, advancing to the bed side, and yet more earnestly looking at her, "I pray not now," he cried, "for thy life! inhumanly as I have treated thee, I am not yet so hardened as to wish thy misery lengthened: no; quick be thy restoration, or short as pure thy passage to eternity!—Oh my Cecilia! lovely, however altered! sweet even in the arms of death and insanity! and dearer to my tortured heart in this calamitous state, than in all thy pride of health and beauty!—"

He stopt, and turned from her, yet could not tear himself away; he came back, he again looked at her, he hung over her in anguish unutterable; he kissed each burning hand, he folded to his bosom her feeble form, and, recovering his speech, though almost bursting with sorrow, faintly articulated, "Is all over? no ray of reason left? no knowledge of thy wretched Delvile?—no, none! the hand of death is on her, and she is utterly gone!—sweet suffering excellence! loved, lost, expiring Cecilia!—but I will not repine! peace and kindred angels are watching to receive thee, and if thou art parted from thyself, it were impious to lament thou shouldst be parted from me.—Yet in thy tomb will be deposited all that to me could render existence supportable, every frail chance of happiness, every sustaining hope, and all alleviation of sorrow!—"

Dr. Lyster now again approaching, thought he perceived some change in his patient, and peremptorily forced him away from her: then returning himself, he found that her eyes were shut, and she was dropt asleep.

This was an omen the most favourable he could hope. He now seated himself by the bedside, and determined not to quit her till the expected crisis was past. He gave the strictest orders for the whole house to be kept quiet, and suffered no one in the room either to speak or move.

Her sleep was long and heavy; yet, when she awoke, her sensibility was evidently returned. She started, suddenly raised her head from the pillow, looked round her, and called out, "where am I now?"

"Thank Heaven!" cried Henrietta, and was rushing forward, when Dr. Lyster, by a stern and angry look, compelled her again to take her seat.

He then spoke to her himself, enquired how she did, and found her quite rational.

Henrietta, who now doubted not her perfect recovery, wept as violently for joy as she had before wept for grief; and Mary, in the same belief, ran instantly to Delvile, eager to carry to him the first tidings that her mistress had recovered her reason.

Delvile, in the utmost emotion, then returned to the

chamber; but stood at some distance from the bed, waiting Dr. Lyster's permission to approach it.

Cecilia was quiet and composed, her recollection seemed restored, and her intellects sound: but she was faint and weak, and contentedly silent, to avoid the effort of speaking.

Dr. Lyster encouraged this stillness, and suffered not any one, not even Delvile, to advance to her. After a short time, however, she again, and very calmly, began to talk to him. She now first knew him, and seemed much surprised by his attendance. She could not tell, she said, what of late had happened to her, nor could guess where she was, or by what means she came into such a place. Dr. Lyster desired her at present not to think upon the subject, and promised her a full account of every thing, when she was stronger, and more fit for conversing.

This for a while silenced her. But, after a short pause, "Tell me," she said, "Dr. Lyster, have I no friend in this place but you?" "Yes, yes, you have several friends here," answered the Doctor, "only I keep them in order, lest they should hurry or disturb you."

She seemed much pleased by this speech; but soon after said, "You must not, Doctor, keep them in order much longer, for the sight of them, I think, would much revive me."

"Ah, Miss Beverley!" cried Henrietta, who could not now restrain herself, "may not *I*, among the rest, come and speak to you?"

"Who is that?" said Cecilia, in a voice of pleasure, though very feeble; "is it my ever-dear Henrietta?"

"Oh this is joy indeed!" cried she, fervently kissing her cheeks and forehead, "joy that I never, never expected to have more!"

"Come, come," cried Doctor Lyster, "here's enough of this; did I not do well to keep such people off?"

"I believe you did," said Cecilia, faintly smiling; "my too kind Henrietta, you must be more tranquil!"

"I will, I will indeed, madam!—my dear, dear Miss Beverley, I will indeed!—now once you have* owned me, and once again I hear your sweet voice, I will do any thing, and every thing, for I am made happy for my whole life!"

"Ah, sweet Henrietta!" cried Cecilia, giving her her hand, "you must suppress these feelings, or our Doctor here will soon part us. But tell me, Doctor, is there no one else that you can let me see?"

Delvile, who had listened to this scene in the unspeakable perturbation of that hope which is kindled from the very ashes of despair, was now springing forward; but Dr. Lyster, fearful of the consequences, hastily arose, and with a look and air not to be disputed, took hold of his arm, and led him out of the room. He then represented to him strongly the danger of agitating or disturbing her, and charged him to keep from her sight till better able to bear it; assuring him at the same time that he might now reasonably hope her recovery.

Delvile, lost in transport, could make no answer, but flew into his arms, and almost madly embraced him; he then hastened out of sight to pour forth fervent thanks, and hurrying back with equal speed, again embraced the Doctor, and while his manly cheeks were burnt with tears of joy, he could not yet articulate the glad tumult of his soul.

The worthy Dr. Lyster, who heartily partook of his happiness, again urged him to be discreet; and Delvile, no longer intractable and desperate, gratefully concurred in whatever he commanded. Dr. Lyster then returned to Cecilia, and to relieve her mind from any uneasy suspense, talked to her openly of Delvile, gave her to understand he was acquainted with her marriage, and told her he had prohibited their meeting till each was better able to support it.

Cecilia by this delay seemed half gratified, and half disappointed; but the rest of the physicians, who had been summoned upon this happy change, now appearing, the orders were yet more strictly enforced for keeping her quiet.

She submitted, therefore, peaceably; and Delvile, whose gladdened heart still throbbed with speechless rapture, contentedly watched at her chamber door, and obeyed implicitly whatever was said to him.

She now visibly, and almost hourly grew better; and, in a short time, her anxiety to know all that was passed, and by what means she became so ill, and confined in a house of which she had not any knowledge, obliged Dr. Lyster to make himself master of these particulars, that he might communicate them to her with a calmness that Delvile could not attain.

Delvile himself, happy to be spared the bitter task of such a relation, informed him all he knew of the story, and then entreated him to narrate to her also the motives of his own strange, and he feared unpardonable conduct, and the scenes which had followed their parting.

He came, he said, to England, ignorant of all that had past in his absence, intending merely to wait upon his father, and communicate his marriage, before he gave directions to his lawyer for the settlements and preparations which were to precede its further publication. He meant, also, to satisfy himself, of the real situation of Mr. Monckton, and then, after an interview with Cecilia, to have returned to his mother, and waited at Nice till he might publicly claim his wife.

To this purpose he had written in his letter, which he meant to have put in the Post-office* in London himself; and he had but just alighted from his chaise, when he met Ralph, Cecilia's servant, in the street.

Hastily stopping him, he enquired if he had left his place? "No," answered Ralph, "I am only come up to town with my lady."

"With your lady!" cried the astonished Delvile, "is your lady then in town?"

"Yes, sir, she is at Mrs. Belfield's."

"At Mrs. Belfield's?—is her daughter returned home?"

"No, sir, we left her in the country."

He was then going on with a further account, but, in too much confusion of mind to hear him, Delvile abruptly wished him good night, and marched on himself towards Belfield's.

The pleasure with which he would have heard that

Cecilia was so near to him, was totally lost in his perplexity to account for her journey. Her letters had never hinted at such a purpose,—the news reached him only by accident,—it was ten o'clock at night,—yet she was at Belfield's—though the sister was away,—though the mother was professedly odious to her!——In an instant, all he had formerly heard, all he had formerly disregarded, rushed suddenly upon his memory, and he began to believe he had been deluded, that his father was right, and that Belfield had some strange and improper influence over her heart.

The suspicion was death to him; he drove it from him, he concluded the whole was some error: his reason as powerfully as his tenderness vindicated her innocence; and though he arrived at the house in much disorder, he yet arrived with a firm persuasion of an honourable explanation.

The door was open,—a chaise was at it in waiting,—Mrs. Belfield was listening in the passage; these appearances were strange, and encreased his agitation. He asked for her son in a voice scarce audible,—she told him he was engaged with a lady, and must not be disturbed.

That fatal answer, at a moment so big with the most horrible surmises, was decisive: furiously, therefore, he forced himself past her, and opened the door:—but when he saw them together,—the rest of the family confessedly excluded, his rage turned to horror, and he could hardly support himself.

"O Dr. Lyster!" he continued, "ask of the sweet creature if these circumstances offer any extenuation for the fatal jealousy which seized me? never by myself while I live will it be forgiven, but she, perhaps, who is all softness, all compassion, and all peace, may some time hence think my sufferings almost equal to my offence."

He then proceeded in his narration.

When he had so peremptorily ordered her chaise to St. James's-square, he went back to the house, and desired Belfield to walk out with him. He complied, and they were both silent till they came to a Coffee-house, where they asked for a private room. The whole way they went, his heart, secretly satisfied of the purity of Cecilia, smote him for the situation in which he had left her; yet, having unfortunately gone so far as to make his suspicions apparent, he thought it necessary to his character that their abolition should be equally public.

When they were alone, "Belfield," he said, "to obviate any imputation of impertinence in my enquiries, I deny not, what I presume you have been told by her self, that I have the nearest interest in whatever concerns the lady from whom we are just now parted: I must beg, therefore, an explicit account of the purpose of your private conversation with her."

"Mr. Delvile," answered Belfield, with mingled candour and spirit, "I am not commonly much disposed to answer enquiries thus cavalierly put to me; yet here, as I find myself not the principal person concerned, I think I am bound in justice to speak for the absent who is. I assure you, therefore, most solemnly, that your interest in Miss Beverley I never heard but by common report, that our being alone together was by both of us undesigned and undesired, that the honour she did our house in calling at it, was merely to acquaint my mother with my sister's removal to Mrs. Harrel's, and that the part which I had myself in her condescension, was simply to be consulted upon a journey which she has in contemplation to the South of France. And now, sir, having given you this peaceable satisfaction, you will find me extremely at your service to offer any other."

Delvile instantly held out his hand to him; "What you assert," he said "upon your honour, requires no other testimony. Your gallantry and your probity are equally well known to me; with either, therefore, I am content, and by no means require the intervention of both."

They then parted; and now, his doubts removed, and his punctilio satisfied, he flew to St. James's-square, to entreat the forgiveness of Cecilia for the alarm he had occasioned her, and to hear the reason of her sudden journey, and change of measures. But when he came there, to find that his father, whom he had concluded was at Delvile Castle, was in the house, while Cecilia had not even enquired for him at the door,—"Oh let me not," he continued, "even to myself, let me not trace the agony of that moment!—where to seek her I knew not, why she was in London I could not divine, for what purpose she had given the postilion a new direction I could form no idea. Yet it appeared that she wished to avoid me, and once more, in the frenzy of my disappointment, I supposed Belfield a party in her concealment. Again, therefore, I sought him,—at his own house,——at the coffee-house where I had left him,—in vain, wherever I came, I just missed him, for, hearing of my search, he went with equal restlessness, from place to place to meet me. I rejoice we both failed; a repetition of my enquiries in my then irritable state, must inevitably have provoked the most fatal resentment.

"I will not dwell upon the scenes that followed,—my laborious search, my fruitless wanderings, the distraction of my suspense, the excess of my despair!——even Belfield, the fiery Belfield, when I met with him the next day, was so much touched by my wretchedness, that he bore with all my injustice; feeling, noble young man! never will I lose the remembrance of his high-souled patience.

"And now, Dr. Lyster, go to my Cecilia; tell her this tale, and try, for you have skill sufficient, to soften, yet not wound her with my sufferings. If then she can bear to see me, to bless me with the sound of her sweet voice, no longer at war with her intellects, to hold out to me her loved hand, in token of peace and forgiveness.——Oh, Dr. Lyster! preserver of *my* life in hers! give to me but that exquisite moment, and every past evil will be for ever obliterated!"

"You must be calmer, Sir," said the Doctor, "before I make the attempt. These heroicks are mighty well for sound health, and strong nerves, but they will not do for an invalide."

He went, however, to Cecilia, and gave her this narration, suppressing whatever he feared would most affect her, and judiciously enlivening the whole by his strictures. Cecilia was much easier for this removal of her perplexities, and, as her anguish and her terror had been unmixed with resentment, she had now no desire but to reconcile Delvile with himself.

Dr. Lyster, however, by his friendly authority, obliged her for some time to be content with this relation; but when she grew better, her impatience became stronger, and he feared opposition would be as hurtful as compliance.

Delvile, therefore, was now admitted; yet slowly and with trepidation he advanced, terrified for her, and fearful of himself, filled with remorse for the injuries she had sustained, and impressed with grief and horror to behold her so ill and altered.

Supported by pillows, she sat almost upright. The moment she saw him, she attempted to bend forward and welcome him, calling out in a tone of pleasure, though faintly, "Ah! dearest Delvile! is it you?" but too weak for the effort she had made, she sunk back upon her pillow, pale, trembling, and disordered.

Dr. Lyster would then have interfered to postpone their further conversation; but Delvile was no longer master of himself or his passions: he darted forward, and kneeling at the bed side, "Sweet injured excellence!" he cried, "wife of my heart! sole object of my chosen affection! dost thou yet live? do I hear thy loved voice?—do I see thee again?—art thou my Cecilia? and have I indeed not lost thee?" then regarding her more fixedly, "Alas," he cried, "art thou indeed my Cecilia! so pale, so emaciated!—Oh suffering angel! and couldst thou then call upon Delvile, the guilty, but heart-broken Delvile, thy destroyer, thy murderer, and yet not call to execrate him?"

Cecilia, extremely affected, could not utter a word; she held out to him her hand, she looked at him with gentleness and kindness, but tears started into her eyes, and trickled in large drops down her colourless cheeks.

"Angelic creature!" cried Delvile, his own tears overflowing, while he pressed to his lips the kind token of her pardon, "can you give to me again a hand so ill deserved? can you look with such compassion on the author of your woes? on the wretch, who for an instant could doubt the purity of a mind so seraphic!"

"Ah, Delvile!" cried she, a little reviving, "think no more of what is past!—to see you,—to be yours,—drives all evil from my remembrance!"

"I am not worthy this joy!" cried he rising, kneeling, and rising again; "I know not how to sustain it! a forgiveness such as this,—when I believed you must hate me for ever! when repulse and aversion were all I dared expect,—when my own inhumanity had bereft thee of thy reason,—when the grave, the pitiless grave, was already open to receive thee,"—

"Too kind, too feeling Delvile!" cried the penetrated Cecilia, "relieve your loaded heart from these bitter recollections; mine is lightened already,—lightened, I think, of every thing but its affection for *you!*"

"Oh words of transport and extacy!" cried the enraptured Delvile, "oh partner of my life! friend, solace, darling of my bosom! that so lately I thought expiring! that I folded to my bleeding heart in the agony of eternal separation!"——

"Come away, Sir, come away," cried Dr. Lyster, who now saw that Cecilia was greatly agitated, "I will not be answerable for the continuation of this scene;" and taking him by the arm, he awakened him from his frantic rapture, by assuring him she would faint, and forced him away from her.

Soon after he was gone, and Cecilia became more tranquil, Henrietta, who had wept with bitterness in a corner of the room during this scene, approached her, and, with an attempted smile, though in a voice hardly audible, said, "Ah, Miss Beverley, you will, at last, then be happy! happy as all your goodness deserves. And I am sure I should rejoice in it if I was to die to make you happier!"

Cecilia, who but too well knew her full meaning, tenderly embraced her, but was prevented by Dr. Lyster from entering into any discourse with her.

The first meeting, however, with Delvile being over, the second was far more quiet, and in a very short time, he would scarcely quit her a moment, Cecilia herself receiving from his sight a pleasure too great for denial, yet too serene for danger.

The worthy Dr. Lyster, finding her prospect of recovery thus fair, prepared for leaving London: but, equally desirous to do good out of his profession as in it, he first, at the request of Delvile, waited upon his father, to acquaint him with his present situation, solicit his directions for his future proceedings, and endeavour to negociate a general reconciliation.

Mr. Delvile, to whose proud heart social joy could find no avenue, was yet touched most sensibly by the restoration of Cecilia. Neither his dignity nor his displeasure had been able to repress remorse, a feeling to which, with all his foibles, he had not been accustomed. The view of her distraction had dwelt upon his imagination, the despondency of his son had struck him with fear and horror. He had been haunted by self reproach, and pursued by vain regret; and those concessions he had refused to tenderness and entreaty, he now willingly accorded to change repentance for tranquility. He sent instantly for his son, whom even with tears he embraced, and felt his own peace restored as he pronounced his forgiveness.

New, however, to kindness, he retained it not long, and a stranger to generosity, he knew not how to make her welcome: the extinction of his remorse abated his compassion for Cecilia, and when solicited to receive her, he revived the charges of Mr. Monckton.

Cecilia, informed of this, determined to write to that gentleman herself, whose long and painful illness, joined to his irrecoverable loss of her, she now hoped might prevail with him to make reparation for the injuries he had done her.

To Mr. MONCKTON.

I write not, Sir, to upbraid you; the woes which have followed your ill offices, and which you may some time hear, will render my reproaches superfluous. I write but to beseech that what is past may content you; and that, however, while I was single, you chose to misrepresent me to the Delvile family, you will have so much honour, since I am now become one of it, as to acknowledge my innocence of the crimes laid to my charge.

In remembrance of my former long friendship, I send you my good wishes; and in consideration of my hopes from your recantation, I send you, Sir, if you think it worth acceptance, my forgiveness.

CECILIA DELVILE.

Mr. Monckton, after many long and painful struggles between useless rage, and involuntary remorse, at length sent the following answer.

To Mrs. MORTIMER DELVILE.

Those who could ever believe you guilty, must have been eager to think you so. I meant but your welfare at all times, and to have saved you from a connection I never thought equal to your merit. I am grieved, but not surprised, to hear of your injuries; from the alliance you have formed, nothing else could be expected: if my testimony to your innocence can, however, serve to mitigate them, I scruple not to declare I believe it without taint.

Delvile sent by Dr. Lyster this letter to his father, whose rage at the detection of the perfidy which had deceived him, was yet inferior to what he felt that his family was mentioned so injuriously.

His conference with Dr. Lyster was long and painful, but decisive: that sagacious and friendly man knew well how to work upon his passions, and so effectually awakened them by representing the disgrace of his own family from the present situation of Cecilia, that before he quitted his house he was authorised to invite her to remove to it.

When he returned from his embassy, he found Delvile

in her room, and each waiting with impatience the event of his negociation.

The Doctor with much alacrity gave Cecilia the invitation with which he had been charged; but Delvile, jealous for her dignity, was angry and dissatisfied his father brought it not himself, and exclaimed with much mortification, "Is this all the grace accorded me?"

"Patience, patience, Sir," answered the Doctor; "when you have thwarted any body in their first hope and ambition, do you expect they will send you their compliments and many thanks for the disappointment? Pray let the good gentleman have his way in some little matters, since you have taken such effectual care to put out of his reach the power of having it in greater."

"O far from starting obstacles," cried Cecilia, "let us solicit a reconciliation with whatever concessions he may require. The misery of DISOBEDIENCE we have but too fatally experienced; and thinking as we think of filial ties and parental claims, how can we ever hope happiness till forgiven and taken into favour?"

"True, my Cecilia," answered Delvile, "and generous and condescending as true; and if *you* can thus sweetly comply, I will gratefully forbear making any opposition. Too much already have you suffered from the impetuosity of my temper, but I will try to curb it in future by the remembrance of your injuries."

"The whole of this unfortunate business," said Dr. Lyster, "has been the result of PRIDE and PREJUDICE.* Your uncle, the Dean, began it, by his arbitrary will, as if an ordinance of his own could arrest the course of nature! and as if *he* had power to keep alive, by the loan of a name, a family in the male branch already extinct. Your father, Mr. Mortimer, continued it with the same self-partiality, preferring the wretched gratification of tickling his ear with a favourite sound, to the solid happiness of his son with a rich and deserving wife. Yet this, however, remember; if to PRIDE and PREJUDICE you owe your miseries, so wonderfully is good and evil balanced, that to PRIDE and PREJUDICE you will also owe their termination: for all that I could say to Mr. Delvile, either of reasoning or entreaty,—and I said all I could suggest, and I suggested all a man need wish to hear,—was totally thrown away, till I pointed out to him his *own* disgrace, in having a *daughter-in-law* immured in these mean lodgings!

"Thus, my dear young lady, the terror which drove you to this house, and the sufferings which have confined you in it, will prove, in the event, the source of your future peace: for when all my best rhetorick failed to melt Mr. Delvile, I instantly brought him to terms by coupling his name with a pawnbroker's! And he could not with more disgust hear his son called Mr. Beverley, than think of his son's wife when he hears of the *Three Blue Balls!* Thus the same passions, taking but different directions, *do* mischief and *cure* it alternately.

"Such, my good young friends, is the MORAL of your calamities. You have all, in my opinion, been strangely at cross purposes, and trifled, no one knows why, with the first blessings of life. My only hope is that now, having among you thrown away its luxuries, you will have known enough of misery to be glad to keep its necessaries."

This excellent man was yet prevailed upon by Delvile to stay and assist in removing the feeble Cecilia to St. James's-square.

Henrietta, for whom Mr. Arnott's equipage and servants had still remained in town, was then, though with much difficulty, persuaded to go back to Suffolk: but Cecilia, however fond of her society, was too sensible of the danger and impropriety of her present situation, to receive from it any pleasure.

Mr. Delvile's reception of Cecilia was formal and cold: yet, as she now appeared publicly in the character of his son's wife, the best apartment in his house had been prepared for her use, his domestics were instructed to wait upon her with the utmost respect, and Lady Honoria Pemberton, who was accidently in town, offered from curiosity, what Mr. Delvile accepted from parade, to be herself in St. James's-square, in order to do honour to his daughter-in-law's first entrance.

When Cecilia was a little recovered from the shock of the first interview, and the fatigue of her removal, the anxious Mortimer would instantly have had her conveyed to her own apartment; but, willing to exert herself, and hoping to oblige Mr. Delvile, she declared she was well able to remain some time longer in the drawing-room.

"My good friends," said Dr. Lyster, "in the course of my long practice, I have found it impossible to study the human frame, without a little studying the human mind; and from all that I have yet been able to make out, either by observation, reflection, or comparison, it appears to me at this moment, that Mr. Mortimer Delvile has got the best wife, and that you, Sir, have here the most faultless daughter-in-law, that any husband or any father in the three kingdoms belonging to his Majesty* can either have or desire."

Cecilia smiled; Mortimer looked his delighted concurrence; Mr. Delvile forced himself to make a stiff inclination of the head; and Lady Honoria gaily exclaimed, "Dr. Lyster, when you say the *best* and the most *faultless*, you should always add the rest of company excepted."

"Upon my word," cried the Doctor, "I beg your ladyship's pardon; but there is a certain unguarded warmth comes across a man now and then, that drives *etiquette* out of his head, and makes him speak truth before he well knows where he is."

"O terrible!" cried she, "this is sinking deeper and deeper. I had hoped the town air would have taught you better things; but I find you have visited at Delvile Castle till you are fit for no other place."

"Whoever, Lady Honoria," said Mr. Delvile, much offended, "is fit for Delvile Castle, must be fit for *every* other place; though every other place may by no means be fit for him."

"O yes, Sir," cried she, giddily, "every possible place will be fit for him, if he can once bear with that. Don't you think so, Dr. Lyster?"

"Why, when a man has the honour to see your ladyship,"

answered he, good-humouredly, "he is apt to think too much of the person, to care about the place."

"Come, I begin to have some hopes of you," cried she, "for I see, for a Doctor, you have really a very pretty notion of a compliment: only you have one great fault still; you look the whole time as if you said it for a joke."

"Why, in fact, madam, when a man has been a plain dealer both in word and look for upwards of fifty years, 'tis expecting too quick a reformation to demand ductility of voice and eye from him at a blow. However, give me but a little time and a little encouragement, and, with such a tutress, 'twill be hard if I do not, in a very few lessons, learn the right method of seasoning a simper, and the newest fashion of twisting words from meaning."

"But pray," cried she, "upon those occasions, always remember to look serious. Nothing sets off a compliment so much as a long face. If you are tempted to an unseasonable laugh, think of Delvile Castle; 'tis an expedient I commonly make use of myself when I am afraid of being too frisky: and it always succeeds, for the very recollection of it gives me the head-ache in a moment. Upon my word, Mr. Delvile, you must have the constitution of five men, to have kept such good health, after living so long at that horrible place. You can't imagine how you've surprised me, for I have regularly expected to hear of your death at the end of every summer: and, I assure you, once, I was very near buying mourning."

"The estate which descends to a man from his own ancestors, Lady Honoria," answered Mr. Delvile, "will seldom be apt to injure his health, if he is conscious of committing no misdemeanour which has degraded their memory."

"How vastly odious this new father of yours is!" said Lady Honoria, in a whisper to Cecilia; "what could ever induce you to give up your charming estate for the sake of coming into his fusty old family! I would really advise you to have your marriage annulled. You have only, you know, to take an oath that you were forcibly run away with;* and as you are an Heiress, and the Delviles are all so violent, it will easily be credited. And then, as soon as you are at liberty,

I would advise you to marry my little Lord Derford."

"Would you only, then," said Cecilia, "have me regain my freedom in order to part with it?"

"Certainly," answered Lady Honoria, "for you can do nothing at all without being married; a single woman is a thousand times more shackled than a wife; for, she is accountable to every body; and a wife, you know, has nothing to do but just to manage her husband."

"And that," said Cecilia, smiling, "you consider as a trifle?"

"Yes, if you do but marry a man you don't care for."

"You are right, then, indeed, to recommend to me my Lord Derford!"

"O yes, he will make the prettiest husband in the world; you may fly about yourself as wild as a lark, and keep him the whole time as tame as a jack-daw:* and though he may complain of you to your friends, he will never have the courage to find fault to your face. But as to Mortimer, you will not be able to govern him as long as you live; for the moment you have put him upon the fret, you'll fall into the dumps yourself, hold out your hand to him, and, losing the opportunity of gaining some material point, make up at the first soft word."

"You think, then, the quarrel more amusing than the reconciliation?"

"O, a thousand times! for while you are quarrelling, you may say any thing, and demand any thing, but when you are reconciled, you ought to behave pretty, and seem contented."

"Those who presume to have any pretensions to your ladyship," said Cecilia, "would be made happy indeed should they hear your principles!"

"O, it would not signify at all," answered she, "for one's fathers, and uncles, and those sort of people, always make connexions for one, and not a creature thinks of our principles, till they find them out by our conduct: and nobody can possibly do that till we are married, for they give us no power beforehand. The men know nothing of us in the world while we are single, but how we can dance a minuet, or play a lesson upon the harpsichord.''

"And what else," said Mr. Delvile, who advanced, and heard this last speech, ''need a young lady of rank desire to be known for? your ladyship surely would not have her degrade herself by studying like an artist or professor?"

"O no, Sir, I would not have her study at all; it's mighty well for children, but really after sixteen, and when one is come out, one has quite fatigue enough in dressing, and going to public places, and ordering new things, without all that torment of first and second position, and E upon the first line, and F upon the first space!''*

"Your ladyship must, however, pardon me for hinting," said Mr. Delvile, ''that a young lady of condition, who has a proper sense of her dignity, cannot be seen too rarely, or known too little.''

"O but I hate dignity!" cried she, carelessly, ''for its the dullest thing in the world. I always thought it was owing to that you were so little amusing;—really I beg your pardon, Sir, I meant to say so little talkative.''

"I can easily credit that your ladyship spoke hastily," answered he, highly piqued, ''for I believe, indeed, a person of a family* such as mine, will hardly be supposed to have come into the world for the office of amusing it!''

"O no, Sir," cried she, with pretended innocence, ''nobody, I am sure, ever saw you with such a thought.'' Then, turning to Cecilia, she added in a whisper, ''you cannot imagine, my dear Mrs. Mortimer, how I detest this old cousin of mine! Now pray tell me honestly if you don't hate him yourself?''

"I hope," said Cecilia, ''to have no reason.''

"Lord, how you are always upon your guard! If I were half as cautious, I should die of the vapours in a month; the only thing that keeps me at all alive, is now and then making people angry; for the folks at our house let me go out so seldom, and then send me with such stupid old chaperons, that giving them a little torment is really the only entertainment I can procure myself. O—but I had almost forgot to tell you a most delightful thing!''

"What is it?"

"Why you must know I have the greatest hopes in the world that my father will quarrel with old Mr. Delvile!"

"And is that such a delightful thing!"

"O yes; I have lived upon the very idea this fortnight; for then, you know, they'll both be in a passion, and I shall see which of them looks frightfullest."

"When Lady Honoria whispers," cried Mortimer, "I always suspect some mischief."

"No indeed," answered her ladyship, "I was merely congratulating Mrs. Mortimer about her marriage. Though really, upon second thoughts, I don't know whether I should not rather condole with her, for I have long been convinced she has a prodigious antipathy to you. I saw it the whole time I was at Delvile Castle, where she used to change colour at the very sound of your name; a symptom I never perceived when I talked to her of my Lord Derford, who would certainly have made her a thousand times a better husband."

"If you mean on account of his title, Lady Honoria," said Mr. Delvile: "your ladyship must be strangely forgetful of the connections of your family, not to remember that Mortimer, after the death of his uncle and myself, must inevitably inherit one far more honourable than a new-sprung-up family, like my Lord Ernolf's, could offer."

"Yes, Sir; but then, you know, she would have kept her estate, which would have been a vastly better thing than an old pedigree of new relations. Besides, I don't find that any body cares for the noble blood of the Delviles but themselves; and if she had kept her fortune, every body, I fancy, would have cared for *that*."

"Every body, then," said Mr. Delvile, "must be highly mercenary and ignoble, or the blood of an ancient and honourable house, would be thought contaminated by the most distant hint of so degrading a comparison."

"Dear Sir, what should we all do with birth if it was not for wealth? it would neither take us to Ranelagh nor the

Opera; nor buy us caps nor wigs, nor supply us with dinners, nor bouquets.''*

''Caps and wigs, dinners and bouquets!'' interrupted Mr. Delvile; ''your ladyship's estimate of wealth is really extremely minute.''

''Why, you know, Sir, as to caps and wigs, they are very serious things, for we should look mighty droll figures to go about bare-headed; and as to dinners, how would the Delviles have lasted all these thousand centuries if they had disdained eating them?''

''Whatever may be your ladyship's satisfaction,'' said Mr. Delvile, angrily, ''in depreciating a house that has the honour of being nearly allied with your own, you will not, I hope at least, instruct this lady,'' turning to Cecilia, ''to adopt a similar contempt of its antiquity and dignity.''

''This lady,'' cried Mortimer, ''will at least, by condescending to become one of it, secure us from any danger that such contempt may spread further.''

''Let me but,'' said Cecilia, looking gratefully at him, ''be as secure from exciting as I am from feeling contempt, and what can I have to wish?''

''Good and excellent young lady!'' said Dr. Lyster, ''the first of blessings indeed is yours in the temperance of your own mind. When you began your career in life, you appeared to us short-sighted mortals, to possess more than your share of the good things of this world; such a union of riches, beauty, independence, talents, education and virtue, seemed a monopoly to raise general envy and discontent; but mark with what scrupulous exactness the good and bad is ever balanced! You have had a thousand sorrows to which those who have looked up to you have been strangers, and for which not all the advantages you possess have been equivalent. There is evidently throughout this world, in things as well as persons, a levelling principle, at war with pre-eminence, and destructive of perfection.''

''Ah!'' cried Mortimer, in a low voice to Cecilia, ''how much higher must we all rise, or how much lower must you fall, ere any levelling principle will approximate us with YOU!''

He then entreated her to spare her strength and spirits by returning to her own apartment, and the conversation was broken up.

"Pray permit me, Mrs. Mortimer," cried Lady Honoria, in taking leave, "to beg that the first guest you invite to Delvile Castle may be me. You know my partiality to it already. I shall be particularly happy in waiting upon you in tempestuous weather! We can all stroll out together, you know, very sociably; and I sha'n't be much in your way, for if there should happen to be a storm, you can easily lodge me under some great tree, and while you amuse yourselves with a tête-à-tête, give me the indulgence of my own reflections. I am vastly fond of thinking, and being alone, you know,—especially in thunder and lightening!"

She then ran away; and they all separated: Cecilia was conveyed up stairs, and worthy Dr. Lyster, loaded with acknowledgments of every kind, set out for the country.

Cecilia, still weak, and much emaciated, for some time lived almost wholly in her own room; where the grateful and solicitous attendance of Mortimer, alleviated the pain both of her illness and confinement: but as soon as her health permitted travelling, he hastened with her abroad.

Here tranquility once more made its abode the heart of Cecilia; that heart so long torn with anguish, suspense and horrour! Mrs. Delvile received her with the most rapturous fondness, and the impression of her sorrows gradually wore away, from her kind and maternal cares, and from the watchful affection and delighted tenderness of her son.

The Egglestons now took entire possession of her estate, and Delvile, at her entreaty, forbore shewing any personal resentment of their conduct, and put into the hands of a lawyer the arrangement of the affair.

They continued abroad some months, and the health of Mrs. Delvile was tolerably re-established. They were then summoned home by the death of Lord Delvile, who bequeathed to his nephew Mortimer his town house, and whatever of his estate was not annexed to his title, which necessarily devolved to his brother.

The sister of Mrs. Delvile, a woman of high spirit and strong passions, lived not long after him; but having, in her latter days, intimately connected herself with Cecilia, she was so much charmed with her character, and so much dazzled by her admiration of the extraordinary sacrifice she had made, that, in a fit of sudden enthusiasm, she altered her will, to leave to her, and to her sole disposal, the fortune which, almost from his infancy, she had destined for her nephew. Cecilia, astonished and penetrated, opposed the alteration; but even her sister, now Lady Delvile,* to whom she daily became dearer, earnestly supported it; while Mortimer, delighted to restore to her through his own family, any part of that power and independence of which her generous and pure regard for himself had deprived her, was absolute in refusing that the deed should be revoked.

Cecilia, from this flattering transaction, received a further conviction of the malignant falsehood of Mr. Monckton, who had always represented to her the whole of the Delvile family as equally poor in their circumstances, and illiberal in their minds. The strong spirit of active benevolence which had ever marked her character, was now again displayed, though no longer, as hitherto, unbounded. She had learnt the error of profusion, even in charity and beneficence; and she had a motive for œconomy, in her animated affection for Mortimer.

She soon sent for Albany, whose surprise that she still existed, and whose rapture at her recovered prosperity, now threatened his senses from the tumult of his joy, with nearly the same danger they had lately been menaced by terror. But though her donations were circumscribed by prudence, and their objects were selected with discrimination, she gave to herself all her former benevolent pleasure, in solacing his afflictions, while she softened his asperity, by restoring to him his favourite office of being her almoner and monitor.

She next sent to her own pensioners, relieved those distresses which her sudden absence had occasioned, and renewed and continued the salaries she had allowed them. All who had nourished reasonable expectations from her bounty she remembered, though she raised no new

claimants but with œconomy and circumspection. But
neither Albany nor the old pensioners felt the satisfaction of
Mortimer, who saw with new wonder the virtues of her
mind, and whose admiration of her excellencies, made his
gratitude perpetual for the happiness of his lot.

The tender-hearted Henrietta, in returning to her new
friends, gave way, with artless openness, to the violence of
untamed grief; but finding Mr. Arnott as wretched as
herself, the sympathy Cecilia had foreseen soon endeared
them to each other, while the little interest taken in either by
Mrs. Harrel, made them almost inseparable companions.

Mrs. Harrel, wearied by their melancholy, and sick of
retirement, took the earliest opportunity that was offered her
of changing her situation; she married very soon a man of
fortune in the neighbourhood, and, quickly forgetting all the
past, thoughtlessly began the world again, with new hopes,
new connections,—new equipages and new engagements!

Henrietta was then obliged to go again to her mother,
where, though deprived of all the indulgencies to which she
was now become familiar, she was not more hurt by the
separation than Mr. Arnott. So sad and so solitary his house
seemed in her absence, that he soon followed her to town,
and returned not till he carried her back its mistress. And
there the gentle gratitude of her soft and feeling heart,
engaged from the worthy Mr. Arnott the tenderest affection,
and, in time, healed the wound of his early and hopeless
passion.

The injudicious, the volatile, yet noble-minded Belfield,
to whose mutable and enterprising disposition life seemed
always rather beginning than progressive, roved from
employment to employment, and from public life to
retirement, soured with the world, and discontented with
himself, till vanquished, at length, by the constant friendship of Delvile, he consented to accept his good offices in
again entering the army; and, being fortunately ordered out
upon foreign service, his hopes were revived by ambition,
and his prospects were brightened by a view of future
honour.

The wretched Monckton, dupe of his own cunning and artifices, still lived in lingering misery, doubtful which was most acute, the pain of his wound and confinement, or of his defeat and disappointment. Led on by a vain belief that he had parts to conquer all difficulties, he had indulged without restraint a passion in which interest was seconded by inclination. Allured by such fascinating powers, he shortly suffered nothing to stop his course; and though when he began his career he would have started at the mention of actual dishonour, long before it was concluded, neither treachery nor perjury were regarded by him as stumbling blocks. All fear of failing was lost in vanity, all sense of probity was sunk in interest, all scruples of conscience were left behind by the heat of the chace. Yet the unforeseen and melancholy catastrophe of his long arts, illustrated in his despite what his principles had obscured, that even in wordly pursuits where fraud out-runs integrity, failure joins dishonour to loss, and disappointment excites triumph instead of pity.

The upright mind of Cecilia, her purity, her virtue, and the moderation of her wishes, gave to her in the warm affection of Lady Delvile, and the unremitting fondness of Mortimer, all the happiness human life seems capable of receiving:—yet human it was, and as such imperfect! she knew that, at times, the whole family must murmur at her loss of fortune, and at times she murmured herself to be thus portionless, tho' an HEIRESS. Rationally, however, she surveyed the world at large, and finding that of the few who had any happiness, there were none without some misery, she checked the rising sigh of repining mortality, and, grateful with general felicity, bore partial evil with chearfullest resignation.

FINIS

The wretched Monckton, dupe of his own cunning and artifices, still lived in lingering misery, doubtful which was most acute, the pain of his wound and confinement, or of his defeat and disappointment; led on by a vain belief that he had parts to conquer all difficulties; he had indulged without restraint a passion in which interest was seconded by inclination. Allured by such fascinating powers, he shortly suffered nothing to stop his course; and though when he began his career he would have started at the mention of actual dishonour, long before it was concluded, neither treachery nor perjury were regarded by him as stumbling blocks. All fear of failing was lost in vanity, all sense of probity was sunk in interest, all scruples of conscience were left behind by the heat of the chace. Yet the unforeseen and melancholy catastrophe of his long arts, illustrated in his despite what his principles had obscured, that even in worldly pursuits where fraud out-runs integrity, failure joins dishonour to loss, and disappointment excites triumph instead of pity.

The upright mind of Cecilia, her purity, her virtue, and the moderation of her wishes, gave to her in the warm affection of Lady Delvile, and the unremitting fondness of Mortimer, all the happiness human life seems capable of receiving:—yet human it was, and as such imperfect! she knew that, at times, the whole family must murmur at her loss of fortune, and at times she murmured herself to be thus portionless, tho' an HEIRESS. Rationally, however, she surveyed the world at large, and finding that of the few who had any happiness, there were none without some misery, she checked the rising sigh of repining mortality, and, grateful with general felicity, bore partial evil with chearfullest resignation.

FINIS.

APPENDIX I

BURNEY'S DRAFT INTRODUCTION TO CECILIA

Burney's draft Introduction to *Cecilia* (British Library Egerton MS 3696, ff. 1–3) has not been previously published. In this transcription, words and phrases cancelled or replaced by Burney have been recorded in footnotes. The Introduction is reproduced verbatim, with no emendation or modernization.

INTRODUCTION

In the early ages of Authorship, Genius instituted the school of Letters, & inspired it's Disciples; but as brightness of parts is no security for vigilance of conduct, from a negligence the most unfortunate for posterity, vanity was suffered to become the self-nominated Patroness of his, thence polluted seminary.

But if Industry is it's own reward, Indolence is no less it's own scourge; vanity soon grew insolent, & Genius disgusted. two parties were formed, & a vigorous[1] contest ensued: on one side, the Founder was animated[2] by all the fire of genuine abilities, on the other, the Patroness was emboldened by all the arrogance of self-sufficiency: but, as it is infinitely more practicable to destroy Beauty, than to grace Deformity, so is it a task far more feasible to repress Merit, than to subdue Ignorance: Genius, therefore, soon quitted the Field, & selecting those few of his favourite Disciples whose intellectual faculties he had rarified by sparks of his own immortal Fire, he withdrew himself from the promiscuous herd of his importunate followers & thence forward secluded himself forever from all such claimants who consider the art of Writing to consist in researches for Flattery, not improvement & Truth.[3]

Meanwhile, vanity, too conceited to be humbled, & too shallow for conviction, proud of the number, & unconscious of the feebleness of her adherents, maintained her Ground, & far from deploring the separation, weakly triumphed in her victory.

Hence originated the 2 sects which, from the infancy of their Institution, to the present Time, have presided in the Literary World, & to which we must attribute the striking inequality of the works with which it is overwhelmed. Hence the redundancy of copious nothings with wh^{ch} the wearried, yet restless Reader is perpetually annoyed; & hence those scarce,[4] but noble productions, wh^{ch} are fostered by the soul of Literature, Genius,

—whose Eye pervades all Nature, whose penetration investigates all art, & whose Breath is spirit, Life, & inspiration.

Every[5] youthful Author, in his first Career, views both the seminaries at an humble distance: he distinguishes the Temple of Genius by its radiance, &, with longing Eyes, & a beating Heart, he gazes at it's height, but sickens at it's distance; each step he advances, he trembles, each Eye he meets, he Blushes: Hope, the flattering seducer of Inexperience, allures him on, & Fear, the doubt-exciting discourager of Timidity, calls him back: he wavers,—yet he proceeds; he repents,—but he never returns! New to the scene before him, it absorbs every faculty of his agitated soul; his accustomed occupations become irksome, his former pleasures, insipid; the smallest praise has power to enchant, the slightest criticism to distract him: Ambition possesses all the Avenues by wh[ch] he might retreat, &, whether hopeless or sanguine, he still pursues the same course; all his ideas of Happiness & of Misery are centred in Fame & Disgrace, & in the *Author*, the *Man* is lost.

At length, he wearries; he sees with wonder the little progress he has made, &, as he casts around his wistful Eyes, the Temple of Vanity, gay, luxurious & attractive, appears in full view, & invites his approach. Struck by it's exterior form & ornaments, & charmed by it's vicinity & easiness of access, he determines upon a closer[6] examination. The nearer he advances, the more beautiful it seems, & his heated Imagination represents its allurements as irresistable. Conceit, in the Habit of Merit, conducts him to the Gate, & Adulation, in the Garb of Candour, makes him welcome. He is delighted with his reception, his Fears give place to wishes, & his Hopes to Expectations; vanity regales him with Food, & he Drinks from the delicious Fountain of Flattery. Intoxication ensues; he loses even his desire of pursuing his Journey; his Eyes, indeed, glance towards the Temple of Genius, but he is too inebriated to perceive its Glory; his feelings are all in favour of Vanity, & he is too much captivated[7] to consider her inferiority.

Such is the fate of all those who mistake Inclination for Ability; & happy is the error! for vain were their toil, & lost their labour; it is not by pursuit, however arduous, that Genius is to be caught; the chosen few on whom he dispences his blessings, receive them unasked, are unconscious of the Gift, possess them without effort, & enjoy them without trouble.

How strange is the infatuation by which we are seduced! how cruel the enchantment by which we are beguiled! When warmest in the pursuit of Glory, we are most liable to Dishonour, & when we think ourselves rising to the summit of Fame, we are most in danger of sinking into the abyss of Ridicule!

But stranger yet is the fascination by which those are entangled, who are neither blinded by self Love, nor allured by Ambition, who are fearfully & feelingly awake to the perils wh· surround them, yet, urged by an impulse irresistable, rather Court than shun them, &, like the ill fated starlings, see the Destruction with which they are threatened[8] yet plunge in to it headlong.[9]

Among the numerous Tribes of this latter sect, who may not improperly be called the *Quakers* of Litterature,[10] the author of the following sheets is classed: but whether the spirit which moves me to write is a Being beneficent, who will countenance & protect me; or whether some malignant Daemon, delighting in mischief,[11] woos me to derision, that he may enjoy my repentance, I know not,——& I fear to learn! My Readers will severally determine for themselves, & to their decisions I must, perforce, submit.

I plead not, alas! for venturing into the World, that I am transported by the wild effusions of Genius; yet I should be most unwilling to suppose myself influenced by the egregious folly of vanity. I am sensible that the Mediocrity of my Talents has distanced me from the first, but I hope that the humility of my Sect has at least guarded me from the second.

I will not, however, attempt a precise investigation of the interior movements by which I may be impelled: the intricasies of the human Heart are various as innumerable, & its feelings, upon all interesting occasions, are so minute & complex, as to baffle all the power of Language. What Addison has said of the Ways of Heaven, may with much more propriety & accuracy be applied to the Mind of Man, which, indeed, is

Dark & Intricate,
Filled with wild Mazes, & perplexed with *Error*.[12]

As the fortunate Editor of Evelina,[13] I may sometimes, perhaps, admit[14] a ray of that Hope which my first Publication wholly obscured from me; yet it shines but faintly, if it shines at all, for I well know that the Success of one work is no security for the safety of another, since not only the annotations of the critics, but even the Approbation of the Friends of the First, frequently prove alike pirnicious to the second; the one by exciting Expectations unreasonable, the other by previously paving the way for severity of Judgement.[15]

Notes

1 *a vigorous*: replaces 'an animated'.

2 *animated*: replaces 'supported'.

3 *consist in . . . Truth*: replaces 'be more the business of the Hands, than of the Heart'.

4 *those scarce*: replaces 'the scarcity'.

5 *Every*: 'Each' is inserted here, but 'Every' is not deleted.

6 *closer*: replaces 'nearer'.

7 *captivated*: replaces 'elated'.

8 *with which they are threatened*: replaces 'to which they are destined'.

9 *headlong*: starlings are peculiar birds in this fabulous context; perhaps the word 'swallows' should be substituted. Burney may be misrecollecting Dryden's *The Hind and the Panther* (1687), with its fable of the Swallows, in which the misguided birds ignore the advent of winter to their certain destruction. Even a man as learned as Dr Johnson still believed that swallows gathered in groups and plunged into streams.

10 *Quakers of Litterature*: the Quakers, the nonconformist religious sect founded by George Fox in 1652, stressed the importance of inward spiritual experience and spoke of being moved by the spirit. The Quakers were so called by others because of their quaking or shaking from religious fervour. Burney puns on the idea of quaking (with timidity) and being moved by an inward spirit.

11 *mischief*: replaces 'mischief and sport, again'.

12 *Error*: in Addison's *Cato* (1713), Portius describes the 'ways of Heaven' as 'dark and intricate, / Puzzled in mazes, and perplex'd with errors' (I. i. 48–9).

13 *Evelina*: in her preface to *Evelina*, Burney presents herself as 'editor' of the letters that comprise the work, a characteristic device in the eighteenth-century epistolary novel.

14 *admit*: replaces an illegible word.

15 *Judgment*: the final paragraph resembles Burney's brief prefatory 'Advertisement' to *Cecilia*.

APPENDIX II

GLOSSARY OF FRENCH TERMS

French terms in *Cecilia* are spelled and accented in a variety of ways. Words here are in modern French spelling; original spellings are retained in the text.

abattu: dejected, cast down.

abîmé: destroyed, ruined.

accablant: oppressive, insupportable.

accablé: weighed down, overburdened.

anéanti: overwhelmed, tired out.

assez de monde: enough people.

assommé: overpowered, oppressed.

au désespoir: in despair.

dégoûté: disgusted.

de grâce: for pity's sake.

douceur: kindness, i.e. tip.

empressement: haste, eagerness.

ennuyé: bored, weary.

enragé: enraged, violent.

fade: dull, insipid.

horreur: horror, dread.

indécidé: undecided, uncertain.

malheur: unhappiness, misfortune.

mon ami: my friend.

mon possible: my best, the best I can.

obsédé: beset, importuned.

parfaitement: perfectly, completely.

partout: everywhere.

quelle honte: what a shame, what a pity.

sans fin: endlessly.

ton: fashion, vogue, modishness.

tout à fait: entirely, completely.

APPENDIX III

LONDON

In the first census of London, 1801, the population stood at just under one million; in 1782 it might be estimated at approximately 750,000. Over ten times larger than its nearest rival, Liverpool, London was by far the biggest city in England and also considerably larger than Paris, the second greatest European city. Much of the action in *Cecilia* takes place in Westminster, the rapidly expanding and increasingly fashionable west end of London. The Harrels' house in Portman Square is on the western outskirts of this fashionable area; beyond is the village of Paddington, where Mrs Belfield owns a small house. After leaving the Harrels, Cecilia stays with the Delviles in St James's Square, at the very heart of the 'polite' western end of town. Further to the east, on the other side of Temple Bar, lies the City of London, the centre of trade and finance, where Briggs has his shabby residence. In the City, too, Cecilia establishes her protégée Mrs Hill in Fetter Lane, and in the City she intends to stay when, much later, towards the end of the novel, she searches for cheap lodgings. The rivalry between the City and Westminster, between middle-class 'citizens' and people of fashion, is manifested in the novel by the mutual contempt of Briggs and Compton Delvile.

Vauxhall Gardens, scene of the greatest set-piece in *Cecilia*, lay to the south of the river Thames. To reach it, Cecilia's party would cross the river at Westminster Bridge. Although the first London Bridge, joining the City to Southwark, dated from Roman times, Westminster Bridge, the second, was completed only in 1750, and the third, Blackfriars Bridge, in 1769.

The following list provides brief descriptions of the various streets and areas of London mentioned in *Cecilia*, with page references to their first appearance in the novel:

33 *Portman-square*: a new, large, highly fashionable square on the western outskirts of London, begun in 1764 but not completed until the 1780s. Frances Burney's acquaintance, the bluestocking Elizabeth Montagu, gave a house-warming party for her new house there at Easter 1782, shortly before the publication of *Cecilia*.

49 *Cavendish-square*: an early Georgian fashionable square close to Regent Street, inhabited by Lady Mary Wortley Montagu,

1731–38, and by Princess Amelia, daughter of George II, 1761–80.

81 *Harley-street*: an elegant street joining Cavendish Square to Marylebone Road. The association with doctors for which the street is now famous began only in about 1845.

96 *St. James's-Square*: since about 1670 the most magnificent square in London, close to St James's Palace and inhabited largely by the aristocracy.

176 *Oxford Road*: now Oxford Street, the principal east–west thoroughfare through London. Tyburn (then the site of the gallows and now the site of Marble Arch) was just to the west of Harrel's residence; Cecilia encounters the mob progressing there as she walks east towards Briggs's house in the City.

181 *Moorfields*: a field to the north of the City, famous for its cheap secondhand bookstalls.

201 *Fetter-lane*: running from Fleet Street to Holborn in the City. An unfashionable but respectable address, appropriate for Mrs Hill. From the mid-seventeenth century the street was well known for its Dissenting meeting-houses.

205 *Swallow-street*: an undistinguished street, running north from Piccadilly to Oxford Street.

215 *within Temple-Bar*: within the City of London, separated from Westminster by a gateway designed by Wren that survived until 1870.

218 *Padington*: normally spelled Paddington; an attractive village to the north-west of London; a haven for exiled French Huguenots in the eighteenth century.

226 *Cavendish-street, Oxford-road*: close to Cavendish Square; an undistinguished address.

339 *Portland-street, Oxford Road*: running from Oxford Street north to Euston Road; a good address, where Belfield would not be ashamed to receive visitors.

588 *Pall-Mall*: a highly fashionable street, running from St James's Street to the Haymarket; known for its coffee houses and expensive shops as well as for its fine houses.

662 *Hyde Park*: the largest of the London parks, extending from Bayswater Road in the north to Knightsbridge in the south, merging with Kensington Gardens to the west. Rotten Row, on the south side of the park, was and still is a favourite riding-place for equestrians.

721 *Soho Square*: south of Oxford Street, built in the 1680s and highly fashionable until the later eighteenth century. In the 1770s its aristocratic residents began to move to other areas, but country dwellers such as Lady Margaret retained their town-houses there. Frances Burney herself lived in nearby Poland Street.

743 *Tottenham Court Road*: running north from Oxford Street to Tottenham Court, Tottenham Court Road soon became a country road passing between fields and market gardens.

767 *a court leading into Piccadilly*: although Piccadilly itself, running from the Haymarket to Hyde Park Corner, was a very fashionable street, leading off it there were many small, insalubrious courts (small areas surrounded by buildings).

826 *Albemarle-Street*: running off Piccadilly; a highly fashionable street with many distinguished residents.

References

James Howgego, *Printed Maps of London, circa 1553–1850*, 2nd edn. (London, 1978).

Ben Weinreb and Christopher Hibbert, *The London Encyclopaedia* (London, 1983).

Henry B. Wheatley and Peter Cunningham, *London Past and Present* (London, 1891).

The Survey of London, 42 vols., in progress (London, 1900–86).

John Cary's map of London, 1782 (listed in Howgego, no. 173), is the best of several contemporary with *Cecilia*; John Harris's map of 1779 (Howgego, no. 170), the date when the action of the novel begins, is also useful.

APPENDIX IV
FINANCE

Most of the coinage of late eighteenth-century England is mentioned in *Cecilia*: in gold the guinea and half-guinea; in silver the crown, half crown, shilling, sixpence, threepence, twopence, and penny; in copper the halfpenny and farthing. There were four farthings to a penny, twelve pence to a shilling, five shillings to a crown, and twenty-one shillings to a guinea. English coinage was truly on the gold standard, and the golden guinea was a handsome and valuable coin. Payments for very large sums were usually made in pounds (£, or *l.* as in *Cecilia*), worth twenty shillings, for which there was no coin; such payments would be made by notes drawn on a bank. For very approximate modern equivalents, amounts should be multiplied by at least sixty; a pound was thus a considerable sum, and more than many workers earned in a week.

As she is not yet of legal age, Cecilia's only income is a yearly allowance of £500, half of which she pays to her guardian Harrel for room and board, leaving her a 'private allowance' or pocket money of £250 (p. 203). When she comes of age at 21, she will inherit both £10,000 in stocks from her father and, unless she transgresses the name clause, a fortune of £3,000 per annum from her uncle. While living with the Harrels, however, Cecilia borrows sums totalling £9,100 from the Jewish money-lender Aaron on three occasions: £600 (p. 190), £7,500 (p. 271), and £1,000 (p. 392). All but £50 of this she lends to Harrel to pay off his creditors. Harrel is acting outside the law in taking, indeed extorting, money from his ward, and the entire transaction with the money-lender is illegal since Cecilia is a minor. Of the borrowed money, Cecilia gives another £40 to Mrs Hill (p. 203), leaving herself with only £10. During her minority she also spends further sums on various objects of charity, such as the Hills and Belfield, on a 'well-chosen collection of books' in which 'she was restrained by no expence' (p. 103), and on a Merlin pianoforte (p. 460), costing around £100 in Merlin's catalogues. These expenses considerably exceed Cecilia's private allowance, but she believes that her other guardians, Compton Delvile and Briggs, will advance her money from her father's £10,000 before she comes of age; both, however, refuse her requests.

After Harrel's suicide, Monckton ostensibly befriends Cecilia by paying Aaron the £9,050 capital that Cecilia owes him, as well as an unspecified, exorbitant (and illicit) amount of interest. Monckton could have urged Cecilia to repudiate the debt, since a minor could not be bound by such a contract; instead he wishes to bind Cecilia to himself. Cecilia will now repay this sum to Monckton, at the normal rate of interest paid on money in a bank (about 3 per cent), after she comes of age (p. 437). When she does obtain her £10,000 from the reluctant hands of Briggs, she exhausts the entire sum by repaying Monckton's principal and interest and by 'settling' with her patient bookseller (p. 766).

Cecilia is now, having come of age, in possession of an estate worth £3,000 a year. For several months after her twenty-first birthday she engages in the construction of her new house, and also spends heavily on acts of charity, guided by Albany. She can spend so much because she relies on a handsome annual income, but after her marriage to Delvile is discovered by Eggleston (p. 853) she has no source of income at all. At the end of the novel, however, Delvile receives a legacy from his late uncle, including a town house and part of an estate, while Cecilia receives the fortune of Delvile's late aunt, enabling the couple to live comfortably and Cecilia to resume some of her charitable works.

APPENDIX V

FASHIONABLE AMUSEMENTS

(Prepared with the assistance of Melinda Finberg)

There were many public places of amusement in Cecilia's London. Vauxhall (formerly termed New Spring Garden) was the oldest of the pleasure gardens; its twelve acres containing shrubbery, statues, and cascades were located across the Thames from Westminster Abbey. The admission fee from 1732 to 1792 was one shilling; a visitor paid more to take supper in one of the supper boxes painted by Francis Hayman, from which one could hear the endeavours of the orchestra (pp. 398–423). The extreme thinness of Vauxhall (or Fox-hall) sliced meat was proverbial. Ranelagh Gardens (p. 286) was in Chelsea; opened in 1742 after Lord Ranelagh's death when his grounds were purchased by an investment syndicate, Ranelagh offered an ambitious and more expensive imitation of Vauxhall. Admission was half a crown; on firework nights, 5 shillings. At the centre of the gardens was a rotunda in rococo style, 150 feet in diameter, admittance to which cost an additional shilling. The rotunda contained the orchestra as well as booths for taking tea and wine. Painting, sculpture, and lighting effects featured among Ranelagh's attractions. The Pantheon, a large building in Oxford Street designed by James Wyatt, was intended to be a winter Ranelagh. Opened in 1772, it housed masquerades, concerts, and ridottos (entertainments consisting of music and dancing) as well as twelve assemblies in a season, for which the subscription was a costly six guineas a year. The Pantheon's central rotunda was modelled on Santa Sophia in Constantinople; smaller rooms and vestibules off the central rotunda permitted separate parties for tea, supper, and cards (pp. 274–89). The Phantheon was destroyed by fire in 1792; in 1937 Marks and Spencer acquired the property, still the site of its Oxford Street store. In 1764 William Almack, formerly a valet to the aristocracy, opened his assembly rooms in King's Street (p. 38). During the reign of George III and the Regency, Almack's insisted upon its exclusiveness, and aristocratic patronesses could decide whether or not a young lady was eligible to attend. Males desiring exclusive social retreats could seek shelter in clubs such as White's or Brooks's (p. 39), where gambling figured as the chief entertainment and huge sums could be won or lost.

As had been the case since the Restoration, London had only two licensed major theatres for the production of plays; these were the Theatre Royal Drury Lane and the Covent Garden Theatre. Garrick ruled Drury Lane as manager and star actor (also director and sometime playwright) from 1747 until his retirement in 1776, when Richard Brinsley Sheridan succeeded him as manager. Covent Garden Theatre was the place of first performance of important works, including plays by Goldsmith and Sheridan. Reconstructed in 1782, Covent Garden seated about 2,500 spectators. The King's Theatre in the Haymarket was originally designed by Vanbrugh in the reign of Queen Anne; after the Licensing Act of 1737 it was barred from producing plays and became the Opera House. It held an audience of about 3,000 persons (pp. 60 and 131). (From 1773 to 1778 this Opera House was managed by two women, the playwright Frances Brooke whom Burney met, and the actress Mary Anne Yates.) There were also several London concert rooms, and subscription concerts were held, like those managed by C. F. Abel and J. C. Bach.

After the New Year, fashionable people would begin to cluster in London (in the 'town', i.e. the west end and Westminster, not the vulgar City). The high season was from the period following Easter to the King's Birthday, celebrated on 4 June. As no public entertainments were allowed during Holy Week, and the courts were not sitting, it was proper to retire to an estate in the country at Easter (p. 199), as during the summer and autumn. There were, however, many more year-round amusements for the wealthy in London than formerly, and private amusements became increasingly various and elaborate. Paying calls had already become a complex system involving personal calling cards and a detailed code of behaviour (pp. 24 and 63); footmen were kept busy delivering messages, cards, and invitations. There were many sumptuous private entertainments to which one could be invited. Dining at home became more and more important; a wealthy man such as Henry Thrale might hire a French cook to prepare fine meals of many courses. As the century wore on, meal times became later and later. Breakfast, a simple repast of bread and butter with tea (or coffee or chocolate), in the style of the present-day Continental breakfast, was taken not at 7 or 8 in the morning but at 9 or 10 or even later. Cecilia, fresh from the country, expects breakfast in the early morning, and is surprised to find that her hosts are not taking breakfast even by 10 o'clock (p. 28). The period between breakfast and dinner was called 'morning'; morning activities could include shopping or paying calls, but most 'morning calls' took place in what we would call the afternoon. Ladies could entertain themselves by going shopping or attending auctions, if only to enjoy a display of goods (pp. 28 and 42–4). A young woman could not go out on such an expedition or for a walk unless chaperoned, or at least accompanied by her maid. It was important to be on time and dressed appropriately for dinner, which was becoming a major social event. Dinner, the main meal of the day, was taken by working people and country gentry at noon, but people of fashion dined later. Richard Steele complained that during his lifetime the dinner hour had crept from 12 o'clock to 3, and much later Horace Walpole was to complain that he did not care for dining at 6. Frances Burney in King's Lynn, Norfolk, in 1768 records that 'we breakfast always at 10 . . . we dine precisely at 2, drink tea about 6—and sup exactly at 9' (*Early Diary*, i. 15). She virtuously worked at her needle during the morning and did not allow herself reading and writing until after dinner. But such a provincial regime would be too simple for the polite world. In town, dinner would be served between 3 and 6, with tea offered afterwards. Tea, as an expensive drink, was itself a sign of conspicuous consumption; a pound of fine tea might cost from two to four times the week's wage of a labourer or artisan. Tea after dinner served much the same function as our after-dinner coffee, but eventually became a meal on its own account, and stuck at 4 or 5 o'clock while the next century's dinner hour moved forward to 7 or 8 o'clock. In Burney's first novel the heroine describes a visitor coming to tea 'near five o'clock, for we never dine till the day is almost over' (*Evelina*, p. 56). Supper, the fourth meal, became increasingly rich and varied, and was also served later and later; at a ball, supper might be served at 2 a.m.

Horace Walpole complained in 1777 that 'the present folly is late hours'. Those who could afford it seem to have stayed up as late as we do, leaving the working poor to observe the sun. It was a sign of wealth to be able to turn night into day. Candles were expensive; fine wax candles such as Cecilia's hosts would use cost about 3 shillings a pound, and a party given at home might cost several guineas in candles alone. The variety of private parties given was something new. As well as offering the older style of dinner party or ball, hostesses could invite guests to a private masquerade or to a 'rout', a large evening party or reception with refreshments but not dinner. Interior decorators were soon to assist the party-giving classes to prettify their homes for an occasion. The Harrels in *Cecilia* are already spending large sums on décor and even special constructions for a party (pp. 100 and 121–4). Of course children were still playing old-fashioned games of the style of 'Puss in the Corner' and 'Hide and Seek' and these too are mentioned in *Cecilia* (pp. 13 and 26), in ironic association with the grown-up games of party-goers, masqueraders, and gamblers.

References

Richard D. Altick, *The Shows of London* (Cambridge, Mass., 1978).
Elizabeth Burton, *The Georgians at Home 1714–1830* (London, 1967).
Charles Beecher Hogan, *The London Stage 1776–1800: A Critical Introduction* (Carbondale and Edwardsville, Ill., 1968).

EXPLANATORY NOTES

We have attempted to supply information about places, customs, activities, and language not necessarily familiar to today's reader, as well as to give complete references for literary quotations. Material covered in the Appendices (see 'French Terms', 'London', 'Finance', and 'Fashionable Amusements') is not included in the Notes. The following works are cited in the Notes by short titles:

Boswell, *Life of Johnson*	*Boswell's Life of Johnson*, ed. George Birkbeck Hill, rev. L. F. Powell, 6 vols. (Oxford, 1934–64).
Burney, *Camilla*	Frances Burney, *Camilla: or, A Picture of Youth*, ed. Edward A. Bloom and Lillian D. Bloom (Oxford, 1972).
Burney, *Diary and Letters*	*Diary and Letters of Madame d'Arblay*, ed. Charlotte Barrett, 7 vols. (London, 1842–6).
Burney, *Early Diary*	*The Early Diary of Frances Burney*, ed. Annie Raine Ellis, 2 vols. (London, 1889).
Burney, *Evelina*	Frances Burney, *Evelina: or, the History of a Young Lady's Entrance into the World*, ed. Edward A. Bloom with the assistance of Lillian D. Bloom (Oxford, 1968).
C2	Frances Burney, *Cecilia, or Memoirs of an Heiress*, 2nd edn. (London, 1783).
Cunnington, *Handbook*	C. Willett and Phillis Cunnington, *Handbook of English Costume in the Eighteenth Century* (London, 1957).
EDD	*The English Dialect Dictionary*, ed. Joseph Wright (Oxford, 1898–1905).
Grose, *Classical Dictionary*	Francis Grose, *A Classical Dictionary of the Vulgar Tongue*, ed. Eric Partridge (London, 1937).
Johnson, *Dictionary*	Samuel Johnson, *A Dictionary of the English Language*, 2 vols. (London, 1755).

OED	*A New English Dictionary on Historical Principles*, ed. James A. H. Murray (Oxford, 1888–1933).
Tilley, *Dictionary*	Morris Palmer Tilley, *A Dictionary of the Proverbs in England in the Sixteenth and Seventeenth Centuries* (Ann Arbor, Michigan, 1950).

VOLUME I

3 *Four Editions in one Year*: three English editions and one Irish edition of *Evelina* were published in 1779.

6 *had by the Dean been entrusted*: 'had been entrusted by the Dean' in C2.

Bury: Bury St Edmunds in the county of Suffolk, to the north-east of London, 72 miles distance via Sudbury on the coach road, according to Daniel Paterson's *A New and Accurate Description of all the Direct and Principal Cross Roads in England and Wales* (London, 1794), pp. 206–7.

10 *Dean her Uncle*: 'Dean' in C2.

11 *humble companion*: usually an indigent gentlewoman hired in effect for room and board to amuse the lady of the house and perform small tasks such as grooming and feeding pets. In *The Wanderer* the heroine herself has an unpleasant job as a companion.

militia . . . red-coat . . . cockade: the militia was a localized voluntary service for home defence only; its members were in no danger of having to fight in the war in America, but could wear military uniform, the British red coat. The captain sports the badge of rank on his hat, the dashing cockade (the word has the same origin as cock's comb) either of ribbons or of feathers.

12 *entered . . . Temple*: to become a lawyer a young man had to study and take residence in one of the Inns of Court in London, such as the Inner Temple or the Middle Temple (either of which may be meant here). These buildings stood on the site once occupied by the Knights Templar.

13 *the least claim . . . age or rank*: as the youngest male present, without claim to status by birth or by profession (for lawyers did not rank high), Morrice should defer to the rest of the company, and take the least comfortable chair. It was an age highly conscious of matters of precedence.

Christmas sports . . . move-all: the company are assembled during the 'Christmas holidays' (p. 10), between Christmas and Epiphany (6 January), during which period it was customary for young and old to join in noisy games which any number could play, such as 'move-all', a game like 'General Post' that entails all parties rushing about in search of a chair.

14 *For common rules . . . mind*: slight misquotation of Jonathan Swift's *Cadenus and Vanessa* (1726): 'That common Forms were not design'd / Directors to a noble Mind' (ll. 612–13).

15 *how infinite . . . God!*: alluding to Shakespeare's *Hamlet*, II. ii. 316–19: 'How infinite in faculty! . . . In apprehension how like a god!'

   the noblest work of God: Alexander Pope, *An Essay on Man* (1733–4), iv. 248.

18 *stopping her, again expressed*: 'stopping her again, expressed' in C2.

19 *bows and smiles*: 'vows and smiles' in C2.

   members of parliament . . . privileges: Morrice is making a joke on the basis of Monckton's preceding phrase, 'privilege of my house', as if he had been referring to the privilege of the House of Parliament, into which the king himself cannot enter without permission, and within which members are free to speak without charge of slander. Among other privileges was immunity from arrest when Parliament was in session. MPs' zealous assertions of their rights are here connected with Monckton's assertion of his right to Cecilia, though he is apparently only asserting the 'privilege' of a host and an old friend.

20 *naturally enough*: 'naturally' in C2.

21 *Violet Bank*: the name of the Harrels' fashionable country villa is reminiscent of phrases in Shakespeare's *Twelfth Night*, I. i. 5–7.

23 *rouged well*: ladies were exhorted by all the conduct books not to apply make-up to their faces, but many did so, and not only older women like the 'painted Jezabel' Madame Duval in *Evelina*. In that novel the fop Mr Lovel makes a similarly sneering speech to the heroine's face: 'I have known so many different causes for a lady's colour . . .' (p. 79).

26 *sigh for . . . desire*: 'covet . . . sigh for' in C2.

Q in the corner: apparently a form of 'Puss in the Corner', a children's game in which four players stand in the corners of a room and change places when they think that the fifth player at the centre is not looking; the player at the centre must try to capture a corner. Cf. *Early Diary*, i. 66.

27 *toûpée*: 'a periwig in which the front hair was combed up, over a pad, into a top-knot . . . also a patch of false hair or a small wig to cover a bald place' (*OED*). Both men and women wore elaborate toupees in the 1770s: 'The toupee was built up over the pads over the forehead to a height often exceeding the length of the face' (Cunnington, *Handbook*, p. 372).

wire-drawing: straining or wresting a meaning, or protracting something to length and thinness, a figurative expression derived from the process of drawing out metal into a wire.

29 *caps*: women throughout the eighteenth century wore a headdress indoors, usually of a fine material pleated and arranged. Caps for the wealthy were expensive confections of lace.

32 *the birth-day*: the king's birthday, celebrated on 4 June.

33 *at the head*: 'being at the head' in C2.

high honour: 'honour' in C2.

34 *to cheapen*: to ask the price of, to bargain for.

witticisms upon recent divorces: divorce cases were highly scandalous, and always dealt with the wife's sexual infidelities. The entire legal process of obtaining a divorce (obtainable only by the husband) entailed the husband's first suing his wife's lover and getting a judgment against him. Such cases of criminal conversation (or *crim. con.*) were salaciously reported in the popular press. Witticisms upon recent divorces would thus be both lewd and antifeminist.

35 *vis-à-vis*: 'a light carriage for two persons sitting face-to-face' (*OED*). The phrase means 'face-to-face'.

39 *macaroni*: 'a fop: which name arose from a club, called the Maccaroni [*sic*] Club, instituted by some of the most dressy travelled gentlemen about town, who led the fashions; whence a man foppishly dressed, was supposed a member of that club, and by contraction styled a Maccaroni' (Grose, *Classical Dictionary*, p. 227).

42 *pompoon*: variant of 'pompon', a bunch of ribbons or threads used to ornament hair, cap, or dress. The same word is used

in Burney's *The Witlings*, Act I, the scene in the milliner's shop, in which Censor asks, 'will you inthrall me in a Net of Brussels Lace? . . . Will you fire at me a Broad Side of Pompoons?'

45 *Custom-house-officers*: customs officials could make life difficult for travellers, and bringing goods purchased on the Continent through ports of entry such as Dover could be time-consuming and costly. Horace Walpole in France, in a letter to Lady Hervey, 21 Nov. 1765, complained that it would hardly be worth while to buy anything: 'I hear of nothing but difficulties; and shall, I believe, be saved from ruin myself, from not being able to convey any purchases into England' (*Correspondence*, ed. W. S. Lewis, 48 vols. (New Haven, Conn., 1937–83), xxxi. 73). Duties might amount to more than the original cost of an article; goods could be impounded until duty was paid. Bribing customs officials was sometimes the preferred solution, and smuggling was also much patronized. Mr Meadows may have done a little smuggling to oblige Miss Moffatt and Miss Larolles.

47 *pretence*: 'apology' in C2.

49 *turning suddenly*: 'turning' in C2.

50 *fair . . . foul one*: perhaps an echo of *Macbeth*, I. i. 11–12; iii. 38.

   resty: sluggish.

   on horseback through the streets: gentlemen rode in coaches or walked through urban streets, or hired a chair in bad weather, but riding was customarily reserved for the Parks and the country, the press of street traffic hindering a rider and endangering a good horse.

51 *send to Astley . . . John*: Philip Astley (1742–1814), a famous equestrian performer, established nineteen equestrian theatres, including the main one, his Amphitheatre Riding House at the foot of Westminster Bridge. Apparently he hired out horses. 'John' refers to the footman who should fetch the horse.

   giving you: 'your having' in C2.

52 *precise*: strict in observing rules, over-punctilious.

54 *finding it*: 'finding' in C2.

56 *a good and faithful delegate*: echo of 'Well done, thou good and faithful servant', Matthew 25: 21.

59 *serious Opera*: an opera with a serious or tragic plot as distinct from *opera buffa*, or comic opera. All opera performances provided dances in the *entr'actes*, and often in the main action.

60 *An Opera Rehearsal*: in August 1789 on a visit at the family seat of the Earl of Mount Edgcumbe, Burney was amused to find a copy of *Cecilia* in which 'the chapter, An Opera Rehearsal, was so well read, the leaves always flew apart to display it' (*Diary and Letters*, v. 46). Lord Mount Edgcumbe was another enthusiast for Pacchierotti, as recorded in his *Musical Reminiscences* (1834).

61 *figuranti*: Italian plural for figure-dancer; *figurante* (p. 135) may be French feminine singular or Italian feminine plural of a noun anglicized as figurant, a recently imported word for a dancer in the corps who describes various figures (movements of the body and movements from place to place) but does not perform as a principal dancer.

63 *festino*: diminutive of Italian *festa*, an entertainment or feast.

formidably stout: not fat, but frightfully brave and aggressive.

waited . . . myself: Miss Larolles says she called upon Cecilia personally, as distinct from merely sending a footman with a card.

64 *Signore Pacchierotti*: Gasparo Pacchierotti (1744–1821), a celebrated castrato singer and an acquaintance of Charles Burney. Frances Burney often met him and greatly admired his singing (see *Early Diary*, I. lxxiv–lxxv, lxxxvii).

65 *Artaserse . . . interesting drama*: on 23 Jan. 1779 a new production opened at the Haymarket of a version of Pietro Antonio Metastasio's *dramma per musica*, *Artaserse*, with music by Ferdinando Gasparo Bertoni. One evening early in January Pacchierotti came to tea at the Burneys' house and sang 'a rondeau of "Artaserse" of Bertoni's', accompanied by Bertoni himself (*Diary and Letters*, i. 130). *Cecilia*'s action runs through 1779 and Burney is faithful to the current events of that year. The heroine could have read Metastasio's play in Italian, but an English version of the 'interesting drama' had been produced by Charles Burney's old master Thomas Arne, with Arne's music, at Covent Garden in 1762.

sono innocente: from an aria in *Artaserse*: Italian for 'I am innocent'.

66 *spectacle*: italics indicate French pronunciation.

ancient music, and Abel's concert . . . the ladies concert: the Earl of Sandwich and other noblemen founded the Concert of Ancient Music in 1776; music of the recent past was performed. Carl Friedrich Abel (1723–87), composer and performer on the viola da gamba, combined with J. C. Bach to give subscription concerts from 1762 until 1781; these concerts were held in the Great Room in Dean Street. The 'ladies concert' presumably refers to an event funded by patronesses, not one in which females acted as public performers.

mignons: plural of original French form of 'minion', meaning darling, favourite, or servile dependent.

67 *make it quite*: 'make it' in C2.

shew the lyons: from the old days when seeing the menagerie at the Tower of London was obligatory for country visitors, the phrase came to mean seeing the sights of London, and then any sights, including celebrated persons.

69 *Albany*: name perhaps suggested by the name of a character in *King Lear*; the manuscript draft indicates that at one point in the novel's development the Delviles' last name was to be 'Albany'. It echoes the sound of 'Albina', the original name for the heroine, and with its associations of candour is thus suitably given to the uncompromising prophet. Burney said her father's favourite character was 'the old crazy moralist' (*Diary and Letters*, ii. 113); contemporaries suggested real analogues whom Burney had not known.

getting his ears cropt: the legal penalty for starting a riot, but Floyer is perhaps thinking of old laws against slander of the nobility.

70 *side scenes*: stage scenery chiefly consisted of a back flat and three pairs of side wings, painted scenes in frames that could be moved along grooves in the stage floor.

71 *Mentor*: in the *Odyssey*, the name of Pallas Athena when disguised as Telemachus' wise male friend; also an important character in de la Mothe-Fénelon's *Télémaque* (1699). The reference here looks forward to the masquerade scene.

a small temporary building: the performance of private theatricals had become increasingly popular, and wealthy families sometimes created their own playhouses for out-of-season amusement. The Harrels cannot afford such a luxury.

72 *half starved*: not pining away for want of food, though that would be true of Mrs Hill, but dying of cold; cf. Miss Larolles, 'one's quite starved', p. 132.

crown . . . double that sum: five shillings to ten shillings.

the new Temple: landscaped gardens were often ornamented with little neo-classical buildings, to make the scenes resemble those in paintings by, for example, Claude Lorraine. The effects can still be viewed at the grounds of great estates such as Stowe and Stourhead. It is ridiculous for the Harrels to plan this kind of thing in the grounds of their little suburban villa.

74 *children are*: 'children' in C2.

77 *the impending destruction of unfeeling prosperity*: quoting Albany's speech above, p. 68.

81 *vapoured*: afflicted by the vapours, from the old humours theory that held that various exhalations of bodily organs were injurious to the health; colloquially, in a fit of depression, in low spirits, sullen or over-sensitive.

82 *its design*: 'his design' in C2.

87 *the unkindness you have suffered*: this scene between Cecilia and Mrs Hill was illustrated by Edward Francesco Burney and the illustration served as the frontispiece to *The Norfolk Ladies Memorandum Book* in 1787.

oh!''—again bursting into tears, ''that: 'oh that' in C2.

90 *assistance . . . hospital*: five great new hospitals were founded in London during the eighteenth century, as well as some specialist hospitals such as the Lying-In Hospital. These were supposed to aid the poor, with the wealthy acting as subscribers. In practice a small fee (sufficiently daunting to a poor patient) was often charged, and some person of means would have to employ money and interest to get a poor person a bed, food, and laundry service, as well as medical treatment.

therefore was: 'was therefore' in C2.

93 *you've*: 'you have' in C2.

dish-clout: dish-cloth, rag for doing the washing-up.

Anan: a meaningless word to designate a stupid sound, like 'Uh?'.

94 *Mogul*: the great Mogul (from 'Mongol') was the European name for the Emperor of Delhi; the term refers to the idea of an excessively wealthy and important person.

snuff-colour suit: jacket and pantaloons of dark tan or brown colour, unfashionable but unlikely to show the dirt.

bob wig: 'a wig having the bottom locks turned up into bobs or short curls' (*OED*). This was 'always an undress wig'

(Cunnington, *Handbook*, p. 91), and by now old-fashioned. Briggs saves money by not sending his wig to a hairdresser. Appearing before Cecilia bald is an almost shocking breach of decorum, as is his combing his wig in front of her.

warmer . . . cast an account: richer . . . reckon an account.

95 *German Duke, or a Spanish Don Ferdinand*: the German nobility were thought ridiculously stiff, while the pride and formality of the Spanish gentleman had long been proverbial.

Don Vampus: a mock name, composed of the Spanish title for one of the knightly class ('Don') and a nonce word derived from 'To vamp' which Grose defines as 'To pawn any thing . . . Also to refit, new dress, or rub up old hats, shoes or other wearing apparel' (*Classical Dictionary*, p. 359). Mr Delvile is as fine as new-furbished goods from a pawn shop, a thing made up out of shreds and patches. Briggs's unexpected soubriquet expresses his view of Delvile as a proud formal old scarecrow.

watch . . . six-pence: watches, expensive and ornamental, were suspended on ribbons or gold chains. Women's watches were suspended from the waist; men's were carried in the fob pocket. Dainty little watches were in fashion at the time, but chiefly for ladies: 'Two watches or a watch and a miniature were the mode' (Cunnington, *Handbook*, p. 404).

sparks: foppish beaux, lightweight suitors.

shoe-buckles . . . Bristol stones: shoe-buckles could be elaborately decorated and inset with precious gems, including diamonds, or they could be ornamented with fake gems such as the rock crystal found in the Clifton limestone near Bristol.

brass gilt over: or ormolu; gilded brass and bronze were used in decorative articles throughout the period. Cf. George Etherege, *The Man of Mode* (1676), II. ii: 'Love gilds us over . . . but soon . . . the native brass appears'.

96 *rent-roll . . . stuck pigs*: when needy gentlemen who hope to woo an heiress are asked for their own proof of property and income (that is, for the list or roll of those renting land from them) these indigent suitors will be dumbfounded. 'To stare like a stuck pig' is a country proverb, from observation of the expression of a pig being killed or 'stuck'.

hard times . . . women chargeable: such sentiments had long been associated with men of the merchant class: they are uttered by middle-class characters in Sir Richard Steele's *The Tender Husband* (1705), in Daniel Defoe's *Moll Flanders* (1722), and in Samuel Richardson's *Sir Charles Grandison* (1753–4). Women might be thought 'chargeable'—heavily charged with expenses—as they not only needed money for housekeeping, clothes, and amusement but also required a prospective husband to tie up some money in settlements and a jointure. Despite the American war, which in Briggs's view makes for a scarcity of buyers in the absence of men, it should not be so difficult to 'get her off', as Cecilia has a large fortune to offer.

100 *coloured ices*: ice-cream or sorbet dyed with vegetable colouring.

Tuesday se'nnight: a week from Tuesday.

a little Orchestra: a little gallery for the band; it will be put up, see reference to 'new gallery', p. 121.

106 *the local cant . . . I know you*: masqueraders were supposed to disguise themselves from acquaintances and find out the identity of others. See Burney's own account of her youthful experience of a private masquerade at the house of a French dancing master in January 1770, where, in 'a close pink Persian *vest* . . . covered with gauze', with 'a wreath of flowers on the side of my head' and a mask, she was given marked attentions by a droll 'Dutchman'. She notes among effective maskers a Witch (who proved to be 'a young officer'), a Shepherd, a Merlin 'who spoke with all the mock heroick . . . which his character could require', and a Harlequin. See *Early Diary*, i. 70–7.

Dominos: a domino is a loose cloak, perhaps modelled on the garment worn by a priest, hence from *dominus*; the cloak was worn with a half mask. 'Dominos' refers to the persons in such garb.

107 *Circassians . . . sultanas*: women could display their charms by appearing as fair ladies of Circassia, presumably as Caucasian slaves for the Sultan's harem, or they could come as the wives of Sultans, in oriental voluptuousness. See Terry Castle, *Masquerade and Civilization*, for fantasies permitted in masquerading.

Hotspur: the hot-tempered young Henry Percy, son of the Earl of Northumberland, as presented in Shakespeare's *1 Henry IV*.

a-kembo: or 'akimbo', hands resting on hips, elbows out.

108 *hair . . . powder*: the well-to-do had their hair dressed with white, grey, yellow, or blue powder, applied with a dredger or a powder-puff; hair powder was made of grain flour: 'The powder had by law to contain starch though this was often

omitted' (Cunnington, *Handbook*, p. 95). The powder, scented with orris-root or something similar, was not cheap at two shillings a pound, and a heavy tax on hair powder in 1795 led to a rapid decline of this fashion.

Don Quixote . . . the admirable Cervantes: Miguel de Cervantes' *Don Quixote*, published in two parts (1605; 1615), had long been admired throughout Europe, and was popular with all classes in England, as Johnson and Mrs Thrale found when they tested the Thrales' servants for knowledge of the novel. The translation into English by Peter Motteux (1700–3) was the version best known. Belfield has carefully studied the novel and has the details of appearance right, including the barber's basin which the Don insisted was the helmet of Mambrino (*Don Quixote*, Part I, ch. xxi). Burney may have identified Belfield with certain aspects of Samuel Johnson, who felt a strong affinity with Don Quixote: 'when we laugh, our hearts inform us that he is not more ridiculous than ourselves, except that he tells what we have only thought' (*Rambler* 2 [24 Mar. 1750]).

109 *and, obsequiously bending to your divine attractions, conjure*: 'and conjure' in C2.

characteristic address: the masquerader speaks in the character of Don Quixote, in the language based on Motteux's version; he is drawing on incidents in which the Don addresses the pretended Princess Micomicona or apostrophizes the imaginary Dulcinea.

black bile: according to the humours theory, an excess of black bile made a person melancholy, acrimonious, and sullen.

my gauntlet: throwing down the gauntlet was the traditional (but by this time archaic) method of issuing a challenge.

110 *victoria*: victory!

Tripping on light fantastic toe: alluding to Milton's 'L'Allegro' (1645), ll. 33–4: 'Come, and trip it as you go / On the light fantastic toe'.

111 *Don Devil*: italics indicate quotation of Belfield's speech above, p. 109.

Goddess of Wisdom and Courage: Pallas Athena, or in the Roman pantheon Minerva, who is badly impersonated by the foolish Miss Larolles.

I'll cross him though he blast me: adaptation of Horatio's speech in *Hamlet*, I. i. 127: 'I'll cross it, though it blast me.'

Harlequin: Harlequin is the perpetual outrageous clown in love with Columbine in the *commedia del arte*. His accoutrements include particoloured spangled garments and a light wooden sword. He was often represented on the English stage in the eighteenth century.

113 *Shylock . . . cut as near the heart as possible*: reminiscence of Shakespeare, *The Merchant of Venice*, IV. i. 230–54.

noisy Mentor: Mentor in the *Odyssey* and *Télémaque* is an advocate of wise deeds, and inimical to loud or foolish words.

Pythagoras . . . disciples: Pythagoras, Greek philosopher of Samos (d. 497 BC), advocated the study and practice of asceticism to liberate the soul from the corruption of the body; his disciples naturally tried to follow his dictates.

proverbially entitled: i.e. 'to give the devil his due', meaning to be just in all cases, or to speak well of a person disliked.

the art of tormenting: phrase probably derived from Jane Collier's *Essay on the Art of Ingeniously Tormenting* (1753).

114 *green stuff*: woollen fabric dyed green.

a rod: a birch rod of long stripped twigs fastened together, used for whipping schoolboys.

breaking out of bounds: a schoolboy's offence, going beyond the school limits or into areas forbidden; figuratively, to transgress set limits.

confusion to all order: apparently quotation of a phrase about riot and rebellion.

country pedagogue: 'pedagogue' in C2.

dead languages: Latin and Greek, taught in boys' schools.

false concord: grammar requires a concord between words in case, number, gender, and person. An inflected language such as Greek or Latin poses many opportunities for an English-speaking person to make errors in relating subject and verb, or verb and object. For such errors in Latin and Greek, schoolboys were routinely given corporal punishment.

water-gruel . . . as a mad-man: insane persons were often kept on a lowering diet, consisting largely of light liquid foods such as gruel, an unexciting watery porridge made of oatmeal (or other grain or flour) and milk or water.

rat-tan . . . called up: an erring student might be called up to the master's desk at the front of the room to receive punishment, such as a whipping on the palm of the hand with a switch made from rattan (from Malay 'ratan'), a light and limber portion of the rattan palm. A student might also be 'called up' merely to recite to the master.

forced phthisical cough: an assumed consumptive or asthmatic wheezy cough.

116 *three-headed Cerberus*: Cerberus, the dog guarding the entrance to Hades, is usually presented as a monster with three heads and the tail of a serpent. In *Aeneid*, vi. 417–25, Cerberus threatens Aeneas but is pacified with a drugged sweet sop by the Sibyl.

black-guard: a term used for dirty working-class urchins such as link boys and, in the eighteenth century, shoe-blacks; figuratively, a person of the criminal class, or an unprincipled rogue.

Budge not . . . budge: Launcelot in *The Merchant of Venice*, II. ii. 17–18: ' "Budge," says the fiend. "Budge not," says my conscience'.

117 *jut*: a jutting out, a protrusion; *OED* gives date of first use in this sense as 1786.

naughty girls: it may have been a common nursery threat to bad children that they would be sent away in the sweep's bag. The amount of nursery and schoolroom language swirling about *Cecilia* is very striking.

poke in: thrust forward head first, with connotations of poking one's nose in and of being confined in a 'poke' or bag.

118 *French beads*: imported glass beads and spangles.

wax candles: wax candles were costly but burned clearly and did not smell bad, as did the cheaper tallow candles.

nick: 'To win at dice, to hit the mark just in the nick of time' (Grose, *Classical Dictionary*, p. 243); here to catch out, see through, and score off the 'spark' or 'trim or smart fellow' (ibid., p. 321).

119 *chouse*: to swindle, to dupe; *OED* cites this as the earliest example.

120 *rentall*: a number of tenancies paying rent; cf. 'rent-roll', p. 96.

old fox,—understand trap: proverbial: 'An old Fox cannot be taken in a snare' (Tilley).

horrid: 'horrible' in C2.

Hope . . . silver anchor: Hope's traditional emblem in

iconography, from the New Testament: 'Which hope we have as an anchor of the soul', Hebrews, 6: 19. The masquerader probably wears a costume like that of Spenser's Speranza, 'clad in blue' with 'a silver anchor' on her arm (*The Faerie Queene*, I. x, stanza 14).

121 *Niobe*: daughter of Tantalus, wife of Amphion; her pride in her children provoked the goddess Latona, whose children Apollo and Diana destroyed all of Niobe's children save one daughter. Niobe in the horror of misfortune turned into a weeping stone; see Ovid, *Metamorphoses*, vi. 148–312.

Apollo: son of Zeus, twin of Artemis or Diana; traditionally presides over the arts and is iconographically represented wearing a laurel crown and bearing a harp.

hautboy: oboe.

Midas: according to legend, Apollo gave King Midas of Phrygia asses' ears, to punish him for preferring the music of Pan to that of Apollo. Midas concealed the ears, but his barber told the secret to the reeds, who told it to the world: see Ovid, *Metamorphoses*, xi. The joke here refers to this 'Apollo' having a bad ear for music.

122 *Goliah*: variant spelling of Goliath, the giant vanquished by the boy David as told in 1 Samuel.

Pallas: Pallas Athena, deity of Athens, whom the Romans identified with Minerva. Customarily portrayed with a helmet, she is the patroness of war, craft, and wisdom.

Edgar . . . Poor Tom's a cold: in Shakespeare's *King Lear* (and in Nahum Tate's version of it which was performed on the eighteenth-century stage) Edgar, the disinherited son of the Duke of Gloucester, pretends to be a mad vagrant beggar (III. iv. 120–89; the line quoted is l. 152). This reference ties in with the general theme of madness in the novel, and parodically reflects various instances of deprivation. A number of characters in the novel have occasion to complain of feeling cold.

consular: pertaining to a consul, one of the two chief magistrates of republican Rome; their sign of office was the *toga praetexta*, a crimson- or purple-bordered or fringed toga, and in public assemblies they carried an ivory wand with an eagle on its top.

Monsieur . . . Ciceron . . . la bonne compagnie: 'Sir, I have the honour to represent Cicero, the great Cicero, father of his

country! but although I have that honour, I am no pedant!—
for heaven's sake, Sir, I speak only French in polite society!'

a plum: since the 1690s, a slang term for £100,000.

123 *less and less*: 'less' in C2.

124 *abhorrence of*: 'aversion to' in C2.

papier machée: should be 'papier mâché', literally 'chewed
paper', a new ornamental substance made of processed paper-
pulp moulded, lacquered, and coloured, used for making
fancy boxes, trays, etc.

126 *hackney chair*: hired sedan chair.

127 *warehouse*: masquerade costumiers called their shops
'warehouses' and some such place as Jackson's Habit-
Warehouse in Tavistock Street, Covent Garden, is meant; see
Castle, *Masquerade and Civilization*, p. 58.

129 *open as day to melting charity*: Shakespeare, *2 Henry IV*, IV. iv.
31–2: 'He hath a tear for pity, and a hand / Open as day for
melting charity'.

interest with Heaven and the poor: cf. the saying 'who gives to the
poor lends to the Lord'. Eighteenth-century charity sermons
emphasize the value of lending to God through charitable
giving as a good investment, since God repays with high
interest and the prayers of the poor for a benefactor are valued
in Heaven.

130 *œconomy*: the older and more proper spelling of 'economy' from
Latin *œconomia*.

131 *golden mean . . . philosopher's stone*: the golden mean is the perfect
medium between extremes, an idea ultimately derived from
Aristotle; the medieval alchemists (philosophers) sought the
stone that would turn base metals into gold.

132 *fixed himself*: stationed himself.

lollops so, that one's quite starved: throws his body about so (thus
obstructing the fire) that one is likely to die of cold.

133 *lolling . . . wainscoat . . . gaping*: lounging up against the wall
and yawning.

get there . . . mortifying: 'have the honour of sliding in; I did *mon
possible*, but it was quite beyond me' in C2. Here sixty-seven
words are cut to sixteen, the longest deletion in the novel's
revision.

a trial to get into the pit: an attempt to find a seat in the main floor
of the theatre, rather than in the gallery or a box.

135 *totally careless*: 'careless' in C2.

    jointured: in possession of a property or income settled on the bride at marriage for her sole use in case of the death of the husband; the ungentle 'gentlemen' could be calculating both the duration of the widows' chastity and their life expectancy, since a widow's death and the reversion of her property could improve the lot of her husband's male heirs.

    fop's alley: the aisle along which gentlemen could walk, talking to each other, surveying the house and admiring the ladies; ladies were supposed to sit decorously and not to patrol the house.

137 *impertinent fellow*: 'fellow' is a term of abuse, signifying low class; 'impertinent' had come to describe the inappropriate speech or behaviour of an inferior to a superior. Floyer insults Belfield by plainly indicating he is no gentleman; by having the Baronet accept his challenge, Belfield in effect does achieve an acknowledgement of his status, though at the cost of his health.

141 *French beads and Bristol stones*: the stranger who came to the masquerade in the white domino quotes Briggs's words at the masquerade, pp. 118–19.

    plum friend: his friend possessing £100,000.

    in ten thousand pounds . . . centred: not identified.

143 *his particular occasions*: alluding to Harrel's words to Arnott, p. 89.

147 *sympathy offensive and defensive*: the speaker does not wish Cecilia and Sir Robert Floyer to feel that an offence to the one is an offence to the other; in his revision of the political phrase 'treaty offensive and defensive' young Delvile jokingly hopes that Cecilia is not engaged to marry Floyer.

    a faithful Esquire: young Delvile remembers that Belfield came to the masquerade as Don Quixote (see pp. 108–28); the comparison of himself to the Don's Esquire would make him a Sancho Panza.

148 *no surgeon*: it was customary in the conduct of duels between gentlemen of high fashion to have a surgeon in attendance who would be sworn to secrecy (as duelling was illegal); Belfield could not afford this attendance and Floyer did not bother with it.

149 *Cecilia's uneasiness*: 'the uneasiness of Cecilia' in C2.

    to church . . . Sunday morning: the emphasis presumably points to the fact that the duel was fought on Sunday morning, as well as to Miss Larolles's paying calls and gossiping on a holy day.

153 *do the honours*: to treat with honour as a guest of the house; the phrase is now a vulgarism but was not one in the eighteenth century.

154 *not with severity . . . candour*: not judging the matter with great strictness but looking at it (and Sir Robert) in an honest manner, impartial and unbiased. The quality of *candour* was highly valued in the eighteenth century; it was the ability to be fair-minded and disinterested, the quality opposed to pride and prejudice.

156 *my regard for her merits they should be answered*: unchanged in all subsequent editions, this ungrammatical construction seems to indicate that some words have been left out. The best correction would seem to be to introduce the words 'is such that' between 'merits' and 'they' ('they' here refers to 'enquiries'). Mrs Delvile will not ask Cecilia any questions that could be considered rude or prying until Cecilia is truly convinced of Mrs Delvile's esteem for her, and then might be willing to answer questions.

157 *am*: 'I am' in C2.

158 *shewy adventurer*: flashy, penniless fortune-hunter.

161 *tender . . . hand . . . fortune*: an offer of his hand in marriage and all his worldly goods; though the Marriage Service had the man endow his bride with all his worldly goods, the law regarding matrimony made the wife's fortune entirely her husband's. Sir Robert wants Cecilia's fortune; the offer of his own is an ironic formality.

raillery: teasing of a flattering kind.

settlement . . . by herself: pre-nuptial contracts involved money settled upon the wife, for an annual allowance and also for an annuity should her husband predecease her. Such contracts were negotiated by lawyers and guardians; it would be unusual and indelicate for Cecilia to dictate the settlement made upon her.

163 *forgetting Bury, its inhabitants and its environs*: a quotation from the second chapter of the novel, p. 13.

now passes . . . then have: 'passes . . . have' in C2.

165 *open*: 'openly' in C2.

herself . . . Sir Robert: 'herself' in C2; twenty-one words are deleted here.

170 *the skin*: 'his skin' in C2.

surgeon . . . physician: the differences were marked and the professions jealously guarded. Only surgeons were licensed to operate, but a physician was of superior status to a surgeon, who worked vulgarly with his hands. A surgeon could extract the bullet and bind the wound, but Belfield also needs a medical practitioner to treat and prescribe for the fever. Either practitioner could be expensive.

171 *eleven o'clock*: as dinner would have taken place in mid-afternoon, Cecilia has indeed made a long call.

VOLUME II

173 *attorney*: 'a properly qualified legal agent practising in the courts of Common Law (as a solicitor practised in Chancery)' (*OED*). The title was abolished in 1873. Lawyers were considered not only greedy ('griping') but low; Harrel uses the term 'gentleman' sarcastically. Dr Johnson once said 'he did not care to speak ill-of any man behind his back, but he believed the gentleman was an *attorney*' (*Life of Johnson*, ii. 126).

174 *round*: large, considerable.

tape and buckram: tape is a strip of cloth used for binding garments; buckram is a cloth (usually linen) stiffened with starch or glue and used in lining or padding. Harrel refers to the cheapest materials in a garment, but both words also have legal connotations, 'tape' referring to red tape tying up legal documents and 'buckram' to a lawyer's bag.

stock: a log or block of wood, hence an insensible or stupid person.

176 *Tyburn . . . mob*: on execution day, which occurred every six weeks or so, a procession of condemned prisoners went in carts from Newgate prison to the gallows at Tyburn (the present site of Marble Arch). 'Mob' was originally a slang term, diminutive of *mobile vulgus*, the easily swayed crowd of plebeians. The word 'execution' is reserved in the novel for legal distraint on goods. Executions ceased to be held at Tyburn in 1783, but hangings continued. Burney would have known Dr Johnson's great essay against execution for offences other than murder (*Rambler* 114, 20 Apr. 1751), which alludes to 'legal massacre'.

French beads and Bristol stones: again quoting Briggs's words about Floyer, pp. 118–19.

177 *Blacking*: Briggs's household manufactures ink from his left-over boot polish.

drap: variant of 'drop'.

black lead pencil: 'pencil' in C2.

178 *polt*: blow, hard knock.

peck of troubles: a vulgar phrase since the sixteenth century for a great deal of trouble.

sich: 'such' in the fifth and subsequent editions.

kennel: a shallow channel in the middle or at the side of a roadway for the conveyance of rainwater, used for refuse of all kinds throughout the eighteenth century.

near: miserly.

nice: fastidious.

sharp: hungry.

179 *patch of brown paper*: vinegar and brown paper, used as a primitive plaster or poultice, as in the nursery rhyme 'Jack and Jill'.

trumpery: trashy, rubbishy.

broke my head: not a fracture but a wound to the skin and flesh of the head.

scrubs: low insignificant persons.

Scrawled: spread the limbs in a sprawling manner.

soused: drenched.

Turner's cerate: a stiff ointment made of 7½ oz each of calamine and wax, added to a pint of olive oil, composed by Daniel Turner (1667–1741) whose cerate is still listed in the *London Pharmacopaeia* in the nineteenth century.

half ruined in vinegar: half-ruined financially by paying for the vinegar in the brown-paper plaster.

180 *jallop*: generally, any purgative medicine, or even any medicine in liquid form.

black lead pencil: 'pencil' in C2.

181 *minor . . . farthing*: a minor could not be legally constrained to pay any debt, even a farthing (the quarter of a penny).

pot-hook: the first hooked strokes or parts of letters made by a child learning to write were called 'pot-hooks'; to Briggs, all books are useless letters, as worthless as a child's first attempts at the alphabet.

186 *no equipage, no establishment*: no coach and horses, no household.

The Spectator, Tatler and Guardian: periodicals conducted by Joseph Addison (1672–1719) and Richard Steele (1672–1729): *The Tatler*, founded by Steele (1709–11); *The Spectator*, produced by Addison and Steele (1711–12); *The Guardian*, founded by Steele (1713). There were numerous reprints of each, and the essays were often recommended to the attention of what Addison calls 'the fair sex', to whom many of the original articles were instructively addressed.

more books . . . you to look into: if Cecilia marries as Compton Delvile would approve, her husband's family seat would include a handsome library; the books in such a library are, however, not for the use of women.

188 *master of it*: Book II and Volume I end here in C2.

189 *the alley*: Change alley (for Exchange alley), the site of deals in stock and gambling speculation.

a Jew . . . taking up money upon interest: the Jews, who had been allowed to live in England for only a little over a hundred years since their expulsion in the Middle Ages, could not serve in universities or government institutions, and laboured under restrictions as to land-holding; a certain fixed number were licensed stockbrokers. Their chief outlet was business and, as elsewhere in Europe, many became money-lenders; they performed a valuable function in the new capitalism. Since the reign of Queen Anne the limit on interest had been officially 5 per cent—often too low for the value of money. Money-lenders who charged higher than legal interest could afford to serve those who would not attract lenders at legal rates. It is a pity that Burney did not go beyond the general stereotype of the Jewish money-lender, drawn chiefly from literature, especially Richard Brinsley Sheridan's *The School for Scandal* (1777) with its Jewish money-lender Mr Moses.

191 *dare say*: 'dare say; I shall pay him off in a very few days' in C2.

194 *blunt her purpose*: italics point out an echo of *Hamlet*, III. iv. 110–11.

195 *only censorious*: only fault-finding for love of finding fault.

200 *ague*: 'an intermitting fever, with cold fits succeeded by hot. The cold fit is, in popular language, more particularly called the *ague*, and the hot the fever' (Johnson, *Dictionary*).

201 *plain work*: plain sewing, as contrasted with embroidery, etc.

202 *dunning him*: hounding him for payment of a bill, as creditors do.

204 *These deeds are mine*: italics emphasize quotation of an internal statement.

208 *up two pair of stairs*: up two flights of stairs, two stories up.

211 *any help*: 'help' in the fifth and subsequent editions.

214 *a linen-draper*: a dealer in cloth or goods by the yard; perhaps Burney thought of this trade because Alexander Pope's father had been a linen-draper.

Eaton: Eton College near Windsor, one of the oldest and by then one of the most aristocratic schools for boys. In the eighteenth century the contemporaries Horace Walpole and Thomas Gray were celebrated old Etonians, demonstrating the value of an Eton education both to aristocrat and to talented poor boy; Gray's father was a scrivener and his mother kept a milliner's shop, yet at Eton he was a friend of Walpole who later took him with him on his Grand Tour. Thus it is not absurd to expect an Eton education to lead to patronage and opportunity.

one of the Universities: there were only two in England, Oxford and Cambridge.

215 *Temple-Bar*: the gateway that marked the entrance to the City.

216 *portions of his daughters*: the money they are each to be given as a dowry or marriage-portion. Each of the Belfield girls is to have £2,000, not a bad inheritance for the time.

217 *The produce*: the profits.

preventing him: 'preventing his' in C2.

218 *Gazette*: the official organ publishing governmental, institutional, and legal news; among other things, it included lists of bankrupts.

annuity: an annual income, presumably produced by the widow's invested jointure.

canvass: a word now largely restricted to the seeking of votes, but in the eighteenth century broadly used for the searching out of individuals for favours, including subscriptions or patronage (as well as votes).

a place at court: Mrs Belfield's expectations are wild, and her notions of life in higher spheres hazy. Young Belfield might have been given some small sinecure post had one of his

upper-class friends brought influence to bear, but such a post
would be a government office, as in the customs or the postal
service; places at court were customarily kept by the
aristocracy for their own kind. It is an added irony that Burney
herself, against all likelihood as against her own wishes, was
to be given 'a place at court' in 1786.

222 *two years . . . unhappiness*: quoting Henrietta Belfield's words to
Cecilia, p. 213.

his sake: 'his use' in the seventh and subsequent editions.

223 *he was sunk*: '*he* was sunk' in C2.

order a bill: put up a notice of rent or sale.

227 *the penny-post*: a letter could be sent anywhere in the London
area for a penny.

the note: 'a note' in C2.

228 *dodging*: following stealthily.

230 *sermons*: young ladies were often enjoined to read improving
sermons, and there were a number of sermon-like conduct
books and sermons written especially for youthful females,
which might well make them look 'demure', works such as Dr
James Fordyce's *Sermons to Young Women* (1766).

240 *felicity unmixed*: 'unmixed felicity' in C2.

250 *a tutor*: wealthy families who sent their sons abroad on the
Grand Tour (usually to France and Italy) customarily sent
with the youth an educated man, capable of continuing the
boy's education and acting as a combination of companion
and guardian.

255 *inartificial evasion*: 'artifical evasion' in the third and subsequent
editions.

259 *held down . . . alliance*: Cecilia remembers and quotes
Monckton's words to her, p. 257.

263 *with his family*: Book III ends here in C2.

265 *she believed . . . suicide*: cf. Evelina and the apparently suicidal
Macartney in *Evelina*, pp. 181–4.

266 *a razor*: the eighteenth-century razor is the kind later called 'cut-
throat', a long bare shaft of edged steel attached to a handle into
which it might be folded. In *The Life and Death of Mr. Badman* (1680)
John Bunyan paints a gruesome picture of a man committing
suicide by cutting his own throat with such a razor.

268 *To rush unlicenced on eternity*: misquotation of a speech by the

Chorus to the suicidal Athelwold in William Mason's poetic drama *Elfrida* (1751): 'Think what a sea of deep perdition whelms / The wretch's trembling soul, who launches forth / Unlicens'd to eternity.'

269 *been bail for his brother*: made payment for his brother-in-law.

270 *to give up her settlement*: having given up the money settled on her at marriage, Priscilla now has no personal means whatsoever, and nothing to live on should Mr Harrel predecease her.

compulsatory: compulsory, extorted under compulsion; by law promises made under duress are not binding.

273 *ten to one*: the odds are 10 to 1.

274 *as if no Orchestra*: the daughter of a musician and friend of many professional performers, Burney resents fashionable inattention to music, as she had already shown in her portrayal of the Branghtons at the Opera, and was to express at more passionate and more satiric length in *The Wanderer*.

275 *soberly, as Lady Grace says*: in *The Provok'd Husband* (a play begun by Sir John Vanbrugh and after his death completed by Colley Cibber in 1728), the sensible Lady Grace tries to persuade the extravagant Lady Townley that it might be possible to follow the town amusements in moderation: 'I would go to Court; sometimes to an Assembly, nay play at *Quadrille*—soberly: I would see all the good Plays; and . . . I might be drawn in once to a Masquerade! And this, I think, is as far as any Woman can go—soberly' (III. i).

276 *forms*: backless benches.

glass: opera glass or monocle.

277 *had spoke*: 'had spoken' in C2.

279 *gothic*: barbarous and old-fashioned.

chronologer of the modes: historian of the eras of fashion.

280 *INSENSIBLISTS . . . VOLUBLE . . . SUPERCILIOUS*: the use of these substantives appears to be Burney's own invention. Of the three, only 'Insensiblist', defined as a nonce word with this passage cited, is recorded as a substantive in *OED*.

happy Triplet: happy threesome (Mr Meadows, Miss Larolles, and Miss Leeson).

JARGONISTS: *OED* cites this as first use.

pains: 'pain' in the third and subsequent editions.

281 *Liliputian vocabulary*: an adjective more properly spelled 'Lilliputian', referring to the tiny inhabitants of Lilliput in the first book of Swift's *Gulliver's Travels* (1726); the 'jargonist' has a stock of words as small for a human vocabulary as the Lilliputians are small for human beings.

285 *a convent*: there were no convents in England.

much lessen your entertainment: corrected to 'not much lessen your entertainment' in the third and subsequent editions.

286 *I sat at the outside on purpose*: a stratagem remembered by Jane Austen's Anne Elliot in *Persuasion*, vol. II, ch. viii.

287 *tooth pick case glass*: toothpick cases could be very elaborate, in ivory, silver, or gold; they often included a mirror on the inside of the lid to assist a gentleman in picking his teeth; cf. Jane Austen, *Sense and Sensibility*, vol. II, ch. xi. The toothpicks encased were often of expensive materials, such as tortoiseshell; see Cunnington, *Handbook*, p. 264.

289 *Like a brave general . . . retreat*: from 'An Epilogue, Spoken by Mrs. Midnight's Daughter', riding upon an Ass dressed in a great Tie-Wig', a popular feature of the stage show 'The Old Woman's Oratory' in the 1750s. See Betty Rizzo, 'Enter the Epilogue on an Ass—By Christopher Smart', *PBSA* 73 (1979), 340–4, and Katrina Williamson (ed.), *The Poetical Works of Christopher Smart*, IV (Oxford, 1987), 264 (and note). This 'Epilogue' (1753) was not published in official editions of Smart's works; Burney's note substantiates recent attribution of the piece to the poet. The 'Epilogue' is boisterous and satiric; the ass represents Dr John Hill, 'whose kicking, caning and de-wigging at Ranelagh the preceding spring none of the wits had forgotten' (Rizzo, p. 342). The part of Mrs Midnight's Daughter was probably a transvestite role, as that of Mrs Midnight certainly was.

Charles Burney was a close friend of Smart (1722–71) during the 'Oratory' period, and continued to befriend the poet during and after his periods of incarceration in a madhouse. Frances Burney records her impressions of Smart in September 1768: 'He is extremely grave, and has still great wildness in his manner, looks, and voice; but 'tis impossible to *see* him and to think of his works, without feeling the utmost pity and concern for him' (*Early Diary*, i. 28). In August 1771 she notes Smart's death in the King's Bench Prison: 'I never knew him in his glory, but ever respected him in his decline, from the fine proofs he had left of a better day' (ibid., 133).

Smart had once presented her with a rose (ibid., 66). The memory of Smart seems to colour the representation of both Belfield and Albany in *Cecilia*, and here Mortimer is also associated with him.

290 *sycophants*: quoting Albany's diatribe, p. 68.

291 *private mad-house*: Christopher Smart, a possible model for Albany (see note to p. 289 above), had been confined in a private madhouse from 1756 to 1757, and again from 1759 to 1763. With certain exceptions such as Bedlam and the new St Luke's Hospital where the humane Dr William Beattie also treated Smart (1757–8), lunatic asylums were privately owned and managed. Inmates could be incarcerated almost at the whim of their relations; even well-meaning treatment for insanity was often violent and sometimes cruel. For a vivid fictional account (and one that Burney would have known) of such a madhouse, see Tobias Smollett's *The Life and Adventures of Sir Launcelot Greaves* (1760–1), ed. David Evans (Oxford, 1973), ch. xxii, pp. 184–91. In Smollett's novel as in Burney's the chief Quixotic male character and the heroine are both called mad.

the honour to cut: Aresby's mixture of polite language and low slang is ridiculous; 'to cut' is slang meaning 'to leave quickly'.

working for the poor: sewing garments for poor people.

292 *more in sorrow than in anger*: *Hamlet*, I. ii. 231.

296 *tradesmen would have been insolent*: 'tradesman would have been so insolent' in C2.

perdition: like other Christians before and since, Burney and Cecilia believe that suicide entails eternal damnation, the state of being eternally lost (perdition), since it is a sin that cannot be repented.

301 *she could do no worse . . . before-hand*: italics indicate quotation of Mrs Harrel's very words.

heartless: disheartened, discouraged.

run of luck: italics indicate quotation of Harrel's own speech, with its gambler's language.

303 *letter*: 'letters' in the fifth and subsequent editions.

304 *noble friend*: quoting Henrietta's earlier speech to Cecilia, p. 248.

involuntary: 'involuntarily' in the seventh and subsequent editions.

307 *son of a steward*: stewards who managed great estates could often make money in illicit or unscrupulous ways and thus rise in the world, like the infamous Peter Walter, or Henry Fielding's Peter Pounce in *Joseph Andrews* (1742).

intention: 'attention' in C2.

308 *oh stop him . . . will nobody stop him*: quoting Cecilia's own words, p. 138.

his own expressions: 'her own expressions' in the fifth and subsequent editions.

315 *keep myself up*: keep going, keep cheerful.

316 *journeyman*: a working man who had completed his apprenticeship but still worked as an employee for a day's wages, and was not a master.

317 *bit of place*: 'bit of a place' in the third and subsequent editions.

genteelness: italics indicate quotation of Mrs Belfield's own vulgar word.

VOLUME III

321 *A Rout*: a fashionable gathering, an evening party.

324 *the dog-days*: the hottest period of the year, commonly said to run from 3 July to 15 August. The name 'arose from the pernicious qualities of the season being attributed to the "influence" of the Dog-star; but it has long been popularly associated with the belief that at this season dogs are most apt to run mad' (*OED*).

325 *jemmy*: spruce, smart, dexterous; 'a low word' (Johnson, *Dictionary*).

326 *hallow*: a cry to attract attention.

327 *frizzling my pate*: crimping the side hair of the wig, to make it frizzy.

328 *a married man*: alluding to Morrice's words that earlier enraged Monckton, p. 83.

330 *her former . . . gaiety*: corrected to 'his' in later editions.

331 *steward of the race*: stewards were appointed to supervise and maintain order at horse-race meetings.

332 *punch . . . rum*: punch could also be made with other spirits, such as brandy or gin. Briggs, however, has been given not punch but lemonade.

a'n't worth a rush: a form of the proverbial 'not worth a straw (rush)'; worth nothing.

the west end of the town: Briggs, living in the City of London, expresses contempt for the fashionable world west of Temple Bar.

jackanapes: 'a pert impertinent fellow, who assumes ridiculous airs; a coxcomb' (*OED*).

333 *casting up*: adding, reckoning up.

tie-wig: a wig in which the hair is drawn back and tied with a ribbon at the nape of the neck. The curls are normally short, but 'in the 70's this might be worn long and flowing' (Cunnington, *Handbook*, p. 247).

334 *a ventilator*: a fan built into a window, replacing stale air with fresh. First introduced in the 1740s, such a fan would be a fashionable 'improvement' to Mr Harrel's room.

337 *seen her in her happier hour*: Pope, 'Epilogue to the Satires, Dialogue I' (1738), l. 29: 'Seen him I have, but in his happier hour.'

339 *rectitude . . . mend*: casuists, theologians who resolved difficult cases of conscience, were proverbial for their sophistry.

340 *all in the wrong box*: proverbial for 'mistaken'; *box* in the sense of place.

341 *down in the mouth*: dejected, dispirited (from having the mouth shaped in a pout).

342 *made but a poor hand of it*: been unsuccessful in making his fortune.

345 *her brother's noble friend*: again quoting Henrietta's description of Delvile as Belfield's 'noble friend'; see pp. 248 and 304.

347 *clients*: others to whom Morrice can offer his services.

348 *while she was sitting with Miss Belfield, her maid told her*: 'while Miss Belfield was sitting with her, she was told by her maid' in C2.

gloves: always worn outdoors by fashionable women, and often worn indoors on formal occasions.

349 *more seemed meant than met the ear*: alluding to Milton, 'Il Penseroso' (1645), l. 120: 'Where more is meant than meets the ear.'

350 *discovery*: in the now obsolete sense of 'disclosure'.

355 *Irish fortune hunter*: English contempt for the Irish in the

eighteenth century is reflected by the gossipmongers' labelling the London-born Belfield an Irishman. There is also a possible allusion to the recent scandal of Andrew Stoney's turbulent marriage to the Countess of Strathmore; see note to p. 477.

rattle: empty talk, gossip; a favourite word of Burney's.

357 *more honoured in the breach than the observance*: *Hamlet*, I. iv. 15–16: 'it is a custom, / More honour'd in the breach than the observance'. Burney quotes the same phrase in *Camilla*, p. 826.

362 *a citizen*: 'a man of trade; not a gentleman' (Johnson, *Dictionary*). Henrietta's father was a linen-draper (see p. 214).

363 *to envy thee*: Book IV and Volume II end here in C2.

368 *it is vain*: 'it is in vain' in C2.

370 *his dagger and his bowl*: alluding to Joseph Addison's *Rosamond: an Opera* (1707), in which Queen Elinor gives her rival, Rosamond, the choice of committing suicide by drinking poison or being stabbed with a dagger: 'Or quickly drain the fatal bowl, / Or this right hand performs its part, / And plants a dagger in thy heart' (II. vi). Rosamond drinks the bowl, but the potion, it transpires, is only a soporific.

372 *belongs to the club; secrets in all things*: there were a number of male clubs and secret societies in England at this time (see Roy Porter, *English Society in the Eighteenth Century* (London, 1982), pp. 172–3). Here, however, both club and secrets may be Briggs's invention.

a broker's: a dealer in second-hand furniture, or pawnbroker.

A close dog, but warm: a stingy rascal, but wealthy.

373 *stuffing and guttling*: gorging and eating voraciously.

bed without any curtains: a respectable eighteenth-century bed would be a four-poster with curtains; this one is either in a state of decay, or else a cheap bed without posts.

like to have you . . . Harrel's had his share: Harrel has received half of Cecilia's annual allowance of £500 as payment for room and board (p. 203). Briggs would make a considerable profit if he were paid a similar sum.

374 *never stand for a trifle*: never come to a stop over a small matter; proverbial for the unimportance of minor details.

smart as a carrot: from the proverbial 'smart as a carrot half scraped' (*EDD*).

380 *one year's income*: i.e. the £3,000 per annum from her uncle's estate.

384 *enamoured even to madness*: perhaps a misrecollection of Iago's words in Shakespeare's *Othello*, II. i. 305–6: 'practising upon his peace and quiet, / Even to madness'.

388 *a post chaise*: a hired carriage seating two to four persons, with the driver riding on one of the horses.

391 *such an office*: such disservice.

400 *Aldermen sucking custards*: aldermen, who together with the Mayor and Corporation had governed the City of London since 1200, were proverbial for their gormandizing at the annual Lord Mayor's Banquet, and for their special relish for custard pies.

I'll fit you for this: I'll punish you for this; quoted in *OED* as an example of the expression. The italics suggest a possible allusion to Hieronimo's well-known remark in Thomas Kyd's *The Spanish Tragedy* (1615), IV. i. 70: 'Why then I'll fit you.'

401 *A man of business . . . joint-stool*: *A Man of Business* is the chapter title. Hobson will as readily do business on a joint-stool, a solidly made stool fitted by a joiner, as on a counter.

mislest: molest.

404 *'cute*: acutely.

408 *a blank*: Simkins misinterprets the Captain's *blank*, giving it the sense of a lottery ticket that wins no prize.

411 *scrubby*: insignificant, shabby; *OED* cites this as the earliest example.

five times five: changed to 'three times five' in the seventh and subsequent editions.

412 *had passed*: 'passed' in C2.

416 *hartshorn*: ammonia, so named whether derived from the horn of a hart or elsewhere; a popular eighteenth-century restorative. 'It is used to bring people out of faintings by its pungency, holding it under the nose, and pouring down some drops of it in water' (Johnson, *Dictionary*).

425 *propriety of mind*: the italics suggest a general conduct-book phrase, or a more specific allusion.

431 *a dun*: an importunate creditor.

433 *what he wished*: quoting Harrel's words in his suicide note, p. 431.

437 *an exorbitant interest*: the rate of interest on the lending of money was legally fixed at 5 per cent; in addition the contract is illegal because Cecilia is still a minor. In *Camilla* the money-lender Clykes offers Camilla, also a minor, a rate of 10 per cent; see p. 760 and note.

the same interest . . . from the funds: i.e. about 3 per cent, the rate of interest that Monckton would receive on his money in a bank ('the funds').

440 *pocket*: until the end of the eighteenth century, when handbags came into fashion, women wore pear-shaped bags as pockets, 'tied round the waist under the dress and accessible through placket holes' (Cunnington, *Handbook*, p. 177).

443 *by quietly*: 'quietly' in C2.

444 *like to*: 'like' in C2.

anotherguess: another sort of.

clear of the world: free of debts.

445 *one's never in*: 'one's in never' in C2.

bills without a receipt to 'em: unpaid bills.

high: overbearing, haughty.

446 *comical*: odd or peculiar behaviour.

447 *lucre*: wealth, without the modern pejorative connotation.

452 *tip the perch . . . stanch . . . blacklegs*: die, like a dead bird falling off its perch (here, commit suicide); staunch, sound; swindlers, sharpers.

the constable: an unpaid citizen, chosen for yearly terms of office. The modern police force, founded by Sir Robert Peel, dates only from 1818.

453 *A good man always wears a bob wig*: Briggs's favourite bob-wig (see p. 94) is an informal, undress wig. Mr Harrel would wear a more elaborate style.

how does he cut up: how much does his fortune turn out to be; *OED* cites this as the earliest example of the phrase.

a twey-case: a case of small instruments, an étui; the only example in *OED*.

bam: a hoax or imposition.

lighted up like a pastry-cook on twelfth-day: pastry shops would do especially good business, and hence be well lit up, on twelfth day, 6 January, on which Epiphany was celebrated. Twelfth-night cakes, large and ornamental, were sold in great numbers.

sweetmeat: a sugared cake, pastry, fruit, etc.

piping, and hopping: loud talking (this use of 'piping' predates the earliest example given in *OED*, 1784); dancing.

a brack: a flaw.

454 *chuse to come in for my thirds*: Briggs still wants his part of Cecilia's allowance of £500 for room and board; see note to p. 373.

gulled: cheated.

petrific: petrifying, i.e. with the quality of turning into stone.

great cry and little wool: proverbial for 'much ado about nothing'.

mere puff and go one: mere emptiness and pretence.

455 *Don Puffendorff*: playing on Briggs's earlier 'Don Puff-about' (p. 95). Samuel Pufendorf (1632–94), a German jurist, was widely read in the eighteenth century; *Puffendorff* here echoes Sterne's *Tristram Shandy* (1760), I. ii: 'Tully, Puffendorff, or the best ethic writers'.

fine: 'smart' in C2.

456 *suited*: 'suitable to' in C2.

ringing a bell . . . a dust-man: a dustman would announce the approach of his refuse cart by ringing a bell and shouting. Briggs implies that Delvile would make more money as a dustman, scavenging refuse, than in contemplating the dust and ashes of the family vault.

457 *at Delvile Castle*: Book V ends here in C2.

no openings . . . beautiful objects: such vistas were highly prized; their absence in the grounds of Delvile Castle exemplifies Delvile's lack of taste.

458 *sometimes he appeared again at tea-time, but more commonly he rode*: 'he commonly continued with him till tea-time, and then rode' in C2.

460 *a Piano Forte of Merlin's*: the pianoforte, resembling the modern piano, dates from about 1709. John Joseph Merlin (1735–1803), a Flemish instrument-maker and inventor, was a friend of Charles Burney, who ordered pianos from him in 1775 and 1777 (see Percy Scholes, *The Great Doctor Burney* (Oxford, 1948), ii. 208–9). In a letter of 16 July 1778, Frances Burney's sister Susan wrote prophetically: 'Merlin sup'd here and was very diverting. (I think you must introduce him in your next work)' (*Early Diary*, ii. 242).

fine work: delicate needlework, embroidery, etc.

461 *the milk of human kindness*: Macbeth's words in *Macbeth*, I. v. 17.

meekly borne: again alluding to Macbeth's words; Duncan 'Hath borne his faculties so meek' (I. vii. 17).

463 *even seized the dead body*: Harrel's body was valuable as a potential means of obtaining ransom money; before a funeral relatives and mourners might be moved to pay off the deceased's debts.

466 *caro sposo*: Italian for 'dear husband'.

468 *presented . . . come out*: presented at court, and thus able to make a formal entry into society; *OED* cites this as the earliest example of this use of *come out*.

472 *the present*: 'this' in C2.

473 *Cecilia!—Madam!—Miss Beverley*: the highly informal *Cecilia* would be appropriate only if Delvile were her husband; the formal *Madam* would be appropriate if he were a stranger. *Miss Beverley*, his third attempt, is correct.

476 *white wine whey*: a medicinal drink consisting of one part of wine to two parts of skimmed milk, with sugar and lemon. A recipe is given in Elizabeth Raffald, *The Experienced English Housekeeper*, 7th edn. (1780), p. 313.

477 *so common for an heiress*: although rare today, the practice of a man's taking his wife's name in marriage so that she could inherit an estate was not uncommon in the eighteenth century. One heiress tied by a name clause similar to that restricting Cecilia was Mary Eleanor Bowes (1749–1800), who took as her first husband the 7th Earl of Strathmore, John Lyon (1767), and as her second husband Andrew Robinson Stoney (1777); both men took the name of Bowes. The Irish adventurer Stoney later provided Thackeray with his model for Barry Lyndon (see the World's Classics edition, ed. Andrew Saunders, pp. xvi–xix). In 1773 Samuel Johnson, in conversation with Boswell, objected vigorously to the name clause: 'An ancient estate should always go to males. It is mighty foolish to let a stranger have it because he marries your daughter, and takes your name' (*Life of Johnson*, ii. 261).

479 *Mr. Newbury's . . . twenty of them*: John Newbery (1713–67) was the most important publisher of books for children and juveniles in the eighteenth century. The twenty volumes referred to here are probably a collection entitled *The World*

Displayed (1759–67), of which a twenty-volume set was listed
in 1781; see Sydney Roscoe, *John Newbery and his Successors: A
Bibliography* (Wormley, Herts, 1973), pp. 274 and 388–9.

480 *a new pamphlet*: a small, unbound publication, usually political
in nature.

482 *a pleurisy*: an inflammation of the membrane enclosing the
lungs; often fatal in the eighteenth century.

484 *a cambric handkerchief about his throat*: Lady Honoria is making
fun of a young man's going out muffled up like an invalid.
Cambric, a fine French linen, would serve better as a
handkerchief to wipe away lovers' tears, as Dr Lyster
observes.

485 *She knew not . . . his heart*: quoting Delvile's words to Cecilia
after the storm, p. 476.

486 *call him to account*: summon him to answer for his conduct; here
with the implication of challenging him to a duel.

487 *Bristol*: Bristol Hotwells, where Delvile will travel to drink the
supposedly medicinal water, features prominently in *Evelina*
(pp. 268 ff.). The Bristol Hotwells season ran from May to
September, avoiding conflict with the season at Bath; the
Delviles will arrive there in early August.

488 *Fidel . . . the faithful animal*: the spaniel is aptly named *Fidel*,
Spanish for 'faithful'.

489 *embroidering a screen*: a favourite occupation for ladies. The
screen was a frame, covered with embroidered cloth, held by
a handle, and used to ward off the heat of a fire or draughts
of air.

494 *a gipsey*: gipsies, a nomadic race, had been present in England
since about 1500. They were subject to frequent persecution;
Delvile's sympathy is uncommon.

     staring: sensational.

495 *full drive*: at full speed.

496 *red and white . . . in a minute*: quoting Lady Honoria's
description of Cecilia, p. 491.

504 *quarrel with him*: in this passage Lady Honoria deftly alludes to
much of the action of *Romeo and Juliet*: the feud between the
Capulets and Montagues; the love of Paris, Romeo's rival, for
Juliet; and the roles of Romeo's friend, Mercutio, and Juliet's
confidante, the Nurse. Cf. reference to *Romeo and Juliet*, p. 68
above.

505 *the sheriff, or the mayor and corporation*: the City of London was

governed by two Sheriffs and the Lord Mayor, who headed the Corporation. The institutions date from the Middle Ages.

box: a small country-house. *Richmond*: now a suburb of London, then an elegant and very fashionable village. Richmond Bridge had recently been built (1777), making the village more accessible from London.

509 *tablets*: a notebook made of stiff sheets fastened together, used for memoranda.

infer: in the sense of 'imply'.

510 *he jests at scars who never felt a wound*: Romeo's words in *Romeo and Juliet*, II. ii. 1: 'He jests at scars that never felt a wound'.

511 *saw masks*: held a masquerade; *OED* cites this as the only example of the phrase.

515 *pap-boat*: 'a boat-shaped vessel for holding pap for feeding infants' (*OED*, which cites this as the earliest example).

516 *the first stage*: the principal routes in England were divided into series of stages, at each of which horses could be changed and travellers taken up or set down.

a slabbering-bib . . . A pin-a-fore: a child's bib (*OED* cites this as the latest example); a protective cover pinned upon the dress in front (*OED* cites this as the earliest example).

517 *the climates*: 'a region of the earth, a "clime"' (*OED*).

521 *rose water*: 'water distilled from roses, or impregnated with essence of roses' (*OED*).

522 *hopeless*: 'desperate' in C2.

524 *prepare*: 'prepare her' in C2.

bring with her Fidel: 'bring Fidel with her' in C2.

525 *side-board of plate*: silver table utensils, contained in a sideboard; *OED* cites this as the only example of 'sideboard' used in the sense of its contents.

a title . . . alliance with Miss Beverley: Lord Derford, in marrying Cecilia, would retain his title, which would be used in place of his new family name of Beverley. The as yet untitled Mortimer, however, would be addressed as Mr Beverley.

VOLUME IV

533 *but too proud*: 'proud' in C2.

535 *old proverb of the ill luck of listeners*: 'Listeners hear no (never hear) good of themselves'; already an 'old proverb' in 1647 (see the *Oxford Dictionary of English Proverbs*).

Ouran Outang, or man-monkey: the name orang-outang, with many variant spellings, derives from the Malay for 'man of the woods'. Oliver Goldsmith calls it the 'wild man of the woods' in his *History of the Earth* (1774), ii. 343, quoted in *OED*.

536 *had happened*: 'happened' in C2.

539 *united*: 'omitted' in C2; 'united' was presumably a misreading of the manuscript.

541 *Norfolk*: the county to the north of Suffolk, hence close to Mrs Charlton's house in Bury.

544 *cried in every market-town*: a form of advertising lost and found property common from the sixteenth to the nineteenth century.

smoke: to make fun of, jest at, ridicule.

fograms: 'an antiquated or old-fashioned person, a fogy' (*OED*). The word was a favourite pejorative of Burney's father and of her friend Samuel Crisp (see *Camilla*, p. 46 and note); the italics here emphasize the private joke.

545 *expresses . . . Scotland or Flanders*: express messages, sent because Lady Honoria's father would fear that she had eloped. Since 1753, Lord Hardwicke's Marriage Act had required the consent of parents or guardians for the marriage of persons under 21. Runaway couples would thus head by road to Scotland, usually to Gretna Green, or by sea to nearby Belgium (Flanders), where marriages could be readily obtained. In 1772 Burney's stepsister Maria Allen had been secretly married in Ypres, Belgium; see *Early Diary*, i. 181.

with him: 'with it' in C2.

546 *with more anger than sorrow*: alluding to Horatio's words in *Hamlet*, I. ii. 231; see note to p. 111 above.

a summer-house in the garden: a simple, airy building, providing a cool, shady place in the summer; often associated with romantic encounters in eighteenth-century novels.

547 *dear Fidel*: quoting Cecilia's words that Delvile has just overheard.

560 *for ever*: Book VI and Volume III end here in C2.

563 *yet is it*: 'yet it is' in C2.

567 *evening came*: 'evening yet came' in C2.

569 *deep a trench . . . raise this pile*: in this elaborate metaphor, Cecilia envisages Delvile's digging a trench as foundation for a large building (*pile*). The sentence is quoted under 'trench' in *OED*.

575 *principal difficulties . . . coming of age*: when Cecilia is 21 she will no longer require the consent of her guardians to marry Delvile.

576 *tremblingly alive*: Pope, *An Essay on Man* (1733–4), i. 197: 'Or touch, if tremblingly alive all o'er, / To smart and agonize at ev'ry pore?'

579 *dressing-room*: a lady's boudoir or sitting room, furnished with books, armchairs, etc; not the bedroom.

583 *you have*: 'that you have' in C2.

584 *and that*: 'that' in C2.

589 *A chaise . . . with post-horses for speed*: a chaise was a light carriage, seating one to three passengers, which could be drawn by one, two, four, or six horses. By ordering fresh horses at each staging post, Cecilia hopes for a speedy journey.

   they was going: 'they were going' in C2.

591 *puddle*: a dialect word, used here to suggest decrepitude. *OED* erroneously cites this as an example of *puddle* in the sense of 'muddler' or 'bungler'.

592 *judge by*: 'judge from' in C2.

593 *devoirs*: dutiful respects, courteous attentions.

594 *to make way for . . . get out herself*: although Morrice believes that there is room for three in the chaise, the third could be seated only with discomfort on a small, folding seat facing backwards.

   This only: 'The only' in C2.

597 *hesitation, she said*: 'hesitation' in C2.

   my lady Notable . . . steward: a 'notable' woman is an over-zealous housekeeper. In Colley Cibber's *The Lady's Last Stake: or, the Wife's Resentment* (1707), Miss Notable, a young heiress, threatens to 'choose a new Guardian' who will let her do as she pleases (II. i). Burney may have a more specific reference in mind.

   register-office keeper: the Universal Register Office was founded by Henry Fielding and his half-brother John in 1750. 'For a small fee, by registering their names with the Office, servants and apprentices would find masters, priests curacies, soldiers commissions, teachers schools, travellers conveyances, borrowers lenders; and those with houses to sell or lodgings to let, or with goods and curiosities to dispose of, could all be satisfied' (Martin C. Battestin, Introduction to Henry Fielding's *Amelia* (Oxford, 1983), p. xxxi). Several other such offices opened later in the century.

fee-simple: 'an estate in land, etc. belonging to the owner and his heirs for ever' (*OED*). Gosport thus suggests that Cecilia's heart is in absolute possession ('in fee-simple').

600 *touching his hat*: OED cites this as the first example of the casual form of raising the hat. It is furnished, appropriately, by the indolent Meadows.

the sale . . . single day: since Mr Harrel has furnished his house lavishly, the auction held there to dispose of his property would take place over several days. Such sales, as Miss Larolles notes, were widely attended by people of fashion.

602 *Portia . . . which is which*: in *The Merchant of Venice*, I. ii, Portia asks her waiting maid Nerissa to name her many suitors; 'and as thou namest them I will describe them; and according to my description, level at my affection'.

upon the scout: spying, watching out.

his hat flapped: with the flap pulled down over his eyes.

605 *cut him up*: censure or criticize him.

acquaintance. All the ton people do so: 'acquaintance, and always finding fault. All the *ton* do so' in C2.

613 *got*: 'she got' in C2.

the Public Office in Bow-Street: an office connected with Bow Street Magistrate's Court. Founded in 1740, the Court became famous under its second Magistrate, Henry Fielding, who organized the 'Bow-Street runners' as a small police force. In 1780 the building was attacked, but not badly damaged, in the Gordon Riots.

614 *in our bond*: again alluding to *The Merchant of Venice*, in which Shylock protests ''tis not in the bond' (IV. i. 261).

627 *the pew-opener*: churches contained closed pews, reserved for particular families, as well as open seating for the remainder of the congregation. Pew-openers were employed as ushers; *OED* cites this as the first example of the phrase.

628 *the glasses*: the windows.

633 *lie upon the road*: spend a night of her journey at an inn.

655 *Mr. Arnott's*: Book VII ends here in C2.

657 *the fears*: 'fears' in C2.

a day labourer: a labourer hired to work by the day; an unskilled worker.

658 *then they*: 'they' in C2.

and that he went: 'and went' in C2.

663 *shaking the dust from my feet*: alluding to Matthew, 10: 14: 'when ye depart out of that house or city, shake off the dust of your feet'.

strole: 'strolled' in C2.

most enlightened of men: Burney's friendship with and admiration for Dr Johnson, reciprocated by his commendation of *Evelina* and *Cecilia*, is manifested in her journals. The Johnsonian passages have been edited by Chauncey Tinker, *Dr. Johnson and Fanny Burney* (New York, 1911). See also Joyce Hemlow, 'Dr Johnson and Fanny Burney—Some Additions to the Record'.

panting after solitude: in his 'Life of Cowley' (1779) Johnson quotes a letter written by Cowley in his retirement, the wretchedness of which he recommends 'to the consideration of all that may hereafter pant for solitude' (*Lives of the English Poets*, ed. George Birkbeck Hill (Oxford, 1905), i. 16).

a cell: a hermit's dwelling, consisting of a single room.

664 *having nothing to do*: in italicizing the phrase, Burney alludes to Harrel's words in his suicide letter, 'the want of something to do', p. 431.

667 *jealous in honour*: quoting Jaques's 'All the world's a stage' speech in Shakespeare's *As You Like It*, II. vii. 152: 'Jealous in honour, sudden and quick in quarrel'.

673 *defalcation*: fraudulent deficiency, shortcoming.

675 *great*: 'greatly' in C2.

683 *going post*: going with speed.

689 *puff*: inflated display, bragging.

690 *gout . . . into his stomach*: gout most commonly affects the extremities, especially the toes and thumbs; a stomach gout is much more dangerous. The disease, associated with over-indulgence in food and drink, was widespread in the eighteenth century, primarily among males; see Pat Rogers, 'The Rise and Fall of Gout', *Times Literary Supplement*, 20 Mar. 1981, p. 315.

694 *Egbert, first king of all England*: Egbert, King of the West Saxons, succeeded to the throne in 802. Although not the titular King of England, before his death in 839 he had conquered much of the country.

696 *he long since said . . . misery of life*: quoting Delvile's words to Cecilia, above, p. 573.

castle-building: from the proverb 'to build castles in the air', i.e. to plan impracticable projects.

I proposed . . . by means of a title: if this proposal were carried out, Delvile would receive a new peerage and thus acquire a new title. He would, however, lose the name 'Delvile' so precious to his father.

697 *unsullied and uninterrupted*: if Delvile were to take the name of Beverley he would remain Lord Delvile, a title his eldest son would assume on succession. His younger sons and his daughters, however, would be known as Beverley.

705 *a native of the West Indies*: of Jamaica, the largest island in the British West Indies. The island was colonized by the British in the mid-seventeenth century; its plantations produced an abundance of sugar, coffee, and cocoa.

708 *Mr. Gosport . . . formerly confined*: see Gosport's words, above, p. 291.

711 *she humbled the oppressor, she exalted the oppressed*: echoing Virgil's *Aeneid*, in Dryden's translation (1697), vi. 1177: 'To tame the Proud, the fetter'd Slave to free'. See Introduction, p. xxxiv above.

a cloud in which she was supported by angels: alluding to the many paintings of Saint Cecilia surrounded by angels. Cecilia is frequently described as an 'angel' in the novel: the musical heroine is given the traditional associations of Saint Cecilia with music.

714 *Miss Charltons*: 'the Miss Charltons' in C2.

VOLUME V

718 *the cheats . . . of stock jobbing*: Johnson memorably defines a stockjobber as 'a low wretch who gets money by buying and selling shares in the funds' (*Dictionary*). After 1773, however, when the Stock Exchange was founded in Threadneedle Street, the buying and selling of stocks and shares became more orderly and respectable.

720 *knew*: 'knew that' in C2.

721 *These*: an abbreviation of the legal term 'these presents', used to denote a document; a usage oddly inappropriate to a personal letter.

722 *the Bookseller*: the eighteenth-century bookseller, such as this one, filled the role of publisher and worked closely in conjunction with authors, commissioning works and advising on what was in vogue.

725 *saluting*: kissing.

you who: 'you' in C2.

726 *the three kingdoms*: of England and Wales, Scotland, and Ireland. The term 'United Kingdom' dates from 1801.

727 *walk with his hat on*: i.e. without raising his hat to his superiors.

728 *speeches was*: 'speeches were' in the fourth and subsequent editions.

stopped in: 'stopped her in' in C2.

731 *family was*: 'family were' in C2.

732 *mistake the thing*: a favourite phrase of Charles Burney; may be a literary allusion.

Grub-Street regiment, of the third story: a witticism beginning an extended military metaphor. Grub-Street writers, hacks named after the London street where many lived, were likely to inhabit small, cheap, third-storey rooms.

736 *a groat*: a coin worth fourpence, withdrawn from circulation in 1662; used loosely to mean a very small sum.

Carthusian . . . mortified so severely: the Carthusians, a secluded order of monks founded in 1084, were noted for their extreme austerity.

Our giants may, indeed, be only windmills: again alluding to Don Quixote's delusions in Cervantes' novel; see note to p. 108.

738 *first I*: 'I first' in C2.

739 *the Dedication . . . pamphlet*: hack writers, in particular, would make full use of the eighteenth-century convention of the elaborate dedication. Swift's *A Tale of a Tub* (1704) parodies the form. In *Rambler* 136 (6 July 1751) Johnson declares that 'Nothing has so much degraded literature from its natural rank, as the practice of indecent and promiscuous dedication'.

741 *was herself*: 'was' in C2.

Mrs. Delvile was recovered . . . melancholy: 'Mrs. Delvile, whose health in her own letter was mentioned in terms the most melancholy, was yet recovered' in C2.

some reproach: Book VIII and Volume IV end here in C2.

with sad civility and an aching head: Pope, 'An Epistle to Dr. Arbuthnot' (1734), ll. 37–8: 'I sit with sad Civility, I read / With honest anguish, and an aking head'.

742 *snap*: 'make a quick or eager catch, at a thing' (*OED*).

a Death's head: an emblem of mortality.

743 *talk to the boards*: with the same sense as the proverbial 'talk to the wind'.

the Tabernacle: a chapel erected by George Whitefield, the Methodist preacher, in 1756, in open fields and close to a large pond. For illustrations of the original building and its successors see *Survey of London*, xxi, pls. 24–6.

744 *one up*: 'up one' in C2.

bob: deceive, cheat.

preparing for the small-pox: i.e. preparing for inoculation against small-pox, at which time physicians recommended a low diet, such as water-gruel. Inoculation is an important topic at the outset of Burney's next novel, *Camilla*; see p. 22 and note.

bit: deceived, taken in.

745 *pomatum . . . plaistered pate . . . bob jerom*: scented ointment for dressing the hair; a head smeared with powder and ointment; the bob wig that Briggs praises above, pp. 452–3.

pig-tail . . . calves of their legs: the pig-tail wig, with a long, dangling queue, was favoured by fops until the 1790s. Cunnington (*Handbook*, p. 248) quotes a couplet from the *Gentleman's Magazine* of 1773; 'Curls on their sides, toupees before, you'll find / With tails like monkies, dangling down behind'.

a damper: something that takes the edge off the appetite. Predates the earliest example (1804) of this use cited in *OED*.

748 *the Great Mogul*: Briggs's symbol of power and wealth; see note to p. 94.

749 *engrossing*: by 'engrossers of wealth' Albany means accumulators, but Hobson interprets the term in a different sense. 'Engrossing' a commodity is buying up the whole supply in an area for the purpose of 'regrating' or reselling it at a higher price. Such monopolizing was illegal; hence Hobson's 'underhand dealings'.

the Lord Chancellor: the highest judicial functionary, who appoints all justices of peace.

a neat income of 2 or 3000 a year: in 1763 Johnson suggested to

Boswell that £600 a year gave a man 'consequence' while £6,000 gave him 'opulence' (*Life of Johnson*, i. 440). Hobson's 'neat income', with a modern equivalent of some £150,000, is closer to opulence than consequence, and similar to the £3,000 per annum conditionally bequeathed to Cecilia by her uncle.

750 *free-born Englishman . . . by the right of Magna Charta*: the Great Charter, obtained from King John in 1215, granted personal and political liberty to all 'freemen' (as opposed to 'villeins') and eventually to all Englishmen.

exulting; even: 'exulting, exulting even' in C2.

niggard cant: mean hypocritical moralizing.

"Give him a whip!" cried Briggs, "sha'n't have a souse": '"Sha'n't have a souse!" cried Briggs, "Give him a whip' in C2. *Souse*: a small coin of negligible worth; from the French *sou*, worth the twentieth part of a *livre*.

Bridewell: a prison for vagrants, prostitutes, etc., who were employed there in beating hemp and picking oakum. The severity of its discipline was notorious.

the chink: ready cash.

sent to the Thames: to relieve overcrowding in London prisons, many convicts were held in hulks (unfitted ships) on the Thames, in extremely arduous conditions.

751 *the poor's rate*: a tax for the relief of the poor, paid by property owners. Its administration was improved by the Poor Law Act of 1782.

Mr. Bounce: a boastful, swaggering fellow. This pre-dates the earliest example (1812) of this use given in *OED*.

good: financially sound. *OED* quotes an example of 1778: 'The whole city of London uses the words *rich* and *good* as equivalent terms.'

don't take me: i.e. 'you don't get my meaning'.

little gold boys: gold coins.

752 *touched*: bribed; Briggs suggests that Albany is in collusion with his objects of charity.

753 *stand*: 'you stand' in C2.

marrowbones: knees.

Chancellor of the Exchequer, or Commissioner of Excise: the highest finance minister; one of the board responsible for the collection of excise duties. Hobson does not share Johnson's detestation of excise: 'a hateful tax levied upon commodities, and adjudged not by the common judges of property, but by wretches hired by those to whom excise is paid' (*Dictionary*). Commissioners could become wealthy by accepting bribes.

grand-dads: pre-dates the earliest example of the word (1819) cited in *OED*.

the sink: the gutter or open sewer.

755 *ire*: 'fire' in C2; presumably an error, but not corrected in subsequent editions.

756 *a cut up*: see notes to pp. 453 and 605; *OED* cites this as the first example of the phrase as a substantive.

end: 'an end' in C2.

cracked in the noddle . . . break out some day: somewhat damaged in the head; he will break out into madness some day.

a complaint has been lodged: a legal metaphor; a formal accusation or charge made before a court.

758 *suffer*: 'to suffer' in C2.

only known by his title: as the Earl of Ernolf is not known by his family name, Derford, it is immaterial to him that it will change to Beverley. The Delviles, in contrast, have long been known by their family name.

763 *he was tied to himself*: because his usurious dealings with Cecilia are illegal; see note to p. 437.

768 *an apothecary*: apothecaries were subordinate to physicians, but ranked above unlicensed medical practitioners. Their 'bill' was not for treatment, for which they were not allowed to charge, but for medicines supplied. Cecilia judges that a physician, who charges a guinea a visit, is an unnecessary extravagance.

770 *the East India Company*: incorporated in 1600, the Company effectively governed India through its monopoly of trade until its dissolution in 1858. Wheatley describes it as 'once the largest and most magnificent Company in the World' (*London Past and Present*, ii. 2).

a clear-starcher . . . plain work-woman: one who stiffens and dresses linen with clear, colourless starch; a needleworker doing plain sewing, as opposed to embroidery.

781 *shilly shally*: *OED* cites this as the earliest use of 'shilly shally' as a verb.

782 *as proud as Lucifer*: proverbial since the late fourteenth century.

783 *rout day*: the day for her fashionable gathering; see note to p. 321. The earliest example cited in *OED* is from Burney's journal for 1775.

   a quart . . . too much: Hobson suggests, obscurely, that one cannot be said to 'know' someone as long as anything about that person is unknown. His mercantile catchphrase is derived from the brewery; a quart or two pints is 0.5 per cent of a hogshead, which contained some fifty gallons.

   ungain: awkward, troublesome.

784 *whisky frisky*: 'light and lively, flighty' (*OED*; the only example).

   Hocus Pocus: a nonsense phrase commonly derived from Protestant ridicule of the words of consecration in the Catholic mass (*hoc est corpus meum*), used generally in reference to magic, conjuration, or mysterious muddle.

785 *I'll*: 'I shall' in C2.

   no stand . . . my entry: I'll not have my hall turned into a hackney coach stand.

786 *a mistake*: Delvile quotes Cecilia's words to himself, p. 760.

789 *over night*: before retiring for the night.

   still might: 'might still' in C2.

790 *by her*: 'from her' in C2.

   evils . . . struggling: the only one of the many internal quotations in *Cecilia* for which Burney provides a page reference, perhaps because of its Johnsonian ring. It is echoed again in the final sentence of the novel.

800 *therefore to*: 'to' in C2.

806 *the South of France*: with its balmy temperatures and plentiful supply of fresh fruit and vegetables, the South of France became fashionable among English travellers seeking to restore their health in the late 1770s and 1780s. Then as now, Nice, Mrs Delvile's eventual destination, was the principal coastal town.

820 *outstepped the modesty of*: alluding to Hamlet's words in *Hamlet*, III. ii. 18: 'o'erstep not the modesty of nature'.

823 *out to nurse*: in the hands of trustees, who would let the properties and thus increase Delvile's wealth.

834 *subject*: 'object' in C2.

838 *Margate*: the channel crossing from Margate to Ostend that the

Delviles undertake is considerably longer than the more popular route from Dover, by which Delvile returns (see p. 888). No explanation is given for Delvile's choice of route.

845 *travelling pistols*: commonly carried to guard against the danger of highwaymen. Delvile had just arrived at Monckton's house, his pistols still charged after a day's journey.

850 *the tender Belvidera . . . curse me*: in Thomas Otway's *Venice Preserv'd* (1682), V. 305–6, Belvidera cries to her husband Jaffeir: 'Oh, call back / Your cruel blessings, stay with me and curse me!'

852 *sufferings from sea-sickness*: Mrs Delvile's crossing takes place in April, a marginal month for those hoping to avoid stormy seas. Seasickness was a frequent complaint among travellers, who crossed the Channel in non-stabilized ships; see Jeremy Black, *The British and the Grand Tour* (Beckenham, 1985), pp. 6–8.

854 *the name of your husband*: if Cecilia reveals that her husband's name remains Delvile, Eggleston will have confirmation that the clause in her uncle's will has been broken.

if you die without children: this clause has not been mentioned before. It is, however, a logical part of the Dean's will, since his desire is not primarily to benefit Cecilia but rather to perpetuate his family name.

856 *now added——*: Cecilia's abortive wedding takes place on 25 September 1779, two days after her 21st birthday. The real wedding takes place in mid-April 1780. Eggleston, however, believes that Cecilia was married in September 1779 and thus owes him not only the few days' income accruing since the date of the wedding, but the whole of the income and interest on it since September. He is willing to go to law over this, as 'eight months share of such an estate . . . is well worth a little trouble' (p. 857).

one female friend . . . another person . . . as father: Mrs Charlton, the female friend, and Mr Singleton, who took Monckton's place in acting as father; see p. 624.

857 *eight months share*: even had the interrupted wedding taken place, this should be only seven months; see note to p. 856.

861 *folding it up . . . Mrs. Mortimer Delvile*: letters were folded on themselves and closed with a seal. Having opened the letter hastily, Cecilia sees the address when she folds it up again.

868 *put her seal*: as a mark of ownership; *OED* cites this as the earliest example of this use.

872 *their from*: corrected to 'their' in C2.

874 *she knew nothing of the route*: the usual route to Nice from Ostend would be via Paris, Lyons, and Marseilles.

876 *A Prating*: 'A Parting' in C2, but this is also the title of ch. viii, Book VIII.

878 *the Daily Advertiser*: founded in 1730, the paper consisted primarily of advertisements, including many on financial matters. It was, therefore, of especial interest to 'a man in business'.

    the law making no proviso to the contrary: Hobson recognizes, grudgingly, that under English law Cecilia is not disqualified from inheriting her uncle's estate simply because she is female.

880 *a pension*: defined by Johnson, before he received his own pension in 1762, as 'an allowance made to any one without an equivalent. In England it is generally understood to mean pay given to a state hireling for treason to his country' (*Dictionary*). State pensions were not, as Simkins supposes, awarded indiscriminately; after five years' arduous service at Court, 1786–91, Burney herself received one of £100 per annum.

881 *a red-letter day*: 'a saint's day or church festival indicated in the calendar by red letters' (*OED*); hence a public holiday.

882 *upon the stilts*: pompous and pretentious; equivalent to the modern 'stilted'.

    rhodomontading: boasting, bragging.

    every man . . . his own carver: proverbial for 'let every man choose for himself'.

    a tap on the shoulder with a writ: i.e. an arrest for debt.

887 *Rumford*: 'about three miles from Bury' (p. 789 above); but no such village in Suffolk exists.

888 *by the light of the lamps*: oil lamps, which were plentiful in London and much admired by foreign visitors.

895 *taking the number of his coach*: London's hackney coaches were numbered from 1 to 1,000; complaints could be made to the central licensing office by giving the offending driver's coach number.

    the Court of Conscience: a small debt court, established in 1517, where citizens could argue a case without a lawyer, before a board of aldermen and councilmen. It was abolished in 1847.

897 *riding habit*: ostensibly a riding costume, but worn as ordinary day or travelling dress: consisting of a jacket, waistcoat, and petticoat. It was highly fashionable in the 1770s and early 1780s; see Cunnington, *Handbook*, pp. 304–10.

Bedlam: the popular name for Bethlehem Royal Hospital, a hospital for the insane from 1547 to 1815, in Moorfields. The patients' ill-treatment was notorious, and until the 1770s the hospital was open as a place of public entertainment. Johnson's visit on 8 May 1775 is recorded in Boswell's *Life of Johnson* (ii. 374–75).

901 *the printer of the Daily Advertiser*: similar advertisements were printed in the *Daily Advertiser* of this period, although announcements of lost and found dogs and horses were more common.

the Three Blue Balls: three blue balls were commonly used as a sign by eighteenth-century pawnbrokers, giving way to the modern golden balls in the early nineteenth century. Burney, however, seems to have coined the title of her pawnbroker's shop; see Bryant Lillywhite, *London Signs* (London, 1972), pp. 555–7.

902 *the feathers . . . to her shoulder*: several of the various styles of riding hat popular in the 1770s and 1780s contained ornamental feathers; see Cunnington, *Handbook*, p. 367.

weep over him!—fly to him and pluck: 'pluck' in C2.

906 *deserve it*: 'deserve it all' in C2.

909 *severe discipline*: starvation, bondage, and even corporal punishment were commonly prescribed for the insane.

910 *who had already*: 'who already' in C2.

912 *enter it*: 'enter' in C2.

invalide: thus spelled in Johnson's *Dictionary* and still common in the late eighteenth century; 'invalid' in C2.

who was now: 'who now' in C2.

920 *you have*: 'have you' in C2.

922 *the Post-office*: from 1678 to 1829 the Post Office headquarters were at Lombard Street in the City. Ralph had been sent by Cecilia to Mrs Hill's, in nearby Fetter Lane, 'to procure her a lodging' (p. 876); hence his accidental meeting with Delvile.

930 *PRIDE and PREJUDICE*: Burney's phrase here has often been noted as the source for the title of Jane Austen's *Pride and Prejudice* (1813).

932 *his Majesty*: i.e. George III, King from 1760 until he became insane in 1811.

933 *take an oath that you were forcibly run away with*: since 1753 the Marriage Act had permitted annulment of forced marriages. In *Camilla*, however, Eugenia refuses to testify in court that her marriage to Bellamy was forced; see p. 842 and note.

934 *as tame as a jack-daw*: the jackdaw, a kind of crow, was tamed by having its wings clipped, and could be taught to imitate human speech.

935 *first and second position . . . . first space*: referring to Lady Honoria's previous comment about dancing a minuet and playing an exercise on the harpsichord. The line and space are those of the musical staff.

of a family: 'of family' in C2.

937 *bouquets*: i.e. nosegays of artificial flowers, very fashionable for women.

939 *her sister, now Lady Delvile*: 'her' refers to Lady Delvile's late sister. Since her estranged husband, Compton Delvile, has become Lord Delvile on the death of his brother, Mrs Delvile is now Lady Delvile.

THE WORLD'S CLASSICS

A Select List

HANS ANDERSEN: Fairy Tales
Translated by L. W. Kingsland
Introduction by Naomi Lewis
Illustrated by Vilhelm Pedersen and Lorenz Frølich

JANE AUSTEN: Emma
Edited by James Kinsley and David Lodge

Mansfield Park
Edited by James Kinsley and John Lucas

J. M. BARRIE: Peter Pan in Kensington Gardens & Peter and Wendy
Edited by Peter Hollindale

WILLIAM BECKFORD: Vathek
Edited by Roger Lonsdale

CHARLOTTE BRONTË: Jane Eyre
Edited by Margaret Smith

THOMAS CARLYLE: The French Revolution
Edited by K. J. Fielding and David Sorensen

LEWIS CARROLL: Alice's Adventures in Wonderland
and Through the Looking Glass
Edited by Roger Lancelyn Green
Illustrated by John Tenniel

MIGUEL DE CERVANTES: Don Quixote
Translated by Charles Jarvis
Edited by E. C. Riley

GEOFFREY CHAUCER: The Canterbury Tales
Translated by David Wright

ANTON CHEKHOV: The Russian Master and Other Stories
Translated by Ronald Hingley

JOSEPH CONRAD: Victory
Edited by John Batchelor
Introduction by Tony Tanner

DANTE ALIGHIERI: The Divine Comedy
Translated by C. H. Sisson
Edited by David Higgins

A complete list of Oxford Paperbacks, including The World's Classics, OPUS, Past Masters, Oxford Authors, Oxford Shakespeare, and Oxford Paperback Reference, is available in the UK from the Arts and Reference Publicity Department (BH), Oxford University Press, Walton Street, Oxford OX2 6DP.

In the USA, complete lists are available from the Paperbacks Marketing Manager, Oxford University Press, 200 Madison Avenue, New York, NY 10016.

Oxford Paperbacks are available from all good bookshops. In case of difficulty, customers in the UK can order direct from Oxford University Press Bookshop, Freepost, 116 High Street, Oxford, OX1 4BR, enclosing full payment. Please add 10 per cent of published price for postage and packing.